PN
2285
N65
1989

Notable women in the
American theatre.

$115.00

DATE			

NOTABLE WOMEN
IN THE
AMERICAN THEATRE

NOTABLE WOMEN
IN THE
AMERICAN THEATRE

A Biographical Dictionary

Edited by
ALICE M. ROBINSON,
VERA MOWRY ROBERTS,
and
MILLY S. BARRANGER

GREENWOOD PRESS

New York • Westport, Connecticut • London

Library of Congress Cataloging-in-Publication Data

Notable women in the American theatre : a biographical dictionary /
  edited by Alice M. Robinson, Vera Mowry Roberts, and Milly S.
  Barranger.
    p.   cm.
    ISBN 0-313-27217-4 (lib. bdg. : alk. paper)
    1. Women in the theater—United States—Biography—Dictionaries.
  2. Theater—United States—Biography—Dictionaries.   3. Performing
  arts—United States—Biography—Dictionaries.   4. Women
  entertainers—United States—Biography—Dictionaries.   I. Robinson,
  Alice M., 1922–   .   II. Roberts, Vera Mowry.   III. Barranger, Milly
  S.
  PN2285.N65   1989
  792′.082—dc20   89–17065

British Library Cataloguing in Publication Data is available.

Library of Congress Catalog Card Number: 89–17065
ISBN: 0–313–27217–4

First published in 1989

Greenwood Press, Inc.
88 Post Road West, Westport, Connecticut 06881

Printed in the United States of America

The paper used in this book complies with the
Permanent Paper Standard issued by the National
Information Standards Organization (Z39.48–1984).

10 9 8 7 6 5 4 3 2 1

Contents

Contributors

Doris E. Abramson, Professor Emeritus, University of Massachusetts in Amherst

Patricia B. Adams, New York City

Lucien L. Agosta, Kansas State University, Manhattan

Mark Hall Amitin, New York City

Patricia Angelin, New York City

Gayle Austin, Georgia State University, Atlanta

Nancy Backes, University of Wisconsin, Milwaukee

Nelda K. Balch, Kalamazoo College, Kalamazoo, Michigan

Rosemarie K. Bank, Kent State University, Kent, Ohio

Barbara Barker, University of Minnesota at Minneapolis

Noreen Barnes, San Francisco, California

Milly S. Barranger, The University of North Carolina at Chapel Hill

Beth R. Barrett, Daniel Webster College, Nashua, New Hampshire

Daniel Barrett, Nashua, New Hampshire

Mike A. Barton, Drake University, Des Moines, Iowa

Linda Ben-Zvi, Colorado State University, Fort Collins

Diane R. Berg, Purdue University, West Lafayette, Indiana

Dwight B. Bowers, Smithsonian Institution, Washington, D.C.

George B. Bryan, University of Vermont, Burlington

H. Edward Bryant III, Western Kentucky University, Bowling Green

James C. Burge, deceased

Morris U. Burns, Colorado State University, Fort Collins

Beverley Byers-Pevitts, University of Las Vegas, Nevada

Diana Serra Cary, Carlsbad, California

Phyllis Scott Carlin, University of Northern Iowa, Cedar Falls

Saraleigh Carney, Pro Bono Publications, New York City

Sue Ellen Case, University of Washington, Seattle

Helen Krich Chinoy, Professor Emeritus, Smith College, Northampton, Massachusetts

Constance Clark, The Princeton Library in New York, New York City

Edna J. Clark, Montgomery College, Rockville Maryland

Vévé A. Clark, Tufts University, Medford, Massachusetts

Ginnine Cocuzza, Performing Arts Resources, New York City

Barbara Cohen-Stratyner, Parsons School of Design, New York City

Ruby Cohn, University of California at Davis

Susan S. Cole, Appalachian State University, Boone, North Carolina

Rives B. Collins, Northwestern University, Evanston, Illinois

Kathleen Conlin, Ohio University, Athens

Audrey Cooper, Westport, Connecticut

Orlin Corey, Anchorage Press, New Orleans, Louisiana

Jerri C. Crawford, University of Missouri, Columbia

Jane Ann Crum, The Catholic University of America, Washington, D.C.

Rosemary Curb, Rollins College, Winter Park, Florida

Marianne Custer, University of Tennessee, Knoxville

Mary R. Davidson, University of Kansas, Lawrence

Jed H. Davis, University of Kansas, Lawrence

Mari W. DeCuir, University of Tennessee, Knoxville

Mary DeShazer, Wake Forest University, Winston-Salem, North Carolina

Caroline Dodge-Latta, Columbia College, Chicago, Illinois

Ellen Donkin, Hampshire College, Amherst, Massachusetts

Gresdna A. Doty, Louisiana State University, Baton Rouge

David Downs, Northwestern University, Evanston, Illinois

Judith Edwards, American Musical and Dramatic Academy, New York City

Harry Elam, University of Maryland, College Park

Mira Felner, Hunter College, the City University of New York

Ann L. Ferguson, Yale University, New Haven, Connecticut

Monica Fernandez, San Antonio, Texas

Mari Kathleen Fielder, Villanova University, Villanova, Pennsylvania

Yolanda Fleischer, University of Detroit, Detroit, Michigan

Winona L. Fletcher, Indiana University, Bloomington

Elizabeth Hadley Freydberg, Kenyatta University, Nairobi

Elinor Fuchs, Emory University, Atlanta, Georgia

Liz Fugate, University of Washington, Seattle

Lou Furman, Washington State University, Pullman

Anamarie Garcia, Phoenix, Arizona

Rosemary Gipson, University of Arizona, Tucson

Lynne Greeley, University of Maryland, College Park

Alexis Greene, New York City

Brenda Gross, Barnard College, New York City

David Hammond, University of North Carolina at Chapel Hill

Laurilyn J. Harris, Washington State University, Pullman

Lynda Hart, University of Pennsylvania, Philadelphia

Fran Hassencahl, Old Dominion University, Norfolk, Virginia

Faye E. Head, Professor Emeritus, University of Georgia, Athens

Louise Heck-Rabi, Wyandotte, Michigan

Erlene Hendrix, Old Dominion University, Norfolk, Virginia

Marilyn A. Hetzel, Metropolitan State College, Denver, Colorado

Pamela Hewitt, University of Northern Colorado, Greeley

Holly Hill, John Jay College, the City University of New York

Ken Holamon, San José, California

W. Kenneth Holditch, University of New Orleans, New Orleans, Louisiana

Robin Holt, Towson State University, Baltimore, Maryland

Jane E. House, Columbia University, New York City

Elizabeth M. Hutton, University of Maryland Baltimore County, Baltimore

Linda Walsh Jenkins, Los Angeles, California

C. Lee Jenner, Rutgers University, New Brunswick, New Jersey

Frances Langford Johnson, San Diego State University, San Diego, California

Anne Hudson Jones, Institute for the Medical Humanities, University of Texas Medical Branch, Galveston

Eugene H. Jones, City Colleges of Chicago, Chicago, Illinois

Janet Juhnke, Kansas Wesleyan, Salina, Kansas

Beth Kalikoff, Eastern Illinois University, Charleston

Carolyn Karis, The Hamlin School, San Francisco, California

Judith Kase-Polisini, University of South Florida, Tampa

Roger Kenvin, Arlington, Virginia

Anton Kiesenhofer, Mount Allison University, Sackville, New Brunswick, Canada

Ann Gavere Kilkelly, Transylvania University, Lexington, Kentucky

Margaret M. Knapp, Oceanside, New York

Richard K. Knaub, University of Colorado at Boulder

Jean Prinz Korf, Rio Hondo College, Whittier, California

Susan Krantz, University of New Orleans, New Orleans, Louisiana

Joanna Halpert Kraus, State University of New York at Brookport

Colby H. Kullman, University of Mississippi, University

Penny M. Landau, Montclair State College, Upper Montclair, New Jersey

Katherine Laris, Columbia University

James Larson, Emmy Gifford Children's Theatre, Omaha, Nebrska

Roberta L. Lasky, University of California at Davis

Florence M. Lea, Sacred Heart University, Bridgeport, Connecticut

Dinah L. Leavitt, Fort Lewis College, Durango, Colorado

William Lindesmith, University of Cincinnati Medical Center, Cincinnati, Ohio

Margaret Linney, Brooklyn College, the City University of New York

Dusky Loebel, Tulane University, New Orleans, Louisian

Felicia Hardison Londré, University of Missouri, Kansas City

Craven Mackie, Southern Illinois University, Edwardsville

Landis K. Magnuson, Saint Anselm College, Manchester, New Hampshire

David Manning, Palmetto, Florida

Sam McCready, University of Maryland Baltimore County, Baltimore

Catherine B. McGovern, Saint Thomas University, Miami, Florida

Marilyn McKay, University of Central Florida, Orlando

Walter J. Meserve, The Graduate School, City University of New York

D. E. Moffitt, Southern Methodist University, Dallas, Texas

Charlotte Kay Motter, Sherman Oaks, California

Donn B. Murphy, Georgetown University, Washington, D.C.

Norman J. Myers, Bowling Green State University, Bowling Green, Ohio

Deborah Nadell, Dance Critic, Norfolk, Virginia

Elizabeth J. Natalle, University of North Carolina at Greensboro

Rose Norman, University of Alabama, Huntsville

Gloria Orenstein, University of Southern California, Los Angeles

Bobbi Owen, The University of North Carolina at Chapel Hill

Georga Larsen Parchem, Ohio State University, Columbus

Vivian M. Patraka,Bowling Green State University, Bowling Green, Ohio

James A. Patterson, University of South Carolina, Columbia

Margaret Patterson, deceased

Merope Pavlides, Trinity University, San Antonio, Texas

Lucille M. Pederson, Professor Emeritus, University of Cincinnati, Cincinnati, Ohio

Jane T. Peterson, New Jersey Institute of Technology, Newark

Rita M. Plotnicki, Lehigh University, Bethlehem, Pennsylvania

Maureen Potts, University of Texas at El Paso

Judith Pratt, Ithaca Collge, Ithaca, New York

Janelle Reinelt, California State University, Sacramento

Vera Mowry Roberts, Hunter College and The Graduate School, the City University of New York

Alice M. Robinson, University of Maryland Baltimore County, Baltimore

Ellen Rodman, L. N. Productions, TV Program Development and Consulting, New York City

Maria Rodriguez, John Jay College, the City University of New York

Harvey Rovine, Wilmington, Delaware

Stacy A. Rozek, University of Texas, Austin

Janet E. Rubin, Saginaw Valley State University, University Center, Michigan

Loren K. Ruff, Western Kentucky University, Bowling green

Betsy Ryan, University of California at Los Angeles

Wendy Salkind, University of Maryland Baltimore County, Baltimore

Robert K. Sarlós, University of California at Davis

Raymond Sawyer, Clemson University, Clemson, South Carolina

Donald Ray Schwartz, Peru State College, Peru, Nebraska

Ingrid Winther Scobie, Texas Woman's University, Denton, Texas

Yvonne Shafer, University of Colorado at Boulder

Olive Stroud Sheffey, University of Virginia, Charlottsville

Reuben Silver, Cleveland State University, Cleveland, Ohio

Barbara Ann Simon, Housatonic, Massachusetts

Susan Harris Smith, University of Pittsburgh, Pittsburgh, Pennsylvania

N. J. Stanley, Indiana University, Bloomington

Cheryl L. Starr, University of Wisconsin, Eau Claire

Susan M. Steadman, Richardson, Texas

Judith L. Stephens, Pennsylvania State University, Schuylkill

Patricia Sternberg, Hunter College, the City University of New York

Jennifer Stock, Hunter College, the City College of New York, New York City

Douglas Street, Bryan, Texas

Rebecca Strum, New York City

Elizabeth Swain, Barnard College, New York City

Jo A. Tanner, the City University of New York

Sister Francesca Thompson, O. S. F., Fordham University, the Bronx, New York

Juli Thompson, University of Hawaii at Manoa, Honolulu

Margaret M. Tocci, University of Maryland, College Park

Linda Tolman, Lakeland College, Sheboygan, Wisconsin

Suzanne Trauth, Montclair State College, Upper Montclair, New Jersey

Jan Frances Triplett, Austin, Texas

Ronald H. Wainscott, University of Nebraska at Lincoln

Frank L. Warner, Loyola University, New Orleans, Louisiana

Margaret B. Wilkerson, University of California at Berkeley

Alan Woods, Ohio State University, Columbus

Jeannie M. Woods, Winthrop College, Rock Hill, South Carolina

Lin Wright, Arizona State University, Tempe

Debra Young

John Wray Young, deceased

Introduction

American theatre, like theatre everywhere, is the reflection of the society that produces it. In the male-dominated societies of past times, intellectuality and creativity were not ascribed to any of the generally acknowledged roles for women: wife/mother, virgin/nun, and whore/outcast. In most of nineteenth-century America, the only acceptable role for women was that of wife/mother, and the great women reformers of the period, like Elizabeth Cady Stanton and Susan B. Anthony, were reviled for their "lack of femininity."

For 2,000 of the 2,500 years of Western theatre, women were not even permitted to assume the female roles in plays written for sanctioned public performance. There have been, of course, women entertainers from the beginning of recorded social history, but the reputations attached to them were frequently unsavory. Regular and sanctioned theatre, like the literary arts, politics, and war, was the province of men. Not until the Restoration in 1660 were women accepted as actresses in the English-speaking theatre, and for many generations before and after that date, in the theatres of France, Italy, and Spain, actresses were required to be the wife, daughter, or mother of a male member of the company. The first professional actress in America was the wife of the company's manager; she is known only as Mrs. Lewis Hallam, her given name entirely obscure. Over the decades, professional actresses struggled to prove that they were respectable working women, not seductive sex symbols who were unfit company for wives and children. Not until the closing years of the nineteenth century was the battle won—though as actress and writer Olive Logan pointed out in 1869, theatre was the single avenue in those days where women could expect to receive equal pay for equal work. From their hard-won position as acceptable performers of female roles, some women proceeded to become playwrights, directors, managers, and designers. But not until the twentieth century, with varying degrees of acceptance, was it possible for a woman to enter one of these non-acting occupations as a career choice. Even today, with the feminist revolution well under way, women encounter closed doors in various areas of theatre work. What is remarkable, then, is that there have been so many women, since the beginning of American theatre, who have been engaged professionally in contributing to its growth and development. In addition to the obvious thousands of actresses, there have been hundreds of playwrights and scores of directors, managers, producers, and designers; there have also been a respectable number of critics, educators, and scholars. No book could hope to cover all the accomplishments of these many women. Though the editors of this volume are dedicated to correcting the historical record to show that, in a male-dominated profession, the contributions of women have been significant (though too often overlooked), the selection of notable women for inclusion here is based on the following criteria:

1. The individual should have been born in the United States or have had the major portion of her career in the United States;

2. The individual's achievements should have been important and significant in the American theatre;

3. The individual should have been influential in her own lifetime in the American theatre; and

4. A pioneering or innovative quality should have characterized the individual's contributions.

We determined that the book would not simply list names and activities but would—to the extent possible—narrate and evaluate these women's lives and accomplishments. Not only would it provide relevant biographical information and bibliographical materials, but it would also describe these women's professional contributions.

The women herein described as "notable" include not only actresses but also producers, playwrights, directors, designers, critics, theatrical agents, managers, patrons, variety entertainers, dancers/choreographers, educators/scholars, and administrators. There are noteworthy persons from the commercial theatre and from regional, experimental, educational, and children's theatres. *Notable Women in the American Theatre* is a demonstration of the widespread activities of women in the American theatre from the earliest times to the present. Many of the women herein have functioned in more than one capacity in theatre; for the convenience of the reader and researcher, we have appended lists of names in the various functional categories.

We express here our profound gratitude to the many women and men who so enthusiastically supported the endeavor by researching and writing the various entries. Their names appear at the end of their essays, and a complete list of contributors appears in the frontmatter.

This project originated in 1981 with Ellen Dowling and Janet Horne, who were then at Texas A & M University. Subsequently, for professional and personal reasons, both found it impossible to continue. The present editors have been working for the past five years to bring the project to completion, and they gratefully acknowledge here the effective preparatory labors performed by Dowling and Horne.

We also gratefully acknowledge Lynda L. Hart, Margaret Knapp, and Lin Wright for their help in finding writers for some of the subjects, as well as Margaret Lynn for her encouragement and material assistance. Finally, we wish to acknowledge financial assistance in partial support of this reference work through grants from the University Research Council at the University of North Carolina at Chapel Hill.

Vera Mowry Roberts
Alice M. Robinson
Milly S. Barranger

NOTABLE WOMEN
IN THE
AMERICAN THEATRE

— A —

ADAMS, Maude (November 11, 1872–July 17, 1953): actress, most famous for her roles in plays by James M. Barrie, was born in Salt Lake City, the only child of businessman James Kiskadden and actress Ansenath Ann (Adams) Kiskadden (known professionally as Annie Adams). Her mother, a member of the Salt Lake City stock company, carried the infant Maude Adams on stage in *The Lost Child* for her first appearance at the age of nine months. The family moved to California in 1874 and settled in San Francisco in 1875. In San Francisco, at the age of seven, "La Petite Maude" made her formal debut in *Fritz* on October 17, 1877. She remained a child actress until 1882. By that time she had grown too tall to play children's roles and was sent to live with her grandmother in Salt Lake City, where she attended the Collegiate Institute. Her schooling there, which lasted little more than a year, was the only formal education Maude Adams ever received.

After the sudden death of her father in 1883, Adams rejoined her mother, then a member of a traveling stock company. Mother and daughter worked in various stock companies until they reached New York in 1888, where Maude Adams made her debut in *The Paymaster*. She played second leads with E. H. Sothern's company and in 1890 was hired by Charles Frohman for similar roles in one of his touring companies. (She was to remain closely associated with Frohman until his death on the *Lusitania* in 1915.) In October 1892 Adams became John Drew's leading lady, remaining with him for four years. While appearing with Drew in *Rosemary*, Adams was seen by James M. Barrie, who adapted his novel *The Little Minister* into a play for her. In 1897, as head of her own company, she was a dazzling success as Barbie in Barrie's dramatization.

Adams became one of the most popular of American star performers for the next two decades, inspiring intense devotion and loyalty on the part of her fans.

Physically slight, she projected qualities of winsomeness and feminine charm and was particularly well suited to the sentimental dramas of Barrie, which formed her major repertory. In *The Little Minister* (1897), *Quality Street* (1901), *What Every Woman Knows* (1908), *The Legend of Leonora* (1914), and *A Kiss for Cinderella* (1916), Adams perfected a stage image of feminine fragility. With Barrie's *Peter Pan* (1905), Adams reached her zenith. Her portrayal of the androgynous hero was, for a generation of playgoers, the personification of graceful youth and the spirit of childhood.

Other important productions for Adams during this period of her greatest success were two plays by Edmond Rostand—*L'Aiglon* in 1910 and *Chantecler* in 1911. As Napoleon's dreamy and ineffectual young son, called L'Aiglon ("The Eaglet"), Adams projected youthful charm and pathos. Her performance as Chantecler, the idealistic rooster who thinks his crowing makes the sun rise, was greeted on one occasion with twenty-two curtain calls. Her personal warmth and charm brought a success to the play that proved impossible to duplicate.

Adams was less successful in plays that made greater histrionic demands. Her only major performance in Shakespeare, *Romeo and Juliet* in 1899, was called "very bad." Adams played two performances as Viola in *Twelfth Night* in 1908 and a single performance as Rosalind in *As You Like It* in 1910. She also performed the role of Joan of Arc in an adaptation of Friedrich von Schiller's *The Maid of Orleans* for a single performance at Harvard Stadium in 1909.

After becoming dangerously ill during the great influenza epidemic of 1918 (while touring in Barrie's *A Kiss for Cinderella*), Adams effectively retired from the stage at the age of forty-five. Her final roles were as Portia to Otis Skinner's Shylock in a tour of *The Merchant of Venice* during the 1931–1932 season and as Maria in a summer stock tour of *Twelfth Night* in 1934.

Adams's final stage performances struck many viewers as retaining the youthful charm and energy of her starring days. In 1934 Adams acted in a series of eight radio broadcasts adapted from her earlier stage successes. Her distinctive voice, which was said to combine enchantingly both tears and laughter, was well suited to the broadcast medium.

In addition to her acting career, Adams was active in technical areas, especially in the realm of stage lighting. She helped oversee the lighting for her starring tours and designed the light bridge at Frohman's Empire Theatre in New York. She spent two years, from 1921 to 1923, working with engineers at the General Electric Company in Schenectady, New York, where she astonished the experts. She developed an incandescent bulb that was widely used in color film. (She failed to patent the invention and refused to sue when her idea was reproduced by others.) During the 1920s she persistently, if unsuccessfully, attempted to film Rudyard Kipling's *Kim*, drafting the scenario herself and traveling to Europe and India to scout locations. Adams never made a film, although there were many offers from various motion picture companies.

Adams began a third career in 1937, at the age of sixty-five, founding the drama department at Stephens College in Columbia, Missouri. She remained active, teaching drama and directing several plays annually until 1947; she then taught part-time until 1950. She died of a heart attack in 1953 at her farm in Tannersville, New York, and was buried in the private cemetery on her Ronkonkoma, Long Island, estate, which she had donated in 1922 to the Cenacle, a Roman Catholic order. Adams never married.

Throughout her life Maude Adams was noted for her reclusiveness; she rarely granted interviews and refused to participate in the usual publicity events expected of stage stars. Her faithful fans respected her privacy.

Throughout her adult life her devoted companion was Louise Boynton, who functioned as Adams's secretary and assistant from 1905 until she died in 1951. Adams periodically retreated to seclusion at the Cenacle convent in New York City, where a room was maintained for her during her starring years; she bequeathed Caddam Hill, her estate at Onteora in the Catskills, to the Cenacle in 1949, in addition to the estate at Ronkonkoma.

Adams's acting career has been well studied, but the impact of her technical work in lighting and of her teaching career at Stephens College has never been fully assessed. Before her death she burned all her private correspondence, except her letters from James M. Barrie. Her surviving papers include the manuscripts of three textbooks written while at Stephens ("The First Steps in Speaking Verse," "The Spoken Verse," and "A Pamphlet on English Speech and English Verse"), comprising the Maude Adams Collection at the Library of Congress, Washington, D.C. Two biographies by Phyllis Robbins, *Maude Adams: An Intimate Biography* (1956) and *The Young Maude Adams* (1959), are by a lifelong fan and friend and contain much valuable personal information. Adams published seven installments of an autobiography (written in the third person), *The One I Knew Least of All*, in *Ladies' Home Journal* from March 1926 through May 1927. Early biographies of less value are Acton Davies, *Maude Adams* (1901), and Ada Patterson, *Maude Adams, A Biography* (1907). Adams figures in many reminiscences and biographies of popular performers, and in popular journalistic essays of the early twentieth century; a complete bibliography of these sources can be found in Stephen Archer, *American Actors and Actresses* (1983). Brief essays can also be found in *Dictionary of American Biography*, Supplement five, 1951-1955 (1977), and *Notable American Women*, Vol. IV: *The Modern Period* (1980).

Alan Woods

ADAMSON, Eve (October 30, 1940?–): contemporary actress and director, notable for founding the Jean Cocteau Repertory Theatre in New York, was born in Los Angeles. Her mother, Julia (Eastmond) Adamson, had been a Powers model and registered nurse. Her father, Harold Adamson, a noted lyricist, wrote such songs as "Time on My Hands" (with Vincent Youmans), "Around the World in 80 Days" (with Victor Young), "Everything I Have Is Yours" (with Burton Lane), and "It's a Most Unusual Day" (with Jimmy McHugh).

After her parents divorced when she was five years old, Adamson, an only child, lived with her mother, moving between Los Angeles and New York. She graduated from the Chadwick School in Los Angeles and studied English at Hiram College in Ohio, the University of California at Los Angeles, and the

University of California at Santa Barbara. "I have always been interested in many, many things," Adamson comments about her schooling. "I think that's why I finally wound up concentrating in theatre, because it's a way of pulling them all together" (Interview, April 30, 1982).

While performing Ismene in a tenth-grade production of Jean Anouilh's *Antigone*, Adamson became interested in theatre; she subsequently played as Katherina, Ophelia, Prospero, and John of Gaunt at the Chadwick School's Summer Shakespeare Festival. While in high school she also studied piano and modern dance and was active in community theatre.

Adamson studied acting in New York with Nola Chilton, who subsequently became a well-known director in Israel. "At that point I was an intense Method actress, which is just what I won't work with now," Adamson recalls (Interview, 1982). After a year she returned to California and started working at small theatres in the Los Angeles area, notably the Circle Theatre. Beginning as a stage manager and working her way into acting, she began to realize that "I wasn't thinking like an actress. I was thinking overview. Simultaneously, at the Circle I directed a couple of staged readings and started a children's theatre in which the children did everything but the writing and directing. I adapted Euripides' *Iphigenia in Tauris* as *Beyond Our Dream* for the children's theatre. George Boroff, the Circle's producing director, was a strong influence on me" (Interview).

For three years Adamson taught English, drama, dance, and creative writing at Happy Valley School—founded by Aldous Huxley and J. Krishnamurti—at Ojai, California. She also performed locally with her own modern dance troupe and wrote poetry, some of which was published in such journals as the *Beloit Poetry Journal* and *Freelance*. In addition, she became theatre and film reviewer for the *Ojai News*. During this period Adamson married actor Warner Jones; after several years the marriage was dissolved.

In her mid-twenties, Adamson moved to Manhattan, where she wrote film reviews for a neighborhood newspaper, *Downtown*; continued to write poetry; and taught English, drama, and dance at Riverside School. She began her New York directing career in 1970 by staging some half-dozen productions at the Mainstream Theatre, an Off-off-Broadway house devoted to producing new plays. When Mainstream's founder gave up the theatre's lease, Adamson took it over and moved to form her own theatre. "By that time," she explains, "I had gotten awfully sick of making silk purses out of sows' ears—of making imperfect new scripts work. Because I had always been involved with the classics, I was really longing to do some, and I was also beginning to move into the notion of repertory" (Interview).

Though Adamson had to find a new theatre when the Mainstream burned, she was able to open the Jean Cocteau Repertory Theatre by June 17, 1971. Her first offering, in a storefront space at 43 Bond Street, was a double bill of Jean Cocteau's *Orphée* and Michel de Ghelderode's *Christophe Colomb*.

Adamson chose "Jean Cocteau" as the name of her theatre because, as she says, "I'd always admired Cocteau's work and his idea of combining all the elements of theatre to make poetry *of* theatre, rather than focusing on language, or poetry *in* theatre. Cocteau was a twentieth-century Renaissance theatre person, so I chose his name. As it evolved, the Jean Cocteau is one of few true repertory companies in that we are committed to a resident company and to a rotating repertory format. We worked on a showcase basis for two years, and then became a non-Equity repertory company'' (Interview). The Cocteau, which moved into the landmark Bouwerie Lane Theatre in 1974, has presented nearly one hundred period and modern classics in its thirteen seasons. Noteworthy among these have been the first professional New York production of Percy Bysshe Shelley's *The Cenci*, the New York premiere of Pierre Corneille's *The Cid* in English, the first English translation of Halper Levick's Yiddish play *The Golem*, the American premiere of Philip Massinger's *The Roman Actor*, and such rarely seen plays as Victor Hugo's *Ruy Blas*, Lord George Byron's *Cain*, Henrik Ibsen's *Love's Comedy*, and Sarah Bernhardt's only play, *The Confession*. The Cocteau has also presented two adaptations—one of them a musical version—of *The Count of Monte Cristo* and the premières of two plays by Tennessee Williams: *Kirche, Kutchen und Kinder* and *Something Cloudy, Something Clear*. (Adamson has directed some seventy of these plays.)

She was a founding member of the Off-off-Broadway Alliance (now called the Alliance of Resident Theatres—New York). Serving as both treasurer and vice president of the organization, she has been a member of its board of directors since its inception. She also served on the original Theatre Development Fund steering committee, which led to the introduction of the Theatre Development Fund discount ticket system.

The Cocteau company consists of some thirteen performers and operates from September through May. The ensemble participates in weekly workshops in acting, dance, speech, mime, and stage dueling. They also have an active apprentice program. Since 1977 the theatre has presented a school day matinee series for high school students, in which the company performs a play from its repertory and actors talk to the students afterwards. "I'm very committed to the concepts of a resident company, to repertory, and to plays that I would define as dramatic poems, plays that resonate," Adamson comments. "I'd like to keep doing what we're doing now, do it . . . better and . . . reach more people with it" (Interview). At the close of the 1988–89 season, Adamson vacated the top post of the company, but remains as Artistic Advisor and director of specific productions.

The material on Eve Adamson is based upon an interview with her in New York City, April 30, 1982. The quotations by Adamson are from that interview. Adamson's work with the Jean Cocteau Repertory Company is reviewed or discussed in ''Rare Company at the Jean Cocteau,'' *New York Times* (August 26, 1977); ''Durable Jacobean Play Revived by the Cocteau,'' *New York Times* (September 16, 1977); ''Shelley's *The Cenci* is Revived,'' *New York Times* (January 28, 1977); ''A Classic Case,'' *Other Stages* (Special Issue, 1980); ''Something Tennessee,'' *Other Stages* (July 30, 1981); ''Tennessee Williams: 'I Keep Writing. Sometimes I am Pleased,' '' *New York Times* (August 13, 1981); ''The Challenge of a Soviet Play,'' *Newsday* (October 9, 1984); and ''Boy/Tractor Dramas Out in USSR,'' *United Press International* (Fall 1984). The Jean Cocteau

Repertory Company is mentioned in the biography of Tennessee Williams, *The Kindness of Strangers* (1984), by Donald Spoto. *Theatre Profiles/3, A Resource Book of Nonprofit Professional Theatres in the United States* (1977) has a short account of the Jean Cocteau Repertory Theatre. Adamson's birth year is not verifiable.

Holly Hill

ADLER, Stella (February 10, 1902–): teacher, actress, director, and prominent member of the Group Theatre, was born into one of the most distinguished families in American theatre. Her father, the eminent tragedian Jacob P. Adler (1855–1926), emigrated from Russia to America at the turn of the century. He was sometimes called "the Henry Irving of the Yiddish theatre." By 1939 over fifteen members of the Adler family were contributing to the Yiddish theatre and the Group Theatre in New York. These included his wife Sarah, who was a successful actress-manager, and eight children: Julia, Florence, Frances, Stella, Luther, Jay, Abe, and Charles.

At the age of four Stella Adler made her stage debut with her father in *Broken Hearts*. In her youth and adolescence, she played in Jacob Adler's repertory company, which featured productions of plays by William Shakespeare, Leo Tolstoy, and Henrik Ibsen as well as other modern and classical playwrights. After attending New York University, Stella Adler studied theatre with her father, Maria Ouspenskaya, and Richard Boleslavsky at the American Laboratory Theatre. By 1919 she was ready for her debut on the London stage in the role of Naomi in *Elisha Ben Avia*. She returned to New York in 1920 to appear in *Martinique*, *The Man of the Mountains*, and the expressionistic *The Insect Comedy; or, The World We Live In* (1922). Adler performed in vaudeville on the Orpheum Circuit for one season and then appeared in the American Laboratory Theatre productions of *The Straw Hat* and *Much Ado About Nothing*. She also toured in Europe and South America with the Yiddish Art Theatre of New York. From 1927 to 1931 Adler played over a hundred roles.

In 1931 Stella Adler became associated with the Group Theatre, the famous organization formed by Harold Clurman, Lee Strasberg, and **Cheryl Crawford**. Adler married director and writer Clurman in 1943, having previously married and divorced Horace Eleascheff. The marriage to Clurman lasted until 1960. Her sometimes stormy participation in the Group Theatre lasted until its dissolution in 1940. Under its auspices she appeared as Geraldine Connelly in *The House of Connelly* (1931), Dona Josefa in *Night Over Taos* (1932), Sarah Glassman in *Success Story* (1932), and Myra Bonney in *Big Night* (1933). She enacted the title role in *Hilda Cassidy* (1933) and performed in *Men in White* (1933). Adler appeared as Gwyn Ballantine in *Gentlewoman* (1934), portrayed **Adah Isaacs Menken** in *Gold Eagle Guy* (1934), and starred in two plays by Group Theatre writer Clifford Odets: she played Bessie Berger in *Awake and Sing* (1935) and Clara in *Paradise Lost* (1935). In 1939 she performed in *Thunder Rock* and *My Heart's in the Highlands*.

In the 1940s Adler appeared as Catherine Carnick in *Sons and Soldiers* (1943), directed *Manhattan Nocturne* (1943), appeared as Clotilde in *Pretty Little Parlor* (1944), directed *Polonaise* (1945), and appeared as Zinaida in *He Who Gets Slapped* (1946). Her film appearances included *Love on Toast* (1938), *The Thin Man* (1944), and *My Girl Tisa* (1948). In 1943 she was associate producer of *DuBarry Was a Lady*. Her later stage work included directing *Sunday Breakfast* (1952) and *Johnny Johnson* (1956). In a London production of *Oh Dad, Poor Dad, Mama's Hung You in the Closet and I'm Feeling So Sad* (1961), she took the role of Madame Rosepettle.

Although she was eager to explore "the craft of acting," Adler chafed against dogmatic adherence to the principles of Constantin Stanislavsky and his "Method" of actor training. She thought that the use of an actor's personal life to call forth emotion displayed on stage was schizophrenic and unhealthy. When she was in Russia in 1933, Adler studied with Stanislavsky, who answered her objections to his theories and techniques by saying, "If the system does not help you, forget it. But perhaps you do not use it properly." She returned to America believing that the Group Theatre's use of the Stanislavsky system had been incorrect. She made a formal report to the Group Theatre members on her understanding of Stanislavsky's technique. Then, openly challenging Lee Strasberg's authority, she began to give acting classes herself. In describing the effect her new understanding of Stanislavsky had on the study of acting in the Group Theatre, she said, "The work was healthier. It was more externalized. It had to do with the circumstances of the play, with using your imagination, which contained all the emotion and all the background that you needed" (*Educational Theatre Journal*, December 1976, p. 509). She continued to act, teach, and direct with the Group Theatre though she still found the organization's male domination stifling.

From 1940 through 1942, Adler taught acting at Erwin Piscator's Dramatic Workshop in the New School for Social Research. She opened her own conservatory in 1949 and has taught and directed there ever since. In 1966-1967 she was adjunct professor of acting at the School of Drama at Yale University; in 1967-1968 she was the head of Yale's acting department. From 1970 until 1972 Adler was again associated with the New School for Social Research, and she now teaches classes at her own studio for the School of the Arts at New York University.

As an actress, Stella Adler moved audiences, critics, and colleagues with the grandeur and imaginative sympathy of her characterizations. **Helen Krich Chinoy** observed that perhaps Adler's "vibrant theatricality, experience, and great personal beauty" made her "not quite at home in the somewhat untheatrical Group." Those who rehearsed or studied with her were impressed by her dedication to the craft of acting. Sanford Meisner called her "a deeply thoughtful" as well as a "brilliant" actress. Her directing and teaching influenced many students of theatre; Margaret Barker said, "Stella Adler taught me more in fewer rehearsals than anyone'' (*Educational Theatre Journal*, December 1976, pp. 503, 506, 522).

Stella Adler published her own book on acting, *The Technique of Acting* (1988). In a special issue of the *Educational Theatre Journal* (December 1976) titled *Reunion* and edited by Helen Krich Chinoy, Stella Adler and other members of the Group Theatre discuss the Group Theatre in separate interviews. Harold Clurman's portrait of Adler in *The Fervent Years* (1945) presents a strikingly individualistic personality. F. Cowles Strickland's *The Technique of Acting* (1956) has a paragraph on Adler; *The New Theatre Handbook and Digest of Plays* (1959), edited by Bernard Sobel, provides a paragraph on the Adler family tree. *The Biographical Encyclopaedia and Who's Who of the American Theatre* (1966), and *Who's Who in the Theatre* (1981) supply detailed accounts of Adler's professional career through 1961 and 1967, respectively. *Notable Names in the American Theatre* (1976) gives a history of her film, theatre, and teaching career until 1972. She is listed in *The Oxford Companion to American Theatre* (1984) and in *Contemporary Theatre, Film, and Television*, Vol. 3 (1986). There is an informative biographical account of Adler in *Current Biography* (August 1985).

Beth Kalikoff

AKALAITIS, JoAnne (June 29, 1937–): director, actress, writer, designer, and moving force in the theatrical company called Mabou Mines, was born in Cicero, Illinois, the daughter of Clement Akalaitis, a supervisor for Western Electric, and Estelle (Mattis) Akalaitis. She grew up in Chicago in what she calls "a heavy Catholic, Lithuanian atmosphere" (*Theatre*, Spring 1984, p. 6). She received her Bachelor of Arts degree in philosophy from the University of Chicago in 1960. She then went to California, where she first pursued graduate work in philosophy at Stanford University; but she soon transferred to the Actors' Workshop of San Francisco, where she worked as an apprentice and technician until 1963. At the Actors' Workshop she met Lee Breuer, **Ruth Maleczech**, and Bill Raymond. Breuer had already distinguished himself as a resident director there, and Maleczech and Raymond were actors. Akalaitis also worked at this time with the San Francisco Mime Troupe, then in their strongly political phase. Soon these four creative persons became members of the San Francisco Tape Music Center, where they made important cultural contacts with visual artists— especially those engaged in Happenings—and also with avant-garde musicians.

In 1963 Akalaitis sought work as an actress in New York and in North Carolina, and late in 1964 she left for Paris with her husband-to-be, Philip Glass, a composer who had received a Fulbright scholarship to study with Nadia Boulanger. In Paris she met two more creative artists who would later become members of Mabou Mines. They were David Warrilow, then editor of the English-language edition of *Réalités* but also a former actor anxious to get back into acting, and Fred Neumann, whom she met at an audition for a film-dubbing assignment. All three eventually became involved in dubbing films, an occupation which increased their awareness and knowledge of microphones and film-dubbing techniques as useful devices in the theatre.

In 1965 Lee Breuer and Ruth Maleczech also happened to be in Paris; there, along with Glass, Raymond, and Neumann, Akalaitis worked informally on Samuel Beckett's *Play* in a Paris theatre workshop. In 1966 she traveled in Asia and later continued to study acting in New York with Mira Rostova and Gene Frankel. In 1969 she returned to France and with Ruth Maleczech attended workshops held by the Polish director Jerzy Grotowski at Aix-en-Provence.

Excited by Grotowski's "poor" theatre, which gave more importance to the actor than to the elements of makeup, costume, lighting, and scenery, Akalaitis, back in New York in 1969, wrote to her friends in Paris suggesting that they all come to New York to form a troupe. Breuer, Maleczech, and Warrilow arrived. They lived with Akalaitis and Glass, all of them taking ordinary jobs to help pay for the making of Lee Breuer's first "animation," *The Red Horse*. Akalaitis says of this association, "It had to do with language and the formalization of material. . . . I had picked up a lot of Joe Chaikin's exercises from Open Theatre workshops, and Ruth and Lee got stuff from the Berliner Ensemble. Ruth and I taught the Grotowski work to David and Lee. So we had some idea about technique that came from all these sources" (*Soho News*, April 29, 1981, p. 10).

An early benefactor of the group was **Ellen Stewart** of La Mama Experimental Theatre Club. She saw *The Red Horse* and supported the performers with a studio and fifty dollars a week each. In the meantime, the group refined *The Red Horse* at Glass's beach house in Nova Scotia, not far from an old mining village with the picturesque name of Mabou Mines. When *The Red Horse* was ready to be presented at the Guggenheim Museum in New York, a formal name for the group was needed, and Akalaitis suggested "Mabou Mines."

So it was that in 1970 Mabou Mines became an important member of the new theatre movement in New York. In the period from 1970 to 1979, Akalaitis also worked on Breuer's *The B-Beaver Animation* and *The Shaggy Dog Animation*. In 1976 she won a *Village Voice* Obie (an award for excellence in the Off-Broadway theatre) for her direction of Samuel Beckett's *Cascando*, and in 1977 she designed, directed, and performed in *Dressed Like an Egg*, a dramatization made from the writings of Colette. For this work she won another Obie and also the American Theatre Wing's Joseph Maharem Award for scenic design. In 1979 she won still another Obie for *Southern Exposure*, a work that she wrote, directed, and designed.

In the 1980s JoAnne Akalaitis has continued her highly individualistic work. She wrote and directed *Dead End Kids: A History of Nuclear Power* (1980), presented by Joseph Papp at the Public Theatre in New York. In 1981 Akalaitis received great critical praise for her direction of Joan MacIntosh in *Request Concert* by Franz Xaver Kroetz. In 1982 she directed Michael Hurson's *Red and Blue*, also produced by Joseph Papp. In 1983 she directed *The Photographer*, a play about Eadweard Muybridge, one of the inventors of the motion picture; and in 1984 she directed *Through the Leaves* by Franz Xaver Kroetz, featuring her friends Ruth Maleczech and Fred Neumann. In the same year Akalaitis directed Beckett's *Endgame* for the American Repertory Theatre in Cambridge, Massachusetts. This production provoked a legal disagreement with Beckett and publisher Barney Rossett of Grove Press because of its radical departure from the written stage directions. Akalaitis and designer Douglas Stein set the play in a demolished subway station instead of the "bare interior" described by the author and also added an overture and incidental music by Philip Glass. The production brought the issue of directorial license to national attention.

Akalaitis directed Jean Genêt's *The Balcony* for the 1985-1986 season at the American Repertory Theatre, Cambridge, using a new translation by Jean-Claude van Itallie and a musical score by Ruben Blades. Akalaitis transferred the play's setting from France to modern Central America in order to examine the fantasy/reality, power, and martyrdom themes in a contemporary context. In February 1986 she directed Franz Xaver Kroetz's *Help Wanted*, presented by Mabou Mines at New York's Theatre for the New City, featuring Ruth Maleczech and Akalaitis herself in a play about people who are castoffs in a disposable-prone society.

JoAnne Akalaitis's work attracts critical respect because she does not settle for traditional, easy approaches. She aims instead for extreme precision and honesty in her work so that even the subtlest nuances communicate themselves fully. Like other members of Mabou Mines, she often employs high-tech devices, mixing sights and sounds in a visual-aural collage. The visual is especially important in her work. She says, "I get most of my ideas from pictures. In fact, all images in the theatre are visual, even the language—it's impossible to read without making pictures in your mind. The crucial thing for me is always to remain true to your images" (*New York Magazine*, February 23, 1981, p. 20).

While continuing to work with the American Repertory Theatre and Mabou Mines, JoAnne Akalaitis has also created a piece about refugees and immigrants called *Green Card*, produced in 1986 at the Mark Taper Forum in Los Angeles. In the fall of 1987 she directed an innovative production of a new translation by Henry J. Schmidt of Georg Büchner's *Leon and Lena* at the Guthrie Theatre in Minneapolis. She will also be directing *Cymbeline* in 1989 for the New York Shakespeare in the Park Public Theatre.

Akalaitis is also writing an opera with John Gibson under grants from the National Endowment for the Arts and the Rockefeller Foundation. The subject will be the Victorians, a topic that has endless fascination for her. She says about this opera, which will focus on Charles Darwin, "It's all part of my general interest in the nineteenth century: sexual repression, women as objects, men who are scientific adventurers, intellectual spirits" (*Theater*, Spring 1984, p. 10). As writer-director, JoAnne Akalaitis premièred the film version of her award-winning play *Dead End Kids*, featuring the founders of Mabou Mines, at the Toronto Film Festival in September 1986. Since Akalaitis is now at the peak of her career, much more work can be expected from her.

For descriptions and reviews of JoAnne Akalaitis's works, see Terry Curtis Fox, "The Quiet Explosions of JoAnne Akalaitis," *The Village Voice* (May 23, 1977); Sally R. Sommer, "JoAnne Akalaitis of Mabou Mines," *Tulane Drama Review* (September 1976);

Xerxes Mehta, "Notes from the Avant-Garde," *Theatre Journal* (March 1979); Xerxes Mehta, "Some Versions of Performance Art," *Theatre Journal* (May 1984). Also see the *New York Magazine* (February 23, 1981) and *The Soho News* (April 29, 1981). JoAnne Akalaitis's play, *Dead End Kids: A History of Nuclear Power*, appears in *Theater* (Summer/Fall 1982). Jonathan Kalb interviews Akalaitis in *Theater* (Spring 1984). Don Shewey has written "The Many Voices of Mabou Mines," *American Theatre* (June 1984) and "A Revue for The Nuclear Era Moves from Stage to Film," *New York Times*, November 9, 1986, II, 15. The controversy over Akalaitis's production of *Endgame* is discussed in the *New York Times* (December 8, 13, 20, and 23, 1984), in *Theatre Crafts* (May 1985), and in *Theater* (Spring 1985). See also *American Theater* (September 1983, November 1985, March 1986, and June 1986). Akalaitis is one of the directors interviewed by Arthur Bartow for his 1988 book, *The Director's Voice*, published by Theatre Communications Group.

Roger Kenvin

AKINS, Zoë (October 30, 1886-October 29, 1958): playwright of considerable success and fame in the early twentieth century, was born in Humansville, Missouri. She was the daughter of Thomas Jaspard and Elizabeth (Green) Akins and the grandniece of Duff Green, who had been appointed in 1829 by President Andrew Jackson to serve as the first public printer in the United States. When Akins was eleven, the family moved to St. Louis, where her father became postmaster. She received her early education at home, but from 1899 to 1901 she attended Monticello Seminary in Godfrey, Illinois, which became the setting for her 1941 novel, *Forever Young*. She had two more years of formal schooling at Hosmer Hall in St. Louis.

From childhood Akins was fascinated by the theatre. One of her early plays was performed by schoolmates at Hosmer Hall. Still in her teens, she became a frequent contributor of feature stories and criticism to *Reedy's Mirror* (St. Louis), primarily because it afforded her the opportunity to meet visiting celebrities like **Julia Marlowe**. At seventeen she joined the Odeon Stock Company, and in 1908 she helped to establish the Juvenile Theatre of St. Louis. In 1909 she went to New York to try her luck at acting and playwriting while supporting herself by writing articles for magazines, including the prestigious *McClure's*, whose editor, Willa Cather, took a friendly interest in her work.

Akins's first book was a collection of verse, *Interpretations* (1911). Her three-act "amorality play," *Papa*, published in 1913, was produced in Los Angeles in 1916 and in New York in 1919. That genre of her own invention was defined in *Town and Country* (December 1, 1916) as "a play in which the characters are depicted as being unaware of the decencies of the real world." *Papa* turns convention upside down with such sly charm and sophistication that the play still seems quite fresh and amusing. Akins's first professionally produced play, *The Magical City*, a one-act free-verse tragedy set in New York, won acclaim as the best of four short plays presented by the Washington Square Players on March 20, 1916.

Akins's long string of popular successes on Broadway began in 1919 with *Déclassé*, starring **Ethel Barrymore**. *Daddy's Gone A-Hunting* (1921) was an absorbing drama of marital infidelity. *The Varying Shore* (1921) unfolded backwards in time telling the story of a fallen woman from her death as the rich old "Sinner's Saint" of Monte Carlo to her flight from a forced marriage at the age of seventeen. Most critics agreed that Akins's finest work was *Greatness*, first produced in New York in 1922 under the title *The Texas Nightingale*. She wrote this comedy about a temperamental, often-married opera singer especially for her friend, actress Jobyna Howland, who also played the leading role in Akins's *O Evening Star!* (1936), a play based upon the true story of **Marie Dressler**'s comeback in motion pictures.

On March 12, 1932, Akins married Captain Hugo Cecil Levings Rumbold, a British painter and set designer, who died of war injuries in November of that same year. Akins continued writing not only her fanciful, sophisticated romances but also adaptations of foreign plays and many screenplays, including those for **Edna Ferber**'s *Showboat* (1931) and the Greta Garbo *Camille* (1936). She won the Pulitzer Prize for *The Old Maid* (1935), her dramatization for the stage of Edith Wharton's story, and it ran for two years at the Empire Theatre, New York. She was working on her memoirs at the time of her death in Los Angeles, at the age of seventy-two.

It is unfortunate that there has been no major biographical or critical study published on Zoë Akins. Although the emotional excesses of some of her works may make them seem outdated, her dialogue often sparkles, and her all-too-humanly frail characters are still capable of capturing one's interest and sympathy. Critic Alexander Woollcott was consistently intrigued by her work, observing, "Whatever she may write for the stage, whatever the perversities of her viewpoint and the caprices of her ever restless and curious imagination, you may be sure of one thing—it will be the play that will count" (*New York Times*, September 1, 1921). Her characteristic manner was best summed up by Oliver Sayler: "Zoë Akins is still the chief romancer of our stage. Voluptuous in taste, sensuous after the unequivocal but reticent manner of the Orient, mistress of sentiment held in leash by sophistication, instinctive warder of words and word sounds, she lavishes her gifts on attenuated tales and on minor tragedies of life's supernumeraries" (*Our American Theatre*, 1923, reprinted 1971, p. 21).

In addition to Akins's writings mentioned above, her works include *The Hills Grow Smaller* (1937, poetry); *Cake Upon the Waters* (1919, novel); and the plays, *Such a Charming Young Man* (one-act, 1916), *Did It Really Happen?* (1917), *Foot-Loose* (1920), *A Royal Fandango* (1923), *The Moon-Flower* (1924), *First Love* (1926), *Pardon My Glove* (1926), *The Crown Prince* (1927), *Thou Desperate Pilot* (1927), *The Furies* (1928), *The Love Duel* (1929), *The Greeks Had A Word for It* (1930), *The Little Miracle* (1935), *I Am Different* (1938), *The Happy Days* (1942), and *Mrs. January and Mr. Ex* (1944). Some of her screenplays besides those mentioned in the text are *Eve's Secret* (1925), *Morning Glory* (1932), and *Desire Me* (1947). The Theatre Collection of the New York Public Library Performing Arts Research Center at Lincoln Center has clippings on Akins, mostly from the 1930s, and the scrapbook of her friend, actress Jobyna Howland, contains other clippings about Akins's plays. Brief biographical references and personality sketches may be found in Edwin Bjorkman's Introduction to *Papa* (1913); *Theatre Arts Monthly* (July 1927); *American Mercury* (May 1928); John Van Doren, *Theatre* (February 1922); *Saturday Review of Literature* (May 11, 1935); *Wilson Library Bulletin* (June 1935); and her *New York Times* obituary (October 30, 1958). Patricia Lee Youngue's entry in *American Women Writers*, Vol. 1 (1979), cites R. A. Mielech, "The Plays of Z. A. Rumbold" (Unpublished Ph.D. dissertation, Ohio State University, 1974) as the only thorough scholarly work on Akins. Akins is listed in *The Oxford Companion to the Theatre* (1983) and *The Oxford Companion to American Theatre* (1984).

Felicia Hardison Londré

ALDREDGE, Theoni Vachlioti (August 22, 1932–): award-winning costume designer, was born in Salonika, Greece, to General Athanasios and Meropi (Gregoriades) Vachlioti. Her father served in the Greek army as surgeon-general and was a member of the Greek parliament. After receiving her early education at the American School in Athens, Aldredge attended the Goodman School of Theatre in Chicago from 1949 to 1952. There she met actor Thomas E. Aldredge, whom she married on December 10, 1953.

Theoni V. Aldredge is one of America's foremost contemporary costume designers. She has designed costumes in almost every arena of the professional entertainment business: plays, films, ballets, operas, and television specials. However, her immense talents have been most evident on the Broadway stage. Aldredge's first professional costume designs were for *The Distaff Side* at the Goodman Theatre in 1950. Throughout the early 1950s she designed for various regional theatres in the Midwest, including not only the Goodman Theatre but Chicago's Studebaker Theatre.

In 1957 Aldredge moved to New York City. She made her costume design debut there with *Heloise* at the Gate Theatre on September 24, 1958, and her Broadway debut with Tennessee Williams's *Sweet Bird of Youth*, for which she created Geraldine Page's costumes. This play opened at the Martin Beck Theatre on March 10, 1959. Seven more Broadway shows preceded her long and productive association in the 1960s with producer/director Joseph Papp and the New York Shakespeare Festival. Her first designs for Papp were for *Measure for Measure* at the Delacorte Theatre in Central Park on July 25, 1960. Since that time she has created costumes for over fifty Festival productions of Shakespeare at the Delacorte outdoor theatre and for some forty modern plays produced by Papp at the Vivian Beaumont Theatre in Lincoln Center, at the Public Theatre, and on Broadway. Aldredge designed costumes for the New York Shakespeare Festival award-winning productions of *Hair* (1967), *Peer Gynt* (1969), *That Championship Season* (1972), *The Cherry Orchard* (1973), *A Chorus Line* (1975), and *Dreamgirls* (1981). Her name is associated with the Broadway premieres of Edward Albee's *Who's Afraid of Virginia Woolf?* (1962) and *A Delicate Balance* (1966), and with significant New York revivals of plays by

Henrik Ibsen, Anton Chekhov, Bertolt Brecht, George Bernard Shaw, **Lorraine Hansberry**, and Samuel Beckett.

In 1984 John Gruen, writing for the *New York Times* (April 8, 1984), called Theoni Aldredge "Broadway's most designing woman." By that year she had entered into the annals of American theatre history. Her costumes had appeared in five shows running on Broadway at the same time (*A Chorus Line*, *42nd Street*, *Dreamgirls*, *La Cage aux Folles*, and *The Rink*), and she belonged to a design team (itself a phenomenon in the New York theatre) that included director/choreographer Michael Bennett, set designer Robin Wagner, and lighting designer **Tharon Musser**. Their collaboration began under Joseph Papp's auspices with *A Chorus Line* in 1975 and has continued through *Ballroom* (1978) and *Dreamgirls* (1981).

Aldredge received Broadway's Antoinette Perry (Tony) Award nominations for *A Chorus Line*, *Dreamgirls*, and *42nd Street*. She won Tonys for her costume designs for *The Devil's Advocate* (1961), *Annie* (1977), *Barnum* (1980), and *La Cage aux Folles* (1983). Moreover, she has garnered numerous Drama Desk and Critics awards, the Theatre World Award (1976), the *Village Voice* Off-Broadway (Obie) Awards for distinguished service to Off-Broadway theatre, and an Academy (Oscar) Award for her costume designs for the film version of *The Great Gatsby* (1974). As one of the theatre's most gifted and respected designers, she has produced over 1,000 costumes.

Designer/historian Douglas A. Russell has said that in many ways Theoni Aldredge's career and her design approach emerged from her early design experiences at the New York Shakespeare Festival's outdoor theatre in Central Park. In those stage productions, he says, the costumes were the major element in the visual design. Russell has written, "Aldredge seemed to have an innate sense of how to design costumes that were not just character clothes but integral visual support for the underlying soul of the play" (*Contemporary Designers*, 1984, p. 20).

She begins the design process by studying the characters and the cast of any given production. She has stated that "good design is design you're not aware of. It must exist as part of the whole—as an aspect of characterization. . . . A performance will suffer if an actor doesn't love his costume, and it's your job to make him love it" (*New York Times*, April 8, 1984). *A Chorus Line*, essentially the story of a Broadway audition, is a good example of Aldredge's design process. Working closely with director/choreographer Michael Bennett and other members of the design team, she closely observed the personalities of the dancers and singers and took numerous photographs of the outfits they wore to rehearsals. She adapted their rehearsal clothes as essential elements of her design. The major transformation came with the "golden chorus line" at the end of the show, which she conceived as a fantasy number using the color of champagne to indicate celebration.

As a designer Aldredge prefers to be part of a true collaboration—a family—where through communication with other team members she knows about every aspect of a production and from that starting point makes her own contributions. Of the designer's role in theatre she is adamant that the costumes are there to serve the producer's vision, the director's viewpoint, and the actor's comfort. She has said of her work, "My aim is to create designs that will make people look alive and comfortable and to give a show a look of unity and inevitability" (*New York Times*, April 8, 1984).

For thirty years Aldredge's career has consistently followed a pattern that embraces Broadway, the New York Shakespeare Festival, and film. If she has a signature as a costume designer, it is threefold: her costumes look deceptively like "clothes"; she insists on the absence of synthetic materials ("a linen suit must really wrinkle!"); and there is a special line and color consciousness adapted from her native Greek culture—vertical columns and certain muted colors of sunset.

Aldredge has written on costume design for *Theatre Crafts*: "Costumes and the Budget," (November/December 1969, reprinted in *The Theatre Crafts Book of Costumes*, 1973). She has also written about herself and her Broadway and Off-Broadway design experiences in Howard Greenberger, *The Off-Broadway Experience* (1971). Articles on Aldredge, including designs, are found in Clarke Taylor, "Costumes That Look Like Clothes: Theoni Aldredge's Recent Works on Stage and Film," *Theatre Crafts* (January/ February 1977); Patricia MacKay, "Redesigning the History of Show Biz," *Theatre Crafts* (October 1980); Patricia Mackay, "*42nd Street*, The Season's First Blockbuster Musical," *Theatre Crafts* (November/December 1980); E. L. Gross, "Network Designer Theoni Aldredge," *Vogue* (August 1978); K. McMurran, "Theater's Top Twofer is Tom and Theoni Aldredge: He Emotes, She Keeps Broadway in Stitches," *People Weekly* (Chicago, June 29, 1981); Peter Carlsen, "Architectural Digest Visits: Theoni V. Al- dredge," *Architectural Digest* (December 1982); Ronn Smith, "*La Cage aux Folles*: It Is What It Is—a Hit!," *Theatre Crafts* (November/December 1983); Patricia MacKay, "The Dream Team on Collaboration or Five Designers in Search of an Author," *Theatre Crafts* (August/September 1982); John Gruen, "She Is One of Broadway's Most De- signing Women," *New York Times* (April 8, 1984); "Leading Lady of Costume Design Is Making News," *Vogue* (October 1983); Douglas A. Russell, "Theoni V. Aldredge," *Contemporary Designers* (1984). Aldredge is listed in *The Biographical Encyclopaedia and Who's Who of the American Theatre* (1966); *Notable Names in the American Theatre* (1976); *Who's Who in Opera* (1976); *Who's Who in the Theatre* (1981); *Who's Who of American Women, 1983-1984* (1983); *Who's Who in America, 1984-1985*; Vol. I (1984); *The Oxford Companion to American Theatre* (1984); and *Contemporary Theatre, Film, and Television*, Vol. I (1984).

Bobbi Owen and
Milly S. Barranger

ALEXANDER, Jane (October 28, 1939–): actress, was born Jane Quigley in Boston, Massachusetts, to Dr. Thomas Bart Quigley and Ruth Elizabeth (Pear- son) Quigley. She was educated at Beaver Country Day School for Girls. Alex- ander's father was a physician and an avocational participant in the University Players on Cape Cod, where he worked occasionally with such theatre professionals as Henry Fonda, James Stewart, and Joshua Logan. Her mother's family was from Nova Scotia and had lived in a poor neighborhood of South Boston.

Alexander began performing as a child when she appeared as Long John Silver in *Treasure Island* in Boston. She went to Sarah Lawrence College for one year and then to the University of Edinburgh in Scotland, where she majored in math with the intention of becoming a computer programmer. She began acting when, after reading general notices in the university's student union, she auditioned and got the lead in *The Plough and the Stars* by Sean O'Casey. Other roles followed, and in 1960 Alexander and the university players participated in the Edinburgh Festival with a performance of Tennessee Williams' *Orpheus Descending*. With increased exposure to the stage, Alexander abandoned her computer programming career.

In 1961 after finishing college, Alexander went to New York, where she worked for a theatrical agent. Discouraged by the thousands of acting resumés that the agent could not handle, she didn't even try to find an agent for herself. However, she did begin seriously to study acting according to the system of Mira Rostova. In class, she met her first husband, Bob Alexander, from whom she acquired her stage name. While studying in New York, she also commuted to Boston to work with Faye Dunaway at Harvard's Loeb Drama Center. There and elsewhere she played in *As You Like It*, *Misalliance*, *Antigone*, and other classics. She thus supported her family, which now included her first son, Jason. In New York Alexander also worked with Paul Sills and the improvisational comedy group Second City, which included Dana Elcar, Alan Alda, and Olympia Dukakis.

In 1966 Alexander accepted an offer to play *Saint Joan* at Arena Stage (Washington, D.C.), under the direction of Ed Sherin. She stayed with Arena Stage for three seasons, doing fifteen productions and learning to perform not only for the evening adult audiences but also for children's matinees. Alexander has said, "The audience at the Arena taught me a great deal. They let me know when they couldn't hear me. Or see me. I learned to trust them. That was how I learned to trust myself, to follow my instincts" (Dworkin, *Ms.*, November 1982, p. 100).

The roles Alexander played at Arena Stage included Major Barbara in George Bernard Shaw's play of the same title, Katrina in *Mother Courage*, and Eleanor Bachman in *The Great White Hope*. Her Washington appearance in *The Great White Hope* led to her Broadway performance in the same play, which became the sensation of the 1968-1969 Broadway season. Directed by Ed Sherin, the play made James Earl Jones and Jane Alexander famous. Alexander played a shy white woman who falls in love with a black prizefighter. Interracial audiences both jeered and cheered the love story. *The Great White Hope* brought Alexander the Drama Desk Award, the Theatre World Award, and the Antoinette Perry (Tony) Award, as well as her film debut in 1969 with James Earl Jones and the original cast. She received an Academy Award (Oscar) nomination for her performance in the film.

In addition to stage and film, Alexander added made-for-television movies to her list of credits in 1971 with *Welcome Home, Johnny Bristol*. Since then she has worked steadily on stage, in films, and in television. She returns regularly to the stage between the making of memorable films (*All the President's Men*, 1976; *Kramer vs. Kramer*, 1979; and *Testament*, 1982). Her television performances have been notable for their treatment of the socially or historically sensitive subjects, such as the private lives of the Roosevelts (*Eleanor and Franklin*, 1976, and *Eleanor and Franklin: The White House Years*, 1977); education for the emotionally disturbed (*A Circle of Children*, 1977); love between women (*A Question of Love*, 1978); and life in a Nazi concentration camp (*Playing for Time*, 1981). She has received Academy Award nominations for *Testament*, *Kramer vs. Kramer*, *All the President's Men*, and *The Great White Hope*. She won television's Emmy Award for her performance as the tough orchestra leader in *Playing for Time* and an Emmy nomination for *Eleanor and Franklin: The White House Years*.

Alexander's stage characterizations have consistently won positive reviews. She has performed regularly since 1971 in comedy, both classic and modern (Mistress Page in *The Merry Wives of Windsor* and Anne Miller in *6 Rms Riv Vu*) and tragedy (Gertrude in *Hamlet* and Lavinia in *Mourning Becomes Electra*). Her characterization of Annie Sullivan in *Monday After the Miracles* (1982) was described in the *New York Times* as showing "convincing fortitude" (December 1982). Her credits are so extensive that, from 1971 to 1982, she has been reviewed at least once a year in the *New York Times*. The worst review has suggested that a characterization is "not quite it," but the best, and there were several of them, adopt adjectives such as "splendid," "superb," and "intelligent." One critic described Alexander's portrayal of Catherine Sloper in *The Heiress*, as "super." He commented on her "bewildered eyes searching for middle distance happiness with a dowdiness she wears the way other women wear chic, as a statement rather than an apology" (*New York Times*, April 21, 1976).

As an actress Alexander has succeeded in a wide range of roles, in the media as well as in the theatre. Michael Kahn, who directed Alexander as Lavinia in *Mourning Becomes Electra*, describes her as "a New England girl. She has a reserved quality. And it's the tension between the outer reserve and what's underneath that makes her so fascinating, that makes her able to play Lavinia and Eleanor Roosevelt and Hedda Gabler" (Dworkin, *Ms.*, November 1982, p. 100). Among her contemporaries, Jane Alexander is surely in the top rank of stage and film actresses.

For biographical and personal information on Jane Alexander, see Cathy Cevoli, "These Women May Change Your Life," *Ms.* (January 1983), and Susan Dworkin, "The Passion for a Thinking Woman's Theatre," *Ms.* (November 1982). Alexander talks about herself and her role as St. Joan in an interview with Holly Hill, "Playing Joan," *American Theatre* (October 1986). Reviews and discussions of the New York production of *The Great White Hope* may be found in the *New York Times* (December 14 and 24, 1967, and October 4 and 13, 1968). See also articles in *Harper's Magazine* (January 1969) and *The Saturday Review* (December 10, 1967). Reviews of *Mourning Becomes Electra* are in the *New York Times* (November 16 and 26, 1972). For a comprehensive list of Jane Alexander's credits, see *Notable Names in the American Theatre* (1976) and *Contemporary Theatre, Film, and Television*, Vol. 1 (1984).

Lynne Greeley

ALLEN, Viola (October 27, 1867-May 9, 1948): actress, was born in Huntsville, Alabama, where her parents, Charles Leslie Allen and Sara Jane (Lyon) Allen, both actors, were on tour. As a young child Viola Allen made several appearances in children's roles, but most of her time was taken up with her education. With her two brothers and her sister, she attended schools in Toronto, Boston, and New York; and as part of her education in literature and rhetoric, she and her father read Shakespeare together.

Allen's stage career began by accident. In 1882 her father was playing Old Rogers in **Frances Hodgson Burnett's** *Esmeralda* at the Madison Square Theatre in New York. The stage manager needed an understudy for Annie Russell, who played the title role. Allen, who had been showing a picture of his fourteen-year-old daughter to members of the company, was encouraged to bring her to the audition. He did, and she was engaged as Russell's understudy. When Annie Russell took a vacation from the long-running play, Viola Allen made her stage debut in the title part at the Madison Square Theatre on July 4, 1882. The following season the three Allens—father, mother, and daughter—toured in *Esmeralda*. While they were playing at the Harlem Opera House in New York, John McCullough, the tragedian, saw the young actress and hired her to play juvenile roles in his company for the 1883-1884 season. During the tour McCullough's leading actress left the company, and Viola Allen took over her roles. She was playing with the popular McCullough the next year when he suffered a physical and mental breakdown during a performance and had to be helped from the stage. McCullough died a year later.

After brief engagements with Lawrence Barrett and Steele MacKaye, Allen became leading lady to Tomasso Salvini, the famed Italian tragedian, playing Desdemona and Cordelia to his Othello and Lear. A brief venture as a starring performer in *Talked About* in 1886 was unsuccessful, and she returned to playing opposite other stars. In the 1888-1889 season she was leading lady for the Boston Museum Stock Company, where she created the role of Gertrude Ellingham in Bronson Howard's Civil War drama, *Shenandoah*, a part she again played in the New York première on September 9, 1889. From 1889 to 1892 she played Lydia Languish in Joseph Jefferson's all-star production of *The Rivals*, in which Jefferson played Bob Acres, William Florence played Sir Lucius O'Trigger, and **Mrs. John Drew** played Mrs. Malaprop.

In 1893 the renowned producer Charles Frohman formed the Empire Theatre Stock Company, and Viola Allen became its leading lady. She stayed with the company for five seasons, receiving acclaim for her performances in *Sowing the*

Wind (1894), *The Masqueraders* (1894), *Michael and His Lost Angel* (1896), and *The Conquerors* (1898). In the American premiere of *The Importance of Being Earnest* in 1895, she played Gwendolyn Fairfax, but the play was poorly received and soon dropped from the repertory. After *The Conquerors* she left the Empire Theatre to become a star on her own.

Allen chose as her first starring play *The Christian*, a dramatization of the popular romantic novel by Hall Caine, which opened in Albany, New York, on September 23, 1898. The play toured for two years, earning a profit of over $500,000 and making Allen one of the best paid performers in the country. She continued her success in other dramatizations of *In the Palace of the King* (1900) and *The Eternal City* (1902). In 1903 Viola Allen began a series of Shakespearean productions. She appeared as her namesake, Viola, in *Twelfth Night* (1904), as Hermione and Perdita in *The Winter's Tale* (1905)—**Mary Anderson** had been the first actress to play both roles in 1887—and as Imogen in *Cymbeline* (1907). Allen's carefully staged Shakespearean productions toured the country and won both critical praise and popular acclaim.

After *Cymbeline*, Allen returned to romantic melodrama, touring in *The White Sister* from 1909 to 1911 with James O'Neill as her co-star. (Another O'Neill, the actor's son Eugene, was an assistant company manager for a brief period.) In 1915 she recreated her role for the first film version of the play. By that time her stage career had begun to wane. Her long-time managing agents, Liebler and Company, had failed in 1913, and she did not appear at all in the 1914 season. In 1916 she co-starred with J. C. Hackett in *Macbeth* and later appeared as Mistress Ford in *The Merry Wives of Windsor*. Her last appearance on the New York stage was on December 1, 1918, in *When A Feller Needs a Friend*, a benefit for war relief.

Following her retirement from the stage, Allen and her husband, Peter Cornell Duryea (a wealthy Kentucky horse breeder whom she had married in 1905), divided their time between Europe and America. She occasionally appeared in benefit productions and also was active in war relief during the Second World War. Duryea died in 1944 after a long illness. In 1946 Allen made her last public appearance when she presented her personal collection of pictures and programs to the Museum of the City of New York. Allen died at her home in New York City on May 9, 1948. She was survived by her two brothers, her sister, and several nephews.

In her thirty-five years on the stage, Viola Allen played over eighty roles. In her most famous plays—*The Christian, The Eternal City, The Winter's Tale*, and *Cymbeline*—she projected a womanly grace that pervaded her characterizations. She was an accomplished, charming performer. Her strong convictions on stage propriety enhanced her audience appeal. She refused to participate in productions that conflicted with her ethical convictions and, in several instances, persuaded authors to change characters to suit her beliefs. People who would not ordinarily go to the theatre would go to see her because they could be sure of moral and uplifting entertainment. She actively participated in managing her own career, selected plays and actors, and occasionally wrote her own press releases. At a time when Shakespeare was not considered commercially viable, she left melodrama to do Shakespearean roles. Whether in Shakespeare or in melodrama, Viola Allen personified gracious womanhood, and to her admirers she was the ideal heroine of the Victorian theatre.

A typescript autobiographical sketch by Allen is in the Theatre Collection of the Museum of the City of New York. A list of Viola Allen's theatrical appearances, compiled by Johnson Briscoe, was printed in the column, "Broadway After Dark," by Ward Morehouse in the *New York Sun* (February 22, 1935). See also the Robinson Locke Collection in the New York Public Library Performing Arts Research Center at Lincoln Center. There are some clippings about her in the Harvard Theatre Collection and in the collection of the Philadelphia Free Library. Some of Allen's correspondence with her manager, George Tyler, is available at the Princeton Theatre Collection. The Rodgers and Hammerstein Archives of Recorded Sound at Lincoln Center have two brief recordings of Allen reciting from Shakespeare. Rita M. Plotnicki has given a detailed account of her career in "The Evolution of a Star: The Career of Viola Allen 1882-1918" (Unpublished Ph.D. dissertation, City University of New York, 1979). Allen's obituary appeared in the *New York Times* (May 10, 1948). Allen is included in Lewis C. Strang, *Famous Actresses of the Day in America*, First Series (1899) and Second Series (1901); John B. Clapp and Edwin F. Edgett, *Players of the Present*, Part I (1899); *Notable American Women*, Vol. I (1971); *Who Was Who in the Theatre*, Vol. I (1978); and William C. Young, *Famous Actors and Actresses on the American Stage*, Vol. I (1975).

Rita M. Plotnicki

ANDERSON, Judith (February 10, 1898–): actress, most famous for her portrayal of Euripides' *Medea*, was born Frances Margaret Anderson-Anderson in Adelaide, Australia, the daughter of James and Jessie Margaret (Saltmarsh) Anderson-Anderson. Neither her English mother nor her Scottish father had a theatrical background; but Frances, the youngest of their four children, decided at the age of seven—when she saw Dame Nellie Melba, the Australian singer, perform—that she wanted to be an actress. Her father, who had once been known as the "Silver King of Australia," lost his money through gambling and left his family when Frances was five. Her mother ran a grocery store to support her children and to send the youngest daughter to two private Adelaide schools, Rose Park and Norwood. Then they moved to Sydney, where in 1915 Frances Anderson-Anderson made her first professional appearance as Stephanie in Julius Knight's production of *A Royal Divorce*. Anderson remained with Knight's company until 1917, appearing in such plays as *The Scarlet Pimpernel*, *Monsieur Beaucaire*, and *The Three Musketeers*. She later toured Australia and New Zealand with E. J. Tait in *Turn to the Right*. In January 1918, armed with a letter of introduction to Cecil B. De Mille and accompanied by her mother, the young actress left Australia for Hollywood. From that day forward, her career has been that of an "American" actress.

After four unsuccessful months, Anderson abandoned her plan to be a Hollywood star and with her mother moved to New York. She haunted the booking agencies with no success until one day, weak from a bout with influenza, she went into one more agency in the hope of finding a place to sit down. She was seen by the manager of the Emma Bunting Fourteenth Street Stock Company, who hired her as an ingénue for the 1918-1919 season. A road tour of *Dear Brutus* with William Gillette followed, together with more work in stock companies. Finally in 1922, billed as Frances Anderson, she appeared on the New York stage with Arnold Daly in *On the Stairs*.

Changing her name to Judith Anderson, she then appeared in *Crooked Square*, *Peter Weston*, and *Patches*. Her first notably triumphant performance in New York was as Elsie Von Zile in Martin Brown's *Cobra* (1924). Her performance caught the attention of David Belasco, and as a result she played in a two-season run of his play *The Dove*, beginning in 1925. After a brief return to Australia in 1927 to appear in *Cobra*, *Tea for Three*, and *The Green Hat*, she returned to Broadway in George Kelly's *Behold the Bridegroom* (1927). In July 1928 Anderson succeeded **Lynn Fontanne** in the leading role of Nina Leeds in Eugene O'Neill's *Strange Interlude*, which she played through the national tour of 1929. The Unknown Woman in Pirandello's *As You Desire Me* (1931) was her next Broadway performance followed by another O'Neill play, *Mourning Becomes Electra* (1932), in which she acted the role of Lavinia, both in New York and on the national tour. Other Broadway productions followed, and in 1935 she received great praise for her performance as Delia in Zoë Akins's Pulitzer Prize-winning drama *The Old Maid*. By this time Judith Anderson was respected as a Broadway star. She had, however, no experience or training in classical drama; therefore, she was somewhat surprised and hesitant when Guthrie McClintic proposed that she play the role of Gertrude in the John Gielgud production of *Hamlet* (1936). She accepted the role and, despite some adverse criticism, established her position as a classical actress. A London appearance at the Old Vic in 1937 as Lady Macbeth opposite Laurence Olivier followed.

In 1939 Anderson successfully portrayed the role of Mary, the mother of Jesus, in *Family Portrait*. In 1940 she played Clytemnestra in Robinson Jeffers's *The Tower Beyond Tragedy*, which she also directed. She then received critical approval for her performance as Lady Macbeth in the Maurice Evans's production of *Macbeth* (1941); and when **Katharine Cornell** revived *The Three Sisters* (1942), she played Olga to high praise.

All of Anderson's prior performances were eclipsed, however, when in 1947, under the direction of John Gielgud, she created the vengeful Medea in Robinson Jeffers's adaptation of Euripides' tragedy. *Medea* was an occasion of many firsts. It was the première of Jeffers's play, Gielgud's first production of a Greek classic, and the first time *Medea* had been done in the modern professional theatre. This role is considered by most critics to be Anderson's most brilliant. For her performance as Medea she received the Donaldson Award, the New York Critics' Award, and the American Academy of Arts and Sciences Award for best speech, and she was named the "First Lady of the Theatre" by the General Federation of Women's Clubs.

Following the success of *Medea*, Anderson again appeared as Clytemnestra in Jeffers's *Tower Beyond Tragedy* (1950). Then, in January 1952, *Come of Age*, in which she had first appeared in 1934, was revived at the City Center in New York. Although she has called The Woman in this poetic musical work based on the life of Thomas Chatterton her favorite part and although considerable effort went into the production, the play was not a success. She played in *John Brown's Body* (1953), toured with Enid Bagnold's *The Chalk Garden* in the role of Miss Madrigal (1956-1957), and played Isabel Lawton in *Comes A Day* (1958). In addition, Anderson performed *Medea* in France, Germany, and Australia. She played Madame Arkadina in *The Sea Gull* at The Old Vic (1960), toured extensively in scenes from her most famous roles, and played the title roles in Maxwell Anderson's *Elizabeth the Queen* (1966) and Shakespeare's *Hamlet* (1968, 1970, 1971), the latter in emulation of Sarah Bernhardt. Her most recent Broadway appearance was in 1982 when a revival of Jeffers's *Medea* ran for a limited engagement with **Zoe Caldwell** as Medea and Anderson as the Nurse. The critic for *The New Yorker* praised Anderson, "who, at eighty-four, is as strong-voiced and commanding a stage presence as ever" (May 17, 1982).

Apart from her career in the theatre, Anderson has appeared in films and on television. Her first film venture, in 1933, was in a gangster picture called *Blood Money*. For the role of the malevolent housekeeper, Mrs. Danvers, in *Rebecca* (1940), she was nominated for an Academy (Oscar) Award. She has since appeared in twenty-four films, including *King's Row* (1941), *Laura* (1944), *And Then There Were None* (1945), *Spectre of the Rose* (1946), *Cat on a Hot Tin Roof* (1958), and *A Man Called Horse* (1970). In her film work she has been particularly successful in unsympathetic, often sinister, roles.

On television Anderson has appeared on the *Hallmark Hall of Fame, Playhouse 90, Play of the Week*, and such specials as *Caesar and Cleopatra* (1956), *The Circular Staircase* (1956), *The Cradle Song* (1956), *Medea* (1959), *Elizabeth the Queen* (1968), and *Macbeth* (1954 and again in 1960). She received two television Emmy awards, one for each of her performances as Lady Macbeth. Finally, Anderson started a new phase of her career when she appeared as a regular performer on the short-lived soap opera *Santa Barbara*, which aired in 1984.

Anderson has been married twice. Her first husband was Benjamin Harrison Lehman, professor of English at the University of California, whom she divorced in 1939. Then, on July 16, 1946, she was married to Luther Greene, a producer, from whom she was divorced on June 26, 1951. She has no children and has lived in California for several years. She has retained her Australian citizenship and in 1960 received her highest honor when she was created Dame Commander of the Most Excellent Order of the British Empire (D.B.E.) in recognition of her "most distinguished contribution to the stage." She is the second Australian-born performer to have attained this title. She has been granted honorary degrees by Northwestern University (1953) and Fairfield University (1964). She was also presented the Dickinson College Art Award in 1960.

Dame Judith Anderson's career has now lasted for over sixty years. In a 1968 interview she said that she regretted not having been the first female Hamlet and not having played St. Joan, Peter Pan, or Phaedra. She has, however, played many of the great female roles. She has appeared in the legitimate theatre, has performed dramatic readings, and has acted in films, on television, and on radio. Although her acting has sometimes been criticized as stilted and mechanical, it has more often been considered brilliant and majestic. Her performance of Medea, likened to "a full cavalry charge across an open plain" (*New Republic*, November 3, 1947), would be sufficient reason for categorizing her as a great emotional actress. She is also one of the great classical actresses of the English-speaking stage; and she may well be, as some critics have claimed, America's greatest living actress.

For further information about Judith Anderson, see "They Stand Out from the Crowd," *Literary Digest* (March 2, 1935); "Portrait as Mary in *Family Portrait*," *Theatre Arts Monthly* (May 1939); and R. Wallsten, "Shakespeare on the Jungle Circuit," *Collier's* (December 9, 1944). Portraits of Anderson appear in *Independent Woman* (December 1937), *Theatre Arts* (April 1939), and *Time* (March 20, 1939, January 26, 1948, and June 7, 1948). Portraits of Anderson in her most famous roles may be seen in *Theatre Arts Monthly* (November 1936), as the Queen in *Hamlet*; *Theatre Arts* (March 1942), as Lady Macbeth; and *Theatre Arts* (November 1947), as Medea. Some useful *New York Times* reviews of her performances include *The Old Maid* (January 8, 1935), *The Three Sisters* (December 22 and 27, 1972), *Medea* (October 21, 1941, and September 14, 1951), *The Tower Beyond Tragedy* (November 27, 1950, and December 10, 1950), *John Brown's Body* (February 16 and 22, 1953), and *Elizabeth the Queen* (November 4, 1966). Jack Gould's review of her *Hallmark Hall of Fame* NBC-TV performance as Lady Macbeth appeared in the *New York Times* (November 21, 1960). See also Daniel Blum, *Great Stars of the American Stage* (1952); Toby Cole and Helen Krich Chinoy, *Actors on Acting* (1954); and Faye E. Head, "Judith Anderson, Actress: An Analysis Based on the Writings of Six Drama Critics," (Unpublished Ph.D. dissertation, Louisiana State University, 1952). Judith Anderson is listed in *Who's Who of American Women, 1958-1959* (1959); *Who's Who in America, 1960-1961* (1961); *Current Biography* (1961); William C. Young, *Famous Actors and Actresses on the American Stage*, Vol. I (1975); *Notable Names in the American Theatre* (1976); *Film Encyclopedia* (1979); *Who's Who in the Theatre* (1981); and *The Oxford Companion to the Theatre* (1983).

Faye E. Head

ANDERSON, Mary (July 28, 1859–May 29, 1940): popular late nineteenth-century actress, was born in Sacramento, California, the older child and only daughter of Marie Antoinette (Leugers) and Charles Henry Anderson. Nothing in her heritage or early background suggested the fame she was to achieve as a leading actress. Her mother, a native Philadelphian of German descent, had been raised according to the most rigorous of Roman Catholic principles in a home where theatre was strictly forbidden. Her father, although from a more liberal background, was often away on business trips in England, a circumstance that prompted her mother to move to Louisville, Kentucky, in order to be closer to her uncle, Father Anthony Mueller. Upon the outbreak of the Civil War, Mary

Anderson's father joined the ranks of the Confederate Army and was killed two years later while fighting at Mobile, Alabama, when his daughter was barely three years old.

For the next five years Anderson's education was guided mainly by Father Mueller, who instructed her in the beliefs of the Roman Catholic faith and prepared her for a life of service. This prospect, however, changed when her mother married Dr. Hamilton Griffin in 1868. He was an army surgeon who had an established practice in Louisville. A passionate lover of the arts, Dr. Griffin encouraged and supported Anderson's early aspirations toward theatre and, in later years, served as her personal adviser and business manager.

Mary Anderson's formal education began under Dr. Griffin's guidance. She attended the Convent of the Ursulines and the Presentation Academy in Louisville, where she was an indifferent student who pursued only those subjects that interested her—reading and music. When she was twelve, her stepfather introduced her to the works of Shakespeare, an event that awakened the serious side of her nature and helped to shape her later career. Lessons in English literature and elocution were begun with Professor Noble Butler of Louisville, and progress was rewarded with tickets to the Saturday matinees at the Louisville Theatre. It was here, at the age of fourteen, that she observed Edwin Booth as Richelieu, an event that marked a major turning point in her life: "I felt for the first time that acting was not merely a delightful amusement, but a serious art that might be used for high ends" (*A Few Memories*, p. 29).

She decided to become an actress and began to work at home to achieve that end. Believing the voice to be of most importance for the actor, she studied James E. Murdoch's *Analytic Elocution* and James Rush's *The Philosophy of the Voice*. She also systematically and conscientiously began to exercise her voice so that by the end of a few months it had become full and strong. Grace of pose and movement, she determined, was next in importance for the successful actress. Extremely tall and awkward for her age, she turned to the Delsarte system of expression to help her with the nonverbal aspects of emotion. Because she admired Booth intensely, she patterned much of her work after him, inclining towards the intellectual school of acting of which he was a proponent. Thus, her later performances were always marked by thoughtful analysis and meticulous planning designed to provide a unified character consistent with the dramatic values of the text.

Her progress was rapid, and her stepfather had her read for the leading actor of the Louisville Theatre, Henry Wouds, who was so impressed that he arranged an interview for her with Charlotte Cushman. In 1874 she traveled to Cincinnati to read for the famous actress, who said that she lacked only method and moderation in the use of her voice and advised her to take lessons from actor George Vandenhoff in New York. Following Cushman's advice, Mary Anderson took ten hourly lessons from Vandenhoff in elocution and in the mechanics of acting. This was virtually the only formal theatrical training she ever had.

Returning to Louisville, she began working with renewed intensity, and on November 25, 1875, at the age of sixteen, she made her debut as Shakespeare's Juliet at Macauley's Theatre. Three months later she was invited back for a week's engagement and, in addition to Juliet, performed the roles of Bianca in *Fazio*, Julia in *The Hunchback*, Evadne in *Evadne*, and Pauline in *The Lady of Lyons*. Appearances in St. Louis, New Orleans, and other southern cities followed.

In 1876 John McCullough invited her to appear at his theatre in San Francisco, an experience she described as "the most unhappy part of my professional life" (*A Few Memories*, p. 74). The company considered her an interloper, and the fashionable actresses laughed at her clothes. Thus ridiculed by the company and berated by the press, she seriously considered leaving the stage. She was dissuaded by Edwin Booth, who encouraged her to continue after witnessing her performances. The discouraging effects of the California engagement were further alleviated by highly successful tours of the South, the West, and Canada. She began the 1877-1878 season with brief engagements in Boston and Philadelphia. On November 12, 1877, she opened in New York at the Fifth Avenue Theatre in the role of Pauline in Edward Bulwer-Lytton's *The Lady of Lyons*. This was followed by appearances in *Evadne*, *Guy Mannering*, *Ingomar*, and *Fazio*.

Although a popular success, Mary Anderson did not succeed in the eyes of the critics during her first New York engagement. In spite of her "fine voice and splendid physique," she was found to be "stilted and declamatory" and "attired in . . . execrable taste" (*New York Leader*, March 31, 1889). During the six weeks in New York, however, she received valuable advice from the playwright and actor Dion Boucicault, critic William Winter, and such leading actors and actresses as Lawrence Barrett, Edwin Booth, Joseph Jefferson, and **Clara Morris**. For the next six years she toured major American cities, constantly adding to her repertoire and popularity.

Mary Anderson made her London debut as Parthenia in *Ingomar* at the Lyceum Theatre on September 1, 1883. She followed this with performances in *The Lady of Lyons*, *Pygmalion and Galatea*, and *Comedy and Tragedy*, the last having been written for her expressly by W. S. Gilbert. Critical reaction to her first Lyceum season was not too favorable. At a time of increasing interest in dramatic realism, the plays in her romantic repertoire were found to be old-fashioned and her acting style out of date. Nevertheless, she proved to be a popular success and was offered the use of the Lyceum Theatre for the following year. There, on November 1, 1884, she introduced her production of *Romeo and Juliet*, which held the stage for over one hundred performances. Following the close of the season, she teamed with Johnston Forbes-Robertson to tour the provinces. He remained with her for four years, later acting Orlando to her Rosalind in *As You Like It* and Leontes to her Hermione in *The Winter's Tale*.

Her production of *Romeo and Juliet* during her second Lyceum season marked the beginning of a new era in her career. Under the influence of many leading performers of the day who were applying a more realistic standard to the works of Shakespeare, she mounted the production lavishly in an attempt to render the visual aspects historically accurate and pictorially pleasing. Emphasis was on the total effect, and Anderson's attempt to modify her declamatory style and subordinate herself to the ideal of the ensemble was viewed favorably by the critics, who noted increasing smoothness and conviction in her acting.

Because of the tremendous success of *Romeo and Juliet*, she was offered the opportunity to appear as Rosalind in *As You Like It* for the benefit of the Shakespeare Memorial Theatre at Stratford-upon-Avon on August 30, 1885. Following an unequivocal success, she toured the production to Leeds, Edinburgh, Glasgow, and Dublin, then followed an eight-month tour of America. Following a year's rest, she performed the dual roles of Hermione and Perdita in *The Winter's Tale*, a historical first. She performed the play at Nottingham on April 23, 1887, to celebrate Shakespeare's birthday, and on September 10 she opened at London's Lyceum Theatre. *The Winter's Tale* held the London stage for one hundred and sixty-four nights. It was the only time in her career that she acted the same play for an entire season. A tour of the production to Ireland and Scotland followed.

During the 1888-1889 season, she returned to New York, where on November 13, 1888, at the Fifth Avenue Theatre, she again played *The Winter's Tale*. Following a six-week engagement, she began an extended tour of major American cities. The strain of the tour was evidently too much for her. On March 16, 1889, she suffered a physical and emotional breakdown during a performance in Washington, D.C., and was compelled to cancel the rest of the season. This was her last professional appearance on any stage. The following year, on June 17, 1890, she married Antonio Fernando de Navarro, a wealthy American sportsman of Basque descent, and settled in Worcestershire, England, where she pursued an active social life. She gave birth to three children: a son who died at birth; another son, José Maria who became a noted Cambridge archaeologist; and a daughter, Elena Antonia.

Although she received many lucrative offers to return to the stage, Anderson never again resumed her professional career. In 1911 she successfully collaborated with Robert S. Hichens on a dramatization of his novel *The Garden of Allah*, but she performed only for charitable purposes. During World War I, in an effort to contribute to the Allied cause, she acted and spoke in many camps and theatres, often accompanied by the popular Shakespearean actor E. H. Sothern. Anderson died of a heart condition on May 29, 1940, at her home in Worcestershire, at the age of eighty.

For the most part, Mary Anderson adhered closely to the classical approach to acting. Contemporary descriptions of the great English actress Sarah Siddons's style—"studied," "proper," "dignified"—could easily be applied to Anderson's acting as well. She consistently selected plays that provided her with roles suited to her personality and temperament and approached her characters on an intellectual rather than an intuitive basis. She then meticulously planned all business in relation to her concept and relied heavily on sculpturesque poses, graceful movements, and dignified action. Her beauty was uncontested. Her features were extremely mobile and were often used to great advantage to express the thoughts and emotions of the characters she portrayed. Her voice was a deep contralto and invariably impressed the critics. John Ranken Towse felt that it "was always one of the most potent weapons in her artistic armory. It was . . . uncommonly full, deep, supple, and melodious" (*Sixty Years of the Theatre*, p. 216). "It was always her predominate charm," said William Winter. "Certain tones in it . . . went straight to the heart, and brought tears into the eyes" (*Other Days*, p. 256). Her personal moral code engendered much respect for her and helped to improve the status of the woman performer but often inhibited the performance of scenes demanding deep passion. In addition, some critics maintained that she never succeeded in overcoming her lack of extensive training and attributed her early retirement in 1889 to the fact that she lost confidence in her abilities.

Although critics were divided in their opinion of her ability, there was no doubt as far as the public was concerned: "Our Mary" was overwhelmingly supported wherever she appeared. From 1884 to 1889 she reigned as America's foremost Shakespearean actress.

Anderson's autobiographies are *Mary Anderson de Navarro, A Few Memories* (1896) and *A Few More Memories* (1936). See also William Winter, *The Stage Life of Mary Anderson* (1886); *Other Days* (1908); and *The Wallet of Time*, Vol. II (1913, reprinted 1969). Articles about her include G. E. Humphreys, "Voice and Emotion: With Reference to the 'Juliet' of Miss Mary Anderson," *The National Review* (February 1885), and William Archer, "Miss Mary Anderson," *The Theatre* (October 1, 1885). Promptbooks, letters, and clippings about Anderson are located in the Folger Shakespeare Library, Washington, D. C., the New York Public Library Performing Arts Research Center at Lincoln Center, the Walter Hampden Memorial Library at the Players Club, New York, and the Theatre Collection of the Museum of the City of New York. See also Raymond Sawyer, "The Shakespearean Acting of Mary Anderson 1884-1889" (Unpublished Ph. D. dissertation, University of Illinois, 1974). Mary Anderson's obituary appeared in the *New York Herald Tribune* (May 30, 1940). She is listed in *Notable American Women* Vol. I (1971), and *The Oxford Companion to the Theatre* (1983).

                                                                                                    Raymond Sawyer

ANGELOU, Maya (April 4, 1928–): poet, playwright, composer, singer, director, stage and screen performer, was born Marguerita Johnson in St. Louis, Missouri. Although her parents, Bailey Johnson (a naval dietician) and Vivian (Baxter) Johnson, figured prominently in her adolescent development, the young Angelou was raised primarily by her grandmother, Ann Henderson, who appears as a central character in her critically acclaimed autobiography *I Know Why the Caged Bird Sings* (1970). After attending public schools in Arkansas and California, Angelou studied dance with Martha Graham, Pearl Primus, and Ann Halprin as well as acting with Frank Silvera and Gene Frankel. She has one son, Guy Johnson, who lives in Sonoma, California, and writes poetry and fiction.

Angelou is best known as an autobiographer and a poet. In her first autobiographical work, which documents her search for identity as black and female, Angelou claims that "if growing up is painful for the Southern Black girl, being aware of her displacement is the rust on the razor that threatens the throat. It is an unnecessary insult" (*I Know Why the Caged Bird Sings*, p. 13). An instant critical success, her first book was nominated in 1970 for the National Book Award. Angelou has published four other autobiographies: *Gather Together in My Name* (1974), *Singin' and Swingin' and Gettin' Merry Like Christmas* (1976), *The Heart of a Woman* (1981), and *All God's Children Need Traveling Shoes* (1986).

Described by critics as "distinctive and energetic," Angelou's poetry further attests to the complexity of the black woman's experience, her intense and intimate assertion of self. Her first collection of poems, *Just Give Me a Cool Drink of Water 'Fore I Diiie*, received a Pulitzer Prize nomination in 1972. Subsequent volumes include *O Pray My Wings Gonna Fit Me Well* (1975) and *And Still I Rise* (1978).

Angelou's career as a playwright and director has been distinguished. In 1954-1955 she performed in *Porgy and Bess* on a twenty-two nation tour sponsored by the United States Department of State, an experience she recounts in *Singin' and Swingin'*. She has appeared in several Off-Broadway plays including *Calypso Heatwave* (1957), Jean Genêt's *The Blacks* (1960) at St. Mark's Playhouse, and *Cabaret for Freedom* (1960) at the Village Gate Theater, a musical review that she wrote, produced, and starred in with Godfrey Cambridge. After performing in *Mother Courage and Her Children* in Ghana in 1964 and in *Medea* in Hollywood in 1966, Angelou wrote three plays: *The Clawing Within* (1966), as yet unproduced; *The Least of These*, a two-act drama produced in Los Angeles in 1966; and *Adjoa Amissah*, a two-act musical that emerged from her experiences as a journalist and performer in Africa in the 1960s.

Angelou made her Broadway debut in 1973 in *Look Away*, a performance for which she received an Antoinette Perry (Tony) Award nomination. Her adaptation of Sophocles' *Ajax* (1976) received critical acclaim when produced at the Mark Taper Forum in Los Angeles. A one-act musical based on her poems, *And Still I Rise*, was first produced in Oakland in 1974. Praising the energy and range of this play, reviewer Janet Boyarin Blundell noted that Angelou, "seemingly unafraid to approach anything, . . . includes comments on aging, the disappointments of love, anger at the abuse of black people, and the everyday aspects of womanhood" (*Kirkus Reviews*, October 1, 1978). The passion and determination that characterize *And Still I Rise* are evident in the title poem's opening lines:

You may write me down in history
With your bitter, twisted lies,
You may trod me in the very dirt
But still, like dust, I'll rise.

On a Southern Journey, Angelou's most recent play, premièred in Charlotte, North Carolina, in 1984. Its pivotal characters are two women, one black and one white, whose inadvertently simultaneous journey "back home" leads first to painful dialogue, then to both tragedy and regeneration. In October 1985 Angelou continued her theatrical challenge of racial and sexual stereotyping by directing two repertory productions of Shakespeare's *Macbeth* at Wake Forest University in Winston-Salem, North Carolina: one starring a black Macbeth and a white Lady Macbeth, the other featuring an all-female cast.

Angelou's accomplishments as a screenwriter, musician, and television performer are many. Among her original screenplays are *Georgia, Georgia*, produced by Independent-Cinerama in 1972; *All Day Long*, an American Film Institute Project of 1974; and, more recently, the television adaptation of *I Know Why the Caged Bird Sings*. She has numerous musical compositions to her credit, among them the scores for her own screenplays and two songs for the film *For Love of Ivy*. As a television personality, Angelou has appeared on many specials and talk shows but is perhaps best known for her role as Kunta Kinte's mother in *Roots*. A member of Actors' Equity and the American Federation of TV and Radio Artists, she is also on the Board of Trustees for the American Film Institute and is one of the few women members of the Directors Guild of America.

Angelou has received many honorary degrees and awards, among them a Yale University Fellowship (1970) and a Rockefeller Foundation Scholarship (1975). In 1976 she was named Woman of the Year in Communications by *Ladies' Home Journal*. A popular lecturer and performer at colleges and universities in the United States and abroad, she is now Reynolds Professor of Humanities at Wake Forest University.

Maya Angelou's name belongs with those of Godfrey Cambridge, **Ruby Dee**, Ossie Davis, **Lorraine Hansberry**, LeRoi Jones (Imamu Amiri Baraka), and **Ntozake Shange** as outstanding black contriʿutors to the American theatre. They have conveyed the pain and the power of the American black experience through the medium of drama. In a recent interview with Claudia Tate, Angelou revealed the essence of her literary and theatrical contribution: "All my work, my life, everything is about survival. All my work is meant to say, 'You may encounter many defeats, but you must not be defeated.' . . . I try to tell the truth and preserve it in all artistic forms" (*Black Women Writers at Work*, p. 7).

Angelou's autobiographies and poetry are published by Random House and Bantam Books; readers wanting more biographical information should consult the autobiographies *I Know Why the Caged Bird Sings* (1970), *Gather Together in My Name* (1974), *Singin' and Swingin' and Gettin' Merry Like Christmas* (1976), and *All God's Children Need Traveling Shoes* (1986). Representative commentaries and reviews can be found in the *New York Times* (February 25, 1980), the *New York Post* (November 5, 1972), *Harper's Bazaar* (November 1972), *Writer's Digest* (January 1975), and *Kirkus Reviews* (October 1, 1978). Useful interviews with her appear in *Vogue* (September 1982); *Essence* (May 1983); and Claudia Tate, *Black Women Writers at Work* (1983). She is included in Sandra M. Gilbert and Susan Gubar, eds., *The Norton Anthology of Literature by Women: The*

Tradition in English (1985). Angelou's work and life are discussed in *Contemporary Authors* (1977), *Who's Who of American Women, 1981-1982* (1982), The *Oxford Companion to American Literature* (1983), and *Who's Who in America, 1984-1985* (1985).

Mary DeShazer

ANGLIN, Margaret (April 3, 1876-January 7, 1958): actress, director, and manager, famous for her productions of Greek tragedies, was born to Timothy Warren Anglin and Eleanor (McTavish) Anglin in Ottawa during her father's term as Speaker of the Canadian Parliament. After her father left Parliament, he moved the family to St. John, New Brunswick, and became a newspaper editor. Her brother Francis, a distinguished lawyer, became chief justice of Canada in 1924.

Margaret Anglin attended convent schools in both Toronto and Montreal and excelled in elocution. Desiring to become a Shakespearean performer, she went to New York and entered the Empire Dramatic School, which was connected with Charles Frohman's Empire Theatre. Frohman saw her in one of the school's productions and hired her to play Madeline West in a revival of Bronson Howard's *Shenandoah*. She made her professional debut in that part at the Academy of Music in New York in September 1894. Following a tour in *Shenandoah*, she played with James O'Neill's company in the 1896 season and with E. H. Sothern's troupe the following year.

In the fall of 1898 Margaret Anglin played Roxanne in Richard Mansfield's production of Edmond Rostand's *Cyrano de Bergerac*, a role that established her as one of the leading young actresses of the day. Frohman hired her to become the leading lady of the Empire Theatre Stock Company, where she appeared in *Mrs. Dane's Defense*, *Diplomacy*, and *The Unforeseen*. From 1903 to 1905 Anglin and the popular actor Henry Miller toured together in an effort to fight the Theatrical Syndicate. As early as 1896 some theatre entrepreneurs, including Charles Frohman, had established the Syndicate. They took over as Syndicate houses the best theatres in the major cities across the country and then demanded that producers and managers book their plays exclusively in those theatres. Thus the Syndicate was able to stifle competition. Many well-known actors such as Joseph Jefferson, James A. Herne, **Minnie Maddern Fiske**, and James O'Neill fought the Syndicate by performing in smaller theatres or even in makeshift spaces. At last in 1905 a rival monopoly was established by the Shubert brothers—Sam, Lee, and Jacob. Under the management of the Shuberts, Anglin toured in *Zira*, her first starring role.

While touring in *Zira*, she appeared in a matinee of a play called *The Sabine Woman* by a University of Chicago English professor, William Vaughn Moody. After securing the rights, Margaret Anglin and Henry Miller brought the revised play to New York. Retitled *The Great Divide*, it opened on October 3, 1906, and became one of the sensations of the season. The stars toured in the play for the next two years. During 1908 Anglin toured Australia in Shakespearean and modern plays.

In 1910, as an independent actress-manager, Margaret Anglin starred in her first production of a Greek tragedy, Sophocles' *Antigone*, at the University of California, Berkeley. For the next eighteen years she included the Greek classics in her repertory, presenting the plays in outdoor theatres or in opera houses. Besides directing the classical plays, she supervised almost all aspects of production. When she appeared as Clytemnestra in *Iphigenia in Aulis* at the Manhattan Opera House in New York in 1921, Alexander Woollcott praised her performance: "The unforgettable part of this evening of Euripides was the splendor of Miss Anglin, the lovely music of her voice and the prodigious, the amazing energy that is hers and hers alone among the actresses of the American stage" (*New York Times*, April 8, 1921).

While preparing for *Antigone*, Anglin met a dramatist and aspiring actor named Howard Hull, whose two brothers, Henry and Shelley, and sister-in-law, Josephine, were also noted actors. Margaret Anglin married Howard Hull on May 11, 1911, in St. Patrick's Cathedral in New York City. Hull assisted his wife thereafter in the management of her company and also performed in many of the productions.

Beginning in 1913, Anglin produced a series of Shakespearean revivals, including *The Taming of the Shrew*, *Twelfth Night*, and *As You Like It*. Besides her Greek and Shakespearean roles, Anglin also appeared in many serious contemporary plays like *The Awakening of Helen Ritchie* and *The Trial of Joan of Arc* and in comedies like *Lady Windermere's Fan* and *A Woman of No Importance*.

An opponent of Actors' Equity Association, Anglin had difficulties with the union over her insistence that her husband be given a role in each of her plays. From 1928 to 1936 she was prevented from appearing in New York though she continued to tour. After returning to the New York stage in *Fresh Fields* (1936), she continued to act, both in New York and on tour, until 1943. Anglin died in a Toronto nursing home on January 7, 1948.

In her nearly fifty years on the stage, Anglin played over eighty parts. Renowned for her emotional roles, she was also highly praised for her appearances in the classics and in comedy. Her revivals of Greek drama not only added to her reputation as an actress but also to her adeptness as a stage director. Thoda Cocroft, who later became publicity manager for Anglin, wrote, "On her own shoulders she loaded the multiple responsibility of directing, staging, selecting a chorus (Greek, not musical comedy), arranging and rearranging business, choosing costumes, supervising electricians, actors, musicians, and stage hands, up to the last detail relating to the performance" (*Great Names and How They Are Made*, reprinted by Young, Vol. I, p. 36). Thus Anglin was not only a great actress but also one of the pioneers of modern directing.

Gordon Johnson, in "The Greek Productions of Margaret Anglin" (Unpublished Ph. D. dissertation, Case Western Reserve University, 1971), provides detailed information on Anglin's Greek revivals. Anglin's publicity manager, Thoda Cocroft, describes working with the actress in Cocroft's book, *Great Names and How They Are Made* (1941).

The New York Public Library Performing Arts Research Center at Lincoln Center has clippings on Anglin's career. She is included in Lewis C. Strang, *Famous Actresses of the Day in America* (1902); Forest Izard, *Heroines of the Modern Stage* (1915); William C. Young, *Famous Actors and Actresses on the American Stage*, Vol. I (1975); and *Who Was Who in the Theatre*, Vol. I (1978).

Rita M. Plotnicki

— B —

BALLARD, Lucinda (April 3, 1906–): costume and scenic designer, was born Lucinda Davis Goldsborough in New Orleans, Louisiana, to Richard Francis and Anna Girault (Larrar) Goldsborough. Her father was a lawyer, and her mother was the political cartoonist known as Doré. She attended Miss McGehee's fashionable girl's school in New Orleans, then trained as an artist in New York at the Art Students' League (1923–1925), in France at the Sorbonne (1928–1929), the Beaux Arts Academy (1928–1930), Paris, the Fontainebleu Academy (1929–1931), and in Hubért, France, with Paul Baudoin. She married William F. R. Ballard on February 6, 1930, and had one son, Robert, and one daughter, Jennifer. The marriage was dissolved in 1938. She married the lyricist Howard Dietz on July 31, 1951, and has one stepdaughter, Liza Dietz.

Ballard began her active career in the professional theatre as assistant to scenic designers, including Norman Bel Geddes, Tony Sarg, and Claude Bragdon. She was in great demand for her exceptional painting abilities. She made her Broadway debut in 1937 as costume and scenic designer for Dwight Deere Wiman's production of *As You Like It* (Ritz Theatre, October 30, 1937). The notices following the opening of *As You Like It* commended her on her excellent use of color, a facet of her design that would often receive the attention of reviewers during her career in the theatre. Ballard had an exceptional eye for color and period detail and put this talent to judicious use in the costumes she created.

During 1940, when the Ballet Theatre was formed in New York, Ballard was appointed technical director for all costumes. She designed costumes for *Les Sylphides* and *Swan Lake*; created scenery and costumes for *Giselle*, *Peter and the Wolf*, and *Quintet*; and supervised the reconstruction of the Bakst-designed ballets.

Perhaps her southern heritage enabled Ballard to capture the costume style for two of America's greatest southern playwrights, Tennessee Williams and **Lillian Hellman**. In 1945 she created memorable costumes for *The Glass Menagerie* and then also designed the costumes for the film version of the play and for the London production. She designed costumes for the Broadway premieres of Williams's *A Streetcar Named Desire* (1947), *Cat on a Hot Tin Roof* (1955), and *Orpheus Descending* (1957). In 1946 she designed the costumes for Hellman's *Another Part of the Forest*. In 1955 she designed costumes for another play set in the South, *The Wisteria Trees*, Joshua Logan's adaptation of Anton Chekhov's *The Cherry Orchard*.

Ballard was not restricted to designing for realistic plays. She designed the costumes for three of America's favorite musicals—*Annie Get Your Gun* and the revival of *Show Boat*, both in 1946, and *The Sound of Music* in New York in 1959 and in London in 1961. Lewis Nichols, writing a review of *Show Boat* in the *New York Times*, commented that "Lucinda Ballard's riotously multi-colored costumes form a brilliant background for life that could be lived nowhere else than in *Show Boat*" (January 6, 1946).

In the 1950s Ballard was perhaps the most famous and sought after of American costume designers. The roster of shows she designed in that decade include a number of almost legendary productions: *The Four Poster* (1951), *Mrs. McThing* (1952), *The Time of Your Life* (1955), *The Dark at the Top of the Stairs* (1957), and *J. B.* (1958).

In recent years Ballard has been less active in the theatre. Recently she designed another Tennessee Williams play, a new production of *The Night of the Iguana*, which was scheduled for Broadway in 1985. Unfortunately, the play did not survive its tryouts and never reached New York.

Lucinda Ballard has received many awards for her work in costume design. In 1945 she received the Donaldson Award for her costumes in *I Remember Mama*. Then in 1947 she was the first winner of the Antoinette Perry (Tony) Award for Costume for her designs in five plays: *Happy Birthday*, *Another Part of the Forest*, *Street Scene*, *John Loves Mary*, and *The Chocolate Soldier*. She was nominated for the Academy (Oscar) Award for her designs for *A Streetcar Named Desire*. Ballard received another Tony Award in 1961 for *The Gay Life* and the New York Drama Critics' Poll Award in 1962. In 1985 the United States Institute for Theatre Technology honored her for a lifetime dedicated to excellence in costume design.

Articles on Lucinda Ballard include "Helpful," *The New Yorker* (November 29, 1947); M. Zolotow, "Designing Woman," *Saturday Evening Post* (September 18, 1948); and " 'Gay Life' Costumes," *Theatre Arts* (November 1961). She is listed in *The Biographical Encyclopaedia and Who's Who of the American Theatre* (1966), *Who's Who of American Women, 1972–1973* (1971), *Costume Design in the Movies* (1974), *Who's Who in the World, 1976–1977* (1976), *Notable Names in the American Theatre* (1976), *Who's*

Who in America, 1978–1979, Vol. I (1978), and *The Oxford Companion to American Theatre* (1984).

Bobbi Owen

BANCROFT, Anne (September 17, 1931–): prominent contemporary actress, was born Annemarie Italiano, one of three daughters of Michael and Mildred (Di Napoli) Italiano, of the Bronx, New York. Though neither of her parents was involved in the theatre, her mother was supportive of her ambition to become an actress. Toward this end, Anne Bancroft studied drama while attending Christopher Columbus High School (1943–1947). After briefly considering a career as a laboratory technician, she continued her studies at the American Academy of Dramatic Arts, New York, with tuition money provided by her mother.

She began to get small parts in television, her first being a Studio One production of Ivan Turgenev's *The Torrents of Spring*. Other early television assignments included such programs as *Danger* and *Suspense*, as well as a continuing part on the Gertrude Berg series, *The Goldbergs*. Her television appearances led to a Twentieth Century-Fox screen test and the offer of a contract.

Her early Hollywood years (1952–1958) cannot be considered a resounding success, either personally or professionally. After selecting the name "Anne Bancroft" from a studio-approved list, she was given the featured role of Richard Widmark's girlfriend in *Don't Bother to Knock* (1952). Audience attention, however, was focused on Widmark's co-star, Marilyn Monroe. Other roles in such films as *Tonight We Sing, Demetrius and the Gladiator*, and *Gorilla at Large* did little to enhance her career. The one exception to the general mediocrity of her roles was *The Last Frontier* (1956), a western in which she played a cavalry colonel's wife.

In 1954 Bancroft had married Martin A. May, a businessman. The marriage ended in 1958. At about the same time Bancroft returned to New York, determined to pursue her studies. At this point she learned of William Gibson's play *Two for the Seesaw* (1958), and by her own admission, she won the part not so much because of her acting ability but because she was able to make herself over into the physical embodiment of the play's heroine, Gittel Mosca. Producer Fred Coe, remembering Bancroft from her previous television works, convinced Gibson and director Arthur Penn that she was the right choice for the part.

For a woman with only a handful of television appearances and several forgettable films to her credit, and with veteran actor Henry Fonda as her co-star, Bancroft found early rehearsals an unnerving experience. In spite of her initial anxiety, Bancroft, with the help of a sympathetic director, developed a memorable character, Gittel, the part-time ballet dancer/part-time beatnik in search of self-respect. The play opened in New York on January 16, 1958. Bancroft was, in the words of the critic of the *New York World-Telegram and Sun*, "a deliriously captivating comic." Other critics agreed, and by the end of that season Bancroft was the winner of a Theatre World Award, the Drama Critics'

Poll Award, and an Antoinette Perry (Tony) Award. (Hollywood, using the same questionable logic that gave Audrey Hepburn *My Fair Lady* and Rosalind Russell *Gypsy*, turned down both Fonda and Bancroft for the film version of *Two for the Seesaw*, signing instead Robert Mitchum and Shirley MacLaine. The film was released in 1962, the season in which Anne Bancroft won an Academy Award for *The Miracle Worker*.)

The next project on which the Gibson-Penn-Coe partnership collaborated was *The Miracle Worker* (1959), a play based on Annie Sullivan's struggle to teach the young Helen Keller. The three men had no doubt that the part of Sullivan, one of the most physically taxing roles of the contemporary theatre, was ideal for Bancroft. To prepare herself for this demanding task, Anne Bancroft spent three weeks studying blind and disturbed children in New York City's Institute of Physical Medicine and Rehabilitation, and she visited the Vacation Camp for the Blind to practice the use of the manual alphabet. In addition, she spent time with her eyelids taped down and wore dark glasses in an effort to understand better just what it would be like to be blind. These efforts paid off handsomely. Both Bancroft and Patty Duke, as Helen Keller, were highly praised in virtually every review. For her portrayal of Annie Sullivan, Anne Bancroft won her second Tony Award and a New York Drama Critics Award.

This time the Gibson-Penn-Coe team was determined that Bancroft would not be cheated out of the chance to re-create her role on film. They produced the film version themselves, retaining Bancroft and Patty Duke. Made in 1962 on a small budget, *The Miracle Worker* was resoundingly acclaimed. In the spring of 1963, Bancroft and Duke won the best actress and best supporting actress Academy (Oscar) awards, respectively. For Anne Bancroft, the occasion was a special triumph, as she had faced strong competition in the nominations of such distinguished luminaries as Bette Davis and **Katharine Hepburn**.

With the success of *The Miracle Worker*, Bancroft seemed to be set for a major film career. Some of her films, like *Seven Women* (1965), *Young Winston* (1972), *Lipstick* (1976), and *The Hindenburg* (1976), are easily forgotten. However, she has had some successes. Her sharply etched portraits of the insecure wife in *The Pumpkin Eater* (Oscar nomination and Cannes Film Festival best actress award, 1964), the predatory matron of *The Graduate* (Oscar nomination, 1967), the aging prima ballerina of *The Turning Point* (Oscar nomination, 1977), and the prioress in *Agnes of God* (Oscar nomination, 1985) have made up for lesser roles.

During this same period in her career, Anne Bancroft also has been active in the theatre. At the time of her Oscar win for *The Miracle Worker*, she was appearing in a New York production of Bertolt Brecht's *Mother Courage and Her Children* (1963). Though the production itself was well received, the reviews for Bancroft were mixed.

Two years later (1965), she played opposite Jason Robards, Jr., in John Whiting's *The Devils*, an adaptation of Aldous Huxley's study of seventeenth-century religious hysteria in France titled *The Devils of Loudun*. The consensus of the critics was that, although her portrayal of the neurotic, sexually obsessed Sister Jeanne of the Angels was technically superb, the play itself failed to provide enough depth to make the hysteria believable.

Bancroft had better luck in the 1967 Lincoln Center revival of **Lillian Hellman**'s *The Little Foxes*. She wisely chose not to model the role on either **Tallulah Bankhead**, originator of the role of Regina, or Bette Davis, star of the 1941 film. The *New York Times* critic found her Regina Giddens possessed of "iron instead of bone in her skeleton, a huskily musical voice that hums a dance of death, and a smile so icy that you almost expect it to melt leaves" (October 27, 1967).

Bancroft did not neglect television during these years. In addition to guest-starring on several musical variety programs and the drama *Jesus of Nazareth*, she starred in her own special, *Annie: The Woman in the Life of Man* (1970). The only woman on the show, Bancroft, aided by a large roster of male guests, portrayed a gallery of the different women that every man finds in his life at some point. Done in a series of sketches—some musical, some comic, some dramatic—her performance can only be described as a tour de force. Deservedly, she won television's Emmy award for that year as best actress in a musical special.

In the 1970s, in addition to *The Turning Point*, she made a cameo appearance in *Silent Movie* (1976), a creation of Mel Brooks, whom she had married in 1964 and by whom she had a son, Maximilian. In *Silent Movie*, her natural flair for comedy, seen on stage in *Two for the Seesaw* (1958) and on her television special, was once again demonstrated. In the late 1970s she was reunited with William Gibson, with whom she had last worked in the poorly received play *Cry of Players* (1968). This time the vehicle was titled *Golda* (1977), based on the life of Golda Meir. Though the play had its weak spots, critics were delighted with Bancroft's performance. The *New York Times* reported that "Miss Bancroft's real accomplishment is her re-creation not of Mrs. Meir's floppy dresses but of her mind and spirit" (November 15, 1977).

In 1980 Bancroft tried her hand at directing, but the film, *Fatso*, was roundly panned by critics and largely ignored by audiences. She has since confined her professional activity primarily to screen work, appearing in such films as *The Elephant Man* (1980); Mel Brooks's ill-advised remake of Ernst Lubitsch's *To Be or Not to Be* (1983), in which she played a role originated by Carole Lombard; the charming, offbeat, little-seen *Garbo Talks* (1984); and the screen adaptation of *Agnes of God* (1985).

Bancroft's career to date has been a patchwork of brilliant performances on both stage and screen coupled with a number of mediocre ones. Yet she has persevered in her chosen profession, and it seems clear that a satisfying number of her characterizations have become definitive ones.

Reviews of *The Miracle Worker* may be found in *Cue* (October 17, 1959), the *New York Herald Tribune* (November 8, 1959), the *New York Times Magazine* (February 9, 1958), *Theater* (December 1959), the *Saturday Review* (November 7, 1959), and the

New York Times (December 20, 1959). See also Lewis Funke, *Actors Talk about Acting*. Further information about Anne Bancroft may be found in *Current Biography, 1960* (1960–1961); *International Motion Picture Almanac* (1960); *Notable Names in the American Theatre* (1976); *Illustrated Encyclopedia of the World's Great Movie Stars* (1979); *Who's Who in the Theatre* (1981); *The Oxford Companion to American Theatre* (1984); and *Who's Who of American Women, 1985–1986* (1986).

William Lindesmith

BANKHEAD, Tallulah Brockman (January 31?, 1902–December 12, 1968): actress, most famous for her role as Regina Giddens in **Lillian Hellman's** *The Little Foxes*, was born in Huntsville, Alabama, into one of the most famous and prestigious political families in the South. Her paternal grandfather, who had been an officer in the Confederate army and a United States senator, was the founder of a dynasty of politicians. Her uncle was also a senator from Alabama, and her father, William Brockman Bankhead, was for a long time in the House of Representatives and served as Speaker of that body from 1936 to 1940. Her mother, Adelaide Eugenia (Sledge) Bankhead, died when Tallulah was only a few weeks old. There was one older child, a sister, also named Eugenia.

The two girls were reared by grandparents, aunts, and their father. It was their father, William Brockman Bankhead, who was adored by both of them and for whose affection they fought until his death. The rivalry between the siblings extended into other areas as well. Eugenia was always beautiful, popular, and an excellent student while her younger sister was, as a child, overweight and an indifferent scholar. Perhaps to compensate for a sense of inferiority, Tallulah Bankhead early became a performer, showing off before family and friends. Her father, always interested in acting, encouraged her in her youthful displays and took the girls to the theatre when they were still very young. The Bankheads were Episcopalians, but the two girls were educated in various Roman Catholic schools. They grew up in Jasper, Alabama, where the family home was located, but spent much time in Montgomery, Alabama, and in Washington, D.C., after their father's election to Congress.

In 1917 Tallulah Bankhead entered a photograph of herself, dressed in such a way as to appear considerably older than her fifteen years, in a contest sponsored by *Picture Play Magazine*. She won first prize: a trip to New York and a role in a film. It is perhaps a tribute to her early dramatic abilities, or at least to her charm, that she was able to convince her father and other family members to let her accept. Accompanied by her Aunt Louise, she left her southern home, hoping to become an actress. In New York, they checked into the Algonquin Hotel, already established as *the* theatrical hotel, and she was soon involved in the filming of *The Wishful Girl* in a role that had been part of the contest prize. However inauspicious that beginning in show business, her father soon used his influence with the Shubert organization to get her a small part in a play called *Squab Farm* (1918). The same year she appeared in another movie in New York, still the center of the film industry in those early years.

Her first speaking part on stage was in *39 East* (1919), in which she played opposite the aspiring young southern actor, Sidney Blackmer. By this time, her Aunt Louise had returned to Alabama, and Bankhead was living alone at the Algonquin. She had been befriended, however, by an established actress, Estelle Winwood, with whom she was to be closely associated for the rest of her life. Winwood introduced her to important theatrical figures of the period, including John and **Ethel Barrymore** and the members of the Round Table at the Algonquin. Alexander Woollcott, at that time drama critic of the *New York Times*, and Frank Crowninshield, editor of *Vanity Fair*, became her regular escorts to plays and other functions and championed her career.

A series of unmemorable plays followed—*Footloose* (1920), *Nice People* (1921), and *The Exciters* (1922), among others. Her big break came when Charles Cochran, a British producer, saw her perform and arranged for her to meet Sir Gerald du Maurier in London. In 1923 she sailed for England, where she was to remain for eight years and achieve fame and popularity. In the du Maurier play *The Dancers*, she became an overnight sensation. Contemporary accounts describe the hordes of her followers—mostly young women, many of them working class—who filled the theatre to capacity to see her in that production and those that followed. With her small (five feet three inches) body, her deep voice strongly tinged with the accent of her southern origin, her large, rather sad-looking eyes, her risqué demeanor, and her striking beauty, she made a lasting impression and became a celebrity who was adored and emulated.

The du Maurier work was followed by *Conchita*, a melodrama in which she played a Cuban dancer; *This Marriage*, a comedy in which she starred with Herbert Marshall and Cathleen Nesbitt, who became a close friend; and *The Creaking Chair*, a mystery in which she played opposite C. Aubrey Smith. Then as later, Bankhead aspired to be a great actress, but at every period of her career she seemed to become caught up in a series of generally mediocre plays. Her popularity, the adoration she inspired in the young women of London in the 1920s and in generations of theatregoers in the decades to follow, was for the most part inspired by her persona, her bearing, and her presence, rather than the performance she was giving, however strong its merits might be. Already, in those early London days, her name was enough to underwrite a production, and this fact sometimes resulted in a play unworthy of her abilities being rushed into production to capitalize on what producers may have imagined to be a passing fancy in the audiences.

During those eight years in London, Bankhead acted in sixteen plays. Of these, perhaps the most significant were Noel Coward's *Fallen Angels* (1925), Michael Arlen's *The Green Hat* (1925), and Sidney Howard's *They Knew What They Wanted* (1926). Presumably by decision of Somerset Maugham himself, she was denied the opportunity to play Sadie Thompson in the original production of *Rain*—a disappointment that remained with her for a long time even though she played the role when *Rain* opened in New York a few years later.

Although Bankhead was making very good money in London, she decided to return to the United States, apparently drawn back by the lure of big money in the movie industry. From that point until her death, she was to be affluent, but she continually played the impoverished artist with her friends. Back in New York, she settled into the Hotel Elysée and began to make undistinguished motion pictures for Paramount, a studio determined to capitalize on her London fame and make her into a new Greta Garbo or Marlene Dietrich (the most popular female screen stars of the day). These early movies, some made in Hollywood, were typical of most of her screen efforts. She was, perhaps because of the somewhat extravagant and stylized form of her acting, much better suited for the stage.

None of these early films was successful. Paramount soon bought out her contract, and she returned to Broadway in *Forsaking All Others* (1933), a comedy whose cast included Ilka Chase and Henry Fonda. It was, unfortunately, a failure, and Bankhead, who had produced it herself, lost a substantial amount of money. The next year she played the role of Judith Traherne in *Dark Victory*, a character later played with considerable success in the movies by Bette Davis. In 1935 Bankhead finally got the chance to play Sadie Thompson in *Rain*, the role that had been denied her in London. The reviews were almost universally good, but the play lasted only a few weeks since theatregoers apparently looked upon it as a mere revival. This was followed by *Something Gay* (1935), which also had a brief run, and *Reflected Glory* (1936), which went on tour after a short stay in New York.

In the summer of 1937 in Connecticut she met John Emery, an actor, and they were married on August 31. The same year they performed together in *Antony and Cleopatra*, with Bankhead as the female lead, Emery as Octavius. The play represented an attempt on her part to fulfill a longtime desire—to create a serious role and be accepted as an actress of stature. Unfortunately, the venture was a disaster, the reviews were devastating, and the play closed after only five performances.

The following year she starred in a successful revival of Somerset Maugham's *The Circle* and toured with her husband in **Zoë Akins's** *I Am Different*. But it was in 1939 that she achieved what was surely her greatest triumph on Broadway when she played Regina Giddens in **Lillian Hellman**'s *The Little Foxes*. For the first time in her twenty-year-old career, she had a serious opportunity to demonstrate that her acting ability involved more than mere stage presence, personality, and that inescapably fascinating voice. As Regina she was controlled, subdued, effective. The critics were properly appreciative, and rave followed rave for her portrayal of one of the most intriguing women in the history of American drama. The play ran for more than four hundred performances in New York, and she received the New York Critics Circle best actress award.

While Bankhead was involved in preparations to take *The Little Foxes* on its long tour, her beloved father, still Speaker of the House of Representatives at the time, died. The loss was a devastating one for her and might have been even more so had she not by then formed a close attachment with **Eugenia Rawls**, who had taken over the role of Alexandra Giddens during the Broadway run. Rawls became for Bankhead the daughter she would never have. Bankhead later was godmother for Rawls's son, and the relationship between her and the younger actress and her family was one of the sustaining elements for the remainder of her turbulent life.

During the war years (1941–1945), Bankhead alternated stage appearances with USO tours to army camps and hospitals. In addition, she actively campaigned for fellow Democrat Franklin Delano Roosevelt. After touring in Arthur Wing Pinero's *The Second Mrs. Tanqueray*, Bankhead appeared on Broadway in Clifford Odets's *Clash by Night*, which received generally bad reviews. In 1942 Bankhead played the second major role of her stage career, the part of Sabina in Thornton Wilder's *The Skin of Our Teeth* (1942). It was a triumphant success for which she won her second Critics Circle actress of the year award. The play, which also starred Frederic March, **Florence Eldridge**, Florence Reed, Montgomery Clift, and E. G. Marshall, was acclaimed by critics and was also a popular success. Bankhead, however, quarreled with the director, Elia Kazan, and with the producer, and insisted on leaving when her contract expired.

It was during this period that she bought a house in Bedford Village, New York, which she christened "Windows" and filled with her entourage: several women who worked for her and assisted her in various ways; old friends such as Estelle Winwood, with whom she was still very close; and the latest young man to whom she had attached herself. Her marriage had ended in divorce (June 13, 1941). Bankhead was never without a love interest for very long.

She began to appear on radio, where her distinctive voice was a strong asset. In the late 1940s and early 1950s she had her own program, *The Big Show*, a memorable variety format in which Bankhead played hostess to an astonishing cast of major stars from all entertainment fields. It was one of radio's last attempts to stop the encroachment of the new and rapidly growing medium of television. Soon people all over the country knew that husky baritone voice, with its heavy southern accent that all the years in London and New York had done nothing to dilute.

In 1944 Bankhead returned to Hollywood for the best film of her career, Alfred Hitchcock's *Lifeboat*, for which she was awarded the New York Film Critics' best actress award. The movie remains one of the best available ways for new generations of audiences to see a vintage performance by a legendary figure of American theatrical history. The role she plays is a flamboyant one, similar to her own persona in real life, but she displays excellent control and delivers a performance, under Hitchcock's careful guidance, that is credible and moving.

After another film, Ernst Lubitsch's *Royal Scandal* (1945), a comedy in which she gave a broad portrayal of Catherine the Great, Bankhead returned to Broadway in Philip Barry's *Foolish Notion* (1945). The play was generally disliked by the critics, but her performance, which was highly praised, caused it to run for more than one hundred performances and then to go on tour. Unquestionably, at this period her name was still a strong attraction to audiences. The following year she appeared in a role she relished, Amanda Prynne, in a touring production of Noel Coward's *Private Lives*, which she brought to Broadway in 1948 for a seven-month run. She starred in 1947 as the queen in Jean Cocteau's *The Eagle Has Two Heads*, in which she delivered an astonishing seventeen-minute soliloquy as her opening lines.

During the next six years, she did no stage plays, working instead on radio and traveling the lecture circuit, although the search for a good script continued. New York audiences saw her again in 1954 in *Dear Charles*, which ran for 150 performances. Critics praised her portrayal of the female lead but regretted that she had not made her return in a play more worthy of her talent. Appropriately, Bankhead was finally given the opportunity to play Blanche DuBois in a 1956 revival of *A Streetcar Named Desire*. Tennessee Williams once said that he had written the play with her in mind, imagining her speaking each of Blanche's lines as he wrote them. Despite the playwright's wishes, however, it was Jessica Tandy who was cast in the original production. Bankhead's appearance as Blanche in the revival proved to be a bittersweet experience. The production, which opened in Palm Beach, Florida, before moving to New York, received the approbation of many of the critics, who commended Bankhead for being able to subdue the forcefulness of her own personality in order to create convincingly a delicate and fragile character, but some of her fans, looking only for a demonstration of Tallulah mannerisms, were evidently disappointed.

Streetcar was to be the last of her major performances on the stage despite the fact that she continued for the remaining twelve years of her life to seek an appropriate role. What followed were a series of mediocre plays, not matched to her abilities. *Eugenia* (1957), an adaptation of Henry James's novel *The Europeans*, ran for only twelve performances, and *Crazy October* (1958), a comedy by James Leo Herlihy, closed out of town. *Midgie Purvis*, a 1961 comedy by **Mary Chase,** which garnered for Bankhead a nomination for the Antoinette Perry (Tony) Award, ran for only twenty-one performances. Her last Broadway vehicle was, sadly and ironically, Tennessee Williams's *The Milk Train Doesn't Stop Here Anymore* (1964). The play, the story of an aging and egocentric actress who had a series of lovers, had apparently been written about Bankhead. That Bankhead failed to recognize the parallels between Flora Goforth and herself is difficult to believe, and yet she wanted the part in this revival of the play, which had been first produced at the Festival of Two Worlds, Spoleto, Italy, in 1962, and in New York in 1963. The *Milk Train* production was a disaster, partly because Tab Hunter played the male lead, but also, surely, because the actress gave a shaky performance. The play closed after only five nights.

By 1964 Bankhead had become dependent on alcohol and drugs, and the remainder of her life was disordered and often unhappy. Her appearances on television, including the Dragon Lady on the *Batman* series, were parodies of the style that had made her famous through the years. Since her early days on stage, her public use of obscenity and some of her behavior had created an aura of scandal about her, and now those actions that some people found offensive became more bizarre, more frequent, and occasionally more public. There were always young men around her—"caddies," she called them—to escort her.

Drunk or sober, however, Bankhead always expected to be treated as a lady in the old southern tradition, and the young men, remunerated though they might be, paid court to her in a way that her ego obviously needed. Remarkably, she was able to meet her professional obligations despite her condition during the last years. The list of her appearances and activities even during the worst times is truly astonishing. Early in her career she had adopted as a motto, "Press on!"; and the volume, range, and variety of her performances on stage, screen, radio, and television attest to the fact that she paid more than lip service to that imperative.

She made one final film, *Die, Die, My Darling*, in 1965; it was a predictable horror film, calculated to capitalize on the popularity of other movies of that genre starring aging and famous actresses. Her performance as a demented religious fanatic and would-be murderess, bent on avenging the death of her son, was in many ways moving and convincing. Her television engagements in the last years included *What's My Line?*, *The Andy Williams Show*, *The Merv Griffin Show*, and *The Smothers Brothers Comdey Hour*. On May 14, 1968, she made her last public appearance on *The Tonight Show*.

Near the end of 1968, she contracted Asian flu, and from that combined with the emphysema that she had had for some time, she developed pneumonia. She died on December 12 at St. Luke's Hospital, two months short of her sixty-seventh birthday.

Tallulah Bankhead was one of that group of celebrities, which includes such diverse types as Garbo, Valentino, Marilyn, and Elvis, who achieved such mythic heights of fame and recognition that they came to be referred to and known by only one name. It is difficult to judge her now: the legend always obscures the reality with such figures. Despite her total lack of formal training in her field, she did master, through instinct or practice or perhaps a combination of the two, many of the elements of that craft, a fact demonstrated by her magnificent creation of the roles of Regina Giddens in *The Little Foxes*, Sabina in *The Skin of Our Teeth*, and, despite the debacle which that production turned out to be, Blanche in *A Streetcar Named Desire*. She possessed also, to a remarkable degree given the excesses of her lifestyle, a discipline in her way of approaching a role and meeting the demanding schedules of rehearsals and performances, even in her declining years when, though ailing and weak, she still yearned to fulfill herself in her chosen profession.

More information about Tallulah Bankhead may be obtained by consulting her auto-biography, *Tallulah* (1952), written with Richard Maney. *Tallulah, Darling* (1980), by Denis Brian, is a superficial biography. Brendan Gill's *Tallulah* (1972), which originally appeared as a profile in *The New Yorker*, is brief but objective and includes a list of all her stage, film, and television appearances. A detailed but critical biography is Lee Israel's *Miss Tallulah Bankhead* (1972). *Tallulah: Darling of the Gods* (1973), by Kieran Tunney, is a sentimental memoir. Her obituary was published in the *New York Times* (December 13, 1968). The Tallulah Brockman Bankhead Collection in the Alabama Department of Archives and History (Maps and Manuscripts Division) contains correspondence and press clippings. There are photographs, letters, and scripts in the Walter Hampden-Edwin Booth Theatre Collection and Library in New York City. Bankhead is listed in *Current Biography, 1953* (1954); *The Biographical Encyclopaedia and Who's Who of the American Theatre* (1966); *Who's Who in the Theatre* (1967); William C. Young, *Famous Actors and Actresses on the American Stage*, Vol. I (1975); *Who Was Who in the Theatre*, Vol. I (1978); *Notable American Women*, Vol. IV; *The Modern Period* (1980); *The Oxford Companion to the Theatre* (1983); and *The Oxford Companion to American Theatre* (1984).

W. Kenneth Holditch

BARNES, Djuna (June 12, 1892–June 18, 1982): poet, novelist, actress, playwright, theatre reviewer, was an experimental playwright of the 1920s associated with the Provincetown Players. Her major work has been compared to that of James Joyce in its use of imagistic language, literary allusions, and unconventional dramatic forms and styles.

Djuna Barnes was the eldest daughter of a resolutely individualistic father, Wald Barnes, and his wife, Elizabeth (Chappell) Barnes. The matriarch of the family was Barnes's grandmother, Zadel Barnes, a well-educated suffragist and teacher. Art, music, literature, and writing were part of the household's daily routine. Wald Barnes was a versatile amateur artist who painted, played several musical instruments, and composed operas. The young Djuna played the banjo, violin, and French horn and also acted and wrote plays for her family. From her birthplace in Cornwall-on-the-Hudson, New York, she went to New York City to study at the Pratt Institute and the Art Students' League. She was torn between painting and writing as career choices.

During her early days in New York, Barnes participated in the bohemian life of Greenwich Village, and in 1920 she became a part of the lively American expatriate scene in Paris. During these years in New York and Paris, she was described by Louis Kannenstine as an "active, sometimes dazzling, always imposing figure in literary and social circles" (Kannenstine, p. 11).

Barnes began her theatrical involvement as an actress in minor roles for the Washington Square Players and the Provincetown Playhouse, but a desire for privacy eventually led her away from performance and into playwriting. From 1919 to 1920 Barnes's one-act play *Three from the Earth* appeared at the Provincetown on a double bill with Eugene O'Neill's *The Dreamy Kid*. During the same season, Provincetown also staged Barnes's *Kurzy of the Sea* and *An Irish Triangle*. In addition, Smith College produced her play *The Dove* in 1926.

During this early period, Barnes, under the pseudonym Lydia Steptoe, also wrote some "Ten-Minute Plays," intended only for reading. Such playlets as *Little Drops of Rain*, *Water-Ice*, *Two Ladies Take Tea*, *The Beauty*, and *Five Thousand Miles* appeared in various magazines but have never been collected or republished. Other one-act plays were published (but never produced) under

Barnes's name: *To the Dogs*, *She Tells Her Daughter*, and *A Passion Play*. Barnes also began two full-length plays during the twenties but eventually abandoned them. Not until 1958 would a three-act drama appear, her densely imagistic and influential *The Antiphon*, produced in 1961 at the Royal Dramatic Theatre, Stockholm, translated by Dag Hammarskjold and Karl Ragnar Gierow. Except for a reading by the Poet's Theatre of Cambridge, Massachusetts, in 1958, initiated by the playwright's admirer Edwin Muir, the play has never been staged in English. Critics, however, most often referred to *The Antiphon* and her novel *Nightwood*, written in 1936, as illustrations of Barnes's genius.

A member of the American Academy of Arts and Letters, Barnes is often classified as a minor experimental writer related to the American expatriates in Paris during the 1920s. Critical opinion of her work has been divided. Her champions have most often been poets or novelists appreciative of her inventive language, her imaginative use of great literary sources, and her experimentation with style and form. Edwin Muir has been the most outspoken champion of Barnes's work, calling *The Antiphon* "one of the greatest things . . . written in our time" (Kinsman and Tennenhouse, p. 56) and citing her use of language as superior to that of James Joyce in richness and vividness of imagery. Contrary to most evaluations, which consider *Nightwood* Barnes's masterpiece, it is Kannenstine's belief that *The Antiphon* is "Djuna Barnes' most compact and definitive work" (Kannenstine, pp. 152–160).

In addition to writing plays, Barnes also served as a theatre reviewer, primarily for the *New York Morning Telegraph* in 1916–1917 and for *Theatre Guild Magazine* from 1929 to 1931. Her illustrated monthly column in the *Theatre Guild Magazine* was first called "Playgoers' Almanack" and was retitled in 1931, "The Wanton Playgoer." Her published writing also includes interviews with such theatre artists as **Rachel Crothers**, Jo Mielziner, Mordecai Gorelik, **Alla Nazimova**, and **Eva Le Gallienne**.

Between 1911 and 1936 Barnes published numerous nontheatrical works: poetry, short stories, novels, magazine articles, and essays, many illustrated with her own drawings. Major publications were *The Book of Repulsive Women* (1915, poems and drawings); *A Book* (1923, poems, short stories, three one-act plays, and drawings); *Ryder* (1928, novel); *Ladies Almanack* (1928, novel); *A Night among the Horses* (1929, a reissue of *A Book* with three additional stories); and *Nightwood* (1936). After *Nightwood*, nothing was published by Barnes until 1958 when *The Antiphon* appeared. Since then, growing interest in the author has resulted in republication of various pieces and the slightly revised *The Antiphon* for inclusion in her *Selected Works*.

Barnes's literary silence between 1936 and 1958 reflected her reclusive lifestyle during that period. Despite her self-described nature in early years as the "life of the party," by 1929 she had begun to withdraw from society. In reply to a journal editor accumulating autobiographical statements from contributors, she wrote, "I am sorry, but the list of questions does not interest me to answer. Nor have I that respect for the public" (Scott, p. 143). Barnes rarely granted interviews, seeming to wish, like a character from her one-act play *The Dove*, that people could escape "biography."

Barnes's influence on modern experimental novelists is indisputable. John Hawkes and Anais Nin have both stated their indebtedness while critics have detected her influence in the writings of William Faulkner, Lawrence Durrell, Isak Dinesen, and Truman Capote. Although her effect on other playwrights is less direct, her unique exploration of character relationships and her emphasis on sound and rhythm are qualities that drama has increasingly embodied. Moreover, since women are central characters in all of Barnes's writings, there is a revival of interest, influenced largely by feminists, in her plays.

Douglas Messerli, *Djuna Barnes: A Bibliography* (1975), provides a compilation of works by and about Barnes. *Djuna Barnes Interviews*, edited by Alyce Barry (1985), contains essays and interview profiles written between 1914 and 1931 and originally published in the *New York Press*, the *New York Morning Telegraph Magazine*, and *The Theatre Guild Magazine*; the collection also contains 23 drawings by Barnes. References in this article are from Lionel Abel, "Bad by North and South," *Partisan Review* (Summer 1958); Djuna Barnes, *A Book* (1923); Djuna Barnes, "A Passion Play," *Others* (February 1918); Djuna Barnes, *Selected Works of Djuna Barnes: Spillway, The Antiphon, Nightwood* (1962); Ruby Cohn, *Dialogue in American Drama* (1971); Richard Eberhardt, "Outer and Inner Verse Drama," *Virginia Quarterly Review* (Autumn 1958); Melvin Friedman, *Stream of Consciousness: A Study in Literary Method* (1955); Louis F. Kannenstine, *The Art of Djuna Barnes: Duality and Damnation* (1977); Clare D. Kinsman and Mary Ann Tennenhouse, eds., *Contemporary Authors* (1974); Howard Nemerov, "A Response to *The Antiphon*," *Northwest Review* (Summer 1958); Henry Raymont, "From the Avant-Garde of the Thirties, Djuna Barnes," *New York Times* (May 24, 1971); and James B. Scott, *Djuna Barnes* (1976). The Djuna Barnes Papers are at the McKeldin Library at the University of Maryland, College Park, Maryland. Barnes's obituary appeared in the *New York Times* (June 20, 1982). Barnes is listed in *American Women Writers* (1979) and *Contemporary Dramatists* (1982).

Erlene Hendrix

BARRANGER, Milly Hilliard Slater (February 12, 1937–): theatre producer, administrator, educator, was born in Birmingham, Alabama. Her mother, Mildred Hilliard, was a dance instructor, and her father, C. C. Slater, was an engineer. After they divorced in 1941, Milly Slater moved with her maternal grandparents to Dayton, a small rural town in southern Alabama, and attended elementary and high schools in nearby Thomaston. Upon graduation, she enrolled in the women's college, Alabama College (now called the University of Montevallo), majored in English, and earned a Bachelor of Arts degree in 1958. A year later she obtained a master's degree in English from Tulane University, where she studied with noted English professors Irving Ribner and Richard H. Fogle. She also enrolled in a seminar in theatre theory and criticism with the founding editor of the *Tulane Drama Review*, Robert W. Corrigan, who invited her to join the journal's staff. Subsequently, Milly Slater continued her graduate studies for the Ph.D. degree in theatre at Tulane in the Department of Theatre and Speech, then chaired by Monroe Lippman, whose dynamic leadership gave the department a national reputation. From 1961 to 1985 she was married to Garic K. Barranger, an attorney, in Covington, Louisiana. They had one daughter, Heather, born in 1966.

After receiving her Ph.D. degree in 1964, Barranger was a Special Lecturer in English at Louisiana State University in New Orleans (now the University of New Orleans) until 1969, when she joined the theatre faculty at Tulane as an assistant professor. Two years later she was appointed chairperson of the department and continued in that position until 1982. During this time she embarked on a new phase of theatre activity by founding and serving as producer for Tulane Center Stage, a professional summer repertory company designed to fill the vacuum created by the demise of the New Orleans Repertory Theatre in 1971. The company's repertory ranged from classics such as *A Midsummer Night's Dream* and *The Rivals* to works by Noel Coward and Tom Stoppard. Barranger also became active in the American Theatre Association and was its national president in 1978–1979. As a faculty member at Tulane, she also published books and a number of papers in dramatic criticism, especially on the works of Henrik Ibsen.

In addition to her position at Tulane, Barranger has held visiting professorships at the University of Tulsa, Yale University School of Drama (scholar-in-residence), and the University of Tennessee, Knoxville, where she held the title of Visiting Lindsay Young Professor in Humanities.

In July 1982 Barranger became a professor and also the chair of the Department of Dramatic Art at the University of North Carolina, Chapel Hill. She is simultaneously the executive producer of PlayMakers Repertory Company, a professional Equity theatre on the campus, and a constituent member of the League of Resident Theatres (LORT). Barranger is the first woman chair of the department. Professor Frederick Koch, who founded this department in 1936, also established the Carolina Playmakers, and assisted such people as playwrights Paul Green and **Betty Smith**. The professional theatre evolved out of the Carolina Playmaker tradition in 1976 and is now part of the national network of regional theatres. Under Barranger's leadership PlayMakers Repertory Company continues the tradition of nurturing new plays as well as producing classical and modern plays.

Barranger's honors include membership in the American Theatre Association College of Fellows (1984) and the National Theatre Conference (1982). She has received the President's Award for outstanding achievement in the performing arts from the University of Montevallo (1979); the Southwest Theatre Conference Award for professional achievement (1978); and the New Orleans Bicentennial Award for achievement in the arts (1976).

Like other women whose theatre careers have developed in educational settings, such as **Hallie Flanagan**, **Vera Mowry Roberts**, and **Patricia McIlrath**, Barranger's career bridges academic administration and theatrical management. She has chaired major theatre programs for over fifteen years and now heads one of a handful of LORT theatre companies located on the campus of a major public university. She rose to leadership in professional organizations (the American Theatre Association and the National Theatre Conference), serving as president of both associations, and continues to publish articles and books on drama and theatre history.

Barranger is the author of four textbooks: *Understanding Plays* (1990), *Theatre: Past and Present* (1984) and *Theatre: A Way of Seeing* (1980; new revised edition, 1986). With Daniel Dodson she co-edited *Generations: An Introduction to Drama* (1971). She has published articles and reviews on modern and Renaissance drama and theatre in *Modern Drama*, *Comparative Drama*, *The Quarterly Journal of Speech*, *The Educational Theatre Journal*, *The Explicator*, *The Southern Speech Communication Journal*, *Theatre Journal*, *The Southern Quarterly*, and *Scandinavian Studies*. Barranger is listed in *The Biographical Encyclopaedia and Who's Who of the American Theatre* (1966), *The World Who's Who of Women* (1973), *Notable Names in the American Theatre* (1976), *Who's Who of American Women, 1977–1978* (1977), *Contemporary Authors* (1978), *Directory of International Scholars* (1980), *Who's Who in the Theatre* (1981), *Directory of American Scholars* (1982), *Directory of International Biography* (1982), and *The Writer's Directory 1984–1986* (1983).

Gresdna A. Doty

BARRYMORE, Ethel (August 16, 1879–June 17, 1959): actress, most famous as Miss Moffat in *The Corn Is Green*, was the daughter of Maurice and Georgiana Drew Barrymore. Her grandmother was that formidable woman of the theatre, **Louisa Lane Drew**, known professionally as Mrs. John Drew. The Lane family can be traced back in English theatrical history to 1752 when they performed as a family of strolling players. Louisa Lane acted professionally in England as a child prodigy. Then in 1827, at the age of seven, she came with her recently widowed mother and an English stock company to America. Her mother married a Philadelphia stage manager, John Kinlock, who turned his stepdaughter into a profitable family asset. As an adult, Louisa Lane Drew developed into an outstanding actress and also successfully managed the Arch Street Theatre in Philadelphia for over thirty years. Her husband, John Drew, Sr., was a comedian, and two of their children, John Drew, Jr., and Georgiana Drew, became actors. Georgiana, known as Georgie, an excellent comedienne, fell in love with a handsome young English actor whose stage name was Maurice Barrymore. He had been born Herbert Blythe in India and was educated at Harrow and Oxford in England before coming to America in 1874. Maurice Barrymore and Georgie Drew were married on New Year's Eve 1876. All three of their children— Lionel, Ethel, and John—became famous actors.

Since their parents were frequently on tour, the three Barrymore children lived with their grandmother in Philadelphia. As a child Ethel Barrymore was placed in the Convent of Notre Dame in Philadelphia, the school that her mother had attended. There she developed a passionate desire to become a concert pianist, sometimes practicing as much as five hours a day. In 1892 Georgie Barrymore's health failed; and the doctors, diagnosing a serious case of tuberculosis, advised her to go to California where the air was drier. Ethel was taken out of school to accompany her mother. The mother and daughter had been only a short time in Santa Barbara when Georgie Drew Barrymore died. Thirteen-year-old Ethel Barrymore had the responsibility of packing her mother's things and arranging for herself and the coffin to be taken back to New York by train. Shortly after Ethel Barrymore returned to school, her grandmother informed her that she would have to start earning her own living. Maurice Barrymore had remarried, and Mrs. Drew had had to give up the management of the Arch Street Theatre. She proposed to tour, playing Mrs. Malaprop with the famous comedian Joseph Jefferson as Bob Acres in a production of *The Rivals*. Ethel Barrymore, not yet fifteen years old, joined the tour to play the small role of Julia. "Acting was, after all," Ethel Barrymore said, "the only thing I could do best" (Alpert, p. 47).

When the tour was over, Ethel moved into a small room next to her grand-mother's room in the apartment that her uncle, John Drew, kept in New York. She began looking for work as an actress. Her uncle, who was at this time considered one of the best of the "modern" actors, especially in drawing room comedies, had just been lured away from the venerable manager Augustin Daly by the younger Charles Frohman. Frohman, to meet the public's demand for "stars," paired John Drew with a new young actress, Maude Adams, in a French farce, *The Masked Ball*, adapted by Clyde Fitch. John Drew was able to secure a small role for Ethel in a second Frohman production called *The Bauble Shop* in 1894. It also starred John Drew and Maude Adams, with Elsie De Wolfe playing a supporting role. Ethel Barrymore was hired as a "tea-tray carrier" and understudy to De Wolfe. When the play went on tour, De Wolfe decided to stay in New York; and Barrymore, though she was not quite sixteen, was allowed to play Lady Kate. In Chicago Barrymore received her first mention by a critic, who wrote, "An opalescent dream named Ethel Barrymore . . . came on and played Lady Kate" (quoted by Alpert, p. 52).

Barrymore appeared in two more of her uncle's plays. In the second, *Rose-mary*, she had a slightly larger part, and audiences were beginning to notice this newest of the Drew-Barrymore family to take the stage. One night while touring in *Rosemary*, her uncle received a telegram from the playwright and actor William Gillette, another Frohman star. Gillette invited Ethel to go to London to appear in the small role of Miss Kittredge and to understudy the leading ingénue role in his play *Secret Service*. Barrymore was delighted with the chance to appear on the London stage.

Though Barrymore played the leading ingénue role in *Secret Service* for only two nights, her continuing role as Miss Kittredge brought her notice in London. One who noticed the beautiful actress was Laurence Irving, son of the great actor Sir Henry Irving. As a result of his son's infatuation, Sir Henry and his co-star Ellen Terry asked Barrymore to remain in England to play Armette in *The Bells*. She was also cast in a play that had been written by Laurence Irving called *Peter the Great*. The two plays were alternated in London and also taken on tour. Though she could not yet be classified as a star, Barrymore was a great social success in London, and her name was frequently mentioned in the social columns.

Upon her return to the United States, Barrymore was taken by her uncle to see Charles Frohman, who gave her a small role in *Catharine* (1899). When the play *His Excellency, the Governor* was about to go on tour (1900), Frohman cast her in the part of a thirty-year-old adventuress. However, it was not until the fall of 1900 that Barrymore was given a starring role. Clyde Fitch, then America's most successful playwright, had two plays running on Broadway and wanted his new play, *Captain Jinks of the Horse Marines*, to appear on Broadway at the same time. *Captain Jinks* is a social comedy exposing the snobbery of New York society, which mistakes Madame Trentoni, played by Barrymore, as a genuine European opera star. In truth, she was born in America, as the action reveals. The play opened in Philadelphia before playing in New York. Despite unfavorable reviews in Philadelphia, Fitch wanted to have three plays on Broadway, so the play was scheduled at the Garrick Theatre for a brief two-week run.

The New York opening of *Captain Jinks of the Horse Marines*, February 4, 1901, made theatrical history. The audiences and the critics praised the new star, and the run of the play was extended first to three months and then to six months. A road tour followed the New York run. Not only was Barrymore's charm as an actress applauded, but during the run of the play a fashion writer noted the development of "a real Barrymore cult among the girls, who model themselves on her" (Alpert, p. 85). Though Barrymore's next few stage parts were meager and gave her little chance to grow as an actress, audiences came to see her, and young girls copied her clothes and her hair styles.

In 1904 Charles Frohman decided to feature Barrymore as a star in London. In *Cynthia*, Barrymore played the role of a young innocent wife. The audiences that came to see her included W. S. Gilbert, Arthur Wing Pinero, and James M. Barrie. The play was not a huge success, and Barrymore returned to the United States to play in *Sunday*, first in New York and then on tour. In 1907 she appeared in *Her Sister*, another drawing room comedy by Clyde Fitch. The critics were beginning to ask if Ethel Barrymore could do nothing more than dress up in fashionable clothes.

In 1908 Barrymore appeared in *Lady Frederick*, first on a tryout tour and then in New York. While performing the play in Boston after the New York run, Ethel Barrymore announced her engagement to Russell Griswold Colt, the son of the millionaire president of the United States Rubber Company, Samuel Pomeroy Colt. They married on March 14, 1909, and Colt went with his new bride on a tour to the West Coast. Shortly before they returned to New York, it was announced in the press that the famous English playwright Arthur Wing Pinero was writing a play called *Mid-Channel* for Barrymore. Charles Frohman also announced that from now on Barrymore would do only strong dramatic parts. The production was postponed until the next season because Barrymore was expecting her first child. In November 1909 Samuel Colt was born. On

February 1, 1910, Barrymore opened in *Mid-Channel*, playing the role of Zoë Blundell, an unhappily married Englishwoman of thirty-seven. With this role, Barrymore put to rest all doubts about her maturity as an actress. Once again Barrymore was the talk of New York.

Barrymore had another acting triumph with *The Shadow*, in which she played the role of a paralyzed woman confined to a wheelchair. While rehearsing *The Shadow*, Barrymore had come across a book of short stories called *Roast Beef Medium* by **Edna Ferber**. She became enchanted with the heroine of the stories, Emma McChesney, a down-to-earth saleslady. Frohman arranged for Edna Ferber and George Hobart to turn the stories into a drama, *Our Mrs. McChesney*, which was a success when presented on the stage. However, Charles Frohman was never to see the play. He was lost on the *Lusitania* when it sank after being struck by a German torpedo on May 7, 1915. No other loss during the war touched Barrymore so much as that of the rotund little producer who had made her a star.

In the summer of 1918 Alf Hayman, the man who had taken over as Barrymore's producer, showed her a new play written by a young woman, **Zoë Akins.** Barrymore was delighted with the play and was looking forward to beginning rehearsals when, early in August 1919, seven New York shows were closed by an actors' strike. The actors were seeking more equitable contracts and better working conditions, including rehearsals with pay and of shorter duration. Barrymore was drawn into the strike and became a leader of the Actors' Equity Group, whose activities finally forced the closing of every theatre in New York. Because of her leadership, she was chosen as one of the people to sign the five-year pact between actors and management that ended the strike.

The strike over, Barrymore went into rehearsal and opened at the Empire Theatre in Zoë Akins's *Déclassée* on October 16, 1919. The play, in which Barrymore played Lady Helen, a slightly tarnished lady, turned out to be one of her greatest triumphs. Night after night she played to standing-room-only houses. With her two hundredth performance she broke the Empire Theatre's all-time box-office record. Then she went on tour with the play. It was during the tour of *Déclassée* that Barrymore became seriously ill from an infection and had to be hospitalized. Also during this period of her life, her marriage with Russell Colt was in difficulty. The Colts separated, and two years later, in 1923, they obtained a divorce.

During the 1920s many actors were moving to California to work in film, but Barrymore gave no thought to deserting the stage. In 1922 she was praised for her performance in Gerhart Hauptmann's *Rose Bernd*, but the play was not successful. Her performance as Shakespeare's Juliet was not a success because the younger **Jane Cowl** was playing the role in New York at the same time, and audiences seemed to prefer the younger actress in the role. One of Barrymore's triumphs was as Lady Teazle, playing with her uncle, John Drew, as Sir Peter, in a production of *The School for Scandal* at the Players' Club's annual revival of a classic. This performance in 1923 was in celebration of John Drew's fiftieth anniversary on the stage. In the cast of *The School for Scandal* was an actor who was making a name for himself, Walter Hampden. Barrymore appeared with him again in 1925 in a repertory of classics; she played Ophelia in *Hamlet* and Portia in *The Merchant of Venice*. Barrymore and Hampden also appeared together in a revival of *The Second Mrs. Tanqueray*, making a critical success but only a moderate commercial success of the Arthur Wing Pinero play written thirty years earlier.

In 1926 Barrymore made her greatest hit of the twenties as Constance Middleton in Somerset Maugham's *The Constant Wife*. The New York performances and the tour of the play kept Barrymore busy for over two years. On December 17, 1928, the new theatre built by the Shuberts on West 47th Street in New York was named the Ethel Barrymore.

Barrymore's two brothers, Lionel and John, were both in Hollywood at this time, and in 1932 they convinced their sister to appear with them in a film. The three Barrymores had appeared together on the same stage in 1906 when Lionel and John had acted together in *Pantaloon*, a curtain-raiser by James M. Barrie, and Ethel had starred in the accompanying production, *Alice Sit-by-the-Fire*, also by Barrie. However, the three actors had never appeared together in the same play. Now the three were to appear in the film *Rasputin and the Empress*. Though Ethel Barrymore did not enjoy the experience, the reviews were good, and press agents began to call the Barrymores the "Royal Family of the American Stage." After the filming, Barrymore hurried back to New York.

The depression years of the thirties were hard times for Ethel Barrymore. She had difficulty getting stage roles and was reduced to playing James M. Barrie's short vaudeville play *The Twelve Pound Look*, which accompanied a feature movie. Not only was she in financial difficulties, but the Internal Revenue Service was pursuing her for nonpayment of taxes. In an effort to gain money she turned to radio. As early as 1928 she had read on the air from one of her successful plays, *The Kingdom of God*. She now began to give occasional performances on the Radio Theatre of the Air and acted as a comedienne on Ben Bernie's popular radio show. In 1936 she began a twenty-six-week series of radio programs of her own on the NBC-WJZ network. Beginning with *Captain Jinks of the Horse Marines*, the series featured Barrymore in revivals of plays in which she had appeared on Broadway. The radio series enabled Barrymore to recover from her financial straits.

In 1937 Barrymore returned to the stage. The occasion was the Theatre Guild's production of Sidney Howard's *The Growth of Yankee Doodle*, a play showing one wealthy family's attempt to deal with the problems presented by the dangerous growth of fascism in the world. The play was not a good one, but all the critics praised Barrymore's portrayal of the gracious head of the family. The next year Barrymore played a 102-year-old woman in *Whiteoaks*, a play based on the *Jalna* novels by Mazo de la Roche. Once again Barrymore won critical praise.

On November 26, 1940, after tryouts in Baltimore, Washington, and Philadelphia, *The Corn Is Green* by Emlyn Williams opened in New York. Williams's autobiographical play about a dedicated teacher, Miss Moffat, "who turns a smutty-faced, surly-mannered Welsh coal miner into an educated man" (*New York Times*, December 8, 1940), became a tour de force for Ethel Barrymore. "Magnificent" was the word most often used by the critics for Barrymore's Miss Moffat. John Mason Brown wrote that she "gives the finest, most thoughtful and concentrated performance she has given in many years" (*New York Post*, November 27, 1940). The critic for the *New York Times* wrote of Barrymore's performance, "She plays it forcefully, but she also plays it with compassion and from now on she can wear Miss Moffat as a jewel in her crown" (November 27, 1940).

In February 1941 the NBC network devoted a half hour of time to celebrate Barrymore's fortieth anniversary as a star. The celebrated years started with *Captain Jinks of the Horse Marines* and went as far as *The Corn Is Green*. In May of that same year Barrymore received the Barter Theatre Award "for the outstanding performance given by an American actress during the current theatre season." The award was presented by Eleanor Roosevelt. Barrymore played Miss Moffat for a total of 461 performances on Broadway before beginning a countrywide tour. In 1944 she interrupted her tour of *The Corn Is Green* to play the role of Ma Mott in the film *None But the Lonely Heart* for which she received the Academy (Oscar) Award for the best performance by an actress.

During the winter of 1944–1945, while playing in New York in *Embezzled Heaven*, Barrymore contracted pneumonia and began to turn her thoughts to warmer climates. After winning the Academy Award, she had received numerous film offers, and now she finally moved to California. In *The Spiral Staircase*, a murder mystery, she played the role of a bedridden elderly woman. She acted with Merle Oberon in *Night Song* and appeared in an Alfred Hitchcock thriller, *The Paradine Case*.

On Barrymore's seventieth birthday, August 16, 1949, the Motion Picture Academy, in cooperation with the NBC radio network, presented a half-hour program as a tribute to the actress. In 1950 she went East to visit her daughter and grandson. She was asked to participate in the American National Theatre and Academy (ANTA) Album, the theatre's annual benefit for itself. She agreed to do a scene from *The Twelve Pound Look*. The performance took place at the Ziegfeld Theatre on January 29, 1950; it was to be Ethel Barrymore's last appearance on the stage.

During the 1950s Barrymore continued to make films, among the best of which were *Portrait of Jennie*, *Pinky* (the first Hollywood movie to treat seriously the interracial problem), *Kind Lady*, and *Young at Heart*. Her last film was *Johnny Trouble*, made in 1956. After 1953 she made several guest appearances on television and even started her own program, acting as hostess on a series called *The Ethel Barrymore Theatre*. When the quality of the scripts failed to satisfy her, she withdrew from the project.

Ethel Barrymore died quietly in her sleep on June 17, 1959. Perhaps Clifton Webb best summed up her life in the theatre: "A queen has died," he sadly noted (Albert, p. 387). Indeed, Ethel Barrymore had long reigned as the queen of the American stage. She was buried beside her two famous brothers in Calvary Cemetery in Beverly Hills.

The Robinson Locke Scrapbooks in the Billy Rose Theatre Collection in the New York Public Library Performing Arts Research Center at Lincoln Center are the best source of information about Ethel Barrymore. *The Cumulated Dramatic Index, 1909–1949* lists articles and books that have been written about the Barrymores. Besides her autobiography, *Memories* (1955), Barrymore wrote "My Reminiscences," *Delineator* (September 1923 through February 1924) and "How Can I Be an Actress?" *Ladies' Home Journal* (March 15, 1911). *The Barrymores* (1964) by Hollis Alpert follows the careers of Ethel, Lionel, and John Barrymore. *Fanfare* (1957) is by Richard Maney, Barrymore's press agent. Articles include Robert Downing, "Ethel Barrymore, 1879–1959," *Films in Review* (August and September 1959); Barbara Birch Jamison, "Ethel Barrymore—In Mid-Career at 75," *New York Times Magazine* (August 15, 1954); and S. J. Woolf, "Miss Barrymore Refuses to Mourn the 'Good Old Days,' " *New York Times Magazine* (August 13, 1939). Montrose J. Moses devotes most of his chapter in *Famous Actor-Families in America* (1906) to the founders of the Drew-Barrymore clan. Lionel Barrymore, with Cameron Shipp, wrote *We Barrymores* (1951). For other family background, see James Kotsilibas-Davis, *Great Times, Good Times: The Odyssey of Maurice Barrymore* (1977). *Who Was Who in the Theatre*, Vol. I (1978), lists the plays in which Ethel Barrymore appeared, and William C. Young reprints some reviews of her performances in *Famous Actors and Actresses of the American Stage*, Vol. I (1975). Reviews of *The Corn Is Green* appeared in the *New York Times* (November 27, 1940; December 1, 1940; May 4, 1943; and May 9, 1943). Barrymore's obituary appeared in the *New York Times* (June 19, 1959). Short biographies of Barrymore are given in *Current Biography 1941* (1942); *Notable American Women*, Vol IV: *The Modern Period* (1980); *The Oxford Companion to the Theatre* (1983); and *The Oxford Companion to American Theatre* (1984). Most sources give the date of Barrymore's birth as August 15, but her birth record in Philadelphia gives August 16, 1879. Some biographies give the date of her death as June 18, but Alpert's biography says that she died on the evening of June 17, 1959.

Catherine B. McGovern
Alice McDonnell Robinson

BARTON, Lucy Adalade (September 26, 1891–May 14, 1979): costume designer, educator, and scholar, was born in Ogden, Utah, the third and youngest child of Jesse Billings Barton and Lucy Eudora Thomas (Bonfield) Barton. The Bartons were a mature couple in their forties (both widowed in previous marriages) when their youngest child was born. Their three-year stay in Utah, where Lucy Barton's father was practicing law and was active in Democratic politics, ended shortly after Lucy's birth, when the family moved to Chicago. Barton was raised in Hinsdale, a Chicago suburb, and her early schooling was at home, supervised by her mother. In 1905 she was enrolled in the Lewis Institute in Chicago, which she attended until 1909, when she spent a school year (1909–1910) at the National Cathedral School in Washington, D.C. Barton's theatrical interests found an outlet in the Anna Morgan School of Expression in Chicago, where she studied voice, oral interpretation, and acting with Anna Morgan and Jesse Harding, both during her schooling at the Lewis Institute and after her return from Washington. She continued her study of advanced oral interpretation with Winifred Woodside-Just in 1913 and 1914. Barton considered using her elocutionary training to follow in her father's footsteps as a lawyer, a plan that apparently did not meet with her mother's approval. She decided to pursue her acting ambitions instead, enrolling in the new drama department at Carnegie Institute of Technology (now Carnegie-Mellon University) in Pittsburgh in 1914. She was one of three students in the class and the only woman.

The theatre program at Carnegie Tech was headed by Thomas Wood Stevens, who became a formative influence in Barton's education and in her later professional life. At Carnegie, Barton also met B. Iden Payne, the Shakespearean director, who would be a favored colleague in the years to come, and William Poël, the English actor/director, who came in 1916 to direct Ben Jonson's *Poetaster*, in which Barton played the part of the young Ovid. Poël's theory and practice of staging Shakespeare was to become a hallmark of Barton's own designs, especially in her collaborations with Payne.

Barton's shift from actress to costume designer was made during the Carnegie years. Her training in design had as its basis a broad liberal arts education, and she continued to advocate a broad spectrum of experience for effective training in costume design and construction. By the time she graduated in 1917, Barton was ready to work professionally in her field under the guidance of Thomas Wood Stevens. She "interpreted" his sketches for pageant costumes to seamstresses and staff who often had little specific theatrical training. She also continued to perform a role she originated at Carnegie—"Truth"—in Stevens's pageant *The Drawing of the Sword*, written to encourage the World War I draft. After touring with this production, Barton designed and supervised the construction of the costumes for a larger Stevens work, *The Red Cross Pageant*, which was presented on Long Island and at Carnegie Hall in New York City. In the summer of 1918 Barton again costumed a pageant for Stevens, titled *Freedom*, which was performed in St. Louis on Independence Day. It was to Stevens that Barton owed much of her own exactness of historical detail, an interest in research, and the important experiences in theatrical pageantry that necessitated the effective, somewhat stylized, but always meticulously accurate, period costumes that became her forte.

In 1919 and 1920 Barton served as a supervisor at Van Horn and Son, a costume rental agency in Philadelphia, but she left because the strong smell of disinfectant bothered her. After this experience Barton returned to academe, where she became an important force in the formative development of costume design programs in this country. From 1920 to 1923 Barton was at the Knox School for Girls in Cooperstown, New York, where, as the only member of a theatre faculty, she taught theatre, diction, and costuming and also wrote, directed, and designed plays for the girls to perform. At this preparatory school she met Ruth Linda Allen, an English teacher, who would be her friend and companion over the next fifty-odd years. Barton and Allen spent a year together in Europe, primarily at Oxford and Bruges. Upon returning to the United States, Barton began teaching at the Irene Weir Art School. During the summers she directed, wrote, or designed pageants. In 1927 she directed pageants in Jamestown, Dunkirk, and Cherry Valley, New York. In 1928 she wrote a pageant, *The Interpreter*, which was presented in Charlottesville, Virginia, and in the same year she designed the costumes for *The Pageant of New Brunswick*, presented in New Brunswick, New Jersey.

In 1929 Barton began teaching at the University of Iowa. Here she was able to concentrate more exclusively on instruction in costume and makeup and on designing for productions directed by E. C. Mabie, B. Iden Payne, Whitford Kane, and Vance Morton. In 1934 she became costume designer for the Globe Theatre at the Chicago World's Fair, working with directors Thomas Wood Stevens, B. Iden Payne, and Theodore Viehman. Her costumes for the shortened versions of eight Shakespearean plays were re-creations of Elizabethan dress. Barton's work with Stevens continued that fall with her designs for the masque in *The Pageant of Old Fort Niagara*, presented at Niagara Falls.

Between the years 1932 and 1940 Barton published the articles, plays, and books for which she is best remembered: *Historic Costume for the Stage* (1936), *Costuming the Biblical Play* (1937), and *Costumes by You* (1940). The last book consisted largely of essays published previously in *Players Magazine* from 1933 to 1940. These books comprise her canon for professional, student, and amateur costume designers. In 1936 and 1937 Barton supervised the Chicago costume shop for the Federal Theatre Project. In 1938 and 1939 she studied with Allardyce Nicoll at Yale University and then transferred to the Graduate Institute of Art History and Criticism at New York University, where she completed a thesis titled "The Designs of Court Spectacles in Sixteenth Century France" and received her Master of Arts degree in 1941.

Her last collaboration with Thomas Wood Stevens was on the pageant *The Entrada of Coronado*, which toured the Southwest from 1940 to 1942. Stevens died shortly thereafter; Barton has left an interesting memoir, "He Thought I Could Do It," in *Educational Theatre Journal* (December 1951), which tells of her work with Stevens and their research and work methods in this pageant in particular. From 1939 to 1952 Barton designed the summer productions of the Michigan Repertory Players at the University of Michigan, Ann Arbor. From 1943 to 1947 Barton taught at the University of Arizona and from 1947 to 1949 at the University of Washington in Seattle. Also during these years she served as costume editor for *Players Magazine* and contributed regularly to *Dramatics Magazine*.

In 1947 Barton began her long and happy tenure at the University of Texas at Austin, having been invited there by B. Iden Payne, then a professor and a director on the theatre faculty. Barton retired in 1961, becoming the drama department's first professor emeritus. At Texas Barton was able to focus on her specialty exclusively, designing the major shows of the season (often six or seven a year), teaching her craft, and urging the development of a major in costume design. In the early fifties the University of Texas became the first public institution to offer a degree in costume design. By the time of her retirement in 1961, Barton had become a seminal force in the education of costume designers and technicians around the country.

In retirement Barton continued to write (*Appreciating Costume*, 1969) and to lecture. She taught occasionally in the 1960s, returning to the University of Texas several times: in 1965, to attend the exhibit of her designs presented by the department; in 1968, to design *The Tempest* for B. Iden Payne (their last collaboration); and in 1971, to lecture and advise the first thesis about her life and work by Jane Morgan. Barton spent her last years in Texas with her companion, Ruth Linda Allen, who died in the mid–1970s. Barton herself died on May 14, 1979.

In addition to the special exhibit of her work in 1965 at the University of Texas, Barton was widely recognized during her lifetime. The Southeastern Theatre Conference named her recipient of their Merit Award in 1957; in 1960 she received the American Educational Theatre Association's Senior Eaves Award in Costuming. In 1961 she was recognized by the Alumni Federation of Carnegie Institute of Technology with an Award of Merit, and the University of Texas established a scholarship in her name in 1961. The National Cathedral School in Washington, D.C., named her an outstanding alumna in the mid–1960s. In 1964 the New England Theatre Conference honored her with a citation "in recognition of her long and illustrious career as a costumer, author, and theatre educator." In May 1971 the United States Institute for Theatre Technology (USITT) gave her a Special Costume Award.

Barton was a scholar and educator whose definitive text, *Historic Costume for the Stage*, has had an inestimable influence on thousands of students. Barton's work and her writings helped to hasten the day when costume designers were at last recognized in educational institutions as artists of equal stature with their scenic design colleagues.

Important works by Barton include *Historic Costume for the Stage* (1936, 1961), *Appreciating Costume* (1969), *Costuming the Biblical Play* (1962), *Costumes by You* (1940), and *Period Patterns*, written with Doris Edson (1942). Among her articles are "He Thought I Could Do It," *Educational Theatre Journal* (December 1951); "A Major in Costume," *Educational Theatre Journal* (March 1950); "Costume Design," *Arts of the United States*, William Pierson and Martha Davidson, eds. (1960); "Costume Design, Theatrical," *Encyclopedia Britannica*, Vol. 6 (1969); "Costumes Are Clothes, Clothes Are Costumes," *Players Magazine* (September-October 1946); "A Cultural Background for the Stage Costumer," *Players Magazine* (November-December 1932); and "Why Not Costume Shakespeare According to Shakespeare?" *Educational Theatre Journal* (October 1967). Barton often contributed to *Players Magazine* during 1939 and from 1944 until 1949 and to *Dramatics Magazine* in 1944 and 1945. Jane Elizabeth Morgan's "An Analysis of the Costume Design Theories of Lucy Barton and Their Relation to the Designs of *Richard III*" (Unpublished Master's thesis, University of Texas at Austin,

1972) contains useful and authoritative biographical information. Morgan's biographical chapter will probably remain the definitive treatment of Barton's life and career and was the primary source for this article. Other sources include the unattributed monograph, *Fifty Years of Curricular Theatre at the University of Michigan* (University of Michigan, Ann Arbor, 1965); "Lucy Barton: The Texas Years. An Exhibition of Costume Designs" (Catalogue of the Exhibition, The University of Texas at Austin, March 1965); Melvin White, "Honoring Lucy Barton," *Players Magazine* (October 1951); and Wayne B. Pevey, "A History of the Department of Drama, 1938–63" (Unpublished Master's thesis, University of Texas at Austin, 1965). What survives of Barton's designs is held in the Barton Collection in the Hoblitzelle Theatre Arts Library at the University of Texas in Austin.

Patricia B. Adams

The BATEMANS. Sidney Frances Cowell Bateman (March 29, 1823–January 13, 1881): playwright, theatre manager, and actress; Kate Josephine Bateman Crow (October 7, 1842-April 8, 1917): actress; Ellen Douglas Bateman Greppo (December 18, 1844–1936): actress; Virginia Frances Bateman Compton (January 1, 1853-May 4, 1940): actress; and Isabel Emilie Bateman (1854-June 10, 1934): actress. The Batemans were a theatrical family active in the United States and England.

Sidney Cowell was born in New York (or New Jersey), the daughter of British-born comedian Joe Cowell (a naturalized American citizen) and his second wife, Frances Sheppard, an American. Educated in Cincinnati, she made her stage debut in New Orleans in *The Unfinished Gentleman* on April 23, 1823. During the 1838–1839 season she was a member of the Camp Street Theatre stock company in New Orleans. In August 1839 she moved with her family to join Sol Smith's company in St. Louis, Missouri, where she met the actor Hezekiah Linthicum Bateman (1812–1875), whom she married on November 10, 1839. Their four daughters became actresses.

For many years Sidney Cowell Bateman was known mainly as the mother of Kate and Ellen, who, billed as the Bateman Children, gained national fame as child prodigies (1846–1856). The two children made an early debut in Louisville, Kentucky, on December 11, 1846, in *Children in the Wood*, when Kate was four and Ellen not quite two years old, replacing two children unable to appear. Three years later they made their New York debut (December 10, 1849) at the Broadway Theatre in scenes from Shakespeare and other plays. Kate played Portia to Ellen's Shylock, Richmond to Ellen's Richard III, and Artaxaminous to Ellen's Bombastes. In 1850 they appeared at Barnum's American Museum, and in 1851 they were part of a Barnum tour of the British Isles, debuting in London at the St. James's Theatre on August 23, 1851. An American tour begun in September 1852 at the New York Astor Theatre took them to Thomas Placide's New Orleans Varieties Theatre in February and March of 1853 and to San Francisco, Sacramento, and California mining towns from April to November of 1854. In California the Bateman Children added to their repertoire two melodramas written for them by their mother, Sidney Cowell Bateman, *Young*

America; or the News Boy and *A Mother's Trust; or California in 1849*. Only one earlier play has been attributed to Sidney Bateman, *The Golden Calf; or Marriage à la Mode* (written in 1850, published in 1857).

A Mother's Trust was the center of a publicity stunt apparently staged by impresario H. L. Bateman, who had offered $1,000 for an original play set in contemporary California to be performed by the Bateman Children. When it became known that his wife had written the winning play (and donated the prize money to an orphanage), newspaper reports were so scathing that Bateman shot and wounded the editor of the *California Chronicle* on the streets of San Francisco. *A Mother's Trust* opened to packed houses on June 28, 1854, at the San Francisco Metropolitan Theatre, and included Edwin Booth in the cast.

Kate and Ellen retired as child actresses in 1856. Ellen married Claude Greppo on March 29, 1860, and retired permanently from the stage. (Her son Francis became an actor, however.)

The year of the Bateman Children's retirement saw the production of Sidney Bateman's most famous play, *Self*, first performed in St. Louis, Missouri, where H. L. Bateman was managing a theatre. The play opened in New York on October 27, 1856, at Burton's new theatre on Broadway and had a successful run. Often compared to **Anna Cora Mowatt's** *Fashion* (1845), which it resembles in plot, *Self* was revived in 1869 by John E. Owens, who bought the rights to the play and made the role of John Unit a star part. Because of its resemblance to *Fashion* and Owens's success with the play, *Self* has retained a minor place in theatre histories to this day.

Kate Bateman, at the age of sixteen, returned to the stage in adult roles, appearing in *Geraldine* in New Orleans in 1859 and then in her mother's dramatization of Longfellow's *Evangeline* in New York in 1860. She went on to play other favorite roles, including Julia in *The Hunchback*, Pauline in *The Lady of Lyons*, Bianca in *Fazio*, and Juliet in *Romeo and Juliet*. The role that made Kate Bateman's fame—the role that she was to play successfully for the next thirty years—was Leah the Jewess in Augustin Daly's *Leah, the Forsaken*, adapted (at H. L. Bateman's suggestion) from S. H. Mosenthal's *Deborah*. *Leah* premièred in Boston on December 8, 1862, and in New York at Niblo's Garden Theatre on January 19, 1863. Kate toured Baltimore and Washington with Daly managing the production and publicity, and on October 1, 1863, *Leah* opened for a long (211 performances) and critically acclaimed run at the Adelphi in London, marking Kate's adult London debut. So successful was the role that Kate eventually bought the rights to the play.

The whole Bateman family joined Kate in her London tour; both Isabel and Virginia made their debuts in London in *Little Daisy* (Her Majesty's Theatre, December 1865). They returned to New York in 1866, where Kate played Leah for six weeks to full houses at Niblo's Garden Theatre. On October 13, 1866, Kate married English physician George Crowe and moved to London, announcing the second of many retirements. Their daughter, Sidney Crowe, debuted as a child actress in 1876, playing little Leah to Kate's Leah.

In 1869 or 1870 the Bateman family moved to London, where H. L. Bateman took over the management of the Lyceum Theatre (1871–1875). With Kate married and her career successfully launched, H. L. Bateman turned to promoting his youngest daughter, Isabel. To this end, Sidney Bateman wrote an adaptation of *Die Grille* (a German version of George Sand's *La Petite Fadette*) called *Fanchette; or The Will o' the Wisp*. Isabel made her adult debut in the title role in Edinburgh (May 1871), opening at the London Lyceum on September 11, with a then little-known actor, Henry Irving. Isabel did not repeat Kate's success, and the Lyceum was in financial straits when Irving convinced H. L. Bateman to produce *The Bells*, a play that made Irving's fame and Bateman's fortune.

After H. L. Bateman's unexpected death from a heart attack (March 22, 1875, during the unprecedentedly long run of Irving's *Hamlet* with Isabel as Ophelia), Sidney Bateman took over the management of the Lyceum. By her own account, her most significant achievements during her three-and-a-half-year tenure (1875–1878), aside from making a profit every year, were the première of Alfred Lord Tennyson's *Queen Mary* (starring Kate Bateman in the title role and Isabel as Elizabeth I) and the production of *Richard III* (with Isabel as Lady Anne, Kate as Queen Margaret, and Irving as Richard III).

During the Lyceum years, the elder Batemans treated Henry Irving as a son; he lodged with them for some time, and Sidney Bateman was godmother to his second son, Laurence Sidney Irving. Moreover, despite Irving's marriage, Sidney Bateman apparently entertained hopes of a match between Irving and Isabel. Isabel was in love with Irving, but he could not get a divorce and, in fact, chafed under the Batemans' selection of plays, supporting casts, and the necessity of co-starring with the Bateman sisters. In the summer of 1878 Irving insisted on his own leading lady—Ellen Terry. The result was that Sidney Bateman turned over the Lyceum lease to Irving (instead of selling the lease at a profit) and took over Sadler's Wells Theatre.

Sidney Bateman made a brave attempt to rejuvenate Sadler's Wells, a theatre that had fallen on hard times. She remodeled the building and reopened the theatre on October 9, 1879, with *Rob Roy*, starring Kate Bateman as Helen MacGregor. As manager, Sidney Bateman had raised funds for the Sadler's Wells venture, but the productions were not successful. In January 1881 she caught a chill waiting for transportation to the theatre and on January 13 died in London of pneumonia. After Sidney Bateman's sudden death, the theatre closed, having incurred a heavy debt through Sidney Bateman's unsuccesful management. Much of Kate Bateman's fortune went toward these debts, and she went into retirement for ten years after her mother's death.

Isabel Bateman continued to act on both London and provincial stages until the Sadler's Wells Theatre's debts were paid off. Her best role and greatest success was as Ophelia to Irving's Hamlet in the 1874–1875 production at the Lyceum. In January 1899 she joined an Anglican sisterhood, the Community of St. Mary the Virgin, of which she became Reverend Mother General in 1920. She died there June 10, 1934, at the age of seventy-nine.

In 1891 Kate Bateman returned to the stage as the Marquise de Bellegarde in Henry James's *The American* and in 1892 opened an acting school in London under her married name of Mrs. George Crowe. In May 1892 she appeared in *Karin* and in November 1892 in *David*. She performed infrequently during the early twentieth century. She played Medea in 1907 and made her last stage appearance in *The Younger Generation* in 1912. She died in London of a cerebral hemorrhage on April 8, 1917.

Virginia Bateman had been less closely allied to Sidney Bateman's fortunes than the other daughters. She had played supporting roles at the Lyceum (appearing with Irving in *The Bells* when she was twelve, under the stage name Virginia Francis) and at Sadler's Wells (1880), but in 1882 she married actor-manager Edward Compton (1854–1918) and became leading lady of the Edward Compton Comedy Company, managing it after his death. The company mainly toured the provinces but sometimes played London, and the Comptons performed at the first Shakespeare festivals at Stratford-on-Avon. Kate's daughter Sidney Crowe joined the Compton Comedy Company in 1889, and four of the five Compton children went on the stage, most notably actress Fay Compton. Virginia Bateman opened a repertory theatre in Nottingham and also founded a Theatre Girls' Club in London for the benefit of needy chorus girls. She died in London in 1940, at the age of eighty-seven.

Laurence Irving's *Henry Irving* (1952) includes photos of Sidney and Isabel Bateman and provides information on the Batemans' Lyceum days. Marvin Felheim's *The Theater of Augustin Daly* (1956) is useful for information on Kate Bateman and *Leah*. For information on Sidney Bateman's early acting career, see William B. B. Carson, *The Theatre on the Frontier: Early Years of the St. Louis Stage* (1932), and John S. Kendall, *The Golden Age of the New Orleans Theater* (1968). The Bateman Children's California tour is discussed by George R. MacMinn in *The Theater of the Golden Era in California* (1941). *Self* is reprinted in Montrose J. Moses's *Representative Plays by American Dramatists*, Vol. II (1925, reissued 1964), with a biographical introduction including an interview with Sidney Bateman's niece Sidney Cowell (daughter of her brother Samuel). Although Sidney Bateman's father, Joe Cowell, wrote a memoir, *Thirty Years Passed among the Players in England and America* (1844), it entirely avoids family matters; none of Cowell's children is mentioned by name. Isabel Bateman wrote *From Theatre to Convent: Memories of Mother Isabel Mary, C.S.M.V.* (Isabel Bateman, 1936). Sidney Bateman's obituary appeared on January 14, 1881, in both the *London Times* and the *New York Times*. Kate Bateman's obituary appeared in the *London Times* (April 10, 1917) and was reprinted in the *New York Times* (April 12, 1917). It was followed by an editorial on Kate Bateman in the *New York Times* (April 13, 1917). Isabel Bateman's obituary appeared on June 13, 1934, in both the *London Times* and the *New York Times*. Virginia Bateman Compton's obituary appeared in the *New York Times* (May 5, 1940) and is the source of her day of birth. Very little information on Ellen Bateman appears in the public record after her retirement from the stage in 1856; no obituary has been found and no date of death. Her date of birth is taken from T. Allston Brown, *History of the American Stage* (1870), but this source is in many respects unreliable. Useful biographical references are to be found in Davenport Adams's *Dictionary of the Drama*, Vol. 1 (1904); the *Dictionary of National Biography*, Vol. I, on Sidney Bateman (1917);

Notable American Women, Vol. I (1971); *The Oxford Companion to the Theatre* (1983) under Bateman and Compton, and *The Oxford Companion to American Theatre* (1984).

Rose Norman

BATES, Blanche (August 25, 1873–December 25, 1941): actress, most notably associated with David Belasco, was born in Portland, Oregon, the first child of Francis Marvin Bates and Eliza (Wren) Bates, both performers in stock companies. The Bateses had acted across the North American continent, eventually settling in San Francisco, where Francis Bates managed a company in which his wife played the leads. An attempt to expand to a chain of stock theatres in the Northwest failed, and the Bates family traveled to Australia in 1874, where the parents achieved great success as visiting stars. In 1879 Francis Bates was murdered in Melbourne in mysterious circumstances; his widow returned to San Francisco with her two small daughters and continued acting.

Blanche Bates was educated in the San Francisco public schools, graduating (the first girl to do so) from the Boys' High School in 1889. A brief marriage (to Milton F. Davis, an army officer) took place in 1890, but the couple separated after four weeks. Bates worked as a kindergarten teacher for several years but then made her debut in San Francisco in *This Picture and That* (August 21, 1893), a benefit performance for L. R. Stockwell, a pioneer western actor-manager and friend of her mother. Blanche Bates then joined Stockwell's company as a regular performer, playing a variety of roles. After an unsuccessful attempt to gain work in the New York theatre, she became the leading lady of T. Daniel Frawley's Denver stock company in the autumn of 1894. Frawley's company eventually toured, and Bates returned to San Francisco to play the leading role in *Sweet Lavender* by Arthur Wing Pinero. Frawley opened the Columbia Theatre in San Francisco on May 13, 1895, with this play. Bates remained with Frawley's company, both in San Francisco and on tour until 1898, when she traveled to New York to seek engagements once more on the East Coast.

Hired by Augustin Daly in the spring of 1898, Bates played second leads for several months. While on leave from Daly, she acted Nora in *A Doll's House* in San Francisco (November 6, 1898). She rejoined Daly to play the adventuress's role in *The Great Ruby* (February 9, 1899), only to resign after the first performance, citing an "uncongenial" atmosphere. The true reasons for her departure were rumored to range from a dispute over gowns to the jealousy of Daly's leading lady **Ada Rehan.**

Bates next played Miladi in *The Musketeers*, followed by a spectacular performance as Hannah Jacobs in Israel Zangwill's *The Children of the Ghetto* (1899), when she reportedly was signed by Liebler and Company to a five-year contract at $20,000 annually. She also attracted the attention of David Belasco, for whom she played the lead in *Naughty Anthony* (January 8, 1900). This farce is now remembered only because, when attendance began to slip after two months, Belasco added a one-act curtain-raiser, *Madame Butterfly* (March 5,

1900), adapted from the story by John Luther Long. With the role of Cho-Cho-San, the deserted Madame Butterfly, Bates achieved the status of a major star, which she was to maintain with a string of Belasco hits over the next decade.

Though tall and large-boned herself, Bates played Cho-Cho-San with such believability that critics and audiences were convinced that she was, in fact, delicate and fragile. Her next role for Belasco, the swashbuckling Cigarette in an adaptation of Quida's *Under Two Flags* (February 5, 1901), therefore stunned audiences through contrast with its predecessor; the play ran almost two years in New York and on tour. Bates returned to a Belasco vision of the Orient for her next role—another Long adaptation, *The Darling of the Gods* (December 3, 1902)—which occupied her for the next three years as the tragic Yo-San. During its tour Bates also performed *Hedda Gabler* and *The Taming of the Shrew* at matinee performances during her starring career in other than popular, commercial theatre pieces.

Belasco provided Bates with yet another contrasting role in her next play, *The Girl of the Golden West* (November 14, 1905). As Minnie, "The Girl," Bates again stunned audiences with the athletic vigor and stamina of her performance. Her last two plays for Belasco, *The Fighting Hope* (September 22, 1908) and *Nobody's Widow* (November 15, 1910), while hugely successful, did not provide Bates with striking roles.

Bates broke with Belasco shortly after her marriage to George Creel, a Denver journalist, on November 28, 1912. With Creel she had two children. However, she remained on the stage and retained her star status until her retirement in 1926, though her vehicles—including *Witness for the Defense* (1913), *Molière* (1919), *The Famous Mrs. Fair* (1919), *The Changelings* (1923), and *Mrs. Partridge Presents* (1925)—never recaptured the excitement or success she had enjoyed with Belasco. Bates's last stage appearance was in 1933 when she played a character role in *The Lake*. She died on December 25, 1941, and was buried in San Francisco.

Blanche Bates achieved her greatest success as Belasco's leading lady and, as was the case with several actresses associated with this director, was not able to duplicate her success after breaking with him. Unlike other Belasco proteges, however, Bates had demonstrated solid professional achievement and capabilities before working with him and was able to maintain her star status, albeit with diminished lustre, once the break had occurred. Her background in western stock companies provided her with a wide-ranging versatility, enabling her to shift from the fragile heroines of Belasco's pseudo-Japanese plays to the battling Cigarette or hard-drinking Minnie with no apparent strain. She was noted for her realistic portrayal of emotions in all of her major characters, an ability that, when combined with the lush sentimentality of Belasco's scripts and productions, helped create lasting impressions on turn-of-the-century audiences.

An incomplete autobiography was published after Bates's death in the *Sacramento Bee*, (May 16, 23, and 30, and June 6 and 13, 1942); otherwise, no complete account of her life or career has appeared though she does figure importantly in the major biographies of Belasco. She was a special favorite of critic William Winter, who discusses her acting in *The Wallet of Time* (1913). Contemporary journalistic accounts are listed in Stephen Archer's *American Actors and Actresses* (1983). Biographical essays appear in *Notable American Women*, Vol. I (1971); *Dictionary of American Biography*, supplement 3 (1973); and *The Oxford Companion to American Theatre* (1984).

Alan Woods

BAYES, Nora (1880?–March 19, 1928): actress in musical comedy and vaudeville, was at the height of her career the highest paid single act in vaudeville. She was born Dora Goldberg in Joliet, Illinois (various sources give Milwaukee, Chicago, and Los Angeles), the daughter of Elias and Rachel (Miller) Goldberg. Little is known of her early life. In 1899–1900 she was apparently living in Joliet, where she was married to her first husband, Otto Gressing, an undertaker. (They were divorced in 1908.) It is thought that she first appeared on the stage in Chicago at the age of eighteen as a vaudeville singer at Hopkins' Theatre and at the Chicago Opera House. Her early career is difficult to trace because she used a variety of first and last names. However, by 1902 she was on the regular vaudeville circuit and performing at Percy Williams's Orpheum Theatre in Brooklyn, New York, where she made Harry von Tilzer's ballad, "Down Where the Wurzburger Flows," into a popular hit. In 1904 she went to Europe. There she appeared in musical comedy and variety shows, opening at the Palace Theatre in London. Returning to America in 1907, Bayes starred in the first Ziegfeld *Follies* (1907) and continued to appear in these revues for several years.

Bayes had a deep, rich voice that communicated emotion so well it moved audiences to laughter or tears with equal ease. She collaborated with her second husband, Jack Norworth, a song and dance man (they were married in 1908 and divorced in 1913), on the lyrics and music of many songs, the best remembered of which is "Shine On, Harvest Moon," featured in *The Follies of 1908*. In 1910 she appeared under the management of Lew Fields in *The Jolly Bachelors*, in which she sang "Has Anybody Here Seen Kelly?" In 1911 she and Jack Norworth appeared in *Little Miss Fix-it*. In 1912 Bayes and Norworth opened at Weber and Fields's new Music Hall in a double bill, *Roly-Poly* and *Without the Law*, in which they introduced the song "When It's Apple Blossom Time in Normandy." In September 1914 Bayes, billed as "The Greatest Single Woman Singing Comedienne in the World," appeared at the Palace Theatre in New York before beginning a thirty-week vaudeville tour.

In 1917 George M. Cohan chose Bayes to sing the first American rendition of "Over There," which she introduced in her own production called *Two Hours of Song*. In October 1918 she opened at the Broadhurst Theatre in New York and then toured in the musical play *Ladies First*. George Gershwin accompanied her on the piano as she introduced the first song he wrote in collaboration with his brother Ira, "The Real American Folk Song." Another song that she popularized was "Oh Johnny! Oh Johnny! Oh!" Bayes's trademark was an ostrich fan, and she delighted in extravagant and outlandish costumes in her stage performances and public appearances. For a short time she organized and managed her own theatre, which opened and closed in 1919 with *Ladies First* (featuring Bayes in the role of Betty Burt). She had to give up the Nora Bayes Theatre because of money problems and her inability to act and manage at the same time.

Bayes's sense of humor was an asset to her stage performances and also came out in personal interviews. She claimed that World War I started because England and Germany could not agree about her singing. She was outspoken, independent in her opinions, and a champion of the underdog. Her strong-willed personality caused managers and other show business personnel to claim she was difficult to work with. Bayes's marital and romantic life was much publicized and commented upon by the public. The press delighted in reporting on what was scandalous behavior for the times. She married five times, first to Otto Gressing, a Joliet businessman. Her second, third, and fourth husbands were Jack Norworth, Harry Clarke, and Arthur Gordon or Gordoni, all performers she had worked with at some point in her career. Her fifth husband was Benjamin Friedland, a wealthy businessman. She adopted three children: Norman, Leanora, and Peter; and she was a great supporter of children's charities. According to one account, she performed two charity benefits the day of the abdominal surgery that eventually led to her death. In her last years she became a Christian Scientist. She died March 19, 1928, in New York City at age forty-seven. She was financially insolvent at her death.

Nora Bayes won her audiences with her freewheeling style, humor, and rich voice. Her peripatetic professional life brought American-style musical comedy and vaudeville entertainment to diverse audiences in both America and Europe. In expressing his sorrow at her death, E. F. Albee, president of the Keith-Albee-Orpheum Circuit, observed, "She was the personification of the ideal vaudeville artist. . . . Her comedy was universal" (*New York Times*, March 20, 1928). The independence of her opinions and her lifestyle raised many disapproving eyebrows but also helped to open up the traditionally limited role into which actresses were cast both on and off the stage.

Nora Bayes wrote "Holding My Audience," which appeared in *Theatre* (September 1917). Other newspaper and magazine articles about her include *Green Book Magazine* (April 1914), *Life* (May 17, 1917), *New Republic* (April 6, 1918), and *The Boston Post* (December 1, 1921). The Robinson Locke Scrapbook collection, volumes 46 and 47, in the New York Public Library Performing Arts Research Center at Lincoln Center contains information about Nora Bayes. There are also clippings in the Harvard Theatre Collection. Obituaries and articles published after her death appeared in the *Evening World* (March 24, 1928), the *New York Times* (March 20, 1928 and December 29, 1929), the *Tribune* (March 20, 1928), and *The Telegraph* (May 13, 1931). Books on vaudeville and musical comedy that contain references to Nora Bayes include: Douglas Gilbert, *American Vaudeville—Its Life and Times* (1940); Sigmund Spaeth, *A History of Popular Music in America* (1948); Joe Laurie, Jr., *Vaudeville* (1953); James J. Fuld, *American Popular Music* (1955); Marjorie Farnsworth, *The Ziegfeld Follies* (1956); and David Ewen, *Complete Book of the American Musical Theatre* (revised edition, 1965). Bayes is listed in

Notable American Women, Vol. I (1971); *Who Was Who in the Theatre*, Vol. I (1978); and *The Oxford Companion to American Theatre* (1984).

Pamela Hewitt

BEL GEDDES, Barbara (October 31, 1922–): stage, film, and television actress most memorable as "Maggie the Cat" in Tennessee Williams's play, *Cat on a Hot Tin Roof*, was born in New York City to pioneering scenic designer Norman Bel Geddes and Helen Belle (Sneider) Bel Geddes. She was educated at the Buxton Country School, the Putney School, and Andrebrook. She made her stage debut at the Clinton Playhouse in Clinton, Connecticut, in a walk-on role in *The School for Scandal* in 1940. That same summer she also appeared in *Tonight at 8:30* and played Amy in *Little Women*.

Barbara Bel Geddes made her New York debut as Dottie Coburn in *Out of the Frying Pan* at the Windsor Theatre on February 11, 1941. After a brief USO tour she returned to Broadway in *Little Darling* (October 1942). In his review for the *New York Times* Brooks Atkinson wrote, "Since her plump debut in *Out of the Frying Pan* two seasons ago, Miss Bel Geddes has become an enchanting creature of less rotundity and greater charm. She has an uncommonly pleasant voice. In addition to that, she is an actress. Whatever you may think of *Little Darling* in other respects, Miss Bel Geddes is in the best of taste" (October 28, 1942).

Little Darling was followed by *Nine Girls* (January 1943), *Yes, My Darling Daughter* (Summer 1943), *Mrs. January and Mr. X* (March 1944), *Deep Are the Roots* (September 1945), *Burning Bright* (October 1950), and *The Moon Is Blue* (March 1951), her first collaboration with the actor Barry Nelson. William Hawkins of the *New York World-Telegram* compared her favorably to Gracie Allen, and John Chapman of the *Daily News* called her "a captivating comedienne" (March 9, 1951).

During the summer seasons of 1952 and 1953 Bel Geddes appeared at the Robin Hood Theatre in Wilmington, Delaware, in a succession of plays produced by her husband, Windsor Lewis. Along with her roles in *The Voice of the Turtle* and *The Respectful Prostitute*, she portrayed Julie in *Lilliom* and Billie Dawn in *Born Yesterday*.

She returned to Broadway in *The Living Room* by Graham Greene. Although Greene's drama was not well received, Bel Geddes was hailed by Brooks Atkinson in the *New York Times* as "an extremely gifted actress" (November 18, 1954). In March 1955 Bel Geddes created the most important role of her career, Maggie in Tennessee Williams's *Cat on a Hot Tin Roof*. Both the actress and the play won nearly universal accolades. Chapman wrote, "No actress was ever more resourceful. . . . She carries almost all of the first act in a monologue" (*Daily News*, March 25, 1955); Walter Kerr in the *Herald Tribune* praised her "lasting and altogether luminous performance" (March 25, 1955).

Bel Geddes next appeared as Mary, the showgirl in Terence Rattigan's *The Sleeping Prince*, directed by Michael Redgrave (November 1956). This appearance was followed by Robert Anderson's *Silent Night, Lonely Night* with Henry Fonda. Walter Kerr wrote, "If the actress's face is childlike, it also has the firm dignity of childhood, and it is astonishing how much invisible terror Miss Bel Geddes can convey through the mask with a faint shake of her head and the tremor of her idle hands" (*Herald Tribune*, December 4, 1959).

Anderson's short-lived drama was followed by the long-running comedy *Mary Mary*, which marked Bel Geddes's second production with Barry Nelson (March 1961). Her personal mannerisms meshed perfectly with the character. Wrote Howard Taubman in the *New York Times*, "Barbara Bel Geddes plays Mary with an agreeably light touch; her quirk of pausing for quick intakes of breath in the midst of phrases, whether a habit or not, seems felicitous here" (March 9, 1961). The summer of 1964 saw Bel Geddes in *The Constant Wife* and *Love and Marriage*. She also appeared in the pre-Broadway tryout of *The Porcelain Year*.

Bel Geddes returned to Broadway in 1967, again with Barry Nelson in Edward Albee's dark comedy *Everything in the Garden* (November 1967). Her last Broadway appearance was in the **Jean Kerr** comedy *Finishing Touches* (February 1973).

Among Barbara Bel Geddes's film credits are *The Long Night* (her film debut, 1947), for which she received an Academy Award (Oscar) nomination as best supporting actress; *I Remember Mama* (1948); *Vertigo* (1959); and *Summertree* (1971). Included in her television appearances are two episodes of *Alfred Hitchcock Presents: Godhorn* and *Lamb to the Slaughter*. In the latter, a favorite among viewers, Bel Geddes plays a homicidal wife who murders her husband by administering a skull fracture with a frozen leg of lamb, which she then roasts and feeds to the detectives investigating the murder. Since 1978 (with the exception of one season, 1984–1985, when she had heart surgery), she has appeared as the matriarch, Miss Ellie, on the prime time soap opera *Dallas*, a role for which she received television's Emmy Award as best dramatic actress.

Barbara Bel Geddes won the Clarence Derwent Award (1946) for her performance as Genevra Langdon in *Deep Are the Roots*. She has two daughters, one each from her marriage to Carl Schreuer (dissolved 1951) and the late Windsor Lewis.

For reviews of Barbara Bel Geddes's performances see the *New York Times* (October 28, 1942; November 18, 1954; and March 9, 1961); the *Daily News* (March 9, 1951, and March 25, 1955); and the *Herald Tribune* (March 25, 1955, and December 4, 1959). See also *Liberty* (November 1947), *Look* (August 19, 1947), and the *New York Post Magazine* (November 8, 1947). Barbara Bel Geddes is included in *Current Biography, 1948* (1949); *The Biographical Encyclopaedia and Who's Who of the American Theatre* (1966); *Notable Names in the American Theatre* (1976); *Who's Who in Hollywood* (1976);

Who's Who in the Theatre (1981); and *The Oxford Companion to American Theatre* (1984).

Robin Holt

BERG, Gertrude (October 3, 1899–September 15, 1966): actress and playwright, creator of the long-running radio and television series *The Goldbergs*, was born Gertrude Edelstein in New York City. She was the only child of Jacob and Diana (Goldstein) Edelstein and the granddaughter of immigrants, all living in immediate proximity in an upper Manhattan Jewish community. Gertrude Edelstein grew up immersed in family and neighborhood ritual, religion, and *yiddishkeit*. She drew all of the characters appearing in her creation *The Goldbergs* from relatives and friends who wandered with ease in and out of each other's homes. Diana Edelstein took care of the home and her daughter while supporting her husband in his various business ventures. Jacob Edelstein seemed like a character waiting for a play to be written about him. An entrepreneur with extravagant ideas about his own importance, he dabbled more or less successfully in restaurant and hotel businesses.

When Gertrude Edelstein was seven years old, her father borrowed money to purchase a hotel resort at Fleischmanns, New York, in the Catskills. Here she learned to entertain the guests not only through courteous service and attention to their needs but also by writing and performing skits, pantomimes, and fortuneteller acts. The guests admired her performances and called for more. Eventually, from these rudimentary attempts, the characters of the "Goldbergs" emerged.

Gertrude Edelstein attended public school in New York at Wadleigh High School and took courses in playwriting at Columbia University. In 1918 she married Lewis Berg, a chemical engineer, who attained some recognition in his field as a sugar technologist. For a while the couple lived on a sugar plantation in Louisiana, but they soon returned to New York City. They had two children: a son, Cherney Robert (born 1922), and a daughter, Harriet (born 1926). When they returned to New York, Gertrude Berg, in hopes of obtaining a weekly radio series, persuaded NBC officials to look at one of her scripts. In 1929 NBC agreed to a trial airing, and *The Rise of the Goldbergs* received enthusiastic response and acclaim. In 1934 the actors in the series began a personal appearance tour of vaudeville houses. In one form or another, *The Rise of the Goldbergs* played almost uninterruptedly for two decades. From 1938 until 1945 it was carried by both NBC and CBS radio. In 1949 the show made the transfer to television with continued success.

The adventures of the Yiddish-accented Molly Goldberg (the playwright always portrayed the role of Molly), her husband Jake, Uncle David, and the teenage children, Rosalie and Sammy, enthralled millions of Americans throughout the years. Berg's popularity was demonstrated when she once canceled a performance due to illness and the radio station received tens of thousands of letters in protest. Throughout the golden age of radio, *The Goldbergs* usually topped the popularity polls, only occasionally coming in second to *Amos 'n' Andy*. Berg seemed able to transfer the Goldbergs successfully to any medium. In 1948 her play *Me and Molly* enjoyed 156 performances on Broadway. In 1951 Berg co-authored and starred in a movie version, titled *Molly*.

Despite her success and renown as a scriptwriter, Berg's chief fame was as an actress. In 1959 she won an Antoinette Perry (Tony) Award for her portrayal of the widowed Mrs. Jacoby at the Shubert Theatre in *A Majority of One* by Leonard Spiegelglass. In 1963 she appeared successfully in *Dear Me, the Sky Is Falling* at the Music Box Theatre. She died suddenly on September 15, 1966, while she was rehearsing for the starring role in *The Play Girls*. Berg's significance rests, however, as she would have preferred, upon her craftsmanship as a radio and television writer and playwright. For several years she was perhaps the most popular dramatist in America, with more people entertained by her work than by that of Eugene O'Neill or Tennessee Williams. Without question she advanced the art of popular American playwriting and paved the way for women in the field.

The best source of information on Berg's professional life is the collection of correspondence, scrapbooks, and radio and television scripts in the Gertrude Berg Collection in the George Arents Research Library at Syracuse University. Berg's own memoir, written in collaboration with her son, Cherney, and appropriately titled *Molly and Me* (1961), is, as one would expect, full of the warmth of her alter ego, Molly Goldberg. Some reviews of her plays can be found in *Commonweal* (March 12, 1948), *The New Yorker* (March 6, 1948), *Newsweek* (March 8, 1948), *Theatre Arts* (April 1948), and *Time* (March 8, 1948). Other articles can be found in *The Saturday Review* (October 8, 1966) and *Readers Digest* (January 8, 1962). Berg's obituary in the *New York Times* (September 15, 1966) provides a good summary biography. For additional information, see *Who's Who in American Jewry* (1938–1939); *The Universal Jewish Encyclopedia*, Vol. 2 (1940); *Who Was Who in the Theatre*, Vol. I (1978); *Notable American Women*, Vol. IV: *The Modern Period* (1980); and *The Oxford Companion to American Theatre* (1984).

Donald Ray Schwartz

BERNSTEIN, Aline Frankau (December 22, 1880–September 7, 1955): first important woman theatrical designer in the United States, was born Hazel Frankau in New York City. She was the elder of two daughters of Rebecca (Goldsmith) Frankau and Joseph Frankau, an actor of German-Jewish ancestry. Her early years were spent in a succession of theatrical boardinghouses. By the time she was seventeen, both her parents were dead, and she had become the ward of her aunt, Rachel Goldsmith. When Tom Watson, a close friend of the family, perceived a definite talent in her drawings, he arranged for her to receive a scholarship at the New York School of Applied Design, where he served as a member of the Board of Directors. There she studied with Robert Henri, one of the most important American painters of the era. Aline Frankau married Wall Street broker Theodore Bernstein on November 19, 1902. They had two children, Theodore (born 1904) and Edla (born 1906).

Bernstein's early artistic expression was in portrait painting, but she also volunteered as a backstage worker at Henry Street Settlement, where the **Lewisohn** sisters (**Alice** and **Irene**) were producing plays and pageants. From 1915 to 1924 Bernstein designed and executed costumes for at least fifteen plays. In 1924 she designed *The Little Clay Cart*, the ancient Indian classic, which received widespread critical acclaim and marked Bernstein's emergence as a major designer of sets and costumes. She had based her design concept on the Rajput style of miniature painting.

In the summer of 1925, Bernstein met the young Thomas Wolfe. Though Wolfe was twenty years younger than Bernstein, they became lovers and for five years carried on a passionate relationship. Bernstein supported the young writer financially for several years, encouraged him in his writing, and acted as his unofficial agent for his first book, *Look Homeward Angel*, which was published in 1928. Wolfe lived in a loft that Bernstein rented in Greenwich Village to use as her office and studio. Though she spent part of nearly every day with her lover, Bernstein continued to live with her husband and family and continued her career as a designer.

Her relationship with Wolfe was often stormy. In 1930, when Wolfe was granted a Guggenheim Fellowship to travel and write in Europe, he tried to end the romance, though he did continue to correspond with Bernstein. When he returned to New York, Bernstein tried to renew the relationship, but Wolfe rejected her. Her despondency over the breakup led her to drink and even to attempt suicide. Finally, with the help of her family, she pulled herself together and immersed herself once again in her work. Bernstein was the model for one of Wolfe's characters, Esther Jack, who appeared in both *The Web and the Rock* (1939) and *You Can't Go Home Again* (1940). She, in turn, used Wolfe's early New York experiences in her own novel *The Journey Down* (1938).

At the Neighborhood Playhouse Bernstein designed expressionistic settings and costumes for the first American production of *The Dybbuk*, a classic Jewish folktale; then she created a series of satiric designs for *The Grand Street Follies*, an annual Neighborhood Playhouse parody of the Broadway season (1924 through 1929). In early 1928 Bernstein began working with **Eva Le Gallienne** at her Civic Repertory Theatre, where she was the resident designer for the next four years. She designed an average of five shows each year and most notably contributed to the Civic Repertory Theatre's operation a unit setting consisting of a skeleton frame that, with the addition of dozens of different inserts, doors, and windows, could accommodate almost any dramatic need.

By 1934 the Neighborhood Playhouse and the Civic Repertory Theatre had closed, and Bernstein turned to the Theatre Guild and other independent producers. In 1934 she designed Herman Shumlin's production of **Lillian Hellman's** first play, *The Children's Hour*. Subsequently, the three worked together on four other Hellman scripts between 1934 and 1949.

In 1935 Bernstein went to Hollywood, where she designed two RKO spectaculars (*She* and *The Last Days of Pompeii*). She then returned to New York.

Over the years she designed Hellman's *The Little Foxes* (1939, sets only), *The Male Animal* by James Thurber and Elliott Nugent (1940, sets only), and Samuel Taylor's *The Happy Time* (1950). From 1943 to 1949 she was an instructor in costume design and consultant to the Experimental Theatre at Vassar College. In 1949, when she was almost seventy years old, Bernstein won an Antoinette Perry (Tony) Award for her costume designs for the opera *Regina*. With unflagging energy, she designed three additional shows that season. Her last project as a theatrical designer was the creation of the costumes for the Off-Broadway production of *The World of Sholom Aleichem* in 1953. She died in New York City on September 7, 1955.

For thirty years Bernstein was an outstanding designer for the theatre. In 1926 she was taken into the Brotherhood of Painters, Decorators, and Paperhangers of the American Federation of Labor; she was the first woman to belong to the Brotherhood. At the time, there was no separate designers' or artists' union. Bernstein was also instrumental in setting up the famous Costume Institute at the Metropolitan Museum of Art, and for the last eleven years of her life she served as its president.

A collection of Aline Bernstein's unpublished notebooks, drawings, and photographs is in the Billy Rose Theatre Collection, New York Public Library Performing Arts Research Center at Lincoln Center. The Houghton Library, Harvard University, contains substantial correspondence between Bernstein and Thomas Wolfe. Bernstein's publications include her autobiography, *An Actor's Daughter* (1941); *The Martha Washington Dollbook* (1945); the novels *The Journey Down* (1938) and *Miss Condon* (1947); *Masterpieces of Women's Costume of the 18th and 19th Centuries* (1959); "Scissors and Sense," *Theatre Arts Monthly* (August 1952); "Off-Stage: A Harp String Breaks," *Vogue* (December 1939); and "In Production," *Atlantic Monthly* (September 1940). *Aline*, a biography by Carole Klein, was published in 1979. "Aline Bernstein: A History and Evaluation" (Unpublished Ph.D. dissertation, Indiana University, 1971) by Mike A. Barton has an extensive bibliography. Other sources on her life and career include Alice Lewisohn Crowley, *The Neighborhood Playhouse* (1959), and Norris Houghton, "The Designer Sets the Stage," *Independent Woman* (May 1946). Her obituary appeared in the *New York Times* (September 8, 1955). Bernstein is listed in *Who Was Who in the Theatre*, Vol. I (1978); *Notable American Women*, Vol. IV: *The Modern Period* (1980); *The Oxford Companion to the Theatre* (1983); and *The Oxford Companion to American Theatre* (1984).

Mike A. Barton

BOESING, Martha Gross (January 24, 1936–): actress, director, librettist, manager, and a leading feminist playwright, is also founding manager of At the Foot of the Mountain, an influential women's theatre collective in Minneapolis. Martha Gross was born in Providence, Rhode Island, to Mary Elizabeth (Jones) Gross of Dorchester, Massachusetts, and Harold Bancroft Gross of Providence. She was the only child of her mother's second marriage. Her mother worked as a secretary for an Episcopalian church; her father was an English teacher at a boys' preparatory school in New England for a few years and then studied law and became head of American Cyanamid's legal department.

After boarding school at the Abbot Academy (Andover, Massachusetts), Martha Gross attended Connecticut College for Women, where she received the Bachelor of Arts degree in English in 1957. In her junior year she wrote her first play, *Accent on Fools*. She earned a Master of Arts degree in English literature from the University of Wisconsin in 1958. In 1959 she married Martin Pierce; the couple attended the University of Minnesota, where Martha Gross Pierce began doctoral work in theatre. She dropped out after a year to work with the Minneapolis Repertory Theatre.

In 1961 she co-founded and directed the Fourth Street Players and the Moppet Players; the latter became the acclaimed Minneapolis' Children's Theatre. In 1962 she took time off to have her first child, a son named Curtis. In 1964 she was back at work in the theatre, becoming associated with Minneapolis' experimental Firehouse Theatre. She worked there for three years as performer, fund raiser, and playwright. Having divorced Martin Pierce, in 1966 Martha Gross married Paul Boesing, a composer, musician, and actor. Over the next four years the Boesings created a number of music-theatre pieces, including *The Wanderer* (1966), an opera commissioned by the Minnesota Opera Company; *Earth Song* (1970), a music drama; and *The Chameleons* (1971), songs and dialogues of marriage. By 1968 the Boesing household had grown to include two daughters, Rachel (born 1966) and Jennifer (born 1968).

In 1972 the family of five moved to Atlanta where the Academy Theatre had commissioned the Boesings to write *Shadows: A Dream Opera*, an experimental work funded by a Martha Baird Rockefeller Foundation grant. The next year Martha Boesing, as playwright-in-residence at the Academy Theatre, wrote *Pimp* (1973) and *Journey to Canaan* (1974). Both plays deal with the fantasies, fears, and needs of women—subjects that would all become overridding themes in her later plays. In June 1974 the Boesings and four other Academy Theatre actors returned to Minneapolis, where they again produced *Pimp* and toured it with Boesing's *The Gelding* (a companion piece for three men) as the first production of their new theatre company, At the Foot of the Mountain. The company toured *Pimp* through the winter and spring of 1975. In the fall Boesing, now separated from her husband, and Jan Magrane produced Boesing's new full-length play, *River Journal*, a modern ''morality musical'' depicting Everywoman's journey through marriage, with music by John Franzer. By 1976 At the Foot of the Mountain became a women's theatre collective, and since that time Boesing's playwriting career has burgeoned. The company, ranging from five to fourteen women, has provided productions of such plays as *Love Song for an Amazon* (1976), *Mad Emma* (1976), *Trespasso* (1977), *The Moon Tree* (1977), *Labia Wings* (1979), *Dora Du Fran's Wild West Extravaganza; or, the Real Lowdown on Calamity Jane* (1979), *The Web* (1981), *Song for Johanna* (1981), *The Last Fire: An Illumination* (1981), *Antigone Too: Rites of Love and Defiance* (1983), and *The Mother of Ludlow* (1983). In addition, the members of the company have worked with Boesing to create *Raped: A Look at Brecht's The Exception and the Rule* (1976), *The Story of a Mother* (1977), *Junkie* (1981), *Ashes, Ashes, We All Fall Down* (1982), and *Las Gringas* (1984).

Today, At the Foot of the Mountain is one of several full-time, professional feminist theatres in the United States. Since 1974 Boesing has supplied most of its plays and given the company its performance style through her singular playwriting. Commissioned in 1981 by the Playwrights' Laboratory in Minneapolis, Boesing wrote her first radio drama, *Song for Johanna*, a poetic, surreal explanation of a woman's decision to leave her family. In collaboration with her company, she also wrote *Junkie*, a participatory ritual drama about addiction (to chemicals, food, sex, commodities, work, and violence) and recovery. Also directed by the playwright, *Junkie* became the highlight of the Gathering—a festival of theatre companies from all over the country held in St. Paul, Minnesota, in August 1981.

Boesing is recognized primarily as a playwright. However, she is also a performer, a director, and a technician. She has said, ''I became a playwright about fifteen years ago, but I was trained in the theatre as an actor, technician, director; and hence to this day I passionately see theatre as a nonliterary art form—a collaborative performance art which takes place in *time*, not in space (as on the page or canvas). Sometimes I call myself an architect of the theatre rather than a playwright'' (from a letter dated June 9, 1981). Boesing's plays successfully balance art, therapy, and politics. Her style is nonrealistic, intuitive, nonlinear, and overtly theatrical. Over the years her work has become more economical and ritualistic.

In 1979 the National Endowment for the Arts awarded Boesing a fellowship. In 1984 the Bush Foundation gave her a writing fellowship, and she resigned from the management of At the Foot of the Mountain.

She continued to reside in Minneapolis and work occasionally with the company on specific plays and projects. In the fall of 1987 she returned to At the Foot of the Mountain to re-create her earlier play, *The Story of a Mother*, with the new multi-ethnic ensemble which had won a Ford Foundation grant to aid in its transition to a more inclusive personnel. By January of 1988 she had returned to her vocation as playwright with another new play, *The Business at Hand*, appearing that month.

Since 1974, as a playwright and as founder of a women's theatre collective, Martha Boesing has immeasurably strengthened feminist theatre in the United States.

Three of Martha Boesing's plays—*The Gelding, River Journal,* and *Love Song for an Amazon*—have been published in *Journeys Along the Matrix: Three Plays by Martha Boesing* (1978). *Pimp* appears in *A Century of Plays by American Women*, edited by Rachel France (1979), and *The Story of a Mother* appears in *Women in American Theatre*, edited by Helen Krich Chinoy and Linda Walsh Jenkins (1980). A brief history of At the Foot of the Mountain and Boesing's involvement in the theatre collective can be found in *Theatre: Past and Present* by Milly S. Barranger (1984). Articles and reviews of works produced by At the Foot of the Mountain appear in Minneapolis newspapers and in *Feminist Theatre Groups* by Dinah L. Leavitt (1980). See also Robert Collins, "A Feminist Theatre in Transition," *American Theatre* (February 1988).

Dinah L. Leavitt

BOLAND, Mary (January 28, between 1880 and 1885—June 23, 1965): actress, famous for her flighty, comic characters, was born in Philadelphia, where her mother, Mary (Hatton) Boland, was accompanying her actor husband, then on tour. William A. Boland was a minor stock actor based in Detroit, Michigan. Mary Boland subsequently grew up in Detroit, where she received a Catholic education at the Sacred Heart Convent. Despite her parents' ardent objections she elected at an early age to follow her father's calling and first appeared on the stage in *A Social Highwayman* in Detroit in 1901. She then spent four years touring and performing with stock companies in Cincinnati, Nashville, Los Angeles, and Providence. On August 28, 1905, she replaced an actress in *Strongheart* by William C. de Mille, at the Savoy Theatre in New York. The first New York production in which she originated a role was *The Ranger* (1907), a melodrama by Augustus Thomas. Within a year after this she was offered a permanent position in the Charles Frohman Company opposite the venerable John Drew. Boland acted in eight productions with Drew, including *Much Ado About Nothing* (1913) and Victorien Sardou's *A Scrap of Paper* (1914), which included **Ethel Barrymore** and **Laura Hope Crews** in the cast. During these years (1908–1914) Boland played both serious and light comic roles. She often portrayed saucy, witty, or sensual women—like Micheline in *Inconstant George* (1909), described by Allen Churchill in *The Great White Way* (p. 76) as "a wild, sensitive, primitive child." While performing with Drew, Boland also made numerous appearances on the vaudeville circuit, which often featured star actors in comic playlets.

Mary Boland earned renown as a highly accomplished comedienne. Her dramatic material ranged from light drawing room comedy to broad farce, from polite melodrama to musicals. Equally significant, however, were her humanitarian contributions during World War I and her efforts for Actors' Equity during the momentous strike of 1919.

For five months during the last year of World War I, Boland toured France with an acting company, traveling in ambulances and working, in Alexander Woollcott's words, "like a horse giving farces and melodramas for homesick Yanks in the great, cheerless base hospitals" of the American Expeditionary Forces (*New York Times*, September 28, 1919). In 1919, although it jeopardized her starring role in the production of *Clarence* just before a Broadway opening, she helped Francis Wilson, Ethel Barrymore, and others lead the professional actors' strike against the Producing Managers Association). This strike brought Broadway theatres to a standstill for thirty days and ended many practices by which managers had long exploited the acting profession. The strike ended on September 6, and on September 20, 1919, Boland appeared as Mrs. Webster in *Clarence*. Her characterization of Mrs. Webster, the stepmother of an irresponsible family, marked a change in her acting style. This hilarious Booth Tarkington play, which elevated Alfred Lunt to stardom and firmly solidified the career of young **Helen Hayes**, also launched Boland's extensive series of variations on madcap, scatterbrained, flighty, frivolous wives and mothers. Her most successful farcical role in the 1920s was Paula Ritter in George Kelly's *The Torchbearers* (1922), a play that wittily satirized the "Little Theatre Movement" sweeping the country at that time. Alexander Woollcott in his *New York Times* review (August 30, 1922) described her performance as that of "a pretty, silly little matron who suffers from the brief but dangerous delusion that she is an emotional actress. Really, last night saw Miss Boland triumph as an utterly delightful comedienne. She had a little glory all her own." Her comic performance as a celebrity-chasing woman who becomes an accidental bigamist in Lynn Starling's *Meet the Wife* (1923) was so memorable that a scene from it was revived by the American National Theatre and Academy for a fund raiser in 1951.

Extensive film commitments reduced the number of her theatre performances in the 1930s and 1940s, but she periodically reappeared on the Broadway stage, sometimes in musicals, to the delight of New York theatregoers. In *Jubilee*, for example, a Cole Porter/Moss Hart musical of 1935, Boland was, according to Brooks Atkinson's *New York Times* review (October 14, 1935), "a carnival of comic delights. For the venom she puts into her moments of shrewish indignation, the sticky unction of her philandering and the general club-lady excitability of her deportment are unconscionably sharp and funny."

Impressed by her comic skills, the Theatre Guild selected the role of Mrs. Malaprop in Richard Brinsley Sheridan's *The Rivals* as a vehicle for her in 1942. Although her relationship with the director **Eva Le Gallienne** was not a happy one, Boland's Mrs. Malaprop left a lasting impression on the critics.

At the end of her long stage career, Boland played what *Time* (July 2, 1965) called "the mother-in-law to end them all" in Don Appell's *Lullaby* in 1954. "Miss Boland's old bat is in her broadest comic style," Brooks Atkinson wrote in the *New York Times* (February 4, 1954), "rattle-brained, dry, bustling and aggressive. After an absence of six years from Broadway, Miss Boland returns as overwrought and mercurial as ever, still the professional comedienne." With *Lullaby* Boland completed her thirty-second Broadway production, a record augmented by many road and stock productions and more than fifty films.

As a Hollywood actress Boland performed in at least ten silent films from 1915 to 1920. She did not return to film until 1931 but remained active until the mid–1940s. Her film roles were not unlike her stage characterizations. On film she presented a myriad of zany mothers and wives. Her most memorable films are perhaps *Ruggles of Red Gap* (1935), a wild comedy with Charles Laughton as Charles Ruggles that broke all box office records up to that time; *The Women* (1939), a delightful, catty comedy with an all-female cast including Norma Shearer, Joan Crawford, Rosalind Russell, and Paulette Goddard; and *Pride and Prejudice* (1940), a comedy in which Boland, playing Mrs. Bennett, a silly, frivolous mother, starred with Laurence Olivier and Greer Garson. Boland made her last film, *Guilty Bystander*, in 1950.

During a fifty-three-year career in theatre and film Boland never married. Dying of an apparent heart attack while asleep in her Essex House suite in New York, she left no immediate survivors. She is buried in Glendale, California.

The best sources of information on Mary Boland are an interview with the actress by John B. Kennedy, "Making Them Laugh," *Collier's* (August 22, 1931), and Daniel Blum, *Great Stars of the American Stage* (1952). For stories and anecdotes that include the actress, see Eva Le Gallienne, *With a Quiet Heart* (1953); Lloyd Morris, *Curtain Time* (1953); Cornelia Otis Skinner, *Life with Lindsay & Crouse* (1976); Maurice Zolotow, *Stagestruck* (1965); Allen Churchill, *The Great White Way* (1962); and Ray Stuart, *Immortals of the Screen* (1965). Significant reviews include Alexander Woollcott, *New York Times* (September 22, 1919; September 28, 1919; and August 30, 1922) and Brooks Atkinson, *New York Times* (October 14, 1935; January 15, 1942; and February 4, 1954). Boland's obituaries appeared in the *New York Times* (June 24, 1965), *Variety* (June 30, 1965), *Time* (July 2, 1965), and *Newsweek* (July 5, 1965). For chronologies of Boland's career, see *The Biographical Encyclopaedia and Who's Who of the American Theatre* (1966); *Who Was Who in the Theatre*, Vol. I (1978); and Ephraim Katz, *The Film Encyclopedia* (1979). See also *A Pictorial History of the American Theatre* (1951) and *The Encyclopedia of the American Theatre 1900–1975* (1980). Boland's birth date is given in different sources as 1880, 1882, and 1885.

Ronald H. Wainscot

BONFILS, Helen Gertrude (November 26, 1889-June 6, 1972): Broadway producer, Denver newspaper publisher, and occasional actress, was born in Denver, Colorado, the second daughter of Frederick Gilmer and Belle (Barton) Bonfils. (The name was pronounced Bone-feece.) She grew up in Denver as the daughter of the wealthy and powerful co-owner of the *Denver Post* newspaper. In her late teens Bonfils went to finishing school at Forest Glen, Maryland, because her father thought that a woman should have a good education and a good speaking voice. Returning to Denver, she led a sheltered life. Her father was convinced that any young men who were interested in her were only after her money, and it was not until he died in 1933 that "Miss Helen," as she was called, was free to find a channel for her energies. Although she held various positions at the newspaper (she was chairman of the board when she died), she left the day-to-day operations to professionals and devoted herself to theatre. She appeared in a small role in *Men in White* in 1934 at Denver's Elitch's Gardens Theatre. Two years later she married the company's director, George Somnes, and the two went to New York where Bonfils financed and her husband directed *Sun Kissed* (March 10, 1937). Somnes then directed *The Greatest Show on Earth* (January 5, 1938). Bonfils co-produced the play and appeared in it as Mrs. Polar under the name Gertrude Barton. Their next three ventures played a total of thirty-six performances: *The Brown Danube* and *Pastoral* in 1939 and *Topaz* in 1947. Bonfils appeared for the one performance of *Topaz* in the role of Baroness Pitart-Verginolies. Somnes died in 1953.

In 1959, with her second husband, Edward Michael Davis (whom she divorced in 1971), and the actress Haila Stoddard, Helen Bonfils coproduced *Come Play with Me*. This was followed by *A Thurber Carnival* in 1960, Bonfils's first notable success as a producer. It ran for 213 performances in two engagements during the year. Bonfils and Stoddard formed Bonard Productions in 1961. *Sail Away* was produced on Broadway at the Broadhurst Theatre in conjunction with Charles Russell that year and with Harold Fielding in a London production the following year (1962). During 1963 Bonard Productions presented *The Hollow Crown*, *The Beast in Me* (in conjunction with producer Morton Gottlieb), and *Chips with Everything* and was a financial backer for *Enter Laughing*. Bonard Productions and producer Donald Seawell, by arrangement with the Royal Shakespeare Theatre, produced *King Lear* and *The Comedy of Errors* for a national tour in 1964, followed by a New York run. Helen Bonfils produced, again in association with Morton Gottlieb, *The White House* and *P.S. I Love You* in 1964, *The Killing of Sister George* in 1966, *Come Live with Me* and *The Promise* in 1967, *Lovers* and *We Bombed in New Haven* in 1968, *The Mundy Scheme* in 1969, and *Sleuth* in 1970.

Bonfils was also a co-producer of the South Shore Players (Cohasset, Massachusetts). She continued her support of Elitch's Gardens Theatre in Denver as well as sponsoring the Denver Post Operas for thirty-eight years until her death. She was made a Daughter of Public Service by the University of Denver in 1951. In 1953 she built the Bonfils Civic Theatre in Denver, and in 1963 she received the Malcolm Glen Wyer Award for her contribution to the Denver theatre scene. Among her humanitarian contributions to the Denver area were the Bonfils Tumor Clinic and the Belle Bonfils Blood Bank. She also financed the building of the Holy Ghost Roman Catholic Church in Denver. On May 21, 1972, she was honored *in absentia* with a St. Genesius Award. **Helen Hayes**, who was also honored at that time, accepted the Award for Bonfils. After a long illness caused by heart complications, Helen Bonfils died at her New York apartment on June 6, 1972.

Even after her death Helen Bonfils continued her involvement in theatre through the Bonfils Foundation, which gave generous support to the Denver Center for the Performing Arts and maintained the Denver Center Theatre Company.

Helen Bonfils is included in the *Biographical Encyclopaedia and Who's Who of the American Theatre* (1966) and *Who Was Who in the Theatre*, Vol. I (1978). Her recent productions are listed under Morton Gottlieb's biography in *Notable Names in the American Theatre* (1976). A discussion of the Bonfils Theatre is found in *The Oxford Companion to the Theatre* (1983). Bonfils's obituary appeared in *The Denver Post* (June 7, 1972) and the *New York Times* (June 7, 1972).

Richard K. Knaub

BONSTELLE, Jessie (November 19, 1871?–October 14, 1932): actress, director, and manager, nicknamed the "Maker of Stars," discovered significant new talent for the theatre and founded one of America's first civic theatres in

Detroit. She was born Laura Justine Bonesteele on a farm near Greece, New York, the eleventh child of Helen Louisa (Norton) Bonesteele and Joseph Frederick Bonesteele, an attorney who turned to farming to support his large family. Always called Jessie by her family, she changed the spelling of her last name early in her career.

Helen Bonesteele had longed for a career on the stage before her marriage. In a six-part autobiographical article in *McCall's Magazine* in 1927, Jessie Bonstelle recounts her mother's visit to a fortuneteller during her pregnancy with Jessie. The gypsy told her mother that she would realize all she had longed for through her daughter. Helen Bonesteele began to groom her daughter to fulfill her dream almost from the cradle, tutoring the toddler in singing, dancing, and recitation. There is an anecdote that the prodigy sang temperance songs from a pulpit at the age of two. She also toured as a child reciter. Despite a bustling household her mother often managed to take Jessie to the theatre in Rochester, where she saw Sarah Bernhardt, **Helena Modjeska**, and **Fanny Janauschek**. In 1880, at the age of nine, the young Jessie joined a touring company in Rochester for her first professional engagement in *Bertha, The Beautiful Sewing Machine Girl*. When the national tour ended in California, Bonstelle returned home to attend the Nazareth Convent School for the only formal education she was to receive. By 1886 she had resumed her career, touring in a one-woman variety act under the management of Edward D. Stair.

Bonstelle's father died in 1890, and her mother six months later. Bonstelle headed for New York and sought out a childhood idol, Fanny Janauschek, who had been one of Germany's most celebrated actresses before her American debut in 1867. Accepted into the aging star's company, Bonstelle toured the South in *Harvest Moon*. She fell in love with the leading man, Alexander Hamilton Stuart, who was several years her senior. They were married in 1893. She claimed to be seventeen at the time, though the birth date on her death record suggests that she was twenty-two. Stuart had been a member of the famed Chestnut Street Theatre Company in Philadelphia in the 1870s and returned to that city in April 1893 as a member of the New Forepaugh Stock Company; Bonstelle joined him in September of that year. Stuart also appeared on Broadway. His last appearance was in a role especially written for him by Clyde Fitch, in the 1910 film *The City*. He died in 1911.

With the Forepaugh Stock Company Bonstelle played secondary roles to leading ladies Fanny McIntyre and Martha Ford, expanding her repertory with each week's new offering and observing stock company management at its finest. Bonstelle periodically left the company to assume more substantial roles in smaller stock companies. For instance, she appeared in Rochester as a leading lady in such demanding roles as Magda, Juliet, Ophelia, Lady Teazle, and Margaret Gautier. During the 1898–1899 season, she was a leading player with the Standard Theatre Stock Company in Philadelphia, which presented melodramas to lower-class audiences. Here Bonstelle starred in such vehicles as *The Stowaway*, *The Unknown*, and *Slaves of Gold*. In the last of these Bonstelle suffered a broken wrist when she fell fifteen feet because a carpenter prematurely allowed a scenic element to drop. A bitter disagreement ensued between Bonstelle and the company manager, John J. Jermon, over his failure to pay her medical bills and his refusal to release her salary until she signed a waiver absolving him of responsibility for the accident. Not surprisingly, Bonstelle did not again appear at the Standard Theatre.

At the turn of the century Jacob J. Shubert put her in charge of a company he and his brothers had acquired in Rochester. This position launched her managerial career. Although she claimed to be the youngest manager at the time, she was not the first woman. Before her, **Laura Keene** had successfully run her own theatre in New York City from 1855 until 1863, and **Mrs. John Drew**, after her husband's death in 1862, had for many years run the Arch Street Theatre in Philadelphia.

In the early years of this century Bonstelle also directed New York stock productions for the Shuberts and for another prominent producer, William A. Brady. She performed in stock in New York and Philadelphia and toured productions in Canada.

In 1906 Bonstelle took on the management of the Star Theatre in Buffalo in addition to the theatre in Rochester. In 1909 she also began managing the Garrick in Detroit. At times she literally commuted among her companies, as both entrepreneur and actress. She espoused stock as the ideal situation for an actress or, at least, the best training ground. When asked why an established leading actress like herself preferred a stock career, she replied, "The actress who has in three seasons played 100 parts is surely better qualified than the actress who has in the same length of time played possibly five parts" (unidentified clipping dated January 29, 1905, in Robinson Locke Scrapbook Collection). With all her stock commitments, Bonstelle still accepted Broadway engagements. In 1908 she appeared in Frederick Paulding's *The Great Question*; in 1909 she was in William Vaughn Moody's *The Faith Healer*; and in 1913 she played in Elizabeth Jordan's *The Lady From Oklahoma*. In 1911 Bonstelle conceived the idea of producing a stage version of Louisa May Alcott's novel *Little Women*. She convinced Marion de Forest to write the adaptation, found a co-producer in William A. Brady, and enlisted Bertram Harrison as co-director. Four national companies toured for a year before the New York opening in 1912. The play had a long and successful run in New York. After the First World War, a London company of *Little Women* was headed in 1919 by American actress Katharine Cornell, daughter of Dr. Peter Cornell, who had in 1906 invited Bonstelle to take over the Star Theatre in Buffalo. As a child Katharine Cornell watched rehearsals, and she eventually became a special protégée of Bonstelle.

In 1912 Bonstelle was invited to manage the first municipal theatre in the United States, in the small city of Northampton, Massachusetts, with co-director Bertram Harrison. The thousand-seat theatre had been built by a philanthropic merchant and donated to the city. Bonstelle selected the repertoire, primarily

Broadway comedies and melodramas. She directed and often played leading roles in the weekly changing bills.

Bonstelle remained with the Northampton Theatre until 1917. For a short time during that period she, **Mary Shaw**, and a few others set about raising a million dollars to establish a national Women's Theatre that would offer good plays at low prices to women in several different cities. Once established in each place, such theatres were to be turned over to the municipalities. The idea failed for lack of capital. But the concept, plus her Northampton experience, convinced Bonstelle that, in spite of the prevailing stock company system, communities could be persuaded to support professional civic theatres.

Because she had for several summer seasons operated a successful stock operation there, she had gained the respect of the Detroit business community. When she approached selected business leaders with her master plan, therefore, they readily supported her, and on January 1, 1925, she opened the Bonstelle Playhouse, which after three seasons of year-round operation became on July 1, 1928, the Detroit Civic Theatre. It was a noncommercial theatre; any profits were to be automatically turned over to the sustaining fund. At the beginning she raised $200,000 in subscriptions, most of it from large investors but $50,000 from one-dollar memberships. She was convinced that the time was "ready for the civic theatre, owned and supported by the people," and she promised to offer "the best in modern and classical drama at a moderate price" (*Theatre*, October 1928). Freedom from financial pressures now allowed Bonstelle—"the petticoated Belasco," as she was sometimes called—to indulge in a more experimental repertoire. She founded the Bonstelle Theatre Guild, presenting the works of Eugene O'Neill, Ferenc Molnar, Carlo Goldoni, and **Edna St. Vincent Millay**, as well as experimenting with modern dress performances of *Romeo and Juliet* and *Hamlet*.

Late in 1928 Bonstelle assessed her career to date: "To January 1, 1927, I had given 3,422 performances in my seventeen years' work in Detroit; I had produced 276 full-length plays, five one-acts, thirteen fantasies, and four children's plays. In addition to managing the various companies, I had myself appeared in 164 roles. Forty-one plays had their initial production in Detroit at the Bonstelle Playhouse in the three years of its existence. I have given nineteen plays their first production on any stage" (*McCall's*, December 1928).

Bonstelle was outspoken in her support of women in all branches of the theatre. She wrote, "I would encourage women playwrights, women managers, women scene painters. . . . Women should have more to do with the theatre. Since two-thirds of theatre audiences are women, it stands to reason that women know better what women want than men do" (*New York Evening Mail*, December 29, 1915). Bonstelle's company also employed women directors: Willamene Wilkes, who later established and directed the Wilkes Theatre in Los Angeles, and Maud Howell, who was Bonstelle's assistant in both Northampton and Detroit.

The Detroit Civic Theatre was conceived as being a vital part of the community. Its functions went beyond play production to include classes in acting, dancing, and technical theatre. There were such extracurricular activities as supper served on the mezzanine, dancing on the stage after performances, art exhibits, and even interdenominational religious services. It was Jessie Bonstelle's boast that she never "went Broadway." She saw stock as the spawning ground for new playwrights and as a training ground for actors. She insisted that "the great value of educational, technical, and artistic results of playing in stock can hardly be overstressed. . . . The value of stock to the actor is immeasurable. It is the only real training school when he is beginning, and the only postgraduate course for him after he has arrived and wants to keep out of the rut induced by long runs and typecasting" (*The Drama*, March 26, 1926, p. 216). It was somewhat ironic, therefore, that Katharine Cornell, some twelve years later in her autobiographical *I Wanted to be an Actress* (1938), appraised her one-time mentor's ability in this way: "She was not a great actress, but an extraordinarily good one for that particular job. . . . She was simply a trouper—right through" (p. 16). Cornell also lauded Bonstelle's discipline and energy, terming her a "human dynamo." Bonstelle had a reputation as a hard taskmaster—but one who never drove anyone harder than herself.

Of all her functions in the theatre over the years, Jessie Bonstelle was most famous for her ability to discover and develop talent in young stage aspirants, some of them amateurs when they first came to her. In addition to Katharine Cornell, other famous performers who received their early training in her companies included Ann Harding, William Powell, Frank Morgan, James Rennie, Josephine Hull, Melvyn Douglas, and Jessie Royce Landis. Winifred Lenihan, later of the Theatre Guild, served an apprenticeship with Bonstelle. Also included were designers Norman Bel Geddes and Jo Mielziner and director Guthrie McClintic. McClintic met Cornell while working for Bonstelle, and the two formed a lifetime partnership, in marriage and in professional life. He often directed her starring vehicles. In *Me and Kit*, his reminiscence of his life with Cornell, McClintic stated, "Miss Bonstelle is an extraordinary woman, tremendously competent as an actress, and the finest of stock managers. . . . She had one of the keenest noses for acting talent I have ever encountered" (p. 190).

In 1932 Bonstelle made a trip to Hollywood, reportedly to discuss directing films as well as to scout the territory for a stock company. She became ill, however, and returned to Detroit, where she died. She was buried in Rochester in Mount Hope Cemetery next to her husband. The Detroit Civic Theatre survived only one season after Bonstelle's death. However, that does not diminish the importance of her pioneering venture in conceiving and founding such an institution. This accomplishment, along with the scores of theatre artists she trained and launched in their careers, establishes her significance in the history of American theatre.

There is a six-part interview appearing in *McCall's Magazine* from September 1928 through February 1929. Although "Helen C. Bennett" by-lined the interview, "The Star Lady," takes the form of an autobiographical narrative by Bonstelle illustrated with several photographs. The Billy Rose Theatre Collection at the New York Public Library

Performing Arts Research Center at Lincoln Center contains the Robinson Locke collection of scrapbooks and portfolios of loose clippings about Bonstelle. There are also clippings in the Harvard Theatre Collection. "America's First Civic Theatre," a contemporary account of the opening of the Detroit Civic Theatre by Sylvia B. Golden, appeared in *Theatre Magazine* (October 1928). *The New York Times Theatre Reviews, 1870–1919* (1976) reprints reviews of Bonstelle's Broadway appearances. In *I Wanted to Be an Actress* (1938), Katharine Cornell discusses the impact of her first mentor upon her early career. Guthrie McClintic also evaluates Bonstelle in his reminiscence, *Me and Kit* (1955). See also Mari Kathleen Fielder, "Forepaugh Stock Company" and "Standard Theatre Stock Company" in *American Theatre Companies*, Vol. 2, ed. Weldon B. Durham (1987), and William Luther Dean, "A Biographical Study of Miss Laura Justine Bonstelle Stuart" (Unpublished Ph.D. dissertation, University of Michigan, 1954). *Notable American Women,* Vol. I (1971), contains an entry on Jessie Bonstelle as does *The Oxford Companion to the Theatre* (1983) and *The Oxford Companion to American Theatre* (1984). Some sources give 1872 as Bonstelle's birth date.

Constance Clark
additions by Mari Kathleen Fielder

BOOTH, Agnes (October 4, 1841?–January 2, 1910): famous leading actress of the last quarter of the nineteenth century, was born Marion Agnes (Land) Rookes in Sydney, Australia. According to her own account, her mother and sister had recently moved from London, leaving her father, a "Captain Rookes of the British Army," in England (*Notable American Women*, Vol. I, p. 202). He died there before Agnes was born, and her mother, Sara (Land) Rookes, then married the Reverend Henry Smeatham, an Anglican clergyman. Agnes began taking ballet lessons at the Victoria Theatre in Sydney when she was ten, primarily as a means of future support, and progressed to dancing and acting at that theatre. Then the family migrated to California, and Agnes and her sister Belle began their careers on the American stage. Agnes Land, as she was billed, first appeared with **Matilda Vining Wood**'s company (February 1858) in San Francisco on a double bill, *The Corsair* and *Popping the Question*. During the next few months she also appeared with the **Ada Isaacs Menken** Company in the sensational *Mazeppa* and even toured the northern California mining camps. She then became a member of the stock company at Maguire's Opera House in San Francisco, where she remained until 1865. On February 11, 1861, Agnes Land married Harry A. Perry, a handsome young actor also with Maguire's; he died in 1863. It was during these years that she met and performed with Junius Brutus Booth, Jr., who was at that time also associated with Maguire's.

In June 1865 Agnes Perry left San Francisco for the East Coast, where she was to live for the remainder of her life. Her stepfather had died, and both her mother and her sister moved east with her. Agnes Perry first appeared in comic roles at the Winter Garden Theatre, New York, with the John Sleeper Clarke Company in October 1865. She joined the Edwin Forrest Company at Niblo's Garden Theatre on November 13, 1865, and played in rapid succession in *Richelieu* (Julie de Mortemar), *Othello* (Desdemona), *Virginius* (Virginia), *Hamlet*

(Ophelia), and *Jack Cade* (Marianne). She finished the season supporting **Kate Bateman** in *Leah*. Her popularity was immediate and her versatility established.

The following season, 1866–1867, she became the leading lady of the Boston Theatre, then under lease to Edwin Booth and John S. Clarke (brother-in-law of Booth). On June 29, 1867, she married Junius Brutus Booth, Jr. (Edwin's brother), who took over the lease and the management of the Boston Theatre at the beginning of the 1867–1868 season. They remained with the Boston Theatre until 1873 when her husband took over the management of Edwin Booth's theatre in New York. During this period in Boston, Agnes Booth (which remained her professional name until her death) appeared with most of the famous actors of the time, played an extensive repertory of classic and modern dramas, and developed the skills that made her one of the most respected and versatile actresses of her day.

The Booth Theatre was in dire financial straits when Junius Booth assumed its management. He reintroduced his wife to New York in a production of *La Femme de Feu*, which earned her critical acclaim as "the most finished and effective emotional actress at present on the metropolitan stage" (Odell, Vol. IX, p. 386) and also gave New York audiences an opportunity to see her in her notably successful role as Lady Constance in *King John*. Years of mismanagement and the Panic of 1873 forced the closing of the theatre and brought financial ruin to Booth. For the next two seasons Agnes Booth toured to help her husband recover his losses. This period culminated in her appearance as Myrrah in the Jarret and Palmer production of *Sardanapalus* by Lord Byron at the reopened Booth's Theatre on August 14, 1876, followed by her performance as Cleopatra in a revival of Shakespeare's play at Niblo's Garden Theatre. Critics called her interpretation of Cleopatra remarkable "for its impressiveness and subtlety" (Clapp and Edgett, p. 45). As a result of these successes, she became the leading lady of the A. M. Palmer Stock Company at the Union Square Theatre. During the 1877–1878 season, she played Lady Maggie Wagstaff in *Pink Dominoes*, Adrienne in *A Celebrated Case*, and other modern roles with the Palmer company. She left Palmer to join the new Park Theatre company of Henry Abbey, appearing in Bronson Howard's comedy, *Old Love Letters* (1878), and creating the role of Belinda, "one of the great and lasting hits of the American theatre" (Odell, Vol. X, p. 600), in W.S. Gilbert's *Engaged* (1879).

In 1881 Agnes Booth joined the Madison Square Theatre company and remained its leading lady (aside from intervals when she quarreled with the management, appeared with other companies, or toured) until 1891. Her first performance as Mrs. Ralston in Sir Charles Young's *Jim the Penman*, one of her most brilliant triumphs and the role that did much to establish the dramatic possibilities of the middle-aged heroine, was given at the Madison Square Theatre on November 1, 1886. In 1891 she temporarily retired from the stage, but in February 1895 she returned to create the title character of *The Sporting Duchess* for Charles Frohman. She then appeared as Rose in *L'Arlesienne* at the Broadway Theatre in 1897. This was her last major appearance, although she was in

Frohman's production of *The Best of Friends* in 1903 and continued to perform for benefits on other special occasions.

Junius Booth died in September 1883. He had spent the last years of his life building Masconoma House, a large hotel in Manchester-by-the-Sea, Massachusetts, which, at his death, was bequeathed to his widow. Although she married John B. Schoeffel (manager of Boston's Tremont Theatre and a partner of the theatrical firm of Abbey, Schoeffel and Grau) on February 4, 1885, Agnes Booth continued to use Masconomo as her summer home and as a profitable business venture. Manchester-by-the-Sea became a mecca for theatrical stars and Masconomo House a popular gathering place. It was there, in 1887, that Agnes Booth directed an outdoor production of *As You Like It*, encouraging other open-air performances in the Northeast.

Following her retirement, Agnes Booth lived in Brookline, a suburb of Boston, and devoted her time to social and domestic activities. She died on January 2, 1910, and was buried at Manchester-by-the-Sea in the Booth lot at Rosedale Cemetery. She was survived by her second husband and two of the four sons she had by Junius Booth. Both sons became actors, but neither achieved outstanding success.

Agnes Booth had, according to Lewis C. Strang, an indisputable claim to the title "America's leading lady." She evidently never wanted or earned the accolade of "star," but she remained the "perfect artist," as the famous French actor Coquelin called her (McKay and Wingate, *Famous American Actors of To-Day*, pp. 231, 232). Overshadowed by her husband's more famous and flamboyant family, she nevertheless deserved the niche she carved for herself in the American theatre. An editorial printed in the *New York Times* following her death best expresses her talent: "Agnes Booth was an actress of commanding skill and rare versatility. Her range comprehended Shakespeare's Cleopatra and Byron's Myrrha as well as the heroines of romantic drama and modern comedy. If deficient in fervor she had dignity, poise, facility of utterance, variety of expression uncommon on the stage in any era" (*New York Times*, January 4, 1910).

The manuscript autobiography of Agnes Booth (fifteen pages, 1889) is in the Walter Hampden Memorial Library at The Players, New York City. More information on Agnes Booth can be found in George C. D. Odell, *Annals of the New York Stage*, Volumes VIII–XV (1936–1949); Frederic E. McKay and Charles E. L. Wingate, eds., *Famous American Actors of Today* (1896); John B. Clapp and Edwin F. Edgett, *Players of the Present*, Part I (1899); Frances E. Willard and Mary A. Livermore, eds., *A Woman of the Century* (1893); Eugene Tompkins, *The History of the Boston Theatre, 1854–1901* (1908); and Stanley Kimmel, *The Mad Booths of Maryland* (1940). Booth's obituaries appeared in the *New York Times* and the *Boston Transcript* (January 3, 1910). The following day an appreciation of her contribution as an actress appeared in the *New York Times* (January 4, 1910). Booth is listed in *National Cyclopaedia of American Biography*, Vol. I (1898); W. Davenport Adams, *A Dictionary of the Drama*, Vol. I (1904, reprinted 1968); *Dictionary of American Biography*, Vol. II (1937); *Who Was Who in America*, Vol. I (1942); *Notable American Women*, Vol. I (1971); and *The Oxford Companion to*

American Theatre (1984). Booth's obituary and some other sources give her birth date as 1846; however, the record of her marriage to Booth gives her age in June 1867 as twenty-five, which would make her birth date 1841.

Faye E. Head

BOOTH, Shirley (August 30, 1907–): stage, film, and television actress best known for her stage roles in *Come Back, Little Sheba* and *A Tree Grows in Brooklyn*, was born Thelma Booth Ford in Manhattan's Morningside Heights. She was the first of two daughters of Albert J. Ford and Virginia (Wright) Ford. Her father was a reserved businessman and her mother a gentle, emotional individual. Their marriage was not a happy one, and when Shirley Booth was in her teens, her parents separated.

Though her family background was hardly theatrical, Booth seems to have made her first public appearance by reciting a short poem at the age of three. From childhood her only ambition was to become an actress. At the age of twelve her formal education ended, and she left school to begin acting with a Hartford, Connecticut, stock company in a play called *Mother Carey's Chickens*. When she was fourteen, she moved to New York and landed a job as an ingénue with the Poli Stock Company. Since her father had forbidden her to use his name, Thelma Booth Ford became Shirley Booth; "Shirley" was from a character she had played and "Booth" was from her own middle name. The separation from her father was now complete; they never spoke to each other again.

In 1925 Booth made her Broadway debut opposite Humphrey Bogart in *Hell's Bells*. After the play closed, she returned to stock. Following the same pattern for the next ten years, she alternated short New York runs with stock company engagements. In New York she was usually cast in minor roles, but she often had starring parts in stock. She highly valued her stock experience: "I could have hung around New York and taken my chances," she said, "but I had to go where people believed in me, and I had to keep acting so I could believe in myself" (*Life*, December 1, 1952, p. 133). At the home of a stock company director in 1929, Booth met a salesman with a theatrical bent named Eddie Poggenburg (later known as Ed Gardner). They married after the play she was rehearsing, *Claire Adams*, opened. Although their marriage was never a smooth one, they developed a warm artistic bond. Booth's influence undoubtedly encouraged Gardner to abandon his sales career to become a director with the WPA Federal Theatre Project. He also rented the Barbizon-Plaza Hotel's little theatre and there presented *Sunday Nights at Nine*, starring his wife.

Producer George Abbott remembered Booth's performance in *Sunday Nights at Nine* when he cast *Three Men on a Horse* in 1935. He gave Booth her first substantial part on Broadway, casting her as the warmhearted gangster's moll, Mabel. The play had a successful two-year run, after which she moved with her husband to Hollywood, where he had been invited to direct the radio show *Ripley's Believe It or Not*. After a year of inactivity on Booth's part, the couple returned to New York in 1939, and she began acting once again. Her appearance in Philip Barry's *Philadelphia Story* (1939) won her at least as much critical praise as that accorded **Katharine Hepburn**, the show's star. From 1940 to 1942 she co-starred in *My Sister Eileen* (1940) while simultaneously performing the role of "Miss Duffy" on her husband's successful radio show. From 1940 to 1950 Booth acted in a wide variety of Broadway shows, including *Tomorrow The World*, *Hollywood Pinafore*, and *Land's End*. For her work in **Fay Kanin**'s *Goodbye, My Fancy* in 1948, she was given the Antoinette Perry (Tony) Award for best supporting actress.

In the midst of this professional success Booth suffered a personal setback in 1942 when Gardner asked for a divorce. Her performances on stage, however, seem not to have been affected, and soon after her divorce she met a young investment broker named William Baker, who was then a noncommissioned officer in the army. They were married four months later. After the war ended and Corporal Baker was discharged, they bought a dairy farm in Bucks County, Pennsylvania, and Shirley Booth divided her time between farming and acting. This period of calm and comfort in her life was shattered when Baker had a mild heart attack. They decided for his health to return to New York. In 1950 the Theatre Guild offered Booth the opportunity to play Lola Delaney in William Inge's *Come Back, Little Sheba*. Reluctantly, she agreed to try out the play in Connecticut. It was an immediate success, and for the first time Shirley Booth was proclaimed a star. She was awarded the Antoinette Perry (Tony) Award for best actress, the Billboard Award, the Barter Theatre Award, and the New York Critics Circle Award for the best performance of the season.

Consistent with her belief that an actress should make you forget everything she has done before, Booth moved from the domestic tragedy portrayed in *Come Back, Little Sheba* to zany musical comedy as fun-loving Cissy in *A Tree Grows in Brooklyn* (1951). So well did Booth succeed in the role that **Betty Smith**, author of the novel from which the play was adapted, said, "She knows more about Cissy than I do" (*Collier's*, June 16, 1951, p. 23). While the play was in rehearsal, Booth's husband died. She missed only two rehearsal sessions and then opened to ecstatic reviews. After a substantial run in the musical, she was invited by Paramount Studios to star in the film version of *Come Back, Little Sheba*. The film was shot in a single month, and Booth seemed to make the transition between stage and screen acting effortlessly. She earned many awards for her film performance, including the Academy (Oscar) Award for the best film actress and the Cannes International Film Festival Award for the world's best actress of 1952.

After this brief but highly successful film venture, she returned to the stage and starred as a lonely spinster in Arthur Laurents's *The Time of the Cuckoo* (1952), garnering another Tony Award for her performance. From 1953 to 1961 she created a number of beautifully detailed, highly praised characters in mediocre plays, such as *By the Beautiful Sea* (1954), *The Desk Set* (1955), and *Miss Isobel* (1957), a series of appearances that prompted reviewer Walter Kerr to ask in anguish, in his review of *Isobel*, "How are we to go on this way—

endless valentines for the girl we all love and endless outrage for the lulus in which she appears?'' (*New York Herald Tribune*, December 27, 1957). She also appeared in three more films: *About Miss Leslie* (1954), *The Matchmaker* (1958), and *Hot Spell* (1958). In 1961 she signed a five-year contract with Screen Gems Television to play the housemaid, Hazel, on the weekly show of the same name. Defending her decision, Booth insisted, ''I think you should do what you believe in and not worry about whether people are going to like it or not.... I knew I'd be criticized'' (*Saturday Evening Post*, September 22, 1962, p. 66). She went on to say that there were few good roles for women in the plays being written and that she would rather be working than waiting for a role. Thus she launched wholeheartedly into yet another medium—and once again triumphed. For her performance as Hazel she received twenty-eight awards, including three television Emmy awards for best continuing performances by an actress in a series (1962, 1963, 1964).

After the *Hazel* series ended, she went to London to make a television adaptation of Tennessee Williams's *The Glass Menagerie*. It was not entirely successful because of a disagreement with the director over character interpretation, though she did win another Emmy as Amanda Wingfield. The next three years were what Booth calls her ''Gobi Desert Period—I did nothing but putter'' (*TV Guide*, May 12, 1973). Then, in 1970, she returned to Broadway to perform in the musical *Look to the Lilies* and in a revival of Noel Coward's *Hay Fever*. Neither play was a financial or critical success. In the spring of 1973 Booth shot half a season of episodes for an ABC comedy called *A Touch of Grace*, but the show was canceled; she turned once again to employ her considerable talents in stock companies.

Some of New York's most severe critics have commended Shirley Booth's acting. Richard Watts of the *New York Post* proclaimed, ''It is not exactly a secret these days that Miss Booth is one of the wonders of the American stage, a superb actress, a magnificent comedienne and an all-around performer of seemingly endless versatility'' (April 20, 1951). *Saturday Review*'s John Mason Brown called her ''one of the most gifted actresses our theatre hosts, ... one of the few who to my knowledge have never been guilty of a bad performance'' (May 5, 1951). The same magazine's movie reviewer, Bernard Kalb, agreed: ''In just one film, she asserts her consummate artistry, her ability to create and sustain a complete character through a variety of emotional conflicts and crises'' (December 27, 1952). John Chapman of the *Daily News* expressed the consensus perhaps most succinctly: ''Shirley Booth is truly something. I suspect she can do anything in the theatre and do it better than anybody else can'' (April 20, 1951).

Helen Hayes, one of Shirley Booth's most faithful fans, said of her, ''She has perfect timing and perfect reading, and she always has complete control of herself, her part and her audience. I have often gone back to watch her a second and a third time, trying to figure out how she does it, because the first time she has made it seem so effortless that I have forgotten I'm watching an actress''

(*Time*, August 10, 1953, p. 64). Booth herself says, "An actress is doing a poor job if the audience sits out there and thinks, 'Boy, I'm watching some acting.' Audiences should feel somebody left a door open by mistake, and they happened to stroll in when something interesting was going on. They should be so free of the feeling they're watching actors that they expect someone to say any minute, 'Hey, get out of here, this is personal' " (*Harvest Years Magazine*, March 1972, p. 49).

Shirley Booth has been called in the theatre a "character" actor. She often did not get the parts she deserved, and she was often cast in mediocre or poorly written dramas. However, despite the mediocrity of many of her vehicles, Booth has always been able to rise above the material by bringing her warmth and vitality to many plays that would have failed miserably without her.

The *New York Theatre Critics Reviews* compilation chronicles Shirley Booth's critical impact on Broadway from the 1935 volume through the 1970 volume. *Time*'s article "The Trouper" (August 10, 1953), Robert Coughlan's extensive piece "New Queen of the Drama" for *Life* (December 1, 1952), James Poling's article "One Touched with Genius" in *Collier's* (June 16, 1951), and Arnold Hanno's "Back from the Gobi Desert" for *TV Guide* (May 12, 1973) all provide interesting and different insights into Shirley Booth's personal and professional life. See also the *New York Post* (April 20, 1951), the *Saturday Review* (May 5, 1951, and December 27, 1952), the *Daily News* (April 20, 1951), the *New York Herald Tribune* (December 27, 1957), the *Saturday Evening Post* (September 22, 1962), and *Harvest Years Magazine* (March 1972). Biographical information may be found in *Current Biography, 1953* (1954); *The Biographical Encyclopaedia and Who's Who of the American Theatre* (1966); *Plays, Players, and Playwrights: An Illustrated History of the Theatre* (1975); *Encyclopedia of the Musical Theatre* (1976); *Who's Who in the Theatre* (1977); *The Film Encyclopedia* (1979); *The Oxford Companion to the Theatre* (1983); and *The Oxford Companion to American Theatre* (1984).

Katherine Laris

BOVASSO, Julie (August 1, 1930–): playwright, actress, director, educator, was born in Brooklyn, New York, the daughter of Bernard Michael Bovasso, a teamster, and Angela Ursula (Padovani) Bovasso. From an early age Julie Bovasso was involved with theatre. At thirteen she made her theatre debut in *The Bells* at the Davenport Free Theatre (August 1943). Joining the Rolling Players from 1947 to 1949, she appeared in plays by Oscar Wilde and Henrik Ibsen. Meanwhile she studied theatre at City College of the City University of New York (1948–1951) and also took acting classes with **Uta Hagen**, Herbert Berghof, Mira Rostova, and Harold Clurman.

During the 1950s and 1960s she acted with major regional theatres throughout the United States. She appeared at the Provincetown Playhouse in June 1950 as Emma in *Naked* and as Countess Geschwitz in *Earth Spirit*; in the title role of *Faustina* for the Living Theatre at the Cherry Lane Theatre and with the San Francisco Repertory Theatre as Anna Petrovna in *Ivanov* in 1952; at the American Shakespeare Festival Theatre in Stratford, Connecticut, as Mistress Quickly in *Henry IV, Part I* in 1962; and at the Chelsea Theatre Center, Brooklyn, as the

Mother in the American première of Jean Genêt's *The Screens* in 1972, for which she received the New York Critics Poll Award. She also performed with the Theatre Workshop in New York, the Playhouse in the Park in Cincinnati, Center Stage in Baltimore, and Café La Mama (now La Mama Experimental Theatre Club) in New York.

In 1953 Julie Bovasso adventurously founded the Tempo Playhouse (in Manhattan), where she produced, directed, and acted in avant-garde plays and introduced to America works by Jean Genêt, Eugène Ionesco, and Michel de Ghelderode. The Tempo, a daring enterprise for a young woman, represented a pioneering movement in the development of Off-Broadway theatre and an early arena in the United States for absurdist plays by European playwrights. For her work Bovasso won a *Village Voice* Off-Broadway Award, known popularly as the Obie, for best experimental theatre (1956). This was followed by an Obie for best actress, which she won for performances as Claire and as Solange in Tempo productions of Genêt's *The Maids* (1956).

During this period she was married to George Ortman (from 1951 to 1959) and then to Leland Wayland (from 1959 to 1964). She taught at the High School for the Performing Arts, New York City (1967–1968); at Brooklyn College Graduate School (1968–1969); at the New School for Social Research, New York City (1965–1971); and at Sarah Lawrence College, Bronxville, New York (1969–1974).

Bovasso's talent as a playwright surfaced when *The Moondreamers*, written in 1963, was produced as a workshop piece at **Ellen Stewart**'s La Mama Experimental Theatre Club in February 1968 and again in December 1969. *Gloria and Esperanza*, a second full-length play, also had two productions—the first at La Mama Experimental Theatre Club in April 1969 and the second at the American National Theatre and Academy (ANTA) in February 1970. Both plays reflect Bovasso's characteristic dramaturgy. Both might be regarded not as full-length plays but as satirical theatre pieces with plot and music. "Camp collage" aptly describes a Bovasso play with its mixture of whimsy, fairy tale, parody, camp, and philosophy. These theatrical collages are constructed out of old songs, stereotypical characters, and stock situations. Girl falls in love with boy of different station or background in *Schubert's Last Serenade*; Esperanza journeys through hell in pursuit of self in *Gloria and Esperanza*; the all-knowing mother tries to solve her daughter's problems by rescuing her from an "evil" husband in *The Moondreamers*.

Bovasso has also written *Down by the River Where Waterlilies Are Disfigured Every Day*, produced by Trinity Square Repertory Company (Providence, Rhode Island) in December 1971 and at the Circle Repertory Company (New York) in 1975; and *Monday on the Way to Mercury Island*, produced by La Mama Experimental Theatre Club in 1971. Her short plays—*Schubert's Last Serenade*, *The Final Analysis*, *Super Lover*, *The Nothing Kid*, and *Standard Safety*—were produced at La Mama Experimental Theatre Club in 1975. *Angelo's Wedding*, written in 1983, was produced in 1985 at the Circle Repertory Company, where she has served as resident playwright.

All of Bovasso's plays have a story line or a plot ornamented by nightmarish events and bizarre images. But, however sprawling the plays may seem, Bovasso maintains her control, and the plays issue as daydreams with sunny moods. Brendan Gill, writing for *The New Yorker* (February 14, 1970), called *Gloria and Esperanza* "a calculatedly incoherent phantasmagoria that always threatens to make our flesh creep but chooses to make us laugh instead—a collision, at once comic and murderous, between the author and the many aspects of our society that arouse her contempt."

In addition to founding theatres and writing plays, Bovasso has worked to encourage productions of new playwrights, especially of women. Toward this end she organized the Women's Theatre Council, composed of **Rochelle Owens**, **Rosalyn Drexler**, **Megan Terry**, **Maria Irene Fornès**, **Adrienne Kennedy**, and herself. In an interview published by *Mademoiselle* (August 1972), Bovasso stated the concept for the group: "The Women's Theatre Council is a nonprofit corporation of women playwrights established for the purpose of developing a professional theatre which will nurture the works of innovative playwrights and reach out to the disadvantaged audience that has not had the chance to experience an authentic contemporary theatre which reflects the spiritual, social, and aesthetic concerns of our times" (pp. 288–289).

The Women's Theatre Council soon evolved into a larger organization called the New York Theatre Strategy. The larger group included the original six playwrights together with Ed Bullins, Tom Eyen, Sam Shepard, Ronald Tavel, Jean-Claude van Itallie, Lanford Wilson, and other playwrights of Off-Broadway and Off-off-Broadway. Bovasso served as president of Theatre Strategy for a time.

During her years in the theatre, Bovasso has garnered a number of significant awards. She has received five Obies; one for best actress (in *The Maids*), one for best experimental theatre work (Tempo Playhouse), and three in 1969 for *Gloria and Esperanza* (best play, best actress, and best direction). She has received a Rockefeller Foundation playwriting grant (1969–1970), a New York State Council on the Arts Grant (1970–1971), and a Guggenheim Fellowship (1971–1972). She was named playwright-in-residence at the Circle Repertory Company (1976). Under the auspices of the United States Department of State she toured Latin America in 1975 with a program of her own works.

Energy, resourcefulness, imagination, and originality have characterized Julie Bovasso's theatrical work. She has worked as actress, playwright, director, and teacher. Through her encouragement other dramatic artists have found their own ways of contributing to the profession, and thanks to her theatrical sensibilities audiences have enjoyed new realms of dramatic experience.

Bovasso's published plays are found in various collections. *The Off-Off-Broadway Book* (1972) contains *Gloria and Esperanza* as well as bibliographic material on Bovasso. *The Best Short Plays 1972* (1972) contains *Schubert's Last Serenade*; and *Plays from the*

Circle Repertory Company (1987) contains *Down by the River Where the Waterlillies are Disfigured Every Day* and also a short biography of Bovasso. *The Best Short Plays 1976* (1976) contains *Standard Safety*. *New York Theater Critics Reviews* (1970) contains collected reviews of Bovasso's plays. Information for this entry was obtained from "Five Important Playwrights Talk About Theatre without Compromise and Sexism," *Mademoiselle* (August 1972), and from a personal interview with playwright **Maria Irene Fornés** in December 1976. Additional information about Bovasso can be found in *Who's Who of American Women 1974–1975* (1973), *Who's Who in the Theatre* (1981), and *The Writer's Directory 1984–1986*.

Carolyn Karis

BRADSHAW, Fanny (December 27, 1900–June 1, 1973): outstanding educator and voice coach/consultant named to the Stratford-upon-Avon Shakespeare Memorial Theatre's Board of Governors in honor of her work with Shakespearean verse, was born in Pittsburgh, Pennsylvania, to John and Laura (Durbin) Bradshaw. She was **Cornelia Otis Skinner**'s cousin. Her father, who had a brief career as an actor, introduced her at an early age to Shakespeare. Between 1915 and 1919 Fanny Bradshaw studied music and singing at the New England Conservatory of Music in Boston, and speech and interpretation at Leland Powers School of the Spoken Word. Even after she had become a teacher herself, she continued her studies. She took literature courses at Columbia University in 1923, studied stage design and color at Grace Cornell's Summer School of Art in 1926, stage and costume design with Norman Bel Geddes in 1928, and phonetic methods of teaching diction with Ida Ward at University College, London, in 1929.

In the early 1920s Fanny Bradshaw acted on stage and radio. Then she began concentrating on teaching speech and interpretation. Her first teaching position was as drama director at Briarcliff-on-the-Hudson from 1923 until 1929, after which she directed speech and dramatics at the Spence School in Manhattan from 1930 until 1960. Among her other teaching affiliations were New York's Nightingale-Bamford School; Tamara Daykarhanova School for the Stage; the Neighborhood Playhouse; the American Theatre Wing; the Dwight School in Englewood, New Jersey; the American Shakespeare Festival in Stratford, Connecticut; the Rice Summer School of Dramatic Art on Martha's Vineyard; and the Apprentice Theatre of the Rockland County Theatre in Suffern, New York.

In 1920 Fanny Bradshaw opened her own studio for dramatic training. She took students and theatre-lovers on summer study tours of England beginning in 1932 and became the founder and director of the Shakespeare Fortnight Hostelry in Stratford-on-Avon in 1935. According to the hostelry brochure, students, educators, and theatre-minded travelers were invited to attend two-week sessions. They were housed in a four-hundred-year-old house, and they engaged in lecture-discussions, informal readings, classes, and rehearsals led by professionals and often conducted in Stratford's Shakespeare Memorial Theatre. Among the hostelry sponsors were John Mason Brown, Joyce Carey,

Charles Coburn, Barry Jackson, **Eva Le Gallienne**, Burns Mantle, B. Iden Payne, and Cornelia Otis Skinner. Thriving for five years, the hostelry was brought to an end by World War II. For her activities in support of Shakespearean drama, Bradshaw was elected in 1957 to the Board of Governors of Stratford's Shakespeare Memorial Theatre, a rare honor for an American.

During the war Bradshaw gave her services to the American Theatre Wing, which maintained in New York City a recreation and entertainment center for servicemen and also sent dramatic troupes to all major war areas. She was one of those chosen to conduct speakers' training classes sponsored by the Women's Action Committee for Victory and Lasting Peace. When the Theatre Wing formed a school in New York City for G.I.'s after the war, Bradshaw taught speech and was part of a faculty that also included **Margaret Webster** and Romney Brent. John Houseman subsequently asked her to teach at Stratford, Connecticut, when the American Shakespeare Festival was founded in 1957.

Bradshaw gave recitals of American and English poetry in the 1930s and was one of three directors of the Spotlight Theatre, a professional experimental group in New York City, in 1940. In 1964 she wrote and co-produced *The White Rose and the Red*, which was directed by Edwin Sherin and played Off-Broadway at Stage 73. The production used essential scenes from the three parts of *Henry VI* and *Richard III*, and, according to Richard F. Shepard in the *New York Times* (March 19, 1964), it did "an expert job of telling the full story." The *Christian Science Monitor* (March 21, 1964) found the play "a powerhouse of emotional depth and dramatic action, gleaning the Bard's richest scenes without loss of his poetry."

Among Bradshaw's students were Hal Holbrook, Earle Hyman, Gregory Peck, **Geraldine Page**, Eli Wallach, Kevin McCarthy, **June Havoc**, Rosemary Murphy, Katina Paxinou, and Akim Tamiroff. With her classes and private students, she adhered to principles that she described to a *New York Evening Post* reporter (November 18, 1933): "Diction is an instrument that should be unnoticed because it is right. If it is overstressed, it loses any interpretive quality. One must grant, though, that a classic reading is appropriate to the old-school romantic plays, even when produced today. . . . On the other hand, so-called 'natural' stage diction can be so natural that you can't hear it ten rows back, or it is a bore if you do hear it." Particularly during the postwar dominance of "Method" theories of acting and the avant-garde approaches of the 1960s, Fanny Bradshaw contributed greatly towards keeping alive a love of and respect for poetry and classical drama in countless students, professionals, and theatregoers. She died in her studio on June 1, 1973. A memorial celebration of her life and work was held in the Manhattan home of Cornelia Otis Skinner.

There is a clipping file under Bradshaw's name in the Billy Rose Theatre Collection of the New York Library Performing Arts Research Center at Lincoln Center, which includes, among other items, the 1933 *New York Post* interview, her hostelry brochure, and her obituaries. Fanny Bradshaw is listed in *The Biographical Encyclopaedia and Who's Who of the American Theatre*, (1966).

Holly Hill

BRADY, Alice (November 2, 1892–October 28, 1939): stage and film actress, creator of Lavinia Mannon in Eugene O'Neill's *Mourning Becomes Electra*, was born in New York City on November 2, 1892, the daughter of William A. Brady and Rose Marie (Rene) Brady. Her father was a successful and respected theatrical producer, whose management of the Manhattan Theatre from 1896 to 1910 produced such notable productions as *Mlle. Fifi*, *Women and Wine*, and *Way Down East*. Later, as an independent producer, he was responsible for all-star revivals of *Uncle Tom's Cabin*, *The Two Orphans*, *Trilby*, and *The Lights of London*. Brady's mother, a French dancer, died when Alice was three years old; the actress Grace George later became her stepmother.

Brady's early education was at the Convents of St. Elizabeth in Madison and in Fort Lee, New Jersey. Over her father's objections, she sought and gained admission to the Boston Conservatory of Music, where she studied for an operatic career under Theodora Irvine. However, she was soon to change her mind and seek a stage career. Although she often appeared in musical theatre productions and films, her musical training was rarely used. She was briefly married to actor James L. Crane and had a son, Donald.

Perhaps the most notable feature of Brady's stage and film career (1909–1939) was her versatility. Theatregoers saw her perform in musical comedy, light farce, and the powerful tragedy of Eugene O'Neill. Moviegoers loved her as a comedienne in a number of "empty-headed dowager" roles, but she received the Academy (Oscar) Award for her dramatic performance in the film *In Old Chicago* (1938).

Brady first appeared on stage in a 1909 production of *As You Like It*, starring Robert Mantell. Her New York stage debut was made two years later, when she was eighteen. The play was a musical, *The Balkan Princess* (Herald Square Theatre, February 9, 1911). In 1912 she appeared in her first nonmusical production, as Meg in an adaptation of Louisa May Alcott's *Little Women*. The producer was her father, William A. Brady, whose parental disapproval of his daughter's chosen career was by this time apparently mollified. Between 1911 and 1915 Alice Brady used her vocal training in a number of Gilbert and Sullivan operettas, usually playing outside New York City and on tour. Other comic and melodramatic roles followed: *Forever After* (1918), *Zander The Great* (1923), and *Lady Alone* (1927).

On October 26, 1931, at the Guild Theatre, Brady played Lavinia Mannon in Eugene O'Neill's adaptation of the Orestes legend, *Mourning Becomes Electra*. John Mason Brown (*New York Evening Post*, October 27, 1931), called the play "one of the most distinguished, if not the most distinguished, achievements of Mr. O'Neill's career." Of the production Brooks Atkinson (*New York Times*,

October 27, 1931) said, "It is played by Alice Brady and Mme. Nazimova with consummate artistry and passion." Garff B. Wilson, in *A History Of American Acting* (1966), noted that Brady was known to the majority of American audiences "only as the scatterbrained, garrulous, middle-aged comedienne of many movies whereas, in truth, she was a versatile performer who played both comedy and tragedy effectively and contributed a superb portrait of the Electra-like Lavinia in Eugene O'Neill's original production of *Mourning Becomes Electra*" (p. 279). Her final stage appearance was in 1934 at the Biltmore Theatre in Los Angeles, where she played Marion Froude in S. N. Behrman's *Biography*.

Brady made her first film appearance in 1914 in *As Ye Sow*, an adaptation of a play that had been produced in 1905 by her father. Although a few silent films followed, it was in the sound era that she became known as a character actress playing supporting roles. Starting in 1932, Brady largely deserted the stage to appear in films for the rest of her life. She was widely noticed in support of Fred Astaire and Ginger Rogers in *The Gay Divorcee* (1934), with William Powell and Carole Lombard in *My Man Godfrey* (1936), and in other films. As the sacrificing but staunch mother of Tyrone Power and Don Ameche in *In Old Chicago* (1938), Brady won an Academy (Oscar) Award for best supporting actress, the highlight of her film career. In the last year of her life, she appeared with Henry Fonda in *Young Mr. Lincoln* (1939).

After a thirty-year career in the theatre and in films, Alice Brady died on October 28, 1939, of cancer, at the LeRoy Sanitarium in New York City. She is buried in the Sleepy Hollow Cemetery in Tarrytown, New York.

Brady's range of roles on stage and in film set her apart from all but a few of her contemporaries. Yet the general public was largely unaware of her name. It was her face that was recognized in scores of plays and films. If she never had the satisfaction of fame, she must be appreciated for her ability to be thoroughly convincing and professional in such a wide range of roles.

The most personalized summary of Alice Brady and her career is found in Daniel Blum's *Great Stars Of the American Stage* (1952). Alice Brady also figures to a small extent in her father's autobiography, *Showman*, published in 1937. A more complete listing of her stage and film credits may be found in the 1939 edition of *Who's Who In the Theatre*, edited by John Parker. See also *Notable American Women*, Vol. I (1971), and *The Oxford Companion to American Theatre* (1984).

Frank L. Warner

BRICE, Fanny (October 29, 1891–May 29, 1951): comedienne, was born Fanny Borach to Jewish immigrant parents in New York City. Her mother, Rose Stern, was an eighteen-year-old girl from Budapest when she married Charles Borach, a Bowery bartender. Fanny was the third of four children born to Rosie and "Pinochle Charlie." When Fanny was still young, Borach's gambling and alcoholism caused her mother to leave him, taking her children—Philip, Caroline, Fanny, and Lew—with her.

Brice began her career as a performer singing in neighborhood streets for pennies. She first stepped onto a stage when she was thirteen. She entered an

"Amateur Night" contest at Keeney's Theatre in Brooklyn in order to avoid the admission charge and charmed the audience with her rendition of "When You Know You're Not Forgotten by the Girl You Can't Forget." That night she took home the first prize, a five-dollar gold piece, and decided to pursue a stage career. Brice continued to enter and win amateur contests in Brooklyn and Manhattan, hoping for an opportunity to audition professionally. In addition, she changed her name from Borach to Brice, the surname of a family friend. As her mother and the other children no longer maintained a relationship with Pinochle Charlie, they too adopted the name Brice.

At age fourteen Brice obtained an audition for a musical being produced by George M. Cohan. She was cast as a chorus girl, but her inability to dance caused her to lose the job. Dancing lessons and perseverance won her the opportunity to join the Traveling Burlesque Company. When the soubrette fainted backstage before an evening performance, Brice went on in her stead. Unable to duplicate the leading lady's singing style, the teen-age Brice performed the selections comically. This performance inaugurated her career as a comedienne.

The following season Brice was hired by Max Speigel to perform in his musical *College Girls*. When Brice learned that she would need a "specialty" act, she convinced songwriter Irving Berlin to provide her with a song. He presented her with "Sadie Salome" and suggested she perform it with a Jewish accent. Once again Brice delighted her audiences, and Speigel quickly signed her to an eight-year contract. While touring with *College Girls*, Brice met and married Frank White in 1909. The marriage was never consummated, and after a failed attempt to have the match annulled, Brice was granted a divorce in 1911.

Brice's performances in *College Girls* were beginning to win her some attention, and in 1910 entrepreneur Florenz Ziegfeld offered her a place in his fourth *Follies*. Brice broke her contract with Speigel (she had been under eighteen years of age when she signed with him) and began her long association with Ziegfeld, becoming not only one of his most popular stars but the performer to set the record for the greatest number of *Follies* appearances.

During her rise to stardom Brice became involved with confidence man Jules (Nick) Arnstein. She lived with him while he attempted to secure a divorce from his wife, Carrie Greenthal, and waited for him while he served a two-year prison sentence in Sing-Sing for grand larceny. Brice and Arnstein were married shortly after his release from prison in 1917; however, the marriage required two ceremonies since Arnstein's divorce had not been finalized at the time of the first. Brice bore Arnstein two children, William and Frances. When his daughter was six months old, Arnstein disappeared from the family's New York apartment after being indicted for masterminding a plot to steal five million dollars from several Wall Street brokerage houses. Arnstein was apprehended and jailed once again. While Brice was awaiting her husband's trial in 1921, she was asked by Ziegfeld to listen to a French song titled "Mon Homme." Channing Pollack had written English lyrics to the ballad, now titled "My Man." On the opening night of the *1921 Follies* her rendition of "My Man" so moved the audience that the song soon became her trademark.

While Brice's marriage was faltering, her career continued to grow. In 1925 producer David Belasco asked her to appear for him in a "straight" play, aptly named *Fanny*. Brice's attempt at a dramatic role was a failure, and New York critics begged her to return to comedy. That same year she learned of Arnstein's infidelity and demanded a divorce, which was finally granted in September 1927.

If "My Man" was Brice's serious trademark, the character of "Baby Snooks" was her comic one. Snooks made her debut at a private party as "Babykins," a precocious child who never failed to outwit the adults with whom she conversed. Babykins appeared publicly for the first time on Broadway in 1930 in *Sweet and Low*, a musical by songwriter Billy Rose, who had become Brice's third husband the previous year. Babykins changed her name to Baby Snooks and reappeared in the *1933 Follies*, providing Brice with yet another success. In 1938, the same year that Brice divorced Rose, Baby Snooks appeared for the first time on the radio and six years later Brice, as Baby Snooks, received her own radio show on CBS.

Brice's career included not only stage work but film and radio work as well. When Brice died in her Hollywood home in 1951 of a cerebral hemorrhage, she had achieved recognition as one of America's finest comediennes. Not only was she an important vaudevillian, but she can certainly also be regarded as one of the most talented female "clowns" of the early twentieth-century American stage, radio, and film.

The one complete biography of Brice is Norman Katkov's *The Fabulous Fanny* (1953). Eddie Cantor writes of Brice in *As I Remember Them* (1963), and Niven Busch, Jr., includes Brice in *Twenty-One Americans* (1930). Several articles are also of interest: "The Feel of the Audience," written by Brice for the *The Saturday Evening Post* (November 21, 1925); "She Couldn't Make Them Cry," *Coronet* (1949); and "Memories of Brice," *Newsweek* (February 16, 1953). Works on the musical theatre of Brice's day include Cecil Smith's *Musical Comedy in America* (1950), Marjorie Farnsworth's *The Ziegfeld Follies* (1956), and David Ewen's *The Complete Book of American Musical Theatre* (1959). Brice's obituary appeared in the *New York Times* (May 30, 1951). Short biographies of Brice appear in *Dictionary of American Biography*, Supplement Five (1946); *Current Biography 1946* (1947); *Who Was Who in the Theatre*, Vol. I (1978); *Notable American Women*, Vol. IV: *The Modern Era* (1980); and *The Oxford Companion to American Theatre* (1984).

Merope Pavlides

BRYANT, Hazel (1939?–November 7, 1983): singer, actress, founder, and artistic director of the Richard Allen Center for Culture and Art in New York, was the daughter of Bishop and Mrs. Harrison Bryant of Baltimore. She had one brother and two sisters. She began her theatrical career as an opera singer, studying at the Peabody Conservatory of Music, Oberlin Conservatory of Music, and the Mozarteum School of Music in Austria. For nearly a decade she toured

Europe and performed in major opera houses in such roles as Mimi in *La Bohème*, Bess in *Porgy and Bess*, and Fiordiligi in *Cosi Fan Tutte*.

Bryant returned to New York in 1962 to try her luck in the nonoperatic theatre. She studied with **Stella Adler** and Harold Clurman and appeared on and off Broadway in *Funny Girl*, *A Taste of Honey*, *Lost in The Stars*, and *Hair*. But the same restrictions she encountered as a black woman in classical opera confronted her in the commercial theatre. Unhappy with the stereotyped roles offered her as a dramatic and musical actress, she established the Afro-American Total Theatre in 1968 in New York.

In 1976 the theatre's name was changed to the Richard Allen Center for Culture and Art. Richard Allen was from Philadelphia and in 1787 had been one of the founders of the African Methodist Episcopal Church. He believed in cooperative economics and encouraged blacks jointly to acquire and maintain capital investments, thereby insuring their personal survival and freedom.

Under Bryant's leadership the Richard Allen Center reflected the diversity and richness of black theatre. Productions have included *The Fabulous Miss Marie*, *The Amen Corner*, *Ms. Griot*, *Second Thoughts*, and a critically acclaimed revival of *Long Day's Journey Into Night* with an all-black cast. Bryant wrote, produced, and directed several musicals, including *Mae's Amees*, *Nativity*, *Sheba*, and *Black Circles*. In its first five years, the Richard Allen Center presented fourteen original musicals.

Donations from the African Methodist Episcopal Church, Avery Fisher Hall, and Exxon Corporation enabled the Richard Allen company to establish permanent quarters in the Lincoln Center area in 1976. The Richard Allen Center for Culture and Art houses the Ira Aldridge Playhouse, the Paul Robeson Concert Hall, the Henry O. Tanner Gallery, the Oscar Micheaux Media Center, and the James Baldwin Library. As Bryant explained to a *New York Times* reporter, "We now and have always needed art centers created for and devoted to the professional mounting of our work" (May 20, 1976).

In addition to her work with the Richard Allen Center, Bryant made numerous concert and television appearances in the United States and Canada and produced musicals for cable television. In 1981 she headed a company that performed *Black Nativity* by Langston Hughes for Pope John Paul II at the Vatican in Rome. Bryant served as a member of the Mayor's Cultural Council and the New York State Council on the Arts and was president of the Black Theatre Alliance from 1974 until 1976. In 1977 she founded the National Arts Consortium to help black arts groups combine their resources. In 1978 Bryant received the Mayor's Award of Honor for outstanding contributions to the arts in New York City. In 1979 she received a special citation from the governor of New York for producing the 1979 Black Theatre Festival at Lincoln Center. In September 1983 Bryant received the Harold Jackman Memorial Award at Columbia University.

In November 1983 Hazel Bryant, who had a history of heart disease, died at the age of forty-four. She had hoped to expand the Richard Allen Center and thus provide a still more conspicuous professional showcase for black talent.

"We want to develop spaces to house our own art forms. We want to claim black musical theatre as a legitimate art form in this culture," she had said (*New York Amsterdam News*, April 28, 1979). By establishing the Richard Allen Center for Culture and Art, Hazel Bryant took a major step toward fulfilling her dream.

Material used in this biographical sketch came from *The Villager* (August 19, 1976), *New York Amsterdam News* (December 21, 1974, and April 28, 1979), *New York Times* (May 20, 1976), *New York Daily News* (January 17, 1977), and press releases in a clippings file at the Billy Rose Collection, New York Public Library Performing Arts Research Center at Lincoln Center.

                                                                Maria Rodriguez

BURGER, Isabel Blogg (October 30, 1902–): specialist in children's theatre and senior adult theatre, was born in Baltimore, Maryland. Her father was Percy Thayer Blogg, who started the first photoengraving company in Baltimore, and her mother was Isabel (Ogier) Blogg. Although born to a life of social privilege, the young Isabel rejected that life and in its place sought intellectual stimulation and service to others. At a time when education for women was novel and deemed by many to be unnecessary, she attended a stimulating private school (Bryn Mawr School for Girls), a private camp (Camp Asquam in Maine), and Johns Hopkins University. She also did graduate work at Johns Hopkins University in 1927, at the University of Minnesota in 1950, and at the Howard School of Social Work in 1965.

Upon graduating from Johns Hopkins University in 1924, Isabel Blogg married T. Terry Burger, who became a prominent pediatrician in Baltimore. They had two children, Thomas and Jane. Dr. Burger lived until 1984.

A significant influence in shaping Burger's approach to working with young people was her study of Greek at Bryn Mawr School under the noted classics scholar Edith Hamilton. The emphasis on balance of body, mind, and spirit became a fundamental component of Burger's creative drama approach. In 1941 Isabel Burger established an experimental drama class on the Johns Hopkins campus, which led to the founding of the Children's Theatre Association in 1943. From its inception, the Children's Theatre Association was a community-oriented and service agency, not a purely theatrical enterprise. At the height of its activity the theatre operated eighteen creative drama classes a week in Baltimore and suburban areas. The objectives of the classes were in human development, not theatre training, the aim being "to develop initiative, self-confidence, well-coordinated bodies, imagination, sensitivity to beauty, and deeper understanding of life and one's fellow men" (Children's Theatre Association Annual Report, October 1946-June 1947).

From the beginning the Children's Theatre Association's goal was to heighten perception of self and others through creative drama techniques. Its unique theatrical feature was its improvisational training. Its underlying impetus was the dynamic personality of the director, who adhered to the concept that one can only teach those whom one loves. It was the combination of these two features that made this theatre an outstanding independent community children's theatre, which received local, national, and international recognition during its twenty-three years under Burger's guidance.

Burger's creative drama technique had its own structural hierarchy, progressing from activity to pantomime, then to dialogue, and finally to story situations. Even stronger than the accent on movement and language facility was Burger's emphasis on the creative use of imagination and emotion. Much of the classroom improvisational material was taken from real-life situations and proved rich in its potential for developing empathy. The first half of Burger's well-known text, *Creative Play Acting* (1950), was an outgrowth of these principles, which she had been testing for nearly a decade. The last half of the book discusses staging formal plays for young audiences and includes her use of improvisation as an integral part of production. (This book was translated by E.J. Lutz and published in Munich, Germany, in 1957, under the title of *Das Schulspiel*.)

At the peak of its activity, the Children's Theatre Association presented ten productions a season. Many of the scripts were Burger's adaptations of literary classics. Of all the productions of the Children's Theatre Association, the one that best embodied the expressed goals of the organization and represented the unique aspects of the Children's Theatre Association was *A Christmas Carol*. For eighteen years (1946–1964) two to eight public performances were done annually. Burger pointed to *A Christmas Carol* as the production most clearly expressing her point of view: "A basic part of my philosophy, in terms of selecting material for use in every aspect of CTA's program, concerned helping children to deepen their understanding of themselves and others, to sharpen their sensitivity to the beauty of nature and of human nature, and to build a strong set of standards for living contributive lives by giving loving service to their fellow men. *A Christmas Carol* speaks eloquently to all these points" (Isabel Burger, letter to the author, November 12, 1970).

In 1966 Burger retired from the Children's Theatre Association, having established a program of live theatre for young audiences, a summer Showmobile, creative drama classes for students eight to eighteen, and college-level training courses for teachers and youth leaders. In addition, she had lectured and given demonstration workshops nationally and internationally.

Burger's strong interest in religious drama led to additional lectures and workshops. The results of her work were published in *Creative Drama in Religious Education* (1977). Since 1977 she has been exploring a totally new field—drama with senior adults—developing a local program called Dynamic Living in Retirement. She is currently drama consultant for the Baltimore County Department of Aging. *Creative Drama for Senior Adults* (1980) is drawn from her dynamic leadership training activities.

Honors accorded to Isabel Burger include a research grant from Delta Kappa Gamma International (1963), the Annual Award of the Greater Baltimore Arts Council for outstanding contribution to the arts (1969), appointment as a Life Fellow of the International Institute of Arts and Letters (1961), the Edwin Strawbridge Award from the Children's Theatre Association of America (1965), a citation from the American Theatre Association for pioneer work with senior citizens (1977), and the Creative Drama for Human Awareness Award from the Children's Theatre Association of America (1980). In 1982 she was made a member of the American Theatre Association College of Fellows, and in 1983 she was presented a Distinguished Service Award by the Baltimore County Medical Association for special service to senior adults. In 1985 Isabel Burger received the Campton Bell Award from the Children's Theatre Association of America for ''a lifetime of outstanding contributions to the field of child drama/ theatre.''

Isabel Burger has been a pioneer in both child drama and drama for senior adults and thus has made significant contributions to American educational theatre.

For information concerning her work, see her published books. Biographical information is contained in *Who's Who in the East*, Vol. 6 (1948); *Who's Who of American Women, 1972–1973* (1971); *The Dictionary of International Biography*, Part I (1974); and *The National Register of Prominent Americans* (1974–1975).

Joanna Halpert Kraus

BURNETT, Frances Eliza Hodgson (November 24, 1849–October 29, 1924): playwright, popular novelist, and children's author, was born in Manchester, England. Edwin Hodgson, her father, was a prosperous dealer in hardware and her mother, Eliza Boond, was from a family in Cheshire. In 1854 Edwin Hodgson died suddenly of a stroke. His wife, left with four young children and a baby yet to be born, decided to continue the family business. Frances was the third of five children. She had two older brothers, Herbert and John George, and two younger sisters, Edith Mary and Edwina. It was the American Civil War (1861–1865) that destroyed the economy of Manchester (a cotton manufacturing center), and in consequence, the business of the Hodgson firm. Eliza Boond Hodgson sold the big house on the outskirts of Manchester and moved the family to a smaller house at Islington Square in the center of Manchester. There, Frances attended the Select School for Young Ladies, which provided her only formal education.

By 1865 economic conditions were so bad in Manchester that when Mrs. Hodgson received a letter from her brother, William Boond, suggesting that the family join him in Knoxville, Tennessee, she moved the family once again. They set sail on the *Moravian* in the late spring. Five weeks later they were in Knoxville, then a little village with one unpaved street lined with wooden houses and log cabins. The Hodgsons moved into a log house in nearby New Market. Frances Hodgson played the piano well enough to help support the family by giving lessons to a few students. She soon opened a school in their New Market home. Near the Hodgson's log home stood the community's largest house, a white frame dwelling belonging to Dr. John M. Burnett, the district physician. The three Burnett girls—Jo, Ann, and Mary—soon became close friends with the Hodgson girls. Their brother, nineteen-year-old Swan Burnett, became fascinated with Frances Hodgson. Swan Burnett, born in 1847 and lamed in childhood by an accident, was a quiet, studious young man preparing to follow in his father's profession. The old doctor's practice, especially after the war, paid poorly; yet Swan Burnett attended Miami Medical College in Cincinnati, Ohio, supplementing his small stipend by writing for newspapers.

Frances Hodgson was fascinated by the stories that appeared in *Godey's Lady's Book* and *Peterson's Magazine*, and when she was eighteen, she sold her first story, "Hearts and Diamonds," which was published by *Godey's Lady's Book* in June 1868. Her writing soon became more than an avocation. When Mrs. Hodgson died on March 17, 1870, Frances Hodgson became the breadwinner of the family, supporting it by a steady stream of conventional stories, easily written and quickly sold to women's periodicals. When her two sisters married and her brothers became self-supporting, Frances Hodgson was able to concentrate more on quality than quantity in her writing. Her first literary success, "Surly Tim," was published by *Scribner's Monthly* in 1872.

Following the completion of his medical studies in 1872, Swan Burnett opened a small office in Knoxville. On September 19, 1873, Frances Hodgson and Swan Burnett were married. Lionel, their first son, was born on September 20, 1874. In order to allow her husband to pursue a career as an eye and ear specialist, Frances Burnett acquired a loan from Charles Peterson of *Peterson's Magazine* to finance his study in Paris (she agreed to pay back the loan by writing stories), and the family moved to Paris. There, a second son, Vivian, was born on April 5, 1875. In addition to writing for Peterson, Burnett sent stories to *Scribner's* and *Harper's* and completed her first novel, *That Lass o' Lowries* (1877), which was so successful that it was dramatized without the author's permission and ran an entire season in London. Outraged at the theft and at what she saw as artistic distortion, Burnett decided to write her own dramatization for the New York stage. Her dramatic version was quickly completed, and negotiations for its production on Broadway were taken up with producer John T. Raymond, who wanted his wife, Marie Gordon, to star in it. The play opened on Broadway in 1878, Burnett's first appearance as a playwright. In 1923 it was made into a motion picture called *The Flame of Life*.

Burnett wrote some fifty novels between 1877 and 1922. She dramatized thirteen of them and involved herself in the rehearsals of all her plays. Her second venture was *Esmeralda* (New York, 1881), written in collaboration with William Gillette. It became a Broadway success and later a 1915 movie starring Mary Pickford. *The Real Little Lord Fauntleroy* (produced in London and New York, 1888), an immensely popular play adapted from her own novel, was filmed in 1921 by United Artists, again as a vehicle for Mary Pickford, who at age twenty-seven acted not only the young lord but his mother as well. (In 1936 it was remade with Freddie Bartholemew in the title role.) Other Burnett plays were *Phyllis* (London, 1889), adapted from her novel *The Fortunes of Philippa Fairfax*; *Nixie* (London, 1890), also titled *Editha's Burglar*, written in collaboration with Augustus Thomas; *The Showman's Daughter* (London, 1892), in collaboration with Stephen Townesend; *The First Gentleman of Europe* (New York, 1897), in collaboration with Constance Fletcher; *A Lady of Quality* (New York, 1897), in collaboration with Stephen Townesend (made into a popular motion picture in 1924); *A Little Princess* (London, 1902), which met with little success on the stage but with great success as a motion picture starring Shirley Temple, and which also was produced as late as 1973 by BBC television; *The Pretty Sister of José* (New York, 1903), produced by Charles Frohman as a vehicle for his star **Maude Adams**; *That Man and I* (London, 1903), from her novel *In Connection with The De Willoughby Claim; The Dawn of a Tomorrow* (New York, 1909), made into a popular motion picture in 1915 starring Mary Pickford; and the *Racketty-Packetty House* (New York, 1912), a play for children adapted from her novel of the same title.

However, it was the publication of *Little Lord Fauntleroy* (1886) that brought Burnett immediate widespread fame and great fortune. Soon translated into a dozen languages, the novel made her a celebrity. Little Lord Fauntleroy was modeled on Vivian, her second son. His photograph was sent to Reginald Birch, the illustrator, who evolved from it the velvet suit with the lace collar and the hair style of long, golden curls. It had been a serious matter when an unauthorized play had been made from *That Lass o' Lowries*, but when E. V. Seebohm made a play from *Little Lord Fauntleroy*, her most valuable property, Burnett decided to fight. In 1888 she won a legal suit against the producers of the unauthorized version in England and established for the first time in that country the right of an author to control the dramatization of novels.

Despite enormous popularity, critical acclaim, a considerable income, and a circle of distinguished friends, Burnett was often restless and unhappy and complained of chronic ill health. The great tragedy of her life was the death of her elder son, Lionel, who became ill with tuberculosis in early 1890 and despite her lavish care died on December 7, 1890, at the age of sixteen. Her chief solace seems to have been the imaginative creation of fictional worlds—where endings were inevitably happy. By 1898 relations with her husband, Swan Burnett, had become so strained that the couple were divorced. The medical career he had established in Washington, D.C., though productive and successful, had in no way matched the fame achieved by his wife. In 1900 she married her frequent collaborator Stephen Townesend, an Englishman ten years her junior, who also had a medical degree but pursued a career in the theatre. Townesend had helped her during Lionel's illness and was her secretary and protégé, as well as her collaborator. The difficulties of this second marriage, which ended in 1902, are described in her novel *The Shuttle* (1907).

From 1898 to 1907 she made her home in Maythem Hall, a medieval castle in Rolvenden, Kent. Her last years were spent at Plandome, Long Island, where she built a magnificent home. Despite chronic illnesses, she continued to write. During her last illness, she sat up in bed writing *In the Garden*, her last story, published in 1925, the year after her death. Frances Hodgson Burnett died on

October 29, 1924, four weeks before her seventy-fifth birthday, and was buried at Roslyn, Long Island.

Not only did Burnett write for a huge audience, but she also fought for the rights of ownership in works of fiction. Her legal action in 1888 to establish her claim to the dramatic rights of her famous story *Little Lord Fauntleroy* effectively stopped unauthorized dramatizations of novels in England. (The 1911 Copyright Act was a direct result of her action.) The Authors' Association of England celebrated her victory at a banquet and presented her with a diamond bracelet and an illuminated memorial inscribed with the names of many leading writers of the time. During her lifetime Frances Hodgson Burnett made a lasting contribution to juvenile literature. Her masterpieces for children, *Little Lord Fauntleroy* and *A Little Princess*, as dramatizations were star vehicles for the stage and motion pictures of her time.

Frances Hodgson Burnett's autobiography is titled *The One I Knew Best Of All* (1893). Biographies of Burnett include Constance Buel Burnett, *Happily Ever After: A Portrait of Frances Hodgson Burnett* (1969); Vivian Burnett, *The Romantick Lady* (1927); Elizabeth Jordan, *Three Rousing Cheers* (1938); and Ann Thwaite, *Waiting for the Party: The Life of Frances Hodgson Burnett* (1974). See also Marghanita Laski, *Mrs. Ewing, Mrs. Molesworth, and Mrs. Hodgson Burnett* (1950), and John Rowe Townsend, *Written for Children: An Outline of English-Language Children's Literature* (1974). Articles about Burnett include Phyllis Bixler Koppes, "Tradition and the Individual Talent of Frances Hodgson Burnett," *Children's Literature* (1978); and "The Literary Spotlight," *Bookman* (October 1922). Her obituary appeared in *The Times* (October 30, 1924). She is listed in *Yesterday's Authors of Books for Children*, Vol. I (1977); *Twentieth Century Children's Writers* (1978); *American Women Writers*, Vol. I (1979); and *Contemporary Authors*, Vol. 108 (1983).

Rosemary Gipson

BURSTYN, Ellen (December 7, 1932–): stage and screen actress and first woman president of Actors' Equity, was born Edna Rae Gillooly, the daughter of a middle-class Irish Catholic family, in Detroit, Michigan. Her parents divorced when she was quite young. Her mother, Corinne Marie (Hamel) Gillooly, remarried several times, and her father, John Austin Gillooly, who had a plumbing business in Detroit, eventually retired to Florida. She had two brothers: the elder (Jack Gillooly) entered the plumbing business in Decatur, Georgia, and her younger brother (Steven Schwartz) became a telephone company employee in California.

The future actress attended Cass Technical High School in Detroit, where she neglected her studies and embarked on a career as a model, working part-time at Hudson's department store. In an interview with Rex Reed she admitted, "I flunked everything and finally dropped out and got married" (*New York Sunday News*, March 9, 1975, p. 7). She has since married three times; each marriage has ended in divorce. In 1950 she married a hometown Detroit boy who was striving to become a poet. She continued to model, first commuting to Dallas, Texas, and then to New York City, where in addition to modeling, she had a variety of jobs: drugstore clerk, fashion coordinator, and television walk-on. By 1953 her first marriage had crumbled under the strain of her many commitments. Her second marriage to Paul Roberts, the director of her first Broadway play, *Fair Game* (1957), produced her only child—a son, Jefferson. In 1957 she moved to Los Angeles with Roberts but returned to New York City with her son when the marriage failed. In 1959 she married Neil Burstyn and took Burstyn as her professional name in 1968 when she began a major film in Paris, *Tropic of Cancer*, directed by Joseph Strick. As her career flourished, her marriage faltered and finally ended in 1976.

Almost as varied as the means by which she supported herself in her early years were the names she used during the period before 1959. She was Keri Flynn for a brief stint as a chorus dancer in a Montreal nightclub, Erica Dean for a Gregory Ratoff-sponsored screen test in 1955, and Edna Rae for a number of minor television assignments that culminated in a regular job on the Jackie Gleason program from September 29, 1956, through June 22, 1957. For the Gleason show she was one of a group of attractive young women who served as decorative background. At the end of the 1957 television season she made a significant career change: she chose a stage career, having heard that the producers needed an ingènue to portray a garment industry model in the Broadway comedy *Fair Game*. This was Burstyn's breakthrough, and playwright Sam Locke remembered her audition in an interview with the *Philadelphia Inquirer*: "We had auditioned hundreds of girls until one day Ellen . . . came into the theatre without an appointment. We let her read and it was like all the corpuscles had been drained from everybody who had tried out. . . . We were supposed to put descriptive phrases on the casting sheet beside the name of each actress who auditioned. I remember that all I wrote next to Ellen's name was 'Wow' with an exclamation mark'' (October 6, 1957). Commenting on how she got the female lead for the Broadway show, she said in the *New York Times* interview, "I got the part because I sparkled, and I smiled good" (March 2, 1975, p. 17).

The critics were enthusiastic over "Ellen McRae's" performance when *Fair Game* opened at the Longacre Theatre on November 2, 1957. When the show closed in May of 1958, she went to California and continued to act on television under the name Ellen McRae. With the auspicious Broadway debut fading into the background, she alternated television work with a summer stock tour in 1960 with James Garner in a production of *John Loves Mary*. In 1964 she was featured in two lackluster films, *For Those Who Think Young* and *Goodbye Charlie*.

Concerned about her growth as an actress, Burstyn left Hollywood for New York in 1964. There she worked on the NBC-TV soap opera *The Doctors* and took acting classes with Lee Strasberg. By 1969 she had joined the Actors' Studio; in 1975 she became a member of the board. The year 1969 also marked the release of *Pit Stop*, her last picture under the name of Ellen McRae. At that time she was considering abandoning her career altogether to give full time to her marriage to Neil Burstyn, but a call from Joseph Strick offering her the part of Mona in an adaptation of Henry Miller's novel *Tropic of Cancer*, to be filmed in Paris, afforded the opportunity to make another new beginning. She appeared in the film under the name of Ellen Burstyn. The film received good reviews and was followed by Paul Mazursky and Larry Tucker's *Alex in Wonderland* (1970), which solidified Burstyn's reputation as an actress of unusual sensibilities. *Time Magazine* called her "lovely and affecting" (January 18, 1971, p. 75). Shortly thereafter she was recommended to film director Peter Bogdanovich, who was casting the citizens of a small Texas town in the early 1950s in his film version of the Larry McMurtry novel *The Last Picture Show*. The director was so impressed with her that he gave her the choice of three important roles. She chose that of Lois Farrow, the sensual wife of a wealthy oilman. Following its screening at the New York Film Festival on October 2, 1971, *The Last Picture Show* received awards from the New York Film Critics and the National Society of Film Critics. The latter voted Ellen Burstyn the year's best supporting actress. A number of film roles followed: *The King of Marvin Gardens* (1972) with Jack Nicholson; *The Exorcist* (1973) with Max Von Sydow, for which she received her second Academy Award (Oscar) nomination for best actress; *Harry and Tonto* (1974) with Art Carney; and Robert Getchell's *Alice Doesn't Live Here Anymore* (1974), receiving an Oscar for her performance as the widowed Alice Hyatt. After a stint on Broadway, she returned to Hollywood to make *Same Time, Next Year* (1978) with Alan Alda; and *Resurrection* (1979) with Sam Shepard.

In 1975, Burstyn returned to Broadway in Bernard Slade's romantic comedy, *Same Time, Next Year* (Brooks Atkinson Theatre, 1975) as Doris, the housewife who from 1951 to 1975 has an annual weekend tryst with her married lover. Writing for *Cue* magazine, **Marilyn Stasio** said that Ellen Burstyn exuded "enough tenderness, compassion, and good humor to melt an ice floe" (March 24, 1975). The same year she received the Oscar for *Alice* she also received the Antoinette Perry (Tony) Award for her performance in *Same Time, Next Year*. Her next Broadway appearances were in Tom Kempinski's *Duet for One* (1981) and in James Roose-Evans's *84 Charing Cross Road* (1982), adapted from the novel by Helene Hanff.

Burstyn's attention has recently turned to directing, particularly in the non-commercial, Off-Broadway theatre. Her first major directorial effort was in 1979 for the Actors' Studio. The production, a comedy by Norman Krasna titled *Bunny*, introduced Catlin Adams as a call girl who makes friends of her clients. In 1980 in the theatre basement of St. Peter's Church, she directed Philip Anglin, the actor who had originally played Elephant Man, in a two-hour monologue titled *Judgment*, a dramatic piece based on a cannibalism incident that took place during World War II.

In 1982 Burstyn became the first woman president of Actors' Equity. That same year, after the death of Lee Strasberg, she and Al Pacino were appointed co-artistic directors of the Actors' Studio. As chairman of its board of directors, she has continued her affiliation with this innovative workshop and has written the preface for the second edition of David Garfield's history titled *The Actors*

Studio: A Player's Place (1984). In 1985 and 1986 she turned again to television. For ABC she co-starred with Marsha Mason in *Surviving* (1985), as the mother of a suicidal teen-ager, and starred in the film *Twice in a Lifetime. The Ellen Burstyn Show* premièred as an ABC series in the fall of 1986.

Burstyn has become a distinguished actress on stage and in film. She has sought out strong female characters, such as Doris in *Same Time, Next Year* and Alice in *Alice Doesn't Live Here Anymore*, who are role models for struggling, independent women. Moreover, as head of the Actors' Equity and as artistic director of one of the major acting studios in America, she has shown a strong commitment to professional leadership.

At the time of her success with *Same Time, Next Year*, several excellent articles on Burstyn were published, including "A Talk with Ellen Burstyn" by Mary Cantwell in *Mademoiselle* (May 1975); "Gillooly Doesn't Live Here Anymore" *Time* (February 17, 1975); and "Ellen McRae Doesn't Live Here Anymore," by Lee Israel for *McCall's* (August 1975). Claudia Driefus wrote an interview for *Mademoiselle* (October 1981) titled "Ellen Burstyn: the Softer Side of a Superwoman." Burstyn wrote the preface to *The Actors Studio: A Player's Place* by David Garfield (New York, 1984). She has biographical entries in *Current Biography, 1975* (1975–1976), *The Oxford Companion to American Theatre* (1984), and *Who's Who of American Women, 1985* (1985–1986). She is listed in *The Movie Makers* (1974); *Women Who Make Movies* (1975); *Who's Who in Hollywood* (1976); *International Motion Picture Almanac* (1976–1980); *The Film Encyclopedia* (1979); *Halliwell's Filmgoer's Companion* (1980); and *A Biographical Dictionary of Film* (1981).

Jerri C. Crawford

— C —

CALDWELL, Zoe Ada (September 14, 1933–): actress of international repute, was born in a working-class district of Melbourne, Australia. Her father, A. E. Caldwell, was a plumber who was extremely interested in the theatre. Her mother, Zoe Caldwell, was herself a singer and dancer who performed in Gilbert and Sullivan operettas. Given her parents' interest in the theatre, the younger Zoe Caldwell did not have to convince them of the value of a stage career, and she began her training in tapdance, ballet, and elocution in childhood. When she was nine, she acted in *Peter Pan* at the Tivoli Theatre, Melbourne. By the age of eleven she interviewed celebrities on her own radio program, and as a teenager she entertained at birthday parties and performed in amateur dramatics in Melbourne. She received academic training at the Methodist Ladies' College, Melbourne.

From 1953 to 1957 Caldwell appeared with the Union Repertory Company, Melbourne, and the Elizabethan Theatre Trust, Sydney, performing classical and native drama. In 1958 a scholarship took her to England and to Stratford-on-Avon, where she began as a walk-on and made her way into the major Shakespeare roles over two seasons. Particularly noteworthy were her portrayals of Bianca to Paul Robeson's Othello, Cordelia to Charles Laughton's King Lear, and Helena in Tyrone Guthrie's production of *All's Well That Ends Well*. Her performance as Helena drew high praise from critic A. Alvarez of the *New Statesman* (April 25, 1959). Pleased with the production as a whole, he singled her out, saying "The major triumph, however, was Miss Zoe Caldwell . . . . She can speak verse not only as though she both means it and understands it but in such a way that it seems perfectly to express all the subtlety, flow, and depth of her feelings. Perhaps her intensity made her wail too much at the beginning, but by the end she had transformed Helena, against all the odds, into one of the most moving of Shakespeare's heroines. On this showing she has the emotional range and intelligence to make her the finest Shakespearean actress of her generation.''

In 1960 Caldwell made her debut in London, playing Ismene in *Antigone* and the whore in *Cob and Leach*, both at the Royal Court Theatre. Early in 1961, at the same theatre, she played Isabella in Tony Richardson's production of *The Changeling* and Jacqueline in *Jacques*. In the summer of that year she was engaged by Tyrone Guthrie to perform at the Stratford Shakespeare Festival, Ontario, Canada. Seeing her portray Rosaline in *Love's Labour's Lost*, Walter Kerr, critic for the *New York Herald Tribune*, took particular notice of the power of her voice. "She flatters a man at nightingale pitch," wrote Kerr, "then drops her voice four out of five registers to cut his heart out" (June 23, 1961).

After the 1961 season Caldwell divided her time during the next two years between the Manitoba Theatre Center, Canada, and her native Australia. On special invitation, she performed in *St. Joan* for the Adelaide Festival of the Arts. She then returned to the Australian companies where she had begun her adult career and performed in contemporary plays by Patrick White and Ray Matthew for the Elizabethan Theatre Trust and the Union Repertory Company.

In 1963 she agreed to appear in the opening season of the Minnesota Theatre Company at the new Tyrone Guthrie Theatre in Minneapolis. On May 12, 1963, Howard Taubman of the *New York Times* said of her performance as Frosine in *The Miser*, "Zoe Caldwell, a little Australian actress who had performed at the English and Canadian Stratfords, contributes a choice comic portrait. As Frosine, the calculating matchmaker . . . her observations on the superior attraction of old men for young women are delivered with such a mischievous air of elaborate conviction that they not only enchant the decrepit Harpagon but are also a highlight of the performance." That same season she also performed Natasha in *The Three Sisters* to considerable critical acclaim.

After engagements in Manitoba, Canada, and the Goodman Theatre, Chicago, in 1964, she returned to Minneapolis's Guthrie Theatre in 1965, repeating Frosine in *The Miser* and playing Millamant in *The Way of the World* and Grusha in *The Caucasian Chalk Circle*. Of her performance as Millamant, Howard Taubman of the *New York Times* (June 2, 1965) commented, "It is better to do Congreve with forces not equal in all the parts than not to do him at all, provided, of course, you have such delightful exemplars as Miss Caldwell to show the irresistible way."

In December 1965 she agreed to understudy **Anne Bancroft** in the Broadway production of John Whiting's *The Devils*. When Bancroft wrenched her back, Caldwell took over the role of Sister Jean, a mad hunchbacked nun, and received ovations for her several performances. In February 1966, she opened on Broadway as Polly in *Gnädiges Frauelein*, one-half of the double bill of Tennessee Williams's *Slapstick Tragedy*, directed by Alan Schneider. The play was not well received, but Zoe Caldwell was awarded a 1966 Antoinette Perry (Tony)

Award for best supporting actress and received critical acclaim from the New York Drama Critics Circle, the *Saturday Review*, and *Theatre World*.

In 1966 she was back in Canada in the Niagara-on-the-Lake Shaw Festival and in 1967 at Stratford, Ontario. At Stratford her interpretation of Cleopatra in *Antony and Cleopatra* prompted Ronald Bryden of the London *Observer* (September 13, 1967) to remark, "To an extent few Cleopatras dare, she played the royal harlot: sexy, foul-mouthed and funny, itching with desire. . . . But she was royal too, with the same animal unselfconsciousness that made her wanton. As her Antony's dead head fell back on her arm, she launched into Shakespeare's lament for the withered garland of war in a crooning howl, like a wolf baying at the moon. The theatre throbbed with wild, furious desolation. Had Lear been a woman, you felt, she could play that too."

Returning to New York, she opened on Broadway with *The Prime of Miss Jean Brodie*, adapted from Muriel Spark's novel. Directed by Michael Langham, the production proved to be a great triumph. Caldwell's performance was favorably compared with that of Vanessa Redgrave, who had starred in the play in London, and she won her second Tony Award, this time for best actress, against such competition as **Colleen Dewhurst**, **Maureen Stapleton**, and Dorothy Tutin.

On May 9, 1968, Caldwell married Robert Whitehead, New York theatrical producer and director. They have two children, William Edgar (b. July 1969) and Charles Albert (b. May 1972).

In May 1970 Caldwell opened in *Colette*, directed by Gerald Freedman, at **Ellen Stewart**'s La Mama Experimental Theatre Club. She portrayed the French writer-actress from age fifteen to eighty. John J. O'Connor of the *Wall Street Journal* (May 8, 1970) wrote that she was "quite simply mesmerizing, giving one of those virtuoso, flamboyant performances that prompt thoughts of legendary actresses of the past." Other critics were disappointed. Nathan Cohen of *The Toronto Daily Star* found her performance eccentric and physically and vocally mannered (July 8, 1970). In the fall of 1970, Caldwell opened in London as Lady Hamilton to Ian Holm's Nelson in Terence Rattigan's *A Bequest to the Nation*. Here she displayed once again her talent for characterization. John Barber of the *London Daily Telegraph* (September 25, 1970) wrote, "Admiration above all for Miss Caldwell whose tart-with-a-heart-of-gold is ribald, funny, touching, ruthless and tender all at once, with all of it only a veneer for the fear of an aging, discarded whore." At the close of the year she was awarded the Order of the British Empire.

Since 1971 she has acted exclusively in the United States—in *The Creation of the World and Other Business* (Broadway, 1972), *Love and Master Will* (The John F. Kennedy Center, Washington, D.C., 1973), *The Dance of Death* (Vivian Beaumont, New York, 1974), and *Long Day's Journey Into Night* (The John F. Kennedy Center and the Brooklyn Academy of Music, New York, 1976). In 1982 she won her third Tony for her performance of the title role in Robinson

Jeffers's adaptation of *Medea*. In this production Caldwell honed her well-known emotional, vocal, and physical powers to move audiences in her portrayal of the betrayed and abandoned Medea. The production was directed by Robert Whitehead and co-starred **Judith Anderson** as the Nurse. In 1983 the production toured Australia. Again with Whitehead directing, Caldwell appeared Off-Broadway in a one-woman show, *Lillian*, adapted by William Luce from the autobiographical works of **Lillian Hellman**.

Caldwell made her debut as a director in 1977 with *An Almost Perfect Person*, which opened on Broadway in October starring Colleen Dewhurst. Dewhurst praised her director in a *New York Post* interview (October 22, 1977), "Zoe makes you feel free to fail, where you all feel highly attractive and supported, . . . which is not always the case, I assure you." In 1979 she directed *Richard II* at Stratford, Ontario, and in 1980, *These Men* at the Harold Clurman Theatre, New York. In 1982 she was the unbilled co-director of the Broadway production of *Othello*, a production originally staged by Peter Coe at the American Shakespeare Festival, Stratford, Connecticut, and starring James Earl Jones and Christopher Plummer. In 1985 she directed *The Taming of the Shrew* for the American Shakespeare Festival student audience program. In the summer of 1986, after three dark seasons, the American Shakespeare Theatre in Stratford, Connecticut, reopened under the artistic direction of Zoe Caldwell, who directed two productions.

Caldwell taught Shakespeare at the Neighborhood Playhouse, and she also served as visiting eminent scholar at Florida Atlantic University in Boca Raton for the 1988–1989 school year. She held the Dorothy F. Schimdt Chair in Theatre, teaching a Shakespeare master class for graduate students and performing a one-woman show for the university.

In addition to her stage career Caldwell has appeared in a number of television programs: *The Lady's Not for Burning*, *Macbeth*, and *The Apple Cart* for CBC-TV; "Catherine the Great" in the *Witness to Yesterday* series for Canada Global TV in 1974; *The Sea Gull* for BBC-TV in 1977; and *Sarah*, the dramatic special on Sarah Bernhardt, directed by Waris Hussein for CBC-TV in 1977. She also played Liesl in *Deptford Trilogy* for CBC-Radio in 1979. For this performance she received the 1981 ACTRA Andrew Allan Award for best acting performance in radio.

Zoe Caldwell has remained dedicated to enhancing the quality of live theatre. Her exemplary and fascinating career as actress and director reveals her dedication to ancient and modern classics (Shakespeare, Congreve, Molière, Shaw, Brecht, Giraudoux, Strindberg, O'Neill, and Chekhov) as well as contemporary writers (Rattigan, Fry, Williams, and Hellman). One of her particular interests has been to play women who have actually lived—Lady Hamilton, Cleopatra, St. Joan, Colette, Sarah Bernhardt, Catherine the Great, Lillian Hellman. In an interview with Margaret Tierney in *Plays and Players* (October 1970) she admitted, "I do like women who've lived. I've done a lot of that, and I always have a good time with those ladies." Caldwell's career is such that other significant acting and directing achievements may be expected in the future.

Interviews with Zoe Caldwell include Ralph Hicklin, "Interview with Zoe Caldwell," *Toronto Globe and Mail* (January 30, 1965); Rex Reed, "A Few Clues to Miss Caldwell," *New York Times* (February 4, 1968); and Margaret Tierney, "Jumping at Lady Hamilton: Zoe Caldwell Talks to Margaret Tierney," *Plays and Players* (October 1970). Critiques of her performances may be found in *Toronto Globe and Mail* (October 15, 1966), *Maclean's Magazine* (July 1967), *Washington Post* (March 3, 1968), *Newsweek* (February 5, 1968), and *After Dark* (July 1970). See also *American Theatre* (March 1986). Short biographical accounts of Zoe Caldwell may be found in *Who's Who in America 1970–1971* (1970); *Notable Names in the American Theatre* (1976); *Who's Who in the Theatre* (1981); *The Oxford Companion to American Theatre* (1984); and *Contemporary Theatre, Film, and Television*, Vol. I (1984).

Jane E. House

CARROLL, Vinnette (March 11, 1922–): actress, playwright, director for stage, television, and film, was born in New York City, one of three daughters of Dr. Edgar and Florence Carroll. After earning a diploma from Wadleigh High School, Carroll attended Long Island University and New York University, graduating with a degree in psychology. She began studying acting at night while employed as a psychologist with the New York City Board of Education's Bureau of Child Guidance.

In 1948 Carroll won a two-year scholarship to Erwin Piscator's Dramatic Workshop at the New School for Social Research. She made her professional debut in 1948 at the Falmouth, Massachusetts, Playhouse, portraying one of the Christians in George Bernard Shaw's *Androcles and the Lion*. The following summer she worked at the Southhold Playhouse in Long Island, playing Addie in *The Little Foxes* and Bella in *Deep Are the Roots*. Carroll went on to study voice with Susan Steele and acting with Margaret Barker, Lee Strasberg, and **Stella Adler**. After completing Piscator's course, she was cast as Ftatateeta in the touring company of Shaw's *Caesar and Cleopatra*. This production was the first in which the role of Ftatateeta was played by a black woman. *Caesar and Cleopatra* opened on June 16, 1959, at the Olney Theatre in Olney, Maryland; Carroll's notices were glowing.

When other substantial roles did not develop, Carroll began preparing a one-woman show based on a concept she had first conceived in 1949. From 1952 to 1957 Carroll successfully toured the West Indies and the United States in this performance, which presented excerpts from the classics, from Broadway plays, and from writings by Edgar Allan Poe, Dorothy Parker, Langston Hughes, and Margaret Walker. By 1955 Carroll was teaching drama at the High School of Performing Arts in New York City, but she also continued to perform her one-woman show. She gave twelve performances in a single season at the Circle in the Square and the Theatre de Lys in New York. Understandably, some of the success of this type of presentation was due to its novelty. "Miss Carroll is the first Negro to enter the one-woman show field," announced a press release by her booking agents Giesen and Boomer of the Columbia Lecture Bureau.

Carroll made her debut on the Broadway stage in 1956 as the "Negro Woman" in the revival of *A Streetcar Named Desire*, starring **Tallulah Bankhead**. Her other Broadway and Off-Broadway credits include *Small War on Murray Hill*, *The Crucible*, *Jolly's Progress*, *The Octoroon*, and *Moon on a Rainbow Shawl*. *Rainbow Shawl*, which depicted back-alley life in Trinidad, opened on January 15, 1962, at the East 11th Street Theatre. Other members of the distinguished cast included James Earl Jones, **Cicely Tyson**, and Ellen Holly. Carroll won a *Village Voice* Off-Broadway (Obie) Award for her portrayal of Sophie Adams.

Her television appearances include *A Member of the Wedding*, *The Green Pastures*, *Sojourner Truth*, and *All in the Family*, as well as several other shows. She was seen in the films *One Potato, Two Potato*, *Up the Down Staircase*, *Alice's Restaurant*, and *The Reivers*.

Carroll has also been directing since 1958, when she staged *Dark of the Moon* with an all-black cast. During the next five years, she also directed Langston Hughes's *Black Nativity* and narrated it in London and on television. Carroll staged the Equity Library Theatre's productions of *Ondine* and *The Disenchanted* in New York. She also staged Langston Hughes's *Prodigal Son* Off-Broadway and in London, Paris, Brussels, and Holland. She had some difficulty finding suitable material for black actors and turned to creating her own material. In 1963 her *Trumpets of the Lord*, a musical adaptation of James Weldon Johnson's *God's Trombones*, ran for 161 performances at the Off-Broadway Astor Playhouse. (In 1966 *Trumpets of the Lord* was selected to represent America at the Théâtre des Nations festival in Paris, headed by Jean-Louis Barrault.) Carroll won a television Emmy Award in 1964 for conceiving, adapting, and supervising the CBS production of *Beyond the Blues*.

For six months in 1967 Carroll was associate director of the Inner City Repertory Company in Watts, Los Angeles. While there she staged *The Flies* and the racially integrated *Slow Dance on the Killing Ground*. Back in New York Carroll organized the Urban Arts Corps (1967), a pilot project of the Ghetto Arts Program of the New York Council on the Arts. The program was designed to train young Puerto Ricans and blacks as performers and to develop opportunities for professionals using materials by black playwrights and composers. According to Carroll, the main function of Urban Arts Corps was to take their work into different communities "to help them find image-building material" (*New York Times*, March 23, 1968). As artistic director, she was responsible for conceiving, selecting, and directing their productions. Now, with a stage on which to present her works and a group of eager young artists to perform them, she entered one of her most creative periods.

Carroll's successful collaboration with Micki Grant began in 1972. Carroll remembers: "Micki came in here and sang her songs, and I knew it was right" (Interview, November 25, 1985). Their first musical was *Don't Bother Me, I Can't Cope* (1972). Their other collaborations include *The Ups and Downs of Theophilus Maitland*, *But Never Jam Today*, *Croesus and the Witch*, and Irwin Shaw's *Bury the Dead* with music added.

Your Arms Too Short to Box with God, one of Carroll's best-known plays, was commissioned by the Italian government to open at the Spoleto Festival during the summer of 1975. On December 22, 1976, *Box* opened at the Lyceum Theatre in New York. This religious musical, showing the Passion, Crucifixion, and Resurrection of Christ, was a hit. The occasion was a landmark in theatre history. "Carroll becomes, with *Box*, Broadway's first black female director," wrote the critic in the *New York Times* (December 19, 1976). The musical received two Antoinette Perry (Tony) nominations. In November 1982 Carroll revived *Box* at the Alvin Theatre in New York with celebrated soul singers Al Green and Patti LaBelle.

Carroll has always maintained that black artists must create a forum where they can work and develop. However, she has also argued that black artists should stop using Broadway to validate their work. Leading the way, she has widened her audience to include areas outside of New York. She sought out the John F. Kennedy Center for the Performing Arts for her musical *When Hell Freezes I'll Skate*, which opened on May 2, 1984, for a five-week run. In October 1985 she presented *The Ups and Downs of Theophilus Maitland* at the Dallas Theatre Center.

Still artistic director of Urban Arts Corps, she has organized the Vinnette Carroll Repertory Company, serving the South Florida area of Miami and Fort Lauderdale. This repertory company first presented her *What You Gonna Name that Pretty Little Baby?*, a celebration of Christ, at the Mount Olive Baptist Church in Fort Lauderdale on December 15, 1985. In 1988 the company moved into a permanent home, a renovated Methodist Church in Fort Lauderdale.

Vinnette Carroll is a distinguished playwright and director. During her nearly forty years in American theatre, she has made significant contributions to black theatre and to black artists. A pioneer black director, she has provided a gateway through which other women can enter. "When I started out in the fifties," recalled Carroll, "there were no black women directors because there were almost no black playwrights and no black theatre to speak of" (*New York Times*, November 17, 1979).

Carroll has been partly responsible for the growth of a new generation of black theatre. Besides helping to train minority theatre people, her musicals have given many black performers the opportunity to work professionally, both here and abroad. Moreover, she has helped launch the careers of actress-singer Jonelle Allen, Marvin Felix Camillo (director of the Broadway play *Short Eyes*), and Sherman Hemsley of television's *The Jeffersons*, among others.

Because of her ability to employ a distinctive black voice, Carroll has acquired a faithful audience. Her black-oriented plays, with religious overtones, bring to the legitimate stage a foot-stomping, hand-clapping, finger-snapping, "can't sit" style in which song and dance draw upon the gospel-soul-jazz tradition. In an early interview, Carroll once declared, "They told me that I had one-third less chance because I was a woman and a third less chance again because I was black, but I tell you, I'm going to do one hell of a lot with that remaining one third'' (S. Patterson, ''Blacks' 'Alice': Lewis Carroll via Vinnette, Broadway Bound Sensation,'' undated clipping in the Billy Rose Theatre Collection). As she predicted, she has done and is still doing ''one hell of a lot with that remaining one third.'' Her honors include a Ford Foundation Grant for Directors, the Los Angeles Drama Critics Award for *Cope*, NAACP's Image Award for Distinguished Direction, the 1975 Audelco Achievement Award, the 1977 Frank Silvera Writers' Workshop Foundation Award, the Harold Jackman Memorial Award, *Ebony Magazine*'s Black Achievement Award, The Golden Circle Award, and induction into the Black Film Makers Hall of Fame.

There is a useful clipping file on Carroll in the Billy Rose Theatre Collection at the New York Public Library Performing Arts Reseach Center At Lincoln Center. Articles by Arthur Pollack and John G. Patterson (unidentified) in that collection give information concerning her early career. Articles in the *New York Times* (March 23, 1968; March 23, 1975; December 19, 1976; and November 17, 1979) comment on Carroll's career and her productions, as do articles in the *New York Herald Tribune* (December 29, 1961), the New York *Daily News* (June 6, 1972), and the *Amsterdam* (New York) *News* (September 30, 1978). See also Carolyn Jack, ''Carroll Has a Mission, a New Home,'' *American Theatre* (November 1988). Carroll is listed in *The Biographical Encyclopaedia and Who's Who of the American Theatre* (1966), *Notable Names in the American Theatre* (1976), and *Who's Who in the Theatre* (1981). Some of the material for this essay was obtained through an interview with Vinnette Carroll (November 25, 1985).

Jo A. Tanner

CARTER, Mrs. Leslie (June 10, 1862–November 13, 1937): actress and star of David Belasco's popular melodramas, was born Caroline Louise Dudley in Louisville, Kentucky. Her father, Orson Daniel Dudley, was a wealthy merchant, and her mother a southern belle. After her father's death, the family moved to Dayton, Ohio, where the young Caroline attended the Cooper Seminary. In 1880, at eighteen, she married Leslie Carter, a Chicago industrialist and son of a wealthy and socially prominent Chicago family. They had one son, Leslie Dudley Carter, who died in 1934.

The Carters' marriage lasted nine years, ending in 1889 in a widely publicized divorce. Caroline Carter's husband had had her judged insane and confined to a private sanitarium. After her release, she sued for divorce, charging extreme cruelty. Her husband countersued for adultery, naming the actor Kyrle Bellew as corespondent. He won both the divorce case and the custody of their son.

After the divorce Carter turned to the stage to earn a living. She went to David Belasco, the famous producer, and begged him to train her for the stage. After intensive training under Belasco's personal supervision, she made her stage debut at the Broadway Theatre in New York on November 10, 1890, starring in *The Ugly Ducking* under the name of Mrs. Leslie Carter. She reportedly chose to use her married name in order to annoy her ex-husband. Whenever she appeared in Chicago, Mr. Carter left town. Advertisements for her plays never appeared on the trains of the Chicago's South Side El, a company in which her ex-husband owned an interest.

The New York critics were not enthusiastic about her first starring role, nor did they praise her in *Miss Helyett*, a musical comedy, the following year. She toured in *Miss Helyett* until 1893, then left the stage for two years to engage in more intensive study. Belasco prepared his next play, *The Heart of Maryland*, especially for her. In this Civil War drama, Carter played Maryland Calvert, whose lover was doomed to die when the evening bell tolled. The play's climactic scene came when she raced up the steps of the tower and, suspended thirty-five feet above the stage floor, swung from the clapper of the bell, muting its sound so her lover would not die. The play opened at the Herald Square Theatre on October 22, 1895. Despite a lukewarm reception by the drama critics, the play became a tremendous hit, establishing Mrs. Leslie Carter as one of America's top stars.

After appearing in *The Heart of Maryland* for three years in both the United States and London, Carter opened in Belasco's *Zaza* on January 9, 1899. Though denounced by clergy as immoral, this dramatization of the life and loves of a music hall singer was another spectacular success. When Carter appeared as Zaza in London, she received public acclaim from the Prince of Wales (later King Edward VII) and other members of the royal family.

DuBarry, Carter's third successive Belasco hit, opened on December 25, 1901. The critic of the New York *Dramatic Mirror* wrote, "The role of DuBarry has been skillfully fabricated to afford Mrs. Carter opportunity for the display of her every talent and accomplishment. . . . In her scenes of anger and passion she rose to higher force than she had ever before shown. Her comedy was her weakest point. The pathetic scenes she managed well, and she lent distinction to the role throughout the performance" (January 4, 1902). *DuBarry* toured for three years. Carter's last play with Belasco, *Adrea*, opened in New York in 1905, but its run was terminated in 1906 when Carter left Belasco's management.

During the summer of 1906 Carter married William Lewis Payne, a fellow actor thirteen years her junior, in Portsmouth, New Hampshire. Belasco had not been informed of the forthcoming marriage and was astonished when he heard of it. He was widely quoted in the newspapers of the time as having said, "I would as soon think of the devil's asking for holy water as of Mrs. Carter taking a husband." The agreement between Carter and Belasco was severed, and the breach between the two was not healed until 1931, shortly before Belasco's death.

Carter was less successful in her acting career following her break with Belasco. After a brief association with another manager, she toured on her own for two years. In 1908 she was forced to declare bankruptcy and had to auction her personal effects. After touring for a few more seasons in plays like *Camille*, *Two Women*, *Magda*, and *The Second Mrs. Tanqueray*, she retired from the stage and bought a villa in France, where she lived for several years.

Carter returned to the stage in 1921 as Lady Catherine in Somerset Maugham's *The Circle*, her most critically acclaimed role. During 1924 and 1925 she appeared in vaudeville. She returned to the legitimate stage in 1926 and toured until 1934, when she went to Hollywood to play character roles in films. In the same year she appeared for the last time on the stage in a revival of *The Circle*. She died in Hollywood on November 13, 1937, of a heart ailment and was survived by her husband and an adopted daughter, Mary Carter Payne.

In turning to the stage for a career, Mrs. Carter took a great risk. She did not have the advantage of a long stage apprenticeship as did most performers of the day. She was fortunate in securing the tutelage of Belasco and worked hard for several years to develop her abilities as an actress. Belasco described her as "a pale, slender girl, with a mass of red hair and a pair of green eyes gleaming under black brows, who alternately wept and smiled, whose gestures were full of unconscious grace, and whose voice vibrated with musical sweetness" (quoted in her obituary, *New York Times*, November 14, 1937). With his help she developed her pleasing voice, her expressive face, and her ability to project deep emotions. She became one of the outstanding actresses of her day and one of the most popular performers at the turn of the century.

Mrs. Leslie Carter's autobiography, "Portrait of a Lady with Red Hair," which appeared in *Liberty* (January 15 through March 19, 1927), is not very reliable. Charles H. Harper, "Mrs. Leslie Carter: Her Life and Career" (Unpublished Ph.D. dissertation, University of Nebraska, 1978) provides a detailed study of her career. She is described in Lewis C. Strang, *Famous Actresses of the Day*, First Series (1899) and Second Series (1901), and in Craig Timberlake's *The Bishop of Broadway: The Life and Work of David Belasco* (1954). See also William Winter, *The Wallet of Time*, Vol. II (1913). Clippings and other primary source material may be found in the Robinson Locke Collection at the New York Public Library Performing Arts Research Center at Lincoln Center, the George Arents Research Library at Syracuse University, the Hoblitzelle Theatre Arts Library at the University of Texas at Austin, the Dayton and Montgomery County Public Library in Ohio, and the Margaret Herrick Library of the Academy of Motion Picture Arts and Sciences in Beverly Hills, California. Carter's obituary appeared in the *New York Times* (November 14, 1937). Mrs. Leslie Carter is included in *Who's Who on the Stage, 1908* (1908); *Who's Who in the Theatre*, Vol. I (1912); *Who's Who in Music and Drama* (1914); *Who Was Who in America*, Vol. I: *1897–1942* (1966); *Notable American Women*, Vol. I (1971); William C. Young, *Famous Actors and Actresses on the American Stage*, Vol. I (1975), and *The Oxford Companion to American Theatre* (1984).

                                                                    Rita M. Plotnicki

CASSIDY, Claudia (1905?–): influential critic for many years on the Chicago *Tribune*, was born in Shawneetown, Illinois, the daughter of George Peter and Olive (Grattan) Cassidy. She earned the Bachelor of Arts degree at the University of Illinois and soon (1925) began to write on the arts for the Chicago *Journal of Commerce*. On June 15, 1929, she married William John Crawford but always thereafter continued to use her maiden name in writing.

She remained with the *Journal of Commerce* as music and drama critic until 1941, writing a daily column called "On the Aisle." When she moved to the *Chicago Sun* in 1941, she continued her "On the Aisle" column. In late 1941 she moved to the music and drama desk of the Chicago *Tribune* and occupied that desk until her retirement in 1965. It was here that she gained her reputation for perspicacity and for incisive criticism. Richard B. Gehman, writing about Claudia Cassidy in 1951, called her "honest, outspoken, fearless, and highly intelligent." He rated her "one of the five most perceptive, informed, and scholarly critics in American journalism. A brilliant phrase-maker, she has the ability to make people continue to read her no matter what they think of her notions and opinions" ("Claudia Cassidy, Medusa of the Mid-west," *Theatre Arts*, July 1951, p. 14).

Though she was often judged to be overly critical, Cassidy fought for what she considered good theatre. Her name is part of the legendary success story of Tennessee Williams's *The Glass Menagerie*, which opened in Chicago's Civic Theatre in 1945. Cassidy called it a "tangible, taut and tentacled play . . . that gripped players and audience alike, and created one of those rare evenings in the theatre that make 'stage struck' an honorable word" (Chicago *Sunday Tribune*, January 7, 1945). When Chicago audiences failed to turn out for this exceptional play, Cassidy led the crusade to convince them to attend an event of first importance in the theatre. As a result of her efforts, *The Glass Menagerie* became a veritable hit, proceeded to Broadway, and became one of the most famous of modern American plays.

During the summer when Cassidy was abroad, she continued her column under the title "Europe on the Aisle" and published a collection of these columns under the same title in 1954. After her retirement, Cassidy functioned as critic-at-large for the *Tribune* and conducted a weekly program on WFMT, Chicago, called *Critic's Choice*. She served on the 1970–1971 committee for the Joseph Jefferson awards, and in 1971 the Goodman Memorial Theatre, Chicago, engaged her to help select plays. In 1973 she became film critic for the *Chicago Magazine*, and a year later its critic-at-large.

Claudia Cassidy was one of the first women to serve as long-term theatre critic on a large metropolitan newspaper, and she did so with insight, verve, and competence.

Claudia Cassidy wrote *Europe on the Aisle* (1954). See also Richard B. Gehman, "Claudia Cassidy: Medusa of the Mid-west," *Theatre Arts* (July 1951), and Marguerite Courtney, *Laurette: The Intimate Biography of Laurette Taylor* (1968). Brief biographical information on Cassidy is contained in *Notable Names in the American Theatre* (1976); M. E. Comtois, *Contemporary American Theatre Critics* (1977); and *The Oxford Companion to American Theatre* (1984).

Vera Mowry Roberts and
Alice McDonnell Robinson

CHAMBERS, Jane (March 27, 1937–February 15, 1983): playwright and prominent feminist, was born Carolyn Jane Chambers in Columbia, South Carolina, to Clarice and Carol Chambers. During her early years the family lived in Orlando, Florida, where she began to write radio scripts for high school and local public stations while keeping up her studies sufficiently to earn several scholarships. In 1954, at the age of seventeen, she entered Rollins College in Winter Park, Florida, intent on becoming a playwright. Soon after her arrival at Rollins, Chambers was producing, writing, and starring in her own television show *Youth Pops a Question*. By 1956 she determined to leave Rollins to study acting at California's Pasadena Playhouse.

The following year Chambers moved from Pasadena to New York, where she appeared in several Off-Broadway productions. She continued her writing career as a reporter for theatrical trade papers and concentrated on playwriting as a member of the Poet's Theater. Although her first play, *The Marvelous Metropolis*, was produced at the 41st Street Theatre, she was unable to earn a living as a writer. She moved to New England to work for Jack Paar's station (WMTW-TV) in Poland Spring, Maine, where she wrote program copy, developed material for Paar, and starred in her own children's show titled *The Merry Witch*. During her years in Maine, Chambers also worked as a teacher and counselor for the Job Corps.

In 1968 Chambers moved back to New York. She continued working for the Job Corps (in New Jersey) and also writing plays. She eventually enrolled in Goddard College, Vermont. There she met Beth Allen, who became her lifelong companion and manager. In 1971, a productive year for Chambers, she received the Rosenthal Award for Poetry; the Connecticut Television Award for best religious drama for her civil rights play, *Christ in a Treehouse*; founded the New Jersey Women's Political Caucus; and completed her undergraduate degree at Goddard.

The following year her play *Tales of the Revolution and Other American Fables* won the Eugene O'Neill Prize and was produced at the Eugene O'Neill Memorial Theatre Center in Connecticut. Shortly thereafter Chambers was instrumental in founding the Women's Interart Center, New York, where her plays *Random Violence*, *Mine!* and *The Wife* were produced during 1973 and 1974. At the same time Chambers also wrote for the CBS-TV soap opera *Search For Tomorrow*, which won her the 1973 Writer's Guild of America Award for daytime serials.

In 1974 Playwrights Horizons in New York produced *A Late Snow*, Chambers's play about the interrelationships of a group of lesbians stranded in a cabin during a snowfall. Chambers was open about her homosexuality and created characters who were equally open about their sexual preferences and lifestyles. She thought that her plays had a universal appeal, whatever their subject matter.

Jane Chambers was now being recognized as both a playwright and a novelist. Her play *Common Garden Variety* was produced at the Mark Taper Theatre Studio in Los Angeles in 1976, her novel *Burning* was published by Jove Press in 1978, and her play *A Late Snow* was published in *Gay Plays* by Avon Press in 1979.

In 1980 Chambers began a relationship with The Glines, a New York-based theatre company dedicated to presenting works about the gay experience. For their First Gay American Arts Festival, Chambers wrote what is considered to be her finest work, *Last Summer at Bluefish Cove*. The play concerns several lesbian couples who vacation at the shore every summer. Central to the action is Lil, who is dying of cancer and is spending her final summer at Bluefish Cove. The play opened at the Westside Mainstage in 1980 and won the Villager Downtown Theatre Award in 1981.

Chambers wrote *Bluefish Cove* after a friend had died of cancer. In late 1981, while rehearsing her new play *Kudzu* for Playwrights Horizons, Chambers fell ill, and it was discovered that she too was battling cancer. Despite terminal illness she continued to write. For the Second Gay American Arts Festival the following year she wrote and directed *My Blue Heaven*, which ran for several months at the Shandol Theatre in New York. *The Quintessential Image* was presented at the Women's Theatre Conference in Minneapolis in the summer of 1983 and toured New York State for the East End Gay Organization for Human Rights. Jane Chambers had died on February 15, 1983, in her Greenport, Long Island, home.

During her brief career Chambers was playwright-in-residence at The Glines; served on the Board of Directors of the Off-off-Broadway Alliance (OOBA); was a member of the planning committee for the Women's Program of the American Theatre Association; and held membership in the Writer's Guild East, Dramatists Guild, Author's League, Actors' Equity, and the East End Gay Organization for Human Rights.

Chambers pioneered in writing plays about homosexuality in the contemporary American theatre. She deserves recognition for a successful writing career and for dedication not only to her art but to the enhancement of human dignity and self-respect for gay people. It was appropriate that on May 10, 1982, nine months before her death, Chambers became the recipient of the Fifth Annual Award of the Fund for Human Dignity, which honors persons who, by "their work or by the example of their lives, have made a major contribution to public understanding and acceptance of lesbians and gay men."

Most of Jane Chambers's plays—*Common Garden Variety, One Short Day at the Jamboree, Kudzu, Curfew!, The Quintessential Image, Eye of the Gull, Deadly Nightshade, Random Violence, The Wife,* and *Tales of the Revolution and Other American Fables*—are unpublished, yet all have been produced. Her published works include *A Late Snow* in *Gay Plays, The First Collection* (1979), *My Blue Heaven* (1981), *Last Summer in Bluefish Cove* (1982), the novel *Burning* (1978, reprinted 1983), and a collection of poetry titled *Warrior at Rest* (1984). Another novel, *Chasin' Jason*, has not been published. In *The Drama Review* (March 1981), Terry Helbing and Emily Sisley discuss Chambers' work in articles titled "Gay Plays, Gay Theatre, Gay Performance" (Helbing) and "Notes on Lesbian Theatre" (Sisley). See also Tish Dace, "New York, New York," *Other Stages* (June 25, 1980), and the *Daily News* (December 23, 1980). Chambers' obituary appeared in the *New York Times* (February 16, 1983). She is listed in *National Playwrights Directory*, 2nd Edition (1981).

Penny M. Landau

CHANG, Tisa (April 5, 1941–): actress, dancer, and artistic director/producer of the Pan Asian Repertory Theatre (New York City), was born in Chungking and came to the United States in 1947. She is the daughter of Ping Hsun Chang and Teresa (Kang) Chang. Her father was a classmate of the Communist premier Chou En-lai, and they acted together in high school productions of Western plays. "Ibsen was a favorite of theirs. Chou played women's parts and my father played men's parts," Chang said (*New York Times*, October 14, 1977). Her father was a career diplomat from the Republic of Nationalist China from 1946 until 1957.

Tisa Chang graduated from the New York High School of the Performing Arts and attended Barnard and City colleges of New York. She trained professionally with Uta Hagen, Alice Hermes, and Jaime Rogers and studied dance with the Thomas-Fallis School and the Martha Graham School.

Although Tisa Chang made a successful career for herself as an actress and dancer, she was disturbed at the limited and stereotyped roles available to Asian artists. In 1975 she formed the Chinese Theatre Group at the La Mama Experimental Theatre Club in the Bowery. Initial productions were adaptations from classical Chinese theatre, such as *Orphan of Chao* and *Return of the Phoenix*. The group began to combine traditional elements of Far Eastern and Western theatrical techniques. Chang's adaptation of *A Midsummer Night's Dream* was set in China and performed bilingually. The success and the reach of the company grew rapidly, and it was incorporated in 1977 as the Pan Asian Repertory Theatre. The theatre encourages the production of new plays exploring Asian-American themes and offers professional workshops and on-the-job experience for emerging talents. In order to expand its audience and introduce Asian-American theatre to the general public, the company now performs entirely in English.

Critics have praised Chang's skill as a director. For instance, one says, "As richly sculpted as these portraits are, their behavior and immediate motivations are always clear and accessible to the Western theatregoer, thanks to the clear-lined direction" (*The Villager*, July 31, 1980). Some of Chang's productions include *Ghosts and Goddesses* (1974), *The Pursuit of Happiness* (1975), *Hotel Paradiso* (1975), *Sunrise* (1980), *Monkey Music* (1980), *An American Story* (1980), *Flowers and Household Gods* (1981), *Bullet Headed Birds* (1981), *Station J* (1982), *Teahouse* (1983), *A Midsummer Night's Dream* (1983), *Empress of China* (1983), and *A Song for a Nisei Fisherman* (1983).

Chang has also directed at the Equity Library Theater, the Lincoln Center Library and Museum of the Performing Arts, the Women's Project at the American Place Theater, and Studio Arena in Buffalo. In addition to her directing and her accomplishments as artistic director of the Pan Asian Repertory Theatre, Tisa Chang has maintained a demanding and successful acting career. She appeared on Broadway in *Lovely Ladies, Kind Gentlemen* (1970) and *The Basic Training of Pavlo Hummel* (1977). Her Off-Broadway credits include *Pacific Overtures*, *Brothers*, *The Love Suicide at Schofield Barracks*, *Sweet Charity*, *The King and I*, *A Funny Thing Happened On The Way To The Forum*, and *The World of Suzie Wong*. Some of her film credits are *Greetings*, *Ambush Bay*, and *Hanky Panky*. Her television performances include *Purge's Place* and *Escape from Iran*.

Chang is married to Ernest Abuba, a professional actor/playwright/director, who has been involved in several Pan Asian Repertory Theatre productions and is a member of the Board of Directors. They have one son, Auric.

In 1981 Mel Gussow, a *New York Times* theatre critic, wrote, "In its four-year history, Chang's company has enriched the New York theatre with stories of Asian-Americans from diverse backgrounds (Chinese, Japanese, Filipino) at the same time that she has encouraged emerging acting and writing talent" (April 21, 1981). It is as if the critic were paraphrasing Chang's own words, "I want to use my heritage to explore new theatrical forms—rather than to espouse ethnicity. I also want to provide the opportunity for Asian-American performers to work on the highest professional level" (*New York Times*, October 14, 1977).

Through the 1984–1985 season the Pan Asian Repertory Company presented twenty-six new plays as mainstage productions. For its proven artistic excellence and its pioneering work, the company has been designated a "Primary Organization" by the New York State Council on the Arts. In 1985 it was awarded a two-year grant for institutional development by the Ford Foundation. Mel Gussow, introducing Tisa Chang at a symposium of the American Theatre Critics Association, said, "The Pan Asian Repertory Theatre, . . . in a very few years, has made tremendous strides in developing plays and actors. The Pan Asian is a broadly ethnocentric company. At the Pan Asian I have seen plays . . . that express a diversity of styles and points of view. Tisa Chang has made audiences 'Pan Asian' conscious, while also brightening many of our evenings at the theatre" (*Newsletter*, April 1985). In 1988 the Pan Asian Repertory Theatre began sending touring productions of past hits and new works into New England and planned to extend their tours into the west and midwest in 1989.

The Billy Rose Theatre Collection, New York Public Library Performing Arts Research Center at Lincoln Center has a limited clipping file on Tisa Chang. Much of the material for this biographical sketch came from reviews, including *The Villager* (July 21, 1980), *The New York Post* (November 19, 1980), *Newsday* (August 19, 1981), the *New York Times* (October 14, 1977; April 8, 1980; April 21, 1981; November 25, 1981; and April 15, 1982), and *ATCA Newsletter* (April 1985). Other information was obtained from production programs and discussions with Tisa Chang. Chang is included in *Contemporary Theatre, Film, and Television*, Vol. I (1984).

Maria Rodriguez

CHANNING, Carol (January 31, 1921–): actress, singer, and comedienne, was born Carol Elaine Channing in Seattle, Washington, the only child of George and Adelaide (Glaser) Channing. Her father was a Christian Science practitioner, lecturer, writer, and editor. Three months after her birth, the family moved to San Francisco. In elementary and junior high school, Carol Channing gained a reputation as the class clown by mimicking the accents and gestures of teachers and fellow students. Channing's size set her apart at a young age. She grew to stand five feet, nine inches tall. Stage-struck since the age of six, Channing first achieved dramatic recognition as a senior in high school when she won first prize in a contest for the best four-minute speech on "What America Means to Me."

In 1938 Channing enrolled in Bennington College, Vermont. During the summer of 1940 she worked briefly at the Tamiment Summer Playhouse in the Poconos but was dismissed because she was too disorganized. The next winter, during the six-week recess at Bennington, she went to New York. There she moved into the YWCA's Studio Club and landed her first job. She made her Broadway debut as a singer in Marc Blitzstein's *No For an Answer*, which opened at the Mecca Temple in January 1941. The show ran for only three days, but Channing received praise in *The New Yorker*. Thrilled by this recognition, she decided to stay in New York. In the fall of 1941 she was cast as an understudy for Eve Arden in *Let's Face It*, but during its nine-month run she replaced Arden only one time.

Channing then married a young novelist named Theodore Nash. This was a sudden and impulsive marriage born out of Channing's loneliness in New York, and it lasted only two years. During that time she played Broadway once again— as a Polish peasant in *Proof Through the Night* at the Morosco Theatre (December 25, 1942). She then appeared in Greenwich Village night clubs and cabarets with little success. Tired of her idle career, Channing left the theatre and in 1946 moved to California where she joined an artists' colony.

Early in 1948 Channing was one of hundreds of actresses in line to audition for a single opening in the Hollywood review *Lend an Ear*. When her turn finally came, Channing informed the director that she could not accurately show what she could do without going through at least a dozen numbers. Six numbers later she was hired. The show opened in California in June of 1948. In December of that year she was married to Alexander Carson, a football player and private detective who cared little for show business. Four days after they were married, *Lend an Ear* opened in New York at the National Theatre (December 1948). The Broadway run was an outstanding success, playing for more than a year. Carol Channing was singled out for special praise.

Although Channing was not yet a star, producers Herman Levine and Oliver Smith agreed to give her a chance in the role of the gold digger Lorelei Lee in *Gentlemen Prefer Blondes*. The show opened in December 1949 and ran for two years on Broadway. Carol Channing became Broadway's new celebrity best known for her rendition of the song "Diamonds Are a Girl's Best Friend." *New York Times* critic Brooks Atkinson said after her première, "Let us call her portrait of the aureate Lee the most fabulous comic creation of this dreary period in history" (December 9, 1949). Another critic called her "the funniest female since **Fanny Brice** and Beatrice Lillie" (*Time*, December 19, 1949, p. 62). *Gentlemen Prefer Blondes* went on tour for two years, opening September 20, 1951, at the Palace in Chicago, and continued to earn rave reviews along the way.

In 1953 Channing replaced Rosalind Russell as Ruth Sherwood in *Wonderful Town*, Leonard Bernstein's musical adaptation of the play *My Sister Eileen*. She played Ruth for six months on Broadway and then went on tour for two years. In 1955 she appeared again in New York, this time as Flora Weems in *The Vamp*, based on the life of the silent screen star Theda Bara. In September 1956 Channing married Charles Lowe, a television writer and producer for a New York advertising agency. In the same year she prepared a nightclub act that featured caricatures of celebrated female entertainers and songs from *Gentlemen Prefer Blondes*. Opening her act at the Tropicana Hotel in Las Vegas in July 1957, Channing took her revue on the road for the next three years. Much of this material was incorporated into a musical called *Show Girl*, which opened at the Eugene O'Neill Theatre on January 12, 1961. After 100 performances of *Show Girl*, Channing returned to the nightclub circuit. In 1962 Channing co-starred in *The George Burns-Carol Channing Show*, a musical revue that also toured for a season. She then toured in the Theatre Guild's production of *The Millionairess* by George Bernard Shaw. After almost ten years of solid touring, Channing was a household name from coast to coast.

In January 1964 this one-woman spectacular opened in the musical *Hello, Dolly!* in the role of the unforgettable Dolly Gallagher Levi. When producer David Merrick offered her the role of Dolly, she agreed only if director Gower Champion, who had hired her for *Lend an Ear* (1948), directed it. Not everyone was convinced she could play the role, and Channing did what few "stars" ever have to do: she auditioned for the role. *Hello, Dolly!* opened at the St. James Theatre in New York on January 16, 1964, with Channing playing Dolly, the widow intent on remarrying into money. Reflecting the critics' unanimous praise, Walter Kerr in the *New York Herald Tribune* commended Channing for bringing to life "all the blowsy glamour of the girls of the sheet music of 1916. She is glorious" (January 25, 1964). *Hello, Dolly!* received the New York Drama Critics Circle Award for the best musical of the 1963–1964 season. It also received ten of the Antoinette Perry (Tony) Awards for 1964. After the Broadway run, Channing toured with the show until 1967, performing the role of Dolly 1,273 times.

Carol Channing made her London debut at the Drury Lane Theatre in April 1970 in a revue titled *Carol Channing and Her Ten Stout-Hearted Men*, for which she was awarded the London Critics Award. In New York in January 1971 she appeared in *Four on a Garden*, a collection of four one-act plays in each of which she played the female lead. In 1974 Channing re-created the role of Lorelei Lee for *Lorelei, or Gentlemen Still Prefer Blondes*. She was nominated for another Tony Award for her performance in *Lorelei*. In 1976 she played Alma in a tryout of *The Bed Before Yesterday*. A year later Channing took up her role of Dolly once again, playing both New York and London over a period of four years (1977–1980). She toured for a short time in the musical revue *Sugar Babies*, which had opened on Broadway October 8, 1979, with Mickey Rooney and **Ann Miller**. Ralph G. Allen, author of the musical's book, revised the show extensively for Channing's national tour, which proved unsuccessful. Audiences preferred the combination of Mickey Rooney and Ann Miller.

In the summer of 1985, while she was once again appearing in *Hello Dolly!*, Channing was visited by **Mary Martin**, her friend for the previous thirty-six years. Martin had been offered a role in a new play, *Legends*, written by James Kirkwood. The comedy is about two bitterly feuding Hollywood screen legends who must share a New York stage. Martin wanted Channing to do the play with her. Channing agreed and the two stars began a six-city American tour, but the planned showings in London and New York did not take place.

Carol Channing has appeared in two films: *The First Traveling Saleslady* (1956) and *Thoroughly Modern Millie* (1957). For her performance in the latter film she won the Golden Globe Award for best actress. Channing has appeared in over fifty television shows as a guest star, including *The Ed Sullivan Show*, *The Perry Como Show*, and *The Dinah Shore Show*. She has been featured in her own specials as well.

Channing is a woman of inexhaustible energy and talent. For forty years she has been entertaining and charming audiences. When Harold Clurman reviewed *Hello, Dolly!* for *The Nation* in 1964, he wrote, "She's a triumph of guilelessness over the facts of life. The audience is grateful to a person so good-humored, so without malice, so openhearted in a world where intelligence alone leads to very different sentiments. Bless her goofiness, we feel like crying. She makes life positively gay because she hears no evil, sees no evil, and will speak no evil. She is a public benefactress" (February 10, 1964, p. 154). The last twenty years have only given added strength to the truth of those words.

Among the many articles about Channing and reviews of her performances are *Cue* (December 25, 1948), New York *Daily News* (December 9, 1949), *Time* (January 9, 1950), *New Republic* (January 2, 1950), *New York World-Telegram* (January 7, 1961), *New York Herald Tribune* (January 17, 1964), *New York Times* (January 17 and January 26, 1964), and *The Nation* (February 10, 1964). Two recent articles about Channing are "High Voltage: Carol Channing," *Vogue* (July 1985), and "Mary Martin and Carol Channing Are Bitchy Superstars in *Legends!*—But Don't Worry, It's All an Act," an interview with D. Wallace, *People Weekly* (December 16, 1985). *Current Biography* for 1964 tells of Channing's early life and career. *The Biographical Encyclopaedia and Who's Who of the American Theatre* (1966) and *Notable Names in the American Theatre* (1976) both give listings of Channing's stage and film credits as well as awards received. Other information can be found in *Theatre World* (1980–1981), *Variety International Show Business Directory* (1981), and *The Oxford Companion to American Theatre* (1984).

Monica Fernandez

CHASE, Mary Coyle (February 25, 1907–October 21, 1981): playwright, best known for her play *Harvey*, one of the four longest-running shows on Broadway and later a successful film starring James Stewart, was born to Mary (Mc-Donough) Coyle and Frank Bernard Coyle in Denver, Colorado. During adolescence she was often amused by her Irish uncles' tales of the myths and legends of the "old country." These tales became a strong influence on her life and her approach to written humor. At the age of eleven she saw her first stage production,

Macbeth. From then on, Mary Coyle was in love with the theatre; she saw all the shows available in the Denver area and read plays and books on playwriting.

Mary Coyle attended Denver public schools and graduated from West High School before the age of sixteen. She majored in classics at Denver University (1921–1923) and also attended the University of Colorado (1923–1924), but she did not remain long enough at either institution to earn a degree. It was not until 1947 that Denver University awarded her an honorary doctorate.

In 1924 Mary Coyle became a reporter for the *Rocky Mountain News*, where she wrote society notes and "sob sister" stories and covered a variety of events. She is said to have chosen newspaper work so that she could "study people, meet life and later put it into plays. . . . I wanted to see how people reacted under stress, how they spoke in times of crisis" (*Rocky Mountain News*, October 23, 1981). Reporters during that period were notorious for working long hours, for drinking too much, and for stopping at nothing to beat a competitor to a story. A close friend, Marge Barrett, described her during the seven years she worked for the paper as flamboyant, fey, daring, and full of Irish superstitions. It was not unusual to see her ride off on the back of photographer Harry Rhodes's motorcycle, wearing a dress and long dangling earrings, to cover a story. When newsworthy individuals did not wish their pictures taken, she was known to steal their photographs to accompany the story.

On June 7, 1928, she married fellow reporter Robert Lamont Chase, who later became associate editor of *The Rocky Mountain News*. Mary Chase left the newspaper in 1931 and subsequently had three sons: Michael Lamont, Colin Robert, and Barry Jerome. She became a free-lance correspondent between 1932 and 1936 for the International News Service and the United Press. She also founded a chapter of the American Newspaper Guild in Denver and became an advocate for the civil rights of Colorado's Spanish-Americans.

Before the great Broadway success of *Harvey* in 1944, Chase had written *Now You've Done It* (1936) for a New York production of the Federal Theatre Project and the script for a motion picture, *Sorority House* (1938). Three more of Chase's plays saw production on Broadway: *The Next Half Hour* in 1945, *Mrs. McThing* with **Helen Hayes** in 1952, and *Midgie Purvis* with **Tallulah Bankhead** in 1961. Plays produced elsewhere include *A Slip of a Girl* (Camp Hill, Colorado, 1941), *Mickey* (Denver, 1953), and *Lolita* (Abingdon, Virginia, 1954). She also wrote *Too Much Business* (1938), *The Prize Play* (1961), *The Dog Sitters* (1963), and *Cocktails With Mimi* (1974).

Chase's renown is largely based on two of her plays—*Harvey* (1944) and *Mrs. McThing* (1952). *Harvey* opened on November 1, 1944, and ran for 1,775 performances on Broadway starring Frank Fay. It was later performed in London and Europe. Universal-International Studios paid one million dollars (an unprecedented fee) for the rights to the script. The movie starred James Stewart as Elwood P. Dowd. The Broadway production of *Harvey* won the 1944–1945 Pulitzer Prize for drama and placed second in the New York Drama Critics Circle Award. "*Harvey* has been translated into every language and has been produced in all but the Iron Curtain countries," reported Frances Melrose of the *Rocky Mountain News* (October 23, 1981). Lewis Nichols of the *New York Times* wrote in November 1944, "Mrs. Chase's play is not composed of haphazard gags, but rather offers a warm and gentle humor." "*Harvey* will be another American winner, another in the long series of American successes in London," claimed Cecil Wilson of *The Daily Mail* (London, January 1949). Mary Chase also was a runner-up for the 1951–1952 New York Drama Critics Circle award for *Mrs. McThing*, which starred Helen Hayes. "It is delightful. Thank Ireland for Mrs. Chase's rich make-believe sense of humor and her compassion for the needs of adults and children," said reviewer Brooks Atkinson of the *New York Times* (February 21, 1952). Atkinson wrote of the play again, "Probably *Mrs. McThing* will not be so sensationally popular as *Harvey* was in every corner of America. But to at least one theatregoer it is a richer play with a broader point of view, a greater area of compassion, and a more innocent sense of comedy," (*New York Times*, March 2, 1952).

After the success of *Harvey*, Chase developed a "mental block," feeling that none of her work compared with that play. In spite of that idea, she continued to write daily, seldom taking as much as a week off. Another noteworthy achievement was the victory over her long-standing alcoholism. Chase led a productive life. She founded and operated the House of Hope, a home for alcoholic women. She was a member of the board of trustees of the Bonfils Theatre and the Denver Center for the Performing Arts. She also belonged to the Christian Science Church, the Honorary Committee of the American National Theatre and Academy, and the Dramatists Guild. She held an honorary life membership in the Women's Press Club of Denver. In 1944 she received the William MacLeod Rains Award from the Colorado Authors League. Among her friends and associates were such luminaries as Helen Hayes, Roger L. Stevens, Robert Whitehead, James Stewart, Tallulah Bankhead, Joe E. Brown, Brock Pemberton, **Dorothy Parker**, Frank Fay, Jules Munshin, Irwin Corey, Fred Gwynn, and Ernest Borgnine, to name a few. Donald R. Seawell, chairman of the board of the Denver Center for the Performing Arts, called her "Colorado's first lady of the theatre" (*Denver Post*, October 21, 1981).

In October 1981 Mary Coyle Chase died at the age of seventy-five following a heart attack. Her body was cremated. In a brief statement her husband said, "She had many wonderful qualities and she lived a very full life."

Acting editions of Mary Chase's plays *Harvey*, *Mrs. McThing*, *Bernardine*, *The Dog Sitters*, and *Cocktails With Mimi* are all available from Dramatists Play Service, New York. Chase's husband and Marge Barrett, theatre critic of the *Rocky Mountain News*, supplied information to the author concerning Chase's life and career. A biographical article on Chase appeared in the *Rocky Mountain News* on October 23, 1981, two days after her death. Chase is included in *American Women Writers* (1979) and *The Oxford Companion to American Theatre* (1984).

Elizabeth M. Hutton

CHILDRESS, Alice (October 12, 1920–): playwright, was born in Charleston, South Carolina, but grew up in New York City's Harlem under the care of her grandmother, the storyteller who first roused Alice's interest in writing and theatre. Basically self-educated, Childress completed two years of high school in Harlem (1934–1936); then in 1939 she helped to found the American Negro Theatre, in which she performed for eleven years. One of her first roles was Titania in *A Midsummer Night's Dream*. She also performed in Abram Hill's *On Striver's Row* in 1940, Theodore Browne's *Natural Man* in 1941, and Philip Yordan's *Anna Lucasta* in 1944.

Conscious of the shortage of good theatrical roles for black women, Childress wrote the one-act play *Florence* in 1949. First performed in a tiny Harlem loft, it excited such critical acclaim that Childress was launched as a playwright. Set in the Jim Crow segregated waiting room of a southern railroad station, the play portrays an encounter between a black woman, identified only as Mama, and a white woman, Mrs. Carter. Across the iron grille that separates the sections, Mama tells Mrs. Carter that she is on her way to New York to fetch her daughter, Florence, who has been finding it difficult to get professional acting roles. Mrs. Carter condescendingly offers to find work for Florence as a domestic. Furious about the white woman's insensitive attitude, Mama decides at the end not to go north but to send her daughter the travel money with the message "Keep trying."

The character of Mama in *Florence* is the first of Childress's many "genteel poor" stage *personae*. Instead of the falsely romantic characters in popular literature, Childress creates intelligent, sensitive, and complex characters who may be impoverished and lacking formal education but whose love of art and learning—along with a fierce personal pride and independence—make them admirable. Like the heroes of classic American literature, Childress's self-educated poor exhibit strength and self-assurance. Unlike most other American heroes, they are usually black, female, and aging.

In 1950 Childress adapted the novel *Simple Speaks His Mind* by Langston Hughes into the play *Just a Little Simple*, which was first performed at the Club Baron Theatre in Harlem. In 1952 Childress had the distinction of being the first black woman to have a play (*Gold Through the Trees*) professionally produced on the American stage at Club Baron. Shortly thereafter Childress negotiated what would prove to be the first all-union Off-Broadway contracts in Harlem with Actors' Equity Association and the Harlem Stagehands Local.

In 1955 Childress wrote *Trouble in Mind*, her first full-length play. On the basis of her own struggles against what she perceived as a racist and sexist theatre system, she created the character Wiletta Mayer, a talented middle-aged black actress cast as the mother of a civil rights activist son, Job, in a play titled "Chaos in Belleville." Wiletta and the white director, Al Manners, clash in their interpretation of the play within the play. A three-act version of *Trouble in Mind* was first produced at the Greenwich Mews Theatre in New York on November 3, 1955, and ran for ninety-one performances. It won the *Village Voice* Off-Broadway (Obie) Award for the best original play produced Off-Broadway during 1955–1956. A shorter two-act version of the play was published in Lindsay Patterson's collection titled *Black Theatre* in 1971.

In 1962–1963 Childress wrote *Wedding Band: A Love/Hate Story in Black and White*. It is a full-length tragedy set in Charleston, South Carolina, in 1918.

The play was given a rehearsed reading in 1963 and then produced professionally at the University of Michigan in 1966. Like *Trouble in Mind*, it was optioned for Broadway several times but never produced because it was considered too controversial. In 1972 Joseph Papp produced it at the Public Theatre in New York, and in 1973 ABC gave the New York Shakespeare Festival production prime-time airing, even though a few local stations refused to broadcast it.

Wedding Band dramatizes the love affair of black Julia and white Herman, barred from each other by South Carolina race laws and the racist fears of their neighbors and relatives. During the three successive days portrayed in the two-act play, Herman, who works as a baker, brings Julia a cake to celebrate the tenth anniversary of their love and a gold wedding band, which she can only wear on a chain around her neck. The crisis of the drama erupts at the end of the first act when Herman comes down with influenza. Lest she be prosecuted for harboring a woman who violates the law against miscegenation, Julia's landlady refuses to call a doctor. When Herman's mother arrives in the second act, the clash between her and Julia escalates to a shouting of racist insults. Herman dies in Julia's arms, imagining that they are sailing on a steamer to New York where they can get married and live openly as husband and wife.

In 1968, before *Wedding Band* had been produced in New York, Childress wrote a short play illustrating racial insensitivity and misunderstanding within the black community. Written for WGBH in Boston, *Wine in the Wilderness* was produced on March 4, 1969, as the first drama in the series *On Being Black* produced by Luther James under a grant from the Ford Foundation. In Bill Jameson's one-room Harlem apartment Bill and two middle-class, college-educated friends exhibit their collective snobbery toward ordinary black people like working-class Tommy, a girl Bill thinks he may use as a model for the third panel of the triptych he is painting. Bill's ideal African queen dominates the central panel, flanked on one side by a black girl in a Sunday dress and on the other by the empty panel on which he will paint Tommy as the lost woman. Tommy forces Bill to recognize that ordinary black women like her are more heroic than his romantic, idealized African queen.

Alice Childress has written several short plays, including a few for children. Two adult plays, *Mojo: A Black Love Story* and *String*, are available from Dramatists Play Service. *Mojo* was first performed in November 1970 at the New Heritage Theatre in Harlem; and *String*, a dramatic adaptation of the story "A Piece of String" by Guy de Maupassant, was presented by the Negro Ensemble Company in New York in 1969. In 1971 Childress published *Black Scenes*, a collection of fifteen scenes from contemporary black plays, including a scene from an unproduced and unpublished play by Childress herself titled *The African Garden*.

Two plays for children were published in 1975 and 1977. *When the Rattlesnake Sounds* dramatizes a scene from the life of Harriet Tubman shortly before the end of slavery. Tubman's strength and bravery renew the flagging spirits of two young women working in a laundry to raise money for the abolitionist cause.

Let's Hear It for the Queen dramatizes from a feminist perspective the nursery rhyme about the Queen of Hearts who made some tarts. The play happily explodes stereotyped sex roles when the Queen's serving maid steps in as defense attorney for the knave accused of tart thievery. In her children's plays as well as her adult plays, Childress shows girls and women to be brave and creative in solving problems.

In 1979 the South Carolina Arts Council commissioned the hour-long musical *Sea Island Song* about the Gullah people living on Johns Island off the coast of South Carolina, where African customs and language are still preserved. "Alice Childress Week" was observed in both Columbia and Charleston for the opening of the musical, which was performed all over the state.

Alice Childress's more recent play, *Moms*, opened in New York at the Hudson Guild Theatre in February 1987. *Moms* tells the story of Jackie (Moms) Mabley, a comedienne who was for fifty years a headliner on the black vaudeville circuit. The play contains many excerpts from "Moms" Mabley's routines and was given a good review by Mel Gussow of the *New York Times* (February 10, 1987).

Despite her lack of formal education, Alice Childress has been the recipient of academic honors. In 1966–1968 she enjoyed an appointment as playwright-scholar to the Radcliffe Institute for Independent Study. In 1984 she received the Radcliffe Alumnae Association graduate award for distinguished achievement. In the same year she served as Artist-in-Residence at the University of Massachusetts, Amherst. There she directed a full-length production of *Gullah!*, an expanded version of *Sea Island Song* for which Childress's husband, Nathan Woodard, wrote the music.

In addition to her plays, Childress has published other works. *Like One of the Family*, a prose study based on conversations with black domestic workers, was published in 1956 and reissued by Beacon Press in 1986. Her juvenile novel, *A Hero Ain't Nothing But a Sandwich* (1973), won the Jane Addams Honor Award for a young adult novel in 1974 and the Lewis Carroll Shelf Award from the University of Wisconsin in 1975. In 1977 her film adaptation of this novel won the Virgin Islands Film Festival Award for best screenplay. The adult novel *A Short Walk* (1979) portrays the ordinary heroism of a black woman born at the beginning of the century and surviving through all sorts of oppression until her death in the 1960s. Her novel *Rainbow Jordan* (1981) narrates the struggle of one teen-age girl to grow into her best self. In 1986 she produced the screenplay, *Portrait of Fannie Lou Hamer*.

Alice Childress currently lives on Roosevelt Island in New York with her husband, Nathan Woodard. She has one daughter, Jean, who is married to Richard Lee.

Most of Childress's dramatic works have been published in periodicals and collections. *Florence* appears in *Masses and Midstream* (October 1950). *Trouble in Mind* appears in *Black Theatre*, edited by Lindsay Patterson (1971). *Wedding Band* appears in *The New Women's Theatre* edited by Honor Moore (1977) and in *9 Plays by Black Women* (1986). *Wine in the Wilderness* appears in *Plays By and About Women*, edited by Victoria Sullivan and James V. Hatch (1973). *Mojo* and *String* are published by Dramatists Play Service, and the two juvenile plays, *When The Rattlesnake Sounds* and *Let's Hear It for the Queen*, are published by Coward-McCann. Interviews with Childress have appeared in *Black World* (April 1967) and in *Freedom Ways* (1966). For a review of *Moms* see the *New York Times* (February 10, 1987). Loften Mitchell mentions Childress several times in his landmark book *Black Drama: The Story of the American Negro in the Theatre* (1966), and Doris E. Abramson devotes a whole section to her plays in *The Negro Playwrights in the American Theatre 1925–1959* (1967). In a chapter of her published doctoral thesis *Feminist Drama* (1979), Janet Brown analyzes *Wine in the Wilderness*. Jeanne-Marie A. Miller discusses several characters of Childress in "Images of Black Women in Plays by Black Playwrights," *College Language Association Journal* (June 1977). In the only full-length article devoted exclusively to Childress, "Unfashionable Realistic Tragedy of American Racism: Alice Childress's *Wedding Band*," *MELUS Journal* (Spring 1981), Rosemary Curb analyzes why the play was not popular when it first appeared and why the characterizations make most American audiences uncomfortable. For a bibliography of Alice Childress's works and works about her, see *More Black American Playwrights—A Bibliography*, compiled by Esther Spring Arata (1978). Childress is included in *Living Black American Authors*, eds. Ann Allen Shockley and Sue P. Chandler (1973); *Notable Names in the American Theatre* (1976); *Selected Black American Authors*, compiled by James A. Page (1977); *Contemporary Literary Criticism*, Vols. XII and XV (1980); *Contemporary Dramatists* (1982); *Who's Who in America, 1984–1985*, Vol. I (1984); *Dictionary of Literary Biography*, Vol. 7: *Twentieth-Century American Dramatists*, Part I (1980); and Vol. 38: *Afro-American Writers After 1955: Dramatists and Prose Writers* (1985).

Rosemary Curb

CHINOY, Helen Krich (September 25, 1922–): theatre historian, actress, and scholar, was born in Newark, New Jersey, the only daughter of Benjamin and Anne (Kalen) Krich, who had separately immigrated to the United States from Russia in their late teens. After their marriage, the couple settled in Newark, where Ben Krich was an automobile dealer and Anne Kalen Krich an activist in community affairs. Here they reared their two children, Aron and Helen, the first of whom later became a therapist and writer. Helen Krich made her stage debut as one of several five-year-olds at Elving's Jewish Theatre under the auspices of the Workingmen's Circle, a Jewish fraternal organization. Fatally "stage-struck" from the day of her debut, she has continued her association with the theatre, in one way or another, throughout her life.

As a child and teen-ager of the Great Depression, she performed with other youngsters for the International Workers Order, where she learned puppetry and basic acting skills: voice, movement, and sense memory. During her high school years she gained performance experience touring locally in political plays, performing on picket lines and in union halls. On visits to Broadway she eschewed popular theatre fare and sought instead plays like *Tobacco Road*, *Of Mice and Men*, and especially *Awake and Sing* by Clifford Odets, which reinforced her preference for social theatre. In addition, as a "child of the thirties" she was fascinated by the work of actors, whose methods were being explored in the

Stanislavsky system, widely taught at that time. Also, her fascination with the director's art grew in part from that decade's concern with making performance unified and meaningful.

Though she contemplated attending the American Academy of Dramatic Arts after graduating from the public schools in Newark, Helen Krich enrolled in New York University, where she graduated with Honors in English in 1943. However alluring summer stock in Maine and professional performance may have been, academic pursuits proved a more powerful attraction. She continued her education at New York University, earning a master's degree as a University Fellow in 1945. Immediately afterwards, she launched a career in college teaching (Queens College, 1945, and Newark Colleges of Rutgers University, 1946–1948). She continued her studies at the Shakespeare Institute in England in the summer of 1947.

She initiated a new career with marriage in 1948 to Ely Chinoy, who became the Mary Huggins Gamble Professor of Sociology at Smith College, until his untimely death in an automobile accident in 1975.

As Helen Krich Chinoy she published *Actors on Acting*, her landmark reference work on acting, which she edited with her sister-in-law, **Toby Cole**, in 1949. In 1953, after the birth of her first child, Michael (who is a television foreign correspondent), Chinoy became a part-time member of the Department of English at Smith College. In the following year she and Toby Cole collaborated again to edit *Directors on Directing*. The same year she gave birth to her daughter Claire Nicole (who is an ethnic dancer). Also in 1956 she joined the faculty of the Department of Theatre at Smith College. She taught there from 1956 to 1960, and again from 1965 to her retirement in 1986. After acquiring her Ph.D. degree from Columbia University in 1963, she taught for a year at the University of Leicester, England. Between 1968 and 1971, she served as chair of the Department of Theatre at Smith, where she was named professor in 1975.

In 1981 Chinoy edited, with Linda Walsh Jenkins, *Women in American Theatre*, which was expanded for republication in 1987. She is currently at work on a comprehensive study of the Greek theatre.

Decades ahead of the women's movement, Chinoy exercised the freedom to choose a double career: wife/mother and professor/scholar. Her honors include a University Fellowship, New York University, 1945; Fellowship, American Association of University Women, 1962–1963; Fellowship, National Endowment for the Humanities, 1979–1980. As a "scholar-humanist" she has directed much of her attention to theatre groups whose contributions to culture have been ignored, and her basic reference works have helped lay the foundation of what we now describe as "performance studies."

Chinoy's publications on performance include *Actors on Acting* (edited with Toby Cole, 1949, 1970, paperback edition, 1980); *Directors on Directing* (edited with Toby Cole, 1953, 1963); and "The Director as Mythagog: Jonathan Miller Talks about Directing Shakespeare," *Shakespeare Quarterly* (Winter 1949). Her publications on the theatre of the thirties include "Reunion: A Self-Portrait of the Group Theatre," *Educational Theatre*

Journal (December 1976); the "Hallie Flanagan Davis" entry in *Notable American Women*, Vol. IV: *The Modern Period* (1980); "The Founding of the Group Theatre" in *Theatre Touring and Founding* (1981); "The Chosen Ones: Passion and Politics in the Group Theatre," Engel Lecture Series Publication, Smith College (1985); and "The Poetics of Politics: Some Notes on Style and Craft in the Theatre of the Thirties," *Theatre Journal* (December 1983). Chinoy's publications on women in American theatre include "Art Versus Business: The Role of Women in the American Theatre," *The Drama Review* (June 1980); "Women in the 1920's" in *Women, the Arts, and the 1920's in Paris and New York*, edited by Kenneth W. Wheeler and Virginia Lee Lussier (1982); and *Women in American Theatre*, edited with Linda Walsh Jenkins (1981, revised edition 1986). For *American Dramatic Companies, A Historical Encyclopedia*, edited by Weldon B. Durham, Chinoy contributed an entry on "The Northampton Players, 1919–1923." In addition Chinoy has written articles and reviews for *Encyclopedia Britannica*, *Enciclopedia dello spettacolo*, *Dictionary of American Biography*, *Theatre Arts Magazine*, *Players Magazine*, and *Modern Drama*. She is listed in *The Biographical Encyclopaedia and Who's Who of American Theatre* (1966); *Notable Names in the American Theatre* (1976); and *Who's Who of American Women, 1983–1984* (1983).

Gresdna A. Doty

CHORPENNING, Charlotte Barrows (January 5, 1873–January 7, 1955): playwright, director, author, teacher, and pioneer in children's theatre, was one of nine children. Her mother, Laura Barrows, was an accomplished pianist. Her father, Allan Campbell Barrows, began his career as a clergyman in Kent and Cleveland, Ohio. He left this career to become a professor of English literature, teaching at Iowa State Agricultural College in Ames and at Ohio State University in Columbus. In 1897 he became dean of Ohio State University's College of Arts, Philosophy, and Science, a post he held until 1901.

As a student at Iowa State Agricultural College, Charlotte Barrows was intrigued by chemistry and physics, but her passion for the sciences was overruled by her interest in history, which she studied during her advanced work at Cornell University. Upon graduating from Cornell in 1894 with a Bachelor of Letters degree, she taught literature at a high school in Springfield, Ohio. Shortly after her move to Springfield she met and married John Charles Chorpenning. This union produced one child, Ruth, born in Springfield on February 11, 1898. John Chorpenning, stricken with tuberculosis, first moved with his family to Denver, Colorado; then moved alone to Mexico. Rather than take her young daughter to Mexico, Charlotte Chorpenning accepted a position as a teacher of literature in 1904 at the State Normal School in Winona, Minnesota.

Encouraged by her husband and the publication of a few short stories, Charlotte Chorpenning submitted a play in 1913 to George Pierce Baker of Harvard University's famed 47 Workshop. She was one of twelve people accepted by Baker that year to study playwriting with him. The course provided her with her first professional experiences in playwriting and directing. *Between the Lines*, which she wrote during her second year at the 47 Workshop, was later produced at the Castle Square Theatre in Boston.

Chorpenning was widowed at the age of 43 and returned from Boston to Winona, where, in her spare time, she wrote and produced plays for community groups. She also worked with community players in Minneapolis and Cleveland. Neva L. Boyd of the Recreation Training School, having heard of Chorpenning's work, asked to meet her. Their meeting resulted in Chorpenning's taking the position of drama director of the Hull House School in Chicago. There she expanded her work with adults to include dramatics with children.

Northwestern University in Evanston eventually absorbed the classes Boyd and her colleagues were conducting. Chorpenning became a member of the School of Speech and was involved in two projects that had determining influences throughout her life. She was asked to direct new scripts written in Theodore Hinckley's playwriting course, a task that gave her experience in adjusting scripts for performances. During this time **Winifred Ward** was organizing the resources of the university, the Evanston Parents-Teachers Association, and the public schools to establish a theatre for children. Because of Chorpenning's background in community dramatics, she was invited to attend these organizational meetings. In 1928 Ward asked Chorpenning to rewrite a *Wizard of Oz* script that the former had found difficult to adapt for children. Shortly afterward, Chorpenning, at Ward's request, wrote her first script for children's theatre, *The Emperor's New Clothes*. Maurice Gnesin of the Goodman Theatre in Chicago saw this play and offered Chorpenning the position of director of plays for children at the Goodman Theatre. She held this position from 1931 until 1952 and for several years conducted classes at Northwestern as well.

Chorpenning's health failed in the summer of 1949. After suffering a nervous breakdown, she was taken east to recuperate at a health camp. Although she never fully recovered, she returned to Chicago and lived for three years with Mary Dodge, a former student. She spent the last years of her life with her daughter and son-in-law, Ruth and James Norris, in the Warwick Valley, New York. Here Chorpenning wrote her famous book, *Twenty-One Years With Children's Theatre* (1954). On January 7, 1955, she died in her home in Warwick at the age of eighty-three.

Chorpenning was one of the first artist/teachers to apply professional standards to children's theatre. Her plays were proved very popular in many children's theatres in the 1930s. Twenty-five plays were eventually published and, even today, are performed by both professional and amateur children's theatre companies. Her *Cinderella*, *The Sleeping Beauty*, *Rumpelstiltskin*, and *Jack and the Beanstalk* are consistently produced for children. During her long career at the Goodman Theatre, Chorpenning staged some eighty productions, taught courses in playwriting, and continued to expand the repertoire of plays for children through her dramatizations. Throughout her tenure as director of children's theatre, she observed young audiences, spoke with parents, exchanged ideas with students, colleagues, and technical staff, and experimented with methods for writing and directing plays for children. She is credited with drawing national attention to the Goodman's children's theatre program.

Chorpenning's book *Twenty-One Years With Children's Theatre* describes her career, her philosophy of writing for young audiences, and such additional topics as acting, directing, and staging for the child viewer. Chorpenning believed that the child's theatre experience should incorporate novelty, beauty, social values, and emotional experiences. Her purpose was to present useful life experiences to children in an entertaining manner. Chorpenning was concerned with the type of story to be used, the attention span of the viewers, and their levels of interest and comprehension. She believed that the best sources for dramatization were fairy, folk, and historical tales. In her plays she included "exercise spots," where children could respond physically to the events of the story. To involve older viewers, she included ideas expressed through dialogue.

Among the honors accorded Chorpenning, two are particularly significant. On June 13, 1952, she was awarded an honorary doctorate in fine arts from the Art Institute of Chicago for her achievements at the Goodman Theatre and elsewhere. In 1956 the Charlotte B. Chorpenning Cup was created to honor outstanding playwriting achievement in children's drama and is presented annually by the Children's Theatre Association of America.

Although busy with her duties at the Goodman Theatre, Chorpenning was generous with her aid to various organizations. For example, she helped the Ohio Farm Bureau to establish its National Cooperative Recreational School. In the summer of 1935 she visited Noble County, Indiana, and worked with rural youth in dramatic experiences. She also helped **Sara Spencer** to establish the Children's Theatre Press (now the Anchorage Press) and served on its advisory board. In 1944 she worked with Ward, Spencer, and **Isabel Burger** in creating the Children's Theatre Conference, now known as the Children's Theatre Association of America. After the Second World War, in the interest of re-educating German youth, she prepared a special report (with Burdette Fitzgerald and Sara Spencer) on "The Value of the Theatre in the Emotional Development of Children" for the Mid-Century White House Conference on Children and Youth held in Washington, D.C., in 1950. Chorpenning contributed to such publications as *Educational Theatre Journal*, *Quarterly Journal of Speech*, *Journal of the American Association of University Women*, and *Journal of Religious Education*. She also assisted the National Progressive Educational Conference, the National Conference of Social Work, and the Association of the Junior League of America, Inc.

It is worth noting that one play written by Chorpenning for adults was professionally produced by the firm of Boothe, Gleason, and Truex. Written in 1926 and based on the cattle wars of her Denver period, *The Sheepman* gave aspiring actor Spencer Tracy his first leading role. The show closed before it reached Broadway.

Chorpenning also gained national attention in 1947 for her playwriting and directing skills during the première season of the Children's World Theatre, a New York-based company. Chorpenning's *Jack and the Beanstalk*, *Many Moons*, *King Midas and the Golden Touch*, *The Indian Captive*, and *Rumpelstiltskin* were consistently produced by this company.

For the television series "The Magic Slate," Chorpenning adapted seven of her plays, including *Tom Sawyer*, *King Midas and the Golden Touch*, and *Jack and the Beanstalk*. Aired in 1950 and 1951 by NBC as a summer replacement, the series earned higher ratings than the shows it replaced.

As a playwright, Charlotte Chorpenning significantly increased the number of plays available for children. Her plays, along with those written by her students, remain in the forefront of dramatic material now being produced for children. As a director, she gave stature to the children's wing of the Goodman Theatre and to the Children's World Theatre. Her guidance through her publications and teaching has aided countless professionals in children's theatre.

An analysis of Chorpenning's life, work, and plays can be found in Janet Rubin's "The Literary and Theatrical Contributions of Charlotte B. Chorpenning to Children's Theatre" (Unpublished Ph. D. dissertation, The Ohio State University, 1978). Relevant texts include Chorpenning's *Twenty-One Years With Children's Theatre* (1954); Maurice Forkert's *Children's Theatre That Captures Its Audience* (1962); and Nellie McCaslin's *Theatre For Children in the United States, A History* (1971). Chorpenning's plays are available from the Anchorage Press, the Coach House Press, Samuel French, and the Dramatic Publishing Company.

Janet E. Rubin

CLAIRE, Ina (October 15, 1892?–February 21, 1985): actress most noted for sophisticated high-comedy roles, was born in Washington, D.C., as Inez Fagan, the younger of the two children of Joseph Fagan Claire of Topeka, Kansas, and Cora B. (Leiurance) Claire.

Claire's father was among the twenty-two government clerks who were killed in the collapse of Ford's Theatre in Washington, D.C., in 1893. Thereafter her mother supported the family by running a boardinghouse. Claire attended public schools and the Holy Cross Academy in Washington, D.C. Her brother, Allen H. Fagan, five years her senior, became an actor and dancer, but served most significantly as stage manager with Broadway producer Charles B. Dillingham.

Ina Claire's first marriage, on July 9, 1919, was to Chicago reporter and music critic James Whittaker; it ended in divorce in 1925. Her second marriage, May 9, 1929, was to silent screen star John Gilbert, and it also finished in divorce two years later. Her third marriage, March 16, 1939, to William Ross Wallace, Jr., a lawyer and financier, lasted until his death in 1975. Claire died in 1985. She had no children.

Ina Claire's career spanned almost fifty years of the American theatre. From 1907 to her retirement in 1954, she achieved preeminence as a performer of sophisticated high comedy. Consistently listed as one of the best-dressed women in the world, Claire enhanced her comic brilliance with an elegant personal style, which established her as a charismatic model for succeeding comediennes. Although her career was divided between Broadway and Hollywood, she made only nine films and always considered herself primarily a stage performer.

Her career began in 1907 when her mother took her out of school and put her into vaudeville as a singing mimic. She made her New York debut on March 13,

1909, at the American Music Hall, where her impersonation of Sir Harry Lauder brought her immediate acclaim. For the next two years Claire continued her popular imitations of celebrities on the Orpheum Circuit and in Keith and Proctor Halls.

In 1911 she advanced to musical comedies, premièring March 6 of that year as Molly Pebbleford in *Jumping Jupiter* at the New York Theatre. Claire was a big success as Prudence in *The Quaker Girl*, which opened October 23, 1911, at the Park Theatre, New York, and ran for 240 performances. This was followed by other light musical fare in 1913 and 1914: *The Honeymoon Express*, *Lady Luxury*, *The Belle of Bond Street*, and *The Girl from Utah*. In the last named play, she made her London debut in the role of Una Trance at the Adelphi on October 18, 1913. Claire returned to the variety stage in *The Ziegfeld Follies* of 1915 and 1916. Here again she showed her imitative skills. Appearing on the bill with such performers as Ed Wynn and W.C. Fields, she mimicked the emotional acting of Jane Cowl and portrayed Juliet in a travesty titled "In the Backyard of the Capulets."

In September 1917 Ina Claire made her straight-comedy debut in the title role of George Middleton and Guy Bolton's *Polly with a Past*, produced and directed by David Belasco at his theatre in New York. This role of French-maid-turned-adventuress established Claire as a fine comedienne and gifted legitimate actress. After 1917 virtually every Broadway comedy Claire appeared in was assured a long run of one to two years. Her success at the Belasco Theatre was followed by 315 continuous performances of *The Gold Diggers*. This popular comedy, about the lovelife of Jerry Lamar, the money-chasing chorus girl, opened at the Lyceum Theatre on September 30, 1919, with Claire in the leading role.

Ina Claire showed her true forte, however, in the drawing room comedies of the 1920s and 1930s. She premièred on September 19, 1921, at the Ritz Theatre, New York, as Monna in the drawing-room comedy *Bluebeard's Eighth Wife*. She reached stardom the following year as Lucy Warriner in *The Awful Truth* at the Henry Miller Theatre. Success followed success with long runs as Denise Sorbier in *Grounds for Divorce* (September 23, 1924), the title role in *The Last of Mrs. Cheyney* (November 9, 1925), and as Lady Grayston in a revival of Somerset Maugham's *Our Betters* (February 20, 1928). Whether portraying a woman scheming to win back her ex-husband, an adorable young jewel thief, or a title-hunting American, Claire illuminated drawing-room comedy with her cosmopolitan style, intelligence, and wit.

Alexander Woollcott, in his review of *Grounds for Divorce* (*New York Sun*, September 24, 1924), acknowledged Claire's development: "From the days when she was a song and dance girl until now when she is one of the most competent and delicately adroit comediennes we have met, her ascent has been interesting and eventful. Oddly enough, it was not until she shook the dust of Mr. Belasco's 'Gold Diggers' from her feet that she suddenly turned into an actress. It was in 'The Awful Truth' that one noted for the first time the growing expertness, the fine coquetry and the tonic sparkle of her playing. And now . . . she gives the kind of perfected and beguiling performance that playwrights pray for and almost never get.''

The actress first left Broadway in 1928 when she followed many other stage performers to Hollywood. Her excellent voice and diction (for which she received a gold medal from the American Academy of Arts and Letters in 1936) were valuable commodities in the new world of talkies. Between 1928 and 1932 Claire made several films, beginning with a film version of *The Awful Truth*. She also appeared in *Rebound*, *The Greeks Had a Name for Them*, and *The Royal Family of Broadway*. The last film, in which she portrayed **Ethel Barrymore**, is considered to be her best.

By 1932 Claire had severed her film contract with Samuel Goldwyn and had ended her second, highly publicized marriage to silent screen idol, John Gilbert. On December 12 she returned to Broadway, opening at the Guild Theatre in S.N. Behrman's comedy *Biography*. Portraying Marion Froude, the portrait artist who creates havoc when she writes an intimate biography of her subjects, Claire returned to her best milieu. In the *New York Post* of December 13, 1932, John Mason Brown said, ''Miss Claire is the ablest comedienne our theatre knows. To watch her, even in such a faltering script, is a joy in itself. Her playing has about it the brilliance of a diamond. It is all sparkle and light. . . . By means of her technical excellence, her intelligence, her dazzling beauty and charm, she adds much, as needs no saying, to Mr. Behrman's script.''

Biography's long run and tour were followed by a London production in which Claire co-starred with Laurence Olivier. Other successes followed these. She appeared again at the Guild Theatre (in 1934), as Madeleine in *Ode to Liberty*, her brother, Allen H. Fagan, also being in the cast. Claire created two other S.N. Behrman sophisticates, Leonie Frothingham in the 1936 production of *End of Summer* and Enid Fuller in *The Talley Method*, 1941. In the intervening years she portrayed Madeline Neroni in *Barchester Towers*, an adaptation of the story by English novelist Anthony Trollope; played the Duchess of Hampshire in *Once Is Enough*; and filmed *Ninotchka* with Greta Garbo.

By the 1940s the kind of roles in which Ina Claire excelled were seldom written. She returned to California, where she lived on Nob Hill in San Francisco with her third husband, William R. Wallace, in a style suitable to the cosmopolitan personality she had so often played. Thereafter she returned to Broadway only twice, finding tremendous success each time. On November 19, 1946, she opened at the Royale Theatre, New York, as Mrs. Paul Espenshade in *The Fatal Weakness*, playing a woman so compliant that she stands by as a rival steals her husband away and then dresses herself up to attend their wedding.

Claire's final Broadway appearance was at the Morosco Theatre as Lady Elizabeth Mulhammer in T.S. Eliot's *The Confidential Clerk*, which opened February 11, 1954. Eric Bentley, in the *New Republic* (February 22, 1954), wrote: ''The theatre is a place where it may be the supreme achievement of a T.S. Eliot to provide a good part for an Ina Claire. In *The Confidential Clerk*, Mr. Eliot has not given Miss Claire the funniest lines she ever spoke, or the most shrewdly characterized, but he has caught the speech rhythms of a rich lady with religious longings, and from these Miss Claire can make the highest of high comedy. Such precise timing, such delicate underlining, such subtle modulation from phrase to phrase and word to word are almost unknown to our stage today.''

In later years Claire expressed regret that she had not been offered a wider range of stage roles. Within her repertoire, however, she was without comparison. Perhaps the best summation of her contribution to the American theatre was expressed in the career retrospective that appeared in *Life* magazine (February 10, 1947): ''More than any other actress, Ina Claire has brought civilized laughter to the United States stage.''

The New York Public Library Performing Arts Research Center at Lincoln Center contains clippings, reviews, programs, and photos of Claire. Other sources include *Life* (February 10, 1947), *New Republic* (February 22, 1954), *Post* (December 13, 1932), *Sun* (September 24, 1924), and *Theatre Arts* (December 1933, February 1937, August 1951, May 1954, and September 1958). Her obituary appeared in the *New York Times* (February 23, 1985). General biographical information appears in *Current Biography, 1954* (1954); *The Biographical Encyclopaedia and Who's Who of the American Theatre* (1966); William C. Young, *Famous Actors and Actresses on the American Stage* (1975); *Notable Names in American Theatre* (1976); and *The Oxford Companion to American Theatre* (1984). Ina Claire maintained that she was born in 1895; however, her obituary and early biographical material give her birth date as 1892.

Jeannie M. Woods

CLARK, Peggy (September 30, 1915–): outstanding Broadway lighting designer, was born Margaret Brownson Clark in Baltimore, Maryland, to Dr. Eliot R. and Eleanor (Linton) Clark. Her father was a professor of anatomy at the University of Pennsylvania, and he and her mother published more than six hundred papers on the circulation of the blood. Peggy Clark graduated from Smith College (cum laude) in 1935 and received the Master of Fine Arts degree in design from Yale University in 1938.

Peggy Clark began her professional career in 1938 as scenic designer for the Green Mansions Summer Theatre in Warrentown, New York. She first worked on Broadway as costume designer for *The Girl from Wyoming* later that same year. During the war years she was co-designer and supervisor for *Stage Door Canteen*, produced by the American Theatre Wing. She became technical director for the Theatre Wing's *Lunchtime Follies* in 1942–1943 and used her sketching talents to draw portraits of wounded soldiers in local hospitals. In another wartime assignment she created sets and lights for the Department of Agriculture's touring production *It's Up to You.*

In 1944 Clark became technical supervisor for designer Oliver Smith and worked on forty-three shows for him over the next twenty-one years. Not only did Clark supervise *On the Town* (1944) for Smith, but she also completed her one Broadway stage management assignment with this show. In 1946 Clark did the complete lighting design for *Beggar's Holiday* on Broadway. Thereafter she won major recognition in her imaginative lighting designs in *Brigadoon* (1947), *High*

Button Shoes (1947), *Gentlemen Prefer Blondes* (1949), *Miss Liberty* (1949), *Paint Your Wagon* (1951), *Pal Joey* (1952), *Peter Pan* (1954), *The Three Penny Opera* (1954), *Plain and Fancy* (1955), *Bye Bye Birdie* (1960), and *Mary Mary* (1961).

After 1950 Peggy Clark added dance lighting design to her many credits; productions included the revolutionary *Fall River Legend*, choreographed by **Agnes de Mille**, and other dances for the American Ballet Theatre. In the summer of 1952 Clark began a nineteen-year association with the Los Angeles Civic Light Opera Association by lighting revivals of *Song of Norway* and *Jollyanna*.

Clark became heavily involved with the New York City Center in 1957, lighting five musical revivals and a new production of *The Glass Menagerie* there. The following year she was chosen to design the lighting for three musicals and a ballet for the Brussels International Exposition.

In 1960 Clark prepared lighting for *The Unsinkable Molly Brown* and *Bye Bye Birdie* on Broadway and became the technical supervisor for *Martha* at the Metropolitan Opera. The next year Jones Beach began producing musicals, and it was Peggy Clark who designed the lights for them, beginning with *Paradise Island*. Most of Clark's work during the 1960s was for the New York City Center, the Los Angeles Civic Light Opera, and Jones Beach.

On January 28, 1960, she married Lloyd R. Kelley, who had been the chief electrician for *Beggar's Holiday* in 1946. Until Kelley's death in 1972, the two worked closely together. After her husband's death, Peggy Clark cut back on most of her professional activities, but she did assume two new lighting projects: one for the Bill Baird Marionette Theatre and another for the Light Opera of Manhattan, most recently *A Night in Venice* (1982) for the latter.

She has taught lighting design at the Polakov Studio and Forum of Stage Design, and on several occasions she has been visiting lecturer and critic at Smith College and the Yale University School of Drama. She has been a member of the United Scenic Artists, Local 829, since 1938 and was its president in 1968–1969. She is a member of the United States Institute for Theatre Technology and was named a fellow in 1978.

Peggy Clark's published works appear in *Theatre Design and Technology*, *Theatre Crafts*, and *Theatre 2*. Her most notable article is "Training the Lighting Designer," *Theatre Crafts* (November/December 1976). For information about Clark, see Jane Ann Crum, "Three Generations of Lighting Designers: An Interview with Peggy Clark Kelley, **Jennifer Tipton**, and Danianne Mizzy," *Theater* (Winter 1985). She is listed in *The New York Times Dictionary of Theatre* (1973); *Notable Names in the American Theatre* (1976); *Who's Who in America, 1982–1983*, Vol. I (1982); *World's Who's Who of Women, 1982* (1982); and *The Oxford Companion to American Theatre* (1984).

Richard K. Knaub

CLIFTON, Josephine (1813?–November 21, 1847): popularly styled "The Magnificent Josephine," was the first American actress to play major roles on the English stage. Some controversy surrounds the date of her birth and her birthplace as well. Various sources give her birth date as either 1813 or 1814. While most reports agree that she was born in New York City, both Charles Durang (*The Philadelphia Stage, From the Year 1749 to the Year 1856*) and the *Enciclopedia dello spettacolo* give Philadelphia as her birthplace. Her father is unknown, and contemporary sources suggest that her mother was a successful brothel keeper. Her real surname may have been Miller. It is known that she had a younger half sister, Louisa Missouri Miller, who also pursued an acting career.

Precise details on Clifton's education are likewise scant. Joseph Ireland (*Records of the New York Stage from 1750 to 1860*) says that she received "the best education that the ill-gotten wealth of an indulgent mother could procure" (Volume II, p. 17). There are also suggestions but no concrete records to prove that she attended St. Joseph Academy in Emmitsburg, Maryland.

Clifton became the protégée of Thomas Hamblin, manager of the Bowery Theatre, New York, who is said to have rescued her from the "Cyprean Sisterhood." Hamblin gave her intensive training for the stage; and as part of his efforts to promote native talent and attract audiences by offering novelty, he presented her as "a young lady of this city" (New York) in her debut as Belvidera in Thomas Otway's *Venice Preserved* on September 21, 1831, at the Bowery Theatre. Her striking physical appearance and considerable charm made her a popular favorite, and Hamblin's promotional ability soon elevated her to the ranks of stardom. By the time she was nineteen, she had built up a formidable repertoire of major roles, had supported the actor Junius Brutus Booth, and had been featured as an attraction against the famous English actors Charles and Fanny Kemble, who were making their first American appearance at the Park Theatre. She had begun at the top and was to remain there for most of her short but spectacular career.

In 1834 Josephine Clifton became the first American-born actress to appear in England, making her London debut in *Venice Preserved* on October 4, 1834, at the Covent Garden Theatre. After a brief engagement at both Covent Garden and Drury Lane, during which she appeared in major roles, she became a regular member of the companies at both theatres, sharing the ingénue roles with Ellen Tree. The London critics, polite but unenthusiastic, found a lack of depth in her characterizations and suggested that Clifton's ambitions exceeded her abilities. It was agreed, however, that she showed much promise and needed only perseverance and continual study to achieve success. She did, in any case, win popularly with audiences.

Clifton remained abroad until March 1836, touring provincial theatres throughout the British Isles. The highly favorable and probably exaggerated reports reaching the United States prepared the public to welcome home an American actress who had conquered England. Her return was a veritable triumph. The consensus was that her acting had indeed improved as a result of her work abroad, and undertaking the rigorous life of a touring star in the United States, she proved to be an immensely popular attraction in both tragedy and comedy.

On August 25, 1837, she appeared at the Park Theatre in the tragedy *Bianca Visconti* by Nathaniel Parker Willis, prize winner in the writing contest for a play in which the principal character was tailored to Clifton's particular abilities. Bianca Visconti became her most celebrated role. Critics praised her subtlety and skill. The *New York Mirror* remarked, "It was a performance full of mind" (August 26, 1837).

Clifton was at the height of her popularity between 1836 and 1843, during which time she travelled west, south, and north, visiting St. Louis and Vicksburg, and giving a command performance in Montreal. During the 1842–1843 season she conducted an extensive tour with Edwin Forrest, playing all the leading female roles in his repertoire. Years after Clifton's death, Forrest was accused in his divorce trial of having committed adultery with her during this tour, a charge never completely substantiated.

In 1838 Clifton's half sister, Louisa Missouri Miller, barely sixteen, was determined to go on the stage and, in spite of Clifton's objections, placed herself under Hamblin's management. A newspaper controversy resulted, in which Clifton was accused of trying to prevent her sister's debut out of jealousy. Clifton replied that she only desired that Louisa not associate with Hamblin. Finally, George Washington Dixon, editor of the scandal sheet *Polyanthis*, printed revelations concerning the earlier activities of the sisters' mother, namely that she had been a brothel keeper. The shock is said to have contributed to Louisa Miller's death shortly after she made her first appearances on the stage and seems to have defamed Clifton herself. The *Dictionary of American Biography* speculates that Clifton may have suffered some sort of nervous disorder as a result of the controversy and that this may have affected her already frail health.

After 1843 records of Clifton's performances become sketchy. It is known that she toured briefly in 1844 with James Anderson during his first American visit, but she seems to have acted very little after that time. In July 1846 she married Robert Place, manager of the American Theatre in New Orleans, and retired to private life. She died suddenly in New Orleans on November 21, 1847.

Much of Clifton's popular appeal appears to have come from her imposing physical stature and her outstanding beauty. She was nearly six feet tall with a figure variously described as majestic and magnificent. Throughout her career it was noted that her beauty alone was usually sufficient to attract an audience, and Clifton seems to have relied on her considerable physical attractions to guarantee her both engagements and attention. The most perceptive assessment of her strengths and shortcomings comes from Joseph Ireland, who noted that "at the time of her death, no other American actress, with the exception of Miss Cushman [**Charlotte Cushman**], had created so wide (we do not add, deep) a sensation" (Ireland, Volume II, p. 18) and contended that, had Clifton combined Cushman's intellect and dedication with her own outstanding physical requisites, she would have "reigned the legitimate empress of our national stage."

Clifton left no personal papers, and there is at present no biography of her. An account of her career must be pieced together from various sources. Among the most useful are

Joseph Ireland, *Records of the New York Stage from 1750 to 1860* (1866–1867, reprinted 1968), and Charles Durang, *The Philadelphia Stage, From the Year 1749 to the Year 1855*, published in the *Philadelphia Sunday Dispatch* (First Series, 1749–1821, beginning in the issue of May 7, 1854; Second Series, 1822–1830, beginning June 29, 1856; Third Series, 1831–1855, beginning July 8, 1860). Durang's *The Philadelphia Stage* may be found in the libraries of the Philadelphia Company, of the Historical Society of Pennsylvania, and of the University of Pennsylvania. Also useful are *Dictionary of American Biography*, Vol. II (1929); George C. D. Odell, *Annals of the New York Stage*, Vols. III and IV (1927–1949); H. P. Phelps, *Players of a Century* (1880); and F. C. Wemyss, *Chronology of the American Stage* (1852). See also Theodore Shank, "The Bowery Theatre, 1826–1836" (Unpublished Ph.D. dissertation, Stanford University, 1956), and Ernest Frederick Meinken, "American Actors in London, 1825–1861: Reception by London Professional Critics" (Unpublished Ph.D. dissertation, University of California, Los Angeles, 1972). Clifton's obituaries appeared in the New Orleans *Daily Picayune* (November 22, 1847) and *The Spirit of the Times*, New York City (December 11, 1847). Josephine Clifton is included in *The Oxford Companion to American Theatre* (1984).

Norman J. Myers

COGHLAN, Rosamond Marie (March 18, 1852?–April 2, 1932): actress and star of the famous Wallack company, was born in Peterborough, Lincolnshire, England, the daughter of Francis and Anna Marie (Kirby) Coghlan. Her father, author and publisher of *Coghlan's Continental Guides* and friend of Charles Dickens and other contemporary men of letters, spent little time with his family. Perhaps this in part accounted for the close relationship between the young Rosamond Marie and her older brother, Charles Francis. Charles Coghlan had been educated for the bar, but he married an actress and abandoned law for the stage. Rosamond Coghlan soon followed in her brother's steps, appearing first at the Theatre Royal, Greenock, Scotland, in 1865. On September 13, 1869, she made her London debut at the Old Gaiety Theatre as Pippo in *Linda of Chamouni*. For the next three years she played in London and in the provinces in featured roles in such plays as *Dotheboys Hall*, *Nicholas Nickleby*, and *Nell Gwynne*. Coghlan came to America in 1871. She appeared on September 2 at Wallack's Theatre in New York as a member of the Lydia Thompson English Burlesque Company, playing the roles of Ixion in *Jupiter* and Mrs. Honeyton in *A Happy Pair*. The youthful, handsome, golden-voiced Coghlan soon left Thompson to become a member of Lester Wallack's company. During the 1872–1873 season she appeared in supporting roles with E. A. Southern in *Our American Cousin*, *Brother Sam*, and *Dundreary Married and Settled*. In April 1873 she returned to England, where she remained for four years, acting in leading roles with Charles Mathews, Barry Sullivan, John Clayton, and the American actor Joseph Jefferson, who may have influenced her to return to America. She came back to America in 1877 to become the leading lady with Wallack's company, where she remained, except for occasional appearances with other companies, until 1885. At this time Wallack's was regarded as one of the leading companies in America. The repertoire included a variety of old and modern comedies and melodramas.

Coghlan, whom the critics considered one of the most elegant actresses on the stage, achieved numerous successes and became one of the most popular stars of New York. Some of her acclaimed roles were as Mrs. Tiffe in *Marriage*, Lady Teazle in *The School for Scandal*, Countess Zicka in *Diplomacy*, Lady Gay Spanker in *London Assurance*, Lydia Languish in *The Rivals*, Nellie Denver in *The Silver King*, and Stephanie in *Forget Me Not*.

In 1882 Wallack moved to a new theatre; however, despite the presence of such stars as Coghlan and her brother Charles, who was by then considered one of America's best comic actors, the stature of the Wallack company steadily declined. Coghlan left Wallack's in the spring of 1885 to launch her own company, but in 1888 she returned to star again as Lady Teazle in *The School for Scandal*, Wallack's final production before his retirement. She also appeared as the Player Queen in a benefit performance of *Hamlet*, which was given for Wallack at the Metropolitan Opera House on May 21, 1888.

On August 14, 1885, the Rose Coghlan Company had been formed and appeared at Niblo's Garden Theatre with *Our Joan*. For a few years Coghlan successfully produced and starred in such plays as *London Assurance*, *The School for Scandal*, *Masks and Faces*, *Diplomacy*, and *Peg Woffington*. In December 1893 she presented the first American production of Oscar Wilde's *A Woman of No Importance*. Her company also produced three plays by her brother: *Jocelyn*, *Lady Barter*, and *The Check Book*. Whether from poor management, poor direction, or other factors, the company failed after a few seasons.

Rose Coghlan turned to vaudeville in 1898 (with the Keith Circuit) to supplement her declining income. She was, however, still appearing in the legitimate theatre. In 1908 she starred with John Drew in *Jack Straw*. She was a member of Winthrop Ames's ill-fated New Theatre Company, an attempt by backers J.P. Morgan, J.J. Astor, the Vanderbilts, and others to found a permanent National Art Theatre. The New Theatre closed in 1911. She toured in such plays as George Bernard Shaw's *Mrs. Warren's Profession* and Somerset Maugham's *Our Betters* and appeared in silent films, including *As You Like It* (1912), *The Sporting Duchess* (1915), and *The Secrets of Paris* (1922). Her last regular New York engagement was as Madame Rabouin in David Belasco's *Deburau* with Lionel Atwill in 1920.

In April 1885 Coghlan married Clinton J. Edgerly, a Boston attorney. He divorced her in September 1890 on a charge of desertion; and on January 7, 1893, she married John Taylor Sullivan, a Boston actor who was for some years the leading actor in her company. They were divorced on June 11, 1904, after having been separated for some years. Coghlan's later years were plagued with domestic and financial troubles. Her brother died in 1899; she declared bankruptcy in 1899 and again in 1915. In April 1922 Rose Coghlan suffered a slight stroke and became critically ill. That same month Sam H. Harris, head of the Producing Manager's Association, arranged a benefit for her and raised ten thousand dollars. This sum was soon depleted, and during the last years of her life she was under the care of the Actors' Fund of America and the National

Vaudeville Artists' Association. She died of a cerebral hemorrhage on April 2, 1932, at St. Vincent's Retreat for Nervous and Mental Diseases at Harrison, New York, where she had been for over four years. She was survived by her adopted daughter, Rosalind Agnes, an actress and the wife of the theatrical producer Richard Pitman; a nephew, Charles Coghlan, Jr.; and a niece, Gertrude Evelyn, also an actress and the wife of Augustus Pitou, Jr.

Rose Coghlan did not become an American citizen until 1902, but her career in this country spanned half a century. "Her name was emblazoned in the lights of Broadway successes more frequently than that of any distinctively comedy actress of her time" (*New York Herald Tribune*, April 6, 1932); yet she died in poverty and obscurity. Various reasons for her decline in popularity have been proposed. Lewis Strang, in his *Famous Actresses of the Day in America*, suggested that she lacked the personal magnetism or charm that might have made an audience give her long-lasting, unquestioning love. Theatre historian George C. D. Odell in his famous *Annals* blamed her eventual failure on bad management. However, the most probable cause was simply the passage of time. Her declamatory style of acting became outmoded, and she was either unable or unwilling to adapt to a more "natural" style.

During her era, however, Rose Coghlan won high praise. Though critics were not always unanimous in their opinions of her, certain facts are irrefutable: she had a magnificient contralto voice; she was one of the great stars of Wallack's company; her interpretations of Rosalind in *As You Like It*, Countess Zicka in *Diplomacy*, Lady Gay Spanker in *London Assurance*, and Lady Teazle in *The School for Scandal* were considered among the best of her generation. An editorial published in the *New York Times* at her death best summed up her career. It stated that in the fields of comedy and melodrama the "wide-eyed, velvet-voiced, caressing, fascinating, divinely smiling Miss Coghlan was unsurpassed" (April 5, 1932).

For contemporary views of Rose Coghlan, see John B. Clapp and Edwin F. Edgett, *Players of the Present*, Part I (1899); Frederick E. McKay and Charles E. L. Wingate, *Famous American Actors of Today*, Vol. II (1896); Lewis C. Strang, *Famous Actresses of the Day in America* (1899); J. Ranken Towse, *Sixty Years of the Theatre* (1916); George C. D. Odell, *Annals of the New York Stage*, Vols. IX-XV (1937–1949); and *Who's Who in the Theatre* (1930). Rose Coghlan's obituary appeared in the *New York Herald Tribune* and the *New York Times* (both on April 5, 1932). Coghlan's death record gives 1852 as her birth date. Other published accounts give the date 1851 or 1853. Coghlan is included in *Notable American Women*, Vol. I (1971); William C. Young, *Famous Actors and Actresses on the American Stage*, Vol. I (1975); and *The Oxford Companion to American Theatre* (1984).

Faye E. Head

COHN, Ruby (August 13, 1922–): critic, scholar, educator, outstanding for her writings on Samuel Beckett and on American theatre, was born in Columbus, Ohio, where her father, Peter Burman, was a veterinary student. Her mother was May (Salesky) Burman. The family moved to New York City, where, she recalls, she "sneaked" into theatres free with the intermission crowd. While still in high school she was plunged into the WPA Federal Theatre. In the afterword to her book *Modern Shakespeare Offshoots* (1976), she describes her excited reaction to . Orson Welles's Federal Theatre production of *Voodoo Macbeth* and its relation to her writings: "I have tried to convey some sense—some small sense—of such excitement when I write about theatre, the most perishable of goods" (p. 393).

Cohn began her academic studies at Hunter College of the City of New York, receiving a Bachelor of Arts degree in 1942. During the Second World War she served in the WAVES. In 1946 she married Melvin Cohn. They were divorced in 1961.

After the war, Cohn lived in Paris and earned a doctorate from the University of Paris in 1952. In 1953 she attended the première of Samuel Beckett's *Waiting for Godot*, which was to affect her career as a scholar and critic. After her return to America, she enrolled at Washington University in St. Louis, where she earned a second doctorate in 1960. "I published my first Beckett article in 1959," she has written, "after it had been rejected by a discriminating editor: 'We like your criticism, but we don't feel your author merits publishing space' " (*Back to Beckett*, p. 3). It was Cohn's seminal study *The Comic Gamut* (1962) that helped to launch Beckett studies in America. Many readers have made their first foray into Beckett's oeuvre with Cohn's book as a guide. To familiarize American readers with Samuel Beckett, Cohn edited special issues of *Perspective* (1959) and *Modern Drama* (1966). She also compiled a *Casebook on Waiting for Godot* (1967) and an international collection of articles called *Samuel Beckett: A Collection of Criticism* (1975).

The best indication of the success of her pioneering studies is provided by the fact that when she wrote her second book on Beckett, a decade after her first, she could count thirty-seven books devoted to "her author." Although she does not say so, almost all cite Cohn's work in their discussions, as do the numerous publications on Beckett that have appeared yearly. In response to an unprecedented groundswell of critical attention, Cohn wrote *Back to Beckett* (1973) in order "to get back to Beckett, to the words of the works," and "to clarify my enthusiasm for Beckett" (pp. 3–4, 6).

The third of her Beckett books, *Just Play* (1980), is dedicated "To Beckett-lovers here and elsewhere/now and otherwise." It focuses on the two areas of dramatic criticism that have continually drawn her attention: the close reading of dramatic texts and the description of Beckett performances. One-third of its 279 pages are devoted to Beckett as director, a topic Cohn is eminently prepared to explore. Besides studying his plays as literature, she has consistently been concerned with their staging—hence she has attended rehearsals, read his director's notebooks, and seen as many productions as possible in England, France, and Germany. Her goal has been "to convey a sense of the live performance" (*Just Play*, p. 230), and her writing is sufficiently vivid to achieve this end.

This ability to bridge the gap in drama criticism between those who talk of text and those who talk of performance is perhaps the most important contribution

Cohn has made to theatre criticism. An example of this balance in her work is her book *Currents in Contemporary Drama* (1969); it discusses theme and language in the contemporary drama of England, France, and Germany, but it is dedicated to six directors "who played these plays." Her study *Dialogue in American Drama* (1971) makes an eloquent case for the power of the word in drama. In *New American Dramatists, 1960–1980* (1982), Cohn champions the written text in the works of twenty-six playwrights.

Cohn is also a highly respected teacher, as well as scholar and critic. Since 1972 she has been professor of comparative drama at the University of California at Davis. She was a fellow of the California Institute of the Arts from 1969–1971 and professor of English and comparative literature at San Francisco State University from 1961 to 1968. She has also taught courses at the University of California at Berkeley and at Santa Cruz, at City College of the City University of New York, at Stanford University, and at the University of Missouri.

Cohn has been the recipient of numerous awards: Fulbright Fellowship, 1949; Guggenheim Fellowship, 1965; National Endowment for the Humanities Summer Seminar Leader, 1978; and Faculty Research Lecturer, University of California at Davis, 1978. She has given lectures on modern drama at over twenty colleges and universities in America, England, and Scotland. Fittingly, she is an associate editor of *Modern Drama* and *Theatre Journal*.

In seven books, over sixty articles, and seven edited book and journal collections, Cohn has consistently reconstructed a personal enthusiasm for a text or a performance and transmitted it through the clarity of her prose. Of Beckett, the author with whom her name is most associated, she has said, "The significance of Beckett's play lies in the precision of its wide human embrace" (*Just Play*, p. 14). It is appropriate to describe the body of dramatic criticism written over the last twenty years by Ruby Cohn as "precise" and "human."

Ruby Cohn has written over sixty critical articles on the theatre. Her book-length studies include *Samuel Beckett: The Comic Gamut* (1962), *Currents in Contemporary Drama* (1967), *Dialogue in American Drama* (1971), *Back to Beckett* (1973), *Modern Shakespeare Offshoots* (1976), *Just Play* (1980), and *New American Dramatists, 1960–1980* (1982). In addition, she has edited the following collections: *Casebook on Waiting for Godot* (1968), *Samuel Beckett: A Collection of Criticism* (1975), and *Dejecta: A Collection of Critical Writings of Samuel Beckett* (1983). Cohn has also co-edited *Twentieth Century Drama* (1966) and *Classics for Contemporaries* (1969). Recently Cohn has written "Twentieth Century Drama" for the *Columbia Literary History of the United States* (1988), was a contributing editor for the Cambridge Guide to World Theatre (1989), and has written "Dramatic Poetry" for the *Princeton Encyclopedia of Poetry and Poetics* (in press). Cohn is listed in *Directory of American Scholars*, Vol. II (1974). Information for this entry was obtained through conversations with and letters from the subject.

Linda Ben-Zvi

COIGNEY, Martha Wadsworth (June 21, 1933–): administrator and director of the International Theatre Institute (ITI) of the United States, was born in New York City to Charles and Martha Clay (Hollister) Wadsworth. She was educated at Vassar College, from which she received the Bachelor of Arts degree in theatre in 1954. For a short time she was in the literary department of the Music Corporation of America. From 1956 through 1959 she was executive secretary of the Actors' Studio. She then became administrative and production assistant to Roger L. Stevens during the period when he was a highly active New York producer and also was starting work on the National Cultural Center in Washington, D.C. (later to be known as the John F. Kennedy Center for the Performing Arts). In 1966 Martha Wadsworth joined **Rosamund Gilder** at what was then the U.S. Center for the International Theatre Institute, where she participated in the process that changed its status to that of an independent organization in 1968. The next year she became its director when Rosamund Gilder retired. On December 27, 1969, she married Dr. Rodolphe Lucien Coigney, then director of the Liaison Office of the United Nations' World Health Organization, and became stepmother to three children.

The International Theatre Institute of the United States, Inc., is the American affiliate of the International Theatre Institute, a nongovernmental organization chartered in 1947 by UNESCO to "promote the exchange of knowledge and practice in the theatre arts." During Coigney's twenty years with the agency, hers has become one of the most visible and familiar American faces to theatre luminaries and groups throughout the world. The institute, under her direction, not only arranges individual learning experiences for foreign visitors and for Americans going abroad but also fosters a cross-fertilization of cultures and ideas by scheduling innumerable conferences and other events that join Americans with other nationalities, here and abroad. Participants share with each other the approaches, philosophies, work habits, and differing processes that grow out of a common theatre passion. This work has brought Coigney and her influence into the lives of many prominent theatre people on the world stage. Meetings of minds have been arranged in familiar settings, as well as less familiar sites like Rumania, Russia, and Poland. In 1984, in cooperation with the Eugene O'Neill Theatre Center in Waterford, Connecticut, she arranged symposia to accompany performances by actors from Denmark, Argentina, China, the USSR, Australia, and France. In 1985 she and the League of American Theatres and Producers aided the Nordic Theatre Council, 150 members strong, in setting up their fourth international conference in Washington, D.C., and New York to study the mixed private and public theatre economy of the United States, meet with American theatre leaders, ask questions, see plays and opera, study theatre training, and exchange views. This last conference typifies the work Coigney's institute arranges and complements. There is no other such advocate of theatre exchange in the world.

In addition to her work with ITI, Coigney has served as president of the National Theatre Conference (1983–1986), as chairperson for the Professional Theatre Panel of the New York State Council on the Arts (1978–1979), as a juror for the Commonwealth Awards since 1984, and as board member for the Theatre of Latin America (1973–1979) and the U.B.U. Repertory Theatre (since

1980). She has been a member of the International Panel of the National Endowment for the Arts (1981), the Curriculum Committee of the National Theatre Institute (since 1982), the Executive Committee of the United States National Commission for UNESCO (1975–1980), and the Performing Arts Committee of the Japan Society (since 1983). She has also been on the Executive Committee of the worldwide International Theatre Institute since 1971 and was elected president of that body in 1987. For her achievements in international theatre exchange, she has been designated by the French government as Officier de l'Ordre des Arts et des Lettres.

The files of ITI, New York City, contain information concerning Martha Coigney's work with that organization. Additional information in this article is from a personal interview with Coigney. She is listed in *Who's Who in America 1984–1985*, Vol. I (1984).

Audrey Cooper

COIT, Dorothy (September 25, 1889–October 20, 1976): educator, administrator, director, pioneered in theatre for young people as co-founder and co-director of the King-Coit School and Children's Theatre, New York City. Dorothy Coit was born in Salem, Massachusetts. Her father, Robert Coit, was an architect and a graduate of Harvard University (1883). Her mother, Eliza ("Lilla") (Richmond) Atwood, studied design at the Boston Museum of Fine Arts. Dorothy Coit was the oldest of four children; she was raised in Winchester, Massachusetts (a suburb of Boston), with her sisters Elisabeth and Mary and their younger brother, Robert.

Dorothy Coit never had formal theatre training, but she cultivated a love for the theatre as well as for music and poetry. After graduating from Winchester High School, she enrolled in Radcliffe College in 1907. Between 1908 and 1911 she became active in the English Club, which met two times each month to discuss original papers written by students and to hear such speakers as George Pierce Baker of Harvard's 47 Workshop. During her Radcliffe years, Coit also belonged to the Idler Club, a theatrical and social club. Short plays or scenes were presented at their meetings along with one major production a year.

Coit received her Bachelor of Arts degree *cum laude* in 1911 and began teaching English and history at the Buckingham School, a private school in Cambridge, Massachusetts, where she met **Edith Lawrence King**. Their first collaborative effort was a production of John Milton's masque, *Comus*, with a class of thirteen-year-old girls. Coit "cut it and edited it and made quite a good play out of it" (Barclay, *New York World-Telegram*, May 7, 1940). King worked with the girls on costumes and scenery. Between 1915 and 1922 they produced and directed *The Tempest*; *Chansons de France, or Divertissements Français* (based on books by Boutet de Monvel); *The Story of Theseus, or The Sword of Attica*; *Ahmed the Cobbler*; *Aucassin and Nicolete*; and *Nala and Damayanti* at the Buckingham School and other locations in Massachusetts and New Hampshire. In the summers (1923–1926) they presented shows in Massachusetts and in Woodstock, New York, with young performers between the ages of three and fifteen.

Despite the success of their collaboration, there came a point at which the two women felt constrained by the conservative and puritanical environment around Boston and longed for a school of their own elsewhere. They relocated in New York City in 1920. In 1921 they mounted *Aucassin and Nicolete* at the 39th Street Theatre with Jane Wyatt and Beatrice Straight among the children in the cast. Critic Alexander Woollcott described the presentation as "pure gold" (*New York Times*, April 9, 1921), and Coit wrote on a copy of the review: "This is what really launched us in New York." In 1923 they opened the unique King-Coit School and Children's Theatre, famous for its carefully mounted theatrical productions and interesting art work, which they operated for the next thirty-five years.

Nonprofessional children, ages three to fifteen, attended the King-Coit School for a few hours a week after regular school and on weekends to study painting, drawing, dancing, acting, history, mythology, and literature. They were the sons and daughters of artists, musicians, poets, theatre people, and dilettanti. Among them were the children of **Helen Hayes**, **Geraldine Fitzgerald**, Herbert Brodkin, **Mildred Dunnock**, Dorothy McGuire, Maxwell Anderson, and George Bellows; the godchildren of **Tallulah Bankhead**; and the grandchildren of Arthur B. Davies, Walter P. Chrysler, and **Aline Bernstein**. Tanaquil LeClercq, Madeleine L'Engle, Jane Wyatt, Jacques D'Amboise, Lee Remick, Zina Bethune, Anne Baxter, and Beatrice Straight also attended the King-Coit School. Scholarships were provided to a few talented, but poor, children.

Edith King, artist and teacher, was responsible for painting and drawing classes, scenery, lighting, and costumes; Dorothy Coit, actress and teacher, supervised the storytelling, acting, diction, pantomime, script adaptations, and directing. Artists Martha Ryther Kantor and Helen Farr Sloan, and dancer Mikhail Mordkin (a colleague of Pavlova) were among their assistants. Some of the best costumers, lighting designers, and musicians in the New York theatre scene at the time also volunteered to assist.

"Perfection at all costs" was the prevailing production attitude. Neither the tuition the children paid (about two hundred dollars a year) nor the ticket sales (usually between three and five dollars each) covered the costs, and support from people like Walter Damrosch, **Katharine Cornell**, **Rosamond Gilder**, members of the J.P. Morgan and Rockefeller families, **Lynn Fontanne**, and Alfred Lunt— and many, many others—was crucial. Besides financial considerations, King and Coit were plagued by theatrical unions, child labor laws, and fire marshals.

The purpose of the King-Coit School and Children's Theatre was not to train children for careers in the professional theatre. Rather, it was to give children a chance to stimulate their imaginations, to learn history, literature, mythology, music, dance, art, and drama after regular school hours, and to bring their studies to fruition in performance. King and Coit integrated the arts through the theatre, and each production was the result of months of preparation. When asked about their work, Coit responded that "culture," which for her implied both a product and a process, was their aim, the result of which would be the "development of the individual child into a person of sensitivity and understanding, who has acquired some taste for quality and some distaste for cheapness and superficiality'' (speech given by Coit, April 13, late 1950s).

Their teaching methods involved Coit's telling the children a tale. Then the children were encouraged to act the story out informally, invent dialogue, or use pantomime. Under King's supervision, they listened to music from the period, danced to the music, drew, painted, and modeled with clay the characters, incidents, or objects in the story. Next, Coit would offer the actual lines of the play as substitutes for the children's improvisations or would speak specific lines while the children pantomimed them. Eventually, words and gestures were memorized. The young people played every role during the preparation period before the actual production. The stylized, elaborate plays were presented before mostly adult audiences, and the children's art work was exhibited throughout the United States and Mexico.

The King-Coit School and Children's Theatre interested the first-string Broadway drama critics. Among them were John Mason Brown, William Hawkins, Henry Hewes, Stark Young, Robert Littell, Alexander Woollcott, Burton Rascoe, John Anderson, and Brooks Atkinson. The critics raved about the humor, the acting, the children's lack of self-consciousness, the beauty, the perfection, and the uniqueness of the performances. John Anderson spoke for many when he wrote in 1935, ''I can say that the productions are unlike anything else. They are very special. . . . There is nothing like the [King-Coit] Children's Theatre'' (*New York Evening Journal*, April 27, 1935). In a letter to Dorothy Coit and Edith King, Lynn Fontanne wrote, ''Mr. Lunt and I went [to the play] and thought it such a rare and wonderful piece of art. The amazing direction of these tiny creatures, we know, is a job requiring as much patience as even Job never knew about. The costumes and decorations, which are the most beautiful we have ever seen on any stage whatsoever, were something you could sit and feast your eyes on for hours'' (letter dated May 2, 1947).

The King-Coit School and Children's Theatre demonstrated the importance of the three D's—dance, drama, and design—in the traditional three R's education of children. It demonstrated, too, that theatre for young people can be an integral part of American theatre.

After thirty-five years the King-Coit School and Children's Theatre closed in 1958. Dorothy Coit continued to teach classes in acting two days a week at various private schools in New York during the winter months. ''I have done a less ambitious type of coaching the last few years, just simple drama with no costumes, scenery, etc.,'' she wrote in 1968 in *The Radcliffe Quarterly* (June 1968, p. 30). During the summers she lived in Bethlehem, Connecticut. She died on October 20, 1976, at the age of eighty-seven. In one obituary, the King-Coit Children's Theatre was referred to as ''a constituent part of New York drama'' (*New York Times*, October 24, 1976).

Dorothy Coit published two books, *The Ivory Throne of Persia* (1929) and *Kai Khosru and Other Plays for Children* (1934). She also wrote ''A Defense of Dramatics,'' *The Rad-*

cliffe Magazine (February 1911), and "Recipe for a Children's Theatre" (no other information available). The most complete study of Dorothy Coit and the King-Coit School and Children's Theatre is Ellen Rodman, "Edith King and Dorothy Coit and The King-Coit School and Children's Theatre" (Unpublished Ph.D. dissertation, New York University, 1980). This dissertation contains an extensive bibliography including numerous unidentified clippings that are in the files of the New York Public Library Performing Arts Research Center at Lincoln Center. Weston Barclay wrote an informative piece, "The Play's the Thing When It Comes to Progressive Education," on the King-Coit collaboration in the *New York World-Telegram* on May 7, 1940. Alexander Woollcott's piece "The Play: *Aucassin and Nicolete*" appears in the *New York Times* (April 9, 1921). On April 13th, one year in the late 1950s (specific year unknown), Coit made a speech to parents whose children were attending the school. Useful magazine articles include: "Aucassin and Nicolete Behind the Footlights," *Vogue* (August 15, 1921); Constance D'Arcy Mackay, "The Most Beautiful Children's Theatre in the World," *The Drama* (February 1924); Dorothy Goggins, "Where Children Study Persian Drama," *Children's Vogue* (February-March 1925); Sheila Mayne, "From Never Never Land to Iran," *Art and Decoration* (December 1925); Catharine Cook Smith, "The Child Actors in the Coit-King Productions," *Theatre Arts Monthly* (September 1927); Richard Hayes, "The Stage: The King-Coit Children's Theatre," *The Commonweal* (May 21, 1954); and Euphemia Van Rensselaer Wyatt, "Nala and Damayanti," *The Catholic World* (June 1954). See also newspaper reviews: John Anderson, "*The Tempest* with Juvenile Cast . . . ," *New York Evening Journal* (April 3, 1933); John Mason Brown, "Two on the Aisle: Boutet de Monvel's Songbooks Charmingly Brought to Life at the King-Coit Children's Theatre," *New York Post* (April 30, 1934); John Mason Brown, "Two on the Aisle: *Nala and Damayanti* As It Is Enchantingly Performed at the King-Coit Children's Theatre," *New York Post* (April 25, 1935); John Anderson, "King-Coit Children's Theatre: Adaptations of East Indian Legend Refreshingly Done by Juveniles," *New York Evening Journal* (April 27, 1935); John Mason Brown, "Two on the Aisle: *Aucassin and Nicolete* at the King-Coit Theatre," *New York Post* (December 30, 1936); Brooks Atkinson, "The Play: Andrew Lang's *Aucassin and Nicolete* Acted by the Children of the King-Coit School," *New York Times* (February 14, 1937); John Anderson, "Children Draw on Blake Poetry for a Play," *New York Journal American* (April 6, 1938); Brooks Atkinson, "The Play: Shakespeare Without Tears," *New York Times* (April 1, 1940); Burton Rascoe, "King-Coit Children Enchant Audience with Thackeray Play," *New York World-Telegram* (December 14, 1942); Sally MacDougall, "Imagination Is the Big Thing for Tiny Actors," *New York World-Telegram and Sun* (April 16, 1953); Louis Sheaffer, "Theaters: The King-Coit Youngsters and Other Theater Matters," *Brooklyn Eagle* (May 7, 1953); and "King-Coit Performances," *New York Herald Tribune* (May 1, 1955). Dorothy Coit's obituary appeared in the *New York Times* (October 24, 1976). Few biographical books contain entries on Dorothy Coit. She is included in *Enciclopedia dello spettacolo*, Vol. III (1956).

Ellen Rodman

COLE, Toby (January 27, 1916–): actress, theatrical agent, and author, was born in Newark, New Jersey, the only daughter of Jacob and Bessie Cholodenko, who named her Marion. She called herself Toby Cole early in her professional career, and that is the name by which she is known in the world of theatre. Her parents had immigrated from the Ukraine to Newark, where her father was a builder. Here they raised their family, which included two sons in addition to Marion. She had her elementary and secondary schooling in the Newark city schools, where she also early showed her talent as an actress and the enthusiasm for theatre that has continued all her life.

Like many talented young people in the depression decade of the 1930s, Toby Cole began her involvement with theatre under the auspices of the Jewish socialist fraternal organization, the Workmen's Circle. She then became active in the "mobile agit-prop" plays done by the Newark Jack London Club and in the productions of the Newark Collective Theatre. A vivacious, copper-haired young woman, she was very effective in such roles as the farmer's firebrand daughter in **Hallie Flanagan**'s *Can You Hear Their Voices?* and Martha in Irwin Shaw's *Bury the Dead*. During its last year of existence, she was a member of the Federal Theatre Project.

As organizational secretary of the New Theatre League in New York from 1939 to its demise in 1941, Toby Cole gave evidence of her theatrical talents and her dedication to a socially committed theatre, as well as her administrative abilities. She had studied acting in 1938 at the New Theatre League School, and now she assisted this umbrella organization for the left-wing, popular-front theatre of the period in its many activities: publication of plays, new play contests, an artists' service bureau for bookings, and the theatre school. It was she who closed the league's office in 1942 and presented its archives to the Theatre Collection of the New York Public Library. Toby Cole was married in 1940 to Ben Irwin, then organizational secretary of the New Theatre League.

In the next decade she was assistant to the producer of the Broadway productions *Counterattack* (1942) and *Finian's Rainbow* (1949); librarian for the American-Russian Institute, New York (1943–1946); registrar for the Tamara Daykarhanova School for the Stage (1946–1947); playreader for Broadway producers Irene Selznick and Kermit Bloomgarden; and producer for Children's Holiday Theatre, New York (1955–1956). In 1946 she married Aron Krich, marriage counselor and writer. Their son, John Kalen Krich, born in 1951, is a writer.

After this varied experience in different aspects of professional theatre, Toby Cole started her own Actors and Authors Agency in 1957. She has represented important actors and directors—Zero Mostel, Sam Jaffe, and Joseph Chaikin, among others. Her agency has been particularly active in encouraging productions of some of the seminal playwrights of the sixties: John Arden, Edward Bond, Ann Jellico, Simon Gray, David Hare, and Trevor Griffiths. She has also been interested in European dramatists—Luigi Pirandello, Eduardo de Filippo, Bertolt Brecht (in Eric Bentley's translations), Peter Handke, and Slawomir Mrozek—and in many American playwrights, among whom the most notable are Sam Shepard, Saul Bellow, and Barbara Garson.

During these busy years she edited a number of books that have become basic reference texts in the important field of "performance studies." These include *Acting: A Handbook of the Stanislavsky Method* (1947), *Actors on Acting* with **Helen Krich Chinoy** (1949, 2nd edition 1970), *Directors on Directing* with Helen Krich Chinoy (1953, 2nd edition 1963), and *Playwrights on Playwriting* (1960).

Since 1973 Toby Cole has had a residence in Venice, Italy, where she edited several collections of valuable historical material in the volumes *Venice: A Portable Reader* (1979), *Florence: Traveler's Anthology* (1981), and *The World's First Ghetto: Venice 1516–1779* (unpublished).

Since 1985 she has also been spending extended periods of time in Berkeley, California, where she is once again arranging productions of socially conscious plays like *The Biko Inquest*. An explication of her life work appeared in the August 1985 issue of the *Bay Area Call Board* in the article "Perspectives: Do Playwrights Need Agents?"

In short, Toby Cole has dedicated her life to the promotion of plays and theatres that speak to the crucial issues of our times.

In 1983 the Toby Cole Archive, the records of her years as a highly regarded theatrical agent, was acquired by the Shields Library of the University of California at Davis. This file contains much material about her career. A file about the New Theatre League is in the New York Public Library Performing Arts Research Center at Lincoln Center. See Cole's "Perspectives: Do Playwrights Need Agents?" in *Bay Area Call Board* (August 1985). Much of the information contained in this essay is from a series of personal interviews with the author. Malcolm Goldstein mentions her briefly in *Political Theatre* (1974). Toby Cole is listed in *The Biographical Encyclopaedia and Who's Who of American Theatre* (1966) and *Notable Names in the American Theatre* (1976).

Helen Krich Chinoy

COLÓN, Miriam (1945?–): actress, producer, and artistic director of the Puerto Rican Traveling Theatre, was born in Ponce and raised in San Juan, Puerto Rico, the eldest of three children. Her father was a dry-goods salesman, but her parents divorced when she was very young, and it was Colón's mother, Josefa Quiles, who had a strong and very positive influence on her career.

Colón first became interested in acting when, at age eleven, she was cast in a junior high school production. A professor from the University of Puerto Rico saw her performance and invited her to observe his classes. By the time she graduated from high school, Colón was a member of the university's theatrical company. A special two-year scholarship enabled her to study with director Erwin Piscator's Dramatic Workshop in New York. Her mother accompanied her and took a job as a seamstress to support the family. After just one audition with Elia Kazan, Miriam Colón was the first Puerto Rican to be accepted at the Actors' Studio. She also studied with various private teachers. She made her Broadway debut in *In the Summer House* at the Playhouse in December 1953, beginning a decade of numerous stage and screen performances.

In 1966 Colón married George P. Edgar (now deceased). In that same year she became involved with a bilingual acting company and performed (in Spanish) René Marqués's *The Oxcart* in New York parks, jails, and storefronts free of charge. Recognizing the need for an ongoing bilingual theatre company, Colón founded the Puerto Rican Traveling Theatre that same year. The company started production in a rented Manhattan loft—a large room with fifty chairs—and lived up to its name by performing in community centers, storefronts, and city parks. They produced dozens of plays by Puerto Rican, South American, European, and American playwrights.

A training unit was established in 1969, and since that time some two hundred youngsters each year have attended bilingual classes in acting, speech, dance, and music. As the activities and scope of the theatre grew, so did the need for a permanent home. In 1974 Miriam Colón saw an abandoned firehouse on West 47th Street and, after two years of intensive work, was granted a long-term lease. Following extensive renovation, the 196-seat theatre was opened in 1981— the first Hispanic theatre ''on Broadway.'' Plays are presented in Spanish and English on alternating days, and in the summer a bilingual production tours neighborhood streets in all boroughs. The latest addition to the theatre's activities has been the introduction of a playwriting unit, which offers free seminars for aspiring writers. With all these activities the Puerto Rican Traveling Theatre fulfills Colón's definition of theatre as ''a vehicle for change, a communicator, as well as entertainment'' (*Interview*, May 1986).

Although she has devoted her chief energies to the company since its inception, Miriam Colón has had a very successful acting career. On Broadway she has appeared in *In the Summer House* (1953), *The Innkeepers* (1956), and *The Wrong Way Light Bulb* (1969). She has also appeared in numerous Off-Broadway productions, including *The Passion of Antigona Perez* (1972) and *Fanlights* (1980), both presented by the Puerto Rican Traveling Theatre. In 1982 Colón was invited to take a production to her own country. There she performed a leading role in *La Calle Simpson* by Puerto Rican playwright Eduardo Gallardo. In 1985 she appeared at the Puerto Rican Traveling Theatre in an English translation of a two-character play, *Orinoco*, by the Mexican playwright Emilio Carballido.

Though she continues to act, Colón now serves primarily as producer of the bilingual plays presented by the Puerto Rican Traveling Theatre. As a producer she uses the name Miriam Colón Edgar. In 1983 she produced *Inquisition* by Spanish playwright Fernando Arrabal, *The Great Confession* by Argentinean writers Sergio de Cecco and Armando Chulak, and *The Oxcart* by Puerto Rican René Marqués. The next year she produced *The Management Will Forgive a Moment of Madness* and *The Accompaniment*. In 1985 Colón co-directed *Simpson Street* and produced *The Dead Man's Agony* and *Orinoco*. These plays were all presented at the company's permanent theatre at 304 West 47th Street. During the summer the touring unit continues to take free-of-charge performances to communities throughout the city.

Colón has also performed in films, including *One-Eyed Jacks* (1961), *The Appaloosa* (1966), *The Possession of Joel Delaney* (1971), *Back Roads* (1981), and *Scarface* (1983). Colón's list of credits also includes roles in over 250 television shows.

Miriam Colón has received many awards and honors. In May 1982 she received the Mayor's Award of Honor for Arts and Culture, presented by New York City's Mayor Edward I. Koch. In August 1982 she received a certificate of appreciation from Mayor Koch in recognition of her contributions to New York's cultural life as founder of the Puerto Rican Traveling Theatre. Colón has also received the Extraordinary Woman of Achievement Award from the National Council of Christians and Jews. She has served on various panels and committees, such as the National Hispanic Task Force and the Expansion Arts Panel of the National Endowment for the Arts.

Miriam Colón states her position on bilingual theatre in these words: "Any knowledgeable theatregoer in New York has to discover that in Argentina, in Mexico, and in Spain, there's a great crop of playwrights that are writing theatre of the avant-garde. If you are a seasoned theatregoer, you should know what's going on in Puerto Rico as well as New York" (*Other Stages*, May 7, 1981). As an accomplished actress, producer, and director, Miriam Colón has made a major contribution to the growth and enrichment of bilingual theatre. As a result of her effort, the Puerto Rican Traveling Theatre has become a major center of Hispanic cultural activity in New York.

There is a clipping file on Miriam Colón in the Billy Rose Theatre Collection in the New York Public Library Performing Arts Research Center at Lincoln Center. Articles about her appear in *El Diario* (June 25, 1981, in Spanish only; and February 11, 1982, in Spanish and English), *Hispanic Arts* (September 1980), *Other Stages* (November 29, 1979, and May 7, 1981), *The Soho News* (April 8, 1981), *The New York Times* (May 29, 1980; August 12, 1980; April 13, 1981; February 5, 1982; and January 27, 1985), *Daily World* (April 6, 1982), *Voice* (February 12, 1985), and *Interview* (May 1986). Colón is listed in *Notable Names in the American Theatre* (1976) and in *Who's Who in the Theatre* (1977).

Maria Rodriguez

COMDEN, Betty (May 3, 1918–): lyricist, playwright, and actress, was born in Brooklyn, the daughter of Leo and Rebecca (Sadvoransky) Comden (some sources give Cohen). Her father was a lawyer and her mother an English teacher. Betty attended the Brooklyn Ethical Culture School, where the students read the classics and frequently dramatized them. Betty liked both the writing and the acting of these plays. At Erasmus Hall High School she continued to write, but rather than trying out for the high school plays, she spent her time at the Clay Club in Greenwich Village. After graduating from high school, she attended New York University, at first studying education but changing to a major in dramatics. She received her Bachelor of Science degree in 1938. Upon graduating, Betty Comden began making the rounds of theatrical agents.

While going from agent to agent she became acquainted with a young man named Adolph Green. He too had attended New York University, though for only a short time. He had been looking for work as an actor in New York for nearly four years, supporting himself as a runner on Wall Street, as a carpet salesman, and in many other jobs. At night he worked with little theatre groups and every summer he went to the Catskill Mountains to provide entertainment in the adult camps there. In the summer of 1938, Green met a shy young girl named Judy Tuvim at one of the summer camps. She was interested in writing and was attracted to the witty Adolf Green. That September, back in New York, Judy Tuvim, while strolling along Seventh Avenue in Greenwich Village, ducked inside a doorway to avoid a sudden downpour. She had stumbled into the Village Vanguard, a coffee house where the patrons read of recited poetry. After becoming acquainted with the manager, Max Gordon, Tuvim volunteered as entertainment her friend Adolph Green and his troupe of actors and singers called Six and Company. Max Gordon gave Six and Company a chance to perform for his customers. After a very unsuccessful "first night" at the Village Vanguard, Adolph Green knew that he had to change both his company and his material. He called on his friend, Betty Comden, to join him. By this time Comden had had some experience working in borough theatre groups and had even played a small part in a subway-circuit production of the 1937–1938 Broadway hit *Having Wonderful Time*. Green also brought in Alvin Hammer, a young man who had been doing monologues in neighborhood nightclubs. Comden brought a musician friend she had known at New York University, John Frank. Judy Tuvim did not want to act, but she volunteered to help backstage. Eventually, she was persuaded to perform because the group needed another woman.

Soon the group realized that they needed new and original material, and, since they could not afford royalties and they could not afford to hire a writer, they decided to write their own scripts. They called themselves the Revuers. Their style of satire was good-natured and was inspired mainly by the entertainment pages of the newspapers. They poked fun at movies, radio, Broadway, and Hollywood. By the spring of 1939, the group had a following of fans and had received brief, but flattering notices from the nightlife reviewers. They had gone from one show every Sunday night to three nights a week and then six. The Vanguard was becoming a popular night club.

In September 1939 the Revuers moved up-town. They were invited to perform at the Rainbow Room, located on one of the top floors of the RCA Building in Rockefeller Center, but their type of humor did not appeal to the conservative audiences at the Rainbow Room. In 1940 they played at Radio City Music Hall for three weeks. Other jobs followed—a weekly program on NBC, engagements at Loew's State, Spivy's, Cafe Society, and several television shows. Toward the end of 1940 they returned to the Village Vanguard, which had been newly renovated by Max Gordon. While playing at the Vanguard they were asked to join the cast of a new musical, *My Dear Public*, written by Irving Caesar. It told the story of the making of a musical, and the Revuers were to play themselves in the play within a play. The musical eventually opened in New York but was not a success, though the Revuers received favorable comments from the critics.

The Revuers now had to go back to the nightclub circuit. They played a successful engagement at the Blue Angel, a cabaret that Max Gordon opened on East 56th Street. After this they went on the road. While in Toronto, they had an offer to play in a film in Hollywood. Green, Tuvim, and Hammer decided to go to Hollywood. Comden also agreed to go because her husband, Steven Kyle, whom she had married in 1942, had been drafted overseas. Kyle, an artist, later became a well-known designer of fabrics and household articles. When the four Revuers arrived in Hollywood, they discovered that the movie they had come to make had been called off. They were able instead to get a booking at the Trocadero. Studio scouts and producers began to stop by to see them, but all of the offers that came from the Hollywood producers were for Judy Tuvim and not for the group. Tuvim at last consented to sign a contract with Twentieth Century–Fox if the Revuers were allowed to appear in a film. The group was added to the movie *Greenwich Village*, to bring an authentic note by performing two of their nightclub sketches. When the film was released, both of the sketches had been cut. Upon her friends' insistence, Judy Tuvim agreed to stay with her contract—her name now changed to **Judy Holliday**. Betty Comden and Adolph Green went back to New York, but Alvin Hammer remained in Hollywood.

In New York, Comden and Green returned to the Blue Angel. One night a long-time friend, Leonard Bernstein, wandered into the nightclub. He wanted to do a full-length show built around the idea of *Fancy Free*, a ballet by Bernstein and Jerome Robbins. He had come to ask Comden and Green to do the book and lyrics. The story, the character development, and the various numbers in the musical which evolved from the collaboration were all Comden and Green's ideas. The new musical was *On the Town*. Even before the book was completed, RKO saw the possibilities of the show and invested in it. Then Metro-Goldwyn-Mayer offered to buy the film rights plus an investment in the stage production. *On the Town* was the first musical comedy bought by Hollywood before it was performed on the stage. The musical opened at the Adelphi Theatre in New York on December 28, 1944. *P.M.*'s Louis Kronenberger called the show "one of the freshest, gayest, liveliest musicals I have ever seen" (quoted in *Current Biography*, 1945). Betty Comden played the lady anthropologist and Adolph Green was the third sailor.

Comden and Green's second musical, *Billion Dollar Baby* (1945), with music by Morton Gould, was not so successful. It was followed by *Bonanza Bound* (1947), with music by Paul Chaplin, and *Two on the Aisle* (1951), with music by Jule Styne. In 1953 they collaborated once again with their friend Leonard Bernstein, writing the lyrics for his *Wonderful Town*, based on the play *My Sister Eileen* by Joseph Fields and Jerome Chodorov. In 1956 Comden and Green wrote the book and lyrics for *Bells Are Ringing*, with music by Styne, specifically to use the talents of Judy Holliday, who, after the successful play and film *Born Yesterday*, was now famous as Billy Dawn, the dumb blond with the squeaky voice. Comden and Green created the character of the telephone operator, Ella Peterson, described in the script as "pretty, warm, sympathetic . . . with a quick mind and a vivid imagination," as a tribute to their good friend (Carey, *Judy Holliday*, p. 190). Though the plot was called "antiquated" by Walter Kerr (*New York*

Times, November 30, 1959), the show was a box-office hit that ran for over two years.

In 1958 Comden and Green performed in *A Party*, a revue based on a collection of their previously written songs and sketches. First presented off Broadway at the Cherry Lane Theatre, the revue was expanded and produced on Broadway at the St. James Theatre with the title *A Party with Betty Comden and Adolph Green*, opening on December 23, 1958. Nearly twenty years later, in February 1977, a new version was produced on Broadway at the Morosco Theatre. Gerald Clarke, writing in *Time* (February 21, 1977), said of their performance: "These comic Prosperos can conjure up whole casts with a mere wink of the eye or shrug of the shoulder . . . Rarely has so much wit and fun been packed into two hours. To cop a line from another song-writer, Cole Porter, what a swellegant, elegant party this is."

Comden and Green wrote the lyrics, with music by Jule Styne, for *Do Re Me* (1960), *Subways Are for Sleeping* (1961), *Fade Out—Fade In* (1964), and *Hallelujah, Baby* (1967). In 1970 they wrote the book for *Applause*, with music by Charles Strouse, based on the film *All About Eve*. The musical brought Lauren Bacall to Broadway and she was the one who received most of the applause. *On the Twentieth Century* (1978), a musical based on the play *Twentieth Century* by Ben Hecht and Charles MacArthur, with music by Cy Coleman, received mixed reviews. Harold Clurman (*Nation*, March 11, 1978) called it "the best in musical comedy that Broadway offers thus far this season." Brendan Gill (*New Yorker*, March 6, 1978) though that the "kindly" satire of Comden and Green did not go with the contempt for mankind of the Hecht–MacArthur play.

Two of Comden and Green's most recent musicals have been unsuccessful,. *A Doll's Life*, a sequel to Henrik Ibsen's *A Doll's House*, represented for them "a venture into more serious subject matter than before." The question of what happened to Nora after she left her husband seemed an interesting one to Betty Comden. Jeremy Gerard in the *New York Times* (September 19, 1982) quotes Comden as saying, "I have had a career all my life. I've also been married, had children. My husband was a totally enlightened man, interested in what I did and a supporter of Adolph and me. But the fact that I had that wonderful thing didn't mean I wasn't aware of what it's like for others." The musical lost money when it tried out in Los Angeles and ran for only five performances when it moved to New York. Frank Rich of the *New York Times* (September 27, 1982) described the play as "a well-intentioned show" that "collapses in its prologue and then skids into a toboggan slide from which there is no return."

Similar negative reviews greeted their 1985 musical, *Singin' in the Rain*. Based on the extremely popular Hollywood film for which they had written the screenplay in 1952, the stage version received scathing reviews. Frank Rich of the *New York Times* (July 3, 1985) wrote, "Once transposed to the stage in realistic terms, the fantasy evaporates even the rain pours down." Douglas Watts of the *Daily News* headed his review "Singing' Down the Drain" (July 3, 1985).

After their second Broadway musical, Comden and Green had made a second, more successful trip to Hollywood. After that they worked on both Coasts. Among their screenplays are *Good News* (1947), *The Barkleys of Broadway* (1949), *On the Town* (1949), *Take Me Out to the Ballgame* (1949), *Singin' in the Rain* (1952), *The Bandwagon* (1953), *Auntie Mame* (1958), *Bells Are Ringing* (1960), and *What a Way to Go* (1964).

Comden and Green have won Tony (Antoinette Perry) Awards for *Wonderful Town* (1953), *Hallelujah, Baby* (1968), *Applause* (1970), and *On the Twentieth Century* (1978). Their story and screenplay for *The Bandwagon* (1953) won an Academy Award nomination, as did their *It's Always Fair Weather* (1955). Their *A Party with Betty Comden and Adolph Green* was awarded a *Village Voice* Off-Broadway (OBIE) Award.

Betty Comden and Adolph Green are seldom mentioned individually. In an interview with them in 1975, the author of the *New Yorker*'s "The Talk of the Town" (May 12, 1975) wrote that "when Comden and Green are talking or inventing they seem to be one doubly alert person." They told him that they thought their partnership had survived because they were both happily married to other people. Betty Comden's husband Steven Kyle has since died, in 1979. They had two children. Adolph Green is married to Phyllis Newman, the actress and director.

For mother than fifty years, Comden and Green have worked together. Harold Clurman has commented on Adolph Green's "ebullient nature" which is somehow "disciplined by Betty Comden's decorous wit" (*Nation*, March 11, 1978). Brendon Gill, in the *New Yorker* (February 21, 1977), speaks of their "acute, affectionately bantering view of human frailty," and says that they "have never lost their freshness, and it is plainly their intention, growing older, never to grow old."

Perhaps the best way to appreciate the sparkling humor of Betty Comden and Adolph Green is to read their scripts or listen to the recordings of their shows. Articles and reviews of their works may be found in the *New Yorker*, *Newsweek*, *Time*, *Saturday Review*, *Nation*, and many other periodicals. There are two biographies of Judy Holliday, both of which chronicle the activities of the Revuers: Will Holtzman, *Judy Holliday* (1982) and Gary Carey, *Judy Holliday, An Intimate Life Story* (1982). Max Gordon's *Live at the Village Vanguard* (1980) also tells about the Revuers. *Current Biography, 1945* (1946) covers the early years of Comden's life. Comden is listed in *Notable Names in the American Theatre* (1976); *Who's Who in the Theatre*, 17th Ed. (1981); *Contemporary Theatre, Film, and Television*, Vol. II (1986); *The Oxford Companion to American Theatre* (1984); *Contemporary Dramatists*, ed. James Vinson, 3rd Ed. (1982), listed under Musical Librettists; *Contemporary Authors*, New Revision Series, Vol. II (1981); and *A Guide to American Screenwriters: The Sound Era, 1929–1982*, Vol. I, Screenwriters, ed. Larry Langman (1984).

Alice McDonnell Robinson

CONNER, Charlotte Barnes (1818–April 14, 1863): playwright and actress, was born in New York City to John and Mary (Creenhill) Barnes, who were both actors. They had come to America from England two years before her birth and established themselves at the Park Theatre, where John Barnes became a perennial favorite in comic roles. Charlotte Barnes was educated for the theatre and first appeared on stage in her mother's arms in *The Castle Spectre* before she was three years old. It was in this same play in 1834 that she made her legitimate debut as Angela at Boston's Tremont Theatre. A more important event in theatre history was her New York debut later that year (March 29, 1834) in the same role while her mother played the part of Evelina.

Shortly thereafter, Barnes's acting career was well under way, and she began to combine her love of writing with her enthusiasm for the theatre. Her first attempt at playwriting was a dramatization of *The Last Days of Pompeii* (1835), based on the novel by Bulwer-Lytton. Then in 1837 she wrote *Octavia Bragaldi; or, The Confession*, first performed in New York in November 1837 and, according to its author, subsequently played more than fifty times in America and England (Preface to *Plays, Prose and Poetry*, 1847). Her dramatization of J. H. Ingraham's novel *LaFitte; or, The Pirates of the Gulf* opened at the New Orleans Theatre in 1837 with the author acting the young romantic male lead.

In 1842 Barnes visited England and, with the help of her mother and father, obtained some engagements, playing Hamlet and Jane Shore as well as the lead in her own *LaFitte*. *The Forest Princess; or, Two Centuries Ago*, Barnes's historical play featuring Jamestown and the Pocahontas legend, was first acted in Liverpool in 1844. In the published version the author expressed her joy in doing the research for the play in the British Museum, then went on to confess that the play did not attract a great deal of attention in the theatre.

In 1847, after her return from England, Barnes married Edmond S. Conner, a fairly popular leading actor in tragedies and melodramas, who became manager of Philadelphia's Arch Street Theatre. That same year she prepared her *Plays, Prose and Poetry* for publication, introducing, she wrote in her preface, "these fruits of girlhood and womanhood's leisure to the reading public" (p. V). In 1848 she adapted a French novel to the stage, calling her play *A Night of Expectations*. The text is not extant. Writing was probably more important than acting to her though she gained a respectable reputation in both careers. The text has not been found of another play in which she acted the lead, *Charlotte Corday* (1851), based on and adapted from Lamartine's *Histoire des Girondins* and Dunamoir and Clairville's *Charlotte Corday*. Conner died at the age of forty-five in New York on April 14, 1863, after a brief illness.

Charlotte Barnes Conner was not a major actress in the American theatre and was never clearly established on the New York stage. It seems that without the reputation of her parents she would not have enjoyed much of a career in acting. According to Joseph Ireland, she was limited by physical defects that, according to his listings, were considerable. (See Ireland, *Records etc.*, 1866 passim). Although she was pleasingly slender and fragile in appearance, her voice was weak and broke when she attempted violent passages. She was at her best, according to Ireland, in male parts such as young Norval in Home's *Douglas* or the young hero, Theodore, in *LaFitte*. She seems to have had some successes as Hamlet, Jane Shore, Juliet, and Lady Teazle.

It is as a playwright that Charlotte Barnes Conner made her greatest contribution to the American theatre. Even then, by her own admission, her early efforts were applauded with an enthusiasm stimulated more by her youth and the reputation of her parents than by her own talents. She revised her plays carefully, however, before publishing them. Highly intellectual, imaginative, and skillful as a writer, she produced two poetic dramas that for their dramatic construction are superior to most such plays written before the Civil War. *Octavia Bragaldi* (1837), a well-structured play with some excellent scenes, is the best of her dramas. Basing her plot on a notorious tragedy of passion that occurred in Frankfort, Kentucky, in 1825—and subsequently inspired more literature than any other American crime—Conner had both Thomas H. Chivers's *Conrad and Eudora* (1834) and Edgar A. Poe's *Politian* (1835) as models for her play. Like Poe she camouflaged her plot with a setting in Milan, Italy, near the end of the sixteenth century. The desertion of the heroine, Octavia, by Castelli, her subsequent marriage to Bragaldi, the challenge, the slander and murder of Castelli at Octavia's instigation, and the climax in which both she and Brigaldi die—all came from the event in Kentucky. Conner brought to this plot her effective theatrical instincts and some good blank verse. As heroic tragedy, *Octavia Bragaldi* has an energy and vitality that set it above most plays written at that time. *The Forest Princess* (1844) is appealing mainly in its final act, which takes place in 1617 in England. During this act Walter Raleigh must answer to King James I for the failure of his expedition, and Pocahontas dreams of returning to America. Both these plays are typical of the poetic drama written in America before the mid-nineteenth century, but Conner's knowledge of practical theatre and her skill in poetic expression make her plays more stageworthy than others. Charlotte Barnes Conner's importance rests on the fact that she was one of the very few women playwrights who wrote successfully for the early nineteenth-century American theatre.

In *A History of the American Drama from the Beginning to the Civil War* (1943), Arthur Hobson Quinn comments on Conner's plays. Joseph N. Ireland provides more particular observations on her work as an actress in *Records of the New York Stage from 1750 to 1860*, Vol. II (1866). George C. D. Odell, *Annals of the New York Stage*, Vol. IV (1928), mentions her work in the theatre as does Charles Durang, *The Philadelphia Stage*, Series 3 (1860). James Rees's *Dramatic Authors of America* (1845) includes Americans who wrote for the stage during the Age of Jackson. For Conner's own reactions to her playwriting, read her preface to *Plays, Prose and Poetry*, published in Philadelphia in 1848. Also helpful in viewing her overall achievements is Hal J. Todd's "America's Actor-Playwrights of the Nineteenth Century" (Unpublished Ph.D. dissertation, University of Denver, 1955). Charlotte Barnes Conner (listed under Barnes) is included *American Authors, 1600–1900*, ed. Stanley J. Kunitz and Howard Haycraft (1938, reprinted 1964); *American Women Writers*, Vol. I (1979); *The Oxford Companion to American Literature* (1983); *The Oxford Companion to the Theatre* (1983); and *The Oxford Companion to American Theatre* (1984).

Walter J. Meserve

COREY, Irene (October 27, 1925–): educator, designer, best known for her spectacular mosaic makeup and costume design for *The Book of Job*, was born Irene Lockridge in Oskaloosa, Iowa, near the farm of her parents, Lawrence L.

Lockridge and Vallie (Click) Lockridge. She had one brother (now deceased), who was four years her senior. Her mother encouraged an interest in sewing, painting, and crafts. The Lockridge family moved in 1937 to Houston, Texas, where Irene graduated from high school with the desire to become a painter. While an undergraduate in the art department at Baylor University in Waco, Texas, Irene Lockridge became interested in theatre. Paul Baker, then head of the theatre program, recognized her talent and encouraged her to continue as a student in his graduate program.

After her graduation from that program, she married her fellow student Orlin R. Corey, and they moved to Kentucky. She took a faculty position in the art department of Georgetown College while her husband taught in the theatre department; she designed the shows directed by her husband, developing there her unique approach to theatrical design. In the early 1950s the Coreys took a sabbatical leave; Irene Corey studied costume design at London's School of Arts and Crafts with Norah Waugh and oil painting in Paris with Raynold Arnuld.

Upon their return to Kentucky, the Coreys created the world-renowned stage production known as *The Book of Job*. Although originally commissioned by the Religious Drama Society of Great Britain, the production first took place at Georgetown College on October 11–13, 1957. Word spread quickly about the unusual choral drama in which the performers wore shimmering mosaic robes, their faces painted to blend harmoniously with their costumes. On May 28, 1959, *The Book of Job* was presented at the Cathedral of the Hills in Pine Mountain State Park, Pineville, Kentucky. The outdoor productions that summer were so popular that the Kentucky Mountain Theatre, Incorporated, was formed to perpetuate the annual summer production of the play in Pine Mountain State Park. To keep up with demands, Corey and her husband co-founded the Everyman Players, which toured the world from 1958 until well into the 1970s. The Everyman Players created and presented not only *The Book Of Job* but also *Romans by Saint Paul*, *Electra*, *The Tortoise and The Hare*, *Reynard The Fox*, *The Pilgrim's Progress*, *Wiley and The Hairy Man*, *The Butterfly*, and *The Tempest* (all designed by Irene Corey). They played at such locations as the Brussels World's Fair (1958), the New York World's Fair (1964), the international festival celebrating the nine-hundredth anniversary of Westminster Abbey (1966), the Netherlands's International Theatre Festival (1970), the Biennale Festival of Venice (1970), and the Nuremburg International Festival (1973). The company undertook six national tours and five international tours as well as three New York City engagements and five television adaptations of their work. These tours, both domestic and foreign, presented Irene Corey's designs on several continents and garnered enthusiastic notices in over nine hundred reviews and articles. The *New York Times*, the *Times of London*, *Life*, *Look*, *Life International*, *Newsweek*, *Horizon*, *Oggi*, *Paris-Match*, the Associated and Reuters Press agencies, and the Asahi Press of Japan contributed to this publicity.

In 1960 the Coreys joined the faculty at Centenary College in Shreveport, Louisiana, where Irene Corey taught design and created scenery and costumes for most of the theatre department's productions. They continued to tour with the Everyman Players. Moreover, in Pineville, Kentucky, for a period of twenty years, *The Book of Job* became an annual summer event at Pine Mountain State Park's natural amphitheatre. From 1960 until 1969 the Corey's base of operations was Shreveport, but their influence on the theatrical profession was worldwide. In the spring of that year they left Centenary College and began giving full attention to establishing new productions for the Everyman Players. They toured almost continuously until 1973, when Irene Corey divorced her husband and settled in Dallas, Texas. In 1974 Irene Corey married John Barr, a painter, model builder, and special effects inventor. He died in 1976.

Corey's career as a designer has continued to flourish and has extended beyond theatre to television, theme parks, and club interiors. But her chief fame was earned during the exciting and innovative days of the Everyman Players. In 1970 this enterprise received the Jennie Heiden Award from the American Theatre Association in recognition of outstanding professional theatre for children. Irene Corey's imagination and her unending quest for new ways to solve old problems have brought delight to audiences around the world and have expanded the dimensions of stage possibilities.

Irene Corey's most fully stated philosophies of design and the theatre can be found in her book, *The Mask of Reality: An Approach to Design for the Theatre* (1968, reprinted 1976). Two plays illustrated with her costume and makeup designs, *Reynard The Fox* (1962) and *The Great Cross Country Race* (1969), have been published by Anchorage Press. Articles by Corey on various aspects of makeup and costuming have appeared in *Theatre Crafts* (May/June 1969 and May/June 1977), *Dramatics* (1976), *Mime Journal* (1975), *Woman's Day* (October 18, 1977), and *Ohio Journal* (Autumn 1979). Her designs have been reproduced in Oscar G. Brockett, *The Theatre, an Introduction* (1964, 2nd edition 1969); George Kernodle, *Invitation to the Theatre* (1971, 2nd edition 1978); Frank M. Whiting, *An Introduction to the Theatre* (1978); Jerry Crawford, *Acting, In Person and Style* (1976, 2nd edition 1979); Milly S. Barranger, *Theatre, A Way of Seeing* (1980); Vera Mowry Roberts, *The Nature of Theatre* (1971); *Creative America* (1962); *The Illustrated Library of the World and Its Peoples*, Vol. 3 (1967); Herman Buckman, *Stage Makeup* (1971); *John Willis' Theatre World*, Vol. 29 (1972); Jed H. Davis and Mary Jane Evans, *Theatre, Children and Youth* (1981); Garry Boham, *The Actor's Guide to MakeUp* (1981); C. Ray Smith, ed., *The Theatre Crafts Book of MakeUp, Masks, and Wigs* (1974); and Nellie McCaslin, *Theatre for Children in the United States: A History* (1971). Articles on Corey's career can be found in *Life* (November 21, 1960), *Horizon* (January 1963), and *Paris-Match* (April 27, 1963).

Ken Holamon

CORNELL, Katharine (February 16, 1893–June 12, 1974): actress and producer, became one of the "stars" of the American stage and was most renowned for her portrayals of Elizabeth Barrett, Juliet, Candida, and Antigone. At her birth in Germany, she weighed scarcely three pounds, and her parents, Peter Cortelyou and Alice Gardner (Plimpton) Cornell, feared that she would not survive. Her father, a physician, had been engaged in postgraduate work in medicine, but soon after the child's birth, he and his wife returned home to Buffalo, New York, where the young Katharine spent her childhood. In 1901 Dr. Cornell gave up the practice of medicine to manage and become part owner of Buffalo's Star Theatre.

Katharine Cornell became "stage-struck" at a young age when she saw **Maude Adams** in *Peter Pan*. Although her father did not take her theatrical aspirations seriously, he did send her to Oaksmere School, a finishing school in Mamaroneck, New York, where she was encouraged to pursue her interest in theatre and in athletics. At Oaksmere she wrote plays and pantomimes, directed performances, and built sets. After completing her schooling, she taught drama there for two years. During her last year at Oaksmere, Edward Goodman was brought from the Washington Square Players to direct a play Cornell had written. By his casual mention that she should let him know if she thought of going into the theatre, Goodman, in effect, launched her career (Cornell, *I Wanted To Be an Actress*, p. 9).

In 1916 she left Oaksmere, took a room in New York, and for two years gained experience with the Washington Square Players before she joined **Jessie Bonstelle's** stock company in Detroit. Recognizing her talent, Bonstelle insisted she take the part of Jo in the London production of Louisa May Alcott's *Little Women* (1919). At the end of the London run, Cornell returned to Bonstelle's company, where the young Guthrie McClintic had been engaged as director. They fell in love, and despite her father's disapproval Cornell married McClintic on September 8, 1921, the year in which her first great role as Sydney in Clemence Dane's *A Bill of Divorcement* catapulted her to stardom. Thereafter, until Guthrie's death from cancer in 1961, the McClintics devoted their lives to the theatre.

It was Alexander Woollcott's enthusiasm for *A Bill of Divorcement* (1921) that initiated Cornell's rise to stardom. In the next two years, she played in *Will Shakespeare*, *The Enchanted Cottage*, *Casanova*, *The Way Things Happen*, *The Outsider*, *Tiger Cats*, and *Candida*. After seeing her in the title role of George Bernard Shaw's *Candida* (1924), Gilbert Seldes predicted that Katharine Cornell was likely to attain prominence in the theatre (Seldes, p. 58). She then starred in *The Green Hat* (1926), a long-running play which, as she says, "gave her a public" (Cornell, p. 81). Following that success, a series of plays—*The Letter* (1927), *The Age of Innocence* (1928), and *Dishonored Lady* (1930)—established her as one of the foremost actresses of the time. Critic Jackson Harvey wrote that "a ceaseless energy" pervaded her performances and that she gave to characters "a subtlety and conviction" by the "aliveness of her art" (Harvey, p. 60). However, by the end of the decade, even her kindest critics were expressing a dissatisfaction with the kinds of plays in which she was appearing. The eminent critic Stark Young deplored the misuse of her talent and urged her to take the risk of doing plays with more dramatic substance (Young, p. 208).

In 1931 to accept the challenge of the critics and perform roles she believed were worth doing, Cornell and her husband formed the Cornell-McClintic Corporation. The new company's first play, Rudolph Besier's *The Barretts of Wim-*

pole Street (1931) with Cornell as Elizabeth Moulton-Barrett, broke all records at the Empire Theatre in New York.

The schedule of Cornell as actress-manager in the following years included an ambitious series of brilliant successes and some costly failures. After closing *The Barretts*, she played in *Lucrece* (1932), which closed in four weeks, losing one hundred thousand dollars. While she was playing in Sidney Howard's *Alien Corn* (1933), the famous critic of the *Transcript*, H. T. Parker, persuaded Cornell to consider the female lead in *Romeo and Juliet*. She was studying the role when Ray Henderson, her publicity manager, convinced her that she should tour. Caught up by his enthusiasm, she consented to undertake a national tour that would cover over 17,000 miles and include 225 performances in 74 towns and cities. The tour's three-play repertory consisted of *Romeo and Juliet* as well as revivals of *Candida* and *The Barretts of Wimpole Street*. The tour was another milestone for her. Receptive audiences of half-a-million people proved that a good company could succeed financially as well as artistically.

At the close of her first tour (1933–1934) Cornell and McClintic began to prepare a second production of *Romeo and Juliet* for her first appearance as Juliet in New York (December 1934). Her performance gained plaudits as well as criticism. **Edith J. R. Isaacs** said her performance had "wiped out the memory of other Juliets." (Isaacs, p. 94). Stark Young, likening her method to that of Eleonora Duse, declared that Cornell's portrayal of Juliet made one believe in love (Young, p. 252). Some critics found fault with various aspects of the production, but on the whole her Juliet was one of the pinnacles of her career.

Her next play, *Flowers of the Forest* (1935), was not successful, but then Cornell appeared in *Saint Joan* (1936), which she also toured. Critics called this one of her finest performances. In 1936–1937 Cornell presented Maxwell Anderson's *The Wingless Victory* and in 1937 a second revival of Shaw's *Candida*. During the war-torn decade of the 1940s, Cornell presented *The Doctor's Dilemma, Rose Burke, The Three Sisters, Lovers and Friends, Candida, The Barretts of Wimpole Street, Antigone, Antony and Cleopatra,* and *That Lady*. The roles were challenging, and reactions to her portrayals were usually favorable. By far the most profoundly inspiring experience for Cornell was that of taking *The Barretts of Wimpole Street* to the G.I.'s on the front lines in the European theatre of battle. Their expressions of appreciation convinced her that she had provided "spiritual ammunition" and "moral uplift" for courageous, lonely American soldiers (Woolf, p. 14). Her company returned home with the assurance that they had contributed something worthwhile to the war effort.

In the 1950s the number of her productions diminished, but she played in *The Constant Wife, The Prescott Proposals, The Dark is Light Enough, The Firstborn,* and a television production of *The Barretts of Wimpole Street* on the twenty-fifth anniversary of its Broadway opening. Her last production was Jerome Kilty's *Dear Liar* (1959). Critics detected an ebbing of her vibrancy, an apparent relaxation of the personal discipline that had enabled her to maintain her youthfulness and agility. At this time, she still had many parts she wanted to play, but the sudden death of her husband in 1961 ended Cornell's career in the theatre. She developed a heart condition, and the remaining years of her life were passed in the company of friends and neighbors at her home "Chip-Chop" on Martha's Vineyard. Her death on June 12, 1974, was the end of an era. Ten days after her death Hobe Morrison remarked in the Passaic *Daily News* that "even before her long lingering illness, her sort of theatre had ceased to exist."

Among those who played with Cornell were Maurice Evans, Charles Waldron, Florence Reed, Brian Aherne, Basil Rathbone, Edith Evans, Mildred Natwick, **Blanche Yurka**, Margalo Gillmore, and a host of others. Cornell promoted such promising young actors as Tyrone Power, Burgess Meredith, Orson Welles, and Marlon Brando. Probably the most impressive ensemble was that which performed *The Three Sisters*, a play that the McClintics agreed demanded "the most flawless casting, the most balanced acting" (*Time*, p. 45). The sparkling cast included **Judith Anderson**, **Ruth Gordon**, Gertrude Musgrove, Edmund Gwenn, Alexander Knox, Dennis King, and Katharine Cornell.

Cornell received many honors and awards. Of the twelve honorary degrees she received, the first was from the University of Wisconsin. The Drama League's Medal was awarded to her in 1935 for her portrayal of Juliet. The Katharine Cornell Foundation, a private charity, was established in 1935. On January 10, 1974, for "her incomparable acting ability" and "for having elevated the theatre throughout the world," she was given the American National Theatre and Academy's National Artist Award (Mosel, p. 16). In April of that year, the Katharine Cornell-Guthrie McClintic Room was dedicated at the New York Public Library Performing Arts Research Center at Lincoln Center.

For over forty years Katharine Cornell gave to the American theatre what Garff Wilson described as "an integrity, devotion, and a standard" that most nearly resembled the ideals of the classic school (Wilson, p. 281). **Martha Graham** said of her that, whenever she left any stage, she seemed to strip it, "leaving the audience a little forlorn and eager for her return," and that her final "exit from the stage of life cannot take away the 'innocence of greatness' " (Mosel, vi). With **Lynn Fontanne** and **Helen Hayes** she was counted as one of the leading actresses of her era.

The main sources of information are Cornell's autobiographies, *I Wanted To Be an Actress*, with Ruth Sedgewick (1938), and *Curtain Going Up* (1943); Guthrie McClintic's autobiography, *Me and Kit* (1955); and the biography *Leading Lady: The World and the Theatre of Katharine Cornell* (1978) by Tad Mosel and Gertrude Macy. Fan letters, news clippings, and press releases are held in the Cornell-McClintic collection at the New York Public Library Performing Arts Research Center at Lincoln Center. Articles in journals and periodicals are extensive: Morton Eustis, "The Actor Attacks His Part—V: Katharine Cornell," *Theatre Arts Monthly* (January 1937); Francis Fergusson, "A Month of the Theatre," *Bookman* (April 1931); Morris German, "A Theatre Portrait: Katharine Cornell," *The Theatre* (January 1960); Marc Goodrich, "Who Is the Best American Actress?" *Theatre Magazine* (December 1925); "Great Katharine," *Time* (April 3, 1939); "To the Ladies," *Theatre Magazine* (April 1930); Anne Herendeen, "The Lady of Two Legends," *Theatre Guild* (April 1931); Edith J. R. Isaacs, "Ring Out the Old: Broadway in Review,"

Theatre Arts Monthly (February 1935); "Katharine Cornell at the War Front," *Stage* (Spring 1945); S. J. Woolf, "When Wimpole Street Went to the Front," *New York Times Magazine* (February 25, 1945); Katharine Cornell and Alice Griffin, "A Good Play Will Always Find a Good Audience," *Theatre Arts Monthly* (May 1954); "Lucrece," *Stage* (February 1933); Richard Maney, "Exile by Choice," *Christian Science Monitor Magazine* (April 20, 1938); Ward Morehouse, "Queen Katharine," *Theatre Arts* (June 1958); Anne Morrow, "Katharine Cornell, a Sketch and a Prophecy," *Woman Citizen* (October 1925); Mary B. Mullett, "Unhappiness Has Its Own Magic," *American Magazine* (June 1926); Ada Patterson, "Two Innocents on Broadway," *Theatre Magazine* (June 1925); Ellery Rand, "A Study in Self-Mastery," *Personality* (July 1928); Gilbert Seldes, "Producers and Playwrights of 1924–1925," *Theatre Magazine* (July 1925); Richard Dana Skipper, "The Play: The Barretts of Wimpole Street," *Commonweal* (February 25, 1931); "The Barretts of Wimpole Street," *Life* (April 16, 1945); "Three Star Classic," *Time* (December 21, 1942); Alexander Woollcott, "Miss Kitty Takes to the Road," *Saturday Evening Post* (August 18, 1934); Stark Young, "Miss Katharine Cornell," *New Republic* (August 18, 1934); and Stark Young, "Katharine Cornell's Juliet," *New Republic* (January 9, 1935). Obituaries and other articles written at the time of Cornell's death include Richard L. Coe, "Cornell: It had to be the Best," *Courier Journal and Times*, Louisville, Kentucky (June 23, 1974); "Katharine Cornell Is Dead," *Daily News* (June 12, 1974); "Katharine Cornell Returns to a Last Spring at Tashmoo," *Vineyard Gazette*, Edgertown, Massachusetts (June 14, 1974); Hobe Morrison, "Obituary," *Herald-News*, Passaic, New Jersey (June 22, 1974); Alden Whitman, "Katharine Cornell Is Dead at 81," *New York Times* (June 12, 1974); and Burgess Meredith, "A Marchbanks Fondly Recalls His Candida," *New York Times* (January 16, 1974). Cornell is included in *Current Biography, 1952* (1953); *The Biographical Encyclopaedia and Who's Who of the American Theatre* (1966); *Who's Who in the Theatre* (1967, 1972); William C. Young, *Famous Actors and Actresses on the American Stage*, Vol. I (1975); *Who Was Who in the Theatre*, Vol. I (1978); *Notable American Women*, Vol. IV: *The Modern Period* (1980); *The Oxford Companion to the Theatre* (1983); and *The Oxford Companion to American Theatre* (1984).

Lucille M. Pederson

COWL, Jane (December 14, 1884–June 22, 1950): actress and playwright, was born Grace Bailey in Boston, Massachusetts. She was the only child of Charles A. Bailey and Grace (Avery) Bailey; her father was a clerk and her mother a trained singer and music teacher. The family moved to Brooklyn when the child was three. There her mother encouraged Jane's artistic pursuits, hoping her namesake might become a concert pianist. Grace Bailey was a student at Brooklyn's Erasmus Hall from 1902 to 1904, during which time she published some of her verses and stories in *Brooklyn Life*.

The illness of her mother prompted her to leave school and to seek employment in the theatre. She was hired by David Belasco and made her debut under the name Jane Cowl on December 10, 1903, playing Miss Derby in *Sweet Kitty Bellairs*. While she played several minor roles in subsequent Belasco productions, Cowl continued her education by attending lectures at Columbia University and studying with Brander Matthews, among others. On June 18, 1906, Cowl married Adolph Klauber (1879–1933), who was at that time drama critic for the

New York Times. Klauber later produced many of Cowl's theatrical ventures. They had no children.

Cowl's early training with Belasco in *The Music Master* and *The Rose of the Rancho* led to her first major role in his 1909 production, *Is Matrimony a Failure?* This experience was augmented by leading roles with the Hudson Theatre Stock Company in Union Hill, New Jersey. In later years she frequently acknowledged the great value of her stock company training. Belasco saw her at Union Hill and told her, "You will be the greatest emotional actress on the American stage" (untitled biography dictated by Cowl to Frank Morse, Installment 1, p. 20, Cowl scrapbook). His prophecy was fulfilled in 1912 with Cowl's success in Bayard Veiller's melodrama *Within the Law*, in which she played Mary Turner, the innocent shop girl sent to jail for a crime she did not commit. Cowl enjoyed equal success as Ellen Neal in a 1915 melodrama, *Common Clay*. Her extremely emotional acting earned her the sobriquet "Crying Jane," but it was widely appealing to prewar Broadway audiences.

At the outbreak of the First World War the lack of suitable scripts and a desire to make a contribution to the war effort prompted Cowl to team up with her friend from Belasco days, Jane Murfin, to write a play about the war. The result was the Broadway hit *Lilac Time* (1916), a sentimental melodrama starring Cowl as Jeannine. Other collaborations by Cowl and Murfin included *Daybreak* (1917) and *Information, Please* (1918). The latter was the première production at the new Broadway house, the Selwyn Theatre, built specifically for Jane Cowl. The two playwrights' next collaboration, published under the pseudonym of Allan Langdon Martin, was the tremendously successful *Smilin' Through*. It opened in December 1919, starring Cowl in the dual roles of Moonyeen Clare and Kathleen Dungannon; it ran a total of 1,700 performances.

Now firmly established as a successful playwright and Broadway star, Cowl determined to extend her range; she rejected popular melodrama and turned instead to the classics. In January 1923 Cowl opened on Broadway in her greatest role—Juliet in Shakespeare's *Romeo and Juliet*. This production, in which Rollo Peters played Romeo, was an immense success, and Cowl was hailed as the finest Juliet of her generation. When the run ended after 174 performances on June 10, 1923, the *New York Times*, in that day's issue, said it was the "longest continuous run of a Shakespearean play at one theatre in the history of the world." Cowl subsequently toured with the play, and in later years she claimed she had performed Juliet 998 times.

The critics adored Jane Cowl, who had dared to attempt a role that had, in recent memory, proved a failure even for the inimitable **Ethel Barrymore**. The *Sun* on January 26, 1923, claimed, "Jane Cowl is the Juliet of our dreams, beautiful, tender, and loving and always a simple, unaffected impersonation of Shakespeare's heroine." The *Tribune* (April 22, 1923) agreed, saying, "Miss Cowl has given the world a Juliet of such spontaneous youth, such virginal purity, such ecstasy of love and loveliness—and given her in terms so modern that no auditor is conscious of attending 'classic drama' when sitting through the performance."

Romeo and Juliet was a highpoint in Cowl's career; in it her abilities came to full flower. She continued to expand her classical range, playing Mélisande in Maeterlinck's *Pelléas and Mélisande* (1923), Cleopatra in Shakespeare's *Antony and Cleopatra* (1924), and Anna in Hans Mueller's *The Depths* (1924). In 1925 she turned to the comedy of Noel Coward and received wide acclaim as Larita in *Easy Virtue* in New York and in London. In his autobiography, *Present Indicative* (1937), Coward described Cowl as being "everything a famous theatrical star is expected to be: beautiful, effective, gracious, large-hearted, shrewd in everything but business, foolishly generous, infinitely kind to lesser people of the theatre, extremely annoying on many small points, and, over and above everything else, a fine actress" (p. 228). Cowl triumphed again in Robert E. Sherwood's *The Road to Rome* (1927), in which she played Amytis, a Roman wife of such charm and intelligence that she turns Hannibal away from the gates of the city. The comedy ran on Broadway for almost two years. In 1929 Cowl played Francesca in a revival of *Paola and Francesca* and the title role in *Jenny*.

Although success followed success, Cowl was aware of the risks in mounting new productions on Broadway. In the November 1927 issue of *Theatre* she spoke out for a strong effort to revive and strengthen the theatre. She noted that the demise of the stock system, which had formerly trained young actors, as well as the public's fascination with the new cinema medium, was contributing to a crisis in the American theatre. She had been impressed with the Moscow Art Theatre when the company appeared in New York in 1923 and was convinced that its artistic achievements were due, in part, to the stable economic subsidy and to an acting ensemble that evolved over an extended period of time. With this example in mind Cowl dreamed of creating a repertory company on Broadway. In 1930, with Leon Quartermaine as her co-star, she starred in a two-play repertory, playing Viola in *Twelfth Night* and Mrs. Bottle in *Art and Mrs. Bottle*. Although these productions were successful, personal circumstances, including mismanagement of her financial matters and the illness of her husband, combined with the exigencies of the Great Depression to discourage Cowl's pursuit of her ideas.

Nevertheless, considerable successes were yet to come in her career. In 1931 she went to the West Coast, where she played Camille in *The Lady of the Camellias*, and the following year she returned to Broadway to co-star with Franchot Tone and Osgood Perkins in *A Thousand Summers*. Also in 1932 she toured as the Lady in *A Man with a Load of Mischief* and played Camille again, this time at Boston's Tremont Theatre. The years 1934–1936 brought double triumphs to Jane Cowl: her portrayal of Lady Violet in the Theatre Guild production of S. N. Behrman's *Rain from Heaven* and her memorable interpretation of Lucy Chase Wayne in *First Lady*. She returned to the Theatre Guild in its production of Thornton Wilder's *The Merchant of Yonkers*, in which, under Max Reinhardt's direction, she created the role of Mrs. Levi. Her later productions included John Van Druten's *Old Acquaintance* on Broadway (1940) in addition to tours and regional productions of *Candida*, *Ring Around Elizabeth*, and *The First Mrs. Fraser*.

While continuing her successful stage career, Cowl wrote two more plays, *The Jealous Moon* (1928, in collaboration with Theodore Charles) and *Hervey House* (written with Reginald Lawrence), directed in London by Tyrone Guthrie in 1935. She also hosted the Jane Cowl radio program weekdays on the Mutual Network for two years, beginning in 1944, and was a featured radio guest star performing for the *RKO Theatre of the Air* (1931), *The Rudy Vallee Show* (1933 and 1939), the *Great Plays* series (1939), and *The Danny Kaye Show* (1944), all on CBS radio. During the Second World War Cowl was co-chair, with Selina Royle, of the New York Stage Door Canteen and considered it one of the most worthwhile accomplishments of her life.

From 1948 to her death in Santa Monica in 1950, Cowl lived in California, where she performed at the La Jolla Playhouse and made several Hollywood films, including *Once More, My Darling*, *No Man of Her Own*, *The Secret Fury*, and *The Story of a Divorce*. On June 22, 1950, she succumbed to cancer, with her lifelong friend, Jane Murfin, at her side.

Jane Cowl's stunning Broadway successes form a major part of her contribution to theatre; historically significant, too, were her ideals and her efforts to encourage the growth and public support of the art. She was an officer of Actors' Equity Association and a member of the board of the Stage Relief Fund. She set up the Sarah Bernhardt Scholarship Fund for young actresses. In articles and lectures she spoke out against gritty realism and was ever ready to plead for a theatre of hope and beauty. In *Theatre* (September 1929) she confirmed her romantic view of the stage, saying, "Surely there is still a place for beautiful writing, for now and then a jeweled phrase, and for a true emotion that springs honestly from the heart" (p. 12).

The Jane Cowl Collection in the New York Public Library Performing Arts Research Center at Lincoln Center includes clippings, reviews, programs, photos, an incomplete biography dictated to Frank Morse, radio scripts, and numerous scrapbooks. Other sources include the *New York Times* (June 10, 1923), the *Sun* (January 26, 1923), *Theatre Magazine* (November 1916 and September 1929), and the *Tribune* (April 22, 1923). Personal information can be found in *The Curtain Falls* by Verner Reed (1935); *Present Indicative* by Noel Coward (1937); and *Then Came Each Actor* by Bernard Grebanier (1975). Cowl's obituary appeared in the *New York Times* (June 23, 1950). General biographical information may be found in *Notable American Women*, Vol. I (1971); William C. Young, *Famous Actors and Actresses of the American Stage*, Vol. I (1975); *The Oxford Companion to the Theatre* (1983); and *The Oxford Companion to American Theatre* (1984).

Jeannie M. Woods

CRABTREE, Lotta (November 7, 1847–September 25, 1924): actress and popular performer, was born in New York City and christened Charlotte Mignon Crabtree. She was the eldest child and only daughter of John Ashworth Crabtree and Mary Ann (Livesey) Crabtree, both English immigrants. Her father was the proprietor of a bookstore, and her mother worked in her family's upholstery business. John Crabtree went to California early in 1852 to search for gold. His wife remained in New York with the children, earning a living for them all. In 1853 John Crabtree wrote that a fortune was all but in his hands and insisted that his family join him, whereupon they sailed for California. They joined Crabtree in an isolated mining camp called Grass Valley, where Mrs. Crabtree ran a boardinghouse for miners. Soon the mining camp had a surprising new resident: the beautiful Lola Montez, actress, dancer, and courtesan, who had entertained European royalty and had now married a miner and moved into a tiny white cottage just below the Crabtree boardinghouse. Accustomed to entertaining and being entertained, Montez found in Lotta Crabtree the perfect outlet for her pent-up energies. She passed on to the little girl much of what she knew about performing. Soon Crabtree was dancing hornpipes, Irish jigs, and clogs. With seeming ease she mastered the exacting *cracovienne*, a tour de force from Montez's own impressive dancing repertoire. Montez also taught Crabtree to ride horseback, and on one of their frequent rides together, Crabtree made her first public appearance as a performer. Stopping at a blacksmith shop to rest, Montez, on a sudden impulse, swept the child to the top of the smithy's anvil. While she clapped her hands and sang the now familiar tunes, Montez coaxed Lotta Crabtree to go through her routines. The miners went wild, throwing their hats in the air and saying they had never seen the likes of "our Lotta."

Immediately after this impromptu debut, the Crabtree family moved still deeper into the wilderness, establishing another boardinghouse in a camp called Rabbit Creek. But Mary Ann Crabtree, determined that her daughter should not neglect her newfound talent, discovered a man named Matt Taylor, owner of a saloon theatre and proprietor of a rustic dancing school. Taylor arranged an audition for Crabtree with "Dr." Robinson, a well-known impresario from San Francisco, who was visiting Rabbit Creek with his daughter, "Little Sue," also a child performer. Lotta Crabtree auditioned for Robinson, but he responded by presenting "Little Sue" alone in a performance across the street from Taylor's saloon theatre. Miffed, Taylor and Mary Ann Crabtree presented little Lotta themselves in Taylor's saloon as a rival attraction. Lotta Crabtree, saucily dressed in bright green silk breeches with matching long-tailed coat made by her mother and silver buckled shoes cobbled by Taylor, danced her favorite jigs and reels to Taylor's guitar accompaniment. Her performance completely routed Robinson and "Little Sue," and the stomping, screaming audience of miners littered the stage with a shower of half dollars, quarters, Mexican silver dollars, gold nuggets, and one fifty-dollar gold piece. These profits convinced Mary Ann Crabtree to put her daughter on the road with Taylor, who could play the guitar and dance and who knew a good fiddler to go with them. The frontier saga of Lotta Crabtree was launched.

No child in theatrical history ever made a more arduous and literal climb to fame. She played remote mining camps where other players feared to go. Here Lotta Crabtree was received like an angel from heaven by crowds of lonely miners. But savage winters forced the little company down out of the mountains and back to San Francisco. There Crabtree played in the lowly "bit" theatres—

mere cleared areas in the backs of stores. She toured in melodramas, mastered the banjo, performed as a minstrel in burnt cork, danced soft-shoe numbers, and sang, all the while perfecting her roguishly delightful and captivating stage personality. She and her mother made two more strenuous tours of the mining camps before Crabtree finally found a place in the legitimate theatres of San Francisco playing in mixed minstrels. She was then seventeen and was billed as "Miss Lotta, The San Francisco Favorite." She had become an irresistible confection of wicked innocence, flirting her skirts in a walk-around as she sang such show-stoppers as "The Captain with His Whiskers Gave a Sly Wink at Me." In 1864, hailed as "The California Diamond," Lotta Crabtree set out with her parents for New York.

In the summer of 1864, she appeared in a variety program at Niblo's Garden Theatre in New York. The critics praised her versatility and especially her dancing and her banjo playing, but they considered her suitable only for music houses and not for first-class theatres. She played briefly in New York and then began touring smaller cities in the Midwest. Gradually, Crabtree and her mother, who always traveled with her, began to add plays to her repertoire—*Nan the Good for Nothing*, *The Pet of the Petticoats*, *Captain Charlotte*, and *The Seven Sisters*, sometimes called *The Seven Daughters of Satan* (a great spectacle). John Brougham, actor and playwright, saw Crabtree and adapted Charles Dickens's *The Old Curiosity Shop* into *Little Nell and the Marchioness*, first produced at a small theatre in Boston in 1866. Then Crabtree went on a tour of the West and South, news of her triumphs reaching New York. Finally, in the summer of 1867, she was offered Wallack's Theatre on Broadway. For six weeks in the middle of a hot summer Crabtree packed the house. Most popular was *Little Nell and the Marchioness*, in which Crabtree played both poor Little Nell and the ragged, dirty, and comic Marchioness. The next year, again at Wallack's Theatre, Crabtree delighted her audiences with *Firefly*, adapted for her by Edmund Falconer from Ouida's *Under Two Flags*. In 1869 Crabtree made a triumphal visit to San Francisco. Upon her return to the East, she opened in Philadelphia in *Heart's Ease*, a farce by Falconer on the gold-rush days. She toured in this play for two years.

For the next two decades, Crabtree remained a highly popular performer on the American stage. Beginning in 1870 she toured with her own company. Two of her later successes were Fred Marsden's *Zip; or Point Lynd Light*, in which she played the light-keeper's daughter, and *Musette; or Little Bright Eyes*, in which she played a gypsy girl. Crabtree's last popular play was *Pawn Ticket 210* (1887), written for her by David Belasco and Clay M. Greene.

Constance Rourke called Crabtree "the hoyden in a dozen aspects" (*Troupers of the Gold Coast*, pp. 203–204). On stage the actress lifted herself to tables and swung her feet. She wore short skirts, she smoked, she played masculine parts. But all these actions became in her performance indescribably comic, and she made millions.

In her personal life Lotta Crabtree had no close friends, never married, and was devoted to her mother and three brothers, whom she put through the finest schools here and abroad. Her father stopped working after his daughter's rise to fame. His chronic drinking eventually caused his wife to send him to England, where he settled in Cheshire on an allowance of five pounds a week for life, boasting to his neighbors that he had really made a killing in the California gold fields.

In 1892, on her forty-fifth birthday, Lotta Crabtree retired from the stage. She was still at the peak of her popularity and looked not a day over thirty. She and her mother moved to an enormous mansion in the New Jersey countryside that they named "Attol Tryst" (Attol, as Mary Ann Crabtree told visitors without fail, was "Lotta" spelled backwards.) In 1905 Mary Ann Crabtree died, a rich woman in her own right, with more than two million dollars in real estate that she had picked up on her daughter's cross-country travels. Lotta Crabtree then purchased the Brewster Hotel in Boston, which she ran for theatrical people. She spent her later years painting watercolors and mourning the loss of her mother, who she insisted was the greatest woman who had ever lived. In 1915 the city of San Francisco honored Crabtree by declaring a "Lotta Crabtree Day." The streets were roped off for blocks around the towering stone fountain that the actress had presented to her adopted city years before. Crabtree died in Boston at the Brewster Hotel on September 23, 1923. She left a fortune of four million dollars to charity and a reputation as a performer with youthful innocence, even in seductive dances and songs, and as a commedienne of immense popularity.

Constance Rourke's *Troupers of the Gold Coast, or the Rise of Lotta Crabtree* (1928) views Crabtree's career against its historical setting, as a part of the California Gold Rush. *Trouping: How the Show Came to Town* (1973) by Phillip C. Lewis is an insightful study of barnstorming in general and contains an account of Lotta and Mary Ann Crabtree. The most carefully documented and complete account of her life is *The Triumphs and Trials of Lotta Crabtree* (1968) by David Dempsey and Raymond Baldwin. An appreciation of Crabtree by Deshler Welch is included in *Famous American Actors of Today*, Vol. II (1896), edited by Frederic Edward McKay and Charles E. L. Wingate. Another contemporary account of Crabtree appears in J. B. Clapp and E. F. Edgett, *Players of the Present*, Part 1 (1899). See also T. Allston Brown, *History of the American Stage* (1870); George C. D. Odell, *Annals of the New York Stage*, Vols. VIII-XIV (1936–1945), and *Woman's Who's Who of America, 1914–1915* (1915). Diana Serra Carey's book *Hollywood's Children: An Inside Account of the Child Star Era* (1979) is useful for Crabtree's childhood experiences. See also Helen Marie Bates, *Lotta's Last Season* (1940); Edmond M. Gagey, *The San Francisco Stage* (1950); and Claudia D. Johnson, *American Actress, Perspective on the Nineteenth Century* (1984). Crabtree's obituary appeared in the *New York Times* (September 26, 1924). The Harvard Theatre Collection has an extensive collection of pictures, clippings, and other materials. Crabtree is listed in *Notable American Women*, Vol. I (1971); William C. Young, *Famous Actors and Actresses of the American Stage* (1975); *The Oxford Companion to the Theatre* (1983); and *The Oxford Companion to American Theatre* (1984).

Diana Serra Cary

CRAWFORD, Cheryl (September 24, 1902–October 7, 1986): producer and director, was born in Akron, Ohio, the only daughter of Robert K. and Luella Elizabeth (Parker) Crawford, who had three sons following the birth of Cheryl.

No one, Crawford has written, in her "nice, normal Midwestern" family had been involved in theatre (*One Naked Individual*, p. 6). Her father was a successful realtor in the quiet Ohio town at the opening of the century, but both he and his wife, who had studied at the Emerson School of Elocution in Boston, did enjoy amateur dramatics, and Cheryl got involved in these as early as the third grade. At Central High School she performed Lady Macbeth's sleep-walking scene on graduation day.

Her interest in theatre intensified at Smith College, where she worked with Professor Samuel Eliot, who inspired her complete commitment to theatre. She astounded everyone with a production of the Indian drama *Shakuntala*, performed in the garden of Smith's famed President William Alan Neilson. She was then invited to stage a play at the historic Academy of Music of Northampton for the fiftieth anniversary of the college. She spent the summer of 1924 with the Provincetown Players on Cape Cod.

From Smith, despite the objections of her parents, she went to the short-lived theatre school organized by the Theatre Guild. It was with the Theatre Guild that she made her Broadway debut in 1926 as Madame Barrio in *Juarez and Maximilian*; she also served as assistant stage manager for the production and assisted Winifred Lenihan, who was directing for the guild student company. Crawford's efforts to find a position in professional theatre as a stage manager met with the rebuff that women were not suited to management positions; they had to be "actresses or nothing." **Theresa Helburn** of the Theatre Guild, however, gave her a crucial opportunity by making her casting director and general assistant on productions.

At the Theatre Guild she met Harold Clurman and Lee Strasberg, who, while playing minor roles, were dreaming of a new kind of theatre that would be socially conscious and based on a continuing ensemble of actors. Although Crawford was happy at the Guild, she was so enticed by the vision later set down by Clurman in *The Fervent Years* (1945) that she left her position to work with them. With her executive ability and shrewd practical know-how, she moved them from talk to action, founding the Group Theatre in 1931. It was first an offspring of the Theatre Guild and then an independent theatre. Embodying during the days of the Great Depression the idea of theatre as an ensemble and socially conscious art form, it became, ultimately, a legend in world theatre annals.

As one of the three directors of the Group Theatre, Crawford performed in many important capacities. She was responsible for the financial and business operations and organized the summers for rehearsal of new plays and study of the Stanislavsky method. She assisted Lee Strasberg in direction of the Group Theatre's first production, Paul Green's *The House of Connelly* (1931), which she had gotten the Theatre Guild to release to them. She directed Dawn Powell's *Big Night* (1933), Clifford Odets's *Till The Day I Die* (1935), and Nelisse Childs's *Weep for the Virgins* (1935). She worked closely with authors on the preparation of their texts and was responsible for bringing Paul Green and Kurt Weill together for the musical *Johnny Johnson* (1936). Not the least of her hard tasks was keeping her fellow directors, Clurman and Strasberg, functioning and working together. She has described the three directors as a "bizarre trio, two Old Testament prophets and a WASP *shiksa*" (*One Naked Individual*, p. 52). By 1937 she had had enough of the difficulties and tensions of life in the Group Theatre, and she resigned to try her hand at producing on her own. Nevertheless, that hectic but glamorous experiment remained one of the major inspirational experiences of her life.

From 1937, when newspapers talked about her as the "producer in skirts," until 1986, when the *New York Times* called her "illustrious," she was an active force as a producer in the professional theatre, where she helped provide over one hundred shows. In the years immediately following her departure from the Group Theatre, she produced on Broadway, among other shows, *Family Portrait* in 1939, starring **Judith Anderson**. At the Maplewood Theatre, New Jersey (1940–1942), she presented weekly productions with major stars such as **Ethel Barrymore**, **Tallulah Bankhead**, Paul Robeson, Walter Hampden, and **Helen Hayes**. It was here that she did her first production of the Gershwin *Porgy and Bess*, which she then offered in New York in 1942. *One Touch of Venus* (1943) with **Mary Martin** and *The Tempest* (1945) with Vera Zorina and Canada Lee followed.

With **Eva Le Gallienne** and **Margaret Webster** she formed the American Repertory Theatre in 1946, which in that year produced Shakespeare's *Henry VIII*, J. M. Barrie's *What Every Woman Knows*, Henrik Ibsen's *John Gabriel Borkman*, George Bernard Shaw's *Androcles and the Lion*, and in the next year Eva Le Gallienne's adaptation of *Alice in Wonderland* and Sidney Howard's *Yellow Jack*. In the next few years she continued the battle for repertory and nonprofit theatre by doing a number of productions for the American National Theatre and Academy (ANTA), among them Bertolt Brecht's *Galileo* (1947) with Charles Laughton and Henrik Ibsen's *Peer Gynt* (1951) with John Garfield.

Over the years Crawford had been an enthusiastic producer of musicals. Among the most notable were *Brigadoon* (1947), *Flahooley* (1951), *Paint Your Wagon* (1951), *Regina* (1949), *Brecht on Brecht* (1962), and *Celebration* (1969). She was particularly proud of having produced four plays by the great playwright Tennessee Williams, of whom she first became aware when he won a prize in a Group Theatre play contest in 1940. She did *The Rose Tattoo* (1951) with Maureen Stapleton and Eli Wallach, *Camino Real* (1953) with Eli Wallach, *Sweet Bird of Youth* (1959) with **Geraldine Page** and Paul Newman, and *Period of Adjustment* (1960) with James Daley and Barbara Baxley.

In 1947 she joined with her former Group Theatre colleagues Elia Kazan and Robert Lewis, both of whom had directed productions for her, to found the Actors' Studio as an "artistic home" for young actors and actresses. From the beginning the Actors' Studio membership has read like a who's who of American stars. Crawford made many contributions to the studio both as a member of its board of directors and as executive producer of its short-lived Actors' Studio Theatre in 1963 and 1964. In these years she was associated with productions of *Strange Interlude*, *Marathon 33*, *Blues for Mr. Charlie*, and *The Three Sisters*. Among her notable productions in the last twenty years have been *Mother Courage and Her Children* (1963) with **Anne Bancroft**, *Collette* (1970) with **Zoe Caldwell**, *Yentl* (1975), and *Do You Turn Somersaults?* (1978). In 1986 she co-produced Sandra Deer's *So Long on Lonely Street*, the latest entry in her fifty-five years of producing. Cheryl Crawford died on October 7, 1986, from complications following a fall.

Cheryl Crawford received the Antoinette Perry (Tony) Award in 1951 for *The Rose Tattoo*. In 1959 she was named Woman of the Year, and in 1964 she was presented an Achievement Medal from Brandeis University. In 1962 she was given an honorary doctorate from her alma mater, Smith College.

Most of the quotations from Cheryl Crawford included in the essay come from her autobiography, *One Naked Individual: My Fifty Years in the Theatre* (1977). Crawford is mentioned in Harold Clurman's *The Fervent Years* (1945, 1985) and his *All People Are Famous* (1974). Other books which mention her are David Garfield, *A Player's Place: The Story of the Actor's Studio* (1980); Foster Hirsch, *A Method to Their Madness: The History of the Actors' Studio* (1984); and Cindy Adams, *Lee Strasberg* (1980). Crawford's obituary appeared in the *New York Times* on October 8, 1986. Crawford is listed in *Current Biography 1945* (1946); *The Biographical Encyclopaedia and Who's Who of the American Theatre* (1966); *Plays, Players, and Playwrights: An Illustrated History of the Theatre* (1975), ed. Marion Geisinger; *Notable Names in the American Theatre* (1976); *Who's Who in the Theatre* (1977); *The Oxford Companion to the Theatre* (1983); and *The Oxford Companion to American Theatre* (1984).

Helen Krich Chinoy

CREWS, Laura Hope (December 12, 1879–November 13, 1942): director, stage and film actress renowned toward the end of her career for her character parts, was born in San Francisco, the second daughter and youngest child of John Thomas and Angelena (Lockwood) Crews. The theatre was very much a part of Laura Hope Crews's background since her mother was a member of the California Stock Company. In 1884 Laura Crews made her stage debut at the age of five in San Francisco; by the age of six she was touring California in such plays as *Editha's Burglar*. At this point there was a hiatus in her career while she attended school in San José, where her family was then living. In 1898 she returned to the stage, playing ingénues for San Francisco's Alcazar Stock Company.

After moving with her mother to New York in 1900, she joined the Henry V. Donnelly Stock Company, playing a variety of roles until she eventually reached leading lady status. (This early training in stock would serve her well in the 1920s.) By 1904 Laura Crews had her first major success on Broadway, appearing in *Merely Mary Ann*, a performance that brought her to the attention of actor-director Henry Miller, who cast her in his production of *Joseph Entangled* (1905). Thus began a professional relationship that lasted until Miller's death in 1926. Crews would later note that Miller's guidance was the single most valuable learning experience of her career. Her most notable performance with Miller was as Polly Jordan in William Vaughn Moody's *The Great Divide* in 1906, in which she supported Miller and **Margaret Anglin**.

By 1910 Laura Hope Crews was becoming well known both in the United States and in England, having made her London debut in *The Great Divide* (1909). The next ten years saw her alternating between classic and contemporary roles, appearing opposite some of the most illustrious names in both British and American theatre. She played Beatrice in *Much Ado About Nothing* (1913) with John Drew and Mistress Page in *The Merry Wives of Windsor* (1916) opposite Sir Herbert Beerbohm-Tree. She also appeared in *Peter Ibbetson* (1917) with Lionel and John Barrymore.

During the 1920s she was at the zenith of her stage career, acting in New York, on tour, and in stock, as well as branching into directing for a short period of time. Though she appeared in many notable plays during this decade, including Noel Coward's *Hay Fever* (1925) and Luigi Pirandello's *Right You Are If You Think You Are* (1927), her greatest stage triumph came in Sidney Howard's *The Silver Cord* (1926). Playing an obsessive mother whose warped love destroys one of her sons, she gave a performance that was heralded by critics as brilliant.

In 1929 Crews joined the migration of stage performers to Hollywood. Her motive for the trip was not to appear in films herself but to coach such silent stars as Gloria Swanson and Carole Lombard in proper diction for the new "talkies." It was not long, however, before she herself appeared in films; her first, ironically enough, was a silent film titled *Charming Sinners* (1929). In 1933 she re-created her stage role in the screen adaptation of *The Silver Cord*. Unfortunately, Crews's age and appearance were obstacles to film stardom. She was middle-aged, short, and plump: neither movie producers nor audiences were prepared to accept her in starring roles. Hollywood's consensus was that she projected an image best suited to comic character parts. A thoroughly professional Crews gave each role in the over thirty films she made in the 1930s the full benefit of her experience and talent. The result was a gallery of memorable vignettes, among them the raucous Prudence in Greta Garbo's *Camille* (1937); a "refined" madam (explaining the disarray of her house with an ingenuous "We had a party here last night!") in Bette Davis's *The Sisters* (1938); and the bogus, gin-swilling clairvoyant opposite Clark Gable and Norma Shearer in *Idiot's Delight* (1939). As fine as these portrayals were, they seemed to be merely a warm-up for a part in a film that the entire nation was waiting to see: *Gone With the Wind* (1939).

The epic search for the right actress to play Scarlett O'Hara and the public's certainty that Clark Gable was the only choice for Rhett Butler are well documented; a far more obscure fact about the film's casting is that Laura Hope Crews was virtually the only serious candidate for the role of Pittypat Hamilton, Scarlett's fluttery, swooning maiden aunt. Like those of Clark Gable, Vivien Leigh, and many other members of the film's large cast, Crews's characterization transcended a role to become an enduring part of an American folk legend. When *Gone With the Wind* was released, Crews received much public recognition. Returning once again to the New York stage in 1942, she joined the cast of the popular hit *Arsenic and Old Lace* as one of the sweetly homicidal Brewster sisters. While appearing in this play, she contracted a kidney disease and, after a short illness, died in New York's Le Roy Sanitarium.

One of the greatest strengths of both the American theatre and the film industry is an ability to find, develop, and use a special breed of talent known as the character actor. Easily identifiable to audiences by face if not by name, these fine players are able to deliver performances that often become the yardstick by which specific character types will thereafter be gauged. Laura Hope Crews's personification of a flighty, dithery maiden lady illustrates this acting strength.

Information on the life and career of Laura Hope Crews appears in William Pratt, *Scarlett Fever* (1977), a well-researched, beautifully illustrated, and highly enjoyable study of the *Gone With the Wind* phenomenon, covering the years 1926–1976. See also Whitney Stine and Bette Davis, *Mother Goddam* (1974), a thorough, salty profile of the career of Bette Davis. Crews's obituary appeared in the *New York Times* (November 14, 1942). There are entries on Crews in *Current Biography, 1943* (1944); *Notable American Women*, Vol. I (1971); *Who Was Who in the Theatre*, Vol. I (1978); and *The Oxford Companion to American Theatre* (1984).

William Lindesmith

CRISTE, Rita (March 12, 1898–): director, educator, and outstanding figure in creative dramatics and children's theatre in the United States, was the third of seven children born to Mary Ann (Carlin) Criste and John Gilbert Criste, in Allegheny, Pennsylvania, where her father owned a lumber company. Rita Criste attended St. Francis Xavier Catholic grade school but went to Allegheny Public High School for its college preparatory course. She was the first Catholic student in the area to make such a move. She graduated with honors and was awarded a scholarship to the Pennsylvania College for Women (now Chatham College). Criste received her Bachelor of Arts degree in 1920 and began teaching high school classes in math, Latin, English, and physical education at a rural school. After two years she moved to a high school in Pittsburgh where, in addition to teaching French and math, she was assigned to direct and produce the annual student play. Up to this time her total theatre experience had been a college course titled "Oral Expression" and several roles in high school and college productions. Directing the high school play rekindled her interest in drama, and after school hours she became actively involved with the Pittsburgh Repertory Company.

Even though she had nearly completed a master's degree in French, Criste applied for and received a Carnegie-Mellon grant to spend two summers at Northwestern University in Evanston, Illinois, to study drama. The summer of 1930 was her first formal introduction to creative dramatics. **Winifred Ward**, the pioneer of creative drama in the United States and professor of theatre at Northwestern, returned to the campus in the fall to find a new graduate student with theatre and teaching experience. Criste had decided to stay in Evanston and complete a degree in drama.

Criste had not foreseen a career of working with children in creative dramatics, but the philosophy of the program coincided with her own teaching beliefs.

Though she never had a formal course in eduation, she was interested in educational theory and the art of teaching. She posed questions, formulated answers, tested her ideas with children, and carefully analyzed her teaching.

In addition to her graduate studies at Northwestern, Criste began teaching creative drama under Winifred Ward's supervision in Evanston's District 65 elementary and junior high schools. In the fall of 1931 she joined the faculty of the Evanston public schools to teach drama to seventh and eighth grade students. In 1940 she received her master's degree in drama from Northwestern. She continued teaching in Evanston schools as well as working on the staff of the Children's Theatre of Evanston.

Criste's career in creative drama took a significant leap forward in 1950 with the retirement of Winifred Ward. Since Rita Criste had worked closely with Ward at Northwestern while a graduate student there and was a member of the staff at the Children's Theatre of Evanston as well as a drama teacher in the Evanston schools, she was Ward's logical successor on the Northwestern University theatre faculty. At Northwestern Criste taught classes in creative dramatics, children's theatre, and interpretation of children's literature. Proof of her effectiveness as a university professor is the large number of her students who became leaders of child drama programs throughout the country.

The 1950s were important years in the growth and development of television, and Rita Criste's drama program in Evanston was featured on national and educational television. In 1958 Dave Garraway's *Wide, Wide World* included a six-minute segment on children's theatre in a special called *American Theatre '58*. The Evanston Children's Theatre shared the spotlight with theatrical figures like Helen Hayes, Peter Ustinov, and William Inge. The Evanston segment included a presentation on the Children's Theatre and several minutes from two creative drama sessions. Though the most publicized, this was not Criste's only venture into television. In 1960 she was involved in an educational television series produced for airborne television, MPATI (Midwest Program on Airborne Television Instruction). The series was titled *All That I Am* and was broadcast live within a 150-mile radius of Chicago. It was later seen on forty-five educational television stations across the country. Criste was the master teacher for sixteen sessions, using first and second grade students; the programs were shown in weekly thirty-minute segments. In 1962 the film *Creative Drama: The First Steps* was released. Co-authored by Criste and Ward, the film featured Criste demonstrating the developmental process of creative drama, using twelve fourth-graders from the Evanston schools.

The decade of the 1960s also included much activity and progress at the Children's Theatre of Evanston. An educational, nonprofit organization, the Children's Theatre of Evanston offered six plays per year, three to children prekindergarten to third grade and three to children in grades four through eight. In addition to providing quality education and entertainment, the theatre offered children an opportunity to experience theatre as active participants. The students acted, made costumes, designed and painted scenery, and performed most of the backstage duties during the productions. This total involvement in theatre was an appropriate culmination to the carefully developed creative dramatics programs and the exposure to theatre the children had experienced in the Evanston schools.

While involved with the activities at the Children's Theatre and teaching at the university, Criste remained as supervisor of drama teachers for District 65 of the Evanston Public Schools. As supervisor, she coordinated a staff of fourteen full-time and three part-time trained creative drama teachers for nineteen elementary and junior high schools. Combining this in-school experience with the opportunities offered at the Children's Theatre, children growing up in Evanston during this period had a unique opportunity for complete involvement in theatre arts.

In 1965 Criste retired as director of the Children's Theatre of Evanston, supervisor of drama for the District 65 schools, and assistant professor at Northwestern. Shortly after retiring she moved to Omaha, Nebraska, and became active in the Omaha Community Playhouse. She also found more time for her international travel, which took her to the Orient as well as Europe and included attendance at several international children's theatre festivals. Through all of this she arranged time to teach creative drama to children and senior citizens and to conduct classes for teachers in Kentucky, Tennessee, and Nebraska. In 1981 she did a television series for children entitled *Strawberry Square* and sponsored by the Nebraska Department of Education.

The Children's Theatre Association of America honored this brilliant, dedicated woman in 1979 for a lifetime of outstanding work in the field by conferring on her the Creative Drama for Human Awareness Award. Arizona State University has instituted the Rita Criste Scholarship for Graduate Study in Child Drama. Criste now lives in Richmond, Virginia.

Rita Criste did not write about her work, and important as she has been in the field of children's theatre, very little has been written about her. Newspaper articles and records of her work are housed in the Special Collections Library at Arizona State University in Tempe as part of the Children's Theatre Association of America Archives. Included in the collection of materials is a taped interview with Criste conducted by Lin Wright in January 1981. Also included are films showing Criste working with children.

Lin Wright and
Cheryl L. Starr

CROTHERS, Rachel (December 12, 1870?–July 5, 1958): director, actress, and successful playwright, best known for her feminist viewpoint prior to the women's movement of the 1960s, was the youngest of three children and the second daughter of two physicians, Dr. Eli Kirk Crothers and Dr. Marie (de Pew) Crothers. Her mother, who studied medicine after the age of forty, became the first woman physician in central Illinois. Born in Bloomington, Illinois, Rachel Crothers came from an affluent, professional family with strong traditional midwestern conservative religious beliefs. At the age of thirteen, with May Fitzwilliam, a childhood friend, she wrote *Every Cloud Has a Silver Lining; or, The Ruined Merchant*, a play in which all five characters were played by Rachel and May. Crothers continued to write short plays for the Bloomington Dramatic Society for several years.

After graduation in 1891 from Illinois State Normal School in Normal, Illinois, she went to Boston and studied at the New England School of Dramatic Instruction, graduating in February 1892. Between 1897 and 1902 she was at the Stanhope-Wheatcroft School of Acting (New York), first as a pupil and later as an instructor. While at Wheatcroft her early one-act plays, *A Water Color*, *Elizabeth*, *Mrs. John Hobbs*, and *Which Way*, were performed by students. The first of her plays to be professionally produced was *The Rector*, which opened at the Madison Square Theatre, New York, on April 3, 1902.

Crothers's professional writing career lasted over thirty-seven years and included approximately thirty-eight plays, twenty-three of which were full-length. She was well versed in most aspects of production. She could write, direct, and act, and she could also design sets, costumes, and props. Crothers acted professionally for several years, working with E. H. Sothern's Company and later with the Lyceum Stock Company. She directed *Myself Bettina* at the encouragement of **Maxine Elliott**, who played the lead. The play opened at the Chicago Powers Theatre in January 1908 and later went to New York. With *A Little Journey*, which opened at the Little Theatre, New York, on December 26, 1918, Crothers began directing professionally and supervising the staging of all her plays. During her later years, she developed a partnership with John Golden, who produced all of her works. She rarely directed the plays of other writers; in fact, her productions of John Kirkpatrick's *The Book of Charm* (1925) and Zoë Akins's *Thou Desperate Pilot* (1927) were failures.

Throughout her career Crothers wrote nearly a play a year, many of them Broadway successes. Her early melodramatic one-acts, often classified as problem plays, were eventually replaced by comedies of manners with sentimental endings. She used a strong heroine as protagonist because she felt women were "more dramatic than men, more changing . . . because of their evolution . . . the most important thing in modern life" (*Boston Evening Transcript*, February 13, 1912). Crothers explored the problems and conflicts affecting women because of their increased education, professional careers, and financial independence. She also explored the effects of divorce. Crothers' career was long; she continued propounding her feminist viewpoint for several decades. Her characters not only demonstrated a given woman's changing attitudes over a period of time but also examined the attitudes in women of different generations. Although she described the psychological and sociological nature of feminist concerns, she insisted she was writing plays for entertainment and disclaimed any conscious effort to chronicle women's causes or evaluate sex roles (*New York Times Magazine*, May 4, 1941).

Crothers's plays written between 1899 and 1914 depicted a heroine in her mid-thirties who is often experienced and successful, who may, by choice, lose her man to a more traditional woman. These heroines aided other women in breaking away from traditional roles. They were often strong, spirited writers or artists and were frequently economically independent. In her early plays women were portrayed with sympathy; they often suffered the consequences of society's restraints. Rhy MacChesney in *Three of Us* (1906) is an independent woman who, although she believes a woman's honor is not determined by a man, ends by marrying so that her younger delinquent brother will have the advantages of a male as head of the house. Bettina Marshall in *Myself Bettina* (1908) challenges the concept that marriage restores a woman's honor. In *A Man's World* (1910) a successful writer rearing a motherless illegitimate child discovers that the man she loves is the child's father and rejects him for his callous behavior. *He and She*, produced in Boston as *The Herfords* in 1912 and revived in 1920 with Crothers playing the lead, is considered one of her better early plays. Ann Herford and Ruth Creel question the inherent inferiority of a woman's role in marriage. Ann, who has won a sculpturing commission that her husband also attempted, decides to give up the commission, not for her husband, but because her daughter needs a mother. Ruth, on the other hand, chooses her career rather than the man who is courting her. In *Ourselves* (1913) Beatrice Barrington, a rich society woman, determined to reform a prostitute, learns the importance of self-help rather than patronage.

Crothers's plays written between 1914 and 1918 follow the format of sentimental drama with women in more conventional roles. In *Young Wisdom* (1914) a situation set up to be a trial marriage turns into a conventional wedding. *Old Lady 31* (1916) offers a sentimental treatment of an elderly couple who enter a nursing home for women because they cannot afford to maintain their own home. The women welcome Abe as a member, but strife ensues and he flees. When he returns he finds the stock he thought worthless is now valuable, and the couple no longer have financial worries.

Many of Crothers's plays written in the 1920s use a comic mode with occasional irony and satire, but they demonstrate the growing conservatism of her feminist viewpoint. Crothers's characters become more ambivalent about women's progress, illustrating some of the difficulties of stepping out of the traditional roles. The New Woman, concerned with self-fulfillment and personal liberty, is seen as a product of a flawed society rather than superior to it. In *Nice People* (1921) Teddy Gloucester, a rich young society woman, becomes embroiled in a scandal and redeems herself by going to the country where she learns the values of hard work and clean living. *Mary the Third* (1923) offers a look at marriage from three generations within the same family. By 1929 a sense of disillusionment pervaded Crothers's heroines in the plays *Let Us Be Gay* (1929), *As Husbands Go* (1931), and *When Ladies Meet* (1932). In her most important work, *Susan and God* (1937), starring Gertrude Lawrence, Susan Trexel is a meddling, bored wife who turns to a new religious cult and alienates others in her attempt to reform them.

Crothers spent five years in Hollywood writing adaptations of her plays: *Old Lady 31*, *Nice People*, *When Ladies Meet*, *As Husbands Go*, *Mother Carey's Chickens*, and *Susan and God*. She retired from active writing in 1937 and moved to Redding, Connecticut. Her later works include *Bill Comes Back* (written in 1945 but never produced), *My South Window* (written in 1950 but withdrawn from production because she felt it was inappropriate because of the outbreak of the Korean War), and *We Happy Few* (written in 1955 but not produced). Rachel Crothers died in her sleep at Danbury, Connecticut, on July 5, 1958.

Crothers was praised for her deft characterizations, skillfully constructed plots, and clever, though occasionally overly sentimental, dialogue. Burns Mantle referred to her as America's first "lady" dramatist (*Contemporary American Playwrights*, p. 105). Brooks Atkinson considered her one of the theatre's most sagacious women, one who had a profound understanding both of the fundamentals of human nature and of the theatre (*New York Times*, October 8, 1937). Crothers paid little attention to criticism. She believed the public was the real critic and the theatre should move people through feelings, not cerebral exercises ("The Construction of a Play," *The Art of Playwriting*, p. 117). Although active in war relief in the teens and poverty relief during the Great Depression, she was never a part of the drama of commitment during the 1930s. Her plays remained apolitical comedies set in a society world. Feminists sometimes attacked her plays, but Crothers responded that she had earned the right to satirize the women's movement and claimed she was laughing with, not at, the feminists, especially the more militant feminists (*New York Sun*, January 4, 1914).

Although she maintained a very private life, Crothers worked with many of the important figures of her time. Her plays were produced by Walter N. Lawrence, Maxine Elliott, the Shuberts, Sam H. Harris, Mary Kirkpatrick, and John Golden. Actors who worked with her included Carlotta Nillson, Maxine Elliott, Chauncey Olcott, **Tallulah Bankhead**, **Katharine Cornell**, Francine Larrimore, Gertrude Lawrence, and **Ethel Barrymore**. Jo Mielziner designed the scenery for *Susan and God* before creating his famous designs for *A Streetcar Named Desire* and *Death of a Salesman* in the 1940s.

During Crothers's life she received many honors. Ida Tarbell included her in the list of "50 Foremost Women in the U.S." (1930). She received the Megrue Prize for *When Ladies Meet* (1933) and the Theatre Club's gold cup for *Susan and God* (1937). The Town Hall Club, which she helped establish in 1920, honored her in 1937. She was awarded the Chi Omega National Achievement Award in 1939. She was a member of the Society of American Dramatists and the Authors' League of America. She was a founder of P.E.N. and an organizer and first president of the Stage Women's War Relief Fund (1918). She belonged to Actor's Theatre (1924) and the Stage Relief Fund (1932), which she organized with John Golden. She was the founder and president of the American Theatre Wing War Service, Inc. (1940), which operated the Stage Door Canteen (1942) and of which she remained executive head until 1950. By reason of her extraordinary output of plays, her all-encompassing involvement in theatre, and the force of her personality, Crothers is remembered as one of the most notable of women in the American theatre.

Crothers's nondramatic writings include several discussions on playwriting: "The Construction of a Play," *The Art of Playwriting* (1928); "The Producing Playwright," *The*

Theatre Magazine (January 1918); and "Troubles of a Playwright," *Harper's Bazaar* (January 1911). She demonstrated her appreciation of the director in "The Future of the American Stage Depends on Directors," *New York Times Magazine* (December 3, 1916). Manuscript collections of significance include three volumes compiled by Irving Abrahamson that are available on microfilm from the University of Chicago Library. The Museum of the City of New York Theatre Collection contains clippings, reviews, and Mrs. Anthony D. Hoagland's bequest of Crothers's memorabilia; included in this collection are several articles by Crothers on her craft and *The Box in the Attic*, a fragment of Crothers's autobiography. Collections at the New York Public Library Performing Arts Research Center at Lincoln Center include the Billy Rose Theatre Collection, which contains some typescripts with significant revisions; the Robinson Locke Scrapbooks, with documents on the first two decades of Crothers's career; and the general Theatre Collection, which includes some photographs. The Library of the American Academy of Arts and Letters, New York City, contains correspondence. Collections of interest in Illinois include the Crothers Scrapbook in Special Collections, Illinois State University Library, Normal, Illinois, and the Crothers file in the Withers Public Library and Information Center, Bloomington, Illinois, which contains clippings from the *Bloomington Daily Pantagraph* from 1893–1958. Secondary sources offering insight into Crothers' career as well as production lists and publication information include Arthur H. Quinn's *A History of the American Drama from the Civil War to the Present Day*, II (1936); "Rachel Crothers, Pacemaker for American Social Comedy," *Theatre Arts Monthly* (December 1932); *McGraw Hill Encyclopedia of World Drama*, Vol. I (1972); and Henry James Forman's "The Story of Rachel Crothers," *Pictorial Review* (June 1931). Eleanor Flexner's *American Playwrights: 1918–1938, The Theatre Retreats from Reality* (1969) offers an analysis of Crothers's plays. Ada Patterson's "Woman Must Live Out Her Destiny," *The Theatre Magazine* (May 1910), offers early insight into Crothers's attitude toward the feminist movement. Marguerite Mooers Marshall's "What Do Women Think of Other Women?"(*New York World* 1915) and "How Far Does a Girl Go Nowadays" (undated reprint of an interview in the *New York World*) can both be found in the Crothers Scrapbook, Special Collections, Illinois State University Library. Charlotte Hughes's "Women Players," *New York Times Magazine* (May 5, 1941), interviews Crothers at the end of her writing career. Contemporary feminist criticism includes Lois C. Gottlieb's *Rachel Crothers* (1979) and two other Gottlieb articles: "Obstacles to Feminism in the Early Plays of Rachel Crothers," *University of Michigan Papers in Women's Studies* (June 1975) and "Looking to Women: Rachel Crothers and the Feminist Heroine," *Women in American Theatre* (1981), ed. Helen Krich Chinoy and Linda Walsh Jenkins. Irving I. Abrahamson's "The Career of Rachel Crothers in the American Theater" (Unpublished Ph.D. dissertation, University of Chicago, 1956) and Sharon P. Friedman's "Feminist Concern in the World of Four Twentieth-Century American Women Dramatists: Susan Glaspell, Rachel Crothers, Lillian Hellman, and Lorraine Hansberry" (Unpublished Ph.D. dissertation, New York University, 1977) trace Crothers' work. J. P. Wearing, *American and British Theatrical Biography* (1979), contains a bibliography. Crothers is listed in *Twentieth Century Authors* (1955); *The Oxford Companion to American Literature* (1965); *The Concise Encyclopedia of Modern Drama* (1964); *Who's Who of American Women 1964–1965* (1964); *American Literature* (1969); *Contemporary American Authors* (1970); *Contemporary American Literature* (1974); *A Concise Encyclopedia of Theatre* (1974); *Encyclopedia of World Literature in the Twentieth Century* (1975); *Notable Names in the American Theatre* (1976); *American Women Writers* (1979–

1980); *Dictionary of American Biography*, Vol. VI (1980); *Dictionary of Literary Biography: Twentieth-Century American Dramatists*, Vol. VII (1981); *The Oxford Companion to the Theatre* (1983); and *The Oxford Companion to American Theatre* (1984). Alternate birth dates of 1871 and more frequently 1878 are given in the various sources. The 1870 date appears in the 1880 U.S. Census and is also given on her death certificate provided by the Connecticut State Department of Health.

Liz Fugate

CUSHMAN, Charlotte Saunders (July 23, 1816–February 18, 1876): actress, singer, and manager, introduced a more natural, intuitive style to the nineteenth-century stage and became famous in America and London for her "breeches" parts (men's roles), particularly that of Shakespeare's Romeo. She was born to middle-class parents in Boston. Her mother, Mary Eliza Babbitt, was probably the greatest influence on her daughter, endowing her with a love of music and singing. Mary Eliza Babbitt had married a widower, Elkanah Cushman, a Boston merchant, in 1815. Their daughter was born a year later. There were three more children: Charles (born 1818), Susan (born 1822), and Augustus (born 1825). Augustus died in a riding accident in 1834; the father died in 1841. But the surviving mother, brother, and sister were an integral part of Cushman's life and career for many years.

Cushman spent her youth at a dreary primary or "dame" school in Boston, followed by a rigid grammar school. By 1825 the family fortunes began to fail, causing a series of moves into less expensive lodgings. Her mother took more and more responsibility for the family, and her father's influence dwindled. Augustus Babbitt, an uncle thirteen years her senior, frequently took her to plays and encouraged her studies in music and theatre. It was in his company that she first saw the English actor William Charles Macready, who was to have an influence on her later career.

To bolster the family fortunes, her mother took over the management of a boardinghouse. In 1829 Cushman, as the eldest child, determined to rescue her family from their fallen fortunes by capitalizing on her talents. She obtained a job as contralto singer at Second Church, where the young Ralph Waldo Emerson was the junior pastor. Though only fourteen at the time, she was already five feet six inches tall and physically mature. She attracted the attention of Robert D. Shepherd, a friend of her father. Shepherd became her patron and arranged with John Paddon, the finest voice teacher in Boston, for a three-year apprenticeship. The agreement was canceled when Cushman went to New York with some family friends for a two-week visit that turned into a three-month stay.

In New York Cushman was fortunate enough to sing duets with Mary Ann Wood and to impress Wood's coach, James G. Maeder, who took on the training of the young Cushman. Maeder married the English actress/singer **Clara Fisher** in 1834, and Fisher's ideas of singing and acting gave Cushman insights that helped her with the growth of her own talent. During this time Cushman was being courted by an old friend, Charles Wiggins, and a new suitor, Charles

Spalding, to whom she may have become engaged. However, her chief interest at this time was in the development of her career and the care of her family. Later she wrote that no one who was an actress should ever marry, and indeed, she never did.

Cushman made a successful operatic debut on April 8, 1835, with the Maeders. She continued to sing through the summer and fall and went with the Maeders to New Orleans in October. Cushman had a range of almost two full registers (a full contralto and almost a full soprano), but the low voice was the natural one. When they went to New Orleans, Clara Maeder, who was a contralto, sang the contralto roles, and the soprano roles were assigned to Cushman. The strain on her voice, coupled with the change of climate, was too much; the high notes failed her, and she was left with a weakened and limited contralto range. In despair, Cushman went to the manager of the theatre who told her that she should become an actress. Tragedian James Barton took on her training and prevailed upon her to appear as Lady Macbeth opposite him on April 23, 1836. Despite her fears and borrowed costumes, she scored a tremendous success and was launched on a new career.

New York attracted the confident Cushman, who wrote to the manager of the Park Theatre to offer her services. The manager suggested that she give him a chance to watch her perform. Insulted by this response, Cushman accepted a three-year contract at the Bowery Theatre and went there with a trunk full of costumes that were not paid for. Disaster struck when the theatre burned down, destroying both her costumes and her hopes. Finally, she was offered a five-week contract in Albany, where she opened in *Macbeth* with Junius Brutus Booth. The engagement was a great success, with a new play every night, ending with *Romeo and Juliet*. The tall, strong, square-jawed Cushman played a number of "breeches" parts, including Hamlet and Romeo. Romeo was to become the most popular of the nearly forty breeches roles she played from 1835 to 1861.

The next important milestone in Cushman's career was her first performance as Meg Merrilies, the gypsy fortuneteller, in an adaptation of Sir Walter Scott's novel *Guy Mannering* on May 8, 1837. She appeared dressed in rags with gray hair, wrinkled skin, and demented eyes. This new interpretation of the role was favorably recalled by critics throughout her career. Cushman continued to perform in New York and Philadelphia and even managed the Walnut Street Theatre in Philadelphia for a year. In the fall of 1843 she appeared in *Macbeth* at Philadelphia's Chestnut Street Theatre with William Charles Macready. The English actor was impressed with her potential, realized her lack of training and experience, and suggested that she go to England. On October 6, 1844, Cushman set sail for England. After several frustrating months, she made her London debut at the Princess's Theatre on February 13, 1845, as Bianca in Henry Milman's *Fazio*, followed by an engagement with Edwin Forrest. Her brother Charles joined her in April and her mother and sister Susan, also an actress, in July.

Cushman went on a tour of the provinces; then she and Susan Cushman were offered the opportunity to perform *Romeo and Juliet* at the Haymarket Theatre with Charlotte Cushman as Romeo opposite her sister as Juliet. They opened on December 29, 1845, and London went wild. The originally scheduled eight performances were extended to eighty. The newspaper reviews were uniformly complimentary about Cushman's masculine appearance and her performance as Romeo. Capitalizing on their tremendous London success, the sisters performed *Ion*. The play was also well received, but most theatregoers preferred Cushman as the passionate Romeo to the effete Ion. In the spring she went to Dublin and then on tour in England. In October 1847 she appeared again as Lady Macbeth and Queen Katherine (*Henry VIII*) opposite Macready.

When Charlotte Cushman returned to America in 1849, after this five-year sojourn in England, she was a star. She again toured the South, where her acting career had begun. In 1850 she made another journey to England, the first of many such returns to the scene of her greatest success. In 1852, tired and sick, she made a series of farewell appearances and retired to Rome. The retirement was a short one, however, for she returned to London to play Romeo again at the Haymarket, ten years after her original English triumph. This time Cushman, who was thirty-nine and looked it, was not so successful in the role. Her return to America in 1857 featured her first appearance as Cardinal Wolsey in *Henry VIII*, one of the more interesting of her breeches roles.

By now breast cancer had become her constant enemy, and Cushman kept retiring and returning to her home in Rome. However, she needed money for her family and activity for her own peace of mind, so she kept going back to the stage. She came home to America when her mother died in 1860; on this trip (in 1861) she played Hamlet in costumes borrowed from Edwin Booth.

During the last years of her life, Cushman, unable to perform on stage, turned to readings of her favorite plays. She was able to sit and read, captivating her audience with her portrayal of all the characters in the plays. An emotional farewell performance at Booth's Theatre, New York, on November 7, 1874, was climaxed by a tumultuous ovation. Vowing that she would kill herself rather than die of cancer, the indomitable Charlotte Cushman finally gave in to her illness and died of pneumonia on February 18, 1876, in Boston. She was buried in Mount Auburn Cemetery, where other theatre personalities, including Edwin Booth, are also buried. In 1907 a Charlotte Cushman Club was established in Philadelphia, in a house containing theatrical memorabilia from her career.

Cushman's acting style was very much influenced by William Charles Macready. She broke with the stilted, chanting style for tragedy then in vogue. She was intense and more natural in delivery because she was more intuitive than trained in technique. She was not the first woman to play breeches parts, but she was certainly one of the most successful. Many who saw her Romeo in London proclaimed her the best Romeo they had ever seen. Charlotte Cushman's strong stage presence was due to her intellect, her moral strength, and her personal magnetism. William Winter, a great fan of Cushman's, said of her, "The greatness of Charlotte Cushman . . . was that of an exceptional because grand and striking personality, combined with extraordinary power to embody the highest ideals of majesty, pathos, and appalling anguish. She was not a great actress merely; she was a great woman'' (*New York Tribune*, February 19, 1876).

The papers of Charlotte Cushman in the Manuscript Division of the Library of Congress provide a valuable source of information and include the memoirs written by Emma Crow Cushman, the wife of Edwin Charles Cushman, Susan Cuchman Merriman's son who was adopted by Charlotte Cushman. The Library of Congress Manuscript Division also contains scrapbooks, photographs, a number of letters addressed to Cushman, and other clippings and similar materials. The most complete and accurate biography of Cushman is *Bright Particular Star: The Life and Times of Charlotte Cushman* by Joseph Leach (1970). Leach incorporates material from the papers as well as from earlier biographies: *Charlotte Cushman* by Clara Ershine Clement (1882); *A Life of Charlotte Cushman* by William Thompson Price (1894); and *Charlotte Cushman: Her Letters and Memories of Life*, edited by Emma Stebbins (1878). These early biographies tend to be incomplete and uncritical, particularly that of Stebbins, Cushman's close companion. Even the collection of Cushman's papers contains only favorable reviews. Other works that refer to Cushman's acting are Laurence Barrett's *Charlotte Cushman, A Lecture* (1889) and a number of works by William Winter, including *The Wallet of Time* (1913), *Other Days* (1908), and *Shakespeare on the Stage*, 2nd Series (1915), which tend to praise her rather uncritically. See also Francis Courtney Wemyss, *Twenty-Six Years in the Life of an Actor and Manager* (1847); T. Allston Brown, *History of the American Stage* (1870); James E. Murdoch, *The Stage* (1880); and Henry Austin Clapp, *Reminiscences of a Dramatic Critic* (1902). Cushman's obituary by William Winter appeared in the *New York Tribune* (February 19, 1876). She is listed in *Dictionary of American Biography*, Vol. I (1904, reprinted 1968); *Who Was Who in America: Historical Volume, 1607–1896* (1963); *The Oxford Companion to American Literature* (1965); *Notable American Women*, Vol. I (1971); William C. Young, *Famous Actors and Actresses of the American Stage* (1975); *The Oxford Companion to the Theatre* (1983); and *The Oxford Companion to American Theatre* (1984).

Susan S. Cole

— D —

DALRYMPLE, Jean (September 2, 1910–): producer, writer, and publicist, was born in Morristown, New Jersey, the only child of George Hull and Elizabeth Van Kirk (Collins) Dalrymple. When Jean Dalrymple was fifteen months old, her mother died, leaving her to reside with her father and grandmother. After her father married Madeline Ross, the daughter of a wealthy Morristown real estate family, Jean spent the next few years moving between her father's homes in Morristown, Philadelphia, and Newark, New Jersey, and her grandmother's home in Morristown. During this time she discovered her talent for writing. Although her formal education ended with grammar school, Dalrymple regularly submitted prize-winning stories and essays to newspapers and magazines. She also devoted herself to writing stories for William S. Hart, the star of many film westerns, and some years later he actually bought one for fifty dollars. Although they never met, the two corresponded for many years.

Dalrymple's father and stepmother eventually moved the family to New York (her father and stepmother had two children, Madge Groves and Ogden), and at sixteen Dalrymple went to work for a Wall Street firm where she found almost immediate success in the financial world. However, she soon left her job on Wall Street to perform in a touring one-act vaudeville play, *Just A Pal*, which she co-authored with Dan Jarrett. With Jarrett and producer Max Tishman, she developed a number of vaudeville skits for such soon-to-be stars as Cary Grant and James Cagney. During this time she completed a successful screen test for Fox Studios; however, instead of accepting the contract offer, she continued touring with the very popular *Just A Pal*.

From 1929 to 1933 Dalrymple worked for producer and director John Golden as a play doctor, general understudy, casting director, and press representative. During this time she married Ward Morehouse (March 30, 1932), the "Broadway

After Dark'' columnist for the *New York Sun*. Although her marriage did not succeed (the divorce decree is dated August 4, 1934), her professional career continued to thrive. From 1937 to 1944 she was a free-lance publicist and concert manager as well as the personal manager of concert and theatre personalities. In 1940 she became the publicity director for the American Theatre Wing.

Dalrymple began her long and successful association with the Broadway stage in 1943 as publicity director for two of the season's biggest hits, *One Touch of Venus* (Imperial Theatre, October 7, 1943) and *The Voice of the Turtle* (Morosco Theatre, December 9, 1943). During the same year she offered to assist Mayor Fiorello LaGuardia in his effort to develop a performing arts center in New York. When the New York City Center of Music and Drama became a reality in 1943, Dalrymple was appointed director of public relations and member of the board of directors. Since the inception of City Center, Dalrymple has been a guiding force in the development and growth of the project. With her new responsibilities she still found time to present a number of Broadway shows: *Hope for the Best* (Fulton, February 7, 1945), *Brighten the Corner* (Lyceum, December 12, 1945), a successful revival of *Burlesque* (Belasco, December 12, 1946), and *Red Gloves* (Mansfield, December 4, 1948). In 1951 she handled the public relations for various productions sent by the United States Department of State to the Berlin Arts Festival in West Germany. While traveling to promote the productions Dalrymple married her second husband, Major General (then Colonel) Phillip de Witt Ginder (November 1, 1951). That same year she produced the *ANTA Album* at the Ziegfeld Theatre in New York City.

Dalrymple became director of the New York City Center Theatre Company in 1953 and in November and December of that year produced a series of plays with José Ferrer: *Cyrano de Bergerac*, *The Shrike*, *Richard III*, and *Charley's Aunt*. Her assignment as director of the Theatre Company did not stifle her other activities for City Center. In 1954–1955 she was producer and press representative for a number of successful productions, such as *What Every Woman Knows*, *The Fourposter*, *The Time of Your Life*, and the Brattle Shakespeare Players' productions of *Othello* and *Henry IV, Part I*. Despite an ever busier schedule, Dalrymple found time to co-author *The Feathered Fauna* with Charles Robinson (produced at the **Margo Jones** Theater in Dallas, Texas, in 1955 and the Elitch Gardens Theatre in Denver in 1957.) At City Center in 1956 she demonstrated her ability to produce successfully a wide range of theatrical fare that included the Orson Welles production of *King Lear* (by arrangement with Martin Gabel and Henry Margolis), a program of pantomime with Marcel Marceau, and revivals of *A Streetcar Named Desire*, *The Teahouse of the August Moon*, *The Glass Menagerie*, and *Mister Roberts*.

In 1957 Dalrymple added still another distinction to her ever growing list of accomplishments at the New York City Center when she became the director of the organization's Light Opera Company. For this company she produced *The Beggar's Opera*, *Brigadoon* (which moved to the Adelphi Theatre), *The Merry Widow*, *South Pacific*, *The Pajama Game*, and *Carousel*. During this time (1957–

1958) the urge to write struck again, and the result was *The Quiet Room* (produced at Wyndham's in London, March 30, 1958, as well as in Austria and Australia). In 1958 Dalrymple coordinated the United States's performing arts presentations at the World's Fair in Brussels, Belgium. Among the many productions arranged there by Dalrymple were the world première of Gian-Carlo Menotti's opera *Maria Golovin*, New York City Center musicals *Wonderful Town* and *Carousel*, and the play *The Time of Your Life* (which she also directed). The musical portion of these events earned a gold medal as the finest presentation at the World's Fair.

In 1959 Dalrymple ventured into the world of television as producer-director of the WNTA Play of the Week series, for which she produced *The Cherry Orchard* and *Crime of Passion*. For the NBC Producer's Showcase she produced *Reunion in Vienna*. In 1960 Dalrymple became the executive director for Paramount's International Telemeter Company (pay television), where she produced Menotti's *The Consul* and administered the Fourth Street Theatre's production of *Hedda Gabler* and the first live television broadcast of a Broadway show, *Show Girl*, from the Eugene O'Neill Theatre.

During the 1960s Dalrymple continued to produce for the New York City Center, most notably *The Servant of Two Masters* by the Piccolo Teatro di Milano (February 23, 1960, in association with Jerry Hoffman) and a Frank Loesser festival in 1966. One of the festival's productions, *Guys and Dolls*, was presented at the White House, Washington, D.C. (March 18, 1967). This was the second of two Dalrymple productions to be seen at the White House; six months earlier (September 14, 1966) she had presented *Moments From Great American Musicals*. In addition to her regular duties at City Center, Dalrymple served as producer and publicist for the center's American Playwright's Series in 1966 and 1967. She produced excerpts from *Fiorello!* for the Governor's Conference Dinner at the White House (Washington, D.C., February 29, 1968) and that same year produced City Center's twenty-fifth anniversary Christmas musical, *Carnival* (December 12, 1968). In 1969 Dalrymple demonstrated that her producing acumen extended beyond musicals and comedies. As executive director of the American National Theatre and Academy, she brought to the ANTA Theatre in New York three productions of the American Conservatory Theatre of San Francisco (*Tiny Alice*, *A Flea in Her Ear*, and *The Three Sisters*), the *Henry V* of the American Shakespeare Festival Theatre of Stratford (Connecticut), *Our Town* from the Plumstead Playhouse of Long Island, and *No Place To Be Somebody* from the New York Shakespeare Festival Public Theatre. During the same year the indefatigable Dalrymple produced *Salute to Alan J. Lerner* for the American Academy of Dramatic Arts and *American Musical Highlights* at the Governor's Mansion in Albany, New York. Her eclectic theatrical taste was evident again in the 1970 season at the ANTA Theater, where these diverse companies performed: National Theatre of the Deaf (*Sganerelle* and *Songs from Milk Wood*), the Playwrights Unit (*Watercolor* and *Criss Crossing*), the La Mama Experimental Theatre Club (*Gloria and Esperanza*), the Phoenix Theatre Company (*The Cherry Orchard*), and the Trinity Square Repertory Company of Providence, Rhode Island (*Wilson in the Promised Land*).

In 1972 Dalrymple co-produced *The Web and The Rock* with her long-time friend **Cheryl Crawford** at the Theatre de Lys (March 19, 1972). From 1972 to 1974 Dalrymple produced the **Agnes de Mille** Heritage Dance Theatre, and in 1974 she co-produced (with Leonard Schlosburg) *Naomi Court* at the Manhattan Theatre Club (May 29, 1974). She presented Agnes de Mille's *Conversations About the Dance* (1974–1975), and in 1978 she produced *The Origin of Species* (Westport, Connecticut, and Shreveport, Louisiana).

Never one to rest on her past achievements, Dalrymple is now president of the Light Opera Company of Manhattan and can be seen regularly on cable television in New York as creator and moderator of the American Theatre Wing seminars. The many awards she has received include an honorary doctoral degree in fine arts from Wheaton College (Illinois, 1959), numerous citations from New York City, the Spirit of Achievement Award from the Albert Einstein College of Medicine (Yeshiva University), the annual "Brava" of the New York Newspaper Women's Club, and the Colonel Jacob Ruppert Award for the City Center productions. Additionally, the Outer Circle critics have cited New York City Center Light Opera Company three times, and for her participation in the Brussels World's Fair she was decorated by the Belgian government as Knight, Order of the Crown. Not surprisingly, Dalrymple has been a member of numerous arts advisory councils such as the Opera Musical Theatre and Theatre panels and the National Council on the Arts at the National Endowment for the Arts, North Carolina School of the Arts (advisory board), Museum of the City of New York (Friends of the Theatre and Music Collection), John F. Kennedy Memorial Cultural Center (charter member of the national advisory council), and the Office of Cultural Affairs (New York City, advisory committee).

Jean Dalrymple's books include her autobiography, *September Child* (1963) and *From the Last Row* (1975), an account of her involvement with the New York City Center of Music and Drama. She has also written *Jean Dalrymple's Pinafore Farm Book* (1971) and *The Folklore and Facts of Natural Nutrition* (with Fay Lavan, 1973). Newspaper and magazine articles about Dalrymple include several in the *New York Times* (July 10, 1956, May 19, 1957, October 5, 1963, September 12, 1968, August 31, 1969, and December 10, 1974); C. Powers, "City Center's Talent Tracker," *Theatre Arts* (February 1956); and "Interesting Women," *McCall's* (March 1969). Bill Smith, *Vaudevillians* (1976), contains an interview with Dalrymple about her career as a vaudeville performer. Additional information may be found in *Current Biography, 1953* (1953); *Notable Names in the American Theatre* (1976); *Who's Who in the Theatre* (1981); *The Oxford Companion to American Theatre* (1984), and *Who's Who of American Women, 1985–1986* (1985).

Harvey Rovine

DAVENPORT, Fanny Lily Gypsy (April 10, 1850–September 26, 1898): actress and theatre manager, was the eldest of nine children born to Edward Loomis Davenport and Fanny Elizabeth Vining in London in 1850. Seven of the nine children survived infancy and all made careers in the theatre. Her father, known as E. L. Davenport, was an American actor who had gone to London in 1847 with **Anna Cora Mowatt** and had enjoyed such success that he was encouraged to stay behind in London when Mowatt returned to America. Davenport married the English actress Fanny Vining and remained in London for seven years, returning to America in 1854. The family settled in Boston, and Fanny Davenport went to school there. Her interest in theatre was all-encompassing, however. In a letter to a friend, she described her first appearance on stage at the age of eight waving a flag while her father's acting company sang "The Star Spangled Banner," at the Howard Athenaeum, Boston, on July 4, 1858. Until the age of fourteen, she performed with her parents in Boston and New York, notably as the young King Charles II of Spain in *Faint Heart Never Won Fair Lady* on February 14, 1862, at Niblo's Garden Theatre in New York.

Davenport soon had opportunities to appear without her parents, and she accepted an offer to play the soubrette roles in the stock company at the Louisville (Kentucky) Theatre in 1864. Her first part was Carline in the musical production *The Black Crook*, and she was a success from then on. From Louisville she went to Philadelphia's Arch Street Theatre, under the management of **Mrs. John Drew**. While performing there she was seen and hired by Augustin Daly, who had recently taken over the management of the Fifth Avenue Theatre in New York. Davenport opened there as Lady Gay Spanker in *London Assurance* by Dion Boucicault on September 19, 1869, with her father playing Sir Harcourt Courtly. The role was a success for Davenport. The critic for the *New York Sun* wrote on March 20, 1877, of the revival of *London Assurance*, "As for Miss Davenport, she is apparently one of the few actresses intended by nature, no less than by art, to play the part of Lady Gay. She is always at her best when she is effusive and rompish. As a hoydenish, impetuous, illogical beauty of this, or any other period, she has no equal in the adjacent ranks of her profession."

During the nine years in which Davenport was leading lady with Daly's company she acted in revivals, new plays, and Shakespeare. In addition to her success as Lady Gay Spanker she triumphed as Lady Teazle in Richard Brinsley Sheridan's *The School for Scandal*. According to Montrose Moses, "Miss Davenport's presence was well adapted to such roles; powerfully but well built, she added to her grace a marked beauty of feature" (*Famous Actor Families in America*, p. 253). Davenport also appeared as Nancy Sykes in *Oliver Twist* and as Madge, the haggish tramp in *Charity*. Her versatility and dramatic power induced Daly to write *Pique*, in which Davenport created the role of Mabel Renfrew. It opened at the new Fifth Avenue Theatre on December 14, 1876, and ran for 238 consecutive performances. During the next season, Daly's last as manager of the Fifth Avenue, Davenport's chief success was as Rosalind in Shakespeare's *As You Like It*. John Rankin Towse wrote that "Fanny Davenport was a lovely Rosalind to the eye, was spirited, arch, gallant and coquettish" (*Sixty Years of the Theatre*, p. 133).

Davenport's success enabled her to take her own company on tour for a few years, during which she continued to act an extensive and varied repertoire.

Then in 1882 she played a brief season in London and elsewhere. Her principal role was Mabel Renfrew in *Pique*, which played under the title of *Only a Woman* with no great success.

The year 1883 marked a significant turning point in Davenport's career. At this time Sarah Bernhardt was appearing in Paris in Victorien Sardou's play *Fedora*, but no American actress had obtained the rights to the play. Davenport managed to obtain the rights and opened the play in New York in 1883. It was an instantaneous success. For five years she performed *Fedora* almost exclusively with only occasional appearances in other plays in her repertoire. According to Jay Benton, Davenport's "impersonation was no imitation of the French actress; it was a forceable, distinct conception of the part. As such it met with approbation from critics, and praise from audiences" (*Famous Actors of Today*, p. 115).

In 1887 Davenport obtained the rights to Sardou's *La Tosca*, which Bernhardt had been playing successfully in France. As *Tosca* the play opened at the Broadway Theatre on March 3, 1888. She followed this with *Cleopatra*, the third of Sardou's plays performed by Bernhardt for which Davenport obtained the American rights. After months of preparation for the elaborate production, *Cleopatra* opened on December 23, 1890, at the Fifth Avenue Theatre. A week later, January 2, 1891, the theatre burned, destroying all of the elaborate scenery and most of the costumes. Davenport and her company were booked to appear in Boston three weeks later, and she was determined to meet the contract. In three weeks the elaborate spectacle was reconstructed, and *Cleopatra* opened on January 27, 1891, at the Hollis Street Theatre in Boston.

Gismonda, which opened in 1894, was the fourth and last of the Sardou/Bernhardt productions performed by Davenport. She reportedly paid Sardou $25,000 for the script; it was an elaborate scenic production and continued to be included in Davenport's repertoire until her death. The roles in Sardou's plays were more serious and emotionally involving than many of Davenport's earlier roles. Arthur Low, in his article in *Poet Lore*, said her Gismonda "was an able, graphic performance; picturesque, of an alluring charm and technical proficiency!" (*Poet Lore*, May-June 1918, p. 359).

After thirteen years devoted almost exclusively to productions of Sardou's melodramas, Davenport attempted a romantic drama about Joan of Arc, *Soldier of Fortune* by Frances Aymar Mathews. It was an unfortunate choice. The public refused to accept the buxom Fanny as Joan, and the production was a failure. She then attempted to revive the Sardou plays to salvage the 1897–1898 season. Her last performance was in *Cleopatra* during an engagement at the Grand Opera House in Chicago. In March 1898 she was forced by illness to close the season. She retired to her summer home in South Duxbury, Massachusetts, and died there of a heart ailment on September 26, 1898, at the age of forty-eight. She was buried in Forest Hills Cemetery, Boston.

Davenport was married twice, first to Edwin H. Price on July 30, 1879. Price was a supporting actor in her company and later became her business manager. They were divorced in 1888. On May 19, 1888, less than a year later, Davenport married her leading man, William Melbourne MacDowell. They purchased the summer home in South Duxbury and named it Melbourne Hall. Davenport died a wealthy woman, despite the failure of *Soldier of Fortune*; she left her estate to her husband.

William Winter described the young Fanny Davenport in *Vagrant Memories* as "a voluptuous beauty, radiant with youth and health, taut and trim of figure, having regular features, a fair complexion, golden hair, sparkling hazel eyes, and a voice as naturally musical and cheery as the fresh, incessant rippling flow of a summer brook" (p. 229). In her mature years, she was well suited to strong, emotional characters such as those of Gismonda, Cleopatra, and Tosca. According to Benton, "the varying phases of Sardou's Tuscan heroine seem almost as if created expressly for her. In the soft, languorous moments, in her cooing petulance, in the rage of jealousy, in her pleading fondness, in her terrible struggles, in the carrying out of her horrible revenge of Scarpia she was always excellent, and oftentimes great" (pp. 117–118).

Davenport was an outstanding and successful actress and manager, who presented new plays to America as well as elaborate productions of old plays. A shrewd businesswoman, she was not afraid to try unusual and demanding roles. The *New York Dramatic Mirror* of April 18, 1879, reviewing a revival of *Pique*, described the success of Fanny Davenport thus: "Of all the actresses now before the public, there is scarcely one presenting such manifold claims to popular attention as does Fanny Davenport. A woman of radiant presence, inheriting her father's great histrionic gifts, and fulfilling the promise given by all of the Davenport family, with restless industry and ambition and the most boundless versatility, she unites all the qualifications of a great star."

Biographical material on Fanny Davenport can be found in *Famous Actors of Today*, edited by Frederick E. McKay and Charles E. L. Wingate (1896), and Amy Leslie, *Personal Sketches* (1906). See also "The Daring Davenport," *Greenbook Magazine* (March 1913), and "Some Childish Memories," *Lippincott's Magazine* (October 1888). Supplementary material appears in George C. D. Odell, *Annals of the New York Stage*, Vols. VI-XV (1931–1949); James Rankin Towse, *Sixty Years of the Theatre* (1916); and Arthur Row, "Great Moments in Great Acting," *Poet Lore* (May-June 1918). Davenport's obituary appeared in the *New York Times* on September 27, 1898. There are clippings and a scrapbook kept by Melbourne MacDowell in the New York Public Library Performing Arts Research Center at Lincoln Center. Short biographies of Davenport appear in Thomas Allston Brown, *History of the American Stage* (1870); *Dictionary of American Biography*, Vol. III (1930–1931); *Who Was Who in America*, Historical Volume 1607–1896 (1966); *Notable American Women*, Vol. I (1971); William C. Young, *Famous Actors and Actresses on the American Stage*, Vol. I (1975); *The Oxford Companion to the Theatre* (1983); and *The Oxford Companion to American Theatre* (1984).

                                                                                            Susan S. Cole

DAVENPORT, Millia Crotty (March 20, 1895–): costume designer and writer, best known for her definitive and pioneering work in the history of costume, was born in Cambridge, Massachusetts, in very comfortable circumstances. Davenport was one of three children; her sister became Jane Joreleman Detomasti, and her brother, Charles Benedict Davenport, died in 1917. Their parents were marine biologists and writers. Her father, Charles Benedict Davenport, notable for his writing on marine biology, was the director of the Station for Experimental Evolution at Cold Spring Harbor, Long Island, New York. Davenport's mother, Gertrude (Crotty) Davenport, was also a biologist and assisted her husband with much of his work and the writing of his books.

When she was fifteen, Millia Davenport went to Paris for a year of study at the Cours au Daasir. She returned to the United States and graduated in 1913 from Huntington High School in New York. She attended Barnard College from 1913 to 1915, Teacher's College of Columbia University from 1915 to 1916, and the New York School of Fine and Applied Arts (Parsons School) from 1917 to 1918. In 1918 she agreed to teach for a year at Parsons. In 1916 she married Arthur Moss, and in 1922 she married Walter L. Fleisher. Both marriages ended in divorce.

Early in her life Davenport decided that she wanted to be around interesting people and the theatre. Little did she realize that the beginning of what was to be an exciting first career in theatre would be at a 1918 party attended by Blanding Sloane, Peter Larsen, and Michael Carmichael Carr (Edward Gordon Craig's first assistant in Florence, Italy). These three and Davenport formed a company that they called the Wits and Fingers Studio for Theatrical Design. Davenport stayed with the group until 1923, designing both sets and costumes.

A trip to Provincetown, where she had gone to visit a friend who was doing costumes for the Provincetown Playhouse, occasioned the next step in her career. While Davenport was there, the friend was injured, and in the true spirit of theatre, Davenport picked up the work to get the show finished. Her abilities as both a designer and a craftswoman were quickly noticed, and she designed for both the Provincetown Playhouse and the Greenwich Village Players throughout the 1920s. Most notably she designed with Robert Edmond Jones at Greenwich Village Theatre *Love for Love* (1925), *The Last Night of Don Juan* (1926), and *The Pilgrimage* (1926). Once recognized, her talent was in demand, particularly on Broadway. One of her important Broadway triumphs was *The Shoemaker's Holiday* (1938) for the Mercury Theatre. The costumes for that production were described by designer Howard Bay as being among the best ever worn on the Broadway stage. Other successes included *Love for Love* (1940), again with Robert Edmond Jones, and *Journey to Jerusalem* (1940). So versatile were her abilities in costume that she not only designed but was under contract at Brooks-Van Horne costume house to do costume construction.

In 1938 she entered into the marriage that was to last the rest of her life. Her husband, Edward E. Harkavy, was a physician and psychiatrist. She now had time to think seriously about the need for a comprehensive reference book on costume design. She began designing less and less, to allow time for research. Originally planned as a "Dictionary of Costume" in one volume, with chart outlines of the development of dress by civilization and century, the book became a survey of European and American dress and styles with a large number of illustrations. World War II made it difficult to obtain the illustrations she wanted for the book. However, Davenport used the time to read more source books and enlarged her original concept about the publication. Thus was born *The Book of Costume* (1948). Containing three thousand illustrations, with details on the source of each illustration and about the history surrounding the people who wore the clothing, the book continues to be the definitive work on the subject. One review of the book said that it used "small colorful details to bring into focus the large outlines of artistic and social history" (*Antique*, February 1949, p. 141). It became the first all-inclusive source of costume plates from original sources. First published in 1948, *The Book of Costume* has never been out of print. Scholars and other researchers have found it valuable, not only because of the plates themselves, but also because of the additional facts Davenport supplies to each plate. The book is a basic reference in the field of costuming for the stage. Upon completion of this work, Davenport, then in her early fifties, withdrew more completely to the private life that she had always cherished. She had done what she wanted to do. Occasionally she would make a public appearance or give a lecture. She could often be found attending a meeting, such as those of the Costume Society of America or the United States Institute of Theatre Technology. In 1981 she was awarded an honorary doctorate from the New School for Social Research and the Parsons School. Though the scholarly work upon which her fame rests was completed in 1948, it remains a unique and important contribution to the theatre in America.

Some of Millia Davenport's personal papers and correspondence are in the private collection of Don Stowell, Tallahassee, Florida. Swatched pencil sketches from some of the Provincetown and Mercury Theatre productions can be found in the Billy Rose Collection of the New York Public Library Performing Arts Research Center at Lincoln Center. A brief biography listing some of the plays designed by Davenport may be found in *Notable Names in the American Theatre* (1976). Reviews of *The Book of Costume* (1948) may be found in the *New York Times* (January 16, 1949), the *San Francisco Chronicle* (January 19, 1949), *Time* (January 10, 1949), and *Antique* (February 1949), as well as other papers and magazines of the period. Some information for this essay was supplied by Don Stowell. Davenport is listed in *The Biographical Encyclopaedia and Who's Who of the American Theatre* (1966), *The Author's and Writer's Who's Who* (1971), and *Notable Names in the American Theatre* (1976).

Mari W. DeCuir

DEAN, Julia (July 22, 1830–March 6, 1868): actress, most famous on the West Coast, came from a theatrical family and received some of her early training in the midwestern circuit of theatres established by her grandfather, actor-manager Samuel Drake. Julia Dean was born in Pleasant Valley, New Jersey, to Edwin Dean and Julia (Drake) Dean, who were also actors. Her mother died when Julia was two years old; her father remarried in 1832 and left his daughter to be raised by his Quaker parents. When Julia Dean was eleven, her father took her from her grandparents and brought her to his home to help her stepmother run the family boardinghouse. Shortly after this move Julia Dean began to appear in small parts with Noah Ludlow's theatre company in the Midwest. During the 1844–1845 season she performed in Mobile, Alabama, as a utility actress. Working with her was a young Joseph Jefferson III, who at that time was also a utility actor, receiving six dollars a week.

In his autobiography Jefferson wrote of Dean with affection and recounted the circumstances that led to her rise from utility actress to leading lady. When the actress who was to play in *Wives as They Were and Maids as They Are* fainted and was unable to go on, the prompter suggested Julia Dean. Years later Jefferson vividly remembered Dean's entrance as Lady Priory: "The gentle eyes are raised, so full of innocence and truth and now she speaks. Who ever thought that Julia harbored such a voice—so low, so sweet, and yet so audible! It sinks deep into the hearts of all who listen. They are spellbound by her beauty, and as she gives the lines with warm and honest power a murmur of delight runs through the house, and from that moment our lovely friend is famous" (*Autobiography*, pp. 147–148).

Dean made her New York debut as Julia in Sheridan Knowles's *The Hunchback* on May 18, 1846, at the Bowery Theatre. She became one of the most popular of young actresses, and the role of Julia one of her most famous. The *New York Herald* (May 18, 1846) reported the popular enthusiasm for Dean, who was still two months short of sixteen: "Gifted by nature with a fine figure—a beautiful and expressive face—a voice of great sweetness and considerable power, the hand of time is alone needed to make her, certainly, one of the greatest and most popular of actresses." Julia in *The Hunchback* remained one of Dean's principal roles. Laurence Hutton considered her to be perfect in the part: "Her light, graceful figure, and beautiful face won for her all the sympathy and interest in the first act that her genius and fire enable her to maintain until the fall of the curtain" (*Plays and Players*, p. 142). Dean followed her success in *The Hunchback* with leading roles in *The Lady of Lyons*, *The Wife*, *The Stranger*, *Romeo and Juliet*, *Pizarro*, *Jane Shore*, *Fazio*, and *Love's Sacrifice*. Her Juliet was considered by many critics to be the best of her time. Several years later she was engaged to perform at a theatre managed briefly by Joseph Jefferson in Charleston, South Carolina. Jefferson wrote of her at that time that she had turned from a "tall, lanky" girl of sixteen into "the graceful figure of a charming woman" (*Autobiography*, p. 149).

In 1855 Dean married Dr. Arthur Hayne, son of Robert Hayne, a senator from South Carolina. Soon there was a separation attended with much public gossip and scandal. As a result, Dean lost her public support. Disheartened and puzzled, she made plans to retire from the stage, but she then accepted an offer to appear in starring roles from her repertoire in San Francisco. She opened at the Metropolitan Theatre on June 23, 1856, and she was an overnight success despite her tarnished reputation. She was adored on the West Coast and played a record thirty nights at the Metropolitan. She performed in many places in California, from Sacramento to the mining camps. She traveled as far north as

Victoria, British Columbia, where she appeared on stage with the very young David Belasco. Dewitt Bodeen claimed that "every man was at her feet—from the coarse Sierra miner to the gilded youth of San Francisco. For almost ten years, she was the star of the West" (*Ladies of the Footlights*, p. 65).

In 1865 Dean left San Francisco on a tour by stage coach with an entire company to Salt Lake City. She opened in *Camille* and was such a hit that she and her leading man, George B. Waldron, were hired to stay the season. The rest of the company, bereft of their stars, set up an opposing theatre; but this competition had no effect on Dean's popularity, and she stayed until June 1866, playing an extensive repertoire of classic and modern plays.

She was finally divorced from Hayne in 1866, and decided to return to New York. But her earlier brilliance seemed to have diminished. Even Hutton, who had admired her so much, wrote, "She was no longer . . . the Julia of the past, but a Julia of the present. . . . We could not but think she had changed her nature with her name" (*Plays and Players*, p. 144). In 1866 or 1867 Dean married James G. Cooper and made her last appearance on stage in October 1867. George C. D. Odell recorded that she was "no longer the radiant star of earlier years, but the saddened woman and rather coarsened artist, whose later work her former admirers deplored" (*Annals of the New York Stage*, Vol. VI, p. 162). She died on March 6, 1868, in New York City, and was buried in Port Jervis, New York.

Dean was a leading actress in America from early youth and was highly regarded for her natural style in such roles as Julia (*The Hunchback*), Juliet (*Romeo and Juliet*), Pauline (*Lady of Lyons*), and Beatrice (*Much Ado about Nothing*). She also originated the roles of Norma (*The Priestess*) and Leonor (*Leonor de Guzman*). William Winter summed up Dean's accomplishments in *Brief Chronicles*: "In person, Julia Dean was tall, stately, graceful, and interesting. Her voice was sweetly plaintive, the soft and gentle expression of her countenance harmonized with her voice, and both fitly expressed a delicate, sensitive, refined, affectionate nature. As an actress, while she always manifested a quick imagination and gave a sense of power, she was not successful in delineating gentle phases of character and emotion and the milder aspects of human experience. . . . Whatever she did was earnestly done. Her soul was in her art, and she neither did nor suffered anything to degrade it" (pp. 75–76).

The information about Dean is scant and scattered. George C. D. Odell's *Annals of the New York Stage*, Vols. V-VIII (1931–1936) documents her New York appearances, especially her performances as Julia in *The Hunchback*. Commentary on her acting is contained in Laurence Hutton's *Plays and Players* (1875) and William Winter's *Brief Chronicles* (1889). Joseph Jefferson's *Autobiography* (1897) relates the times that Dean and Jefferson worked together. The major source of biographical material is Dewitt Bodeen's chapter on Dean in *Ladies of the Footlights* (1937). There are scattered references to her in Noah M. Ludlow, *Dramatic Life as I Found It* (1880), and in William Winter, *The Life of David Belasco* (1918). For an account of her California career, see Walter M. Leman, *Memories of an Old Actor* (1886), and Edmond M. Gagey, *The San Francisco Stage: A History* (1950). For her Salt Lake City season, see George D. Pyper, *The Romance of an Old Playhouse* (1828). Julia Dean's obituary appeared in the *New*

York Times (March 17, 1868). There are numerous clippings about Dean in the theatre collections of Harvard University, the Boston Public Library, and the New York Public Library Performing Arts Research Center at Lincoln Center. Biographies of Dean appear in Thomas Allston Brown, *History of the American Stage* (1870); *Dictionary of American Biography*, Vol. III (1930–1931); *Who Was Who in America*, Historical Volume 1607–1896 (1963); *Notable American Women*, Vol. I (1971); William C. Young, *Famous Actors and Actresses on the American Stage*, Vol. I (1975); and *The Oxford Companion to the Theatre* (1983).

Susan S. Cole

DEE, Ruby (October 27, 1924–): actress and social activist, was born in Cleveland, Ohio, as Ruby Ann Wallace. Her parents were Marshall and Emma (Benson) Wallace. Her father was a railroad porter and her mother a public school teacher. When she was still a child, Ruby Dee and her family, which included two sisters and a brother, moved to Harlem in New York City. There she attended Public School 119. In the evenings, under their mother's leadership, the family would read and recite great works of poetry and literature.

Even in her early years Dee was determined to be an actress. At Hunter High School and then at Hunter College in New York City, she pursued her interest in the theatre. While in college she worked as an apprentice at the American Negro Theatre on West 135th Street. The American Negro Theatre was at that time the home of young, talented black actors like Harry Belafonte and Sydney Poitier. Dee helped in the box office, worked as a stagehand, and appeared in minor roles. After graduating from Hunter College in 1945 with a Bachelor of Arts degree in Romance languages, she began to put more effort into her acting career. Eventually she studied with Morris Carnovsky (1958–1960) and at the Actors Workshop with Paul Mann and Lloyd Richards. In February 1946, however, she had already appeared on Broadway in *Jeb* by Robert Ardrey. The play's run was a brief nine performances. Still, Dee's reviews were good. Most important, the play brought her together with actor Ossie Davis, who would later become her husband. In June 1946 she took over the title role in the all-black Broadway production of *Anna Lucasta*. Ossie Davis was also in the cast. A nationwide tour ended in California, where the notices were so good that there was talk of a movie version of the play. Indeed a movie of *Anna Lucasta* was made; however, it featured an all-white cast. On December 9, 1948, Ruby Dee and Ossie Davis were married. They have been professional and creative partners ever since. In an interview Dee said of their relationship, "Our creative vision is the cement in our lives" (*Parade*, December 6, 1981). The couple have had three children: Guy, Nora, and LaVerne.

Dee's reputation increased when she appeared as Ruth in **Lorraine Hansberry**'s award-winning *A Raisin in the Sun*, which opened to universal acclaim at the Ethel Barrymore Theatre, New York, on March 11, 1959. During the run of *A Raisin in the Sun*, husband and wife again appeared together when Ossie Davis briefly replaced Sydney Poitier, who had Hollywood obligations. Next

Dee appeared with Davis in the Broadway production of *Purlie Victorious*, a satire on racial segregation in the South, written by Davis. It opened at the Cort Theatre on November 28, 1961, and ran for 261 performances. A film version titled *Gone Are the Days*, again featuring Davis and Dee, was released in 1963. After it failed at the box office, it was released under the original title, *Purlie Victorious*.

Dee's film career began in 1950 when she played opposite the renowned baseball player in the movie entitled *The Jackie Robinson Story*. That same year she was featured in the film *No Way Out*. A series of movie appearances followed: *Tall Target* (1951), *Go Man Go!* (1954), *Edge of the City* (1957), *St. Louis Blues* (1958), *Take a Giant Step* (1959), *Virgin Island* (1960), *A Raisin in the Sun* (1961), *Gone Are the Days* (1963), *The Incident* (1967), and *Uptight* (1968). For *Uptight*, Dee not only acted but also collaborated on the film script, which was adapted from the novel *The Informer* by Liam O'Flaherty. In 1972 she starred with Harry Belafonte and Sydney Poitier in the film *Buck and the Preacher*. In 1975 she was in *Countdown at Kusini*.

Dee's profound interest in the classics led her in 1965 to the American Shakespeare Festival in Stratford, Connecticut. There she became the first black actress to appear with the company in major roles when she portrayed Katherina in *The Taming of the Shrew* and Cordelia in *King Lear*. The following year her classical repertoire expanded when she played Cassandra in Aeschylus' *Agamemnon* and Iris in Aristophanes's *The Birds* at the Greek Theatre in Ypsilanti, Michigan. Nine years later, in June 1975, as part of the New York Shakespeare Festival, she played Gertrude to Sam Waterston's Hamlet at the Delacorte Theatre in Central Park.

One of her finest theatrical achievements came earlier when she was featured opposite James Earl Jones in Athol Fugard's South African drama *Boesman and Lena*. The play opened at the Circle in the Square Theatre on June 22, 1970. Clive Barnes wrote in the *New York Times*, "Ruby Dee as Lena is giving one of the finest performances I have ever seen" (June 23, 1970). Of this character Dee once said, "I understand Lena. I relate to her particular reality because it is mine and every black woman's" (*New York Times*, July 12, 1970). She received both a *Village Voice* Off-Broadway (Obie) Award and a Drama Desk Award for her memorable portrayal of Lena. Two years later she again received accolades for her portrayal of Julia Augustine in **Alice Childress**'s play *Wedding Band*, a powerful drama of interracial love. Dee had first played the role in December 1966 at the Lydia Mendelssohn Theatre in Ann Arbor, Michigan. In October 1972 she effectively re-created the part of Julia on the stage of Joseph Papp's Public Theatre in New York.

Ruby Dee has made numerous appearances on both television and radio. In 1955 she was featured on the radio program *This is Nora Drake*. In 1960 she appeared on the television show *Actors Choice* and in a WNTA Play of the Week titled *Seven Times Monday*. During the 1960s and 1970s Dee made several guest appearances on different television specials. In 1974 she and her husband did a program called *The Ossie Davis and Ruby Dee Story Hour* on the National Black

Network. More recently, she appeared in the ABC mini-series *Roots II*. In February 1981, Dee and Davis began a thirteen-week series on PBS aptly titled *With Ossie and Ruby*. The show featured a variety of guest artists and attempted to explore black contributions to popular culture. It has been rerun several times since its initial airing.

In addition to her long and active theatrical career, Ruby Dee has dealt with political issues. In her early years she spoke out in defense of Julius and Ethel Rosenberg. Because of their support of radical social issues, Dee and Davis were blacklisted during the McCarthy era of the 1950s. But this criticism has not deterred them from fighting injustice. Dee has been active in a variety of organizations, including the NAACP, CORE, the Christian Leadership Conference, and the Negro American Labor Council. During the turbulent sixties she was active in raising money for the legal defense of civil rights workers. She also held benefits for the Black Panthers and has worked to combat drug abuse.

Neither her activism nor her artistry has gone unnoticed or unrewarded. In 1970 she and Davis received the Frederick Douglas Award from the Urban League for bringing "a sense of fervor and pride to countless millions." Operation PUSH awarded Dee its Martin Luther King, Jr., Award in 1972. In 1975 Actor's Equity Awarded Ruby Dee and Ossie Davis the Paul Robeson Citation for their "outstanding creative contributions in the performing arts and society at large." At the 1980 Audelco Awards they received the Board of Directors Award for their forty years of creative and political activity. In 1988, the same year in which Ruby Dee played on Broadway in Ron Milner's *Checkmates*, she was inducted into Broadway's Hall of Fame for all-time great performers.

Ruby Dee and her husband have remained constantly active and committed. In the 1970s and 1980s they toured colleges and institutions with shows that emphasized the power and beauty of black culture. With all three children grown and active in various careers, Dee continues to work on her own and with her colleague and husband on a variety of creative ventures and social issues.

Ruby Dee has written an anthology of poetry titled *Glow Child* (1972) and an unpublished play, *Take It from the Top* (1979). Reviews and articles about Dee can be found in *The New Yorker* (April 8, 1961), the *New Republic* (July 25, 1970), the *New York Sunday News Magazine* (June 1, 1961, and July 19, 1970), the *New York Post* (April 13, 1961, and July 25, 1970), *Ebony* (December 9, 1979), *Good Housekeeping* (April 1981), *Parade* (December 1981), and the *New York Times* (June 23, 1970; July 12, 1970; March 2, 1980; October 9, 1980; November 17, 1980; and February 13, 1981). See also Elton C. Fax, *Contemporary Black Leaders* (1970). Dee is listed in *The Biographical Encyclopaedia and Who's Who of American Theatre* (1966); *Notable Names in the American Theatre* (1976); *Who's Who in the Theatre* (1981); and *Contemporary Theatre, Film, and Television*, Vol. I (1984).

                                                                                              Harry Elam

DE MILLE, Agnes (1905?–): dancer, choreographer, and pioneer in modern dance, was one of the first women to choreograph Broadway musicals, most notably *Oklahoma!*, *Carousel*, and *Brigadoon*. Agnes de Mille was born in New

York City to William de Mille, a film producer, and Anna (George) de Mille, the daughter of Henry George, the famous American economist. When Agnes was nine years old, her family moved to Hollywood where her uncle, Cecil B. de Mille, was a motion picture director. Agnes de Mille graduated cum laude with a degree in English from the University of California, Los Angeles. Not until after graduation did she seriously consider dance as a career. She began to study with Theodore Koslov and then with Marie Rambert, who told her, "You are a dancer only from the ankles down—five inches—not enough!" (*Speak to Me, Dance with Me*, p. 52). Nevertheless, de Mille persisted. She studied further with Antony Tudor and Tamara Karasavina and became a proficient ballet dancer, although she seemed from the outset of her career most interested in creating character sketches, which many considered to be "choreographic acting."

In 1925 her parents divorced, and she and her sister Margaret and her mother moved back to New York City. De Mille's first New York performance was in MacKlin Marrow's production of Mozart's *La Finta Giardiniera* in 1927. One of her first concerts as a choreographer was at the Guild Theatre in 1928, where she presented themes that were forerunners of those she would develop in future years, particularly in the famous *Rodeo*. A piece that caught the flavor of the free-spirited West was an American dance called *'49*. Other productions were *Hymn*, choreographed to Bach's *Jesu, Joy of Man's Desiring*, and *Harvest Reel*, a piece with the flavor of folk dances. She also displayed a keenly developed sense of comedy in such solo sketches as *Ballet Class* and *Stage Fright*. In 1929 de Mille had her first professional success as a theatrical choreographer when she was hired to stage the dances for the Hoboken revival of the melodrama *The Black Crook*. Originally produced in 1866, *The Black Crook* is often regarded as a forerunner of musical comedy, although the dance sequences tended to be mostly ornamental. As the musical comedy form developed over the years, dance, song, and dialogue tended to remain separate units. De Mille's prime contribution to musical theatre would be the use of dance to communicate, to convey information too elusive for words, or to explore depths of character.

In 1934 de Mille returned to Hollywood at the request of Cecil B. de Mille to participate in the dance sequences of his elaborate production of *Cleopatra*. De Mille was to have performed an Egyptian dance on a platform built on the back of a bull. She withdrew from the film, however, after differences arose concerning the interpretation, execution, and filming of the dances. A series of disappointments were to follow, including her involvement with the Leslie Howard-Norma Shearer film version of *Romeo and Juliet* (1937), where her filmed dances ended up on the cutting-room floor. The next year she presented a dance concert at the Hollywood Bowl. It consisted of a series of folk dances and a re-creation of *Harvest Reel*, all works with an American flavor. She would later say of her use of these themes, "I have never consciously tried to create 'American' ballets; but, after all, I am American and the native characteristics must come through in all that I do" (*Dancemagazine*, April 1965).

De Mille spent the 1937–1938 season in England where she helped form a ballet troupe called Dance Theatre in Oxford and also choreographed the Cole Porter hit *The Nymph Errant*, which starred Gertrude Lawrence.

Returning to New York, de Mille staged the dances for Leslie Howard's *Hamlet* (1936) and the Ed Wynn musical comedy *Hooray for What?* (1937). She also staged the dances for *Swingin' the Dream* (1939), a jazz version of *A Midsummer Night's Dream*. In 1939 she joined the staff of a new dance company in New York, Ballet Theatre (now known as American Ballet Theatre). As both choreographer and performer with the company, she had the opportunity to create and direct her own dances. During her first season with this company, she choreographed *Black Ritual*, the first ballet of a classic American ballet company to be danced by all black dancers. She then established a company of her own and began a national tour. One of the hits of the tour was a morality play, *Three Virgins and a Devil*. De Mille not only choreographed the piece but also danced the lead role.

In 1941 the famous Ballet Russe de Monte Carlo toured the United States. Serge Ivanovitch Denham, who headed the tour, wanted to include an American dance choreographed by an American. He asked de Mille if she had such a dance. Remembering a cowboy dance sequence that she had created in London, she devised a scenario for *Rodeo*, insisting that Aaron Copland compose the music for the dance. *Rodeo* was presented on October 16, 1942, at the Metropolitan Opera House with de Mille dancing the role of the cowgirl. She had had to teach the classically trained dancers of the Ballet Russe to walk and act like American cowboys, but the dance was a great success, receiving twenty-two curtain calls from the shouting and applauding audience. In *Rodeo*, de Mille achieved a new dimension somewhere between literal movement and choreographic stylization. By taking the simple aspects of ordinary life, then developing and stylizing the gestures, de Mille established her reputation as an innovator in dance. As the dance critic John Martin said of *Rodeo*, "In nothing she has previously done has Miss de Mille exhibited so much pure choreographic skill and resourcefulness" (*Current Biography, 1943*, p. 167).

Rodeo was a foreshadowing of greater things to come. Her choreographic approach in *Oklahoma!* launched the modern era of Broadway musical theatre. De Mille's choreography for the Richard Rodgers/Oscar Hammerstein II musical *Oklahoma!*, produced by the Theatre Guild on March 31, 1943, at the St. James Theatre, ended an era of dance as divertissement having little or nothing to do with plot. The most revolutionary dance aspect was the dream ballet depicting a pleasant daydream that turns into a nightmare when the hero instead of the villain is killed. The dance probed into the characters' hidden thoughts, adding to the dimensionality of the plot. Another de Mille innovation was the device of juxtaposing dancers as dream counterparts to the actual characters, a technique much used since that time. Other dances equally delightful in *Oklahoma!* included *Many a New Day*, *Kansas City*, *All 'er Nothin'*, and *The Farmer and the Cowman*. Each served as a vehicle to enhance the story line. Critical reaction to *Oklahoma!* was enthusiastic, and the show ran for 2,212 performances. De Mille's ballets, danced to Richard Rodgers's music, were "the biggest hit of the show," according to the *New York World-Telegram*'s critic, Burton Rascoe (April 1, 1943). Olin Downes, the well-known music critic, said that de Mille's dances were "not only acceptable to the average theatregoer who would be bored to death by classical ballet but something he can get excited and shout about." Downes also felt that de Mille was "one of the richest and most indigenous talents the dance has yet uncovered" (quoted in *Current Biography, 1943*, p. 167).

While de Mille was preparing the dances for *Oklahoma!*, which opened only five months after *Rodeo*, she was also planning her own wedding. On June 14, 1943, three months after *Oklahoma!* opened, she married Walter Foy Prude. They subsequently had one son, Jonathan. They continue to maintain their home in New York City's Greenwich Village.

Agnes de Mille was one of the first women choreographers to work on Broadway. Since the enormously successful première of *Oklahoma!* in 1943, de Mille has choreographed *One Touch of Venus* (1943), *Bloomer Girl* (1944), *Carousel* (1945), *Brigadoon* (1947), *Gentlemen Prefer Blondes* (1949), and *Paint Your Wagon* (1951). The most important single development in the Broadway musical since the Second World War has been the elimination of clean-cut distinctions between dramatic movement and choreography, and Agnes de Mille can take credit for being the initiator of this unified production style. "In their natural setting dances draw on the whole atmosphere, the smell and the sound of the place, the food, the watchers—take all this away and the steps seem bare and stripped. You have to suggest the environment theatrically," de Mille says (*Dancemagazine*, October 1971).

Despite her successes, de Mille has not devoted herself entirely to Broadway musicals. In 1944 she created *Tally-Ho* for the Ballet Theatre and danced the part of the errant wife herself. In 1948 she choreographed the ballet *Fall River Legend*, a series of scenes from the life of Lizzie Borden, and directed *The Rape of Lucretia*, an opera by Benjamin Britten. In 1953–1954 she toured with her own dance company, the Agnes de Mille Dance Theatre, visiting 126 cities in twenty-six weeks. In 1955 she choreographed the movie version of *Oklahoma!* and the next year she danced in *Rodeo* at Covent Garden in London.

De Mille continued to be very active during the 1960s. In 1962 she once again supervised the dances for a revival of *Brigadoon*; in 1963 she choreographed the musical *110 in the Shade*; and in 1965, when Ballet Theatre celebrated its twenty-fifth year with a special production, she was represented with four ballets. In 1966 she was commissioned by Lincoln Center for the Performing Arts in New York to create major works for television. In 1969 she was invited as the guest of the Soviet government to be the only American representative on the panel of judges for the International Ballet Competition held in Moscow.

De Mille had long lamented the lack of an American national dance company to preserve and present the native dances of the United States. In 1973 she founded the Heritage Dance Theatre at the North Carolina School of the Arts. In late 1973 the company set out on a series of tours with programs including folk and historical dances and ballets reflecting American themes.

In 1975 de Mille suffered a massive cerebral hemorrhage that left her right side partially paralyzed. She learned to write with her left hand and to walk with the aid of a cane. Only fourteen months after her stroke, she was able to stand on the stage of the New York State Theatre at Lincoln Center to acknowledge the ovation given for the American Ballet Theatre's world première of *Texas Fourth*, her piece for the American bicentennial. A year later she narrated the Joffrey Ballet's production of her lecture-demonstration, *Conversations About the Dance*, which was televised by the Public Broadcasting Service in 1980.

De Mille was co-founder and president (1965–1966) of the Society of Stage Directors and Choreographers. She was a member of the National Advisory Council of the Performing Arts in 1965–1966. She has been awarded honorary doctorates from twelve universities: Mills College (1952), Smith College (1954), Western College (1955), Hood College (1957), Northwestern University (1960), Goucher College (1961), Clark University (1962), the University of California, Los Angeles (1964), Franklin and Marshall College (1965), Western Michigan University (1967), and Nasson College (1970). De Mille has also received many awards: the Donaldson Award in 1943, 1945, and 1947; the *Mademoiselle* Merit Award in 1944; and the New York Critics Award in 1945 and 1947. She was named Woman of the Year in 1946 by the American Newspaper Women's Guild. She received the Antoinette Perry (Tony) Award for best choreographer in 1947 and 1962, the Lord and Taylor Award in 1947, the Dancing Masters Award of Merit in 1950, the *Dancemagazine* Award in 1957, the Woman of the Year Award from the American National Theatre and Academy (ANTA) in 1962, and the Capezio Award in 1966. In 1976 she received the Handel Medallion, New York City's highest award for achievement in the arts, and in 1979 the Arnold Gingrich Memorial Award from the Arts and Business Council. In 1980 she was presented the John F. Kennedy Center Career Achievement Award and the Bank of Delaware Commonwealth Award for distinguished lifetime service to the theatre, and in 1982 she was given the Elizabeth Blackwell Award honoring outstanding women in the arts and sciences. In 1986 Agnes de Mille was presented a National Medal of the Arts by President Ronald Reagan at the White House. Hers is truly a unique and distinguished career.

Agnes de Mille has written three autobiographical books: *Dance to the Piper* (1952), *And Promenade Home* (1958), and *Reprieve* (1981). Her other books include *To a Young Dancer* (1960), *The Book of the Dance* (1963), *Lizzie Borden: A Dance of Death* (1968), *The Dance in America* (1971), and *Speak to Me, Dance with Me* (1973). Biographical information can be found in "The Grande Dame of Dance" in *Life* (November 15, 1963). "Twenty Years of *Oklahoma!*" by Donald Duncan in *Dancemagazine* (March 1963) contains information about her innovations in musical theatre, primarily in *Oklahoma!*. See also *Dancemagazine* (November 1974) for information concerning her contributions to musical theatre. A list of her works, although not comprehensive, and a discussion of her use of folk art and American themes can be found in *Time* (October 26, 1953) and in *Theatre Arts* (October 1944), respectively. Further information can be found in *Dancemagazine* (April 1965 and October 1971) and *Time* (February 25, 1974). See also Jane McConnell, *Famous Ballet Dancers* (1955), and Hope Stoddard, *Famous American Women* (1970). There is a biographical article on de Mille in *Current Biography, 1985* (1985). Shorter biographical sketches may be found in *Notable Names in the American Theatre* (1976); *Who's Who in the Theatre* (1981); *Who's Who in America, 1984–1985* (1984); and *The Oxford Companion to American Theatre* (1984).

Deborah Nadell

DESMOND, Mae (March 29, 1887–July 13, 1982): early twentieth-century actress and manager, was born Mary Veronica Callahan in Philadelphia's poor Southwark community, the third of eight children of Irish immigrants Michael and Annie (Kennedy) Callahan. Her father, adhering to the precepts of his former profession as a hedge (unofficial) teacher in his native rural County Cork, stressed oral recitation as the primary teaching method for his children. Keen memory and a heightened sense of delivery already punctuated Mary Callahan's talent when she began acting in church theatricals as a young teen-ager. Her exposure to professional theatre took place in Philadelphia's local stock companies or resident theatres, which provided a weekly change of bill for family-oriented, local audiences. Generally, a resident stock company was comprised of an ensemble of approximately fifteen actors in typed roles who performed in one theatre for a season of anywhere from twenty to forty-five weeks. Several of the most successful troupes were headed by female managers or actress-managers.

Mary Callahan joined Philadelphia's most prestigious stock organization, the Chestnut Street Theatre's Orpheum Players, as an extra and made an unscheduled debut on September 23, 1907, in Clyde Fitch's *The Cowboy and Lady* when the troupe's leading lady was suddenly hospitalized. Mary Callahan's week as "leading lady" earned for her a place as a regular player with the company under the stage name Mae Desmond. Manager Grant Laferty, assessing her real name as too reminiscent of Irish peasantry, created for her another Irish name designed to evoke images of landed gentry and baronial estates. "Mae Desmond" was a name well suited to the actress's Irish beauty—dark curls, milky skin, round face, and upturned nose. Mae Desmond remained on the Orpheum Players' roster for two seasons, during which she became the troupe's leading ingénue.

Marriage to fellow Philadelphia actor Frank Fielder (1884–1980) in September 1908, and the birth of their sons, Frank Raymond in March 1910 and John Richard in March 1912, forced the couple to seek employment in the scant markets available to married acting couples. They performed with the Gus A. Forbes Stock Company in Duluth, Minnesota, and later with Forbes's Brooklyn troupe and the Gotham Players. Both Desmond and Fielder attained leading player status during their three-year tenure with the Gotham Players (1910–1913).

Between 1913 and 1917 Desmond was the leading lady of the Metropolis and Prospect Theatres in the Bronx, New York, in Scranton, Pennsylvania, and on tour in the Northwest and Midwest. In the spring of 1917 she returned to Brooklyn's Own Stock Company at the Grand Opera House. The difficulty of obtaining concurrent employment finally compelled Mae Desmond and Frank Fielder to create and manage their own theatre. They secured the lease on Schenectady's Van Curler Opera House from the Shubert brothers and created the Mae Desmond Players, so named because of Desmond's renown in regional stock circles. The troupe with Desmond and Fielder in the leading roles opened on April 7, 1917, with Cleves Kinkead's drama *Common Clay*. Desmond played a role that was emblematic of her stage persona: beautiful, innocent, and unpretentious but always successful in climbing social and financial ladders. The troupe's large, weekly changing repertory included such plays as *Rebecca of Sunnybrook Farm*, *Pretty Peggy*, *In Old Kentucky*, and *Polly of the Circus*.

The Mae Desmond Players appealed to middle-class audiences seeking respectable family entertainment. Desmond and Fielder presented themselves as a modest, hard-working married couple with family and small business priorities. They published a weekly newsletter full of folksy humor and homespun philosophy, and Desmond was often seen around town arm-in-arm with her younger sister, Bernice (Anna) Callahan, the troupe's ingénue. Desmond sporadically gave lectures between the acts on subjects such as motherhood and met often for a picnic or Sunday dinner with the local, all-female Mae Desmond Fan Club. From the start the company performed to full houses. The Shuberts, however, reclaimed the Schenectady Theatre as a touring facility for the main fall-winter 1917–1918 season, and the Mae Desmond Players moved to the Mozart Theatre in Elmira, New York. When Schenectady's theatre again became available in February 1918, the Mae Desmond Players returned to it.

Although contractually bound to appear in Schenectady for the ensuing 1918–1919 season, Desmond and Fielder secured Philadelphia's Orpheum Theatre in the fall of 1918 after spending the summer at Poli's Theatre in Scranton. Always intent on making a theatrical career in their native city, they split the company's personnel between the two cities that year and relocated in Philadelphia permanently in 1919. The troupe catered to the Germantown area's middle and lower-middle classes, often Roman Catholic and of Irish, British, and German descent. Irish-American theme plays, such as *Peg O' My Heart*, *The Daughter of Mother Machree*, and *Little Peggy O'Moore*, were scheduled occasionally, but the dramas usually focused on themes of upward mobility and respectability. Desmond also expanded her talents for light romantic comedy. She assumed more of the vivacious, spunky characters in such plays as *Adam and Eva*, *Polly with a Past*, and *Daddy Long Legs* and perfected the stylized antics of such bedroom farces as *Up in Mabel's Room* and *Parlor, Bedroom, and Bath*. The troupe remained at the Orpheum for three highly prosperous seasons (1918–1921). A bitter dispute with theatre owner J. Frederick Zimmerman over his share of the receipts finally compelled the Mae Desmond Players to vacate the theatre.

In the fall of 1921 Desmond opened at Philadelphia's lavish Metropolitan Theatre at Broad and Poplar Streets. Although basically unsuited to the small scope of typical stock company productions, this theatre was the city's only available facility at the time. The season there ultimately was financially unrewarding, since the expenses for extra personnel, spectacular scenery, and advertising to fill the 3,500-seat house drained much of the profits. However, playing at the Metropolitan elevated Mae Desmond to city-wide celebrity status; she was invited to share her personal philosophy on beauty and fashion in the major newspapers and to lend her name to local business ventures and products.

The Mae Desmond Players next moved to Philadelphia's People's Theatre in the fall of 1922, renaming it the Desmond Theatre. Located at Kensington Avenue and Cumberland Streets in the city's largest textile mill district, the theatre serviced primarily lower middle-class and working-class audiences; it periodically staged benefits for local Catholic parishes and charities and emphasized the ethnic appeal of Irish and Catholic plays. In 1924 Desmond celebrated her two-thousandth stage performance. When she bore her third child, Richard Michael, in April 1925, she distributed photos of herself and the infant to audience members, thus emphasizing her commitment to family values and domestic priorities. The Mae Desmond Players achieved their greatest financial success during their four years at the Desmond Theatre, and Desmond and Fielder used some of their profits to sponsor a stock company of black actors at Philadelphia's Dunbar Theatre.

From 1921 to 1925 Desmond's company had played summer seasons at West Philadelphia's Cross Keys Theatre and, having had an established audience there, had no trouble securing the lease on the nearby William Penn Theatre, located at 41st Street and Lancaster Avenue, when they lost the Desmond Theatre to motion pictures. They remained at the William Penn for the next three seasons, 1926–1929, during which time a young Clifford Odets received his initial theatrical training as an actor of general utility and juvenile roles with the organization. Desmond's fourth son, William, was born in August 1928. However, the innocent, youthful, optimistic roles on which she had built her career were becoming unsuitable to both her advancing age and the more sophisticated times. She shifted to more mature leading roles and dramas like *Rain*, *Kongo*, and *The Green Hat*, which were popular in the 1920s, but the success of her company dwindled. Resident stock companies were on the decline throughout America at this time, as sound motion pictures took over theatres and as dire economic conditions following the 1929 stock market crash made financing exceedingly difficult.

Desmond was forced to vacate the William Penn Theatre in the winter of 1929, when several of her company members induced the theatre's owners to transfer the lease to them on more favorable terms. For the first time in eleven seasons, she was left without a theatre in Philadelphia. Brief seasons of the Mae

Desmond Players followed in the Delaware Valley area—at Camden's Towers Theatre, Wilmington's Playhouse, and Lancaster's Fulton Opera house—and in Scranton. In 1931 Desmond, attempting to meet changing tastes, returned to the Philadelphia stage with a new resident company, the Locust Street Theatre Players Guild. Occasionally manager Desmond played secondary roles to Broadway and Hollywood visiting stars, including Jean Arthur, Lou Tellegan, **Mrs. Leslie Carter**, Madge Bellamy, and Guy Bates Post. The company presented recent Broadway releases, most often urbane and stylish comedies. Despite critical praise this venture endured for only one season. Desmond continued to keep a smaller company active sporadically throughout the 1930s, primarily by booking resort theatres at the New Jersey beaches and in the Pocono Mountains and by adapting the old stock company repertory for radio on Philadelphia's WIP and WDAS stations. In 1939 Desmond briefly sponsored a semiprofessional troupe at the suburban Drexel Hill Playhouse.

The Mae Desmond School of Theatre opened in 1937 on Philadelphia's Chestnut Street, and out of this enterprise grew the Mae Desmond Children's Theatre, which officially premièred in 1941 and, after 1945, played weekly at the city's Town Hall. This children's company became yet another Philadelphia theatrical institution, often playing twelve performances per week at local schools and community centers. The troupe, in which Desmond and Fielder assumed character roles in plays written or adapted by their sons, Frank and Richard (the latter became a well-known Hollywood screen and television writer-producer), also toured the mid-Atlantic states.

Desmond and Fielder continued their children's theatre but gradually diminished their activity until 1969, when the couple retired at age eighty-two and eighty-six, to their home in Willow Grove, Pennsylvania. Ill health forced them to take up residence at a nearby Doylestown nursing home in 1979, where Fielder died on December 24, 1980, and Desmond followed, less than two years later, on July 12, 1982. She was ninety-five.

Mae Desmond, aided and supported by her husband, played in and managed professional theatre for Philadelphians for over fifty years, longer than virtually any other artists associated with the city's theatrical history. On the occasion of her death, the *Philadelphia Inquirer* proclaimed, "For an era, she was theatre" (August 9, 1982). This actress-manager was early twentieth-century Philadelphia's most renowned local performing arts personality and the longest standing proprietor and manager of a resident company relying on its own ensemble, not visiting stars, to entertain local audiences. For an era, it was Mae Desmond who insured the city's maintenance of a professional regional stage.

The best sources of information about Mae Desmond are Mari Kathleen Fielder, "Mae Desmond and Her Players: The Public Presentation of a Stock Company Actress, 1917–1929" (Unpublished Masters thesis, Ohio State University, 1976); Mari Kathleen Fielder, "Mae Desmond Players," *American Theatre Companies*, Vol. 2, edited by Weldon B. Durham; and Mari Kathleen Fielder, "Theatre and Community in Early Twentieth-Century Philadelphia: The Mae Desmond Players, 1917–1932" (Unpublished Ph.D.

dissertation, University of California, Los Angeles, 1986). See also "Wooing a Local Audience: The Irish-American Appeal of Philadelphia's Mae Desmond Players," *Theatre History Studies* 1 (1981), and Harry Harris, "On Stage at 80 and 77," *Philadelphia Inquirer Sunday Today Magazine* (March 28, 1965). In the Philadelphia Theatre Collection, Free Library of Philadelphia, see *The Germantown Telegraph, New York Dramatic Mirror, Philadelphia Inquirer, Philadelphia North American, Philadelphia Public Ledger, Schenectady Gazette*, and the *Scranton Republican*. There are scrapbooks, programs, photographs, promptbooks, playscripts, posters, and publicity releases of the Mae Desmond Players in the personal collection of Mari Kathleen Fielder.

Mari Kathleen Fielder

DEWHURST, Colleen (June 3, 1926–): actress, director, and theatre activist, most noted for her roles in plays by Eugene O'Neill, was born in Montreal, Quebec (Canada). The tomboyish Colleen often accompanied her father, a well-to-do Canadian athlete, to sports events. Her mother was a devout Christian Scientist, and although Colleen Dewhurst does not practice the religion herself, she has said that "everything I like about myself comes from the religion, and when I get in a bad bind, my mind goes back to it" (*Time*, January 21, 1974). Before her parents divorced during her adolescence, the family had traveled a great deal, mostly in the United States, moving when Colleen was seven to the first in a series of midwestern towns. Dewhurst attended fifteen schools in twenty years. She enrolled in Downer College for Young Ladies, a Milwaukee finishing school, leaving after a year or so but not before discovering that acting had displaced all earlier ambitions to become a journalist. She told reviewer Rex Reed that at Downer she wrote and directed a school play, got "fed up" with the lead, kicked her out, and played the role herself (*Conversations in the Raw*, p. 118).

In 1946 Dewhurst moved to New York, where she studied at the American Academy of Dramatic Arts with Joseph Anthony and Harold Clurman. In those first years in New York she held many jobs to support herself and pay for classes. From time to time she worked as a switchboard operator, usher, and instructor at a weight-reducing gymnasium. At the American Academy of Dramatic Arts she met James Vickery, and they were married in 1947. The marriage ended in divorce in 1959. The following year she wed actor George C. Scott, with whom she had two sons, Alexander and Campbell. She and Scott were divorced in 1963, remarried in 1967, and divorced once again in 1972.

After summer stock engagements and appearances as Julia Cavendish in *The Royal Family* in an American Academy of Dramatic Arts production at the Carnegie Lyceum in October 1946, Dewhurst began her professional career with a small role in the January 1952 revival of Eugene O'Neill's *Desire Under the Elms*, directed by Harold Clurman, at the ANTA Playhouse in New York. She did not appear on Broadway again until January 1956, when she played both a Turkish concubine and a virgin of Memphis in *Tamburlaine the Great* at the Winter Garden.

Her early career was encouraged by Joseph Papp, the producer whose abundant energies developed the New York Shakespeare Festival and later created the Public Theatre. Her first part in a Papp Shakespeare production was as Tamora in *Titus Andronicus* at the East Side Amphitheatre in the summer of 1956. She subsequently played Katherina in *The Taming of the Shrew* (also 1956), Lady Macbeth at the Belvedere Lake Delacorte Theatre in Central Park (August 1957), and Cleopatra in two separate productions of *Antony and Cleopatra*, at the Heckscher Theatre (January 1959) and the new outdoor Delacorte Theatre (June 1963). The *Antony and Cleopatra* production was taped for broadcast over CBS-TV. In the summer of 1972 she returned to the New York Shakespeare Festival at the Delacorte to portray a sympathetic Gertrude in *Hamlet*.

Dewhurst played a variety of challenging roles Off-Broadway in addition to her Shakespearean performances. A September 1956 revival of *Camille* at the Cherry Lane Theatre featured Dewhurst as the heroine. The following December her appearance as the Queen in a revival of Jean Cocteau's *The Eagle Has Two Heads* at the Actors' Playhouse proved sufficiently impressive, combined with her portrayal of Katherina in *The Taming of the Shrew*, to earn her a *Village Voice* Off-Broadway (Obie) Award. In yet another revival, Dewhurst played Mrs. Squeamish in *The Country Wife*, which opened at the Adelphi in November 1957 and subsequently moved to the Henry Miller Theatre on Broadway; she had previously played Mrs. Dainty Fidget in the production's successful Washington, D.C., run. In 1958 Dewhurst received a Theatre World Award for her performance as Laetitia in Justus Mayer's *Children of Darkness*, starring George C. Scott and directed by José Quintero at the Circle in the Square. Walter Kerr wrote of her performance: "One must stand in honest awe of Colleen Dewhurst's sultry-mouthed, stony-eyed trollop; as bad girls go, she is a beauty to be remembered" (*New York Herald Tribune*, March 1, 1958).

While Off-Broadway audiences were becoming increasingly familiar with the tall, husky-voiced actress, Dewhurst's appearances on Broadway were far less frequent. The Broadway-bound *Maiden Voyage* by Paul Osborn, with Dewhurst as Penelope, opened and closed in the winter of 1957. She had better luck with the American premiére of Albert Camus's *Caligula* in February 1960, playing Caesonia—her first major Broadway role—at the 54th Street Theatre. The following November, after the curtain rose on *All the Way Home* at the Belasco Theatre, the *New York Post*'s Richard Watts called Dewhurst's creation of Mary Follett "one of the most beautiful performances of recent seasons" (December 11, 1960). A critical success, the Tad Mosel play finally established Dewhurst, who won both the 1961 Lola D'Annunzio Award and an Antoinette Perry (Tony) Award as best actress. She portrayed Phoebe Flaherty in Alice Cannon's *Great Day in the Morning*, directed by José Quintero, which opened at Broadway's Henry Miller Theatre in March 1962. Although this play, which deals with an Irish-American family in St. Louis in 1928, was not well received, Dewhurst's performance was greatly admired. Howard Taubman, reviewing the show in the

New York Times, wrote, "As a marvelously big, slovenly, truculent, and sentimental Phoebe, she is virtually a one-woman show" (March 29, 1962).

Dewhurst has long been associated with the work of Eugene O'Neill. She told Rex Reed, "I love the O'Neill women. They move from the groin rather than the brain. To play O'Neill you have to be big. You can't just sit around and play little moments of sadness or sweetness. You cannot phony up O'Neill" (*Conversations in the Raw*, p. 119). In January 1963 she opened in the Circle in the Square revival of *Desire Under the Elms*, playing Abbie Putnam opposite George C. Scott. Both received *Village Voice* Off-Broadway (Obie) awards for their performances. Four years later, she portrayed Sara Melody in *More Stately Mansions*, directed by José Quintero and produced from O'Neill's incomplete manuscript. This larger-than-life struggle between two women (Ingrid Bergman played the mother-in-law) had its American première in Los Angeles in September 1967 before opening in New York at the Broadhurst Theatre the following October. Dewhurst's interpretation of a third O'Neill woman, the tortured Christine Mannon in Circle in the Square's November 1972 production of *Mourning Becomes Electra*, earned a Drama Desk Award.

Dewhurst's most famous O'Neill characterization, however, proved to be that of Josie Hogan in *A Moon for the Misbegotten*, which opened on Broadway in December 1973 at the Morosco Theatre. A critical and popular success, with Jason Robards, Jr., as James Tyrone and José Quintero as director, *A Moon for the Misbegotten* garnered a number of awards for Dewhurst, including the Antoinette Perry (Tony) Award, the Drama Desk Award, the Theatre World Award, and the Sarah Siddons Award. After twenty-seven years in the theatre, Colleen Dewhurst had her first uncontestable Broadway hit.

When presented at the Ahmanson Theatre in Los Angeles in November 1974, *A Moon for the Misbegotten* gained Dewhurst the Los Angeles Drama Critics Award. In addition, the production reached a nationwide audience when broadcast by ABC Theatre in 1975. T. E. Kalem, writing in *Time* (January 14, 1974), said, "No woman has been big enough for the part before, not only physically but in the generosity of the heart, mind, and spirit which Josie must convey." Walter Kerr wrote of the radiant actress, "It is difficult to take your eyes off Miss Dewhurst, whether she is smiling or in fury" (*New York Times*, January 13, 1974).

José Quintero had twice previously directed her in this role: once at the Festival of Two Worlds in Spoleto, Italy, during the summer of 1958; again in October 1965 at the Studio Arena in Buffalo, New York. Dewhurst attributed much of her success as Josie Hogan to Quintero, who "makes you break through, and releases something for you." This "breaking through" is the only way to play O'Neill, who strips his characters "until he's down to the marrow" (interview with Chris Chase in the *New York Times*, February 17, 1974).

When Papp's Public Theatre celebrated O'Neill's birthday with a staged reading of *O'Neill and Carlotta*, by Barbara Gelb (October 1979), Dewhurst joined Jason Robards, Jr., **Geraldine Fitzgerald**, and others for this special event.

Dewhurst, who played Carlotta opposite Robards's O'Neill, said upon this occasion that O'Neill's female characters were "taken a lot from Carlotta's personality and their relationship. I love his women—passionately. They're women who, instead of making a simple mistake, create a tragedy; they do it big—they march right into the gale" (*New York Times*, October 15, 1979). In addition to Dewhurst's numerous performances in plays by O'Neill, she is actively encouraging wider production of O'Neill's plays by professional companies in the United States.

Another major American dramatist, Edward Albee, has also provided challenging roles for Dewhurst. She created the part of Miss Amelia Evans in Albee's adaptation of *The Ballad of the Sad Cafe*, from the novel by **Carson McCullers**, at the Martin Beck Theatre (October 1963); the production was a critical, if not a financial, success. She later won a Drama Desk Award for her portrayal of the Mistress in *All Over* by Edward Albee, which opened at the Martin Beck Theatre in March 1971. In a Broadway revival directed by the playwright, she portrayed Martha opposite Ben Gazzara's George in Albee's best-received play, *Who's Afraid of Virginia Woolf?*, at the Music Box Theatre (April 1976). This was the second time she had played the raucous, bullying, discontented Martha; she had toured in the role during the summer of 1965.

In addition to her distinguished performances in plays by Albee and O'Neill, Dewhurst has performed a wide variety of roles for both commercial and not-for-profit theatres as well as for movies and television. Notable among these are her appearance as Hester in Athol Fugard's *Hello and Goodbye* at the Sheridan Square Playhouse in 1969, for which she won a Drama Desk Award; the title character in the Vivian Beaumont Theatre production of *The Good Woman of Setzuan* in 1970; Nel Denton in *The Big Coca-Cola Swamp in the Sky* at the Westport (Connecticut) Country Playhouse in 1971; and Margaret in the world première of *Artichoke* by Joanna Glass at the Long Wharf Theatre in 1975. In Boston she played Alice in August Strindberg's *The Dance of Death* and returned to Broadway as Irene Porter in *An Almost Perfect Person* by Judith Ross, which opened at the Belasco Theatre in October 1977. In October 1978 she appeared briefly in the role of **Lillian Hellman** in Eric Bentley's *Are You Now or Have You Ever Been?*, which opened at the Promenade Theatre in New York; she then played a limited engagement at the Public Theatre in February 1979 as Ruth Chandler in Thomas Babe's *Taken in Marriage*. Two additional Broadway appearances were *The Queen and the Rebels* at the Plymouth Theatre in September 1982 and her huge success the next year as a Russian emigré in a revival of *You Can't Take It With You*, directed by Ellis Rabb at the Plymouth Theatre. According to Frank Rich, "It's a cameo role, but Miss Dewhurst, functioning as a cleanup hitter, knocks every laugh clean out of the park" (*New York Times*, April 5, 1983).

On January 29, 1987, Dewhurst opened at the Public Theatre in New York in the one-woman play *My Gene*, written by Barbara Gelb, a biographer of Eugene O'Neill. Dewhurst plays Carlotta Monterey, O'Neill's widow. The play is set in a hospital room where the aging Carlotta is under psychiatric care. She reminisces, sometimes lucidly, "and at other times assaulted by the hallucinations of her mental decay and the obsessions of her married life" (*New York Times*, January 25, 1987).

Though her primary allegiance is to theatre, Dewhurst has appeared frequently on television and in movies. In 1950 she played a role in *Burning Bright* and starred in *Medea* on WNTA-TV. Her first film role was in 1959 in *A Nun's Story*. Her portrayal of Aldonza in *I, Don Quixote* (CBS, 1960) won a Sylvania Award. A selective list of television and film credits includes *Man on a String* (film, 1960), *No Exit* (WMTA, 1961), *The Crucible* (CBS, 1967), *My Mother's House* (WNET, 1967), *You Are There: The Trial of Susan B. Anthony* (CBS, 1972), *Annie Hall* (film, 1977), *When a Stranger Calls* (film, 1979), *Studs Lonigan* (NBC, 1979), *Guyana Tragedy: The Story of Jim Jones* (CBS, 1980), *Tribute* (film, 1980), and *Alice in Wonderland* (WNET, 1983). Dewhurst has also appeared in episodes of such television series as *Alfred Hitchcock Theatre*, *Ben Casey*, *Dr. Kildare*, *The Virginian*, and *Love Boat*. In addition, she served as a host for the 1977 PBS series *The American Short Story*.

Dewhurst has also tried her hand at directing. *Ned and Jack*, a play about the dramatist Edward Sheldon and the actor John Barrymore, had an unsuccessful run at the Hudson Guild Theatre in May 1981. She had become interested in the drama on seeing it two years earlier at Stratford, Ontario, and had worked with Canadian playwright Sheldon Rosen on revisions. Despite good reviews in Stratford, the production's Broadway attempt closed after one performance. Her second directorial effort took her to Connecticut during the summer of 1984, where she worked with the National Theatre of the Deaf on *All the Way Home*, the play for which she had won a Tony Award twenty-four years earlier. Dewhurst returned to classical repertory as Madame Arkadina in the revival of Anton Chekhov's *The Sea Gull*, directed by Peter Sellars for the American National Theatre and Academy (ANTA) in its new home at the John F. Kennedy Center for the Performing Arts in Washington, D.C., in 1986. Dewhursts's long association with Eugene O'Neill's plays continued in 1988 when she performed the leading roles in *Long Day's Journey Into Night* and *Ah, Wilderness*, first at the Yale Repertory Theatre, and then at the Neil Simon Theatre in New York for the first International Festival of the Arts.

In recent years Dewhurst has often been engaged in public causes. She participated in the "Night of 100 Stars," written and produced by **Hildy Parks** as a centennial celebration for the Actors' Fund of America (Radio City Music Hall, February 14, 1982). Her spring 1985 schedule included an April reading from Golda Meir's prose for the Zionist Federation's "Opportunities in Israel," and soon thereafter she was one of several performers who participated in the twelfth annual Solidarity Sunday for Soviet Jewry. A vice chair of the group called Save the Theatres, Dewhurst has been very active in the fight to preserve New York theatre buildings. In fact, she was arrested along with others during a 1982 demonstration to stop the wrecking ball from demolishing the Helen

Hayes and Morosco theatres. A year later, in July 1983, she was a speaker at the renaming of the Little Theatre on West 44th Street for **Helen Hayes**. In March 1984 she was among the speakers at a public hearing regarding plans to rebuild Times Square.

Dewhurst has received wide recognition for her talents and contributions to American theatre. In 1972 she received an honorary doctorate in fine arts from Lawrence University (which had merged with Downer College). She was elected to the Theatre Hall of Fame in 1981 and named president of Actors' Equity Association in 1985. She served on the Theatre Advisory Panel at the National Endowment for the Arts 1986–1987. In 1986 she was awarded the Eugene O'Neill Birthday Medal for enriching the world's understanding of the playwright.

The epitome of the modern successful actress, Dewhurst has performed brilliantly in both classic and contemporary plays in a variety of theatre settings and has also maintained a lively commitment to social and artistic causes. She is truly a great lady of the American theatre.

The largest number of articles about Colleen Dewhurst appeared after her December 1973 opening in *A Moon for the Misbegotten*; they include "It's a Rich Play, Richly Performed," *New York Times* (January 13, 1974); "Gorgeous Gael," *Time* (January 11, 1974); and "Colleen has Broadway 'Moon'-Struck," *New York Times* (February 17, 1974). Among informative earlier pieces are "Cleo in the Park," *Theatre Arts* (July 1963), and "Great Day in the Morning," *Theatre Arts* (June 1962). A Rex Reed interview with Dewhurst first appeared in the *New York Times* (November 12, 1962) and was reprinted in a slightly different version in *Conversations in the Raw* (1969). Dewhurst's directing debut is praised in "Theatre: Colleen Dewhurst Directs 'Ned and Jack,' " *New York Times* (May 22, 1981), and in "Sassy Parody and Dead-End Drama," *New York Times* (May 31, 1981). See also the article on Dewhurst and her performance in *My Gene* in the *New York Times* (January 25, 1987). Dewhurst is listed in Earl Blackwell's *Celebrity Register* (1973); *Current Biography, 1974* (1974); *Notable Names in the American Theatre* (1976); *Actors' Television Credits*, Supplement I (1978); *Who's Who in the Theatre* (1981); *Who's Who in American Theatre Now* (1981); *The Oxford Companion to the Theatre* (1983); and *The Oxford Companion to American Theatre* (1984).

Susan M. Steadman

DORO, Marie (May 25, 1882–October 9, 1956): actress and leading lady to William Gillette, was born Marie Kathryn Stuart, the daughter of Virginia (Weaver) Stuart and E. H. Stuart, a prominent Wall Street lawyer in Duncannon, Pennsylvania. The stage name Doro is a contraction of the nickname "Adorato," by which her family knew her. Marie Doro was preparing for Vassar College at Mrs. Brown's School on Fifth Avenue, New York, when she persuaded her father to let her try for the stage. She had already been a performer. As a child of twelve, for example, she had given a piano concert. In adult life she continued to play the piano and published several songs she had written. She also wrote plays.

Doro made her stage debut in 1901 in a stock company in St. Paul, Minnesota, as Katherine in *Aristocracy*. After several roles in stock and two years of acting on the road, she debuted in New York in *The Billionaire* (1903). Charles Frohman spotted her and added her to those to be groomed for stardom. She appeared in a flurry of engagements over the next few years, including J. M. Barrie's *The Admirable Crichton* (1904), produced by William Gillette's company. In 1905 she played her first title role in *Friquet*. That year she also debuted in London in *The Dictator* with William Collier. Her rapid rise culminated in the title part opposite William Gillette in his own play *Clarice* (1905), and that same year she performed in a revival of Gillette's *Sherlock Holmes*. There were constant rumors of a romance between Doro and Gillette. They were, in fact, lifelong friends.

Doro achieved a major success as Carlotta in *The Morals of Marcus* (1907), which she played first in Boston, then in New York. After *The Richest Girl* (1909) Doro returned to London in *The Climax*. When this failed, she impulsively announced her retirement, but on her return to New York she was persuaded to take the lead in Gillette's *Electricity* (1910). Following a tour of *A Butterfly On The Wheel*, she appeared in the highly praised revival of *Oliver Twist* in 1912. Doro later claimed that Oliver was her favorite role. Certainly her delicate frame and soulful eyes made her perfect for the part of Charles Dickens's waif. Later the same year Doro, who had played small parts in musicals early in her career, performed in Gilbert and Sullivan's *Patience*.

In 1913 Doro appeared in *The New Secretary* in New York and *The Scarlet Band* and *The Bill* in London, as well as in Victorien Sardou's *Diplomacy*. In this play she co-starred with Gillette. When *Diplomacy* moved to New York, however, Doro coached the young actor Elliot Dexter to be her co-star. A relationship developed, and the two were secretly married in 1915. They were both signed up at this time to make films for the Famous Players Company. After six weeks of shooting in Palm Springs they finally announced their marriage, but it lasted only a few years. Doro never remarried.

Her technique of practicing subtle nuances of facial expression in a mirror to prepare for her roles no doubt served Doro well as a silent screen actress. Her beauty was also an asset, and she became a popular film star. Her films included versions of her stage roles in *The Morals of Marcus*, *Oliver Twist*, and *Diplomacy*. After only two years she complained of the poor artistic standards of the American film industry and returned to the stage in *Barbara* (1917). She made her final appearance on Broadway in *Lilies of the Field* (1921). She retired to private life while still at the height of her career, still a beauty, and still very much in demand. Long afterwards she died of a heart ailment in New York at the age of seventy-four.

Doro was awarded unusual honors during her career. She was the first American actress to give a command performance at Windsor Castle. She played *Diplomacy* before England's royal family in 1914. She was the first American to be awarded the Legion Commandatora, given by King Victor of Italy in 1920.

In the course of a twenty-year career, Marie Doro rose in critical esteem from a novelty—a professional beauty and dilettante—to a major dramatic star, holding her own in the company of such actresses as **Mrs. Fiske**, **Ethel Barrymore**, and **Laurette Taylor**. Early reviews concentrated on her beauty and personal charm. "Little Miss Doro" was described as "elfin" and compared to "a Dresden china doll." Interviewers expressed surprise at finding an erudite and witty woman behind her stage personality. The *New York Times* review of *Oliver Twist* described the movie's star as "a lovely and highly sympathetic little Oliver" (February 27, 1912). Later its reviewer of *Diplomacy* noted, "Miss Doro, who never looked lovelier, is entirely charming" (October 21, 1914). In 1917 the *New York Times* critic gave her this accolade for her role in *Barbara*: "Miss Marie Doro has quite found herself. . . . By some magic, her girlish prettiness and charm have been touched with the flame of a real beauty—a beauty that is as compelling as it is exquisite and unaffected" (November 6, 1917).

The Players' Collection scrapbook and the Robinson Locke scrapbooks in the New York Public Library Performing Arts Research Center at Lincoln Center are uncollated, but contain assorted clippings, programs, articles, and interviews about Marie Doro. Daniel Blum's *A Pictorial History of the Silent Screen* (1953) contains several photos from films produced between 1915 and 1919. Blum's *A Pictorial History of the American Theatre* (1981) has performance photos dating from 1904 to 1921. Blum's *Great Stars of the American Stage* (1952) provides brief biographical sketches, portraits, and production photos. Her obituary appeared in the *New York Times* on October 10, 1956. Biographical information about Doro may be found in *Enciclopedia dello spettacolo* (1954–1966); *The Green Room Book: or, Who's Who on the Stage* (1906); *Who's Who on the Stage, 1908* (1908); *Who's Who in Music and Drama* (1914); *Who's Who in the Theatre* (1930); *Theatre World, 1956–1957 Season*, Vol. 13 (1957); *Who Was Who in the Theatre*, Vol. I (1978); and *The Oxford Companion to American Theatre* (1984).

                                                                                      Constance Clark

DOUGLAS, Helen Gahagan (November 25, 1900–June 28, 1980): actress, opera singer, and politician, is best remembered for her role in a vicious political campaign in 1950, when she lost her bid for United States senator from California to Richard M. Nixon. Helen Gahagan was one of five children, the older of two daughters, born to Walter Hamer Gahagan, a wealthy, politically conservative engineer, and his cultured, musical wife, Lillian (Mussen) Gahagan. She grew up in Brooklyn, New York, near fashionable Prospect Place. From early childhood, she spent her time either entertaining her siblings and girlfriends (often from a makeshift stage on top of her father's billiard table) or drifting off into imaginary worlds where she pretended to be a variety of characters. In Fairlee, Vermont, where the Gahagans summered, Helen Gahagan's mother insisted on voice, dance, and piano lessons for her daughter. At Brooklyn's Berkeley Institute, the Capon School in Northampton, Massachusetts, and Barnard College (1920–1922), Gahagan made a name for herself in dramatics. She showed no interest in political events, except when she tried to sell war bonds from the New York Public Library steps. These efforts ended quickly when her activities were discovered by her father.

In the spring of 1922, her Berkeley Institute mentor, director-dramatist Elizabeth Grimgall of New York's Inter-Theatre Arts, Inc., produced a dramatization of an Irish legend that Helen Gahagan and a friend had written for a drama class at Barnard College. This production set off a rapid chain of events that led to two small parts for Gahagan in Off-Broadway productions and then to a three-year contract with Broadway producer William A. Brady. The key turn in events came when producer John Cromwell persuaded the actress Grace George, wife of William A. Brady, to see Gahagan's performance as Sybil Harrington in *Manhattan* (1922). Grace George conveyed her enthusiasm for the young actress to her husband, who had a reputation for recognizing young talent. Brady then had the difficult and unpleasant task of persuading Gahagan's father to let her leave college to try her wings on Broadway. Mr. Gahagan adamantly opposed his daughter's driving determination to have a theatrical career, but he lost the battle. As her first Broadway role Gahagan played the lead in *Dreams for Sale* (1922). Although the play, by Pulitzer Prize-winning playwright Owen Davis, proved a disaster and closed after thirteen performances, it launched Helen Gahagan as the most sensational debut of the season. Even Alexander Woollcott acknowledged that Gahagan had beauty and talent. Her instant success was all the more unusual as her theatrical experience had been limited to high school and college plays.

For the next three years, Gahagan played leading roles either in Brady productions or on loan to other producers. Her roles included Paula in Ferenc Molnar's *Fashions for Men* (1922), Jean Trowbridge in *Chains* (1923), and Leah in an all-star revival of the popular *Leah Kleschna* by C. M. S. McLellan (1924). The noted **Jessie Bonstelle** staged the play, and **Minnie Maddern Fiske**, for whom the play was originally written, assisted her. Critics consistently ranked Gahagan as one of the most promising actresses, often likening her to **Ethel Barrymore**.

Despite this considerable success, Gahagan felt increasingly restless and dissatisfied with the roles Brady offered her. She wanted more intellectual stimulation than commercial theatre offered and often spoke of moving into directing, playwriting, or producing. Despite her successful career, her personal life continued to be quite circumscribed. Her protective father insisted that the family chauffeur escort her daily to and from the theatre. Feeling that she had only tenuous bonds with her professional colleagues, Gahagan used her free time to take dancing, music, and diction lessons. She also read biography and science extensively. In 1925 she terminated her contract with William A. Brady. She then did challenging leading roles in two brief runs: the German expressionist play *Beyond* (1925) by Walter Hasenclever, produced by the nonprofit Provincetown Players, and a Hungarian play, *The Sapphire Ring* (1925) by Laszlo Laketos, at the Morosco Theatre. In August 1925 she agreed to play Lady Caroline Dexter in Rosalie Stewart's production of *The Enchanted Cottage*. Although unsure of her eventual goal, she signed a five-year contract with the well-established producer George Tyler, with hopes of better roles. Her relationship with Tyler became a very close one both personally and professionally. Her first play with Tyler, *Young Woodley* (1925), proved a major box-office hit (260 performances) and drew considerable attention to Gahagan, her male lead (the temperamental Glenn Hunter), and the young British playwright John Van Druten. In her role as the schoolmaster's wife at a British boarding school who falls in love with one of the students, Gahagan demonstrated that she had matured as an actress. Although her interests were shifting to opera she agreed to do two more plays with Tyler: critically and financially successful revivals of Arthur Wing Pinero's *Trelawney of the Wells* (1927) and Victorien Sardou's *Diplomacy* (1928).

By 1928 Gahagan was seriously committed to a career in opera. Her European opera debut took shape in two tours, 1929 and 1930, when Cehanovska (her Russian/American opera coach) felt her new pupil was ready to appear in some of the smaller European opera houses. Singing Tosca, Manon Lescaut, Aida, and Santuzza (in *Cavaleria Rusticana*) with some success in Europe, she decided to return to the United States where she felt she could earn more money, but an interview with the Metropolitan Opera Company in late 1929, between the two European trips, proved disappointing. She cut short her 1930 tour because of her father's illness and agreed to play a role in Lili Hatvany's play *Tonight or Never* (1930), produced by David Belasco. Belasco had worked for over a year to get Gahagan to accept the part of a frustrated opera singer in this romantic comedy. He cast a young actor from Jessie Bonstelle's company, Melvyn Douglas, as the male lead. Gahagan and Douglas fell in love even before the show opened and were married during its run. In August of 1931 the couple moved to Hollywood; Samuel Goldwyn had bought the movie rights to *Tonight or Never* for Gloria Swanson and hired the entire cast, but not Helen Gahagan, for the film.

In retrospect, it is clear that her marriage to Douglas refocused Helen Gahagan's sense of a professional career. From 1931 to 1937 she accepted only starring roles that she found satisfying, because of a diminished need to support herself and because of the birth of two children, Peter (born 1933) and Mary Helen (born 1938). In 1932 she played the leading role in Otto Harbach and Jerome Kern's *The Cat and the Fiddle* with the Los Angeles Civic Light Opera at the Belasco and Curran Theatre in San Francisco, and in 1934 she acted in two Broadway plays written by Dan Totheroh: *Moor Born*, in which she played Emily Brontë, and *Mother Lode*, in which she played opposite her husband, who was fast becoming a Hollywood leading man. She played a dramatic Queen Mary opposite **Helen Hayes** as Elizabeth I in a lengthy national tour of Maxwell Anderson's *Mary of Scotland* (1934). Gahagan made one film in her lifetime: H. Rider Haggard's *She* (1935). Although the reviews were generally uncomplimentary, over thirty years later the film won a national award as one of the classic horror films.

Gahagan's final Broadway play, *And Stars Remain* (1936), preceded a return to Europe for a series of singing engagements, climaxed by an appearance at the Salzburg Festival in August 1937. During this tour, she observed first hand the Nazi activities in Germany and Austria and, for the first time, developed a sensitivity for issues beyond her own immediate life and family. When she reached home, she and her husband joined the Hollywood anti-Nazi league, and Helen Gahagan gradually found herself drawn into the political arena. By 1940 she was totally immersed in the volatile climate surrounding national politics to the exclusion of opera or theatre.

Helen Gahagan Douglas's interest in politics had first been aroused by the political controversies surrounding the Dust Bowl migrants to California during the 1930s. This interest led to a friendship with Franklin and Eleanor Roosevelt and to the post of Democratic National Committeewoman from California (1940–1944). In 1944 she ran for Congress with Roosevelt's blessing from a Los Angeles district that embraced parts of Hollywood's fashionable Wilshire Boulevard, Chinatown, a variety of ethnic and blue-collar neighborhoods, and the largest black community in the West. She won and was reelected in 1946 and 1948, each time by an increased margin, with her strongest support coming from organized labor and blacks.

Helen Gahagan Douglas's influence on national policy came not from a powerful legislative position in Congress but from her reputation as a forceful and articulate public speaker. As early as 1940 the Democratic National Committee included Douglas in a key group that campaigned nationally for the party. While in Congress, Douglas found herself deluged with hundreds of invitations to speak at mass rallies, universities, and national and state meetings of liberal organizations. Her superb speaking ability and her persuasive style had their roots in her stage career.

After Helen Gahagan Douglas was defeated for the United States Senate by Richard M. Nixon in 1950, she combined her three career interests in a variety of ways. She did one more play, *First Lady* at New York City Center (1952), but for a number of years she toured small cities and towns singing German lieder and reading Emily Dickinson poems. She continued to accept speaking engagements on political topics, particularly on nuclear disarmament, and intermittently campaigned for presidential and state Democratic candidates. Despite breast cancer, she embarked in 1974 on the writing of her autobiography, *A Full Life*, published two years after her death.

Helen Gahagan Douglas's particular combination of theatrical, operatic, and political careers was unusual. While she never fulfilled predictions that she would some day join the ranks of the leading stars of the American stage, her total career was a brilliant one that was guided by her own choices—first in theatre, then in opera, and finally in politics.

Helen Gahagan Douglas's papers are to be found in the Carl Albert Congressional Research Center, Western History Collection, University of Oklahoma. Documents on her theatrical period are in the New York Public Library Performing Arts Research Center at Lincoln Center. Materials on the political period are located in numerous manuscript collections, particularly the Bancroft Library at the University of California, Berkeley;

the Franklin Delano Roosevelt Library, Hyde Park, New York; and the Library of Congress, Washington, D.C. Although a wealth of journalistic articles have been written over the years on Douglas, little scholarly material exists with the exception of the 1950 campaign. Ingrid Winther Scobie, "Helen Gahagan Douglas and Her 1950 Senate Campaign with Richard M. Nixon," *Southern California Historical Quarterly* (Spring 1976), includes a number of references to the primary and secondary material on the campaign. Douglas wrote a number of articles on political issues during the 1940s, but little during her theatre period. See "To Audiences," *The Drama: A Monthly Review* (July 1923). Her esteem and affection for Eleanor Roosevelt resulted in a memorial volume, *The Eleanor Roosevelt We Remember* (1963). See also Ingrid Winther Scobie, "Helen Gahagan Douglas and the Roosevelt Connection," in Joan Hoff-Wilson and Marjorie Lightman, eds., *Without Precedent: The Life and Career of Eleanor Roosevelt* (1984). Helen Gahagan Douglas's autobiography, *A Full Life* (1982), is a well-written account. Two oral history programs include substantial information on her: the regional Oral History Office at the Bancroft Library in Berkeley and the Indiana University Oral History Program on Melvyn Douglas, which includes many references to Helen Gahagan Douglas. Douglas is listed in *Current Biography, 1944* (1945); *Who's Who in America, 1974–1975* (1975); *Who's Who of American Women, 1975–1976* (1975); *Who Was Who in the Theatre*, Vol. I (1978); and *The Oxford Companion to American Theatre* (1984).

Ingrid Winther Scobie

DRAKE, Sylvie (December 18, 1930-): one of the few women theatre critics for a major metropolitan newspaper, was born in Alexandria, Egypt, the only child of Robert Franco and Simonette (Barda) Franco. Her father was a cotton broker and a stockbroker. She grew up and was educated in Alexandria and attributes her interest in theatre and poetry to a secondary school English teacher who had wanted to become an actress and who devoted much personal time to nurturing her students' interest in the arts and literature.

Few persons can pinpoint exactly when they decide upon their future careers, but Sylvie Franco made her choice when her teacher took her English class to Cairo during the Second World War to see John Gielgud in a production of *Hamlet*, which he was touring for the British equivalent of the American U. S. O. Following that magical evening, though she was only fifteen years of age, Sylvie Franco knew her life must be spent in some aspect of the theatre. Upon graduation from the English Girls' College in Alexandria she matriculated at Oxford and Cambridge universities and earned an Oxford and Cambridge Higher Certificate with distinction in French and English literature.

Pursuing her interest in theatre, Sylvie Franco emigrated to the United States in 1949, where she enrolled at the Pasadena Playhouse, California, as an acting and directing major. In 1952 she married actor Kenneth K. Drake, from whom she was divorced in 1972. Both of her children have chosen careers in theatre. Her daughter, Myriam Jessica, is an actress who has worked most recently with the South Coast Repertory Theatre in Costa Mesa, California. Her son, Robert Ira, a stage manager, has worked in Denver and at the Old Globe Theatre in San Diego, California. In 1973 Drake married Ty Jurras, a public relations man.

In 1950 Sylvie Drake acted Off-Broadway. When she returned to the Los Angeles area, she worked in little theatres and acted and directed from 1953 to 1956 at the Stage Society, a company composed of actors who made their living in the film and television industries but formed their own group in order to work in live theatre.

While she was raising her family, Drake began her career as a writer. She joined the Writers' Guild of America in 1960 and wrote for television from 1960 to 1971. She became a noteworthy drama critic, working for the Los Angeles *Canyon Crier* from 1968 to 1972 and on assignment for the *Los Angeles Times* from 1969 to 1971. She joined the drama staff of the *Times* as a full-time columnist and critic in 1971. There she has remained, becoming one of America's leading theatre critics. Fluent in Italian and French as well as English, she has translated Paul Claudel's *The Tidings Brought to Mary* and Jean Anouilh's *Traveler Without Luggage*.

In 1968 Drake returned to the Pasadena Playhouse to complete work on a master's degree in theatre arts. Drake is interested in educational as well as professional theatre and has often been a guest speaker at conventions of the American Theatre Association and the California Educational Theatre Association. For her work with the American College Theatre Festival she has received both the Gold and Silver Medallions of Excellence awarded jointly by the Amoco Oil Company and the John F. Kennedy Center for the Performing Arts.

Drake was president of the Los Angeles Drama Critics Circle in 1979 and 1980 and is currently on the Executive Board of the American Theatre Critics Association. She received the Beverly Hills Theatre Guild "Bravo" Award in 1983. In November of 1985 she was a delegate to the International Theatre Critics Association World Congress in Rome. For the *Los Angeles Times* Drake reviews approximately eighty plays and musicals each year and writes about one hundred columns, features, and interviews. She exerts a major influence on West Coast theatre, especially in the Los Angeles area.

Information for this essay was obtained through the Public Relations Department of the *Los Angeles Times* and by a personal interview with Sylvie Drake. Drake is listed in *Who's Who in America, 1984–1985* (1984).

Charlotte Kay Motter

DRAPER, Ruth (December 2, 1884–December 30, 1956): actress renowned as a performer of solo dramatic material throughout the Western—and also in the Eastern—world, was born into the patrician family of Dr. William Henry Draper in New York City, the next to youngest in a household of eight children. The two eldest, a girl and a boy, were born to Draper's first wife, Elizabeth Kinnicutt; the others, three boys and two girls, to his second spouse, Ruth Dana, daughter of Charles A. Dana, editor of *The New York Sun*. The youngest Draper, Paul, was the only other child with a lifelong bent toward performance. He sang occasionally in major concert halls in the United States and England and with his wife created an artistic and literary salon in their London home. Their son,

Paul, Jr., became a dancer, who occasionally appeared in later years on bills with his aunt Ruth Draper.

Life in the Drapers' uptown Manhattan household was spirited but orderly, eclectic but refined. The children were often under the direction of governesses and tutors, yet rarely far from the concerned care of doting parents. Celebrated guests and heady conversation charged the atmosphere, and full schedules of lessons and cultural outings enriched the environment in which the children matured. Ruth Draper began at an early age to regale her siblings by mimicking teachers and acquaintances. Her amusing portrayals were encouraged by her parents, who brought dinner guests to the nursery to be entertained by the precocious family mimic. Aside from two years (1894–1896) at Miss Spence's School in Manhattan, Ruth Draper was educated by private tutors.

In adolescence her impersonations grew into drawing-room recitations, and in her twenties she began to put them into writing. The incidental satiric observations were lengthened, and serious dramatic overtones began to appear. Now she was asked to perform for friends at informal parties and weekend sojourns in the country. Increasingly conscientious about these efforts, she refined her skills in long rehearsals. With no coaching in elocution or stage deportment, she developed her talent alone. Experimenting continually, she pruned and polished as she shaped her performances to fit her scripts and adjusted the scripts to suit her performances. Caricatures born of nursery revels were meticulously fleshed out as nuances of gesture and inflection replaced the broad strokes.

Eventually her portfolio of personality sketches became a gallery of richly detailed portraits, and Ruth Draper was increasingly in demand. Manhattan hostesses vied to present the charming and mercurial young performer. Appearances at charity benefits soon followed and then performances before larger and more varied gatherings. With ample material for a full evening's entertainment, Draper was no longer an added feature but the whole attraction. She had "come out" as a debutante in 1903 and now moved assuredly through Manhattan society. Facility in foreign languages and extensive travel put her at ease abroad as well. She was, however, becoming concerned about her role in a milieu that sanctioned few life choices for women. She mused—in flowery and rather melancholy verse—about her destiny. Should she turn her fascinating avocation into a professional career? She was being persuaded toward the latter course by family friends, including the famed pianist Ignace Paderewski. Furthermore, she had been encouraged by the New York success of Beatrice Herford, a British actress who played humorous monologues at various times from the 1890s to the 1930s. Draper was also inspired by Chinese theatre traditions employed in the play *The Yellow Jacket* in 1912: with mime, few properties, and the audience's imagination, the stage leapt to life. It remained for the English novelist Henry James, who had seen her work, to frame the elegant summons that endorsed her move into a performance career, "You have woven your own very beautiful little Persian carpet. Stand on it!" (quoted by Zabel in *The Art of Ruth Draper*, p. 51).

In 1914 Draper began taking paid engagements as well as giving benefits for the war effort in towns all across America. She traveled with a few shawls, hats, canes, and handbags, which, with a chair or table against a neutral backdrop, comprised almost the whole of her scenic investiture. In 1916 she made an insignificant debut in a Broadway show and appeared in an evening of short plays. She never again joined other actors in a traditional play nor acted words other than her own.

On January 29, 1920, she made her London debut as a professional monologist. She was an immediate and enormous success. Bookings all across Canada and again across the United States followed, with an appearance in the Blue Room of the White House for President and Mrs. Warren G. Harding and a command performance at Windsor Castle in 1926. Draper toured for the next thirty years in America, Italy, Poland, Denmark, and France, and eventually in such remote and romantic theatre venues as India, Australia, and Singapore.

She brought her monologues to Broadway for the first time in 1928, appearing eight times each week for nineteen weeks, thereby breaking previous records for a solo performance in the New York theatre. Private presentations for Sarah Bernhardt and Eleanora Duse followed; and she received plaudits from celebrities in and out of the theatre all over the world, many of whom became acquaintances and friends. She became particularly close to the anti-Fascist poet Lauro de Bosis, whose death in his plane following a daring leaflet-dropping mission was a great sorrow to her. She established a lectureship in his honor and helped friends of his who fled Mussolini's regime.

A usual Draper program consisted of short and longer monologues chosen from her large repertoire. Where more than one character spoke in a piece she presented them in sequence, never attempting dialogue between characters. Her exquisitely detailed delivery, which seemingly filled the stage with characters and action, was her great strength. "The Italian Lesson," perhaps her most famous selection, is typical in its powerful delineation of multiple characters, although only Draper speaks. She portrays an elegant matron who, undaunted by the intrusions of a frenetic morning—servants, children, telephones, and a puppy—pursues her lesson in Dante. A similar but more deeply poignant character appeared in "Three Women and Mr. Clifford," a trio of monologues detailing the complex web of love and deceit that enmeshes a wealthy man's wife, his mistress, and his secretary. Although Mr. Clifford never speaks, his character is, by implication, etched as penetratingly as the other three. Another trilogy, from the opposite end of the social scale, "Three Generations in a Court of Domestic Relations," presents the touching breakup of an immigrant family. Other pieces take place at parties and dances, hospitals, and railway stations, with Draper appearing as a dressmaker, governess, charwoman, miner's wife, lady of the Spanish court of Philip IV, and various other characters.

Having opened yet another of her many engagements in New York City on Christmas Day of 1956, she played two performances on Saturday, returned to her apartment, on December 30 and died in her sleep.

Draper received the first of several honorary degrees, the Master of Arts from Hamilton College at Clinton, New York, in 1924 at the suggestion of alumnus Alexander Woollcott. She was named Doctor of Fine Arts in 1941 by the University of Maine and Doctor of Humane Letters by Smith College in 1947. In 1951, at a private audience at Buckingham Palace, King George VI conferred on her the insignia of Honorary Commander of the Most Excellent Order of the British Empire. She received the honorary Doctorate of Laws from the University of Edinburgh the same year and in 1954 received an honorary Doctorate of Law from Cambridge University. A year after her death she was honored with a memorial exhibition tracing her career through portraits, photographs, posters, letters, and other memorabilia, including the few well-worn stage properties and shawls with which she had created her remarkable gallery of characters.

Thirty-five of Draper's monologues have been carefully edited and published with extensive biographical notes by Morton Dauwen Zabel in *The Art of Ruth Draper* (1960). Zabel identifies another fifteen pieces that remained incomplete—apparently never finished or performed—at the time of Draper's death. Other early monologues are mentioned by title in theatre programs but have apparently been lost. Neilla Warren has edited *The Letters of Ruth Draper, 1920–1956* (1979). See also Iris Ougo, "Ruth Draper and Her Company of Characters," *Cornhill Magazine* (Winter 1957–1958). A shorter version of the same article appears in *The Atlantic Monthly* (October 1958). Reviews of Draper's work may be found in John Ciardi, "The Genius of Ruth Draper," *Saturday Review* (October 14, 1961); Francis Hackett, "Miss Ruth Draper," *New Republic* (March 23, 1921); and Alexander Woollcott, *Going to Pieces* (1928). An interview with Draper appeared in *The New Yorker* (March 6, 1954). On May 5, 1982, actress Patrizia Norzia opened at the Cherry Lane Theatre in New York, presenting a program of the monologues under the collective title *Cast of Characters*. Norzia played a brief run, changing monologues at various performances as Draper had done. The best recordings of Draper's achievements are the ones she herself made for the Spoken Arts label, New Rochelle, New York. Draper's obituary appeared in the *New York Times* (December 31, 1956). Biographies of her appear in *Notable American Women*, Vol. IV: *The Modern Period* (1980); *The Oxford Companion to the Theatre* (1983); and *The Oxford Companion to American Theatre* (1984).

Donn B. Murphy

DRESSLER, Marie (November 9, 1869–July 28, 1934): stage and screen actress and vaudeville performer, was born Leila Marie Koerber in Cobourg, Ontario, Canada. She was the younger of two daughters born to Alexander Rudolph and Anne (Henderson) Koerber. She was twice married: on May 6, 1894, to George Francis Hoppert, whom she divorced in 1896, and about 1911 to James H. Dalton, her manager, who died in 1921. She died from cancer in 1934 in Santa Barbara, California, and was buried in Forest Lawn Memorial Park, Glendale.

A plump, awkward child, Leila Koerber discovered that she could attract amused attention by exaggerating her clumsiness. She found solace in entertaining others, and having determined that "fate cast me to play the role of the ugly duckling with no promise of swanning," she decided to become a come-dienne, to play "my life as a comedy rather than the tragedy many would have made of it" (*The Life Story of an Ugly Duckling*, p. 2). It proved a wise choice, for by the time she died, she had become one of Hollywoo-d's best-loved stars, renowned for her portrayals of strong, self-sufficient, humorous older women.

Since her father, an impoverished musician of uncertain temperament, had a habit of first attracting and then alienating his pupils, Leila Koerber's family lived in chronic poverty, moving from town to town in Canada and the United States. As a teen-ager, Leila was fiercely determined to seek a job in order to improve her mother's financial situation, and having no formal education, she decided to pursue a career as a circus performer. She was diverted, however, by a newspaper advertisement recruiting actors for a second-rate dramatic stock company touring in Michigan. She answered the ad and found herself at age fourteen the leading lady of a group of touring performers managed by the actor Robert Wallace. Because of her father's opposition to using the family name on stage, she took the name of her aunt, Marie Dressler, and in 1886 launched her professional career with an appearance as Cigarette, the camp follower, in the dramatization of Ouida's novel *Under Two Flags*.

She subsequently found chorus work in touring light opera companies managed by Jules Robert Grau and Frank Deshon. She had a natural singing voice but discovered that she was "too homely for a prima donna and too big for a soubrette" (*The Great Movie Stars*, p. 177). Therefore, she concentrated on playing character parts such as Katisha in *The Mikado*. She spent a grueling three-year engagement with the Bennett-Moulton Opera Company, which toured the northern central states and New England. With this company she learned a new comic opera every week, eventually playing thirty-eight different operatic parts, ranging from the leading roles to older character women. By age twenty she was a seasoned stage veteran with a following.

She made her New York debut at the Fifth Avenue Theatre on May 28, 1892, as Cunigonde in *The Robber of the Rhine*, a romantic comedy with music by Maurice Barrymore. The play closed after five weeks, however, and Marie Dressler, by this time supporting her entire family (including her mother, father, sister, brother—in-law, and two elderly aunts) sang songs nightly at the Atlantic Garden in the Bowery and at Koster and Bial's Music Hall while desperately seeking other acting jobs.

Her breakthrough came when she was chosen to support Lillian Russell in both *The Princess Nicotine*, which opened in November 1893, and *Girofle-Girofla* in March 1894. She had several other New York engagements but scored her first major personal success when she created the role of music hall singer Flo Honeydew in *The Lady Slavey* (February 1896); because of that role she became widely known as a first-rate musical comedienne. The musical played for four years, both in New York and on tour; but when illness finally forced Dressler to leave the show in Denver, she found that obligations to her family once again strained her financial resources. Soon she was working in shows like

The Man in the Moon (1899), *Miss Prinnt* (1900), and *The King's Carnival* (1901). She played in musicals, burlesques, and comedies and then decided to try her luck in vaudeville. In 1905 she joined comedian Joe Weber at Weber's Music Hall and was featured in such vaudeville reviews as *Higgledy-Piggledy* (1904) and *Twiddle-Twaddle* (1906). Energetic and inventive and never averse to falling down, standing on her head, or in any other way making herself ridiculous in order to amuse audiences, she was as great a success in vaudeville as she had been in musical comedy. She toured with Weber in 1906 and then made her first appearance in London at the Palace Theatre on October 28, 1907, in a variety show. She scored a great personal triumph at both the Palace and the Coliseum, but when she tried in 1909 to put on a production of two American musicals, *Philopoena* and *The Collegettes*, British audiences found them unamusing. She returned to New York in 1909, bankrupt and severely ill with an ulcerated throat.

Nevertheless, she was acting again in a few months, and a year later she was established in the greatest success of her stage career, *Tillie's Nightmare* (1910). For two years she played the role of Tillie Blobbs, the boardinghouse drudge who dreams of richer worlds, singing "Heaven Will Protect the Working Girl," a song forever afterwards associated with her. After *Roly Poly* (1912) she attempted to produce her own review, *Marie Dressler's All Star Gambols*, but it lasted only eight performances, and she eventually went to Los Angeles for a rest. While there, she was offered a new challenge—a film role. She was approached by Mack Sennett and Bauman of Keystone Pictures and offered a part in a movie. Never afraid to experiment, Dressler accepted, and the result was *Tillie's Punctured Romance* (1914). The cast included Mabel Normand and an unknown comic actor named Charlie Chaplin, whom Dressler is said to have selected for the film. No expense was spared (six reels instead of the usual one or two), and *Tillie's Punctured Romance* was a great hit with audiences. Dressler followed it with a succession of other films such as *Tillie's Tomato Surprise* (1915) and *Tillie Wakes Up* (1917), but they had little success and her film career seemed destined for oblivion.

Meanwhile, she threw herself into the war effort. She made hundreds of speeches, sold millions of Liberty Bonds, and entertained servicemen, always paying her own expenses. When the war was over, she displayed the same wholehearted determination in fighting to establish Actors' Equity Association. She helped to found the Chorus Equity Association, of which she was president, and championed the actors' strike of 1919. Newspapers referred to her as "strike heroine," but she found herself persona non grata with important managers, and her career languished. Offers came less and less frequently, and the public, caught up in the postwar craze for youth and beauty, seemed to have little use for an overweight, aging comedienne. She obtained a few stage roles in shows such as *The Dancing Girl* (1923) and made some one-reel comedies in France, but she was in financial straits when Allan Dwan offered her a small part in a 1927 film, *The Joy Girl*. Then Frances Marion, a top MGM scenarist whom

Dressler had befriended years earlier, fashioned a screenplay for her, *The Cal-
lahans and the Murphys* (1927), and convinced Irving Thalberg to produce it.
Marie Dressler was signed on at $1,500 a week; and though the picture was
withdrawn because of protests from Irish pressure groups, other supporting parts
followed in the films *Bringing Up Father* (1928), *The Divine Lady* (1929), and
Chasing Rainbows (1930). Her career slowly gained momentum. "There is no
such thing as age," she said (*The Life Story of an Ugly Duckling*, p. 233), and
at a time of life when others contemplated retirement, she set out to win new
audiences and conquer the world of film.

She regained stardom in the film of Eugene O'Neill's *Anna Christie* (1930).
Frances Marion persuaded Thalberg to let Dressler test for the role of Marthy,
the waterfront hag, a serious part unlike those she had played thus far. Such
shrewd theatre managers as Herbert Beerbohm-Tree and Augustin Daly had
always maintained that she had great potential as a serious actress, and she now
got a chance to prove them right. Greta Garbo, the film's star, is said to have
been impressed by her work, and so were the critics and MGM, who now offered
Dressler a contract. Dressler was a success in the film, but, as Richard Griffith
said, "What to do with an ugly old woman who had, none could say how, stolen
a picture from Greta Garbo?" (*The Movie Stars*, p. 86). She became typed as
a worldly wise, battered mother figure and was teamed with Polly Moran in
slapstick comedies like *Caught Short* (1930) and *Politics* (1931) and with Wallace
Beery in sentimental comedies like *Min and Bill* (1930) and *Tugboat Annie*
(1933). She was a star again, commanding a salary of $5,000 a week, winning
in 1931 the Academy (Oscar) Award for best actress for her performance in *Min
and Bill*, and topping the popularity polls in both the *Motion Picture Herald* and
the *Hollywood Reporter* as the biggest box-office draw in the films of 1933.
Though she was already suffering from cancer, some of her finest work was
done during her last years as she brought fifty years of experience and skill to
Dinner at Eight (1933) and *Christopher Bean* (1933). By the time she died,
MGM was billing her as "The World's Greatest Actress," and she was still at
the top of the popularity lists.

Dressler's position in film history is unique. In an age supposedly dedicated
to glamour, she proved that one need not be young or beautiful to succeed with
the public. At a time when the unknown and untrained were pushed forward as
stars, she demonstrated the advantages of decades of rigorous stage training. As
an actress she was a master of technique, improvisation, facial expressiveness,
and comic timing, and she was able to adjust the broadness of her effects to the
size of any theatre or medium. "Her appeal was universal," said *Photoplay* in
tribute to her (*The Great Movie Stars*, p. 179). She said of herself, "I am not
afraid, for fear means death, and I know that the reaching-out, giving-out part
of me—that part that likes to make people laugh and cry and be happy—can
never die" (*The Life Story of an Ugly Duckling*, p. 234).

Dressler left two autobiographies: *The Life Story of an Ugly Duckling* (1924) and *My
Own Story* (1934). Lewis C. Strang writes about her early career on the stage in *Prima*

Donnas and Soubrettes of Light Opera and Musical Comedy in America (1900). There are clippings about Dressler in the Harvard Theatre Collection. Her obituary appeared in the *New York Times* (July 29, 1934). Dressler is listed in *Who's Who on the Stage, 1908* (1908); *Dictionary of American Biography*, Vol. XL, Supplement One (1944); Bernard Griffith, *The Movie Stars* (1970); *Notable American Women*, Vol. I (1971); *A Biographical Dictionary of Film* (1976); *Who Was Who in the Theatre*, Vol. II (1978); *The Oxford Companion to the Theatre* (1967); and *The Oxford Companion to American Theatre* (1984).

Laurilyn J. Harris

DREW, Louisa Lane, better known as Mrs. John Drew (January 10, 1820–August 31, 1897): actress and manager of the Arch Street Theatre in Philadelphia, was born in London. A child of actors, Louisa Lane was on stage as a babe in arms. Following the death of her father, Thomas F. Lane, about 1825, Louisa and her mother, Eliza Trenter (or Trentner) Lane, emigrated to the United States. Louisa Lane made her American debut at Philadelphia's Walnut Street Theatre on September 26, 1827, as the Duke of York in Junius Brutus Booth's production of *Richard III*. She first appeared in New York at the Bowery Theatre on March 8, 1828, as Little Pickle in *The Spoiled Child*. As a child star, Louisa Lane appeared with noted actors of the day in Philadelphia, Baltimore, New York, Albany, Providence, Boston, Natchez, New Orleans, St. Louis, Louisville, Cincinnati, and other cities.

Eliza Trenter Lane had married John Kinlock, the manager of the Walnut Street Theatre, and late in 1831, Louisa Lane and the Kinlock family left for Jamaica. John Kinlock and a baby died there of yellow fever, so Louisa, her mother, and the two Kinlock daughters, Georgiana and Adine, returned to the United States in 1832.

At twelve Louisa Lane moved into more adult parts, acting with her mother in companies along the eastern seaboard. By 1835 she was playing such roles as Maria in Richard Brinsley Sheridan's *The School for Scandal* at the St. Charles Street Theatre in New Orleans. In March 1836 Louisa Lane married Henry Blaine Hunt, whom she described as "a very good singer, a nice actor, and a very handsome man of forty" (*Autobiographical Sketch of Mrs. John Drew*, p. 77). They were divorced in 1847, and Hunt died in 1854 after a respectable but undistinguished career. Under the name Louisa Lane Hunt, she toured as leading lady with her mother, half sister, and brother-in-law throughout the South, Midwest, and East, acting with all the major stars and for all the major managers of the time, including Edwin Forrest, Junius Brutus Booth, Ellen Tree, James H. Caldwell, Sol Smith, F. C. Wemyss, James F. Murdoch, William Macready, James H. Hackett, and Charles Kean. She sang opera and operetta and danced ballet, but she was best known and most admired as a comic actress. She moved with ease between star tours and engagements as a leading stock actress. In June of 1848 she married George Mossop, a supporting player and a specialist in Irish roles. He died in October of 1849 after a short illness. Louisa continued to act as Mrs. Mossop, the name under which she had been hired, until April 1851, when her July 1850 marriage to her third and final husband, John Drew, was revealed. She was thereafter known as Mrs. John Drew. Considered second only to Tyrone Power, John Drew (1797–1841) was a noted actor in Irish parts until his untimely death from "congestion of the brain" in 1862 at the age of thirty-five. John and Louisa Lane Drew had three children: Louisa Eliza Drew Mendum (December 7, 1851-May 17, 1889), who never went on the stage as an adult; John Wheatley Sheridan Drew (1853–1927), a famous actor of drawing-room comedy and for many years one of Augustin Daly's "big four" stars; and Georgiana Drew Barrymore (1855–1893), who had a successful though brief acting career and was the mother of Lionel, John, and **Ethel Barrymore**. In addition, Louisa Lane Drew adopted the daughter of her half sister, Georgiana Kinlock Stephens, who died in 1864 after an unremarkable acting career. The daughter, Adine Stephens, died in 1888. She also adopted Sidney Drew White (1863–1919), son of John White and Maria Drew; under the name Sidney Drew he had considerable success in vaudeville and films.

Louisa Lane Drew's major contributions to the American theatre as actress and manager span the decades from 1850 to 1890. In the 1850s, she toured with her half sister Georgiana, with her mother Mrs. Kinlock (who retired in 1855 and died in 1887), and with John Drew and his brother Frank. She was a leading lady and star throughout the Midwest and East. From 1853 to 1855 she performed at the Arch Street Theatre in Philadelphia under the management of John Drew and William Wheatley. As she moved into older leading parts—Gertrude rather than Ophelia, Lady Teazle rather than Maria—she continued to play mostly comic repertory (from fifty to eighty parts a season) with great success. In 1861 Drew took over the lease of Philadelphia's Arch Street Theatre, which she managed until 1892. She maintained a company of actors there until 1879, after which the Arch Street Theatre served primarily as a road house for touring combinations, though still under her lease and management.

The first eleven years, 1861 to 1872, were the most successful for Drew at the Arch Street Theatre. During that time its company rivaled Lester Wallack's in New York and the Boston Museum's in excellence. The company was augmented by visiting stars in moderate runs; and young stock actors were hired, encouraged, and trained by Mrs. Drew. Many of these actors credited their subsequent successes to Louisa Drew. Her revivals of the comic classics—Goldsmith, Sheridan, Shakespeare—were particularly praised, as was the quality of her management. This was a period of relentless work for her. She labored to choose popular plays, to put together a skilled company of actors, to stave off her competition, and to support her many dependents. After 1872, because of changing theatrical conditions, the number of visiting stars increased, combination companies began to appear, and the quality of the resident players declined. John and Georgie Drew, who had debuted with their mother's company, went on to work for Augustin Daly (John in 1875 and Georgie in 1876). Drew continued to star at her own theatre and occasionally went on tour, but she began to give up day-to-day management.

In 1880, while continuing to hold the Arch Street theatre, Drew began a series of star tours as Mrs. Malaprop in *The Rivals* with Joseph Jefferson as Bob Acres. Even though on tour, she remained faithful to the Arch Street Theatre stockholders, hiring managers and appearing there in starring engagements. Her Lady Teazle in *The School for Scandal* was still praised in 1885, though she was then sixty-five years old. She and members of her family continued to appear at the Arch Street Theatre, and she toured with a company managed by Sidney Drew. The tours with Jefferson ceased temporarily with his "retirement" in 1892. According to her autobiography, receipts were poor when she returned that year to Philadelphia, and at age seventy-two she decided to give up the Arch Street Theatre's lease. The tributes and testimonials that accompanied her retirement from management attested to the respect and affection that people felt towards her in Philadelphia and in the profession.

With the period of her greatest achievement as stock actress, manager, and star behind her, Drew spent the years from 1892 until her death in 1897 assembling her memoirs, touring for Charles Frohman and Sidney Drew, acting with Joseph Jefferson, and living with her son John Drew, Jr., in New York. Thomas Allston Brown records that her colleagues called her "the best stage director ever seen" (*Famous American Actors of Today*, p. 133). Frank Stull said of her management that she did it "better than any man in the country" (*Lippincott's Monthly Magazine*, March 1905), and countless other actors who worked for her attested to her talent as manager and as teacher of acting. The reviews of her own acting ability were overwhelmingly favorable from the time of her assumption of adult leading roles (indeed of her child acting as well) until her death. She was, moreover, respected and affectionately regarded by those who worked with and for her. With grace and humor she sustained a long professional life in the theatre.

Biographies of Louisa Lane Drew include Dorothy E. Stolp, "Mrs. John Drew, American Actress and Manager, 1820–1897" (Unpublished Ph.D. dissertation, Louisiana State University, 1953) and Mrs. Drew's own *Autobiographical Sketch of Mrs. John Drew* (published posthumously, 1899). She is discussed in other stage-related biographies, such as Joseph Jefferson, *The Autobiography of Joseph Jefferson* (1897); Otis Skinner, *Footlights and Spotlights* (1923); Lester Wallack, *Memories of Fifty Years* (1889); John Drew, *My Years on the Stage* (1921); Lionel Barrymore, *We Barrymores* (1951); Ethel Barrymore, *Memories* (1955); and Gene Fowler, *Goodnight Sweet Prince* (about John Barrymore, 1944). Other sources include **Clara Morris**, *Life on the Stage* (1901); Clara Morris, "The Dressing Room Reception Where I First Met Ellen Terry and Mrs. John Drew," *McClure's Magazine* (December 1903); A. Frank Stull, "Where Famous Actors Learned Their Art," *Lippincott's Monthly Magazine* (March 1905); Montrose J. Moses, *Famous Actor Families* (1906); F. E. McKay and Charles E. L. Wingate, *Famous American Actors of Today* (1896); and Rosemarie K. Bank, "Louisa Lane Drew at the Arch Street Theatre: Repertory and Actor Training in Nineteenth-Century Philadel,phia," *Theatre Studies* (1977–1978/1978–1979). The Robinson Locke Scrapbooks of the Theatre

Collection in the New York Public Library Performing Arts Research Center at Lincoln Center contain clippings about Mrs. Drew. She is included in T. Allston Brown, *History of the American Stage* (1870, reissued 1969); *Who Was Who in America*, Historical Volume (1963); *Notable American Women*, Vol. I (1971); William C. Young, *Famous Actors and Actresses on the American Stage*, Vol. I (1975); *The Oxford Companion to the Theatre* (1983); and *The Oxford Companion to American Theatre* (1984).

Rosemarie K. Bank

DREXLER, Rosalyn (November 25, 1926–): playwright, novelist, painter, was born Rosalyn Selma Bronznick in the Bronx, New York, where her father, George Bronznick, was a pharmacist and her mother, Hilda (Sherman) Bronznick, a secretary. Because her father's cousin was married to Chico Marx, Rosalyn as a child saw all the Marx Brothers movies. These films left a lasting influence that was to surface later in the language and style of her plays. Although her family was too poor to attend Broadway theatre, Rosalyn enjoyed the vaudeville skits that played at no extra cost after the showing of a movie in those days.

In her youth Rosalyn Bronznick felt clumsy and weird. She labeled herself an outsider. To relieve these feelings of inadequacy she started writing because she had power over words. Unable to stop her parents' arguments, she wrote down their mutual accusations and presented them "as a court record." Her parents, of course, tore them up. This experience, she says, taught her that "writing has an effect and is disposable" (*New York Times*, February 27, 1975).

Rosalyn's mother wanted her daughter to become an actress. At nine or ten Rosalyn won a scholarship to study acting with Erwin Piscator at his Dramatic Workshop in New York, but she quit after one lesson. Later, she dropped out of high school and is largely self-educated.

In 1946 she married Sherman Drexler, a painter and professor at City College of the City University of New York. She has two children, Rachel (born 1947), who is an actress, and Danny (born 1958), a musician. Early in their marriage Drexler made a tour of southern and midwestern states as a lady wrestler under the name of Rosa Carlo, "The Mexican Spitfire." Her novel *To Smithereen* (1972) recounts the semi-autobiographical story of a young woman who became a wrestler to please her art-critic lover who found women wrestlers were a sexual "turn-on." A later musical play, *Delicate Feelings* (produced at the Theatre for the New City in 1984), features two lady mud wrestlers.

In 1961 Drexler started her first play *Home Movies* as a secret project to amuse herself. She was influenced by Eugene Ionesco's *The Bald Soprano*, which expressed in play form the type of weirdness she herself felt. (Up until this time she had written a diary that later became the novel *I Am the Beautiful Stranger*, published in 1965). The favorable comments of some friends about *Home Movies* encouraged her to take the play to the Judson Poets' Theatre in Greenwich Village, where it was first produced in March 1964. With the support of Orson Bean, *Home Movies*, called the "first musical of the absurd," moved in May

1964 to the Off-Broadway Provincetown Playhouse. It won the 1964 *Village Voice* Off-Broadway (Obie) Award for most distinguished Off-Broadway play. In addition to writing plays and novels Drexler was also painting, creating sculpture, and writing short stories, feature articles, movie reviews (for the *New York Times*), and screenplays. At the time her first play was receiving its première production, a showing of her paintings occurred at the Kornblee Gallery in New York. She has been described as "a lightning creator. Painting, sculpture, literature leap from her like tongue-flicks from a chameleon" (*Newsweek*, March 30, 1964, p. 53). Asked why she wrote, Drexler answered, "I'm writing because that's the place that I can express myself and say what I really feel and think about" (*Mademoiselle*, August 1972, p. 289). Her plays, "written in the tradition of the Marx Brothers and the Beatles, . . . aim at upsetting some of man's hallowed applecarts" (*Line of Least Existence and Other Plays*, back cover). Her success with *Home Movies* brought her to the conclusion that "a play can be what you want to say. It can be anything. So I wrote down a whole list of things a play could be—time of day, what you eat, anger, history, anything. It just opened everything up for me, so I wrote a lot of plays very fast" (*The Massachusetts Review*, Winter/Spring 1972, p. 267).

According to Richard Gilman (Introduction to *Line of Least Existence*, p. ix), a motto for all her plays might be this line from the play *Least Existence*: "Don't you know that appearance is everything and style is a way of living?" Gilman also noted, "All the truths she has to offer are contained in the appearance of her plays, in her style—the words and gestures she selects, the way her imagination chooses to live publicly. Imagination equals style equals play" (Introduction to *Line of Least Existence*, pp. ix-x). A later work, *She Who Was He*, produced in New York in 1973, diverges from her usual approach. Set in pre-Biblical times, the play, about the murder of Queen Hatshepsut, puts aside hijinks and "leaves the modern and concrete for . . . the eternal seriousness of myth" (Arthur Sainer in *Contemporary Dramatists*, p. 204). A closer look at three of Drexler's plays reveals her themes and techniques. In *Home Movies*, a pseudo-religious, sexually stimulated woman is depressed over her exercise-crazed husband's death and her daughter's desire to abandon her virginity "with one fell swoop of the moopen." A cast of characters flickers through to sympathize and to eulogize the husband, who in the end is delivered alive to her home in a large wooden closet. He challenges his wife to a wrestling match as sexual foreplay. In *Hot Buttered Roll* (produced in 1966 by the New Dramatists' Committee in New York), a billionaire engages a crew to give him a kick that will break his sex-o-meter. The play hops from sweetness to savagery (literally from Jewel, the female bodyguard, to Savage, the purveyor of burly girls) as the billionaire seeks his kicks and the crew struggles to capture the billions. In *The Line of Least Existence* (produced March 1968, at Judson Poets' Theatre, with music by Al Carmines), Dr. Toloon-Fraak, a psychiatrist-pimppusher, employs Ibolya, a "groupie," in his undercouch drug-and-sex-trafficking operation. Ibolya acts out Fraak's sex fantasies and gives birth to smuggled drugs. At home, Mrs. Toloon-Fraak has an affair with Andy, the hip-talking dog with sunglasses. In *Softly, and Consider the Nearness* (produced in 1973 by the New York Theatre Strategy but written about 1964), Nona, a solitary office clerk, courts and marries her walking and talking television; she unites herself with its world—its blue light is her blue heaven. Drexler's novels—*Cosmopolitan Girl* (1974), *Starburn* (1977), and *Bad Guy* (1982)—likewise echo her plays' characters, events, and themes.

Drexler's plays have not been as extensively produced as she would wish, but some have enjoyed London productions (e.g., *Hot Buttered Roll* and *The Line of Least Existence*). The New Dramatists' Committee, the New York Theatre Strategy, the Milwaukee Repertory Theatre, and the Theatre for the New City have been major producers of Drexler's plays. In 1979 the Theatre for the New City produced *The Writer's Opera*, a comedy inspired by the life of Suzanne Valadon and her son Maurice Utrillo and depicting the woman as artist and mother. Drexler received a second Obie for *The Writer's Opera*. Theatre for the New City also produced *Graven Image* in 1980 and *Delicate Feelings* in 1984.

Drexler is a member of the New Dramatists, the New York Theatre Strategy, the Dramatists Guild, P.E.N., and Actors' Studio. She was also a member of the short-lived Women's Theatre Council (formed in 1972), which included **Megan Terry**, **Maria Irene Fornés**, **Rochelle Owens**, **Adrienne Kennedy**, and **Julie Bovasso**. Drexler received Rockefeller Foundation grants (1965, 1968, and 1974), a MacDowell Fellowship (1970–1971), and an Emmy Award for writing excellence from the Academy of Television Arts and Sciences for *The Lily Show*, a Lily Tomlin special.

In 1975 a film about Drexler appeared at the Whitney Museum, New York. The sixty-minute film *Who Does She Think She Is?* was directed by Patricia Jaffe and Gaby Rogers and starred Drexler. It presented her family and daily life, her fantasies, her singing, and an interview with Jack Kroll of *Newsweek*. Several of Kroll's reviews summarize the general critical view of Drexler as a talented artist and writer (*Newsweek*, February 9, 1970, and April 1, 1968). He finds her "a playwright with a brilliant gift, not only for language, but for making language work on many levels with the ease and excitement of a Cossack riding his horse everywhere but in the saddle" (February 9, 1970, p. 95). "She has the great and necessary gift of fashioning a new, total innocence out of the total corruption that she clearly sees. With a lot of laughs!" (April 1, 1968, p. 88). Drexler has been called the first Marx Sister or "Kafka as interpreted by the Marx Brothers" (*New York Times Book Review*, June 28, 1970, p. 5). In 1985 Rosalyn Drexler was one of eight playwrights named by the Rockefeller Foundation to receive grants to support residencies with professional theatres. Through the grant Drexler has been associated with the Theatre for the New City, New York, where her play *Green River Murders* opened in April 1986. In 1988 the Magic Theatre of Omaha produced another new Drexler play, *The Heart that Eats Itself*.

Drexler's plays *The Line of Least Existence, Home Movies, The Investigation, Hot Buttered Roll, Softly, and Consider the Nearness*, and *The Bed Was Full* appear in the collection titled *The Line of Least Existence and Other Plays* (1967). *The Off-off-Broadway Book*, edited by Albert Poland and Bruce Mailman (1972), contains *Home Movies* and background information. *Collision Course*, edited by Edward Parone (1969), contains *Skywriting*, which is also contained in *A Century of Plays by American Women*, edited by Rachel France (1979). *Transients Welcome* (1986) includes three 1985 Obie Award-winning plays: *Room 17C, Lobby,* and *Utopia Parkway*. Plays not included in the above publications are *Invitation* (1971), *Message from Garcia* (1971), *Was I Good?* (1971), *She Who Was He* (1973), *The Writer's Opera* (1979), *Graven Image* (1980), and *Delicate Feelings* (1984). Also of interest are articles by Rosalyn Drexler in the *New York Times*: "Where Are the Women Playwrights?" (May 20, 1973), "Notes on the Occasion of Having 'Line of Least Existence & Other Plays' Remaindered at Marboro Book Shops" (November 7, 1971), and "She's Glad 'The Emigrants' Came" (October 22, 1972). Drexler's "Seeking the Life of Most Existence" appeared in the *Village Voice* (April 4, 1968). Other articles of interest include Jack Kroll, "Looking for Ibolya," *Newsweek* (April 1, 1968); Jane Goulianos, "Women and the Avant-Garde Theatre: Interviews with Rochelle Owens, Crystal Field, Rosalyn Drexler," *The Massachusetts Review* (Winter/ Spring 1972); Nora Sayre, "A Visit with Rosalyn Drexler at the Whitney," *New York Times* (February 27, 1975); and "Five Important Playwrights Talk About Theatre Without Compromise and Sexism," *Mademoiselle* (August 1972). Mel Gussow's review of *The Writer's Opera* appeared in the *New York Times* (March 16, 1979), and his review of *Graven Image* also appeared in the *New York Times* (May 17, 1980). Sylviane Gold's review of *Delicate Feelings* was in *The Wall Street Journal* (August 1, 1968). Rosalyn Drexler is listed in *Contemporary Dramatists* (1982), *Contemporary Literary Criticism* (1974), *Modern American Literature* (1976), *Contemporary Authors* (1979), *World Authors 1970–1975* (1980), and *The Writer's Directory 1984–1986* (1983).

Carolyn Karis

DUFF, Mary Ann (1794?–September 5, 1857): actress, was born Mary Ann Dyke in London. She began her career at the Dublin Theatre, Ireland, as part of a dancing trio with her two sisters, Ann and Elizabeth. They were the daughters of an Englishman in the service of the East India Company. Little else is known of their father, except that he died abroad, leaving his family impoverished. Under their mother's supervision, the girls were trained by D'Egville, the ballet master of the King's Theatre, London, and made their debut in 1809 in Dublin. Later that year, Irish poet Thomas Moore fell in love with fifteen-year-old Mary Ann Dyke and composed verses for her. She did not return his affections, and Moore later married her sister Elizabeth. Several years later, her younger sister Ann married William Murray, brother of Mrs. Henry Siddons and manager of the Theatre Royal of Edinburgh. Ann Dyke Murray died shortly after her marriage.

In 1810 Mary Ann Dyke met John R. Duff, an actor born in Dublin who had been a classmate of Moore's at Trinity College. John Duff, who had been a law student at Trinity before entering the theatre, was offered a position at the Federal Street Theatre in Boston under the management of Snelling Powell and James Dickson. He proposed marriage to Mary Ann Dyke; she accepted, and they sailed for America in July 1810, shortly after their marriage. Duff made her

American debut at the Federal Street Theatre on December 30, 1810, as Juliet to her husband's Romeo. Her acting was then viewed as stilted and not forceful enough, but Powell and Dickson felt that she had some promise and offered her a position with the company. During the next two years, she performed many roles, including Desdemona and Ophelia, and created one of her greatest parts, Jane Shore, in Nicholas Rowe's tragedy of that name.

In 1812 the Duffs moved to Philadelphia and joined the William Warren and William Wood Company, spending September through May in Philadelphia at the Chestnut Street Theatre and June through August touring Washington, D.C., Baltimore, and Alexandria, Virginia. They remained with this company until 1817, when they returned to Boston, and John Duff became manager of the Federal Street Theatre. When Duff made her first appearance in Boston in 1818 after several years' absence, critics noticed a definite improvement in her acting. Motivated by her husband's illness and fearful of being forced to work on her own without his guidance, Duff exhibited a concentration and a talent heretofore unseen by her public. As a result, her career soared and she began to perform with the greatest actors of her time. Thomas Abthorpe Cooper, Junius Brutus Booth, Edwin Forrest, and Edmund Kean praised her talents as a great tragic actress. She became the favorite of audiences with her dramatic portrayals of Juliet, Lady Macbeth, Jane Shore, Belvidera in *Venice Preserved*, Mrs. Beverly in *The Gamester*, and her greatest triumph, Mrs. Haller in Kotzebue's *The Stranger*. She made her New York debut in 1823 at the Park Theatre with Junius Brutus Booth and continued to play there, in Boston, and in Philadelphia.

In a landmark case in 1827, the Duffs were sued for breach of contract by Henry Wallack, who argued that the Duffs were under contract to him and were therefore his "valuable property." The Duffs said that no such contract existed between them and Wallack and that they should be able to choose the theatres in which they worked and the roles they played. The judge ruled in their favor. It was the first time that actors, rather than the theatre manager, had been granted the right to control their own careers. It was during this time that Duff was favorably compared with the prominent British actress Sarah Siddons and often referred to as the "American Siddons." The first such comparison appeared in the *New York Mirror* (June 1826), which likened their acting styles and repertoire, both having played Jane Shore, Isabella, Lady Randolph, Belvidera, Mrs. Haller, and Lady Macbeth. Physical similarities were also noticed though the resemblance was not close. Duff was said to have the finest eyes since Mrs. Siddons, and it was said that at times Duff's face took on a "Siddonian" look that prompted audiences and critics to imagine that Mrs. Siddons was performing rather than Duff.

The Duffs traveled to London in 1828, and the "American Siddons" gave a series of performances at Drury Lane. Although London was her birthplace, both the press and Duff herself considered her an American actress. Despite some anti-American feelings in the British press, though, her reviews were quite favorable. Later that year, the Duffs returned to America and again performed in Boston, New York, and Philadelphia.

On April 28, 1831, John Duff died, and Mary Ann Duff was left as the sole support of her seven children: Mary, James, John, Eliza, Thomas, William, and Matilda. Her previous successes insured her employment, but since touring offered marginally higher pay, she began to tour the South and the Midwest. On one of those tours she received a commendation for aiding the victims of a cholera epidemic aboard the Mississippi riverboat on which she was traveling. In 1833, despondent over her financial situation and the loss of her husband, and under medication for depression, she married the actor Charles Young. The marriage was annulled shortly after, Duff claiming that her state of depression and drug-induced confusion had caused her to accept Young's proposal.

Three years later, Duff married Joel G. Seaver, an attorney. They moved to New Orleans; and Duff, retaining her stage name, continued her career there and in St. Louis with the Ludlow and Smith Company. She went into semi-retirement in 1837 and, following several performances in 1839, entered private life as Mrs. Joel Seaver. She came out of retirement for two benefit performances in April 1846, the last recorded performances in her career.

In 1850, at her husband's request, Duff, now Seaver, renounced the theatre and her childhood Catholicism and converted to Methodism, becoming a teacher in the Sabbath School and a member of the Temperance Society. In the next two years, four of her seven children died: Mary and John in 1851, James and Eliza in 1852. All had been actors. Mary Ann Seaver (or Sévier, as Seaver called himself in French New Orleans) continued to live a quiet life in New Orleans in virtual obscurity until 1854, when her husband's political views on slavery forced them to leave the area. Duff arrived alone in New York City in late 1854 to live with her youngest daughter Matilda (Mrs. I. Reillieux) at 36 West 9th Street. No member of Matilda's family knew that Mrs. Seaver was the famous actress. Mary Ann Duff died of cancer on September 5, 1857, at the age of sixty-three.

Duff was buried on September 6, 1857, in Greenwood Cemetery, Brooklyn, New York. A simple stone, "Mother and Grandmother," marked the plot. Thomas Thatcher Duff, the last surviving child of Mary Ann and John R. Duff, was an actor and theatre manager for many years, associated with the New Greenwich, Chatham, and Bowery theatres in New York.

The career of Duff spanned twenty-nine years. She was one of the first great actresses of the American stage. Her unique acting style, which borrowed much from Edmund Kean and Junius Brutus Booth, combined classic and romantic elements. Duff managed to raise and support seven children while enjoying a full theatrical career. Her greatest attribute was her ability as a tragic actress to create believable, sympathetic, and agonizing characters. She excelled in parts that required extreme emotion. It was said of her that she must have suffered greatly in her personal life in order to project such sorrow on the stage. Duff was respected and praised by her fellow actors. Booth called her the greatest actress in the world; and Kean proclaimed her the finest leading lady he had appeared with in America and superior to his British costars as well. She is remembered as "the American Siddons."

Mrs. Duff and "Notices of Mrs. Duff" were written by the noted historian of that time, Joseph Norton Ireland, and contain a great deal of information on Mary Ann Duff's life and career. *Mrs. Duff* (1882) was part of the American Actor series published by James R. Osgood. "Notices of Mrs. Duff" is an unpublished, handwritten manuscript. The only copy is in the Brander Matthews Dramatic Library at Columbia University in New York City and contains the background material used in the published book. George C. D. Odell mentions Duff in Vols. II, III, and IV of *Annals of the New York Stage* (1927–1949). See also Noah M. Ludlow, *Dramatic Life As I Found It* (1880), and Lewis C. Strang, *Players and Plays of the Last Quarter Century* (1902). Garff Wilson in *A History of American Acting* (1966) and in a short piece in *Educational Theatre Journal* (March 1955) discusses her acting style. Lael Woodbury in "Styles of Acting in Serious Drama on the Nineteenth Century Stage" (Unpublished Ph.D. dissertation, University of Illinois, Champaign-Urbana, 1954) describes Mrs. Duff and her acting style. The most recent work on Duff is Penny M. Landau, "The Career of Mary Ann Duff, the American Siddons, 1810–1839" (Unpublished Ph.D. dissertation, Bowling Green State University, 1979). Mary Ann Duff is included in T. Allston Brown, *History of the American Stage* (1870, reissued 1969); *Dictionary of American Biography*, Vol. III (1958–1959); *Who Was Who in America*, Historical Volume (1963); *Notable American Women*, Vol. I (1971); *The Oxford Companion to the Theatre* (1983), and *The Oxford Companion to American Theatre* (1984).

Penny M. Landau

DUNHAM, Katherine (June 22, 1912–): pioneering dancer, choreographer, manager, anthropologist, and writer in ethnic dance theatre, was born in Joliet, Illinois, and grew up in Glen Ellyn, a suburb of Chicago, and in the city itself. Her mother, Fanny June (Buckner) Taylor, was of French-Canadian and native American heritage. Her father, Albert Millard Dunham, traced his ancestry to the Malagasy Republic and to West Africa. Raised in an atmosphere of music in the home, Katherine Dunham also lived for a time with relatives who were actively engaged in vaudeville. When she chose dual careers in anthropology and dance, Dunham united her multiple heritage through research on and performance of Caribbean culture, itself a mixture of various ethnic strains.

Katherine Dunham's long theatrical career can be divided into three stages: training and research (1926–1939); American and world tours (1939–1967); and community service (1967 to the present). In the first period, she was inspired by her elder brother's example to attend the University of Chicago and participate in avant-garde theatre. Having himself experienced obstacles to growth and advancement because of race, Albert Dunham, Jr., carefully prepared the way for his younger sister by encouraging her to join the Little Theatre Group of Harper Avenue, a rival of the then well-known Cube Theatre. He felt the stage provided a forum for the active expression of black creativity. Katherine Dunham taught dance at the Little Theatre, and a friend, Ruth Attaway, taught drama. Their productions drew guests like musician Louis Armstrong, actor Canada

Lee, writers Frank Yerby, James Farrell, and Langston Hughes, painter Charles White, and one of the primary movers of the Harlem Renaissance, Alaine Locke. At the time, Dunham was majoring in anthropology at the University of Chicago, where she was influenced by the anthropologist Robert Redfield and by Melville Herskovits, chairman of the Department of African Studies at Northwestern University, Evanston.

Dunham's university studies in anthropology were combined with dance and theatre education off campus. In the same row of artists' studios that housed the Harper Avenue group, Dunham met Mark Turbyfill and Ruth Page of the Chicago Opera who, with Ludmilla Speranzeva, became her primary teachers. Speranzeva's influence was profound. A Kamerny-trained modern dancer from Russia, she emphasized equally dance and theatre techniques. During this period under the Turbyfill-Page tutelage, Dunham's Ballet Négre presented *Negro Rhapsody* at the annual Chicago Beaux Arts Ball (1931). In 1934 Dunham danced a solo in Ruth Page's *La Guiablesse* at the Chicago Civic Opera. For the remainder of the 1930s, Dunham continued her experiments in ballet and modern dance, seeking through her anthropological research a choreographic style suited to the Afro-American sensibility. Seven young women, the Negro Dance Group, assisted her in these performances. Quite unexpectedly, during one of their concerts, a member of the Rosenwald family discovered Dunham's young talent. Encouraged by Redfield, the writer and psychoanalyst Erik Fromm, and the renowned scholar Melville Herskovits, and with support from the Rosenwald Foundation, Dunham spent eighteen months in the Caribbean observing and participating in the dance culture of Jamaica, Martinique, Trinidad, and Haiti. Her master's thesis, entitled ''Form and Structure in the Dance,'' focusing primarily on the dances of Haiti, was completed in June of 1939. Her research trip led to doctoral studies in anthropology that became the basis for the unique Afro-American style that Dunham created.

Upon her return from the Caribbean, Dunham participated in an evening of dance at the Young Men's Hebrew Association of New York in 1937. Assembled for that occasion were the foremost performers of authentic Afro-American dance. Edna Guy, a student of Hanya Holm, danced to Negro spirituals. Assadata Dafore from Sierre Leone performed African ritual dances; Dunham and Archie Savage presented Caribbean works. In 1938 Dunham choreographed for *Run Lil' Chillun* in Chicago and for the Chicago Federal Theatre Project. There she met John Pratt, costume designer and painter, with whom she collaborated on her first full ballet, *L'Ag'Ya*, named after the foot fighting dances she had observed in Martinique. Dunham and Pratt were married in July 1941 and have continued their partnership in the theatre. In 1940 Dunham faced a dilemma: to continue the doctorate in anthropology or join the musical *Cabin in the Sky*. Ultimately, she chose the theatre.

During the second period of her career, the Dunham Company played on Broadway in revues produced by Sol Hurok and toured the nation as well as fifty-seven other countries between 1943 and 1965—the year of their final professional appearance. The center from which the activity emanated was the Dunham School of Dance and Theatre, established in New York in 1945. Specializing in primitive rhythms, voice, acting, and dance ethnology, the school influenced several generations of prominent theatre people, among them Peter Gennaro, Marlon Brando, José Ferrer, Arthur Mitchell, Walter Nicks, Chita Rivera, and Eartha Kitt. The first film performance choreographed by Dunham was *Carnival of Rhythm* in 1939; it was followed by *Star Spangled Rhythm* and *Pardon My Sarong* (1942), *Stormy Weather* (1943), *Casbah* (1948), *Botta e Risposta* (1950), *Mambo* with Sylvana Mangana (Italy 1954), *Liebes Sender* (Germany 1954), *Musica En la Noche* (Mexico 1955), *Green Mansions* (1958), and *The Bible* with John Huston (Italy 1964).

From 1965 to the present, Dunham's work in theatre has ranged from the international to the local. She was a Department of State representative to the First World Festival of Negro Arts in Dakar, Senegal (1966). On her return home, she began her long association with Southern Illinois University's Performing Arts Training Center in East St. Louis, Illinois. During the anxious 1960s Dunham, as director of the center, used her theatre and dance techniques with disadvantaged youths in the ghetto of East St. Louis. She instructed them on how to see other cultures and their own from within. While dancing, her students reproduced—and thereby became acquainted with—those gestures that make a culture unique and those that bind it to universal rhythms. Since 1968, Dunham has worked largely with a semi-professional company of dancers and a community theatre group called the Kutana Players. With poet-in-residence Eugene Redmond, she wrote *Ode to Taylor Jones* (1968), a play based on an incident during which a local resident and his wife were killed in an automobile accident. Recently the Katherine Dunham Museum, which houses her collection of African, Asian, and Caribbean art as well as costumes and memorabilia from her stage career, was opened in East St. Louis. Performances at Carnegie Hall (1979) and a television documentary *The Divine Drumbeats* (1980) for the *Dance in America* series have reconstructed the Dunham style on stage and screen. For these events three generations of her dancers, trained in Dunham technique, were reunited.

Dunham technique, now a part of American dance vocabulary, is Afro-American art in motion, drawing upon the isolation of body parts that she saw in African-devised dancing (*New York Times*, June 8, 1986). Having evolved with Dunham during her years of research, teaching, and travel in Africa, the West Indies, and South America, the technique can be divided into three distinct styles: the fundamental, based on primitive rhythms danced close to the earth; the lyrical, with softer movements; and the martial, influenced especially by karate and other Asian combative forms which Dunham witnessed during her tour of Japan in 1958. Dunham's technique, founded on the observation of various cultures, is the hallmark of her innovation in dance theatre. Her theatre pieces were not reproductions of authentic rituals but artistic transformations capable of communicating the feel and function of dances from other cultures. Long before national folkloric troupes from the Third World began to tour, the Dunham Company had paved the way for African American folklore in the theatre. Over the years Dunham has staged an astonishing array of some 115 theatre pieces.

Of Dunham's major ballets, attention must be drawn to *L'Ag'Ya* (1938), a story of love and revenge set in Martinique; *Rites de Passage* (1943), a danced ritual of puberty, fertility, and death; *Shango* (1945), a reenactment of Trinidadian cult practices; and *Southland* (1950), a dance documentary of lynching in American society. Her major shows include *Tropics* and *Le Jazz Hot* (1940), *New Tropical Revue* (1943), *Carib Song* (1945), *Bal Nègre* (1946), and *Caribbean Rhapsody* (1948). At the Metropolitan Opera in 1964, Dunham was asked to provide the choreography for the Verdi opera *Aida*. In 1972 she directed and choreographed a presentation in Atlanta of Scott Joplin's folk opera *Treemonisha* with musical arrangement by T. J. Anderson. The last major Dunham Company show was *Bamboche* (1962), a Haitian revue of sacred and secular dances, which included on the program members of the Royal Troupe of Morocco.

Katherine Dunham's career has served as a model in American modern dance and dance theatrical history. A humanist in the tradition that speaks of "art for life's sake," she was given the *Dancemagazine* Award in 1969, the Albert Schweitzer Award in 1979, the John F. Kennedy Center Honors in 1983, and the Samuel H. Scripps American Dance Festival Award in 1986. Her devotion to inner city communities in East St. Louis, to the elderly, and to youth is one of her most valued achievements. She has engendered in all of them a sense of beauty and has given budding artists an opportunity to enter the field as well-trained dancers and well-rounded human beings. The Dunham Company, supporting itself throughout, was one of the few unsubsidized dance groups significant to American dance and theatre history. As one of the great pioneers in restoring the black cultural heritage to American dance and to the American musical theatre, Katherine Dunham brought African-derived dances to American audiences who had never seen them before on stage. She formulated an independent modern-dance technique (known as the Dunham technique) born of emotional impulses and a desire to transpose authentic rituals into the mainstream of American dance.

The Katherine Dunham archives are located at the Katherine Dunham Museum in East St. Louis and at Morris Library, Southern Illinois University, Carbondale. A collection of articles, scrapbooks, and a guide to visual materials are in the Dance Collection in the New York Public Library Performing Arts Research Center at Lincoln Center, New York. A selection of Dunham's published writings include "The Negro Dance," *The Negro Caravan* (1941); *Journey to Accompong* (1946); "The Dances of Haiti," *Acta Anthropologica* (1947); *A Touch of Innocence* (1959); *Island Possessed* (1969); and *Kasamance* (1974). Biographies of Dunham include Ruth Biemiller, *Dance: The Story of Katherine Dunham* (1969); Terry Harnan, *African Rhythm, American Dance* (1947); Ruth Beckford, *Katherine Dunham: A Biography* (1979); and James Haskins, *Katherine Dunham* (1982). Significant critical writings on Dunham's contributions to theatre and dance may be found in Richard Buckle, ed., *Katherine Dunham, Her Dancers, Singers, and Musicians* (1949); Lynne F. Emery, *Black Dance in the United States from 1619–*

1970 (1972); VéVé A. Clark and Margaret B. Wilkerson, *Kaiso: Katherine Dunham, An Anthology of Writings* (1978); Joyce Aschenbrenner, *Katherine Dunham; Reflections on the Social and Political Contexts of Afro-American Dance* (1981); VéVé A. Clark, "Katherine Dunham's *Tropical Revue*," *Black American Literature Forum* (1983); and Anna Kisselgoff, "Dunham Has Been a Controversial Pioneer," *New York Times* (June 8, 1986). Dunham is listed in the major guides to modern black dance and in *Current Biography, 1941* (1942); *Biographical Encyclopaedia and Who's Who of the American Theatre* (1966); *Notable Names in the American Theatre* (1976); and *Who's Who in the Theatre* (1981).

Vévé A. Clark

DUNNOCK, Mildred Margaret (January 1, 1900–): character actress, best known for her creation of the stage roles of Linda Loman and Big Mama in *Death of a Salesman* and *Cat on a Hot Tin Roof*, was born in Baltimore, Maryland, to Florence (Saynook) and Walter Dunnock, president of the Dumari Textile Company. She began her education in Baltimore's public schools and credits her interest in the stage to a Western High School English teacher who forced her to overcome her shyness to play the part of Gwendolyn Fairfax in Oscar Wilde's *The Importance of Being Earnest*. While pursuing a Bachelor of Arts degree in English at Goucher College in Baltimore, Dunnock played leading men because of her thin build and height of five feet six inches. Dunnock's father overrode her theatrical aspirations, and she began teaching, "the only career besides marriage for a Southern girl" (*New York Sunday News*, January 13, 1952).

Dunnock taught at the Friends' School in Baltimore and acted in her spare time with the Vagabond Players and with the Johns Hopkins University troupe, where she played opposite John Van Druten in his *The Return Half*. She moved to New York to teach at the Friends' School in Brooklyn and to pursue a master's degree at Columbia University. Her involvement with Columbia's Morningside Players was "just for fun," but in 1932 their production of *Life Begins* moved to Broadway, propelling her into a second career in earnest (Goucher College *Program*, January 28, 1963). On August 21, 1933, Dunnock married Keith Urmy, a Chemical Bank executive whom she characterized as "a conventional man" (*New York Times*, September 24, 1976). From 1934 to 1938 Dunnock balanced her teaching schedule with summer stock at the Westchester Country Playhouse in Mt. Kisco, New York. She also did *The Eternal Road* (Manhattan Opera House, January 7, 1937), played Agnes Riddle in *The Hill Between* (Little Theatre, March 11, 1938), and toured in *Herod and Marianne* (1938). The birth of a daughter, Mary Melinda Urmy, in May 1939 interrupted her acting career for a season.

Dunnock's most significant roles came in the 1940s and early 1950s on Broadway. She created the role of Miss Ronberry in Emlyn Williams's *The Corn is Green*, which starred **Ethel Barrymore** (National Theatre, November 26, 1940). With **Lillian Hellman** directing, she originated the role of the shrinking Lavinia Hubbard in *Another Part of the Forest* (Fulton Theatre, November 20, 1946).

She played Madame Tsai in *Lute Song* with **Mary Martin** (Plymouth Theatre, February 6, 1945), Rose in *Foolish Notion* with **Tallulah Bankhead** (Martin Beck Theatre, March 14, 1945), and Etta Hallam in *The Hallams* (Booth Theatre, March 4, 1948). Dunnock made her film debut as Miss Ronberry in the Warner Brothers' production of *The Corn is Green* in 1945. The decade concluded with the première of Arthur Miller's *Death of a Salesman* at the Morosco Theatre (February 10, 1949) and the 742 subsequent performances. Lillian Hellman had suggested Dunnock to the producer, who informed the wispy Dunnock that she wouldn't fit the part of the long suffering Linda Lomen. Dunnock auditioned anyway, in full padding to match the playwright's description, but played the role without padding when the burly Lee J. Cobb was cast as the lead. Brooks Atkinson applauded: "Mildred Dunnock gives the performance of her career as the wife and mother—plain of speech but indomitable in spirit" (*New York Times*, February 11, 1949). Dunnock repeated her role for the 1951 Columbia picture, and Bosley Crowther titled her performance "simply superb, as she was on the stage" (*New York Times*, December 21, 1951). Dunnock herself called Linda Loman "one of [her] finest experiences" (*Cue*, May 23, 1970).

Dunnock followed *Salesman* with *In the Summer House*, directed by José Quintero and starring **Judith Anderson**. Critic William Hawkins characterized *Summer House* as Dunnock's "finest job of acting" (*New York World-Telegram and Sun*, December 30, 1953). She returned to the Morosco in 1955 for the première of Tennessee Williams' *Cat on a Hot Tin Roof*. This was a gratifying development, as Dunnock was exchanging her image as a fluttering, timorous woman for the character of Big Mama. Walter Kerr praised her as "startlingly fine in an unfamiliar sort of role: the brash, gravel-voiced outspoken matron" (*New York Herald Tribune*, March 25, 1955). Brooks Atkinson added, "An actress of modesty and great purity of spirit, Miss Dunnock has thus spoken the minds of the two leading dramatists of the forties. They are lucky to have been so scrupulously deputized" (*Broadway*, p. 400).

Dunnock's roles escalated in number in the 1950s and 1960s as she explored regional theatre and film. Most notably, Dunnock appeared with the American Shakespeare Festival, the Goodman Theatre, the Repertory Theatre of Lincoln Center, and the Festival of Two Worlds in Spoleto, Italy, where she created the role of Vera Ridgewood Condotti in Tennessee Williams' *The Milk Train Doesn't Stop Here Anymore* (July 10, 1962)—a role she repeated on Broadway in 1963. At the Théâtre du Nouveau Monde in Montreal, Dunnock portrayed her favorite character, Mary Tyrone in *Long Day's Journey Into Night*, which she repeated in 1966 at the Long Wharf Theatre in New Haven. Her movies included *The Girl in White* (MGM, 1952), *Viva Zapata!* (Twentieth Century-Fox, 1952), *The Jazz Singer* (Warner Brothers, 1953), *Love Me Tender* (Twentieth Century-Fox, 1956), *Peyton Place* (Twentieth Century-Fox, 1957), *Butterfield 8* (MGM, 1960), *Sweet Bird of Youth* (MGM, 1962), *Youngblood Hawke* (Twentieth Century-Fox, 1964), *Behold a Pale Horse* (Columbia, 1964), and *Whatever Happened to Aunt Alice?* (Cinerama, 1969).

From 1967 to 1970 Dunnock alternated between the Long Wharf and the Yale Repertory Theatre in New Haven. In May 1970 she played Sido to **Zoe Caldwell**'s *Collette* at **Ellen Stewart**'s La Mama Experimental Theatre Club, New York, and in December, Clair Laines in Marguerite Duras's *A Place Without Doors* at the Off-Broadway Stairway Theatre. She played a leading role in *Days in the Trees* (1976) and appeared in *Ring Around the Moon* at the famous Circle in the Square Theatre in New York. The following year she played Madame Pernelle in the Circle's *Tartuffe*.

Dunnock's television credits are substantial. They include *Alfred Hitchcock Presents*, *Philco Playhouse*, *Kraft Television Playhouse*, *The Defenders*, *The F.B.I.*, *Omnibus*, *Inner Sanctum*, *Ghost Story*, and *Death of a Salesman* for CBS. When asked which medium she preferred, Dunnock laughed and said, ''I love to work!'' However, she added that on stage ''the actor controls the medium much more than other forms. . . . And it can only happen at that moment'' (*Cue*, May 23, 1970).

Dunnock has studied with Maria Ouspenskaya, Lee Strasberg, Tamara Daykarhanova, Robert Lewis, Elia Kazan, and **Uta Hagen**. She is a member of Actors' Equity, SAG, and AFTRA; has served on the council of the American Educators' Association; and since 1949 has belonged to the Actors' Studio. Because of her friendship with Lillian Hellman, Elia Kazan, and Arthur Miller she suffered brief blacklisting in the 1950s. Until the 1960s her work included teaching at Spence School, Masters' School, Milton Academy, Brearley School, Barnard College, and Yale University School of Drama. Dunnock believes that her acting and teaching careers have been ''made possible by an undemanding, encouraging husband . . . and my own energy and need. It has given me many lives to live'' (Goucher College *Program*). Reviewers have often commented on Dunnock's modesty, suggesting that the characters she plays are always better known than the actress. To this observation she has replied, ''I like to play parts that are not like myself. I'm not in the least bit exciting. I'm an ordinary person in an ordinary life, but in my imagination there's no stopping me'' (*New York Times*, September 1976). Mildred Dunnock's consistently fine contributions to the American theatre, whether in the classroom, on stage, or in film, hint at the breadth of her extraordinary career.

The New York Public Library Performing Arts Research Center at Lincoln Center (NYPL/LC) has several files on Dunnock, including reviews and programs from her many performances. The best summaries of Dunnock's thoughts about the theatre can be found in Warren Hoge, ''Mildred Dunnock is 'Ordinary' Only Until She Gets on Stage,'' *New York Times* (September 24, 1976), and Glenn Loney, ''In the Words of Mildred Dunnock,'' *Cue* (May 23, 1970). For the tribulations involved in the casting of *Death of a Salesman*, see Wanda Hale, ''Her Wish for Film Role Was Granted,'' New York *Sunday News* (January 13, 1952); Helen Ormsbee, ''Mildred Dunnock Almost Missed Her Biggest Role,'' *New York Herald Tribune* (undated clipping NYPL/LC); and Mary Day Winn, ''The Triple Player,'' *Baltimore Sun* (June 12, 1949). The Goucher College *Program* for the dedication of the College Center (NYPL/LC), January 28, 1963, also contains biographical material. Dunnock is mentioned in *Who's Who in America, 1984–1985*

(1985); *Who's Who in American Theatre* (1981); *Who's Who of American Women, 1975–1976* (1976); *Notable Names in the American Theatre* (1976); *International Motion Picture Almanac, 1975–1976* (1976); *The Oxford Companion to the Theatre* (1983); and *The Oxford Companion to American Theatre* (1984).

Stacy A. Rozek

E

EAGELS, Jeanne (June 26, 1890?–October 3, 1929): stage and film actress, whose most famous role was that of Sadie Thompson in *Rain*, was born in Kansas City, Missouri, the second of six children of Edward and Julia (Sullivan) Eagels. Her carpenter father traced his ancestry not from Spanish blood as often noted but maternally to the Irish and paternally to the French. Her mother, born in Boston, was descended from the Irish through both parents.

Christened Amelia Jean and reared in the Roman Catholic faith, Eagels reportedly ended regular church attendance after her first communion. Her early education fluctuated between parochial and public schools, as financial resources dictated. In interviews she often boasted of only a year and a half of formal education, but this seems unlikely. Numerous tales paint a colorful childhood for this lanky, blue-eyed tomboy who possessed a vivid imagination and a fiery temperament, though not always the physical constitution to back them up. Traditionally, her appearance as Puck at age seven in an amateur Kansas City production of *A Midsummer's Night Dream* is cited as her stage debut. Her biographer insists that her debut occurred at age eleven, which seems more probable.

Few conclusive statements can be made about her adolescent years. Employment as a stock girl and then as a cash girl in a local department store is known. Some information suggests that she frequently took on bit parts and limited touring engagements with area theatre companies, most notably the O. D. Woodward Stock Company. Employment in the office of Al Mackensen's local casting agency further whetted the ambitions of this stage-struck teen-ager. The desire was gratified when Dubinsky Brothers Tent Repertoire Company hired her at age fifteen to tour in a musical extravaganza, *Pickings from Puck*. She worked her way into the position of leading lady, acting roles such as Little Eva, Little

Lord Fauntleroy, Juliet, and Camille. She stayed with the company nearly six years, touring throughout the Midwest. Because of this early touring she would later acquire the nickname "Bernhardt of the Sticks." Some sources suggest that she married the eldest of the Dubinsky brothers, Morris, and bore him a son.

With her striking beauty and with considerable theatre experience behind her, Jeanne Eagels made her way to New York in 1911, believing herself destined to be great. More than another decade would pass before she enjoyed a brief but brilliant reign as one of America's leading actresses. Shortly after her arrival in New York, director Richard Carle cast her as Miss Renault in the musical farce *Jumping Jupiter* (1911). Roles in support of Billie Burke and Julian Eltinge followed, along with the lead in *The Outcast* as it toured the South and the New York "subway circuit" (theatres in the city's various boroughs). In 1916 and 1917 she played opposite George Arliss in *Paganini* and *The Professor's Love Story*; he later praised her "unerring judgment and artistry" (*Up the Years from Bloomsbury*, p. 271).

Her first film experience came in 1913 in *The Bride of the Sea*. She gave her days to various New York movie studios and her nights to the Broadway stage. Her silent Thanhouser productions of *The World and the Woman* (1916), *Fires of Youth* (1917), and *Under False Colors* (1917) were undistinguished, but the World Productions release of *The Cross Bearer* (1918), generally received a positive response. She reputedly used stimulants and sedatives to cope with the emotional and physical demands that her torturous work schedule placed upon her increasingly frail body.

In 1918 she experienced her first unqualified stage hit, *Daddies*, produced and directed by David Belasco. Her portrayal of Ruth Atkins, a French war orphan adopted by a confirmed bachelor, won for the production its run of forty-three weeks. Three subsequent roles in as many years failed to elicit the acclaim of *Daddies*. However, the enthusiasm that greeted her next characterization more than compensated for the three meager years. Unquestionably her greatest critical and popular success occurred with the première of John Colton and Clemence Randolph's *Rain* on November 7, 1922, at the Maxine Elliott Theatre. As Sadie Thompson, the rowdy San Francisco harlot who seduces a minister, she achieved "toast of the town" status during the play's 648 Broadway performances. John Corbin's review summarized the acclaim: "Miss Eagels . . . rises to the requirements of this difficult role with fine loyalty to the reality of the character and with an emotional power as fiery and unbridled in effect as it is artistically restrained" (*New York Times*, November 8, 1922). After the New York run she made a triumphant national tour for an additional two years (1925 and 1926).

She ended months of public speculation by marrying Edward H. ("Ted") Coy on August 26, 1925. However, the New York banker, once an all-American football star from Yale, failed to furnish a stabilizing influence in her life; rumors of an impending rift surfaced within a year. Within less than three years, the marriage was terminated by divorce on the uncontested grounds of cruelty.

On March 21, 1927, Jeanne Eagels played her final role for the legitimate stage—Simone, a rich woman who falls in love with a man hired to masquerade as her paramour in a French farce entitled *Her Cardboard Lover*. Brooks Atkinson pinpointed fundamental weaknesses in her performance: "The ironic caprices of a temperamental Parisian lady do not trip lightly from her fingertips, and her voice and gestures lack the subtle grace imperative for such a part" (*New York Times*, March 22, 1927). With typical determined effort and diligent study, Eagels improved her performance during the run to make it one that historians rank among her finest. Following one hundred performances of *Her Cardboard Lover* on Broadway and during preparations for the play's tour, she completed the silent film *Man, Woman and Sin* (1927). One reviewer captured, perhaps unwittingly, the harsh reality of the last years of her life when he noted that the "camera may have been cruel in some scenes. Miss Eagels looks haggard in spots contradicting . . . [her] description in the subtitles" (*Variety*, December 7, 1927). Claiming illness due to ptomaine poisoning, she canceled a week of performances of *Her Cardboard Lover* in Milwaukee as well as another week in St. Louis. Shortly thereafter the company disbanded, and, after hearings in early April 1928, Actors' Equity barred her from appearing with other members of the association until September 1929 and ordered her to pay a fine equal to two weeks' salary (approximately $3,600), a harsh ruling that surprised many in the theatre community. During this long exile from the stage, she turned to successful engagements in vaudeville and motion pictures. Her debut in sound films came in *The Letter*, a 1929 Paramount release, based upon the Somerset Maugham story of the same name. Her performance as Leslie Crosbie, considered an acting triumph, earned her an Academy (Oscar) Award nomination for best actress.

In early September 1929 Eagels underwent an operation at St. Luke's Hospital in New York for cornea ulcers caused by sinus infection. She improved rapidly and left the hospital after ten days. But in less than two weeks her life ended during a visit to New York's Park Avenue Hospital, where she had been receiving regular treatments for a "nervous disorder." On October 3, 1929, while awaiting a consultation with her physician, a convulsion seized her, and she collapsed and died almost instantly. A preliminary autopsy identified the cause of death as alcoholic psychosis, but the city toxicologist cited the official cause as an overdose of chloral hydrate, a powerful nerve sedative and soporific that fatally depressed her heart. Following a requiem mass at St. Vincent's Catholic Church in Kansas City, she was buried at the Calvary Cemetery. At the time of her death she was not yet forty years old. Her last film, *Jealousy*, was filling movie theatres throughout the country, and she had been planning her reappearance on stage in a Sam Harris production of *Storm Song*.

In a written eulogy John D. Williams, her director in *Rain*, praised her thorough apprenticeship in the tent theatres, her keen sense of listening on stage, her careful and controlled diction, and her unflagging loyalty to the author's intent (*New York Times*, October 12, 1929). Legend has it that early in her career she refused a job offer from Florenz Ziegfeld by retorting, "I'm a dramatic actress." Indeed, no one ever questioned her realistic portrayals of emotional intensity. Outside the theatre she often exhibited erratic behavior touched off by volatile emotions, leading some to consider her more the actress off the stage than on. Nevertheless, her natural ability to strike a fine balance of fire and discipline in her roles brought justified acclaim to her meteoric career.

Edward Doherty's *The Rain Girl* (1930), a biography with a sensational bent, was originally published as a serial in *Liberty* magazine. Doherty insisted on Kansas City, 1890, as her place and date of birth. (Some sources list her birth in Boston in 1890 or 1894, but no evidence has been found to support these claims.) There are many reviews of her work in the *New York Times* from 1917 to 1930. Among them are reviews of *Rain* (November 8, 1922), *Her Cardboard Lover* (March 22, 1927), and the film *Man, Woman and Sin* (December 7, 1927). Stan Cornyn, *A Selective Index to Theatre Magazine* (1964) lists reviews in *Theatre Magazine*. See also *Variety Film Reviews*, Vols. 1–3 (1983); Einar Lauritzen and Gunnar Lundquist, *American Film Index 1908–1915* (1976); and *American Film Index 1916–1920* (1984). Hollywood's contribution to her memory is the exploitative 1957 film *Jeanne Eagels*, reviewed in *Life* (March 11, 1957). Eagels is mentioned in Ward Moorehouse, *Matinée Tomorrow* (1949), and George Arliss, *Up the Years from Bloomsbury* (1927). She is listed in *Notable American Women*, Vol. I (1971); William C. Young, *Famous Actors and Actresses on the American Stage*, Vol. I (1975); *Who Was Who in the Theatre*, Vol. II (1978); and *The Oxford Companion to American Theatre* (1984).

Landis K. Magnuson

ELDRIDGE, Florence (September 5, 1901–): actress and frequent co-star with husband Fredric March, was born in Brooklyn, New York, the daughter of James Eldridge and Clara Eugenie McKechnie. Her formative education took place at the Girls' High School in Brooklyn.

Florence Eldridge's professional debut on the New York stage was as a chorus member in *Rock-A-Bye Baby* (Astor Theatre, May 22, 1918). She subsequently appeared in the national tour of *Seven Days Love* and the New York production of *Pretty Soft* (Morosco Theatre, 1919). She first appeared with the Theatre Guild in October 1921 in its production of *Ambush*, a grimly realistic domestic drama in which she played the promiscuous daughter of a Jersey City clerk.

The role that finally brought her to prominence on Broadway was that of Annabelle West, a young heiress forced to spend a terrifying night in a gloomy mansion in order to claim her inheritance, in John Willard's *The Cat and the Canary* at the National Theatre in February 1922. The special effects—sliding panels, clutching hands, voodoo incantations, and disappearing bodies—made the play the prototype of the many "Let's-scare-the-heroine-to-death" melodramas that followed it. *The Cat and the Canary* ran for a very successful 349 performances.

Later that year she appeared as the stepdaughter in the first American production of Italian playwright Luigi Pirandello's masterpiece, *Six Characters in Search of an Author* (Princess Theatre, October 30, 1922), but it was not an outstanding commercial success. *Six Characters* was followed by a succession of forgettable melodramas and comedies: *The Love Habit* (March 14, 1923), *The Dancers* (October 17, 1923), *Cheaper to Marry* (April 15, 1924), *Bewitched* (October 1, 1924), and *Young Blood* (November 11, 1924). In the last she appeared with Helen Hayes. On February 2, 1926, Eldridge opened at the Ambassador Theatre as Daisy Buchanan in the stage adaptation of F. Scott Fitzgerald's *The Great Gatsby*, under the direction of George Cukor, who subsequently was to earn greater laurels in film. She followed this production with roles in the comedy-drama *A Proud Woman* (Maxine Elliott's Theatre, November 15, 1926) and in the more melodramatic *Off-Key* (February 8, 1927).

Florence Eldridge married actor Fredric March (1897–1975) on May 30, 1927, and began one of the American theatre's great acting partnerships, similar to those of Alfred Lunt and **Lynn Fontanne** and of Hume Cronyn and **Jessica Tandy**. Working initially with the Theatre Guild, Eldridge and March toured in the Theatre Guild's 1927–1928 productions of *Arms and the Man*, *Mr. Pim Passes By*, *The Silver Cord*, and *The Guardsman*, the last of which had starred the Lunts on Broadway.

Back in New York Eldridge appeared in the comedy *An Affair of State* (Broadhurst Theatre, November 19, 1930) and as Julie Rodman in *Days to Come* (Vanderbilt Theatre, December 12, 1936), an early **Lillian Hellman** play about class warfare in a midwestern factory town. *Days to Come* closed after seven performances, and Eldridge's next play, *Yr. Obedient Husband* (in which she appeared with Fredric March), had only eight performances after opening on January 10, 1938.

The next year, however, her career turned a corner. She and March starred in the George S. Kaufman and Lorenz Hart drama *The American Way* (Center Theatre, January 21, 1939). It ran 244 performances and helped to establish the reputations of the Marches and the playwrights. *The American Way* was followed by *Hope for a Harvest* (November 26, 1941), a drama by **Sophie Treadwell**, produced by the Theatre Guild. Again, the Marches starred together, but the production ran for only 38 performances.

On November 18, 1942, Fredric March and Florence Eldridge opened in that milestone in American drama, Thornton Wilder's *The Skin of Our Teeth*, at Broadway's Plymouth Theatre. The play, which won the Pulitzer Prize for drama that year, also starred **Tallulah Bankhead** and Montgomery Clift and was the first Broadway success for director Elia Kazan. Eldridge played Mrs. Antrobus in the dazzling cast. Wrote John Anderson in the *Journal-American*: "Fredric March plays Mr. Antrobus with deep sincerity and simplicity. Florence Eldridge is better at the fatuous humors of the eternal housewife than with the rest of it, and Florence Reed provides a vivid and fascinating sketch of a boardwalk fortune teller. Tallulah Bankhead is irresistibly comic and entertaining . . . " (November 19, 1942).

Eldridge and March next appeared in **Ruth Gordon**'s comedy *Years Ago* (December 3, 1946), which ran a respectable 206 performances, followed by a disastrous epic called *Now I Lay Me Down to Sleep* (March 2, 1950), which closed after only 44 performances. The *Journal-American* panned it as "self-conscious, arty and pretentious" (March 3, 1950).

The Marches were more successful in their next venture, the Arthur Miller adaptation of Henrik Ibsen's *An Enemy of the People* (December 29, 1950). Of her performance as the loyal Mrs. Stockmann, Brooks Atkinson of the *New York Times* wrote, "Florence plays the less ferocious part of the wife with a pleasant womanliness that acquires conviction as the play develops. For the character of Mrs. Stockmann sharpens with the experience of the play and Miss Eldridge sharpens with it" (December 29, 1950). On March 17, 1951, Eldridge opened as Rose Griggs in Lillian Hellman's *The Autumn Garden* at the Coronet Theatre. William Hawkins of the *New York World-Telegram and Sun* described Eldridge's portrait of the General's wife thus: "She acts this ridiculous woman with no thought of being comical or piteous. The result is an uncannily real person" (March 8, 1951).

Just as the great acting team of Alfred Lunt and Lynn Fontanne capped their careers with one of the century's masterworks (Friedrich Duerrenmatt's *The Visit*), Fredric March and Florence Eldridge crowned their careers in Eugene O'Neill's greatest play, *Long Day's Journey into Night*, which premièred at the Helen Hayes Theatre on November 7, 1956. As James and Mary Tyrone in O'Neill's lacerating autobiographical drama, the Marches made acting history. John McClain of the *Journal-American* wrote, "As the mother, Florence Eldridge gives the most commanding and incisive performance of her career" (November 8, 1956). Directed by José Quintero, *Long Day's Journey* won both the New York Drama Critics Circle Award and the Pulitzer Prize. The critic Walter Kerr wrote, "Florence Eldridge makes the downward course of an incapable mother utterly intelligible. She does not have the deep resonant notes that will sustain her woman through the blinding, tragic center of the play; she cannot quite fight fury with fury. Yet there is a hidden delicacy that is often touching in the shallow gaieties and transparent pretenses of a convent girl who could not survive the world" (*New York Herald Tribune*, November 8, 1956).

In July 1957 the Marches appeared in *Long Day's Journey* at the Theatre of Nations Festival in Paris. Eldridge carried with her the New York Drama Critics' Poll Award for her performance as Mary Tyrone. In the spring of 1965 Eldridge and March, at the request of the United States Department of State, assembled a series of concert readings that they toured overseas to Italy, Greece, Egypt and elsewhere in the Middle East.

Florence Eldridge and Frederic March's film credits include their debut, *Studio Murder Mystery* (Paramount 1929), *Les Miserables* (United Artists 1935), *Mary of Scotland* (RKO 1936), *Another Part of the Forest* (Universal 1948), *Act of Murder* (MGM 1948), *Christopher Columbus* (Universal 1949), and *Inherit the Wind* (United Artists 1960).

Although March died in 1975, Florence Eldridge continues to live in Los Angeles. She has received an honorary Doctor of Humanities degree from Elmira College. In 1964 she also became a Timothy Dwight fellow in Arts and Letters.

Eldridge excelled in roles illustrating the loyal, quietly steadfast wife. Though she sometimes frustrated directors (notably Robert Lewis, who directed *An Enemy of the People*) with her desire to be "sympathetic" to the audiences, she succeeded admirably. In her last film, *Inherit the Wind*, she played opposite March as Sara, the dutiful wife of Matthew Harrison Brady, who is modeled closely after William Jennings Bryan. Based on the famous Scopes "monkey trial," the film also starred Spencer Tracy as the defense lawyer modeled after Clarence Darrow. In one scene Tracy as an old friend of the Bradys takes Sara aside and tells her that he never thought her husband would have made a great President, "but I'd have voted for him as king, just so we could have you as queen." This line of dialogue is a fitting coda to Florence Eldridge's place in the American theatre.

Critical comments on Florence Eldridge's work are to be found in reviews of her various performances, most notably in the New York *Journal-American* (November 19, 1942, and November 8, 1956), the *New York Times* (December 29, 1950), the *New York World-Telegram and Sun* (March 8, 1951), and the New York *Herald Tribune* (November 8, 1956). Biographical information on Eldridge may be found in *Current Biography, 1943* (1944); *The Biographical Encyclopaedia and Who's Who of the American Theatre* (1966); *Who's Who in the Theatre* (1972); *Notable Names in the American Theatre* (1976); *Who Was Who in the Theatre*, Vol. II (1978); and *The Oxford Companion to American Theatre* (1984).

Robin Holt

ELLIOTT, Maxine (February 5, 1868–March 5, 1940): actress and theatre manager, star of the early twentieth century, was born Jessie C. Dermot, the second of six children of Tom and Addie (Hall) Dermot of Rockland, Maine. Her Irish father changed his name from MacDermot to Dermot after he came to New England around 1850. In addition to three brothers, she had two sisters: Gracie, who died in infancy, and May Gertrude, who went on to a celebrated stage career and married the famous English actor Johnston Forbes-Robertson. Jessie Dermot's father, a sea captain, was often away on sailing trips, and her mother suffered from bouts of mental illness; consequently, as the eldest daughter, Jessie assumed much responsibility in the Dermot home. A lively and direct child, she did not yield easily to the constraints of New England life. Her relationship at age fourteen with a man ten years her senior caused concern in the Dermot family, and Jessie was sent on a sea voyage to South America and Spain with her father. On her return she was enrolled in Notre Dame Academy, a convent school in Roxbury, Massachusetts.

During a visit to New York, Jessie Dermot met George MacDermott, a New York lawyer, and married him sometime around 1884. They separated only a few years later, however, allegedly because of MacDermott's excessive drinking and physical abuse of his wife. After the failure of her marriage Jessie Dermot went to San Francisco to stay with her father and his new wife, Isabelle Paine. (Her mother had continued to suffer from mental illness until her death in a state asylum in 1888 at the age of forty-five.) Although welcomed by her father and stepmother, Jessie was restless in San Francisco. Her experiences in New York had made her aware of the opportunities available to women—especially on the stage. As she later said, "The stage offers bigger prizes to a woman than any other profession, and for those lucky enough to gain the prizes, life presents a broader horizon and many of the agreeable perquisites of success" (*Theatre Magazine*, July 1908, p. 202).

Considered a great beauty with her black hair, dark eyes, and ivory skin, Jessie Dermot saw that a stage career held obvious promises for her. Although she later spoke of beauty as only a "fifth wheel," it was clearly an asset for her as a young woman with no acting experience. She returned to New York and enrolled in Dion Boucicault's acting classes. Fortunately, Boucicault took a liking to his new student and offered encouragement and advice—even helping choose her stage name, Maxine Elliott, to replace the more pedestrian Jessie Dermot. Following Boucicault's death, just a few months after Elliott's arrival, the aspiring actress presented herself to A. M. Palmer, who cast her in the English company of Edward S. Willard. Her first appearance was in the role of Felicia Umfraville in Henry Arthur Jones's *The Middleman* on November 10, 1890, at Palmer's Theatre in New York City. After this debut, Elliott was cast in minor roles with the Willard troupe for the next three seasons. In 1893 Elliott played at the American Theatre under the management of T. Henry French; this additional experience helped her gain a second leading lady position with **Rose Coughlan**'s company in 1894. By this time, Gertrude, Maxine's sister, had come to New York and was also given a place in the company. Friction between Elliott and Rose Coughlan developed during the company's New York run, and Elliott was eager to find another position. Not surprisingly, she jumped at an invitation from Augustin Daly to join his company in 1895.

Elliott's acceptance into Daly's company was a major step forward in her career. Her debut in the Daly company was in the title role of *Heart of Ruby*, a Japanese fantasy. Throughout the next year she played both leading and minor parts, including her first Shakespearean role, Silvia in *Two Gentlemen of Verona*. When the company traveled to London in the summer of 1895, Elliott received favorable reviews and much attention from the press. Despite success with Daly, however, she became irritated with the manager after the company's return to New York when Daly withdrew *The Two Escutcheons*, a production that was doing very well with Elliott in the female lead, and replaced it with a new play for Ada Rehan. Upset by this move, Elliott resigned from Daly's company on January 27, 1896.

In June of that year, she joined the San Francisco company of T. Daniel Frawley. Elliott hardly had time to settle into her new position, however, before the well-known comedian Nat Goodwin arrived in San Francisco en route to a tour in Australia. Enchanted by Elliott when he met her at a dinner party, Goodwin offered her a place in his company at double her salary—raising it to $150 per week—and agreed to take on her sister, whose stage name was Gertrude Elliott. Always one to maximize opportunities, Elliott left Frawley's company and set sail for Australia. Her success in Australia came at the expense of Blanche Walsh, Goodwin's leading lady at the time. Unwilling to share star billing with Elliott, Walsh left the company. Her departure from the tour, and the subsequent discovery by the press that both Elliott and Goodwin had instituted divorce proceedings against their respective spouses, sparked a major scandal in the press. Though the timing of the divorce petitions had been coincidental, Elliott was placed in the unpleasant position of appearing to have a romantic involvement with Goodwin. To quell the rising scandal, both Elliott and Goodwin decided to announce their engagement—not necessarily intending to follow through with a wedding. When they returned to the United States, however, there was no end to the speculation in the press concerning their relationship and engagement. They finally acquiesced and were married at the Hollenden Hotel in Cleveland on February 10, 1898.

While in Australia, Elliott played leading roles in a variety of plays: *The Nominee*, *In Mizzoura*, *David Garrick*, and *An American Citizen*. On their return to the United States, Elliott and Goodwin continued their tour for a season and a half with great success. They departed for England in May 1898, where they spent the summer in a new home, Jackwood Hall, which Goodwin had insisted on buying for his wife. The following season American audiences saw them in a new play by Clyde Fitch, *Nathan Hale*, another hit for the pair, in which Elliott played Alice Adams, Hale's fiancée. They returned to England that summer in another Fitch play, *The Cowboy and the Lady* (1899), a western romance that did not fare as well, and after poor notices it was quickly replaced by *An American Citizen*. Elliott and Goodwin toured the United States for five more seasons together; their most popular production, *When We Were Twenty-One* (1900) by Henry V. Esmond, was their mainstay for four years.

In September 1903 Elliott made her first independent venture in Clyde Fitch's *Her Own Way*, signifying both a professional and personal break from Nat Goodwin. It had become increasingly difficult to find plays with starring roles to suit both performers; appearing in different plays gave them greater opportunities. At the same time, their personal relationship was disintegrating; Elliott's interests were centered upon her social life with the English elite, while Goodwin found relief in less fashionable friends and in drink. The professional split of 1903 was followed by divorce in 1908.

Her Own Way was a triumph for Elliott both in the United States and in London. She next appeared in another Fitch play, *Her Great Match* (1903), which brought further acclaim. Although her future roles met with varied responses, her star stature remained unquestioned. With an interest in financial security and independence, Elliott assumed control of her appearances, and her increasing wealth testified to her good business sense. By now, however, her interest in the stage had dwindled, and she placed much more value on time spent with the English social set and with her sister's growing family, the Forbes-Robertsons. The financial gains from acting, rather than love for the theatre, were the major motivation for Elliott's remaining on the stage. Between 1907 and 1911 she starred in *Under the Greenwood Tree*, *Myself—Bettina*, *The Conquest*, *The Chaperon*, and *The Inferior Sex*. After two years away from the stage (1911–1913), she returned to the theatre in *Joseph and His Brethren*, a lavish London production by Sir Herbert Beerbohm-Tree in 1913.

In partnership with the Shubert organization, Elliott had opened in 1908 the Maxine Elliott Theatre on West 39th Street in New York City—an achievement in which she took great pride. The rumor that J. P. Morgan helped finance her in the project was widespread, but like many of the myths that surrounded the beautiful actress, it was never substantiated. Wanting a comfortable, well-equipped theatre, she personally supervised its construction. To accommodate the intimacy of modern plays, Elliott limited her theatre to 725 seats—a small house by Broadway standards. The theatre opened on December 30, 1908, to a distinguished first-night audience with Elliott starring in *The Chaperon*.

A year after her divorce from Goodwin, Elliott bought Hartsbourne Manor in Hertfordshire, England, where she entertained the elite of society including Winston Churchill, tennis champion Tony Wilding (with whom she reportedly had a romantic involvement), and Lord Curzon (whose offer of marriage she refused). The years at Hartsbourne from 1909 until the war were filled with tennis, bridge, and elaborate dining. When the First World War came, Maxine Elliott was determined to play an active role. She devised a plan to transport food and other supplies by barge to an unoccupied section of Belgian territory. Her plan was a success; the barge *Julia*, with Elliott in charge, operated from February 1915 to May 1916, serving some three hundred and fifty thousand people. Elliott's dedication earned her a decoration from the king of the Belgians.

Maxine Elliott's return to the stage and her venture into films between 1917 and 1920 were due, in large part, to her desire to restore her wealth, which had been drained during the war years. She made two films for Goldwyn Pictures, *Fighting Odds* and *The Eternal Magdalene*, in 1917. Following these films she took the stage part of Lady Algernon Chetland in *Lord and Lady Algy*, co-starring with William Faversham. Following a successful tour of this production, Maxine made her last stage appearance. In 1920, at her own theatre, she played Cordelia in *Trimmed in Scarlet* by William Hurlburt. The play ran for only two weeks, and with its closing Maxine Elliott's career came to an end.

The remainder of Elliott's life was spent entertaining her many friends, enjoying her homes, and indulging herself in food, pets (including her much beloved pet monkey, Kiki), and her major pastime, bridge, which she had played incessantly for years. Growing tired of Hartsbourne, she had her final home, the Château de l'Horizon, built on the Riviera near Cannes. After two years of work, the house was finished in 1932, complete with a water chute leading from the swimming pool down the rock cliffs to the sea. She died at the Château of a heart attack on March 5, 1940. Maxine Elliott was buried in the Protestant Cemetery of Cannes, leaving an estate of one million dollars to her family.

Capitalizing on her beauty, sharp business sense, ambition, and personal charisma, Maxine Elliott became one of the greatest stars of her day. Although her beauty remained a major factor in her stardom, she was credited with being a competent, polished performer. She managed her career, built her own theatre, and acquired great fame and wealth—achievements that are a testament to the ability of women to gain independence and respect in the American theatre.

The best source of information about Maxine Elliott is *My Aunt Maxine* (1964), an objective, well-researched biography by her niece, Diana Forbes-Robertson. Biased, but of interest, is Nat C. Goodwin's *Nat Goodwin's Book* (1914). Other books that discuss Elliott are Lewis C. Strang, *Famous Actresses of the Day in America*, First Series (1899) and Second Series (1901), and Margherita A. Hamm, *Eminent Actors in Their Homes* (1902). Valuable articles and interviews include Ada Patterson, "Beautiful Maxine Elliott: An Interview," *Theatre Magazine* (November 1903); "Army Relief Work in a Canal Barge," *New York Times* (February 7, 1915); Ionia Scherer, "America's Only Actress-Manager," *Green Book Album* (April 1909); Lucy France Pierce, "Will Maxine Elliott Return To Us?" *Green Book Magazine* (December 1912); "Maxine Elliott's Advice to Stage-Struck Girls: 'Don't,' " *Theatre Magazine* (July 1908); Alan Dale, "Maxine the Magnificent," *Cosmopolitan* (May 1912); Ada Patterson, "At Home with Maxine Elliott," *The Green Book Album* (January 1911); Alexander Woollcott, "The Truth About Jessica Dermot," *Cosmopolitan* (October 1933, reprinted in *The Portable Woollcott*, 1946); Maxine Elliott, "How I Built My Theatre," *Woman's Home Companion* (April 1909); and Carol Hughes, "The Strange Story of Maxine Elliott," *Coronet* (December, 1952). There is also material on Elliott in the Robinson Locke Collection of Dramatic Scrapbooks at the New York Public Library Performing Arts Research Center at Lincoln Center. Her obituary appeared in the *New York Times* on March 7, 1940. She is included in *Notable American Women*, Vol. I (1971); William C. Young, *Famous Actors and Actresses on the American Stage*, Vol. I (1975); *Who Was Who in the Theatre*, Vol. II (1978); *The Oxford Companion to the Theatre* (1983); and *The Oxford Companion to American Theatre* (1984).

Ann Ferguson

EMMONS, Beverly (December 12, 1943–): lighting designer, was born in Sudbury, Massachusetts, the daughter of Howard W. and Dorothy (Allen) Emmons. Beverly's father was a scientist and teacher at Harvard University, where he was instrumental in developing the field of fire research. Her early interest in performing arts led her to Sarah Lawrence College in 1961, where she studied dance with Bessie Schoenberg. During a college summer spent backstage for the American Dance Festival at Connecticut College, she was directly influenced by watching **Jean Rosenthal**'s and Tom Skelton's work as lighting designers for dance. She received a Bachelor of Arts degree from Sarah Lawrence College in 1965 and began studying design with Tom Skelton at the Lester Polakov School of Theatrical Design. She married Peter Angelo Simon, a photographer, on October 17, 1980. They have one daughter, Annie Corinne.

Beverly Emmons' career in lighting design has included work in commercial, noncommercial, and experimental theatre, as well as modern dance, opera, and performance art, with such diverse directors as Joseph Chaikin, Richard Foreman, Peter Hall, and Robert Wilson. From 1965 to 1968 she was the lighting designer and stage manager for the Merce Cunningham dance troupe. From 1968 to 1975 she assisted various other lighting designers, including Tom Skelton and Jules Fisher. Her first Broadway design was Bette Midler's *Clams on the Half Shell Revue* (1975). Major recognition as a designer came with the highly influential 1976 Metropolitan Opera production of Robert Wilson's *Einstein On The Beach* (as well as its 1985 revival at the Brooklyn Academy of Music), for which she received the Lumen Award. In 1978 she worked with Joseph Chaikin on the New York Shakespeare Festival production of *The Dybbuk*.

During the next few years the focus of her work shifted to Broadway and resulted in three Antoinette Perry (Tony) nominations for achievement in lighting design: in 1979 for *The Elephant Man*, in 1980 for *A Day in Hollywood/A Night in the Ukraine*, and in 1983 for the Royal Shakespeare Company production of *All's Well That Ends Well*. In 1980 she was awarded a special *Village Voice* Off-Broadway (Obie) Award in recognition of her outstanding professional achievement. The following year, 1981, her lighting design for *Amadeus* with British designer John Bury won her a Tony Award.

Emmons's most recent work reflects her ongoing interest in experimental approaches to dance and theatre. Her work with choreographer **Meredith Monk** (an association that dates back to their undergraduate days) includes *Juice*, *16 mm. Earrings*, and *Quarry*. The collaborative performance art piece *The Games* was another outcome of her work with Monk and Ping Chong. She participated in East European director Lucian Pintilie's critically acclaimed productions of *Tartuffe* at the Guthrie Theatre in Minneapolis and *The Wild Duck* at Arena Stage, Washington, D.C. Her credits in opera include lighting design for *Rigoletto* at the Welsh National Opera and Mozart's *Cosi Fan Tutte* under the direction of Liviu Ciulei.

Other projects have included the lighting design for Robert Wilson's Rome section of *the CIVIL WarS* at the Brooklyn Academy of Music in December 1986, and the lighting for the Broadway production of *Stepping Out: A Play with Dancing* (Golden Theatre, December 1986) and for Wilson's production of *Salome* at La Scala, Milan, in 1987. Liviu Ciulei chose Emmons to do the lighting for his 1987 production of *Coriolanus* at the McCarter Theatre in Princeton, New Jersey. In early 1988 Emmons did the lighting design for the American première of German playwright Harald Mueller's award-winning play *Deathraft* at the Cleveland Play House.

Beverly Emmons has called herself a "less is more" designer. The American theater has undergone a transitional stage in visual design. The heavy saturation of color and glamour of the pre–1960s has been replaced by a "minimalist" framework, typified by the use of white light and fewer lighting instruments. Emmons' background in dance may have convinced her that the human figure is of primary importance on the stage. As she has said, "Lighting is not about the way a set sits there, it's about the way two actors stand and look at each other" (*Theatre Crafts*, March 1986, p. 22). She is adamant that rigid preconceptions have no place in the collaborative nature of the design process. Emmons' career to date has many similarities to that of **Jennifer Tipton**, especially their original interest in dance and their remarkable ability to work successfully, as their profession requires, in diverse theatrical media.

Works by Beverly Emmons are "Lighting Modern Dance," *Theatre Design and Technology* (October 1970); "Lighting for the Dance," *Theatre Crafts* (September 1973); and "Americans Abroad," *Theatre Crafts* (March/April 1977). Works about Beverly Emmons are G. M. Loney, "Recreating *Amadeus*: An American Team Recreates John Bury's Designs," *Theatre Crafts* (March 1981); and Rob Baker, "Visual Recall: Beverly Emmons' Working Pragmatism," *Theatre Crafts* (March 1986).

Jane Ann Crum

ENTERS, Angna (April 18, 1897?–February 25, 1989): pioneering mime, dancer, author, director, teacher, and painter, was born Anita Enters in Milwaukee, Wisconsin. She was the only child of Edward W. and Henrietta (Gasseur-Styleau) Enters. Upon completing the fine arts course at the Milwaukee Normal School, Angna Enters went to New York in 1919 to begin study at the Art Students League. While earning her living as a free-lance advertising illustrator, she began taking dance lessons from Michio Ito, the Japanese dancer who, in Hellerau at the Jacques Dalcroze Institute, had been trained in "eurythmics"—a system in which the artist learns to experience music kinesthetically by responding physically to the rhythms of musical compositions. Ito had also developed his own gestural system to create interpretive dances with ten basic gestures, each one having its male and female variations. Enters studied eurythmics and traditional Japanese Geisha dancing with Ito. In February 1921 Enters became Ito's professional dancing partner, performing a program of music interpretations and traditional Japanese dances.

In the summer of 1922 Enters appeared on Broadway when Ito was hired to produce Raymond Hitchcock's revue, titled *Pinwheel Revel*. In addition to leading a group dance, *Ecclesiastique*, Enters performed several solos of her own creation: *Le Petit Berger*, *Feline*, and *A Tribute to Gauguin*.

In 1923 Enters left Ito to concentrate on her development as a solo performer. In 1926, after several years of sharing concert stages with other performers, usually musicians and singers, Angna Enters presented her *Compositions in Dance Form*, an evening of solo performance assisted by pianist Madeleine Marshall. She toured her solo program across the United States and Europe for more than thirty years until her retirement in the mid-sixties. Retitled *The Theatre of Angna Enters*, her repertoire included more than 250 dance-mime compositions, each with a costume designed and often constructed by Enters. She also frequently selected and arranged her own music.

Enters adhered to no one performance technique. Instead she allowed each image to develop into its own theatrical form. This deliberate lack of identifiable technique gave her great freedom and variety when creating a dance-mime composition. As a result of her eurythmic/dance background many of her early compositions were a development of a mood or concept in the form of dance. *Feline*, danced to Claude Debussy's Prelude No. III, explored the feline qualities of a woman's sensuality. Other compositions were nearly pure pantomime, suggesting a time, place, or situation. *Le Petit Berger*, also danced to music by Debussy, was a pantomime of the Little Shepherd being startled awake and then drowsing back to sleep. As she became more involved in psychological exploration, her characters' actions and behavior suggested a deeper, more complex life beyond the brief vignette. The prostitute in *Aphrodisiac-Green Hour*, the corrupt *Boy Cardinal*, the young woman in *Vienna Provincial* revealed their personalities and life situations in the space of a few minutes.

In 1929 Enters had begun writing professionally. She contributed essays on the art of mime and dance in addition to articles and letters on the Spanish Civil War to such magazines as *Drama*, *The Dance Magazine*, *Twice a Year*, and *The New Masses*. Her autobiographies include *First Person Plural* (1937); *Silly Girl* (1944), a fictionalized autobiography of her childhood and early performing career; and *Artist's Life* (1958). She also wrote a play in collaboration with Louis Kalonyme, *Love Possessed Juana* (1939) and co-wrote a novel with him, titled *Among the Daughters* (1955), a story about love and ambition in the arts and theatre worlds of New York. Her last book, *Angna Enters On Mime* (1966), is a compilation of journal entries, lesson plans, and observations on her experiences.

In addition to performing and writing, Enters was also a remarkable visual artist. In 1933 her paintings and drawings were first exhibited in New York. Costume renderings, paintings of her dance-mime compositions, portraits of performing artists, and still lifes formed a large portion of her art work. She has exhibited in New York's Metropolitan Museum of Art and the Museum of Modern Art in addition to one-woman shows throughout the United States, Canada, and Europe. As a model she has been the subject of several well-known visual artists, including Isamu Noguchi, Walt Kuhn, and John Sloan.

Enters received her first Guggenheim Foundation Fellowship in 1934. With this award she studied ancient mime in Greece and, with a second award in 1935, studied dance in Egypt and the Near East. This research resulted in a large body of drawings and paintings, several new mime compositions based on religious themes, and a revival and revision of *Pagan Greece*, Enters's only evening-length composition cycle.

From the early 1940s to the early 1950s Enters was a contract writer for Metro-Goldwyn-Mayer. Film scripts attributed to her include *Lost Angel* (1944), *Tenth Avenue Angel* (1946), and *You Belong to Me* (1950). She also created and staged the *commedia dell'arte* sequences for the film *Scaramouche* (1952).

In 1946 the Houston Little Theatre invited Angna Enters to direct and design a production of her play *Love Possessed Juana*. The following year the group produced her unpublished play *The Unknown Lover*. Enters directed and designed Garcia Lorca's *Yerma* for the University of Denver in 1958 and Jean Giraudoux's

The Madwoman of Chaillot for the Dallas Theatre Center in 1962. Other directing assignments were in conjunction with artist-in-residence programs at Baylor University (1961–1962) and Wesleyan University (1962–1963) during which Enters taught classes in mime for actors. She last taught at Pennsylvania State University in 1970.

In July 1936 Enters married Louis Kalonyme, art critic for *Art and Decoration*. After his death in 1961 she curtailed her touring and performing schedule. In 1974 she became incapacitated and entered a nursing home. Agna Enters died February 25, 1989, in Tenafly, New Jersey.

Angna Enters's dance-mime compositions combined the esthetics of concert art dance with the piquancy of her special point of view. Through her influence, the world concert stage, Broadway, and the cinema blended mime into the American modern dance.

Works by Angna Enters include *First Person Plural* (1937), *Love Possessed Juana* (1939), *Silly Girl* (1944), *Among the Daughters* (1955), *Artist's Life* (1958), and *Angna Enters on Mime* (1965). Very little has been written about Angna Enters. See Ginnine Cocuzza, "Angna Enters: American Dance-Mime," *The Drama Review* (December 1980), and Ginnine Cocuzza, "First Person Plural: A Portfolio from the Theatre of Angna Enters," *Women and Performance* (Spring/Summer 1983). Angna Enters' personal papers, including many photographs and drawings, are in the Dance Collection at the New York Public Library Performing Arts Research Center at Lincoln Center. Enters' obituary appeared in *Variety* (March 8–14, 1989). Short biographical accounts of Enters appear in *Current Biography, 1940* (1940); *The Biographical Encyclopaedia and Who's Who of the American Theatre* (1966); *The Oxford Companion to the Theatre* (1967); *Notable Names in the American Theatre* (1976); *The Biographical Dictionary of Dance* (1982); and *The International Encyclopedia of Dance* (1983). Enters changed her birth date on all of her biographical material. Most sources give Enters's date of birth as 1907. However, her birth certificate gives the date as April 18, 1897).

Ginnine Cocuzza

EVANS, Dina Rees (June 19, 1891–January 20, 1989): drama educator and director, was born in Chicago, Illinois, the youngest of the four children of Elizabeth (Rees) and David E. Evans, a Presbyterian/Congregational minister. She had two older brothers and one sister who died at the age of three months. When seventy-two years old, Dina Rees Evans married Harvey Shaw, a retired railroad engineer; he died three years later.

For a woman who claimed, "The only thing I did was to love my kids" (Dole Interview, 1983), Dina Rees Evans's contributions to the theatre world were many. She earned the first doctoral degree in theatre education granted in the United States (1932). She was an exceptional high school teacher, a leader in the American Theatre Association, and the organizer and director of Cleveland's civic theatre, Cain Park. After retiring from that position she became active in senior adult theatre.

In her book, *Cain Park: The Halcyon Years* (1980), Evans revealed that she could not act, dance, or sing—yet her interest in dramatic art began when she recognized in play production a powerful teaching tool. In an interview with

Donald Doyle she stated, "The discipline given by theatre is the paramount reason for it. Drama develops personality" (1983). This philosophy permeated her contributions to the world of theatre.

Evans began her teacher training at Northland College in Ashland, Wisconsin. She completed her Bachelor of Arts degree at the University of South Dakota. After graduation she went on to teach Latin and German in several high schools, where she usually directed the "senior play."

With the intention of enrolling in classes to improve her play production skills, Evans attended the University of Iowa in the summer of 1926. Professor E. C. Mabie persuaded her to pursue a master's degree in dramatic art, which she did, receiving her degree in 1929. Her thesis, titled "A Preliminary Study of Play Production in the Secondary Schools," was a survey of high schools to determine student and teacher involvement in dramatic art. She was fascinated, though not surprised, by the answers she received to the question, "What do you consider the most important outcome (note: not objective) of your students' participation in dramatic activities?" Many replied that a transformation of personal characteristics, attitudes, and social behavior occurred. This had already been Evans's own personal experience. Sixteen years of teaching had convinced her that drama was a remarkable educational tool.

This hypothesis became the basis of her doctoral research at the University of Iowa. While studying for the degree she was offered a teaching job at Cleveland Heights High School, and it was during this teaching that she conducted the research for her dissertation. A psychologist selected for her a class of "misfits," mostly unhappy students who were delinquents. After repeating the study twice at the insistence of her dissertation committee, she reported data in "A Preliminary Study of Play Production in the Secondary Schools" that showed that these delinquent students had moved toward the norm on her scale. At the oral defense of her study she had to overcome the prevalent attitude that the arts were not academic. Her persuasive dissertation led the University of Iowa to offer a Ph.D. degree in theatre and similar degrees in all of the arts. She later confessed that had she known the future status of the arts in American universities depended on her success, she might not have had the fortitude to undertake such a program.

Evans lived chiefly in Cleveland until 1958. During these years she firmly established herself as a drama and English teacher at Cleveland Heights High School. There she organized the "Heights Players," one of her greatest achievements. Students started as freshmen and worked their way from apprenticeship to become journeymen, masters, and national thespians. They had their own theatre, wrote and directed their own plays, and held critiques. Many of the participants later became theatre professionals.

While in Cleveland Evans also organized and directed the very successful civic theatre Cain Park, which included a children's theatre as well as an adult theatre. The idea for the park, named after the mayor who strongly supported the venture, was born in 1934 when Evans decided to produce a play combining civic theatre performers with her youthful Heights Players. The first production,

A Midsummer Night's Dream, was performed outdoors in a ravine and was a resounding success. After much hard work Evans opened Cain Park Theatre in August of 1938. The facility grew to include a 4,000-seat outdoor auditorium and a three-story office building. Within seven years, with the support of the local news media, Cain Park Theatre grew to be a vital part of Greater Cleveland.

In 1941, under Evans's guidance, a children's theatre, named the Alma Theatre after the mayor's wife, was built at Cain Park. Designed with integral workshops, it had four theatres: one for marionettes, one for hand puppets, one for shadow puppets, and one for actors. The facility included a building to house the already existing children's school of the theatre. It was the first and only permanent stage of its kind and the first large permanent puppet theatre in America. Under the direction of Kenneth Graham, the children's theatre expanded to include not only drama with children but also drama for children. The philosophy of the theatre was not to train child actors but to develop personalities.

In addition to developing the Cain Park children's theatre, Evans became involved with national children's theatre events. She attended the meeting called by **Winifred Ward** to establish the Children's Theatre Conference (now the Children's Theatre Association of America). Evans's involvement in professional organizations included the American Theatre Association and the Secondary School Theatre Association (SSTA). She was instrumental in establishing SSTA and served as its chairperson in 1937.

Evans retired as executive director of Cain Park Theatre in 1950 but presided over the children's theatre wing through 1958. Upon her full retirement in 1958 she moved to Youngtown, Arizona, where she founded theatre groups, directed, wrote plays, and worked tirelessly in support of theatre for senior citizens. She died there on January 20, 1989 at the age of ninety-seven.

For information on Dina Rees Evans and the Cain Park civic theatre, see her book *Cain Park: The Halcyon Years* (1980). Other information is available in the Children's Theatre Archives at Arizona State University in Tucson, notably a taped interview with Evans conducted by Donald Doyle in 1983. Her obituary appeared in *The Cleveland Plain Dealer* on January 22, 1989.

Anamarie Garcia

EVANS, Mary Jane Larson (April 7, 1923–): educator and children's theatre playwright and director, was born in Superior, Wisconsin, to Hazel (Newland) and Lionel H. Larson. The family, which included one brother, moved frequently as her father, an employee of the J. C. Penney Company, was transferred to various midwestern communities. She attended public schools in Marquette (Michigan) and Manitowoc (Wisconsin), and Ely Junior College (Minnesota), before being admitted to Northwestern University in Evanston, Illinois. While at Northwestern, Mary Jane Larson had the opportunity to study with **Winifred Ward**, the outstanding pioneer of children's theatre in America, and in 1944 she was awarded a Bachelor of Science degree in the School of Speech. There followed a period of teaching, directing, and additional study at Western Reserve University, during which time she worked as a children's theatre staff member with **Dina Rees Evans** at Cain Park in Cleveland Heights, Ohio, developed an experimental drama program at Sunbeam School for Crippled Children in Cleveland, and in 1953 was hired as director of the Junior Civic Theatre of Kalamazoo, Michigan. A 1946 marriage to Harrison Wills-Watkins ended in divorce, and she returned to school to pursue advanced work in theatre.

A teaching assistantship in children's theatre was offered her at Michigan State University in 1954. Upon earning her master's degree in theatre in 1955, she continued at Michigan State as an instructor in the children's drama program, teaching courses in speech and theatre, directing productions for children with both college students and children, and leading creative drama sessions with child participants. During this period, she became a colleague of Jed H. Davis, another children's theatre specialist, with whom she was to collaborate in later publications.

Her teaching and administrative career took an important step forward in 1959 when she accepted an appointment to develop the children's drama program at the newly established San Fernando Valley State College (now California State University, Northridge). In her extended tenure there she served the theatre program as department chair and as director of graduate studies. As coordinator of the children's theatre and the creative drama faculty she developed an extensive curriculum for undergraduate and graduate students which has since been recognized for its excellence by the Children's Theatre Association of America. She concurrently established an exemplary production program for child audiences, and her productions regularly tour the Los Angeles area under the auspices of Junior Programs of California. She has been a visiting professor at California State University, Long Beach; and she has pursued additional graduate training at the University of Minnesota and at the University of Wisconsin, Eau Claire. In 1970, she was promoted to full professor at California State University, Northridge.

Shortly after arriving in California, she renewed an acquaintance with Robley Dwight Evans, a fellow worker at Cain Park and nephew of Cain Park's chief administrator, Dina Rees Evans. They were married in December of 1961, and a son, David Rees, was born in 1964. Robley Evans is now an administrative law judge for the state of California.

Evans has contributed extensively to the field of theatre and drama for and with children. Collaborating with Jed H. Davis and using the pen name Mary Jane Larson Watkins, she wrote her first book, *Children's Theatre: Play Production for the Child Audience* (1960), to a large extent based on her Michigan State years. Their second book, *Theatre, Children and Youth* (1982), reflected the broader experience of her professional career at California State University, Northridge, and elsewhere. An experienced playwright for children's theatre, she co-authored *Tales from Hans Christian Andersen* with Deborah Anderson. In addition, from 1968 to 1972 she was children's theatre editor for the *Educational Theatre Journal*.

Her long-term dedication to the work of the Children's Theatre Association of America began when she attended its opening meeting, called by Winifred Ward at Northwestern in 1944. Subsequently she has held many offices in the association, including secretary, governor of several regions, member of the Board of Governors, and administrative assistant to the director. She took part in the association's 1977 conference on "Theatre Education for Public Schools," held at the Wingspread Conference Center (Racine, Wisconsin). She has served as a member of the Executive Committee of the International Children's Theatre Association's United States Center (now ASSITEJ/USA).

Her service among professional theatre educators continued with the American Theatre Association, where she was a member of the Executive Committee and Board of Directors. In 1977 her stature in the field of children's theatre earned membership for her in the American Theatre Association's College of Fellows. Evans has given of her expertise not only to the American Theatre Association and to the Children's Theatre Association of America but to the California Educational Theatre Association, where she has held offices and spearheaded a 1974 publication on the *Drama/Theatre Framework for California Public Schools*.

Evans's educational program at Northridge won the Children's Theatre Association of America's 1981 **Sara Spencer** Award and has been certified by that association to receive Winifred Ward scholars, who are chosen annually from a nationwide competition. Her production of *Reynard the Fox* was selected in 1972 by a panel of national critics as first alternate for presentation at the Congress of the International Children's Theatre Association and was the only university production in the country to be so honored.

In a keynote address to the 1980 meeting of the Children's Theatre Association of America, Mary Jane Evans manifested the perceptive and analytical powers for which she has been much admired. In her speech, "Perceptions/Generalizations/Image Making—Challenges to Theatre for Children in the 80s," Evans insisted that children's theatre must never be cheap or second-best but always stimulating, imaginative, and of the highest caliber. Her lifelong devotion to excellence in theatre for children exemplifies the standards she wants the profession to pursue.

Mary Jane Evans's books written in collaboration with Jed H. Davis include *Children's Theatre: Play Production for the Child Audience* (1960) and *Theatre, Children and Youth* (1982). She wrote the chapter titled "Theatre for Children—Art Form or Anarchy" in *Theatre for Young Audiences* by Nellie McCaslin (1978). Evans's speech, "Perceptions/ Generalizations/Image Making—Challenges to Theatre for Children in the '80s," has been printed in the *Children's Theatre Review* (1980). Evans is listed in *Notable Names in the American Theatre* (1976); *Who's Who of American Women, 1977–1978* (1977– 1978); and *Who's Who in the West, 1978–1979* (1978).

Jed H. Davis

EYTINGE, Rose (November 21, 1835–December 20, 1911): leading actress of the New York stage in the 1860s and 1870s, is thought to have been the daughter of David and Rebecca Eytinge of Philadelphia. Her father was a language teacher and translator. The Eytinge name was familiar to Philadelphians at the time, since there were four Jewish merchants of that name operating in the city, two of whom were Dutch immigrants. However, their relationship to Rose Eytinge's family is unclear. Rose Eytinge had at least one sibling, a brother named Samuel D., also an actor (d. 1859).

Eytinge received an informal education at home, first in Philadelphia and later in Brooklyn. Her stage career began at the age of seventeen when she joined the Geary Hough stock company in Syracuse, New York, on the recommendation of the elder Charles Parsloe, a New York agent. Her first notable role was that of Melanie in Dion Boucicault's *The Old Guard* (1855). Billed as a leading lady in 1855, she appeared in Albany, New York, at the Green Street Theatre, managed at that time by David Barnes. She subsequently married Barnes; their one daughter, Courtney, eventually married comedian John T. Raymond. Barnes and Eytinge were divorced before 1862.

In May of 1864 Eytinge acted for the first time with Edwin Booth at Niblo's Garden Theatre in New York. *The Fool's Revenge* was Tom Taylor's adaptation of Victor Hugo's *Le Roi S'Amuse*; Eytinge portrayed Fiordelisa. That same year she was engaged as leading lady by Orlando Tompkins, Ben Thayer, and Henry C. Jarrett of the Boston Theatre. Her tenure there was short; she broke her contract after refusing to play a minor role while a visiting actress received star billing. E. L. Davenport and J. W. Wallack, who were starring at another Boston theatre, immediately offered her a position acting with them. Together they produced *Othello* and stage adaptations of Alfred Lord Tennyson's *Enoch Arden* and Walter Scott's *Lady of the Lake*. At the close of the Boston engagement the company went on tour, playing in Philadelphia, Baltimore, and Washington, D.C. President Abraham Lincoln attended several of Eytinge's performances and later invited her to the White House, where, upon meeting her, he said, "So this is the little lady that all us folks in Washington like so much?" (*The Memories of Rose Eytinge*, pp. 76–77).

From 1865 to 1868 she continued to expand her repertoire. With Edwin Booth she appeared in *Richelieu* at the Winter Garden Theatre in New York. At Wallack's Theatre she first played Nancy Sykes, which became one of her most noted and frequently performed roles, in the adaptation of *Oliver Twist* with E. L. Davenport as Bill Sykes and J. W. Wallack as Fagin. During the same engagement she acted with Wallack and Davenport in Bayle Bernard's *The Iron Mask*. The trio received glowing reviews. The *New York Times* critic wrote: "It is difficult to speak [of them] without exaggeration. Three such artists on the stage in any one scene . . . must necessarily lead to decided results, but one could hardly anticipate such positive perfection" (June 13, 1865).

Following her engagement at Wallack's Theatre she acted at the New York Theatre with John K. Mortimer in Augustin Daly's *Griffith Gaunt*, based on Charles Reade's novel. Her creation of the part of Laura Cortlandt in Augustin Daly's *Under the Gaslight*, also at the New York Theatre, was so well received that she was offered the position of principal actress at Wallack's Theatre for the 1868–1869 season. In that one season at Wallack's she won acclaim as Lady Gay Spanker in Dion Boucicault's *London Assurance*, Beatrice in *Much Ado About Nothing*, and Kate in *She Stoops to Conquer*. She had become, as George C. D. Odell stated, "the most beautiful and talented young actress then on the American stage" (*Annals of the New York Stage*, Vol. VIII, p. 269).

Eytinge's career was interrupted in November 1869 by her marriage to Colonel George H. Butler, a journalist who became United States Consul General to Egypt several months later. She lived abroad three or four years and had two children. Colonel Butler was a dissolute and violent man, and Eytinge left him in 1873 to return to America. Although she had intended to forgo acting she was approached by Sheridan Shook and A. M. Palmer to join the Union Square company in New York, an offer she accepted in 1873. In her autobiography she states, "Thus it fell out that after I had thought my stage career was ended I did my highest and my best dramatic work, playing for the first time, among other parts, Lady Macbeth, Cleopatra, Hermione, Rose Michel, Gabrielle Le Brun, Felicia, and Miss Multon" (*The Memories of Rose Eytinge*, pp. 214, 215). She created the roles of Armande, the dissatisfied wife, in Boucicault's *Led Astray*; Marianne, the outcast, in *The Two Orphans*; and Rose Michel, a mother who protects her daughter at great cost, in the play of the same name, all at the Union Square Theatre. *Led Astray* and *Rose Michel* enjoyed runs of six months each and were considered two of her best vehicles; *The Two Orphans*, on the other hand, starred Eytinge for only a fortnight since she refused to share star billing with another leading lady, Kate Claxton. Eytinge was replaced in the part.

In 1876 she formed her own touring company and began appearing in *Rose Michel* in major American cities. In San Francisco she first appeared in what became her most famous role, Cleopatra in *Antony and Cleopatra*. She returned to New York to appear in Shakespeare's play at the Broadway Theatre, opening on November 26, 1877. The part was a great favorite with the actress, possibly because of her familiarity with the Egyptian setting; moreover, the temperamental and fiery character of Cleopatra was much like her own. William Winter, evaluating the production, wrote, "No other actress appearing on our stage, in my remembrance . . . has given a more acceptable performance of [Cleopatra]" (*Shakespeare on the Stage*, 3rd series, p. 460). Eytinge continued for the next year almost exclusively in that role.

In January 1880 she appeared as Gervaise at the Standard Theatre in *Drink* opposite Cyril Searle, with whom she had toured for some time. They were married later that year; however, the relationship did not endure past 1884. In 1880 she was warmly praised on the London stage, where she appeared as Nancy Sykes in *Oliver Twist* at the Olympic Theatre. Although such prominent figures as Wilkie Collins, Charles Reade, Tom Taylor, and the young Charles Dickens urged her to continue acting in London, her stay there was brief. By February 1881 she had returned to New York to open in *Felicia*. It was her first appearance on the New York stage in five years and the last important role of her career.

As she turned to teaching and writing, Rose Eytinge's appearances on stage became less frequent, and in 1890 she virtually retired from acting. The same year she opened an acting school in New York and published a novel, *It Happened This Way*. Her play, *Golden Chains*, preceded publication of her autobiography, *The Memories of Rose Eytinge* (1905). She returned to the stage to appear in productions of *The Helmet of Navarre*, *Frocks and Frills*, and *Mary of Magdala*. Her last performance was in 1907 in *The Bishop's Carriage*. After spending several years as an invalid, she died in 1911 at the Brunswick House, Amityville, Long Island, under the care of the Actors' Fund of America.

Rose Eytinge was one of America's favorite actresses of the 1860s and 1870s. With dark hair and eyes and an ample figure she was considered a beauty. Quick to anger and unpredictable by nature, she often quarreled with actors and managers and broke contracts. Although she did not stay with one company or management for an extended period, she always felt indebted to E. L. Davenport and J. W. Wallack and acknowledged that had their partnership continued past 1868, she would probably have remained with them. The *New York Clipper* called her "one of the brightest lights of the American stage" (December 30, 1911), and her high standing in the eyes of theatre managers and the general public is evidenced by her claim to have been the first woman on the American stage to command a three-figure salary. In her most famous roles—Nancy Sykes, Lady Gay Spanker, Rose Michel, and Cleopatra—she proved to be an actress of considerable versatility and emotional range.

By far the best resource is *The Memories of Rose Eytinge* (1905), an autobiography with lengthy discussions of her stage career, though little is revealed about her personal life. George C. D. Odell documents her New York performances in his *Annals of the New York Stage*, Vols. VII-IX (1936–1937), and Eugene Tompkins and Quincy Kilby include her in their *History of the Boston Theatre, 1854–1901* (1908). William Winter's appreciation of her Cleopatra appears in his *Shakespeare on the Stage* (1916). Obituaries and appreciative articles after her death include the *New York Clipper* (December 27 and 30, 1911), the *New York Tribune* (December 21, 1911), the *New York Times* (December 21, 1911), and the *New York Herald* (December 21 and 23, 1911). There are clippings about Eytinge in the Harvard Theatre Collection. She is included in T. Allston Brown, *History of the American Stage* (1870); John Bouve Clapp and Edwin Francis Edgett, *Players of the Present*, Part I (1899); *Who Was Who in America*, Vol. I 1897–1942 (1966); *Notable American Women*, Vol. I (1971); William C. Young, *Famous Actors and Actresses on the American Stage*, Vol. I (1975); *The Oxford Companion to the Theatre* (1983); and *The Oxford Companion to American Theatre* (1984).

                                                                    Beth R. Barrett

— F —

FERBER, Edna (August 15, 1885–April 16, 1968): celebrated novelist, short-story writer, and playwright, was the younger of two daughters born to Jacob Charles and Julia (Neumann) Ferber of Kalamazoo, Michigan. Jacob Ferber had come to America from Oyeso, Hungary, at the age of seventeen. When Edna Ferber was thirteen her father began losing his eyesight because of an atrophying optic nerve. By the time she was sixteen he was totally blind, leaving the management of the family's general store to his wife, who ran it for thirteen years. To Edna Ferber's mind her father, who died in 1909, was "completely engulfed by his family of three energetic, high-vitality females—my mother, my sister and myself" (*A Peculiar Treasure*, p. 15).

Julia Ferber, her mother, was born in Milwaukee, Wisconsin. She was a strong-willed individual who aggressively took control of the family's welfare when her husband's blindness prevented him from doing so. Ferber described her mother as possessing "all the great human virtues" and cited her as one of the four women who strongly influenced her "thinking" and "conduct of life." Jane Addams, Ida Tarbell, and Lillian Adler were the other three (*A Kind of Magic*, p. 124).

Edna Ferber's childhood was nomadic, the family moving from Kalamazoo, Michigan, to Chicago, Illinois, to Ottumwa, Iowa, back to Chicago, to Appleton, Wisconsin, and again to Chicago. Chicago later served as a home base for Ferber, but Ottumwa and Appleton had the greatest impact on the young Edna Ferber. She never forgot the anti-Semitic treatment she underwent in the Iowa coal-mining town, though as an adult she saw her seven years there as "stringent, strengthening years" that gave her "a solid foundation of stamina, determination, and a profound love of justice" (*A Peculiar Treasure*, p. 31). Although she did not practice the Jewish religion, she was fiercely proud of her Jewish heritage and lashed out against anti-Semitism throughout her career.

Reading and theatregoing occupied much of the young Edna Ferber's free time. From the age of seven to seventeen she read at least one book a day by such authors as Charles Dickens, Mark Twain, O. Henry, George Eliot, and Guy de Maupassant. The theatre was an important part of her life, as she noted in *A Peculiar Treasure*: "Certainly, I have been stage-struck all of my life" (p. 25). She was enchanted as a young girl with performances given by her maternal grandfather who used cardboard characters on a cardboard miniature stage he had made. The theatre served as a refuge during the family's Iowa years. She explained, "I suppose it was color, escape in that dour, unlovely world" (*A Peculiar Treasure*, p. 54). In addition to attending performances whenever possible, Edna and her sister performed plays in the family's woodshed. Ferber's love affair with the theatre continued at Ryan High School in Appleton, where she played leading roles in the school plays.

After winning first place in the Wisconsin State Declamatory Contest as a high school senior, Ferber decided to go to the Northwestern University School of Elocution in Evanston, Illinois. She later admitted that this decision was probably formed in part by a hidden desire for a career on the professional stage. Because her father's income could not support her college education, she described herself plaintively as a "blighted Bernhardt" (*A Peculiar Treasure*, p. 102). As she noted, "I didn't want to be a writer . . . .The stage was my one love" (*A Peculiar Treasure*, p. 101). Nevertheless, upon graduation Ferber secured a job as the first woman reporter for the *Appleton Daily Crescent*. She lost that job because a new city editor preferred a male reporter who could "cover more varied ground" (*A Peculiar Treasure*, p. 128). Ferber then accepted an offer to join the *Milwaukee Journal*. Three and a half years of hectic police court reporting and celebrity interviewing played havoc with Ferber's health. In early 1909 anemia and exhaustion forced her to give up her reporter's beat and return to Appleton to recuperate. She fully intended to return to the *Journal*, but during her convalescence she began her career as a short-story writer and novelist.

In 1909 she finished her first novel, *Dawn O'Hara*, published in 1911, and sold her first short story, "The Homely Heroine," to *Everybody's Magazine*. After moving to Chicago, Ferber produced a series of short stories with plots and characters drawn from that milieu. In 1912 a collection of these stories, *Buttered Side Down*, was published. In that same year Ferber wrote her first Emma McChesney story, a tale of a traveling saleswoman, published in *The American Magazine*. This story and subsequent ones featuring McChesney were enthusiastically received and gained for Ferber a national reputation. The stories were collected and published in three separate volumes: *Roast Beef Medium: The Business Adventures of Emma McChesney* (1913); *Personality Plus: Some Experiences of Emma and Her Sons* (1914); and *Emma McChesney and Co.* (1915).

Many successful books were to follow the McChesney series, both short stories and novels. Foremost among her total of twelve novels were *So Big* (1924), *Show Boat* (1926), *Cimarron* (1930), *Saratoga Trunk* (1941), *Giant* (1952), and *Ice Palace* (1958). Eight of her novels were made into films: *Fanny Herself* in 1921; *So Big* in 1925, 1932, and 1953; *Show Boat* in 1929, 1936, and 1951; *Cimarron* in 1931 and 1961; *Come and Get It* in 1936; *Saratoga Trunk* in 1945; *Giant* in 1956; and *Ice Palace* in 1960. Two collections of short stories were also the bases for films: *Gigolo* in 1926 and *Mother Knows Best: A Fiction Book* in 1928. Individual short stories made into films were *Our Mrs. McChesney* in 1918, *Classified* in 1925, *The Home Girl* in 1928, and *Old Man Minick* in 1932.

Ferber's career as a playwright began in 1914. Upon returning from her first European trip, she agreed to collaborate with George V. Hobart on a play based on the McChesney character. Titled *Our Mrs. McChesney*, it opened at the Lyceum Theatre, New York, on October 19, 1915. While pleased that the play was produced by the Charles Frohman organization, Ferber was unhappy with the choice of **Ethel Barrymore** for the McChesney role. She was also disappointed with the script itself, describing it as "clumsy, inept and spiritless" (*A Peculiar Treasure*, p. 217). Despite Ferber's feelings about the play, it had a respectable run of 151 performances.

Five years elapsed before Ferber's next playwriting venture. Her collaborator this time was Newman Levy, a Chicago lawyer she had met on the return voyage of her European trip in 1914. The play, *$1200 a Year*, was Levy's idea. The comedy's plot centered on a $1200-a-year university professor who lived in a town where steel workers received twenty-five dollars a day. It was a failure, closing a week after its opening in Baltimore. Ferber realistically said, "The play wasn't really bad. It just wasn't good enough" (*A Peculiar Treasure*, p. 249). She was grateful for the opportunity the play gave her to work with producer Sam Harris. In later years he would produce her more successful plays (also collaborations), *Dinner at Eight* and *Stage Door*.

Ferber's one solo venture into playwriting was for the Provincetown Players in 1924, an adaptation of her short story titled *The Eldest*. Playwright George S. Kaufman entered Ferber's life as a collaborator and friend in 1924 when he asked her in a letter if she would like to collaborate with him on writing a play based on her short story, *Old Man Minick*. Although Ferber was highly skeptical that this story possessed stageworthy material, she jumped at the chance to work with Kaufman: "If George had approached me with the idea of dramatizing McGuffey's First Reader I'd have been enchanted to talk about it" (*A Peculiar Treasure*, p. 283). It was the beginning of a working relationship that would produce six plays over the next twenty-four years: *Minick*, 1924 (141 performances); *The Royal Family*, 1927 (345 performances); *Dinner at Eight*, 1932 (232 performances); *Stage Door*, 1936 (169 performances); *The Land Is Bright*, 1941 (79 performances); and *Bravo*, 1948 (44 performances).

Although Ferber claimed that plot in itself did not interest her, she initiated the plot ideas for four of the six plays that she wrote with Kaufman. *Stage Door* and *The Land is Bright* were the only scripts for which she did not originate the plot idea. Ferber was more interested in characterization. Critics and biographers generally credit Ferber with plot and character development in her collaborations with Kaufman and give Kaufman credit for the dialogue and playwriting expertise. In his biography of Kaufman, Howard Teichmann claimed that Ferber stretched Kaufman as a playwright: "With Miss Ferber, Kaufman's plays always had a larger variety of plot and a broader spectrum of color and characterization. Their plays darted back and forth between drama and comedy. Although he wrote an occasional drama with [Marc] Connelly or [Moss] Hart, Ferber made him dig deeper into what he called 'the rich, red meat of playwrighting' " (*George S. Kaufman, An Intimate Portrait*, p. 91). Scott Meredith, another Kaufman biographer, included Ferber along with Connelly and Hart in discussing the three best of Kaufman's twenty-two collaborators (*George S. Kaufman and His Friends*, p. 257). Of Ferber's six collaborations with Kaufman, four were successes: *Minick*, *The Royal Family*, *Dinner at Eight*, and *Stage Door*. All had successful Broadway runs and were made into films. *Minick*, *The Royal Family*, and *Dinner at Eight* also received successful London productions. Burns Mantle honored *Minick*, *The Royal Family*, and *Stage Door* by including them in his *Best Plays of the Year* series.

George Oppenheimer, in reviewing the 1966 revival of *Dinner at Eight*, probably best evaluates the contribution of the Ferber and Kaufman team to the American theatre: "George S. Kaufman and Edna Ferber wrote an entertainment rather than an earth-shattering contribution to the art of drama, but it is intricately and wonderfully constructed, filled with bright dialogue and its characters are varied and, for the most part, absorbing today as well as yesterday" (*Ferber, A Biography*, p. 44). Although regarded principally as a novelist, Ferber wrote, each time in collaboration, a group of plays that were successfully produced on Broadway. She did so in a period of American theatre history when few women playwrights were represented on the New York stage.

Edna Ferber died of cancer in New York City at the age of eighty-three, never having married.

Edna Ferber's autobiographies are *A Peculiar Treasure* (1939) and *A Kind of Magic* (1963). Biographies on Ferber and Kaufman are Julie Goldsmith Gilbert, *Ferber, A Biography* (1978); Malcolm Goldstein, *George S. Kaufman, His Life, His Theatre* (1979); Scott Meredith, *George S. Kaufman and His Friends* (1974); and Howard Teichmann, *George S. Kaufman, An Intimate Portrait* (1972). Ferber's obituary appeared in the *New York Times* on April 17, 1968. The Edna Ferber Papers are at the State Historical Society of Wisconsin. There is a clipping file in the Billy Rose Theatre Collection at the New York Public Library Performing Arts Research Center at Lincoln Center. Ferber is listed in *The Biographical Encyclopaedia and Who's Who of the American Theatre* (1966); *The Oxford Companion to the Theatre* (1967); *Who's Who in the Theatre* (1967); *McGraw-Hill Encyclopedia of World Drama* (1972); Myron Matlaw, *Modern World Drama: An Encyclopedia* (1972); *Who Was Who*, Vol. 6, *1961–1970* (1972); *Who Was Who in the Theatre*, Vol. I (1978); *Notable American Women*, Vol. IV, *The Modern Period* (1980); *American Women Writers*, Vol. II (1980); *Dictionary of Literary Biography*, Vol. IX:

American Novelists, 1910–1945, Part 1 (1981); *The Oxford Companion to American Literature* (1983); and *The Oxford Companion to American Theatre* (1984). Ferber's date of birth is recorded in her mother's diary and confirmed by the Michigan Department of Health. She habitually cut two years from her age; therefore, her birth date is often given as 1887.

Morris U. Burns

FICHANDLER, Zelda Diamond (September 18, 1924–): producing director at Arena Stage in Washington, D.C., has been recognized, along with **Margo Jones** and **Nina Vance**, as a matriarch of the regional theatre movement in America. Her thirty-five-year career with Arena Stage chronicles her impact on American regional theatre. Fichandler's contribution to American theatre is inextricably bound to her role as producing director of Arena Stage, which she founded with Edward Mangum and others in 1950.

Fichandler was born in Boston, the first of two daughters of Harry and Ida (Epstein) Diamond. Her father, who had been brought to Boston as an infant by his Russian immigrant parents, became a scientist and inventor; the United States Army named its Harry Diamond Laboratories in his honor. Fichandler grew up in Washington, D.C., where she graduated from Woodrow Wilson High School in 1941. She received her Bachelor of Arts degree (Phi Beta Kappa) in 1945 from Cornell University in Russian language and literature. In 1950, the same year Arena Stage was founded, she received her Master of Arts degree in dramatic arts from George Washington University.

Zelda Diamond had married Thomas C. Fichandler on February 17, 1946. During their early married years, Tom Fichandler, an economist, was head of Twentieth Century Fund's Washington office, but he was involved with Arena at its inception, first in the role of business manager and then as executive director, the position from which he retired in 1986. When the idea to start a professional theatre in Washington was conceived in 1949, Zelda Fichandler was a graduate student of Edward Mangum's at George Washington University. The founding group consisted of Edward and Mary Mangum, Tom and Zelda Fichandler, Albert Berkowitz, and **Vera Mowry Roberts**. They pooled their resources, incorporated, and sold shares of stock in order to convert the old Hippodrome movie house at Ninth Street and New York Avenue into a 247-seat theatre-in-the-round. Fichandler says that she owes her early interest in arena staging to **Margo Jones**, "who took the time to talk to a frightened young girl to encourage her objectives and stiffen her right arm" (Diamonstein, p. 123).

Since 1952 Fichandler has held the position of producing director at Arena Stage. After producing fifty-five plays in five years, Arena Stage closed the Hippodrome theatre in July 1955. The 1955–1956 season was spent looking for a new theatre building. Arena Stage, needing more space, expanded to a 500-seat arena theatre by converting the ice storage room of an old brewery into a new home. Nicknamed the "Old Vat" (in imitation of the Old Vic), this theatre housed forty productions. It closed in 1961, when the company moved to a building designed by architect Harry Weese on the shores of the Potomac River, one of the earliest modern regional theatres built specifically as such and not converted from another type of building. The new theatre had 750 seats (later increased to 811) surrounding all four sides of the stage. This building, with the addition of the Kreeger Theatre in 1971, is still the home of Arena Stage.

By the late 1950s, Arena Stage had become a part of the American regional theatre movement. In 1957 W. McNeil Lowry of the Ford Foundation visited regional theatres around the United States, including Arena Stage, and set up a network of communication among them. Arena Stage transformed itself into a nonprofit institution, the original shareholders donating their holdings. Fichandler wrote her first grant proposal to the Ford Foundation in 1958. She was later to become known among her peers as a wizard at grant writing. In the meantime, the Arena, the Alley Theatre in Houston, and Actors Workshop in San Francisco were the first theatres awarded Ford Foundation grants enabling them to pay $200 a week to each actor in their companies. During the 1960s Fichandler expanded this idea, initiating many projects to further the growth of her company. With a 1965 grant from the Rockefeller Foundation, she started a three-year program for the training and development of the acting company, including courses in acting technique, movement, mime, dance, fencing, and makeup. For the 1967–1968 season, she attempted a rotating repertory system, which unfortunately proved too expensive and was jokingly dubbed ''Fichandler's Folly.'' She experimented with an interracial company for the 1968–1969 season with the aid of another Ford Foundation grant.

During the 1967–1968 season, Arena Stage presented the world première of Howard Sackler's *The Great White Hope* and gained national recognition when the production was moved to Broadway. This production did much to alter the course of professional theatre in America; since the commercial success of *The Great White Hope*, regional theatres have become recognized as a major spawning ground for new plays and new playwrights. In the ensuing years Arena Stage has premièred many plays that later went on to Broadway and national acclaim, including *Moonchildren* by Michael Weller, *Indians* by Arthur Kopit, *Raisin* (the musical version of **Lorraine Hansberry**'s *A Raisin in the Sun*), *The 1940s Radio Hour* by Walton Jones, and *K 2* by Patrick Meyers. As recently as the 1982–1983 season Fichandler directed the world première of *Screenplay* by Istvan Orkeny.

In September 1973, under the auspices of the United States Department of State, sixty-eight members of Arena's company, including Fichandler, traveled to the USSR, touring productions of *Our Town* and *Inherit the Wind* in Leningrad and Moscow. This venture made Arena Stage the first resident American company ever to appear in the Soviet Union. During this tour, Fichandler saw the Soviet play *The Ascent of Mount Fuji* by Aitmatov and Mukhamedzhanov in Moscow, and she later directed its American première at Arena Stage in 1975. Fichandler also served as a delegate to the 1974 International Theatre Institute Conference in Moscow. The company made its second international tour in 1980 to the Hong Kong Arts Festival, performing Arthur Miller's *After the Fall*, again directed by Fichandler.

In May of 1976 Fichandler and Arena Stage received the Antoinette Perry (Tony) Award, for the regional theatre's general stature and achievement. This Tony—the first one awarded to a theatre outside New York—recognized the importance of regional theatres in the United States and the contributions of Fichandler and others like her to the expansion and decentralization of American theatre.

Fichandler's activities in the theatre came to extend beyond her association with Arena Stage. In the 1970s she served as a visiting professor at the University of Texas in Austin and as professor of theatre arts at Boston University. In September 1984 she became chairperson of the acting and directing department of New York University's Tisch School of the Arts (simultaneously retaining her position as Arena's producing director). In addition to her role as teacher, Fichandler has lectured at colleges and universities all over the United States and delivered numerous speeches on the art of the theatre to various organizations. She has also helped shape the development of the American theatre through her work in professional associations. She has been actively involved with the Theatre Communications Group (TCG) since its inception in 1961. She is a past member of TCG's Executive Committee and a past member of the board of the American National Theatre and Academy (ANTA). Currently, she is a contributing editor to TCG's *American Theatre Magazine*.

During her career at Arena Stage, Fichandler has encouraged and inspired the work of thousands of theatre artists. Arena Stage has invited many guest directors over the years, including Alan Schneider, who first came to Arena to direct *The Glass Menagerie* in 1951 and returned often until his death in 1984. Numerous actors began their careers at Arena, such as George Grizzard, Pernell Roberts, Lester Rawlins, **Jane Alexander**, and James Earl Jones.

The range of awards Fichandler has received attests to her reputation as a matriarch of the regional theatre. She has received honorary doctorates from Hood College, Georgetown University, George Washington University, and Smith College. In 1971 she received the Margo Jones Award for significant contributions to the dramatic arts through her presentation of new plays. She has been awarded citations from the United States Institute of Theatre Technology, the Southeastern Theatre Conference, and the National Theatre Conference. She has been recognized as the Washingtonian of the Year and the Woman of the Year, and in 1985 she received the Commonwealth Award for Distinguished Service in Dramatic Arts. For her direction of Arthur Miller's *The Crucible* at Arena Stage in 1988, she received Washington's Helen Hayes Award as best director of that year.

Zelda Fichandler has guided Arena Stage to its status as one of America's foremost regional theatres. In the last thirty-five years, she has directed forty-five plays and produced over three hundred. All her work has centered on her belief in the theatre and its value for humankind. ''A theatre or a training institution," she says, "is, in fact, a laboratory and what we are studying is human life and especially the motions of the human heart. . . . Theatre, to me, is an aspect of the humanist tradition, is rooted in our capacity for empathy and identification, and takes its appeal from the universal desire of people to know their own essence" (*Performing Arts Journal*, pp. 93, 95).

The best history of Zelda Fichandler and the development of Arena Stage is Julius Novick's article "The Theatre" in *The Performing Arts and American Society* (1978). B. A. Coyne, "A History of Arena Stage, Washington, D.C." (Unpublished Ph.D. dissertation, Tulane University, 1965) traces the theatre from its beginnings to 1965. Two interviews provide enlightening details about Fichandler's values and ideas: Barbaralee Diamonstein, *Open Secrets: Ninety-four Women in Touch with our Time* (1972), and Shirlee Henningan, "The Woman Director in the Contemporary Professional Theatre" (Unpublished Ph.D. dissertation, Washington State University, 1983). Other articles of interest are Ben Cameron and James Lee, "Arena Stage: Interviews with Zelda Fichandler, David Chambers, and Thomas Fichandler, *Theater* (1979); Richard L. Coe, "Washington's First Lady of Theatre," *Theatre Arts* (1963); and Dorothy B. Magnus, "Matriarchs of the Regional Theatre," *Women in American Theatre* (1981). The majority of Zelda Fichandler's speeches are in the author's private collection, but a few have been published. These include "A Humanist View of Theatre," *Performing Arts Journal* (1983), "Theatres or Institutions?" *Theatre 3* (1970) and "Still No Roses" (July-August 1983) and "A Test of Resonance, a Test of Life" (January 1982) in *Theatre Communications*. See also "The Essential Actor," *American Theatre* (March 1986) and *Theatre Profiles 7* (Theatre Communications Group, 1986), and "Casting for a Different Truth," *American Theatre* (May 1988). Joseph W. Zeigler's *Regional Theatre: The Revolutionary Stage* (1973) includes a short history of Zelda Fichandler and Arena Stage and a description of *The Great White Hope* production. Fichandler is listed in *The Biographical Encyclopaedia and Who's Who of the American Theatre* (1966); *Plays, Players, and Playwrights: An Illustrated History of the Theatre* (1975); *Notable Names in the American Theatre* (1976); *Who's Who in the Theatre* (1981); and *The Oxford Companion to the Theatre* (1983).

N. J. Stanley

FIELDS, Dorothy (July 15, 1905–March 28, 1974): lyricist, librettist, and screenwriter noted for her skill in speech and characterization in musical form, was born in Allenhurst, New Jersey. She was the youngest child of Lewis Maurice Schoenfeld, better known as Lew Fields, a vaudeville comic and producer, and Rose (Harris) Fields. Her father was a second-generation Polish immigrant with little formal education.

Lew Fields was opposed to show business careers for his four children; however, only the elder daughter Frances shunned a theatrical career. In the early 1920s, encouraged by her playwright-brothers Joseph and Herbert, Dorothy Fields's ambition was to become an actress. Thwarted by her father's intervention, she turned her attention to writing poetry and was persuaded by composer J. Fred Coots to become a lyricist. In 1925 Fields married Dr. J. J. Wiener, a Manhattan surgeon. The marriage was dissolved in 1932. While on the staff at Mills Music Company, Fields began an eight-year collaboration with Jimmy McHugh. While their first effort, the 1927 song titled "Our American Girl," proved disastrous, the two achieved success in the same year with material they devised for black performers at Harlem's famous Cotton Club. The team's first Broadway score was for the revue *Blackbirds of 1928*. Among the popular songs to emerge from this venture were the humorously suggestive "Diga-Diga-Doo" and "I Can't Give You Anything But Love," both of which revealed Fields's ability to approximate common speech patterns in lyrics. In 1930 *The International Revue* included her songs "Exactly Like You" and "On the Sunny Side of the Street," sung by Gertrude Lawrence and Harry Richman.

Between 1932 and 1938 Fields worked primarily in Hollywood, writing memorable lyrics for largely forgettable screen musicals. During this period she and McHugh produced "Don't Blame Me," "I Feel a Song Comin' On," and "I'm in the Mood for Love." Other Hollywood collaborators included Nacio Herb Brown, Max Steiner, and, most notably, Jerome Kern. Fields devised songs with Kern for the films *Roberta* (1935), *Joy of Living* (1938), for which she co-authored the screenplay, and *Swing Time* (1936). "The Way You Look Tonight," from *Swing Time*, won for her the 1936 Oscar Award for best song from the Academy of Motion Picture Arts.

Returning to New York in the late 1930s, Fields began two partnerships. The first was her marriage to dress manufacturer Eli Lahm in 1938, which lasted until Lahm's death in 1958. The marriage produced a son, David, born in 1941, and a daughter, Eliza, born in 1944. The second partnership was a professional association with Arthur Schwartz to create the score for *Stars In Your Eyes* (1939). In 1941 Fields entered another career in the theatre by joining her brother Herbert as co-librettist for eight musicals. Their earliest collaborations were libretti devised around the songs of other composers. *Let's Face It!* (1941), *Something for the Boys* (1943), and *Mexican Hayride* (1944) featured songs by Cole Porter, while the landmark musical comedy *Annie Get your Gun* (1946) had a score by Irving Berlin. Concurrent with her assignments as a co-librettist, Fields discovered her true métier in developing the craft of the dramatic lyric for the book musical. Early examples of these efforts are apparent in the scores for *Up in Central Park* (1945), written with Sigmund Romberg, and *Arms and the Girl* (1950), a collaboration with Morton Gould.

Lyric characterization within the convention of popular song structures dominates the remainder of Fields's work for the Broadway stage. Teaming again with Arthur Schwartz in the 1950s, she wrote songs for *A Tree Grows in Brooklyn* (1951) and *By the Beautiful Sea* (1954), both tailored for the talents of **Shirley Booth**. The songs for *Redhead* (1959), with Albert Hague, and *Sweet Charity* (1966), with Cy Coleman, were designed expressly for **Gwen Verdon**. Although these four shows were largely star vehicles, Fields's lyrics emerged as on-target evocations of the interior thoughts and emotions of their respective heroines. Fields's last musical, *Seesaw* (1973), reunited her with Cy Coleman. The brashly contemporary score reveals her ear for colloquial speech as well as her dramatist's instinct for delineating characters in lyric form.

In early 1974 Dorothy Fields died of a heart attack in her Manhattan apartment. She left unfinished a number of projects, as well as a legacy that includes scores for thirteen Broadway shows, over five hundred songs written for films and television, and a number of libretti and screenplays. She was the first female lyricist to receive an Oscar (1936), an Antoinette Perry (Tony) Award (1959), and membership in the Songwriters' Hall of Fame (1971).

Fields's lyrics, a number of which remain in print, are the major source of information about her work. Recordings of her Broadway works currently available are *Blackbirds of 1928*, *Arms and the Girl!*, *A Tree Grows in Brooklyn*, *By the Beautiful Sea*, *Sweet Charity*, and *Seesaw*. Many of the libretti are available in manuscript in the Billy Rose Theatre Collection in the New York Public Library Performing Arts Research Center at Lincoln Center. Biographical material appears in Max Wilk, *They're Playing Our Song* (1973), and in Fields's obituary in the *New York Times* (March 29, 1974). Additional information for this essay was supplied by conversations with Raymond Marcus, Fields's nephew. Fields is included in *Current Biography, 1958* (1958); *The Biographical Encyclopaedia and Who's Who of the American Theatre* (1966); *Who's Who in the Theatre* (1972); *Notable American Women*, Vol. IV: *The Modern Period* (1980); and the *Oxford Companion to American Theatre* (1984).

Dwight B. Bowers

FISHER, Clara (July 14, 1811–November 12, 1889): child prodigy, then leading actress for a seventy-year career, was born in London, the sixth and youngest child of Frederick George Fisher, a librarian, auctioneer, amateur actor, and theatre enthusiast. At age five, Clara Fisher was allowed to join her two older sisters, Caroline and Amelia, in classes taught by the dancing master Dominic Corri. Corri adapted David Garrick's piece *Lilliput* so that all the roles with the exception of Gulliver could be played by his small female charges. Representatives of Drury Lane Theatre saw a rehearsal and added it to their repertory of afterpieces. On December 10, 1817, Clara Fisher made her professional debut in this burletta. A passage from the last act of *Richard III* (from the tent scene to the death) was interpolated for her to speak; she was the hit of the production, which ran on alternate nights for several weeks. She was next offered a similar role including the *Richard III* scene at Covent Garden in a pantomime called *Harlequin Gulliver*, in which she worked with the famous clown Joseph Grimaldi. Again Fisher made a great hit and was taken on tour to fulfill engagements offered by managements all over Britain. She added to her repertoire portions of Shylock and Young Norval (from John Home's *Douglas*) and other adult roles as well. Since the heyday of Master Betty ten years before, as she wrote in her *Autobiography* (1897), there had been no precocious children upon the stage, and she had the whole field to herself.

For the next several years Fisher continued learning and performing Shakespearean and other adult roles and the short afterpieces she described as her favorites in which she played several characters. Among her performances were the Four Mowbrays in *Old and Young*, seven parts in *The Invisible Girl*, and five parts in *Actresses of All Work*. In all of these she introduced popular songs and dances to display her developing talents. In 1823 Clara Fisher's father signed a three-year contract for her with Robert Elliston at Drury Lane for such suitable children's roles as Little Pickle in *The Spoiled Child*. In 1825 William Charles Macready cast her as Tell's son Albert in the first production of Sheridan Knowles's play *William Tell*. In 1827, perhaps considering her waning popularity as a child star, Fisher's father accepted an offer from Edmund Simpson of the Park Theatre, New York, for American appearances. Her last performance in England took place in Liverpool while the family was awaiting a ship to America. A local manager prevailed upon Fisher to play one performance opposite Junius Brutus Booth. She played Rosalie Summers, and he played Reuben Glenroy in *Town and Country*.

Clara Fisher's American debut took place at the Park Theatre on September 11, 1827, when she was sixteen years old. She played Albina Mandeville in *The Will*, a rather ponderous melodrama that was enlivened, however, by her interpolation of a song, "Hurrah for the Bonnets of Blue," over which the audience was wildly enthusiastic. The evening concluded with her Four Mowbrays. The enormous success of this and succeeding performances in a similar range of characters established her firmly in the favor of American audiences. During her first years in America, Clara Fisher toured, accompanied by her mother, to every theatre center in the United States. Her repertoire soon included Juliet, Ophelia, and other Shakespearean heroines, as well as modern parts such as Pauline in *The Lady of Lyons*. Particular favorites were Clara Douglas in *Money*, Letitia Hardy in *The Belle's Stratagem*, and the title role in *Clari, the Maid of Milan*. She had a quality of natural believability in all she did, and the innate poise of a veteran performer in this charming child endeared her to American audiences. Her popularity and fame increased with every performance. The actor-manager Joe Cowell wrote of her first appearance in Baltimore: "The captivating Clara Fisher . . . played with me for six weeks to a succession of overflowing houses. Nothing could exceed the enthusiasm with which this most amiable creature was received everywhere. 'Clara Fisher' was the name given to everything it could possibly be applied to: ships, steamboats, racehorses, mint juleps, and negro babies" (*Thirty Years Passed Among the Players*, p. 82).

On December 6, 1834, Clara Fisher married the composer and voice coach James Gaspard Maeder, and in their remarkably successful union her career continued to flourish. Her husband encouraged her musical talents and wrote for her an opera, *Peri, or the Enchanted Fountain*. She had already sung both Cherubino and Susanna in Mozart's *Marriage of Figaro*, and as Mrs. Maeder she added more operatic roles to her repertoire, including Agatha in *Der Freischutz*. Although her voice seems not to have been of true operatic caliber, she performed in operas with John and **Matilda Wood**, John Sinclair, John Braham, and other famous singers of the time. The historian Joseph Norton Ireland declared, "Clara Fisher appeared to every advantage that a thorough knowledge of music with a limited extent of voice permitted." He continued, "Her best vocal efforts were found in those ballads to which her inimitable expression gave a lasting popularity'' (*Records of the New York Stage*, Vol. I, p. 539).

Fisher was most effective in light and eccentric comedy; Ireland called her ''the most perfect and finished actress that has ever trod the American stage. Though not conventionally beautiful, her vivacity and femininity were captivating'' (Ireland, Vol. I, p. 538). She was admirable in breeches parts (men's roles), having ''rather a *penchant* for male attire,'' wrote a newspaper critic (*New York Mirror*, September 12, 1829). Viola was one of her greatest successes, and she was the Fool to William Charles Macready's King Lear in his American seasons. According to Laurence Hutton, she played Hamlet on at least one occasion. Since childhood she had also played modern male roles, such as Young Norval in *Douglas* and the masculine parts in the multicharacter farces like *Old and Young*. She did not often essay tragedy, but her Ophelia was considered one of her finest creations, and she played it to the Hamlets of Charles Kemble, Charles Kean, Edwin Forrest, James Murdoch, and James Caldwell. In other roles, classic and modern, she was at times the leading lady for Thomas Abthorpe Cooper, George Vandenhoff, James H. Hackett, and Frank Chanfrau (Liza to his famous Mose the Fireboy). She was one of the favorite visiting stars of the Ludlow-Smith Mississippi Valley theatre circuit. Noah Ludlow wrote of her, ''Then came the gem of the season, Miss Clara Fisher, at that time the finest comedy actress in the United States, and the most fascinating woman, on the stage or in private life, that I remember to have ever met in the profession'' (*Dramatic Life As I Found It*, p. 375).

During the depression years after the panic of 1837 (in which Fisher lost, through the collapse of the United States Bank, the fortune she had been accumulating since childhood), she suffered, like many other theatre people of the time, a lapse in her career. Her last performance at the Park Theatre was in a benefit for her oldest sister Mrs. Vernon (Jane Marchent Fisher) in 1844; soon thereafter she and her husband moved to Albany. She appeared only occasionally in New York; a notable date was May 10, 1849, when she played the First Singing Witch in the performance of Macready's *Macbeth*, which was halted by the Astor Place Riot. In 1851 Clara Fisher and her husband returned to live in New York. She played a season at Brougham's Lyceum Theatre and began an occasional association with the opera company of Madame Thillon at Niblo's Garden Theatre. When possible, Fisher continued playing with the best stock companies, such as the Globe Theatre in Boston and **Louisa Lane Drew**'s Arch Street Theatre in Philadelphia, and sometimes she toured. In periods when she was not performing, she offered lessons in elocution and acting to young ladies aspiring to theatrical careers.

By 1856, as Fisher was in her middle years, she began to assume the line of business called the ''old women.'' For the next thirty years she continued performing, finding a whole new range of roles she could present with extraordinary success. She became known for such characters as Mrs. Candour, Prudence to **Matilda Heron**'s *Camille*, and Juliet's Nurse. She played the Nurse to the Romeo and Juliet of Maurice Barrymore and **Helena Modjeska** in the final performance given at Booth's Theatre on May 10, 1883. She continued to act until the end of that decade, mostly in the touring companies of Augustin Daly. In her last performance, concluding a theatre career of more than seventy years, she played Mrs. Jeremiah Joblots in Daly's production of *The Lottery of Love* at Ford's Theatre, Baltimore, in 1889.

Clara and James Maeder had a happy marriage and were the parents of seven children. Two, Edward and Helen, died in infancy. The eldest daughter, Clara, married a British physician, and the other four were variously connected with the theatre: Frank, in his youth an actor, became a well-known theatrical agent; Mollie was a popular soubrette in theatres in the South and West; James was a talented artist; and Frederick was an actor and playwright. James died in his young manhood, but the others lived long and productive lives. Their father, James G. Maeder, died in 1876.

As a remarkable actress, Clara Fisher gave to the American theatre a standard of freshness and vivacity not easily matched. Her extraordinary gifts, her innate good taste, her naturalness and charm were a revelation to audiences when she first appeared in the United States, and her increasing versatility and thorough professionalism in everything she did kept them enchanted with the many roles she played throughout one of the longest careers on the nineteenth-century stage. Her hoyden romps as a girl delighted the theatregoers. Though, according to critics of the time, she never managed to perform the perfect lady, she captured throughout her career those rough-diamond qualities of many a role in a way that was totally believable. As a child, her Little Pickle and, as a mature woman, her Prudence and Juliet's Nurse were remembered vividly and with matching admiration. Her varied talents adapted well to the diverse circumstances and the evolving styles of theatre during her lengthy career on the stage.

The last few years of Clara Fisher's life were spent in quiet retirement at her home in Harlem, and she died at the home of her daughter Mollie (Mrs. Edward S. Post) in Metuchen, New Jersey. An Episcopal burial service was conducted for her there, and she was buried at Woodlawn Cemetery, New York City.

Clara Fisher's *Autobiography of Clara Fisher Maeder* (1897) is a charming, if somewhat loosely organized, reminiscence containing an excellent introduction by its editor, Douglas Taylor. There are clippings about her in the Harvard Theatre Collection. Many memoirs and other theatrical books of the period refer to her. These include Joe Cowell, *Thirty Years Passed Among the Players in England and America* (1844); Laurence Hutton, *Curiosities of the American Stage* (1891); Noah Ludlow, *Dramatic Life As I Found It* (1880); Walter M. Leman, *Memories of an Old Actor* (1886); Henry Phelps, *Players of a Century: A Record of the Albany Stage* (1880); and Joseph F. Daly, *The Life of Augustin Daly* (1917). Her New York performances are recorded in George C. D. Odell's *Annals of the New York Stage*, Vols. III-XIII (1928–1940), and with more extended commentary in Joseph Norton Ireland's *Record of the New York Stage From 1750 to 1860* (1866). See also Brander Matthews and Laurence Hutton, eds., *Actors and Actresses of Great Britain and the United States*, Vol. III (1886), and T. Allston Brown, *History of the American Stage* (1870). Fisher is included in *Notable American Women*, Vol. I (1971); *The Oxford Companion to the Theatre* (1983); William C. Young, *Famous Actors and Actresses on the American Stage* (1975); and *The Oxford Companion to American Theatre* (1984).

Eugene H. Jones

FISKE, Minnie Maddern (December 19, 1865–February 15, 1932): actress, playwright, director, producer, and champion of Henrik Ibsen in America, was born in New Orleans, the only child of Thomas W. and Elizabeth (Maddern) Davey. Thomas W. Davey was a self-educated Welsh immigrant who, beginning as a callboy in a theatre, became manager of a theatre touring company. In 1858 he married Elizabeth ("Lizzie") Maddern, an actress-musician and member of a strolling concert troupe composed of her parents and their seven children.

The Daveys christened their daughter Marie Augusta Davey, but she appeared on stage as Minnie Maddern. At the age of three, she was singing and dancing during act intervals for the touring company that her father managed and her mother performed in. While the company was appearing in Little Rock, Arkansas, the three-year-old Minnie made her formal acting debut when another visiting company used her as the Duke of York in Shakespeare's *Richard III*. Shortly after this appearance, she portrayed the Crown Child in Shakespeare's *Macbeth* in New Orleans for the Irish tragedian Barry Sullivan. Not long afterward, Tom Davey left the family, never to return. Mother and daughter went to New York, where on May 30, 1870, at the age of four, Minnie Maddern appeared at the French Theatre in *A Sheep in Wolf's Clothing*, which starred Carlotta LeClercq. She continued to work steadily as a child performer, appearing as Willie Leigh in Dion Boucicault's *Hunted Down* (with **Laura Keene**), Prince Arthur in *King John* (with John McCullough), Mary Morgan in *Ten Nights in a Barroom*, Hendrick and Meenie in *Rip Van Winkle* (with Joseph Jefferson), Eva in *Uncle Tom's Cabin*, and Ralph Rackstraw in *Pinafore*. When she was twelve she graduated to playing older women, including the Widow Melnotte in *The Lady of Lyons*. Between engagements her education took place in convents in Cincinnati and St. Louis. By 1879 Minnie Maddern's parents were dead, and she went to live with her mother's sister, Emma Stevens.

Her debut as an adult actress occurred on May 15, 1882, at Abbey's New Park Theatre, New York, where at age sixteen she appeared as Chip in *Fogg's Ferry*, a comedy-melodrama by Charles Collaban. The New York papers heralded her performance, the *Sun* making a prophecy that she would more than fulfill: "She has a native gift and disposition to her calling that will not be denied expression and which, if afforded any occasion of growth and development, cannot fail to make her a thoroughly popular artist in her line of small comedy. She made a better impression than has been made by any debutante in years" (*Mrs. Fiske, Her Views on the Stage*, pp. 210–211). After a successful New York run, the play embarked on a national tour through 1883. Touring her New York successes was a practice Fiske would follow throughout her career. Her purpose was twofold: to bring good theatre to people throughout the country and to earn a living.

During the run of *Fogg's Ferry*, she married Legrand White, an accomplished musician who had joined the play's orchestra in order to woo her. They commissioned Howard Taylor to write her next play, *Caprice*. It was the first of a number of plays to be written for her, and it gave early evidence of the support she would give new playwrights. Her performance as Mary Baxter in *Caprice* is most remembered for her singing of "In the Gloaming," a song that became a popular ballad for decades. The play, which toured throughout 1884, hardly outlasted the Whites's marriage. Their separation followed the production's close. They were divorced on June 25, 1888. Within two years, on March 18, 1890, she married Harrison Grey Fiske, editor of the New York *Dramatic Mirror*. He eventually became her manager, adapted two French one-act plays for her to appear in (*The White Pink* and *Marie Deloche*), and wrote an original script for her titled *Hester Crewe*. Immediately after the wedding, however, Mrs. Fiske left the stage for almost four years and began writing one-act plays, like *The Rose*, *The Eyes of the Heart*, and *A Light from St. Agnes* (eventually adapted into an opera by Frank Harling), and full-length plays like *Fontenelle* (in collaboration with Paul Kester). After her return to the stage, her playwriting skills proved useful in "doctoring" scripts written for her, such as *Leah Kleschna* by C. M. S. McLellan, *Erstwhile Susan* by Marian de Forest, *Mis' Nelly of N' Orleans* by Laurence Eyre, *Helena's Boys* by Ida Erlich, and *Against the Wind* by Carlos Drake.

On November 20, 1893, Mrs. Fiske (as she was always thereafter known) returned to the stage in the title role of her husband's play, *Hester Crewe*. The première at the Tremont Theatre in Boston was not a success, but her appearance as Nora Helmer in Henrik Ibsen's *A Doll's House* in a single benefit performance at the Empire Theatre in New York on February 15, 1894, began a long series of major successes. She proceeded to champion the Norwegian playwright's work in New York and on the road throughout the rest of her career, both by producing his plays with her husband and by appearing in them. Besides Nora in *A Doll's House*, she appeared as Hedda in *Hedda Gabler*, Rebecca West in *Rosmersholm*, Lona Hessel in *Pillars of Society*, and Mrs. Alving in *Ghosts*. Strongly attracted by Ibsen's realistic dramatizations of modern problems, she encouraged new American playwrights to write in the same manner. For her, Ibsen was an "inspiration": "And if now I speak much of Ibsen, it is because he has been my inspiration, because I have found in his plays that life-sized work that other players tell us they have found in Shakespeare" (*Mrs. Fiske, Her Views on the Stage*, p. 60).

After *A Doll's House*, Mrs. Fiske's next major triumph was as Tess in Lorimer Stoddard's adaptation of Thomas Hardy's novel *Tess of the D'Urbervilles*, which opened in New York on March 2, 1897. The production had a successful run and a national tour; it was both a critical and a popular success. The opposition of Fiske and her husband to the monopolistic Theatre Syndicate during a twelve-year period (1897–1909) meant that on her tours Mrs. Fiske played in many inferior theatres and on improvised stages. In New York, to combat the syndicate, the Fiskes leased the Manhattan Theatre in 1901, and they mounted productions there that were noted for their ensemble playing and their rejection of the star system. Their opening production was a new play by **Anne Crawford Flexner** called *Miranda on the Balcony*. Of the star system Mrs. Fiske once said, "The successful actress who seeks to have in her company any but the very best players to be had should be calmly and firmly wiped out" (*Mrs. Fiske, Her Views on the Stage*, p. 143). In 1904, three years after leasing the Manhattan Theatre, the Fiskes formed the Manhattan Theatre Company, whose goal was to bring together the best group of actors in America. The company continued into 1914. The opening vehicle of the company was a revival of Langdon Mitchell's *Becky Sharp*, which Mrs. Fiske had first introduced in 1899.

In addition to acting with the company, Mrs. Fiske frequently functioned as director, a task she had performed before the company's formation and after its demise. As director she strove for ensemble playing, noting that a production should possess a "perfect harmony, . . . one on a par with the performance of a well balanced orchestra" (*A History of American Acting*, p. 235). The fact that she was usually a featured performer in the plays she directed apparently had no effect on her ability to give focus to her supporting players. George Arliss, later to become a famous actor, noted an interesting problem after his first season with the company: "Our greatest difficulty at this time was to prevent her from effacing herself. She was so interested in getting the best out of everybody else that she always seemed to regard herself as a negligible quantity in the play" (*Up the Years from Bloomsbury*, p. 215). Mrs. Fiske prodded actors to search out honest projections of their emotions and cautioned them not to rush their execution. Her attention to detail in rehearsal impressed Beatrice Sturges, who, after watching her conducting a rehearsal, wrote, "Nothing is too small for the eye and attention of Mrs. Fiske—whether it be the gesture of an actor, a detail in the stage setting or lighting, a tone of voice, or a strain of music—and it is her watchful care and artistic sense that have made her company a model one to see" ("Mrs. Fiske: Actress Manager," *Public Opinion*, May 20, 1905, p. 778). Her attention extended to the house as well as to the stage; Archie Binns, one of her biographers, relates the story of her rehearsing the Shubert Theatre ushers in their jobs during an engagement in Kansas City.

By 1906 the Fiskes had given up their lease of the Manhattan Theatre, since David Belasco and the Shubert Brothers, both now in opposition to the syndicate, provided the Fiskes with good New York theatres for their company and their productions. On November 19, 1906, at the Lyric Theatre in New York, they presented Langdon Mitchell's new play, *The New York Idea*, written for and directed by Mrs. Fiske. It had been tried out in Chicago and St. Louis, and then it played in New York for sixty-six performances before it went on tour. The play is the best social comedy written in America up to that time and has since had several revivals. In 1909 the syndicate offered the Fiskes the use of any syndicate theatre on independent terms. At that time Mrs. Fiske was on tour in Edward Sheldon's *Salvation Nell*, which she had directed and in which she played the title role. This highly successful production, written by Sheldon while he was a member of George Pierce Baker's Workshop at Harvard, again illustrates Fiske's continuing support of new American playwrights. Mrs. Fiske made theatrical successes of three more original scripts: *Mrs. Bumpstead-Leigh* by Harry James Smith in 1911, *The High Road* by Edward Sheldon in 1912, and *Mis' Nelly of N'Orleans* by Laurence Eyre in 1919. She ventured briefly into films in 1913, recreating her role of Tess in *Tess of the D'Urbervilles* for Daniel Frohman, one of her old enemies from the syndicate days. In 1915 she created the role of Becky Sharp in a film of *Vanity Fair* for the Edison Company. The films were partially undertaken to bring financial solvency to the Fiskes, whose struggle with the syndicate had proven financially draining. In 1911 Harrison Fiske was forced to sell the *Dramatic Mirror*, and in 1914 he declared bankruptcy. By this time the Fiskes' marriage had "become a business partnership with mutual affection" (*Mrs. Fiske and the American Theatre*, p. 285).

Fiske's last years on the stage were spent touring revivals of her previous hits and playing in renowned classics—Richard Brinsley Sheridan's *The Rivals* in 1924 and 1930 and Shakespeare's *The Merry Wives of Windsor* and *Much Ado About Nothing* in 1927. She performed for the last time in Chicago in November of 1931 in *Against the Wind*, a play written for her by Carlos Drake. She was in ill health while the production was being rehearsed and had to leave the cast after sixteen performances. She returned to her home in Hollis, New York, where she died of chronic endocarditis on February 15, 1932. During her last decade, she had received several honors: the League of Women Voters 1923 Award as one of the twelve greatest living American women, an honorary degree from Smith College in 1926 for being "the foremost living actress," an honorary degree from the University of Wisconsin in 1927 for her services to the American stage, and the Good Housekeeping Award in 1931 as one of the twelve greatest living women.

Fiske's acting career encompassed more than six decades. During that time she was heralded by Alexander Woollcott as "the loftiest artist on the American stage" (*New York Times*, January 19, 1916, p. 12). The theatre historian Garff B. Wilson notes that "before the theories of the Moscow Art Theatre gained currency in America, Minnie Maddern Fiske was teaching similar principles and applying them in her productions" (*A History of American Acting*, p. 227). She advocated the honest projection of emotion,, but she was also insistent on being in absolute control on stage and having everything planned: "Anyone may achieve on some rare occasion an outburst of genuine feeling, a gesture of imperishable beauty, a ringing accent of truth, but your scientific actor knows how he did it. He can repeat it again and again and again. He can be depended on" (*Mrs. Fiske, Her Views on the Stage*, p. 79). Critics praised the naturalness and simplicity of Mrs. Fiske's acting and the intellectual understanding she brought to her characters. Her detractors noted a coldness and a repressed quality in her emotional projection and some lack of clarity in her vocal delivery. No one, however, could fault the range of roles she played in the course of her career. As Lewis C. Strang noted in *Famous Actresses of the Day in America*, she had appeared "in a range of impersonations far more comprehensive than any covered by any player of her age on the American stage'' (p. 121). She seemed equally at home in classical or modern plays, in comedy or tragedy.

Fiske's contributions to the American theatre went beyond creating a vast range of characters during a sixty-year career. She also vigorously fought against the Theatre Syndicate, gave encouragement to new playwrights, introduced Ibsen to America, developed audiences' taste for ensemble acting, aided in the development of young actors working in her company, and fostered a natural style of acting. In an editorial published shortly after her death, the *New York Times* aptly described what Fiske's passing meant to the American theatre: ''To lose Mrs. Fiske is to lose an actress who kept the theatre at its high estate'' (February 17, 1932, p. 24).

Books on Minnie Maddern Fiske's career include Archie Binns (in collabor‚ation with Olive Kooken), *Mrs. Fiske and the American Theatre* (1955), and Frank Carlos Griffith, *Mrs. Fiske* (1912). See also George Arliss, *Up the Years from Bloomsbury* (1927); Norman Hapgood, *The Stage in America, 1897–1900* (1901); Gustav Kobe, *Famous Actresses and their Homes* (1905); Lewis C. Strang, *Famous Actresses of the Day in America*, Second Series (1902); Frederic Edward McKay and Charles E. L. Wingate, eds., *Famous American Actors of Today*, Vol. II (1896); Garff B. Wilson, *A History of American Acting* (1966); Alexander Woollcott, *Mrs. Fiske, Her Views on the Stage* (1917); Beatrice Sturges, ''Mrs. Fiske: Actress Manager,'' in *Public Opinion* (May 20, 1905); and Alexander Woollcott, ''Second Thoughts on First Nights,'' *New York Times*, February 27, 1916. Mrs. Fiske's obituary appeared in the *New York Times* on February 17, 1932. There are clippings about her in the Harvard Theatre Collection. Many of her papers, correspondence, and prompt books were presented to the Library of Congress in 1962. She is included in *Notable American Women*, Vol. I (1971); William C. Young, *Famous Actors and Actresses on the American Stage* (1975); *Who Was Who in the Theatre: 1912–1976*, Vol. I (1978); *The Oxford Companion to the Theatre* (1983); and *The Oxford Companion to American Theatre* (1984).

Morris U. Burns

FITZGERALD, Geraldine (November 24, 1914–): outstanding actress and director, was born in Dublin, Ireland, to Edward and Edith Fitzgerald. Her father was a lawyer of some repute and his law firm, D. & T. Fitzgerald, has been immortalized by a reference in James Joyce's *Ulysses*. One of her brothers became a lawyer; another is a doctor. She had one sister who died in 1971. Fitzgerald attended a convent school in London, England, for her elementary education, and in 1928, after she had entered high school in Dublin, she began attending classes at the Dublin Art School. Even though she saw herself as a painter, her teachers evidently did not; she turned to acting almost by chance. Her aunt, Shelah Richard, was a well-known Irish actress of the Abbey Theatre and once took her niece to a rehearsal at Dublin's Gate Theatre where Richard was making a guest appearance. Shelah Richard's husband, the playwright Denis Johnston, was one of the directors of the Gate Theatre. By her own account (*New York Times*, June 13, 1971), Fitzgerald was mistaken by Hilton Edwards, the artistic director of the Gate, for an actress, was accused of being late, and was told to get on the stage and start reading. She did so and thus began her distinguished career.

Fitzgerald married her first husband, Edward Lindsay-Hogg, in November 1936. This marriage produced one son, Michael Lindsay-Hogg, who is currently a director of British stage, television, and film. In 1937, looking for an opportunity to advance her career, Fitzgerald and her husband came to America. She was first cast in New York in 1938 by Orson Welles as Ellie Dunn in George Bernard Shaw's *Heartbreak House*. The Mercury Theatre, where the play was being staged, had a financially poor season; consequently, *Heartbreak House* soon closed, and Fitzgerald and her husband went on to Hollywood.

In 1939 Fitzgerald played the role of Isabella Linton in Samuel Goldwyn's movie production of *Wuthering Heights*. Her performance won her an Academy Award (Oscar) nomination as best supporting actress. Her second movie role in Hollywood was that of the confidante of Bette Davis, the dying heroine, in *Dark Victory* (Warner Brothers, 1939). These two roles, according to most critics, remain her best performances in film. From 1939 to the mid–1940s, Fitzgerald played largely secondary roles in numerous films, mainly because of her insistence that she have six months off every year to work in the theatre. This practice hampered her film career, but it provided her with the professional refreshment and sense of integrity that she insisted she needed.

In 1943 Fitzgerald won critical acclaim for her role as Rebecca in Irwin Shaw's play *Sons and Soldiers* (1943), directed by Max Reinhart and introducing Gregory Peck. The story is about a young woman who, when told she should not have her baby for health reasons, lies down on the couch and dreams of the life of this baby. As Wilella Waldorf remarked in the *New York Post* (May 5, 1943), "In less talented hands, Rebecca might sometimes become a nauseating, embarrassing bore. But Miss Fitzgerald turns loose all of her Irish art, her Gaelic charm, her brilliant theatrical skill, on this difficult role, and proves genuinely enchanting in it." *Sons and Soldiers*, however, was not a financial success, and neither was her next play, *Portrait in Black*. The latter production closed during its pre-Broadway tryouts in the winter of 1945–1946.

At this time, the marriage of Geraldine Fitzgerald and Edward Lindsay-Hogg ended. Soon after, in September 1946, she married a business executive, Stuart Scheftel, the original creator of the Pan American building and chairman of the New York City Youth Board. Their daughter, Susan Scheftel, now works in New York City as a psychologist.

Abandoning Hollywood, Fitzgerald went into a period of retirement, from which she emerged in early 1955 in order to portray Jennifer Dubedat in a revival of George Bernard Shaw's *The Doctor's Dilemma* at the Phoenix Theatre, New York. Her performance was acclaimed by the critics. Brooks Atkinson commented that Geraldine Fitzgerald "is a beautiful and affecting wife" (*New York Times*, January 28, 1955), and John McClain praised her as "radiant and compelling" (*New York Journal American*, January 12, 1955).

From 1955 to 1969, Fitzgerald played a number of stage roles, including Goneril in Orson Welles's production of *King Lear* at New York City Center in January 1956; the distressed wife of a nuclear scientist in *Hide and Seek* at the

Ethel Barrymore Theatre in 1957; Gertrude in the American Shakespeare Festival's production of *Hamlet* at Stratford, Connecticut, in the summer of 1958; a faded ex-vaudeville entertainer in a revival of William Saroyan's *The Cave Dwellers* at the Greenwich Mews Theatre in October 1961; and the Third Woman in a one-act play called *Pigeons* at the Cherry Lane Theatre in March 1965. In none of these roles, however, did Fitzgerald attract widespread critical notice.

Not until the fall of 1969 when Fitzgerald agreed to play Essie Miller in a revival of Eugene O'Neill's *Ah, Wilderness!* at Ford's Theatre in Washington, D.C., were her true talents acknowledged again. Perhaps the most triumphant of her stage performances, however, was her portrayal of Mary Tyrone in Eugene O'Neill's *Long Day's Journey Into Night*, which opened at the Promenade Theatre in New York in April 1971. Typical of the critics' praise is that of Tom Burke in *The New York Times*; "Geraldine Fitzgerald in *Long Day's Journey Into Night* abruptly brought the critics to their knees and audiences to their feet cheering the artistry with which she expands the tiny stage of the Promenade Theatre in the revival of *Long Day's Journey Into Night*" (June 13, 1971). For her stunning performance, she won the New York Drama Critics' Poll Award for the 1970–1971 Off-Broadway season and also shared in the 1971 Vernon Rice Award.

Since 1971 Fitzgerald has distinguished herself as Juno Boyle in Sean O'Casey's *Juno and the Paycock* at Catholic University in Washington, D.C.; in Peter Nichols's *Forget-Me-Not* at the Long Wharf Theatre in New Haven, Connecticut; as Amanda Wingfield in Tennessee Williams' *The Glass Menagerie* at the Walnut Street Theatre in Philadelphia in 1975; and as the first woman to play the Stage Manager in Thornton Wilder's *Our Town* in the 1976 Williamstown Theatre Festival in Massachusetts. In February 1987 Fitzgerald opened at Lincoln Center in the play *I Can't Remember Anything*, presented along with *Danger: Memory*, two one-act plays by Arthur Miller. Between stage engagements Fitzgerald renewed her interest in Hollywood, acting in such movies as *Watch on the Rhine* (1943), *Ten North Frederick Street* (1958), *The Pawnbroker* (1965), *Rachel, Rachel* (1968), *The Last American Hero* (1973), *Harry and Tonto* (1974), and *The Pope of Greenwich Village* (1984). Beginning in 1951, Fitzgerald has also appeared in numerous television films and specials.

Fitzgerald's greatest successes on the stage have been her mother roles, to which she brings compassion, versatility, and a strength of character that never becomes sentimental. One of her finest assets as an actress is the lovely Irish lilt of her speaking voice, which she controls with a proper sense of stress and timing. Indeed, at the age of fifty-five she began taking singing lessons and at fifty-nine, she launched a nightclub act. As she admits in a *Newsweek* interview (November 22, 1976), she first considered singing "a sort of stepchild" but now gives it equal weight with her acting. Her most successful performances are "songs of the streets," as she calls them. Apart from her nightclub bookings, she has also sung her street songs at New York's Lincoln Center and at the Circle in the Square.

In recent years Fitzgerald has turned her many talents to writing, producing, and directing. In 1968, when the mayor of New York City asked the city's Arts Council, of which she was a member, to help the people in ghetto areas, she collaborated with a Franciscan monk, Brother Jonathan Ringkamp, on a modernized version of *Everyman* called *Everyman and Roach*. The production took place on a corner of Surf Avenue in Coney Island, and the turnout was so huge that the sidewalks could barely contain the audience. The response was so enthusiastic that she and Brother Jon formed the "Everyman Company" and wrote an updated satirical rock opera version of *Macbeth*. As she explained to Tom Burke in a *New York Times* interview (June 13, 1971), "I've always believed that theatre should belong to everyone, like water, air, fire; that it cannot be elitist, arcane, and that anyone who needs to share it must simply go and do so." For her work with New York City street theatre, Fitzgerald was given a Mayor John V. Lindsay Award in 1969, the Handel Medallion award (New York City's highest cultural recognition) in 1973, and an honorary Doctor of Fine Arts degree conferred by Adelphi University in 1973.

In 1980 Fitzgerald became a director and has since directed *Mass Appeal* by Bill C. Davis; *Long Day's Journey Into Night* with a black company (Earle Hyman, Gloria Foster, Al Freeman Jr., and Peter Faronic James); *The Threepenny Opera* with Elly Stone; *Take Me Along*, also with a black company; *The Return of Herbert Bracewell* with Milo O'Shea; and a new musical, *To Whom It May Concern* by Carol Hall (lyricist/composer of *Best Little Whorehouse in Texas*). In 1986 she was inducted into the Theatre Hall of Fame along with nine other notables, including Rosemary Harris, having served over twenty-five years on Broadway. Fitzgerald continues to contribute to American theatre her courage, energy, intelligence, and Irish charm.

The two longest articles on Geraldine Fitzgerald are contained in the *New York Times* (June 13, 1971) and *Newsweek* (November 22, 1976). A summary of reviews of her New York performances can be found in *New York Times Theatre Reviews*. A review of *I Can't Remember Anything* appeared in the *New York Times* (February 9, 1987). She is listed in *The Biographical Encyclopaedia and Who's Who of the American Theatre* (1966); *Current Biography, 1976* (1976); *Notable Names in the American Theatre* (1976); *Hollywood Players: The Forties* (1976); *Who's Who in Hollywood, 1900–1976* (1976); *The Film Encyclopedia* (1977); *Who's Who in the Theatre* (1981); and *Contemporary Theatre, Film, and Television* (1984).

Maureen A. Potts

FLANAGAN, Hallie (August 27, 1890–July 23, 1969): director, administrator, educator, playwright, theatre historian, and producing director of the Federal Theatre Project, was born in Redfield, South Dakota, the first of three children, to Frederic Miller and Louisa (Fisher) Ferguson. Her mother came from a large German family in Illinois and was a quiet, gentle woman who painted pastels and devoted herself to the family. Her father, of Scottish ancestry, worked at various business enterprises and moved the family several times before they settled in the college town of Grinnell, Iowa. According to Flanagan, the two most useful values given to her by her family were a belief in the equality of men and women and an ability to accept change.

Hallie Mae Ferguson received a public school education and graduated from Grinnell College in 1911. A fellow student was Harry Hopkins, who would later call upon her to direct the Federal Theatre Project. After Hallie Ferguson had taught for a year at Sigourney High School, she married John Murray Flanagan on December 25, 1912, and moved with him to St. Louis, where he worked for an insurance firm. She settled into a happy marriage and devoted her attention to her children: John, born in 1915, and Frederic, born in 1917. In 1918 her husband was admitted to a sanitarium in Colorado Springs for the treatment of tuberculosis; he died a year later. During his hospitalization, she and the children moved back to Iowa. Faced with the need to support her sons and aging parents (her father had suffered a severe financial loss in 1918), she returned to the high school classroom. Flanagan also assisted a professor at Grinnell College who gave lessons in voice, fencing, and dance. In 1919 she convinced the head of Grinnell's English Department that her experiences in college dramatics and her high school teaching experience qualified her to teach courses in drama. Little by little she built a theatre program at Grinnell. Although she was encouraged to seek an acting career, she felt writing and teaching would allow her more time with her children. In 1920 she published a play, *The Curtain*, that not only won a $100 prize in the Des Moines Little Theatre Contest but brought her an invitation to attend, as production assistant, George Pierce Baker's famous 47 Workshop for Playwrights at Harvard University. Her excitement over this honor was tempered by the tragic death in 1922 of her seven-year-old son from spinal meningitis. Gathering her courage and using the funds from her husband's insurance policy, Flanagan packed up her possessions and journeyed east to Cambridge along with five-year-old Frederic. Not only did she participate in the 47 Workshop, but she also earned a master's degree from Radcliffe College and in 1924 wrote a satirical comedy, *Incense*, with which Baker opened his first season at Yale University in 1925. Baker encouraged her to continue writing, but finances demanded that she return to teaching as an associate professor of drama at Grinnell (1924–1925). One of her courses, "Basic Communication," had evolved into the Grinnell Experimental Theatre, and she began a season of productions that would precipitate her return to the East as an associate professor at Vassar College to establish an experimental theatre there in the fall of 1925. Her work at Vassar was soon interrupted when in the spring of 1926 she undertook, with a Guggenheim Foundation grant, a comparative study of European theatre; she was the first woman to receive a Guggenheim grant.

As she investigated the relationships between theatre and European governments, she found that theatres in general had a paucity of ideas and seemed unwilling to interpret or even grapple with the issues confronting postwar Europe. Only in the Soviet Union was theatre attempting to become an instrument for social change. Flanagan was profoundly impressed by the workshops of Constantin

Stanislavsky's students, Vsevelod Meyerhold and Alexander Tairov, and their experiments with new artistic forms and innovative methods of acting. Later, Flanagan would deplore Communism, for it soon subverted theatre to the ends of indoctrination. But in the fall of 1926 she was challenged to return with renewed effort to the Vassar Experimental Theatre. Her book *Shifting Scenes of the Modern European Theatre* (1928) is a record of her Guggenheim investigation.

The Vassar theatre under Flanagan in the years 1925 to 1942 gained a reputation as one of America's leading experimental theatres. Broadway critics journeyed up from New York for major productions, theatre leaders abroad were impressed, and Vassar students devoted enthusiastic energy to their director. The theatre produced not only student plays but also the classics, new American plays, and experimental forms of theatre. Most innovative were the productions of Shakespeare's *Antony and Cleopatra* (1934), Chekhov's *The Marriage Proposal* (1933)—first seen as a realistic drama, then as an expressionistic and constructivist drama all in the same evening—and *Can You Hear Their Voices?* (1931). This play, written by Flanagan and a former student, Margaret Ellen Clifford, was experimental in both content and its use of the documentary form. Based on Whittaker Chambers's account of the Arkansas drought and the plight of dirt farmers there, *Voices* was a forerunner of the Federal Theatre's Living Newspaper, which created drama out of narratives, voice-overs, factual information, charts, and statistics. The play received notice outside Vassar and was presented across the country by various groups. *Theatre Guild Magazine*, which usually reviewed only professional theatre productions, found the Vassar production worthy of comment and noted how strongly the play had affected audiences. The play was unabashedly propagandistic and, as the *Times* critic observed, "a play in which propaganda did not defeat drama, as usually happened, because it was all propaganda—scaring, biting, smashing propaganda" (*New York Times*, May 10, 1931).

Flanagan's Vassar years are chronicled in her book *Dynamo: The Story of a College Theatre* (1943). In 1930 she returned briefly to the Soviet Union with a group of students to attend a theatre festival. In February 1934 Harry Hopkins asked her to come to New York to discuss the problem of unemployed actors. Flanagan was sailing the next week to England where she was to direct the theatre at Dartington Hall during a leave of absence from Vassar. She also planned to visit theatres in Italy, Sicily, Africa, and Greece and continue the examination of European theatre begun earlier. She had just married Vassar's Greek professor Philip H. Davis, a widower with three young children; consequently, the trip was also a honeymoon for her. Davis proved to be very supportive of Flanagan's work and vision.

After her European trip, Hallie Flanagan accepted Harry Hopkins's offer (in 1935) to come to Washington, D.C., to direct the Works Progress Administration (WPA) Federal Theatre Project; she was imbued with the idea that the project not only would supply financial relief to the unemployed but would create a viable theatre nourished by the soil of each region where it operated and would affect the artistic and social values held by the people of that region. The national theatre Flanagan proposed was based upon community theatres that would join together in a "federation of theatres" under the auspices of the federal government. She consulted with Elmer Rice, playwright and director of the Theatre Alliance, and with E. C. Mabie at the University of Iowa. Ideas were exchanged at the National Theatre Conference in Iowa in July 1935, where Hopkins promised a "free, adult, uncensored theatre." Flanagan wrote in *Arena: The History of the Federal Theatre* (1940), "I took this declaration seriously . . . and this is the kind of theatre we spent the next four years trying to build" (p. 29).

The task was not easy. Not only was theatre suffering from economic problems associated with the depression, but it was losing audiences to radio and film. Road companies and vaudeville had all but disappeared. Broadway, subservient to the box office, to its own star system, and to the demands of unions and producers, insinuated in its advertising that theatre outside New York was less than professional. President Franklin D. Roosevelt, aware of the situation in commercial theatre, wisely wanted the Federal Theatre Project headed by a non-Broadway person. Flanagan proved to be a good choice.

During the years 1935 to 1939, she emerged as a forceful yet gentle administrator who believed that the program should do more than supply work for actors or bring culture to the masses. She envisioned a theatre that would be experimental and that would foster regional and local sources of talent and plays. For her, this theatre would be uniquely American, reflecting the economic and social forces of modern life. Such a theatre, she hoped, would create new, loyal audiences who would continue to support theatre in their communities after federal funds ceased. By 1936 some 12,500 people were employed, presenting plays in six different languages to weekly audiences of 350,000 in nearly thirty states. Some 839 plays were produced, including musicals, Shakespeare, contemporary drama, ethnic plays, marionettes and puppets, vaudeville and circuses, children's theatre, and religious drama. The program promised no discrimination, and black theatre was promoted, much to the dismay of some southern senators. Those who contributed to or got their start with the Federal Theatre are among the list of theatre "greats." Playwrights include the established Elmer Rice and T. S. Eliot and newer writers such as Arthur Miller. Directors Orson Welles and Joseph Losey, designers Howard Bay and Ben Edwards, and innumerable actors got their start or continued to build their careers. A major negotiating coup by Flanagan was to persuade George Bernard Shaw and Eugene O'Neill to release their plays for reduced royalties.

Flanagan was convinced that the theatre must respond to the social and economic realities of the 1930s. Toward that end she encouraged socially relevant plays, but government officials wanted safe plays. Presentations that aroused the most controversy were productions of the "Living Newspaper," which documented such social issues as slum housing in *One-Third of a Nation* (1939), the farmer's plight in *Triple A-Plowed Under* (1936), and labor's efforts to organize in *Injunction Granted* (1936). A nationwide opening on October 27, 1936, in twenty-one theatres in seventeen states of *It Cannot Happen Here*, written by Sinclair Lewis and John C. Moffitt, seemed appropriate to Flanagan because it was "material of our own age and country and was a play by one of our most distinguished American writers, based on a burning belief in American democracy" (*Arena*, p. 120). The show, an indictment of fascism and communism, received warm reviews and played 260 weeks in various theatres in English, Spanish, and Yiddish. News stories and editorials, however, argued that the production proved the Federal Theatre Project was Communist, New Deal, subconsciously Fascist, or merely a tool to re-elect Franklin D. Roosevelt. To Flanagan, it proved that the Federal Theatre could take a show and open it simultaneously across the country and that the theatre could be one of the forces to keep democracy alive.

In 1937, after much criticism, the funds of the Works Progress Administration were cut. The impact upon the Federal Theatre Project was devastating: reorganizations occurred; censorship loomed over the future of the productions and the project's magazine, *Federal Theatre*; and some directors left the project. The bulk of Flanagan's time was now spent not in theatre work but in preventing people and forces outside the theatre from blocking the production of plays. As Walter Hart, director of the New York project, wrote to Flanagan in a letter of resignation, "Every time a play is produced by the Federal Theatre, a major miracle has passed" (*The Federal Theatre, 1935–1939*, p.130). He resigned from exhaustion after thirty-five miracles.

By the autumn of 1938, that major miracle to save the Federal Theatre Project from its critics in Congress was not forthcoming. Over the summer, the project had come under congressional attack, instigated by Martin Dies's House Committee to Investigate Un-American Activities. Dies's committee tried to show that Flanagan, because of her early interest in Russian theatre, was a Communist, and that some of those employed in the Federal Theatre Project were also Communists. Flanagan testified; others also defended the project. The tiny soft-spoken redhead from Vassar College persisted but was denied a final statement; her brief in defense of the project was not printed, as promised, in the published reports of the hearings. By the simple expedient of not renewing its appropriation, Congress shot down the Federal Theatre Project on June 30, 1939, giving its director only a month to wind up its vast affairs. Flanagan returned to Vassar still carrying the vision of a socially relevant yet entertaining national theatre. She secured funding from the Rockefeller Foundation to write *Arena* (1940), a history of the Federal Theatre. In that same year her husband died suddenly. Flanagan remained at Vassar until 1942, mounting in 1941 a widely acclaimed production of T. S. Eliot's *Murder in the Cathedral*. In her earlier visit to England in 1934, Eliot had promised her this play about Thomas à Becket, and it had also been one of the Federal Theatre's many successes. In 1942 Smith College offered her a position as an academic dean and professor in a new theatre department, a post that provided her with an opportunity to develop her ideas about general education. She served as dean from 1942 to 1946 and then continued in the theatre department until she was stricken by Parkinson's disease and forced to retire in 1955.

Flanagan continued to stress at Smith an interdisciplinary theatre. To that end she and her students wrote new plays, among them a documentary about nuclear power, $E = MC^2$. The play, a collaboration between science and art with science faculty helping to assemble materials, raised the question as to whether the atomic bomb would work for or against its masters. Harold Clurman, critic for the *New Republic*, saw the play as a double reminder that living newspaper could be exciting theatre and that university theatres were cradles of experimentation. He found the performance "altogether engaging as a show" and suggested that it was comparable to a medieval play that ought to be given in schools, union halls, factories, libraries, and other free public places across the United States even when critics were not lauding it to be art or "one of the season's ten best plays" (*New Republic*, July 5, 1948).

Brandeis University gave Flanagan a Creative Arts Award in 1957; Grinnell and Williams Colleges awarded her honorary degrees. In 1968 the National Theatre Conference, an organization of theatre leaders that she helped to found, gave her their first annual citation. She died in Old Tappan, New Jersey, on July 23, 1969.

Flanagan brought abundant energy and organizational skills to the Federal Theatre Project and a vision of theatre as a means of communicating ideas and fostering understanding and unity among people. To her, theatre was more than a repository, a museum to preserve plays, an art form, or a medium of entertainment and diversion. Flanagan wrote in *Arena* that by giving citizens a forum for free expression and offering access to the arts and tools of a civilization that they themselves are helping to make, a theatre is at once an illustration and a bulwark of the democratic form of government.

Many of Hallie Flanagan's ideas can be gleaned, along with autobiographical details, from her three books: *Shifting Scenes of the Modern European Theatre* (1928), *Arena* (1940), and *Dynamo: the Story of a College Theatre* (1943), and from various articles written by her, many of which appeared in *Theatre Arts Monthly*. The Billy Rose Theatre Collection in the New York Public Library Performing Arts Research Center at Lincoln Center houses Flanagan's personal papers, which include not only correspondence but photographs, scrapbooks, articles, and reviews. Additional materials can be found in the archives at Smith and Vassar colleges. Her stepdaughter, Joanne Davis Bentley, has Flanagan's autobiographical notes from 1948 and has recently published *Hallie Flanagan: A Life in the American Theatre* (1988). Excerpts from the book are printed in "Hallie's Project," *American Theatre* (June 1988). Of the books about the Federal Theatre Project, Jane DeHart Matthews, *The Federal Theatre, 1935–1939: Plays, Relief, and Politics* (1967), is the best source of biographical information. Other books, Willson Whitman, *Bread and Circuses* (1937), and John O'Conner and Lorraine Brown, *Free, Adult, Uncensored: The Living History of the Federal Theatre Project* (1978), are primarily histories of the Federal Theatre Project. Additional information is in the Federal Theatre Project's records in the Research Center at George Mason University, Fairfax, Virginia. One doctoral dissertation by Barbara Mendoza, "Hallie Flanagan: Her Role in American Theatre, 1924–1936" (Unpublished Ph.D. dissertation, New York University, 1976), covers her work as an educator. Flanagan's obituary appeared in the *New York Times*

(July 24, 1969). An entry on Flanagan by **Helen Krich Chinoy** appears in *Notable American Women*, Vol. IV: *The Modern Period* (1980). She is listed in *The Biographical Encyclopaedia and Who's Who of the American Theatre* (1966); *Plays, Players, and Playwrights: An Illustrated History of the Theatre* (1975); *Notable Names in the American Theatre* (1976); *Who's Who in the Theatre* (1977); *The Encyclopedia of World Theater* (1977); *The Entertainers* (1980); *The Oxford Companion to the Theatre* (1983); and *The Oxford Companion to American Theatre* (1984).

Fran Hassencahl

FLETCHER, Winona Lee (November 25, 1926–): leading theatre educator and author, was born to Henry Franklin and Sarah Belle (Lowdnes) Lee in Hamlet, North Carolina, the youngest in a clergyman's family of fourteen. Winona Lee's formal education began in the segregated public schools of Hamlet, where she walked five miles a day, past two white schools, to Capital Highway School for her first six years of education. In 1939 the family decided that its youngest member should get the best high school education possible and sent her to Greensboro, North Carolina, to live with her sister Lillian and attend Dudley High School there. The high school years at Dudley provided the groundwork for Winona Lee's later years of involvement in art, drama, student government, and newspaper activities. She was able to spend time also with her only living grandparent, Martha Lee, a former slave, who was nearly one hundred years old when her youngest granddaughter came to know her. Winona Lee's mother and grandmother both died in 1942.

Upon graduation from high school in 1943, and with several scholarships in hand, Winona Lee enrolled at Johnson C. Smith University in Charlotte, North Carolina, where she became a leader in student government, in the honor society, and in newspaper and drama activities. She majored in English, speech, and theatre, graduating *magna cum laude*. After graduation, she joined her brother, Kenneth, as teacher-secretary in his new Radio and Electronics School at Winston-Salem. After three years, however, she decided to go to graduate school to study theatre, choosing to attend the University of Iowa because of its outstanding theatre program and the presence there of E. C. Mabie, a distinguished theatre educator. She completed her work for the master's degree in August 1951 with a thesis consisting of the design for a production of **Anna Cora Mowatt's** *Fashion*. She accepted a teaching assignment at Kentucky State University in Frankfort, Kentucky. It was a position in the Department of English with an opportunity to develop a program in speech and theatre. In less than a year after her arrival in Frankfort, she married Joseph G. Fletcher, a professor of English there, and from their union was born one daughter, Betty.

For several years at Kentucky State University, Fletcher ran a one-woman drama program, developing and teaching speech and theatre courses and managing, directing, and producing plays. Between 1951 and 1978, she directed, costumed, designed, produced, and sometimes acted in well over fifty theatrical productions ranging from *Antigone* to *Hallelujah, Baby!* and from *Hamlet* to

Run, Little Chillun. She also planned the auditorium-theatre area of the new arts building and worked closely with the architects during the design and construction of the modern facility. Upon its completion in the mid–1960s, the building became a showplace for the community as well as the university. During the 1950s and 1960s, Fletcher spent her summers teaching, directing, and/or costuming in summer theatres in Missouri, Indiana, and Kentucky. She also became active in the National Association of Dramatic and Speech Arts, which sponsored talented black youths in summer theatre experiences and training under the auspices of Lincoln University. These summer activities encouraged talented theatre students from black colleges to pursue careers in the profession, and many of these former students are now successful educators, actors, directors, and designers.

In 1962 Fletcher interrupted her tenure at Kentucky State to pursue doctoral studies at Indiana University, Bloomington, with two more distinguished theatre educators, Hubert C. Heffner and Lee Norvelle. She completed the degree in 1968. While continuing her work at Kentucky State, she returned briefly to Indiana University in 1971 to design and teach courses in black drama for its pioneering Afro-American studies department. In 1978, when her husband retired, Fletcher moved permanently to Bloomington, where she is professor of theatre and Afro-American studies and associate dean of the College of Arts and Sciences at Indiana University.

Fletcher has pioneered in the research, design, and teaching of courses in black theatre and drama. Since receiving her doctoral degree she has advocated the recognition of the contribution of blacks to the theatre. Her own profound sense of ethnic pride has stimulated students, colleagues, and audiences in this and other countries to research, understand, and appreciate black theatre. The rediscovery of lost materials from the Federal Theatre Project of the 1930s has prompted Fletcher to take a special research interest in blacks and women in the project. She has shared her expertise as a visiting professor, lecturer, panelist, and writer with audiences at many colleges and universities at home and abroad and at national and regional conventions. In 1982 she participated as one of four United States delegates to the 5th World Congress on Drama in Education in Villach, Austria, sponsored by the International Association of Amateur Theatre.

In 1978 on a grant from the Kentucky Humanities Council, Fletcher conceived and implemented a pilot project with Frankfort senior citizens titled ''Making Theatre Work for Older Americans.'' In 1980 Fletcher was named coordinator of the American College Theatre Festival/Black College Technical Assistance Project, a special outreach effort of the John F. Kennedy Center's Cultural Diversity Committee designed to increase the number of blacks participating in national theatrical activities by strengthening theatre education and production in black colleges. Fletcher has served as executive secretary for the National Association of Dramatic and Speech Arts (1958–1962) and is a member of the editorial boards of *Encore* and *Players Magazine*. She chaired the screening committee for theatre of the Council for International Exchange of Scholars

(1975–1979) and was the first black appointed to the Kentucky Arts Commission (1976–1982). She has also served on the theatre advisory board of the Indiana Arts Commission (1971–1981), the task force of the Black Playwrights Project at the John F. Kennedy Center (1977–1981), and the American Theatre Association board of directors (1959–1960 and 1978–1981). From 1974 until 1977 she chaired the American Theatre Association's Black Theatre Program and from 1979 to 1980 was President of the University and College Theatre Association. In 1979 the American Theatre Association bestowed one of its highest honors on Fletcher by naming her to the College of Fellows "in recognition of continuous and outstanding meritorious service to the educational theatre of the nation."

With a broad interest in American theatre in general but with particular emphasis on a multiracial, multicultural approach to studying theatre, Fletcher has published articles in the *Quarterly Journal of Speech*, *Southern Speech Journal*, *Encore*, and *Players Magazine*. In 1974 she and Errol Hill of Dartmouth College co-edited a special curriculum issue of the American Theatre Association's Black Theatre *Bulletin*. Her article "Black Drama in Traditional Courses" strongly suggested that instructors of American modern and contemporary drama should "broaden and enrich" courses with discussions and analyses of black plays and their writers, performers, and producers. Fletcher's essay "Who put the 'Tragic' in the Tragic Mulatto?" in *Women in American Theatre* (1980) examined the dilemma of "racial admixture," candidly pointing out that the real tragedy of the half-white/half-black person is the difficulty, if not impossibility, of determining where black leaves off and white begins. Fletcher's "Consider the Possibilities: An Overview of Black Drama in the 1970s" appeared in *Essays on Contemporary American Drama* (1981).

Fletcher's determination to secure the rightful recognition and appreciation of blacks and women and their contribution to American theatre has had a great impact on American educational theatre. She is a woman who gets things done. The manner in which she goes about accomplishing her tasks may best be described by the following citation that was delivered at her induction into the American Theatre Association's College of Fellows: "She is a power for good in any endeavor. Always willing to serve wherever needed and under the most trying circumstances, she exerts a calming influence on the potentially volatile passions of theatre people, welding them together for the good of the whole."

Information on Winona Lee Fletcher's professional career was gathered from the files of the English Department of Kentucky State University, the files of the Afro-American Studies Department of Indiana University, and her personal files in Bloomington. She discusses her early life in "Offshoots," a history of her family, co-authored with her sister Lillian Lee Humphrey in 1971 (and as yet unpublished). In addition to the articles mentioned above, she has also written a biography of black playwright Ted Shine for the *Dictionary of Literary Biography* (1981). Selected articles appear in *Encore* (1960), *Players Magazine* (1960 and 1961), *Southern Speech Journal* (April 1968), *Educational Theatre Journal* (1976 and 1977), and *Theatre News* (April 1978). Fletcher is listed in *The Directory of American*

Scholars, Vol. II (1982); *The International Scholars Directory* (1972); *Who's Who of American Women, 1979–1980* (1979); and *World Who's Who of Women* (1982).

Olive Stroud Sheffey

FLEXNER, Anne Crawford (June 27, 1874–January 11, 1955): playwright best known for *Mrs. Wiggs of the Cabbage Patch*, was born in Georgetown, Kentucky, the daughter of Louis G. and Susan (Farnum) Crawford. She lived in Kentucky until she entered Vassar College, from which she graduated with a Bachelor of Arts degree in 1895. At Vassar, Flexner began to consider playwriting as a career, but she delayed going to New York to pursue a career for two years. During those two years she worked as a tutor in Louisville, Kentucky, where she met her future husband, the well-known educator Abraham Flexner, and married him in 1898. The couple had two daughters; the younger of them, Eleanor, is a respected writer, who has published books on drama and the women's suffrage movement.

In 1901 Flexner's first play, *Miranda on the Balcony*, was produced by **Minnie Maddern Fiske** as the first production in her Manhattan Theatre in New York. In 1903 Flexner adapted *Mrs. Wiggs of the Cabbage Patch* for the stage. This somewhat liberal dramatization of Alice Hegan Rice's novel soon became Flexner's most popular play. It was produced at the Savoy Theatre, New York, on September 3, 1904, and ran for 150 performances. Mrs. Wiggs, played by Madge Carr Cook, is that endearing, eternally optimistic country woman who loves nothing better than helping others to lead better lives. In succeeding years, several of Flexner's plays were produced in New York, generally to receptive audiences who found that her gifts for dialogue, sentiment, and comedy largely overcame the standardized plot situations of her plays. In one play of that period, *The Marriage Game* (1913), a single woman, mistakenly invited on a cruise with three couples, shares her insights on marriage.

Flexner's two most ambitious plays, *All Soul's Eve* (1920) and *Aged 26* (1936), reveal best her imagination and dramatic skills. In *All Soul's Eve*, produced at the Maxine Elliott Theatre in New York, Flexner's heroine is Alison Heath, the wife of an architect and the mother of a young son. Shortly before her death, Alison welcomes an Irish girl named Norah into her home; after Alison is killed in an automobile accident, her spirit transfers to Norah in order to save the life of the young boy, who has fallen desperately ill. (Both female roles were played by one actress, Lola Fisher.) Although the play is in some ways a hackneyed combination of sentimentality, spiritualism, and superstition, the undertaking nonetheless testifies to Flexner's ambitious attempt to present serious questions to her audience while maintaining the theatricality necessary for successful dramatic entertainment.

Her last play, *Aged 26*, was produced at the Lyceum Theatre in New York in 1936 and chronicles the last few months of John Keats's life. Again, the ambition of Flexner can be seen in her serious attempt to incorporate the language of Keats's poetry into the drama. The play seemed stilted in places and received a mixed review in the *New York Times*. The reviewer praised the motives of the author, the skill of the actors, the competence of the director, and the beauty of the sets, but he complained that "Mrs. Flexner has written the dialogue in a style of literary impressionism, quaint, a little pompous, always formal. Her characters are walking lexicons of literary style" (December 22, 1936).

Critics have noted Flexner's serious, ambitious approach to her theatrical work. Abraham Flexner's autobiography manifests his respect for his wife, and Eleanor Flexner's *Century of Struggle* (1959) recognizes her mother's dedication to her profession: "Her life was touched at many points by the [suffrage] movement whose history I have tried to record . . . . She marched in the New York suffrage parades. She made her mark as a playwright at a time when such an achievement was still unusual for a woman" (dedication).

Flexner's plays include *A Man's Woman* (1899), *Miranda on the Balcony* (1901), *Mrs. Wiggs of the Cabbage Patch* (1903), *A Lucky Star* (1909), *The Marriage Game* (1913), *Wanted—An Alibi* (1917), *The Blue Pearl* (1918), *All Soul's Eve* (1920), and *Aged 26* (1936). For biographical information about Anne Crawford Flexner, see Abraham Flexner's *I Remember: An Autobiography* (1940); *Reader's Encyclopedia of American Literature* (1962); W. J. Burke and Will D. Howe, *American Authors and Books*, Third Revised Edition (1972); *Who Was Who in the Theatre*, Vol. II (1978); and *The Oxford Companion to American Theatre* (1984).

Susan Krantz

FLORENCE, Malvina Theresa Pray (April 19, 1830–February 18, 1906): actress famous for her Yankee and Irish-American characterizations, was born Anna Theresa Pray in New York City and grew up in a theatrical family. Samuel Pray, her father, worked backstage at various New York playhouses; he was killed on April 22, 1848, when struck by a falling curtain drum during a fire at the Broadway Theatre. Of the four daughters raised by him and his wife Anna (Lewis) Pray, three danced on stage while in their teens. Maria, the eldest, began her career in 1842 and later became popular as Mrs. Barney Williams, a spirited comic actress. A younger daughter, Louisa, made her debut in 1849 and later married George Browne, an actor in Lester Wallack's company. The fourth daughter, Julia, never appeared on stage. The daughters Pray enjoyed remarkable longevity: her sisters all outlived Malvina Theresa, who died at age seventy-five.

Since the three dancers were all billed at approximately the same time as "Miss Pray," there is some confusion about the date of Malvina Pray's stage debut. George C. D. Odell (Volume V) lists her as one of the milliners in *The Milliner's Holiday* at the Olympic Theatre in New York on October 14, 1844; Mrs. Barney Williams, however, believed her sister first performed three years later. She is easier to trace after July 1847 when she adopted her professional name of Malvina Pray. At age sixteen she married actor Joseph Littell. A daughter, Josephine, was born about 1848, but the couple was divorced toward 1850. Meanwhile, Malvina Pray became a prominent entr'acte dancer at many New York theatres and was a featured dancer at the Lyceum Theatre under John

Brougham (1851) and James W. Wallack (1852–1853). During this engagement she met William J. ("Billy") Florence, a popular Irish comedian; they were married on January 1, 1853.

Basing their repertoire on the Irish boy and Yankee girl made popular by Mr. and Mrs. Barney Williams, with whom they had a sometimes hostile rivalry, the Florences undertook a new career as a starring team. They first appeared together in New York on June 13, 1853, at Purdy's National Theatre in *Ireland as It Is* and *The Yankee Gal*. Soon they embarked on a tour of American cities, filling two- or three-week engagements, as they would throughout most of their careers. Malvina Florence, acting primarily in Irish or Yankee farces and burlesques (many of them written by her husband), gained a reputation as an impersonator, sometimes representing as many as seven characters in one play. She also had a fine voice, and her song "Bobbing Around" from *The Yankee Housekeeper* sold over 100,000 copies.

A turning point in her career occurred on April 28, 1856, when she won instant acclaim at London's Drury Lane Theatre in *The Yankee Housekeeper* and *Mischievous Annie*. After an initial engagement of fifty nights, the Florences began a successful provincial tour that included the major cities of England, Scotland, and Ireland. Returning to America in August 1856, they drew on their overseas publicity and its financial profit to establish their reputation as leading representatives of Irish-American comedy. On July 5, 1858, they brought their extensive collection of farces and burlesques to Wallack's Theatre, New York, for the first of many summer seasons. Their one misfortune during these eventful years was the death of their only daughter in infancy.

In the early 1860s, when their preferred style of comedy began to decline in favor, the Florences expanded their range of characters. In July 1861 Mrs. Florence played Susan Nipper to her husband's Captain Cuttle in *Dombey and Son*. A more significant achievement took place on November 30, 1863, when they presented the American première of Tom Taylor's *The Ticket-of-Leave Man* at the Winter Garden Theatre with Malvina Florence appearing as Emily St. Evremond. These two plays long remained staples of their repertoire, as did T. W. Robertson's *Caste*, in which Malvina Florence first played Polly Eccles on August 5, 1867, at the Broadway Theatre. Continuing their practice of starring guest appearances, the Florences alternated these three pieces with their stock of Irish-American farces, adding in 1875 their most famous vehicle, *The Mighty Dollar*. Malvina Florence's portrayal of Mrs. General Gilflory was generally considered her finest performance; except for Matilda Starr in *Facts*, it also marked the last substantial addition to her repertoire. For the next thirteen years the Florences toured with their own supporting company through America and Europe, relying almost exclusively on their established favorites. Mrs. Florence retired temporarily in 1888, the year her husband began his renowned partnership with Joseph Jefferson. She had been living in London for some time when her husband died in Philadelphia on November 19, 1891.

Mrs. Florence returned to live in America, and in 1893 she conducted a farewell tour of principal American cities in *The Mighty Dollar*. On January 10 of that year she married George Howard Coveney, an English actor and playwright who had been a member of the Florences' company. The marriage ended in separation three years later, and Malvina Florence declared in her will that Coveney was to have no share in her estate of $100,000 since he had never contributed to her support. Coveney later contested the will. Her last years were spent living comfortably in a New York boardinghouse until 1905, when she lost her eyesight and was stricken with Bright's disease. She died two months later. She was buried beside William Florence in Greenwood Cemetery, Brooklyn.

Although her reputation has been overshadowed by that of her husband Billy Florence, she was clearly the major partner in their early years. When they first ventured to London in 1856, it was her performance that made them overnight celebrities. "She literally sparkles with vivacity," a reviewer exclaimed of her Yankee housekeeper portrayal (*The Times*, May 1, 1856). Unlike her predecessors who had acted abroad, Mrs. Florence did more than mimic the distinctive manners and language of her native country. Instead she presented original character types and invested them with a wild abandon that the English found charming and refreshing. Her ability to maintain these same high spirits through a rapid succession of characters was also the chief attraction of her demanding protean performances. When she moved to legitimate drama, she was most successful playing characters who with boisterous humor undercut snobbery or affectation. Although she created at least two major roles on the American stage (Polly Eccles and Emily St. Evremond), she was remembered more as a buoyant, energetic, irresistibly funny personality and as a pioneer in expanding the range of farcical and burlesque roles available to women.

Of the few published sources that discuss Malvina Florence's, as distinct from her husband's career, the most helpful are George C. D. Odell, *Annals of the New York Stage*, Vols. V-XIV (1931–1945) and William Winter, *The Wallet of Time*, Vol. I (1913). The obituaries in the *New York Times* (February 19, 1906) and *New York Clipper* (March 3, 1906) fill in the details of her private life. See also Brander Matthews and Laurence Hutton, *Actors and Actresses of Great Britain and the United States*, Vol. V (1886); Frederic E. McKay and Charles E. L. Wingate, eds., *Famous American Actors of Today* (1896); and Joseph N. Ireland, *Records of the New York Stage from 1750 to 1860*, 2 vols. (1866–1867). There are numerous clippings about the Florences in the Theatre Collection, Houghton Library, Harvard University. Malvina Florence is included in T. Allston Brown, *History of the American Stage* (1870); Robert L. Sherman, *Actors and Authors With Composers Who Helped Make Them Famous* (1951); *Who Was Who in America*, Historical Volume (1963); and *Notable American Women*, Vol. I, (1971).

Daniel Barrett

FONTANNE, Lynn (December 6, 1889?–July 30, 1983): actress, who, with her husband, Alfred Lunt, was long associated with the Theatre Guild, was born in Woodford, Essex, England. Throughout her life, she was notoriously coy about her exact birth date, but the consensus of her biographers seems to hover around 1889. She was the fifth daughter of Jules Pierre Antoine Fontanne and Ellen (Thornley) Fontanne. Her French father, a designer of printing type, was a poor businessman but was blessed with a placid temper; he most enjoyed tinkering with homemade inventions and reading aloud to his daughters from Charles Dickens and William Shakespeare. Her Irish mother was the complete opposite of Jules Pierre. She was gifted with a sharp tongue and a quick temper. Their daughters, Fontanne once recalled, left home as quickly as they could.

It was from her father that Lynn Fontanne acquired a taste for elegant clothes and fine literature. From him she learned to recite Shakespearean monologues and in his company received her formal introduction to the theatre: *The Merchant of Venice* at the Lyceum, starring Henry Irving and Ellen Terry, the most notable London theatre acting partnership of the nineteenth century. Then in her late fifties, Terry enjoyed being what she called an "encourager" to well-bred young ladies with an ambition in the theatre. In September 1905, a friend of Terry's arranged an audition for Lynn Fontanne. While a maid served the famous actress breakfast in bed, Terry bade the awkward, somewhat angular girl to "do something," and Lynn audaciously recited "The quality of mercy is not strained . . . " from *The Merchant of Venice*. Whether struck by the young girl's talent or by her conceit, Terry took her on as a student for approximately a year and arranged for her professional debut in the chorus of a Christmas pantomime of *Cinderella* (December 26, 1905).

Sometime in 1906, Terry dismissed Lynn Fontanne with two letters of introduction—one to Drury Lane Theatre and the other to the great actor-manager Sir Herbert Beerbohm-Tree. Fontanne went to work as a professional actress in London's West End and began establishing a reputation as a promising comedienne. In 1910, she made a brief and unsuccessful New York appearance in *Mr. Preedy and the Countess*. In the fall of 1914, she met **Laurette Taylor**, the most successful American actress of her day, who was then on tour in London with *Peg o' My Heart*. She took Fontanne under her wing and brought her to the United States as a member of her own company. Fontanne appeared in four productions with Taylor and profited by the experience and the exposure. Thanks to Laurette Taylor, Lynn Fontanne made her second, and this time successful, New York appearance on November 27, 1916, in *Harp of Life* at the Globe Theatre. Fontanne achieved genuine stardom in her own right in the comedy *Dulcy*, co-authored by George S. Kaufman and Marc Connelly (1921). The *New York Times* critic Alexander Woollcott wrote, prophetically, of her performance that "she can do great things and perhaps she will" (August 14, 1921). Two years before, in May 1919, Fontanne had met Alfred Lunt, who scored his first great success that year in Booth Tarkington's *Clarence*. They were married in May 1922 in a civil ceremony in New York, borrowing the two dollars necessary for the license from the witnesses. They appeared together for the first time in *Sweet Nell of Old Drury* in 1923, but it was not until *The Guardsman* (1924) that they became known as "the Lunts" and linked their fortunes with the rising star of the Theatre Guild.

The Guild, founded in 1919, was an outgrowth of the Washington Square Players in Greenwich Village and aspired to be New York's "art theatre." Though in the years before 1924 it had produced several artistic successes, primarily with British and European plays, it was not until Ferenc Molnar's comedy *The Guardsman*, starring the Lunts, that it had a financial as well as an artistic success. The production made money for the Guild. Between 1924 and 1949 the fortunes of Lynn Fontanne and Alfred Lunt were synonymous with that of the Theatre Guild. The Lunts appeared in twenty-three Guild productions during those years, many of them the Guild's most commercially successful productions. Among the playwrights whose works they presented were George Bernard Shaw, Eugene O'Neill, Maxwell Anderson, Robert Sherwood, and S. N. Behrman. In most, though not all, of these plays the Lunts appeared together.

Lynn Fontanne's most notable Theatre Guild performances include Eliza Doolittle in *Pygmalion* (1926), Jennifer Dubedat in *The Doctor's Dilemma* (1927), and Katherina in *The Taming of the Shrew* (1935). These were performances in revival productions. She also created a significant number of roles in new American plays, notably Elizabeth in Maxwell Anderson's *Elizabeth the Queen* (1930) and Nina Leeds in O'Neill's *Strange Interlude* (1928). Of her performance in Anderson's play the *New York Times* drama critic Brooks Atkinson wrote: "The word noble has few friends these days, but it is a word that likes her. It explains somewhat the aura that she casts about this tormented Queen. So noble it shall be for the transcendence of Miss Fontanne's acting" (November 2, 1930).

The Lunts also created the leading roles in three plays by Robert Sherwood. Fontanne appeared as Elena in *Reunion in Vienna* in 1931. It was a frothy romantic comedy set against an austere authoritarian regime. In 1936 she created the role of Irene in Sherwood's brittle anti-war comedy *Idiot's Delight*, for which Sherwood won the Pulitzer Prize. The playwright again won a Pulitzer for *There Shall Be No Night* (1940), his heroic drama of Finnish resistance in which Fontanne created the role of Miranda Valkonen (the play incidentally gave the young Montgomery Clift his first significant stage role).

Among Lynn Fontanne's other significant roles in the later 1930s were Madame Arkadina in Anton Chekhov's *The Sea Gull* and Alkmena in S. N. Behrman's adaptation of Jean Giraudoux's *Amphitryon 38*. In 1938–1939 the Lunts went on a nationwide tour with a repertory of *Amphitryon 38*, *The Sea Gull*, and *Idiot's Delight*. The next season they toured with *The Taming of the Shrew* and the following one with *There Shall Be No Night*. Fontanne's last appearance with the Theatre Guild was in S. N. Behrman's adaptation of *I Know My Love* in November 1949.

During their association with the Theatre Guild, Fontanne and Lunt occasionally left those auspices for independent productions. In 1933 they performed in Noel Coward's successful comedy *Design for Living* and in 1935 in his drama *Point Valaine*, which was not particularly well received. Coward and the Lunts were lifelong friends. Another excursion away from the Guild was for Terence Rattigan's *O! Mistress Mine* in 1946. Three years after leaving the Guild the Lunts again teamed with Noel Coward in his play *Quadrille*, which opened first in London and then in New York. This was followed in 1956 with *The Great Sebastians*, a play written for them by Howard Lindsay and Russel Crouse.

For nearly fifteen years the Lunts had appeared almost exclusively in comedies, some of minor literary distinction. These vehicles dismayed many of their admirers. Brooks Atkinson, in reviewing *The Great Sebastians*, wondered aloud what they could do if they selected a script as subtle and skillful as they were. Then in 1957 the British director Peter Brook offered them the principal roles in Friedrich Duerrenmatt's *The Visit*. Their first appearance in this dark, absurdist tragedy of revenge and corruption was grimly received when it opened in England on Christmas Eve, 1957. On its New York première, however, in the newly remodeled Globe Theatre, renamed the Lunt-Fontanne, *The Visit* was acclaimed as a fitting culmination of a great stage partnership. Walter Kerr, in the *New York Herald Tribune*, wrote of Fontanne's performance, "the malice is implacable, even when it is invisible, a source of enormous chillingly felt strength. This is as much mesmerism as acting" (May 6, 1958). *The Visit* marked the last stage appearance of the Lunts. Fontanne starred on television as the cockney charwoman in James M. Barrie's *The Old Lady Shows Her Medals*, which was presented in 1963 on the final installment of the *United States Steel Hour*. Then she and Lunt played together in Emmet Lavery's historical drama of Oliver Wendell Holmes, *The Magnificent Yankee*, on NBC's *Hallmark Hall of Fame* in 1965. Both won Emmy awards for their performances. Fontanne's last role was as the Dowager Empress on a television adaptation of *Anastasia* (*Hallmark Hall of Fame*, 1967). In February 1970 the Lunts and their old friend Noel Coward appeared on *The Dick Cavett Show* on ABC. They returned to their quiet retirement in the house they had occupied for nearly forty years, the farm called Ten Chimneys in Genesee Depot, Wisconsin. In 1980, three years after Alfred Lunt's death, Fontanne emerged briefly to receive the John F. Kennedy Center Lifetime Achievement Award. It was her last public appearance. On Saturday, July 30, 1983, Lynn Fontanne died.

Fontanne is remembered today as a gifted performer, particularly adept at a device called dovetailing, whereby she and Lunt could overlap their lines on stage and manage to make the words of both characters intelligible. Her acting technique had little to do with Stanislavsky's famous "Method." She delved into the psychology and motivation of the character only after she had learned the lines by rote, and she considered vocal expressiveness to be the foundation of her work as an actress. Yet she seemed to treasure the advice of her first acting teacher Ellen Terry: "Pay no attention to the diction or the reading, but fill your mind with the thoughts of the character and let the words come out of your mouth" (*Actors Talk About Acting*, p. 27). In her sixty-two-year career, Lynn Fontanne typified a style of acting—that of a sophisticated, highly skilled perfectionist—and enjoyed a period in the American theatre distinguished to a large extent by highly polished comedies of wit and grace. If she was criticized in her career, however, it was largely for appearing to waste her talents in trivial comedies. Yet, a certain legacy seemed to linger. When the Actors Studio played its first full season on Broadway in 1963, it opened with O'Neill's *Strange Interlude*, starring **Geraldine Page** in the role that Lynn Fontanne had created 34 years before.

In addition to the John F. Kennedy Center Award, Lynn Fontanne received the Presidential Medal of Freedom in 1964, a special Antoinette Perry (Tony) Award from the American Theatre Wing in 1970 (both shared with Lunt), and honorary Doctor of Letters degrees from Dartmouth College, Yale University, and New York University.

Although she belonged to an American theatre that valued magic and glamour more than it does today, she was a serious craftsman who kept her public and private lives very separate. Her remarks to the designer Cecil Beaton (who designed *Quadrille*) perhaps best embody her attitude towards her profession: "Why do we do this—all in the name of fun? It's never fun. It's damned hard work and we fight a lot, but it's interesting and exciting, and if we win through it will all have been worthwhile" (Obituary, *Washington Post*, July 31, 1983).

The principal biographical source for Lynn Fontanne (and Alfred Lunt as well) remains Maurice Zolotow's 1965 biography *Stagestruck*, though it is marred by the conspicuous absence of a bibliography. Of great value, however, is Philip M. Runkel's *A Bibliography of Alfred Lunt and Lynn Fontanne* (1978). A more recent biography is Jared Brown, *The Fabulous Lunts* (1986). Extensive interviews with the Lunts are included in *Actors on Acting*, edited by Toby Cole and Helen Krich Chinoy (1970) and *Actors Talk About Acting*, edited by Lewis Funke and John E. Booth (1961). For information on the Theatre Guild and the Lunts' contribution to its success, see Lawrence Langner's memoir, *The Magic Curtain* (1951). The Lunts' scrapbooks and production photos are in the New York Public Library Performing Arts Research Center at Lincoln Center. Letters, scripts, and papers are in the Library for Theatre and Film Research, State Historical Society at Madison, Wisconsin. Letters from the Lunts to Alexander Woollcott are in the Houghton Library at Harvard. Other papers are in the Theatre Guild Collection at Yale University and the Theater Arts Library at the University of Texas in Austin. There is a biographical account of Fontanne in *Current Biography, 1941* (1941). She is listed in *The Oxford Companion to American Literature* (1965), *The Biographical Encyclopaedia and Who's Who of the American Theatre* (1966), *Notable Names in the American Theatre* (1976), *Who's Who in the Theatre* (1977), *The Oxford Companion to the Theatre* (1983), and *The Oxford Companion to American Theatre* (1984).

Robin Holt

FORD, Harriet French (1863?–December 12, 1949): playwright most notable for her newspaper play *The Fourth Estate* was born in the village of Seymour, Connecticut, not far from New Haven, where she attended public schools. Several teachers and a minister regarded young Hattie as a gifted child and worked closely with her on elocution, drawing and painting, piano, and voice. Her parents, Samuel and Isabel (Stoddard) Ford—both New Englanders and strict Episcopalians—were not happy about their daughter's desire to become an actress, but they finally allowed her to enroll in the Boston School of Oratory. She quickly realized that "elocution" was not the same as acting and proved to her mother, by selling a poem to a magazine ("At Sunset," published in *Outing*, January 1885), that she was independent enough financially to go to New York.

In New York she studied at the American Academy of Dramatic Art and the Empire School of Acting. One of her teachers was David Belasco, who predicted stardom for her but failed to prepare his pupil for the realities of seeking work in the theatre. Nearly destitute, she persuaded William Gillette to assign her a chorus part in his 1887 dramatization of H. Rider Haggard's *She*. When Belasco discovered his protégée in the chorus, he recast her as the burned and shriveled "She," who emerges from the fire in the last few minutes of the play, her entire body frightfully made up, to writhe and die on stage. A speaking role followed, that of Hippolyta in a production of *A Midsummer Night's Dream* that opened in Chicago.

Struggling for ten years to win recognition as an actress, Harriet Ford gave readings and musical recitals, toured as assistant in **Loie Fuller**'s Humorous Ballad Concerts, performed three seasons as leading woman for Sol Smith Russell, and played one season with **Clara Morris**. A London acting engagement was not successful for her; but that year she wrote the prize-winning poem "Back from the Dead" in the *New York Herald*'s competition in England for the best poem celebrating the return of explorer Henry M. Stanley from Africa. Returning to New York she was now determined to become a writer and published a book of dramatic sketches, *Me an' Methusaler and Other Episodes* (1895). A verse monologue she wrote for Mrs. Sarah Cowell LeMoyne's drawing-room readings led to Harriet Ford's first produced play, *The Greatest Thing in the World* (1900, with Beatrice de Mille), in which Mrs. LeMoyne starred.

The box-office success of *A Gentleman of France* (1901) was assured by the popularity of its stars, Kyrle Bellew and Eleanor Robson, but Harriet Ford later ruefully described her play as "the last of the swashbucklers." Two decades later she and Eleanor Robson (now Mrs. August Belmont) would collaborate on a mystery play, *In the Next Room* (1923).

For several years Harriet Ford supported herself as a play reader for Liebler and Company, a New York producing firm. She was also a willing but self-effacing "mender" of other people's plays. In 1909 she collaborated with Joseph Medill Patterson, founder of the *New York Daily News*, on *The Fourth Estate*, which has been called "the first of the modern newspaper plays." Its fourth act, set in a composing room at press time, featured four typesetting machines in noisy operation on stage; it brought tumultuous applause and shouts of approval from its opening night audience. Patterson and Ford repeated their success with *A Little Brother of the Rich* (1909), a comedy based upon Peterson's more serious book about a money-mad society.

Harriet Ford's most effective collaborative work was with magazine storywriter Harvey O'Higgins. He had never written a play when she approached him with the idea of basing a murder mystery drama on a series of articles O'Higgins had written with the renowned detective William J. Burns. She also won Burns's cooperation, grilling him daily about his real-life adventures and studying his up-to-date techniques of crime detection, which provided authentic bits of stage business—like thumbprinting—to intrigue the audience of *The Argyle Case* (1912). *The Dummy* (1914), also written with O'Higgins, was based upon his

"Detective Barney" stories. *Polygamy* (1914) was a mildly controversial play that looked behind the scenes of Mormonism. Two months after its opening, the authors added a comic curtain raiser to that production: *The Dickey Bird*, about the downtrodden American husband, or "the sad story of a male Nora." Harriet Ford's other collaborations with O'Higgins included *Mr. Lazarus* (1916), in which **Eva Le Gallienne** played the ingénue; *On the Hiring Line* (1919), a comedy about "the servant problem," featuring **Laura Hope Crews**; and *Main Street* (1921), based on the Sinclair Lewis novel.

Another notable collaborator with Harriet Ford was Fannie Hurst. Their *Land of the Free* (1917), loosely based upon Mary Antin's *The Land of Promise*, is the story of a Russian-Jewish immigrant girl, from her breathless first impressions of America to disillusioning revelations about sweatshop conditions and contract-labor laws, to marriage and a home on Washington Square. Like many of Harriet Ford's plays, it flirts with social issues but does not directly confront them. Although 1924 was the year of her last professionally produced play, *Sweet Seventeen* (with Leonidas Westerveldt, John Clements, and Harvey O'Higgins), she continued to write plays, mostly innocuous one-act comedies, published by Samuel French. In 1930 she married Dr. Forde' Morgan (1865–1938), medical director of Sterling Products Company. She died in 1949 at 86, after a two-month illness.

Harriet Ford was highly regarded in the theatrical profession, especially during the 1910 to 1920 period. Soft-spoken, yet strong-willed and energetic, she brought out the best in all her collaborators. After she had become a successful playwright, she remembered her own early difficulties and made a point of helping young women who wanted to go on the stage by introducing them to her producers. Although her plays have not withstood the test of time, they are better than much of what filled the stage in her day and are distinguished by her painstaking background research and her ability to incorporate carefully observed human touches. She was a member of the Dramatists Guild and the Authors' League of America.

The New York Public Library Performing Arts Research Center at Lincoln Center has a clippings file on Harriet Ford that includes useful early profiles such as the one in *The Baltimore News Day* (February 22, 1900). Ford is featured in a number of magazine articles, most notably Lucy Pierce France, *Green Book Magazine* (May 1912); John Ten Eyck, *Green Book Magazine* (August 1913); Ada Patterson, *Theatre Magazine* (July 1914); and Wendell Phillips Dodge, *Strand Magazine* (May 1915). Ford's obituary appeared in the *New York Times* (December 14, 1949). A fairly complete list of her plays appears in the Felicia Hardison Londré entry on Ford in *American Women Writers*, Vol. 2 (1980). See also *The Oxford Companion to American Theatre* (1984).

Felicia Hardison Londré

FORD, Ruth Elizabeth (1912?–): actress and playwright, was born in Hazelhurst, Mississippi, the daughter of Charles Lloyd Ford and Gertrude (Cato) Ford. Her father was involved in the hotel business, and her mother was a painter. Her older brother is Charles Henri Ford, the poet and filmmaker. She received her high school education at Our Lady of the Lake High School in San Antonio, Texas, and then enrolled in All Saints Episcopal Junior College. After attending Mississippi State College for Women (Jackson) for a while, she transferred to the University of Mississippi (Oxford), where she earned the Bachelor of Arts and the Master of Arts degrees. It was during her days at the University of Mississippi that she made one of the most important contacts of her career as an actress and playwright. In 1933 she was dating Dean Faulkner, a young Oxford, Mississippi, resident, who introduced her to his brother, William Faulkner. Thus began a close friendship that was to endure until the famous novelist's death in 1962 and was to influence the creation of one of Faulkner's most innovative works and one of Ford's most important roles.

In 1937, her university education completed, Ford moved to New York and began a career in the theatre that has continued until recent years. Under the tutelage of her brother Charles Henri and the painter Pavel Tchelitchew, both of whom she has credited with having shaped her career in those early years, she made her first professional appearance. Her debut vehicle was *Ways and Means* (1937) at the Ivoryton Playhouse in Connecticut. Shortly thereafter she joined Orson Welles's Mercury Theatre and made her first New York appearance as Jane in *The Shoemaker's Holiday*. This was followed by performances in *Danton's Death* (1938), *Swingin' the Dream* (1939), *The Glass Slipper* (1940), *No Exit* (1946, 1950), and *This Time Tomorrow* (1947). In 1943 she starred in the première of *You Touched Me* by Tennessee Williams and Donald Windham at the Pasadena Playhouse in California, then in 1945 at the Booth Theatre in New York. She toured the United States in 1946 playing Roxanne in *Cyrano de Bergerac*, and in June 1949 she played Ophelia in *Hamlet* at Kronberg Castle in Denmark. Subsequent American stage performances included *Clutterbuck* (1949), *The House of Bernarda Alba* (1951), *Island of the Goats* (1955), and Sabina in *The Skin of Our Teeth* (1955).

It was in 1957 that her association with William Faulkner reached its fulfillment. For years she had been urging the novelist, whenever they met, in New York or in Hollywood, to produce a play suitable for her talents; and he, expressing his admiration for her determination to succeed as an actress, had promised all along that such a project would be forthcoming. In 1951 he had completed the manuscript of *Requiem for a Nun*, a sequel to his novel *Sanctuary*. An experimental novel in which the three acts of a play alternate with prose fiction chapters, *Requiem for a Nun* was not one of Faulkner's most successful achievements, but the execution was daring and innovative, and much of the work exhibits the distinctive elements of his genius. Almost immediately after he had completed the novel, Faulkner was in New York working with Ruth Ford on the stage adaptation. Not until six years later, however, did Ford star in the play she had inspired, after it had already been performed in France in an adaptation by Albert Camus. Ford's debut in *Requiem for a Nun* as Temple Drake occurred at the Royal Court Theatre in London on November 26, 1957. For that performance, she received a nomination for the London Drama Critics'

Award. A little over a year later, Faulkner's play opened in New York at the John Golden Theatre (January 20, 1959) with Ford again in the lead opposite her husband Zachary Scott as Gavin Stevens. The play was never critically acclaimed, but it represents an interesting collaboration between a major American writer and an actress friend, and Ford's performance was a powerful one.

After *Requiem for a Nun*, Ford's career was devoted mostly to playing character roles on stage and screen. Her movie career, which began in 1941, included performances in *Wilson, Dragonwyck, Keys of the Kingdom, Act One,* and *Play It As It Lays*. On stage, she performed as Mommie in Edward Albee's *The American Dream* at the Festival of Two Worlds in Spoleto, Italy, in 1962. Two years later she played the Witch of Capri in New York to Tallulah Bankhead's Flora Goforth in *The Milk Train Doesn't Stop Here Anymore*. She performed thereafter in *Any Wednesday* (1965), *Dinner at Eight* (1966), *The Grass Harp* (1971), *A Breeze from the Gulf* (1973), and *Poor Murderer* (1976). She was Madame Arkadina in *The Sea Gull* in Chicago (1977) and Juliana Bordereau in *The Aspern Papers* (1978).

Ford was first married to Peter Van Eyck, by whom she had a daughter, Shelley, her only child. That marriage ended in divorce, and on July 6, 1952, she was married to Zachary Scott, the screen star. Scott died in 1965, and Ford has not remarried. She has continued to reside in New York and has not made stage appearances in recent years.

Although Ford's career as an actress has not been that of a superstar, she has distinguished herself in portrayals that have consistently drawn praise from drama critics. Her rich southern voice and her commanding stage presence have combined to produce admirable portrayals of characters by three southern authors: William Faulkner, Tennessee Williams, and Truman Capote. Without her urging through a period of some fifteen years, it is doubtful that Faulkner would ever have written *Requiem for a Nun*, the play for which Ford is most likely to be remembered.

Requiem for a Nun: A Play from the Novel by William Faulkner, adapted for the stage by Ruth Ford, was published in 1959. Reviews of *Requiem for a Nun* appeared in the *New York Times* (January 31, 1959, and February 8, 1959). A review of *The Milk Train Doesn't Stop Here Anymore* appeared in the *New York Times* on January 2, 1964. Information about Ruth Ford may be found in *The Biographical Encyclopaedia and Who's Who of the American Theatre* (1966), *The Celebrity Register* (1973), *Notable Names in the American Theatre* (1976), and *Who's Who in the Theatre* (1977). *Who's Who in the Theatre* gives July 1920 as her birth date.

W. Kenneth Holditch

FORNÉS, Maria Irene (May 14, 1930–): playwright and director, was born in Havana, Cuba, the youngest of six children of Carlos Luis and Carmen Hismenia (Collado) Fornés. Her father, a government clerk, did not believe in formal education; instead he spent his afternoons educating his children and encouraging them in the arts. Maria Irene attended school from the third to the sixth grade only. After her father's death, Fornés, her mother, and a sister emigrated to the United States in 1945. In New York she eked out a living as a factory worker, waitress, translator, usher, export clerk, and office clerk. She also painted flowers on trays and designed textiles. Then, at a folk dance at the New School for Social Research, she met a man who introduced her to the Greenwich Village environment, and in 1949 she began studying painting at night classes. Scraping together funds, she studied at the Provincetown School with Hans Hoffman and then went to Europe for three years. She confessed in an interview that she never liked painting but made herself do it (*The Drama Review*, December 1977).

While in Paris, Fornés saw productions of Samuel Beckett's *Waiting for Godot* and *Endgame*, an experience that would later influence her career choice. Back in New York after her European stay, she shared an apartment with **Susan Sontag**. At that time neither wrote, but they often talked about writing and compulsively exchanged ideas. One day Fornés, remembering the plays she had seen in Paris, sat down to write her first play. It was called *Tango Palace*, and she finished it in nineteen days. Shortly after, she wrote *The Widow* (1960) in Spanish, based on letters of her great aunt. *The Widow* was produced by the New York Actors Studio in 1961. After a friend told Herbert Blau, the director of the San Francisco Actors Workshop, about the play, it was presented under its original title of *There! You Died* by his group on November 29, 1963. The Firehouse Theatre in Minneapolis produced a revised version (January 22, 1965) under the auspices of the Office of Advanced Drama Research of the University of Minnesota; its director, Arthur Ballet, was a leading sponsor of new theatre and new playwrights. On the same bill was a production of *The Successful Life of 3* designed and directed by Fornés. A series of performances presented by the Open Theatre followed at the Sheridan Square Playhouse in New York beginning on March 15, 1965. Fornés, who had no formal dramatic training nor had read any plays except Henrik Ibsen's *Hedda Gabler*, thus became a playwright and moved into the world of contemporary playwrights and Off-off-Broadway theatre. She became associated with the Open Theatre, with the Judson Poets' Theatre, and with La Mama Experimental Theatre Club.

Fornés had one early experience with Broadway theatre. After winning critical acclaim and a *Village Voice* Off-Broadway (Obie) Award for distinguished playwriting in 1965 for *The Successful Life of 3* and *Promenade*, both produced at the Judson Poets' Theatre on April 9, 1965, her play *The Office* (written in 1964) was selected for Broadway production under the direction of Jerome Robbins with **Elaine May** as star. The play previewed in April 1966 but never officially opened. Although Fornés did not make it on Broadway, her work and her playwriting have continued to earn recognition and critical support. Her work belongs to the world and style of Off-off-Broadway. She has won five Obies since 1965, more than any playwright except Sam Shepard and Samuel Beckett.

In the introduction to *The Winter Repertory 2: Maria Irene Fornés, Promenade and Other Plays* (1971), Richard Gilman stated, ''Miss Fornés is a dramatist of almost pure imagination whose interest in writing plays has little to do with making reports on what she's observed, in parodying society or behavior, or in dramatizing what already exists in the form of ordinary emotion or experience'' (pp. 1–2). To him, Fornés is neither interested in nor writes plays about communication problems; rather she writes plays about multiple possibilities of human relationships, not necessarily in real time or space, but in her own stage time and space. She wishes the audience to see and understand people and their relationships as she does. Using transformations, cinematic techniques, and a Marx Brothers comedy style, she writes plays that captivate audiences and make them feel, even if they do not understand.

Each play by Fornés is unique. Either the characters, situation, or the style differs markedly in each new production. *A Vietnamese Wedding* (1967) resembles ritual more than it does conventional drama. It is constructed as a re-enactment of a traditional Vietnamese betrothal and marriage ceremony but calls upon the audience to participate in the performance. *The Red Burning Light* (1968) reflects the style of a music hall or a circus entertainment. *The Successful Life of 3* (1963) is a vaudeville skit that uses film techniques, namely double takes, non sequiturs, freezes, and blackouts. *Tango Palace* seems to be a schizophrenic trip through the mind of a man who needs to make a decision. *Promenade* is a takeoff on old Shubert musicals and operettas. *Aurora* (1974) uses tricks with words and slapstick and characters from three centuries who die only to be revived again. *Féfu and Her Friends* (1976) uses an environmental approach to present a reunion of eight women who unveil their hopes, regrets, yearnings, and ideas about the world. *Eyes on the Harem*, which opened at INTAR (International Arts Relations) in New York on April 24, 1979, and won the *Village Voice* Off-Broadway (Obie) Award, tours the domestic history of the Ottoman Turks in a ''collage of music, movement, tableau'' (Edith Oliver, *The New Yorker*, May 7, 1979, p. 131) with a focus on the unspeakable cruelty of the Ottoman Empire, especially to women. In January 1982, the Theatre for the New City presented *A Visit*, a comedy based on Victorian erotic literature. *Newsweek* described the play, which used a ceramic phallus and bosom, as stylish, tasteful, and ''faithful to the paradox of Victorian pornography'' (January 25, 1982, p. 73). In *Mud*, presented at the Playwright's Conference at Padua Hills in July 1983, the wife of a poor, slowwitted, and ailing farmer tries to better herself with the aid of a neighbor, but she ends up burdened with the care of both her husband and the neighbor. *The Danube*, presented at the American Place Theatre in March 1984, uses Berlitz-style language and phrasing in short vignettes that ''deal with the decline and fall of Western civilization, the destruction of the environment, and the prospect of nuclear holocaust'' (Frank Rich, *New York Times*, March 13, 1984). *No Time*, a short location piece presented at the Padua Festival, July 1984, has an upper-class Latin American army family and the audience look down upon a scene in which a young girl is brutally beaten to death. *The Conduct of Life*, a one-act play written and directed by Fornés at the Theatre for the New City in March 1985, continues the Hispanic focus with a play about corruption in Latin America. Herbert Metgang considered the ''onstage proceedings numbing'' but applauded the ''cumulative power'' of the play ''as a feminist statement'' (*New York Times*, March 21, 1985). Fornés's multi-language plays include *Cap-a-Pie* (1975), based on the experiences, fantasies, and remembrances of the Hispanic actors who made up the cast in the production at INTAR in New York in May of 1975, and *Baboon* (with Word Baker and Dan Early of the Cincinnati Playhouse, October 6, 1972), which employs psychodrama techniques to present a theatrical piece formed from the dreams of actors. In 1985 Fornés adapted for the stage Anton Chekhov's short story ''Drowning,'' which was premièred by the Acting Company at the Krannert Center for the Performing Arts, Champaign-Urbana, Illinois (September 19, 1985). In March 1986 Fornés wrote and directed *Joan of Arc* for the Theatre for the New City. In May 1986 she wrote the book and lyrics for *Lovers and Keepers* and directed this musical for INTAR.

Fornés describes her approach to playwriting in the December 1977 issue of *The Drama Review*. Although she does not start writing with an idea or formulated thesis, plays may be generated from the file of scribbles and character phrases that she maintains. For her, the first draft of a play writes itself. At some point, ''the characters became crystallized. When that happens, I have an image in full color, technicolor. . . . When it finally happens, the play exists; it has taken its own life and then I just listen to it'' (*The Drama Review*, December 1977, pp. 27–28).

In addition to writing plays, Fornés has frequently directed her own plays, including *The Successful Life of 3* at the Firehouse Theatre, Minneapolis, in January 1965. In December 1968 she directed a revised version of *Molly's Dream* for the New Dramatist's Workshop. For *Féfu and Her Friends* the link between directing and playwriting was very close. Since Fornés selected the location of the New York Theatre Strategy production (May 5, 1977) before she had finished writing *Féfu*, the play's structure and development were influenced by her conception of the space to be used—the rooms of the Relativity Media Lab. This play represents a change in Fornés's cinematic style of writing and directing. During the second act of the three-part play, the audience is divided into four groups and led into rooms of Féfu's home to view ''close-up'' the characters and their environment. The play with its environmental approach was a critical success.

Besides playwriting and directing, Fornés has been instrumental in providing the means for other playwrights to arrange for productions of their works. She was part of the Women's Theatre Council, which began in 1972 and included **Megan Terry**, **Julie Bovasso**, **Rochelle Owens**, **Rosalyn Drexler**, and **Adrienne Kennedy**. This group was superseded by the New York Theatre Strategy (formed 1972–1973), for which Fornés served as president and provided a meeting place in her Greenwich Village apartment. This larger group included the six women playwrights plus Ed Bullins, Tom Eyen, Terrence McNally, Robert Patrick, Sam Shepard, Ronald Tavel, Jean-Claude Van Itallie, Lanford Wilson, and others. With this group Fornés produced and directed several plays, including her greatest critical success, *Féfu* (which was also produced by the American Place Theatre on January 8, 1978), for which she received Obies both as a playwright and as a director.

In addition to six Obies, Fornés has received grants from the Whitney Foundation (1961–1962), the Yale ABC Fellowship in Film Writing (1967–1968), the Rockefeller Foundation (1971), the Centro Mexicano de Escritores (1962), the Guggenheim Foundation (1972), the New York State Council on the Arts (1972 and 1976), the National Endowment for the Arts (1974), and the American Academy and Institute of Arts and Letters (1985). In addition, Fornés was one of five writers who won the Playwrights U.S.A. Award for outstanding work produced in a noncommercial theatre during the 1983–1984 and 1984–1985 seasons. She was given an award for her translation of *Cold Air* by the Cuban writer Virgilio Piñera. Fornés has had the satisfaction of having her plays presented in Amsterdam, London, Stockholm, and at the Festival of Two Worlds in Spoletto, Italy.

Maria Irene Fornés possesses an amazing versatility as a playwright and director. After almost three decades of writing for the theatre she has reached a time in her life ''when my work is following its most mysterious and personal course and it has become more political'' (*American Theatre*, September 1985, p. 15). This openness to ideas, change, and originality has earned Fornés an important place in the American contemporary theatre. Her newest play is *Abingdon Square*.

Fornés's plays have been collected in *The Winter Repertory 2: Maria Irene Fornés's Promenade and Other Plays* (1971) and in *Maria Irene Fornés's Plays* (1986), which has a preface by Susan Sontag and contains *Mud*, *The Danube*, *Sarita*, and *The Conduct of Life*. *The Off-off-Broadway Book* (1972), edited by Albert Poland and Bruce Mailman, contains *Molly's Dream* and a short biography. *The Performing Arts Journal* (Winter 1978) contains *Féfu and Her Friends* and an interview with Fornés by **Bonnie Marranca**. *A Century of Plays by American Women* (1979), edited by Rachel France, contains the script of *Dr. Kheal* and a brief biography; *The Best of Off-off-Broadway (1969)*, edited by Michael Smith, contains *Dr. Kheal*; *Playwrights for Tomorrow*, Vol. II (1967), contains *Tango Palace*; and *The New Underground Theatre Anthology* (1968), edited by Robert Schroeder, contains *Promenade*. Fornés's translation of *Cold Air* by Virgilio Piñera is in *New Plays U.S.A. 3*, edited by James Leverett and M. Elizabeth Osborn (1986). Fornés's dramatization of Anton Chekhov's short story ''Drowning'' has been published in *Orchards* (1986). *The Drama Review* (December 1977) contains an interview with Fornés about her playwriting methods. *Twentieth Century American Dramatists*, Part I (1981), edited by J. Mac Nicholas, contains an article on Fornés by Phyllis Mael. Also of interest are Robert Pasolli's *A Book on the Open Theatre* (1972) and reviews and articles, especially from the *New York Times* and the *Village Voice*. Fornés talks about writing in ''Five Important Playwrights Talk About Theatre Without Compromise and Sexism'' in *Mademoiselle* (August, 1972) and in ''Women's Work: **Tina Howe** and Maria Irene Fornés Explore the Woman's Voice in Drama'' in *American Theatre* (September 1985). A recent interview with Fornés is included in *Interviews with Contemporary Women Playwrights*, edited by Kathleen Betsko and Rachel Koenig (1987). There is a collection of Fornés's papers and reviews of productions of her works in the New York Public Library Performing Arts Research Center at Lincoln Center. Other material for this entry was obtained in an interview with Maria Irene Fornés in December 1976. Fornés is listed in *Notable Names in the American Theatre* (1976); the *National Playwrights Directory* (1977); *Contemporary Dramatists* (1973 and 1977); *The ASCAP Biographical Dictionary* (1980); *Dictionary of Literary Biography*, Vol. 7; *Twentieth Century American*

Dramatists (1981); *Who's Who in America, 1984–1985* (1984); and *Contemporary Theatre, Film, and Television* (1984).

Carolyn Karis

FRANKEN, Rose Dorothy Lewin (December 28, 1895–June 22, 1988): successful playwright and director of popular domestic dramas, was born in a small town near Fort Worth, Texas. She was the youngest of two girls and two boys born to Michael and Hannah (Younker) Lewin. Rose Lewin's parents separated when she was a small child, and her mother took the children to what was then her family home in New York City's Harlem. Grandparents, aunts, uncles, and cousins were ever present; but the youngest child felt particularly close to her mother and her sister Florence. Her father became a visiting stranger who occasionally arrived unannounced, leaving his youngest daughter in a state of shock and sadness. "A disrupted family is hard on children," she later wrote in her autobiography (*When All Is Said and Done*, p. 49).

She went to the School of Ethical Culture and was admitted to Barnard College. In 1914, shortly before she was to begin classes, however, Rose Lewin married Dr. Sigmund Franken, whom she had met at her sister's wedding the previous summer. He was an oral surgeon and seven years her senior. The first ten months of their married life were spent in a sanitarium on Lake Saranac, where he began his fight with tuberculosis, which plagued him for the rest of his life. There is no doubt that Dr. Franken was the single most important influence on Rose Franken's life and art. He fathered her three sons: Paul (b. 1920), John (b. 1925), and Peter (b. 1928). He also nurtured her early writing career. After the publication of her first novel, *Pattern* (1925), he urged her to try playwriting. The result was *Another Language*, which opened on Broadway in April 1932. It had previously been shown at a summer theatre in Greenwich, Connecticut, which also did her frequently optioned but never commercially produced play, *Fortnight*. In the autumn of 1932 *Another Language* opened in London with Edna Best and Herbert Marshall in the leading roles. It received an unusual amount of critical attention and praise. Shortly after the London opening, Sigmund Franken died (December 17, 1932).

Like several other novelists and playwrights of the period, Rose Franken went to Hollywood. There she polished her writing skills by turning other people's stories into movie scripts. She also learned how to deal with producers and how to protect her own interests while meeting their demands. In 1937 she married William Brown Meloney. Meloney, a lawyer as well as a writer, was an executive of the *New York Herald Tribune*'s *This Week Magazine*. Shortly after their marriage they returned to New York City. Franken and Meloney collaborated in writing magazine serials "under a flock of pseudonyms," one of them being "Franken Meloney" (*When All Is Said and Done*, p. 219). One of the stories she wrote on her own was "Claudia and David" (1939), the beginning of a popular *Redbook Magazine* serial. In 1941 she returned to Broadway as playwright and director of the play *Claudia*, which was destined to be a long-running hit, with 722 performances during its two Broadway runs and many more on the road here and abroad. An earlier radio series and two films were based on the Claudia stories. John Golden produced *Claudia*, and Rose Franken credits him with much of its success. William Meloney produced the four Broadway plays that followed.

Franken wrote nine plays. These included *Mr. Dooley, Jr.*, a collaborative one for children, written with her aunt Jane Lewin and published in 1932, and the still unproduced plays *Fortnight* and *The Wing*. Of the six that were on Broadway between 1932 and 1948, four were named by Burns Mantle among the ten best plays of their respective seasons. They were *Another Language* (1931–1932), *Claudia* (1940–1941), *Outrageous Fortune* (1943–1944), and *Soldier's Wife* (1944–1945). The two plays with shorter runs and less critical acclaim were *Doctors Disagree* (1943–1944) and *The Hallams* (1947–1948). In all her plays, Franken wrote about marriage, family relationships, the maturing of persons, and the clash of life styles. Though she is best known for *Claudia* and its naive heroine, it should be said that in all her plays there is a dark side that lends complexity to simple situations and sentimental characters. *Another Language* is a play about a stultifying middle-class family, the Hallams; *Claudia* is the story of a childlike wife's need to break from her attachment to her mother; *Outrageous Fortune* is a psychological drama about anti-Semitism and homosexuality; and *Soldier's Wife* is about personal and career adjustments after a husband's return home from war. *Doctors Disagree* is about a woman doctor scorned professionally because she is a woman and scorned as a woman because she is a doctor. *The Hallams* picks up the story of the family, first depicted in *Another Language*, at a later date in their history.

Some critics have dismissed Rose Franken as a writer of "matinee shows," a woman writing for an audience of women. Lewis Nichols of the *New York Times* was one of those critics, but he was forced to acknowledge that her matinee shows frequently did very well in the evening, too (October 15, 1944). Brooks Atkinson has referred to her "evocative writing" (*New York Times*, May 15, 1932), and George Jean Nathan wrote that she had "a gift for making the apparently casual internally dramatic" (*The Entertainment of a Nation*, p. 38).

Like **Rachel Crothers** before her, but without Crothers's formal training, Franken directed her own plays. She had a keen eye for casting and could get good performances from inexperienced as well as experienced players. Some of the actors who appeared in one or more of her plays were Margaret Hamilton, Dorothy Stickney, **Mildred Dunnock**, Dorothy McGuire, Phyllis Thaxter, Donald Cook, Maria Ouspenskaya, Glenn Anders, John Beal, Martha Scott, and Lili Darvas.

Rose Franken lived in retirement for about ten years, first in New York City and then in Tucson, Arizona, until her death in 1988. She went on writing, as she said, "to keep my mind alive." As recently as 1985, she spoke of a novel in the planning stages, and she even hoped to write the second installment of her autobiography. The first, *When All Is Said and Done*, was published in 1963. She never gave up the hope that a play she wrote in 1971, *The Wing*, would someday be produced.

The best source of information about Rose Franken is her autobiography, *When All Is Said and Done* (1963). The Rose Franken Papers, a gift of Franken in 1966, are catalogued and arranged in Collections of Correspondence and Manuscript Documents at Columbia University's Butler Library. Included are correspondence related to her plays, original typescripts, drafts of plays and novels, manuscripts and clippings. There are Franken clippings in the Billy Rose Theatre Collection, New York Public Library Performing Arts Research Center at Lincoln Center. The *New York Times* is the best source for pieces written by her about her plays (July 27, 1941, and November 21, 1943). Samuel French has published all of her plays with the exception of *Doctors Disagree*. Burns Mantle's *Best Play* volumes contain useful information and portions of the plays. Scattered references to Rose Franken are to be found in John Gassner, *The Theatre of Our Times* (1954); Lawrence Langner, *The Play's The Thing* (1960); George Jean Nathan, *Encyclopaedia of the Theatre* (1940) and *The Entertainment of a Nation* (1943); and Judith Olauson, *The American Woman Playwright: A View of Criticism and Characterization* (1981). A good bibliography of her works is provided in *Who's Who, 1985–1986* (1985). See also *The Oxford Companion to American Theatre* (1984).

Doris E. Abramson

FRINGS, Ketti (1915?–February 12, 1981): playwright, screenwriter, and novelist, was born in Columbus, Ohio, the daughter of Guy Herbert Hartley and Pauline (Sparks) Hartley. She was named Katherine. Her father, a paper box salesman, did a great deal of traveling and took his wife and two daughters with him. Thus, before she was in her teens, Katherine had lived in thirteen cities, from New York to Oregon. She attended Lake School for Girls in Milwaukee, Wisconsin, and later went one year to Principia College in St. Louis. She won a literary prize at the age of twelve and a silver medal at thirteen for recitation. Her love of acting set her on a playwriting career. She began her professional career as an advertising copywriter in a department store in Newark, New Jersey, and then went on to work as a publicist, a columnist, a radio scriptwriter, and a movie magazine ghostwriter under the name of Anita Kilgore. But it is as a playwright and a screenwriter that she is best known.

In the mid–1930s she went to the South of France to write a novel, and there she met Kurt Frings, a lightweight boxer who was working in France and Belgium. They were married March 18, 1938, but had to spend two years in Mexico before the German-born immigrant could migrate to the United States. He gave her the name of "Ketti." They settled in Hollywood where he became an agent. They had two children, Peter and Kathi (Mixon). They were later divorced.

Frings's first novel, *Hold Back the Dawn* (1942), was based on her experiences in Mexico. A year later it was adapted as a screenplay by Charles Brackett and Billy Wilder and was produced by Paramount, starring Charles Boyer, Olivia de Havilland, and Paulette Goddard. Her first critical and popular success as a screenwriter was her adaptation of William Inge's *Come Back, Little Sheba* in 1952; it earned an Oscar for **Shirley Booth**. In 1955 her screenplay for *The Shrike*, based on the play by Joseph Kramm and starring José Ferrer and June Allyson, was highly successful. Other screenplays include *Guest in the House* (1944), *The Ac-*

cused (1949), *File on Thelma Jordan* (1949), *Because of You* (1952), *About Mrs. Leslie* (1954), and *Foxfire* (1955). For several of these she served also as co-director. Her second novel, written in 1944, was *God's Front Porch*. Her other works include *Let the Devil Catch You* (1947) and short stories for *Good Housekeeping*, *Collier's*, *Woman's Home Companion*, and *The Saturday Evening Post*.

Her first Broadway play, *Mr. Sycamore*, based on a story by Robert Ayr and starring Lillian Gish, ran for only nineteen performances at the Theatre Guild (1942), a fact that did not worry her too much as she considered it a learning process. Brooks Atkinson liked this gentle fantasy and thought it quite original. In 1957 her adaptation of Thomas Wolfe's novel *Look Homeward, Angel* opened at the Ethel Barrymore Theatre with Anthony Perkins, Jo Van Fleet, and Hugh Griffith and ran for 564 performances. It won the Pulitzer Prize in 1958 as well as the New York Drama Critics Circle Award. Other plays of hers appearing on Broadway were *The Long Dream* (1960), adapted from a novel by Richard Wright and produced by **Cheryl Crawford**; *Walking Happy* (1966), a musical version of *Hobson's Choice* by Harold Brighouse; *Judgment At Nuremberg* (1970), based on the motion picture by Kramer and Mann; and in 1978 a musical version of *Look Homeward, Angel* in collaboration with Peter Udell. Frings's last work, a play titled *My Genius, My Child*, covering a period in the life of Eugene O'Neill, won the Harold C. Crain Award for Playwriting in 1981, given through the Drama Department at San José State University in California, where it was performed in October 1981, eight months after Frings's death.

Ketti Frings was named Woman of the Year in 1958 by the *Los Angeles Times* and in 1959 was given the distinguished achievement award of Theta Sigma Phi, an honorary journalism sorority. She also received the Martha Kinney Cooper Ohiana Award from the Library Association in 1958. As a professional writer she spent ten to twelve hours a day at the typewriter when she was at the height of her career. Critics described her writing as competent and workmanlike with a wide range of material: suspense, melodrama, fantasy, and romance. Her greatest accomplishment was the adaptation for the stage of Wolfe's voluminous novel. She took the 626 pages and compressed them into two hours of playing time, reduced the host of characters to nineteen, and cut the novel's time span to weeks. In the words of Richard Watts, Jr., in the *New York Post* (November 29, 1957), "She captured the letter and the spirit of the Wolfe novel in completely dramatic terms and has given it truth, richness, abounding vitality, laughter, and compassion, and enormous emotional impact." Brooks Atkinson wrote that she had "mined a solid drama out of the craggy abundance of *Look Homeward, Angel*. What Thomas Wolfe could never do, Ketti Frings has done admirably" (*New York Times*, November 29, 1957).

At the time of her death in Los Angeles on February 11, 1981, Ketti Frings was a member of the Screenwriter's Guild, the Dramatists Guild, and the League of New York Theatres.

For reviews of Frings's dramatization of *Look Homeward, Angel* see the *New York Times* (November 29, 1957) and the *New York Post* (November 29, 1957). Some biographical information about Ketti Frings is included in "First of the Month" in *The Saturday Review* (September 6, 1958). The sources disagree on the year of Frings's birth. *Current Biography, 1960* (1960–1961) tells of Ketti Frings's early years. See also *Ohio Authors and Their Books*, edited by W. Coyle (1962). Frings is listed in *The Biographical Encyclopaedia and Who's Who of the American Theatre* (1966); *Notable Names in the American Theatre* (1976); *Who's Who in America, 1978–1979* (1978); *American Women Writers*, Vol. II (1979); and *Contemporary Authors*, Vol. 101 (1981).

Nelda K. Balch

FULLER, Loie (January 15, 1862–January 1, 1928): designer, dancer, actress, producer, playwright, and inventor, was born Marie Louise Fuller in the bar of a relative's public-house in Fullersburg, Illinois, a township established by her grandfather, Jacob W. Fuller, some sixteen miles from Chicago. Her parents, Reuben and Delilah, both had theatrical associations, and as a baby, Loie would be taken to engagements where her father was in demand as a fiddler. In her autobiography, *Fifteen Years of a Dancer's Life* (pp. 20–24), she claims she made an unscheduled stage appearance at the age of two and a half, saying a prayer and reciting "Mary Had a Little Lamb" in the Chicago Progressive Lyceum, while at four she made her scheduled acting debut, as Little Reginald in a Chicago stock company production, *Was She Right?*

The family moved to Chicago early in her childhood and little is known of her education, but during the next twenty years she was a temperance lecturer, gave readings of Shakespeare, toured with Buffalo Bill (1883), produced her own play, *Larks*, appeared in Chicago in Gounod's *Faust*, sang at the Chicago Music Festival, and played parts in stock companies, alternating roles in *The Shaughraun* (1878), *Twenty Days* (1883), *Our Irish Visitors* (1886), and *Humbug* (1886) with appearances in vaudeville. She specialized in boy roles and in 1886 she had the title role in Nat Goodwin's *Little Jack Sheppard* at the Byron Theatre, New York, receiving a fair salary of $75 a week. In 1887 she also took the title role in *Aladdin*, at the Standard, a production which featured dances in which she wore a diaphanous garment similar to the one that she was to make famous a few years later.

Thus it was with considerable theatre experience that she embarked on a tour of the West Indies (1888), but the excursion was a financial disaster and she was only rescued from bankruptcy by the intervention of William Hays, a wealthy Colonel. In return for settling her debts of $9,200, he persuaded her to sign a marriage contract with him (1889). Soon after, she set off for London to appear in *Caprice*. The production was short-lived but she had the good fortune to replace Letty Lind in the successful *Carmen-up-to-Date*. The role featured a skirt dance, a specialty dance created by Kate Vaughan, and she made the most of the opportunity to study the dance in exact detail.

Her return to New York in 1891 heralded the "discovery" which was to alter her life. While preparing a scene in *Quack M.D.*, a scene in which she was to appear hypnotized, she wore a translucent Chinese silk skirt, given to her by an English army officer. As she twirled around the stage at an out-of-town performance she mesmerized the audience who responded, "It's a butterfly!" and then, "It's an orchid!" (Fuller, p. 31). In New York, the play was not successful but the skirt dance was, and soon she was invited to present the dance as a solo, accompanied by the popular song "Loin du Bal." She then performed in a silk dress with a pattern of snakes around the hem, and as she danced the snakes appeared to be alive. Thus the dance was christened the *Serpentine* by the director of the Casino Theatre.

She was then contracted to appear in the new musical extravaganza *Uncle Celestin* (1892), and so she set about developing the *Serpentine*, extending it with a series of movements and exploring the possibilities of different colored lights playing on the swirling folds, so that in performance only her spiralling, gossamer form was lit on the darkened stage. Her dance, in which the skirt appeared to take on a form all of its own, was the sensation of the opening performance, reviewers acknowledging the impact of her lighting and the diaphanous costuming. Imitators sprang up overnight, but though many danced well, no one had her success, because not only did they not have her lighting resources and expertise, but they could not infuse the dance with her quality of artistry.

In 1892, at the height of her success, she sued for divorce when she discovered her husband was already married. Her suit was successful but the publicity was hurtful, and as much to escape from that as to widen her artistic horizons, she sailed for Europe, performing first in Germany and then in Paris, at the Folies Bérgère.

No one could have predicted the impact of the *Serpentine* and her other dances on the Parisian social and art world. Her arrival coincided with the Art Nouveau movement and the emergence of the Symbolists, who were evolving new art theories based on image, color, and light. Instead of the traditional dance in tights and short muslin skirt, she captivated with her uncorseted body, her bare arms and legs, and the swirling mass of drapery, all combining to create an extraordinary illusion of perfection, where the dancer was inseparable from the dance and where the artist and the medium united to create an image of total art. The next few months, when she became "La Loie," the *doyenne* of Paris, were arguably the most important of her life. The Folies Bérgère became a mecca and her dancing inspired tributes from the most distinguished artists and writers of her day, among them Baudelaire, Mallarmé, Alexander Dumas *fils*, Anatole France, Rodin, Toulouse Lautrec, Arthur Symons and W. B. Yeats. Extra performances were given, and matinees were arranged for women and children so that they did not have to attend the infamous Folies Bérgère at night.

Despite the adulation (flowers were showered on the stage at most performances), she worked arduously and incessantly to devise new dances, many of them based on natural forms—*Butterfly* (1892), *Clouds* (1893), and *Flower Dance*—and to develop, with the assistance of her mother, who accompanied her everywhere, and her brother, Burt, who provided knowledge of stage lighting and technical expertise, her voluminous and ingenious costumes and lighting effects. By 1893 she had patented a device which allowed her to extend her dance movements through the insertion of aluminum or bamboo wands into the folds of the costumes, so that, by 1895, she was able to manipulate 500 yards of fine silk in *The Lily of the Nile*, the fabric appearing to cover the whole stage, radiating ten feet from her body in all directions and rising to 20 feet in the air.

She no longer danced to popular songs; now she used the music of the classical composers: Beethoven, Mozart, Gluck, Chopin, Schumann, Schubert and Liszt. Lighting became increasingly important; she employed an army of electricians, working to more and more complicated cues and instructions. She experimented not only with directional lighting but also with changing colors; she began to mix colors as in a prism, so that with the rhythm of the music the colors changed, and with each change the image altered, and what was a rainbow became a lily, which in turn became a rose. For these effects she rehearsed with scrupulous attention to detail, nothing being left to chance, and while she danced she cued her technicians with nods and toe taps and the most subtle body gestures and sounds. All her entourage were sworn to secrecy and, lest her designs be lost or stolen, her mother carried them to and from the theater in a handbag. Such was her popularity that the management of the Folies Bérgère effected costly alterations to the stage so that she might incorporate her most novel effect, illuminating herself from below with powerful lights shining up through a glass plate set into the floor.

Thus the *Fire Dance* (1894) became the sensation in an already impressive repertoire, directly inspiring Toulouse Lautrec's famous lithograph. And as Sally R. Sommer writes in her article "Loie Fuller," she "readily embraced both the critics' mystical esthetic and their praise. She absorbed their eloquent definitions and theories and applied them to her art" (*Drama Review*, p. 58). She returned frequently to the United States, where she became the highest paid performer in vaudeville when she appeared at Koster and Bial's Music Hall in New York in 1896. On later visits she no longer played in the vaudeville houses but in the more dignified atmosphere of the Opera Houses of Boston and New York (1909).

But is was in Paris that she continued to receive her greatest acclaim and that she made her permanent home. There she was accepted into the highest social group, the *haute monde*, being received by monarchs and nobility, and making guest appearances at important charity affairs and balls. She never remarried, but she devoted time to special friendships with other women, among them Gabrielle Bloch and, most notably, Queen Marie of Rumania, a friendship which generated much public comment. She remained faithfully devoted to her mother, even cancelling a tour of Russia at the last minute because of her mother's illness, a cancellation that took most of her considerable earnings, and left her extremely poor for the rest of her life.

She sought, too, the company of scientists to increase her technical knowledge of light and electricity, including Camille Flammarion, the noted astronomer who arranged for her to be admitted into the French Astronomical Society. Excited by the possibility of using radium as a light source she contacted Marie and Pierre Curie, offering them a tribute with her dance, *The Fairy of Light*. They advised her it was not possible to use, as she had hoped, radium to create the wings of a butterfly on stage, but they encouraged her experiments with phosphorescent salts as a source of natural light. Despite losing part of her hair in an explosion, she discovered that by painting fabric with the salts she could produce a rich glow of light on a dark stage hung with black velvet curtains. Thus emerged the *Radium Dance*, dedicated to the Curies, in which a disembodied image appeared to be floating in space.

She was always a woman of extraordinary generosity, launching the European careers of Isadora Duncan and Maud Allen, and she never lost her entrepreneurial and pioneering spirit: she realized the importance of the new composers, Debussy, Scriabin, Fauré, Wagner, Darious Milhaud and Stravinsky, introducing their work into her programs; she formed a company of young dancers to extend the range of her work; she explored the possibilities of creating dances in *found* spaces out-of-doors, where the effects were produced by the natural resources of wind, sunlight and shadow, moonlight, grasses, and trees; and she promoted two companies of Japanese actors and dancers, among them Sado Yacco, and made the first of her experimental films in 1904. And always she was aware that she had stumbled upon a new art form, not dance, not theatre, but a form in which the dancer was a living, moving artifact existing in space, color, and light.

With characteristic zeal she threw herself into the war effort in 1914, often performing at the front line, but when the war was over in 1918 her professional appearances became more and more infrequent. She devoted her time to her friends, her troupe of dancers, and to her experiments, so that with her last stage appearance in the London premiere of her *Shadow Ballet*, in 1927, she could still excite the audience with her daring innovations. She died of pneumonia in 1928 and was buried in Père Lachaise Cemetery in Paris.

Her dance company continued to tour for ten more years but gradually as her reputation declined the company found they were unable to continue. Since then her work has been given scant attention and her contribution to the development of the theatre arts inadequately acknowledged. Her experiments in stage lighting are sufficient to place her among the great innovators, Gordon Craig and Adolphe Appia, while her influence on less conventional forms of twentieth century theatre has yet to be fully documented.

To my knowledge there is no major biography of Loie Fuller in English. The best sources of information are her autobiographical essays, *Fifteen Years of a Dancer's Life* (1913, 1977) and "Eighteen Years of Dancing," *Green Book Album* (March 1910), and the excellent biographical essay by Claire de Morinni, "Loie Fuller—the Fairy of Light," *Chronicles of the American Dance*, ed. Paul Magriel. Fascinating technical information may be obtained in Sally R. Sommer, "Loie Fuller," *The Drama Review* (March 1975), while other biographical essays include: Lillian Moore, "Loie Fuller," *Notable American Women* (1971); Jennifer S. Uglow, ed., *Dictionary of Women's Biography* (1989); and Elizabeth Kendall, *Where She Danced* (1979). Frank Kermode writes authoritatively about the significance of the dance to the Symbolists in "The Dancer," *Romantic Image* (1957), while pictures and drawings of Loie Fuller are featured in Margot Fonteyn, *The Magic of Dance* (1979).

Sam McCready

— G —

GALE, Zona (August 26, 1874-December 27, 1938): playwright, novelist, short-story writer, and essayist, was born in Portage, Wisconsin, a small river town that remained her lifelong spiritual home and was, under various fictitious names, the setting of many of her novels and plays. The only child of Charles Franklin and Eliza (Beers) Gale, she was a ninth-generation American, descended from colonist Richard Gael, who had settled in Watertown, Massachusetts, in 1640. Her great-great-grandfather Henry Gale had fought in the Battle of Lexington in 1777 and participated in Shay's Rebellion in 1787. Her father, a locomotive engineer for the Chicago, Milwaukee and St. Paul Railroad, instilled in the sheltered, delicate child his homespun philosophy of human perfectibility. Her well-read and overprotective mother was, until her death in 1923 at the age of seventy-seven, the dominant influence in Zona Gale's life.

When she was eight, Zona Gale decided that she would be a writer, and at fourteen she told her friends that she would marry William Llywelyn Breese, a Portage youth ten years her senior. Both predictions came true, though her marriage to Breese did not take place until June 12, 1928, when she was fifty-three years old and he was a wealthy, widowed Portage manufacturer with a nineteen-year-old daughter. Her brief engagement to poet Ridgely Torrence in 1904 was broken off under pressure from her mother, but her loving regard for Torrence persisted until her death.

Zona Gale's early sentimental stories, written during her Portage public school years and during her four years (1891–1895) at the University of Wisconsin, Madison, have never been published. After graduation, she moved to Milwaukee and became a reporter for the *Evening Wisconsin* and later for the *Milwaukee Journal*. Although frail in appearance, she won her colleagues' respect by her persistence and energy and maintained a following among readers through the human warmth in her reporting. Among her more interesting assignments were her interviews of touring theatrical celebrities like Ellen Terry and Sir Henry Irving. She also worked toward her Master of Arts degree in literature, which she completed at the University of Wisconsin in 1899.

In 1901 Zona Gale was employed by the *New York Evening World*, which she left to become Edmund Clarence Stedman's secretary during the summer of 1902. This position gave her the opportunity to concentrate on free-lance and fiction writing and brought her several important literary friendships. Of her first attempt at playwriting only the title survives; *A Garret in Gotham* was accidentally destroyed by a chambermaid. In a departure from her early predilection for writing about beauty and romance, she experimented with a story based upon personal experience and written in a simpler manner. Its acceptance by *Success* in 1903 marked the beginning of her long, successful career as a writer of popular realistic fiction. In addition to hundreds of short stories and articles, she published twenty-two volumes of fiction, mostly characterized by local color and by wry observation of the trivial lives of small-town Wisconsin people. The popularity of *Friendship Village* (1908), her first collection of stories about an idealized town, resulted in four sequel volumes.

During her New York years Zona Gale sent two-thirds of her income to her parents, and she built them a large house on Edgewater Place overlooking the Wisconsin River. After winning the $2,000 first prize in *The Delineator*'s short fiction contest, Gale decided to go back to Portage to try to concentrate on her writing career. From 1911 on, she lived in Portage and visited New York for two months each winter. Her initial return to Wisconsin coincided with the beginning of her active interest in social issues; she lectured often on behalf of women's suffrage, pacifism, better labor conditions, and Senator Robert M. LaFollette's Progressive party movement. From 1923 to 1929 she served on the University of Wisconsin Board of Regents, and she offered scholarships in creative writing.

In 1910 University of Wisconsin professor Thomas Dickinson organized the Wisconsin Dramatic Society, which was in the vanguard of the little theatre movement in America. Gale encouraged that effort with a gift of $500 and with written contributions to the group's periodical, *The Play-Book*. At Dickinson's request for a one-act play "beating with one human emotion taken from the simple life of a village . . . with just a little tear and smile in it" (*Grassroots Theater*, p. 88), she wrote *The Neighbors* (1912), the play most frequently performed by the society (which later became the Wisconsin Players). In October 1917, the Wisconsin Players took their production to the Neighborhood Playhouse in New York, where it was well enough received to appear a few weeks later on a bill of one-act plays produced by Washington Square Players. Gale arranged for *The Neighbors* always to be available for royalty-free production by the Wisconsin Players and by any theatre group that would plant a tree for each performance in the community where the play was presented. She added in a letter to Professor A. M. Drummond concerning his New York State Fair theatre of 1919: "Furthermore, it is understood that the producers, the cast, and the audience at such a performance shall all be neighbors to everyone, as long as they live" (*Grassroots Theater*, p. 16).

When Zona Gale's 1919 novel *Miss Lulu Bett* (about a spinster trapped by her financial dependence on her sister's family, for whom she cooks and slaves) became a best seller, producer Brock Pemberton encouraged her to dramatize it, which she did in ten days. Pemberton's initial reaction to the script was to be echoed in critical responses to it: "The play has the same direct, incisive quality the book had; it cuts to the quick, and lays bare the lines of the character. In its simplicity, sincerity, and reality it strikes a new note in the theatre. I don't recall anything that approaches it" (*Still Small Voice*, pp. 143–144). The play-wright then begged one unusual concession from her producer: a Wisconsin Players production of *Miss Lulu Bett* was authorized in Milwaukee before the New York opening. The production that opened at the Belmont Theatre in New York on December 27, 1920, was warmly welcomed by critics and audiences; only Alexander Woollcott of the *New York Times* expressed reservations about the dramatization. Some controversy was generated by Gale's decision a few weeks later to alter the play's ending from the ambiguous tableau of a newly liberated woman facing an uncertain future to a more conventional "happy ending." Gale explained her revision in a statement to the *New York Tribune* (January 21, 1921), and the play went on to a 600-performance run and won the Pulitzer Prize.

In 1924 she dramatized her 1918 novel *Birth*, which is generally considered her best work. The play *Mr. Pitt*, produced by Brock Pemberton with Walter Huston in the title role, had a disappointing six-week run on Broadway. It is the story of a traveling pickle salesman who is truly goodhearted but socially hopeless even by the standards of the affection-starved spinsters of a small midwestern town. It succeeds, as do her earlier plays, in giving theatrical value to the commonplace language of ordinary people. She also published several plays that were not professionally produced: *Faint Perfume* (1934, a dramati-zation of her 1923 novel of the same title), *Uncle Jimmy* (1922), *Evening Clothes* (1932), and *The Clouds* (1932).

Zona Gale received honorary degrees from the University of Wisconsin in 1929, Rollins College in 1932, and Wooster College in 1935. She was a lifelong vegetarian, and she always had a strong mystical bent. Having studied Oriental religion and philosophy, she was delighted to accept in 1937 the Japanese gov-ernment's invitation to visit Japan with her husband; it was her only trip abroad. The following year she had begun writing her autobiography when she became ill and died of pneumonia in a Chicago hospital.

Gale's contribution to American drama is best expressed in terms of her regionalism. According to Robert Gard, "It is impossible to estimate the effect of Zona Gale's writings on the feeling of Wisconsin people for Wisconsin places." Her accomplishments, he continues, "threw playwriting and theatre in general into a very favorable light in the state" and "made subsequent drama development easier in Wisconsin'' (*Grassroots Theater*, pp. 16–17). In broader terms, Ludwig Lewisohn wrote, ''Now it is not too much to say that no other American dramatist has succeeded in so fully and richly transferring to the stage the exact moral atmosphere of a class, a section, and a period, as Miss Gale'' (*The Nation*, February 2, 1921).

Zona Gale's *Miss Lulu Bett* has been recently reprinted in *Plays by American Women 1900–1930* (1986), edited by Judith E. Barbour. August Derleth's *Still Small Voice* (1940) is a thorough and affectionate biography of Zona Gale. Another book-length study is Harold P. Simonson's *Zona Gale* in the Twayne series (1962). Anecdotal sketches of interest are Keene Sumner, *The American Magazine* (June 1921); *Bookman* (April 1923); and Henry James Forman, *Wisconsin Magazine of History* (Autumn 1962). Gale's obituary appeared in the *New York Times* (December 28, 1938). Her letters to Ridgely Torrence are located in the Princeton University Library. The Theatre Collection of the New York Public Library Performing Arts Research Center at Lincoln Center has a clippings file, but Gale's own papers are housed at the State Historical Society of Wisconsin. Biographical data is included in *The National Cyclopaedia of American Biography*, Vol. 8 (1927) and Vol. 30 (1943); *Notable American Women*, Vol. II (1971); Mary Bretisprecher, *American Women Writers*, Vol. 2 (1980); and *The Oxford Companion to American Theatre* (1984).

Felicia Hardison Londré

GERSTENBERG, Alice (August 2, 1885-July 28, 1972): playwright and novelist, was born in Chicago, Illinois. Her parents, Erich and Julia (Wieschendorff) Gerstenberg, were both native Chicagoans, and Alice spent her youth there, attending Kirkland School. Upon graduation, she attended Bryn Mawr College, where she developed an interest in writing fiction. Her early novels include *A Little World* (1908), *Unquenched Fire* (1912), and *The Conscience of Sarah Platt* (1915). In 1915 she also wrote her first full-length play, a dramatization of *Alice in Wonderland*, which played at the Booth Theatre and at the Fine Arts Theatre in New York. Her next play, *Overtones*, is also her most famous. Edward Goodman directed the 1915 New York performance by the Washington Square Players, and Lily Langtry starred in the subsequent London production. Gerstenberg expanded the play to three acts and directed the longer version at the Powers Theater in Chicago.

Overtones features the lives of two women, Harriet and Margaret. The action is conventional, representing the conflicts inherent in each woman's situation: Harriet marries for money and wants love; Margaret marries for love and wants money. By placing the two actions side by side, Gerstenberg created a compelling irony and revealed the subconscious selves of the two women.

Overtones was published in *Ten-One Act Plays* (1921), Gerstenberg's second collection, along with *Pot Boiler (The Dress Rehearsal)*, which she entered in the Little Theatre Tournament in New York in 1923. The *New York Times* reviewer stated merely that the production was interestingly staged and played and that it met with the approval of the audience. Mild praise though this was, the short mention was more positive than others she would receive. When her collaboration with Herma Clark titled *When Chicago was Young* premièred in her hometown, it was called a formless chronicle play. The première of *Victory Belles*, a play concerning the plight of women in wartime as they search for husbands, fared even worse; a reviewer recorded it as one of the most embarrassing evenings on Broadway.

Despite the bad reviews, Gerstenberg not only continued writing plays but became a notable name in dramatic circles. Eugene O'Neill claimed to be influenced by the psychological dimensions of her characterizations. She always seemed ready to try experimental techniques in writing and staging her plays. She was a charter member of the Chicago Little Theatre and used her pen and influence to promote the openings of other amateur theatres around the country. With Annette Washburne she established the Chicago Junior League Theatre for children and served for a while as its director. In her enduring efforts to make drama accessible to the public, to make theatres available to fledgling playwrights, and to write experimental plays, she was most notable in founding the Playwrights Theatre of Chicago (1922). Designed to give local playwrights a chance to produce their plays, the theatre remained in operation until 1945. Gerstenberg was recognized for her work in American drama in 1938 when she won the Chicago Foundation for Literature Award. She died in Chicago in 1972. Although her continuing literary reputation is based chiefly on *Overtones*, Gerstenberg's enthusiasm for the little theatre movement and for new playwrights was a significant influence on the developing American theatre.

Alice Gerstenberg's plays include the adaptation of *Alice in Wonderland* (1915), *Ten One-Act Plays* (1921), *Four Plays for Four Women* (1924), dramatization of Lillian Bell's story *The Land of Don't Want To* (1928), *Overtones* (1929), *Comedies All* (1930), a dramatization of Charles Kingsley's *Water Babies* (1930), *Star Dust* (1931), *When Chicago Was Young* (with Herma Clark, 1932), *Glee Plays the Game* (1934), *Within the Hour* (1934), *Find It* (1937), *The Queen's Christmas* (1939), *Time for Romance* (1942), *Victory Belles* (with H. Adrian, 1943), *The Hourglass* (1955), *Our Calla* (1956), *On the Beam* (1957), and *The Magic of Living* (1969). Gerstenberg is mentioned in Wieder David Sievers's *Freud on Broadway* (1955). She is included in *Who's Who of American Women, 1966–1967* (1965); *American Literary Yearbook* (1919, 1968); *American Authors and Books* (1972); *Women's Who's Who in America* (1914, 1976); *Who Was Who Among North American Authors* (1976); and *American Women Writers*, Vol. II (1980).

Debra Young

GILBERT, Anne Jane Hartley (October 21, 1821–December 2, 1904): actress noted for playing character parts, was the youngest of three children born to Samuel Hartley, a printer, and his wife, a descendent of a farming family named Colborn, in Rochdale, Lancashire, England. When a series of misfortunes, including an argument with his father, cost Samuel Hartley his property and income, he moved his family to London. When she was twelve years old, Anne Hartley entered the ballet school at Her Majesty's Theatre, receiving free training in return for appearing in crowd scenes there and at the Drury Lane Theatre. She gradually improved her position in the *corps de ballet* and had advanced to the "first four" when in 1846 she married George Henry Gilbert, a dancer and stage manager. For the next three years they toured the provincial cities, where Mrs. Gilbert, as she was known, appeared as solo dancer for the first time. In 1849, on the advice of friends, the Gilberts emigrated to America where they intended to make their living as Wisconsin farmers. The next year their first son, George, was born.

When the farming venture failed, the Gilberts moved to Milwaukee and then to Chicago, where they joined John B. Rice's company in 1850 or 1851. Mrs. Gilbert's primary duty was dancing in large ballets and entr'actes, but she also took small acting parts, her first being the fairy in *The Cricket on the Hearth*. Soon after, her husband's dancing career was ended by a fall through a stage trap door. Thereafter, he served as prompter and stage manager, and Mrs. Gilbert was forced to assume more acting responsibilities. By 1857 when they were members of John Ellsler's company in Cleveland and Cincinnati, she was identified with the parts of elderly or "heavy" women. She played Lady Creamly in *The Serious Family* and Mrs. Hardcastle in *She Stoops to Conquer*, but she made her first hit in 1860 enacting three burlesque characters in John Brougham's *Pocahontas*. The following year, her willingness to undertake diverse and challenging roles led to her playing Lady Macbeth to Edwin Booth's Macbeth at Lewis Baker's theatre in Louisville. Meanwhile, she continued to specialize in older character parts. Her midwestern apprenticeship ended in 1864 when, having received five offers from eastern managers, she accepted an engagement as "first old woman" at **Matilda Vining Wood**'s Olympic Theatre in New York.

After making her debut on September 19, 1864, as Baroness Freitenhorsen in *Finesse*, Mrs. Gilbert regularly performed the eccentric or querulous old women of the standard dramas and comedies as well as adaptations of Charles Dickens's novels. When Matilda Wood left New York after June 1866, Mrs. Gilbert moved to the Broadway Theatre managed by George Wood and later by Barney Williams. There in August 1867, she created her first major role—the Marquise de St. Maur in T. W. Robertson's *Caste*. She later played opposite Edwin Forrest in a series of Shakespearean dramas. On January 12, 1867, G. H. Gilbert died in New York of consumption; Anne Gilbert never remarried and retained throughout her career the stage name of Mrs. G. H. Gilbert.

With the closing of the Broadway Theatre, Gilbert began her long association with Augustin Daly, first appearing at the Fifth Avenue Theatre on August 16, 1869, as Mrs. Kinpeck in Robertson's *Play*. Three weeks later she performed with James Lewis in Robertson's *Dreams* and thus began a stage partnership with Lewis that would last almost thirty years. Between 1869 and 1877 Gilbert continued to portray comic elderly women, but under Daly's direction she also expanded her range of characters. Her most memorable role was the sinister, dumb, partially demented cook, Hester Dethridge, in Daly's adaptation of Wilkie Collins's *Man and Wife* (1870). When Daly was forced to surrender the Fifth Avenue Theatre in 1877, Gilbert left his company to remain in New York and care for her critically ill son George; he died in late 1877 or early 1878. Meanwhile, she acted at A. M. Palmer's Union Square Theatre, toured with James Lewis under the management of Henry E. Abbey, and performed for two seasons at Abbey's New Park Theatre. One year after the opening of the new Daly's Theatre in New York, Mrs. Gilbert rejoined her former manager, appearing there on September 21, 1880, with Lewis in *Our First Families*. Later that year she was featured in *Needles and Pins* with Lewis, **Ada Rehan**, and John Drew; "The Big Four," as they came to be called, were thereby established as a starring ensemble with the Daly company, enjoying both a privileged status and tremendous popularity with the public. For the next twenty years, "Grandma" Gilbert (a nickname supplied by Daly) portrayed the crusty spinster or nagging wife in such hits as *The Passing Regiment*, *7 –20–8*, *A Night Off*, and *The Railroad of Love*. Her fame extended not only throughout the United States but to England, where Daly frequently took his company, and the Continent. Despite Drew's departure in 1892 and Lewis's death in 1896, Gilbert remained with Daly until he died in 1899.

Although she considered retiring at that point, she was soon lured back to the stage by Charles Frohman to create the part of Aunt Susan in *Miss Hobbs* on September 7, 1899. She performed periodically at his Lyceum and Garrick theatres for five years, usually in support of Annie Russell, until 1904 (her farewell season) when Frohman commissioned Clyde Fitch to write a new play for her. On October 24, 1904, in what was both her first starring engagement and last role, Mrs. Gilbert, at age eighty-three, appeared in *Granny*. Five weeks later, four days after *Granny* had opened in Chicago, she died at her hotel from a brain hemorrhage suffered during her customary cold-water bath. She was buried next to her husband in Greenwood Cemetery, Brooklyn.

For the last thirty years of the nineteenth century, Mrs. Gilbert was regarded as the foremost representative of older character women on the American stage. Her greatest physical assets were a long, homely face especially conducive to comedy and a voice, praised till the end of her career for its clarity and melodiousness. Two qualities of her acting were most notable. Her training as a dancer gave her a gracefulness of movement and gesture that made her characterizations seem spontaneous and unaffected. When the Daly company visited London in 1886, Clement Scott, critic and staunch advocate of the English theatre, wished that English comedians would observe Gilbert's professional approach and improve their own style. Above all, she was concerned with "thinking myself into a part" (*The Wallet of Time*, Vol. I, p. 205) and strictly observing the author's original conception of a character. Through meticulous attention to detail, Gilbert created a gallery of characters who were at once distinct individuals yet endowed with the freshness and charm of her personality.

Although sketchy and anecdotal, *The Stage Reminiscences of Mrs. Gilbert* (1901) is a candid, insightful autobiography of this normally reticent actress. Insiders' views of her work with Daly can be found in Joseph Francis Daly, *The Life of Augustin Daly* (1917); John Drew, *My Years on the Stage* (1922); and Drew's article, "Recollections of Mrs. Gilbert," *Harper's Weekly* (January 21, 1905). *Clyde Fitch and His Letters*

(1924) reprints some of the correspondence concerning *Granny*. A laudatory review of her career is included in William Winter, *The Wallet of Time*, Vol. I (1913). Other contemporary accounts of Anne Hartley Gilbert appear in John Bouve Clapp and Edwin Francis Edgett, *Players of the Present*, Part 1 (1899), and T. Allston Brown, *History of the New York Stage* (1903). Her obituary appeared in the *New York Tribune* (December 3, 1904). See also George C. D. Odell, ed., *Annals of the New York Stage*, Vols. VII-XV (1931–1949). Gilbert is included in *Dictionary of American Biography*, Vol. IV (1931–1932); *Who Was Who in America*, Vol. I: *1897–1942* (1966); *Notable American Women*, Vol. II (1971); *The Oxford Companion to the Theatre* (1983); and *The Oxford Companion to American Theatre* (1984).

Daniel Barrett

GILDER, Rosamond (1891?–September 6, 1986): founder of the International Theatre Institute, editor and critic for *Theatre Arts Magazine*, and first woman to hold membership in the New York Drama Critics Circle, was born Janet Rosamond de Kay Gilder in Marion, Massachusetts. She was the fifth of five living children of Richard Watson and Helena (de Kay) Gilder. Her father was editor in chief of *Century Magazine*, a published poet, and a social and political reformer. He urged the passage of the International Copyright Act, was active in the formation of a free kindergarten on a city-wide basis, and, along with Jacob Riis, aroused the public conscience regarding slum conditions in New York tenement buildings. Helena Gilder was a painter, one of the founders of the American Art Association (the Society of American Artists), and helped establish the New York Philharmonic Society. Rosamond Gilder was greatly influenced by both of her parents and by her aunt, Jeannette Leonard Gilder, who co-founded and edited the *Critic* from 1881 to 1906. Frequently, visitors to the Gilder household included writers such as Rudyard Kipling, Robert Browning, Mark Twain, and Walt Whitman; artists such as John Singer Sargent, Celia Beaux, Homer St. Gaudens, and John La Farge; architect Stanford White; reformer and newspaperman Jacob Riis; business and industry giants such as J. P. Morgan and Andrew Carnegie; United States Presidents Grover Cleveland and Theodore Roosevelt; and actors and actresses Joseph Jefferson, **Helena Modjeska**, and Eleonora Duse.

Rosamond Gilder is best known for her work with the international theatre community. In 1947 she helped to found the International Theatre Institute, an organization dedicated to the exchange of knowledge and practice in theatre arts in order to promote better understanding among all nations. She was immediately appointed director of the United States Centre of the ITI (the U.S. Centre was the foreign affairs branch of the American National Theatre and Academy). Her most important achievement was keeping the U.S. Centre alive from year to year (until she finally guided it to independence in 1968) so that its potential could be realized. The U.S. Centre concentrated on three areas: exchange of persons, exchange of companies, and exchange of information.

From its inception the U. S. Centre's Exchange of Persons Program functioned along two major lines: first, creating scholarships to enable students from foreign countries to come to the United States to study American theatre, and second, setting up a consultation service for foreign theatre artists visiting America and American theatre artists going abroad.

The main purpose of the Exchange of Companies Program was to facilitate the travel of theatrical companies between countries: a foreign company touring the Unites States or an American company venturing abroad. In 1951 the first visit occurred when Louis Jouvet and the Théâtre de l'Athénée played Molière's *L'Ecole des Femmes* at the American National Theatre and Academy (ANTA) playhouse in New York. The next February the theatrical pendulum swung back toward Europe as Gertrude Stein's and Virgil Thompson's *Four Saints in Three Acts* was taken to Paris under ANTA sponsorship. Eventually this international program proved so successful that it was taken over by the Department of State. The Exchange of Information Program extended to other ITI centres, to foreign embassies, and to individuals; it also disseminated information on all phases of American theatre, especially on script rights, books, and publications.

In 1955 Rosamond Gilder was elected vice chairman of the ITI Executive Committee, and in 1963 she was elected president and reelected in 1965, presiding over the twelfth ITI Congress held in New York City in 1967. What had been the U.S. Centre became in 1968 the International Theatre Institute of the United States, Inc., and she was elected president of its board of directors. In 1969 she turned over active direction of the center to her associate, **Martha Coigney**.

Rosamond Gilder is also recognized for her work in theatrical criticism, publishing, and research. In 1931 she published her unique and perceptive record of landmark women in the history of acting, *Enter The Actress*. She began her association with *Theatre Arts Magazine* in 1936 (although she had previously written for it), stayed on to become associate editor, resident drama critic, and finally editor upon **Edith Isaacs**'s retirement in 1946. In 1948 *Theatre Arts* was combined with *The Stage* (a Theatre Guild publication), and in 1964 the magazine was discontinued. During this time she was also elected to membership in the New York Drama Critics Circle, its first and for a time its only woman member.

In July 1925, Rosamond Gilder wrote, ''The clearest insight that can be obtained into the mysteries of this art [of acting], an insight which dies with its creator—dies indeed with the moment of creation—is through the eyes of the observer who has recorded his impressions for our benefit'' (*Theatre Arts*, July 1925). She recorded her impressions of the contemporary theatrical scene both in her monthly dramatic reviews for *Theatre Arts Magazine* and in her book *John Gielgud's Hamlet* (1937). She subtitled her *Hamlet* ''a record of performance.'' After watching Gielgud's *Hamlet* at least thirty times, she compiled a play-by-play description of the action that occurred on stage, including every facet of vocal and physical interpretation, ''a regie-book in narrative form'' (*John Gielgud's Hamlet*, pp. 2, 6). The Shakespearean text and her commentary upon it appear facing one another on opposite pages. Walter Prichard Eaton in the *New York Herald Tribune* declared that Rosamond Gilder ''had given an enduring record of how *Hamlet* emerged on the stage in a famous 20th century version and what a fine actor and able director felt as its most important values" (November 28, 1937). In writing her 1937 *John Gielgud's Hamlet*, she followed the dictum of her statement on "the role of the observer." She merely reported, allowing herself to serve as a medium by means of which a great actor's performance was faithfully and accurately recorded for posterity.

From 1938 to 1948 in the service of *Theatre Arts Magazine*, however, she extended "the role of the observer" to that of commentator and evaluator—in short, to that of dramatic critic. In her view the critic's function extended far beyond responsibility to the individual artist. It also encompassed a relationship to the public and to society as a whole (*Theatre Arts*, May 1946, pp. 256–257). She was to write that the critic must serve as a scourge compelling all concerned to "try to understand more clearly the satanic workings of the world around [them] . . . and attempt, at least, to use . . . their gifts to elucidate its meanings and thereby contribute . . . toward a better future" (*Theatre Arts*, April 1945, p. 203).

In 1948 Rosamond Gilder enlarged her work in publication when she was appointed as one of four members of the ITI Editorial Board under whose auspices were published the ITI bulletin *World Premières* and *World Theatre Magazine* (the two were combined in 1963 and ceased publication in 1969). In 1967, concerned that there was no record of current American theatre, she launched with the help of the U.S. Centre the publication of a yearbook called *Theatre 1*. It continued until 1973 with the issue *Theatre 5*.

Her research contributions included her work with the Works Progress Administration Federal Theatre Project. In 1935 she was appointed head of the Bureau of Research and Publications. **Hallie Flanagan** in *Arena* (1940) stated that Gilder's bureau and *The Federal Theatre Magazine* it engendered explored "lines of theatre activity never before attempted in this country or so far as I know in any country" (p. 63). Under her leadership approximately 1,300 plays were analyzed and catalogued to aid in play selection, and extensive research was done on the American theatre. This research led to the preparation of an intensive day-by-day chronology of plays produced in New York covering the period between the records kept by George C. D. Odell (up to 1894) and Burns Mantle (beginning in 1900), and to the discovery of the first comic opera in America, *The Disappointment; or, The Farce of Credulity* (1767).

In 1932, as editorial secretary of the National Theatre Conference, Rosamond Gilder compiled *A Theatre Library*, a bibliography from which could be created the nucleus of a theatre library. Four years later, she published with George Freedley *Theatre Collections in Libraries and Museums*, a handbook to help theatre people locate material in their field. The handbook emphasized the location of American and European collections of "fugitive" theatrical material, that is, programs, playbills, prints, pictures, photographs, clippings, manuscripts, and so forth. Gilder and Freedley chose to emphasize the visual rather then the literary aspect of a theatre collection because they firmly believed that such visual material not only aided new theatrical production but became "the ultimate guardian and preserver of its immortal life" (*Theatre Collections in Libraries and Museums*, pp. 7, 2).

Rosamond Gilder received much critical acclaim and many honors, including a scholarship in 1955–1956 to study in Paris; the Sixth American Educational Theatre Association Award of Merit in 1961 as an "emissary extraordinary from the American Theatre to World Theatre and hostess without peer to theatre visitors from the whole wide world"; the Kelcey Allen Award in 1963 for her contributions to the American theatre; and the Cross of Officer of the Order of Arts and Letters of the French Republic in 1964 for her lifelong devotion to the art of the theatre. She was also named a Fellow of the American Theatre Association. Rosamond Gilder died on September 6, 1986, after a long period of failing health.

Gilder often defined drama as a "thing done," a definition consistent with her conviction that an active stance is the only possible choice in life. In line with this belief she transformed her principal interest into a vocation. The transformation was not easy. She lacked talent in the ordinary avenues of the practitioner—she was not an actress, playwright, director, or producer. Despite these supposed limitations, her theatrical career was filled with action, with things done, things accomplished, things achieved. Her energy found expression in criticism and, most especially, in the conviction that drama should stir its listeners to action. This conviction, coupled with childhood memories of the voices and portrayals of great actors and actresses who succeeded in stirring her imagination, led her to dream of a theatre that would reassume the place in society it once held in ancient Greece. If theatre could not hope to clothe itself again in religious trappings, it could at least recapture the underlying function and significance it has always held regardless of religious overtones—the magic communion, the magic involvement that occurs between actor and audience. Rosamond Gilder attempted to begin this chain reaction of understanding by taking direct action herself, reaching out to others, showing the extent of her involvement by the depth of her commitment to international artists and theatre. Because of her devotion to the theatre and her untiring and ceaseless work for its emerging community of nations, Rosamond Gilder will be remembered as one of America's best cultural ambassadors.

Books by Rosamond Gilder include *Enter the Actress* (1931, reprinted 1960), *John Gielgud's Hamlet: a Record of Performance* (1937), and *A Theatre Library* (1932). With George Freedley she compiled *Theatre Collections in Libraries and Museums* (1936). Gilder edited *Letters of Richard Watson Gilder* (1916) and *Theatre Arts Anthology* (1950). She translated *My Life* by Emma Calve (1922) and edited *Theatre Arts Magazine* from 1938–1948. Articles about Gilder include "The Lady is a Critic," *Women in American Theatre*, edited by **Helen Krich Chinoy** and Linda Walsh Jenkins (1981); "Rosamond Gilder's Contributions to International Theatre," *Southern Theatre* (Spring, 1977); and Caroline Dodge-Latta, "Rosamond Gilder and the Theatre" (Unpublished Ph.D. dissertation, University of Illinois, Champaign, 1973). Gilder is included in *Current Biography*,

1945 (1945); *The Biographical Encyclopaedia and Who's Who of American Theatre* (1966); *Notable Names in the American Theatre* (1976); *Who's Who in the Theatre* (1977); and *The Oxford Companion to American Theatre* (1984).

Caroline Dodge-Latta

GISH, Dorothy (March 11, 1898-June 4, 1968): film and stage actress, was the second daughter born to James Lee (Leigh) Gish and Mary Robinson (McConnell) Gish. James Gish was a traveling salesman from Pennsylvania when he met Mary McConnell in Urbana, Ohio; soon they were married. On October 14, 1896, their daughter **Lillian** was born in Springfield, Ohio. The Gish family moved to Dayton, Ohio, when Lillian was one year old. It was here that Dorothy Gish was born. When Dorothy was six months old, her father again packed up the family and moved to Baltimore, Maryland, where he operated a theatre concession stand. The year 1900 found the Gish family in New York City where James Gish abandoned his wife and two daughters. Mary Gish leased an old apartment house and rented out rooms to young ladies, many of whom were actresses. She also operated a concession stand at Brooklyn's Fort George Amusement Park. Mary Gish located her wayward husband, but after several attempts at reconciliation she finally obtained a legal separation and custody of the two girls. James Gish did not reappear again in their lives.

Dorothy Gish had only three years of formal education, two of them in public school and one in a boarding school. In 1902 when she was four years old, she appeared for the first time on the stage when an actress, Dolores Lorne, who lived at the Gish rooming house, asked if Dorothy could appear as "Little Willie" in a road company production of *East Lynne*. There were also roles available for Mary Gish and six-year-old Lillian.

After the road show of *East Lynne*, Dorothy Gish toured the next season with a show called *Her First False Step*. She made her New York debut in *Dion O'Dare* (1907), followed by performances in road companies of popular melodramas of the day such as *Mr. Blarney From Ireland, Editha's Burglar, At Duty's Call*, and *The Volunteer Organist*. The Gish family would alternate between road shows and operation of their mother's concession stand. In Brooklyn they met a young girl about Lillian's age named Gladys Smith who worked in the theatre. Gladys Smith's family boarded at the Gish house for several years; they moved away when Gladys's career began to develop. Sometime later, during one of their tours, the Gish family saw a silent film, *Lena and the Geese* (1911), and recognized their friend Gladys. Upon their return to New York City, the Gish family asked about her at the Biograph Studios at 111 East Fourteenth Street and were surprised to learn that Gladys Smith had changed her name to Mary Pickford. Pickford introduced her friends to her director, D. W. Griffith, who offered them work as extras in his studio at five dollars each per week. They eagerly accepted, since this was a larger sum per week than they had ever received on the road.

In 1912 Griffith decided to cast sixteen-year-old Lillian and fourteen-year-old Dorothy Gish as regulars in a film called *An Unseen Enemy*, their first feature film. Griffith preferred Lillian to Dorothy, and Dorothy was used in lead parts only at the insistence of her sister. Dorothy Gish may not have been a Griffith star, but she was a persistent presence. She acted in sixty-one films for Griffith before landing a star contract in 1915. That same year the Griffith film company moved to California where injury in an automobile accident briefly interrupted Dorothy's career. In 1917, with World War I a reality, Griffith decided to make a film called *Hearts of the World*, starring Lillian Gish and Constance Talmadge. At her sister's urging, however, Griffith was persuaded to cast Dorothy Gish instead of Talmadge as the Little Disturber, a vagabond minstrel in war-ravaged France. Gish was required to wear a black-bobbed wig (which she hated) that ultimately became her trademark and made her a popular star. *Hearts of the World* gave Gish the fame she deserved, and though she was offered a million dollar contract from Paramount-Artcraft to do fifteen pictures in two years, she turned the offer down in order to remain a Griffith star. Ironically, the films she made (for less money) were released by Paramount-Artcraft.

During her "black-wig comedy period" Gish spotted a young, talented Italian actor who she felt would become a star some day. Though she convinced Griffith to use him in *Out of Luck* (1919), the director felt the actor was too foreign-looking to be accepted by American audiences and used him again only as a dance partner for a current new female star in the live prologue sequences to the downtown Los Angeles premières of *Scarlet* and *The Greatest Thing in Life*. The actor was Rudolph Valentino.

The next major film that brought Dorothy Gish success was *Remodeling Her Husband* (1920), directed by her sister Lillian, who claimed no one had yet discovered her sister's on-screen potential. **Dorothy Parker** wrote the screenplay for the film, which also starred James Rennie, a young actor from Toronto, Canada, who had worked on Broadway shortly before his arrival in Hollywood. After the film was completed, Rennie and Dorothy Gish were married on December 20, 1920. Gish and her husband worked on two additional pictures together, *Flying Pat* (1920) and *Clothes Make the Pirate* (1925). They were divorced in 1935. *Orphans of the Storm* (1922) was the last Griffith film in which both Gish sisters appeared and was Dorothy Gish's last great film success.

By 1925 the "child-woman" character developed by the Gish sisters and Mary Pickford had become unfashionable, and Dorothy Gish's career in films was in jeopardy. Then a Hollywood miracle happened; Howard Wilcox offered Gish a contract, and she made five films for him: *Nell Gwyn* (1926); *London* (1927), *Tip Toes* (1927), *Mme. Pompadour* (1927), and *Wolves* (1930), released in the United States as *Wanted Men* (1936). *Wolves* was Gish's first talking picture.

Gish returned to the theatre in 1928 to work on a Broadway production of *Young Love*, starring Gish and her husband James Rennie and directed by George Cukor. The play previewed in Rochester, New York, and then moved to Broadway at the Masque Theatre. Brooks Atkinson said, "Miss Gish plays her part admirably, with intelligence, skill, and a variety that neatly accents the points of the farce. Nothing could be more amusing than her crushed and despairing exit'' (*New York Times*, October 21, 1928). *Young Love* was set to tour after the New York run but was canceled when the Philadelphia Censorship Committee banned its performance in Philadelphia. So the show went to London instead. While in London Gish appeared in the film *Wolves* (1930). It was not well received, and she returned to Broadway to star in *The Inspector General*, which opened at the Hudson Theatre on December 17, 1930, but closed after only six performances. Atkinson felt the play was ''only temperately amusing,'' but said ''Dorothy Gish, as the mayor's timid daughter, translates one frantic love scene on the settee into expert comedy'' (*New York Times*, December 24, 1931). In 1931 Dorothy Gish appeared in three plays. In March she played Leo in the Theatre Guild's presentation of *Getting Married* by George Bernard Shaw. Atkinson thought the play ''long and tedious'' but complimented Gish for capturing the humor as she portrayed the covetous wife (*New York Times*, March 31, 1931). Her next play was a revival of *The Streets of New York* by Dion Boucicault, presented by Lawrence Langer's New York Repertory Company at the Forty-Eighth Street Theatre in repertory with Henrik Ibsen's *The Pillars of Society*. In 1932 Gish succeeded Patricia Collinge in *Autumn Crocus* and then, after a short hiatus, returned to Broadway in the 1934 production of *Brittle Heaven* by Vincent York, playing the spinster poet Emily Dickinson. Brooks Atkinson was once again impressed, citing Gish's talent for ''one of those mettlesome performances that recommend her strongly to the admiration of theatregoers'' (*New York Times*, November 14, 1934).

In 1936 Gish appeared in a New Rochelle, New York, production of *The Bride Shines On* by W. Cotton. Two years later she joined Mildred Natwick and José Ferrer on Broadway for E. B. Ginty's *Missouri Legend*, playing the middle-class Mrs. Howard with ''just the right sort of pout and spirit,'' according to Atkinson (*New York Times*, September 20, 1938). The following year, she displayed ''one of the keenest notions of character'' (*New York Times*, December 1, 1939) as Aaronetta Gibbs in *Morning's at Seven* by Paul Osborn. The play opened at the Longacre Theatre on November 30, 1939. In 1940 Gish decided to join a touring company production of *Life With Father*, taking over the role of Vinnie for Dorothy Stickney, who was ill. At the time, her sister Lillian was also playing Vinnie in another touring company's production of the play. When Dorothy became ill in San Francisco, Lillian was called in to take over the role.

Dorothy Gish returned to Hollywood in 1944 to make her first American talking picture, *Our Hearts Were Young and Gay* (playing Mrs. Otis Skinner); she followed this film appearance with *Centennial Summer* (1946). In the same year she appeared on Broadway in *The Magnificent Yankee* by Emmet Lavery at the Royale Theatre. As Mrs. Holmes, Gish made ''a complete character,'' according to the ever-observant Atkinson, who admired her performance as ''the apparently easy-natured woman who rules the Justice with kindness, but firmly'' (*New York Times*, January 23, 1946). Four years later Gish was starring on

Broadway again, as Mrs. Gillis ("a very fine victim," Atkinson called her) in Dinelli's thriller *The Man* at the Fulton Theatre (*New York Times*, January 20, 1950). She went back to Hollywood in 1951 to play the mother's role in *The Whistle at Eaton Falls*.

The Gish sisters teamed up again in the 1956 summer stock run of Enid Bagnold's *The Chalk Garden*, the first time since childhood that they had performed on stage together. After this production Dorothy Gish's health began to deteriorate, and eventually she lost interest in everything. The sisters returned to Masillon, Ohio, where they had spent some of their youth, in an effort to help Gish regain her vigor. She decided to accept an offer to do a television show, but before rehearsals were over, another actor replaced Gish at her own request. Then in 1963 she made her last film, *The Cardinal*. After the filming her condition worsened and Dorothy went to a sanitarium. After some time there, Gish suffered a stroke and contracted bronchial pneumonia. Lillian was present when Dorothy Gish died on June 4, 1968, at the age of 70. She was cremated and her ashes placed in the family crypt at St. Bartholomew's Protestant Episcopal Church on Park Avenue, New York City.

Dorothy Gish was an influential actress who helped shape the public's view of women on stage and in movies. She held her own with such greats as Lillian Gish, D. W. Griffith, Lionel Barrymore, Mary Pickford, Dorothy Parker, and Joshua Logan, always demonstrating her ability to rise above a less than perfect script and give the audience a performance they would not soon forget.

An excellent selection of photographs of Dorothy Gish appears in *Great Stars of The American Stage* (1952, 1959) by Daniel Blum. Dewitt Bodeen writes of his personal memories of Dorothy Gish in his book *More From Hollywood* (1977), and *Hollywood's Children* by Diana Serra Cary provides a fascinating glimpse into Gish's childhood during the silent film era. Lillian Gish has written about her sister and family in her two autobiographies, *The Movies, Mr. Griffith and Me* (1967) and *Dorothy and Lillian* (1973). An acidic analysis of the female role and image in film is explored by Marjorie Rosen in her book *Popcorn Venus* (1973), and Howard Wilcox relates amusing stories in his autobiography *25,000 Sunsets* (1967, 1969). See also Anthony Slide, *The Griffith Actresses* (1973). Dorothy Gish discusses her own career in *Ladies' Home Journal* (July 1925), *Time* (June 17, 1968), and *Newsweek* (June 17, 1968). See also Richard L. Williams, "The Gallant Gish Girls," *Life* (August 20, 1951). Dorothy Gish's obituary appeared in the *New York Times* (June 6, 1968). Biographical sketches of Dorothy Gish are included in *Current Biography, 1944* (1945); Robert L. Sherman, *Actors and Authors With Composers Who Helped Make Them Famous* (1951); *The Biographical Encyclopaedia and Who's Who of the American Theatre* (1966); *Who's Who in the Theatre* (1967), *Notable American Women*, Vol. IV: *The Modern Period* (1980); and *The Oxford Companion to American Theatre* (1984).

David Manning

GISH, Lillian Diana (October 14, 1896?–): film, stage, and television actress, film director, and writer, was born in Springfield, Ohio, the daughter of James Lee Gish, a candy merchant, and Mary Robinson (McConnell) Gish. Her parents' families were early settlers in the American colonies; her mother's forbears included President Zachary Taylor and Samuel Robinson, an influential Ohio politician and state senator. One year after Lillian Gish was born the family moved to Dayton, Ohio (where her sister **Dorothy Gish** was born), and later to Baltimore, Maryland, where her father went into business with Edward Meixner. Two years later her father moved again, to New York, hoping to find more lucrative work. When his family joined him, however, he deserted his wife and two children, leaving them to fend for themselves. Gish had little formal education, and apart from short periods in schools in Baltimore and St. Louis she was educated privately by her mother and by the many actors with whom she toured as a child.

To earn a living for herself and her children, Mary Gish ran a theatrical boardinghouse and a concession stand in a Brooklyn park. Soon the children and their mother were offered roles in road companies. Billed as "Baby Lillian," Lillian Gish made her professional debut in the melodrama *In Convict's Stripes* (1902), in Rising Sun, Ohio. For the next seven years she toured sporadically throughout the United States, often traveling alone, with a Masonic emblem pinned to her lapel by her mother so that fellow Masons would take care of her. The plays were many and of limited literary merit; among them, *Her First False Step*, *At Duty's Call*, *The Child Wife*, and the *Little Red School House*. Although the family's circumstances were often difficult, it is likely that through these experiences Lillian Gish developed those qualities of dedication, resilience, and determination that were to become her hallmark later on. There were occasional periods of some financial security, such as when Mrs. Gish opened an ice cream parlor in East St. Louis, thus enabling Lillian to attend the nearby Ursuline Convent. When the shop burned down, without insurance, the family was forced to move again. An early friendship with the Smith family in New York yielded unexpected benefits when the eldest child, Gladys, who had changed her name to Mary Pickford and become a star of the silent cinema, introduced the sisters, Lillian and Dorothy, to the director D. W. Griffith. He hired the sisters, and Lillian made her screen debut in *An Unseen Enemy* (1912), directed by Griffith. Apart from the stage role of Fairy Morganie in *A Good Little Devil* (1931), directed by David Belasco, she worked exclusively in film for the next seventeen years, mainly with Griffith. With his teaching and encouragement she developed her skills of dancing, voice, and movement, and extended her general knowledge. Griffith demanded thorough research into all aspects of setting and character, and Lillian Gish was an avid student. She also attended the Denishawn School of Dancing, so that, as she claims in her autobiography, *Lillian Gish, The Movies, Mr. Griffith, and Me* (1969): "within a few years my body was to show the effects of all this discipline; it was as trained and responsive as that of a dancer or athlete" (p. 100). After acting in a score of one- or two-reel films, directed by Griffith for the American Mutoscope and Biograph Company of New York— among them, *The Musketeers of Pig Alley* (1912), *The Mothering Heart* (1913), and *Judith of Bethulia* (1914)—she went with Griffith to the Mutual Film Corporation where she made *Home Sweet Home* (1914) and *The Sisters* (1914). Then she embarked on the first of the roles that established her stature as a screen actress: Elsie Stoneman in *The Birth of A Nation* (1915), the Civil War epic that became not only an instant commercial and artistic success but a landmark in the history of the art of the film. A succession of films followed, emphasizing the pure, self-sacrificing heroine pitted against enormous odds of brutality and hardship: *Hearts of the World* (1918), *Broken Blossoms* (1919), *Way Down East* (1920), and *Orphans of the Storm* (1922). Of her acting in *Way Down East*, John Barrymore wrote to Griffith, "I merely wish to tell you that her performance seems to me to be the most superlatively exquisite and poignantly enchanting thing that I have ever seen in my life.... It is great fun and a great stimulant to see an American artist equal, if not surpass, the finest traditions of the theatre" (*Life and Lillian Gish*, p. 163). By 1933 Lillian Gish had become a star, earning the titles, "Queen of the Silent Screen" and "Duse and Bernhardt of the Screen."

Many testify to the enormous courage of the actress, her willingness to work long hours under atrocious conditions, and her refusal to compromise any detail for the quality of the work. After watching her filming in a snowstorm and ninety-mile-an-hour gale for a whole day, Henry Carr wrote, "That blizzard scene in *Way Down East* was real. It was taken in the most God-awful blizzard I ever saw.... Lillian stuck out there in front of the cameras. D. W. [Griffith] would ask her if she could stand it, and she would nod. The icicles hung from her lashes, and her face was blue. When the last shot was made they had to carry her to the studio" (*Life and Lillian Gish*, p. 157). In 1922 after *Orphans of the Storm* was finished, Griffith found he could no longer afford to pay her what she was worth out of the modest budgets he received, so he advised her to work with other managements. She joined Inspiration Films, though not before directing a film for Griffith, *Remodeling Her Husband* (1920), starring her sister, Dorothy. After two films for the Inspiration Company, *The White Sister* (1923) and *Romola* (1924), she joined MGM, where she made five films in two years, for a salary of $800,000: *La Bohème* (1925), *The Scarlet Letter* (1926), *Annie Laurie* (1927), *The Enemy* (1928), and *Wind* (1928). A proposed sixth film was abandoned, but her work in these films had attracted the attention of theatre practitioners worldwide. Vladimir Nemirovich-Danchenko of the Moscow Art Theatre wrote to her, "I want once more to tell you of my admiration of your genius.... A combination of the greatest sincerity, brilliance and unvarying charm, places you in the small circle of the first tragediennes of the world" (*Life and Lillian Gish*, p. 240).

Suddenly, almost without warning, the "talkies" arrived in Hollywood in 1929 and dealt a death blow to the art form in which Lillian Gish had excelled. She made one "talkie," *One Romantic Night* (1930), then returned to New York to her first love, the legitimate stage, which she had deserted years before for the silent cinema. She had matured as an actress, and she was anxious to prove herself on the stage. Her performance as Helena in Jed Harris's production of *Uncle Vanya* (Cort Theatre, New York, 1930) was universally applauded, drawing from critics the same enthusiasm as had greeted her finest screen roles. As Charles Darnton noted in the *New York Times*: "When the presence of her filled the stage like light flooding through a window into a room, she was so luminous that the others faded into the background" (April 16, 1930). She did not fare so well in her next role, *Camille* (1932), directed and designed by Robert Edmond Jones. Generally the critics thought her miscast, while Stark Young in the *New Republic* commented that her performance "had not the necessary technical skill behind it," and added, "As an actress she is, so far, better suited to a role that will be seen but briefly on the stage" (January 4, 1933).

Gish was to prove the criticism ill-founded with a series of characterizations in major roles, all demonstrating her unusual stage presence and versatility, including the role of Effie Holden, loosely based on Lizzie Borden, in *9 Pine Street* (1933), Christina Farley in *The Joyous Season* (1934), and the Young Whore in *Within the Gates* (1934), a performance that so delighted the author, Sean O'Casey, that he wrote to her, "A bad thing well done can never feel success; a good thing well done can never feel failure" (*The Movies, Mr. Griffith, and Me*, p. 323).

After an absence of ten years Gish was persuaded to return to films in *The Commandos Strike At Dawn* (1943). Then followed *Miss Susie Slagle's* (1946), *Duel in the Sun* (1947), *Portrait of Jennie* (1948), *The Night of the Hunter* (1955), *The Cobweb* (1955), *Orders to Kill* (1958), *The Unforgiven* (1960), *Follow Me, Boys* (1966), *Warning Shot* (1967), *The Comedians* (1967), and her hundredth motion picture, *A Wedding* (1978), directed by Robert Altman. She continued working in films, however, with some regret. She found them much less exciting than in the silent era when she had been involved in every facet of the production. Now she found "acting in films was largely a matter of doing what you were told and collecting your salary" (*The Movies, Mr. Griffith, and Me*, p. 345). Nor could cinema replace the stage, and she returned to it in 1947 to play Marquise Eloise in *The Marquise* (1947), Leonora in James M. Barrie's *The Legend of Leonora* (1947), Katerina Ivanova in *Crime and Punishment* (1947) with John Gielgud, Mabel in *Miss Mabel* (1950), the half-crazy Ethel in John Patrick's *The Curious Savage* (1950), and the world-weary Carrie Watts longing for home in Horton Foote's *The Trip to Bountiful* (1953), of which Harold Clurman wrote, "Lillian Gish seems to me to be better in *A Trip to Bountiful* than in any other play in which I have seen her" (*The Nation*, November 21, 1953).

Gish played a summer season with her sister, Dorothy, in *The Chalk Garden* (1956), then played in Berlin with a program of Tennessee Williams one-acts, *Portrait of a Madonna* and *The Wreck of the 5:25* (1957). The next year she created the role of Agatha in the American première of T. S. Eliot's *The Family Reunion*. Then followed Catherine Lynch in Tad Mosel's *All the Way Home* (1960). She succeeded Gladys Cooper as Mrs. Moore in *Passage to India* (1962) and performed Mrs. Mopply in George Bernard Shaw's *Too True To Be Good* (1963); the Nurse in the American Shakespeare Festival Theatre's *Romeo and*

Juliet (1965); the Empress of Russia in *Anya* (1965), the short-lived musical on the life of Anastasia; and Margaret Garrison in *I Never Sang For My Father* (1968). In 1969 and 1970 she toured Russia, western Europe, and the United States with the one-woman concert program *Lillian Gish and the Movies—the Art of Film 1900–1928*, then played Marina in Mike Nichol's production of *Uncle Vanya* (1973) and performed in the revue *A Musical Jubilee* (1975).

Since 1948 she has become known to a wider contemporary audience through her television appearances: *The Late Christopher Bean* (1948), Grandma Moses on *Schlitz Playhouse of Stars* (1952); *The Day Lincoln Was Shot* (1956); *The Spiral Staircase* (1961); *Arsenic and Old Lace* (1969), in which she co-starred with her close friend **Helen Hayes**; *Sparrow* (1978); *Love Boat* (1980); and *Thin Ice* (1980). She also hosted on PBS a collection of early movies entitled *The Silent Years* (1975). Her most recent professional work, however, has been on film, in *Hambone and Hillie* (1984) and as the cantankerous but beguiling mother in Alan Alda's *Sweet Liberty* (1986). In 1987 she appeared with Bette Davis, Vincent Price, and Ann Sothern in *The Whales of August*. Most recently, in 1988, Gish could be heard on the new recording of the Jerome Kern-Oscar Hammerstein musical *Show Boat*. This new version includes music and song left off the original recording or cut from the show before its Broadway run in 1927.

Despite her fragile appearance, Lillian Gish continues to lead a healthy, active life working for special causes like the preservation of films, especially the work of D. W. Griffith and other eminent pioneers in cinema history. Recently she helped to raise funds for film preservation at the George Eastman House, Rochester, New York, and participated in the Lincoln Center Film Society's tribute to Elizabeth Taylor (1986). She continues to travel and visited Expo '86, where she attended the première of the Jeanne Moreau film about the life and career of Lillian Gish.

Gish has received many honors. They include an Honorary Oscar (1971) from the Academy of Motion Picture Arts and Sciences, the Handel Medallion (1973), the United Service Organization's Woman of the Year Award (1978), the Medal of Arts and Letters (France, 1983), and the American Film Institute's Life Achievement Award (1984). The French film director François Truffaut dedicated his film *Day for Night* (1973) to Lillian and Dorothy Gish because "they were the first real actresses of the American cinema." She has been honored by the Smithsonian Institute (1986) and the Museum of the City of New York (1986). Academic awards include honorary degrees from Rollins College, Holyoke College, and Bowling Green State University. Her publications include *Lillian Gish, An Autobiography* (1968), *Lillian Gish, The Movies, Mr. Griffith and Me* (1969), and *Dorothy and Lillian Gish* (1973).

Gish's career spans the twentieth century, from the era of the silent screen to the sophisticated films and television of today, from the quaint melodramas and one-night stands as a child actress to the theatre classics and Broadway. She has always pursued her career with the utmost integrity and dedication and, despite many offers, has never married. "A good wife has a twenty-four-hour-a-day job, while acting has required me to work up to twelve or fourteen hours a day. I didn't ruin any dear man's life, and I'm grateful for that" (*New York Times*, May 11, 1986). She is a "great" who has worked with "greats," and yet all who meet her are impressed with her modesty, her graciousness, her unflagging enthusiasm, and her radiant beauty. As Brooks Atkinson says in his introduction to her autobiography, "She began as a trouper; she is a trouper now" (*The Movies, Mr. Griffith and Me*, p. ix).

The most informative accounts of Lillian Gish's film and theatre career may be found in her books *Lillian Gish, The Movies, Mr. Griffith, and Me* (1969) and *Dorothy and Lillian Gish* (1973). The biography by Albert Bigelow Paine, *Life and Lillian Gish* (1932), is also useful, but it deals mainly with her silent screen career, while Richard Schickel's authoritative biography *D. W. Griffith, An American Life* (1984) contains many references to her relationship with the great director. See also Anthony Slide, *The Griffith Actresses* (1973). Significant reviews of her stage performances may be found in the *New York Times Reviews* (1970). See also Stark Young, "Dame Aux Camélias," *New Republic* (January 4, 1933), and Harold Clurman, *The Nation* (November 21, 1953). Feature stories on Lillian Gish have appeared in the *New York Daily Post* (April 17, 1969), the *New York Times* (December 27, 1960, and May 11, 1986), and *Newsday* (January 6, 1974). See also Richard L. Williams, "The Gallant Gish Girls," *Life* (August 20, 1951). A recent interview with Gish appears in *Interview* (September 1987). Lillian Gish is included in Robert L. Sherman, *Actors and Authors With Composers Who Helped Make Them Famous* (1951); *The Biographical Encyclopaedia and Who's Who of the American Theatre* (1966); William C. Young, *Famous Actors and Actresses on the American Stage*, Vol. I (1975); *Notable Names in the American Theatre* (1976); *Current Biography, 1978* (1978–1979); *Who's Who in the Theatre* (1981); *Who's Who of American Women, 1983–1984* (1983); *The Oxford Companion to American Theatre* (1984); and *Who's Who, 1986–1987* (1986). Among authors there is some disagreement over Lillian Gish's year of birth. *Who's Who in the Theatre* (1981) and *Famous Actors and Actresses of the American Stage* (1975) show the year as 1893, while *Who's Who* (1986) and *Notable Names in the American Theatre* (1976) claim the year as 1899. The biographer Albert B. Paine gives 1896, a date also supported by *Current Biography, 1978* (1978–1979) and Richard Schickel in *D. W. Griffith, An American Life* (1984).

Sam McCready

GLASPELL, Susan (July 1, 1876?–July 17, 1948): playwright, actress, director, co-founder of the Provincetown Players, novelist, and short-story writer, was born in Davenport, Iowa. Although the Scott County Registrar's Office listed no birth certificate for her, the 1880 Iowa Census noted a four-year-old Susie Glaspell, a five-year-old Charles, and a one-year-old Frank, children of Elmer S. and Alice (Keating) Glaspell residing at 502 Cedar Street, Davenport, Iowa. Therefore, Glaspell was apparently six years older than the 1882 date that her biographies have traditionally indicated. The earlier date was also substantiated by Drake University, which listed her age at the time of admission in 1897 as 21.

In her youth, Glaspell spent summers on a farm with an aunt, and as an adult she lived for periods of time in Colorado, New York, France, England, and Greece. While all these locales appeared in her writing, Davenport has been the most consistent source of inspiration for her. "I have never lost the feeling that this is my part of the country," she wrote (*Twentieth Century Authors*, pp. 541–542).

Glaspell was educated in the Davenport public schools and began her writing while still in grammar school. In 1896, two years after her graduation from high school, she started a column called "The Weekly Outlook" for the *Davenport Morning Republican*, under the by-line Susie Glaspell, the name she used throughout her life. One of her earliest articles was devoted to proper audience etiquette in the theatre. In 1897 she enrolled at Drake University in Des Moines, Iowa, in the liberal arts curriculum. While at Drake University she served as literary editor for the college newspaper, received first prize in an oratory contest, and supported herself by writing for the *Des Moines Daily News*. In June 1899, one day after receiving her Bachelor of Arts degree from Drake, she went to work full-time for the newspaper. She covered the State House and also wrote a feature column called "The News Girl," in which she developed the persona of a young, naive, earnest woman who reacts effusively to the world around her.

The idea that she could support herself solely by her writing seemed bold. However, from 1901 until her death in 1948—with the brief exception of the years 1936–1938, when she served as director of the Works Progress Administration Federal Theatre Project in the Midwest—Glaspell was consistently able to publish her writing and generate sufficient income to support not only herself but often her husband. In a career that spanned forty-seven years, she wrote and published fifty short stories, nine novels, and thirteen plays.

In 1904, back in Davenport once more after a year's stay at the University of Chicago, Glaspell began to write short stories about a fictional city called "Freeport," patterned after Davenport. By the time she ended the series in 1922, she had written twenty-six stories. Glaspell's fame soon began to spread: she was interviewed as a celebrity by the local magazine, the *Trident*, and she gained the attention and envy of the young intellectual community of Davenport by winning a $500 prize from *Black Cat* magazine for a short story. By 1909 Glaspell had become a member of the Monist Society, founded by George Cram Cook as an organization for forward-thinking intellectuals. Cook, a member of one of the leading Davenport families, had studied at the Universities of Iowa, Harvard, and Heidelberg, had been a professor at Iowa and Stanford universities, and was an editor, journalist, critic, novelist, and poet. He would later become Glaspell's husband.

In 1909 Glaspell published her first novel, *The Glory of the Conquered*, based on her experiences in Chicago. Taking the advance payment for the novel, she traveled to Europe with her close friend Lucy Huffaker, stopping in Holland and Belgium and eventually settling in Paris for six months. On her return in June

1909, she made a side trip to Colorado but came back to Davenport in January (1910) to begin work on her second novel, *The Visioning*. On April 14, 1913, Susan Glaspell and George Cram (Jig) Cook, now divorced from his second wife, were married by the mayor of Weehawken, New Jersey. Glaspell was thirty-seven at the time. In addition to a collection of short stories titled *Lifted Masks* (1912), she had published two novels and was well on her way to completing a third, *Fidelity* (1915). She had not yet tried her hand at drama.

The world into which the Cooks moved in 1913 was one of great activity and experimentation. In both Greenwich Village, where they spent the winters, and Provincetown, Massachusetts, where they lived in the summer, their friends—writers, artists, and journalists—were fomenting those cultural and social changes that were to affect subsequent generations in America. In 1911 Abbey Theatre Players (Dublin) had toured America, and according to Glaspell, they provided the inspiration for the founding of the Provincetown Players. By 1915 a few experimental theatres had begun to form in America. Glaspell and Cook wrote a one-act spoof on Freudianism, *Suppressed Desires* (1914), for one of these—the Washington Square Players (New York)—but it was "too special" even for this experimental theatre. That summer, on the beach of Provincetown, the Cooks and their friends Hutchins Hapgood and his wife and Neith Boyce decided, at Boyce's suggestion, to perform it themselves. On the evening of July 15, 1915, two plays were presented in the Hapgood living room: *Constancy* by Boyce and *Suppressed Desires* by Glaspell and Cook. By the end of that summer the group had convinced their friend Mary Vorse to allow them the use of her wharf studio, where the two plays were repeated along with *Contemporaries* by Wilbur Steele and *Change Your Style* by Cook. Thus ended the first season of the yet-to-be-named Provincetown Players.

By the summer of 1916 the group had a name, a subscription list, and a new addition—Eugene O'Neill. Glaspell had invited the young O'Neill to perform a reading of his work, and it was she who, after hearing *Bound East for Cardiff*, announced that their theatre's purpose was to foster new playwrights. That summer, besides this O'Neill play, the Provincetown Players offered in the wharf theatre O'Neill's *Thirst*, a revival of *Suppressed Desires*, Glaspell's new work *Trifles*, and five other new plays, including *Winter's Night* by Boyce and *The Game* by Louise Bryant. At the end of the successful season, Cook, with the enthusiastic backing of his friend Jack Reed, the journalist and one of the supporters of the group, decided that the theatre would be taken with them when they returned to New York for the winter. In New York, Cook rented a theatre that was to be called the Playwright's Theatre, first situated at 139 Macdougal Street and later at 133, where it came to be called the Provincetown Playhouse. Glaspell was one of the most active members of the Provincetown Players. In the seven years of its existence, it produced one hundred plays by fifty-two authors. Susan Glaspell contributed eleven, exceeded only by O'Neill's fifteen.

Founded to give American playwrights a chance to work out their ideas freely, as the first "Subscription List" stated, the Provincetown Players were committed to maintaining an amateur status. Accordingly, each member was expected to direct, to stage, and frequently to act in his or her own production. Glaspell proved to be a fine actress. The French director Jacques Copeau, visiting America in 1917, saw a production of *The People*, in which Glaspell played the role of the Woman from Idaho. He praised her acting in a speech to the Washington Square Players, citing her naturalism and moving depiction of character. Besides her role in *The People*, Glaspell played Henrietta in *Suppressed Desires*, Mrs. Hale in *Trifles*, Mrs. Root in *Close the Book* (1917), Abbie in *Bernice* (1919), the Cheated One in *Woman's Honor* (1918), and Allie Mayo in *The Outside* (1918), and then took over the role of Madeline in *The Inheritors* (1921) from the star Ann Harding.

By 1922 after the successes of O'Neill's *The Emperor Jones* and *The Hairy Ape*—both plays moving from Greenwich Village to Broadway—Cook felt that success had made the experimental nature of the theatre no longer viable, the amateur status no longer possible. In March he formally called a halt to the group and set sail for Greece with Glaspell. (Activities at the Provincetown Playhouse on Macdougal Street would continue, under other auspices, for many years.) For almost two years, Glaspell and Cook enjoyed their life in Greece, but in January 1924, Cook unexpectedly died.

Glaspell returned to America in February 1924, settling once more in Provincetown. There she met Norman Häghejm Matson, a young writer, seventeen years her junior, with whom she lived for the next seven years. With him she co-authored her next play, *The Comic Artist*. She also returned to fiction once more, producing three novels in three years: *Brook Evans* (1928), *Fugitive's Return* (1929), and *Ambrose Holt and Family* (1930). The novelist/playwright Zoë Akins made *Brook Evans* into a film titled *The Right to Love*. Glaspell also edited and supplied one of three introductory essays for *Greek Coins* (1926), a collection of Cook's poetry that she edited; and she wrote the story of Cook's life, the remarkable biography titled *A Road to the Temple* (1927). In 1931 she received her most important literary honor: the Pulitzer Prize for her play *Alison's House*, based on the Genevieve Taggart biography of the life of Emily Dickinson, which was presented by the Civic Repertory Company, directed by and starring **Eva La Gallienne**.

After her separation from Matson—who married the nineteen-year-old-daughter of one of Glaspell's friends—she became head of the Midwest Bureau of the Works Progress Administration Federal Theatre Project in Chicago, holding this position from 1936 to May 1938. During this time she received over six-hundred plays and was instrumental in the production of many works, including Arnold Sundgaard's *Spirochete*, *White Fog* by the black playwright Theodore Ward, and an all-black *Swing Mikado*, which had the distinction of being the longest-running Gilbert and Sullivan *Mikado* since 1908.

By mid–1938 Glaspell was once more in Provincetown writing fiction. Before her death she produced three more novels: *The Morning is Near Us* (1939), chosen as a Literary Guild selection; *Norma Ashe* (1942); and *Judd Rankin's*

Daughter (1945). She also wrote a story for children, *Cherished and Shared of Old* (1940). Her life during these years was active, and she maintained close ties with many writers, including John Dos Passos and Edmund Wilson. She died in July 1948 at the age of seventy-two.

Glaspell was not afraid of challenging ideas that appeared to be sacrosanct even among her peers. Her first play, *Suppressed Desires*, satirizes the craze for the then new psychoanalysis that was sweeping Greenwich Village. In *Trifles*, Glaspell depicts events and conditions that induce a farm wife to kill her husband. In *The Outside* two women—a sophisticated city woman named Mrs. Patterson, and her servant, a local woman named Allie Mayo—struggle toward some meaning to the life they share on the outer reaches of Provincetown Harbor. The same theme of female camaraderie appears again in Glaspell's most directly feminist one-act play, *Woman's Honor*, which makes the point that men defend a woman's honor because it gives them a sense of heroism and reinforces a woman's dependence and confinement. Women seeking to live freely, unfettered by male domination, societal restriction, or personal cowardice, are the most dominant concerns in the six full-length plays that Glaspell wrote: *Bernice* (1919), *Inheritors* (1921), *The Verge* (1921), and *Chains of Dew* (1922)—all written for the Provincetown Players—and *The Comic Artist* (1928) and *Alison's House* (1931), both written after Glaspell's return from Greece. These plays focus on a fully developed female heroine. Next to those dominant women, the men with whom they live—husbands, fathers, lovers—are painfully lacking in vigor and intelligence. They are portrayed as incapable of understanding the women and, for the most part, resentful of certain women's superiority and independence.

Although similar in theme, Glaspell's six full-length plays offer a wide variety of dramatic forms. *Bernice* and *Alison's House* are mood pieces. *Inheritors* is an historical epic, spanning forty years in the lives of two families. *Chains of Dew* and *The Comic Artist* are comedies.

Glaspell's greatest achievement in the theatre was her play *The Verge* (1921), depicting a woman's mental breakdown. It is the first totally expressionistic play on the American stage, predating O'Neill's *The Hairy Ape* by several months. In it Glaspell uses sound effects, lighting, and scenery to indicate the state of mind of her heroine, Claire Archer, a woman who experiments with plants in order to create new forms of life for herself. It is Glaspell's most daring and most engaging work both structurally and thematically. Like her contemporary Eugene O'Neill, Glaspell faced the task of creating new modes of presentation—intellectual debate, naturalism, expressionism, and symbolism—in order to expand the limits of the theatre she had inherited and to make it reflective of a changing society.

Plays (1987), edited by C. W. Bigsby, contains Glaspell's works for the theatre. Her *Trifles* has been reprinted in *Plays by American Women, 1900–1930* (1986), edited by Judith E. Barbour. For Glaspell's comments about herself, see *The Road to the Temple* (1927). There is a large collection of Glaspell and George Cram Cook papers, diaries, letters, and clippings in the Berg Collection of the New York Public Library Performing Arts Research Center at Lincoln Center. Some letters and clippings are in the Eugene O'Neill Collection, Barrett Library, University of Virginia. The most valuable source of information about Glaspell's life and fiction is Marcia Noe, "A Critical Biography of Susan Glaspell" (Unpublished Ph.D. dissertation, University of Iowa, 1976). Less complete is Arthur Waterman, *Susan Glaspell* (1966). There is an excellent annotated bibliography of critical assessments of Glaspell's plays compiled by Gerhard Bach, *Susan Glaspell und die Provincetown Players* (1979). The bibliography and comments at the end of this book are in English, although the principal assessments are in German. Glaspell's place in American theatre is discussed in Isaac Goldberg, *The Drama of Transition* (1922); Ludwig Lewisohn, *Drama and the Stage* (1922, reprinted 1966); Ludwig Lewisohn, *Expressionism in America* (1932); and Arthur Hobson Quinn, *A History of the Drama*, Vol II (1927). For background on Glaspell's early years in Iowa, see Floyd Dell, *Homecoming* (1933); Bartholow V. Crawford, "Susan Glaspell," *Palimpsest*, (Dec. 1930); and Clarence A. Andrews, "Parnassus on the Prairie," *A Literal History of Iowa* (1972). For a discussion of Glaspell's life in Greenwich Village and Provincetown, see Hutchins Hapgood, *A Victorian in the Modern World* (1939). For a discussion of Glaspell's relation to the feminist movement, see June Sochen, *The New Woman: Feminism in Greenwich Village, 1910–20* (1972). On Glaspell and the Provincetown Players, see Helen Deutsch and Stella Hanau, *The Provincetown: A Story of a Theatre* (1931); Arthur Waterman, "Susan Glaspell and the Provincetown," *Modern Drama* (Sept. 1964); and Gerhard Bach, "Susan Glaspell: Provincetown Playwright," *The Great Lakes Review*, IV (Winter 1978). For Glaspell's connection to Eugene O'Neill, see Louis Shaeffer, *O'Neill: Son and Playwright* (1968) and *O'Neill: Son and Artist* (1972). For Glaspell's relation to other playwrights, see Cynthia Sutherland, "American Women Playwrights as Mediators of the 'Women's Problem,' " *Modern Drama* 21 (December 1978). For a discussion of Glaspell's use of Freudianism on the stage, see W. David Sievers, *Freud on Broadway* (1955). Glaspell's obituary appeared in the *New York Times* (July 28, 1948). She is discussed in Stanley J. Kuntz, ed., *Living Authors* (1931); *Twentieth Century Authors* (1942); *Who Was Who*, Vol. 4 *1941–1950* (1964); *The Oxford Companion to American Literature* (1965); *Notable American Women*, Vol. II (1971); Myron Matlaw, *Modern World Drama: An Encyclopedia* (1972); *American Women Writers*, Vol. II (1980); *Dictionary of Literary Biography*, Vol. IX, *American Novelists, 1910–1945*, Part 2 (1980); *The Oxford Companion to the Theatre* (1983); and *The Oxford Companion to American Theatre* (1984). Glaspell's birth date is often given as 1882.

Linda Ben-Zvi

GORDON, Ruth (October 30, 1896-August 27, 1985): exuberant comic actress, playwright, and screenwriter, best remembered as the original Dolly Levi in *The Matchmaker*, was born Ruth Gordon Jones to Clinton and Annie (Ziegler) Jones in Wollaston, Massachusetts. She spent her childhood in Quincy, Massachusetts, where her father was employed by Mellin's Food Company. After graduating from Quincy High School she studied acting at the American Academy of Dramatic Arts in New York for a term, leaving when she was told she had no promise; she then began the arduous task of finding an acting job on her own.

She visited numerous producers' offices for several months; after repeatedly hearing "nothing at present," she was finally hired to play Nibs in *Peter Pan* in December 1915. Gordon toured with the company after the New York engagement. For the next few years she acted in various touring companies, mainly in the Midwest. In 1921 she married her leading man in *Seventeen*, Gregory Kelly, and at one point opened with him the Gregory Kelly Stock Company in Indianapolis. Gordon returned to New York in 1923 to act in *Tweedles*, which the *New York Times* noted was "admirably acted" (August 14, 1923). In *Mrs. Partridge Presents* (1925) she received more individual praise for her comic pauses and timing, and in that same year she delighted audiences by her comic mannerisms in *The Fall of Eve*—her rapid walk, jerky arm movements, and comically blank face. Her acting in *Saturday's Children* (1927) was in the same comic vein but with an added seriousness. She impressed Brooks Atkinson by playing her role "with a curiously subtle penetration." He wrote, "Her face wears the same comically vacant expression, and occasionally her gestures recall the awkward arm-thrusts." He added that she was convincing in her portrayal of the character "as an earnest, deadly serious young lady," a woman "who has come up hard against the wall of life" (*New York Times*, January 27, 1927). In 1929 she was admired by critics for her sensitive rendering of Serena in *Serena Blandish*. Indeed, with the exception of her performance as Lily Malone in *Hotel Universe* (1930), Gordon was praised continually throughout her career, receiving special mention for her talents even in such unsuccessful plays as *The Wiser They Are* and *A Church Mouse* (1931). Atkinson noted that she was "one of the most thoroughly individual of our comediennes," one who "has progressed from trickery into conscious method" (*New York Times*, September 18, 1932). Both *Here Today* (1932) and *Three-Cornered Moon* (1933) were likewise well received.

Gordon departed completely from the comic tradition in 1934 to play in *They Shall Not Die*, based on the Scottsboro case, one of the most significant controversies of the time. F. Raymond Daniell, a reporter for the *New York Times*, covered the trial and found the fictitious characters and their situation, as portrayed in the play, to be a close reflection of places, events, and people he had witnessed (*New York Times*, March 4, 1934). It was a mark of her growing dramatic versatility that Gordon was successful in the dramatic role of one of the assaulted women.

Gordon played in *A Sleeping Clergyman* (1934) and *The Country Wife* (1935). In January 1936, she played Mattie in *Ethan Frome*, receiving reviews that described her as an outstanding actress, not just a fine comedienne. Atkinson, who over the years followed her career in the *New York Times*, wrote in 1936, "Miss Gordon has evoked one of the most completely imagined persons I have ever seen on stage. The quantity of detail is enormous; the variety of mood is astonishing; the anguish over the broken dish is piercing. . . . From *Mrs. Partridge Presents* to *Ethan Frome* is a measure of Miss Gordon's tremendous accomplishment on the American stage" (*New York Times*, February 2, 1936).

In October of 1936, Gordon won critical acclaim abroad playing Mistress Pinchwife in *The Country Wife*, her first appearance on the London stage and the first time an American appeared in an Old Vic production. The audience at the Old Vic enjoyed her carefully crafted awkwardness—the comic mannerisms that had been delighting American audiences for years. In the following year, back in New York, she received mixed reviews for her portrayal of Nora in Thornton Wilder's adaptation of *A Doll's House*; some reviewers thought she overplayed in the first half, yet **Lynn Fontanne**, after one of her own performances of *Amphitryon 38*, encouraged her audience not to miss Gordon's performance. In 1939 Gordon met Garson Kanin, director and playwright, who was to become her second husband, Gregory Kelly having died in 1927. In 1942, the year that she and Kanin were married, she appeared in *The Strings, My Lord, Are False* and in *The Three Sisters*, in which she was considered superb as Natasha.

Over the next few years Gordon wrote three plays and acted in two of them: *Over Twenty-One* (1944), *Years Ago* (1946), and *Leading Lady* (1948). The successful *Over Twenty-One*, a flip comedy, ran for 221 performances. *Years Ago*, an autobiographical play, was considered amusing. But *Leading Lady*, co-authored with Garson Kanin, in which Gordon again acted, was judged uneven and closed after eight performances. Also in 1948 Gordon and Garson Kanin began writing screenplays, a more successful venture for Gordon than playwriting. Gordon and Kanin were nominated for an Academy (Oscar) Award in 1947 for *A Double Life*, and won the Box Office Ribbon Award as well as an Oscar nomination for *Adam's Rib* (MGM, 1949).

Not until the 1954–1955 season, when she played Dolly Levi in Thornton Wilder's *The Matchmaker*, did Gordon match her earlier success in *The Country Wife*. *The Matchmaker* was first presented for the Edinburgh Festival in 1954, where major flaws in the last two acts were apparent. Director Tyrone Guthrie did some drastic cutting and eliminated the chaos of the third act by the time the play was brought to London. It was a triumphant success, repeated when the comedy came to New York in 1955, again starring Ruth Gordon, whom Atkinson described as "sweeping wide, growling, leering, cutting through her scenes with sharp gestures, filling in every corner with a detail or a sardonic observation. . . . The performance is epochally funny" (*New York Times*, December 6, 1955). Gordon gave 1,078 performances of *The Matchmaker*, impressing her colleagues with her careful preparation for each performance.

Gordon's next few roles were disappointing after the acclaim she had been accorded in *The Matchmaker*, perhaps because there could never be another role that so perfectly suited her exuberant comic style. In 1960 *The Good Soup*, directed and adapted by her husband, was poorly received, though her performance was described as "amusing" (*New York Times*, March 3, 1960). Little attention was paid to her London performance in *A Time to Laugh* (1962); then in 1963 she appeared in **Lillian Hellman**'s *My Mother, My Father, and Me*, playing with "baleful accuracy" (*New York Times*, March 25, 1963) the role of Rona Halpern. In 1965 she again acted in a work she adapted, *A Very Rich Woman*, receiving negative reviews for both her acting and the play, which closed in less than two weeks. In 1966, however, Gordon's role was described as "done magnificently" (*New York Times*, October 7, 1966) in *The Loves of Cass McGuire*. Two years later she received an Oscar for her role as Minnie Castevet in the film *Rosemary's Baby* and the American Academy's Award of Achievement for 1968, an award especially gratifying since she had been told years earlier by the Academy's president that she had no talent.

In 1971 Gordon appeared in the film *Harold and Maude*, the story of a morbid nineteen-year-old boy obsessed with death and an elderly woman who teaches him the value of life. This film achieved cult status among college students. Gordon also played Clint Eastwood's feisty, shotgun-toting mother in *Every Which Way But Loose* and *Any Which Way You Can*.

Although the play *Dreyfus in Rehearsal*, which was adapted and directed in 1974 by Garson Kanin, received mixed reviews, Gordon's performance was pleasing; some critics were "vastly satisfied" (*New York Times*, October 27, 1974). In *Mrs. Warren's Profession* (1976), Gordon started off the season poorly. Clive Barnes described her performance as "absolutely deplorable. . . . She resorts to cheap comic effects, her voice is as monotonous as a subway, and her style is nonexistent" (*New York Times*, February 19, 1976). Yet a month later Walter Kerr reviewed her performance more favorably. While agreeing that the role called for a younger woman, Kerr found her acting improved; as Mrs. Warren in debate with her daughter, Gordon "marshals her arguments forcibly, warmly, directly. It's eyeball to eyeball, mannerism kept to a minimum" (*New York Times*, March 21, 1976).

In 1985 Ruth Gordon died of a stroke in her home on Martha's Vineyard at the age of eighty-eight. In her autobiography *Ruth Gordon: An Open Book* (1980) she wrote of herself as a "visceral legend," which indeed she was. She was an active part of the American theatre for over fifty years, helping to define the expression of comedy on the twentieth-century stage. Her most memorable achievements were her renditions of Mattie in *Ethan Frome*, Mistress Pinchwife in *The Country Wife*, and Dolly Levi in *The Matchmaker*. Those who worked with her were impressed with her conscientiousness and her professionalism. Although she wrote plays, screenplays, autobiographies, and a novel and showed herself skilled as a speaker on the lecture circuit and on televised talk shows, she will be remembered as an actress, an exuberant comedienne, whose completely imagined characters thrilled many.

Gordon has discussed her career, her marriages, and her son, Jones Harris, in three interesting autobiographies: *Myself Among Others* (1971), *My Side* (1976), and *Ruth Gordon: An Open Book* (1980). Reviews and articles about Gordon may be found in *Theatre Arts* (December 1946), the *New York Post* (August 2, 1969, and May 8, 1971), the *New York Times* (October 17, 1965, and June 9, 1968), the *New York Magazine* (October 5, 1969), and *Newsday* (June 8, 1971). Gordon's obituary appeared in the *New York Times* (August 28, 1985). Gordon is included in *Who's Who in America, 1970–1971* (1970); *Current Biography, 1972* (1972, 1973); *A Companion to the Theatre: The Anglo-American Stage from 1920*, edited by Robin May (1973); *The Biographical Encyclopaedia and Who's Who of the American Theatre* (1966); *Notable Names in the*

American Theatre (1976); *American Women Writers*, Vol. II (1980); *Who's Who in the Theatre* (1981); and *The Oxford Companion to American Theatre* (1984).

Linda Tolman

GRAHAM, Martha (May 11, 1894?–): pioneering dancer, choreographer, and theorist, was one of three daughters born in Allegheny, Pennsylvania, to George Graham, the son of an Irish immigrant, and Jane Beers, who traced her ancestry back to Miles Standish of *Mayflower* fame. Graham's heritage, consequently, was a mixture of the God-fearing Puritan pioneer and the tempestuous, quick-tempered Black Irish. Both branches of the family were staunchly Presbyterian. Her father, a graduate of Johns Hopkins University, was an "alienist" or psychologist. Martha Graham learned from her father that movement does not lie and that one always reveals oneself through movement. Graham later called this her first dance lesson.

In 1908 the family moved to Santa Barbara, California. Shortly thereafter, Graham's father took her to a dance concert given by Ruth St. Denis, one of the first modern dancers. "From that moment on my fate was sealed. I couldn't wait to learn to dance as the goddess danced," Graham recalled (*Frontiers of Dance*, p. 5). Her father, staunch Presbyterian that he was, objected to such a life for his daughter, and she was unable to pursue her interest in dance until after his death in 1914.

At the age of twenty-two, Graham enrolled at Denishawn, the dance school established in Los Angeles by Ruth St. Denis, "the goddess" of her childhood, and Ted Shawn. There she studied various dance forms and styles, including Oriental, Spanish, primitive, and anything else that caught the fancy of St. Denis and Shawn. Although St. Denis felt that Graham did not have the body of a dancer, Graham soon became a student-teacher at the school. While studying at Denishawn, she was able to work with other notable pioneers of modern dance such as Doris Humphrey and Charles Weidman.

In 1920 Martha Graham made her professional debut, dancing a leading role in Ted Shawn's *Xochitl*. Some years later she was seen by John Murray Anderson, who hired her as a featured dancer of the Greenwich Village Follies. After two seasons, however, she tired of performing Oriental and Moorish roles and left the Follies to experiment with new movement concepts. Early in her career, Graham had declined an opportunity to study with Mary Wigman in Germany, feeling that she must explore and discover that unknown "something" herself. She now seized the opportunity to experiment choreographically while teaching at the Eastman School of the Theatre (a division of the Eastman School of Music) in Rochester, New York. Her experiments resulted in a concert of her own works on April 18, 1926, at the Forty-eighth Street Theatre in Manhattan. The performance boasted a wide variety of pieces, ranging from *The Maid with the Flaxen Hair* and *Gypsy Portrait*, to *Clair de Lune*, the pieces being set to music by Franck, Schumann, Schubert, Brahms, Debussy, Scriabin, and others.

Disliking the label "modern dance" and feeling that dance should be concerned with everyday life and should reflect its time, Graham dubbed her new style "contemporary." The inspirations of her pieces included such topics as war, poverty, and neuroses. Her philosophy demanded an abandonment of ballet, which she felt lacked realism, focus, and depth. "My quarrel was never with ballet itself but that, as used in classical ballets, it did not say enough, especially when it came to intense drama, to passion. It was that very lack that sent me into the kind of work I do, so that I could get beyond the surface and to that inner world," she said (*Frontiers of Dance*, p. 56). After her revolutionary discarding of ballet, Graham borrowed elements from her predecessors in modern dance, incorporated them into her own style, developed her own movement vocabulary, and gave it all her personal signature. Graham's initial public concerts were frequently ridiculed rather than acclaimed by audiences that did not understand her unique artistic expression. Accustomed to the beauty of ballet, the public judged her dances ugly and stark. Works such as *First Revolt, Heretic, Vision of Apocalypse, Immigrant,* and *Four Insincerities* were a marked departure from the fantasy of ballet.

Graham set out to discover and develop movement that suited her small, atypical dancer's body. For many years, both the public and most critics found her movement language outrageous, if not comic. As Graham's dances dealt with the struggle of good and evil in humanity, she required a vocabulary of movement to convey her message. "When you are very upset, you have a sinking feeling inside you. So as a dancer I showed on the outside what was happening on the inside—my whole body sank or fell to the floor" (*Frontiers of Dance*, p. 53). One device Graham used to convey emotion was breathing. She translated this concept into a "breath-length," a measure that replaced the metric count in her choreography. The dynamics revealed through controlled uses of the breath became an integral, essential element of the Graham technique. The controlled use of breathing generated the excitement in the type of theatre she created. Various elements of drama could be heightened or diminished according to the tension, or release of tension, signified by the breath.

In 1930 Graham founded the Dance Repertory Theatre in New York, where she and her troupe of dancers performed for a number of years. In 1932 she was awarded a Guggenheim Fellowship to study in Mexico for a summer, the first time a dancer had been so honored. During the summer of 1935, she helped establish a summer dance festival for those interested in modern dance and its development. While at the festival site in Bennington, Vermont, she staged the movement and dances for several plays, one being the **Katharine Cornell**-Guthrie McClintic production of *Romeo and Juliet*. Her theories that breath and movement could be used to reveal the inner person significantly influenced actors for both stage and screen.

At the 1940 Bennington Dance Festival, she presented her first dance-drama, a biography of Emily Dickinson titled *Letter to the World*. "This was the first time in the history of the theatre that movement, poetry, music, costumes, and decor were combined. In this piece she showed the various facets of Emily Dickinson's personality by using a different dancer for each facet'' (*Dance-magazine*, November 1966, p. 64). John Martin, the *New York Times* critic, praised her revised version as ''a bold venture into entirely new territory for the dance'' and ''a work of pure genius'' (*Current Biography, 1961*, p. 183).

This production began the development of her ''theatre of dance.'' She proceeded to develop an entire series of portraits contrasting the inner and outer characteristics of various characters and showing what Graham calls their ''interior landscapes.'' Graham and the ballet choreographer George Balanchine collaborated on one of these portraits, a dramatic characterization of Mary, Queen of Scots. Working independently of each other, they produced a two-section ballet called *Episodes*, which premièred at New York's City Center in May of 1959. Among the many subsequent dances she has produced are *Acrobats of God, Night Journey*, and *Cave of the Heart*, all inspired by Greek drama and legend.

Always short of money, Graham was the recipient of a $25,000 gift from Katharine Cornell and other friends who wished to help support the school Graham had established. Others who supported her productions included the Baron de Rothschild and the Guggenheim and Elizabeth Sprague Coolidge foundations.

During her extensive career, Graham choreographed over one-hundred pieces, including *Seraphic Dialogue, Diversion of Angels,* and *Appalachian Spring. Lamentation*, one of her earlier works, incorporated movement to make fully visible the tortures one suffers in sorrow. The single performer was encased in a long tube of purple elastic cloth, a stark dramatic form of theatrical costuming. An example of the dramatic effectiveness of the movement she created can be seen in *Night Journey*. Of the cry uttered by Jocasta (in the story of Oedipus) at the moment of her undoing, Graham said, ''I felt that when Jocasta became aware of the enormity of her crime, a cry from the lips would not be enough. It had to be a cry from the loins themselves, the loins which had committed sin'' (*Frontiers of Dance*, p. 107).

Indeed, Graham can be considered basically a dramatist through dance. Her dances seldom deal with plot development. They are, rather, dramas of character. Complemented by costumes, sets, properties, lights, and music, characters share their emotions with the audience. Graham relates an entire story by entering a protagonist's mind and showing various facets of character. She often does this by using several dancers to portray different aspects of the same person. The fusion of decor, lighting, and costume with movement and drama have become all-important in Graham's development of a total theatre approach. She incorporates three-dimensional sets into the choreography. For instance, the twisted, uneven structure representing the bed in *Night Journey* serves as a resting place, an erotic torture rack, and the site of sin. The sculptor Isamu Noguchi has designed sets for a number of Graham's dances. Aaron Copeland, Norman Dello Joio, Samuel Barber, and Gian-Carlo Menotti are among those who have composed music for her dances. Costumes are incorporated into her choreography as well. In a piece titled *Voyage*, for instance, she used costumes to suggest fertility. The couple performs a duet in which the woman wears a dress of black and light green with a long train. After the man wraps himself in this train, the woman steps up on his right leg, pivots her body away from him and arches out from his body. Thus, the phallic symbol is made vivid through the creative and theatrical use of costume. Graham is clearly concerned not only with movement but with an expansion into a total theatrical presentation. She is truly a theatre artist, an artist who has succeeded in creating a new art form and training a new kind of performer to achieve her ends.

In 1948 Graham married Eric Hawkins, the first male dancer in her company. Years later, after their divorce, he established his own modern dance company. In 1954 Graham and her company made a highly successful four-month tour of Europe. In 1956 they performed for sixteen weeks throughout the Near and Far East, and Graham gave lecture-demonstrations in Athens, Rome, and Paris. Two years later she choreographed her first full-length work, *Clytemnestra*, which premièred April 1, 1958, at the Fifty-fourth Street Theatre in New York. "It proved to be a fairly overwhelming work," stated John Martin, assessing the dance's impact two years later, "and it has lost none of its power. On the contrary, . . . it has become richer and deeper and even more engrossing" (*New York Times*, April 26, 1960).

In 1957 the film *A Dancer's World* was produced by Nathan Kroll through a grant from the Mellon Foundation and the Baron de Rothschild Foundation. The film, originating out of the Pittsburgh public broadcasting station, WQED, was a documentary danced by the Graham Company and narrated by Graham herself. It garnered Peabody and Ohio State awards as well as awards from several European film festivals. Several films have since been made of her works, including *Appalachian Spring, Night Journey,* and *Seraphic Dialogue*.

The Martha Graham School of Contemporary Dance, based in New York, attracts dance students from all over the world. In addition to teaching at her own school, Graham has taught at the Neighborhood School of the Theatre and the Juilliard School of Music and has given lecture-demonstrations throughout this country and abroad.

Graham, a slender five feet, three inches, exudes an intense, magnetic presence on and off the stage. She is totally dedicated to furthering dance and its message to all humankind. She has been the recipient of several honorary university degrees and countless awards. These include the Henry Hadley Medal for distinguished service to American music; the New York City's Handel Medallion (the city's highest honor for the arts); the *Dancemagazine* Award (1957); and the Capezio Dance Award (1960), one of the most prestigious awards in the field of dance.

At the *Dancemagazine* Award ceremonies in April 1957, she spoke of communication, whether in dance or the spoken word, as the world's great need. As a performer, teacher, and choreographer, and as the creator of a new dance technique, Martha Graham is considered by many to be a genius. She is the first woman in history to have developed an entirely new form of theatre based on dance. This dance form has revolutionized theatre because her raw materials are the drama of human emotion. **Agnes de Mille** calls Martha Graham a great craftswoman in the theatre and compares Graham's contribution to that of Eugene O'Neill.

Among the many reviews of Martha Graham's work see *Dancemagazine* (November 1965, May 1967, August 1968, and May 1977). Sources probing Graham's total theatre concept and Graham the dramatist include *Dancemagazine* (November 1966 and December 1963) and *Theatre Arts* (May 1947). Articles on her revolutionary technique can be found in *Dancemagazine* (May 1966) and *Newsweek* (April 7, 1958). See also Walter Terry, *The Dance in America* (1956) and *Frontiers of Dance* (1975). Graham is included in *Who's Who in the Theatre* (1957); *Current Biography, 1961* (1961–1962); *Who's Who in America, 1962–1963* (1962); *The Biographical Encyclopaedia and Who's Who of the American Theatre* (1966); *The Dance Encyclopedia*, edited by Anatole Chujoy and P. W. Manchester (1967); Don McDonagh, *The Complete Guide to Modern Dance* (1976); *The Encyclopedia of Dance and Ballet*, edited by Mary Clarke and David Vaughan (1977); and Barbara Naomi Cohen-Stratyner, *The Biographical Dictionary of Dance* (1982). *The Bibliographic Guide to Dance: 1975*, Vol. I (1976), lists photographs, films, videotapes, and taped interviews with Graham.

Deborah Nadell

GREENWOOD, Jane (April 20, 1934–): costume designer, was born in Liverpool, England, the only daughter of Florence Sarah Mary (Humphries) and Harold Greenwood, a haulage contractor, later an officer in the British Army. During World War II she was evacuated to Wales. There she spent many hours with her maternal grandmother, Sarah Humphries, who taught her to sew and knit, as well as to make doll clothes. When she returned to Liverpool after the war, a widowed aunt who lived with the family encouraged her to go to the theatre. Together, they attended the many theatrical, operatic, and dance programs available in the city of Liverpool.

After graduation from Merchant Taylor's Girls' School, Greenwood attended the Liverpool Art School. Finding her work "too dramatic," her teachers advised her to go to the Central School of the Arts and Crafts in London, a school known for its training of theatre artists. It was at this school, which she attended on a scholarship, that she first began to appreciate period authenticity and accuracy in design. One of her teachers, Norah Waugh, was writing *Corsets and Crinolines* (1954) at the time and involved the students in working on the patterns. Greenwood learned from Waugh the importance of correct period silhouette. "One of the most important aspects of my training was realizing that there was a very definite change in silhouette which had nothing to do with the human figure. It had to do with what was put on the human figure" (*Theatre Crafts*, March 1985, p. 25). Greenwood graduated from the Central School in 1957 with a thorough knowledge of the cutting and construction of period clothes.

Sent from the Central School for an interview at the Oxford Repertory Theatre, she was hired immediately—it was her first professional position as a costume designer. Her first production there was Luigi Pirandello's *Henry IV*. Conditions at the Oxford Playhouse were very primitive, and Greenwood began her professional life with "a ping pong table, an iron and a lot of old clothes" (*Theatre Crafts*, March 1985, p. 87). She had to rent the costume stock to students for parties in order to raise enough money to purchase a sewing machine.

From the Oxford Rep, she first came to America via Canada at the invitation of **Tanya Moiseiwitsch** who was so impressed with her skills that she invited Greenwood to be a draper at Canada's Stratford Shakespeare Festival. Once again, Greenwood found herself in a situation where period accuracy and detail were important since the audience sat close to the theatre's thrust stage with its minimal scenery.

In 1962 Greenwood was offered a job by Ray Diffen (who had set up the original costume shop at Stratford) in New York City. This position began not only Greenwood's American career but a new phase of her personal life. In September 1963 Greenwood married Ben Edwards, a well-known Broadway set designer. They had been introduced quite informally when a fire in Edwards' building caused him to seek shelter in the building where Greenwood was living. At about this same time, Greenwood decided to turn once again to costume design. Her first production was Carson McCullers's *The Ballad of the Sad Café* (1963), which was produced and designed by Edwards, who helped the fledgling costume designer to get into the New York market after her years as a draper. There followed a series of productions both on Broadway and in regional theatre. Notable among those productions were John Gielgud's *Hamlet* with Richard Burton, *More Stately Mansions* with Ingrid Bergman and **Colleen Dewhurst**, and *The Prime of Miss Jean Brody* with **Zoe Caldwell**. The last two plays won her Best Play citations and nominations for New York Drama Critics awards. *More Stately Mansions* also won for Greenwood an Antoinette Perry (Tony) nomination for best costume design.

During this very productive professional period in her life, Greenwood and her husband bought a house on Nineteenth Street in New York City and there raised two daughters: Sarah, born May 19, 1964, and Kate, born October 16, 1965. As children, Sarah and Kate spent many hours in the musical comedy stock on the sixth floor of the Brooks-Van Horne costume company shop, while Greenwood worked several flights below on various productions. Subsequently, both girls worked as wardrobe assistants in summer theatres.

Greenwood's more recent Broadway credits include *Hay Fever* (1970), *A Moon for the Misbegotten* (1973), *Cat on a Hot Tin Roof* (1974), *Who's Afraid of Virginia Woolf?* (1976), *West Side Waltz* (1981), *Medea* (1982), *Plenty* (1983), *La Bohème* (1984) with Linda Ronstadt, *Lillian* (1985) with Zoe Caldwell, *So Long on Lonely Street* (1986), *The Knife* (1987), *Ah Wilderness* (1988), and *Our Town* (1988).

Regional theatre work comprises another area of impressive credits for Greenwood. Especially notable are the twenty-three productions for the American Shakespeare Festival in Stratford, Connecticut. These include *Twelfth Night* (1966), *The Three Sisters* (1969), *Othello* (1970), *Measure for Measure* (1973), *Romeo and Juliet* (1974), and *King Lear* (1975). Other regional credits show her venturing far not only geographically but stylistically: *Beyond the Horizon* (McCarter, Princeton, New Jersey, 1974), *California Suite* (Ahmanson, Los Angeles, 1976), *The Heiress* and *The Winter's Tale* (McCarter, Princeton, 1976–1977), *A Month in the Country* (McCarter, Princeton, 1978), *Mary Stuart* (Guthrie Theatre, Minneapolis, 1980), *Garden of Earthly Delights* (Lenox Arts Center, New York City, 1984), and *Rainsnakes* (Long Wharf, New Haven Connecticut, 1985).

Greenwood has also designed for motion pictures and television. Her television credits include *Look Homeward, Angel*; *Kennedy*; and *Johnny Bull* (1983). Her films include *Arthur* (1981), *The Four Seasons* (1981), *Tender Mercies* (1983), *Weatherby* (1985), and *Sweet Liberty* (1986).

As Jane Greenwood's reputation for fine, solid work grew, a very special recognition followed. From 1976 to 1986 she was head of the costume design program at the Yale Drama School. The free exchange with her students helped keep her work fresh and "daring." This interaction gained such importance that she remarked, "I used to think that I just [would] go there on Wednesdays, but then I started going on Fridays, too!" (Personal interview, December 2, 1985).

Even though Greenwood is a master of period research and period style, as well as a skillful interpreter of the blending of period with contemporary, she feels that her most significant contribution to the field is that she "keeps working." For her, each production has its own value and its own special method for coming to life that she must find.

An excellent article that provides many insights into Jane Greenwood's development and design philosophy is Susan Lieberman, "Designers on Designing: Jane Greenwood," *Theatre Crafts* (March 1985). There is also an interview with Greenwood and two other prominent designers in *Theater* (Fall/Winter 1981). See also "Jane Greenwood, Costumes for *More Stately Mansions*," *Theatre Crafts* (November/December 1967). Greenwood provided additional information in an interview on December 2, 1985. Lists of Greenwood's many productions may be found in *Notable Names in the American Theatre* (1976) and *Who's Who in the Theatre* (1981).

Mari W. DeCuir

——H——

HAAGA, Agnes Marie (January 11, 1916–): educator, recreation leader, author, actress, director, was born in Memphis, Tennessee, to Oscar John and Agnes (Gallagher) Haaga. Her father was a cotton grower of German ancestry. Her mother, of Irish descent, was a story writer. From her parents, Haaga inherited both a concern for people and a love of the arts. Agnes Haaga was the second of nine children. Even when she was a small child, drama was an integral part of her life. At the age of eight she staged a dance drama to celebrate the birth of a younger sister. Before the age of ten she had directed and acted in a neighborhood production of *Madame Butterfly*, whose receipts replenished the city's milk fund for babies.

An important figure in Agnes Haaga's childhood was Minnie Wagner, superintendent of the Recreation Department of the Memphis Park Commission. The Memphis recreation program had gained national recognition for its imaginative arts projects; as a participant in Wagner's program, Haaga had further opportunities for her interests and skills to grow. She was to have further associations with the recreation department later in her career.

In 1930, while still attending public school, Haaga entered the James Lee Academy of Arts (now the Memphis Arts Academy). Here she met another person who was to have a major impact on her life, Florence McIntyre, the academy's director. The academy provided training in all the arts for hundreds of persons of all ages. The instruction, by practicing artists, was free, allowing all the children of the Haaga household a chance to explore the arts during the depression years. While at the academy Haaga had experiences in creative drama and children's theatre that strongly influenced her later career choices. The academy planned to produce *The Emperor's New Clothes*, and Haaga, then in high school, auditioned for the play. To her surprise the auditions were not formal script readings, but improvisations. This process impressed her. Upon questioning the director, she found that this type of theatre was called "creative dramatics," which the director had learned while a student at Northwestern University under **Winifred Ward**. Agnes Haaga then decided to go to Northwestern and study with Ward. However, her plans were temporarily thwarted by the depression and her father's death. Instead, she found employment as a member of Minnie Wagner's recreation staff and worked her way through Siena College (1933–1936), a Dominican school for women in Memphis.

Once out of college, her desire to act was so strong that she headed for New York. She studied acting at the Provincetown Studio in New York City and spent three summers with a theatre in Clinton Hollow, New York. While studying and working as an actress, Haaga directed drama activities for girls at the Lower West Side Center in Manhattan, sponsored by the Children's Aid Society of New York. She found her work with children to be more rewarding than her acting career, and in 1942, she returned to Memphis and became the director of drama at the Park Department.

In 1947 Haaga began her long involvement with the Children's Theatre Association of America (CTAA) when an exhibit of the drama/theatre program of the Memphis Recreation Department was displayed at a national meeting of that group. She eventually became an active participant and one of the association's leaders. In the summer of 1947, she realized her long-time dream and went to Northwestern University to study with Winifred Ward, at that time the leading authority in creative dramatics and children's theatre in America.

Winifred Ward recommended Agnes Haaga for a new position opening in Seattle, Washington: a program in creative dramatics and the related arts to be co-sponsored by the University of Washington and the Junior League of Seattle. Incentive for the program came from a Junior League volunteer, Ruth G. Lease. Except during the years of 1951–1952, when she returned to Northwestern to study for and receive her master's degree, Haaga remained at the University of Washington as director of creative dramatics and later chair of the Child Drama Department until her retirement in 1977. At the university she developed one of the most comprehensive children's drama/theatre programs in the country. The graduate program met the demands of professionals in education, theatre, and recreation, as well as the special needs of the disabled. In addition, the success of the Child Drama Department program in developing adult theatre audiences has attracted leading talents to Seattle's professional theatre community.

When Haaga retired, she and her long-time associate at the University of Washington, **Geraldine Brain Siks**, were honored by the university, their colleagues, and their friends from all over the world for their dedication to the development of child drama. At that time Seattle's Junior Theatre Program established the Agnes Haaga/Geraldine Siks Scholarship Fund in recognition of the efforts and achievements of both women.

Haaga's impact on child drama can be measured by her publications and by the amount of time and energy she has given to serve organizations that came to define the role of child drama in America. Her first book, *Supplementary Material for Use in Creative Dramatics with Younger Children* (1952), was the initial step in a long-range research program on background materials for creative drama work. It was an innovative text containing actual accounts of children involved in developing their own drama activities, a format often followed in subsequent books on the subject. In addition to her own book, she contributed chapters to *Children's Theatre and Creative Dramatics* (1981), edited by Geraldine Brain Siks and Hazel Dunnington; *Go Adventuring: A Celebration of Winifred Ward* (1977), edited by Ruth Beall Heinig; and *Children and Drama* (1981), edited by **Nellie McCaslin**.

Haaga's dedication to advancing the theory and practice of child drama can best be seen through her service to the Children's Theatre Association of America. Haaga has served as the association's national director, chaired numerous committees, and represented the organization on the executive board of the American Theatre Association. In 1960 she was a representative to the White House Conference on Children and Youth. In 1964 she headed the American delegation to the First International Congress on Theatre for Children and Youth in London and was a member of the ad hoc committee to draw up the resolutions for the creation of the International Association of Theatre for Children and Young People (ASSITEJ). She also has been an advisor to the National Recreation Association, an organizer and developer of workshops for Camp Fire and Girl Scout leaders, and a representative of the Friends of the John F. Kennedy Center for the Performing Arts on the Advisory Council for Arts Coalition Northwest, and she is the first trustee emeritus for the Pacific Arts Center. She was instrumental in establishing the Winifred Ward Memorial Scholarship Fund and was its chairperson when the first award was presented in 1978.

Her services and contributions to the child drama field, to the University of Washington, and to her community have received recognition. Among her many honors are the first annual **Charlotte Chorpenning** Award in 1956, offered by the Children's Theatre Association of America for her university's outstanding program in children's drama; the Phi Beta Honor from the National Professional Fraternity of Music, Speech, and Drama in recognition of Haaga's noteworthy support of those fields; the National Recreation Association Citation in 1963 for her invaluable contribution to the recreation movement; a title conferred in 1972 as Fellow of the American Theatre Association in honor of her continuous and outstanding service to theatre in America; the American College Theatre Festival Award of Excellence in 1974, presented by Standard Oil Company for her significant contribution to the development of college drama; the Alliance for Arts Education Certificate of Appreciation in 1977 for her work in and support of the arts in education; the Creative Drama for Human Awareness Award in 1977, presented by the Children's Theatre Association for outstanding achievement and service in the field; and CTAA's Special Recognition Citation for her

services as fund raiser and finance chairperson of the Winifred Ward Scholarship
Fund (1980). In 1983 the Children's Theatre Association of America presented
its first Campton Bell Award to Agnes Haaga for "a lifetime of outstanding
contributions to the field of child drama/theatre." In May 1985 Agnes Haaga
and her colleague Geraldine Brain Siks received the Seattle Children's Theatre
"Honor Role" Award for their "enormous contribution to Seattle Children's
Theatre, to the world of children's theatre, and to the Seattle theatre community."

Agnes Haaga is most proud of her role in developing the professional organizations that have helped establish child drama as a major element in educational
institutions and professional associations, including the Children's Theatre Association of America, the International Association of Theatre for Children and
Young People, and the academic program at the University of Washington.
Haaga attributes her prominence in the field to the gifts and efforts of others.
However, her determination, spirit, and devotion to young people are, in no
small way, a factor in the rise of child drama to a legitimate and integral part
of education and the arts in America.

Agnes Haaga's book is *Supplementary Material for Use in Creative Dramatics with
Younger Children* (1952). She has contributed chapters to *Children's Theatre and Creative
Dramatics*, edited by Geraldine Brain Siks and Hazel Dunnington (1981); *Go Adventuring:
A Celebration of Winifred Ward*, edited by Ruth Beall Heinig (1977); and *Children and
Drama* (1981), edited by Nellie McCaslin. She has contributed material for two books
by Geraldine Siks: *Creative Dramatics, An Art for All Children* (1958), *Drama with
Children* (1977), and to *Master Teachers of Theatre: Observations on Teaching Theatre
by Nine American Masters*, edited by Burnet M. Hobgood (1988). Haaga has also contributed articles to the *Educational Theatre Journal* (December 1956, October 1957, May
1958, and December 1964), *Children's Theatre Review* (December 1978, Winter 1981,
and October 1984), *Recreation* (May 1951), *Dramatics* (May 1951 and March 1955),
and *American Peoples Encyclopedia* (1953). Additional information about Haaga may
be found in *The Biographical Encyclopaedia and Who's Who of American Theatre* (1966)
and "Special Center Index, 1951 to 1975," *Children's Theatre Review*, 30, No. 1 (Winter
1981). Much of the material on which this article is based is taken from the personal
collection of Agnes Haaga and the records of the University of Washington, Seattle.

                                                                    Lou Furman

HAGEN, Uta (June 12, 1919–): actress, teacher, was born in Goettingen,
Germany, the second child of Oskar F. L. Hagen, an art historian and accomplished musician, and Thyra (Leisner) Hagen, a concert singer. Postwar conditions in Germany were grim; and in 1925, when Oskar Hagen was offered a
professorship at the University of Wisconsin at Madison, the family emigrated
to the United States. On his sabbaticals Hagen took his family back to Europe,
where they visited art galleries, theatres, and museums. As a result, Uta Hagen
became as familiar with European culture as with American culture.

Life in Madison also proved to be culturally rich, with artists and intellectuals
constantly visiting the Hagen household. Thyra Hagen continued to sing and
even branched into theatre, playing Marguerite opposite Oskar Hagen's Faust

in a university production. As a child Uta Hagen also appeared on the university stage; at age fifteen she played beside her real-life brother, Holger, in a production of Noel Coward's *Hay Fever*. The university also provided a rich source of training for Hagen, who studied dance with visiting artists such as Harold Kreutzberg (with whose company she also toured) and **Hanya Holm**. In addition Hagen studied piano and recorder with private teachers.

Hagen's first love, however, was the theatre. According to her memoir, *Sources* (1983), her determination to become an actress began at age six, when she witnessed a performance of George Bernard Shaw's *Saint Joan* in a Berlin theatre. From then on she was fascinated by the theatre. In 1936, when she graduated from University High School, Hagen applied to the Royal Academy of Dramatic Art (RADA) in London. RADA initially rejected her but eventually admitted her to its Preparatory School, where she studied for one semester. During Christmas vacation Hagen returned to Madison, where, at the insistence of her father, she enrolled in the university.

During the spring of 1937 in what was to be her first and only semester of college, she wrote to **Eva Le Gallienne** (who seemed to Hagen to share her love of the European repertory) requesting an audition. Le Gallienne, by then a major figure in the American theatre, granted Hagen's request and was sufficiently impressed by the young actress to cast her as Ophelia in the upcoming production of *Hamlet* at the Cape Playhouse in Dennis, Massachusetts. Hagen's Ophelia drew praise from the Boston critics and from Le Gallienne, who invited the young actress to return in September as a member of a new repertory company. While this company failed to materialize, Le Gallienne remained a faithful mentor to the young actress.

Hagen then persuaded her parents to allow her to try her luck in New York. Her mother opposed the move, fearing that her daughter might stagnate artistically without further training. Hagen was adamant, however. RADA had not lived up to her expectations, and she was equally skeptical of what American drama schools had to offer. Finally, the family reached a compromise: Hagen would go to New York with $250 and return when and if her money ran out.

By Christmas the money was gone, but she had been signed with a casting agency and had made some valuable initial contacts, with the help of her father (who knew Lee Simonson and Thornton Wilder) and Le Gallienne. In January her parents allowed her to return to New York, and on March 28, 1938, she made a successful Broadway debut as Nina in the Alfred Lunt-**Lynn Fontanne** production of Anton Chekhov's *The Sea Gull*. When the show closed for the summer, Hagen went to Connecticut to play summer stock. There she met and fell in love with her leading man, José Ferrer. Hagen had been asked to rejoin the Lunts in September for a national tour of *The Sea Gull* and other plays. Prior to the Boston opening, however, she was summoned back to Madison, where her mother, who had been seriously ill, was dying. Two weeks after the death, Hagen returned to the company. She had not recovered from the loss, however, and she found the strain and loneliness of the tour unbearable. The Lunts refused to release her from her contract. They finally grudgingly agreed to release Hagen from all plays on the tour except for specific performances of *The Sea Gull*.

Two months later, Hagen married José Ferrer. There were two ceremonies, one on December 8, 1938, in a Catholic church and the other ten days later in the Little Church Around the Corner, an ''actor's'' church, where, out of respect for Hagen's father and her late mother, they had an Episcopalian service. Shortly after the marriage, Hagen starred on Broadway in Charlotte Armstrong's *The Happiest Days*. The critics disliked the play but praised her performance; as a consequence she received a number of film offers. Hagen was not particularly interested in making movies or in leaving her new husband, so when Hollywood invited her, she insisted that they also consider Ferrer. They went west but decided not to make films and returned to New York. In 1939 they appeared together on Broadway in Maxwell Anderson's *Key Largo* with Paul Muni. The play received mixed reviews, but Hagen was praised for her ''eloquence'' in the role of Alegre d'Alcala. They did not, however, do the national tour, since Hagen had become pregnant. On October 15, 1940, Hagen gave birth to their first and only child, Leticia Thyra. Although she initially intended to give up her career after the baby was born, Hagen soon became frustrated with full-time motherhood. In May of 1941 she rejoined her husband for the New York City ''subway circuit'' tour of *Charley's Aunt*, which had been a great vehicle for Ferrer on Broadway.

In the early days of their marriage, Hagen and Ferrer dreamed of becoming a creative team like the Lunts and were determined not to let their careers separate them. They appeared together at Suffern County Playhouse in *The Male Animal* and *The Guardsman*, which had been a successful vehicle for the Lunts. Ferrer next directed Hagen in *The Admiral Had A Wife*, a show that closed before its Broadway opening. The couple was not really recognized as an acting team, however, until S. M. Herzog's *Vickie* (1942), when they were hailed out of town as ''the second Lunts.'' But in New York, the critics praised Ferrer and Hagen's individual performances without allusion to their ability as an acting team. They next played Desdemona and Iago in America's first integrated production of *Othello*, starring Paul Robeson and directed by **Margaret Webster**. The show opened on Broadway in 1943 to great acclaim. Although generally well received, Hagen's performance was felt by some critics to be too one-dimensional. **Rosamond Gilder**, for instance, observed in *Theatre Arts*: ''The only positive element she brings to the scene is her fair fragility, but Desdemona is much more than fair and frail'' (December 1943, p. 702).

Although her Desdemona was less than an artistic triumph, Hagen's dedication to the production distinguished her as an actress of great conscience. It separated her from actresses who, fearing controversy, had refused the role. Hagen, having been raised in a liberal college community, had not anticipated the negative reactions that the integrated casting would cause; nonetheless, when circumstances demanded it, she rose to the occasion. Shocked by the prejudice encountered by Paul Robeson and by the hate mail she herself received, she took action. Political work became a priority, and she began to make speeches and do benefits not only for civil rights but for a wide variety of causes. Her political activism would later work against her when in the 1950s the House Un-American Activities Committee would investigate her "communist" background.

As the production of *Othello* ended, so did Hagen's marriage to Ferrer. His career was soaring while Hagen's was virtually at a standstill. Their dream of working together had dissolved, and in the fall of 1946 they separated, divorcing two years later. Meanwhile, Hagen was cast as the ingénue lead in *The Whole World Over*, a Soviet comedy by Konstantine Simonov, directed by Harold Clurman. Working with Clurman was a revelation for Hagen, who discovered that she had always worked externally, creating a mask for her character behind which she could hide. Clurman introduced Hagen to a more internal way of developing a character and, in doing so, reawakened her love for acting. "He took away my 'tricks,' " she wrote in *Respect for Acting* (1973), her handbook on the subject (p. 8).

The Whole World Over also introduced Hagen to Herbert Berghof, a distinguished actor and teacher, who was to be her second husband. Berghof helped her further to develop her acting technique and encouraged her to teach. In 1945 Berghof had opened his own acting studio, and in 1947 Hagen began to teach and act there. After her divorce from José Ferrer, she married Herbert Berghof on January 25, 1951.

In 1948 the Players from Abroad Company had signed Hagen to play opposite Albert Basserman, a renowned German actor, in a German language production of *Faust* and in Ibsen's *The Master Builder*. That same year, she took over the role of Blanche DuBois from **Jessica Tandy** in *A Streetcar Named Desire*. With the help of Harold Clurman, who directed the national tour, Hagen gave performances that were likened by critics to **Laurette Taylor**'s Amanda in *The Glass Menagerie*. The critical acclaim that Hagen received for *Streetcar* caused her career to surge forward. In 1950 she was cast as Georgie in Clifford Odets's *The Country Girl* and gave what many critics agreed was her best performance to date. For Georgie, she received the Donaldson Award, the Antoinette Perry (Tony) Award, and the New York Drama Critics *Variety* Poll Award. The next year she played the part that had first inspired her to become an actress, Shaw's *Saint Joan*. The production ran into difficulties, however, when the Theatre Guild, its producer, came under fire for hiring two alleged "communists," Hagen and director Margaret Webster. In 1952 Hagen returned to the stage to play Tatiana in Robert Sherwood's *Tovarich*. In 1956 she took on the dual leading role of Shen Te in the New York première of Bertolt Brecht's *The Good Woman of Setzuan*. That same year she played Natalia Petrovna in Ivan Turgenev's *A Month in the Country* both on stage and on television.

Her most memorable role was, perhaps, that of Martha in Edward Albee's *Who's Afraid of Virginia Woolf?* (1962), for which she again received a Tony Award and the *Variety* Poll as well as the Outer Circle Award. When she re-created the role in London in 1964, her portrayal of Martha was voted best female performance by the London critics.

After a twelve-year absence from the New York stage, during which time she had been teaching at the Herbert Berghof Studios, Hagen returned in 1980 in *Charlotte*, a play about Goethe's mistress that she and Berghof had translated from the German. *Charlotte* was essentially a one-woman show with Charles Nelson Reilly playing the silent husband. In 1985 she starred in the title role in Shaw's *Mrs. Warren's Profession* at New York's Roundabout Theatre. In 1986 Uta Hagen was awarded a Liberty Medal by New York City's Mayor Koch.

Hagen's contribution to the theatre lies not only in her stage work but also in her writing and in her teaching (Jack Lemmon, Jason Robards, Jr., and **Geraldine Page** were among her pupils). Her first book, *Respect for Acting* (written with Haskell Frankel and published in 1973), is a handbook for actors. Its basic premise is that acting is an art and a social offering; actors are not born but made, and talent brings with it responsibility. The book traces Hagen's own struggle with acting techniques and gives both practical and philosophical advice to the budding actor. Her 1983 *Sources* gives additional information about her life and her career. Hagen has earned her place in American theatre as an actress/ teacher wholly devoted to her craft.

The best biographical material on Uta Hagen can be found in Susan Spector, ''Uta Hagen: The Early Years'' (Unpublished Ph.D. dissertation, New York University, 1982), which deals with Hagen's life and career from 1919–1951. Biographical and theatre references may also be found in *Respect for Acting* (1973) and *Sources* (1983) by Uta Hagen. Hagen's experience with Eva Le Gallienne is described in Susan Spector and Steven Urkowitz, ''Uta Hagen and Eva Le Gallienne,'' *Women in American Theatre* (1981), edited by **Helen Krich Chinoy** and Linda Walsh Jenkins. There is a chapter on Uta Hagen in Rex Reed, *Conversations in the Raw* (1969). There is an interview with Hagen in *Playing Joan: Actresses on the Challenge of Shaw's Saint Joan, Twenty-Six Interviews* by Holly Hill (1987). See also *Theatre Arts* (November 1951) and *Time* (May 10, 1963). Clippings, scrapbooks, programs, and photographs can be found at the New York Public Library Performing Arts Research Center at Lincoln Center, in the collection of Theatre Guild Documents at Yale University, and in the Margaret Webster Theatre Collection at the Library of Congress in Washington, D.C. Hagen also has extensive personal archives. For further biographical information see *Who's Who of American Women, 1958–1959* (1958); *International Celebrity Register* (1959); *Who's Who in America, 1962–1963* (1962); *Current Biography, 1963* (1963–1964); *The Biographical Encyclopaedia and Who's Who of American Theatre* (1966); *Notable Names in American Theatre* (1976); *Who's Who in the Theatre* (1981); and *The Oxford Companion to American Theatre* (1984).

Brenda Gross

HALLAM, Eliza Tuke (1764?–1806?): leading actress in early America's foremost company for twenty years, is presumed to be American by birth. Eliza Tuke had appeared with Hallam's Old American Company for several years and had been the long-time companion of its leading man and manager, Lewis

Hallam, Jr., when she married him in Philadelphia, January 14, 1793, one month after the death of his estranged first wife, Sarah. He had been acting since his arrival in America in 1752 at the age of twelve when Lewis Hallam, Sr., launched "The Company of Comedians from London" in Williamsburg, Virginia.

The earliest known reference to Eliza Tuke appears in the list of members of the company reorganized by Hallam in 1784 after his return from Jamaica, where he had spent the Revolutionary War years. (The theatre had been outlawed by the Continental Congress of 1774.) She may have appeared earlier, however; she may have been the actress identified only as "Young Lady" who played Lady Frances Touchwood in Hallam's production of *The Belle's Stratagem* in Kingston, Jamaica, in 1781.

After a season in Philadelphia, the Old American Company settled into the John Street Theatre in New York in 1785, though they returned to play at Philadelphia's Southwark Theatre and also toured Baltimore and Richmond. Lewis and Eliza Tuke Hallam remained with the company until the 1805–1806 season, when a new incoming manager, Thomas A. Cooper, failed to renew their contracts.

William Dunlap, co-manager of the Old American Company from 1796 to 1799 and sole manager from 1799 to 1805, assessed Eliza Hallam in his *History of the American Theatre* as "young, comely and awkward. She afterwards became an actress of merit and improved in beauty and elegance" (p. 157). Her early reviews were not encouraging. An acerbic New York critic complained, "A manager's partiality has exposed that girl to a profession which to a woman can never be respected but by talent" (Wright, p. 219). As she gained experience and moved up in the company, critics noted her improvement, and she became quite a popular comedienne—as a soubrette rather than a leading lady. A typical role in her line was Cherry in George Farquhar's *The Beaux' Stratagem*. She was also a successful Lady Teazle in Richard Brinsley Sheridan's *The School for Scandal*. In 1804 she played Olivia in the first American performance of *Twelfth Night*.

Although a leading member of America's foremost company for twenty years, Eliza Hallam's claim to fame, unfortunately, is that she provoked the rupture in the company that finally resulted in her husband's giving up his share in the management in 1797, thus ending a forty-five-year tradition. In 1794 a young and talented actor, John Hodgkinson, bought a partnership in the company. He and his wife soon began to overshadow the Hallams in both repertoire and popularity. Whether or not this was the cause of Eliza Hallam's bout with "intemperance" at this time, by 1797 her frequent drunkenness affected her ability to perform and touched off backstage altercations. She was finally withdrawn from the stage at Hodgkinson's insistence. Shortly after, Eliza Hallam made an unscheduled appearance on-stage in the midst of Hodgkinson's performance in the comedy *The Fashionable Lover*. Dressed in black, she advanced to the footlights and begged the audience's permission to read a statement in her defense. She accused Hodgkinson of persecution. He was hissed off the stage on this occasion but was returned to the company by popular demand. On the occasion of her reappearance as Lady Teazle, she recited an apology in verse that concluded:

> On your indulgence still, I'll rest my cause
> Will you support me with your kind applause?
> You verify the truth in Pope's fine line —
> "To err is human; to forgive, divine."

(Dunlap, p. 386)

But soon after this victory Eliza Hallam had a relapse. Her husband, once the most prominent actor in America, had at the age of fifty-seven declined in skill as well as popularity. He relinquished his management at the end of the season, and when the company moved into the new Park Theatre in 1798, the Hallams were reengaged only as hired actors.

The final dismissal of the Hallams occasioned criticism of the new management from the press and public. On June 2, 1806, Lewis Hallam gave his farewell performance in New York in George Coleman and David Garrick's *The Clandestine Marriage*. Eliza Hallam played Mrs. Sterling in the benefit, her last known performance. Lewis Hallam gave two more benefits in Philadelphia, where he died in 1808. Eliza Hallam was then in her early forties. There are no further records for her, and the date of her death is unknown.

A portrait of Eliza Tuke Hallam in her youth shows an oval face with large eyes and a rosebud mouth, surrounded by a head of thick curls. In her heyday she inspired the following poem:

> Here beauty calls you at her enchanting name.
> What bosom feels not a restless claim?
> 'Tis Youth accosts you, whose persuasive strain,
> On years like yours can never call in vain: —
> 'Tis more—'tis love in these pictures shown,
> And fain would teach to make its joys your own.
> From scenes like these then, who could absence brook,
> When called by Love and Beauty and Miss Tuke.

(Seilhamer, p. 361)

William Dunlap presents a biased eyewitness account of Eliza Tuke Hallam's career in *History of the American Theatre* (1832). *Revels in Jamaica* (1937) by Richardson Wright documents the Hallam Company's stay there from 1775 to 1784, during which time Eliza Tuke may have first appeared. Arthur Hornblow, in *A History of the Theatre in America* (1919), discusses Eliza Hallam's dismissal from the American Company and documents her other appearances through 1804. George Seilhamer provides her most thorough biography in *History of the American Theatre Before the Revolution* (1888). George C. D. Odell's *Annals of the New York Stage*, Vol. 2 (1928) lists Mrs. Hallam's roles. Thomas Pollack's *The Philadelphia Theatre in the Eighteenth Century* (1933) contributes a record of the wedding announcement of Lewis Hallam, Jr.

Constance Clark

HALLAM, Mrs. Lewis, Sr. (d. 1774): leading actress in Colonial America for twenty-two years, and yet her maiden and proper names are unknown. The Hallams were a virtual theatrical dynasty in the English theatre from the 1730s. There were at times as many as a half dozen Hallams in a given company, and the custom of not listing first names on playbills adds to the difficulty of sorting them out. A Hallam genealogy gives "Miss Rich" as a tentative maiden name for Mrs. Lewis Hallam, later Mrs. Douglass, since she is said to have been related to John Rich, manager of Covent Garden. The first certain reference to "our" Mrs. Hallam, however, is as Miranda in Susannah Centlivre's *The Busy Body* at the New Wells Theatre on Leman Street in Goodman's Fields, London, February 9, 1745. It is noted as "being the first time of her performing on that stage" (*Theatre Survey*, May 1970, p. 23). It is unlikely this was her debut, since she shortly became a mainstay of the company, carrying a full line of twenty-three major roles. She had also been married to Lewis Hallam for some time; her daughter (Helen?) would have been seven years old, Lewis Jr. four, and Adam two. She may have already been an actress when Hallam met her. Though she is presumed to have been born in London, her career may have taken her to the provincial theatres in Bristol, Bath, or Birmingham before her London stage appearance.

As first leading lady at the New Wells Theatre, Mrs. Hallam played Angelica in William Congreve's *Love for Love*, Imoinda in Thomas Southerne's adaptation of Aphra Behn's novel *Oroonoko*, Miranda in *The Tempest*, Monimia in Thomas Otway's *The Orphan*, and many other roles. As an ingénue she specialized in the softer, more sentimental heroines, with an occasional departure into a femme fatale such as Milwood in George Lillo's *George Barnwell; or, The London Merchant*. She chose Desdemona in *Othello* for her benefit performance just before the New Wells Theatre went bankrupt in 1751. Her husband, Lewis Hallam, whose usual line was as a low comedian, played Iago. One of the causes of the company's demise was the harassment they had been subjected to for years for operating in violation of the Licensing Act of 1737, which had outlawed all theatres in London except the two patent houses, Drury Lane and Covent Garden.

That turn of events gave birth to manager William Hallam's scheme of sending a company, headed by his brother Lewis, to the New World. Taking their three eldest children with them, the Hallams embarked on a sailing ship in the spring of 1752. They brought a company of ten addditional actors, sundry properties and costumes, and a repertoire of twenty-four plays, ranging from Shakespeare's tragedies to contemporary farces by David Garrick. Rehearsals were conducted on deck (weather permitting) during the six-week crossing. "The Company of Comedians from London" opened at Williamsburg, Virginia, September 15,

1752, with Mrs. Hallam making her American debut as Portia in *The Merchant of Venice*.

After a successful season at Williamsburg, the Hallams moved on to New York where they built a theatre on Nassau Street and managed to open after some civic and religious opposition. After her opening performance as Indiana in Richard Steele's moralistic comedy *The Conscious Lovers*, Mrs. Hallam marked the occasion with an original epilogue addressed "To the Ladies." The next year, in Quaker Philadelphia there were petitions and even rioting against the theatre. Mrs. Hallam again spoke an epilogue in defense of the moral efficacy of stage plays. They played in Plumstead's Warehouse, refurbished as a theatre.

After a season in Charleston from October through December 1754, the company sailed for Jamaica, which was a thriving colonial center known to be receptive to players. In fact, there was a troupe already there, whose ranks had been depleted by yellow fever. This company and the Hallam Company joined forces. When Lewis Hallam himself succumbed and died in 1756, Mrs. Hallam appointed an actor from England, David Douglass, as manager. After two years she married Douglass, and they returned to the mainland. Douglass, an efficient and enterprising manager, is said to have been a gentleman by descent and education. Lewis Hallam, Jr., now eighteen, was promoted to leading man of the revamped company, actually playing Romeo to his mother's Juliet. Although Mrs. Hallam, now Mrs. Douglass, gradually gave up her ingénue roles to other actresses, assuming more stately parts such as Gertrude in *Hamlet*, she did not relinquish Juliet until 1766.

Obtaining with difficulty a permit back in New York, the company opened in January 1759 with Mrs. Douglass as the pathetic heroine in Nicholas Rowe's *Jane Shore*. There followed seasons in Philadelphia, Annapolis, Williamsburg, and Newport, developing a "circuit" for the company. In 1763 the successful troupe further ingratiated itself with its public, when, sensitive to growing anti-British, prerevolutionary sentiments, it changed its name to the American Company.

In 1764 the Douglasses visited England again, presumably to recruit new talent for the company. Mrs. Douglass would have had the opportunity to see her daughter Isabella, whom she had left behind and who was now the famous Mrs. Mattocks of Covent Garden who had debuted in 1761 as Juliet.

Yet another Hallam appeared as a leading lady in the American Company after the Douglasses' return to America in 1765. This is said to be Nancy, the daughter of William Hallam. This Miss Hallam, a gifted singer and actress, was extremely popular with the public. Poems were published in her praise, and the eminent painter Charles Wilson Peale painted her portrait as Imogen in *Cymbeline*, one of the many "breeches" parts that were her trademark.

Toward the end of her career Mrs. Douglass handed even her mature leading roles, such as Lady Macbeth, over to others, and she played character parts thereafter. Her last known performance was as Lady Rusport in Richard Cumberland's *The West Indian* in Charleston in 1773. The season had been a successful one, but Mrs. Douglass had been ill during much of it. A premature obituary was printed in Rivington's *Gazette*, and Mrs. Douglass was thus able to learn in her lifetime the esteem in which she was held. It read: "Last week died at Philadelphia Mrs. Douglass, wife of Mr. Douglass, manager of the American Company of Comedians, mother of Mr. Lewis Hallam and of Mrs. Mattocks, of Covent Garden Theatre, and aunt of Miss Hallam; a lady who, by her excellent performances upon the stage and her irreproachable manners in private life, had recommended herself to the friendship and affection of many of the principal families on the Continent and in the West Indies" (Seilhamer, p. 338). In fact, Mrs. Douglass died in a house near Philadelphia's Southwark Theatre in 1774, sometime before the Continental Congress's banning of public entertainments. She had been complaining for quite a while of a "hurt she received in the theatre" (Seilhamer, p. 339).

There is only one eyewitness report of Mrs. Hallam/ Douglass's acting, and that observation was made very late in her career. In Alexander Graydon's *Memoirs* she is described as "a respectable matron-like dame, stately or querulous as occasion required, a very good Gertrude, a truly appropriate Lady Randolph (in John Home's *Douglas*) with her white handkerchief and her weeds; but then, to applaud, it was absolutely necessary to forget, that to touch the heart of the spectator had any relation to her function" (*Memoirs*, p. 76). William Dunlap, who knew Lewis Hallam, Jr., reported in his *History of the American Theatre*: "The writer has heard old ladies speak, almost in raptures, of the beauty and grace of Mrs. Douglass and the pathos of her personation of Jane Shore" (p. 40).

Mrs. Hallam/Douglass's contribution to the American theatre speaks directly through her story. She and her manager-husbands broke the ground to establish theatre in the New World, and through their tenacity developed a theatregoing public. Mrs. Hallam/Douglass played to audiences as disparate as Cherokee royalty and George Washington; she was dubbed the "Queen Mother of the American Stage" (Wright, p. 43). Through her own personal example she made the once-suspect theatre respectable. Finally, her son, Lewis Hallam, Jr., became the most prominent and popular actor of his time, carrying on the family tradition into the nineteenth century.

Philip Highfill, Jr.'s article "The British Background of the American Hallams," *Theatre Survey* 11 (May 1970), describes Mrs. Hallam's importance in the Goodman's Fields Company in London, listing her roles. William Dunlap's *History of the American Theatre* (1832), a contemporary account, is anecdotal and opinionated but remains the primary source for the history of the company and characters of its members. Hugh Rankin's *The Theatre in Colonial America* (1965) traces the Hallam Company from their arrival in 1752 to their departure for Jamaica in 1775, by documentation from colonial newspapers, playbills, and litigations. Arthur Hornblow's *A History of the Theatre in America* (1919) treats the Hallam Company through their return from Jamaica in 1785. George O. Seilhamer's *History of the American Theatre Before the Revolution*, Vol. I (1888), is a well-documented account with painstaking research for missing information on Mrs. Hallam, including a complete list of her known roles. In *Revels in Jamaica*

(1937), Richardson Wright culled island records, histories, and Jamaican newspapers to fill out the account of the two Hallam visits in 1755 and 1775. George C. D. Odell's *Annals of the New York Stage*, Vol. I (1927), records Mrs. Hallam's New York appearances. See also Dorothy C. Barch, ed., *William Dunlap, Diary* (1930); Thomas C. Pollock, *The Philadelphia Theatre in the Eighteenth Century* (1933); and Arthur Hobson Quinn, *A History of the American Drama From the Beginning to the Civil War* (1943). Mrs. Hallam is listed in *Notable American Women*, Vol. II (1971); *The Oxford Companion to the Theatre* (1983); and *The Oxford Companion to American Theatre* (1984).

Constance Clark

HANKS, Nancy (December 31, 1927–January 7, 1983): arts advocate, federal official, foundation executive, and first woman chair of the National Endowment for the Arts, was born in Miami Beach, Florida, daughter of Bryan Cayce and Virginia (Wooding) Hanks. Nancy Hanks attributed her interest in public service to her father, a successful investment attorney and onetime president of Florida Power and Light Company, who was active in civic affairs. The older of two children, Nancy survived her younger brother, who was killed in an automobile accident at the age of eighteen.

During her school years the family moved to Montclair, New Jersey, where she attended high school. When her family subsequently moved to Texas, Nancy Hanks remained behind to attend Duke University in Durham, North Carolina. Before she graduated magna cum laude with a Bachelor of Arts degree in political science in 1949, she spent one summer at the University of Colorado, her parents' alma mater, and another at Oxford University in England.

In 1951, two years after her graduation from Duke, she took a position in the Office of Defense Mobilization. Then in 1953 she joined the staff of the President's Advisory Committee on Government Organization and became secretary to Committee Chairman Nelson Rockefeller. When Rockefeller was named undersecretary of the Department of Health, Education, and Welfare, Hanks joined the HEW staff as his secretary (1953–1954) and accompanied him as his assistant when he moved to the Special Projects Office of the White House in 1955. She remained Rockefeller's assistant until 1959; when he left government service, Hanks joined the staff of the Rockefeller Brothers Fund, where she worked from 1956 until 1969. In addition to serving there as staff coordinator for several projects, she coordinated the landmark study *The Performing Arts: Problems and Prospects*, through which she acquired an impressive grounding in the performing arts. The conclusions of the study were not surprising: private enterprise, individual benefactors, and government at all levels must unite to subsidize the arts and to make them available to all citizens of the United States if its cultural heritage is to survive.

Meanwhile, the federal government had created the National Council on the Arts in 1964 and the National Endowments for the Arts and for the Humanities in 1965. President Lyndon B. Johnson appointed Roger L. Stevens, theatrical producer and arts patron, to chair both the council and the Arts Endowment.

Stevens had proved a potent lobbyist for the formation of these organizations, but neither he nor the Democratic administration had succeeded in wresting more than a miniscule appropriation from the Congress.

With the election of President Richard M. Nixon and the return to power of the Republican party came the obvious need for a new endowment chairman, one closer to the hearts of Republican politicians than the well-known Democratic fund raiser Stevens. In 1967 Nancy Hanks had been elected chair of the Associated Councils of the Arts, a nonprofit organization serving state and community arts councils and national arts institutions. A Republican, well known in arts administration circles, and experienced in the ways of government and foundation operation, Hanks was not only a logical choice for the federal post but a serendipitous one. Energetic, intelligent, dedicated to her work, Hanks would succeed in unlocking the pockets of the United States Congress.

In 1969 Nixon appointed Hanks to a four-year term as chair of both the National Council on the Arts and the National Endowment for the Arts. Hanks found herself in charge of an organizational budget so small as to be laughable by government standards. (For fiscal year 1969 the NEA appropriation was $7,756,875.) Her first task, therefore, was to persuade Congress and the President to increase the agency's funding. In addition to her considerable persuasive skills and her understanding of the political process, Hanks had personal access to the President through Leonard Garment, special assistant to Nixon, a former professional musician, and a personal friend of Michael Straight, Hanks's deputy. Though during his campaign Nixon, in response to a questionnaire from the National Council on the Arts and Government (an arts lobby), had declared that the arts were primarily an individual matter to be fostered by local and private efforts, Hanks and Garment persuaded Nixon not only to request but to support increased funding. In 1971 President Nixon declared his support publicly and issued a memorandum to all government agencies and departments asking for an all-out effort by each organization to determine how it might both help and benefit from the arts. When Hanks's first term expired, Nixon reappointed her and gave a public endorsement of her work.

In the congressional arena Hanks was a master lobbyist. She understood that Congress responded to constituent demands. After one congressman complained that constituents did not seem particularly concerned about the arts since they never wrote expressing interest, Hanks had notices placed on the seats of theatres and concert halls to generate a landslide of appeals to the reluctant congressman. After sifting through his mail, he shed his reluctance. She and her deputy Michael Straight wined and dined congressmen, using the opportunity to explain the endowment's programs, its goals and accomplishments, and its impact in the appropriate congressional district. Hanks made sure that senators and representatives were notified of grants awarded in their districts, so that they could take credit for benefits to their constituents. Her tactics paid off. The endowment's budget grew to almost $100 million during her two terms as chair, and that growth was directly attributed to her efforts.

Perhaps her greatest accomplishment was her successful defense of government's financial support of the arts without censorship of their content. On several occasions the endowment faced public and congressional attack because the work of a grantee was judged to be tasteless, offensive, or lacking in artistic merit. Hanks argued and won the case that the endowment's mandate provided for the creative independence of the grant recipient, and this victory greatly reduced any public relations damage to her organization.

An indefatigable worker, Hanks made the endowment the focus of her life, with virtually every waking hour given to its management. She gathered about her a cadre of dedicated allies. Program directors were selected from ranks of practicing artists, arts administrators, and educators. The team had a sense of pioneer spirit, for they were creating a new organizational structure and designing programs such as no federal agency had ever administered. In later years those involved in this burst of creative energy would refer to Hanks's eight-year tenure as the golden years of the endowment. At the completion of her term in 1977, Hanks's name and the agency had become practically synonymous.

Under Nancy Hanks the endowment expanded its concept of the arts by establishing funding categories for museums, architecture and environmental arts, and expansion arts. "Expansion arts" was the designation for support of the artistic expressions indigenous to particular segments of the society, such as minorities, American Indians, and rural and inner-city dwellers. In addition, the program activities for the more traditional art forms (music, dance, and theatre) multiplied. Hanks was particularly proud of the expansion of the Artists-in-Schools Program, which permitted artists, actors, sculptors, filmmakers, poets, and musicians to visit schools throughout the country and introduce students to the arts and artists.

The endowment's encouragement and assistance in the creation of state arts councils and its financial support of theatres across the country rather than just in the traditional commercial theatre center of New York City were key factors in the growth and expansion of American regional theatre. Grants were provided for the production of new plays, for staff and audience development, and for educational and community service. With theatres as with all arts organizations, Hanks and the endowment encouraged management to emphasize long-range financial planning and facilitated such efforts. While matching grants forced theatres to develop local funding sources, they also stimulated local recognition and support by signifying the endowment's interest.

When she left the chairmanship in 1977 upon the election of Democratic President Jimmy Carter, she did not want to take on another equally demanding full-time position. She chose instead to divide her time among a wide range of activities—many associated with education and the arts, but a significant number emphasizing her interest in the environment.

In 1962 Hanks had had a mastectomy. A decade later the cancer recurred, but Hanks refused to be intimidated. She continued her grueling work schedule and acknowledged her condition only to a few close friends. Even during her last hospitalization, she continued to speak in terms of future plans. She succumbed to cancer at age fifty-five on January 7, 1983, at Columbia Presbyterian Hospital in New York City. Though Hanks made her home in Washington, D.C., she was buried in the family plot at Gatesville, Texas, in a private ceremony. Memorial services for Nancy Hanks, an Episcopalian, were held at the Cathedral of St. John the Divine in New York, the National Cathedral in Washington, D.C., the Mark Taper Forum in Los Angeles, and at her beloved Duke University; these were attended by statesmen, politicians, educators, and representatives of the world of the arts for which she had labored so earnestly. In a memorial tribute to Hanks, **Ruth Mayleas**, director of the endowment's Theatre Program under Hanks, attributed the growth and development in the field of theatre during Hanks's tenure to the increased funding and enlarged visibility that Hanks brought to the arts.

At the time of her death Hanks was vice chairman of the Rockefeller Brothers Fund and a director of Conoco, Incorporated, the Equitable Life Assurance Society of the United States, and Scholastic, Incorporated. In addition she was regent of the Smithsonian Institution, a trustee of Duke University and the Conservation Foundation, a director of Arts International, and a member, director, or trustee of fifteen other organizations.

She held twenty-six honorary degrees from colleges and universities such as Princeton, Yale, Radcliffe, Notre Dame, and the Conservatory of Music of Puerto Rico. Among her many awards were the Smithson Medal of the Smithsonian Institution, the Bronze Medallion from the City of New York, and the Golden Baton Award from the American Symphony Orchestra. The honor that she would perhaps have appreciated most was awarded posthumously. On February 15, 1985, Congress passed legislation designating the renovated Old Post Office building and its grounds as the Nancy Hanks Center, commemorating the time and energy she had spent in saving it from demolition and in encouraging its renovation.

Nancy Hanks's personal papers are deposited with Duke University. "The Friends of the Nancy Hanks Center" are completing oral histories that will also be housed at Duke. "The Friends" have prepared an orientation program and a film, *All But Condemned* (Vision, Inc.), about Hanks and the center. Hanks's official papers from her years at the National Endowment for the Arts have been deposited at the National Archives. Copies of some of Hanks's speeches and press clippings may be found at the library of the National Endowment for the Arts. A recent biography is *Nancy Hanks: An Intimate Portrait* (1989) by Michael Straight, who was Hanks's deputy chairman during her two terms at the National Endowment for the Arts. Margaret Wyszomirski of Georgetown University's Department of Government is working on a biography of Hanks. Secondary sources are somewhat limited. The most lengthy treatment to date of Hanks's years at the endowment is contained in *The Arts at a New Frontier* (1984) by Fannie Taylor and Anthony L. Barresi. Michael Straight, Hanks's deputy chairman, offers insights into some of the colorful events and problems faced by Hanks and the endowment in his book, *Twigs for An Eagle's Nest: Government and the Arts 1965–1978* (1979). Two articles are helpful: "She's an Artist at Getting Money for the Arts," by Andrew Glass in the

New York Times (December 14, 1975), and "Nancy Hanks, Nancy Hanks," by Laurence Leamer for the *Washingtonian* (March 1977). Hanks's own published writings include "Government and the Arts," *Saturday Review* (February 28, 1970); "The Arts in America: A Single Fabric," *Museum News* (November 1973); "In Support of Freedom," *Parks and Recreation* (August 1971); "Shall We Ration the Arts?" *Foundation News* (March 1968); "The Arts in the Schools—A Two-Hundred-Year Struggle," *American Education* (July 1975); "The Arts: National Resources," *Cultural Affairs* (Spring 1970); and "The University and the Arts," Office of Information Services, Texas Technical University, Lubbock, Texas, which is the first address of the Alcoa Distinguished Lecture Series sponsored by Alcoa Foundation, April 7, 1975. Nancy Hanks is included in *Who's Who of American Women, 1975–1976* (1975), and *Current Biography, 1971* (1971–1972).

Margaret M. Tocci

HANSBERRY, Lorraine (May 19, 1930–January 12, 1965): celebrated black playwright, was born in Chicago, Illinois, and died in New York City at the age of thirty-four after a scant six years in the professional theatre. Her first produced play, *A Raisin in the Sun*, has become an American classic, enjoying numerous productions since its original presentation in 1959 and many professional revivals during its twenty-fifth anniversary year in 1983–1984. The roots of Hansberry's artistry and activism lie in the city of Chicago, her early upbringing, and her family.

Lorraine Vivian Hansberry was the youngest of four children; seven or more years separated her from Mamie, her sister and closest sibling, and two older brothers, Carl Jr. and Perry. Her father, Carl Augustus Hansberry, was a successful real estate broker who had moved to Chicago from Mississippi after completing a technical course at Alcorn College. A prominent businessman, he made an unsuccessful bid for Congress in 1940 on the Republican ticket and contributed large sums to causes supported by the NAACP and the Urban League. Hansberry's mother, Nannie Perry, was a school teacher and later ward committeewoman who had come north from Tennessee after completing teacher training at Tennessee Agricultural and Industrial University. The Hansberrys were at the center of Chicago's black social life and often entertained important political and cultural figures who were visiting the city. Through her uncle, Leo Hansberry, professor of African history at Howard University, Hansberry made early acquaintances with young people from the African continent.

Despite the Hansberrys' middle-class status, they were subject to the racial segregation and discrimination characteristic of the period and were active in opposing it. Restrictive covenants, in which white home-owners agreed not to sell their property to blacks, created a ghetto which was known as the "Black Metropolis" in the midst of Chicago's South Side. Although large numbers of blacks continued to migrate to the city, restrictive covenants kept the boundaries static, creating serious housing problems. Carl Hansberry knew well the severe overcrowding in Black Metropolis. He had, in fact, made much of his money by purchasing large, older houses vacated by the retreating white population and dividing them into small apartments, each one with its own kitchenette. Thus he earned the title "kitchenette king." In *A Raisin in the Sun*, Lorraine Hansberry used this type of apartment as the setting for her play, with the struggle for better housing as the driving action of her plot.

Hansberry attended public schools, graduating from Betsy Ross Elementary School and then from Englewood High School in 1947. Breaking with the family tradition of attending southern black colleges, Hansberry chose to attend the University of Wisconsin at Madison, moving from the ghetto schools of Chicago to a predominantly white university. She integrated her dormitory, becoming the first black to live at Langdon Manor. The years at Madison gave sharper focus to her political views as she worked in the Henry Wallace presidential campaign and in the activities of the Young Progressive League, becoming president of the organization in 1949, during her last semester there. Her artistic sensibilities were heightened by a university production of Sean O'Casey's *Juno and the Paycock*. She was deeply moved by O'Casey's ability to universalize the suffering of the Irish without sacrificing specificity and later wrote: "The melody was one that I had known for a very long while. I was seventeen and I did not think then of writing the melody as I knew it—in a different key; but I believe it entered my consciousness and stayed there" (*To Be Young, Gifted and Black*, p. 87). She would capture that suffering in the idiom of the Negro people in her first produced play, *A Raisin in the Sun*. In 1950 she left the university and moved to New York City for an education of another kind.

In Harlem she began working on *Freedom*, a progressive newspaper founded by Paul Robeson, and turned the world into her personal university. In 1952 she became associate editor of the newspaper, writing and editing a variety of news stories that expanded her understanding of domestic and world problems. Living and working in the midst of the rich and progressive social, political, and cultural elements of Harlem stimulated Hansberry to begin writing short stories, poetry, and plays. On one occasion she wrote the pageant that was performed to commemorate the *Freedom* newspaper's first anniversary. In 1952 while covering a picket line protesting discrimination in sports at New York University, Hansberry met Robert Barron Nemiroff, a white student of Jewish heritage who was attending the university. They dated for several months, participating in political and cultural activities together. They married on June 20, 1953, at the Hansberry family home in Chicago. The young couple took various jobs during these early years. Nemiroff was a part-time typist, waiter, Multilith operator, reader, and copywriter. Hansberry left the *Freedom* staff in 1953 in order to concentrate on her writing and for the next three years worked on three plays while holding a series of jobs: tagger in the garment industry, typist, program director at Camp Unity (a progressive, interracial summer program), teacher at the Marxist-oriented Jefferson School for Social Science, and recreation leader for the handicapped.

A sudden change of fortune freed Hansberry from these odd jobs. Nemiroff and his friend Burt d'Lugoff wrote a folk ballad, "Cindy Oh Cindy," which quickly became a hit. The money from that hit song allowed Hansberry to quit her jobs and to devote full time to her writing. She began to write *The Crystal Stair*. This play about a struggling black family in Chicago would eventually become *A Raisin in the Sun*.

Drawing on her knowledge of working-class blacks who had rented from her father and with whom she had attended school on Chicago's South Side, Hansberry wrote a realistic play whose theme was inspired by Langston Hughes, who, in his poem "Harlem," asks: "What happens to a dream deferred . . . Does it dry up like a raisin in the sun . . . Or does it explode?" Hansberry read a draft of the play to several colleagues. On one such occasion Phil Rose, a friend who had employed Nemiroff in his music publishing firm, optioned the play for Broadway production. Although he had never produced a Broadway play before, Rose and co-producer David S. Cogan set forth enthusiastically with their fellow novices on this new venture. They approached major Broadway producers, but the "smart money" considered a play about blacks too risky a venture for Broadway. The only interested producer insisted on changes in director and cast that were unacceptable to Hansberry. So the group raised the cash through other means and took the show on tour without guarantee of a Broadway house. Audiences in the tour cities—New Haven, Philadelphia, and Chicago—were ecstatic about the show. A last minute rush for tickets in Philadelphia finally made the case for acquiring a Broadway theatre.

A Raisin in the Sun opened at the Ethel Barrymore Theatre on March 11, 1959, and was an instant success with both critics and audiences. New York critic Walter Kerr praised Hansberry for reading "the precise temperature of a race at that time in its history when it cannot retreat and cannot quite find the way to move forward. The mood is forty-nine parts anger and forty-nine parts control, with a very narrow escape hatch for the steam these abrasive contraries build up. Three generations stand poised, and crowded, on a detonating-cap" (*New York Herald Tribune*, March 22, 1959). Hansberry became a celebrity overnight. The play was awarded the New York Drama Critics Circle Award in 1959, making Lorraine Hansberry the first black, the youngest person, and the fifth woman to win that award.

In 1960 NBC producer Dore Schary commissioned Hansberry to write the opening segment for a television series commemorating the Civil War. Her subject was to be slavery. Hansberry thoroughly researched the topic. The result was *The Drinking Gourd*, a television play that focused on the effects that slavery had on the families of the slave master and the poor white as well as the slave. The play was deemed by NBC television executives as too controversial and, despite Schary's objections, was shelved along with the entire project.

Hansberry was successful, however, in bringing her prize-winning play, *A Raisin in the Sun*, to the screen a short time later. In 1959, a few months after the play opened, she sold the movie rights to Columbia Pictures and began work on drafts of the screenplay, incorporating several new scenes. These additions, which were rejected for the final version, sharpened the play's attack on the effects of segregation and revealed with surer hand the growing militant mood of blacks. After many revisions and rewrites, the film was produced with all but one of the original cast and released in 1961. The film was widely acclaimed and was invited for screening at the Cannes Film Festival in 1961.

In the wake of the play's extended success, Hansberry became a public figure and popular speaker at a number of conferences and meetings. Among her most notable speeches is one delivered to a black writers' conference sponsored by the American Society of African Culture in New York. Written during the production of *A Raisin in the Sun* and delivered March 1, 1959—two weeks before the Broadway opening—"The Negro Writer and His Roots" is in effect Hansberry's credo. In this speech, now published in *The Black Scholar* (March/April 1981) as an essay, Hansberry declares that "all art is ultimately social" and calls upon black writers to be involved in "the intellectual affairs of all men, everywhere." As the civil rights movement intensified, Hansberry helped to plan fund-raising events to support organizations such as the Student Non-violent Coordinating Committee (SNCC). Disgusted with the redbaiting of the McCarthy Era, she called for the abolition of the House Un-American Activities Committee and criticized President John F. Kennedy's handling of the Cuban Missile Crisis, arguing that his actions endangered world peace.

In 1961, despite the many requests for public appearances, a number of which she accepted, Hansberry began work on several plays. Her next stage production, *The Sign in Sydney Brustein's Window*, appeared in 1964. Before that, however, she finished a favorite project, *Masters of the Dew*, adapted from the Haitian novel by Jacques Romain. A film company had asked her to do the screenplay; however, contractual problems prevented the production from proceeding. The next year, seeking rural solitude, she purchased a house in Croton-on-Hudson, forty-five minutes from Broadway, in order to complete work on *The Sign in Sidney Brustein's Window*.

Early in April 1963, Hansberry fainted. Hospitalized at University Hospital in New York City for nearly two weeks, she underwent extensive tests. The results suggested cancer of the pancreas. Despite the progressive failure of her health during the next two years, she continued her writing projects and her political activities. In May of 1963, she was invited to join writer James Baldwin, singers Harry Belafonte and Lena Horne, and other individuals, both black and white, in a meeting in New York City with Attorney General Robert Kennedy to discuss the escalating protests and violence in the South. She also organized a meeting in Croton to raise funds for SNCC and a rally to support the southern freedom movement. Although her health was in rapid decline, she greeted 1964 as a year of glorious work. On her writing schedule, in addition to *The Sign in Sidney Brustein's Window*, were *Les Blancs*, *Laughing Boy* (an adaptation of the novel into a musical), *The Marrow of Tradition*, *Mary Wollstonecraft*, and *Achnaton*, a play about the Egyptian Pharoah. Despite frequent hospitalization and bouts with pain and attendant medication, she completed a photo-essay for a book on the civil rights struggle titled *The Movement: Documentary of a Struggle for Equality* (1964).

Then, in March of 1964, she quietly divorced Robert Nemiroff, formalizing the separation that had occurred several years earlier. Only close friends and family had known; their continued collaboration as theatre artists and activists masked the reality of their personal relationship. Those outside their close circle would learn about the divorce only when Hansberry's will was read in 1965.

Throughout 1964, hospitalizations became more frequent as the cancer spread. In May she left the hospital to deliver a speech to the winners of the United Negro College Fund's writing contest for which she coined the now-famous phrase, "Young, gifted and black." A month later she left her sickbed to participate in the Town Hall debate, "The Black Revolution and the White Backlash," at which she and her fellow black artists challenged the criticism by white liberals of the growing militancy of the civil rights movement. She also managed to complete *The Sign in Sidney Brustein's Window*, which opened to mixed reviews on October 15, 1964, at the Longacre Theatre. Critics were somewhat surprised by this second play from a woman who had come to be identified with the black liberation movement. Writing about people she had known in Greenwich Village, Hansberry had created a play whose cast was primarily white and whose theme called for intellectuals to get involved in social problems and world issues.

On January 12, 1965, Lorraine Hansberry's battle with cancer ended. She died at University Hospital in New York City at the age of thirty-four. Her passing was mourned throughout the nation and in many parts of the world. The list of telegrams and cards sent to her family read like the Who's Who list of the civil rights movement and the American theatre. *The Sign in Sidney Brustein's Window* closed on the night of her death.

Hansberry left a number of finished and unfinished projects; among them: *Laughing Boy*, the book for a musical adapted from Oliver LaFarge's novel; an adaptation of *The Marrow of Tradition* by Charles Chesnutt; a film version of *Masters of the Dew*, adapted from Jacques Romain's novel about Haiti; sections of a semi-autobiographical novel, *The Dark and Beautiful Warriors*; a number of essays, including a critical commentary written in 1957 on Simone de Beauvoir's *The Second Sex* (a book that Hansberry said had changed her life); and many other works. In her will she designated her former husband, Robert Nemiroff, as executor of her literary estate.

Hansberry's reputation has continued to grow since her death in 1965 as Nemiroff, who owns her papers, has edited, published, and produced her work posthumously. In 1969 he adapted some of her unpublished writings for the stage under the title, *To Be Young, Gifted and Black*. The longest-running drama of the 1968–1969 Off-Broadway season, it toured colleges and communities in the United States during 1970–1971; a ninety-minute film based on the stage play was first shown in January of 1972.

In 1970 Nemiroff produced on Broadway a new work by Hansberry, *Les Blancs*, a full-length play set in the midst of a violent revolution in an African country. Nemiroff then edited *Les Blancs: The Collected Last Plays of Lorraine*

Hansberry, which was published by Random House in 1972 and contained *Les Blancs*, *The Drinking Gourd*, and *What Use Are Flowers?*, a short play on the consequences of nuclear holocaust. In 1974 *A Raisin in the Sun* returned to Broadway as *Raisin*, the musical, produced by Robert Nemiroff; it won an Antoinette Perry (Tony) Award.

In 1987 *A Raisin in the Sun*, with original material restored, was presented at the Roundabout Theatre in New York, the Kennedy Center in Washington, D.C., and other theatres nationwide. In 1989 this production was presented on national television. In March 1988 *Les Blancs*, also with much of the original script restored, was presented at Arena Stage in Washington, D.C., the first professional production in 18 years.

Hansberry made a very significant contribution to American theatre, despite the brevity of her theatrical life and the fact that only two of her plays were produced during her lifetime. *A Raisin in the Sun* was more than a simple "first," to be commemorated in history books and then forgotten. The play was the turning point for black artists in the professional theatre. Authenticity and candor combined with timeliness to make it one of the most popular plays ever produced on the American stage. The original production ran for 538 performances on Broadway, attracting large audiences of whites and blacks alike. Also, in this play and in her second produced play, Hansberry offered a strong opposing voice to the drama of despair. She created characters who affirmed life in the face of brutality and defeat. Walter Younger in *A Raisin in the Sun*, supported by a culture of hope and aspiration, survives and grows; and even Sidney Brustein, lacking cultural support, resists the temptation to despair by a sheer act of will, by reaffirming his link to the human family.

With the growth of women's theatre and feminist criticism Hansberry has been rediscovered by a new generation of women in theatre. Indeed, a revisionist reading of her major plays reveals that she was feminist long before the women's movement surfaced. The female characters in her plays are pivotal to the major themes. They may share the protagonist role as in *A Raisin in the Sun*, where Mama is co-protagonist with Walter. Or a woman character may take the definitive action as in *The Drinking Gourd*, in which Rissa, the house slave, defies the slave system (and black stereotype) by turning her back on her dying master and arming her son for his escape to the North. In *The Sign in Sidney Brustein's Window*, Sidney is brought to a new level of self-awareness through the actions of a "chorus" of women—the Parodus Sisters. Likewise, the African woman dancer is ever present in Tshembe Matoeseh's mind in *Les Blancs*, silently and steadily moving him to a revolutionary commitment to his people. Hansberry's portrayal of Beneatha as a young black woman with aspirations to be a doctor, and her introduction of abortion as an issue for poor women in *A Raisin in the Sun* signaled early on Hansberry's feminist attitudes. These and other portrayals of women challenged prevailing stage stereotypes of both black and white females and introduced feminist issues to the stage in compelling terms. Recently uncovered documents revealing Hansberry's sensitivity to homophobic attitudes have further stimulated feminist interest in her work. As more of her papers are released by Robert Nemiroff for publication, the full scope of Lorraine Hansberry's work can be appreciated and assessed.

A recent reprint of *A Raisin in the Sun* and *The Sign in Sidney Brustein's Window*, edited by Robert Nemiroff (1987), contains restored material to both scripts, a foreword by Nemiroff, an appreciation by Frank Rich, and critical essays by Amiri Baraka and John Braine. Hansberry's published works appear in various English language editions (as well as in French, German, Japanese, and other languages). The uncompleted *Toussaint* appears in *9 Plays by Black Women*, edited by Margaret B. Wilkerson (1968). Selected periodical articles and other publications include: "Willy Loman, Walter Lee Younger and He Who Must Live," *Village Voice* (August 12, 1959); "On Summer," *Playbill* (June 27, 1960); "This Complex of Womanhood," *Ebony* (August 1960); "Images and Essences: 1961 Dialogue with an Uncolored Egghead Containing Wholesome Intentions and Some Sass," *Urbanite* (May 1961); "Genêt, Mailer and the New Paternalism," *Village Voice* (June 1, 1961); "A Challenge to Artists," *Freedomways* (Winter 1963); "The Black Revolution and the White Backlash (Transcript of Town Hall Forum)," *National Guardian* (July 1964); "The Nation Needs Your Gifts," *Negro Digest* (August 1964); "The Legacy of W. E. B. DuBois," *Freedomways* (Winter 1965); "Original Prospectus for the John Brown Memorial Theatre of Harlem," *Black Scholar* (July/August 1979); "The Negro Writer and His Roots: Toward a New Romanticism," *Black Scholar* (March/April 1981); "All the Dark and Beautiful Warriors," *Village Voice* (August 16, 1983); and "The Buck Williams Tennessee Memorial Association," *Southern Exposure* (September/October 1984). Audiovisual materials include "Lorraine Hansberry Speaks Out: Art and the Black Revolution" (record album), Caedmon Records (TC 1352, 1972); "Lorraine Hansberry: The Black Experience in the Creation of Drama," Princeton, New Jersey, Films for the Humanities (1976); *A Raisin in the Sun*, film (1961, distributed by Swann Films); and *To Be Young, Gifted and Black*, ninty-minute film (Production of NET, Educational Broadcasting Corp., 1972). The most extensive Hansberry bibliography to date is "Lorraine Hansberry: Art of Thunder, Vision of Light," *Freedomways* (special volume, fourth quarter, 1979). Hansberry is discussed in Loften Mitchell, *Black Drama: The Story of the American Negro in the Theatre* (1967), and C. W. E. Bigsby, *Confrontation and Commitment: A Study of Contemporary American Drama 1959–1960* (1968). She is included in *Current Biography, 1959* (1959–1960); *Who's Who of American Women, 1964–1965* (1963); *The Biographical Encyclopaedia and Who's Who of the American Theatre* (1966); *Who Was Who in America*, Vol. 4, *1961–1968* (1968); Michael Anderson, et al., *Crowell's Handbook of Contemporary Drama* (1971); *McGraw-Hill Encyclopedia of World Drama* (1972); Myron Matlaw, *Modern World Drama: An Encyclopedia* (1972); Robin May, *A Companion to the Theatre: The Anglo-American Stage from 1920* (1973); James A. Page, *Selected Black American Authors* (1977); *American Women Writers*, Vol. II (1980); *20th Century American Literature* (Great Writers Library, 1980); and *Dictionary of Literary Biography*, Vol. 7, *Twentieth-Century American Dramatists*, Part I (1981).

Margaret B. Wilkerson

HARDWICK, Elizabeth (July 27, 1916–): theatre critic, editor, novelist, essayist, and first woman to receive the George Jean Nathan Award for dramatic criticism, was born in Lexington, Kentucky, daughter of Eugene Allen and Mary

(Ramsay) Hardwick. She holds both bachelor's and master's degrees from the University of Kentucky, Lexington, and did further graduate work at Columbia University in New York City (1939–1941). She married poet Robert Lowell in 1949, and they had one daughter, Harriet. They divorced in 1972.

A well-known figure in artistic and literary circles, Elizabeth Hardwick has published novels, short stories, critical articles, and theatre reviews. She served as theatre critic for the *New York Review of Books* and *Vogue* magazine chiefly in the sixties and seventies. She edited an edition of William James's letters (1961) and eighteen volumes of *Rediscovered Fiction by American Women* (1977). In 1947, she was awarded a Guggenheim Fellowship in fiction and in 1967 received the George Jean Nathan Award for dramatic criticism—the first woman ever to be so honored. Since 1964, she has been adjunct professor of English literature at Barnard College in New York City. She holds an honorary degree from Smith College (1973) and in 1977 was elected to the Academy and Institute of Arts and Letters.

In March 1963, to fill the gap left by the printers' strike in New York City, she became one of the founding editors of the *New York Review of Books*, for which she remains advisory editor and a frequent contributor. For many years she also wrote essays and short stories for *The Partisan Review*, *The New Yorker*, *Vogue*, *Harper's*, and other magazines. Four of her short stories were chosen for reprinting in *Best American Short Stories* (1946, 1947, 1949, 1960).

From her earliest theatre reviews, Hardwick inveighed against the single influential daily critic for the *New York Times*, who wielded unprecedented power over the Broadway theatre. She called the power of such reviewers as Walter Kerr "a tyranny both peculiar and unnecessary" (*New York Review of Books*, October 20, 1966, p. 4).

Hardwick's theatre reviews were sharp and insightful, tending more to literary and sociological concerns than to performance values. However, in the 1960s she reviewed both Broadway and Off-off-Broadway theatre, prophesying the end of the **Lillian Hellman**-Tennessee Williams-Edward Albee era on Broadway with the appearance in 1965 of Peter Brook's production of *Marat/Sade*, with its inmates in tub-gray institutional smocks speaking of the deepest sexual fantasies of our time.

As a reviewer she also traveled Off-Broadway to Lincoln Center and to the lofts and churches of Greenwich Village in Manhattan. As early as 1967 she wrote of playwright Sam Shepard's prodigious "literary talent and dramatic inventiveness" (*New York Review of Books*, April 6, 1967, p. 6). Moreover, she praised the new style of Tom O'Horgan and Jerzy Grotowski at **Ellen Stewart**'s La Mama Experimental Theatre Club.

More recently, Hardwick has turned her critical sensibility to women writers and to women as dramatic characters. In *Seduction and Betrayal: Women and Literature* (1974), she discussed three of Henrik Ibsen's heroines: Nora Helmer, Hedda Gabler, and Rebecca West. "Ibsen seemed to have felt," she wrote, "a troubled wonder about women that made his literary use of them peculiar, original, and tentative—like a riddle'' (p. 34). Analyzing Ibsen's major female characters, she considered Nora Helmer's problem (in *A Doll's House*) as one of money; Rebecca West's (in *Rosmersholm*) as one of survival; and Hedda Gabler, always Ibsen's most intriguing heroine, as a figure of coolness and style. She wrote, ''*Hedda Gabler* is a strange play, about a stranger. What is wrong with her? Everything is wrong with her morally. She has no particular virtue to recommend her, but she does have an advantage, the advantage of style .... Hedda is cool—in the older sense of the word. She is not, by the exercise of control, disguising turbulence or ambition, or even need. Her indifference is real. She is not in love. No one in the play has deeply stirred her feelings. The failure or inability to care for anyone is the first condition of her nature ... It is the basis of her style'' (p.53).

Hardwick reappraised the ''radical undercurrent'' in Ibsen's realistic plays in relation to his choice of feminine characters. ''What newly strikes us about Ibsen may be just what we had a decade or so ago thought was stodgy about him— he sees women not only as individual characters and destinies caught up in dramatic conflict but also as a 'problem.' He seems alone, so far as I can remember, in suggesting that he has given thought to the bare fact of being born a woman'' (p.37).

Hardwick's reappraisal in 1974 of Ibsen's major female characters against the background of the contemporary feminist movement is her most recent work on the literature of the theatre. However, her theatre criticism written largely in the 1960s, in which she assessed a changing New York theatre scene and for which she received the George Jean Nathan Award for dramatic criticism, assure her a significant position among critics of the contemporary theatre scene.

Hardwick's major published works include novels: *The Ghostly Lover* (1945), *The Simple Truth* (1955), and *Sleepless Nights* (1979); collected essays: *A View of My Own* (1962), *Seduction and Betrayal* (1974), *Bartleby in Manhattan and Other Essays* (1983); and edited collections: *Selected Letters of William James* (1961) and eighteen volumes of *Rediscovered Fiction by American Women* (1977). Her major theatre criticism is to be found in *Vogue* during 1963 and 1964 and in the *New York Review of Books* between 1966 and 1983. Principal among these are reviews of Peter Weiss's *Investigation* (1966), Edward Albee's *A Delicate Balance* (1966), Harold Pinter's *The Homecoming* (1967), Sam Shepard's *La Turista* (1967), Arthur Kopit's *Indians* (1969), and Jerzy Grotowski's theatre (1970), and studies of Henrik Ibsen's women (1971–1983). Interviews with Elizabeth Hardwick include: Richard Locke, ''Conversation on a Book,'' *New York Times Book Review* (April 29, 1979); Francine Du Plessix Gray, ''Elizabeth Hardwick: A Fresh Way of Looking at Literature—And at Life,'' *Vogue* (June, 1979); and Joan Didion, ''Meditation on a Life,'' *New York Times Book Review* (April 29, 1979). She is also mentioned in Steven Gould Axelrod, *Robert Lowell: Life and Art* (1978). Hardwick is listed in *American Authors and Books, 1640 to the Present Day* (1972), *Who's Who of American Women, 1974–1975* (1973), *World Authors, 1950–1970* (1975), *International Authors and Writers Who's Who* (1977), *The Blue Book: Leaders of the English Speaking World* (1979), *Dictionary of Literary Biography* (1980), *Novels and Novelists* (1980), *American Women Writers*, Vol. II (1980), *Contemporary Literary Criticism* (1980),

Contemporary Authors (1981), *Current Biography, 1981* (1981–1982), *Who's Who in America, 1982–1983*, Vol. I (1982), and *The Writer's Directory, 1984–1986* (1983).

Milly S. Barranger

HARRIS, Julie (December 2, 1925–): leading stage and television character actress, was born in Grosse Pointe Park, Michigan, to William Pickett and Elsie (Smith) Harris. She was named Julie Ann. Her father was an investment banker, wealthy enough to pursue mammalogy as an avocation and to become associate curator of mammals at the University of Michigan's Zoology Museum. Her mother was trained as a nurse. Julie Harris grew up with two brothers.

From an early age she was determined to be an actress. Harris has admitted that assuming other identities through acting was her compensation for looking plain. Throughout her childhood and adolescence she believed herself to be skinny and awkward, and she was self-conscious about the braces on her teeth. While her mother wanted her to become involved in the social life of the affluent Detroit suburb in which they lived, all Harris really cared about were drama classes and after-school drama activities. She took singing and dancing lessons and, with her mother, went to performances of ballet and children's theatre. She became a movie addict and avid reader of biographies of great performers. At the age of ten she began attending performances of road companies that played the Cass Theatre in Detroit, enjoying the performances of such stage stars as Helen Hayes, Alfred Lunt and **Lynn Fontanne**, **Katharine Cornell**, Maurice Evans, and Al Jolson. She remembers vividly **Ethel Waters** singing "Taking a Chance on Love" in *Cabin in the Sky*. Years later, she would play her first important role with Ethel Waters in **Carson McCullers'** *The Member of the Wedding*.

At seventeen her parents sent her to a finishing school in Providence, Rhode Island, but later allowed her to transfer to Miss Hewitt's Classes, a New York school that offered a course in drama. Her summers were spent at a theatre camp in Steamboat Springs, Colorado, run by **Charlotte Perry** and **Portia Mansfield**. There she studied acting with Perry and dance with Valerie Bettis. With the encouragement of Charlotte Perry, Julie Harris auditioned for and was accepted into the Yale University School of Drama in the fall of 1944. During the spring term she took a leave of absence to make her Broadway debut in *It's a Gift* (1945). The play had a short run, and she went back to finish the year at Yale but did not return the following fall. Instead she became a working actress, playing walk-ons with the Old Vic Company and a series of small speaking roles. She was accepted as a member of the Actors Studio and earned a Theatre World Award as the most promising personality of the 1948–1949 season for the role of Ida Mae in the Actors Studio production of *Sundown Beach*.

Her career as an important character actress began in 1950. Except for a serious illness in 1982, she has performed constantly, mostly on the stage, where she has earned an unprecedented five Antoinette Perry (Tony) awards as best actress, and on television, where she has been a two-time Emmy winner. She has made films and records. While the majority of her appearances have been as the star of realistic dramas, she has acted Restoration comedy on Broadway and Shakespeare in Central Park and in Stratford, Canada. She has even appeared in musical comedy. Her most outstanding roles have been highly eccentric, independent characters whom she has made likable by her charm and by the clarity and forcefulness with which she illuminated their personalities: Emily Dickinson, Mary Todd Lincoln, Joan of Arc, Sally Bowles, and her first great success, Frankie Addams.

Harris was twenty-four years old when she played the twelve-year-old Frankie in Carson McCullers's *The Member of the Wedding* (1950). Her slight stature helped her portray the gawky, neurotic tomboy who wants to join her brother's impending wedding, honeymoon, and life thereafter. While reviewers found the material undramatic, more a novella than a play, they lauded Harris and fellow actors Brandon de Wilde and Ethel Waters. Brooks Atkinson (*New York Times*, January 6, 1950) praised Harris's "extraordinary performance—vibrant, full of anguish and elation, by turns rumpled, unstable, egotistic and unconsciously cruel." Robert Coleman (*Daily Mirror*, January 6, 1950) called her work "a bravura performance, an acting tour de force. It won cheers from the audience." It also won Harris the Donaldson Award.

Her next role was that of Sally Bowles in *I Am a Camera*, John Van Druten's adaptation of Christopher Isherwood's *Berlin Stories*. The *New York Journal-American* review (Robert Garland, November 29, 1951) summed up the critical consensus for the production in its headline: "Julie Harris Held Better Than Play." As Garland noted, "Sally Bowles is as far removed from . . . Frankie Addams as any character could be." Walter Kerr's praise (*New York Herald Tribune*, November 29, 1951) is perceptive: "In every scene of pretense, in every gay birdlike gesture, there is always the shadow of the heartbreaking figure Sally Bowles really is." Christopher Isherwood recalled meeting Harris for the first time, costumed as Sally Bowles for a publicity photo session: "This was not simply an actress dressed up as one of my characters. Here was something other, an independent presence which Julie, under John's [Van Druten] direction, had mediumistically produced" (*Isherwood*, by Jonathan Fryer, p. 242). The producers of *I Am a Camera* evidently agreed, for at the play's fiftieth performance, Julie Harris's name was placed above the title of the play on the theatre marquee; she was now a certified Broadway star. Her performance was recognized with the Donaldson Award, the New York Drama Critics Circle Award, and the Antoinette Perry (Tony) Award as the best actress of the 1951–1952 season. After the New York run Harris toured with *I Am a Camera* for eight months.

Although Julie Harris's talents contributed clearly to the artistic and box office success of both *The Member of the Wedding* and *I Am a Camera*, they did not sustain her next Broadway appearance in Jean Anouilh's *Mademoiselle Colombe* (1954). It ran less than two months, but Harris, in the title role, was again praised as a rare actress. Anouilh also provided Harris with her next vehicle: the role of Joan of Arc in **Lillian Hellman**'s adaptation of *The Lark* (1955). The play, using flashbacks to tell its story, characterizes a woman who, though her inspiration is divine, must call upon all the intelligence, physical strength, and charm she can muster. Reviewers devoted paragraphs of praise to Harris's performance. Perhaps the most graphic response (*New York Herald Tribune*, November 18, 1955) was Walter Kerr's: "Julie Harris has the precise combination of country-girl naiveté and irresistible boisterousness to speak this particular piece. There isn't a languid bone in her wired-together body, and she has a voice that would do credit to the noisiest kid on anybody's city-block. She can listen to a tune out of nowhere and begin stomping her boots on the earth with childlike suddenness; she can throw back her head—with its tomboy haircut that seems carved to her face—and say 'I know I'm proud' with a dazzling honesty; and she can rub her knees in fear and perplexity when she is finally brought to trial without losing an ounce of the ragamuffic dignity that has helped her crown a king.'' Harris played Joan in New York and on tour through the end of 1956. In all, she received five best actress awards for *The Lark*, including her second Tony.

After these four successes Harris entered a period of more than a decade that brought little commercial success, though her work continued to be highly regarded. The period from *The Lark* to *Forty Carats* (1968), her next important success, is marked by what appears to be a conscious effort to broaden her experience by playing a variety of theatrical styles and literary genres. Appearances included the hoydenish title role in William Wycherley's Restoration comedy *The Country Wife* (1957); *The Warm Peninsula* (1959); *Romeo and Juliet* and *King John* in 1960 at the Stratford Shakespeare Festival, Canada; and *Little Moon of Alban* (1960) in New York. This play of the Irish troubles of 1919–1922 had first appeared on television, and Harris's performance won an Emmy. Her next production was a comedy-mystery imported from Paris, *A Shot in the Dark* (1961), in which Harris played a saucy maid accused of killing her chauffeur lover. She then played a vaudevillian in **June Havoc**'s *Marathon '33* (1963), Ophelia in *Hamlet* (1964) in a New York Shakespeare Festival performance in Central Park, and a comically insecure actress in a slight play, *Ready When You Are, C. B.!* (1964). Perhaps then it was no surprise when she appeared in the musical *Skyscraper* (1965), based on Elmer Rice's *Dream Girl*. All reviewers admitted Harris was a nonsinger, but they also agreed, as Norman Nadel (*New York World-Telegram and Sun*, November 15, 1965) wrote, the "fault is tolerable, however, in that she is such a good actress, and such an enthusiastic worker that she gets the idea of a song across, if not all the lyric grace." Though *Skyscraper* was not a commercial success, her next production was. *Forty Carats*, an adaptation by Jay Allen of a French comedy, starred Harris as a chic forty-year-old divorcee who becomes romantically involved with a young man of twenty-two. Reviewers found the play contrived and its jokes on the generation gap forced, but audiences came, in large part to see Harris in the role that won her a third Tony as best actress of the 1968–1969 season. Walter Kerr (*New York Times*, January 5, 1969) called her "fetching from first to last and great fun." Richard Watts, Jr. (*New York Post*, December 27, 1968) believed she had "never looked as beautiful," and had "never been more skillful as a deftly charming comedienne."

After appearing with the now defunct New Orleans Repertory Theatre under the direction of June Havoc in a revival of *The Women* (1970), Harris created the role of Anna in Paul Zindel's *And Miss Reardon Drinks a Little* (1971) on Broadway. In two respects *Miss Reardon* resembled Harris's early successes: the play was primarily character sketches devoid of clear conflict, and Harris's part was that of a neurotic woman. She received mixed notices, but the play had a healthy national tour, in part due to the audience appeal of Julie Harris's name. She returned to New York the next season to appear in a suspense play about the supernatural, *Voices* (1972). It was a quick failure. She next appeared as Mary Todd Lincoln in *The Last of Mrs. Lincoln* by James Prideaux, for which she won a fourth Tony. In addition to the Tony, she again won the Drama Critics Circle Award and the Donaldson Award. It would be four years before Harris had another success and another Tony. In the interim she appeared in Hugh Leonard's *The Au Pair Man* (1973), which was a two-character comedy of bons mots and sight gags, and in a sentimental comedy, *In Praise of Love* (1974) by Terrence Rattigan.

The Belle of Amherst (1976) was a new high point in a career that had provoked superlatives for over thirty years. The idea of a one-woman show based on the life of the reclusive poet Emily Dickinson struck many reviewers as inherently unpromising. Yet mere dry fact could not contradict the force and inner truthfulness of Harris's impersonation that had grown out of her twenty-year interest in the poet. The performance prompted Walter Kerr (*New York Times*, June 17, 1976) to reconsider the entire career of the "tiniest tower of strength on Broadway." She played 117 performances at the Longacre Theatre, New York, an impressive run for a one-person show. Her characterization of Emily Dickinson earned Julie Harris a fifth Tony Award; no other actress has been so honored. She then toured America with the show and played London's Phoenix Theatre (1977).

Harris appeared next in New York in Ira Levin's period comedy, *Break a Leg* (1979), which played only one performance. During the 1981 Christmas season she opened in *Mixed Couples*. Though the production might have had a run despite mixed reviews, it closed on January 3, 1982, after nine performances because Harris required immediate hospitalization. She underwent surgery on January 9, 1982, at the Memorial Sloan-Kettering Cancer Center for a serious illness, detected early, according to her husband, William Carroll. Harris recovered from the operation to play Charlotte Brontë in *Currier Bell Esquire*, a one-woman play by the author of *The Belle of Amherst*, for a limited run in Los Angeles during that same year. She has not acted on Broadway since her illness. Instead, she returned to television to create the character Lilimae Clements, the second-rate country singer, on the CBS series *Knots Landing*. In 1988 she took the role of Miss Daisy with the national touring company of Alfred Uhry's 1987 Pulitzer Prize winning play, *Driving Miss Daisy.*

Julie Harris's recent television work was preceded by regular appearances throughout the 1950s and 1960s. For both television and movies, she re-created some of her important stage roles and attempted new characterizations as well. *The Belle of Amherst* was presented on PBS in 1976, while *The Lark* had been a feature on the *Hallmark Hall of Fame* series in 1957. Harris's other television appearances sponsored by Hallmark were highly esteemed: *Johnny Belinda* (1958), *A Doll's House* (1959), *Pygmalion* (1963), and *Anastasia* (1967). She was twice awarded an Emmy for her *Hallmark Hall of Fame* characterizations in *Little Moon of Alban* (1958) and *Victoria Regina* (1961). She re-created two other stage roles for films: *The Member of the Wedding* (1952) and *I Am a Camera* (1955). As she did on stage, she pursued a variety of roles on film. She played the teen-ager Abra in *East of Eden* (1955); the title character in a Dublin Abbey Players film, *The Poacher's Daughter* (1960); a neurotic spinster in a ghost story, *The Haunting* (1963); a dope addict and entertainer in *Harper* (1966); and the brains behind a football stadium holdup in *The Split* (1968). Harris's work was cited for special praise in *Requiem for a Heavyweight* (1962), where she played a compassionate employment counselor, and in *Reflections in a Golden Eye* (1967).

Harris has been married three times. She married Jay I. Julien, a lawyer and producer, in 1946. They were divorced in 1954. That same year she married stage manager Manning Gurian, by whom she had a child, Peter Alston Gurian, in 1955. Her second marriage ended in divorce in 1967. She married writer William Erwin Carroll in 1977. Harris believes it is easier for a man to act and be married than it is for a woman because the necessary separations are more difficult, and she speculates that her earlier marriages might not have failed had she not been an actress. Harris wrote *Julie Harris Talks to Young Actors* (1971), a compendium of practical advice, reminiscence, and exhortation intended for adolescents. In the conclusion, she wrote: "Acting is a unique profession. I won't say it is any better or worse than other kinds of work, only that it is different. It is more than a craft, more than an art form, more than a way of earning a living. It is, as many actors have said many times, a way of life. And a very demanding way of life" (p. 141).

Harris's memoir, *Julie Harris Talks to Young Actors* (1971), was written with Barry Tarshis; Walter Kerr's assessment of her career (*New York Times*, June 17, 1976) is particularly illuminating, as is the feature article by Robert Berkvist (*New York Times*, April 29, 1979). Other reviews include the *New York Times* (January 6, 1950; January 5, 1969; and June 17, 1976), *The Daily Mirror* (January 6, 1950), the *New York Journal-American* (November 29, 1951), the *New York Herald Tribune* (November 29, 1951, and November 18, 1955), the *New York World-Telegram and Sun* (November 15, 1965), the *New York Post* (December 27, 1968), and *Newsweek* (October 30, 1967). For a full list of stage, film, and television credits, see *Current Biography, 1977* (1977–1978) and *Who's Who in the Theatre* (1981). Harris is listed in *The Biographical Encyclopaedia and Who's Who of the American Theatre* (1966); *Notable Names in the American Theatre* (1976); *Who's Who in America, 1976–1977* (1976); and *The Oxford Companion to American Theatre* (1984).

James A. Patterson

HARRIS, Rosemary Ann (September 19, 1930–): stylish actress of Broadway and repertory companies, was born in Ashby, Suffolk (England), to Stafford Berkley Harris and Enid Maude Frances Campion. When she was less than six months old, her father moved the family to India where he was stationed as a group captain in the Royal Air Force. Rosemary Harris and her older sister, Pamela, grew up in India, attending schools there. The family returned to England during World War II, and Rosemary Harris lived for a time with her grandmother in Cornwall. In 1946 she made her first amateur appearance on stage in John Drinkwater's *Abraham Lincoln* at the Westwing School in Penzance. She intended to become a nurse but dropped out of nursing school after a year for lack of funds. She joined the Phoenix Players of the Bognor Regis Repertory in 1949 and made her professional debut at the Roof Garden Theatre in *Winter Sunshine*. She played more than thirty roles in weekly stock for the next nine months. The following year she appeared in some forty roles with the Falcon Players Company in Bedford. During 1951 she performed with Winwood Productions in Margate and Eastbourne and the Penzance Repertory Company. Thus began a career that was to be distinguished in England and in America for continuous work with repertory companies.

In 1951 Harris enrolled in the Royal Academy of Dramatic Art in London. She won the academy's Bancroft Gold Medal and a contract with H. M. Tennant that gave her walk-ons and understudy assignments in London's West End. One day a young actor asked her to read with him while he auditioned for a role in an American play. As a result, Moss Hart chose her for the part of Mabel, a girl reared in a British colony, in *The Climate of Eden*. Thus, her first professional appearance in a substantial role took place not in London but in New York at the Martin Beck Theatre on November 6, 1952. *The Climate of Eden* won Harris the *Theatre World* Award as "one of the most promising actresses of the year" (*Current Biography, 1967*, p. 162). Producers then cast her in a London production of *The Seven Year Itch*, which opened at the Aldwych on May 14, 1953, and ran for about a year.

A motion picture contract followed in MGM's British-produced *Beau Brummel*, released in 1954. Meanwhile, she toured that year in England, Scotland, Ireland, and France with the stage production of T. S. Eliot's *The Confidential Clerk*. In late 1954 she returned to repertory with the Bristol Old Vic Company, portraying Elizabeth Proctor in *The Crucible*, Isabel in *The Enchanted*, and several Shakespeare heroines. In September 1955 she joined the London Old Vic Company, playing Desdemona to Richard Burton's and John Neville's Othello, performed on alternate nights. She played Cressida in the company's modern dress production of *Troilus and Cressida*, which came to New York's

Winter Garden Theatre in December 1956. Following the tour, she stayed in the United States, saying, "There are no good parts for women in the English theatre nowadays. . . . I don't want to spend the rest of my life playing Shakespeare" (*Current Biography*, p. 162).

Broadway next saw Harris as Hilde, the unsuspecting hired companion, in the psychological melodrama *Interlock* at the American National Theatre and Academy (ANTA) Theatre in February of 1958. Although the play closed after only four performances, Harris's acting won praise from critics, including Brooks Atkinson of the *New York Times*. Then in December she co-starred as Zelda Fitzgerald with Jason Robards, Jr., in *The Disenchanted* for a 189-performance run at Broadway's Coronet Theatre.

Searching for more variety and contrast, Harris sought out opportunities in television and again in repertory. During 1957 she appeared in the television production of *The Prince and the Pauper*, on CBS-TV's *Dupont Show of the Month*, on NBC's *Hallmark Hall of Fame* production of *Twelfth Night*, and in two productions of CBS-TV's *Alfred Hitchcock Presents*. In 1958 she earned a nomination for an Emmy Award in *Wuthering Heights* for the *Dupont Show of the Month*. But it was repertory that offered the variety of roles she feels is necessary to an actor's development. In the summer of 1959 with the Group 20 Players, a repertory company at Wellesley, Massachusetts, she played Ann Whitefield in George Bernard Shaw's *Man and Superman* and the title role in James M. Barrie's *Peter Pan*, among other parts. At Wellesley she met Ellis Rabb, an actor and director who was staging some of the Group 20 productions. They married on December 4, 1959. A month later Rabb formed his own repertory company, the Association of Producing Artists (APA). Harris became APA's leading actress for the next six years, taking one leave of absence from the company in 1967. She appeared in more than thirty APA productions. During March and April of 1962 at the Folksbiene Playhouse in New York she enchanted Off-Broadway audiences as Lady Teazle in *The School for Scandal*, as Nina in *The Sea Gull*, and as the lisping Virginia in George M. Cohan's *The Tavern*. These performances earned her the *Village Voice* Off-Broadway (Obie) Award.

Harris returned to England in 1962 to play in revivals of John Ford's *The Broken Heart* and John Fletcher's *The Chances* for the inaugural season of the Chichester Festival Theatre with Laurence Olivier as artistic director. There she portrayed Yelena in Anton Chekhov's *Uncle Vanya* with a notable cast including Michael Redgrave, Joan Plowright, Peggy Ashcroft, and Olivier himself. Taped for television, the production was seen in the United States in 1967 on National Educational Television. When Laurence Olivier became head of the National Theatre Company in 1963, he restaged *Uncle Vanya* with the Chichester cast. Harris played other National Theatre productions including Ophelia in *Hamlet* (1963) and Woman One in Samuel Beckett's *Play* (1964).

When Harris rejoined APA for the 1964–1965 season, the company had suffered financial losses and spent some time in residence at the University of Michigan, Ann Arbor, before affiliating with the New York Phoenix organization, where it found a home at the Phoenix Theatre on East 74th Street. Here Harris enhanced the 1964–1965 season as Violet in *Man and Superman*, Natasha in *War and Peace*, and Judith in Jean Giraudoux's *Judith*. After closing a fifth fall season in Michigan in 1965, APA-Phoenix moved to the Lyceum Theatre on New York's West Side. The revival of George S. Kaufman and Moss Hart's *You Can't Take It With You* was an acclaimed hit largely because of Rosemary Harris's portrayal of Alice, the lovelorn daughter.

Again seeking diversity, Harris returned to Broadway in triumph in March 1966 as Eleanor of Aquitaine in *The Lion in Winter*, in which she co-starred with Robert Preston. Harris drew rave notices as the multifaceted Queen Eleanor. Stanley Kauffmann described her as "the marvel of the evening" (*New York Times*, March 4, 1966). Walter Kerr applauded Harris as "giving one of the ten or twelve best performances you are likely to run across in a lifetime" (*New York Herald Tribune*, March 20, 1966). For her performance as Eleanor, she won an Antoinette Perry (Tony) Award as best dramatic actress. However, the *play* fared less well and closed its run at the Ambassador on March 3, 1966, a month later. Harris rejoined the APA Company in a West Coast tour, and in the 1966–1967 season in New York she repeated her earlier successes in *The School for Scandal* and *War and Peace*.

Harris has also had a remarkable career in United States and Canadian television. Her roles include a pacifist Brooklyn schoolteacher in *Mary S. McDowell* on NBC's *Profiles in Courage* (November 1964) and Elvira in Noel Coward's *Blithe Spirit* on NBC's *Hallmark Hall of Fame* (December 1966). Since that time she has appeared in television productions of *Othello*, *The Prince and the Pauper*, *Twelfth Night*, *Wuthering Heights*, *Notorious Woman*, *Holocaust*, *The Chisholms*, and *To the Lighthouse*, the latter for the BBC, 1984. In addition, she has appeared in such films as *Beau Brummel*, *The Shiralee*, *A Flea in Her Ear*, and *The Boys From Brazil*.

Harris has often said in interviews that repertory is her favorite form of theatre because she prefers diversity in roles to a long run in a single role. Her career, however, has vacillated between repertory companies and the commercial theatre, between London and the United States. At the Billy Rose Theatre, New York, she played Anna in Harold Pinter's *Old Times* (November 1971); at the Vivian Beaumont, New York, she performed Portia in *The Merchant of Venice* (March 1973) and Blanche DuBois in *A Streetcar Named Desire* (April 1973); for the Brooklyn Academy of Music she triumphed as Julie Cavendish in *The Royal Family*, which moved to the Helen Hayes Theatre on Broadway in December 1975. Between 1977 and 1979 she appeared with the BAM Theatre Company, the Williamstown Theatre Festival, and the John F. Kennedy Center for the Performing Arts. Returning to New York in 1980, she played Madame Arkadina in *The Sea Gull*, directed by Andrei Serban, at the Public Theatre (November 1980); Barbara Jackson in *Pack of Lies*, directed by Clifford Williams, at the Royale Theatre (February 1985); and Judith Bliss in *Hay Fever*, directed by Brian Murray, at the Music Box Theatre (December 1985). In September 1986 she returned to London's National Theatre to appear in *The Petition*. In 1988 she appeared in a televised version of Eugene O'Neill's *Strange Interlude* with Glenda Jackson and José Ferrer.

Some years ago Rosemary Harris remarked with characteristic modesty: "I believe it's bad form to talk about one's art. I just like to pin mine to a wall and watch it bleed" (*Time*, December 9, 1966, p. 76). In an interview with *Time* she spoke about acting: "I don't know anything about what is supposed to be 'the real me.' I guess that's why I'm an actress—a chameleon on a tartan." Her voice has been described as "all champagne in the comedies, [which] darkens to cognac in the heavier roles." She has been said to command a "physical plasticity beyond the magic of makeup men," a "body actress, ruling the stage with grace and power and actually seeming to lean into her lines" (*Time*, December 9, 1966, p. 74).

Harris does not take on a part until she has read deeply into the period and thoroughly comprehended it. While she does not disown Stanislavsky, she refuses, nevertheless, to study Stanislavsky's approach to preparing a role because she does not want "to pluck out the heart of the mystery." Asked about the satisfaction of almost a lifetime spent in the theatre, she remarked, "If a performance has gone well that is the elation. That is what sends me singing up the stairs to my dressing room. Not the applause. I feel released and high and spent and fulfilled. If I've worked well and the tensions are gone—then I'd be perfectly happy if somebody called, 'Five minutes,' and we started all over. I'd be ready to go" (*Time*, December 9, 1966, p. 76).

After eight years of marriage, Rosemary Harris and Ellis Rabb divorced. On October 21, 1967, she married John Ehle, a North Carolina novelist. They have one daughter, Jennifer, and make their home in Winston-Salem, North Carolina.

Long regarded as one of the finest repertory actresses at work on the American stage, Rosemary Harris in recent years has expressed a preference for playing comedy to playing tragedy. After her first "commercial hit" in *The Royal Family* with Eva Le Gallienne and Ellis Rabb, Harris has appeared largely in such comedies as *The Sea Gull*, *Pack of Lies*, and *Hay Fever*, always to critical acclaim. In an interview with the *New York Times* (February 11, 1976) she said, "To be quite honest, comedy is less wear and tear. . . . If I had a choice, and had to do eight performances a week . . . I would find it too much to do tragedy. I become physically exhausted. . . . In comedy you don't have to refill your vessel."

Interviews with Rosemary Harris may be found in *Life* (May 6, 1966); *New York Herald Tribune* (April 11, 1966); *New York Post* (February 4, 1957); *New York Times* (April 4, 1965; February 11, 1976; and January 19, 1986); *Newsweek* (May 19, 1958); and *Time* (December 9, 1966). She is listed in *The Biographical Encyclopaedia and Who's Who of the American Theatre* (1966), *Current Biography, 1967* (1967–1968), *A Concise Encyclopedia of the Theatre* (1974) by Robin May; *Notable Names in the American Theatre* (1976); *Halliwell's Filmgoer's Companion* (1980); *International Motion*

Picture Almanac (1980); *Who's Who in the Theatre* (1981); *The Oxford Companion to the Theatre* (1983); and *The Oxford Companion to American Theatre* (1984).

                                                                          Milly S. Barranger

HAVOC, June (November 8, 1916–): actress, director, and playwright, has laughingly described her first involvement in theatre as follows: "Well, I didn't do anything until I was two" (personal interview, 1981). Born in Canada by mistake (her family did not make it back to their Seattle home in time for her birth there) to John Olaf and Rose (Thompson) Hovick, Havoc is the sister of the late Louise Hovick, professionally known as **Gypsy Rose Lee**. Havoc's mother, Rose, had always wanted to be an actress, and seeing that her older daughter, Louise, had little aptitude for either singing or dancing, she turned her energies and frustrations onto her daughter June. John Hovick, a farmer and newsman, was strongly opposed to his wife's plans for his younger daughter, but after a heated argument, Rose Hovick moved her daughter to her parents' home where she and her mother talked June's grandfather into paying for her ballet lessons; her mother also booked her into local clubs and lodges. By the time she was four, June Havoc had appeared in numerous Hal Roach films and completed a season of dramatic stock with the famous Duffy Players of San Francisco. These were the days of vaudeville and the Keith-Orpheum Circuit. By the age of seven, "Dainty Baby June, the Darling of Vaudeville" was earning over $1,500 per week on a three-year contract. Success, though, was not to last. By the age of eleven Havoc had became an awkward and gangly adolescent. Dainty Baby June was no longer a baby and was no longer dainty, no matter how Rose Hovick tried to make her so. The nation's economy, heading toward the depression, also affected vaudeville. "The theatres we played now were shabby, the audiences sparse. There were long stretches of layoffs. I wandered around the different cities alone. I knew something awful had happened to everything" (*Early Havoc*, p. 139). Havoc's feelings were not shared by her mother, who persistently peddled Dainty June from one dying vaudeville house to another. The vaudevillians, Havoc's greatest early influence, were no longer flourishing. With no formal education, a mother who scoffed at suggested professional training, and the depression closing the doors of the vaudeville houses, Havoc, then almost fourteen, ran away from her mother, her sister, and the "Act." "I felt that it would never come back, that it was over, that I had to go out and find a new world," she said (Fleischer interview, 1981). Her new life began with the sadistic world of the dance marathon—ironically, yet literally, dancing for survival. Havoc retells this adventure in her first autobiographical work, *Early Havoc*. Cited by critic Dorothy Parker as "a genuine slice of Americana," the book later served as the scenario for Havoc's play *Marathon '33*, produced in 1963.

From 1933, when she danced for 3,600 consecutive hours (as recorded in the *Guinness Book of World Records*), to her Antoinette Perry (Tony) nomination in the 1963–1964 New York theatre season, Havoc retained the survival instincts nurtured in the marathons and applied them directly to her life. Much of this period from 1933 to 1957 is recounted in the second installment of her second autobiographical book *More Havoc* (1980). At eighteen she decided that she wanted a child but without the problems of marriage, since she had tested that ground earlier. Her daughter, April, was born in April 1935. Within a year of April's birth, Havoc made her debut in the musical *Forbidden Melody*, noted in the *New York Herald Tribune* as "the small girl [who] stopped the musical . . . for two encores on opening night" (*More Havoc*, p. 182). Although Havoc was a hit, the play was a flop. She had made it to New York, but there was no assurance she could stay. In late 1936 she married Stanley Gibbs and settled into a domestic role that maintained her for nearly a year. By 1938 Havoc was ready to return to the theatre, this time accompanied by April. After playing a role in *The Women*, written by **Clare Booth Luce**, in Chicago, Havoc had a string of supper club dates, summer stock, and winter stock. In the summer of 1938 and again in 1939, Havoc appeared in productions at the Starlight Theatre in New York State: *Yes, My Darling Daughter*, *Tonight at 8:30*, *Mary's Other Husband*, and *Spooks*. Also, at the huge Jones Beach Theatre, Havoc performed the role of Irene in *Irene, Sally and Mary*. Her involvement with the Theatre Arts Committee also began around this time. "TAC was composed of thoughtful theatre people who felt strongly about sharing their political viewpoints" (*More Havoc*, p. 195). It was here that she met Mike Todd, who would later direct her in *Mexican Hayride*.

The year of 1941 brought *Pal Joey*, which Havoc calls "my overnight stardom that took all my life since the age of two to reach" (*More Havoc*, p. 206). Although it was her first major success, *Pal Joey* also marked Havoc's "major blunder," because she left the hit show to go to Hollywood. From 1941 to 1943 Havoc appeared in a variety of screen roles, none of which brought her Hollywood stardom. In 1944 she returned to New York to play the role of Montana in Mike Todd's production of *Mexican Hayride*. After that she had no difficulty getting roles on Broadway. She played the title role in Rouben Mamoulian's production of *Sadie Thompson*, Venetia Ryan in *The Ryan Girl* for the Theatre Guild, Ferne Rainer in *Dunnigan's Daughter*, and Georgina Allerton (succeeding Haila Stoddard) in *Dream Girl*. At Westport Country Playhouse Havoc performed the title role in *Anna Christie* and Amy in *They Knew What They Wanted*. Throughout the forties Havoc acted in many films in addition to her legitimate stage work, the most memorable film being *Gentleman's Agreement* (1947).

In 1950 Havoc succeeded **Celeste Holm** as Irene Elliot in *Affairs of State*; then she left the New York stage for six years to work in the infant medium, television, and its parent, radio. She performed in over three-hundred radio programs and acted in the respected *Kraft Television Theatre*, *Studio One*, and *Celanese Playhouse*. Twice Havoc had her own television show, *Willy* (CBS, 1952–1955) and *More Havoc*, a talk show. She made numerous guest appearances and television pilots.

With the development of regional theatres, Havoc found many opportunities. At the American Shakespeare Festival in Stratford, Connecticut, she played Queen Jocasta in Cocteau's *Infernal Machine* (1958), Titania in Shakespeare's *A Midsummer Night's Dream* (1958), and Mistress Sullen in Farquhar's *The Beaux' Stratagem* (1959). She also performed the role of Jonne de Lyn in *The Warm Peninsula* at the Helen Hayes Theatre, New York. During the early 1950s she also began her directing career, though she does not recall the first show she directed except that it was during a summer tour. She recalls, "I would gather up a good old play, fix it, cast it, and tour it. It was so successful I kept doing it when I had a chance" (Fleischer interview, 1981). The 1950s brought the successful publication of her article "Old Vaudevillians, Where Are You?" in *Horizon* and the first installment of her autobiography *Early Havoc* (1959).

Her international reputation was established in 1961 when, by invitation of the Department of State under President John F. Kennedy's cultural program, Havoc toured thirty-two countries in Europe, Asia, and Latin America with the American Repertory Company's production of *The Skin of Our Teeth*. Havoc played Sabina and Helen Hayes was Mrs. Antrobus. In South America Havoc received an award as best foreign actress for 1961.

The 1960s were a time filled with triumph for Havoc. Her play *Marathon '33* was nominated for an Antoinette Perry (Tony) Award in several categories including best play and best director, with the lead, **Julie Harris**, nominated for best actress. Thus Havoc established herself as a playwright and director as well as an actress. She found acting success as Millicent Jordan in Tyrone Guthrie's revival of *Dinner at Eight* in 1966. In 1967 she was invited by director Stuart Vaughan to be a guest star for the New Orleans Repertory Theatre, performing the role of Mrs. Malaprop in Sheridan's *The Rivals*. Her recorded activities as director, besides her work with *Marathon '33*, begin with Edward Albee's *A Delicate Balance*, in which she also performed the lead role, Agnes. By 1969 Havoc had accepted the position of artistic director of the New Orleans Repertory Theatre, succeeding Stuart Vaughan. Between 1969 and 1971 she directed and also starred in many New Orleans productions: *Luv*, *The Women*, *The Threepenny Opera*, *A Streetcar Named Desire*, *The Fantasticks*, *The Skin of Our Teeth*, and *As You Like It*. In 1971 Havoc resigned her post as artistic director because "the funds available for the coming season were not sufficient for what she [regarded] as first-class theatre" (*New York Times*, August 28, 1972).

Havoc's directing, acting, and writing credits continued to mount throughout the seventies. She starred in and directed the touring productions of Paul Zindel's *The Effect of Gamma Rays on Man-in-the-Moon Marigolds* and Neil Simon's *The Gingerbread Lady* in 1972. At the Tyrone Guthrie Theatre in 1973 her third play, *I, Said the Fly*, had its première production with Havoc playing the leading role, Fanny Brads. Her fourth play, *Oh, Glorious Tintinnabulation*, received a workshop production directed by Havoc at the Actors Studio in 1974. It was the last show she directed. Havoc continued performing as an actress in *Twigs*

(Chicago, 1975), for which she was nominated for Chicago's Jefferson Award as best actress, in *Habeas Corpus* on Broadway, and in *The Tax Collector* at the Clarence Brown Theatre in Knoxville, Tennessee. By 1978, though, she had become disillusioned with the theatre: "I'm out of love with the theatre now. I don't want to act anymore and I don't want to write any more plays. The theatre will have to show itself to be interesting before I go back to it. I've found my own place at Cannon Crossing and I'm at home in it" (*New York Times*, March 28, 1978). Havoc turned her energy, love, and attention to an eight-acre complex, Cannon Crossing, a pre-Civil War village near Wilton, Connecticut, which she has restored, uncovering the grace and beauty of the general store, post office, grist mill, and other treasures. Cannon Crossing welcomes thousands of visitors who browse daily through eleven quaint shops filled with everything from antiques to delicious homemade food.

By 1980, however, Havoc saw the publication of her second autobiographical volume, *More Havoc*, and began guest appearances on television specials and talk shows like the *Dick Cavett Show*. She appeared in Allan Carr's film *Can't Stop the Music* with the Village People. In 1982 she was lured back to Broadway with the role of Miss Hannigan in the long-running Broadway musical *Annie*.

Havoc would like to have a company of her own again "with a little more money this time" (Fleischer interview, 1981). In her sixties, she looks at least ten years younger and has the vitality of anyone thirty years old. Her vitality and love for the theatre have extended to the underprivileged young. In 1968 Havoc initiated a program, Youthbridge, for which the Connecticut legislature appropriated $104,000 to teach theatre crafts to underprivileged children in the state. Havoc gathered notables like Tyrone Guthrie, Paul Newman, and Joanne Woodward to "share the joy of making a living in show business" (*New York Times*, August 2, 1968).

Havoc's career has spanned sixty-five years, touching almost every form of American entertainment, including the multifaceted roles of actress, director, and playwright; she has found success on the Broadway stage in each. Her career is matched by few women in the American theatre. Havoc accomplished these feats by following her own advice: "If you have dreams you're going to have to be ready to make those dreams appear" (Fleischer interview, 1981).

Information on June Havoc's life through the early 1950s appears in her two autobiographical works, *Early Havoc* (1959) and *More Havoc* (1980). Some of the more important newspaper and magazine reviews and articles about Havoc have appeared in the *New York Times* (May 15, 1942; June 8, 1942; and October 23, 1942), *Look* (May 5, 1953), and *Time* (June 1, 1959). John Gassner discusses her production of *Marathon '33* in *Dramatic Soundings* (1968). Havoc's directorial techniques are discussed by Yolanda Fleischer in "An Assessment and Analysis of Contemporary American Women in Professional Directing through the Study of Selected Directors" (Unpublished Ph.D. dissertation, Wayne State University, 1983). Havoc is listed in Carlyle Wood, *TV Personalities: Biographical Sketch Book* (1954); George Oppenheimer, ed., *Passionate Playgoers* (1958); *The Biographical Encyclopaedia and Who's Who of the American Theatre* (1966); John E. DiMeglio, *Vaudeville, U.S.A.* (1973); James Robert Parish and Lennard DeCarl,

Hollywood Players: The Forties (1976); *Who's Who in the Theatre* (1981); and *Contemporary Authors*, Vol. 107 (1983).

Yolanda Fleischer

HAYDON, Julie (June 10, 1910–): actress most famous for her role as Laura in *The Glass Menagerie*, was born Donella Lightfoot Donaldson in Oak Park, Illinois, where her father, Orren Madison Donaldson, published three West Coast newspapers, *Oakleaves*, *Forest Leaves*, and *The Austenite*. Orren Donaldson came from Scotch-Irish Vermont stock. The New England Methodist upbringing given him by his parents, the Reverend Sylvester and Phoebe (Tabor) Donaldson, engendered a deep idealism that influenced his life. The motto of his newspapers was "The Public Press, no less than Public Office, is a Public Trust." Donaldson married West Chicagoan Ella Marguerite Horton, who was his editorial assistant and fifteen years his junior. Her family was of Dutch stock on her father's side and English on her mother's side. Her mother's family claimed kinship to George Washington through the Lightfoots of Virginia. Ella Marguerite Horton's mother, Ella Lightfoot Horton, was an actress and musician in her youth. Julie Haydon's mother also was a singer and pianist and later a music critic on her husband's Hollywood newspaper *Hollyleaves*.

Orren Donaldson moved his family to California for his wife's health when Donella was nine years old. They settled in what was then the close-knit small community of Hollywood. There Donella, also called "Donny," explored the Hollywood hills with her older brother Sabin Tabor and her younger sister Miriam Eleanor, "Mimi". Young Donny adored Sabin. He had already begun constructing fast automobiles then and is now one of the Grand Old Men of the Indianapolis 500. The two sisters attended Madame Gordon's School for Girls. Upon finishing school, Donella worked in an art shop by day and took dramatic classes at Neely-Dickson School in Los Angeles by night. Never far from the theatre, Donella performed roles with the Hollywood Drama Club, with Howard Ralston's stock company, and at the Hollywood Playshop.

Donella Donaldson began her professional career with **Minnie Maddern Fiske**'s 1929 West Coast tour of *Mrs. Bumpstead-Leigh* and *The Lower Depths*. She was soon noticed by film studio executives and began a screen career at the age of twenty-one with MGM's *The Great Meadow* (1930), in which she played Nancy Perry, a young pioneer mother. Subsequently, RKO signed her, under the name Julie Haydon, as a full contract player. She did ten films for Radio Pictures, including *Symphony of Six Million* (1932); *Thirteen Women* (1932) with Irene Dunne and Myrna Loy; *The Conquerors* (1932) with Ann Harding; *King Kong* (1933), in which she provided Fay Wray's scream; and *The Age of Innocence* (1934) with Irene Dunne. The next year her father died, his newspapers having succumbed to the Great Depression. Dissatisfied with Edgar Selwyn's attempt to mold her into another Ann Harding, Haydon cut her long blond hair. In consequence she was relegated to Tom Keene westerns for the remainder of her tenure at RKO.

Meanwhile, Haydon made a stage appearance opposite Francis Lederer in *Autumn Crocus* (1931), played Titania in Max Reinhardt's fabled production of *A Midsummer Night's Dream* (September 1934) at the Hollywood Bowl, and accepted the lead in the independent art film *From Dawn to Dawn* (1931). This last endeavor, though hissed and booed in Los Angeles, became something of a cult favorite, enjoying a long run at the Little Carnegie Cinema in New York and bringing Haydon to the attention of playwright Philip Barry. Barry invited her to make her Broadway debut as Hope Black in his play *Bright Star*. *Bright Star* had not been a hit in Boston (1934). While Barry was doing rewrites, Haydon received a call from Ben Hecht and Charles MacArthur to play the poetess Cora Moore to Noel Coward's evil publisher in their now classic film, *The Scoundrel* (1935). It was during filming on Long Island that Haydon met critic George Jean Nathan, whom she married twenty years later. *Bright Star* finally opened at the Empire Theatre in New York (1935) but ran for only five performances. Since Haydon was now her mother's sole support, she accepted a contract with MGM in Hollywood to appear as the elder sister with Lionel Barrymore and Mickey Rooney in the first Hardy Family film, *A Family Affair* (1937).

Finally, frustrated by the lack of movie roles suited to her talents, Haydon returned to New York City. She spent the summer of 1937 doing stock in Massachusetts. George Jean Nathan went up to see her work and suggested that she would be right for the part of Brigid, the Irish servant girl, in Paul Vincent Carroll's *Shadow and Substance*, then being produced by Eddie Dowling. The play opened at the John Golden Theatre in January 1938. It won the New York Drama Critics Award, and it was the beginning of a fruitful association with Dowling. After appearing with Edward Everett Horton in *Springtime for Henry*, which opened the famous Bucks County Playhouse, New Hope, Pennsylvania, in the summer of 1939, Haydon rejoined Dowling in William Saroyan's *The Time of Your Life*. Her lyrical performance as the prostitute Kitty Duval helped the play to win the Drama Critics Circle Award and also the offer of the Pulitzer Prize for 1939 (Saroyan did not accept the Pulitzer Prize). Haydon spent the following summer at Cape May Playhouse, New Jersey, playing in *Shadow and Substance*, *Invitation to a Voyage*, *The Showoff*, *Cradle Song*, and Saroyan's *Sweeney in the Trees*.

William Saroyan's beautiful short play *Hello, Out There* was teamed with G. K. Chesterton's *Magic* for an Eddie Dowling/Julie Haydon Broadway run at the Belasco Theatre in the fall of 1942. This was followed by a New York run and a six-month tour of *The Patriots*, in which Haydon played Patsy Jefferson. This was her fourth Drama Critics Circle Award play. In 1944, Tennessee Williams' *The Glass Menagerie* was taken on for production by Eddie Dowling when he decided to abandon rehearsals of Sean O'Casey's brilliant but bitter anti-British play *Purple Dust*. Haydon traded the role of Avril in the O'Casey play for Williams's fragile Laura, and theatre history was made. The play opened at the Chicago Civic Theatre on the day after Christmas 1944 and then moved to New York, opening at the Playhouse Theatre on March 31, 1945. Lewis Nichols of the *New York Times* wrote, "Tennessee Williams' simple play forms the frame-work for some of the finest acting to be seen in many a day. . . . Julie Haydon, very ethereal and slight, is good as the daughter" (April 2, 1945).

Other Broadway roles created by Haydon were Cicely in *Miracle in the Mountains* and Libeth Arbarbane in *Our Lan'*, both in 1947. She toured as Celia Cople-stone with the national company of T. S. Eliot's *The Cocktail Party* (1951) and played the pre-Broadway tryouts of *Springboard to Nowhere* (1950) and *The Intruder* (1952–1953). In 1955 Haydon married the dean of American drama crit-ics, George Jean Nathan. He had guided her career during seventeen years of close friendship. After Nathan's death in 1958 at the age of seventy-six, his wife established libraries in his honor in Riverdale, New York, and then in Gramercy Park, New York City. George Jean Nathan had always thought that the future of the American theatre lay in the universities. Following his death, Haydon criss-crossed the country lecturing in programs based on Nathan's forty-five books of dramatic criticism or on the literary figures she had known through Nathan and in her own right. She also appeared in plays as a guest artist at Catholic University, Harvard, Florida State University, St. Mary's College, Notre Dame University, and many other universities and colleges. During this time Haydon did some ra-dio and television work and in 1962 appeared in the pre-Broadway tryout of *Mr. Broadway*. Haydon has also served as consultant for the opening of Paul Baker's Frank Lloyd Wright Theatre in Dallas (1965) and was with Jay Broad's Theatre in Atlanta, Georgia (1966). In 1967 she began a ten-year "run" as actress-in-resi-dence at the College of St. Teresa in Winona, Minnesota. Using this women's liberal arts college as her base, Haydon continued to make appearances at other colleges and theatres in plays and programs of readings. In 1980 she portrayed Amanda in *The Glass Menagerie* (for perhaps the fifteenth time—each with a dif-ferent director and approach to the play and the character) at the Lion Theatre (now the **Judith Anderson**) on Theatre Row, New York City.

Julie Haydon Nathan has since been rejecting performance offers in favor of administering her husband's critical legacy, teaching, and writing her own mem-oirs. She continues as a member of the actors' guilds: Actors' Equity Association, the Screen Actors Guild, and the American Federation of Television and Radio Artists.

Julie Haydon is now at work writing her memoirs, hoping to publish them in 1988. Her papers are being collected by Patricia Angelin. Most of the information for this essay is from interviews with Haydon and her family. Partial credit listings for Haydon may be found in James Robert Parish, ed., *Actors' Television Credits: 1950–1972* (1973) and in John Weaver, ed., *Forty Years of Screen Credits 1929–1969* (1970). Julie Haydon is listed in *Who's Who in the Theatre* (1957); *The Biographical Encyclopaedia and Who's Who in the Theatre* (1966); *Notable Names in the American Theatre* (1976); *The Oxford Companion to American Theatre* (1984); and *Contemporary Theatre, Film, and Televi-sion*, Vol. I (1984).

Patricia Angelin

HAYES, Helen (October 10, 1900–): actress, often called the "First Lady of the American Theatre," was born to Francis Van Arnum Brown and Catherine Estelle (Hayes) Brown in Washington, D.C. Helen Brown eventually adopted her mother's family name as her stage name. She saw her first play, *The Merry Widow*, from the balcony of the National Theatre in Washington and reports that following the performance she clung to the seat and refused to leave, hoping that it would start over again. Since that time she never left the theatre.

With some slight training in dance and elocution but encouraged in her innate mimetic skill by her stage-struck mother, she made her first stage appearance on January 22, 1905, impersonating "The Gibson Girl" at Washington's Belasco Theatre in a matinee of *Jack the Giant Killer*. Later that year she joined the Columbian Players, a stock company at the Columbia Theatre, where she portrayed Prince Charles in *A Royal Family*. Over the next few years she appeared in a number of plays with this company, including *Prince Chap* and *A Poor Relation*. She also played in *The Barrier*, and she would later return from New York to play the title role in *Little Lord Fauntleroy* (1911) in Washington, D.C.

Precocious member of a boisterous Irish family, Helen Hayes was especially influenced by the imagination of her colorful and much-beloved grandmother, "Graddy" Hayes, a robust storyteller with a gift for verbal caricature. Her grandfather was the nephew of singer Catherine Hayes, "The Swan of Erin," who sang in Ireland, at Albert Hall in London, and for American miners during the gold rush of 1849. Her father spent much of his time on the road as a salesman for a meat-processing plant. Her vivacious, moody, and erratic mother devoted considerable time to her own theatrical ambitions—occasionally appearing as a comedienne with repertory touring companies.

With her mother as chaperon, Helen Hayes went to New York under the aegis of actor-producer Lew Fields. She made an immediate success appearing with him as "Little Mimi" in *Old Dutch*, a musical that opened on November 22, 1909, at the Herald Square Theatre. This event marked the Broadway debut of "Helen Hayes Brown." The following year she appeared in another musical with Fields, *The Summer Widowers*. She was then seen in *The Never Homes* (Broadway Theatre, October 15, 1911) and on tour in *The June Bride*. Next she appeared with John Drew in *The Prodigal Husband* (Empire Theatre, September 7, 1914). During this period she completed her schooling, tutored by the Sisters of the Sacred Heart Academy in Washington. She returned to her hometown from 1915 to 1917 to appear with the Poli Players. In 1917 and 1918, now a petite young woman in braids, she toured as *Pollyanna*.

Back in New York she did two plays in 1918: *Penrod* and the very successful *Dear Brutus*. She traveled to Washington for *On the Hiring Line* and then returned to New York in 1919 to act with Alfred Lunt in *Clarence*. She played in one or more Broadway attractions in each of the next ten years, most often starring as a sweet if impish darling in light romantic comedies, many tailored to her talents. Their titles tell all: *Bab* (Park Theatre, October 18, 1920), *Golden Days* (Gaiety Theatre, November 11, 1921), *To the Ladies* (Liberty Theatre, February 20, 1922), *We Moderns* (Gaiety Theatre, March 10, 1924), and *Dancing Mothers* (Booth Theatre, August 11, 1924) were among them. She embodied the vivacious spirit of the carefree "twenties" and was adored by reviewers and public for the gallery of "cute" sweethearts and charming flappers she created. At her zenith as an ingénue, however, some friends and critics began to question whether she was capable of artistry beyond the winsome characters she had made so popular. Urged by the actresses Ruth Chatterton and **Ina Claire**, she undertook voice and technique studies with Frances Robinson Duff and later Constance Collier, who often accompanied her during the first week of rehearsals on a new play. Hayes seriously rethought her approach to acting, developing a greater consciousness of her own method. Dissatisfied with her ability to move on-stage, she added interpretive dance, fencing, and boxing lessons to her schedule. With a firmer command of her art, she was able to move successfully from contemporary comedies to Oliver Goldsmith's *She Stoops to Conquer* in 1924 and George Bernard Shaw's *Caesar and Cleopatra* in 1925. This play was the first attraction of the Theatre Guild, and it was greeted with critical acclaim. The following year Hayes appeared as Maggie Wylie in *What Every Woman Knows*, and in 1927 she began a three-year run as Norma Besant, the doomed flapper, in *Coquette* on Broadway and on tour.

In 1928 Hayes married playwright Charles MacArthur, author with Ben Hecht of *The Front Page*, which opened the same year. Though she did not appear in this original production, she revived the play many years later. "Charlie" MacArthur was already established as a well-known newspaperman, playwright, screenwriter, and bon vivant in Manhattan literary and artistic circles. Witty, debonair, iconoclastic—undisciplined, sometimes quarrelsome, occasionally haunted by alcohol and depression—he was the great love, challenge, and inspiration of Hayes's life. Surviving the stresses of their careers—hers continuously successful, his erratically so—this difficult but apparently rewarding marriage lasted until Charles MacArthur's death in 1956 at the age of sixty. Their daughter Mary was born February 15, 1930, studied at the American Academy of Dramatic Art, and in 1946 appeared with her mother in *Alice Sit by the Fire* at the Bucks County Playhouse, at the Olney Theatre in Maryland, and on tour. She appeared again with her mother in a tryout of *Good Housekeeping* in 1949, during which she died suddenly of polio. The MacArthurs' adopted son, actor James Gordon MacArthur, was born in Los Angeles on December 8, 1937, and educated at Harvard. As a child he made his debut in *The Corn is Green* with his sister in 1945 and was also in *Life with Father* in 1953. His chief career has been in films and on television, notably in the series *Hawaii Five-O*.

In the 1933–1934 season Hayes played Mary Stuart in *Mary of Scotland* in New York and on tour. A second historical role, Queen Victoria in *Victoria Regina* (Broadhurst Theatre, December 26, 1935), proved to be the great triumph of her career. The Drama League of New York awarded to her the medal for the most distinguished performance of the season. Building a tour-de-force portrayal in which she aged from maiden to widow, she dazzled Broadway for two seasons and toured coast-to-coast for two more. Producer Gilbert Miller estimated that her performance was seen by two million people.

Upon her return to New York she revived several of her past successes and appeared as Viola in the Theatre Guild's production of *Twelfth Night* (St. James Theatre, November 19, 1940) with Maurice Evans. She had an outstanding success in *Harriet* from 1943 to 1945, portraying Harriet Beecher Stowe in New York and on tour. In 1947 Hayes appeared in *Happy Birthday* by her friend **Anita Loos**; she then went to London to play in *The Glass Menagerie* (Haymarket Theatre, July 28, 1948).

In 1950 Hayes appeared in Joshua Logan's adaptation of Anton Chekhov's *The Cherry Orchard*, set in the American South and called *The Wisteria Trees*. A series of revivals of her past successes and an outstanding performance in the new comedy *Mrs. McThing* (1952) followed. She next played *The Skin of Our Teeth* in Paris and New York, followed by *The Glass Menagerie*, *Time Remembered*, and *A Touch of The Poet*—the latter in a Broadway theatre named for her.

At the request of the United States Department of State she embarked on a tour of Israel, South America, and thirteen European capitals, playing *The Glass Menagerie* and, opposite George Abbott, *The Skin of Our Teeth* (1960–1961). On her return, Hayes joined Maurice Evans in a program of Shakespearean recitations (1962–1963). She was invited to appear at the White House, where in 1964 she gave a program of *First Ladies*. In that same year she established a Helen Hayes Repertory Company with which she toured for the next several seasons, and again under Department of State auspices. In Japan she appeared on television in *The Glass Menagerie*.

Hayes next performed with the APA/Phoenix Repertory Company, where in 1967 she had a great success as the mother in George Kelly's *The Show-Off*, playing the role both in New York and on tour. She announced as her stage farewell the play's production in 1969 in Washington at the National Theatre, but she was persuaded to continue acting. It was also in 1969 that she appeared in her late husband's play *The Front Page* as Mrs. Grant, the character reputedly based on Hayes's own mother. In 1970 she appeared in *Harvey*. In 1971 she did make her last stage appearance to date in Washington at the Catholic University of America in *Long Day's Journey Into Night*.

Although only five feet tall and weighing about one hundred pounds, Helen Hayes has reigned on the American stage for sixty-five years. She achieved stardom as a child, an ingénue, a serious actress, and a character comedienne. Her most singular success was in the role of the regal Queen Victoria (*Victoria Regina*), remarkable in view of her slight stature and the fact that her acting was distinguished not by grandeur but first by charm and later by homey simplicity. The pert insouciance that she portrayed in the dashing heroines of her early career matured into vulnerability juxtaposed with a kind of bedrock emotional solidity and common sense. She was able to enlist great audience sympathy while simultaneously conveying a reassurance that everything could turn out right in a world blessed with a few sturdy, frank, and delightful optimists like herself.

As a child, Hayes appeared in a number of short silent films with titles like *Jean and the Calico Doll* (1910), made by Vitagraph Studios in New Jersey. In 1932 she was awarded the gold "Oscar" of the Motion Picture Academy of Arts and Sciences as best actress for her performance in a screenplay written by her husband, *The Sin of Madelon Claudet* (1931). Her other films include *The Weavers of Life* ("my first and my worst," 1917), *The White Sister* (1923), *Arrowsmith* (1931), *Another Language*, *Night Flight*, *A Farewell to Arms* (1932), *What Every Woman Knows* (1934), *My Son, John* (1951), and *Anastasia* (1956). Returning to films after her retirement from the New York stage, she won an Academy (Oscar) Award in 1970 as best supporting actress for *Airport*. This was followed by a series of light comedies including *Herbie Rides Again* (1974) and *One of Our Dinosaurs Is Missing* (1975).

The *Helen Hayes Theatre* was heard on radio in 1940–1941. Several of her stage successes were repeated on television (*Mary of Scotland*, *Dear Brutus*, and *The Skin of Our Teeth*), and she has made television appearances in other plays (*The Twelve Pound Look*) and in pieces written for that medium (*Christmas Tie* and *Drugstore on a Sunday Afternoon*). She won television's Emmy Award in 1954.

Helen Hayes served as honorary president of the American Theatre Wing and was president of the American National Theatre and Academy from 1951 to 1953. She has been active on behalf of arts and humane causes in recent years. She testified before the U.S. Congress on the needs of aging citizens, an issue she addressed in a notable television documentary called *No Place Like Home*, in which in 1981 she disagreed with the White House Conference on Aging. In 1986 she was a recipient of the Presidential Medal of Freedom Award at the White House.

Helen Hayes has received honorary degrees from Princeton, Columbia, Brown, Denver, Brandeis, and New York universities and from the Carnegie Institute of Technology (now Carnegie-Mellon University), and Hamilton, Smith, Elmira, and St. Mary's colleges. She has received the Medal of the City of New York and the Medal of Arts of Finland. In 1952 she won the Sarah Siddons Award, and in 1974 she was named USO Woman of the Year. The Helen Hayes Theatre on 45th Street (the former Fulton), named in her honor in 1955, was demolished in 1982 to make way for a hotel complex, but another New York theatre was quickly rechristened with her name. In 1981 Hayes was among those upon whom honors were conferred by the John F. Kennedy Center for the Performing Arts. Her likeness by Furman Finck has been received as an official portrait in the National Portrait Gallery of the United States and is displayed in the Helen Hayes lobby of the National Theatre in Washington, which she serves as honorary chair. In June 1987 Helen Hayes was presented the first George S. Kaufman Award for Lifetime Achievement in the Theatre. This award was established by the Pittsburgh Public Theater. In May 1988 Hayes was herself a presenter of awards at the Helen Hayes Awards ceremony honoring outstanding achievement in the professional theatre in Washington, D.C. At this ceremony, American

Express paid special tribute to Hayes with a screen presentation which chronicled her nearly 80-year career on the stage, screen, and radio. In August 1988 Helen Hayes was one of twelve recipients of the annual National Medal of Arts award presented by President Reagan for artistic excellence. In October 1988 Hayes traveled to Maxwell Anderson's hometown, Stamford, Connecticut, for a centenary celebration of the playwright's birth. Hayes was the national chair for the Anderson anniversary.

A declared Republican and a Roman Catholic, Hayes resides in Nyack, New York, taking cameo roles in film and television, and making occasional public appearances for causes in which she believes.

Making her debut as a child, Helen Hayes played on Broadway almost annually for fifty years, frequently in more than one play per season, many of them written for her. Thereafter, she continued occasional appearances on stage, in films, and on television for nearly thirty more years, becoming a plausible contender for the title "First Lady of the American Theatre."

Hayes's book, *A Gift of Joy*, written with Lewis Funke (1965), is a pleasant romantic memoir and anthology of "favorite" inspirational quotations, bits of poetry, and speeches from roles she has played. Its airy glimpses of her years in the theatre pique the curiosity but do not satisfy. *On Reflection*, written with Sandford Dody (1968), is more autobiographical—reporting selected highlights and distresses of her life. It is, however, impressionistic and anecdotal. With Anita Loos, Hayes wrote *Twice Over Lightly* (1972), an affectionate salute to life in Manhattan. She can be heard on the Joy Recording Studio disc *Actors Talk On Acting* and seen in the film *Helen Hayes: Portrait of an American Actress*. A recent biography of Hayes is Kenneth Barrow, *Helen Hayes: First Lady of the American Theatre* (1985). *Life* (November 1963) contains a pictorial tribute to Hayes. *The Americans*, a book of interviews by David Frost, contains an interview with Hayes; and she is included in Margaret Case Harriman, *Take Them Up Tenderly, A Collection of Profiles* (1944). Stephen M. Archer lists many other magazine articles that have been written about Helen Hayes in his *American Actors and Actresses* (1983). Helen Hayes is included in *Current Biography, 1956* (1956–1957); *The Biographical Encyclopaedia and Who's Who of the American Theatre* (1966); *The Penguin Dictionary of the Theatre*, Revised edition (1970); *Notable Names in the American Theatre* (1976); William C. Young, *Famous Actors and Actresses on the American Stage*, Vol. I (1975); *Who's Who in the Theatre* (1981); *The Oxford Companion to the Theatre* (1983); and *The Oxford Companion to American Theatre* (1984).

Donn B. Murphy

HELBURN, Theresa (January 12, 1887–August 18, 1959): producer, actress, and critic, long associated with the Theatre Guild, was born to Julius Helburn and Hannah (Peyser) Helburn on West 46th Street in New York City, in the area that was later to become her "life and home." The west forties were then, and remain today, the hub of the theatrical district. Although she was enchanted by the theatre at an early age, Helburn by her own admission took a long time finding her place as a theatrical producer. The fact that her family was not in "show business" may have had some bearing on that slowness to assume what she called her "wayward quest." Her father was a Boston leather merchant, who was home only on weekends, and her mother was an educator, who ran an experimental school in the basement of their home, which was by that time in the east nineties. Although her parents introduced her to the Broadway scene at the age of nine when she saw **Ada Rehan**'s company perform four Shakespearean plays, she was not permitted or encouraged to attend the theatre on a regular basis. Despite, or perhaps because, the theatre was a forbidden fruit or at best a holiday delicacy, Theresa Helburn yearned for a place in it, though she did not know what her place would be.

In her childhood she attended the Horace Mann School in New York City; then she acquired a finishing school education at Miss Winsor's in Boston (where her family moved in the 1890s). Finally she attended college at Bryn Mawr. It was here that Helburn first tried her hand at producing plays. Taking on the role of producer for all the class plays and plunging into directing, acting, and writing them as well, she found this immersion in theatre to be the most rewarding experience of her college years. After graduating with honors from Bryn Mawr in 1908 and after suffering and recuperating from the first of many occurrences of ill health, Helburn temporarily focused on playwriting as her primary goal. To develop her craft she enrolled in 1909 in George Pierce Baker's famous English 47 Workshop at Radcliffe College of Harvard University. Here she first met her future Theatre Guild partner, Lawrence Langner, as well as future associates Lee Simonson, Philip Moeller, Maurice Wertheim, and two great playwrights, Eugene O'Neill and Philip Barry. For the next eight to ten years she concentrated on writing plays and poetry. Although her works in both of these media were published and she became an active member of the Poetry Society of America, neither her plays nor her poetry achieved critical acclaim. Several decades had to pass before she could admit that she was a second-rate writer.

Like most young women of her social class she made her debut, then taught drama at Miss Merrill's Finishing School in Mamaroneck (where she first met and worked with **Katharine Cornell**). She participated briefly in the women's suffrage movement, then worked as a theatre critic. She also journeyed several times to Paris where she explored French art, theatre, poetry, and dance, meeting such luminaries as writer **Gertrude Stein**, painter Mary Cassatt, and dancer Isadora Duncan. She was impressed by the fact that the arts were subsidized in France and were an integral part of education. She dreamed of revolutionizing and reorganizing the arts in America so that society might be permeated and enriched by them. It was, however, 1914 and the beginning of World War I, so Helburn returned to America.

By 1915 Helburn had begun to gravitate toward a career in professional theatre, joining Lawrence Langner and other former members of Baker's 47 Workshop in forming the Washington Square Players. Growing out of a village playreading group and lasting only two short years, the Washington Square Players became the forerunner of the Theatre Guild. The Players were the first theatre group in

America to support actively the works of new playwrights, and the first American theatre group to advocate a noncommercial subscription audience. In 1918, when the Theatre Guild "rose from the ashes" with a solid core of the former Washington Square Players, its goal was to produce new plays of "artistic merit." Although it ultimately hoped to work with American playwrights, the guild first used European drama to set its artistic standards and to provide a model to inspire the growth and development of American dramatic literature and repertory. Helburn was at first on the periphery of both of these groups but became the executive director of the guild soon after its birth. Although the group was originally run on a cooperative basis by its board of directors (Lawrence Langner, Lee Simonson, Philip Moeller, **Helen Westley**, and Maurice Wertheim), Helburn and Lawrence Langner were from the outset the organization's principal producers. Helburn herself shouldered the major responsibility for play selection, casting, and play doctoring; she was the executive in charge of guild policy and decision making, the kind of position rarely achieved by women in those days. The beginning of her work with the Theatre Guild coincided with her marriage to John Baker "Oliver" Opdycke in 1919. Thus began at approximately the same time her two lifelong loyalties: to the guild and to her marriage. Opdycke died in 1956.

The Theatre Guild's first two plays were Jacinto Benavente's *The Bonds of Interest* and St. John Ervine's *John Ferguson* in 1919. The latter was a great success and established the Theatre Guild as a major art theatre and producing organization; and with Helburn at its helm, it began the education of the American theatregoing public in new and challenging dramatic fare. This introduction of the work of new writers, both European and American, to the American stage was one of Helburn's greatest services. During the guild's first decade, the production of such works as *The Adding Machine*, *Jane Clegg*, *Heartbreak House*, *Caesar and Cleopatra*, *Pygmalion*, *RUR*, *The Guardsman*, *They Knew What They Wanted*, *Marco Millions*, and *Strange Interlude* brought Theresa Helburn and the Theatre Guild to their peak as a world-renowned theatre producer and producing organization. Although the first four seasons consisted almost exclusively of European plays, the guild, true to its goals, had by the end of its first decade shifted its production heavily in favor of American plays. In this first decade, the Theatre Guild made theatrical history. In the 1920s it built its own theatre, moving from the Garrick on 35th Street to what is now the Virginia Theatre on West 52nd Street. In this home through the 1930s it rode on the crest of these earlier historic successes. Some of its productions in this period included *Saint Joan*, *Elizabeth the Queen*, *Green Grow the Lilacs*, *Mourning Becomes Electra*, *Ah! Wilderness*, *Mary of Scotland*, *Idiot's Delight*, *Amphitryon 38*, *Biography*, *The Sea Gull*, and *Porgy and Bess*. Although the repertoire of both decades reads even now like exciting choices for modern repertory theatres, the brutal fact was that the expenses of operating the guild's new theatre, coupled with the choice of plays that did not generate money, put the guild in severe debt. It became apparent that its early halcyon days as an experimental art theatre were rapidly drawing to a close.

Helburn remained committed to the guild and its survival. When the Theatre Guild's board of directors had to be abandoned in the mid–1930s, she and Lawrence Langner assumed equal responsibility as co-directors. Escalating debts and production costs forced them for the first time to accept investments and backing from outside sources. Their commercial liaison with Philip Barry and **Katharine Hepburn** in the production of the very successful *The Philadelphia Story* in 1939 put them on a firmer financial footing, but from then on the guild became no different from any other Broadway commercial producing organization. Nevertheless, Helburn proceeded to demonstrate that commercial theatre need not be synonymous with inane plays; starting with the Hepburn vehicle in 1939, the guild produced many outstanding shows including *Oklahoma!*, *Carousel*, *Allegro*, *The Iceman Cometh*, *Come Back, Little Sheba*, *As You Like It*, and *Picnic*. Unfortunately, the financial failures in this period generally outweighed these successes, the worst period being in the early 1940s when the guild had a record sixteen consecutive failures before *Oklahoma!* charmed Broadway in 1943.

The history of Helburn and the Theatre Guild is the story of the coming of age of American theatre. The members of the board of directors who guided the Theatre Guild started with the idea of creating an art theatre that would produce plays that would not be presented in the commercial theatre. It is unfortunate that in the struggle for survival their utopian spirit of experiment could not be sustained. Helburn herself terminated her active duties with the organization in 1953 and died in Weston, Connecticut, in 1959, but her years of sacrifice and dedication have given the American theatre a great legacy. The early success of the guild provided a body of American dramatic literature; more importantly, it made the American theatre an open and a growing theatre. Although Helburn never realized her own dream of a successful training school working in tandem with the Theatre Guild or her vision of repertory theatres in the major cities in America, these concepts have come to fruition since her death through the nationwide membership of the League of Resident Theatres.

Besides her contributions in shaping American drama and American repertory, Helburn gave many artists their start through the Theatre Guild. The list of those she nurtured includes George Bernard Shaw and Eugene O'Neill, Alfred Lunt and **Lynn Fontanne**, Richard Rodgers and Lorenz Hart, **Agnes de Mille**, **Cheryl Crawford**, and Harold Clurman and Lee Strasburg (who later made their own theatre history with the Group Theatre and, much later, the Actors Studio).

In recognition of her outstanding contributions to the American theatre, Helburn was awarded honorary degrees from Tufts, Franklin and Marshall, and Columbia universities. Although Helburn called her career ''a wayward quest,'' she was an outstanding producer—one of the few, with Cheryl Crawford and **Eva Le Gallienne**, to demonstrate that theatrical producing is not an exclusively male pursuit, but one in which women can be increasingly successful.

The best source of information about Theresa Helburn is her autobiography, *A Wayward Quest* (1960). Walter Eaton's *The Theatre Guild: The First Ten Years* (1929) contains a chapter written by Helburn. Helburn's published plays are *Allison Makes Hay* (1919) and *Enter the Hero* (1919). Marya Mannes's "Behind the Throne," *The New Yorker* (December 6, 1930), gives a colorful portrait of Helburn. Roy Waldau's *Vintage Years of the Theatre Guild* (1972) contains a complete bibliography of the Theatre Guild. Discussions of Helburn's career appear in Glenn Hughes, *A History of the American Theatre* (1951); Brooks Atkinson, *Broadway* (1970); Oscar G. Brockett and Robert R. Findley, *A Century of Innovation: A History of European and American Theatre and Drama Since 1870* (1973); Kenneth Macgowan and William Melnitz, *The Living Stage* (1955); Helene Hanff, *Underfoot in Showbusiness* (1961, 1980); Oliver M. Sayler, *Our American Theatre* (1923); Margaret Webster, *Don't Put Your Daughter on the Stage* (1962, 1972); and *The Theatre Guild Anthology* (1936), with an introduction by the board of directors of the Theatre Guild. Additional information can be found in the Theatre Collection of the New York Public Library Performing Arts Research Center at Lincoln Center and in most books containing information on the Theatre Guild. The manuscripts of Helburn's plays are contained in the Bryn Mawr College archives. Some of her professional correspondence can be found in the Theatre Guild Collection at the Yale College of American Literature, Beinecke Library. The Harvard Theatre Collection and the Radcliffe Theatre Archives also have useful information. Helburn's obituary appeared in the *New York Times* (August 19, 1959). She is included in *Current Biography, 1944* (1945), listed along with Lawrence Langner; *Who's Who in the Theatre* (1957); *Who Was Who in America: Vol. 3: 1951–1960* (1966); *Who Was Who in the Theatre* (1978); *Notable American Women*, Vol. IV: *The Modern Period* (1980); and *The Oxford Companion to American Theatre* (1984).

Jennifer Stock

HELD, Anna (March 18, 1865?–August 13, 1918): musical comedy star and vaudeville comedienne, was born in Warsaw, Poland (some sources say Paris). Sources give differing dates for her birth. She was the youngest of eight (her memoirs say eleven) children of Maurice (or Shimmle) Held, a glovemaker, and his wife, Yvonne Pierre or Helene Held. When her father became ill, the family moved to Paris and opened a small restaurant in which Anna worked. Later she curled ostrich feathers, sewed buttonholes, and made fur caps in various Parisian shops. After her father's death, Anna and her mother moved to London. Held began her theatrical career in the chorus of the Princess Theatre in London, though she had made a minor debut in Paris in 1889 in that forerunner of the music hall called the café-concert. There she had sung in Spanish, French, German, and Polish, but it was her pantomimic ability that made her performances popular. After her stage debut in London, she returned to Paris, performing at the El Dorado and the La Scala cabarets. She appeared throughout Europe—from music halls in Amsterdam to cabarets in Scandinavia, Germany, and Hungary. In 1894 at Trouville, France, she secretly married Maximo Cerrara, a fifty-year-old South American.

Anna Held became famous as a music-hall singer in every capital of Europe. She entertained at the homes of aristocrats and royalty, and she was the subject of two Toulouse-Lautrec lithographs. Her great European popularity drew the attention of the American producer Florenz Ziegfeld, who succeeded in signing her to a contract where other producers like Hammerstein, Rice, and the Kiralfy Brothers had failed. Ziegfeld brought Held to America; the two were known publicly as Mr. and Mrs. Ziegfeld. Held made her American debut at the Herald Square Theatre in New York on September 21, 1896, in *A Parlor Match*. For the next several years Held and Ziegfeld were inexorably linked together. Although she was a famous European music-hall entertainer, it took Ziegfeld's touch to bring her fame as a star of the American musical. Her popularity was due, in part, to her beauty and her style. Her voluptuous figure and lively countenance, coupled with her resonant voice and perfect clarity of diction, had an overwhelming effect on audiences. All of her biographers agree that when she sang "Won't You Come and Play Wiz Me?" it was a unique moment in the American musical theatre. The song became her trademark and promoted the idea of the naughty, teasing French doll. Ziegfeld packaged and sold his doll to American audiences so well that she became a cult figure. There were "Anna Held corsets, facial powders, pomades, Anna Held Girls, Anna Held eyes, and even Anna Held cigars" (*Ziegfeld, the Great Glorifier*, p. 33).

Her shows were considered "outrageously naughty," and when "she toured, the whole nation was alerted" (*The World of Flo Ziegfeld*, p. 22). Between 1896 and 1913 Ziegfeld tailored a series of light musical farces for her, including *A Parlor Match*, *La Poupée*, *Papa's Wife*, *The Little Duchess*, *Mam'selle Napoleon*, *Higgledy Piggledy*, *The Parisian Model*, *Miss Innocence*, and *Follow Me*. These farce pieces featured Held as a not-so-innocent heroine who was usually the victim of some misunderstanding or a mistaken identity. The slight plots were often reworked from earlier French domestic farces. Each show contained recurring elements such as elaborate dance numbers, a bit of plot, and lots of girls. But Anna Held was not afraid of female competition; "sumptuously gowned, rolling her eyes, lifting her skirts," Held would conclude each performance with "Won't You Come and Play Wiz Me?" (*The World of Flo Ziegfeld*, pp. 21–22). Her charming French accent and Gallic style, besides the naughty song that was her unique trademark, assisted Ziegfeld in the development of his highly successful revue format. It was Held's Parisian charisma that infused Ziegfeld's Follies with the style and motif that made them so unique. Anna Held was, indeed, the first "Ziegfeld Girl." Sadly, however, as his star ascended, her star waned. In 1913, after a series of bitter fights, Held and Ziegfeld parted. She sued him for divorce; but it was discovered in court that no legal marriage had ever taken place between them, and she was recognized only as his common-law wife. After she left Ziegfeld, her popularity waned. In 1918 she died in New York City.

As Held had aged, the Ziegfeld beauties seemed to grow younger and younger. It was the ultimate irony that, as Ziegfeld began stressing an American look in order to glorify an "American beauty," Held, who was so distinctly European, finally lost her place in the Ziegfeld Follies and in the American theatre. Nonetheless, her brief career exemplified that form of musical theatre entertainment that captivated the American public under the impresario Florenz Ziegfeld.

Anna Held's purported memoirs, *Anna Held and Flo Ziegfeld*, are actually a somewhat sensationalized account of Held's life written by her daughter, Lianne Carrera, and translated by Guy Daniels (1979). Information about Held is found in Eddie Cantor and David Freedman, *Ziegfeld, the Great Glorifier* (1934), and Randolf Carter, *The World of Flo Ziegfeld* (1974). Anna Held wrote about herself in "My Beginnings," *Theatre* (July 1907). See also Felix Isman, *Weber and Fields* (1924); Bernard Sobel, *Broadway Heartbeat* (1953); Cecil Smith and Glenn Litton, *Musical Comedy in America* (1981); Ethan Mordden, *Broadway Babies* (1983); Martin Gottfried, *In Person: The Great Entertainers* (1985); and Gerald Bordman, *American Musical Review: From the Passing Show to Sugar Babies* (1985). Held's obituary appeared in the *New York Times* and the *New York Tribune* (August 13, 1918). There are clippings about her in the Harvard Theatre Collection. Anna Held's biography is given in Walter Browne and E. deRoy Koch, *Who's Who on the Stage, 1908* (1908); John Parker, ed., *The Green Room Book, or Who's Who on the Stage, 1909* (1909); Dixie Hines and Harry Prescott Hanaford, eds., *Who's Who in Music and Drama* (1914); John Parker, ed., *The New Dramatic List: Who's Who in the Theatre* (1916); Robert L. Sherman, *Actors and Authors With Composers Who Helped Make Them Famous* (1951); *Notable American Women*, Vol. II (1971); *Who Was Who in the Theatre*, Vol. II (1978); and *The Oxford Companion to American Theatre* (1984). James T. Nardin, writing in *Notable American Women*, states that Held's death record gives her birth year as 1877 and her obituaries give 1873. However, he indicates that a letter in the *New York Times* (April 22, 1956) from Dr. Jacob Shatzky of the YIVO Institute for Jewish Research affirms 1865 as the correct year of her birth.

Marilyn McKay

HELLMAN, Lillian Florence (June 20, 1905?–June 30, 1984): playwright and director, was born in New Orleans, Louisiana, as the only child of Julia (Newhouse) Hellman and Max Bernard Hellman, a traveling salesman of German-Jewish ancestry. When Lillian was six, the family suffered severe financial reverses. They then moved to New York to live with the Newhouse family but for many years spent six months of each year in New Orleans with Max Hellman's two sisters. Lillian grew up in two worlds, adjusting to different schools, until she graduated from Wadleigh High School in New York in 1922. She attended New York University from 1922 to 1924 and studied for one semester at Columbia University in 1924 before ending her formal education.

Hellman's upbringing in two vastly different cities and family environments influenced her work. While remaining metropolitan in her approach to character, she uses the South as a backdrop in four of her best plays, including *The Little Foxes* (1939), *Another Part of the Forest* (1946), *The Autumn Garden* (1951), and *Toys in the Attic* (1960). Hellman was also influenced by two additional factors: the social differences between the Newhouse and Hellman families and her own position as an only child. She disliked the upper-middle-class Newhouses and their attitudes toward money, but she was fond of the colorful Hellmans and their eccentric acquaintances. She was conscious of her role in the adult power games she witnessed as a child and early on developed a rebellious and independent spirit. Her sense of morality and justice and her fierce independence pervade all her work; she is often compared to Henrik Ibsen as a champion of social and political causes.

In 1924 Hellman began work as a reader and editor at Horace Liveright, Inc. At this time she met Arthur Kober, a theatre press agent, whom she married on December 31, 1925, a marriage which lasted until 1932. During these seven years Hellman wrote book reviews for the *New York Herald Tribune*, read playscripts for Herman Shumlin, and wrote a number of short stories that she considered unpublishable. She wrote no plays, although she met many people connected with the theatre. The Kobers went to Europe twice, where Hellman wrote for the *Paris Comet*. In 1929 she thought of studying in Bonn, Germany, but was repelled by evident anti-semitism; the experience helped to shape a political attitude that later surfaced in her two war plays, *Watch on the Rhine* (1941) and *The Searching Wind* (1944). In 1930 the Kobers went to Hollywood, where Arthur Kober was a scriptwriter and Hellman was a reader for MGM. She was not enthusiastic about her job or about Hollywood, but she did meet and enjoy the company of S. J. and Laura Perelman, Nathanael West, and William Faulkner. It was also in a Hollywood restaurant that she met the mystery/detective writer, Dashiell Hammett, thirteen years her senior, who became her lifelong companion and one of the greatest influences on her life.

Hellman moved back to New York in 1931. Her liaison with Dashiell Hammett intensified, and an amicable divorce from Arthur Kober followed in 1932. An unpublished play on which Hellman collaborated with Louis Kronenberger was completed in 1932 and titled *Dear Queen*. Two short stories were published in 1933 and 1934, while at the same time Hellman began composing *The Children's Hour*, the first play she was to produce. Hammett's influence on Hellman's work began with *The Children's Hour*. He had recommended that Hellman read William Roughead's *Bad Companions*, which contained a story called "Closed Doors; or, The Great Drumsheugh Case." The story centered on a troublesome child in a boarding school who maliciously tells her wealthy patron aunt that her two teachers are lesbians. The aunt persuades other parents to withdraw their children from school. The teachers bring a libel suit against the aunt, but they lose the case, and their careers are utterly ruined. Hellman kept the basic story line and completed the manuscript in May of 1934. Herman Shumlin agreed to direct the play, and **Aline Bernstein** designed the settings. On November 20, 1934, *The Children's Hour* opened at the Maxine Elliott Theatre on Broadway and ran for 691 performances, the longest run of any of Hellman's twelve stage plays. While the critics all agreed that the third act was weak, the play was a hit. Audiences were fascinated by the taboo topic, the tense pace of the action, and the intense study of slander and self-righteousness. The play was banned in Boston and in London and stirred controversy in Chicago. When it was revived in 1952 at the Coronet Theatre, it ran a respectable 189 performances. Brooks Atkinson reviewed it again, calling it "still powerful and lacerating" and claiming that "Miss Hellman has never written so tersely and accurately" (*New York Times*, December 19, 1952, p. 35).

Many of Hellman's characteristic trademarks appeared first in *The Children's Hour*: awkward, embarrassing, or violent confrontations between characters; interrupted scenes with unfinished business to heighten tension; dialogue sprinkled with sharp quips and quick wit; sparing use of biographical character detail; settings that include elegant living rooms for family or intimate action; and the frequent presence of a dignified older woman character (Moody, pp. 43–47).

On December 15, 1936, Hellman's second play, *Days to Come*, again directed by Shumlin and with scenery by Aline Bernstein, opened at the Vanderbilt Theatre. While politically and socially informed, the play was a failure and ran for only seven performances. Failure was a bitter pill for Hellman to swallow, and it was two years before her next play appeared. In the meantime she wrote a screenplay and several newspaper articles and toured Paris, Moscow, and Spain. On this trip she met Ernest Hemingway and witnessed firsthand the civil war in Spain. Her sympathy for the Spanish Loyalist cause intensified. In 1937 and 1938 Hellman wrote nine drafts of *The Little Foxes*. She considered it her most difficult play to write. She recalls in *Pentimento* that it was during the writing of this play that she depended most on Dashiell Hammett's support and constructive criticism. He did not "approve" of the play until the eighth draft. *The Little Foxes*, set in the turn-of-the-century South, is direct criticism of members of Hellman's mother's family. The Newhouses are cast in the roles of the scheming, heartless Hubbards, capitalists who take advantage of the dying southern aristocracy and cheap labor (black as well as white). On February 15, 1939, *The Little Foxes* opened at the National Theatre in New York; it ran a successful 410 performances. Herman Shumlin again directed, Aline Bernstein designed the costumes, and **Tallulah Bankhead** starred in the role of Regina Hubbard. George Jean Nathan, reviewing the play, wrote that Hellman "indicates a dramatic mind, an eye to character, a fundamental strength, and a complete and unremitting integrity that are rare among her native playwriting sex" (*Newsweek*, February 27, 1939).

In 1940 *The Little Foxes* went on national tour, and Hellman journeyed to Philadelphia to cover the Republican National Convention. With Hitler's rise to power and American involvement in World War II looming in the near distance, Hellman began to work on the first of two politically-informed plays, the strongly anti-fascist *Watch on the Rhine*. It premièred on April 1, 1941, at the Martin Beck Theatre in New York, again under the direction of Herman Shumlin with costumes by **Helene Pons**. It ran for 378 performances, winning the New York Drama Critics Circle Award. Many critics considered *Watch on the Rhine* the most substantial, and one of the most powerful, war plays of the period. In 1942 a special edition of the play with a foreword by Hellman's close friend, **Dorothy Parker**, was published to raise funds for the Joint Anti-Fascist Refugee Committee. On April 12, 1944, Hellman's fourth play, and her second war play, premièred at Broadway's Fulton Theatre. *The Searching Wind* ran for 318 performances and was the last Hellman play directed by Shumlin. The play was Hellman's *post hoc* analysis of America's moral failures in the events leading to World War II.

In her next play Hellman returned to the Hubbard family twenty years earlier to establish the events and motives for *The Little Foxes*. On November 20, 1946, *Another Part of the Forest* opened at the Fulton Theatre under Hellman's own direction. The play ran through April of 1947 for 191 performances. It is set in 1880 and deals with the inception of middle-class greed after the Civil War, signaling death to the southern aristocracy. The Hubbards establish themselves at the expense of an ineffectual aristocracy, and the scene is set for what we already know in *The Little Foxes*. In 1948 Hellman was a major participant at the Progressive party convention supporting Henry Wallace for President. In October of that year, she flew to Europe to interview Marshall Tito. By spring 1949, having attended the Cultural and Scientific Conference on World Peace, Hellman had been labeled by the American press as a pro-Communist sympathizer.

Hellman's adaptation of Emmanuel Roblaas's play, *Montserrat*, opened on October 29, 1949, at the Fulton Theatre and continued for sixty-five performances. Directed originally by Hellman and then by Harold Clurman, the play won the Vernon Rice Award for direction. On March 7, 1951, Hellman's favorite play, *The Autumn Garden*, opened at the Coronet Theatre in New York. It was dedicated to Dashiell Hammett and was directed by Harold Clurman. Brooks Atkinson reviewed the play by saying, "This is Miss Hellman at the peak of her talents—observant, sympathetic, honest, and alert. Nothing is forced. Everything is lucid" (*New York Times*, March 8, 1951). The play again embodies Hellman's favorite theme of human responsibility and moral choice. Like *The Little Foxes* and *Another Part of the Forest*, it has been characterized as "a Chekhovian drama," in which characters discuss life at length.

The years 1951 through 1953 were difficult ones in Hellman's personal life. Dashiell Hammett was jailed for six months for contempt of court in connection with questioning on the Civil Rights Congress, which was considered a pro-Communist organization. Hellman was subpoenaed in 1952 to appear before the House Committee on Un-American Activities (HUAC). Her famous response to Committee Chair John S. Wood was typical of Hellman's spirit: "I cannot and will not cut my conscience to fit this year's fashions" (*Scoundrel Time*, p. 93). Hellman was blacklisted. She was forced to sell her beloved farm in Pleasantville, New York, lost revenue from screenplay royalties, and suffered economically for some time. Hammett returned from jail a sick man and never recovered physically. *The Children's Hour* was revived in 1952 for 189 performances at the Coronet Theatre, and many critics saw it as a pertinent metaphor for the times.

Between 1953 and 1959, Hellman edited *The Selected Letters of Anton Chekhov* and wrote adaptations of Jean Anouilh's *The Lark* and of Voltaire's *Candide*, both of which were produced. In 1955 she moved to Martha's Vineyard, which would be her summer home until her death. In 1957 she began work on *Toys in the Attic*. Directed by Arthur Penn, *Toys in the Attic* opened at Broadway's Hudson Theatre on February 25, 1960. It won the New York Drama Critics Circle Award and ran for 556 performances. Robert Brustein hailed Hellman as a "playwright in the true Ibsenite tradition" (*New Republic*, March 14, 1960, p. 23) and said that "her work is constructed with all the rigidity and tensile strength of a steel girder. Nothing is superfluous" (p. 22). *Toys in the Attic* is set in New Orleans and concerns the sexual and economic interests of a family in the decaying southern culture. Again, it challenges the audience to consider questions of justice and responsibility. It was Hellman's last major play.

Dashiell Hammett died in January 1961. That spring Hellman taught at Harvard University and received an honorary degree from Wheaton College in Massachusetts as well as the Brandeis University Creative Arts Medal in Theatre. In 1963 Hellman's last play opened at the Plymouth Theatre for seventeen performances. It was called *My Mother, My Father, and Me* and was based on Burt Blechman's novel, *How Much?* As she was disillusioned with the economics of the Broadway theatre, Hellman's career as a playwright came to a close with this production, but her career as a writer was by no means over. She continued to cover major events around the world and traveled frequently. She taught at the Massachusetts Institute of Technology, Yale, and the University of California in Berkeley, and she spoke at many other college campuses.

In 1969 Hellman published *An Unfinished Woman*, the first of three popular memoirs, which won the National Book Award. In 1973 her second memoir appeared titled *Pentimento: A Book of Portraits*, and in 1976 *Scoundrel Time* was published. In 1980 a novella appeared titled *Maybe: A Story*. Her last book, co-authored with Peter Feibleman, is a cookbook called *Eating Together: Recipes and Recollections* (1984) that treats one of Hellman's favorite pastimes—cooking.

On June 30, 1984, Lillian Hellman died of cardiac arrest at Martha's Vineyard. She was buried at Abel's Hill Cemetery on that island. Much of her four-million-dollar estate was placed in two funds: one named after Dashiell Hammett to promote writing from a leftist, radical viewpoint, and the other named after herself to promote "educational, literary, or scientific purposes and to aid writers regardless of their national origin, age, sex, or political beliefs" (*Boston Globe*, July 21, 1984, p. 18).

Hellman is considered a major playwright in contemporary America. Social justice dominates her work. She has been compared to Ibsen and Chekhov, while also criticized as melodramatic and apologetic. She showed expert craftsmanship in her writing, though her life and her plays provoked controversy. Her preoccupation with American southern culture appears in four of the plays, and her use of lesbianism, fascism, capitalism, and racism suggests what sorts of moral and political issues Hellman experienced in her own life or observed in the lives of her friends. Apparent in her work are the disparate influences of the avaricious Newhouse family, of her kindly black nurse, Sophronia, of the politically and sexually liberated Dashiell Hammett, of the wry and witty Dorothy Parker, and of many others, including William Faulkner and Ernest Hemingway. Hellman was truly an American playwright whose breadth of character delineation and importance of theme transcend both North and South. Her ideology and her preoccupations place her work at the cutting edge of America's social consciousness.

Hellman's twelve plays are available in a single volume titled *The Collected Plays* (1972). Her memoirs can be read in another volume titled *Three: Collected Memoirs* (1979). The chapter from *Pentimento* called "Theatre" is particularly relevant to the study of Hellman as a dramatist. Hellman's last book, *Eating Together: Recollections and Recipes* (1984), which Peter Feibleman helped her prepare, contains delightful reminiscences about New Orleans life along with stories from her experiences in Europe and the last years of her life on Martha's Vineyard. There are literally hundreds of newspaper and journal reviews of Hellman's plays. Regular coverage of all her plays can be found in the *New York Times*, *The New Yorker*, *The Nation*, *Time*, *Newsweek*, and *The New Republic*. There are three bibliographies: Steven H. Bills, *Lillian Hellman: An Annotated Bibliography* (1979); Mark Estrin, *Lillian Hellman: Plays, Films, Memoirs* (1980); and Mary Marguerite Riordan, *Lillian Hellman: A Bibliography, 1926–1978* (1980), all containing references to Hellman's own work, writings about Hellman, and graduate studies on Hellman. Major sources of information are the clipping file in the New York Public Library Performing Arts Research Center at Lincoln Center and the manuscript collection at the University of Texas in Austin, which is the major repository for Hellman's papers. Manfred Triesch's *The Lillian Hellman Collection at the University of Texas* catalogs holdings through 1966. There are two critical biographies: Richard Moody, *Lillian Hellman: Playwright* (1972), and Doris Falk, *Lillian Hellman* (1978); and her authorized biography by William Wright has the title *Lillian Hellman: The Woman Who Made the Legend* (1986). Two recent books about Hellman are Carl Rollyson, *Lillian Hellman: Her Legend and Her Legacy* (1988), and Peter Feibleman, *Lilly: Reminiscences of Lillian Hellman* (1988). Both of these books are reviewed by Marsha Norman in "So Much Rage" in *American Theatre* (January 1989). Hellman's political and personal life are also treated in John Phillips and Anne Hollander, "The Art of the Theatre I: Lillian Hellman: An Interview," *The Paris Review* (1965). Hellman's introduction to *The Big Knockover: Selected Stories and Short Novels of Dashiell Hammett* (1966) gives insights into her view of Hammett. Marsha Norman has two articles: "Articles of Faith: A Conversation with Lillian Hellman," *American Theatre* (May 1984), and "Lillian Hellman's Gift to a Young Playwright," *New York Times* (August 26, 1984). Hellman's birth date is given either as 1905 or as 1906. Her obituary appeared in the *New York Times* (July 1, 1984). Among the many reference books which contain biographical information about Lillian Hellman are *Twentieth Century Authors*, First Supplement (1955); *Who's Who in America, 1960–1961* (1960); *Current Biography, 1960* (1960–1961); *The Biographical Encyclopaedia and Who's Who of the American Theatre* (1966); *Contemporary Authors*, Vols. 13–16, First Revision (1975); *Notable Names in the American Theatre* (1976); *Contemporary Dramatists* (1977); *American Women Writers*, Vol. II (1980); *Dictionary of Literary Biography*, Vol. 7, *Twentieth-Century American Dramatists*, Part 1 (1981); *Who's Who in the Theatre* (1981); *The Oxford Companion to the Theatre* (1983); and *The Oxford Companion to American Theatre* (1984). *The Dictionary of Literary*

Biography, Yearbook: 1984 (1985) contains tributes paid to Hellman by John Hersey, Patricia Neal, and Richard Wilbur.

Elizabeth J. Natalle

HENIGER, Alice Minnie Herts (1870?–September 28, 1933): producer, director, writer, and acclaimed founder of professional children's theatre in the United States, was born in New York City to Henry B. and Esther Herts. After a public school education in New York and matriculation at the Normal College of New York City (now Hunter College), she traveled abroad to continue her studies at the Sorbonne in Paris. Returning to New York City, Alice Herts began to work in the city's immigrant communities, pioneering early social welfare programs. In her capacity as social worker and program innovator, she founded and became the long-time treasurer of New York's Lenox Hill Settlement. While involved with Lenox Hill, Herts became aware of the need for an outlet for the dramatic instincts of children. Hoping to promote her ideas, she accepted a position as manager of the entertainment department of the multifaceted Educational Alliance of New York City. The Educational Alliance, located on Manhattan's Lower East Side, offered services to newly arrived immigrants, most of whom were from Russia and Eastern Europe. The entertainment department had been in operation for years but had been largely ineffectual. Convinced of the recreational, creative, and educational values of theatre for both adults and children, Heniger transformed her department into a producing organization that would bring live drama to its audiences and would upgrade and expand the existing body of playscripts for child audiences.

In 1903 her program officially became the Children's Educational Theatre, and with this official recognition began the American children's theatre movement as it is known today. To make her theatrical programs more cohesive, she hired Emma Sheridan Fry, long associated with the American Academy of Dramatic Art. The Children's Educational Theatre opened in October of 1903 with Shakespeare's *The Tempest*; all the acting roles except Ariel were performed by adults. So great was the enthusiasm for live theatre from the largely immigrant audience on the Lower East Side, that, at five cents a seat, the performances sold out weeks in advance, and over a thousand copies of the playscript were purchased from local booksellers by patrons anxious to read the play before seeing its performance.

The reaction both to the idea of live theatre and to *The Tempest* in particular was enough to motivate major renovations in the theatre facility the following summer. A new stage was constructed, and better facilities and technical provisions were readied. The first full season began in 1904 with adult evening performances of *As You Like It* (trading on the initial momentum gained with the earlier *Tempest*) and the melodrama *Ingomar*. Sunday matinees were arranged for children—the same actors played **Frances Hodgson Burnett's** *A Little Princess* and William de Mille's *The Forest Ring* under the direction of Jacob Heniger.

Drawn to the project by similar theatrical philosophies for the young, Heniger would become Herts's business partner and husband.

A Little Princess had several child actors portraying characters, and to its rehearsals Alice Herts brought a significant new approach—one that pioneered later advances in adult actor training. Instead of giving the child actors lines and a set way to deliver them, Herts allowed for exploration of the character, his manners, emotions, environment, and motivation. As a result, the performances were of a level of sophistication and artistry heretofore rarely seen from such young talent. As Herts recalled in her book *Children's Educational Theatre* (1911), "The physical exercise seemed always to be suggested by the mental and spiritual attitude toward the assumed character, and thus there was no mechanized learning of lines. The sense of kinship with the character, the feeling which involved its creation from within, were appealed to and the character gradually took concrete human shape" (p. 19). It was an approach like that of Constantin Stanislavsky, who in 1903 was yet to be discovered by the American theatre. Thus began theatre addressed specifically to children. The Children's Educational Theatre, while primarily an adult producing organization, conscientiously promoted quality theatrical entertainment for a largely juvenile audience. One of the Theatre's outstanding productions was a dramatization of Mark Twain's *The Prince and the Pauper*, for which Herts obtained permission from Twain himself. *The Prince and the Pauper* premièred in 1907 and was a rousing success. Mark Twain (Samuel Clemens), invited to the performance with friend William Dean Howells and others, was so impressed with the show and with Alice Herts's concept of theatrical performance for children that he became a vocal supporter and active member of the theatre's organizing board through the duration of its short career.

In June 1908 the theatre, having grown beyond the limits of the Educational Alliance, incorporated as an independent enterprise under the title of the Educational Theatre for Children and Young People. It included Herts and Clemens among its newly appointed directors. During that summer the new theatre conducted acting, voice, and music classes for children and adults, and in December opened its first Sunday matinee productions with a revival of the successful *A Little Princess*. Although finances were meager, for a time all seemed well. In 1909, however, Herts became ill and was unable to continue her normal production pace. The city enacted a Sunday ban on dramatic performances, thus wiping out the group's lucrative Sunday matinee formula. The pioneering theatre ran out of money and closed at the end of 1909. Alice Herts recuperated from her illness but thereafter left further theatrical production to stronger producers. After two years, a new group emerged from the ashes of the disbanded troupe. Without any direct input from Alice Herts, the Education Players, as they were called, sought to build upon her original principles of theatre for children, and they had a modicum of success.

Alice Minnie Herts, who had some years before marrying her partner Jacob Heniger, left commercial theatre production for a teaching position in 1913 with the Extension Teaching Department of New York's Columbia University. She remained at Columbia for several years, frequently augmenting her teaching with lectures and publications on her philosophy of theatre for children and the short-lived but influential Children's Educational Theatre project. Her major book, *Children's Educational Theatre*, delineating her philosophy and chronicling her theatre work was published in 1911; it was followed seven years later by her equally perceptive treatise, *The Kingdom of the Child* (1918).

Alice Minnie Herts Heniger withdrew from the public eye in the late twenties. Her health deteriorating, she grew content to become "Mrs. Jacob Heniger," spending much of her time with her husband at their summer retreat in Casco, Maine. There she died on September 28, 1933, not many days before the thirtieth anniversary of her first *Tempest* performance. She left a bequest to Hunter College to fund an annual award to a student excelling in work with children, and that award is still being given.

While it is likely that her name and theatre company are known today to only a few theatre historians and to even fewer producers and performers, Alice Minnie Herts Heniger is, nevertheless, rightly to be regarded as founder of the professional children's theatre movement in the United States, and all discussion of the history of children's theatre must begin with her 1903 debut production. Her productions and educational philosophies and goals were revolutionary at the time; yet they became the recognized prototypes for the development of the form as we know it today. Her insistence on quality dramatic literature coupled with quality performance, her quite contemporary methods of rehearsal and of approaching characterization, and her ability to inspire people like Mark Twain, William Dean Howells, and noted academics of the age to the possibilities and realities of quality theatre for the young, make Alice Minnie Herts Heniger not only the uncontested founder of American children's theatre but one of the first true pioneers of modern children's theatre pedagogy and production in the United States.

Very little biographical information exists detailing Heniger's life and activities before and after her direct involvement with the Children's Educational Theatre. She is listed (as Herts, Alice Minnie) in John W. Leonard's edition of *Woman's Who's Who of America, 1914–1915* (1914, reprinted in 1976), and her obituary is noted in the *New York Times*, under "Mrs. Jacob Heniger" (September 29, 1933, p. 22), but each is of little use to interested scholars. Her ideas and place in the children's theatre movement are discussed in Nellie McCaslin's *Theatre for Children in the United States: A History* (1971). In order to understand the theatre, philosophy, and milieu of Heniger, one needs to examine *The Children's Educational Theatre* by Alice Minnie Herts (1911), and her other work, *The Kingdom of the Child*, written under the name of Alice Minnie Herts Heniger (1918).

Douglas Street

HENLEY, Mary Beth (May 8, 1952–): playwright and actress, is the second of four daughters of Charles Henley (now deceased), a lawyer who served terms in both houses of the Mississippi legislature, and Lydy (Caldwell) Henley. Beth was born and reared in Jackson, Mississippi, where her mother appeared in amateur theatre productions.

As a senior in high school Beth Henley enrolled in an actor's workshop with the New Stage Theatre in Jackson and went on to receive an undergraduate degree in dramatic arts (1974) from Southern Methodist University in Dallas, Texas. Although she considered herself an actress rather than a playwright, Henley wrote her first play at SMU as a class assignment, a one-act called *Am I Blue*. Set in New Orleans, it concerns two lonely adolescents who meet in the French Quarter. When *Am I Blue* was produced at SMU, the program listed the author under a pseudonym. *Am I Blue* was first produced professionally by the Hartford Stage Company on October 19, 1981. *Variety* (November 4, 1981) called it "achingly funny and sad, . . . rich with piercingly accurate adolescent dialogue that goes straight to the heart." It was staged again in 1982 by the Circle Repertory Theatre in New York City.

Following graduation from SMU Henley spent a year studying for a master's degree at the University of Illinois, Champaign-Urbana, before heading for Los Angeles to work as an actress. The frustration of pursuing acting as a career led her, in 1978, back to playwriting. That play, *Crimes of the Heart*, was co-winner of the Great American Plays competition of the Actors Theatre of Louisville for 1977–1978. In early 1979, Actors Theatre became the first of four regional theatres to mount *Crimes of the Heart*, leading to its New York première at the Manhattan Theatre Club for a limited Off-Broadway run on December 9, 1980. The production moved to Broadway on November 4, 1981, for a run of 535 performances at the John Golden Theatre.

Crimes of the Heart is a three-act play set in the middle-class kitchen of the McGrath house in the town of Hazelhurst, Mississippi. The play encompasses just two days in the lives of the McGrath sisters. Critic John Simon (*New York Magazine*, November 16, 1981) called Henley "a new playwright of charm, warmth, style, unpretentiousness and authentically individual vision . . . [who] restores one's faith in the theatre." The daily newspaper reviews were nearly unanimous in their enthusiastic praise of the play. Frank Rich (*New York Times*, November 5, 1981) wrote that Henley mines "a pure vein of Southern Gothic humor worthy of Eudora Welty and Flannery O'Connor. The playwright gets her laughs not because she tells sick jokes, but because she refuses to tell jokes at all. Her characters always stick to the unvarnished truth, at any price, never holding back a single gory detail. And the truth—when captured like lightning in a bottle—is far funnier than any invented wisecracks."

In April 1981, the Pulitzer Prize for drama was awarded to *Crimes of the Heart*, the only play to win the prestigious award prior to a Broadway opening. Henley was the seventh woman to receive the Pulitzer and the first to be so honored in twenty-three years. The play also garnered the George Oppenheimer/ *Newsday* Playwriting Award and the New York Drama Critics Circle Award for best new American play.

Henley's next full-length play, *The Miss Firecracker Contest*, is also set close to home, in Brookhaven, Mississippi, where her mother was born. *The Miss Firecracker Contest* premièred at the University of Illinois and opened later the same month, on October 30, 1981, at the Studio Arena Theatre, Buffalo, New York. After productions at the Victory Theatre in California, the New Stage Theatre in Jackson, Mississippi, and the Steppenwolf Theatre in Chicago, the two-act comedy began an Off-Broadway run at the Manhattan Theatre Club's hundred-seat theatre on May 27, 1984. A month later, the play was moved to the Manhattan Theatre Club's larger theatre where it played for another month. Then the production was transferred to the West Side Arts Theatre, New York, where it continued its run under a commercial management. Like *Crimes of the Heart*, this second play is a comedy of eccentric character with a pronounced Gothic vision. Frank Rich (*New York Times*, May 28, 1984) generously praised *The Miss Firecracker Contest*, noting how the play's characters try to escape their unhappy pasts and discover "what you can reasonably hope for in life." Most reviewers thought the dialogue was inventive and that the characters were lovingly drawn, but not all notices were favorable. Douglas Watt (*Daily News*, May 28, 1984) believed the author "should have given more time to this play. The idea is good, and so is much of the execution, but the parts don't quite mesh."

Henley's third full-length play premièred New Year's Day, 1982, at the Hartford Stage Company, Connecticut; then *The Wake of Jamie Foster* opened on Broadway at the Eugene O'Neill Theatre on October 14, 1982. The play is a series of scenes from the funeral of a man who is killed four months after leaving his wife for another woman. His death is the result of being kicked in the head by a cow one night while boozing in a field with his overweight mistress. Like Henley's other plays, *The Wake of Jamie Foster* is set in Mississippi, this time in Canton. Critical response was uniformly unfavorable. The author was accused of recycling the southern Gothic territory she explored in *Crimes of the Heart* and of reworking many of the same characters. The writing was characterized as desperate and chaotic, lacking in structural and thematic soundness. *The Wake of Jamie Foster* closed after 12 performances.

Another comedy, *The Debutante Ball*, premièred April 9, 1985, at the South Coast Repertory in Costa Mesa, California. Henley described the play as more baroque and perhaps not so accessible as *Crimes of the Heart*. The debutante ball for Teddy Parker occasions a family gathering at her stepfather's mansion in Hattiesburg, Mississippi. Teddy fears the ball, but her mother, Jen Dugan Parker Turner, believes it is a way for the family to bury its unsavory past and take its rightful place in society. Jen, it seems, was once jailed for murdering her former husband with a frying pan. The ball and the reunion end in disaster, but Henley offers some hope for her eight characters. The production was staged by Stephen Tobolowsky, the director who guided *The Miss Firecracker Contest* to success.

In August of 1986, Henley premièred a workshop production of *The Lucky Spot* at the Williamstown Theatre Festival in Massachusetts. The play then played Off-Broadway at the Manhattan Theatre Club, opening on April 28, 1987. Also in 1986 Henley ventured into film. She wrote the film adaptation of *Crimes of the Heart* (1986) and co-wrote with David Byrne the screenplay of *Nobody's Fool* (1986). In 1989 she wrote the screenplay for *Miss Cracker*, a film adapted from her play, *The Miss Firecracker Contest*. Also in 1989 she premiered *Abundance* at South Coast Repertory in Costa Mesa, California.

Henley still considers herself an actress. Shortly before the Broadway opening of *Crimes* she played a bag lady in a small-scale Los Angeles production. As an actor/playwright, Henley is part of a small trend in recent American theatre that includes Sam Shepard, Christopher Durang, and Bill C. Davis. She believes that being an actress is part of her strength as a playwright and that she learned playwriting not from a college course but "from acting and reading plays. . . . It gives you a feeling for what's theatrical . . . " (*New York Times*, October 25, 1981, p. 22). Even so, she has yet to appear in one of her own plays. She shares a West Hollywood home with Stephen Tobolowsky, director and musician.

Despite a resemblance seen by several commentators, Henley claimed that she had not read novelist Flannery O'Connor's works until a critic noted the similarities. "There's a vividness to Southern life, a sense of humor mixed with a sense of tragedy," Henley believes, that accounts for the likeness. Returning to Mississippi, "I get off the plane and all the stories are just incredible. All sorts of bizarre things that are going on. It's in the air. Oh, Lord, the stories I hear . . ." (*Saturday Review*, November 1981, p. 44). Being southern, she maintains, is not a limitation to the playwright and neither is being female. "Women's problems are *people's* problems. There are certain subjects I mightn't get into, simply because I don't have the necessary knowledge, but I don't think my being a woman limits my concerns" (*New York Times*, October 25, 1981, p. 22). Henley told Hilary DeVries of *The Christian Science Monitor* (October 26, 1983) that she starts with "an idea of what I want to write about, like a funeral, a beauty contest, or somebody in the family getting thrown in jail, and then I do a lot of thinking about the characters who are in the event and what happened to them before that. Then, when I actually sit down to write the play, it just comes real fast, almost like automatic writing." Henley claims to do little reworking of her plays.

While Beth Henley's career is considered early in its development, she already ranks with **Lorraine Hansberry** as a Pulitzer Prize winner for drama and with **Lillian Hellman** as winner of a New York Drama Critics Circle Award for best new play. Moreover, she is counted among a number of new American playwrights emerging from the nonprofit regional theatre into the commercial Broadway theatre. Also, she upholds the tradition of the southern literary heritage transposed into the drama for which Tennessee Williams and **Carson McCullers** are exemplary.

The quotations by Beth Henley are from five feature articles in the *New York Times* (October 25, 1981), *Newsday* (October 18, 1981), *Saturday Review* (November 1981),

Time (February 8, 1982), and *The Christian Science Monitor* (October 26, 1983). See also Benedict Nightingale, "A Landscape That Is Unmistakably By Henley," *New York Times* (June 3, 1984), and Samuel G. Freedman, "Beth Henley Writes a Real, Real Personal Movie," *New York Times* (November 2, 1986).

James A. Patterson

HEPBURN, Katharine Houghton (November 8, 1907–): stage and film star, was born in Hartford, Connecticut, to Dr. Norval Thomas Hepburn and Katharine Martha (Houghton) Hepburn. Her father, a Southerner from Virginia, was educated at Randolph-Macon College and Johns Hopkins University. He became a distinguished surgeon on the staff of the Hartford Hospital, specializing in urological surgery and pioneering the study of sexual hygiene. Her mother, whose socially prominent family founded Corning Glass Works and moved from Buffalo to Boston, was a graduate of Bryn Mawr and Radcliffe colleges. She was committed to the suffragette movement, pioneered as an advocate of birth control, and picketed the White House in the interest of better working conditions for women. There were six Hepburn children: an elder brother, Tom, who died at fifteen; Katharine Hepburn; two younger sisters, Marion and Margaret; and two younger brothers, Richard and Robert. Katharine Hepburn attended the Hartford School for Girls, the coeducational Oxford School (Hartford), and Bryn Mawr College, Pennsylvania (1924–1928), where she engaged in campus theatricals and decided to become an actress. Later, she studied acting and voice with Frances Robinson-Duff, dancing with Michael Mordkin, and Shakespeare with Constance Collier. She married Ludlow Ogden Smith, a Philadelphia socialite, on December 12, 1928. The marriage was dissolved on May 8, 1934. There were no children. Over the years her name has been linked romantically with Howard Hughes, Leland Hayward, and Spencer Tracy, but she has never remarried.

Hepburn's career in theatre began with appearances in college productions before her first professional engagement with the Edwin H. Knopf Stock Company in Baltimore in *The Czarina* (1928) as lady-in-waiting to **Mary Boland**'s Catherine the Great. Her next production that same year was *The Big Pond*, staged as a pre-Broadway tryout in Great Neck, Long Island. In *A Special Kind of Magic* she relates: "I put on my face and did the first scene, including a rather long speech, after which the audience burst into applause. Quite right, I thought. But then I got excited and began to deliver my lines faster and faster, and by the time I was into the second act, nobody could understand a word I said. After the play, I didn't think people appreciated me enough, and we went back to New York, and the next day I was fired" (p. 73).

On November 12, 1928, at the invitation of producer Arthur Hopkins, Hepburn made her Broadway debut as Veronica Sims in *These Days* at the Cort Theatre. This eight-night run was followed by Hepburn's involvement in Philip Barry's *Holiday* (Plymouth Theatre, November 16, 1928). She understudied the role of Hope Williams but never had the opportunity to perform it. In 1929 Hepburn toured for five weeks as Grazia in *Death Takes a Holiday* but was fired after quarrels with director Lawrence Marston. Hopkins recommended Hepburn to Theresa Helburn at the Theatre Guild, where casting director **Cheryl Crawford** offered her an understudy position in the Theatre Guild's production of Ivan Turgenev's *A Month In The Country*. The play starred **Alla Nazimova** and opened on March 17, 1930. By April she had replaced the actress playing Katia, the maid. She spent the summer of 1930 at the Berkshire Playhouse in Stockbridge, Massachusetts, and appeared in *The Admirable Crichton*, *The Romantic Young Lady*, and *Romeo and Juliet*. That fall, British playwright Benn W. Levy cast her in his play, *Art and Mrs. Bottle* (Maxine Elliot Theatre, November 18, 1930), starring **Jane Cowl**. During rehearsals he fired her, then rehired her after auditioning fourteen other actresses. The next season, Hepburn was fired once again, this time from Philip Barry's *The Animal Kingdom* (Broadhurst Theatre, January 12, 1932). She was fired after only one week, because the production's star, Leslie Howard (co-producer with Gilbert Miller), could not tolerate her bossy manner and, according to Hepburn, the fact that she was taller than Howard.

Dauntless Hepburn persevered. On March 11, 1932, she opened in the starring role of Antiope in *The Warrior's Husband* (Morosco Theatre), but her usual quarrelsomeness got her fired and rehired twice before the play opened. This production established her as a Broadway star. On July 1, 1932, she went to Hollywood, where she would soon gain worldwide recognition as one of the finest movie stars of all time. Interspersed among her film roles were several performances on Broadway, on tour, and in regional theatres. Her stage roles have included Stella Surrege in *The Lake* (Martin Beck Theatre, December 26, 1933); *Jane Eyre* (for the Theatre Guild, New Haven, Connecticut, and touring, 1936–1937); Tracy Lord in *The Philadelphia Story* (Shubert Theatre, March 28, 1939); Jamie Coe Rowan in *Without Love* (St. James Theatre, for the Theatre Guild, November 10, 1942); Rosalind in *As You Like It* (Cort Theatre, for the Theatre Guild, January 26, 1950, and on tour); and The Lady in *The Millionairess* (Shubert Theatre, October 17, 1952, and in London at the New Theatre, June 27, 1952). In 1957 she played Portia in *The Merchant of Venice* and Beatrice in *Much Ado About Nothing* at the American Shakespeare Festival in Stratford, Connecticut; in 1960 she acted Viola in *Twelfth Night* and Cleopatra in *Antony and Cleopatra* at the same theatre. Hepburn played Coco Chanel in *Coco*, her first musical on Broadway at the Mark Hellinger Theatre on December 18, 1969. She appeared as Mrs. Basil in Enid Bagnold's *A Matter of Gravity* at the Broadhurst Theatre on February 3, 1976, and as Margaret Mary Elderdice in Ernest Thompson's *West Side Waltz* at the Ethel Barrymore Theatre, New York, on November 19, 1981.

Hepburn's most critically acclaimed stage performance was that of Tracy Lord in Philip Barry's *The Philadelphia Story*. The play was rewritten specifically for her by the author as a custom-made showcase. Brooks Atkinson of the *New York Times* said of Hepburn: " . . . she plays with grace, jauntiness, and warmth—

moving across the stage like one who is liberated from self-consciousness and taking a pleasure in acting that the audience can share'' (March 29, 1939).

Hepburn will certainly be remembered as a film star, having the unique distinction of being nominated for twelve Academy awards (Oscars) as best actress and receiving four for the films *Morning Glory* (1933), *Guess Who's Coming to Dinner?* (1967), *The Lion In Winter* (1968), and *On Golden Pond* (1981). Certainly another of her most memorable performances was with Humphrey Bogart in *The African Queen* (1951). She has also played dramatic roles on television, including Amanda Wingfield in *The Glass Menagerie* (1973), Agnes in *A Delicate Balance* with Paul Scofield (1974), Jessica Medlicott in *Love Among The Ruins* with Laurence Olivier (1975), and Miss Moffat in *The Corn is Green* (1979).

The casual assessment might be that Hepburn's stage career has been eclipsed by her film career. In fact, her special contributions to the American theatre are notable. George Bernard Shaw wrote *The Millionairess* for Hepburn. Philip Barry rewrote *The Philadelphia Story* for her. Both plays have enjoyed successful revivals. Hepburn's film success in *Woman of the Year* (1942) served as the basis of the popular Broadway musical *Woman of the Year* in the 1980s, and at the age of sixty-four, after a hiatus of five years, she returned to Broadway and critical acclaim in *West Side Waltz* (1981), playing Margaret Mary Elderdice, a contentious elderly woman battling loneliness. During her long and often turbulent career, she has played with distinction a variety of roles—both classic and modern—on stage, screen, and television. In addition, she has been a self-assured, outspoken, confident, and socially conscious woman of great and inspiring individuality. Her immense visibility and her unquestioned triumphs have made her one of the great modern stars of the American theatre. Tribute was paid to her and another favorite star, James Stewart, at an October 1987 gala staged by the Actor's Fund of America to raise money for people from the theatre community who are in financial distress.

Books written about the life and career of Katharine Hepburn are *Kate: The Life of Katharine Hepburn* by Charles Higham (1975), *Katharine Hepburn: A Hollywood Yankee* by Gary Carey (1983), and *A Remarkable Woman: A Biography of Katharine Hepburn* by Anne Edwards (1985). Roy Newquist's *A Special Kind of Magic* (1967) is a book of interviews with Hepburn, her director, and her co-stars in *Guess Who's Coming to Dinner?* Other sources of information on Hepburn's life are the *New York Times Theatre Reviews* and magazine articles such as ''Kate Hepburn: My Life and Loves'' by Ralph G. Martin in *Ladies Home Journal* (August 1975), and Hepburn's article, ''Hooked On John Wayne,'' which appeared in *TV Guide* (September 17, 1977). An article on the Hepburn family, ''The Hepburns,'' by Oliver O. Jensen, appeared in *Life* (January 22, 1940). Also see Larry Swindell, *Spencer Tracy: A Biography* (1969); Homer Dickens, *The Films of Katharine Hepburn* (1971); Garson Kanin, *Tracy and Hepburn* (1971); Alvin H. Marill, *Katharine Hepburn* (Pyramid Illustrated History of the Movies, 1973); John Simon, *Singularities* (1975); and James Spada, *Hepburn: Her Life in Pictures* (1984). Katharine Hepburn is included in *The Biographical Encyclopaedia and Who's Who of the American Theatre* (1966); *Current Biography, 1969* (1969–1970); William C. Young, *Famous*

Actors and Actresses on the American Stage, Vol. I (1975); *Notable Names in the American Theatre* (1977); *The Film Encyclopedia* (1979); *Who's Who in the Theatre* (1981); *The Oxford Companion to the Theatre* (1983); *The Oxford Companion to American Theatre* (1984); and *Contemporary Theatre, Film, and Television*, Vol. I (1984).

Barbara Ann Simon

HERNE, Chrystal Katharine (June 17, 1882–September 19, 1950): actress, best known for her realistic portrayal of regal women, the most famous being George Kelly's *Craig's Wife*, was born in the Boston suburb of Dorchester. She was the second of four children (three daughters and one son) of James A. Herne (1839–1901) and **Katharine (Corcoran) Herne** (1857–1943), both of whom had outstanding careers in the theatre. As playwright and actor, her father pioneered the new realistic drama in America in the tradition of Henrik Ibsen. His play *Margaret Fleming* (1890) is considered the most realistic American drama of the nineteenth century for its confrontation of social issues. Chrystal's parents made their reputations by acting in the plays her father wrote; she was named after the role her mother played in *Hearts of Oak*. Of the other three children, only Chrystal's older sister Julie became an actress. Her younger sister Dorothy married drama critic Montrose Moses.

Chrystal Herne was educated in private schools in Boston and New York, where her family moved in 1892, but was, as she confesses in her autobiography, a poor scholar. From an early age Chrystal dreamed of becoming a star. Encouraged by her father, she made her first appearance in his play *The Reverend Griffith Davenport* at the Lafayette Square Opera House, Washington, D.C., on January 16, 1899. Her New York debut followed on January 31, 1900, when the same play opened at the Herald Square Theatre. After touring with *Griffith Davenport*, Chrystal Herne appeared with her sister in her father's popular comedy *Sag Harbor*, first in Boston, then Chicago, and finally on September 27, 1900, at the Republic Theatre in New York. Shortly thereafter, producer George Tyler offered her the leading role in a touring revival of *The Christian*; then she toured in *Sag Harbor* for several months after her father's death in 1901.

The next period of Herne's career is remarkable for its diversity. In 1902 she joined the company of her childhood idol, E. H. Sothern, and performed two minor roles, including the Player Queen in *Hamlet*. She left Sothern to play the lead in a melodrama which failed. Next, she played Hippolyta in *A Midsummer Night's Dream* for Nat C. Goodwin. Her first important role on Broadway was in Clyde Fitch's *Major André* (1903). "She has lots of faults," wrote Fitch, "but those I've seen can be easily cured" (*Clyde Fitch and his Letters*, p. 235). The play was a failure, running only a few performances in November 1903, and Chrystal's acting was adversely criticized. However, her season in Nat Goodwin's company gave her excellent training in the techniques of farce and light comedy, thus improving her range and her skills.

The turning point in Chrystal Herne's career came when the actor Arnold Daly chose her to be his leading lady in a series of plays by George Bernard Shaw at the Garrick Theatre in New York. In September and October 1905, Herne played the title role in *Candida*, Gloria in *You Never Can Tell*, Nora in *John Bull's Other Island*, and Vivie Warren in the first American production of *Mrs. Warren's Profession*. The latter play aroused a furor. After a tryout performance in New Haven, the actors were ordered to leave town. In New York the cast was jailed on opening night. The play was not repeated though the actors were acquitted several months later.

In January 1906, Herne made her only appearance on a foreign stage, acting in London with Henry Irving in a melodrama, *The Jury of Fate*. The play was a failure, and she returned to New York, where she rejoined Daly's company, playing Raina Petkoff in George Bernard Shaw's *Arms and the Man* in April 1906. The following September in Boston she played the Lady in *The Man of Destiny*, her last significant work with Daly. From December 1906 to January 1907, Herne's brief experience with an experimental group at the New Theatre in Chicago expanded her repertory. She had roles in plays by Gerhart Hauptmann, Hermann Sudermann, Arthur Wing Pinero, and Victorien Sardou, and in a revival of her father's *Margaret Fleming*. The next several years were spent in commercial productions on Broadway, the most successful being Israel Zangwill's *The Melting Pot* (September 1909). Herne's performance contributed to its long run (139 nights). As one reviewer noted: "She played with tact, with feeling, and with conviction in scenes that only delicate art could save" (*New York Times*, September 7, 1909). By the time she played Mrs. Clayton in Augustus Thomas' *As a Man Thinks* (March 1911), she had become an excellent actress. Critics praised her performance in this play, which, like *Margaret Fleming*, dealt with the double standard in marriage. Thomas himself wrote, "What impressed me about her work as Mrs. Clayton was the expression of mental alertness, the constantly emotional and thinking personality" (*The Print of My Remembrance*, p. 452).

On August 31, 1914, Herne married Harold Stanley Pollard, chief editorial writer of the *New York Evening World*, a marriage that appears to have been entirely happy. The following December she acted in a drama about Mormonism called *Polygamy*, which ran 163 performances. In Harley Granville-Barker's production of Euripides' *The Trojan Women* (May 1915), she played Cassandra. A milestone in the revival of interest in classical drama in America, Granville-Barker's work was staged in stadiums at Harvard and Yale universities and City College of New York. The most important role Herne played in the next few seasons was that of Lady Grayston in Somerset Maugham's *Our Betters* (March 1917). This scheming and unsympathetic character had been turned down by **Ethel Barrymore**.

In 1917 Herne joined the Stage Women's War Relief, organized by **Rachel Crothers**, Josephine Hull, Dorothy Donnelly, and Louise Closser Hale. As a result of her association with this group, many of her subsequent roles were in plays written by women. In January 1920, she appeared in Rita Weiman's *The Acquittal*, a murder mystery that enjoyed a successful run on Broadway and prompted Kenneth MacGowan to write that Herne was "perhaps the greatest emotional actress in America" (*I Remember Me*, p. 157). In December 1923 she portrayed a black woman in *Roseanne* by Nan Bagby Stephens at the Greenwich Village Theatre. She returned to Broadway to play the role of Minnie Whitcomb in Rachel Crothers's *Expressing Willie* in April 1924, a critical and popular hit that amassed the longest run (293 performances) of any play with which she was associated.

The role that brought her greatest fame, however, and for which she is best remembered, was that of the vengeful Harriet Craig in George Kelly's *Craig's Wife*, which opened in October 1925 and won a Pulitzer Prize in 1926. Years later, critic John Mason Brown recalled Herne's performance as one of the most enduring images of the theatre in the twenties. Herne impressed him as "ice-cold and strong when . . . she played the archetype of the terrible woman whose only passion is the neatness of her house" (*Dramatis Personae*, p. 11). Unfortunately, most of the roles Herne played after *Craig's Wife* were merely weak imitations of Harriet Craig. None was successful. With little fanfare, she gave her final performance in a murder mystery, *A Room in Red and White*, in February 1936. Her retirement was spent in the Pollard family home in Cambridge, Massachusetts. She was taken ill in August 1950 and died "of a malignancy" on September 19 at Boston's Massachusetts General Hospital.

Chrystal Herne's acting style was marked by restrained emotion, somewhat in the tradition of **Matilda Heron** and **Clara Morris**, but tempered by the realistic drama in which she usually appeared. In her unpublished autobiography she declared, "The one real gift I had in the theatre was a power to move people emotionally." Reviews often note her fine voice, physical beauty, and graceful movement. Although she never became a major star, she was a highly competent actress who helped to win an audience for the new drama that presented unsympathetic characters and dealt with social issues.

The major source of information about Chrystal Herne's life and career is her unpublished autobiography, "I Remember Me" (1947). The manuscript is in the Queens College Library, New York City. There are brief references to Chrystal Herne in *The Print of my Remembrance* (1922) by Augustus Thomas; *Clyde Fitch and his Letters* (1924), edited by Montrose Moses and Virginia Gerson; and "The Theatre in the Twenties," written by John Mason Brown in 1951 and included in his *Dramatis Personae*. There are two biographies of her father, James A. Herne: *James A. Herne: The Rise of Realism in the American Drama* (1964) by Herbert J. Edwards and Julie A. Herne and *James A. Herne, The American Ibsen* (1978) by John Perry. One of the best portraits of Chrystal Herne appears in *The World Today* (May 1908). Her obituary was printed in the *New York Times* (September 20, 1950). There are a number of clippings about the Herne family in the Harvard Theatre Collection. Chrystal Herne is listed in *Who's Who in the Theatre* (1947); *Notable American Women*, Vol. I (1971); and *The Oxford Companion to American Theatre* (1984).

Craven Mackie

HERNE, Katharine Corcoran (December 8, 1856–February 8, 1943): actress and wife of actor-playwright James A. Herne, most famous for her performance in the title role of *Margaret Fleming*, was born in Ballyleeks, County Cork,

Ireland. She was the first child of Michael Corcoran, a schoolteacher, and Mary (Nolan) Corcoran. There were three younger children, Edward, Elizabeth, and Mollie. In 1860 the family emigrated to the United States, settling in New York City. During the Civil War, Michael Corcoran was wounded in battle, captured by the enemy, and sent to Libby Prison. He managed to escape from prison, but his health was ruined, and he died in a Washington military hospital a few months before the end of the war. Mary Corcoran was left with four children to support, and the poverty of the family was extreme. Eight-year-old Katharine tried to make money by selling newspapers and flowers and sometimes even shoveling snow. As a child Katharine was an avid reader, and she had a facility for learning poetry that surprised her mother. She loved the theatre and frequently managed to slip past the doorman to watch plays from the back of the gallery. In this way she saw Edwin Booth, Lawrence Barrett, Joseph Jefferson, Lester Wallack, **Lotta Crabtree**, Lucille Western, and James A. Herne.

When Katharine Corcoran was sixteen, her mother's brother came from Ireland and began to look after the family. He obtained a soldier's widow's pension for Mary Corcoran and a substantial amount of back pay, whereupon they all moved to San Francisco. When Katharine decided that she wanted to be an actress, she enrolled as a pupil of Mrs. Julia Melville, who saw possibilities in seventeen-year-old Katharine, giving her a rigorous two years of acting training. At the end of the two years, Julia Melville asked her friend James A. Herne if he would hear her pupil perform. Katharine, not knowing that Herne was present, did a scene from Sheridan Knowles's *The Love Chase*. A few days later Herne offered Katharine the leading part of Peg Woffington in a performance of *Masks and Faces* for his own benefit night. Both the public and the critics were impressed by the young actress, and shortly thereafter Herne asked Katharine to be his leading lady on a tour of the West Coast cities. After their return to San Francisco, on April 2, 1878, Katharine Corcoran married James A. Herne.

Herne and his partner, David Belasco, made Katharine Herne the leading lady of their Baldwin Theatre Company, of which James O'Neill was a member. Herne and Belasco collaborated on adaptations of foreign plays, staging them in the spectacular manner that would become Belasco's trademark. They took their 1879 presentation of *Chums*, based on an English melodrama called *The Mariner's Compass*, on a tour that ended in Chicago. Here, Herne bought out Belasco's share of the play, renamed it *Hearts of Oak* at Katharine Herne's suggestion, and made a great success of it. Although it was a melodrama, it also had a sense of quiet realism, simple characters, and colloquial dialogue. Katharine Herne played Chrystal.

The first season of *Hearts of Oak* ended in Boston. Bostonians liked the play, and the Hernes liked Boston and decided to make their home there, buying a house in the suburb of Ashmont. Their first child, Julie Adrienne, was born on October 31, 1880. In the next few years two other girls, Chrystal and Dorothy, were born.

At Katharine Herne's urging, Herne wrote his first original play: a historical drama of the American Revolution called *The Minute Men of 1774–75*, with the charming role of Dorothy Foxglove written especially for his wife. The play opened at the Chestnut Street Theatre in Philadelphia on April 6, 1886. It played in New York, Boston, and Chicago; but it was not a success, and Herne lost all the money he had made on *Hearts of Oak*.

The next season, while touring his always successful *Hearts of Oak*, James Herne began work on his next play, *Drifting Apart*, which opened at the People's Theatre, New York, on May 7, 1888, with James playing Jack Hepburne and his wife playing Mary Miller. Although the play was attacked by the critics, the Hernes took it on tour, performing in the popular-priced houses located in the poorest sections of cities. One January afternoon in 1889, an unknown and penniless teacher at a small school of oratory in Boston was given a ticket to see the play at a second-rate house in Boston. This teacher, Hamlin Garland, was deeply impressed by the play. "Mrs. Herne's acting of Mary Miller was my first realization of the compelling power of truth . . . . Here was tragedy that appalled and fascinated like the great fact of living. No noise, no contortions of face or limbs, yet somehow I was made to feel the dumb, inarticulate, interior agony of a mother. Never before had such acting faced me across the footlights," he wrote (Garland, "Mr. and Mrs. Herne," *The Arena*, October 1891, p. 545). Garland was to become a much beloved friend of the Herne family. He was convinced that Katharine Herne was one of America's greatest actresses.

In spite of the financial failure of *Drifting Apart*, James Herne, encouraged by his wife, went on to write his best and most realistic play, *Margaret Fleming*. In the spring of 1890 he presented it for three nights in Lynn, Massachusetts, but neither the Boston managers nor the New York managers were interested in it. At last, upon the suggestion of William Dean Howells, the Hernes decided to do the play themselves in the tradition of the *Théâtre Libre* in Paris. They rented Chickering Hall, a small concert hall above the Chickering Piano show rooms in Boston. At their own expense, they altered the stage and installed lights and scenery. While James Herne was casting and rehearsing the play, Garland publicized it and wrote in the newspapers about Boston's own Théâtre Libre.

Margaret Fleming opened on May 4, 1891, before a very distinguished and enthusiastic audience. The play ran for two weeks, but the general public did not support it. Several other attempts were made to present the play, but always it failed to please the general audiences and the critics. Only those who were interested in the "new" drama of Henrik Ibsen and August Strindberg defended the play. William Winter, the influential New York critic who hated the plays of Ibsen and any touch of realism in the drama, led the attack on *Margaret Fleming*.

The role of Margaret Fleming was Katharine Corcoran Herne's greatest characterization. "Mrs. Herne was specially marvelous in the title-part, and the close of the play had a touch of art which up to that time had never had its equal on our stage," wrote Garland (*Roadside Meetings*, p. 75). "The power of this story, as presented in Mr. Herne's everyday phrase, and in the naked simplicity of

Mrs. Herne's acting of the wife's part, was terrific,'' wrote Howells (*Harper's*, August 1891, p. 478).

During the summer of 1888, Katharine Herne and the children had spent a summer holiday on the New England sea coast, and Katharine Herne urged her husband to use the little town of Lemoine as a locale for his next play, *Shore Acres*. For himself he wrote the part of Uncle Nat Berry, and for his wife he wrote the role of Uncle Nat's niece, Helen Berry. *Shore Acres* opened at McVicker's Theatre in Chicago on May 23, 1892, then opened at the Boston Museum Theatre in February 1893, and at Miner's Fifth Avenue Theatre in New York in October. It was a great success. Even William Winter liked the play. In December *Shore Acres* moved to Daly's Theatre, where attendance had sagged while Augustin Daly managed a new theatre in London. *Shore Acres* ran at Daly's Theatre from Christmas Day 1893 until May 1894. At last free from financial troubles, the Hernes were able to buy a summer home, named Herne Oaks, on Peconic Bay, Long Island. On October 11, 1894, their son, John Temple Herne, was born. Katharine Herne, now busy with her family, stayed at home while James Herne toured *Shore Acres* for the next five years.

In 1894 a friend of Katharine Herne, Helen Gardener, had published a novel, *An Unofficial Patriot*, about the life of her father, a Methodist circuit preacher in Virginia, who afterward became a chaplain and guide with the Union forces during the Civil War. Mrs. Gardener asked James Herne to dramatize the novel. He completed the script during the summer of 1898, with roles for himself as the Reverend Griffith Davenport and for Katharine as his wife. Katharine Herne supervised the purchase of period furniture and costumes for the play and helped to direct the ensemble scenes. The play, *The Reverend Griffith Davenport*, opened at the Lafayette Square Opera House in Washington, D.C., on January 16, 1899, then in New York on January 31, where it ran for twenty nights. Although critics and audiences found the play somewhat static, all were in agreement on the fine acting of James and Katharine Herne. William Archer, the London critic, called it ''the most interesting, the most artistic, the most characteristic, and, above all, the most truly American thing I saw in the American theatre'' (*London Tribune*, May 26, 1906, p. 2). Unfortunately, the play was a financial failure, and like *Margaret Fleming* it was shelved.

At Herne Oaks, James Herne wrote his last play, *Sag Harbor*, its characters based on the simple folk along the Long Island sound. This was James Herne's only play that did not have a character written especially for his wife. When the play opened at the Park Theatre in Boston on October 24, 1899, it was an instant success. A successful road tour followed the Boston closing, but the play was not well received in New York. During the road tour of the play, James Herne became very ill. He returned home, but pleuro-pneumonia weakened his heart; on June 2, 1901, he died.

Five years after her husband's death, Katharine Herne was hired as one of the directors of the New Theatre in Chicago, an ''art house'' supported by culturally minded citizens of Chicago, who hoped to present plays of worth and to do away with the star system. There Katharine Herne staged a revival of *Margaret Fleming* with her daughter **Chrystal Herne** playing Margaret. This time the play was applauded by the critics, but the New Theatre failed in its purpose and closed; Katharine Herne retired from active theatre life.

In 1909, a fire destroyed Herne Oaks. The manuscripts of both *Margaret Fleming* and *The Reverend Griffith Davenport* were burned. Acts III and IV of *Griffith Davenport* have since been found and published. In 1914 Katharine Herne wrote down *Margaret Fleming* from memory, and the play was presented during the summer of 1915 with Julie Herne playing Margaret. In 1929 Katharine Herne made a few changes in the script before it was printed in Arthur Hobson Quinn's *Representative American Plays*.

Katharine Corcoran Herne died at the River Crest Sanitarium in New York City on February 8, 1943, following a long illness. She was eighty-six. Chrystal and Julie Herne continued their acting careers, Chrystal achieving more success than Julie.

Katharine Corcoran Herne progressed, along with her husband, from the old melodramatic style of acting to one of realism and inner emotion. She had a musical and expressive voice, and Howells said of her art, "I have never seen so many subtle expressions appearing in the lines of a woman's countenance" (*Roadside Meetings*, p. 83). James A. Herne was America's first playwright to emulate the realistic style of Henrik Ibsen, and Katharine Herne was his collaborator in the writing, directing, and staging of his plays, as well as the inspiration and the model for his three-dimensional women characters—Dorothy Foxglove, Mary Miller, Margaret Fleming, Helen Berry, and Katharine Davenport. J. J. Enneking wrote after James Herne's death, "From no one did Mr. Herne receive so much inspiration, sympathy, and help as from his devoted and accomplished wife, Katharine Herne, who ever understood and encouraged him" (Garland, Enneking & Flower, "James A. Herne," *Arena*, September 1901, pp. 285–286).

Information concerning Katharine Corcoran Herne is included in publications about James A. Herne: *James A. Herne: The Rise of Realism in the American Drama* by Herbert J. Edwards and Julie A. Herne (1964); *James A. Herne, The American Ibsen* by John Perry (1978); Julie Herne's introduction to *Shore Acres and Other Plays* (1928); Chrystal Herne's "Some Memories of My Father" in *Green Book* (April 1909); Arthur Hobson Quinn's chapter on Herne in *A History of the American Drama from the Civil War to the Present Day* (1927, revised 1936); and Montrose J. Moses, *The American Dramatist* (1925, reissued 1964). Hamlin Garland has written a chapter, "James A. and Katharine Herne," in *Roadside Meetings* (1930); "Mr. and Mrs. Herne" in *Arena* (October 1891); "On the Road with James A. Herne" in *Century* (August 1914); and along with J. J. Enneking and B. O. Flower, "James A. Herne: Actor, Dramatist, and Man" in *Arena* (September 1901). William Dean Howells describes the production of *Margaret Fleming* in his "Editor's Study" in *Harper's* (August 1891) and discusses *Drifting Apart* in "Editors Study" in *Harper's* (June 1890). For another contemporary view of Katharine Corcoran Herne see John Bouve Clapp and Edwin Francis Edgett, *Players of the Present*, Part 1 (1899). There is a collection of newspaper clippings, photographs, and other information about the Herne family in the Harvard Theatre Collection. Alice M. Robinson has written about the first production of Margaret Fleming in "James A. Herne and his 'Théâtre Libre' in Boston," *Players Magazine* (Summer 1973). Katharine Corcoran Herne is included in *Who Was Who in America: Historical Volume 1607–1896* (1963) and *The Concise Oxford Companion to the Theatre* (1972).

Alice McDonnell Robinson

HERON, Matilda (December 1, 1830–March 7, 1877): outstanding actress, praised for her definitive performance of *La Dame aux Camélias*, was born in Laughlin County in Londonderry, Ireland, the youngest of five children of John and Mary Heron. When she was twelve years old, her father moved his family from their small farm in Ireland to Philadelphia, where he became a merchant. There, Alexander, her favorite brother, developed into a successful businessman, becoming president of the Heron line of coastal steamers. In this new home city, Matilda Heron attended a private academy auspiciously near the Walnut Street Theatre which she often attended. Her enthusiasm for theatre led her to study elocution with Peter Richings, who groomed her for her theatrical debut. On February 17, 1851, at the Walnut Street Theatre, she played Bianca in Henry Hart Milman's tragedy *Fazio*. Encouraged by her reviews, she played other romantic parts in stock companies, including Juliet at the National Theatre, Washington, D.C., opposite **Charlotte Cushman** as Romeo. The comedian James E. Murdoch, with whom she played in Boston, was instrumental in securing for her an opportunity to act in San Francisco. She was greeted there with wild enthusiasm on her opening night, December 26, 1853. She was also courted by all the gilded youth of the city until she secretly married Henry Herbert Byrne, a lawyer, in St. Patrick's Church on June 10, 1854. The cause of their divorce in the same year is not known, but her career continued.

In the winter season of 1854–1855, Heron again played Bianca in *Fazio*, this time in London at the Drury Lane Theatre. Later that season she attended a performance of *La Dame aux Camélias* in Paris, and her brother suggested that she translate the play, titled *Camille*, as a vehicle for herself. The younger Alexandre Dumas had written the play for Eugénie Doche, a spiritual beauty who gave the role a romantic interpretation. Before bringing the play to New York, Heron presented it in St. Louis and in other cities with increasing success in the role.

When she played *Camille* at Wallack's Theatre in New York, opening on January 22, 1857, she was an explosive success. According to the *New York Herald* critic, she produced striking effects with electric rapidity. She was not the first American actress to play Marguerite Gautier, the courtesan who sacrificed her own happiness for the benefit of her lover. Jean Davenport had appeared in a censored version of *Camille*, which was then a very daring play. Heron's version was candid. Her style was naturalistic, less refined than that of the actresses who preceded her. Heron's Marguerite Gautier was generally acknowledged to be the greatest on the American stage. Later, after her brilliant year as the star of *Camille* in New York, Heron married Robert Stoepel, an orchestra leader and composer, on December 24, 1857. They had one child, Helene, known professionally as Bijou Heron (1862–1937) in her career as a child actress. Bijou Heron later married the actor Henry Miller, and their son was theatrical producer Gilbert Heron Miller. Matilda Heron ended her second marriage in 1869.

Toward the end of her life, the impoverished Matilda Heron was showing premature old age and diminished capacities. In 1874, after a benefit performance given for her at Niblo's Garden Theatre, she said that she had outlived all her relatives except her small daughter. She died at her home in New York City in 1877. She was forty-six. Her funeral services were held at the players' favorite Little Church Around the Corner, and she was buried in Greenwood Cemetery, Brooklyn.

Although Heron was attractive, with dark hair, flashing dark eyes, and a pure complexion, she was not conventionally beautiful. She achieved her effects on stage by the force of her intelligence and by a magnetism admired even by critics who found her coarse and her accent too Celtic. Instead of idealizing Marguerite Gautier, she portrayed this character as a suffering, passionate woman, in a way that William Winter, in his obituary article, hinted was a reflection of Heron's own tempestuous life.

In her triumphant season in New York in 1857, the height of her career, she also played *Medea* in her own translation of Ernest Legouve's *Médée*. Whether she was dying for love or killing for love, she successfully conveyed the emotional storms of her stage characters. Her career proceeded, with reasonable success, for eight years after 1857 in New York, London, and on tour, as she played, whenever she could, the lost woman. Matilda Heron's example influenced such people as the emotional actress **Clara Morris** and helped inaugurate the realistic theatrical style of the early twentieth century.

Contemporary views of Matilda Heron may be found in Brander Matthews and Laurence Hutton, *Actors and Actresses of Great Britain and the United States* (1886); William Winter, *Brief Chronicles* (1889); and T. Allston Brown, *History of the American Stage* (1870). *History of Camille as Performed by Matilda Heron for Over One Thousand Nights* (1864) is a reprint in pamphlet form of an article that originally appeared in the *Missouri Republican* (St. Louis). A copy of this is in the California State Library at Sacramento. See also Alberta Lewis Humble, "Matilda Heron, American Actress" (Unpublished Ph.D. dissertation, University of Illinois, Urbana, 1959), and Merle L. Perkins, "Matilda Heron's Camille," *Comparative Literature* 7, no. 4 (1955). Matilda Heron's obituary appeared in the *New York Times* and the *New York Herald* (March 8, 1877). There are letters, portraits, and other material in the Harvard University Theatre Collection. George C. D. Odell, *Annals of the New York Stage*, Vols. VI-X (1931–1938) gives a record of her performances. Heron is listed in *Who's Who in America, Historical Volume 1606–1896* (1963); *The Dictionary of American Biography*, Vol. IV (1931–1932); *Notable American Women*, Vol. II (1971); William C. Young, *Famous Actors and Actresses on the American Stage*, Vol. I (1975); *The Oxford Companion to the Theatre* (1983); Donald

Mullin, *Victorian Actors and Actresses in Review* (1983); and *The Oxford Companion to American Theatre* (1984).

Mary R. Davidson

HILL, Ann Geddes Stahlman (April 15, 1921–): arts administrator, children's theatre director, long associated with the Nashville Children's Theatre, was born in Nashville, Tennessee, one of two daughters of James Geddes Stahlman and Mildred Thornton (Rhett) Stahlman. Her father was publisher of the newspaper *The Nashville Banner*; and her sister, Dr. Mildred Stahlman, is a physician who still practices medicine in Nashville. A 1939 graduate of Ward Belmont High School, Nashville, Ann Stahlman became a Phi Beta Kappa member and in 1943 received a Bachelor of Arts degree magna cum laude from Vanderbilt University. After graduation from college she joined the United States Navy in the newly created Women Appointed for Volunteer Emergency Service (WAVES). After training at Smith and Mount Holyoke colleges, she was stationed in New Orleans, Louisiana, from 1943 until 1946 as a communications officer, holding the rank of lieutenant, junior grade. On September 23, 1947, she married George de-Roulhac Hill, a advertising and public relations director now deceased. There are four children—Mary Geddes Sanders (b. 1948), George R. Hill Jr. (b. 1950), Margaret Hill Whitaker (b. 1952), and Thomas Stahlman Hill, (b. 1954)—and five grandchildren.

Ann Hill first became involved in theatre in 1947 when, as part of her service in the Junior League, she was asked to design costumes for the Nashville Children's Theatre. She subsequently became its treasurer (1954 to 1956) and president (1956 to 1958). She led the fund-raising campaign that earned $250,000 to build a new theatre. When the new theatre opened in 1960, the Nashville Children's Theatre became the second children's theatre in the nation to have its own building. Although she was increasingly involved with regional and national theatre activities, she continued to work toward the development of the Nashville Children's Theatre into a resident professional theatre and school, now called the Nashville Academy Theatre (NAT). Hill was instrumental in gaining recognition for NAT, which has received invitations to perform at the John F. Kennedy Center for the Performing Arts in Washington, D.C., and at the International Maytime Festival in Ireland in 1978. During the trip to Ireland, the theatre also received invitations to perform in Wales, England, Switzerland, for the United States Army in Germany, and at the International Association of Theatres for Children and Youth (ASSITEJ) International Congress in Madrid. In 1979, as a tribute to her contributions, the main stage of the Nashville Academy Theatre was named the Ann S. Hill Auditorium.

Hill has consistently worked toward the development of excellent quality standards in theatre for young people. In 1969 she was elected president of the Children's Theatre Association of America (CTAA), a division of the American Theatre Association. She was chair of the Winifred Ward Scholarship Committee from 1978 to 1980 and chaired its Scholars Selection Committee. She is also a long-standing trustee of the Children's Theatre Foundation.

Hill became dean of the American Theatre Association (ATA) College of Fellows for 1980–1982 after years of service to that organization. She was elected its first vice president for administration from 1972 to 1973, becoming president-elect in 1974 and president in 1975. She was also on the board of the American National Theatre and Academy (ANTA) from 1963 to 1969.

Hill attended the first meeting of the International Association of Theatres for Children and Youth (ASSITEJ) in London in 1964 and returned home to help found the U.S. Centre of ASSITEJ as a committee of CTAA. She became its first executive secretary. During her term as president of CTAA (1972), the U.S. Centre for ASSITEJ hosted the Fourth International Congress of ASSITEJ, in Albany, New York, the first such conference ever held in the Western Hemisphere. She has been a United States delegate to ASSITEJ festivals and congresses in Moscow, the Hague, Venice, Montreal, and Madrid.

Hill has also served regional and state theatre associations. She was elected president of the Southeastern Theatre Conference (SETC) for 1962–1963. In 1973 she received the SETC award for distinguished service to southern theatre. Hill was a founder of the Tennessee Theatre Association in 1968 and received its Distinguished Service Award in 1975. She was a member of the Theatre Advisory Panel of the Tennessee Arts Commission from 1968 until 1976 and a member of the Tennessee Alliance for Arts Education from 1978 until 1982.

Hill has always patronized and supported the arts in her home community of Nashville. In 1978 she became a founder and board member of the Nashville Institute for the Arts and held the position of vice chair in 1979–1980. She has been on the boards of the Nashville Junior League, the Tennessee Fine Arts Center and Botanical Gardens, the Garden Club of Nashville, the Symphony Guild, and the Nashville Arts Council. She served on the Cultural Affairs Committee of the Chamber of Commerce from 1978 to 1982.

Hill was a reporter and drama columnist for *The Nashville Banner* from 1964 to 1971 and has had articles published in *Children's Theatre Review*, *Southern Speech Journal*, and *Southern Theatre*. The *Nashville Banner* published in pamphlet form a collection of her previously printed newspaper articles, titled *European Children's Theatre and the Second Congress of the International Children's Theatre Association* (1968).

In 1975, Hill was the recipient of the American Theatre Association's Jennie Heiden Award for exceptional service to children's theatre. Ann Hill is an outstanding volunteer arts administrator, who has dedicated her life to the development of the American theatre for children at state, regional, national and international levels. One of a few dedicated volunteer arts administrators who contribute selflessly, totally, and efficiently, she has left her distinctive mark with every theatre organization she has served.

Information about Ann S. Hill can be found in *The Biographical Encyclopaedia and Who's Who of the American Theatre* (1966); *World's Who's Who of Women, 1974–1975*

(1974–1975); *Notable Names in the American Theatre* (1976); and *Who's Who of American Women, 1977–1978* (1977–1978).

Judith Kase-Polisini

HOLDEN, Joan Allan (January 18, 1939–): playwright of the San Francisco Mime Troupe, was born in Berkeley, California. Her father, William Allan, was descended from Scotch-Irish and Pennsylvania-Dutch farmers. He attended Alexander Meiklejohn's Experimental College at the Universi,ty of Wisconsin, trained in economics, and became a civil servant. Holden's mother, Seema (Rynin) Allan, was the daughter of Russian-Jewish immigrants; she was born in New York City but grew up in Los Angeles. A journalist and psychiatric social worker, she wrote *Comrades and Citizens: Everyday Life in the USSR* (1935). Holden's parents met and were married in Moscow in 1932. Holden has a younger brother, Stuart Allan, a geographer-cartographer, author of the *Atlas of Oregon* and *Atlas of California*. Educated at the University of California, Berkeley, and Reed College, Oregon, Joan Allan married actor Arthur Holden in 1958, separated from him in 1968, and was divorced in 1980. With actor and director Daniel Chumley, she has three daughters: Katy (b. 1972), Sophie (b. 1973), and Lilly (b. 1979), all born in San Francisco.

Like predecessors Shakespeare and Molière, playwright Joan Holden has been privileged to rely on a specific company as the consistent outlet for her writing. Her husband Arthur Holden, an actor with the San Francisco Mime Troupe, had "volunteered" his wife to adapt Carlo Goldoni's *L'Amant Militaire* for an anti-war performance in 1967. The following year she adapted the early Ruzzante (stage name for Angelo Beolco) plays from the Italian for the same purpose. In 1970 the troupe members established themselves as a collective whose main purpose was to perform political plays in the parks of California's Bay Area. Joan Holden emerged as the troupe's main dramatist.

Her first play for the new collective was *The Independ-ent Female* (1970), which has also been widely played by other groups. Unlike her earlier adaptations patterned on *commedia dell'arte*, her feminist play was patterned on melodrama. Both forms manipulate the old formula of Greek New Comedy, with a pair of lovers overcoming an obstacle to their union. In *commedia* the obstacle is a stock comic type—Pantalone, Il Dottore, Il Capitano. In the Mime Troupe's modified *commedia* these masked acrobatic figures are satirized as representatives of capitalism; in Holden's modified melodrama the obstacle seems to be a young woman's subjection to a traditional sex role, but she triumphs rejecting her sexist lover and declaring her independence as a woman.

As Holden's *The Independent Female* profits from the modern melodrama of soap opera, her *Dragon Lady's Revenge* (1971) uses the comic strip to condemn American intervention in the internal affairs of Long Penh, a punning reference to Vietnam: "We are there because we desperately want to get out!" Similarly, *San Fran Scandals* (1973) employs musical comedy to expose the scandalous greed of real estate operators at the expense of the aged and indigent, and *Frijoles* (1975) uses farce to reveal how multinational trusts exploit both American workers and those of the Third World, even robbing them of *frijoles*, or beans.

In the 1980s, for the first time, Holden carried a single protagonist through more than one play. The title character of *Factperson* (1980) is an old bag lady with the magic power of citing facts that contradict the lies of the media. The ubiquity of both facts and their bearer was slightly confusing, and in 1981 (*Factwino Meets the Moral Majority*) Holden aimed facts at the lies of the fundamentalist Moral Majority; in a return to the comic strip format she used Superman to create Factwino. The old magical bag lady is renamed the Spirit of Information, who can endow even the most unlikely character with facts, and the particular character she selects is an old wino. Not only does he spout facts, but he has the power to make people think—a power that is granted him on condition that he remain sober: "If you booze it, you lose it." Handily and hilariously triumphant over the Moral Majority, Factwino is captured by a fearful two-headed monster, Armageddonman, and like a Superman comic strip, the play ends suspensefully, with his fate in doubt.

In 1982 Holden followed up with *Factwino vs. Armageddonman*. "The double-headed dealer of doom," or the military industrial powers, keep Factwino submissive by keeping him drunk. An android is his jailer, and she programs Factwino to discourage "peaceniks." However, another wino learns of the dastardly conspiracy and liberates his buddy, foiling the vicious plot. Although the two *Factwino* plays (with musical accompaniment and clever lyrics) revert to comic strip form, the third play in the sequence, *Factwino: The Opera* (1985), reflects a shift in Holden's dramaturgy that she dates back to *False Promises* (1976). In preparing that play, Holden did meticulous research into American underground history—the contributions of labor, women, minorities—to achieve heightened realism in her working-class characters. Similarly, the final view of Factwino humanizes him. No longer a Superman clone, Factwino is revealed to be Sedro F. Wooley, a radical newscaster from Cleveland, who became a wino when he was fired. Since the bag lady, Spirit of Information, washes her hands of miracles, Wooley has to develop his own strength, and we share his new self-recognition: "Everybody has to find their own power." There are no magic solutions.

Although some of these summaries may sound like agitprop, Holden's scripts are invincibly humorous and celebratory, with audiences hissing the villains but sharing the confusions of the increasingly realistic working-class characters. In this vein her deepest play to date is *Steeltown* (1984). Not unlike David Hare's play *Plenty*, Holden's drama moves from a disillusioned present to a hopeful past. She stipulates that the first act is to be played as farce and the second act as a 1940s romantic musical. The farce recalls Chaplin's *Modern Times* when steelworkers, smitten with contemporary consumerism, betray their union's achievements and overwork for overtime. Aware of the dehumanization in the deunionization, a Steeltown wife leaves her husband, and a ghetto black prophesies in the streets for non-unionized labor. Act II, which takes place at the end of World War II, ends with their success and the marriage of the couple we have seen separating in Act I. Holden's message is that everybody must find his or her own power.

In 1986 Holden's musical, *Spain*, about the Spanish Civil War was presented at the Los Angeles Mark Taper Theatre. Then in 1988, four years after *Steeltown*, Holden looked back at another significant time in American history—the 1960s in *Ripped van Winkle*. The plot is borrowed from Washington Irving, but the texture is pure Holden. The twentieth-century Rip overdoses on drugs, and, awakening in the 1980s, he believes the liberating revolution has taken place. But one by one, the harsh (but hilariously staged) realities of Reaganomics slap him down. He and we have been ripped off of our egalitarian dreams.

Through her nearly annual contributions to the Mime Troupe's performances in the parks, Holden has evolved a pungent, witty style. Based on current problems and popular forms, her plays employ credible or caricatured characters who play short scenes of lively dialogue and acrobatic physicality. Often punctuated by songs, the dramas are scaled to a small collapsible stage that is the trademark of the San Francisco Mime Troupe. Although Holden wrote these plays anonymously for about a decade, she is now garnering accolades as a playwright. Her irreverent radicalism is gaining recognition, and she has given lectures, courses, and workshops on her own inimitable approach to playwriting. Minorities, labor unions, and feminist groups have cherished her teaching, and they in turn nourish her plays.

Gradually, Holden's remarkable comic gift is winning acclaim—in 1981 the Bay Area Critics' Circle Award for a script musical (*Factwino Meets the Moral Majority*) and in 1982 *Dramalogue's* award for an outstanding musical script (*Americans*). Invited in 1984 to lecture at an International Theatre Conference at the University of East Anglia, England, and sponsored in 1985 by the International Theatre Institute to give workshops in Israel, Holden has finally been honored nationally at home—with a 1984–1985 Rockefeller Foundation Fellowship. She has recently been appointed a contributing editor of *American Theatre*.

Joan Holden's plays include: *L'Amant Militaire* (1967), *Ruzzante* (lost, 1968), *The Independent Female* (1970), *Seize the Time* (1970), *The Dragon Lady's Revenge* (1971), *San Fran Scandals* (with Steve Friedman, 1973), *The Great Air Robbery* (1974), *Frijoles* (1975), *Power Play* (1975), *False Promises* (1976), *Hotel Universe* (with Daniel Chumley, 1977), *Electrobucks* (with Peter Solomon, 1978), *Factperson* (1980), *Americans, or Last Tango in Huahuatenango* (1981), *Factwino Meets the Moral Majority* (1981), *Steeltown* (1984), *Factwino: The Opera* (1985), and *Spain/36* (1986). A number of Holden's plays have been published in the San Francisco Mime Troupe volume, *By Popular Demand* (1980). Critical studies of her work include William Kleb, "*Hotel Universe*: Playwriting and the San Francisco Mime Troupe," in *Theater* (Spring 1978), and Ruby Cohn, "Joan Holden and the San Francisco Mime Troupe," in *Drama Review* (Spring 1980). A brief account of her work can be found in *New American Dramatists 1960–1980* (1982) by Ruby Cohn. Holden is included in *Contemporary Dramatists* (1982).

                                                                                                                    Ruby Cohn

HOLLIDAY, Judy Tuvim (June 21, 1922–June 1, 1965): actress and legendary Billie Dawn in *Born Yesterday*, was born Judith Tuvim in New York City. Her maternal grandmother, Rachel Gollomb, had emigrated from St. Petersburg in 1892 with her husband and four children and settled in New York's Lower East Side. Soon after their arrival, the husband died and a son was killed in a boating accident, leaving Rachel Gollomb to bring up her three remaining children—Joe, Helen, and Harry—alone. On June 17, 1917, Helen, the middle child, married Abe Tuvim, a native New York Jew and a socialist. The young couple moved in with Rachel Gollomb, who openly disapproved of Abe. Judy Tuvim was born five years later, on June 21, 1922.

As the one grandchild, the young Judy Tuvim was forced to heed not only natural parents but also the stern matriarchal gaze of her grandmother and additional parenting from her uncle. This intense family involvement continued throughout her life. Abe Tuvim fled the suffocating Gollomb environment in 1928, though he and Helen never formally divorced.

Judy Tuvim attended P.S. 150 in Sunnyside, Queens, from 1928 until 1934, and was identified as an exceptionally able student. Throughout her elementary schooling, she distinguished herself in the school's drama and literary clubs. In the fall of 1934, she enrolled in Julia Richmond High School, an all-girls public school where she worked on the school magazine *Bluebird*, wrote poetry, and became involved in drama activities, including direction of the senior play. She graduated at sixteen, first in her class, in January 1938. Upon leaving high school she considered entering the Yale School of Drama but was one year below the minimum entrance age. Instead, she took a job as a switchboard operator at the Mercury Theatre for five dollars a week; here she quickly drew attention to herself by mistakenly cutting everyone off and then bursting into tears.

Judy Tuvim's entrance into show business resulted from her habit of roaming Greenwich Village during her off hours. One evening, in order to avoid a rainfall, she ducked into the Village Vanguard, a basement club on Seventh Avenue South frequented by neobohemians and self-styled poets. The proprietor, Max Gordon, immediately realized that she was out of place and, in order to protect her from the poets, sat down with her and chatted. In the conversation Gordon mentioned that he needed a nightclub act. Judy Tuvim said she could get one together, and within days the Revuers were born. The members included Tuvim, Adolph Green, Al Hammer, **Betty Comden**, and John Frank. The group stayed together for about six years (John Frank dropped out after three) and earned themselves a reputation as a quintessential New York Village song, dance, and skit act.

In 1944 the group went to Hollywood to do a spot in a film version of *Duffy's Tavern*, a popular radio show, and to play a booking at the fashionable Hollywood nightclub, the Trocadero. The picture was canceled, leaving the group to concentrate on the nightclub performance. Here Judy Tuvim was "discovered" and signed on at Twentieth Century-Fox. Her first feature role was in *Winged Victory*, where she played Ruthie, the New York Jewish wife of a young air force cadet. During this period she changed her name from Tuvim to Holliday. By the end of 1944, Holliday was back in New York. Her first venture into live theatre came in 1945, when she played Alice, a goodhearted tramp, in a story about three veteran navy pilots on a four-day leave in San Francisco. The play, titled *Kiss Them For Me*, received mixed reviews, but Holliday was awarded a Clarence Derwent Award for best supporting performance. The next year, when Jean Arthur bowed out of the pre-Broadway run of *Born Yesterday*, a new play written by Garson Kanin and produced by Max Gordon (not the Max Gordon of the Village Vanguard), Holliday was offered the part of Billie Dawn, the uneducated, streetwise, sassy mistress of junkyard tycoon Harry Brock. She was brilliant in the role, and the play opened at the Lyceum Theatre to rave reviews on February 4, 1946. It ran for a total of 1,642 performances, firmly establishing Holliday's career as a comic actress, but also, unfortunately, presenting her in a stereotypical role from which she was never quite able to emerge.

During the long run of *Born Yesterday*, Holliday became reacquainted with David Oppenheim, a clarinetist of some repute, whom she married on January 4, 1948. The marriage was at first a happy one, producing a son, Jonathan, on November 10, 1952. Divorce ended the marriage, however, in March 1957. The couple remained friends, and Oppenheim provided a great deal of support for Holliday during her final illness.

The Broadway run of *Born Yesterday* proved so successful that Harry Cohn was determined to buy the movie rights, despite a running feud between himself and author Garson Kanin. He paid an astounding one million dollars for the play and began to look around for another actress to play Billie Dawn. Meanwhile Kanin and his wife, **Ruth Gordon**, were preparing a screenplay for Spencer Tracy and **Katharine Hepburn** called *Adam's Rib*. Kanin, Tracy, and Hepburn hatched a conspiracy to include a role for Holliday. Thereafter, MGM signed her on to play the part of Billie Dawn. The film version of *Born Yesterday* was released in late December 1950 and co-starred Broderick Crawford. For her stunning performance she received an Academy (Oscar) Award in 1950 and a seven-film contract from Columbia Pictures.

Before beginning work on her next film, however, Judy Holliday was cast by City Center in New York in a revival of Elmer Rice's *Dream Girl*, a whimsical comedy about the far-ranging fantasies of Georgina Allerton. Her performance in this play was favorably compared to her playing of Billie Dawn, probably because she had become so indelibly associated with the character of Billie Dawn that she was to be measured against this character the rest of her career. In fact, the run of movies in which Columbia starred Holliday during the 1950s were all variations on the dumb blonde stereotype. *The Marrying Kind*, written by Ruth Gordon and Garson Kanin and directed by George Cukor, was released in

March 1952. Even though the story gave Holliday a wider scope for her talents than did *Born Yesterday*, and even though Florence Keefer had little in common with Billie Dawn, the critics still made the connection. In 1954 Kanin and Cukor again collaborated to produce *It Should Happen To You*, a contrived comedy about a fame-hungry young woman named Gladys Glover. The story depended heavily on slapstick comedy and sight gags, and whatever life the film had came from the talents of its three principals, Judy Holliday, Jack Lemmon, and Peter Lawford. *Phffft*, which also came out in 1954, was even more contrived and, without George Cukor's directing, mindless and silly. *The Solid Gold Cadillac*, a story about a minor idealistic shareholder who uncovers corruption at the top rung of a major corporation, was a much better film, and Holliday received warm reviews for her portrayal of Laura Partridge. Her last film for Columbia (the seven-film contract was never completed) was a dreary story called *Full of Life* (1956), which offered little for Holliday's talents and was dismissed by Bosley Crowther, film critic for the *New York Times*, as glib and sentimental.

During the 1950s Holliday was also deeply involved in clearing her name of communistic accusations. Throughout her lifetime she had voted liberal, had signed peace petitions, and had permitted her name to be used for sundry civil rights causes. Because of her socialist leanings, she was fair game for Joseph McCarthy-type witch hunts that were prevalent during that decade. She was subpoenaed by the Senate Internal Security Subcommittee to testify on the matter of her own involvement in subversive infiltration of the entertainment industry. She appeared before them on March 26, 1952, and, even though she was terrified, she refused to name names. Instead, she covered up her acute intelligence and played the wide-eyed, misguided innocent, calling herself "irresponsible and slightly—more than slightly—stupid." Apparently, she was highly successful because a *Newsweek* article (October 6, 1952, p. 38) reporting on her testimony observed that Holliday seemed "just a dumb blonde offstage too." As *Ms.* magazine gleefully stated, "she Billie Dawned them with vengeance" (December, 1976, p. 92). Her name was cleared and she was removed from the blacklist, but the damage to her career had been considerable. She was still under contract to Columbia pictures, but her entry into radio, television, and serious theatre was stifled.

The last real success Holliday experienced came in 1956 when she was signed to play in a Broadway musical written by Betty Comden and Adolph Green called *Bells Are Ringing*. The story centered on a goodhearted switchboard operator who solves everyone's problems but her own. Though the material was thin, Holliday was brilliant. As Brooks Atkinson, the *New York Times* theatre critic, observed, "nothing has happened to the shrill little moll whom the town loved when Miss Holliday played in *Born Yesterday*. The squeaky voice, the embarrassed giggle, the brassy naiveté, the dimples, the teetering walk fortunately remained unimpaired" (November 30, 1956). The play ran until mid-December 1958 and was an outstandi,ng box-office success. For her work in the play, she won an Antoinette Perry (Tony) Award in 1957. The film version, directed by Vincent Minnelli and adapted by Betty Comden and Adolph Green, was released by MGM in 1960. Once again, while censuring the thin show and unexceptional music, the critics praised Holliday as a great comedienne who saved a mediocre musical with her consummate acting skill.

During the early 1960s Holliday starred in two more Broadway productions, neither of which was successful. In the course of her career, she had raised the role of the uneducated wide-eyed female to the level of a popular classic, almost a prototype. It was a part eminently suited to her talents, and she played it to perfection. But she was also anxious to do a more serious role. Her chance came when she heard that Stanley Young had written a stage script from Marguerite Courtney's biography of her mother, **Laurette Taylor**. Holliday had long admired Taylor's portrayal of Amanda in Tennessee Williams' *The Glass Menagerie*, and she actively campaigned for the part. After much negotiation she was given the lead, and rehearsals for *Laurette* began in the late summer of 1960. The production was doomed from the beginning: the adaptation simply did not work on the stage, and Young refused to change a word. Other writers were called in, but nothing helped. The pre-Broadway trials in New Haven and Philadelphia made it evident that the play was mediocre, but its fate was sealed when a doctor, called in to treat Holliday's recurring laryngitis, found a lump in her left breast, at which discovery she quickly left the show, returned to New York, and underwent a partial mastectomy.

By 1963 Holliday felt physically and emotionally well enough to try another play. She appeared in the musical *Hot Spot*, a satire about an inept Peace Corps volunteer. Lyrics were by Martin Charnin and music by Mary Rodgers, daughter of Richard Rodgers. The show was plagued with problems but opened on Broadway on April 17, 1963, after a disastrous pre-Broadway run in Washington and Philadelphia and a record fifty-eight previews at the Majestic Theatre in New York. Even though Holliday gallantly did her best, it was not enough. *Hot Spot* closed on May 20 with fewer performances than previews.

Judy Holliday spent the last two years of her life battling financial problems and failing health. The cancer recurred in her right breast and was inoperable. She gradually retreated from public appearances and finally had to be hospitalized on May 26, 1965. She died on Monday, June 7, 1965, at Mount Sinai Hospital, New York City, just two weeks short of her forty-third birthday. At her funeral, on June 9, the eulogy was delivered by Algernon Black, president of the Ethical Culture Society. She was buried that same day in Westchester Hills Cemetery, near Valhalla, New York.

At periodic intervals throughout her life, Holliday attempted to use her considerable intelligence and skill with language in areas other than acting. During her marriage to David Oppenheim, she was surrounded by musicians and tried her hand at songwriting. Her association with jazz musician Gerry Mulligan toward the end of her life gave her another opportunity with lyric writing, and one of their lyrics, "It Must Be Christmas," was picked up by Dinah Shore for her annual network Christmas show in 1959. Holliday was actively working on some lyrics with Gerry Mulligan for a musical version of Anita Loos's play *Happy Birthday* when she died. The musical has never been produced; but it should be, suggests Gene Lees in an article in *High Fidelity*, because Holliday's songs are "brilliant" (January 1977, p. 18).

Perhaps Judy Holliday's greatest contribution to American culture, however, is her decency as a human being. In an age when movie stars were idolized and returned that adulation with self-centered imperiousness, she was remarkably without ego. In the words of Algernon Black, who delivered her eulogy: "Every once in a while a human being lives among us who for intelligence, aliveness, charm, dignity, and grace seems to be of the gods. . . . It will take time to appraise what she meant to us and our generation."

There are two recent biographies of Judy Holliday: Gary Carey, *Judy Holliday: An Intimate Life* (1982), and Will Holtzman, *Judy Holliday* (1982). Numerous articles have appeared in popular magazines. Among the more important are *Newsweek* (January 1, 1951; June 21, 1965; October 6, 1952; and June 27, 1960), *Colliers* (June 15, 1946, and January 26, 1952), *Saturday Evening Post* (December 31, 1955), *Life* (April 14, 1958; April 9, 1951; and April 2, 1951), *New York Times Magazine* (March 4, 1951, and March 3, 1946), *Holiday* (September 1951), *Ms.* (December 1976), *High Fidelity* (January 1977), *McCall's* (October 1957), *Vogue* (October 1, 1960), and *The New Yorker* (March 2, 1951). George Cukor commented on Holliday's career in Roddy McDowell's book *Double Exposure* (1965), and her winning of the Oscar is covered in George Likeness, *Oscar People* (1965). She is also mentioned in Ray Stuart, *Immortals of the Screen* (1965). For information on reviews of her films and plays, see *The New York Times Film Reviews*, *The New York Times Theatre Reviews*, and *The New York Theatre Critics Reviews*. There is a clipping file on Holliday in the Billy Rose Theatre Collection, New York Public Library Performing Arts Research Center, at Lincoln Center, and another in the Harvard Theatre Collection. Her obituary can be found in the *New York Times* (June 10, 1965) and in *Time* (June 18, 1965). Judy Holliday is included in *Who's Who in the Theatre* (1961); *Current Biography, 1965* (1966); *The Biographical Encyclopaedia and Who's Who of the American Theatre* (1966); *Who Was Who in America: Vol. 4: 1961–1968* (1968); and *The Oxford Companion to American Theatre* (1984).

Maureen Potts

HOLM, Celeste (April 29, 1919–): stage and film actress, originator of Ado Annie in *Oklahoma!*, was born in New York City to Theodor Holm, an insurance adjuster, and Jean (Parke) Holm, an artist. She graduated from Francis W. Parker High School in Chicago and attended the University of Chicago from 1932 to 1934, studying dramatic art. She studied acting with Benno Schneider (1938–1941) and voice with Clytie Hine Mundy (1940–1945). After three short and unsuccessful marriages (to Ralph Nelson, Francis E. H. Davies, and A. Schuyler Dunning), she has been married to actor Wesley Addy for many years. Holm made her first stage appearance at the Orwigsburg Summer Theatre in Deer Lake, Pennsylvania, in June 1936; she played Roberta Van Renssalaer in *The Night of January 16*. Her first professional role was as Lady Mary in *Gloriana*, at the Little Theatre in New York City on November 25, 1938. In February 1940, she took over the role of Mary L in William Saroyan's *The Time Of Your Life*, at the National Theatre in New York.

Holm's first great success was in creating the role of Ado Annie in Richard Rodgers and Oscar Hammerstein's *Oklahoma!* (St. James Theatre, March 31, 1943). Holm recalls the experience of being cast and of playing for servicemen going overseas on an LP recording, "Celeste Holm Gives a Very Personal Tribute to OKLAHOMA!" (Original Cast Records OC–8129). Burns Mantle said, "Celeste Holm is happy in her first musical comedy role" (*New York Daily News*, April 1, 1943). Burton Rascoe was more rhapsodic: "Among the principals, Celeste Holm simply tucked the show underneath her arm and just let the others touch it. This is an astounding young woman, Miss Holm. . . . When you see and hear her sing the rather naughty song, 'I Can't Say No,' you are in for a tickling thrill. And you just wait for her next number, which happens to be 'All 'er Nothin',' a bell-ringing hit. . . . Miss Holm, with her fresh beauty, has too much talent to be quite credible" (*New York World-Telegram*, April 1, 1943).

Following this success, Holm starred in Harold Rome's *Bloomer Girl* (Shubert Theatre, October 5, 1944). In this musical she played Evelina Applegate, friend and supporter of Dolly Bloomer, who not only scandalizes the town by wearing "bloomers" but also involves herself in abetting escaped slaves.

A major change in role-type came with the revival of Eugene O'Neill's *Anna Christie* (City Center, New York, January 1952). John McClain said, "Miss Holm, not heretofore regarded as a serious emotional actress, gave what I consider a performance of great depth and conviction as Anna Christie" (*New York Journal-American*, January 10, 1952). John Chapman said, "I suppose interest will center in Miss Holm's portrayal of Anna. . . . I think Miss Holm is excellent; she plays quietly, almost casually, but she can summon dramatic effects where they are needed and her sincerity is absolutely convincing. It is an individual and intelligent approach to the role" (*New York Daily News*, January 10, 1952).

Other major stage roles include Camilla Jablonski in *Invitation To a March* (Music Box Theatre, October 1960) and Lady Rumpers in *Habeas Corpus* (Martin Beck Theatre, November 1975). In 1952 she took over the lead role of Anna Leonowens in *The King and I* and in 1967 took over the role of Mame Dennis in the musical *Mame*. A major disappointment was the production of the musical *The Utter Glory Of Morrissey Hall*, which opened at the Mark Hellinger Theatre on May 3, 1979; there was no second performance. In 1979 Celeste Holm impersonated the author Janet Flanner in a solo show, *Paris Was Yesterday* (Harold Clurman Theatre, December 19, 1979), written by Paul Shyre. Her most recent stage appearances have been Off-Broadway and in regional theatre. She and her husband, Wesley Addy, appeared in *With Love and Laughter* (Harold Clurman Theatre, June 2, 1982), which was billed as "an evening of varied theatre by 22 authors." In the same 1982–1983 season she played the role of Judith Bliss in a revival of Noel Coward's *Hay Fever* for the Center Theatre Group at the Ahmanson Theatre in Los Angeles.

Celeste Holm has received numerous awards for her work in films. Her first film was *Three Little Girls in Blue* (1946). She received an Academy Award (Oscar) as best supporting actress for her 1947 film *Gentlemen's Agreement*. She was nominated for the same award for both *Come To The Stable* (1949) and *All About Eve* (1950). Her later films have been musicals: *High Society* in 1956 and *Tom Sawyer* in 1973.

Celeste Holm has been a member of the governing board of the World Federation of Mental Health, an active participant in the activities of UNICEF, and has served on the National Council of the National Endowment for the Arts. She is currently head of the Film and TV Commission for the state of New Jersey. She is interested in educational theatre, occasionally appearing as a guest artist on college campuses and speaking at conferences. Beautiful, generous, and talented, Celeste Holm has portrayed a variety of characters that have added an undeniable sparkle to the modern American theatre.

Some reviews of *Oklahoma!* and Celeste Holm's Ado Annie are in the *New York Daily News* (April 1, 1943) and the *New York World-Telegram* (April 1, 1943). Reviews of her Anna Christie appeared in the *New York Journal-American* (January 10, 1952) and the *New York Daily News* (January 10, 1952). Listings of her career activities may be found in *The Biographical Encyclopaedia and Who's Who of the American Theatre* (1966); Charles Eugene Claghorn, *Biographical Dictionary of American Music* (1973); Stanley Green, *Encyclopedia of the Musical Theatre* (1976); *Notable Names in the American Theatre* (1976); James Robert Parish and Lennard DeCarl, eds., *Hollywood Players: The Forties* (1976); David Ragan, *Who's Who in Hollywood, 1900–1976* (1976); Ephriam Katz, *The Film Encyclopedia* (1979); *Halliwell's Filmgoer's Companion* (1980); Richard Gertner, ed., *International Motion Picture Almanac* (1980); *Who's Who in the Theatre* (1981); *The Oxford Companion to American Theatre* (1984); and *Contemporary Theatre, Film, and Television*, Vol. I (1984).

Frank L. Warner

HOLM, Hanya (1893–): dancer, and director-choreographer of major works for theatre, was born Johanna Eckert in the town of Worms-am-Rhein in Germany, and moved as a small child to Mainz, a colorful city where the local German dialect is peppered with French words. Carnival time in Mainz provided Holm's first look at dance. Her father was Valentin Eckert, a wine merchant from a family of Bavarian brewers. Her mother, Maria (Moreschel) Eckert, was an amateur chemist who registered several patents for scientific inventions.

The young Johanna Eckert (Hanya was a nickname, and she later chose Holm because it went well with her first name) was sent to the Convent der englischen Fräulein a school chosen by her mother for its progressive teaching and small classes. Here she gained a respect for knowledge and creative ability, an iron discipline, and a belief in perfection. At ten Holm started traveling to Frankfurt-am-Main to the Hoch Conservatory for piano lessons and music appreciation. After graduation from the conservatory she attended the Dalcroze Institute in Hellerau, where she studied rhythm as part of her music education. She became a teacher of the Dalcroze method and explored the use of physical expression beyond the mere realization of rhythm. This exploration led her to Dresden to join the classes of Mary Wigman, a German modern dancer who was gaining a reputation for original movement that explored inner drama.

Mary Wigman has been called the Eleonora Duse of the dance; she met resistance at first for her internal themes but went on to be widely respected in dance circles, to tour on her own, and to form a nucleus of dedicated dancers who expanded on her method. Holm's first composition that brought her to the attention of Wigman was called "Egyptian Dance," and Wigman says she "recognized in it a sure feeling for style and a sense for clear organic structure" (Sorell, *Hanya Holm*, p. 17). By 1928 Holm was the chief instructor at the Wigman school in Dresden. Before going to Dresden she had married painter-sculptor Reinhold Martin Kuntze; the marriage ended in divorce soon after their only son, Klaus, was born. After moving to Dresden with her son, she changed her name to Hanya Holm. She danced the Princesse in Igor Stravinski's *l'Histoire du Soldat*, which she choreographed in Dresden in 1929, and co-directed with Wigman *Totenmal*, a choric anti-war work.

When Sol Hurok, the great American impresario, sent Mary Wigman on a tour to the United States and decided to open a school of the Wigman technique in New York, Hanya Holm was chosen to head that school. She came to America in 1931. After a year Hurok tired of running a school, a very different proposition from running a tour, and Holm undertook to carry on herself. There was some feeling in America at that time that Mary Wigman had not protested sufficiently against the new Nazi regime; as a result, her name was dropped, and the school became the Hanya Holm School.

Holm remained in America and began learning about the country as a whole, having her first association with the West and Midwest through teaching at **Charlotte Perry** and **Portia Mansfield**'s camp near Steamboat Springs, Colorado. The school in New York still held to the Wigman principles, but the themes gradually changed from dark German mysticism to the vitality and freshness of American optimism. Holm established herself as a teacher first and then as a dancer and choreographer. She pioneered in teaching improvisation in dance, and her classes included anatomy, percussion, numerous other ideas associated with all artistic media, and the history of art. She toured a series of demonstration programs in midwestern colleges in the 1930s.

Holm's willingness to become a part of the new dance movement in America, rather than maintain the superiority of its European roots, contributed to her acceptance in what was then the fledgling yet vital modern dance movement. In the early thirties **Martha Graham** dominated modern dance in America, closely followed by Doris Humphrey, Charles Weidman, and **Helen Tamaris**. In the summer of 1934 the Bennington School of the Dance brought together the three great schools of modern dance—Graham, Holm, and Humphrey/Weidman. From 1934 to 1939 this electric combination served both to enlighten and confuse students with its potpourri of creativity. Holm believed that when her method was properly absorbed, the technical development could never lead to a single style; on the contrary, it liberated the inner personality and gave it the freedom to find itself.

In 1937, Holm choreographed at Bennington her first major work, titled *Trend*. She used the music of Wallingford Reigger and Edgard Varese with designs by Arch Lauterer. *Trend* won the *New York Times* award for the best dance composition of the year, and dance critic Walter Terry praised Holm's gift for abstract design in modern dance and called her the equivalent of George Balanchine in classical ballet. Between 1936 and 1944 Holm choreographed her most famous pure dance works, including *Metropolitan Daily*, which had the distinction of being the first televised dance work (1939); *Tragic Exodus* (awarded the *Dance-magazine* award for best group choreography in modern dance, 1938–1939); *They Too Are Exiles* (1939); and *Namesake* (1939). She performed these works with her own company, which was considered more lyrical than the other schools of modern dance. The Holm style is often spoken of as more "feminine" dancing. Holm herself was known for delicacy and expressive lyricism and impressive fleetness as a dancer—quick footwork and lightness combined with strength and drive, which in no way contradicted the lyricism. She had extraordinary skill as a dancer, though she was never considered a "great performer."

At the end of World War II, Holm could no longer afford to keep her company together. She had injured her back, but by then she had gained a reputation as a choreographer as well as a dancer and a teacher, and she began experimentation with dance and the spoken word. More and more humor began to surface in her work, and her dances became choreographically entertaining—humor in dance form was to become one of her great assets. In 1941 Holm began her association with Colorado College in Colorado Springs, an association that was celebrated in a dance festival in her honor in 1965 and that continues to this day.

A transition point between choreography for pure dance and choreography for theatre pieces came when Holm created *The Eccentricities of Davy Crockett*, the third of three Ballet Ballads in 1948. This piece was closely followed by *Kiss Me, Kate*, the Broadway musical that won the New York Drama Critics Award for 1948–1949, and several works that were not commercial successes but brought good notices for Holm. She felt that even the failures were worthwhile, that she learned something and was able to contribute to shows such as *Where's Charley?* (1948), *Out of this World* (1950), *The Liar* (1950), and *Christine* (1960). Dance critic Walter Terry, reviewing *Kiss Me, Kate*, said that Holm has "the rare gift of making each dancer look as if he knew exactly what he was doing." *Kiss Me, Kate* was the first complete choreographic score to be preserved through labanotation, which allows dances to be rehearsed on the basis of notation and gives property rights to the choreographers for their work.

During the 1950s Holm choreographed *My Darlin' Aida* (1952), *The Golden Apple* (1954), the film *Vagabond King* (1954), *Reuben-Reuben* (1955), and *My Fair Lady* (1956), for which she is most remembered in the popular mind. To get the proper atmosphere for the play, she traveled to London, going to the early morning Covent Garden market. Wolcott Gibbs of *The New Yorker* said that Holm staged "at least two dances that struck me as being as lovely as dreams." Brooks Atkinson said she "has blended the dance numbers into the story so unobtrusively that they seem like extensions of the general theme in terms of motion." John Martin said that Holm deserved high praise because she enriched the Shavian didacticism rather than canceling it out, a difficult task since "dance is the fullest basic medium of the lyric theatre" (Sorell, *Hanya Holm*, p. 122). Holm won an Antoinette Perry (Tony) Award nomination for her choreography for *My Fair Lady*. In 1960 Holm choreographed *Camelot*, and once again her choreography received rave reviews. In 1966 she staged the musical numbers for *Anya*, a musical based on the story of Anastasia. Holm subsequently staged the musical numbers for revivals of *My Fair Lady* (1964 and 1968) and *Kiss Me, Kate* (1965) for the New York City Center Light Opera Company.

Outside of New York, Holm was the stage director for the Central City Opera House première of *The Ballad of Baby Doe* (1956) and for the opera *Orpheus and Eurydice* (1959), presented in Vancouver and Toronto. For television she choreographed *Pinocchio* (1957).

Holm has won many awards, among them the Honor Award for the women's division of the Federation of Jewish Philanthropies and the Centennial Citation for Distinguished Service from the state of Colorado. She is a fellow of the International Institute of Arts and Letters and a member of the Society of Stage Directors and Choreographers. She is demanding as a teacher, bringing to her teaching a whole philosophy of life that she verbalizes as she teaches. Her method relies on natural movement, movement based on the structural and functional capabilities of the body, and time, space, and energy. As recently as 1982 the Don Redlich Dance company performed her work *Ratatat* at the Theatre of the Riverside Church in New York City. Reviewer Jack Anderson likened it to another of her recent works, *Jocose*, and said that it follows a trend in Holm's work to become choreographically more cheerful with each passing year. Since her arrival from Germany in 1931, Hanya Holm has been a major force in American dance.

The best source of information about Holm is Walter Sorell, *Hanya Holm, The Biography of an Artist* (1969). This is a factual, comprehensive biography of Holm's dance achievements, reviews, and a chronology of her life, but it gives little sense of the person behind the achievements. Major Holm works are covered in John Martin's *Introduction to the Dance* (1939, republished in 1965), *Modern Dance* (1962), and *America Dancing* (1968). See also Jack Anderson's "Hanya Holm Asks and Answers," in *Dancemagazine* (August 1965). The Colorado Dance Festival is covered in *Colorado College Magazine* (Fall 1965). Hanya Holm as an educator is discussed in "The Dance, the Artist-Teacher, and the Child," in *Progressive Education* (1935), and in "Trend Grew upon Me," by Hanya Holm, in *Magazine of Art* (March 1938). Hanya Holm is included in *The Biographical Encyclopaedia and Who's Who of the American Theatre* (1966); Anatole Chujoy and P. W. Manchester, eds., *The Dance Encyclopedia* (1967); *Who's Who of American Women, 1972–1973* (1973); *Notable Names in the American Theatre* (1976); Don McDonagh, *The Complete Guide to Modern Dance* (1976); *The Concise Oxford*

Dictionary of Ballet (1977); Mary Clarke and David Vaughan, eds., *The Encyclopedia of Dance and Ballet* (1977); *Who's Who in the Theatre* (1981); Barbara Naomi Cohen-Stratyner, *Biographical Dictionary of Dance* (1982); and *The Oxford Companion to American Theatre* (1984).

Judith Edwards

HOWARD, Cordelia (February 1, 1848–August 8, 1941): actress, famous as the first Little Eva in *Uncle Tom's Cabin*, was born in Providence, Rhode Island. Her mother, Caroline Emily (Fox) Howard, had appeared in children's roles in Boston, New York, and throughout New England. She became a member of the Boston Museum Company and there met George C. Howard (George Howard Cunnabell), whom she married at the age of fifteen. In 1846, George Howard organized a family troupe, the Howard-Fox Dramatic Stock Company, which settled in Providence. Cordelia Howard was the second of eight children. She made her debut on the stage as a fairy sprite in a dramatic ballet, *The Mountain Sylph*, at the age of two and a half. In June 1851, the Howards joined George L. Fox at Purdy's National Theatre in New York, and in September George Howard leased Peale's Museum Theatre in Troy, New York, and attempted to win an audience there.

Because the works of Charles Dickens were highly popular, it occurred to George Howard that a play based on *Oliver Twist* might find a ready-made market. Also, because it hymned a morally uplifting theme it might overcome the devout Christian's deep-seated aversion to "Satan's Palace," as the legitimate theatre was referred to by the faithful of the time. Within a day of opening, Howard was still unable to find a child to play the role of Little Dick, a four-year-old inmate of the orphanage from which Oliver is running away. At last, in desperation, he decided to thrust his own four-year-old daughter Cordelia into the part.

Dressed in boys' clothes, her face whitened with chalk to make her appear consumptive, and set down beside a little pile of dirt with a small spade in her hand (she was digging a fellow orphan's grave), Cordelia seemed to grasp the essence of the dramatic farewell scene, and her father was consoled by the fact that she had a mere four lines to remember. On opening night, with her parents watching nervously from the wings, Little Cordelia Howard suddenly responded to Oliver's "I'll come back and see you someday" by bursting into loud, un-rehearsed sobs. Then, in a positively heart-melting voice she delivered one of the greatest ad-libs in theatre history: "It won't be any use, Olly dear! When you come back I won't be digging little graves." (Here she tossed a bit of dirt with her small shovel.) "I'll be in a little grave myself!" (*Trouping*, p. 57).

An echoing gasp of sorrow swept the audience and a thrill went down George C. Howard's spine. The child was an actress. She deserved something better than Little Dick's paltry lines. Immediately he began casting about in his mind for a likely vehicle to showcase his daughter's talent, and he hit upon the answer to all his prayers: Harriet Beecher Stowe's *Uncle Tom's Cabin*. Not only did it have a high moral message in its anti-slavery theme that was sure to attract pious abolitionists as patrons; it also had an appealing child's role—Little Eva—whose redemptive death capitalized on the current vogue of glamourizing the high rate of childhood mortality. Tears that might not be shed at home by heroic mothers and manly fathers might flow freely in the protective darkness beyond the kerosene footlights.

Howard guessed right. Although Harriet Beecher Stowe had already piously refused to cooperate in bringing her book to the stage, Howard did not worry about the copyright. His wife's cousin, George L. Aiken, had the script completed in a week. The play opened on the evening of September 27, 1852, with Cordelia starring as Little Eva and with her mother as Topsy. It ran one hundred nights in Troy, and then, in July of 1853, Howard moved the production to New York. Audience response was so great that the company was forced to add two matinees daily, and soon they found themselves giving eighteen performances a week and eating their meals in costume between shows.

Uncle Tom's Cabin was a hit such as the American theatre had never seen before, and it was destined to change the very image of that theatre as well. In what amounted to a veritable embarrassment of riches, George Howard discovered that his play also qualified as a genuine religious drama, thereby breaking the long-standing preachers' ban against stage productions. Now, because of its humanitarian theme, and especially because of Cordelia's appeal, attending a performance of *Uncle Tom's Cabin* became an obligation of conscience for uncounted thousands of devout Christians of all denominations who had hitherto shunned the proscenium arch as the very gate of Hell. To her everlasting glory, little Cordelia had succeeded where giants of the stage such as Joseph Jefferson, Edwin Forrest, and even the formidable Booths had failed. She made theatregoing respectable.

After *Uncle Tom* closed in New York on May 13, 1854, the Howards toured the major cities of the East and the Midwest, returning occasionally to New York. Cordelia Howard added a few other children's roles to her repertoire, but it was as Little Eva that she became famous. In 1856–1857 the Howards played at the Marylebone and Strand Theatres in London and in Edinburgh and Dublin. Upon their return to the United States, they once again took to the road. Then they appeared at Barnum's American Museum in New York in a shortened version of the play called *The Death of Little Eva*. Cordelia Howard also appeared as Pearl in Aiken's dramatization of Nathaniel Hawthorne's *The Scarlet Letter* and as Mary in *Ten Nights in a Barroom*. She played Little Eva for the last time at the Howard Athenaeum in Boston on October 8, 1861. That December she retired from the stage. She was thirteen.

Cordelia Howard completed her education at a Cambridge, Massachusetts, school for girls. On June 21, 1871, she was married to Edmund Jesse MacDonald, the propietor of a bookbindery in Cambridge. The Howards continued to tour, with Caroline Fox Howard continuing to play Topsy. On George Howard's death in 1887, Caroline Fox Howard went to live in Cambridge, where she died in 1908.

In 1933, some eighty-one years after her debut in the original *Uncle Tom's Cabin*, Cordelia Howard MacDonald was invited to the Player's Club in New York to attend a special all-star revival, with the great Otis Skinner starring as Tom. "Well, they did give me an ovation Monday eve," the eighty-five-year-old actress wrote to her family after the event. "Mr. Skinner made a speech and said the original Little Eva was present and pointed to my box. The applause broke forth and I had to bow to the audience." She also confessed that it had been many years since she had received the plaudits of an audience, "And do you know, I rather liked it!" (*Trouping*, p. 58). In a very touching gesture, she placed the bouquet of four dozen red roses presented to her by the Players on the grave of her mother and father in Mount Auburn. Cordelia Howard MacDonald died in 1941, of a cerebral hemorrhage, at Bourne, Massachusetts, where she was visiting a brother. She is buried in Mount Auburn Cemetery in Cambridge.

Cordelia Howard's career is especially noteworthy in that she was associated throughout her life with a single play, the most successful single hit in American theatrical history. *Uncle Tom's Cabin* continued to be performed on some stage in the nation for ninety years. She also brought about the conversion to stage entertainment of an entire generation reared to shun all dramatic presentations. But she deserves the further distinction of being America's very first child star.

The best source for details of the life of Cordelia Howard is Phillip C. Lewis, *Trouping: How the Show Came to Town* (1973). Having himself "trod the boards" when traveling tent shows and touring repertory companies were in their twilight years, he brings great empathy to little Cordelia and her entire family. He also includes excerpts from the early *Tom Shows* and other scripts that make it possible to reconstruct the dialogue as delivered on stage. Cordelia Howard MacDonald wrote "Memoirs of the Original Little Eva," which appears in *Educational Theatre Journal* (December 1956). See also George C.D. Odell, *Annals of the New York Stage*, Vols. VI-VIII (1931–1936); Henry P. Phelps, *Players of a Century* (1879); and Harry Birdoff, *The World's Greatest Hit* (1947). There are playbills and clippings in the Harvard Theatre Collection, the Seymour Collection (Princeton University), and the Performing Arts Research Center of the New York Public Library at Lincoln Center. Cordelia Howard is included in T. Allston Brown, *History of the American Stage* (1870); *Notable American Women*, Vol. II (1971); and *The Oxford Companion to American Theatre* (1984).

Diana Serra Cary

HOWE, Tina (November 21, 1937–): playwright, grew up in a literary family; her father and aunt were authors; her grandfather was a poet and biographer. She says, "I never thought about getting married or motherhood. I just thought about trying to keep up my end of the family and trying not to disgrace [them]" (Personal interview with Tina Howe, December 1978). She was born and grew up in New York City. Her father, Quincy Howe, was a news commentator, editor, and historian. A pioneer in radio and television news commentary, he worked for CBS radio and ABC television. Her mother, Mary (Post) Howe, was a painter, who exhibited in the New England area. Howe's grandfather was an Episcopal bishop in Pennsylvania. She has one brother, Quincy Howe, who resides in Connecticut.

Howe was educated at private grammar schools in New York City. She attended the Brearly School through grade four and the Chapin School for grades five through seven. At this point her family left New York because her father took a faculty position at the University of Illinois School of Journalism. Tina Howe graduated from the University High School in Urbana, Illinois, which she describes as "a wildly experimental" laboratory school connected with the University of Illinois (Personal interview, January 1982).

Her first real exposure to theatre and the performing arts took place in Urbana at the high school, which had a "wonderful director of production," and the university, which had "an outstanding music department" (Interview, 1982). There she studied piano and became a serious music student. She attended Bucknell University from 1955 to 1957 and Sarah Lawrence College from 1957 until graduation in 1959. While she was a student at Sarah Lawrence her first play, *Closing Time*, was produced. It was directed by **Jane Alexander**, a friend and fellow student, who at the last moment took over the leading role. Howe says everyone at the college thought she was a genius because she had written the play that she terms "an awful, incredibly pretentious piece about the end of the world" (Interview, 1982). The year after Howe graduated from college, she lived in Paris, studied at the Sorbonne, and wrote her first full-length play. Written in capital letters, the play was never shown to anyone.

In 1961 Howe married Norman Levy, a historian and novelist. While he was completing college and graduate school, she did further graduate work at the University of Chicago; was an editor for the college division of Scott, Foresman publishers; and taught high school English (both college preparatory classes and slow learners) in Maine and then in Wisconsin. While teaching high school (Monona Grove, Wisconsin, from 1965 to 1967), she seriously began writing plays. Howe says that because she knew something of theatre she was made head of the drama department. She accepted the position on condition that she be allowed to produce her own plays. During this time she wrote five one-act plays. Howe claims that it was in high school auditoriums that her ability as a playwright was developed and tested.

Howe fuses various art forms into her dramas. She writes in an avant-garde style similar to that used in the *Sprechstücke* of Peter Handke and some of the recent work of Samuel Beckett (Pevitts, Ph.D. dissertation, 1980). Her plays are farcical and absurd, and her center of action is frequently a visual metaphor. As one of the major epiphanies of her life she lists seeing Eugene Ionesco's *The Bald Soprano* in Paris in 1960 and realizing that mayhem could be put on stage (Interview, 1982). Howe believes that when we are most moved, we are silent

(*American Theatre*, September 1985, p. 12). She has created silent visual images in each of her four major plays: *Museum*, *The Art of Dining*, *Painting Churches*, and *Coastal Disturbances*. These visual images are frequently silent metaphors for the meaning. Although not a painter in our everyday understanding of this visual arts term, Howe is a strong visual artist. Her visual orientation contributes to the creation of the total environment of the play. Frank Rich comments on Howe's ability to make dramatic connections between art and life (*New York Times*, February 9, 1983). The critic T. E. Kalem has called her work Chekhovian (*Time*, February 21, 1983, p. 74). Indeed, the plays of Tina Howe explore the roles of women as artists. Her four major plays move in setting from a large public space in *Museum*, to an intimate restaurant in *The Art of Dining*, to the even more private sector of a family living room in *Painting Churches*, to New England beaches in *Coastal Disturbances*. Fascinated with exotic settings and artistic processes, Howe feels one contribution she makes to the theatre is in bringing large public places to life, finding the dramatic tension and surprises in such public spaces as museums (Interview, 1982). While the playwright explores the artistic process in her writing, she also questions the life process with her comic sensibility and candor.

The Nest, her first professionally produced play, was first presented at Act IV in Provincetown, Massachusetts, in 1969. The play moved to the Mercury Theatre, Off-Broadway, in April of 1970. Produced by Ann McIntosh, Honor Moore, and Thayer Burch, it ran for one performance and closed. *Birth and After Birth* is an absurdist play with a vicious view of the family unit in contemporary society: mother, father, and son. It is a grotesque comedy of a young woman who has submitted herself to a life of oppression in the home. The play was produced at the Gotham Art Theatre in New York in 1974 with the playwright directing. It was subsequently published in *The New Women's Theatre*, edited by Honor Moore, in 1977. Howe has said that both of these plays (*The Nest* and *Birth and After Birth*) represented her own "antic vision on the stage of what it meant to be a woman" (*American Theatre*, September 1985, p. 12).

Her next play produced Off-Broadway was *Museum*, which explored the role of women as artists. The play had been first presented in the spring and summer of 1976 at the Los Angeles Actors' Theatre, directed by Ralph White with a cast of forty-four. It was then produced for a limited run by Joseph Papp, and directed by Max Stafford-Clark, at the New York Shakespeare Festival in 1977. It had a subsequent production during the 1980 season at the Terrace Theatre, John F. Kennedy Center for the Performing Arts, Washington, D.C. Howe's center of action in *Museum* is frequently the "creation of a visual metaphor through the image of silence" (Pevitts, p. 168). *The Art of Dining*, like *Museum*, has an unconventional setting. The setting for *Museum* is a gallery in a museum; *The Art of Dining* is set in a small chic restaurant and the female artist is a chef. Howe's *The Art of Dining*, a tour de force and her "favorite play," was co-produced by the New York Shakespeare Festival at the Public Theatre, under the direction of A. J. Antoon, in the fall of 1979. The production then went to the John F. Kennedy Center for the Performing Arts, Washington, D.C., opening December 20, 1979, for a five-week run. The play was then produced at the Berkeley Repertory Theatre in California and directed by Robert Moss, opening on December 11, 1985, for a limited engagement. For this production Howe rewrote the last scene of the play, an endeavor that she says makes the play finally "work" (Interview, 1985). The Milwaukee Repertory Company also produced *The Art of Dining* in the 1985–1986 season.

Painting Churches, for which Howe received a *Village Voice* (Obie) Award in 1983, was produced by the Second Stage at the South Street Theatre in January 1983. The play, conventional within its living room setting but not with its images of art-as-life and life-as-art theme, opened at the Lambs Theatre in the fall of 1984 for a substantial run. The play was produced by **Elizabeth McCann** and **Nelle Nugent** and directed by Carole Rothman. Howe has said several times that women as artists fascinate her. In *Museum* the woman artist's materials are "found materials." So are the materials of the painter as a young girl in *Painting Churches* who found her "own materials" out of which to create art and who, without encouragement from her parents, found her own "very strong abilities" as an artist. The playwright, like her character Mags in *Painting Churches*, is "safely hidden" behind her art (Interview, 1985). *Painting Churches* received a British production in 1988.

Coastal Disturbances opened at the Off-Broadway Second Stage in November 1986 and transferred to Broadway's Circle in the Square in February 1987. Directed by Carole Rothman, the play is set on a New England beach in August and deals with the disturbances of love among four generations of vacationers gathered on a private Massachusetts beach. Reviewing for the *New York Times*, Frank Rich says that *Coastal Disturbances* is "distinctly the creation of a female sensibility, but its beautiful, isolated private beach generously illuminates the intimate landscape that is shared by women and men" (November 20, 1986). Howe's newest play, *Approaching Zanzibar*, was produced Off-Broadway at Second Stage in 1989.

Careful examination of Howe's work is most important for understanding her as a theatre artist. In explaining her comic style and sensibility, Howe says that her "antic vision" developed from desperation within her family; she was always trying to keep her "head above water" because everyone in her family was so bright and productive. Therefore, she became a clown in order to be recognized. She claims a strong physical resemblance to her Aunt Helen, from whom, she says, her comedic gifts come. Helen Howe "scandalized" Boston by becoming a comedienne, a monologist in the tradition of Ruth Draper, who toured the country with her solo act and performed twice in the White House (Interview, 1985).

Included in the major epiphanies of her life were growing up close to the Metropolitan Museum of Art and learning that art was to be enjoyed, not revered, and going to Marx Brothers movies with her "staid New England parents and screaming with laughter with them in the darkness" (Interview, 1982). Howe explains that she is "preoccupied by the mysteries of the artist." She asks: "What must an artist go through to produce [her] work?" She says that she wants to "explore the more oblique metaphors of our lives" (Pevitts, p. 172). With her plays she explores these life processes through art, and she questions both art and life with humor and candor.

Tina Howe's article on her own playwriting, "Antic Vision," was published in *American Theatre* (September 1985). Her play *Birth and After Birth* is in *The New Women's Theatre*, ed. Honor Moore (1977). The book *Three Plays* (1984) includes *Museum*, *The Art of Dining*, and *Painting Churches*. *Coastal Disturbances, Four Plays by Tina Howe* (1989) contains the three mentioned plays as well as *Coastal Disturbances*. Articles about Howe include T. E. Kalem, "Singing the Brahmin Blues," *Time Magazine* (February 21, 1983); Frank Rich, "Theatre: Bostonian Life in 'Painting Churches,' " *New York Times* (February 9, 1983); "From Tina Howe, 'Coastal Disturbances,' " *New York Times* (November 20, 1986); and Beverley Byers-Pevitts, "Feminist Thematic Trends in Plays Written by Women for the American Theatre: 1970–1979" (Unpublished Ph.D. dissertation, Southern Illinois University, 1980). A recent interview with Howe is in *Interviews with Contemporary Women Playwrights*, Kathleen Betsko and Rachel Koenig, eds. (1987). Tina Howe is included in *National Playwrights Directory* (1981); *Contemporary Authors*, Vol. 109 (1983); and *Who's Who of American Women, 1984–1985* (1984).

Beverley Byers-Pevitts

HUNTER, Kim (November 12, 1922–): actress, most famous as Stella Kowalski in *A Streetcar Named Desire* by Tennessee Williams, was born Janet Cole to parents Donald and Grace Cole of Detroit, Michigan. She had one brother, nine years older than she. Her father, a consulting engineer, died when she was three. In 1938 her family moved to Miami Beach, Florida, where she graduated from high school in 1940. It was in Miami Beach that she began taking acting lessons and performing with the local stock companies, making her stage debut in 1939.

Janet Cole was working for the Pasadena Playhouse in California when David O. Selznick saw her and signed her as a contract player. At that time she took the stage name of Kim Hunter. While filming the Selznick production *Tender Comrades* (1943), she met her first husband, Captain William Baldwin. It was a storybook romance: he was a twenty-three-year-old marine flier; she was a twenty-one-year-old Hollywood starlet. They met while he was touring the RKO studios, and they were married two months later amidst much publicity. The marriage was dissolved in 1946 just after the birth of their daughter Kathryn. On December 20, 1951, Hunter married her second husband, the actor Robert Emmett. They have one son, Sean Emmett, and her daughter Kathryn assumed the last name of her stepfather.

Hunter is best known as the original Stella in Tennessee Williams's play, *A Streetcar Named Desire*. She was invited to read for the role by producer **Irene Selznick** at a time when she was unemployed and recently divorced. The play opened in New York in 1947 and ran two and a half years. In 1952 Hunter went to Hollywood to film the screen version. For the stage production, she received the Donaldson Award for best supporting actress and the *Variety* New York Critics Poll Award. For the film production she received an Academy (Oscar) Award for best supporting actress, as well as the *Look* Award and a Golden Globe Award. This play was Hunter's Broadway debut and, in its stage and screen versions, made her an instant star. Shortly after the film was released, however, she was caught up in the Joseph R. McCarthy congressional investigations of Communist activities in the American film industry, and thereafter she never received the offers that normally come after such a phenomenal success.

Although her film work was limited in the 1950s, she continued to do stock and some New York stage work, notably the 1952 Broadway revival of **Lillian Hellman**'s *The Children's Hour*. In 1951 she received the New York Drama Critics Circle Award for her performance opposite Claude Rains in Sydney Kingsley's dramatization of the Arthur Koestler novel *Darkness at Noon*.

Her film career received a brief boost in 1968 with her portrayal of the psychiatrist in *Planet of the Apes*. She made two sequels, *Beneath the Planet of the Apes* in 1970 and *Escape from the Planet of the Apes* in 1971. Most of her work during the 1970s, however, was for television, and she received Emmy nominations in 1977 for an episode of *Barretta* and in 1980 for a limited role on *The Edge of Night*.

She continues to perform supporting roles in high quality stage productions. In 1981 she played the mother to **Eva Le Gallienne**'s grandchildren in *To Grandmother's House* and in 1982 the artist's model Irene in a revival of Henrik Ibsen's *When We Dead Awaken*. Her most innovative work has been for regional theatres such as the Yale Repertory Theater (*Faulkner's Bicycle*, 1985) and the American Place Theater (*Territorial Rites*, 1983). *Territorial Rites* was presented as part of the American Place Theater's Women's Project series, and *Faulkner's Bicycle*, after its run at the Yale Repertory, opened the first festival of regional plays in the American Theater Exchange Program at the Joyce Theater, New York. In 1987 Hunter participated in a staged reading of Robert Perring's *A Cup of Change* at the White Barn Theatre in Westport, Connecticut.

Hunter is a prime example of a working actress who has made a career in supporting roles as a consistent performer, dedicated to her craft. She is a member of the Academy of Motion Picture Arts and Sciences, the American National Theatre and Academy (ANTA), and the Actors Studio. She goes where there is work and has a list of credits several pages long in all the media—Broadway, summer stock, touring companies, regional theatres, as well as television, films, recordings, and lectures. Having lost her ingénue years to McCarthyism, she concentrates on character roles, but even here her youthful appearance sometimes becomes a detriment. One critic commented that Hunter was too young to be a mother in *Faulkner's Bicycle*, even though she was over sixty years old at the time.

The majority of articles on Kim Hunter were written during the early 1950s, the most substantial one being "Talented Hunter," written by Dee L. Katcher for *Collier's* (March 1952). There are three interesting pictorials: "Kim for Success," *Vogue* (April 1, 1955), remarking on the number of young actresses named Kim; "England's Miss America," *American Magazine* (April 1947), celebrating her selection to star in *Stairway to Heaven*; and "Marine Takes a Wife," *Life* (March 13, 1944), on her wedding to William Baldwin. A recent, though limited, interview can be found in the *Wall Street Journal* (January 23, 1981). There are biographical entries on Hunter in *Current Biography, 1952* (1953); *The Biographical Encyclopaedia and Who's Who of the American Theatre* (1966); *Notable Names in the American Theatre* (1976); *Who's Who in Hollywood* (1976); *The Film Encyclopedia* (1979); *Halliwell's Filmgoer's Companion* (1980); *International Motion Picture Almanac* (1980); and *Who's Who in the Theatre* (1981).

Jerri C. Crawford

——— I ———

IRWIN, May (June 27, 1862–October 22, 1938): variety and vaudeville star, singer, and actress, and member of Augustin Daly's company, was born Georgia Campbell in Whitby, Ontario, Canada. Her father, Robert E. Campbell, failed in business when Georgia, thirteen, was in school at St. Cecilia Convent, Port Hope, Ontario. Georgia's mother, Jane (Draper) Campbell, then took her and her older sister Ada out of the convent school and, seeking to support the family, propelled them into show business. They had previously sung together in the Episcopal church choir and had frequently performed duets. On this slight foundation their mother built a stage career for them, remaining dominant in their lives for many years. May Irwin said in 1897, at the age of 35, "I never make a move without consulting her, and if she doesn't like a song, that settles it" (*Dramatic Mirror*, February 27, 1897).

The sisters worked together in variety theatres (the equivalent of music halls) for eight years, beginning in 1875 in Buffalo, New York, for Daniel Shelby, who was responsible for their professional names, "May and Flo, the Irwin Sisters." They played the variety circuit in Cleveland, St. Louis, Cincinnati, and other cities; and finally in 1877 they became popular attractions in vaudeville for Tony Pastor in New York, appearing in his versions of Gilbert and Sullivan favorites. With Pastor they were billed as "Infantile Actresses, Vocalists, and Character Artistes." The Irwin Sisters act broke up in 1883 when May Irwin made the transition from vaudeville to Broadway in Augustin Daly's company. It was a step toward a career as one of the top comediennes of the American stage in the 1880s and 1890s. With Daly's company she supported such famous players as **Ada Rehan**, John Drew, and Otis Skinner. She became known especially for her comic servant roles, including Susan in *A Night Off* and Lucy in *The Recruiting Officer*. Though she left Daly in 1887, partly because there was more money in variety shows, she did not stay away from the legitimate theatre for long. In 1893, Charles Frohman hired her to act with Henry Miller in *His Wedding Day* and *The Junior Partner*; she became a special favorite in a travesty of Oscar Wilde's *Lady Windermere's Fan* called *The Poet and the Puppets*, in which she sang the popular song "After the Ball." She gained star status in the 1895 production of John J. McNally's *The Widow Jones*. A famous scene from this play, a prolonged kiss between May Irwin and John C. Rice, was filmed in close-up for Thomas Edison's "Vitascope" in 1896. It was the first "shocker" of early motion pictures and was denounced by the clergy of the day.

Irwin continued to perform through the early decades of the twentieth century. She succeeded because she willingly combined a cheerful and magnetic personality, a big voice, and a natural intuition for comedy. "Merry," "jolly," and "irrepressible" were the most common epithets used for her by contemporary reviewers. Lewis C. Strang called her "the personification of humour and careless mirth, a female Falstaff, as it were, whose sixteenth century grossness and ribaldry has been refined and recast in a nineteenth century mould" (*Famous Actresses of the Day in America*, p. 174). Plays written especially for her were *Madge Smith, Attorney* (1900); *Mrs. Black is Back* (1902); *Mrs. Wilson, That's All* (1906); *Getting a Polish* (1910) by Booth Tarkington and Harry Leon Wilson; *Widow by Proxy* (1913); and *No. 13 Washington Square* (1915). A special performance of the last of these was done in Washington, D.C., for President Woodrow Wilson and his cabinet, after which Wilson is said to have remarked that he would like to appoint Irwin his "Secretary of Laughter."

Irwin is remembered not only as a fine comedienne but as a singer, since she regularly introduced new songs in plays written for her or produced by her. Many of these songs were labeled "coon songs," or "shouting songs," as they featured Irwin's interpretation of Afro-American singing, picked up, she said, from listening to black servants. Such songs, which lie on the border between the old minstrel music and the new ragtime, became the craze in the 1890s. In *The Widow Jones* (1895) she introduced the popular "Bully Song," sometimes called the first ragtime song, but in the lyrics and style of the "coon song." Other examples of this noisy and spirited (and to a modern view, racist) genre that May Irwin popularized were Ben Harney's "Mister Johnson, Turn Me Loose," which she sang in 1896 in John J. McNally's *Courted into Court*; "Mamie, Come Kiss Your Honey Boy," her own composition introduced in McNally's *A Country Sport* in 1893; and the "Frog Song," sung in *The Swell Mrs. Fitzwell* and written for her by Henry Du Souchet in 1897. Irwin also popularized many other hit songs of the day, including "A Hot Time in the Old Town," "I Couldn't Stand to See My Baby Lose," and "You've Been a Good Old Wagon but You Done Broke Down."

Irwin is also known among American theatre professionals as a successful businesswoman. She had a hand in writing and producing some of the plays she acted in, she made wise investments in New York real estate, and she successfully managed her dairy farm on one of the Thousand Islands in the St. Lawrence River. Some commentators estimate that she made more than a million dollars in these various enterprises. In any event, upon her death in 1938 she was one of the wealthiest women associated with the theatre.

May Irwin was married at age sixteen to Frederick W. Keller, a businessman. She bore two sons, Walter and Harry, before her husband's death in 1886. More than twenty years later, on May 26, 1907, she married her agent Kurt Eisfeldt, who then became her business manager. She retired in 1922 to her farm in Clayton, New York, after making her last Broadway appearance in *The 49ers* (1922). She made a final appearance in a 1925 "Old Timers' Week" at the Palace Theatre. She died in New York City of chronic myocarditis in 1938 at the age of seventy-six and was buried in Kensico Cemetery, Valhalla, New York.

During May Irwin's long theatrical career (nearly half a century), she received acclaim in variety entertainment and vaudeville, in straight and musical comedy, and in management. A vaudeville star, popular comic actress, and admired "coon shouter" of the day, May Irwin made a mark worthy of memory in the history of the American theatre.

For contemporary views of May Irwin, see Amy Leslie, *Some Players* (1899) and Lewis C. Strang, *Famous Actresses of the Day in America* (1899). William C. Young's *Famous Actors and Actresses of the American Stage*, Vol. I (1975), reprints several articles and reviews about Irwin, including one by Irwin herself on "The Business of the Stage as a Career." Irwin's vaudeville career is emphasized in Anthony Slide's *The Vaudevillians: A Dictionary of Vaudeville Performers* (1981) and David Ewen's *The Life and Death of Tin Pan Alley* (1964). Her contributions as a singer are detailed in Sigmund Spaeth's *History of Popular Music in America* (1948) and denounced in William J. Schafer and Johannes Riedel's *The Art of Ragtime* (1973). A good collection of Irwin portraits can be found in Daniel Blum's *Great Stars of the American Stage: A Pictorial Record* (1972) and William Cahn's *The Laugh Makers: A Pictorial History of American Comedians* (1957). There are clippings about Irwin in the Harvard Theatre Collection. Her obituary appeared in the *New York Times* (October 23, 1938) and in *Variety* (October 26, 1938). There is no full biography of May Irwin; but see a brief general overview in *Dictionary of American Biography* (1958), though the article by Alan S. Downer contains some inaccuracies. See also *Notable American Women*, Vol. II (1971); *Who Was Who in the Theatre*, Vol. III (1978); *Victorian Actors and Actresses in Review*, ed., Donald Mullin (1983); *The Oxford Companion to the Theatre* (1983); and *The Oxford Companion to American Theatre* (1984).

Janet Juhnke

ISAACS, Edith Juliet Rich (March 27, 1878–January 10, 1956): theatre critic who edited *Theatre Arts* magazine between 1918 and 1946, was born in Milwaukee, the third child in a family of five girls and one boy, to Adolph Walter Rich and Rosa (Sidenberg) Rich. The family resided in Milwaukee, part of a small group of Hungarian emigrants. Adolph Rich worked his way up from selling glasses to becoming owner of a prosperous shoe factory. The maternal side of the family moved from the lace business in Breslau (Prussia) to become successful stockbrokers and realtors in Manhattan, New York.

Edith Juliet Rich was educated in Milwaukee's public schools, graduating from East Side High School with above average marks. She was granted a Bachelor of Arts degree from Milwaukee-Downer College in 1897 with exceptional merit in English composition. This distinction led to her writing career, first as a reporter for the Milwaukee *Sentinel* and then as its literary editor in 1903. During this period she met Lewis Montefidretu Isaacs, a New York lawyer and free-lance composer. Early in their relationship, she collaborated with Lewis Isaacs on a children's operetta patterned after the style of the Brothers Grimm. Edith Rich and Lewis Isaacs were married on November 28, 1904, and moved to New York, beginning a long and fruitful life together until his death in 1944. The couple had three children: Marian (b. 1906), Lewis (b. 1908), and Hermine (b. 1915).

Isaacs worked all her adult life as a professional writer. Besides becoming a drama critic for the financially troubled *Ainslee's Magazine* (1913), she contributed articles to such periodicals as *Ladies' Home Journal* and *The Delineator*, often signing her name under the pseudonym "Mrs. Pelham." As a free-lance reviewer, Isaacs had sent Sheldon Cheney, editor of *Theatre Arts*, reviews of *The Big Show*, one of the Hippodrome extravaganzas, as well as *The Century Girl, The Cohan Review of 1916, Robinson Crusoe, Jr.*, and in 1918 *The Ziegfeld Follies*. In 1918 Cheney invited Isaacs to join the editorial board of *Theatre Arts*.

By 1922 Edith Isaacs' expertise in editorial feature writing (her style was both informal and witty) gained her the editorship of *Theatre Arts*, and in 1924 the magazine moved from quarterly to monthly publication. Isaacs reinvested portions of her salary in *Theatre Arts*, a move that culminated in her becoming the magazine's chief stockholder. She is credited with broadening the spectrum of *Theatre Arts* to include related areas of dance, mime, and music. Isaacs was the editor of *Theatre Arts* until 1946. At that time **Rosamond Gilder** became the editor. In 1948 *Theatre Arts* was combined with *The Stage* (a Theatre Guild publication), and finally in 1964 the magazine was discontinued.

Isaacs gave her support to the year's emerging new directors, actors, and playwrights by bringing their work to public attention through the pages of *Theatre Arts*. Among those newcomers featured were Eugene O'Neill, Thornton Wilder, William Saroyan, **Martha Graham**, Robert Edmond Jones, Jo Mielziner, and Donald Oenslager, John Mason Brown, and Rosamond Gilder, who succeeded her as editor. Isaacs was characterized by her staff as "an able administrator" who frequently suggested seminal ideas during casual conversation to guide an author (*Notable American Women*, Vol. IV, p. 370).

One of Isaacs's ultimate goals was to work toward the emergence of a national theatre. Her efforts toward that end were fruitful, in that the National Theatre Conference was officially chartered in 1925, followed by the American National Theatre and Academy (ANTA) in 1935. She also consulted with **Hallie Flanagan** when the network of regional theatres was being set up under the auspices of the Works Progress Administration Federal Theatre Project (1935–1939). During the 1920s and 1930s Isaacs combined her activities in the theatre with the growing national concern for social reform by supporting the rise of black culture. Among her projects was the Blondiau Theatre Arts Collection of Primitive African Art, which she sponsored with Alain Locke. This was the first major collection of its type to be shown in New York. After the exhibition Isaacs had the collection divided between Howard University in Washington, D.C., and the Schomburg Center for Research in Black Culture (part of the New York Public Library). She also devoted the August 1942 issue of *Theatre Arts* to "The Negro in American Theatre."

Isaacs's ability in management and economics kept her in the forefront of the theatre's practical as well as aesthetic battles. Not only was she instrumental in founding the National Theatre Conference but she led the group from 1932 until 1946. She was also one of the prime movers in 1935 who presented President Franklin D. Roosevelt with a request to charter the American National Theatre and Academy (ANTA). The purpose was to create a "national theatre to bring to the people throughout the country their heritage of the great drama of the past and the best of the present, which has been too frequently unavailable to them under existing conditions" (ANTA Charter, 1935). ANTA remains to this day the only theatre organization chartered by Congress. The charter carried with it no federal subsidy and the organization's budget was to be maintained through private subscription. Isaacs helped to organize ANTA's first official Board of Directors and Professional Advisory Committee and was its first vice president.

After 1951, afflicted by crippling arthritis which had plagued her for over twenty years, Isaacs retired to a nursing home in White Plains, New York. She died there in January 1956 following a stroke. In 1958 a Theatre Arts Project for East Harlem was established in her honor at the James Weldon Johnson Community Center.

For twenty-five years Edith Isaacs was a leading force in the American theatre as editor of the international theatre magazine *Theatre Arts* and as one of the chief organizers of the American National Theatre and Academy. Her considerable gifts as a theatre, dance, and music critic called attention to a new generation of theatre artists who were to shape the American theatre for half a century.

Among the books Edith Isaacs edited and wrote are *Theatre: Essays on the Arts of the Theatre* (1927), *Plays of American Life and Fantasy* (1929, a collection of plays that had been published in various issues of *Theatre Arts*), *The American Theatre in Social and Education Life: A Survey of Its Needs and Opportunities* (1932), *Architecture for the New Theatre* (1935), and *The Negro in the American Theatre* (1947, 1968). Her obituary appeared in the *New York Times* (January 11, 1956). For additional information, see Kenneth Macgowan and William Melnitz, *The Living Stage* (1955), and Glenn Hughes, *A History of the American Theatre, 1750–1950* (1951). Isaacs' papers are at the Wisconsin

Center for Theatre Research in Madison. There is a clipping file in the Billy Rose Theatre Collection at the New York Public Library Performing Arts Research Center at Lincoln Center. Isaacs is listed in Robin May, *A Companion to the Theatre: The Anglo-American Stage from 1920* (1973); *Notable American Women*, Vol. IV: *The Modern Period* (1980); *The Oxford Companion to the Theatre* (1983); and *The Oxford Companion to American Theatre* (1984).

H. Edward Bryant III

—— J ——

JACKSON, Esther (September 3, 1922–): theatre scholar and educator, was born in Pine Bluff, Arkansas, the daughter of Napoleon F. and Ruth (Atkinson) Jackson. At the age of twenty, she received her Bachelor of Science degree from the Hampton Institute, Hampton, Virginia. After two years as an instructor of English, she attended Ohio State University where she received a Master of Arts degree in 1946. For ten years she taught as an assistant professor of speech and drama at Hampton Institute (1946–1949) and at Clark College, Atlanta, Georgia (1949–1956). In 1956 she returned to Ohio State University, where she received her Ph.D. degree two years later.

During the following years, Jackson was engaged in many activities related to scholarly research and higher education. She was a John Hay Whitney fellow, 1956–1957, and a Fulbright senior research fellow in England, 1960–1961. Upon her return to the United States she was appointed professor of English at Clark College and in 1962 became professor and chairperson in the department of speech and drama at Clark. In 1967 she was honored with a second Fulbright award as a lecturer for American drama at the John F. Kennedy Institute at the Free University of West Berlin. Immediately thereafter she received a Guggenheim fellowship for American drama. From 1969 to the present she has been professor of theatre and drama at the University of Wisconsin at Madison.

Aside from her university affiliations, Jackson has served in the following capacities: specialist in theatre education in the United States Office of Education, 1964–1965; education director of the New York Shakespeare Festival, 1965–1966; associate editor for the *Quarterly Journal of Speech*, 1966–1969, 1971–1974; associate editor for the *Educational Theatre Journal*, 1970–1973; vice president of the American Theatre Association, 1972–1974; and chairperson of the Executive Committee of the Division on Drama in the Modern Language Association.

Her principal fields of research include American theatre and drama and dramatic theory and criticism. She is best known for her book on Tennessee Williams. *The Broken World of Tennessee Williams* (1965) has been acclaimed by Alan Stambusky as "the most thoroughly competent critical appraisal of the major characteristics of the dramatic form of the inimitable Tennessee Williams" (*Quarterly Journal of Speech*, December 1965, p. 472). Jackson has covered a wide field of America drama and theatre in subsequent publications. In her article "Maxwell Anderson: Poetry and Morality in the American Drama," Jackson discusses the importance of Anderson's contribution to the development of American stage language (*Educational Theatre Journal*, March 1973). In a collection of essays titled *LeRoi Jones (Amiri Baraka)* (1978) Jackson traces Baraka's intellectual development as poet, playwright, and theorist and stresses his contribution to the growth of the American drama as an "indigenous kind" (*Imamu Amiri Baraka*, ed. Kimberly W. Benston, p. 36 and p. 41).

In a volume of essays titled *Eugene O'Neill: A World View*, Jackson's chapter, "O'Neill The Humanist," explores the playwright's struggle between secular and religious humanism at a time when "faith in science" challenges "the very humanity of man." Discussing O'Neill's shift between the two concepts of humanism, she arrives at a form, "tragic humanism," which encompasses both seemingly contradictory concepts (*Eugene O'Neill: A World View*, ed. Virginia Floyd, 1980, pp. 253, 256).

As an outstanding scholar in the field of modern American theatre and drama, Esther Jackson has made significant contributions. She has also served the United States Office of Education, scholarly journals, and professional associations at a time when few black women were so distinguished in the field of theatre research.

Publications of Esther Jackson include *The Broken World of Tennessee Williams* (1965) and contributions to *Das Amerikanische Drama von den Anfangen bis zur Gegenwart* (1972); Alan Downer, ed., *The American Theatre Today* (1967); John M. Reilly, ed., *Twentieth Century Interpretations of "Invisible Man"* (1970); Louis Findelstein, ed., *Social Responsibility in the Age of Revolution* (1971); and Walter Meserve, ed., *Studies in "Death of a Salesman"* (1972). Jackson has also contributed to *Revue d'Histoire du Théâtre* and *The Educational Theatre Journal*. She is included in *Contemporary Authors*, Vols. 13–16 (1975), and in *Directory of American Scholars*, Vol. 2 (1982).

                                                                Anton Kiesenhofer

JANAUSCHEK, Fanny (July 20, 1830–November 28, 1904): actress famous in classic revivals, particularly Lady Macbeth, was born Francesca Romana Magdalena Janauschek in Prague, Czechoslovakia, the fourth of nine children. Her father was a tailor and her mother a theatre laundress. At first she studied both piano and voice, but an accident to her hand made it impossible to continue with the piano. At the Prague Conservatory where she studied voice, a professor persuaded her to study acting as well. She made her debut in Prague at the age of sixteen and went on to play with several companies in small cities for several months. At the age of eighteen she was hired as leading woman at the Stadttheater in Frankfurt. She remained there for ten years, performing classic revivals and touring extensively throughout Germany, Austria, and Russia. The King of Bavaria, who was a great patron of the arts, showered honors on her besides engaging her for a four-month *Gastspiel* in Munich. She signed a three-year contract to play at the Royal Theatre in Dresden, but became dissatisfied and made a personal appeal to King John of Saxony to be released from her contract. This was granted with the provision that she return each season for four weeks. Throughout her years in Europe, Janauschek played the principal cities. Her repertoire included Grillparzer's *Medea*, Schiller's *Mary Stuart* and *Joan of Arc*, Goethe's *Faust* and *Egmont*, and Shakespeare's *Macbeth*. She received the highest praise and admiration for her acting ability, and honors and jewels were showered on her everywhere she performed.

In 1867 Janauschek was brought by Jacob Grau to the United States, where she remained until her death in 1904. She opened in New York on October 9 at the Academy of Music in Franz Grillparzer's *Medea*, which she performed in German while the rest of the cast supported her in English. The next day, the *New York Times* reported on the performance: ''Mlle. Janauschek has a handsome figure and a sumptuous presence, aided by features that are in every sense expressive. . . . A human tenderness blending with an Eastern picturesqueness of gesture, and a refined sentiment prominent throughout every scene were the remarkable features of Mlle. Janauschek's *Medea*'' (October 10, 1867).

After this engagement at the Academy of Music, Janauschek and the company toured the United States until the end of the 1867–1868 season. She acted exclusively in German in a number of plays from her repertoire including *Medea*, *Brunhilde*, Mosenthal's *Deborah*, Scribe's *Adrienne Lecouvreur*, and Lessing's *Emilia Galotti*.

The following season she appeared on several occasions as Lady Macbeth with Edwin Booth. Booth had tried to sign her for the season, but she decided that she would be unable to learn the roles in English. As a result of her warm reception in the United States and at the pressing suggestion of Augustin Daly, Janauschek began to study English intensively. On October 9, 1870, exactly three years after her first American appearance, Augustin Daly presented Janauschek at the Academy of Music in *Deborah*, performed in English. The critic for the *New York Daily Tribune* commented on Janauschek's English speaking debut: ''That Madam Janauschek was a great actress nobody . . . is unaware, who ever saw her play Deborah or Mary Stuart or Medea in the German language. . . . Last night she acted an English part, and surprised everybody by the accuracy of her speech'' (October 10, 1870).

Janauschek followed *Deborah* with performances of *Mary Stuart*, *Brunhilde*, and *Medea* in English. When she played Lady Macbeth to Walter Montgomery's Macbeth, the *New York Herald* praised Janauschek as a leading American tragic actress: "Mlle. Janauschek's Lady Macbeth was one of the finest histrionic displays witnessed in this city for many years and deservedly won a cordial recognition from a refined and critical assemblage" (October 18, 1870).

After several seasons Janauschek's control of the English language was complete, though she always had a noticeable foreign accent. According to John Clapp, this "has in no way hindered or even marred the dramatic effect of her acting" (*Players of the Present*, p. 173). *The Dramatic Mirror* commented that "she had a strong accent, which she never entirely conquered, but her art was so splendid that all faults of pronunciation were forgiven her" (December 10, 1904).

Brunhilde and Lady Macbeth were considered her best roles. According to John Rankin Towse: "She endowed it [Brunhilde] with a majestic dignity and thoroughly heroic passion. Her imperious carriage, fiery declamation, and noble gesture contributed to a most imposing and picturesque effect. . . . Her Lady Macbeth was murderous in her ambition and energetic in the prompting of her husband to murder, but she loved him passionately and, in her own tigress fashion, tenderly" (*Sixty Years of the Theatre*, pp. 210, 211).

Janauschek toured the United States for several years, adding Shakespeare's *Henry VIII* and *The Winter's Tale*, as well as modern plays, to her repertoire. The most important addition was the role of Meg Merrilies in the adaptation of Sir Walter Scott's *Guy Mannering*. She received considerable acclaim as the old gypsy woman, but she often regretted adding the role to her repertoire because it "established her in the public mind as a far older woman than she was" (*The New York Dramatic Mirror*, December 10, 1904).

Janauschek spent 1874 to 1880 in Europe with a short season in England in 1876, but she was not a popular success there. By the 1890s the American public had lost its taste for Janauschek's grand style of tragic acting, and she lost both her popularity and her fortune. She refused to forsake the classical roles in favor of the popular sentimental roles of the French melodrama or to change her acting style. During the last ten years of her career she had few engagements, except in supporting roles. In 1894–1895 she played the Countess de Linières in support of Kate Claxton in *The Two Orphans*. Beginning in the fall of 1895 she gave in to the hated melodrama and appeared as Mother Rosebaum in *The Great Diamond Robbery* for two seasons. She tried an unsuccessful tour in *What Dreams May Come*, a romantic drama by Paul Kester, in 1898. In the intervals between roles she gave readings from the classic drama and delivered speeches on various aspects of dramatic art.

In 1900 Janauschek suffered a stroke that paralyzed her. Her fellow actors raised $5,000 to help her, but she was so destitute that finally her rich costumes and jewels were sold. When she died in 1904, she was alone and destitute; her fellow actors provided money for her funeral. Phillip Hale in 1896 had claimed that Janauschek was the last of the actors of the grand style in which classical roles were enacted with grandeur and heightened passion. "There is not one to be compared now to Janauschek in the breadth and the finish, nobility and the sweep of her art'' (*Famous American Actors of Today*, p. 24). The comparison of Janauschek to **Charlotte Cushman** was inevitable because of their physical similarities, acting style, and the portrayals of Lady Macbeth and Meg Merrilies. John Rankin Towse claimed that Janauschek's interpretation of Lady Macbeth, ''fully as strong if less savage than Cushman's, manifested the redeeming quality of feminine devotion'' (*Sixty Years of the Theatre*, p. 211).

Fanny Janauschek was an actress with a strong and expressive face and a deep and vibrant voice. Her personal energy unleashed the powerful passions of the larger-than-life classical characters she portrayed. Audiences were held by this power as well as the sincerity of her performances, whether done in German or English. Her tremendous energy was reflected in the task of her undertaking to learn English within three years so that she could play to win larger audiences than those who had already received her so warmly.

Phillip Hale has summarized the reasons for her tremendous appeal: ''The noble expressiveness of her face, the stateliness of her figure, the same reserve of strength in repose, the grace and the intensity of her gesture, these were natural gifts, enlarged by training, controlled by artistic intelligence'' (*Famous American Actors of Today*, Vol. I, p. 23).

Biographical material on Fanny Janauschek can be found in an interview with Janauschek that appeared in the *Dramatic Mirror* (August 4, 1894) and in Phillip Hale's chapter on Janauschek in *Famous American Actors of Today*, edited by Frederic Edward McKay and Charles E. L. Wingate (1896). Comments on her acting are all highly uncritical and tend toward adulation; they appear in Hales's articles as well as in *Sixty Years of the Theatre* by John Rankin Towse (1916) and *Across My Path: Memories of People I Have Known* by LaSalle Corbell Pickett (1916), who was a great admirer of Janauschek. See also George C. D. Odell, *Annals of the New York Stage*, Vols. VIII-XV (1936–1949). Janauschek's obituary was in the *Dramatic Mirror* (December 10, 1904). Janauschek is listed in *Dictionary of American Biography* (1932–1933, revised 1960–1961); *Who Was Who in America*, Vol. I, *1897–1942* (1966); *The Oxford Companion to the Theatre* (1967); *Notable American Women*, Vol. II, (1971); William C. Young, *Famous Actors and Actresses on the American Stage*, Vol. I (1975); *Victorian Actors and Actresses in Review*, ed., Donald Mullin (1983); and *The Oxford Companion to American Theatre* (1984).

Susan S. Cole

JANIS, Elsie (March 16, 1889–February 27, 1956): variety artist and ''Sweetheart of the A. E. F.'' in the First World War, was born Elsie Janet Bierbower in Marion, Ohio, the daughter of John and Jane Elizabeth (Cockrell) Bierbower. She was known throughout her childhood as ''Little Elsie.'' Her mother, remarkable as a young woman for her beauty, had narrowly missed a theatrical career of her own. Given the times, however, and even allowing for Jane (or Jenny, as she was called) Cockrell's ambition and forceful nature, the American Midwest was not particularly conducive to such unorthodox aspirations; it is not surprising that she married a railroad clerk after her brief stint as a milliner.

Following the birth of her first child, Percy, who disappointed his mother by being a boy, Jenny Bierbower was determined that her second child would be a girl who would fulfill all the dreams that she herself had never realized. As a consequence she made it a point to see every first-rate actor, singer, dancer, and entertainer who came to town, thereby exposing her unborn daughter to theatrical prenatal influences. In later years she confided to her daughter that she had been convinced her daughter would possess the eloquence of **Helena Modjeska**, the versatility of **Maggie Mitchell**, and the elfin alertness of **Lotta Crabtree** (*So Far, So Good*, p. 14). At the age of five "Little Elsie" Bierbower played Little Willie in *East Lynne*, weeping and dying in the best nineteenth-century "angelic child" tradition. Her mother saw to it that her daughter recited for guests at tea parties, carried the ring at weddings, and performed at church socials. By the time she was ten a photographer had lopped off the ungainly Bierbower name and changed Janet to Janis, and Elsie Janis was on the road to vaudeville accompanied by her mother.

John Bierbower refused his permission for such a career, whereupon his wife sued for divorce and won custody of both children. On a dare she wired a theatre owner in Buffalo, New York, who was notorious for his gambling instincts, that he could have the services of Little Elsie Janis for only $125 a week. Such a salary was unheard of in those days, even for an entire family of traveling thespians. But Jenny Bierbower craftily added the proper lure: "However, you pay her *only* if she makes good. *If not, you don't pay her a dime!*" Unable to risk losing his reputation as a gambling man, Mike Shea wired back, "Bring her on!" (*So Far So Good*, p. 19). Ten-year-old Elsie Janis proved a dynamo on stage, dazzling both Mike Shea and Buffalo audiences with her nonstop impersonations and on-stage quick changes. She imitated well-known stars of the day—an astonishing number of them—and with uncanny accuracy. She was renowned for her takeoffs on George M. Cohan, **Ethel Barrymore**, Harry Lauder, and Eddie Foy. She would step behind a screen for a costume change on stage, and slicking back her hair and putting on a jaunty straw hat, she would reappear as Maurice Chevalier after having just dismantled the queenly image of Ethel Barrymore. One of her most vivid impersonations was that of the divine Sarah Bernhardt. She played Camille on a chaise longue, in a peignoir of pink velvet, trimmed with a pink feather boa, and in a pink spotlight. Janis spoke French fluently. This impersonation was doubly poignant because it had been Madame Sarah's farewell role, which she had played lying down, because her leg had been amputated not long before. Elsie Janis had a way of imparting all this "prehistory" to the audience as she dressed for the upcoming role, carrying on a chatty monologue. Then, after a brief pause, she stepped into the role and literally seemed to "become" the person.

While her singing voice remained on the brassy side and her dancing was more ragged than smooth, Janis possessed an unerring sense of comedy that eventually made her one of the greatest ad lib artists of her time. In 1906 she appeared on Broadway in *The Vanderbilt Cup*, followed by *The Hoyden* (1907), *The Fair Co-Ed* (1909), *The Slim Princess* (1910), and *The Lady of the Slipper* (1912).

In 1913 Janis was offered a movie contract by the Hobart Bosworth Studio in Hollywood, which paid her $30,000 a picture and the use of a private Pullman parlor car to and from the coast. She was one of a handful of American performers who became as popular in Paris and London as in New York and Hollywood. In London she appeared in *The Passing Show of 1915* opposite British actor Basil Hallam, with whom she fell in love. But with the outbreak of war in Europe, Hallam joined the Royal Flying Corps, was shot down in a balloon over France, and was killed instantly. Having been persuaded by her mother to postpone marriage until after the war was over, Janis was devastated, and friends believed that the tragedy shadowed her life thereafter.

When the United States entered the conflict in 1917, Janis asked for and obtained official permission from the Allied armies to visit troops at the front line. Throughout the following eighteen months Janis and her mother found their way through mud and rain, riding in every kind of vehicle that could get them to the troops. Once arrived at a camp, a hospital, or a reasonably safe trench, Janis sang her heart out for the American, Canadian, French, and Australian soldiers. Even though she felt that her life after the war would be anticlimactic, instead her career skyrocketed during the postwar years. After the 1919 Armistice, she produced, directed, wrote, and starred in a musical revue called *Elsie Janis and Her Gang* (Gaiety Theatre, 1922). The troupe, all former soldiers, were amateurs trained to perform as professionals.

Later in the 1920s, Janis toured the Keith-Orpheum circuit as one of the highest-paid vaudeville entertainers of all time. Jenny Bierbower saw to it that her daughter got top pay, top billing, and the star treatment but had few serious relationships with men. *Puzzles of 1925* (Fulton Theatre, 1925) was one of her typical fast-paced, extravagantly costumed revues with Cyril Ritchard and Walter Pidgeon appearing at the onset of their careers.

In 1930, at the age of forty-one, Elsie Janis retired from the stage, bought a home in Beverly Hills, California, and turned to writing for the screen. Scarcely six months later Jenny Bierbower died of pneumonia. Within six months of her mother's death, on December 31, 1931, Janis married a twenty-six-year-old actor named Gilbert Wilson. The marriage lasted less than a year. They separated, but neither filed for divorce.

When reporting her death in Beverly Hills, just nine days short of her sixty-seventh birthday, *Variety* called Elsie Janis one of the all-time greats of American show business. An international star during the First World War and a ''Sweetheart'' to the American Expeditionary Forces, she remained popular thereafter and was popular in vaudeville and in musical comedy, especially for her singing and her brilliant impersonations of well-known stage personalities.

The major source for the life of Elsie Janis is her own candid, amusing autobiography, *So Far, So Good* (1932). However sharply she has portrayed the theatre world of her childhood, the book tends to dramatize too much the efforts her mother and she herself made to launch her career. Abel Green, *Show Biz: From Vaude to Video* (1951), includes fragmentary references to Janis's career, as do Charles and Louise Samuels, *Once Upon a Stage: The Merry World of Vaudeville* (1974), and Martin Gottfried, *In Person: The Great Entertainers* (1985). Diana Serra Carey's *Hollywood's Children: An Inside Account of the Child Star Era* (1979) gives perhaps the most detailed eye-witness account of the mother-daughter relationship between Elsie Janis and Jenny Bierbower. Elsie Janis's obituary appeared in the *New York Times* (February 28, 1956). Janis is included in *Who's Who in the Theatre* (1952); William C. Young, *Famous Actors and Actresses on the American Stage*, Vol. I (1975); *Who Was Who in the Theatre*, Vol. III (1978); and *The Oxford Companion to American Theatre* (1984). Most reference books give Janis's death date as February 28, 1956. However, her obituary in the *New York Times* (February 28, 1956) states that she died "last night."

Diana Serra Cary

JELLIFFE, Rowena Woodham (March 23, 1892–): co-founder and co-executive director (from 1915–1963) of Cleveland's Karamu House and Karamu Theatre, was born in Albion, Illinois. She was the first of two daughters (her sister was named Alberta) born to John Franklin Woodham and Minnie (Sax) Woodham. Her father, a graduate of Valparaiso University in Indiana, was a farmer but, because of poor health, left farming to become county clerk of Edwards County, Illinois. Her mother, born in Minnesota, was educated at Fairfield Ladies' Seminary in Fairfield, Illinois. Her paternal grandfather, George Woodham, was one of the founders of Albion, a "sister colony" to Robert Owens's New Harmony, one of several social and communal experiments in utopian living established in the United States in the nineteenth century. Her maternal grandparents, Sarah Gorman and John George Sax, had immigrated to Albion from Europe in 1848. The colony was primarily Episcopalian, though the Woodhams and a number of other members were agnostics. Rowena Woodham's mother was an experienced horsewoman and knew the countryside well. When widowed, she applied for the United States rural mailman's job. Because of opposition to a woman's holding this full-time post, she was able to get a job only as a substitute mail carrier.

Rowena Woodham completed the eighth grade, and then went to the Southern Collegiate Institute at Albion, a preparatory school founded by Oberlin College graduates who hired women to give inspiring, invigorating instruction there. She entered Oberlin in 1910, graduating with a degree in psychology in June 1914. At Oberlin she met her husband and partner in life and work, Russell Wesley Jelliffe. He was the son of Charles Wesley Jelliffe and Margaret Ward and was born (one of five brothers) in Mansfield, Ohio, on November 19, 1891. Jelliffe and Rowena Woodham were married in Ravinia, Illinois, on May 28, 1915; they had one son, Roger Woodham Jelliffe, born in Cleveland on February 18, 1929, who became a research cardiologist and a professor at the Medical School of the University of Southern California. Russell Jelliffe died on June 7, 1980, in Cleveland, Ohio.

While a student at Oberlin, Rowena Jelliffe became president of the Equal Suffrage League and stumped for suffrage for some two years on weekends away from college. She often spoke from the back of trucks for the Ohio suffrage movement.

After graduation from Oberlin, Rowena and Russell Jelliffe both received graduate scholarships in sociology at the University of Chicago. As part of their graduate work they did a housing study on the South Side while headquartered at Jane Addams's Hull House. Their Hull House experience, which involved almost daily contact with Jane Addams, served to strengthen their democratic and egalitarian orientation. They used Chicago's John Crerar Library to research northern and eastern cities where they might themselves establish a racially integrated social-educational-cultural center. They believed Cleveland—then a socially and politically progressive city—might be such a location. An offer from the Men's Club of Cleveland's Second Presbyterian Church brought them there in 1915 after they had completed their master's degrees. Then, at East 38th and Central, in the "Roaring Third" Ward, they established a neighborhood center called the Play House Settlement, which later took the name of Karamu House. Karamu (from Swahili, meaning "place of enjoyment at the center of the community") is now located at East 89th and Quincy Avenue in Cleveland's inner city.

The story of Karamu House and Karamu Theatre is the story of Rowena and Russell Jelliffe. So close were these two in their life work that a distinction between the work and achievements of one and those of the other is virtually impossible.

Fortified by the sociopolitical opinions of Oswald Garrison Villard, editor of *The Nation*, by the friendship and opinions of people like Charles and Mary Beard, James Weldon Johnson, and John Dewey, and by the artistic support of Lynn Riggs, Jasper Deeter, and Adele Nathan, the Jelliffes prepared themselves for the work ahead. They went to New York to study with Robert Milton of the John Murray Anderson School of Theatre and Dance and with **Martha Graham**. In Cleveland, they lived in a cottage behind Karamu House and began by offering children's activities to the community, thereby attracting the parents and thus permitting the establishment of an even wider range of social and cultural services.

Karamu House has from its inception been an arts-oriented community center, not a professional theatre, or a neighborhood house in the traditional sense. In the early years it also served the social needs of the citizenry, many of whom were recently arrived southern blacks, attracted north by offers of employment in burgeoning war industries. The arts grew in significance, and the Karamu Theatre, though only one enterprise of Karamu House, became its most prominent feature and the chief way in which the public—local, national, and international—has learned of Karamu.

In the early years the Jelliffes were part of an informal network with Hedgerow Theatre, Paul Green and the Carolina Playmakers, the Provincetown Playhouse, and New York's Hudson Guild with its Cellar Theatre. Rowena Jelliffe has often pointed out that these theatre companies all influenced each other and were tremendously important to each other.

Perhaps the most significant contribution of Karamu and the Jelliffes was their insistent focus on arts for black people: theatre, dance, the plastic and graphic arts. The Jelliffes were firm in their belief that developing talent and strengthening self-esteem would lead to the kind of interpersonal and interracial relations that a racially troubled America needed. Blacks had to enter the mainstream of American life as qualified artists or just plain citizens. Rowena Jelliffe, who directed almost all of the Karamu Theatre plays for nearly thirty years (besides acting as co-director of Karamu House), established a policy of interracial casting. Black actors and black playwrights were drawn to Karamu, which premièred a wider variety of plays, musicals, and operas than any other area theatre.

The result of the Jelliffes' efforts, seen some seventy years later, is impressive. The philosophical base of Karamu remains valuable and unique. As a community arts center, Karamu has been training and preparing hundreds of thousands of people, black and white, through programs of all kinds, including classes, group activities, exhibits, and productions, to become both makers and consumers of the arts. To the Jelliffes, those of their performers and viewers who found careers in the arts, even those who achieved some measure of prominence, were not more important than those thousands who moved in less glamorous walks of life, but who were somehow personally enriched by their artistic experiences. Karamu has certainly spread the notion of black artistic talent and enhanced America's receptivity to it. Woodie King, Jr., professional theatre producer and director, is one of many who have paid tribute to Karamu Theatre for the inspiration it conveyed and for the quality of theatre training Karamu alumni have displayed in New York and elsewhere. Langston Hughes, a Karamu House member who was active in visual arts while still a high school student, is one of the best known alumni. His plays were developed at Karamu, frequently premièred there, and often revived there. Others who carried their Karamu training and experience into the wider theatre world, or were influenced and inspired by Karamu, include **Alice Childress**, John Marriott, Clayton Corbin, Robert Guillaume, Al Fann, Seth McCoy, Charles Brown, Reuben and Dorothy Silver, Ken Frankel, Ron O'Neal, Tom Brennan, Gilbert Moses, Minnie Gentry, Dave Connell, Dick Latessa, and William T. Brown.

Rowena and Russell Jelliffe have received many local and national citations and awards. These honors include the Charles Eisenman Award from the Jewish Welfare Association (1941), the Human and Race Relations Award from the National Conference of Christians and Jews (1941), the Honor Award of the City of Cleveland (1960), the Honor Citation from the National Association of Negro Professional Women's Clubs (1960), the Distinguished Service Award from the United Appeal of Greater Cleveland (1961), the Human Relations Award of B'nai Brith (1963), and the Distinguished Service Award of the National Association for the Advancement of Colored People (1976).

Since her retirement in 1963 Rowena Jelliffe continues to live in Cleveland and remains a valuable source of information, insight, and inspiration to many—friends and strangers—who visit her to renew old acquaintances or seek advice on current projects. Succeeding directors of Karamu House have all counseled with her, and she continues an active interest and involvement in the affairs of Oberlin College.

The Jelliffes sought no personal publicity, even shunned it, though Karamu over the years has proved a magnet for writers of articles, books, theses, and dissertations. John Selby's *Beyond Civil Rights* (1966) is an affectionate and moving history of Karamu and the Jelliffes. Noerena Abookire's "Children's Theatre Activities at Karamu House in Cleveland, Ohio, 1915–1975" (Unpublished Ph.D. dissertation, New York University, 1981) is a thorough piece of research, emphasizing Karamu's children's theatre activities. Reuben Silver's "A History of the Karamu Theatre of Karamu House, 1915–1960" (Unpublished Ph.D. dissertation, Ohio State University, 1961) is a comprehensive history of the Jelliffes and the theatre at Karamu from the perspective of the institution's philosophical basis. The many articles written about Karamu House and the Jelliffes include "Karamu House, Negro Arts Center in Cleveland, is a Milestone of Racial Amity," *Life* (June 18, 1951); Virginia Carville, "The Key to Karamu House," *Extension* (March 1956); Clayton Fritchey, "Karamu," *Junior Red Cross Journal* (December 1941); Carol Hughes, "Cleveland's Cradle of Talent," *Coronet* (July 1946); "The Story of Karamu House," *The Negro Review* (September 1953); and "A Picture Tour of Karamu," *Onyx* (Cleveland, May 9, 1959). Jelliffe is listed in *The Biographical Encyclopaedia and Who's Who of the American Theatre* (1966) and *Notable Names in the American Theatre* (1976).

Reuben Silver

JOHNSON, Georgia Douglas (September 10, 1886–May 14, 1966): poet, playwright, and composer, won national recognition initially as the first black female poet of the twentieth century. Born in Atlanta, Georgia, to George and Laura (Jackson) Camp, Georgia Johnson was educated in the public schools of the city and completed the "normal course" at Atlanta University before studying music at the Oberlin Conservatory in Ohio. Upon completion of her studies at Oberlin she taught in the Atlanta school system. On September 28, 1903, she married Henry Lincoln Johnson, who later became a prominent lawyer and politician. President William Howard Taft appointed her husband to the post of recorder of deeds in the District of Columbia and the Johnsons moved to Washington, D.C., in 1909. Georgia and Henry Johnson had two sons, Henry Lincoln, Jr. (b. June 21, 1904), who recently retired as a practicing attorney in Washington, and Peter Douglas (b. January 21, 1906), whose career as a physician ended with his death as a young man.

Before her husband's death in 1925 the Johnsons, Congregationalists and Republicans, were active pioneers in the social, political, and literary life of Washington. Georgia Johnson was a participant and leader in most of the organizations in the Washington area committed to concerns of women and minorities, and occasionally she accepted speaking engagements on these topics. She regularly contributed poems and children's stories to *The Liberator, The*

Messenger, Opportunity, and the *Crisis* magazines, and maintained membership in the Civic Club, The League of Neighbors of New York, and The Crisis Guild for Writers and Artists.

The Johnsons' home on "S" Street in Northwest Washington, which Georgia Johnson named Half-Way House, became the meeting place for many literary figures of the day, including W. E. B. Du Bois, Alain Locke, Langston Hughes, William Stanley Braithwaite, Zora Neal Hurston, May Miller Sullivan, Jessie Fauset, Willis Richardson, Countee Cullen, S. Randolph Edmonds, and Owen Dodson. Leading political figures, both black and white, also enjoyed the hospitality of Half-Way House during the famous Saturday Evening Soirees. One guest, J. C. Byars, Jr., was particularly fascinated to watch Georgia Johnson, who worked eight hours a day in the Department of Labor, wield by the force of her personality and her writings an important influence on both races (*Black and White,* p. 42).

By 1928 her books included three volumes of poetry, *The Heart of A Woman and Other Poems* (1918), *Bronze* (1922), and *An Autumn Love Cycle* (1928). These three volumes contain the bulk of Johnson's more than two hundred poems. Inspired by her mentor, William Stanley Braithwaite, she became one of the "Genteel School" of writers, whose lyric poems are often compared with those of Sara Teasdale. She set many of her poems to music and enjoyed singing and playing them on the piano for friends who visited her home. Critics recognized and commended her for the message sung throughout her writing: "May the saving grace of the mother-heart save humanity" (Alain Locke and Jessie Fauset, *Crisis,* February, 1923, p. 161).

The poems in Johnson's first volume were said to "transcend the bonds of race." They were written at a time when many blacks felt a need for "raceless literature" to prove equality. Four years later, when *Bronze* appeared, Johnson had begun to feel the spirit of the "New Negro Renaissance"; and the point of view from which she wrote became "the heart of a colored woman aware of her social problems" (Dover, *Crisis,* December 1952, p. 634). Critics of *Bronze* were captured by the strange force of its burning enthusiasm: "She speaks for the colored people of America. . . . Never have they . . . found a voice at once more delicate and clear" (*Opportunity,* July 1923, p. 218).

In 1925, after her husband's death, Johnson found herself with two college-age sons and new responsibilities. She expressed her greatest fear to a reporter from *The Pittsburgh Courier* that she simply would not have time to complete all the work she had planned (July 7, 1928). She was at the time employed full-time as commissioner of conciliation in the United States Department of Labor. Her sons transferred from Dartmouth College to Howard University in Washington, D.C., to reduce expenses, and Johnson rushed home from her job each day to write poems and plays in her "spare time." In an interview in 1927, she said that she had been influenced by friends to try her hand at writing drama and had found it "a living avenue" (*Opportunity,* July 1927, p. 204). She obviously did not mean to imply that she could make a living by writing plays.

Whatever else the New Negro Renaissance may have done for blacks, it did very little to improve the black playwright's chance to get a play produced on the commercial American stage of the 1920s and 1930s. Johnson's affiliation with W. E. B. Du Bois and the newly formed Krigwa Players and her close contacts with pioneers of drama such as Willis Richardson, May Miller, and S. Randolph Edmonds at Howard University and Morgan State College in Baltimore were influences that brought her talents to the world of theatre. Johnson's first known attempt at playwriting was motivated by the anti-lynching campaign following the First World War. The play, *Sunday Morning in the South* (1924), her best-known play, is set in the early twenties and depicts the death of a young black man who is wrongly accused of raping a white woman and is lynched by an angry mob before his grandmother can prove his innocence.

Protest themes about rape and lynching, along with the social status of black women and of their mulatto sons, dominates all of her dramatic writing. Her next drama, *Blue Blood*, was produced by the W. E. B. Du Bois Krigwa (an acronym for Crisis Guild of Writers and Artists) Players in New York, Washington, and elsewhere between 1926 and 1928. May Miller Sullivan and Frank Horne (singer Lena Horne's uncle) performed in the New York production of *Blue Blood*, which treats the shocking discovery by a mulatto couple about to get married that they have the same white father. The play was selected by Frank Shay for publication in *Fifty More Contemporary One-Act Plays* (1928).

Johnson's third drama, *Plumes*, won the *Opportunity* First Place Drama Award in 1927—a sum of $60.00 and publication by Samuel French Publishers. Johnson's ability as a writer of folk drama is best displayed in this short play about the conflict of a poor southern mother who must decide whether to spend her life savings of $50.00 on an operation that may not save her daughter's life or to use that money to bury her in style complete with plumes on the heads of the horses drawing the hearse. The use of folk tradition and superstition to complicate the mother's decision reminded critics of the modern Irish folk plays that revealed the nobility of mankind through the suffering and defeat of the Irish peasant. *Plumes* was hailed as "one of the few plays to be written in this country that proved itself a worthy heir to the 'universals' of folk drama" (France, *A Century of Plays by American Women*, 1979, p. 75).

Shortly after the publication of Johnson's third volume of poetry in 1928, the country was hit by the depression. Within a few years President Franklin D. Roosevelt's New Deal and the Works Progress Administration provided the first federally sponsored and supported theatre—the Federal Theatre Project (1935–1939)—under the direction of **Hallie Flanagan**. The project encouraged new plays of social protest, and Johnson submitted at least five plays to it, but none was accepted for production. Three of the plays dealt with the rape and lynching of blacks, and two were historical sketches of slaves' attempts to escape to freedom. In addition to *Sunday Morning in the South*, which Johnson submitted in several versions, *Blue-eyed Black Boy* and *Safe* were her other dramas on rape and lynching rejected by the Federal Theatre. In *Blue-eyed Black Boy*, an innocent mulatto man is charged with attempted rape and is about to become the victim of the lynch mob, when his mother, in desperation, appeals to the governor "to look into his blue eyes and remember 20 years ago." The governor remembers, and the lynching is stopped. *Safe* is set in 1893 in the cottage of a black southern family. A young wife awaiting the birth of a child is overcome by the sounds of a crazed lynch mob dragging a sobbing black boy to his fate. The boy's agonizing cries shatter the expectant mother's composure. She goes into labor and delivers her child. The healthy cry of the newborn babe is heard in the other room, followed shortly by the emerging doctor's announcement that a fine son has been born—only to be choked to death by its mother when she discovers it is a son. The mother's agonizing cries of "Safe—safe—now he's safe from the lynchers" punctuate the silence as the curtain descends. Johnson's short plays are tightly structured dramas with compressed action. Themes of racial identity and social protest dominate her writing.

Negro History in Thirteen Plays, edited by Willis Richardson and May Miller (1935), preserves for posterity two of Johnson's attempts to capture black history for the theatre. *Frederick Douglass* and *William and Ellen Craft* concern the efforts of slaves to escape to the North. Other plays credited to Georgia Johnson are *The Starting Point* and *Attacks*, but there are no existing copies.

Johnson, disheartened by the reception of her efforts to bring serious matters of black life to the American stage, gave up playwriting and returned to writing poetry in the 1940s. Johnson's last book, *Share My World* (1962), was privately published by a friend, N. Wright Cuney.

With the coming of the Second World War she joined others in the support of the American war effort. For the next two decades she remained active in the literary, social, and political life of Washington, campaigning for Thomas E. Dewey in the 1944 presidential election. In 1965 Atlanta University conferred on her the honorary degree of Doctor of Literature.

As one of the pioneers of playwriting and production among blacks in the 1920s, as one of the earliest playwrights to treat serious subjects of the black experience, as a molder of literary thought during the New Negro Renaissance, and as one who brought the universals of folk drama to public attention, Georgia Douglas Johnson has earned a place of recognition in early twentieth century literature and in the American theatre. Her busy life was ended by a stroke, and she died quietly at Freedman's Hospital in Washington, D.C., on May 14, 1966.

Dramas by Georgia Douglas Johnson appearing in print include *Plumes*, published by Samuel French in 1927, and also printed in Judith E. Barbour, *Plays by American Women 1900–1930* (1986), Rachel France, *A Century of Plays by American Women* (1979), and Victor Calverton, *Anthology of American Negro Literature* (1929); *Blue Blood*, in Alain Locke and Montgomery Gregory, *Plays of Negro Life* (1927); *Frederick Douglass* and *William and Ellen Craft*, in Willis Richardson and May Miller, *Negro History in Thirteen Plays* (1935); and *Sunday Morning in the South*, in James V. Hatch and Ted Shine, *Black Theatre U. S. A.* (1974). Typescripts of *Blue-Eyed Black Boy* and *Safe*, as well as three of the above dramas, are in the Federal Theatre Archives at George Mason University in Fairfax, Virginia, where the reader's comments and criticism of the plays have been preserved. There is little published material about Johnson's life and career. For insights into her life and thoughts see her introduction to her poems in Countee Cullen, *Caroling Dusk* (1927); the interview, with photograph, in *Opportunity* (July 1927); and the article in *The Pittsburgh Courier* (July 7, 1928). See also Cedric Dover, "The Importance of Georgia Douglas Johnson," *Crisis* (December 1952); Erlene Stetson, "Rediscovering the Harlem Renaissance; and Georgia Douglas Johnson, 'The New Negro Poet,' " *Obsidian* (Spring 1979). James V. Hatch and Ted Shine's, *Black Theatre U. S. A.: 45 Plays by Black Americans* (1969) provides some insights into her life. Rosey Poole's *Beyond the Blues* (1969) gives a final look at the seventy-two-year-old Johnson. A recent article on Johnson is Winona L. Fletcher, "From Genteel Poet to Revolutionary Playwright: Georgia Douglas Johnson," *The Theatre Annual*, Special Issue: Women in Theatre (1985). For an extensive listing of reviews and criticism of her work that appeared regularly from 1905 until 1966, see *Black American Writers Past and Present: A Biographical and Bibliographical Dictionary*, Vol. II (1975). Copies of Johnson's books and plays are housed in the Arthur G. Spingarn and Jessie E. Moorland Collections at Howard University, Washington, D.C., and the Schomburg Collection of the New York Public Library.

Winona L. Fletcher

JONES, Margo (December 12, 1912?–July 24, 1955): director and originator of the regional theatre movement in the United States, known for her arena-style staging at Theatre '47 in Dallas, was born Margaret Virginia Jones to Richard Harper Jones and Pearl (Collins) Jones in Livingston, Texas. Since her father was a lawyer, she said it was the live drama that she watched in the courtroom that prompted her to become a stage director. When she attended Texas State College for Women in Denton, the drama courses were crowded with aspiring actresses, but Margo Jones was the only student interested in directing. Because there was no possibility at the time of taking a graduate degree in directing, she took her master's degree in psychology (1932), using Henrik Ibsen's *Hedda Gabler*, *The Lady from the Sea*, and *When We Dead Awaken* to illustrate her thesis titled "The Abnormal Ways Out of Emotional Conflict as Reflected in the Dramas of Henrik Ibsen." Immediately upon graduating, she took a clerical job at the Southwestern School of Theatre in Dallas, although her ambitions exceeded such a position. After a year in Dallas, she left to enroll in the Pasadena Playhouse Summer School of the Theatre. That fall, Jones secured her first directing assignment; she directed Ibsen's *Hedda Gabler* for the Ojai Community Players in Ojai, California. Soon after her year at Ojai, she took a trip around the world as companion and secretary to a wealthy woman. Starting from the West Coast, she avidly explored theatre at every port of call en route. She reached New York in the fall of 1935, where she became inspired by the work of the Group Theatre.

A short time later, Margo Jones returned to Texas to work as assistant director of the Houston Federal Theatre Project, co-sponsored by the Houston Recreation Department. After a few months, that venture collapsed, and Jones next journeyed to the Moscow Art Festival to write a series of feature articles for the *Houston Chronicle*. Upon her return, the Houston Recreation Department offered her a job teaching playground directors to do plays with children. Late in 1936, she persuaded the Recreation Department to allow her to use a small building, where square dancing was held three days a week, to stage plays with adults. When permission was granted, she announced in the press the formation of the Houston Community Players, which opened in December 1936 with Oscar Wilde's *The Importance of Being Earnest*; it ran for two nights. Since the building was available to the Houston Community Players for only two nights a week, the second production, Elmer Rice's *Judgment Day*, was played, appropriately, in a local courtroom. *Merrily We Roll Along*, *Hedda Gabler*, and *Squaring the Circle* were also produced during that first season; and six plays were planned for the second season. The repertoire of the Houston Community Players relied heavily on the classics; this was characteristic of all Margo Jones's directing and producing career.

In 1939 Margo saw theatre-in-the-round demonstrated at a convention in Washington, D.C., and recognized it as a form uniquely suited to small theatres. Until this time the Community Players had been unable to mount plays in the summer because of the heat; but in the summer of 1939, using the theatre-in-the-round format, they were able to mount a play on the mezzanine floor of an air-conditioned hotel in Houston. That summer Margo Jones directed six plays in this fashion and became forever a champion of theatre-in-the- round (or arena staging) for small theatres.

With the advent of the Second World War, Jones found it increasingly difficult to produce plays with volunteers who could not devote their full time and energies to the production, so she accepted a faculty position for two years in the drama department of the University of Texas at Austin, where she directed three new plays and worked in several in-the-round productions.

In the same year, she staged Tennessee Williams' *You Touched Me* (1943) at the Pasadena Playhouse with **Ruth Ford** in the leading role. Jones also formulated an idea for a new theatre: a professional repertory company of full-time professional theatre workers to perform new plays and classics. The company would include several resident playwrights. She mentioned her idea to John Rosenfield, drama editor and critic of the Dallas *Morning News*, who suggested Dallas as a desirable site for such a theatre. From Jones's viewpoint, Dallas was a logical choice for a regional theatre. It was located in a newly rich, pioneering part of the United States, and Jones had already produced theatre there with the Dallas Little Theatre, which had closed in 1941. Rosenfield's encouragement and subsequent introduction to people who might be interested in the project brought Jones's theatre to fruition.

In the spring of 1944 she applied for a Rockefeller Foundation fellowship, submitting a program outlining her aims to observe professional and nonprofessional theatres in order to gain a reasonably complete picture of the current American theatrical scene and to watch the best designers and directors at work.

It was also to be a search for a repertory company of twenty artists. In addition, she hoped to find new playwrights, whose work she expected to read at the rate of three plays daily for a year. In August of 1944 while she was directing Tennessee Williams' *The Purification* in addition to two other scripts at the Pasadena Playhouse, Jones was notified that she had been granted the Rockefeller fellowship; but in November of 1944 she was called to New York to co-direct, with Eddie Dowling, Tennessee Williams' *The Glass Menagerie*. She relinquished the fellowship in favor of the Broadway experience. Once the play opened in 1945, Jones returned to Dallas and proceeded to gather the forces essential to creating her new theatre.

In February 1945 she went to see Mrs. Eugene McDermott, a member of the prize-winning, nonprofessional Dallas Little Theatre, which had won the Belasco Cup in 1924, 1925, and 1926 at the Little Theatre Tournament in New York. The theatre had been liquidated in good financial condition in 1941, and it left a committee instructed to "entertain any proposals to revive the community theatre in Dallas." It was to Mrs. McDermott, then, that Jones presented her proposal to establish a "permanent, professional, repertory, native theatre in Dallas," and offered her plan that called for subsidy, subscriptions, and a board of directors. Mrs. McDermott wrote Jones a check for $10,000 on the spot. When Jones left the meeting, the groundwork for the organization of a board of directors comprised of forty-eight Dallas citizens, for incorporation by the state of Texas as a nonprofit professional repertory theatre (Dallas Theatre Incorporated), and for a financial campaign to raise $75,000 had been laid. Moreover, Jones asked that a budget be prepared by a business manager in consultation with the managing directors and that it cover all expenses required for opening the theatre and operating it for a season. This meticulously thought-out program can certainly be described as a procedural blueprint for establishing almost any theatre. The project was definitely underway in 1945, but progress was slowed when the building that had been selected was condemned by the Department of Buildings as unfit for use.

While the search for a suitable building was being made, Jones went to New York to direct Maxwell Anderson's *Joan of Lorraine* (1946), starring Ingrid Bergman. Later, she spent three weeks in New York, where she hired Mannian Gurian as business manager, hired eight actors, and optioned four plays. Finally, an attractive modern building of stucco and glass bricks was located at Dallas's Fair Park. It was air-conditioned and suitable for theatre-in-the-round with a playing area of twenty-four by twenty feet. All the papers were signed, at last, with the approval of the State Fair Association and the Dallas Department of Parks. On June 3, 1947, Jones opened Theatre '47 with William Inge's *Farther Off From Heaven* (the title later became *The Dark at the Top of the Stairs*). The first season ran for ten weeks with a cast of eight and a repertoire of five plays in a modified repertory form for eight weeks, and then in the ninth and tenth weeks all five plays (*Farther Off from Heaven, How Now, Hecate, Hedda Gabler, Summer and Smoke*, and *Third Cousin*) were featured in repertory. At the end of the season, Theatre '47 had enough funds to start Theatre '48 with a twenty-week plan.

As the company gained in stature, the repertoire, the cast, and the season increased with each successive year. In June 1953 Jones reported a successful seventh season of thirty weeks and announced her plan to enlarge the repertoire from eight to nine plays.

Before they became known in New York, plays by playwrights like William Inge, Joseph Hayes, Irving Phillips, Ronald Alexander, Jerome Lawrence, and Robert E. Lee were being produced in Dallas. In ten seasons Jones moved six plays from Dallas to Broadway. Jones presented the first of these, *Summer and Smoke*, at the Music Box Theatre, New York, on October 6, 1948. The critics' reception was not enthusiastic, with Brooks Atkinson for the *New York Times* blaming the play's failure on Margo Jones's direction rather than on the play's deficiencies (Donald Spoto, *The Kindness of Strangers*, p. 151). One of the most memorable of Jones's Broadway successes was Jerome Lawrence and Robert E. Lee's *Inherit the Wind*, a 1954–1955 success in Dallas that moved directly to Broadway. With the assistance of New York producer Herman Shumlin, Jones's production opened on April 21, 1955, and became theatre history.

In ten seasons Jones produced and/or directed one hundred plays, including classics and new scripts. She broke the ground for the regional theatre movement, popularized arena staging, and launched a sizable number of young playwrights on the path to success. Jones's concepts for regional theatre and arena staging were adopted by **Nina Vance** of the Alley Theatre, Houston, and by **Zelda Fichandler** of the Arena Stage, Washington, D.C.

In November 1954 Dallas's civic leaders gave Margo Jones a tenth anniversary luncheon in the Hotel Adolphus. New York producer/playwright Howard Lindsay delivered the principal tribute. After several other speakers had lauded Jones and recounted her achievements, Mayor R. L. Thornton, on behalf of the Dallas City Council, presented her with an achievement plaque.

During her brief ten-year professional career, she aroused the interest of many people. Brooks Atkinson and Howard Taubman wrote articles on her arena stage and her regional repertory company for the *New York Times* and kept a watchful eye on the fortunes of Theatre '47 through 1955. Others evincing keen interest were Norris Houghton (*But Not Forgotten*, 1971), who had come down from New York to see her Community Players in Houston and applauded her productions, especially the classics.

Thus things stood when, less than three months after the triumphant Broadway opening of *Inherit the Wind*, Margo Jones was overcome by fumes rising from her carpet that had been cleaned that day with carbon tetrachloride by the management of the hotel where she resided. She was rushed to the hospital and died eleven days later on July 25, 1955. The official record showed the cause of death as ''acute kidney failure and acute necrosis of the liver caused by carbon tetrachloride.'' Margo Jones was buried on July 26, 1955, in Livingston, Texas. Her theatre persevered for another four years but finally closed in 1959.

In her honor, the Margo Jones Award was established by Jerome Lawrence and Robert E. Lee "to be given each year to the *person* or *theatre* displaying the most initiative and producing important new works of dramatic literature in that year." The award is devotedly maintained by the authors of *Inherit the Wind*, whom Jones discovered. On August 28, 1956, Nina Vance dedicated the première of James Lee's *Career* at the Alley Theatre to "the late Margo Jones, producer, director, and good friend of the young playwright." Zelda Fichandler named Margo Jones as the person who had influenced her most in her decision to launch the Arena Stage in Washington, D.C.

Over everything Margo Jones did in the theatre, she cast a mantle of vitality, skill, and confidence. She brought to her task as producer and director an extraordinary acumen in play selection. She set out to become a professional director and to establish a regional theatre in order to confirm her belief that people throughout the country wanted theatre. She maintained that every city with a population of over one-hundred-thousand could sustain a theatre and that it was the responsibility of competent theatre people to go into such an area and create a fine theatre.

When Margo Jones died, she left a theatre that had never operated under an Actors' Equity contract, had never relied on previous Broadway hits, had never received grants (federal or foundation); yet her theatre had always been solvent, had played successfully both classic and new plays, had provided opportunities for actors as well as new playwrights, had established regional theatre firmly in the public consciousness, and had clearly marked the road for current and future regional theatre enterprise.

Theatre-in-the-Round (1951) by Margo Jones is a good source of information. Articles in *Theatre Arts*, *Variety*, *New York Times*, and *Dallas Morning News* from 1945 to 1956 are replete with information on Margo Jones's Theatre '47-'56 and her activities on Broadway. *Regional Theatre: The Revolutionary Stage* (1973) by J .W. Ziegler is a rather slanted, superficial, and condescending account of Margo Jones and her achievements. Donald Spoto, *The Kindness of Strangers: The Life of Tennessee Williams* (1985) traces the relationship between the playwright and the director. See also Don B. Wilmeth, "A History of the Margo Jones Theatre" (Unpublished Ph.D. dissertation, University of Illinois, Urbana, 1964). The files of the Dallas Public Library contain production information, scripts, correspondence, and business records. There are clipping files in the Billy Rose Theatre Collection, Performing Arts Research Center of the New York Public Library at Lincoln Center, and in the Harvard Theatre Collection. Jones's obituary appeared in *Theatre Arts* (July 1955), *Time* (August 8, 1955), and the *New York Times* (July 25, 1955). No birth certificate is available, but the death certificate contains biographical information as well as facts surrounding her death. Some sources give her birth date as 1913. Jones is listed in *Who Was Who in the Theatre*, Vol. III (1978); *Notable American Women*, Vol. IV: *The Modern Period* (1980); *The Oxford Companion to the Theatre* (1983); and *The Oxford Companion to American Theatre* (1984).

Florence M. Lea

— K —

KANIN, Fay Mitchell (1916?–): playwright, screenwriter, television writer, producer, and actress, was born in New York City and grew up an only child in Elmira, New York. Her father, David Mitchell, was a department store manager, and her mother, Bessie (Kaiser) Mitchell, had retired from being a vaudeville entertainer in favor of marriage and family. When Fay Mitchell was thirteen, she won the New York State Spelling Championship. One of her cherished pieces of memorabilia is a picture of herself receiving the award from the then governor of New York, Franklin D. Roosevelt, thus beginning a relationship with the Roosevelts that extended through his presidency.

While still in high school at the Elmira Free Academy, she wrote for the local *Star Gazette* and edited the year book. After high school graduation in 1933, Fay Mitchell entered Elmira College as an English and drama major. While enrolled there she wrote and produced a children's show on local radio. In 1936 her parents moved to California, and she transferred to the University of Southern California for her senior year, receiving a Bachelor of Arts degree in 1937.

Upon graduation, she was hired as a writer at RKO Studios by a producer who was interested in encouraging talented young people. Her first writing job ended when the producer left the studio shortly after hiring her. However, she stayed on in the studio's story department as a reader, earning $25 a week, a position that lasted two years. While on the Studio lot she took every opportunity to learn about filmmaking. While at RKO, Mitchell acted and wrote plays for the RKO Studio Players, a group doing theatre productions on the RKO lot. She also was introduced to a studio writer, Michael Kanin, who asked her to marry him on the very day they met. She took it as a joke, but they were married a year later on April 7, 1940. They spent their honeymoon in Malibu working on their first screenwriting collaboration, *Sunday Punch*, which was produced by

MGM Studios in 1942. Also in 1942 Michael Kanin, in collaboration with Ring Lardner, Jr., won the Academy (Oscar) Award for the screenplay, *Woman of the Year*.

Playwright and director Garson Kanin is Fay Kanin's brother-in-law, and his late wife, **Ruth Gordon**, was her sister-in-law. Fay and Michael Kanin had two sons, Joel and Josh. Joel died of a tumor at the age of 13. Josh, born in 1950, is a film editor and university cinema instructor. There are two granddaughters, Laurel, born in 1974, and Jessica, born in 1982.

During the early 1940s Fay Kanin wrote a screenplay from William Dodd's *Ambassador Dodd's Diary* and Martha Dodd's *Through Embassy Eyes* for Twentieth Century-Fox and Otto Preminger. It was to be a movie detailing the rise of the Nazis in Germany as seen by then American ambassador to Germany, William Dodd, and his daughter. Though it was not produced, it impelled Kanin to join the war effort in an active way. For over a year she wrote and produced for the Office of War Information a radio program titled *The Woman's Angle*. The purpose of this program was to educate women in order to elicit their support of the war effort.

In 1948, in her first attempt at playwriting, Kanin had a Broadway hit in *Goodbye My Fancy*. Opening at the Morosco Theatre on November 17, it was co-produced by Michael Kanin and starred Madeleine Carroll, **Shirley Booth**, Conrad Nagel, and Sam Wanamaker, who also directed it. Some years later, it was repeated at the Pasadena Playhouse in California, and Kanin herself acted the leading role.

After *Goodbye My Fancy* the Kanins collaborated on three plays: *His and Hers*, which opened at the 48th Street Theatre, New York, on January 7, 1954; *Rashomon*, based on the stories of Ryunosuke Akutagawa and the film *Rashomon*, which opened at the Music Box Theatre, New York, on January 27, 1959; and the book for a musical, *The Gay Life*, which opened November 16, 1961, at Broadway's Shubert Theatre. In addition to the plays and the film already listed, the Kanins wrote the screenplays for *My Pal Gus* (Fox, 1952), *Rhapsody* (MGM, 1954), *The Opposite Sex* (MGM, 1956), *Teacher's Pet* (Paramount, 1958), *The Right Approach* (Fox, 1961), *The Swordsman of Siena* (MGM, 1962), and *The Outrage* (MGM, 1964) based on the play *Rashomon*. *Teacher's Pet* won an Academy (Oscar) Award nomination for best screenplay. The film version of *Goodbye My Fancy* was produced in 1951, although Fay Kanin did not write the screenplay. After twenty years of successful collaboration, the Kanins decided it was healthier for their development as writers and for the marriage for them to pursue separate professional careers.

Early in the 1970s when movie studios were embracing disaster movies about sharks and outer space, Fay Kanin turned to writing television drama, finding there a more receptive atmosphere for the exploration of relationships and strong personal and social themes. Her first television film was *Heat of Anger*, starring Susan Hayward, which aired on CBS, March 3, 1972. It has been credited as a contributing factor in the emergence of strong women as protagonists in television dramas because Hayward played the role of a successful woman lawyer with a male law partner. *Tell Me Where It Hurts* aired on CBS on March 12, 1974, and repeated on August 27. In this drama a middle-aged woman, played by **Maureen Stapleton**, finds herself feeling useless after her children are grown. She begins talking to other women in an informal group, and the talking frees them to effect changes in their lives. She sets out to find her own place in the world and at the same time re-educates her husband, whom she loves, to accept her new role. *Tell Me Where It Hurts* won an Emmy Award for best original television drama as well as the Christopher Award.

Hustling, based on Gail Sheehy's investigation of prostitution in New York City, was produced in 1975 on ABC, starring Lee Remick and Jill Clayburgh. In an interview in the *Montreal Gazette* (June 11, 1982), Kanin is quoted as saying, ''When I was asked to write it, . . . I said to ABC that if I was expected to write a pantywaist movie about prostitution, I just didn't want to do it. I asked them, 'Are you willing to be as forthright about this subject as television will allow?' '' In this article Bruce Bailey goes on to say: ''Kanin did her own research, riding around in the van as the police did their nightly hooker round-ups.'' Kanin continues: ''At first they [the prostitutes] tried to bait me by deliberately using crude language. But after they saw me back night after night, they got to know me and they finally understood that I was trying to make an honest, accurate movie.'' Kanin was also associate producer on this project. *Hustling* was aired on February 22, 1975, and repeated on November 14. It won the Writer's Guild Award for best original television drama that year.

In 1979 *Friendly Fire* aired on ABC, starring Carol Burnett and Ned Beatty. It is a story of an actual Iowa family who wage a private war with the army over their right to know the truth behind their son's accidental death by American artillery in Vietnam. Kanin wrote and co-produced it with Philip Barry. *Friendly Fire* won the Emmy Award for the best television film, the San Francisco Film Festival Award in the same category, and the Peabody Award.

In 1978–1979 Kanin and Lillian Gallo formed a production company to make films for television and movies. They became the only female team to be under an exclusive contract to a television network: ABC. The Kanin-Gallo company produced *Fun and Games*, which aired in 1980. Starring Valerie Harper, it dealt with the sexual harassment of a woman in a factory job. *Heartsounds*, adapted from a book by journalist Martha Lear and produced for Norman Lear and ABC Pictures, was Kanin's next project as writer and co-producer. It starred James Garner and Mary Tyler Moore and aired in September 1984. *Heartsounds* won the second Peabody Award for Kanin and received three Emmy nominations. In 1985 Fay Kanin returned to Broadway as the author of the book for the musical *Grind* with Larry Grossman as composer and Ellen Fitzhugh as lyricist. Directed by Hal Prince, it starred Ben Vereen. *Grind* received seven Antoinette Perry (Tony) nominations, including one for Kanin as author.

In addition to writing, Kanin has appeared briefly as an actress in *Tell Me Where It Hurts* and in the feature film, *Rich and Famous*. From 1971 to 1973

Kanin was president of the screen branch of the Writer's Guild of America, West, the first woman elected to that position in twenty years. In the early 1970s, Fay and Michael Kanin were members of the Steering Committee of the American College Theatre Festival in the Southern California-Arizona-Nevada region. This involvement led to the founding of the National Student Playwriting Awards by Michael Kanin. In 1979 Fay Kanin delivered the keynote address at the national convention of the American Theatre Association meeting in San Diego. She is a trustee of the American Film Institute and a director of Filmex Corporation. In 1979 Kanin was elected as the twenty-second president of the Academy of Motion Picture Arts and Sciences, which awards the Oscars. She served four terms in that office. Bette Davis has been the only other woman to hold this position; she served for one month during the Second World War. Since 1983 Kanin has served as vice president of the academy, and as its representative she has traveled extensively abroad. In 1981 she accompanied the first five major American films to be seen in China in over a generation. Through this trip to China, as well as journeys to the Soviet Union and most of Western Europe, Kanin has become the principal woman ambassador of American films in the world today.

In addition to the awards listed above, Kanin won the Writers' Guild's prestigious Val Davies Award in 1975, the Carrie Chapman Catt Award from the League of Woman Voters in 1980, the Crystal Award from Women in Film in 1980, and, most recently, the Internationalism Award from American Women for International Understanding in 1982. She was also awarded a Doctor of Humane Letters by Elmira College, New York, in 1981.

Kanin's outstanding contribution has been to write about contemporary subjects pertaining to the problems of women or contemporary problems for both sexes as seen through the eyes of women. In her first play, *Goodbye My Fancy*, a congresswoman is faced with the choice of marrying her former lover at the price of compromising her deepest beliefs and ideals, a sacrifice she is not willing to make. The play was written at a time when most women saw marriage as their only choice in society.

Fay Kanin has been a model for women working in theatre, films, and television and an inspiration to women writers in particular. She has managed successfully to combine marriage, family, and career. She has always worked in professions largely dominated by men. She was quoted in an article in *People Magazine* (April 21, 1980) as saying, "No one ever told me I couldn't be anything I wanted to be."

For further information about Fay Kanin see Ursula Vils, "Reshaping Heroines Image," Los Angeles *Times* (February 9, 1972); Nan Robertson, "Fay Kanin Makes it Big on Her Own," *The Times Record* (Brunswick, Maine, September 17, 1979); James Powers, "Dialogue on Film: Fay Kanin," *American Film Magazine* (March 1980); Aljean Harmetz, "Fay Kanin at the Helm for Academy Awards," *New York Times* (April 2, 1980); and "To the Top," *People Magazine* (April 21, 1980). An interview with Fay and Michael Kanin was printed in the *Los Angeles Times Home Magazine* (February 15,

1981); Patricia McCormack of UPI interviewed Fay Kanin for "Budget Cuts in the Arts?" which appeared in newspapers throughout the country on September 30, 1981; and an interview with Kanin appeared in the *New York Times* (March 3, 1982) under the title "Academy of Motion Picture Arts and Sciences will present for the first time Special Certificates to all 141 Oscar nominees, Academy President Fay Kanin comments." Bruce Bailey wrote an article in the *Montreal Gazette* (June 11, 1982) titled "Screenwriter Fay Kanin is tuning in to television dramas." Fay and Michael Kanin have donated their archival material to the University of Wyoming, where it is catalogued at the campus library. Fay Kanin is listed in *The Biographical Encyclopaedia and Who's Who of American Theatre* (1966); *Notable Names in the American Theatre* (1976); and *Who's Who of American Women, 1981–1982* (1981).

Jean Prinz Korf

KEANE, Doris (December 12, 1881–November 25, 1945): actress, essentially noted for a single role in Edward Sheldon's *Romance* (1913) played throughout her long stage career, was born Dora Keane to Joseph Keane and Minnie Florence Ricaby (Winter) Keane, near St. Joseph's, Michigan. She was one of five children: May, the eldest, two others who died in their pre-teens, and Horace, the youngest. Her great grandmother, Sarah Cogswell, established, along with Emma Willard, the first girls' school in New York, and her grandmother, Dr. Mary Sudworth Winter, was the third woman physician in America. When Joseph Keane died, his family moved to Chicago, where Dora Keane began her education. Subsequent schooling included two years at a Quaker school in Pennsylvania, two years at the Convent de l'Assomption near Paris (1899–1901), and two years at Franklin Sargent's American Academy of Dramatic Arts (1901–1903) in New York.

Since her parents were actors, Doris Keane first appeared on the stage at the age of two. Under the stage name of Little Dora, she played the part of Little Meenie in her father's adaptation of *Rip Van Winkle*. Her first New York appearance came at the American Academy of Dramatic Arts, where she played Isabel Warland in *The Twilight of the Gods* (1902) and the following year played the lead in *Mrs. Dane's Defense* (1903). Upon leaving the American Academy in pursuit of a professional career, she sought out producer Charles Frohman, who cast her in her first professional role as Rosa for a December 2, 1903, production of *Whitewashing Julie*. That same December, she appeared as Yvette in *Gypsy* (1903). During the 1904–1905 season she toured in *The Other Girl*, and in September 1905 she opened at New York's Empire Theatre opposite John Drew in *DeLancy*. Of her performance, one critic said that she possessed an unusually vivid and charming stage presence. Upon her mother's death, Doris Keane retired briefly from the stage. Although Charles Frohman suggested that she take a longer rest, that June (1906) she joined the George Fawcett Stock Company in Minneapolis. There she performed every night (including Sundays) and two afternoons a week and appeared in a new show every week. She gained valuable experience in such productions as *Friends*, *A Social Highwayman*, *The Middle*, and *Peaceful Valley*. After leaving the Fawcett Stock Company, she secured the role of Rachel Neve in *The Hypocrites*, which opened August 1906 at the Hudson Theatre, New York, and was her first real success. A year later she was given star billing when *The Hypocrites* premièred in London at the Hicks Theatre. Upon her return to America she played Juanita opposite Holbrook Blinn in *The Rose of the Rancho* at Elitch Gardens Theatre, Denver, Colorado (1908); Billy in *The Likes O' Me* at New York's Garrick Theatre (September 1908); Margaret Ellen in *His Wife's Family* with Edward Harrigan and Arnold Daly at Wallack's Theatre, New York (October 1908); and Joan Thornton in *The Happy Marriage* at the Garrick Theatre, New York (April 1909). At this time she was anticipating a new play that Clyde Fitch was writing for her, but his unexpected death at the age of forty-nine brought Doris Keane to a point of despair about her career. That August, however, she opened in the role of Sonia Kritchnofe in *Arsène Lupin*, and in September 1909, she played Adrienne Morel in Gladys Unger's *Decorating Clementine*. For the second time in her career, Doris Keane returned to London to repeat her New York performance, opening in *Decorating Clementine* at the Globe Theatre in November 1910. Upon returning to New York, she considered the part of Egypt Komello in Edward Sheldon's *Egypt*, but decided against it. Always on the lookout for the role that would make her a star, she bided her time with parts such as Hope Summers in *Our World* (Garrick, New York, February 1911); Bess Marks in *The Lights O' London* (Lyric, New York, May 1911) with Douglas Fairbanks, Holbrook Blinn, and William Courtney; Tress Conway in *The Warning* (Boston Theatre, October 1911); Deronda Deane in *Making Good* (Fulton Theatre, New York, February 1912); and Mimi in *The Affairs of Anatol* with John Barrymore (Little Theatre, New York, October 1912).

During the run of *The Affairs of Anatol*, Doris Keane began rehearsing the part of Margherita Cavallini, the great opera star who, in Edward Sheldon's *Romance*, forsakes her clergyman lover rather than ruin his career. She determined to make this role the biggest of her career. Keane first hesitated to take the part because of her prior romantic relationship with Sheldon, which she had broken off in May of 1901. Sheldon assured her that he would not cause her any problems if she would only play the part he had written especially for her. *Romance* premièred in Albany, New York, in early February 1913 before its New York opening at the **Maxine Elliott** Theatre on February 10, 1913. The play proved a milestone in American theatre and drama. The Shuberts sold the play to Charles Dillingham, who in turn successfully toured *Romance* throughout the United States. In 1915 he presented the play in London, where its command performance before Queen Mary enabled it to last for 1,049 performances. Except for two performances, Doris Keane played the role of Cavallini for every production in both the United States and England. (*Romance* had the longest run of all American plays transferred to London, until 1942, when *Arsenic and Old Lace* surpassed it with 1,332 performances.)

Doris Keane remained in London after the closing of *Romance* and in September 1918 appeared as Roxana Clayton in the *Roxana* production that ran for nine months. At Ellen Terry's suggestion, Doris Keane co-starred with her in *Romeo and Juliet* in April 1919. Although Doris Keane's Juliet did not meet with favor, part of the problem lay with Ellen Terry who improvised her lines because she had not learned them. After *Romeo and Juliet* closed, Doris Keane returned to the United States.

In February 1921 Keane opened in a revival of *Romance* at the Playhouse in New York. Of this production a *New York Times* reviewer wrote, "Miss Keane paints the passionate Cavallini with a hundred varied touches. It is a performance rich in detail, one that makes the play live despite its quite apparent theatricalness. New York, like London, probably will be willing to go to see it just as long as Miss Keane cares to play it" (March 1, 1921). Alexander Woollcott wrote, "After eight years one revisits it a trifle apprehensively, only to find that the play has lost not a whit of its great charm and that Doris Keane's La Cavallini is as fascinating as ever" (*New York Times*, March 6, 1921).

In 1920 Doris Keane repeated her role for the movies. Greta Garbo later re-enacted the role on film in 1930. From 1926 throughout the 1940s, *Romance* flourished on every continent in the world and in 1948 was presented in a musical version titled *My Romance*. Doris Keane's legendary performance made her one of the most admired personalities of her time. Patrons would buy a year's pass to *Romance* in order to be assured a seat. Many saw the production more than once; some saw it five to ten times, and one person saw the play sixty-three times. At the close of *Romance* in 1918 Doris Keane married her leading man, actor Basil Sydney (Rafferty). The marriage was dissolved in 1925, and the divorce was finalized in 1926.

During the 1921 New York revival of *Romance*, Edward Sheldon readied *The Czarina* for Keane. *The Czarina* opened January 1922 at the Empire Theatre, New York, and the role of Catherine the Great was Keane's second greatest success in her long career. That same year she became chairperson of the American Committee for the Relief of Russian Children. In March 1924 she opened in Eugene O'Neill's *Welded*, playing the role of Eleanor Owens in a manner that critics called masterful. Her next part was that of Aurelie in *Starlight* (San Francisco, September 1924), which went to New York's Broadhurst Theatre in March 1925. Throughout 1926 and 1927, Doris Keane toured England in yet another revival of *Romance*. Her last performance was in April 1929 at Los Angeles' Belasco Theatre, where she played the roles of Elvira Moreno and Captain Veneno in *The Pirate*.

Keane spent the remainder of her life in seclusion, devoting her energies to the reading and studying of English and Indian philosophic writings. She died of cancer on November 25, 1945, at the LeRoy Sanitarium, New York, at the age of sixty-three. Her body was cremated, and her ashes were buried on Martha's Vineyard, Massachusetts. She is survived by one daughter, Ronda Keane, an actress.

The career of Doris Keane, whom critics saw as one of the most talented actresses of her generation, spanned twenty-six years and two continents.

There is no complete biography of Doris Keane. Extensive primary source material was used for this entry, including an interview with Ronda Keane in May 1982 and Keane's unpublished diary. For reviews of *Romance*, see the *New York Times* (March 1 and 6, 1921, and November 4, 1926). For reviews of *Welded*, see the *New York Times* (March 18 and 23, 1924). There are many references to Doris Keane in Eric Wollencott Barnes's biography of Edward Sheldon titled *The Man Who Lived Twice* (1956). Keane's obituary was published in the *New York Times* (November 26, 1945). Keane is listed in *The Green Room Book of Who's Who on the Stage, 1909*, ed. John Parker (1909); *Who's Who in Music and Drama*, ed. Dixie Hines and Harry Prescott Hanaford (1914); *Who's Who in the Theatre* (1939); Robert L. Sherman, *Actors and Authors with Composers Who Helped Make Them Famous* (1951); *Who Was Who in America, 1943–1950*, Vol. 2 (1966); *Who Was Who in the Theatre*, Vol. III (1978); and *The Oxford Companion to American Theatre* (1984).

Loren K. Ruff

KEENE, Laura (1826?–November 4, 1873): actress, theatre manager, director, and playwright, was born Mary Frances Moss in London, England, in a year variously given as 1820, 1826, 1830, and 1836. A statement by one of her daughters gives 1826 the most authority. Her immediate family seems to have had no connection with the theatre, her father being a carpenter and builder. An aunt, however, had married into the Yates family, which had earned a considerable reputation on the English stage a generation earlier, and an uncle owned and operated an art gallery on St. James Street near the Palace Theatre.

Mary Frances Moss seems to have had little or no formal education, but she is said to have been a voracious reader; she also spent much time in and about her Uncle Taylor's art gallery, and some say she was trained for the stage by her Aunt Yates. In her late teens she married Henry Taylor, a London tavern keeper, and her first child, Emma, was born in 1845. Three years later she gave birth to a second daughter, Clara. Shortly thereafter, her husband was convicted of a felony and sent to a penal colony in Australia. Since her father now also disappears from the record, it is presumed that he died about this time. Perhaps this double calamity forced the twenty-five-year-old Mary Frances Taylor to seek a livelihood on the stage. Her first appearance of record was as Juliet with a company in Surrey on August 26, 1851. She was now called Laura Keene. The surname was assumed by both daughters, and her mother was buried as "Janet Keene" in New York in December 1872.

Laura Keene made her first appearance in London at the Olympic Theatre on October 28, 1851, as Pauline in Bulwer-Lytton's *Lady of Lyons*. That she was thus included in Henry Farren's "splendid company" that year would seem to indicate that she was no novice or that she had an outstanding talent. She was, by all accounts, a beautiful woman, with a slight but graceful body, rich auburn hair, and large, expressive eyes. By May 12, 1852, she was appearing at the Lyceum Theatre in London in *The Chain of Events*. The Lyceum was then under the managership of the famous Madame Lucia Elizabeth (or Lucy Eliza) Vestris and her husband, Charles James Mathews. Keene's engagement there may have resulted either from Vestris or Mathews's seeing her at the Olympic (a theatre where they had both been playing when they were married in 1838) or from the close friendship of the older Mathews and Yates families. In any event, the influence of the person and career of Madame Vestris on the future course of Laura Keene's life was considerable; one of Keene's cherished possessions was an ivory miniature of the older actress/manager.

It is presumed that James W. Wallack, on one of his thirty-four transAtlantic trips, saw Keene performing at the Lyceum and engaged her for the company with which he opened Wallack's Theatre in New York City in the fall of 1852. Keene made the journey to America in the summer of 1852, and except for a short interlude in Australia, the rest of her career is American. She was accompanied to America by her mother and her two small daughters. The children (henceforth to be known publicly as Keene's "nieces") were placed in a convent school in Washington, D.C., after which Keene and her mother went to New York. At this point Keene, born and raised a Calvinist, took instructions and joined the Roman Catholic Church.

Wallack's Theatre opened on September 8, 1852, and Laura Keene first appeared as the company's leading lady on September 21, 1852, when she played Albina Mandeville in Frederick Reynold's *The Will*. The next night she played Lydia Languish in Richard Brinsley Sheridan's *The Rivals*, with John Brougham playing O'Trigger and Lester Wallack (James's son) as Jack. That season she also played Beatrice (*Much Ado About Nothing*), Portia (*The Merchant of Venice*), Rosalind (*As You Like It*), Kate Hardcastle (*She Stoops to Conquer*), as well as parts in contemporary plays. She was credited by the press and the public as contributing significantly to the conspicuous success of Wallack's season, *The Albion* declaring, "She will spoil the critics' trade, if she continues thus adding laurels upon laurels to her brow" (Odell, *Annals of the New York Stage*, Vol. VI, p. 218).

Not far into her second season at Wallack's—on November 25, 1853 (as related by Lester Wallack in his memoirs)—she unaccountably failed to appear for a performance of *The Rivals*, having left New York for Baltimore, where she opened the Charles Street Theatre (more formally known as Howard's Atheneum and Gallery of Art) on December 24, 1853, as manager and star. She thus became one of the two first female managers in the history of the American theatre, if we count the two-year stint of **Catherine Sinclair** (the divorced wife of Edwin Forrest) which began on the same date in San Francisco. As to what led to this abrupt maneuver on Keene's part, viable conjecture is that (aside from her desire to emulate Madame Vestris), her acquaintance with John Lutz helped inspire the Baltimore venture. Lutz was from a well-to-do mercantile family in Washington, D.C.—a person with whom Keene fell in love and whom she married in 1860. The Baltimore season lasted until March 2, 1854, by which time fifteen productions had been mounted, including not only Shakespeare but light comedy, farce, and melodrama. Besides Keene, the company included

E. A. Sothern, Kate Saxon, and Charles Wheatleigh, and it was declared by critics to be the best thus far seen in Baltimore.

By April 1854 Keene was in San Francisco, appearing in a brief and unfortunate engagement at Catherine Sinclair's Metropolitan Theatre, then moving swiftly in June of that year to managership of the Union Theatre. San Francisco's press and public hailed her productions as outstanding, and records show that the house was constantly full. But by July 31, 1854, she was on her way to Australia, in a company that included Edwin Booth, to play in Sydney and in Melbourne for the rest of the year. Evidently John Lutz had proposed marriage, but her legal husband was somewhere in Australia. It is not known whether she found Henry Taylor, but the record shows that she did not marry Lutz until 1860, when Taylor (if not found) could be presumed dead.

By early 1855 she was back in San Francisco managing the American Theatre and presenting a largely Shakespearean repertory laced with a sprinkling of parodies, burlettas, and extravaganzas. Although apparently successful in this endeavor, she headed back to New York City that fall, having been away for just about two years. Having had successful terms as a manager in both Baltimore and San Francisco, she was ready to assume a serious, long-term career as a manager in what had become the theatrical capital of the United States—in competition with two outstanding managers there: William E. Burton and her old mentor James W. Wallack, each of whom had his own theatre and a considerable reputation.

Her first full season as manager in New York took place at the Metropolitan Theatre, which she rented, refurbished, and rechristened "Laura Keene's Varieties." The opening was announced for December 24, 1855, with *Prince Charming* as the main attraction and *Two Can Play at That Game* as the afterpiece. Her new company included three prominent performers who left Burton to join her. It cannot be established that this defection had anything to do with the vandalism, but her scenery was irreparably slashed the day before her announced opening. Consequently, the delayed opening on December 27, 1855, presented an early play of Dion Boucicault, *Old Heads and Young Hearts*. On December 29, Keene herself appeared as Peg Woffington in *Masks and Faces*. The season lasted until June 21, 1856, and included four premières of new works and at least eighteen other productions. The roster was chiefly one of light comedies and melodramas with an occasional Shakespeare, Sheridan, or Goldsmith. On May 26, 1856, Keene played the title role in John Brougham's adaptation of *Jane Eyre*, and it was remarked in the notices that she "had been ill." On June 16 she appeared as Clarissa Harlowe, and her benefit, which closed the season on June 21, saw her performing Lady Teazle in *The School for Scandal*. A noteworthy event of the season had been the presentation on February 22 of ten specially designed and mounted tableaux in honor of George Washington. The season was universally acclaimed an artistic success—and it was successful financially as well. But the competition was not to be outdone. Because of a legal loophole in her lease, Burton was able to buy the Metropolitan, which he did—and Keene was homeless.

Undaunted, she engaged John Trimple to build her a new theatre seating 1,800 at 624 Broadway (near Broome Street), at a price of $74,000 plus interest, to be paid off at the rate of $12,000 per year for seven years. Throughout that seven-year obligation—until May 9, 1863—the Laura Keene Theatre housed the only true stock company in New York. Long after rival companies had succumbed to the star system, Keene maintained her company without stars in a varied repertory. Her refusal to adhere to the then prevalent custom of casting to a line of parts (she once cast Joseph Jefferson as Puck and E. A. Sothern as Lord Dundreary) contributed to the development of several notable acting careers. Not only Jefferson and Sothern were members of her company, but also (at one time or another) Ada Clifton, **Rose Eytinge**, Marion McCarthy, Mary Wells, A. H. Davenport, Charles Wheatleigh, F. C. Weymss, A. C. Walcott, Charles Couldock, **Agnes Robertson**, and Dion Boucicault. She fostered native American playwriting talent, presenting premières of many plays, notably Boucicault's *The Colleen Bawn* on March 29, 1860, Oliver Bell Bunce's *Love in '76* on February 28, 1857, and J. G. Burnett's *Blanche of Brandywine* on April 22, 1858. On occasion she offered money prizes for acceptable new plays, and Arthur Hobson Quinn credits her as being very influential in making New York theatre "more hospitable to native plays that had merit as literature as well as possibilities of stage success" (*A History of the American Drama from the Beginning to the Civil War*, p. 367).

By all accounts, Keene was also extraordinarily concerned with scenery, costume, and stage direction. She took great pains to see that her productions were skillfully and beautifully mounted. Extravaganzas like *The Elves* or *The Statue Bride* (1858) and the spectacular burlesques of *The Seven Sisters* and *The Seven Sons* (1861) exploited all possible stage mechanisms and were immensely successful with audiences. The *New York Times* in 1862 credited her with "a wealth of fancy and artistic finish that has never been equalled or even approached at any other New York theatre" (quoted by Creahan, p. 686). Joseph Jefferson reports that, even in those plays primarily set indoors, she spared no expense. "Nothing but the best ever entered her theatre" he says (Jefferson, p. 142) and this included real lace curtains in the meticulously realized box sets. Yet such was her managerial ability that she successfully weathered the panic of 1857 (which thrust Burton permanently out of managing and damaged Wallack) by, as Jefferson again says, displaying "great taste and judgment in making cheap articles look like expensive ones." She also spent more money on advertising than her fellow managers and, during her career as manager of Laura Keene's Theatre, introduced Wednesday and Saturday matinees so successfully that they became standard in theatre practice. Though devoted to the idea of repertory, she was not unmindful of the virtues of the consecutive playing of a single piece. In practically every season, one or more productions ran consecutively: in her first season at the new theatre, *The Elves* ran from March 16 to July 4, 1857;

Boucicault's *The Colleen Bawn* ran for 38 consecutive performances in the spring of 1862; and *The Seven Sisters* ran for 177 in the fall of that year. Tom Taylor's *Our American Cousin* (so closely identified with Laura Keene's memory because she was playing it at Ford's Theatre on the night President Abraham Lincoln was shot) played from January 9, 1862, through February 22 in consecutive performances. Thus Keene was an early precursor of a type of production that would eventually be the death of repertory—the long-run show.

Keene's executive ability was evident not only in financial management, publicity, settings, costumes, and in training of actors but in directing her company. She was universally known as "the Duchess"—a term of admiration mixed with awe and sometimes with resentment of her autocratic behavior. Although she was not above sewing costumes and painting scenery when necessity demanded, she was inflexible in rehearsal discipline and spared neither herself nor her cast in the preparations for performance. She was evidently at her best directing comedy; but, as Joseph Jefferson relates, the arrangement of large cast stage pictures sometimes eluded her. Nevertheless, she was obviously successful in her activities to the point where the *New York Herald Tribune* in 1862 said her theatre "compares with the best in the city, not even excepting Wallack's" (September 12, 1862).

High points of those seven seasons (not mentioned above) were the following: in 1856–1857, her portrayal of Rosalind in *As You Like It*; in 1857–1858, spectacular productions of *The Sea of Ice* and *The Corsican Brothers* and a production of *The Merry Wives of Windsor,* with James H. Hackett as Falstaff; in 1858–1859, the first presentation of *Our American Cousin* and a much praised production of *A Midsummer's Night's Dream*; in 1859–1860, Tom Taylor's *House and Home* and Dion Boucicault's *The Trial of Effie Deans*; in 1860–1861, immensely successful productions of *The Imaginary Invalid* and *The Beggar's Opera*; in 1861–1862, the appearance of a play written by Keene, *The Mac-Carthy; or The Peep of Day*; and in 1862–1863, *She Stoops to Conquer, Rachel the Reaper*, and an extravaganza called *Blanchette; or, The Naughty Prince and the Pretty Peasant*. These are only highlights of seasons consisting of from ten to twenty plays each.

By March 23 of 1863, Keene had begun a series of farewell performances. She presented *Our American Cousin*, which finally ended on May 9, closing her career as actor-manager per se. It is perhaps worth noting here that Keene's daughter Emma had died on February 23, 1863, as the result of a backstage accident, while she worked as a minor actor and assistant stage manager with a company in New Haven. **Matilda Vining Wood**, who had presented a series of performances at the Laura Keene Theatre from January 6 to March 16, 1863, took over the house in the fall of that year, renaming it the Olympic.

Keene voluntarily left New York management while still considered successful (she later thought her leaving had been a mistake), and departed for a six-year-long career as a touring star under her own management. In that time she played not only Washington, D.C., Boston, Philadelphia, and New Haven but nearly every other major city east of the Mississippi. The fateful performance of *Our American Cousin* on April 14, 1865, was the final night of a two-week stand at Ford's Theatre, which had also included *She Stoops to Conquer*, *The School for Scandal*, *The Story of Peggy* (Woffington), and Keene's own script, *The Workmen of Washington* (which she had also copyrighted under the titles *The Workmen of Boston*, *The Workmen of Chicago*, and so on, while she toured those cities plus St. Louis, Cincinnati, Buffalo, Louisville, Nashville, and New Orleans). She was, of course, arrested (along with John Ford, the theatre proprietor) after the assassination; but her husband's political connections in Washington secured her release. John Lutz, whom she had married in 1860, traveled with her on her tours until he died in 1869.

After the death of her husband, Keene again tried to establish herself as manager of a standing theatre company. She took over the Chestnut Street Theatre in Philadelphia, remodeling and refurbishing it for a short but unsuccessful season, which lasted from September 20, 1869, to the end of January 1870. To recoup her fortunes, she set out on an extensive tour to the South and West that took her as far as Minneapolis. In the early months of 1871, she was back in New York for two more attempts to form standing repertory companies, both of which ended in failure. Her last appearance was in *Hunted Down* at Wood's Museum on April 27, 1872. That the illness from which she finally died—consumption—had begun as early as the late 1850s is evidenced in various published references to sundry "illnesses" through the 1860s. But as late as 1871 she was engaged in the new venture of co-editing and publishing with Emma Webb Nirert a *Fine Arts* magazine, in one issue of which she praised Edwin Booth's tour-de-force in playing the roles of Brutus, Cassius, and Antony in his *Julius Caesar* of that season. Through the winter and spring of 1872–1873 she also toured widely as a lecturer on the fine arts, accompanied by her daughter Clara, who enlivened the lecture presentations with her soprano solos. This lecture tour was undertaken immediately after the death of Keene's mother, and Keene herself must have been aware of her own impending end. Her final performance on any stage was in Tidioute, Pennsylvania, where she performed two short comedies, *The Morning Call* and *The Stage-Struck Barber*, on July 4, 1873.

During the summer of 1873 she sold off the property at 34 Bond Street that she and her family had called home since their arrival from England in 1852, as well as the farm in New Bedford, Massachusetts, which her earnings in theatre had enabled her to acquire. Toward the end of summer, she moved to a small house in Montclair, New Jersey, taking up there once again a religious affiliation with the Church of the Immaculate Conception. She died on November 4, 1873, and was buried in the cemetery attached to that church. In April of 1876, her remains were moved to the family plot in the Greenwood Cemetery, New York, where the headstone still reads—in its entirety—"Laura Keene, died 1873."

The words spoken at her funeral might well stand as her enduring epitaph: "No braver, steadier, abler soldier ever battled in the ranks of art than Laura

Keene. No captain ever planned better or laboured more perseveringly or with more success. Her inflexible energy and perseverance had few equals in any walk of life'' (Obituary, *New York Herald*, December 16, 1873).

There is one full-length biography of Laura Keene: John Creahan's *The Life of Laura Keene* (1887). References with particular points of view are to be found in these works by three of her contemporaries: Joseph Jefferson's *Rip Van Winkle: The Autobiography of Joseph Jefferson* (1889), Walter Leman's *Memories of an Old Actor* (1866), and Lester Wallack's *Memories of Fifty Years* (1889). Her various productions are documented in such works as Edmond M. Gagey's *The San Francisco Stage: Its History* (1950); Joseph N. Ireland's *Records of the New York Stage from 1750 to 1860* (1866–1867); George C. D. Odell's *Annals of the New York Stage*, Vols. VI and VII (1930); and J. Thomas Scharf's *Chronicles of Baltimore* (1874). Dorothy Jean Strickland has written "Laura Keene, Nineteenth Century American Actress-Manager" (Unpublished master's thesis, University of Arizona, 1961); there is a copy in the Theatre Department of the Museum of the City of New York. There is a collection of Keene's letters and legal papers at the Library of Congress in Washington, D.C. Her lengthy obituary appeared in the *New York Herald* (December 16, 1873). Keene is included in *Dictionary of American Biography*, Vol. V (1932–1933, renewed 1960–1961); Robert L. Sherman, *Actors and Authors with Composers Who Helped Make Them Famous* (1951); *Who Was Who in America, Historical Volume 1607–1896* (1963); *Notable American Women*, Vol. II (1971); William C. Young, *Famous Actors and Actresses on the American Stage*, Vol. II (1975); *Victorian Actors and Actresses in Review*, ed. Donald Mullin (1983); *The Oxford Companion to the Theatre* (1983); *The Oxford Companion to American Theatre* (1984); and Claudia D. Johnson, *American Actresses: Perspective on the Nineteenth Century* (1984).

Vera Mowry Roberts

KELLOGG, Marjorie Bradley (August 30, 1946–): scenic designer, was born in Boston, Massachusetts, the eldest of five children of Mary Bradley (Langdon) Kellogg and Jarvis Phillips Kellogg, a corporate lawyer. The Kellogg family, who settled in Connecticut in the early 1900s, is of Scotch-Irish descent. The Langdons came from England, landing at Stonington, Connecticut, in 1624, and the Bradleys, a Boston family, trace their ancestry to the English who arrived with the *Mayflower* in 1620. In the middle of the nineteenth century, the Bradleys became part of the lucrative boot and shoe manufacturing industry in Massachusetts, eventually selling their business shortly after World War II.

Marjorie Kellogg spent a comfortable childhood in the quiet lobster-fishing village of Scituate, a suburb of Boston, attending the Derby Academy in nearby Hingham through the sixth grade. In 1958 the family moved to New York City where Marjorie was educated for a year at the Rudolf Steiner School and then enrolled in Brearley, a socially and academically prestigious girls' school from which she graduated in 1963.

In the ninth grade at Brearley, Marjorie Kellogg joined an amateur theatre group that called itself the 93rd Street Playhouse and performed in a friend's living room. Because of an ability to draw, she began designing scenery for her youthful co-Thespians and also for productions at Brearley. She became increasingly enamored of theatre and in the fall of 1963 entered Vassar College in

Poughkeepsie, New York, where she felt she would receive both a substantive liberal arts education and a solid grounding in stagecraft. She minored in art history and majored in theatre, involving herself in all aspects of the stage from acting to costume, lighting, and set design. Summers were spent as a production and technical assistant at Joseph Papp's New York Shakespeare Festival, which was in its first years at the outdoor Delacorte Theatre in Central Park. During the summer of 1964, Kellogg built stage properties and ran props during performances; when the property master left in mid-season 1965 she was given the position. In 1966 she worked as a scenic painter under Ming Cho Lee, at that time the festival's principal scenic designer, who encouraged her to pursue a design career.

A disciplined, intellectually curious student, Kellogg graduated from Vassar in 1967 (Phi Beta Kappa and summa cum laude). The following autumn she entered the Master of Fine Arts degree program at the University of California in Los Angeles but returned to New York in 1968 to begin a two-year apprenticeship with Ming Cho Lee. Thus, in an unusual career choice for a designer of her generation, Kellogg has never received a graduate degree, preferring instead to learn drafting and other necessary skills in the training ground of a designer's studio. In 1969 Kellogg passed her examination for entrance to the United Scenic Artists of America union in three areas: costume, lighting, and set design.

In terms of her artistic and professional development, Kellogg's first significant design assignment was Off-Broadway for the New York Shakespeare Festival Public Theatre. There, in 1970, she created the setting for Dennis J. Reardon's *The Happiness Cage* which inaugurated the Estelle R. Newman Theatre. George Oppenheimer, reviewing the production for *Newsday*, wrote, "The hospital set by Marjorie Kellogg, on various levels and in various rooms, is the high point of the evening" (*Newsday*, October 5, 1970). Richard Watts of the *New York Post* described the setting as "brilliant" (*New York Post*, October 5, 1970), and Clive Barnes, who did not like the play, nevertheless wrote in his *New York Times* review that the setting was "so real that you feel you ought to be able to get the price of your seat back from Blue Cross" (*New York Times*, October 5, 1970).

Kellogg received the majority of her first jobs in the regional theatres. Since 1970 she has designed for the Arena Stage in Washington D. C., the Goodman Theatre in Chicago, the Guthrie Theatre in Minneapolis, and the Long Wharf in New Haven, Connecticut. In 1975 at New York City's Circle in the Square (uptown), Kellogg designed the setting for the first major revival of Arthur Miller's *Death of A Salesman*, directed by and starring George C. Scott. Critics complained that the Circle in the Square's oblong thrust stage was the wrong choice for Miller's play yet generally praised Kellogg for adapting her design to the exigencies of a difficult playing space. Indeed, Kellogg has demonstrated a skill for imaginative use of the unconventional stage spaces that abound in regional theatres, ranging from Arena's central playing space with audiences on four sides to the Guthrie's proscenium-thrust stage.

Major stages in the growth of Kellogg's reputation as a scenic designer were her first Broadway show, *The Poison Tree* (1976), followed by the 1978 Broadway productions of the musical *The Best Little Whorehouse in Texas* and Hugh Leonard's drama *Da*. *Da* won the Antoinette Perry (Tony) Award for best play of the season. Critics praised Kellogg's design for *Da*, applauding the flexible design elements that expressed the play's constant juxtaposing of past and present. Critics also praised Kellogg's multilevel design for *The Best Little Whorehouse in Texas*, citing Kellogg's skill at creating a set that was both functional and aesthetically imaginative. Douglas Watts wrote, "Majorie Kellogg's unit set—consisting of mostly brass-colored pipes and rails and red-carpeted stairs and platforms (with a special receding and advancing one for the band stage center)—suits the action perfectly" (*Daily News*, April 18, 1978).

Critics have tended to compliment Kellogg on the realistic ambience of her settings, a fact that has led to her reputation as one of the American theatre's realist designers. Kellogg has refused to categorize herself in this fashion, pointing, for example, to the nonrealistic set for *The Best Little Whorehouse in Texas* and to an outrightly abstract production of *A Midsummer Night's Dream*, created for the Denver Center Theatre Company's 1979–1980 season. Described by Kellogg as a "sensual nightmare," the setting was all black carpeting and velour. Nonetheless, it is as a designer of realist settings that Kellogg is usually hired, and it is her ability to create environments that have a realistic sensibility without being earthbound that has made her a unique designer in the contemporary professional theatre. Commenting on contemporary realistic designers Kellogg has said that they are not putting reality on the stage anymore but rather they are interpreting reality. Arnold Aronson has remarked that the key to Kellogg's art is the "interpretive selection of elements from the real world used to create an emotional impact on the stage" (*American Set Design*, p. 55).

In addition to being a stylistic influence in her field, Kellogg has been a catalyst in the regional theatre movement and a leader among women designers. One of her most significant contributions has been as a ground-breaker in a branch of American theatre that, with the exception of **Aline Bernstein** in the 1920s and 1930s, has traditionally been dominated by men. Kellogg's continued representation in regional theatre, and both on and off Broadway, has become an incentive to fledgling women designers who look to Kellogg as a model for their own careers.

In regional theatre Kellogg has been one of a group of scenic designers that includes John Lee Beatty, Karl Eigsti, and David Jenkins, who began their careers when regional theatres were burgeoning and have continued to work in that area. Kellogg still designs predominantly for the regional scene: recent productions include *American Buffalo* (1981) and *Open Admissions* (1982) at the Long Wharf Theatre, New Haven; *Hedda Gabler* and *Steaming* at the Hartman Theatre, Stamford, Connecticut; *Present Laughter* at the Circle in the Square,

New York (1982); *A Mad World, My Masters* at the La Jolla Playhouse, California; *A Private View* at the New York Shakespeare Festival (1983); *Old Times* at the Roundabout Theatre, New York; and *Requiem for A Heavyweight* (1984) and *Self Defense* (1987) at the Long Wharf. In recent years her frequent collaborators have been costume designer Jennifer von Mayrhauser and lighting designers Pat Collins, Richard Nelson, and Arden Fingerhut.

Since *The Best Little Whorehouse in Texas* (1978), her designs have been seen on Broadway in *Steaming* by Nell Dunn (1982) and the revival of *Arsenic and Old Lace* by Joseph Kesselring (1986).

In addition to her theatre career, Kellogg has also worked in film and television, notably for the *Theatre in America* series on the Public Broadcasting Service, for which she designed the Hartford Stage Company's production of Edward Albee's *All Over* in 1976 and Tom Cole's Vietnam drama *Medal Of Honor Rag* for American Playhouse (1981).

Kellogg is the author of *A Rumor of Angels* (1983), a science fiction novel, and in 1985 she took a temporary sabbatical leave from the theatre to write a two-volume work of science fiction called "Lear's Daughters," scheduled to be published by New American Library. However, her chief fame is as an excellent designer for the theatre.

Sources about Kellogg include an interview with the designer by Alexis Greene titled "I Never Dream about Scenery," *Vassar Quarterly* (Fall 1980), and an interview with Kellogg and John Lee Beatty, also by Alexis Greene, "There's No Such Thing as Realism," *American Theatre* (March 1988).

Alexis Greene

KENNEDY, Adrienne (September 13, 1931–): playwright, was born Adrienne Lita Hawkins in Pittsburgh, Pennsylvania, but grew up in Cleveland, Ohio. Her father, Cornell Wallace Hawkins, was a social worker; her mother, Etta (Haugabook) Hawkins, was a teacher.

Adrienne Hawkins attended Ohio State University, graduating with a Bachelor of Arts degree in 1952. She did graduate study at Columbia University between 1954 and 1956. In 1953 she married Joseph C. Kennedy; they were divorced in 1966. Her two children are Joseph (b. 1955) and Adam (b. 1962). Joseph is a composer and pianist.

Sometime in 1951 Adrienne Kennedy started writing plays but received no recognition until she joined Edward Albee's Playwright's Workshop in New York City in 1962. For *Funnyhouse of a Negro*, written in 1962 and produced Off-Broadway at the Cherry Lane Theatre in 1964, Kennedy won a *Village Voice* Off-Broadway (Obie) Award for distinguished playwriting and then a Guggenheim Fellowship for a year in England.

Kennedy cites Tennessee Williams and Edward Albee as major influences on her works. At first she tried to write plays imitating Tennessee Williams (*The Pale Blue Flower*, 1956, is an early example). Success came when she shifted from realism to a more surrealistic technique in *Funnyhouse of a Negro*. Moreover, the realization that a one-act structure best suited her talent and ideas relieved her earlier fear that a three-act structure was requisite to successful playwriting. Four one-act plays—*The Owl Answers* (1963), *A Lesson in Dead Language* (1964), *A Rat's Mass* (1965), and *A Beast Story* (1966)—quickly followed.

Kennedy's plays deal with personal conflicts and emotional distress. In an interview with Lisa Lehman, Kennedy stated that this inner psychological confusion was her "own particular, greatest conflict" and that she had struggled for over five years to find a suitable expression for this theme (*The Drama Review*, December 1977, p. 47). Finally, "the idea just suddenly exploded" in *Funnyhouse* into the character of Negro-Sarah, who talks with her created other selves: Queen Victoria, the Duchess of Hapsburg, Jesus, and Patrice Lumumba. In *The Owl Answers*, the tortured Sarah becomes "She who is Clara Passmore who is the Virgin Mary who is the Bastard who is the Owl." The character of Clara continued as Rat Sister Kay in *A Rat's Mass*. Director and actor Joseph Chaikin later made this technique of character transformation the foundation for *Solo Voyages*, a production presented at the Interart Theater in New York (1985), which interwove passages from *Owl*, *Rat*, and *A Movie Star Has to Star in Black and White* (1980).

Adrienne Kennedy confesses that her writing is "an outlet for inner, psychologic confusion and questions stemming from childhood. I don't know any other way. It's really figuring out the 'why' of things" (*The Drama Review*, December 1977, p. 42). She believes she could not write the way she does were she not black. "The feeling of being a part of a minority is very strong inside me," she said during an interview with Ruthe Stein (*San Francisco Chronicle*, January 31, 1980). Her parents read to her as a child from the works of black writers. "I'm very happy about the fact that I am black. I just feel it's a blessing in allowing me to express how I feel." Kennedy notes that all her works are autobiographical because that is "the only thing that interests me." However, autobiography in Kennedy's works is metamorphosed by dreams, images, and symbols into poetic, surrealistic plays. Her works focus on three main themes: (1) the struggle of being black in a white world, or of being half-black, half-white in an unfriendly world; (2) the search for identity; and (3) the female rite of passage and its attendant agony. This last theme forms the special focus of *A Lesson in Dead Language* (1964), which begins with the line "Lesson I Bleed."

As a poetic writer Kennedy is unique among black playwrights, who often tend to write plays of social realism. Her complex dramas are states of mind. They are masterworks of economy and intensity and are characterized by lyric dialogue and penetrating insights. *Cities in Bezique, A Lesson in Dead Language, A Rat's Mass*, and *Funnyhouse* offer insight into socially produced schizophrenia. *Funnyhouse* derives its title from her recollection of an amusement park she frequented during childhood in Cleveland, at whose entrance towered a gigantic laughing white-faced figure that became for the playwright a symbol of white

America, ridiculing and mocking American blacks. *Funnyhouse* presents the hallucinations of a black girl trapped in a world where black is evil and white is good. Emory Lewis considered *Funnyhouse* "a scorching report on the agony of being black in a hostile world" (*Stages*, p. 158). In *The Owl Answers* Clara is a teacher in Savannah who comes to New York each summer to pick up men on the subway. The subway forms the constant symbol for the journey through the life, mind, and emotions of the girl who suffers so much because she is the illegitimate daughter of a black cook and a rich white man in Georgia. The play has been described by Edith Oliver as a "fantasy of a forbidden and culturally glorious white world, viewed with a passion and frustration that shred the spirit and nerves and mind of the dispossessed heroine." Oliver has best summarized Kennedy's plays as "extraordinary short dramas, compounded of poetry, terror, and wit" (The *New Yorker*, January 25, 1969, p. 77).

Adrienne Kennedy has become a prolific and celebrated writer. She has written stories for magazines, two novels, and poems such as *Sun* (1969), inspired by the murder of Malcolm X. In 1966 Kennedy wrote with John Lennon and Victor Spinetti *The Lennon Play: In His Own Write*, an adaptation of works by Lennon. The first production of *The Owl Answers* at the White Barn Theatre, Westport, Connecticut (1966), was sponsored by **Eva Le Gallienne**, Ralph Alswang, and **Lucille Lortel**. The New York Shakespeare Festival Public Theatre, under the auspices of Joseph Papp, gave an impressive and stimulating production of *Cities in Bezique*, composed of two one-acts, *The Owl Answers* and *A Beast Story*, in 1959. *An Evening with Dead Essex* (1973) and *A Movie Star Has to Star in Black and White* (1976) were both produced in New York. In May 1980, the Empire State Youth Theatre Institute in Albany, New York, produced *A Lancashire Lad*, a play commissioned by the institute for its children's theatre program. *A Lancashire Lad* used the framework of a fictionalized account of the childhood of Charlie Chaplin (renamed Willy Grinby) to present a story about the abuses of childhood that can wound a person for life. The play, neither condescending in its approach nor sentimental in its tone, "enthralled adults and children" (Frank Rich, *New York Times*, May 21, 1980).

Kennedy has received two Rockefeller grants (1967–1969, 1970), a Guggenheim Award (1967), a New England Theatre Conference grant, a grant from the National Endowment for the Arts (1973), and commissions to write plays for the New York Shakespeare Festival, the Empire State Youth Theatre Institute, and for the Royal Court's Theatre Upstairs; a scenario for Alvin Ailey's dance company; and an opera libretto. She has lectured on playwriting at Yale University and Brown University, and has served as chancellor's distinguished lecturer at the University of California, Berkeley (1980). A founding member of the Women's Theatre Council formed in 1972 with **Megan Terry**, **Rosalyn Drexler**, **Rochelle Owens**, **Maria Irene Fornés**, and **Julie Bovasso**, she is now a member of the New York Theatre Strategy. A quiet, reclusive woman, Adrienne Kennedy is an original and imaginative surrealistic playwright whose work has received major critical attention.

People Who Led to My Plays (1987) is an autobiographical book of recollections and reflections on the influences which have shaped Kennedy's writing. The book was reviewed by Margo Jefferson in "Portrait of the Artist as a Young Woman," *American Theatre* (July/August 1987). Kennedy has also written "Becoming a Playwright" for *American Theatre* (February 1988). Kennedy's published plays are *Funnyhouse of a Negro, Samuel (1969); Cities in Bezique: Two One-Act Plays: The Owl Answers and A Beast Story (1969); A Lesson in Dead Language* in *Collision Course*, ed. Edward Parone (1968); *A Rat's Mass* in *New Black Playwrights* (1968), ed. William Couch, Jr.; *The Lennon Play: In His Own Write* (1972); *Sun* in *Scripts 1* (November 1971) and in *Spontaneous Combustion: Eight New American Plays*, ed. Rochelle Owens (1972); and *Funnyhouse of a Negro* in *Woman as Writer* (1978) by Jeannette L. Webber and Joan Grumman. Her unpublished works include *The Pale Blue Flower* (1956), *Boats* (1969), *An Evening with Dead Essex* (1974), *A Movie Star Has to Star in Black and White* (1980), and *A Lancashire Lad* (1980). An interview with Kennedy is included in *Interviews with Contemporary Women Playwrights*, ed. Kathleen Betsko and Rachel Koenig (1987). Articles on Kennedy include Edith Oliver, "Cities in Bezique," *The New Yorker* (January 25, 1969); "Where Are the Women Playwrights?" *New York Times* (May 20, 1973); "A Growth of Images," *The Drama Review* (December 1977); "She Got Her Own Place in the Sun," *San Francisco Chronicle* (January 31, 1980). See also Emory Lewis, *Stages: The Fifty-Year Childhood of the American Theatre* (1969); Doris E. Abramson, *Negro Playwrights in the American Theatre, 1925–1959* (1969); *Black Theater U.S.A.*, ed. James V. Hatch and Ted Shine (1974); and Rosemay K. Curb, "Lesson I Bleed," *Women in American Theatre*, ed. **Helen Krich Chinoy** and Linda Walsh Jenkins (1981). Kennedy is listed in *Crowell's Handbook of Contemporary Drama* (1971); *Contemporary Dramatists* (1973); *Notable Names in the American Theatre* (1976); *Black American Playwrights, 1800 to the Present: A Bibliography* (1976); *Selected Black American Authors* (1977); and *Contemporary Authors* (1979).

Carolyn Karis

KERR, Jean (July 10, 1923–): widely produced playwright and author of humorous essays and books, was born Brigid Jean Collins, the first of the four children of Thomas J. and Kitty (O'Neill) O'Neill, Irish Catholic immigrants who had settled in Scranton, Pennsylvania. Her father was a construction engineer with a wry wit and a lusty baritone voice. Her mother, born in County Cork, was a second cousin to playwright Eugene O'Neill and from age five an enthusiastic playgoer.

"Spelunkers of the writer's mind will find no dark pockets in Jean Kerr's memories of her girlhood," wrote John McPhee (*Time*, April 14, 1961, p. 83). "Norman Rockwell might have painted it, showing an oversized white clapboard house . . . beside . . . a tall elm tree with a tall young girl high in its branches eating an apple and reading a book." If there is any shadow in the portrait, it is cast by the height to which the future playwright grew during her teens. "You can't imagine how agonizing it was to be tall in Scranton," she recalls (*Newsday*, February 4, 1979). The antic perspective that would prompt a reviewer to name her one of the funniest women writers of her generation developed partly in compensation for her height. "It was either that or . . . ," she explains, "I mean,

I was *five-eleven*, and I never got any shorter, although I did get wider.'' (*Newsday*). The calamities of her reign as Marywood Seminary's Queen of the May, picked because she was the only girl in school tall enough to crown a statue of the Blessed Virgin, would become comic literary capital, as would her later quest for a maternity dress large enough to fit her. ''Manufacturers,.'' she wrote, ''seem to operate on the unquestionably sound premise that a woman who takes a size eighteen is already in sufficient trouble and has no business getting pregnant.'' (*How I Got to be Perfect*, p. 23).

In 1941, during her sophomore year at Marywood College in Scranton, Walter Francis Kerr, a young drama instructor from Catholic University in Washington, D.C., attended a campus production of *Romeo and Juliet* of which Jean Collins was stage manager. A carpenter's son from Evanston, Illinois, he was ten years older and three inches shorter than Jean Collins, who shunned men under six feet. However, despite their difference in height, they were married on August 9, 1943, two months after her graduation from Marywood. Over the years, the couple produced six children (Christopher, twins John and Colin, Gilbert, Gregory, and Katharine). As writers they produced both jointly and separately a stream of plays, books, essays, and articles.

Jean Kerr credits her father with prompting her playwriting career. ''I decided to write plays,'' she alleges in one of her humorous essays, ''spurred on by a chance compliment my father had paid me years earlier. 'Look,' he exploded one evening at the dinner table, 'the only damn thing in this world you're good for is *talk*.' By talk I assumed he meant dialogue—and I was off'' (*How I Got to be Perfect*, p. xv). Her new husband had a more direct influence. ''He didn't exactly lock me in my room like Colette's husband,'' she says, ''but just about.'' He also shared the diaper duties, typed her manuscripts, and critiqued her work-in-progress. ''There's no use being modest about it,'' she says, ''he was terrific.'' (*Newsday*).

Her first play, written in collaboration with her husband, was an adaptation of Franz Werfel's novel *The Song of Bernadette*. Like her other early works, it was first produced at Catholic University, where Jean Kerr earned her master's degree in 1945. The play reached the Belasco Theatre on Broadway in 1946 but lasted only three performances. Her first solo effort was *Jenny Kissed Me* (Hudson Theatre, 1948), a comedy starring Leo G. Carroll that lasted twenty performances. Looking back on this experience, Jean Kerr later recalled, ''Louis Kronenberger wrote in *Time* with a felicity it took me only ten years to appreciate, that 'Leo G. Carroll brightens up Mrs. Kerr's play in much the same way that flowers brighten a sickroom'. . . . I don't know why this and similar compliments for Leo G. Carroll didn't stay my hand forever.'' (quoted in *Current Biography*, 1958, p. 222).

Undeterred, Jean Kerr wrote ten plays between 1949 and 1980, namely *Touch and Go*, originally *Thank You, Just Looking*, written with Walter Kerr (Broadhurst Theatre, 1949); two sketches, ''My Cousin Who?.'' and ''Don Brown's Body,.'' for *John Murray Anderson's Almanac* (Imperial Theatre, 1953); *King of Hearts*, written with Eleanor Brooke (Lyceum Theatre, 1954); *Goldilocks*, written with Walter Kerr (Lunt-Fontanne Theatre, 1958); *Mary, Mary* (Helen Hayes Theatre, 1961); *Poor Richard* (Helen Hayes Theatre, 1964); *Finishing Touches* (Plymouth Theatre, 1973); and *Lunch Hour* (Ethel Barrymore Theatre, 1980). Two of her plays were made into movies. *King of Hearts* was filmed as *A Certain Smile* (Paramount, 1958) with Bob Hope. *Mary, Mary* was made into a film by Warner Brothers (1963) starring Debbie Reynolds.

By 1961 Kerr's name had become a household word. Her humorous essays were appearing in *Reader's Digest, Ladies' Home Journal, Saturday Evening Post, Harper's*, and other leading periodicals; she had published two best-selling collections of humor titled *Please Don't Eat the Daisies* (1957) and *The Snake Has All the Lines* (1960); *Mary, Mary*, starring **Barbara Bel Geddes**, was a Broadway hit; and in April 1961 her picture appeared on the cover of *Time*. Two more humor collections followed: *Penny Candy* (1970) and *How I Got to Be Perfect* (1978).

Meanwhile, Walter Kerr had left Catholic University in 1949 to become drama critic for *Commonweal* (1950–1952), the *New York Herald Tribune* (1951–1966), and the *New York Times*, where, after a year, he confined himself to Sunday theatre critiques from 1967 until his retirement in 1983. Consequently, Jean Kerr became not only a nationally known writer but also "One Half of Two on the Aisle." As Broadway regulars on both sides of the curtain, the Kerrs reputedly served Ira Levin as prototypes for his 1960 Broadway comedy, *Critic's Choice*, which featured Henry Fonda as a major drama critic faced with reviewing his playwright-wife's flop. The Kerrs could also see themselves on screen, played by Doris Day and David Niven, in the movie version of *Please Don't Eat the Daisies* (Warner Brothers, 1963), and on television when the book became an NBC series (1965–1967).

In 1955 the Kerrs moved to the Larchmont home immortalized by Jean Kerr as "The Kerr-Hilton." Built by a wealthy automobile inventor, the house is "a brick and half-timber Tudor-Spanish architectural error," sprouting turrets, cupolas, and gargoyles in every direction. It is topped by a thirty-two-bell carillon. Today the bells no longer chime the perfect excerpt from *Carmen* that once rang the children (those famous daisy-eaters) home from play. Squirrels frisking in the tower have unstrung several notes, adding an even more eccentric air to an already improbable dwelling. Jean Kerr selected the house because it had "space near the kitchen for a washer, a dishwasher, a freezer, a dryer, and a large couch where I could lie on sunny days and listen to them all vibrate." (*Newsday*). It was the freezer that started her writing short humor pieces. During the run of *King of Hearts*, *Vogue* asked her to write an article related to the show. "I didn't want to do it," she recalls, "but I needed a freezer, couldn't afford one, and they were paying $200. You know, I still have that freezer" (*Newsday*).

Like her own life, ricocheting by commuter train between Manhattan and Larchmont, Kerr's humor is predicated on incongruities. She juxtaposes Arnold Toynbee and the Waring Blender, Soren Kierkegaard with the Bendix, all with a light, charming touch. Essays on plumbers, carpenters, dry cleaners, children, husbands, and household pets are shuffled with anecdotes about the theatre: going to it, writing for it, rewriting for it, collaborating in it, surviving it. She is also a wicked parodist and a mistress of the "skewed." platitude, as when an aging matinee idol in *Mary, Mary* describes his recent departure from Hollywood as "the sinking ship leaving the rats."

John McPhee calls her "one of the pleasantest humorists now working, a woman who can transform the ordinary vicissitudes of life into laughter, expertly turning next-to-nothing into molehills." (*Time*, April 14, 1961, p. 82). The writer to whom he thinks her most akin is Robert Benchley. "They share,." he says, "the same gently shrugging quality that utterly precludes malice, the same preoccupation with the bizarre edges of the commonplace, the same disarming penchant for self-deprecation, as when the ample Mrs. Kerr compares herself to 'a large bran muffin' or Benchley calls himself 'Sweet Old Bob, or sometimes just the initials.' "

Given the easy flow of her articles, it is surprising to learn that Jean Kerr is a notorious procrastinator. She will read the label on a bottle of Milk of Magnesia rather than face a blank page. She is what is known in journalistic circles as a "bleeder,." someone for whom every sentence emerges agonizingly slowly. "Any idiot should be able to write 200 words about anything in a week,." she believes. "That I can't do it is my cross. If my entrance into eternity depended on it, I couldn't do it. Actually the essays you see in print didn't take any time to speak of—it's the versions I threw out that took the time. The only thing I can do fast is write dialogue. I can write dialogue on any subject in the world, three pages in ten minutes. The only trouble is most of it has to be thrown out. *Poor Richard* (1964), for instance, took me two years to write. And the more I know, the slower I get. I know the chill factor now, the failure probabilities." (*Newsday*).

Kerr served for twenty-five years on the Council of the Dramatists Guild, was honored by the National Institute of Science, and has received honorary degrees from Fordham and Northwestern universities. Jean and Walter Kerr were honored with the Laetare Medal from Notre Dame University. For almost three decades, Jean Kerr was not only a beloved writer of humorous essays but a very successful author of comedies for the stage. Her place in the annals of American playwriting would seem to be secure.

For additional information about Jean Kerr, see *Time* (March 17, 1961, and April 14, 1961); *Life* (April 24, 1954, and February 24, 1958); and *Theatre Arts* (March 1961). *Newsday Sunday Magazine* (February 4, 1979) contains a lengthy interview with Kerr by the author of this essay. Kerr is included in *Current Biography, 1958* (1958); *The Biographical Encyclopaedia and Who's Who of the American Theatre* (1966); *Contemporary Authors*, Vol. 5–8 (1969); *World Authors, 1950–1970* (1975); *Notable Names in the American Theatre* (1976); *American Women Writers*, Vol. II (1980); *Who's Who in the Theatre* (1981); *Contemporary Theatre, Film, and Television*, Vol. I (1984); and *The Oxford Companion to American Theatre* (1984).

C. Lee Jenner

KESSELMAN, Wendy (February 12, 1940–): playwright, was born in New York City, the only daughter of Leo and Nancy (Tow) Spiegel. She received her secondary education at Dalton School in New York and earned a Bachelor of Arts degree from Sarah Lawrence College. Following her graduation from college Kesselman was the recipient of a Fulbright grant to Paris, where she studied art history, Greek mythology, and poetry.

Kesselman began her career as a professional singer, songwriter, and author of such children's books as *Emma, Flick, Time for Jody, Angelita, There's A Train Going By My Window,* and *Joey.* In 1975 she was commissioned by the New York State Council on the Arts to write a play for children. She adapted *Becca,* her short story about a young boy, Jonathan, who owns a menagerie of animals: a parrot, salamander, grasshopper, and bullfrog (all played by adult actors) which he keeps in cages. His most prized possession, however, is his doll Becca, who walks, talks, sings in French and, most importantly, says "I love you" when he squeezes her. In the course of the action, Becca grows rebellious, refusing to be a doll. Later Becca and her cheering chorus of animals unite to oppose their little master and leave to live on the edge of the forest. The action of this musical is punctuated with Kesselman's haunting songs, such as "We're Stuck," sung by the animals, and "Sometimes I'm Lonely," sung by Becca. At the play's end, Becca returns, but not as Jonathan's doll.

Becca received productions at the Interart Theatre, New York, in 1977, and at the Brooklyn Academy of Music in 1978. The fairytale play was produced in the spring of 1987 as part of a two-day Children's Theatre Symposium in Indianapolis and then won top honors at the Indianapolis Children's Theatre Playwriting Competition. Although the play was written about and for children, critics appreciated the mature and dark statement in Becca's awakening consciousness of herself not merely as a doll but as an autonomous human being. The symbolic undertones were clear. Becca's decision to fight back was made during her imprisonment in a closet where she chose to remain forever in preference to being a "doll" again. When Becca emerged she was transformed from Jonathan's plaything into a confident girl with her own individuality.

Although Kesselman did not set out to imbue *Becca* with serious ethical implications, the moral density of her later work is apparent in this seminal first play. In 1981 Kesselman wrote *Merry-Go-Round,* a one-act play commissioned by Actors Theatre of Louisville, Kentucky. This play focused on the reunion of a man and woman who grew up together as children. It was subsequently produced by the 78th Street Theatre Lab in New York in 1983.

Kesselman has also adapted *The Juniper Tree,* subtitled *A Tragic Household Tale,* for production by the Music Theatre Performing Group at the Lenox Arts

Center in Stockbridge, Massachusetts (1982 and 1983), and by St. Clement's church in New York City (1983). *Maggie Magalita* is a play about a thirteen-year-old Latin American girl who has lived with her mother in America since she was seven. At the play's opening she has been fully assimilated into American culture, even changing her name from Magalita to Maggie. Maggie's repressed Spanish background is awakened by the arrival of her Latin-American grandmother, who guides Maggie to resolve the conflict between her new life and her cultural heritage. *Maggie Magalita* was first performed at the John F. Kennedy Center for the Performing Arts, Washington, D.C., in 1980 and became part of their national tour in 1984. The play was then scheduled for production at New York City's Lambs Theatre in 1986.

Kesselman's interest in grandmother/granddaughter relationships carries over into her play *I Love You, I Love You Not*, a delicately rendered and emotionally powerful drama about a woman who survives the holocaust and her thoroughly American granddaughter who nonetheless lives with vaguely felt fears of and anger about her family's past. The girl's parents wish to forget their past and disclaim their ethnic origins; the grandmother silently remembers and cherishes the few remaining customs that bind her to Jewish history. Originally commissioned as a one-act play by Actors Theatre of Louisville under a Ford Foundation grant in 1982, it was subsequently produced as a full-length work by New York's Ensemble Studio Theatre (1983) and by Theatre for a New Audience (1985).

Kesselman is best known for her play *My Sister in This House*, based on the same incident that inspired Jean Genêt's *The Maids* in 1947. Kesselman spent several years painstakingly researching the history of the infamous "Murder in Le Mans" in which two household servants (also sisters), Christine and Lea Papin, brutally murdered and mutilated the bodies of their employers, Madame and Mademoiselle Lancelin. Although Kesselman does not refrain from presenting the crime in all its horror, her play explores the complexity of the sisters' psychological history and all four women's circumstances as victims of class and sex discrimination. *My Sister in This House* shows not only the horror of the women's crime but the brutality inflicted upon the sisters by employers who for seven years spoke to them only in commands. The play was first produced during the Fifth Annual Festival of New American Plays at Actors Theatre of Louisville in 1981. It debuted in New York at the Second Stage in the 1981–1982 season. To date it has received over fifty productions throughout the United States and in Yugoslavia, Ireland, Greece, Canada, Australia, and Hong Kong.

Kesselman has been awarded numerous honors in the arts: four musical theatre awards from American Society of Composers, Authors, and Publishers (known popularly as ASCAP) for the scores of *Becca*, Bertolt Brecht's *The Caucasian Chalk Circle*, *The Juniper Tree*, and *My Sister in This House*. She has received the following grants: Meet the Composer, 1978, 1982–1983; Commission for Young Audiences, New York State Council on the Arts, 1975; National Endowment for the Arts Fellowship, 1979–1980; Guggenheim Fellowship, 1982–1983; a McKnight Fellowship, 1985–1986; and an Artists Foundation of Massachusetts Fellowship, 1986. In 1980 she received the Sharfman Playwright Award for *Maggie Magalita* and the Playbill Award for *My Sister in This House*. In 1981 she was awarded the Susan Smith Blackburn Prize, the most prestigious award given to a woman playwright in the English-speaking world, for *My Sister in This House*, which also received Honorable Mention in the National Play Awards.

Kesselman has been helping young playwrights, and in 1988 she acted as one of the advisers to the four young playwrights under the age of 19 who had been selected from more than 600 entrants for productions and staged readings of their plays. Their plays were presented at the Dramatists Guild's seventh annual Young Playwrights Festival in October at Playwrights Horizons in New York.

Kesselman currently lives in Wellfleet, Massachusetts, where she is working on a new play, *Now I Lay Me*. Now in mid-career, Kesselman is among a number of women who are making significant contributions to American theatre.

My Sister in This House, *The Juniper Tree*, and *A Tragic Household Tale* are published by Samuel French Publishers. Scripts of her other plays are available through New Dramatists Play Service. For an account of the historical incident that inspired *My Sister in This House*, see Janet Flanner's "The Murder in Le Mans" in *Paris Was Yesterday 1925–1939* (1972). See also Helene Keyssar's *Feminist Theatre* (1985), Mel Gussow's comments in the *New York Times* (March 29, 1981) on the production of *My Sister in This House* by Actors Theatre of Louisville, and Frank Rich's review of the Second Stage production in the *New York Times* (November 23, 1981).

Lynda Hart

KIM, Willa (1930?–): costume designer, was born in Los Angeles, California, the eldest of six children. She attended Los Angeles City College and studied painting on a scholarship at the Chouinard Institute of Art in the Westlake district (now the California Institute of the Arts). In 1955 she married writer and illustrator William René du Bois. Of Korean descent, she was cited in 1983 as Asian Woman of Achievement by the Asian American Professional Women.

Kim's design career began in the Off-Broadway theatre and subsequently branched out into dance and opera for both stage and television. Her costumes for the world première of Robert Lowell's *The Old Glory*, which also inaugurated New York's American Place Theatre, first brought her prominence and she received a *Village Voice* Off-Broadway (Obie) Award for costume design for the 1964–1965 season. Kim relates that director Jonathan Miller "wanted the costumes to look like political cartoons of the seventeenth and eighteenth century, and in order to do that, I went to the pen drawings, engravings, wood blocks, and etchings of the era. I began with white costumes for a 'paper' quality, and I drew on them. Unfortunately, dry cleaning left only a faint memory of what had been painted" (Interview, November 12, 1985).

Kim's design techniques for *The Old Glory* proved to be pioneering efforts in the field. Of her results she has said, "I did all the pioneering in the use of painted costumes, possibly as a result of my training as a painter: I had no formal education as a designer.'' In order to spare herself the ordeal of repainting each costume, she searched for "a permanent medium, so that once the costumes were done, the drawing would be there for the life of the costume. This led me to the technique of impregnating printed fabric. The disadvantage, of course, is if you make a mistake, it is there forever" (Interview).

Among Kim's early efforts were costume designs for Arnold Weinstein's *Red Eye of Love* (Provincetown Playhouse, New York, June 12, 1961); *Fortuna* (Maidman Theatre, January 3, 1962); Edwin Harvey Blum's *The Saving Grace* (Writers' Stage Theatre, April 19, 1963); Robert Joffrey's ballet *Gamelan* (premièred in Leningrad, USSR, 1963); *Have I Got a Girl For You!* (Music Box Theatre, New York, December 2, 1963); Adrienne Kennedy's *Funnyhouse of a Negro* (East End Theatre, January 14, 1964); the New York Shakespeare Festival Mobile Theatre production of *A Midsummer Night's Dream* (June 29, 1964); Edward Albee's *Malcolm* (Shubert Theatre, New York, January 11, 1966); and, with scenic designer Howard Bay, the costumes for the pre-Broadway tryout of *Chu Chem* (Locust Theatre, Philadelphia, November 15, 1966; it closed there November 19, 1966).

She received the Drama Desk Award (1969–1970) for her design for **Maria Irene Fornés'** *Promenade* (Promenade Theatre, June 4, 1969) and for Sam Shepard's *Operation Sidewinder* (Vivian Beaumont Theatre, March 12, 1970).

After a decade of working both on and off Broadway, she began designing for ballet companies because, as she said, "at least they'll last a season" (Interview). Between 1962 and 1971 she designed costumes for Glen Tetley's ballets *Birds of Sorrow* (1962) and *Game of Noah* (1965) and for Robert Joffrey's American Ballet Theatre productions of *Gamelan* (1963), *Brahms Quintet* (1969), and *Ontogeny* (1971).

Again in 1971 Kim pioneered in the use of a new fabric for theatrical and dance costumes. For Margot Sappington's *Weewis* (October 27, 1971) she first used the material lycra spandex. "I had gone to the Nylon Institute to see all the stretch fabrics made for underwear and corsets," she said, "and I chose lycra spandex." Joffrey called the effect "electrifying—everyone wanted to know how the dancers got into them because there were no zippers, and how they fit so closely to the body" (Interview). Also in 1971 Kim designed the costumes for the American première of Jean Genêt's *The Screens* at the Chelsea Theatre Center, Brooklyn (June 12, 1972). For this achievement she received the Joseph Maharam Foundation Award, the Drama Desk Award, and the *Variety* New York Drama Critics Poll Awards. In a profile for the *New York Times*, John Duka commented on "the remarkable rag-and-hoop dress designed for . . . 'The Screens,' for which, in a flash of resourcefulness, she also designed dresses from old umbrellas" (September 3, 1981). By the time she designed Joffrey's *Remembrances* in October 1973, she remarked, "I got bolder and bolder in my combination of things. In one costume, I had ten different kinds of fabric (for different effects) which all had to be paintable" (Interview).

On Broadway Kim has been responsible for the costume designs for *Lysistrata* (1972), Tom Stoppard's *Jumpers* (1975), *Goodtime Charley* (1975), and Bob Fosse's *Dancin'* (1978). For the last three productions she received Antoinette Perry (Tony) Award nominations for best costume design, and for *Sophisticated Ladies* (1981) she received a Tony Award for best costume design. That same year she received an Emmy for her work on *Dance in America*, a television production of Michael Smuin's *The Tempest*, which she had designed for the San Francisco Ballet.

Her other television credits include costumes for *St. Patrick's Day* (November 25, 1964), *The Forced Marriage* (January 8, 1965), and *The Beautiful People* (January 28, 1965), all for the Esso Repertory Theatre on National Educational Television; and Smuin's *A Song for Dead Warriors* for the San Francisco Ballet and *Dance in America*.

She has also designed sets and costumes for the Stuttgart Ballet's *Daphnis and Chloë* (June 12, 1975) as well as for *Le Rossignol* and the American première of Menotti's *Help, Help the Gobolinks* for the Santa Fe Opera Company.

In 1985 she was represented on Broadway by Andrew Lloyd Webber's *Song and Dance*, starring Bernadette Peters, and in 1986 by the revival of Eugene O'Neill's *Long Day's Journey Into Night*, directed by Jonathan Miller and starring Jack Lemmon. In 1986 she designed the costumes for the revival of *The Front Page* at Lincoln Center, and in 1988 she created 1920s period costumes for Broadway's *Legs Diamond*.

Willa Kim, one of the most prolific and sought after designers today for both dance and theatre, has been a remarkable pioneer in the use of new materials, fabrics, and painting techniques as applied to costume design and construction.

All quotations from Willa Kim used in the article are from a personal interview by the author (November 12, 1985). Other information about the designer can be found in "Costumes: From Tutu and Toe Shoes to Leotard and Tights," *Theatre Crafts* (September 1973); "Designers for the Dance," *Dancemagazine* (February 1967); and "Designers on Design: Willa Kim," *Theatre Crafts* (March 1989). See also John Duka, "She Made 'Ladies' Look Sophisticated," *New York Times* (September 20, 1981); Deborah Jowitt, "Willa Kim," the *Village Voice* (May 1, 1978); Janice Ross, "San Francisco: Two Views of San Francisco Ballet," *Dancemagazine* (May 1980); John Simon, "Airborne Ellington," *New York Magazine* (March 16, 1981); and Henwell Trecuit, "'Tempest' May Be the Flashiest Treat in Years," San Francisco *Sunday Examiner and Chronicle* (May 11, 1980). Kim's costume designs are frequently reproduced; see the covers of *Horizon Magazine* for July 1977 and May 1978, *The Dance Calendar* for 1980, and Herbert Migdoll's *Dancers Dancing* (1978). Kim is listed in *Notable Names in the American Theatre* (1976).

Saraleigh Carney

KING, Edith Lawrence (October 9, 1884–April 7, 1975): co-director of the King-Coit School and Children's Theatre, was born in Boston and grew up in the suburb of Chelsea, Massachusetts, with her younger sister, Marian Elizabeth. King's father, Edwin, who died at a young age, was an importer, and her mother,

Ellen Augusta (Hough) King, was for many years a librarian at Massachusetts Institute of Technology in Cambridge. The family was Protestant, but King converted to Roman Catholicism as an adult.

King graduated from Chelsea High School and attended the Rhode Island School of Design. Under a cooperative program with Brown University she was enrolled as a special student at the Women's College at Brown from 1903 to 1905. Her primary interest was painting and drawing, and her friendship with Charles and Maurice Prendergast, both estimable American artists, contributed to her life and style. Maurice Prendergast painted her in "Portrait of a Girl With Flowers" (c. 1915) and in "La Rouge" (c. 1913).

King exhibited her works in the historic 1913 Armory Show in New York, the first full-scale introduction of modern art to Americans, that encouraged the acceptance of modern American artists as equal to the Europeans. The group of American artists known as "The Eight" exhibited their works and, eventually, five of "The Eight" became associated with the King-Coit School and Children's Theatre.

Between 1908 and 1910 King found her way to the private Buckingham School in Cambridge, Massachusetts, where she taught painting and drawing and met **Dorothy Coit**. At this school King collaborated with Dorothy Coit in a production of John Milton's masque, *Comus*, with a class of thirteen-year-old girls. Coit cut and edited the masque, and King worked with the girls in creating the costumes and scenery. This was the first of many such collaborations. Between 1915 and 1922 they produced and directed *The Tempest*, *Chansons de France* or *Divertissements Français* (based on books by Boutet de Monvel), *The Story of Theseus; or, The Sword of Attica*, *Ahmed the Cobbler*, *Aucassin and Nicolette*, and *Nala and Damayanti* at the Buckingham School and other locations in Massachusetts and New Hampshire. During the summers (1923–1926) they presented shows in Massachusetts and in Woodstock, New York, with children between the ages of three and fifteen.

In 1920 the two women moved to New York City. In 1921 they presented *Aucassin and Nicolette* at the 39th Street Theatre. Alexander Woollcott, critic for the *New York Times*, described the presentation as "pure gold" (April 9, 1921). In 1923 they opened the King-Coit School and Children's Theatre, which became an integral part of the New York theatre scene from 1923 to 1958. King taught drawing and painting and was also responsible for the theatre's costumes, scenery, and lighting. Coit supervised the diction, storytelling, pantomime, and acting classes as well as the adaptation of scripts and the direction of the plays.

King considered the teaching of art to children a serious matter. Beginning with the subject of the play to be produced, art from the specific period and culture was studied and visits to museums were made. The children drew for weeks before painting; then their choice of colors was limited to those typical of the time and place of the play that eventually would be produced. The settings for the plays were almost always inspired by the art of the period and the culture from which the play came. The completed design often provided a multilevel playing space, as for *Aucassin and Nicolette*, *Kai Khosru*, and *Nala and Damayanti*. The set design for *The Golden Cage* replicated a William Blake watercolor, and *The Rose and the Ring* was played in a circular format. The costumes were often made from painted rather than dyed materials in order to achieve specific colors, and the children's bodies—not just faces—were painted, too. Makeup and hair designs were treated as integral parts of the costuming. King also gave meticulous attention to the lighting for each play.

The children's work was occasionally exhibited as cover designs on programs or in small ways on the sets and properties. For the most part, however, professionals created the music, scenery, costumes, props, and makeup for the King-Coit Theatre. The children's paintings were also exhibited in the foyers of theatres in which King-Coit productions were given in other locations in New York and elsewhere.

The King-Coit productions, supervised and designed by Edith King, were lauded by many of the leading theatre critics of the day. Author and children's theatre practitioner Constance D'Arcy Mackay wrote that King-Coit productions had "set a new standard for scenic and costume design in child-drama" (Mackay, "A Children's Art Theatre in America," unidentified clipping, King-Coit Scrapbook, New York Public Library Performing Arts Research Center at Lincoln Center). Critic John Anderson wrote, "It is a dream-world theatre, more of a spell-bound picture book than drama" (*New York Journal-American*, April 6, 1938.) Stark Young best summarized the effect of this remarkable children's theatre when he wrote that the setting and costumes in King-Coit productions were the best, most varied, delightful, and beautiful in New York (*New York Times*, April 27, 1925).

After thirty-five years the King-Coit School and Children's Theatre closed in 1958. Edith King retired and went to live in Southbury, Connecticut, where she died at her home on April 7, 1975, at the age of ninety-one. The talent of this gifted visual artist helped to raise the King-Coit Children's Theatre productions to a level competitive with the adult theatre in New York at that time.

There are approximately twenty volumes of Edith King's photographs and designs in the New York Public Library Performing Arts Research Center at Lincoln Center. There are other volumes of her designs at the Harvard University Library. The most complete study of Edith King and the King-Coit School and Children's Theatre is Ellen Rodman, "Edith King and Dorothy Coit and The King-Coit School and Children's Theatre" (Unpublished Ph.D. dissertation, New York University, 1980). This dissertation contains an extensive bibliography including numerous unidentified clippings that are in the files of the New York Public Library Performing Arts Center at Lincoln Center. For a listing of some of the many magazine and newspaper articles and reviews see the bibliography at the end of the essay in this volume on Dorothy Coit. Edith King's obituary appeared in the *New York Times* (April 9, 1975).

Ellen Rodman

KRAUSE, Alvina E. (January 28, 1893–December 31, 1981): theatre educator and eminent teacher of acting, was born into the dairy farming family of Charles Frederick Krause and Caroline (Tesch) Krause in New Lisbon, Wisconsin.

Charles Krause had migrated from Germany in the 1860s to settle in Wisconsin, where Caroline Tesch's grandparents had come years earlier from their native Bavaria. There were five children: Edward (b. 1870?), Emma Marie (b. 1873?), Otelia (b. 1875), Johanna (b. 1883?), and Alvina (b. 1893). The three eldest worked on the family farm, while Johanna took a job with the town newspaper and cared for the much younger Alvina.

Graduating from the local high school in 1912, Alvina Krause briefly attended the University of Wisconsin, Madison, and then enrolled at the School of Oratory at Northwestern University, Evanston, Illinois, where she completed the two-year course in 1916. She then spent several years teaching in high schools at various locations, including Seaside, Oregon (where Johanna Krause had moved with her husband, following brother Edward who had gone west in the 1890s), and Springfield, Missouri, where she met her lifelong friend and theatre co-producer, Lucy McCammon.

The School of Oratory became the School of Speech, and Krause returned to Northwestern to earn Bachelor of Science and Master of Arts degrees in speech. A year's teaching in 1929–1930 at Hamline University in Wisconsin culminated in the directing of a Molière play, which won first place in a summer theatre competition held at Northwestern. As a result, Dean Ralph Dennis invited Krause to take a position on the faculty of the School of Speech. She accepted and stayed for thirty-three years.

During her tenure at Northwestern, Krause expanded the one-semester acting class to a full three-year course. The first year's work focused on developing students as creative artists. Voice and movement, sensory perception, imagination studies, sculpture, painting, the novel, music—all such training developed one fundamental acting skill: understanding and creating of character. Second-year students worked from the art of characterization to the art of dramatization. Greek tragedy, William Shakespeare, Anton Chekhov, Henrik Ibsen, and George Bernard Shaw provided the basis for the consideration of the actor as playwright. The last year concentrated on the principles of style: the actor as communicator. Students tackled Molière, Bertolt Brecht, Luigi Pirandello, genre studies, and the best of contemporary playwrights. To complement classroom study and to provide her students with intensive work in directing as well as acting, Krause established an extracurricular workshop series of one-act and full-length productions. Then in 1945 with Lucy McCammon, Krause established a summer theatre at Eagles Mere, Pennsylvania. Junior and senior students formed the company—actors, directors, designers, technicians—producing nine plays in ten weeks every summer. In its twenty seasons, the Playhouse mounted nearly two hundred productions, including eighteen plays by Shakespeare, sixteen by Shaw, five by Ibsen, three by Chekhov, four by Molière, seven musical comedies, an opera, an original revue, several original plays, and works by contemporary playwrights. By the time of her retirement in 1963, Alvina Krause had realized fully her vision of creating a comprehensive program of training in all aspects of theatre art.

In the decade following her retirement, Krause spent much of her time traveling, lecturing, and leading workshops across the country. The University of South Dakota in Vermillion produced a series of videotapes of her teaching. She received an honorary doctorate from Doane College, Nebraska. She produced the Harper Theatre Repertory in Chicago and directed productions for two summers at the Pacific Conservatory of the Performing Arts in Santa Maria, California. In 1971 she moved to Bloomsburg, Pennsylvania, to live with McCammon, then retired from her teaching post at Bloomsburg State College. The following year Krause began private teaching in her home. Her life's dream, she once said, was to see a theatre firmly established in every community in America. In 1977 she and her students took a step toward realizing that dream by forming the Bloomsburg Theatre Ensemble. By the time of Krause's death of heart failure in 1981, the BTE had built a theatre for its productions, had created a Theatre Arts in the Classroom program of workshops and demonstrations for high schools, had formed a touring company for the eastern and mid-Atlantic states, and had established a complete educational program of theatre training for area students.

Shunning publicity throughout her life, Krause consistently refused offers to work for the commercial theatre or to write texts on acting or theatre. She preferred to devote her time to teaching. She received medals in honor of her work: the American College Theatre Festival Award for Excellence, the Hazlett Memorial Award for excellence in the art of theatre, Bucknell University Award for outstanding contribution to theatre, and Northwestern University's Presidential Medal. Lee Strasberg of the Actors Studio called Alvina Krause the best teacher of acting in America, and British actor John Gielgud is reported to have said that Alvina Krause was America's best-kept theatre secret. After her death, Krause's body was cremated and the remains were taken to her hometown of New Lisbon, Wisconsin.

The Bloomsburg Theatre Ensemble in Bloomsburg, Pennsylvania, has a collection of Krause's extensive rehearsal and production notes for the twenty Eaglesmere Theatre seasons as well as Krause's informal notes and essays to her classes over the years. An unpublished dissertation by David Press, "The Acting Teaching of Alvina Krause: Theory and Practice" (Carnegie-Mellon, 1972), attempts a detailed analysis and evaluation of Krause's teaching. A brief essay by David Downs and excerpts from an interview by Billie McCants can be found in *Women in American Theatre*, edited by **Helen Krich Chinoy** and Linda Walsh Jenkins (1981). Articles by Randy Testa, *Secondary School Theatre Journal* (Spring 1977); William Weggner, *Theatre Journal* (May 1977); and Neal Weaver, *Ballroom Dance* and *After Dark* (March 1968), offer personal insights into the nature of Krause's teaching and her effect on American Theatre.

David Downs

KRUPSKA, Dania (August 13, 1923–): dancer, choreographer, and director, was born in Fall River, Massachusetts. She was enrolled in the Lankenau School for Girls in Philadelphia by her father, the Reverend Bronislav Krupska, a minister of the Polish National Catholic Church, and her mother Anna (Niementowska) Krupska, a concert pianist and music teacher. After early coaching from her mother, she began to perform as a child ballerina in Philadelphia. At age six, accompanied by her mother, she began a series of summer tours of Europe, performing as an American prodigy named "Dania Darling." During these seven years of European touring she continued her ballet training in the United States with Ethel Phillips (1932–1934) and the Mikhail Mordkin Studio from 1932 to 1939, and in Paris with Lubov Egorova. In later years she also studied ballet, jazz, and Afro-Caribbean dance at the Aubrey Hitchens Studio and with Syvilla Fort. She studied acting and directing with Robert Lewis, a famous New York acting teacher.

As an adolescent, Krupska performed with many American ballet companies, among them the [Catherine] Littlefield Ballet, the Chicago Opera, and George Balanchine's American Ballet Theatre. She also danced with the ballet troupes of Chester Hale (in Frank Fay's vaudeville act of 1939) and with Florence Rogge at the Radio City Music Hall. Krupska made her acting debut in the mute role of Belinda in the national touring company of *Johnny Belinda* in 1941.

In 1943 she began a long association with **Agnes de Mille**. Until 1945 she danced the role of Laurey during the "Dream" portion of the Broadway production and the national tour of *Oklahoma!* She assisted de Mille on *Allegro* (1947), *The Rape of Lucretia* (1948), *Gentlemen Prefer Blondes* (1949), and *Paint Your Wagon* (1951). Krupska also worked on the Ballet Theatre production of de Mille's *Fall River Legend* (1948) and performed the pivotal role of "The Accused" as a guest artist with the company. She served as Michael Kidd's assistant for *Can Can* in 1954 and was standby for Zizi Jeanmaire in Roland Petit's *The Girl in Pink Tights* until she was injured while appearing for the star.

Since her first solo Broadway assignment in 1951 in the musical entitled *Seventeen*, from Booth Tarkington's novel, Krupska has become one of the theatre's most active women choreographers. She has received many plaudits for her staging of dance numbers in "book musicals," in which choreography is required to advance the plot and not interrupt it. In the refreshing social and comic dances that she inserted into *Seventeen*, critics praised her for avoiding the traditional ballet and dream sequences. Her second show, *The Shoestring Revue* (1955), was her first solo choreography credit, bringing her to the attention of the producers of the operatic musical *The Most Happy Fella*, which opened in 1956. Despite mixed reviews for the musical in 1956 and again in the 1959 and 1979 revivals, she was praised for both the social dance numbers and the stylized movement sequences such as the "Oooh, My Feet" opening number. In 1960 she created, to music by Dave Brubeck, an original work for Ballet Theatre, called *Pointes on Jazz*.

Other Broadway productions that Krupska choreographed include *Her Carefree Heart* (1957), *The Happiest Girl in the World* (1961), *That Hat!* (1964), *Rugantino* (1964), and *A Report to the Stockbrokers* (1975). Two other book musicals—*Her First Roman* (1968), based on George Bernard Shaw's *Caesar and Cleopatra*, and *Rex* (1976)—brought her good personal notices despite general adverse comments on the shows. Krupska is also known for staging and directing revivals of the classic musicals from Broadway's past. For the New York City Center she choreographed revivals of *Oh, Kay* (1960), *Show Boat* (1961), and *Fiorello* (1962). She also directed and choreographed revivals for New York's Equity Library Theatre, the Dallas State Fair, the St. Louis Municipal Opera, and European opera houses.

During the years when New York was the center for television production, Krupska choreographed extensively for such series as *The Buick Hour*, *Omnibus*, and special programs, including Cyril Ritchard's *H.M.S. Pinafore* (1959).

Krupska has a son, Brian, from her marriage to Richard LaMarr and a daughter, Tina Lyn, from her marriage to actor Ted Thurston. She lives in East Hampton, New York.

From her days as a youthful ballerina to the present, Dania Krupska has been an important figure in American theatrical dance. She learned flexibility in form and technique from her work with the popular ballet-based precision routines of Chester Hale and Florence Rogge, and honesty and selectivity in choreography from her tenures with Agnes de Mille and Michael Kidd. Appreciated for their originality and verve, her contributions to Broadway shows, in both original productions and revivals, have been viewed as exceptionally appropriate to plot, format, and milieu.

Dania Krupska is listed in *The Biographical Encyclopaedia and Who's Who of the American Theatre* (1966); *Who's Who of American Women, 1974–1975* (1973); *Notable Names in the American Theatre* (1976); *Dance Encyclopedia* (revised 1978); and *Biographical Dictionary of Dance* (1982).

Barbara Cohen-Stratyner and
Barbara Barker

KUMMER, Clare (1873?–April 22, 1958): playwright and songwriter, was born Clare Rodman Beecher into the same family as Harriet Beecher Stowe and Henry Ward Beecher. Her marriage to Frederick Arnold Kummer was later dissolved. Her second husband was Arthur Henry, cousin of the popular actor William Gillette. Kummer's daughter Marjorie performed in a number of her mother's plays.

Kummer began her professional career as a songwriter with ''The Summerland Song,'' published in 1901, and followed this with several songs a year until 1906, when she had her first popular hit, ''Dearie.'' In 1912 she began a second career as a playwright with one of her most popular works, *Good Gracious, Annabelle!*, produced October 31, 1916, by the decade's most perceptive producer, Arthur Hopkins, at the Republic Theatre in New York. For the next decade and more, Kummer was a highly successful playwright with a show on Broadway almost every year. On October 31, 1918, *Be Calm, Camilla* opened at New York's Booth Theatre for a successful run. Other well-received comedies were *A Successful Calamity* (Booth Theatre, February 5, 1917), written as a vehicle for William Gillette, and *Rollo's Wild Oat* (Punch and Judy Theatre,

November 7, 1920), written for her son-in-law, Roland Young. These plays were followed by others not so notable, including several adaptations of foreign plays and a 1924 Florenz Ziegfeld adaptation of *Good Gracious, Annabelle!* called *Annie, Dear*, which opened at the Times Square Theatre on November 4.

In 1926 *Pomeroy's Past* (Longacre Theatre, April 19) received good reviews, and in 1933 Kummer had her last hit, *Her Master's Voice* (Plymouth Theatre, October 23). This domestic comedy about a young couple and a bothersome mother-in-law was produced by Max Gordon and featured **Laura Hope Crews**. Although Kummer wrote several more original plays and another adaptation, these received little attention. Her 1944 play *Many Happy Returns* (Cole Playhouse, January 5) was poorly received by the New York critics and lasted only three performances.

Kummer was known even in her early career for the weakness of her plots, but a *New York Times* review of *Pomeroy's Past* (1926) explains that "an abundant and buoyant wit" and "a distinct note of summer madness" made her popular and successful nonetheless (April 20, 1926). Although the worst of her plays were contrived, overplotted, and heavy-handed, most of her work contained a subtle humor that charmed audiences. Her characters generally were well-to-do, eccentric people who could not quite adapt to modern life. For example, *Rollo's Wild Oat* is a comedy about a wealthy and restless young man whose one desire is to play Hamlet, which he does opposite an Ophelia whose one desire is to sew initials into clothing. Kummer's skill with repartee usually more than compensated for her lack of plot construction.

In 1964 *Her Master's Voice* was once again performed; one critic deemed it "antique stuff, not much better or worse, for that matter, than some of those family situation comedies that may be seen free on television" (Lewis Funke, *New York Times*, December 28, 1964). Nonetheless, in her day Kummer's work was both distinctive and popular enough for Alexander Woollcott to claim that she was "the only American playwright with a style so recognizable that you could spot her authorship by listening to a single scene" (*New York Times*, January 23, 1921).

Clare Kummer's plays include *The Opera Ball*, with Sydney Rosenfeld (1912), *Good Gracious, Annabelle!* (1916), *A Successful Calamity* (1917), *The Rescuing Angel* (1917), *Be Calm, Camilla* (1918), *Rollo's Wild Oat* (1920), *Bridges* (1921), *The Choir Rehearsal* (1921), *The Robbery* (1921), *Chinese Love* (1921), *Roxie* (1921), *The Light of Duxbury* (1921), *The Mountain Man* (1921), *Banco* (from the French, 1922), *One Kiss* (from the French, 1923), *Madame Pompadour* (American version, 1924), *Pomeroy's Past* (1926), *Amourette* (1933), *Her Master's Voice* (1933), *Three Waltzes*, with Rowland Leigh (1937), *Spring Thaw* (1938), and *Many Happy Returns* (1944). Kummer is listed in *The ASCAP Biographical Dictionary of Composers, Authors and Publishers* (1966); *Contemporary American Authors* (1970); *Notable Names in the American Theatre* (1976); *Who Was Who in the Theatre*, Vol. III (1978); and *The Oxford Companion to American Theatre* (1984).

Duskey Loebel

— L —

LAMB, Myrna (August 3, 1935–): playwright, was born in Newark, New Jersey, the first of two daughters of Melvin A. and Minna (Feldman) Lamb. Her mother worked as a saleswoman for most of her life, while her father worked as a sheriff's officer by day and a musician by night, playing in bands, circus shows, nightclubs, and other settings. The musical background Lamb received from her father led her to direct her writing efforts toward musical theatre. At eight, she wrote her first play and continued to write, produce, and direct plays through her formative school years. Myrna Lamb's marriage at the age of seventeen produced two daughters, Joellen Epstein, a painter, and Ilsebet Tebesli, an actress.

At twenty Myrna Lamb began an acting career in New Jersey, performing with the Actors' Mobile Theatre. Throughout the late 1950s she often worked several jobs simultaneously while she studied at the New School for Social Research, New York; she was a bookseller, bakery saleswoman, medical receptionist, librarian, bookkeeper, newspaper editor, and secretary. She was also a political activist in the civil rights movements of the 1960s. Her schooling included many years of course work in writing, theatre, and directing at the New School for Social Research; two or three years of liberal arts courses at Rutgers University in Camden, New Jersey; and acting courses from Brett Warren and Howard da Silva at the Actors' Mobile Theatre. During this period Lamb continued to write, although her first play was not produced until 1969.

Lamb's plays can be distinguished by the variety of techniques and styles she used: multimedia effects involving dance, film, and visual projections; popular music within operatic forms; song in Brecht-style; distortion, parody, and exaggeration; compression of time and dislocation of chronology; and ritualization of action. Her dramas depict strong emotion and conflicts, physical violence (often handled symbolically), and the negative effects of sex roles, class divisions, corporate ethics, and the industrial/military complex. Her metaphorical, highly charged language seeks a visceral as well as cerebral response to these topics.

Lamb's early plays are generally credited with being the first performed and published feminist plays of the recent wave of American feminism. In a *Village Voice* article titled "Who Is Fairest of Them All?" (May 28, 1970), Vivian Gornick described Lamb as the "first true artist of the feminist consciousness." Lamb's early cycle of short plays investigate the sexual politics of abortion, the nature of marriage, the economics of sexuality, the dehumanizing effect on both sexes of socialization based on gender, and women's dependence on sexual desirability in contemporary society. *Scyklon Z: A Group of Pieces with a Point* (1969) is the collective title of six one-act plays designed to be performed in a cycle. They include *But What Have You Done For Me Lately?*, *Monologia*, *Pas de Deux*, *The Butcher Shop*, *The Serving-Girl and the Lady*, and *In the Shadow of the Crematoria*. The New Feminist Theatre in Manhattan, one of the early feminist theatre groups, began with performances of *Scyklon Z*. They then presented the cycle in its entirety at the Film-Maker's Cinematheque, New York, from September through November of 1969. Subsequently, it was performed by other repertory groups and was broadcast by the Feminist Repertory Theatre of Cambridge on Boston radio.

Lamb began to write full-length plays in 1970 with *Mod Donna; A Space-age Musical Soap Opera with Breaks for Commercials*, credited with being the first feminist musical to achieve widespread recognition. With music by Susan Hulsman Bingham, *Mod Donna* was first produced on May 1, 1970, at the New York Shakespeare Festival Public Theatre, New York, and was directed by Joseph Papp. (For the next five years Papp was to be an important influence on Lamb's career.) *Mod Donna*'s soap opera plot involved mate-swapping among "have" and "have-not" couples in "supersuburbia." In 1971 *Mod Donna* was one of five international plays chosen by the Biennale de Paris committee for performance in October of 1971 at the Théâtre of the Biennale de Paris by Collectif de Travail Théâtral (COLTRA I) and was translated by Georges Roiron and directed by Syn Guerin.

Other short plays by Lamb, written in 1972, include the monologue *I Lost a Pair of Gloves Yesterday* and *Two Party System*. *I Lost a Pair of Gloves Yesterday* was written in response to the death of Lamb's father. Lamb performed the monologue several times, and it was also produced by the One Act Theatre Company of San Francisco in San Francisco in 1972. *Two Party System* was performed at the Interart Theatre, New York, in 1974 as part of a collage containing earlier Lamb works, collectively titled *Because Said So*.

Lamb's next long play was *Apple Pie* (first version copyrighted in 1974), an opera with libretto by Lamb and music by Nicholas Meyers. First performed in a workshop version at the Public Theatre's Other Stage in 1975, and then by the Centre for Theatre Research, New York, also in 1975, it was given its first full production in 1976 at the Public Theatre, and was directed by Joseph Papp.

The work is completely sung. Its sequence of music scenes includes a range of styles from German cabaret and operatic parody to blues, ragtime, and rock. Another completely sung work by Lamb is *The Sacrifice* (1977), an oratorio re-creating Iphigenia's story from Greek legend with music composed by George Quincy. The première took place at the American Academy of Music and Dramatic Art, New York, in 1977.

Crab Quadrille, another full-length play, was first performed in 1976—with incidental music by Nicholas Meyers—at Interart Theatre, New York, under the direction of Margot Lewitin. A play about betrayal and survival set in a beach house on the New Jersey shore, *Crab Quadrille* takes a humorous look at fast-food franchises, hippie entrepreneurs, adolescent vandals, pollution, male executives who pirate the work of female employees, and liberals with Sixties sexual mores and Seventies business ethics.

In 1978 the Interart Theatre produced *Olympic Park*, directed by Georgia Fleenor. In this play Lamb presents working-class Newark during the Second World War through the eyes of fifteen-year-old Violet Grey as revealed in the contents of her diary. In 1980 the Interart Theatre produced Lamb's *Yesterday is Over*. Nicholas Meyers, Lamb's long-time collaborator, composed the music, and Margot Lewitin again directed. The play was inspired by the lives of the Dolly sisters, fraternal twins who ranked among the reigning stage beauties of the 1910s and 1920s.

Other projects by Lamb include *With a Little Help From My Friends*, produced in 1974 at Town Hall Theatre, New York. This collage of works by writers and composers lasted three hours and included works by such playwrights as **Rochelle Owens**, **Jane Chambers**, and **Rosalyn Drexler** as well as by Lamb. Lamb also created *Ballad of Brooklyn* (1979), a celebration of Brooklyn life beginning in the 1600s, adapted and structured from archival material. It was presented in 1979 by Brooklyn Rediscovery and the Brooklyn Academy of Music with Margot Lewitin directing.

Myrna Lamb has received a number of grants and fellowships: a 1971 Biennale de Paris production grant for *Mod Donna*; a 1972 Rockefeller Foundation Fellowship to be playwright in residence at the New York Shakespeare Festival Public Theatre; a 1973 Guggenheim Fellowship for creative work in theatre; National Endowment for the Arts Music Program grants in 1974 and 1975 for libretti (one for *Apple Pie* and one for *Mother Ann*); and, from 1976 to 1977, a New York Shakespeare Festival Public Theatre "Playwrights on Payroll" grant.

Myrna Lamb is best known as a feminist playwright responsible for some of the earliest and strongest theatrical expressions of women's concerns in contemporary American. Her vision has been described as angry, painful, unrelenting, and intensely personal. While some have viewed Lamb as an important creator of revolutionary theatre who challenges her audience with a new view of political, social, and human reality, many reviewers have consistently expressed confusion and hostility toward her work. Nevertheless, because she has strong feelings about her message, she writes as a bold pioneer: first, in the creation of a new form of serious musical drama that resembles neither Broadway musicals nor traditional opera; second, in the expression, by means of first-person narrative, of the world view of her adolescent and middle-aged female protagonists. Lamb thus brings innovation to both the form and the content of contemporary theatre.

Plays by Lamb can be found in *The Mod Donna and Scyklon Z: Plays of Women's Liberation* by Myrna Lamb (1971), which also includes a twenty-one-page introduction by Lamb. *But What Have You Done For Me Lately?* and *The Serving Girl and the Lady*, along with an introduction to them by Anselma dell 'Olio, are in *Women in Sexist Society: Studies in Power and Powerlessness*, ed. Vivian Gornick and Barbara K. Moran (1971). *In the Shadow of the Crematoria*, with an introduction by Anselma dell 'Olio, appears in *Women's Liberation: Blueprint for the Future* (1970). *I Lost A Pair of Gloves Yesterday* can be read in *The New Women's Theatre: Ten Plays by Contemporary American Women*, ed. Honor Moore (1977); and excerpts from *Apple Pie*, along with a prose piece from Lamb titled "Female Playwright: Confessions of a Fallen Woman," appear in *Woman as Writer*, ed. Jeannette L. Webber and Joan Grumman (1978). Also, *The Second Wave: A Magazine of the New Feminism* (1971) contains an interview with Myrna Lamb by Linda Thurston, and the 1972 issue contains Lamb's statement on abortion, "On the Sanctity of Life." Lamb's plays are discussed in Charlotte Rea, "Women's Theatre Groups," *The Drama Review* (June 1972); Margaret Lamb, "Feminist Criticism," *The Drama Review* (September 1974); Stuart W. Little, *Enter Joseph Papp: In Search of a New American Theatre* (1974); Vivian Gornick, *Essays in Feminism* (1978); Dinah Luise Leavitt, *Feminist Theatre Groups* (1980); Patti P. Gillespie, "American Women Dramatists, 1960–1980," *Essays on Contemporary American Drama*, ed. Hedwig Bock and Albert Wertheim (1981); and Judith Olauson, *The American Woman Playwright: A View of Criticism and Characterization* (1981). Myrna Lamb is listed in the *National Playwrights Directory* (1977).

Vivian M. Patraka

LANSBURY, Angela Brigid (October 16, 1925–): actress both on stage and in film, was born in London into a family in which politics and the theatre were apparently given an equal emphasis. Her mother, Moyna (Macgill) Lansbury, was a stage and screen actress, who encouraged her children to follow her calling. Her father, Edgar Isaac Lansbury, was not only a lumber dealer but the mayor of Poplar, a district in East End London, while her grandfather, George Lansbury, was a noted pacifist, who headed the Labor Party from 1931 to 1935. As a child and young adult, Lansbury wanted to pursue a career in politics, but the pressure which her mother had apparently exerted upon her and her siblings ultimately won out. An older half sister, from her mother's earlier marriage to producer and actor Reginald Denham, was later to marry actor Peter Ustinov. The two younger twin brothers, Bruce and Edgar, became producers of television shows, movies, and plays.

When Angela Lansbury was ten years old, her father died, and the family moved to Hampstead, an area on the outskirts of London. Shortly thereafter, the war began, and her mother offered her the option of being sent away into the country for safety or remaining at home and studying acting. Choosing the latter, she studied during the day with a tutor at home and attended formal classes in the evening. She had been enrolled at the South Hampstead High School for Girls from 1934 to 1939 and entered the Webber-Douglas School of Dramatic Arts in 1939.

In 1940 when the German blitz intensified over London, Moyna Lansbury decided to move the family to the United States, under the sponsorship of an American family, the Charles T. Wilsons. Here the young actress chose to remain even after the war, and in 1951 she became a naturalized citizen.

Under a scholarship arranged by the American Theatre Wing, she studied for a time at the Feagin School of Drama and Radio in New York City. She had perfected some impersonations, and in 1942 she took a summer engagement in a Montreal nightclub doing impressions of Beatrice Lillie, among others. When her mother decided that same year to move to Los Angeles, Angela Lansbury followed. She worked there as a salesgirl until she learned in 1943 that M.G.M. needed a young Englishwoman to act in a movie version of Oscar Wilde's novel *The Picture of Dorian Gray*. Louis B. Mayer, impressed by her audition for the part, gave her a seven-year contract that paid five hundred dollars a week. Her first role was her memorable portrayal of Charles Boyer's Cockney maid in *Gaslight*, for which she won her first Academy (Oscar) Award nomination for best supporting actress.

For more than twenty years film was to dominate her acting career. She remained under contract with M.G.M. from 1943 to 1950 and afterwards was a free-lance actress working for several producers. In her films, some good, some bad, she played a long list of supporting roles, often as the villainous antagonist of major stars of the time. She was a sister to Elizabeth Taylor in *National Velvet* (1944), a music-hall entertainer in *The Picture of Dorian Gray* (1945), and one of *The Harvey Girls* (1945). Her movies also include *The Private Affairs of Bel Ami* (1947), *Till the Clouds Roll By* (1946), *State of the Union* (1948), and *The Three Musketeers* (1948). In the last of these, she had wanted the part of Lady de Winter but saw it go instead to Lana Turner while she was assigned the role of evil Queen Anne. By this time she had been stereotyped: the evil, or at least immoral, tramp or the lower-class Englishwoman. In *Samson and Delilah* (1949), for example, she was a cruel Philistine, and in *Kind Lady* (1951) she portrayed a vicious young woman who with Maurice Evans imprisons an ailing and aged **Ethel Barrymore** in her own home.

During these Hollywood years, she had married Richard Cromwell, an actor, but the union ended in divorce after less than a year. On August 12, 1949, she married Peter Pullen Shaw, an agent, and they had two children, Anthony P. (b. 1952) and Deirdre A. (b. 1953). Meanwhile, her career of supporting roles continued, gaining her praise from critics, admiration from a growing circle of fans, but no serious consideration as a major actor from important directors. However forgettable the films might be—and they included entries such as *The Court Jester* (1955), *The Reluctant Debutante* (1958), and *The Summer of the Seventeenth Doll* (1959)—she left her stamp on them. There were exceptions to the mediocre: she held her own easily as Minnie Littlejohn, the middle-aged mistress, opposite Orson Welles in *The Long Hot Summer* (1958); and in *The Dark at the Top of the Stairs* (1960) and *All Fall Down* (1961) she brought powerfully to life very strong female characters that demonstrated what she could have been doing all along with the proper material. Some films that are otherwise without distinction were made memorable by her remarkable portrayals: for example, that of a malevolent and power-hungry mother in *The Manchurian Candidate* (1962) and of a wonderfully elfish mother to Elvis Presley in *Blue Hawaii* (1962).

Almost two decades after her arrival in the United States, she made her debut on Broadway in a stage play. On April 11, 1957, she opened as Marcelle opposite Bert Lahr in *Paradiso*, a farce by Georges Feydeau and Maurice Desvallieres. Though the production received critical praise, its run was brief, and she returned to Hollywood for several years. In 1960 producer David Merrick persuaded her to return to New York to play the mother of easy virtue in *A Taste of Honey*. Both the play and Lansbury received the plaudits of critics, and the audience response assured a year-long run. The Stephen Sondheim musical *Anyone Can Whistle* in 1964, however, in which she played Cora Hoover Hoople, was quite another story; it closed after only nine performances.

It was in 1966 that Angela Lansbury finally received the role that she had needed to establish her as a major actress on the American stage. After its success as a novel, a stage play, and a movie, Patrick Dennis's *Auntie Mame* had been turned into a musical with book by Jerome Lawrence and Robert E. Lee and music by Jerry Herman. After Rosalind Russell, **Mary Martin**, and **Ethel Merman** had turned down the part, a search of several months ensued. Lansbury, who had never seen either the stage or the screen version of the play, was nevertheless determined to have the part of the sophisticated bohemian who had already become a figure of American folklore. She campaigned actively for the role, auditioning twice and finally issuing an ultimatum that either she would have the producer's decision at once or she would return to Hollywood. Fortunately for the actress and for themselves, the producers chose to give her the part that day; *Mame* became a hit and Lansbury moved into the ranks of major dramatic stars. In preparation for the part, with its vigorous dancing and its multiple costume changes, she undertook a strenuous regimen of diet and exercise, and when *Mame* opened May 24, 1966, at the Winter Garden Theatre, it was clear to critics and audiences alike that she was fully qualified for the task at hand. She received critical acclaim not only for her acting but for her singing and dancing, with some critics expressing surprise that she was possessed of all these talents that had until then gone untapped. Within a month after its opening, she had been awarded an Antoinette Perry (Tony) Award for best actress in a musical. She remained with the show in New York and on national tour until 1968.

The following year she portrayed the Countess Aurelia in *Dear World*, a musical adaptation of *The Madwoman of Chaillot*. Although it ran in previews for a lengthy time, its official Broadway stay was short, since it was popular neither with critics nor with audiences. Nevertheless, Lansbury won her second Tony Award for her performance. In 1971 she played the title character in *Prettybelle*, and the following year on January 13 made her London debut with the Royal Shakespeare Company as the mistress in Edward Albee's *All Over*. In 1973, continuing an association with composer Stephen Sondheim that had begun with *Anyone Can Whistle* nine years before and was to continue in the future, she took part in *Sondheim: A Musical Tribute* in New York. The same year she played the part of Rose in a revival of *Gypsy* in London, a role that she re-created in New York the following year and for which she was honored with her third Tony Award for best actress in a musical. Subsequently, she played Gertrude in *Hamlet* at the National Theatre in London in 1974 and Anna in a revival of *The King and I* in 1979.

Her work with Stephen Sondheim produced its most impressive results in 1979 when she was chosen to play Mrs. Lovett, the female lead opposite George Hearn in *Sweeney Todd*. This surprising musical was based on the grisly story of "The Demon Barber of Fleet Street," who in Victorian London slaughtered customers and ground them up to be cooked in meat pies by Mrs. Lovett. The play gained wide acceptance from critics and audiences alike, with numerous supporters arguing that it transcended the status of mere musical and moved into the realm of grand opera. Lansbury, once again playing the lower-class Englishwoman, but this time as a star, was more strongly praised than ever and received her fourth Tony Award for this performance. The show was later taped for showing on public television.

Through the years of her association with Broadway, she continued to make movies now and then, including memorable portrayals in *Death on the Nile* (1978), *The Lady Vanishes* (1979), and the cinema version of Joseph Papp's production of *The Pirates of Penzance* (1982), in which she created a wonderful Little Buttercup. In the more than forty years since *Gaslight*, she has made close to one hundred films, many of them unmemorable, but all improved by her performances. Often, of course, those roles were beneath her talents, but some of the characters she created have become a part of movie legend. She has garnered a total of three Oscar nominations and two Hollywood Foreign Correspondents Association Golden Globe awards for her film work.

In addition to her Broadway work and her films, she has been involved with various touring shows and stock theatres, and has appeared frequently on television. In 1984 she began her own television series, starring as Jessica Fletcher in the highly popular *Murder, She Wrote*. In this series Lansbury is a practical Yankee mystery writer who each week is asked to solve an improbable murder case. Her solid, down-to-earth approach rescues the program from being merely an imitation of myriad other detective dramas of the past and makes even the implausible and simplistic plots seem somehow credible.

Angela Lansbury has proven, in more than four decades of work in the American entertainment industry, to be one of the finest and most dependable of character actresses. She herself has acknowledged that there was always the quality of the comedienne about her and that she was perhaps in the early years not suited for young starring roles. Her particular virtues seem to have made her ideal for character parts, and, indeed, when she finally reached stardom, it was in portrayals of women who could still be labeled "characters": Mame, Rose in *Gypsy*, Mrs. Lovett in *Sweeney Todd*.

Lansbury and her husband, to whom she has been married for thirty-seven years, live in Los Angeles.

Some reviews in the *New York Times* for Angela Lansbury's performances include *Hotel Paradiso* (April 21, 1957), *A Taste of Honey* (October 5, 1960), *Mame* (May 25, 1966), *Dear World* (February 7, 1969), and *Sweeney Todd* (March 29, 1979). See also the *New York Post* (July 9, 1966) and *Life* (June 17, 1966). Also useful is Helen Ross, *The Player: Profile of an Art* (1962). Biographical sketches of Lansbury are included in *The Biographical Encyclopaedia and Who's Who of the American Theatre* (1966); *Current Biography, 1967* (1967–1968); *Notable Names in the American Theatre* (1976); *Who's Who in America, 1980–1981*, Vol. II (1980); *Who's Who in the Theatre* (1981); *Contemporary Theatre, Film, and Television*, Vol. I (1984); and *The Oxford Companion to American Theatre* (1984).

W. Kenneth Holditch

LAWSON, Kate Drain (July 27, 1894–November 20, 1977): scenic and costume designer, technical director, actress, and theatre administrator, was born Kathryn Drain in Spokane, Washington, to James Andrew Drain, an attorney and a banker, and Ethel Mary (Marsland) Drain. In 1910 Kate Drain attended school at the Laurels, Canterbury, England, but graduated from Western High School in Washington, D.C., three years later. During the First World War she drove an ambulance for the American Red Cross in France, where she met another ambulance driver, playwright John Howard Lawson. On November 20, 1918, they were married. One son was born, Alan Drain Lawson, who became an artist and a motion picture technician. In 1924 the marriage was dissolved. Kate Lawson never remarried, and although divorced for fifty-two years at the time of her death in 1977, she had told this writer in 1975 that she never stopped loving John Howard Lawson. Kate Drain Lawson died in her sleep at the Motion Picture Retirement Home in Woodland Hills, California, November 20, 1977.

Kate Drain Lawson's career in the theatre began in the years following the First World War while she was in Paris studying at various art schools. Her first stage appearance was as a dancer in an experimental group that produced *Orpheus in Hades* at the Grand Opera in Paris in 1921. After returning to the United States she had her first experience on Broadway as design assistant and assistant stage manager for *Malvaloca*, the première show at the re-opening of the 48th Street Theatre, October 2, 1922. In the next two years, Lawson assisted the designer of three other plays at the 48th Street Theatre: *Neighbors* (December 26, 1923), *The New Englander* (February 7, 1924), and *Macbeth* (March 15, 1924). She was the costume designer for *Old English* at the Ritz Theatre (December 23, 1924).

In 1925 the Theatre Guild beckoned and she became its technical and art director, remaining in that position until 1931. In addition to her other duties with the Theatre Guild she acted in two of their productions: *The Chief Thing* in 1926 and *The Garrick Gaieties* in 1930. In 1929 she was the technical director for the London Theatre Guild production of *Caprice* at the St. James Theatre. During the summer of 1929 she designed the costumes for the Berkshire Playhouse productions at Stockbridge, Massachusetts, of *Lute Song* and *Right You Are, If You Think You Are*.

In 1932 **Katharine Cornell** was planning a tour of her productions of *Candida*, *The Barretts of Wimpole Street*, and *Romeo and Juliet*. She hired Lawson as technical director, and when the tour ended Lawson continued in that position for the December 1934 revival of *Romeo and Juliet* at the Martin Beck Theatre, opening December 20, 1934. In February of 1934 Virgil Thomson's *Four Saints In Three Acts* was produced at the 44th Street Theatre under the direction of John Houseman. Sets and costumes were designed by Florine Stettheimer. Houseman hired Kate Drain Lawson to execute the difficult design. In *Run-Through* (1972), Houseman described Lawson at that time as "solid, professional, devoted, bossy and harassed" but added that "without her Florine's designs might have never reached the stage" (p. 105).

While continuing to design costumes and settings for productions in New York City as well as nearby summer stock companies, in 1936 Lawson became head of the Bureau of Research and Publication for the Works Progress Administration Federal Theatre Project. The bureau, set up to be a communication center for the project, issued a weekly production calendar, reproduced reviews, and sent photos, designs, and models throughout the country on request. Lawson succeeded **Rosamund Gilder** as bureau head. In 1937 the Federal Theatre put Lawson in charge of its technical division, a position that included supervising the shops and warehouses. In *Arena* (1940), **Hallie Flanagan** described Lawson as having "cool common sense" when everyone else was in a state of jitters over the production of Sinclair Lewis's *It Can't Happen Here* (p. 123). On May 1, 1935, Brooks Atkinson, in a review of *To See Ourselves* in the *New York Times*, wrote: "Kate Drain Lawson has surrounded the acting with cheerfully colored scenery." On October 18, 1938, in a review of *Knights of Song* he said, "Kate Lawson has designed costumes bold enough for a large-scale musical comedy."

In 1939 Lawson went to Los Angeles and in the years before the Second World War designed costumes for productions at the Biltmore Theatre, for the Los Angeles Civic Light Opera at the Los Angeles Philharmonic Auditorium, and for the British War Relief production of *Tonight at 8:30* presented at the El Capitan Theatre in Hollywood in 1940. In the summer of 1942 David O. Selznick produced a season of summer theatre at the Lobero Theatre in Santa Barbara under the direction of John Houseman. Lawson was the technical director and designed the costumes. But the Second World War had started, and once again Lawson heeded the call to duty and became an American Red Cross worker in India. By 1945 she was staff director of the Entertainment Production Unit of

Special Services in Calcutta and in that capacity supervised the production of thirty-two shows. Upon her return from India, Lawson became, in 1947–1948, technical director of Pelican Productions, founded by John Houseman. The company settled in the newly built Coronet Theatre in Los Angeles, and Lawson ordered whatever was necessary to furnish the small theatre. The first play produced by Pelican was the West Coast première of Thornton Wilder's *The Skin of Our Teeth* with Lawson as scenic designer. The second production was the world première of Bertolt Brecht's *Galileo* starring Charles Laughton. Lawson was responsible for the technical direction and business management, but Laughton and Brecht were the final artistic arbiters. In *Front and Center* (1979), Houseman described Lawson's difficulty in dealing with Brecht, whose demands, according to Houseman, were great and were made without regard for budget restrictions (pp. 235–236). Another Pelican production was *Dark of the Moon*. Lawson designed both the costumes and the lighting, "which was much admired" (*Front and Center*, p. 250).

In addition to her design work and her technical and administrative duties in the theatre, Lawson acted in several films, including *Ladies of the Big House* (Paramount, 1932); *Torchy Blaine* and *Girls On Probation* (Warner, Brothers 1938); *Remember the Night* (Paramount, 1940); *Phantom of the Opera* (Universal, 1943); *King of the Cowboys* (Republic, 1943); *Every Girl Should Be Married* (RKO, 1948); *Thelma Jordan* and *The Bride of Vengeance* (Paramount 1949); *M* (Columbia Studios, 1951); and *How To Marry A Millionaire* (Fox, 1953.)

At the beginning of the 1950s Lawson turned her attention to the infant television industry and organized NBC's West Coast television costume department. Between 1951 and 1956, she was the costume designer for the *Colgate Comedy Hour*, and for twenty-five years she designed costumes for Bob Hope's shows until her retirement in 1976.

In the early 1960s Lawson commandeered the El Capitan Theatre on Hollywood's Vine Street and began an annual month-long children's theatre festival. Both professional and nonprofessional actors volunteered their talents, and Lawson, as she reigned over those festivals, reveled in the youth who participated there and who were in the audience.

In 1969 when the American College Theatre Festival (ACTF) was organized, Lawson was a member of the Steering Committee for the Pacific South Region. She played a major role in bringing professional actors, producers, and directors into the festival as judges and advisors in the region. Her interest was so great that from 1969 to 1974 she saw every show entered in the festival in Southern California. As a result of her involvement, Lawson realized the importance of college and university theatre production and decided to do what she could to encourage the student artist-designer. Consequently, she contributed cash prizes for outstanding costumes and scenic designs by students in productions entered in the Pacific Region of ACTF. Lawson personally selected the winner through her attendance at the shows, but when she was no longer able to see the productions in person, she based her award decisions on slide submissions. The young winners were invited to her home to receive their checks and a critique of their work. Today, the Southern California Educational Theatre Association carries on design scholarships in her name and memory.

Lawson was an officer on the executive committees of most of the many professional groups to which she belonged. She was a member of Actors' Equity Association and on its West Coast Advisory Board from 1956 to 1976. She was a member of the Screen Actors' Guild and the American Federation of Television and Radio Artists. She was an active and influential member of the American National Theatre and Academy, serving on its National Board, as director of Region One from 1960 to 1961; and Secretary of the Greater Los Angeles ANTA Chapter from 1960 to 1961. Other memberships included the American Theatre Association and the Children's Theatre Association of America, as well as the Southern California Educational Theatre Association. She was a life member of United Scenic Artists (Local 892); the Costume Designers Guild, of which she was secretary from 1957 to 1958; the Radio and TV Women of Southern California; and the Scene Designers Club of New York City, which she served as treasurer from 1935 to 1936.

Lawson was elected a Fellow of the American Theatre Association and was honored with the Merit Award from the Radio and TV Women of Southern California in 1958. She received the Dance Business Guild of America Award for 1961–1962, the Monte Meacham Award of the Children's Theatre Association of America in 1963, and the Distinguished Service Award for contributions to educational theatre from the Southern California Educational Theatre Association in 1973. Lawson also received the China-India-Burma Campaign Ribbon for her Second World War service in India with the American Red Cross from 1943–1946.

Kate Drain Lawson was one of the outstanding women in technical theatre and theatrical design in America. She was one of the few whose hard, ceaseless, and highly creative labors broke through the tangled undergrowth that for centuries had impeded or prohibited the contributions of women to the complete spectrum of theatre art.

Much of the information about Kate Drain Lawson was obtained by the author through personal conversations with Lawson from 1960 through 1977 and from interviews with John Houseman and Elizabeth Talbot-Martin. Information about Lawson may also be found in Roy Waldaw, *The Vintage Years of the Theatre Guild, 1928–1939* (1972); John Houseman, *Front and Center* (1979) and *Run Through* (1972); Hallie Flanagan, *Arena* (1940); and Katharine Cornell, *I Wanted to Be an Actress* (1938). *New York Times* reviews which mention Lawson as costume or scene designer include reviews of *The Chief Thing* (March 23, 1926), *Mr. Pim Passes By* (April 19, 1927), *R.U.R.* (February 18, 1930), *The Garrick Gaieties* (June 5, 1930), *Valley Forge* (December 11, 1934), *To See Ourselves* (May 1, 1935), *Caesar and Cleopatra* (August 22, 1935), *A Slight Case of Murder* (September 12, 1935), *Eden End* (October 22, 1935), *Love From a Stranger* (September 30, 1936), *A Point of Honor* (February 12, 1937), *Knights of Song* (October 18, 1938), *Meet the People* (December 26, 1940), and *Anna Christie* (August 10, 1941). Lawson is listed in *The Biographical Encyclopaedia and Who's Who of the American Theatre* (1966) and *Notable Names in the American Theatre* (1976).

Jean Prinz Korf

LECOMPTE, Elizabeth Alice (April 28, 1944–): director, was born in New Jersey, the second of four children of Frank M. LeCompte, an engineer, and Elizabeth S. LeCompte. After attending public school in New Jersey, she graduated from Skidmore College, Saratoga Springs, New York, in 1966 with a Bachelor of Science degree in applied art and art history. Before her association with director Richard Schechner and the Off-off-Broadway Performance Group on Wooster Street, LeCompte alternately produced charcoal drawings in a New York studio, worked in a community theatre on weekends, and ran a paperback book store in Saratoga Springs. She is the mother of one child, Jack Frank Dafoe, born June 9, 1982.

LeCompte's theatrical career began Off-off-Broadway in 1964 at the Café Lena, where she worked as a waitress and also worked on plays staged by John Wynn Evans. After meeting Spalding Gray, an actor who later became one of her major collaborators, and after seeing the Performance Group's production of *Dionysus in '69*, LeCompte joined Schechner's company. She soon became attached to The Performance Group's way of creating as a theatre collective. Although she disagreed with Richard Schechner's aesthetics on environmental performance, she remained with the Performance Group functioning as note taker, stage manager, adviser, and contributor to the company's music, photography, and graphics. Although she never really enjoyed acting, she did perform frequently with the group. She appeared in *Commune* (1971), *Tooth of Crime* (1972–1973), *Mother Courage* (1974), *The Marilyn Project* (1975), and *Cops* (1978).

In the middle of her acting career with the Performance Group, Elizabeth LeCompte, Spalding Gray, Jim Clayburgh, and others began developing theatre pieces that merged autobiographical materials with language and highly structured visual and aural images. Their collaborations resulted first in a trilogy titled *Three Places in Rhode Island*: *Sakonnet Point* (1975), *Rumstick Road* (1977), and *Nayatt School* (1978). *Point Judith*, which won a the *Village Voice* Off-Broadway (Obie) Award in 1980, was considered an epilogue to the trilogy. However, with the addition of *Route 1 & 9*, the work, as critic Don Shewey of the *Village Voice* has stated, "demands to be reconsidered as a quintet of related theatre pieces, taking in the full sweep of life from cradle to grave and embracing the most basic dualities—male/female, art/reality, black/white" (November 11, 1981).

With the disbanding of the Performance Group in 1980 and the official placement of its successor, The Wooster Group, under her artistic direction, Elizabeth LeCompte continues to defy attempts to label either her process or her aesthetics. She has collaborated with Spalding Gray and also with Ken Kobland, an independent filmmaker in New York. Interested primarily in structure, she regards herself as an architect, a choreographer, and a composer of theatre pieces.

Elizabeth LeCompte and Spalding Gray founded the Wooster Group as early as 1975. As artistic director, LeCompte makes "theatrical collages" out of gathering objects that take on "special meanings" as they are placed in new contexts. As she develops a theatrical piece with the performers, they collect such raw materials as nondramatic texts, plays, private recordings, film, music, and dance. In rehearsal she watches the performers transform the material into a complex theatrical event. The Wooster Group's second trilogy, *The Road to Immortality*—composed of *North Atlantic* (1984), *L.S.D.* (1984), and *Saint Anthony* (1987)—illustrates the group's way of working with diverse cultural materials. In *L.S.D.*, Timothy Leary, the 1960s drug guru, debates with G. Gordon Liddy, the 1970s Richard M. Nixon aide, against the background of quasi-flamenco dancers performing on video monitors.

LeCompte's work is disturbing and controversial in the following way: she encourages spectators to deal with issues, but never from a clearly defined point of view. The eight major pieces created and performed since 1975 are, according to David Savran, "unique in the American experimental theatre for their combination of intellectual rigor, theatrical flair, and aesthetic and political radicalism" (*American Theatre*, December 1986, p. 20). From the beginning, the group has addressed such social issues as suicide, racism, and victimization of women. Moreover, the Wooster Group's radical politics has often created difficulties with funding agencies. *Route 1 & 9* was embroiled in a bitter controversy with the New York State Council on the Arts over the use of blackface. In a radical reworking of Thornton Wilder's *Our Town*, live performance, telephone conversation, and televised images were juxtaposed with varying degrees of mediation. Two white actors in blackface performed a vicious parody of stereotypical black ghetto behavior. The council deemed the piece "racist" and threatened to terminate its support, but distinguished artists, critics, and producers intervened with the council to insure continued funding for the Wooster Group. LeCompte is aware that to force audiences to deal with racist images directly—without mediation by a narrative voice—is to evoke controversy.

The Road to Immorality represents a shift in LeCompte's (and the group's) work from cultural confrontation to collective autobiography. *Saint Anthony* enacts the recent history of the Wooster Group in the guise of a story about the trials of an itinerant theatre group. As a director, LeCompte's position is usually that of "the hidden person" in the company. For *Saint Anthony*, she modified her working procedures by constructing a strong narrative line about an itinerant theatre troupe rehearsing *The Temptation of Saint Anthony* in a seedy hotel room. The theatrical collage draws on work by Gustave Flaubert, Saint Anthony, and Lenny Bruce to contemplate the various identities of death: cessation of consciousness, transfiguration, absence. "When performed in its entirety," according to David Savran, "*The Road to Immorality* will stand revealed as a psychic journey for the performers and, for their audience, as a spiritual and political passage through American culture'' (*American Theatre*, December 1986, p. 22).

The Wooster Group under LeCompte's artistic leadership has taken its place in the mainstream of radical theatre in America. Unlike many experimental theatres, the Wooster Group does not position itself outside the history of culture. Instead, it launches a vigorous critique of ideology through cultural events to expose the contradictions in American society. In performance, the group refuses to ally itself with political or aesthetic dogma.

Despite its controversial position in American theatrical experiments, the Wooster Group was named one of eight theatre companies awarded in 1984 a five-year Continuing Ensemble Grant from the National Endowment for the Arts. Between November 1986 and March 1987, the Wooster Group has acknowledged its own history by giving at the Kitchen and the Performing Garage in New York City retrospective performances of *Route 1 & 9*, *L.S.D.*, *Saint Anthony*, and *North Atlantic*. In 1985 LeCompte and the Wooster Group collaborated with playwright/director/designer Richard Foreman to produce *Miss Universal Happiness*, a play about Latin American politics. In 1988 the Wooster Group received a grant from the National Endowment for the Arts Inter-Arts Program for a collaborative work to be created by LeCompte, Foreman, composer Butch Morris, and film-maker Ken Kobland.

Elizabeth LeCompte's work in the theatre has evolved from her special perspective not only as a visual artist, a conceptual thinker, and a woman but as an iconoclast. By refusing to bow to tradition and to a defined viewpoint, she envisions each new work as developing its own aesthetic. She has commented, ''I'm a child of the information age. I'm excited about the tremendous amount of information coming in from various media and I want my work in the theater to reflect and make use of that data. . . . I love and honor the old realist tradition, but I also subvert it'' (*New York Times*, January 11, 1987, p. 14).

As assistant director to Richard Schechner with the Performance Group (1970–1975) and since then, as artistic director of the Wooster Group (1975-), LeCompte has remained at the forefront of alternative theatre in the United States for almost twenty years.

Reviews of LeCompte's directing appear in the *Village Voice* (November 11, 1981) and the *New York Times* (October 29, 1981). Articles by Elizabeth LeCompte include ''The Making of a Trilogy,'' *Performing Arts Journal* (Fall 1978); ''The Wooster Group, Inc., Presents *Point Judith*,'' excerpts from her notebook published in *Zone* (Spring/Summer 1981); and ''Who Owns History?'' *Performing Arts Journal* (January 1981). See also Richard Schechner, *Environmental Theater* (1973) and David Savran, *The Wooster Group: When Worlds Collide* (1986) or *Braking the Rules: The Wooster Group* (1988, a reprint in paperback of *The Wooster Group: When Worlds Collide*). The Wooster Group is discussed by David Savran in ''Terrorists of the Text: The Wooster Group mounts a retrospective of its fiercely original works,'' *American Theatre* (December 1986), and Roger Copeland, ''Avant-Garde Stage: From Primal Means to Split Images,'' *New York Times* (January 11, 1987). In addition, materials for this essay were gathered from the files of the Theatre Collection of the New York Public Library Performing Arts Research

Center at Lincoln Center and from an interview with LeCompte conducted on August 16, 1982, in New York City.

Kathleen Conlin

LEE, Franne (December 30, 1941–): theatrical designer, was born in the Bronx, New York City, the daughter of Martin Newman, a tool-and-die maker, and Ann (Marks) Newman. She began her studies at the University of California at Berkeley as an art student and spent one summer at City College of the City University of New York. Ambitious to be a painter, she went to the University of Wisconsin at Madison, where she was soon recruited as a scenic painter; she changed her degree program to theatre, receiving her Master of Fine Arts degree in design.

In 1961 she married Ralph Sandler, a teacher of English in Wisconsin and now head of the University Arts Center at Madison. They have a daughter, born on May 21, 1962, Stacy Michael Sandler Feldman, a recent graduate of New York University in lighting design; and a son, born December 14, 1964, Geoffrey Dylan Sandler, an art curator in Madison. The marriage ended in 1967.

Under the name Franne Newman, she designed costumes for Philadelphia's Theatre of the Living Arts productions of *Harry, Noon and Night* (November 28, 1969) and *A Line of Least Existence* (January 24, 1970). There she met Eugene Lee, set and lighting designer, with whom she lived and worked for the next decade. Arnold Aronson noted in *American Set Design* (1985), "Through the 1970s, most of [Eugene] Lee's work was done in collaboration with Franne Lee. While the credits generally read 'Sets by Eugene Lee' and 'Costumes by Franne Lee,' the collaboration was usually more complex and not so easily classified" (p. 74). Together they designed the Manhattan Project's *Alice in Wonderland* production (October 8, 1970), directed by André Gregory, and for this accomplishment they shared the 1970–1971 Drama Desk Award for most promising new designer; the production is amply documented in the volume *Alice in Wonderland: The Forming of a Company and the Making of a Play* (1973), written by the Manhattan Project.

In the same season, the Lees designed Edward Bond's play, *Saved* (Brooklyn Academy of Music, October 28, 1970; Cherry Lane Theatre, November 13, 1970). Billed as Franne Lee, she also designed the costumes for the Trinity Square world première of *The Good And Bad Times of Cady Francis McCullum and Friends* (Providence, Rhode Island, February 17, 1971), for which Eugene Lee designed sets and lights.

The Lees spent the next season with director Peter Brook, co-designing in 1971 *Orghast* with Jean Monod at the Shiraz Festival, Iran, in 1971 and playwright Peter Handke's *Kaspar* in Paris in 1972. On their return to the United States, they co-designed the Manhattan Project's *Endgame* (1972), directed by André Gregory at the Trinity Square Playhouse, and with Roger Morgan directing, they co-designed *Dude* at the Broadway Theatre (October 9, 1972). "If [the *Dude* production] is at all memorable," wrote Suzy Kalter in a profile on the couple for *People Magazine*, "it is for the eight tons of dirt Eugene dumped on center stage" (February 11, 1979, p. 79). Franne Lee's next project was costumes for Richard Schechner's production of Sam Shepard's *The Tooth of Crime* (the Performing Garage, March 7, 1973). Following the birth of their son, William Tuttle Lee, on September 12, 1973, the couple next tackled Harold Prince's production of Leonard Bernstein's *Candide* at the Brooklyn Academy of Music (December 11, 1973), for which Eugene Lee created an environment by restructuring the theatrical space and audience-actor relationships; Franne Lee designed the sets and costumes.

She describes their collaborations as "beginning with the conceptualization of the piece—how will people look at it. Why are they coming to look at this piece prior to dealing with specific ideas. Living together, we talked about the work all the time. With *Candide*, we asked, 'Is it a carnival? Is it a circus? What is the mood?' Getting a general feeling for placement and environment was where we started" (*People*, February 11, 1979, p.79). The production moved to the Broadway Theatre (March 10, 1974), which once again was transformed into an environmental space.

Director Hal Prince, in his memoir *Contradictions* (1974), writes of his introduction to Franne Lee: "She brought me a tattered black leather valise in which she had crammed bits of fabric, remnants from old costumes, old clothes, a piece of a shawl, an antimacasser from the back of a Victorian chair, a codpiece, a comb, a flower, a swatch of mattress ticking. Everything in the show would be made out of something used (later, when I had a series of run-throughs, one friend spotted it: 'You cannot get those "whites" in less than fifty years of washing.'), and that would give it the feeling that we had emptied a closet, unlocked an attic trunk, a multiplicity of events, times, places. She put three or four of these pieces on my desk and told me that they looked like the character of the Old Lady. Another collage, Cunegonde. If I put one next to another, against a third, I began to see the characters emerging. Something meshed, something seemed right about that kind of thinking. Now that I've seen how she executes her rather primitive sketches, I am surprised how sophisticated and detailed the work is. And witty" (p. 198). For *Candide*, Franne Lee won a citation in *Best Plays*, the Joseph Maharam Foundation Award, the Drama Desk Award, and an Antoinette Perry (Tony) Award for costume design, and shared with Eugene Lee the Maharam, Drama Desk, and Tony awards for set design. Designer **Jane Greenwood** has observed, "I think Franne Lee is singularly responsible for people having the nerve at a time when budgets do not allow anything to be made from scratch to make a collage that has a wonderful sense of design. Her *Candide* is an innovation that should be mentioned" (*Theater*, Fall/Winter 1981, p. 77).

Subsequent projects included designing costumes for *Love For Love* (Helen Hayes Theatre, November 11, 1974); *Gabrielle* (world première, Studio Arena, Buffalo, December 9, 1974); *The Skin of Our Teeth* (the John F. Kennedy Center, Washington, D.C., July 1975; Mark Hellinger, September 9, 1975); Hal Prince's production of *Ashmedai* (1976) at the New York City Opera; *Some of My Best Friends* (Longacre Theatre, October 25, 1977); and *The Girl of the Golden West* (Chicago Civic Opera, 1978).

The Lees' next successful Broadway collaboration with Hal Prince was *Sweeney Todd, the Demon Barber of Fleet Street* (Uris Theatre, March 1, 1979). "Once the initial ideas were presented, for example, with *Sweeney*, it was an attitude, a look for the time," she recalls. "There was a division of labor: Eugene was drafting and at the scene shop, while I was shopping, finding hand props, signs, set dressing, because I was the one who was out" (Personal interview, November 21, 1985). For *Sweeney Todd*, she received Tony and Drama Desk awards for costume design. She also designed *Sweeney Todd* for television and again when it was produced at the New York City Opera in 1984.

In 1975 the couple turned to television with Eugene Lee, creating the sets for NBC's original *Saturday Night Live* while Franne created the Bees and made visible Dan Ackroyd's concept for the Coneheads. That involvement led to designs for the production of *Live From New York: Gilda Radner* (Winter Garden, August 2, 1979), for which the Lees co-designed sets and costumes for both the stage and television versions. The Lees' personal and professional collaboration came to an end in April of 1980. Since that time, Franne Lee has designed costumes for *The Mooney Shapiro Songbook* (Morosco Theatre, May 3, 1981); Botho Strauss's *Three Acts of Recognition* (New York Shakespeare Festival Public Theatre, April 6, 1982, directed by Richard Foreman); *Rock 'n Roll: The First 5,000 Years* (St. James Theatre, October 24, 1982); Shel Silverstein's *Wild Life* (May 2, 1983); three one-acts including Elaine May's *Hot Line*; David Mamet's *The Disappearance of the Jews*, and Shel Silverstein's *Gorilla* (Goodman Studio, Chicago, June 14, 1983). She designed sets and costumes for *Streetheat* (Studio 54, January 26, 1985) and Paul Foster's *The Dark and Mr. Stone* (La Mama Experimental Theatre Club, November 18, 1985).

For television she has designed costumes for the *Paul Simon Special*, *The Scarlet Letter*, *Edith Wharton Specials*, *100 Years of American Pop*, *Breakfast, Lunch and Dinner*, and Emo Phillips's *Cinemax Comedy Special* (Fall 1985), as well as sets for *Comedy Zone* and the 1984 Radio City Music Hall Christmas Special with Mr. T. For film she designed costumes for Paul Simon's *One Trick Pony*, John Sayles's *Baby It's You*, Dorothy Puzo's *First Sundays in Exile*, and sets and costumes for Alan Nicholls's *Dead Ringer* and David Wheeler's *The Local Stigmatic* with Al Pacino. She has also contributed sets and costumes to music videos for Carly Simon and Meatloaf.

Franne Lee has long had an interest in quick change art (design that facilitates almost instant transformations), and has incorporated this in her work, particularly in *Candide*, *The Mooney Shapiro Song Book* (in which five actors played eighty-five parts), and *Rock 'n Roll: The First 5,000 Years*. Sheryl Flatow, in the May 1985 *Playbill*, writes, "One characteristic that recurs in [Lee's] best work [is her] humor." Lee firmly believes in having fun with her costumes, all the while serving the piece. Lee says, "The thing that is really important in design is that you have to have your own point of view . . . . My point of view is that people go to the theatre or to the movies or watch television to be entertained. I'm part of the entertainment, and I think a humorous attitude is important'' (*Playbill*, Vol. III, May 1985, p. 99).

Indeed, in summarizing Lee's career in her biographical note for *The Mooney Shapiro Song Book*, Sheryl Flatow quipped, "Her costumes have been seen in such productions as *The Scarlet Letter* on PBS, . . . Paul Simon's movie *One Trick Pony*, and on most of the 'bag ladies' at Grand Central Station.'' Whether designing in collaboration or solo, whether creating scenery or costumes, Franne Lee has become one of America's most creative and adventuresome designers.

Much of the information about Franne Lee is from an interview with her on November 21, 1985. Additional information about Franne Lee and her designs may be found in *Alice in Wonderland: The Forming of a Company and the Making of a Play* (1973) by the Manhattan Project and *American Set Design* (1985) by Arnold Aronson. See also Rick Davis, "Three American Designers: An Interview with Jane Greenwood, Ming Cho Lee and Michael Yeargan," *Theater* (Fall/Winter 1981); Sheryl Flatow, "The Art of Costume Design," *Playbill*, Vol. III (May 1985); Suzy Kalter, "On the Move: If Success Goes to Their Craniums, There's Room: Franne and Eugene Lee Designed the Cone-heads,'' *People Magazine* (February 11, 1979); Laurence Shyer, "The Theatre of Eugene Lee,'' *Theater* (Winter 1982); and Hal Prince, *Contradictions: Notes on Twenty-Six Years in the Theatre* (1974). Lee is listed in *Notable Names in the American Theatre* (1976).

Saraleigh Carney

LEE, Gypsy Rose (January 4, 1914?–April 26, 1970): variety performer, actress, and author, was born Rose Louise Hovick, the eldest child of John Hovick, a newspaperman, and his wife Rose (Thompson) Hovick. The specific location of Rose Louise Hovick's birthplace on the West Coast is unknown, and her birth date is also a matter of approximation. When her parents divorced, she was taken along with her younger sister, Ellen June (better known as the actress-author **June Havoc**), to live in Seattle with her Thompson grandparents. Though their formal education was neglected, both girls were given music and dance lessons. They made their stage debut as children at a local Knights of Pythias lodge to which their grandfather belonged. The act was well received, and their mother was encouraged to arrange bookings at other lodges in the Seattle area.

In 1922 the girls were on the Pantages vaudeville circuit, billed as *Baby June and Her Pals*. Within two years, the act, which now included six boys and various animals, had metamorphosed into *Dainty June and Her Newsboy Songsters* and was booked onto the prestigious Orpheum circuit. As the title implies, the star was June, a talented dancer who was also billed as "the pint-sized Pavlova.'' Compared to her petite blonde sister, Rose Louise was an overweight, good-natured girl struggling gamely through her allotted scenes, the highlight of which was her singing "I'm a hard-boiled Rose,'' dressed in boy's clothes.

After June eloped with one of the newsboys, the act was quickly restructured with Rose Louise as its star. The new all-girl revue was titled *Rose Louise and Her Hollywood Blondes*. Bookings became scarce as the new "talkies'' and the financial depression started vaudeville's decline. By 1929, after having made over a thousand dollars a week at the peak of their popularity, the Hovick company found themselves virtually without funds.

At this time Mrs. Hovick, a woman who concealed a ruthless iron will beneath a superficial charm, booked the troupe into a burlesque house, and one burlesque engagement followed another. In Toledo, Ohio, the phenomenon known as "Gypsy Rose Lee" made her first appearance. The star of the show had been arrested, and as a substitute the fifteen-year-old Rose Hovick performed her first solo strip as Gypsy Rose Lee. Embarrassed by her height, her general ungainliness, and by what she felt was a lack of talent, she ended her act by demurely wrapping the curtain around herself. (The business with the curtain plus the tossing of a rose attached to a garter into the audience would soon become her trademark.)

By 1931 Gypsy Rose Lee was a star. She had headlined at Minsky's burlesque house in New York; by 1936 she had starred in the Ziegfeld Follies. Perhaps because of the memories of her drab parts in vaudeville, Gypsy Rose Lee was determined to make her act as elegant as possible. Having lost her baby fat, she used her height to advantage, developing an imposing carriage. In addition, her costumes were glamorous, costly creations, which she shed with a maximum of style and taste and a minimum of vulgarity; the term "strip tease" could well have been coined for her.

Seemingly overnight she became very much her own person (a development that her mother would never forgive for the rest of her life), as well as a theatrical personality. The reason for her enormous appeal can be traced to both her zest for life and her realistic appraisal of her own merits and deficiencies: she stressed the former and made good on the latter. While reveling in her stardom, she never, for example, tried to conceal the fact that her education had been haphazard. She had a lively, inquiring mind and while touring the country in her vaudeville days became an avid reader. The thought of a stripper who could discuss philosophy and literature delighted members of the intelligentsia both in this country and in Europe. Indeed, Richard Rodgers and Lorenz Hart paid homage to this paradox in their classic musical number "Zip!" in *Pal Joey* (1940).

In 1937, Gypsy Rose Lee had one of her few career setbacks. Anxious to capitalize on her name, Hollywood offered her a contract. Eager though the film industry was to star her in pictures, care was not taken to find appropriate vehicles for her. In two years she made five films, none of which was successful. At this period (1937) she married her first husband, Arnold R. Mizzy, a dental supply manufacturer. The marriage was childless and ended in divorce in 1941.

By 1940 Lee was back in New York, appearing in *The Streets of Paris* at the New York World's Fair. Two years later, she enjoyed her biggest stage success *Star and Garter*. But her most important professional achievement of the early 1940s was the publication of her first book, a mystery titled *The G-String Murders*. Published in 1941, it became a best seller. Given her innate respect for books and writers, the fact that she had become a successful published author gave her a sense of true accomplishment. Another book, *Mother Finds a Body*, followed in 1942, and she wrote a play, *The Naked Genius*, a year later. The play enjoyed a brief popular success but was closed by its producer, Mike Todd, after a month's run. The author's fame, however, was enough to assure a sale of the film rights to Twentieth Century-Fox while the play was still in rehearsal.

Despite her professional success, Lee's personal life was turbulent during the 1940s. A second marriage in 1942 to actor Alexander Kirkland ended in divorce in 1944. That same year, her only child, a son named Erik, was born. It was not until 1971, one year after her death, that director Otto Preminger admitted that he was Eric's father. Finally, in 1948, Lee was married for the last time to painter Julio De Diego; and though their marriage lasted until 1955, it, too, ended in divorce.

Throughout the 1940s and 1950s the multiple careers of Gypsy Rose Lee flourished. She made a few successful films, including *Stage Door Canteen* (1942), *The G-String Murders* (1943), and *Belle of the Yukon* (1944), and she returned to the stage. Though the heyday of burlesque was ending, Lee could still be counted on to draw huge crowds, both in burlesque houses and in nightclubs. In addition, she kept up a steady flow of articles on numerous subjects to such diverse publications as *The New Yorker* and *Collier's*. But her most successful literary effort of this period was the publication of *Gypsy: A Memoir* (1957). While not strictly an autobiography, the book, written with great warmth and humor, is a vivid backstage portrait of life on both the vaudeville and burlesque circuits. Seeing the book's potential as a musical, producers David Merrick and Leland Hayward bought the rights and commissioned Jule Styne, Stephen Sondheim, and Arthur Laurents to do the music, lyrics, and book. The result was *Gypsy* (1959), one of the best of the 1950s musicals. Starring **Ethel Merman** (in perhaps her greatest role) as Rose Hovick, and Sandra Church as Gypsy, the play was both a critical and a popular hit. The filmed version was released in 1962 with Natalie Wood in the title role and with Rosalind Russell as her mother.

Though she retired from burlesque runways in the 1950s, Lee continued to be active professionally. She made several cameo screen appearances, guest-starred on television series, and was even the hostess of her own syndicated talk show. Her warm personality, tart observations, and down-to-earth outlook won her many new admirers in the 1960s. It may have come as a surprise to some of the post-World War II generation that this statuesque woman with the marvelous flair for clothes had a long history of involvement in liberal causes. Already in the mid–1930s, for example, Gypsy Rose Lee supported the Loyalists in the Spanish Civil War, a stand that earned her a subpoena from Martin Dies's notorious congressional committee. The subpoena was rescinded, and she did not have to appear.

Her death from lung cancer in 1970 robbed the American entertainment scene of one of its true originals. Though it is easy to dismiss Gypsy Rose Lee as simply a successful stripper, she was much more. Like **Mae West**, she was one of the first women to be able to make people aware that an appreciation of sex and of the human body was both healthful and good. Beyond that, however, she was able to share with others through her writing the humor and inconsistencies of her own life, and of human life in general. The theatre and her story have been immortalized in one of the American theatre's best musicals, *Gypsy*.

Additional information about Gypsy Rose Lee may be found in her autobiography, *Gypsy: A Memoir* (1957), and in her sister June Havoc's book *Early Havoc* (1959). Gypsy Rose Lee also wrote "Mother and the Knights of Pythias," which appeared in *The New Yorker* (April 10, 1943), and "Just Like Children Leading Normal Lives" in *The New Yorker* (July 3, 1943). See also the musical *Gypsy* by Arthur Laurents (1959). Her obituary appeared in the *Los Angeles Times* (April 27, 1970) and the *New York Times* (April 27 and 28, 1970). There is a clipping file in the Billy Rose Theatre Collection in the New York Public Library Performing Arts Research Center at Lincoln Center. Lee is listed in *Current Biography, 1943* (1944); *The Biographical Encyclopaedia and Who's Who of the American Theatre* (1966); *Notable American Women*, Vol. IV, *The Modern Period* (1980); and *The Oxford Companion to American Theatre* (1984).

William Lindesmith

LE GALLIENNE, Eva (January 11, 1899–): actress, director, producer, translator, and playwright, was born in London into a cultured and educated family. She was surrounded by art and literature from her youth. Her father was the noted poet Richard Le Gallienne. Her mother, Julie (Norregaard) Le Gallienne, who was born in Denmark, left Richard Le Gallienne when Eva and her sister Hesper were quite young, taking the children with her, and supporting them by running a hat shop and working as a journalist. In Paris Eva Le Gallienne was educated at the College Sevigne, which prepared girls to attend the Sorbonne. Traveling between France, Denmark, and England made Le Gallienne a very sophisticated young lady whose knowledge of English, French, and Danish proved very useful to her career in the theatre. She was drawn to the theatre as a very young girl and was particularly impressed by the acting of Sarah Bernhardt. Lacking the money to buy Bernhardt's 800-page *Mémoires*, she borrowed it from a friend and copied the entire book by hand. Another actress who influenced her greatly was British actress Constance Collier, known for her teaching as well as her acting. As a young girl, Le Gallienne received her first lessons from Collier while visiting family friends.

Eva Le Gallienne suffered a major disappointment at the age of twelve when she was forced to turn down William Faversham's invitation to travel to America to play Lucius in *Julius Caesar* with Collier as Portia. Instead she was sent to an English boarding school, where she played Lord Burleigh in a play about Queen Elizabeth. Her professional debut occurred at the age of fifteen when she "walked on" as Collier's page in Maurice Maeterlinck's *Monna Vanna* (July 21, 1914). She then studied at Herbert Beerbohm-Tree's academy in London (it became the Royal Academy of Dramatic Art). She was hailed as a "brilliant new comedienne," playing the role of a cockney servant in *The Laughter of*

Fools at the Prince of Wales Theatre in May 1915. In July of that year she played in a Red Cross benefit performance of *Peter Ibbetson* organized by Constance Collier, who continued to advise her through the early part of her career.

In 1915 Eva Le Gallienne set off for America accompanied by her mother, hoping to play in the American production of *The Laughter of Fools*. When this production did not materialize, she accepted the role of a black maid in *Mrs. Boltay's Daughters* (1915). In 1916, she played a cockney servant in *Bunny*, followed by her first major role in the production of *The Melody of Youth*, which ran for four months. The success of the play led to prosperity for the first time in her career and to a role in *Mr. Lazarus* (1916), which toured Washington, D.C., Chicago, and other cities. Her next venture was not successful: she was fired from the production of Owen Davis's *Mile-a-Minute Kendall* (1917) after receiving bad notices. After this setback, she toured in 1917 to the West Coast in *Mr. Lazarus* and played roles on the coast in *The Cinderella Man* and Augustus Thomas's *Rio Grande* (with the playwright directing through a megaphone). She returned to New York with hopes of playing in a version of Ferenc Molnar's *Liliom*. Again the production did not materialize, and again she was without work.

Le Gallienne then played several minor roles in a series of plays, performing with such stars as **Maxine Elliott** and **Ethel Barrymore**. She spent two seasons in support of Ethel Barrymore and felt that this period of time working with the great artist of the American stage was very important to her development. She toured playing Ethel Barrymore's daughter, the Duchess of Burchester, in *The Off Chance* (1918–1919). Returning to New York Le Gallienne again sought work, playing occasionally in films for ten dollars a day, and in the unsuccessful Irish play *Lusmore* in 1919. In her next success, she played a French girl (speaking only French) and danced as **Elsie Janis**'s partner in the 1919 production of *Elsie Janis and Her Gang*. Turning from musical comedy to her first love, the legitimate stage, she performed with small success in the play *Tilly of Blooms-bury* but with great success opposite Sidney Blackmer in Arthur Richman's *Not So Long Ago*, which opened triumphantly in New York in 1920. In the next year she fulfilled a dream by playing her first starring role as Julie in Molnar's *Liliom* with Joseph Schildkraut. The play was such a success that it was moved from the Garrick Theatre to a larger theatre and ran for over a year. During this run Le Gallienne's thirst for new challenges and hard work was satisfied by a special matinee of a Maeterlinck play, *Aglavaine and Selysette* (1921), which foreshadowed her later interest in unusual plays and unconventional productions. She toured in *Liliom* (1922–1923) after the New York run, but failing health forced her to leave the production. Following a period of rest she returned to to Europe for the first time in seven years, joining her mother in London. She visited several cities, met Molnar in Vienna, and returned to New York to perform *Liliom* for another season.

In 1923 Le Gallienne performed one of her most memorable roles, that of the princess in Molnar's elegant comedy *The Swan*. The role provided her with a wonderful acting opportunity as well as the chance to go to Europe to buy her gowns. In London she saw Eleonora Duse perform. The great Italian actress impressed her, and a friendship developed between the two, one at the end of a great career and the other at the beginning. Many years later Le Gallienne wrote a moving biography of Duse (*The Mystic in the Theatre*, 1966), describing with sensitivity and skill the loveliness of her acting and personality. During the successful run of *The Swan*, Le Gallienne did some matinee performances of Gerhardt Hauptmann's *Hannele* in 1924. Another special matinee was a performance in French in Bataille's *La Vierge Folle* in the same year.

When the Actors' Equity Association strike cut short the run of *The Swan*, Le Gallienne decided to go to Jasper Deeter's experimental Hedgerow Theatre in Moylan, Pennsylvania. There she played her first Ibsen roles: Mrs. Solness in *The Master Builder* (1923) and later Hilda Wangel in the same play (1925), which she also directed. She became one of the foremost interpreters of Henrik Ibsen's plays in America and made notable translations of several of the plays in the years that followed. The experience at Deeter's theatre was one of the steps that led Le Gallienne to her dream of forming a repertory theatre in imitation of European models.

In the 1925–1926 season Le Gallienne starred with Egon Brecher in the Actors' Theatre production of Arthur Schnitzler's *The Call of Life*. This play was not successful but led to Brecher's agreement to play Solness in special matinees of *The Master Builder*. The success of this venture encouraged them to increase the number of matinees and then move the production to regular performances. She and Brecher rehearsed Ibsen's *John Gabriel Borkman*, which was presented in special matinees with great success. The two plays were taken on tour for the rest of the season, and Le Gallienne continued to make plans for a repertory theatre.

That same year she established the Civic Repertory Theatre, which opened October 25, 1926. It was one of the major events in the American theatre in the twentieth century. Le Gallienne renovated an old theatre that had appeared unfashionable in its location on New York's 14th Street west of 6th Avenue. Here she directed and acted in such classics as Anton Chekhov's *The Three Sisters*, *The Cherry Orchard*, and *The Sea Gull*; William Shakespeare's *Twelfth Night* and *Romeo and Juliet*; the adaptation of Lewis Carroll's *Alice in Wonderland*; Henrik Ibsen's *The Master Builder*, *John Gabriel Borkman*, and *Hedda Gabler*; and James M. Barrie's *Peter Pan* (in which she played Peter and took her curtain call by flying over the heads of the audience into the balcony). These plays were performed in New York and on tour, and many of the plays produced were seen in America for the first time. Le Gallienne demonstrated her conviction that success was attainable with challenging and unusual plays, and she drew audiences to plays for which everyone predicted disaster. Here, and throughout her career, she proved her concept that theatre is art, not commerce, and she achieved commercial success with plays dubbed "box office poison." As one of her activities at the Civic Repertory Theatre she also offered free classes to young actors. During the second season she was awarded the *Pictorial Review* prize for her important work. Despite popular and critical success, there were financial difficulties, and in 1933 the theatre was disbanded. At this time Le Gallienne wrote her first autobiography, *At 33* (1934), which contains a passionate defense of the repertory system.

During the time she operated the Civic Repertory Theatre, Le Gallienne lived in an apartment in the theatre building. She also purchased property in Weston, Connecticut, where she did much of the writing and translating that occupied the time not spent on acting or directing. In 1931, while attempting to deal with a faulty hot-water heater, she suffered serious injury to her hands when the heater exploded. Following her hospitalization and slow partial recovery, Le Gallienne returned to Europe, visited her mother, and settled in Paris for a few months. Here, on a whim, she joined a circus (her identity unknown to the ringmaster and others) and worked with the famous Fratellini Brothers. She learned much from these highly skilled clowns and also studied fencing as part of her effort to exercise her fingers as much as possible. When she returned to the United States in 1932 she had to undergo several operations on her hands to restore their full usefulness.

In the following years, Le Gallienne played many notable roles and performed in outstanding productions in New York and elsewhere. She acted the role of Napoleon's son in Rostand's *L'Aiglon* (1934) both in New York and on tour, played "four-a-day" in vaudeville in a one-act sketch, and toured again with *Camille, The Women Have Their Way,* and *Rosmersholm* in repertory (1935). Well received outside New York City, the company's opening received bad notices in the city and lost money during the run. For a time thereafter, Le Gallienne returned to the healing quiet of Weston, acting occasionally on radio, studying, and planning for the future. In 1936 she appeared in the nearby Westport Country Playhouse (where she has often acted and directed since) in the Restoration comedy *Love for Love.*

In 1937 Le Gallienne performed *Hamlet,* one of her most unusual roles. The play was presented at the Cape Playhouse in Dennis, Massachusetts, for eight consecutive performances after two weeks of rehearsal. The young **Uta Hagen** played Ophelia, and with Le Gallienne's encouragement, training, and advice she, like her mentor, became an outstanding actress and teacher. Following the commercial failure of *Madame Capet* (1938) in New York, Le Gallienne began plans for a tour of *Hedda Gabler* and *The Master Builder* in repertory. While preparing for this tour Le Gallienne again earned money by performing in vaudeville, this time in the balcony scene from *Romeo and Juliet* on a bill that included comics Smith and Dale, the impersonator Elsie Janis, and the strip tease artist Maxine de Shone.   Performances of *Private Lives* in 1939 were followed by the tour of the two Ibsen plays, often performed under difficult conditions in inadequate theatres. The tour began in Hartford, Connecticut, and went to cities such as St. Cloud, Minnesota ("they finally procured me a bucket of water to wash my hands") and Rock Hill, South Carolina ("entirely sold out"). In all the cities she found audiences responding positively to the performers and to Ibsen's plays. "The audience was marvelous—warm, intelligent, and eager; deeply enthusiastic and grateful. *There* is the great reward!" (*With a Quiet Heart*, pp. 183–184).

In 1940, disappointed by her failure to find a play she wished to act or direct, Le Gallienne set out on a lecture tour throughout the country. In the next few years she acted in many outstanding plays (some for the Theatre Guild) and particularly enjoyed the success of Anton Chekhov's *The Cherry Orchard* (1944), in which she again appeared with Joseph Schildkraut. For several years she had been planning to return to the repertory plan, and in 1946 she co-founded the American Repertory Theatre with her long-time friend **Margaret Webster** and the producer **Cheryl Crawford**. This partnership followed the success of the three women's work on Shakespeare's *The Tempest* in 1945. Passing by the more familiar and popular classics, the trio began with *John Gabriel Borkman*, Shakespeare's *Henry VIII*, and James M. Barrie's *What Every Woman Knows*. The rehearsals were exciting and challenging, but the company was beset by problems with the unions and the high costs of costumes. Finally, the absence of strong support from the critics and severe financial problems led to the abandonment of the repertory system. *Androcles and the Lion* was performed as a single production. The company revived *Alice in Wonderland*, which played for a long run. As usual, Le Gallienne emphasized the positive results of this attempt at establishing the kind of theatre she loved: "We left the International Theatre at the end of May; it was a sad leave-taking. In spite of all our trials and tribulations, the memories that remain of our season there are happy ones. The experience of repertory had been a revelation to those of the company who had never known it, and the young people all felt that those months had taught them more than they could have learned in many years of ordinary theatre work" (*With a Quiet Heart*, p. 281).

In the years from 1948 to 1951 Le Gallienne engaged in "recital tours," which were lectures with scenes from plays performed by the actress and one or more actors. She also performed in *The Corn is Green* (1950) on the summer circuit and in New York City. She next presented a radio program that was highly popular, since she had built up a large audience throughout the country during her years of touring. At this time she began to write her second autobiography, *With a Quiet Heart* (1953), in which she stated, "I cannot tell whether there is any longer a place for me in the American theatre. There are times when I doubt it" (p. 301).

Fortunately for the American public, Le Gallienne went on with her work in the theatre. Acting in many productions and touring the country year after year, she brought high quality theatre to the country as a whole. Her theatrical activities ranged from the solo reading of *An Afternoon with Oscar Wilde* at the Théâtre de Lys in 1957 to the role of Queen Elizabeth in *Mary Stuart* at the Phoenix Theatre in the same year. From 1955 on she appeared on television in various productions, including *Alice in Wonderland* for the *Hallmark Hall of Fame* in 1955, *Thérèse Raquin* for *Playhouse 90* in 1972, and *Memories of Duse* for *Camera Three* in the same year. With undiminished energy she established the National Repertory Theatre in 1959 and toured until 1964 playing in *Mary Stuart*, *Elizabeth the Queen*, *The Sea Gull*, and Jean Anouilh's *Ring Around the Moon*. She also directed *Liliom* and *Hedda Gabler* for the tours in 1964 and 1965. Returning to Connecticut, she co-produced a number of plays at the White Barn Theatre in 1966. In 1968 she worked with the Association of Producing Artists at the Lyceum Theatre in New York, acting in Eugène Ionesco's *Exit the King* and in Chekhov's *The Cherry Orchard* in her own translation. She performed at the American Shakespeare Festival in Stratford, Connecticut, in *All's Well That Ends Well* in 1970. In 1975 she directed Ibsen's *A Doll's House* at the Seattle Repertory Theatre. At seventy-six she performed on Broadway with **Rosemary Harris**, Ellis Rabb directing, in the revival of George S. Kaufman and Moss Hart's comedy about the Barrymores titled *The Royal Family*. Her great experience in the theatre, her wit and elegance, and her comic technique combined to make her performance in the role of Fanny Cavendish a high point in New York during the 1975–1976 season and on national tour in 1976–1977.

Despite her advancing age Le Gallienne, like Fanny Cavendish, continued to be excited about theatre and to believe in the value of performing outside New York. In 1980 Le Gallienne performed in *To Grandmother's House We Go* in Houston, Texas, and received an Antoinette Perry (Tony) nomination for her performance when the play ran in New York in 1980–1981. During this period the film *Resurrection*, for which she received an Academy (Oscar) Award nomination, was released. Le Gallienne amazed audiences by her continuing vivacity and creative energy when she revived *Alice in Wonderland* in 1982. In this production she played the White Queen and made a flying entrance, calling up memories of her triumphant performances as Peter Pan.

Living in her home in Weston, surrounded by a beautiful garden, Eva Le Gallienne writes, translates, corrects proofs, and plans the future. A great symbol of courage and imagination, she is also a gracious and modest woman, living simply and displaying kindness and generosity to those who visit her. Regardless of hardship and personal tragedy, she has pursued the highest ideals in the theatre and has refused to give in to commercial demands or easy solutions. She is one of the most admired women in the American theatre. Her numerous honors include honorary degrees from ten colleges, Tufts University and Smith College among them; the Women's National Press Club's Outstanding Woman of the Year Award (1947); the Norwegian Grand Cross of the Royal Order of St. Olaf (1961); American National Theatre and Academy (ANTA) awards (1964 and 1977); the American Theatre Association's Citation for distinguished service to the theatre (1973); an Emmy Award (1978); and the Achievement in Arts Award from the Connecticut Commission on the Arts (1980), to list only a few. In 1986 Eva Le Gallienne was the recipient of a National Medal of Arts presented by President Ronald Reagan at the White House.

Clipping files with reviews of Eva Le Gallienne's productions are in the collection of the New York Public Library Performing Arts Research Center at Lincoln Center. From 1921 to the present Le Gallienne has been a prolific writer. Her work includes articles such as "What is Wrong with the Theatre," *Woman Citizen* (April 1921); "Sarah Bernhardt and Eleonora Duse," *Stage* (April 1933); and "Repertory . . . When?" *Theatre Arts* (September 1958). Her close relationship with Eleonora Duse is described in *The Mystic in the Theater* (1966), and she has given a full picture of her life and career in articles; two books, *At 33* (1934) and *With a Quiet Heart* (1953); and interviews, including Yvonne Shafer's "Acting in Ibsen: An Interview with Eva Le Gallienne," *Ibsen News and Comment* (1981), and "Women in Ibsen: Yvonne Shafer talks with Eva Le Gallienne about Acting in Ibsen," *Theatre Communications* (February 1982). Articles such as Robert Benchley, "Eva Le Gallienne's Repertory Theatre," *Life* (January 11, 1929), and May Sarton, "The Genius of Eva Le Gallienne," *Forum* (Summer 1973 and Winter 1974), have appeared, but there is no standard biography. Le Gallienne has received praise for her translations, which include *Six Plays of Henrik Ibsen* (1957), *The Wild Duck and Other Plays* (1961), *Seven Tales of Hans Christian Andersen* (1959), and *The Spider and Other Stories* (1980). Complete listings of her roles, awards, and publications appear in *The Biographical Encyclopaedia and Who's Who of the American Theatre* (1966) and *Who's Who in the Theatre* (1981). She is also included in *The Oxford Companion to the Theatre* (1983) and *The Oxford Companion to American Theatre* (1984).

Yvonne Shafer

LE NOIRE, Rosetta Burton (August 8, 1911–): actress, singer, playwright, and artistic director, was born in New York City to Harold and Marie (Jacques) Burton. Her father was from the West Indies and was the first licensed black plumber in New York State. He also served as a Republican leader in New York's twenty-first Assembly District for more than fifty years. "We lived on Strivers Row, those blocks in the 130's between Lenox and Seventh Avenue," Le Noire told a *Sunday News* reporter (February 1, 1976). "If you had a government post, or were a doctor or lawyer, you bought a tree-shaded brownstone, the symbol of success. No mistress of such a house went to get so much as a box of salt without wearing gloves and a hat. I do miss the niceties."

Rosetta Burton attended New York City's High School of Commerce and Hunter College and received her professional training at the American Theatre Wing (1950). Her parents wanted her to be a nurse, but her godfather, dancer Bill "Bojangles" Robinson, encouraged her to pursue a career in the theatre. So at fifteen she became a chorus girl performing with her godfather. She began her career with the idea of performing African songs and dances. This desire led her to the Works Progress Administration's Federal Theatre Project, where she appeared as the First Witch in *Macbeth* (1936) and later in *Bassa Moon* (1936). Her Broadway debut was as Peep-Bo in Mike Todd's production of *The Hot Mikado* at the Broadhurst Theatre in 1939. This was the start of a very active and successful acting career.

Le Noire's Broadway credits include *Anna Lucasta* (1944), *Mister Johnson* (1956), *Tambourines to Glory* (1963), *I Had A Ball* (1964), *A Streetcar Named Desire* (1973), *The Sunshine Boys* (1973), *Blues for Mister Charlie* (1974), *God's Favorite* (1974), and *The Royal Family* (1976). Her Off-Broadway credits are *Show Boat* (1951 and 1966), *Supper For The Dead* (1954), *Take A Giant Step* (1956), *The Bible Salesman* (1960), *South Pacific* (1961), *Cabin In The Sky* (1964), *The Name Of The Game* (1967), *A Cry of Players* (1968), and *Lady Day* (1972). She has also acted in several films, including *Anna Lucasta* (1958) and *The Sunshine Boys* (1975). She first came to television in 1954, and since then has appeared extensively on programs such as *Ryan's Hope*, *The Royal Family*, *Another World*, and *A World Apart*.

Le Noire has also written several critically acclaimed plays: *Come Laugh and Cry with Langston Hughes* (1976), *Reminiscing with Sissle & Blake*, written with Louis Johnson (1973), *House Party* (1971), and *Soul: Yesterday and Today* (1970). She has received the Frank Silvera Writer's Workshop Award for playwriting.

In 1968 an event occurred that had a profound effect on Le Noire: "Four years ago," she later writes, "I was standing in a hallway near a classroom in a Harlem church. There was a shout. Who do we love? We love Black. Who do we hate? We hate Whitey" (*New York Amsterdam News*, February 19, 1972). This incident prompted Le Noire to establish a theatrical company that would focus on uniting rather than dividing people of different cultural and ethnic backgrounds. Thus, the AMAS (Latin for "you love") Repertory Theatre was founded in 1969. The company has focused on musical theatre, and its productions have included *Bubbling Brown Sugar* (1975), *Bojangles* (1976), *Dunbar* (1980), *The Crystal Tree* (1981), and *Blackberries* (1985). In addition to presenting original showcases each season, a summer touring unit visits nursing homes and senior centers in New York City's five boroughs. The company also offers comprehensive training programs, including the Eubie Blake Children's Theatre for adolescents, the Adult Workshop for professionals and beginners, and the Community and Outreach Program, which provides instruction at regional schools and other sites.

Rosetta Le Noire's recent musicals have been highly acclaimed. In 1977 she received the Audelco (Audience Development Committee) Award for superior and sustained contribution to the performing arts and again, in 1982, as an outstanding pioneer. In 1985 she was cited by the New York City Council for her commitment and contributions to the community and the same year received the Pierre Toussaint Medallion for excellence and success in her chosen field. In February 1989 Le Noire became the first recipient of an annual award that will bear her name. The award, established by Actors' Equity Association, will be presented each year to a person or institution for "artistic contributions to the universality of the human experience in the American theatre." Le Noire was cited for her long-term commitment to the concept of non-traditional casting and multiracial production. Despite her many theatrical achievements, the personal price Le Noire paid to pursue her craft was often great. She had one son, William, from her first marriage to William Le Noire, which ended in divorce. Her second husband, Edgar Brown, died in 1973. "I remember touring and the nights I sat alone in the train station with my bags at my feet because they wouldn't let me in a hotel, or looking up a preacher to see if he knew a colored family who'd take me in. And stars like Dorothy McGuire and Eileen Heckart walking streets to find a restaurant where we could eat together'' (*Sunday News*, February 1, 1976). Yet, she is not bitter nor dismayed. As the name of her theatrical company indicates, AMAS equals You Love. As founder and artistic director of AMAS Repertory Company, Rosetta Le Noire received New York Mayor Edward Koch's Award of Honor for Arts and Culture in November 1986. The award cited Le Noire's "passionate commitment to a theatre that is color-blind.''

Material contained in this biographical sketch came from an extensive clipping file in the Billy Rose Theatre Collection in the New York Public Library Performing Arts Research Center at Lincoln Center. Brief but informative articles on Le Noire are found in the *New York Sunday News* (February 1, 1976), the *New York Amsterdam News* (February 19, 1972), and *Back Stage* (May 2, 1980). Some of her critical notices appear in the *Cleveland Press* (September 12, 1961), the *Dallas Morning News* (August 8, 1963); the *New York Herald Tribune* (May 27, 1961; April 16, 1963, November 4, 1963; and January 22, 1964), the *Wall Street Journal* (March 1, 1963, and November 4, 1963), the *New York Times* (January 22, 1964, and April 26, 1964), and *Variety* (October 29, 1975, and December 24, 1975). She is cited in *The Biographical Encyclopaedia and Who's Who of the American Theatre* (1966); *Notable Names in the American Theatre* (1976); *Who's Who in Hollywood, 1900–1976* (1976); *Who's Who in the Theatre* (1972, 1977); *Directory of Blacks in the Performing Arts* (1978); and *More Black American Playwrights: A Bibliography* (1978).

Maria Rodriguez

LESLIE, Amy (October 11, 1855–July 3, 1939): drama critic, was born Lillie West in West Burlington, Iowa, to Albert Waring West and Kate (Webb) West. Her father, a pioneer newspaper editor in Indiana and Iowa, founded and edited the *Burlington Hawkeye* and was also a local banker. After attending St. Joseph's Academy in St. Joseph, Missouri, Lillie West graduated in 1876 from St. Mary's Academy near South Bend, Indiana, where she received the gold medal from the conservatory of music.

With some training from the Chicago Conservatory of Music, Lillie West became a performer in light opera and, while with the Grayman Comic Opera Company, became known for her performance as Amelia in *Olivette*. She made her New York City debut as Fianetta in *La Mascotta* at the Bijou Theatre on May 5, 1881. The opera played over one hundred performances in New York, and Lillie West became a popular attraction.

In 1880, while playing in *La Mascotta*, she married Harry Brown, a member of the company, and together they toured the country for several years in light opera companies. Their only child, Frank Brown, died of diphtheria when he was four. At the time of her son's death, Lillie West Brown, who was the prima donna in *Castles in the Air* with DeWolfe Hopper, retired from the stage and returned to her family, then living in Chicago. The Browns were later divorced.

When she settled in Chicago, after her separation from her first husband, Lillie West began her newspaper career. At her mother's urging she submitted some sketches to a Chicago *Daily News* column titled "What One Woman Sees." She used the pseudonym "Amy Leslie," a name she selected at random. The editor, T. H. White, liked her work so much that he hired her as the paper's drama critic, and she remained drama critic of the Chicago *Daily News* for forty years, from 1890 to 1930.

Amy Leslie's prose style can be seen in her review of **Viola Allen**'s performance in *The Winter's Tale*, which played Chicago in 1905. "As the unhappy queen of Sicilia," she wrote, "Miss Allen was frail, touching, and conscientious without reaching any of the sculptural splendors within the heart of the great role." Her remarks were often quite pointed. In an 1895 review titled "The Massacre of 'The Foundling,' " she described the star, Cissy Fitzgerald, as "plain" and wrote that "she cannot dance a step and doesn't pretend to know how to act." Writing of John Barrymore's first stage appearance in Chicago, she said, "The part of Max was essayed by a young actor who calls himself Mr. John Barrymore. He walked about the stage as if he had been all dressed up and forgotten" (Chicago *Daily News*, October 31, 1903).

In July of 1901, Amy Leslie married Franklin Howard Buck, the bell captain at the Virginia Hotel, after a romance that was followed by all of Chicago. Years younger than his wife, Buck later became known as Frank "Bring 'em Back Alive" Buck for his jungle expeditions. The couple were divorced in 1916.

Women reporters were scarce in the 1890s, and female drama critics, especially on major metropolitan newspapers, were almost unknown. Amy Leslie's forty-year career was unique. One colleague, George Ade, with whom she had once shared a desk, commented when she retired, "Think of a woman going to the theatre several times a week for at least forty years and keeping her girlish enthusiasm for the drama . . . and lavishing upon a languishing art a glittery and figurative vocabulary that was always ebullient and never seemed to repeat" (Obituary, *New York Herald Tribune*, July 4, 1939). Another co-worker, Ben Hecht, wrote, "She was a delight to read. . . . Her prose was ornate and endless. . . . But unlike most moralists who take to criticism our Amy was never vicious. Derogatory reviews were rare in the *Daily News*, for the rhapsodies of adulation were Amy's forte. Given half an excuse Amy gave birth to a sunrise of words. No drama critic I have read since, not even Alexander Woollcott, could swoon as madly in front of the footlights as our Amy Leslie" ("Wistfully Yours," *Theatre Arts*, July 1951, p. 13).

Amy Leslie retired from her post on the *Daily News* in 1930. In her later years she suffered from arteriosclerosis and a brain tumor. She died at her home in the Parkway Hotel in Chicago at the age of eighty-three.

In forty years of dramatic criticism Amy Leslie chronicled in her unique prose a rich theatrical epoch. As the first important woman critic on a major American metropolitan newspaper, she opened a way for other women to follow, and was herself an influential figure in the American theatre for four decades.

Amy Leslie was the author of three books: *Amy Leslie at the Fair* (1893), *Some Players* (1899), and *Gulf Stream*, her memoirs (1930). Information on her career is included in William James Robertson, "Drama Criticism and Reviewing in Chicago, 1920–1930" (Unpublished Ph.D. dissertation, University of Wisconsin, 1964). Leslie is mentioned in Frank Buck, *All in a Lifetime* (1941), and Alson J. Smith, *Chicago's Left Bank* (1953). See also Ben Hecht, "Wistfully Yours," *Theatre Arts* (July 1951) and Alexander Woollcott, "In Memoriam: Rose Field," *Atlantic Monthly* (May 1939). Leslie's obituary notices appeared in the Chicago *Daily News* (July 5, 1939), the *Chicago Tribune* (July 4, 1939), and the *New York Times* (July 4, 1939). Amy Leslie is listed in *Who's Who in America, 1899–1900* (1899); *Women's Who's Who in America, 1914–1915* (1914); *Who's Who in the Theatre* (1939); *American Authors and Books, 1640–1940* (1943); *Who Was Who in America*, Vol. IV: *1961–1968* (1968); *Notable American Women*, Vol. II (1971); and *The Oxford Companion to American Theatre* (1984).

Rita M. Plotnicki

LEWISOHN, Alice (April 17, 1883–January 6, 1972): actress, director, writer, producer, and **LEWISOHN, Irene** (September 5, 1892–April 4, 1944): dancer, choreographer, director, producer, co-founders of the Neighborhood Playhouse, were born in New York City, the eighth and tenth children of Leonard and Rosalie (Jacobs) Lewisohn. Their father, born in Hamburg, Germany, had come to the United States in 1865. He became a principal founder of the American Smelting and Refining Company and the Amalgamated Copper Company. Their mother was from a New York banking family; she died in 1900 and their father died two years later, leaving each of his ten children with a legacy of over two million dollars.

The sisters were privately educated and encouraged in philanthropic and artistic pursuits. Before his death their father had introduced them to the pioneering social work of Lillian Wald at the Henry Street Settlement on New York's Lower East Side, and the sisters subsequently became leaders in the settlement's clubs and classes. At the same time, they pursued their own artistic training. Alice, intrigued by the possibilities of poetic drama, studied acting with Sarah Cowell LeMoyne and in 1906 made her professional debut as Phene in a short-lived production of Robert Browning's *Pippa Passes*. Irene, who was interested in dance and movement, studied Japanese Noh drama during a trip to the Orient with Lillian Wald in 1910. In 1912 Alice formed a dramatic group at the Henry Street Settlement. The first production of the Neighborhood Players, as the group was called, was *The Shepherd*, a drama by Olive Tilford Dargan set in pre-Revolutionary Russia. Over the next two years the players offered four more plays, including John Galsworthy's *The Silver Box*.

Encouraged by the success of their amateur group, the Lewisohns announced that they would build a small theatre at their own expense. The Neighborhood

Playhouse, erected on the corner of Grand and Pitt Streets, opened in February 1915. The first production at the new theatre was *Jephthah's Daughter*, a dance drama created by Alice and Irene Lewisohn to music by Lilia Mackay-Cantell. During the twelve years of its existence the Lewisohn's Neighborhood Playhouse offered the most varied theatrical seasons in New York. Two productions that won critical praise were *The Little Clay Cart* (1924), a Hindu play, and *The Dybbuk* (1925), a folk play of the Yiddish theatre. In addition to plays by authors such as Joyce, Yeats, Shaw, Chekhov, and Andreyev, the playhouse presented dance dramas based on the folk dances of various countries and examples of such non-Western theatre forms as Japanese Noh and Burmese Pwe. The Lewisohns were intimately involved with the creation of these productions, Alice as director and actress in the dramatic offerings, and Irene as choreographer and dancer in the dance dramas and non-Western theatre forms. The sisters also supervised scenery, lighting, and costumes, using the knowledge and the materials they had brought back from their trips to Europe and the Orient.

Since the Neighborhood Playhouse was conceived as an integral part of the Lower East Side community as well as a showcase for new styles of theatrical production, it was used on weeknights to show motion pictures of a higher caliber than those being exhibited in many of the neighborhood's nickelodeons. However, the changing economics of the film business forced the Lewisohns to abandon this part of the theatre's operation in 1920 as too costly. Beginning in 1922 the playhouse presented an annual satirical revue called *The Grand Street Follies*. Originally offered at the end of the season as a bonus production for the playhouse's subscription patrons, the *Follies* attracted so much favorable comment that they were frequently moved to Broadway after their run at the playhouse.

In December 1924 Alice Lewisohn married Herbert E. Crowley, an artist who had designed the settings for an earlier playhouse production. Her work at the playhouse continued briefly.

Despite its artistic success, the playhouse never achieved financial solvency. At the end of the 1926–1927 season the Lewisohns reluctantly admitted that they could no longer afford to absorb the playhouse's financial losses, and it closed on May 31, 1927. Irene Lewisohn remained active, however, in various facets of theatre. Shortly after the playhouse closed, she created the first of a series of "orchestral dramas" in which dance was blended with symphonic music. The first such piece was choreographed to Ernest Bloch's symphonic poem, "Israel." It was performed at the Manhattan Opera House in 1928 by the Cleveland Symphony Orchestra and a company of dancers that included **Martha Graham**, Doris Humphrey, and Charles Weidman. Similar concerts were presented under Irene Lewisohn's direction in 1930 and 1931.

In 1928 the Neighborhood Playhouse School of the Theatre was inaugurated with Irene Lewisohn as adviser and **Rita Wallach Morgenthau** as director. The school still functions today as an important training ground for young actors.

In 1937 Irene Lewisohn founded the Museum of Costume Art that, after her death, became the Costume Institute of the Metropolitan Museum of Art in New

York City. The basis of the collection was the many native costumes and materials that the Lewisohns had gathered in their travels. Irene remained active in the work of the school and the Museum of Costume until her death from cancer in 1944.

The closing of the playhouse brought Alice Lewisohn's theatrical career to an end. In the early 1930s she moved to Zurich, Switzerland, to study with psychoanalyst C. J. Jung. In the mid–1930s she obtained a divorce from Herbert Crowley; there were no children. Alice died in Zurich in 1972.

The productions of the Neighborhood Playhouse, so different from those of the Broadway theatre of the time, or of the other "art" theatres like the Provincetown Playhouse and the Theatre Guild, were a reflection of the Lewisohns' artistic beliefs and interests. Besides introducing works by European and American playwrights who had difficulty getting their plays produced in the commercial theatre of the day, the playhouse brought non-Western dramatic forms to New York audiences for the first time and broke new ground in the integration of music, dance, and spoken dialogue. Through the playhouse's productions and through their own personal philanthropy the Lewisohns encouraged such theatre artists as designers **Aline Bernstein** and Donald Oenslager, directors **Agnes Morgan** and Richard Boleslavsky, and dancers Martha Graham, Louis Horst, Charles Weidman, and Doris Humphrey. The Neighborhood Playhouse School, founded to carry out the artistic principles of the Lewisohns in the training of young actors, produced dozens of successful actors and actresses.

Perhaps the most unique contribution of the Lewisohn sisters to the American stage was their belief that theatre could flourish among the poorer classes clustered in the Lower East Side of Manhattan. While the other art theatres appealed primarily to New York's intelligentsia, the Lewisohns proved that good theatre could transcend economic, social, and even language barriers. Their refusal to abandon their neighborhood audiences after the playhouse had become a *succès d'estime* attracting primarily uptown spectators speaks eloquently of the Lewisohns' commitment to their original ideal of a "neighborhood playhouse."

Primary source materials are available at the Theatre Collection of the New York Public Library Performing Arts Research Center at Lincoln Center. Some of these materials are also available at the Library of the Neighborhood Playhouse School of the Theatre. A major published source is Alice Lewisohn Crowley, *The Neighborhood Playhouse: Leaves from a Theatre Scrapbook* (1959). Also useful are the Neighborhood Playhouse sections of Kenneth Macgowan, *Footlights Across America* (1929). Biographical data on Irene Lewisohn is included in *Notable American Women*, Vol. II (1971). Information about Alice Lewisohn is listed in *The Biographical Encyclopaedia and Who's Who of the American Theatre* (1966). See also *The Oxford Companion to the Theatre* (1983) and *The Oxford Companion to American Theatre* (1984).

Margaret M. Knapp

LINKLATER, Kristin (April 22, 1936–): actress and innovator of a widely acclaimed process of voice training, was born in Edinburgh, Scotland, one of four children of Eric and Marjorie (MacIntyre) Linklater. Both parents were Scots, with a dash of English, Dutch, and Swedish blood. Marjorie MacIntyre had studied acting at London's Royal Academy of Dramatic Art (RADA) before marrying Eric Linklater at the age of twenty-four. Eric Linklater became a prolific writer, the author of twenty-three novels (three of them best sellers), ten plays, numerous short stories, children's stories, and essays.

Kristin Linklater lived on the Orkney Islands until she was ten, and then in Easter Ross, Scotland. As a young girl she was a fine pianist, and her mother hoped she would pursue music. Her older sister became a painter, and two younger brothers became writers. Kristin, however, had been smitten by theatre. She had acted in school, performing Romeo at age sixteen at the Downe House School, Newbury, Berkshire, England. However, she received no formal acting training until she enrolled at the London Academy of Music and Dramatic Art (LAMDA). At LAMDA she studied under the innovative vocal coach Iris Warren. In the 1950s English actors were noted for the virtuosity of their voices, but all too often their performances lacked genuine feeling. Warren developed a process to make the voice expressive of true emotions by connecting the voice to the actor's entire psychological and physical being. Kristin Linklater did exceedingly well with Warren's techniques, though she had no intention then of pursuing vocal training as a career. She completed school and spent two years acting in the Byre Theatre, a repertory company in St. Andrews, Fife, Scotland. However, when LAMDA's principal, Michael Macowan, asked her to return to LAMDA as Iris Warren's voice assistant, Linklater agreed, and soon became intrigued with the actor's use of the voice.

She had much success training actors under Warren, but she was struck by how much more curious American actors were about the connection between the acting process and the voice than were the English. Fascinated with the vitality of the theatre in the United States, she moved to New York City in October 1963 and set up a studio. Keeping New York as her base, she was teaching, within six months, at the Stratford Shakespeare Festival Theatre, Stratford, Ontario, and at the Tyrone Guthrie Theatre in Minneapolis. By 1968 she was also working with the Lincoln Center Repertory Company, the Negro Ensemble Company, and the Open Theatre—all in New York City. In 1965 she ran a training program for voice teachers funded by the Rockefeller Foundation. Before coming to the United States she had studied nothing scientific about the human body, but Americans began asking her to justify her approach; so she studied anatomy and physiology. She discovered that everything she read only reinforced what she already knew from hands-on experience with actors. In 1968 she began teaching in the theatre program of the New York University School of the Arts and remained there as master teacher of voice for eight years.

In the early 1960s American actors were still studying elocution and speech, to train their voices. Linklater's process, inherited from Iris Warren, was aimed at releasing the actor's natural voice, rather than controlling it or making it conform to some idea of standard speech. Although each of her exercises isolated an area of vocal production, that is breathing, resonance, tongue release, they all created an integrated psycho-physical process. The actor was asked to employ imagery to connect language with emotions. As her method developed, she worked more specifically to get actors to understand the direct psychological roots, within the family or the environment, that caused the lack of vocal expressiveness. By the early 1970s she had formed the Working Theatre, a foundation-supported program to train actors to teach a unified approach to voice, acting, and movement. Her methods were then being taught in professional actor-training schools all over the country by people she had trained directly. In addition, she toured, offering workshops to students and teachers. For years she resisted writing a book, feeling that her method was meant to be conveyed orally. Nevertheless, there was great demand for some codification of her system, and in 1976 she published *Freeing the Natural Voice*. In that same year, her son Hamish Eric was born.

In 1978 Linklater joined with British director Tina Packer to form a classical theatre company called Shakespeare and Company in Massachusetts. With Packer as artistic director and Linklater as director of training, the two women formed a small company of English and American actors and housed them at novelist Edith Wharton's former estate, the Mount, in the Berkshire mountains of Lenox, Massachusetts. They developed a unique and rigorous rehearsal process requiring actors to immerse themselves in the language, imagery, and ideas of Shakespeare and his time. They stressed that the actor must strive, not for a generalized beautiful sound, but for a personal and emotional connection with each spoken word. As stated in the company's program literature, their goal was "to build and sustain a permanent, professional theatre company on American soil, performing the works of Shakespeare in a way which revitalizes the classic experience for audiences of all ages."

In accordance with their artistic beliefs Linklater and Packer have established an ongoing training program for their own company of actors and an annual intensive four-week workshop for theatre professionals; they continue to provide workshops and lectures wherever they perform on tour. They are also responsible for the creation of an innovative program known as "Shakespeare in Schools," where a company of actors is sent into high schools and elementary schools to offer performances, workshops, and directing services. Funded by the Commonwealth of Massachusetts, the program has met with success in schools throughout the Northeast.

With Shakespeare and Company, Linklater was able to return to acting. She performed a wide range of roles, including Lady Macbeth (1983 and 1985), Maria in *Twelfth Night* (1981), the Nurse in *Romeo and Juliet* (1981), and Hippolyta in *A Midsummer Night's Dream* (1978). At the same time, her professional acting extended to Emilia in *Othello* (1979) at Atlanta's Alliance Theatre and Queen Margaret in *Richard III* at the Repertory Theatre of St. Louis (1980). She also served as a dialect coach and understudy to Cicely Tyson in the Broadway revival of *The Corn is Green* in 1983, during the run of which she replaced Tyson for five performances.

By 1985 Linklater had traveled extensively, conducting voice and acting workshops in Europe and the United States. She created a solo performance of poetry, both classical and modern, which she performed with her individual workshops. Along with her professional acting career, she continued to train American students, professional actors, and teachers. Kristin Linklater's career as a voice teacher and actress has been of major significance to the American theatre; however, she is most renowned for her unique approach to training the actor's voice.

The chief source on Linklater's vocal production methods is her book, *Freeing the Natural Voice* (1976). For further information about the formation of Shakespeare and Company, their rehearsal process and productions, see the *New York Times* reviews of August 28, 1983, by Helen Dudar, and September 7, 1984, by Enid Nemy. Biographical material for this essay was obtained through a personal interview with Linklater.

                                                                    Wendy Salkind

LOGAN, Olive (April 22, 1836–April 27, 1909): actress, playwright, journalist, lecturer, and nineteenth century feminist, was born in Elmira, New York, where her father, an actor, was then performing. Cornelius Ambrosius Logan was well known for his performances of Yankee characters on stage and for authorship of several extremely successful farces. His chief fame was in the South and West. Her mother was Eliza Akeley (or Acheley). When Olive Logan was a few years old, her father became a stage manager in Cincinnati. Olive had been the third child; eventually there were eight: six girls and two boys. Thomas grew up to become a successful criminal lawyer; Cornelius became a physician and twiced served as Minister to Guatemala. All six of the daughters were at one time or another on the stage.

Olive Logan was educated at the Wesleyan Female Seminary in Cincinnati but was frequently pressed into child's parts in productions playing at her father's theatre. When five years old, she played the wordless parts of Cora's child in *Pizarro* and Damian's child in *Damian and Pythias*. A few years later she had a speaking part as the Duke of York in *Richard II*. After the death of her father, she joined the Arch Street Theatre in Philadelphia, then under the management of William Wheatley and John Drew. Her official "adult" debut there was as Mrs. Bobtail in the farce *Bobtail and Wigtail* in 1854.

Olive Logan, however, was not totally committed to acting as a profession, and after a short stay in Philadelphia, she was off to England to study at a school for women. She would not return for eight years, during which time she was entirely out of the life of the theatre. After graduating at the head of her class, she went to Paris and, in 1857, married Edward DeLile (sometimes given as Henry A. Delille), a writer who later became a Chevalier of the Legion of Honor.

At the age of twenty-one, Logan was a familiar of the court of Louis Napoleon, receiving petitions from visiting Americans and writing amusingly of her experiences for both French and English journals. This picturesque experience ended, however, "in the second year of the rebellion," she says. She returned to the United States in July 1863 and resumed her career in the theatre by writing a sensational melodrama called *Evaleen*, which was produced at Wallack's Theatre, New York, early in 1864 with Logan in the cast. That fall and winter, for seven months, she was on the road throughout the South and West, playing Louisville, Cincinnati, Nashville, Columbus, Chicago, Indianapolis, Cleveland, and Milwaukee. Olive Logan not only played in *Evaleen* (now called *The Felon's Daughter*), but she also played Juliet in *Romeo and Juliet*, Julia in *The Hunchback*, and a variety of other roles. Her mother accompanied her on this trip, which was arduous because of the war but gave Logan much material that she later used in writing for publication.

Back in New York, Logan divorced DeLile in 1865 and the next year made her last appearance as an actress in the melodrama *Sam* at the Broadway Theatre, then managed by her brother-in-law George Wood. It was counted a great success, running for a hundred performances. She later said that in each stage appearance she played a star and that, in a week, she never earned less than a hundred dollars and sometimes as much as a thousand. But, at the age of twenty-nine, she decided to make her future career as a writer. Perhaps the success of her first book, *Photographs of Paris* (1866), was a persuasive factor. A series of prose sketches based on her own experience of Paris, it earned praise for her from the elder Dumas. She had also become interested in other things: the status of women, women's rights, and the invasion of what she called the "leg business" into theatre.

When in 1861, in the United States, **Adah Isaacs Menken** in flesh-colored tights made a sensation in *Mazeppa*, Logan had been abroad. She was in New York, though, during the phenomenon of *The Black Crook* at Niblo's Garden Theatre, which began in September 1866 and lasted for sixteen months. The scantily clad dancers offended Logan's high ideals for theatre, and she wrote an article titled "The Leg Business," which appeared in the journal *The Galaxy* (August 1867). So great a volume of letters—pro and con—arrived at the office of *The Galaxy* that Logan was led to apologize to the editor.

About this time, evidently, Artemus Ward (Charles Farrar Brown), the great humorist, suggested that she try the lecture circuit, and she decided to do so. She prepared a lecture on the theatre and tried it out in New York with enough success to persuade her to "take it on the road." During the next year she appeared in such places as Monmouth, Illinois; Piqua, Ohio; St. Paul, Minnesota; Wabasha, Minnesota; and other such places in "the West," sometimes giving her lecture on theatre and sometimes reading from the poets and from Charles Dickens. The tour occurred during the fall, winter, and spring of 1867–1868.

Back in New York Logan continued her writing and used the Author's Guild as her professional address. In 1869 her book *Apropos of Women and Theatres* was published, and Susan B. Anthony invited her to be a featured speaker at the American Equal Rights Association Convention at Steinway Hall, New York, on the evening of May 12, 1869. Elegantly dressed and speaking forcefully for about twenty minutes, she voiced her convictions that women could and should "advance boldly," doing whatever hand or brain enabled them to do, even entering "the arena of politics." It was a wildly successful speech, interrupted incessantly by applause, with a standing ovation at its close. It was reported widely in the press though in somewhat distorted fashion, since the emphasis in the press was given to a single sentence that deplored the displacement in the theatre of "well-trained, well-qualified, decent" actresses by the vogue for "brazen-faced, stained, yellow-haired, padded-limbed creatures" (as quoted in *Packard's Monthly*, July 1869). She was speaking in a larger context of employment for women, but the statement provoked a storm of publicity which led her to write long letters to the *New York Times* and other newspapers and to compose a "definitive" article which was accepted and published by *Packard's Monthly* (July 1869). She called it "The Nude Woman Question," and it was fueled not only by her previous writing but by the arrival in New York of Lydia Thompson and her British Blondes in the notorious production of *Ixion, or the Man at the Wheel*. Again the newspapers entered the battle, most of them supporting Logan's call to excise this lewd entertainment from the theatre. Logan was a national celebrity, and the Blondes soon left New York to tour the country. Logan returned to her writing and publishing; in addition to short stories and articles in various magazines, her book *Before the Footlights and Behind the Scenes* was published in 1870. In 10 months she traveled over 50,000 miles to deliver 170 lectures from Boston to Minnesota.

Also in 1870, Augustin Daly produced her play *Surf*; it appeared not only in New York but in Philadelphia. Nine years later he also produced her comedy *Newport*. Meanwhile, at the height of her fame, in 1871, she married William Wirt Sikes, who was appointed American consul at Cardiff, Wales, and she went abroad with him. She continued to write, publishing articles in *The London World*; another book on the theatre, *The Mimic World* (1871); and two novels, *Get Thee Behind Me, Satan* (1872) and *They Met by Chance* (1872). When her husband died in 1883, she remained in England, writing and editing while two more of her plays were produced at the Princess Theatre. Her list of written work would eventually total fifty plays, eleven books, and innumerable magazine articles.

She married again at fifty-three; her husband, the thrity-three-year-old James O'Neill was, by royal grant, permitted to call himself James O'Neill Logan. The couple returned to America in the mid–1890s, but in 1906 Logan appeared in court charging her husband with nonsupport for squandering money on alcohol. Lady Cook, a friend from the days in England, took the aging Logan back to London in 1907. In 1909, having been committed, at the last, to an insane asylum, Logan died at the age of seventy-one.

The best sources of materials about Olive Logan are three of her own books, *Apropos of Women and Theatre* (1869), *Before the Footlights and Behind the Scenes* (1870), and *The Mimic World* (1871). These volumes reprint many of her articles and articles written by others about her. The *Galaxy* correspondence is in the Manuscript Collection of the New York Public Library. Her later career is chronicled by William Winter in *The Wallet of Time* (1913). See also Marvin Felheim, *The Theatre of Augustin Daly* (1956), and George C. D. Odell, *Annals of the New York Stage*, Vols. VI-XI (1931–1939). Jean Taylor discusses Logan in "Representative Women in the American Theatre" (Unpublished master's thesis, University of Texas, Austin, 1950). *Notable American Women* (1971) contains a short biography of Logan as does *The Oxford Companion to American Theatre* (1984).

Vera Mowry Roberts

LOOS, Anita (April 26, 1888 or 1893–August 18, 1981): screenwriter, playwright, and novelist, was born in Sissons (now Mount Shasta), California. She was the second of three children born to newspaperman R. Beers and Minnie Ella (Smith) Loos. Her elder brother Clifford became an eminent physician, one of the founders of group medicine; her younger sister Gladys died of peritonitis at the age of eight. Anita Loos graduated from Russ High School in San Diego but was largely self-taught, voraciously reading a formidable array of library books. As a teen-ager she married Frank Pallma, the son of a band leader, in order to escape parental authority, and left him approximately twenty-four hours later. In 1919 she married director John Emerson, who died in 1956 after an eighteen-year mental illness. She herself died at age eighty-eight (some sources cite ninety-three) of a heart attack in New York City.

Her feckless father, whose career "linked smalltime journalism with low-grade theatrical ventures" (*A Girl Like I*, p. 20), proved precarious as a source of income, and the family moved around a good deal in California. While in San Francisco, R. Beers Loos decided to put his daughters to work as child actresses to augment the family fortunes. Anita Loos's first stage appearance was in the title role of *Little Lord Fauntleroy*. She played in a number of stock company productions, at times acting with traveling companies in their local presentations, and at times going off with them on tour. Often she found herself the family's chief source of income. This early experience in the theatre left her permanently disenchanted with acting as a profession. She once described it as "a pointless exhibitionism" and "a low form of endeavor" (*A Girl Like I*, p. 131 and *Cast of Thousands*, p. 1).

She found writing infinitely more interesting. Around the age of eight she wrote her first piece for publication, an advertisement in verse for floor polish, which appeared in a children's magazine and won her five dollars. At thirteen, she began to write short paragraphs for a New York newspaper, the *Morning Telegraph*, and was soon a regular paid contributor. Meanwhile, her father had become manager of a stock company that ran short films between the acts of plays. Entranced by the relatively new art form, and realizing that "every film must require a plot," she decided to write one herself. As she said in her autobiography, "My sole preparation for a career was to buy a fountain pen and a large yellow pad" (*A Girl Like I*, p. 150). She sent her scenario, signed "A. Loos," to the American Biograph Company, whose address she found on a film can. Biograph promptly sent a check for twenty-five dollars to "Mr. Loos," and Anita was launched as a screenwriter. The first of her scripts to be filmed was *The New York Hat* (1912), directed by D. W. Griffith and starring Mary Pickford and Lionel Barrymore. This early success was quickly followed by others. Between 1912 and 1915 she wrote more than a hundred scripts, only four of which were rejected by Biograph. Her income steadily grew. By 1916, *Wild Girl of the Sierras* brought her one hundred dollars; *Calico Vampire* earned two hundred dollars; *Stranded* was sold for three hundred dollars. Characteristically, however, she refused to take her now lucrative career very seriously. "I had never thought of myself as a writer," she recounts. "While I loved to work on plots, I looked on them as crossword puzzles—frustrating when they failed, but rewarding when dramatic unities began to unfold which indicated they were going to work out" (*A Girl Like I*, p. 237). T. E. Dougherty, the scenario editor at Biograph, was anxious to meet his prolific author and invited her to come to Hollywood in January 1914. He and director Griffith stared unbelievingly at Anita Loos, who stood four feet eleven inches, weighed about ninety pounds, and looked like a child. However, her wit and intelligence impressed them, and she became a staff writer at Biograph Studio at fifty dollars a week (plus extra money for any script accepted). While there, she produced numerous half-reel farces for actress Fay Tincher, plus longer scripts for stars such as **Lillian** and **Dorothy Gish**, Mae Marsh, Constance Talmadge, and Mary Pickford; and her script *His Picture in the Papers* (1916) launched Douglas Fairbanks as a film star. More importantly, she pioneered the art of subtitling, which, before her innovations, tended to be highly simplistic. She provided subtitles for *Macbeth* (1916), which were credited jointly to William Shakespeare and Anita Loos; her captions for Griffith's masterpiece *Intolerance* (1916) are considered classics of the genre. Thereafter, she was asked to subtitle every film Biograph turned out.

She married film director John Emerson, an insecure hypochondriac who began to list himself as co-author of her scripts and to appropriate her earnings. Eventually, the couple moved to New York, financed by Paramount to produce films during World War I. While there, she wrote two Broadway comedies, *The Whole Town's Talking* (1923) and *The Fall of Eve* (1925). She became friendly with intellectuals such as H. L. Mencken and drama critic George Jean Nathan and gradually stopped writing for films. In 1925, however, she achieved international fame with the novel *Gentlemen Prefer Blondes*. Originally a character sketch conceived as a spoof of her friend Mencken's infatuation with a mindless blonde, *Gentlemen Prefer Blondes* first appeared as a series of installments in *Harper's Bazaar*. Published as a book in 1925, the novel ran through eighty-five editions and through translation into fourteen languages, including Chinese. Novelist Edith Wharton called it "the great American novel (*at last!*)," and Aldous Huxley was "enraptured" by it (*Cast of Thousands*, p. 257 and p. 205). Philosopher George Santayana, asked to name the "best philosophical work by an American," cited *Gentlemen Prefer Blondes* (*A Girl Like I*, p. 274). Loos rewrote the book as a popular play in 1926. It also became the basis for two films, one featuring Ruth Taylor and Alice White (1928), the other starring Marilyn Monroe and Rosalind Russell (1953); and two musical comedies, *Gentlemen Prefer Blondes* in 1949 and *Lorelei* in 1974, both starring **Carol Channing**. The royalties were substantial, and in 1926 Anita Loos decided to give up her writing career to live a private life with Emerson.

However, Emerson's investments proved less than sound. When the stock market crashed in 1929, Loos found herself without funds, and in December 1931, she was called back to Hollywood with an offer from MGM to write a film script for producer Irving Thalberg. The film was *Red-Headed Woman* (1932), which catapulted Jean Harlow to fame and, incidentally, resulted in a more stringent censorship code for films. Thalberg was pleased with Loos's work and offered her a two-year contract at $2,500 a week. Emerson joined her, insisting on a contract, too. His behavior grew more and more irrational as her work proved more successful than his; and diagnosed as a manic depressive, he spent the last eighteen years of his life in a sanitarium. Loos continued to write, and her more notable scripts from this period include *Biography of a Bachelor Girl* (1934), featuring Ann Harding and Robert Montgomery; *San Francisco* (1936), with Clark Gable, Jeanette MacDonald, and Spencer Tracy; and *The Women* (1939), based on the **Clare Boothe Luce** stage production and starring Norma Shearer, Joan Crawford, and Paulette Goddard. She also produced other memorable stage plays, such as *Happy Birthday* (1946), a comedy for **Helen Hayes** that ran for 564 performances, and her adaptation of Colette's novel *Gigi*, which brought Audrey Hepburn to stardom in 1951. Her last film script was the musical version of *Gentlemen Prefer Blondes* in 1958; her last stage work was *Lorelei* in 1974, yet another adaptation of her famous novel.

In addition to over two hundred film scripts, four novels, five musicals, and ten plays, Anita Loos wrote two entertaining and informative autobiographies: *A Girl Like I* (1966) and *Kiss Hollywood Good-by* (1974), both of which deal with her film career. She also wrote an affectionate guide to New York City, *Twice Over Lightly*, with Helen Hayes in 1972; a commentary on her friends in Hollywood, *Cast of Thousands* (1977); and, finally, *The Talmadge Girls* (1978), describing the rise to stardom of Constance and Norma Talmadge in the silent film era.

As a playwright, screenwriter, and international celebrity, Anita Loos proved that a woman could thrive in the manic world of Hollywood and New York show business. She had a combination of brains and talent and a gift for survival that kept her busy and successful while numerous other famous writers fled from Hollywood in dismay or turned to drink out of frustration. Her refusal to take anything very seriously kept her from being overawed, and her self-described "fascination over all things great and small" (*Cast of Thousands*, p. 236) kept her work from becoming stale or overly contrived. Her use of screen captions raised subtitling to an art form, and her crisp, witty dialogue made a genuine contribution to both sound films and stage plays. As a child, she had feared only boredom and vowed to avoid it all her life. She succeeded admirably.

Anita Loos's autobiographies are *A Girl Like I* (1966), *Kiss Hollywood Good-by* (1974), and *Cast of Thousands* (1977). For comments on Loos, see also *The New Yorker* (December 28, 1946), *Theatre Arts* (November 1950), and *Time* (August 26, 1946). At her death Alden Whitman wrote "Anita Loos Dead at 93: Screenwriter, Novelist," *New York Times* (August 19, 1981). She is listed in *Twentieth Century Authors*, First Supplement (1955); *The Biographical Encyclopaedia and Who's Who of the American Theatre* (1966); *Contemporary Authors*, Vols. 21–22 (1969); *Who's Who in America, 1972–1973*, Vol. II (1972); *Current Biography, 1974* (1974–1975); *Notable Names in the American Theatre* (1976); *American Women Writers*, Vol. III (1981); *Who's Who in the Theatre* (1981); *Dictionary of Literary Biography Yearbook 1981* (1982); *American Humorists, 1800–1950*, Part 1 (1982); *The Oxford Companion to American Literature* (1983); *Dictionary of Literary Biography*, Vol. 26, *American Screenwriters*, Vol. II (1984); and *The Oxford Companion to American Theatre* (1984).

Laurilyn J. Harris

LORD, Pauline (August 13, 1890–October 11, 1950): actress, notable for roles in O'Neill plays, was born to Edward and Sara (Foster) Lord in Hanford, California, while the family was living on a fruit farm in the San Joaquin Valley. The father of this family of three girls and one boy was a hardware merchant who had migrated to California from Delaware in the early 1880s. The family moved to San Francisco, where Pauline attended the Holy Rosary Academy in Woodland. There her lifelong interest in theatre was whetted by a school play and by trips to Saturday matinees in San Francisco. She studied acting at the Alcazar Theatre School and made her professional debut there at the age of thirteen as the maid in *Are You a Mason?*, with the Belasco Stock Company. The popular comedian Nat Goodwin saw her in the play and invited her to look him up if ever she got to New York.

After the San Francisco earthquake and fire, Lord went to New York, where she surprised Goodwin by taking him up on his offer. He put her in his touring company, but she left it to return home while it was performing in New Orleans. However, she went back to New York where she joined another company touring in Springfield, Massachusetts, and Milwaukee, Wisconsin. Her first New York appearance was in 1912 as Ruth Lenox in *The Talker* by Marian Fairfax. This play was successful, but the next seven or eight plays in which she appeared were not. In 1917 she appeared in *The Deluge* as Sadie, a woman of the streets. The play lasted only a few weeks, but Lord received favorable notices and impressed director Arthur Hopkins with her acting ability. She appeared in *Under Pressure* (1917); *Out There* (1917) with an all-star cast composed of George M. Cohan, **Laurette Taylor**, and **Minnie Maddern Fiske**; *Our Pleasant Sins* (1919); *Night Lodgings* (1919), with Hopkins as producer; and *Big Game* (1920). In 1920 she also appeared in *Samson and Delilah*, another Hopkins production, in which the critics praised her acting.

Pauline Lord's first outstanding success came in the title role of Eugene O'Neill's play *Anna Christie* on November 2, 1921, at the Vanderbilt Theatre. At first, O'Neill was not happy with the casting, but Lord's immediate success once the play opened made history. From Broadway the play went on tour in the United States and then opened in London on April 10, 1923, where its reception was overwhelming. The ovation at London's Strand Theatre lasted a half hour; the audience sang "For She's a Jolly Good Fellow" and mobbed her dressing room. The play was called the greatest success of the London stage in twenty years. Critics mentioned her "breathless voice," her realistic acting that was "not acting at all." Brooks Atkinson wrote of the "elusive, tremulous, infinitely gifted Pauline Lord" (*Broadway*, p. 198).

In 1924 she was a tremendous success as Amy in Sidney Howard's *They Knew What They Wanted*. Her other truly great role of the decade was that of Nina Leeds in Eugene O'Neill's *Strange Interlude*, a role she took over from **Lynn Fontanne.** She toured in the play during 1928 and 1929. Lord also appeared in *Trelawny of the Wells* (1925 and 1927), *Sandalwood* (1926), *Mariners* (1927), *Spellbound* (1927), and *Salvation* (1928). In 1932 she appeared in three other plays: *Distant Drums*, *The Truth About Blayds*, and *The Late Christopher Bean*, in which she scored considerable success. In 1934 and 1935 she made two films: *Mrs. Wiggs of the Cabbage Patch* and *A Feather in Her Hat*. Then she returned to the stage in 1936 to create perhaps the most complex character of her career, Zenobia, in the dramatization of Edith Wharton's novel *Ethan Frome*. Stark Young titled his critique of the play, "Miss Lord's Day" and pointed out that Miss Lord "tops everything, the story, the play, the scene, the acting . . . . Her performance has a miraculous humility, a subtle variety and radiation and shy power that are indescribable. . . . She must have a role that suits her, one in which she feels right. When she does so, there is no other player who can bring into it such tragic elements, such bite, or so sharp a stain of life" (*Immortal Shadows*, pp. 179–180). Raymond Massey and **Ruth Gordon** formed the rest of the triangle in that production. In 1939 Pauline Lord toured Australia with two rather slight pieces. Later she appeared in *Suspect* (1940), *Eight O'clock Tuesday* (1941), and *The Walrus and the Carpenter* (1941). Her last appearance was as Amanda Wingfield in the national touring company of *The Glass Menagerie* in 1947 at the Plymouth Theatre, Boston.

Pauline Lord was an artist but not a public figure. There are few interviews with her on record though her picture appeared frequently in magazines. She was described as being petite, five feet two inches, and possessing a mop of tawny hair, a straight little nose, wistful, velvety eyes, and a soft, sweet voice. Her manner was hesitant, at times timid and vague with an elusive quality that fascinated her audiences as well as her friends. She was married secretly to an advertising executive, Owen B. Winters, on April 27, 1929, at Elton, Maryland, just before going abroad on a tour, but was divorced two and a half years later on October 26, 1931. While driving to Tucson with a friend in 1950, she was in an automobile accident. Taken to a nearby hospital in Alamagordo, New Mexico, she there contracted bronchopneumonia and died. Her ashes were buried in the Kensico Cemetery, Valhalla, New York.

When the Moscow Art Theatre was leading the way in realistic acting and when many American actresses were bringing their personalities to the stage, Pauline Lord was developing her unique kind of realistic portrayal of emotion, called by interviewer Elizabeth Shepley Sergeant "a betrayal of emotion" (*Free Under the Andes*, p. 146). Early in her career she began searching for the essence of the art and built her own technique of communicating it to the audience. Arthur Hopkins encouraged her to do whatever she felt like doing on the stage, sensing that it would be valid, and so freed her from conventional techniques. "If there is such a thing as Absolute Truth that is what she achieves," he said later in her career (*Free Under the Andes*, p. 154). "It is acting that is not acting; poignancy that comes from deep wells." She herself confessed to her interviewer that she could never act unless she was unhappy or nervous. "On stage I know exactly what I am about. . . . I have to study, struggle, get to rock bottom. . . . But finally I see every word, every action; every intonation, every movement is clear to me" (*Free Under the Andes*, p. 151).

In preparation for her role as Anna Christie she observed the prostitutes on 10th Avenue, but eventually she modeled the character on a department store clerk who waited on her and who projected a "beaten soul . . . tired to death." Joseph Wood Krutch, after seeing her in *Spellbound*, wrote that she was "the most extraordinary temperament to be seen in our theatre . . . . She does not so much interpret as live upon the stage the character of certain specific tragically bewildered women" (*Nation*, November 30, 1927). Stark Young wrote, "I should say, after much thought in the matter, that the greatest single moment I ever saw was that first scene in *Mariners* when Miss Lord as the wife comes down the stairs." He was praising her at that time in his review of *Strange Interlude* and went on to say, "When Miss Lord appears in a realistic piece, no matter how inferior the play may be, it should be taken as a theatrical event of the first rank" (*Immortal Shadows*, p. 178).

In her own way Pauline Lord contributed to the development of realistic acting in the United States. Along with intensive study she depended upon inspiration and intuition to create images that lingered for years in the minds of her audiences.

Pauline Lord is discussed in Ashton Stevens, *Actorviews* (1923); Elizabeth Shepley Sergeant, *Fire Under the Andes* (1927); Stark Young, *Immortal Shadows* (1948, reprinted 1973); and Brooks Atkinson, *Broadway* (1970). See also Joseph Wood Krutch, "Pauline Lord," *Nation* (November 30, 1927). William C. Young reprints some reviews of her plays in *Famous Actors and Actresses on the American Stage*, Vol. II (1975). Her obituary appeared in the *New York Times* (October 12, 1950). She is included in *The New Theatre Handbook and Digest of Plays* (1959); *Notable American Women*, Vol. II (1971); *Dictionary of American Biography*, Supplement Four 1946–1950 (1974); *Who Was Who in the Theatre*, Vol. II (1978); and *The Oxford Companion to American Theatre* (1984).

Nelda K. Balch

LORTEL, Lucille (1902?–): producer and owner of the Lucille Lortel Theatre, New York, formerly the Theatre de Lys, was born and grew up in New York City. She began her theatrical career as an actress in the 1920s, when, after studying in Berlin with the American drama teacher Arnold Korf and with Max Reinhardt, she returned to New York to play a cameo role in the Theatre Guild's production of George Bernard Shaw's *Caesar and Cleopatra* (1925), with **Helen**

Hayes. A blossoming acting career, which included a leading role both on stage (1928) and screen (1930) in *The Man Who Laughed Last* with Sessue Hayakawa, was interrupted in 1931 when she married Louis Schweitzer, a chemical engineer whose fortune came from the production of paper for American cigarettes. Although she continued to make movie shorts, she effectively retired from acting.

The end of this first career, however, was the beginning of her notable roles as producer, artistic director, theatre owner, and theatre patron. Her second career started by chance in 1947 when she offered to stage a reading of a friend's play in the large barn on her husband's estate at Westport, Connecticut. The success of the reading of Philip Houston's *Painted Wagon* (1947) before a distinguished theatrical audience prompted the establishment of the White Barn Theatre, founded by Lucille Lortel to present theatrical productions with the emphasis on originality and quality, and to try out new plays "sheltered from premature exposure in the commercial theatre" (Interview, May 1985). During the first two seasons the presentations were no more than readings; but in 1949 Lortel, newly returned from a survey of theatre in Europe and captivated by the idea of the English Club theatre, remodeled the White Barn and mounted full productions of each play for a limited number of performances, a practice that has been continued each season. Since 1947 the White Barn has premièred scores of plays, among them Sean O'Casey's *Red Roses for Me* (1948), Eugène Ionesco's *The Chairs* (1957), John Whiting's *Saint's Day* (1957), Federico Garcia Lorca's *Blood Wedding* (1958), Archibald MacLeish's *The Music Crept by Me Upon the Waters* (1959), Langston Hughes's *Shakespeare in Harlem* (1959), Ukio Mishima's *Three Modern Japanese Noh Plays* (1960), Edward Albee's *Fam and Yam* (1960), Samuel Beckett's *Embers* (1960), Murray Schisgall's *The Typists* (1961), Athol Fugard's *Blood Knot* (1964), and Paul Zindel's *The Effects of Gamma Rays on Man-in-the-Moon Marigolds* (1966). Featured directors and performers have been Sidney Lumet, Gene Frankel, Eric Bentley, Zero Mostel, **Sada Thompson**, **June Havoc**, Milo O'Shea, Eva Marie Saint, **Kim Hunter**, Geoffrey Holder, and Rod Steiger.

In 1950 Lortel turned her attention to New York City and produced Christopher Fry's *A Sleep of Prisoners* (1951) at the St. James Protestant Episcopal Church on Madison Avenue. In 1955 she acquired her own New York base at the Theatre de Lys and began a long ownership of this Off-Broadway theatre—called by Brooks Atkinson the best stage in town—with Bertolt Brecht's *The Threepenny Opera* (1955–1961), starring Lotte Lenya. The production ran for seven years, winning an Antoinette Perry (Tony) Award for the best Off-Broadway show and the record for the longest running play in that theatre. To maintain her commitment to new and original playwrights, to actors and directors, Lortel began another significant contribution to New York theatre: the American National Theatre and Academy (ANTA) Matinee Series (1956–1975), held on Tuesday afternoons in the Theatre de Lys, enabling distinguished performers and those less well-known to try out roles they would not otherwise have a chance to play. New playwrights were also given the opportunity to see their works performed, and the theatregoing public to see experimental work often combining music, poetry, and dance. From the outset Lortel was determined the series should remain free of commercial influence. Her restless searching for fresh material and talent led her to meetings with the giants of European theatre: Sean O'Casey, Eugène Ionesco, Jean Genêt, and Samuel Beckett. By presenting some of their earliest American productions, the matinee series anticipated the influence these Europeans would have on the development of the American theatre in the 1960s and 1970s.

In its twenty-year history this innovative series welcomed a distinguished and talented collection of actors, among them, Helen Hayes, **Mary Morris**, Sybil Thorndyke, Lewis Casson, Cathleen Nesbitt, Richard Burton, Viveca Lindfors, Clarence Derwent, Siobhan McKenna, Anne Jackson, Estelle Parsons, **Marian Seldes**, and Anne Pitoniak. Many of the plays became Off-Broadway successes, including John Dos Passos's *USA* (1956), adapted by Paul Shyre, Anne Porter's *Pale Horse, Pale Rider* (1957), Langston Hughes's *Shakespeare in Harlem* (1959), George Tabori's *Brecht on Brecht* (1961), and Athol Fugard's *Hello and Goodbye* (1968). The extraordinary success of the ANTA Matinee Series was principally due to the single-mindedness of Lucille Lortel, her timing, her unerring instinct for the right material, her personal dynamism that drew so many talented people of the theatre to work for her without regard for monetary benefit, and her willingness to take risks. As she herself said in an interview for *Fifty Plus Magazine*, "If you love the theatre, you must be innovative. You must try new ideas and new faces. That's the only way the theatre can develop" (June 1980, p. 24).

Lortel has also achieved many successes as co-producer of award-winning shows, among them Sean O'Casey's *I Knock at the Door* (1957) and *Cock-A-Doodle-Dandy* (1958); Jean Genêt's *The Balcony* (1960); Athol Fugard's *Blood Knot* (1964); **Marsha Norman**'s *Getting Out* (1979); Sam Shepard's Pulitzer Prize-winning *Buried Child* (1979), Lanford Wilson's *Angels Fall* (1983); Samuel Beckett's *Ohio Impromptu, Catastrophe, What Where* (1983), and *Rockabye* (1984); and William T. Hoffman's *As Is*, nominated for a Tony Award as the best play of 1985. Some of these productions have been seen at the Library of Congress, where Lucille Lortel has been invited to make an annual presentation of a significant work, the latest being *Sprechen Sie Brecht?* (1985), a revue based on the writings of Bertolt Brecht and Kurt Weill. In 1988 Lortel produced, in association with American Playhouse Theater Productions and Yale Repertory Theater, Lee Blessing's two character play, *A Walk in the Woods*. The play was presented at the Booth Theater. Later it was presented in London, starring Sir Alec Guinness and Edward Herrmann, and in Moscow with the original Broadway cast.

In recognition of her contribution to the theatre Lucille Lortel has received many awards and honors, not only from her peers but from the City of New York and the world of academe. These include a *Village Voice* Off-Broadway (Obie) Award for "fostering and furthering the spirit of theatrical experiment" (1958); the Greater New York Chapter of ANTA Award in 1959, 1961, and

1962 for "pioneering work fostering playwrights, directors, and actors;" and the first **Margo Jones** Award (1962) for "significant contribution to the dramatic art and hitherto unproduced plays." In 1975 she was celebrated both by the city of New York and the League of Off-Broadway Theatres and Producers for her distinguished achievements; in 1979 she received the Villager Award for the longevity of her pioneering spirit; and in 1981 the Museum of the City of New York honored her with an exhibition proclaiming her the "Queen of Off-Broadway," a title given to her in 1962 by Richard Coe of the *Washington Post*. This exhibition was presented in an area of the museum that remains the Lucille Lortel Gallery, in permanent recognition of her contribution to the theatre. Most recently she received the first annual Lee Strasberg Lifetime Achievement in Theatre Award (1985), presented to her at a Gala Thirtieth Anniversary Celebration of the Theatre de Lys, renamed in 1981 the Lucille Lortel Theatre. Also in 1985, the University of Bridgeport honored her with a doctoral degree, and she established the Lucille Lortel Fund for New Writers at Yale Repertory Theatre. In 1988, she endowed the Lucille Lortel Chair in Theatre at The Graduate School of the City University of New York.

Lucille Lortel's enormous service to the contemporary theatre is summed up by John Willis in his dedication of the thiry-eighth volume of *Theatre World* (1981/1982): "To Lucille Lortel, whose vibrant spirit and untiring efforts have made immeasurable contributions to all components of the theatre by discovering and encouraging new talent, and whose devotion to Off-Broadway provided the impetus for its proliferation."

Most of the information in this biography was obtained in a personal interview with Lucille Lortel in New York, in May 1985. On that occasion she gave the author of this essay two privately published brochures, *Thirty Years of the White Barn Theatre* (n.d.) and *Twenty Years: Lucille Lortel's Matinee Series at the Theatre de Lys* (n.d.). These provide lists of plays, players, dates of performances, together with important statements of policy and artistic objectives. See also the periodicals *Fifty Plus* (June 1980), and *Stages* (April 1984). An interview with Lucille Lortel also appears in the *New York Times* (April 8, 1981). Lortel is listed in *The Biographical Encyclopaedia and Who's Who of the American Theatre* (1966); *Notable Names in the American Theatre* (1976); *Who's Who in the Theatre* (1981); and *Current Biography, 1985* (1985–1986).

Sam McCready

LUCE, Clare Boothe (April 10, 1903–October 9, 1987): playwright, author, and prominent public figure, was born in an apartment on Riverside Drive in New York City. Her father, William Franklin Boothe, an itinerant violinist, came from one of the older families in America. Her mother, Ann Clara Snyder, was the daughter of Bavarian immigrants and aspired to a career in the theatre. Because William Boothe was Baptist and Ann Snyder was Roman Catholic, both families disapproved of the marriage. Born of this union were David and Clare. As their families had feared, the marriage did not last; William Boothe, always a poor provider, left his family when Clare was eight.

Ann Snyder Boothe worked at whatever jobs she could find to earn a meager living for her children and herself. Despite hardship, she was determined that her son and daughter should better themselves. Her gifts to them were always books because she felt that knowledge, culture, and hard work were the keys to success. And she expected her children to succeed.

By 1914 Ann Snyder Boothe had made enough money to put her son into a military academy in Wisconsin and to take her daughter on a trip to Europe, where, living cheaply in Paris, they spent hours in the Louvre, went to operas, concerts, and the theatre. In 1915 Mrs. Boothe sent her daughter to the Cathedral School of St. Mary's (Episcopal) at Garden City, New York. From 1917 to 1919, Clare Boothe attended the Castle School in Tarrytown, New York. During those two happy years she avidly read the classics, studied French, and excelled as a swimmer and field hockey player. Upon graduation she had completed her formal education, the equivalent of secondary school. Because college was out of the question for financial reasons, Clare Boothe got a job in New York. When Ann Boothe married physician Albert Elmer Austin in 1919, her situation improved considerably; and Boothe's new stepfather invited her to accompany him and her mother on a trip to Europe, this time first class. Among the notable persons she met on this trip were **Jane Cowl**, the Barrymores, Otis Skinner, and Mrs. O. H. P. Belmont, who interested Clare in the Women's Party.

Through friends Clare Boothe met George Tuttle Brokaw, a wealthy New York bachelor more than twice her age. On August 10, 1923, they were married; and, a year later, Clare Brokaw gave birth to a daughter, Ann Clare. After six years, the marriage ended in divorce, and Clare Boothe set out to fulfill her dream of becoming a writer. She convinced editors at *Vogue* to hire her and in 1929 became an editorial assistant. Later, she moved on to *Vanity Fair* as associate editor and then managing editor. In 1935, the year Brokaw died, she married Henry R. Luce, president of *Time*, who was to become editor-in-chief of *Time-Life-Fortune*. In 1939 Clare Boothe Luce lost her mother in an automobile accident; in 1944 her daughter Ann, a student at Stanford University, was also killed in an automobile accident in Palo Alto, California, and in 1948, her brother David lost his life in a plane crash. But her marriage to Henry R. Luce lasted for thirty-two years, until his death in 1967.

Clare Boothe Luce made several attempts at acting and studied briefly at **Clare Tree Major**'s School of the Theatre in New York City. When she was a child, her mother had taken her to meet David Belasco, who hired her as an understudy to Mary Pickford. She also had played a bit role in a film. Again, in 1945, while a congresswoman, Luce appeared in *Candida* at the Stamford (Connecticut) Theatre to replace the star who was ill. But acting was the only venture she undertook at which she was unsuccessful. She had written several plays in her early years, including *O Pyramids* (1933), but her first to be produced on Broadway was *Abide With Me* (1935), a story of mental cruelty and murder. Theatrical success came when her third play, *The Women*, a satire on society women, opened in New York in December 1936, and ran for 657 performances. Made into a movie in 1939, it featured a host of well-known stars: Norma Shearer, Joan Crawford, Paulette Goddard, Rosalind Russell, **Mary Boland**, and others.

Adapted as a musical under the title of *Opposite Sex*, it was filmed again in 1956. *Kiss the Boys Goodbye* (1938), which she intended as a political allegory about fascism in America, was taken as a parody of the search for Scarlet O'Hara. First produced in 1938, it was adapted as a musical in 1941. In 1939 *Margin for Error*, a comedy-melodrama concerning the murder of a Nazi agent in the United States, was produced. It, too, was made into a film in 1943. Her movie about two nuns, *Come to the Stable* (1949), with **Celeste Holm** and Loretta Young, received an Academy (Oscar) Award nomination. Her play *Child of the Morning*, about a Brooklyn Catholic family whose daughter decides not to follow her family's plans for her life in the convent, was produced in 1951 and again in 1958.

Inspired by Henrik Ibsen's classic drama in which Nora Helmer slammed the door "that was heard around the world," Luce wrote the one-act *Slam the Door Softly*. The play, first titled *A Doll's House—1970*, was published in *Life* (October 16, 1970). In 1971, under the new title *Slam the Door Softly*, it was produced at the Mark Taper Forum, Los Angeles. The play is about the 1970s woman who has read Betty Friedan's *Feminine Mystique* and Simone de Beauvoir's *Second Sex*. Frustrated with having her husband think of her in terms of a female rather than as a person, she announces that she is leaving him. Neither heeding to nor comprehending her need to respect herself a little, he fails to persuade her that she cannot leave. "I'm not bursting with self-confidence, Thaw," she says. "I do love you. And I also need . . . a man. So I'm not slamming the door. I'm closing it . . . very . . . softly."

All but Luce's first play, *Abide With Me*, were written after her marriage to Henry Luce. Since he did not care for the theatre, she began to turn her attention more and more to politics and world affairs. In 1940 she wrote her second book, *Europe in the Spring*, and eventually gave up playwriting. She served twice as congresswoman from Connecticut and became the first woman to hold an important diplomatic post when she was appointed United States ambassador to Italy. She has been a newspaper columnist and a journalist, a war correspondent, the first woman on the House Military Affairs Committee, a regular contributor to journals and magazines, as well as an accomplished, sought-after public speaker. For her service to the nation and the world at large many honors and awards have been bestowed upon her.

Of the plays Clare Boothe Luce has written, she will be best remembered for *The Women*, the play that first won her acclaim as a playwright. Although many critics disliked the play for its shocking portrayal of women, it has been produced in eighteen foreign countries and translated into eleven languages. Over 250,000 women have played in performances of it. Her intention, said Luce, "was to satirize a very small, special group of rich, idle, social female parasites. My aim was to write a clinical, sober-sided, if impolite, genre study of Manhattan manners" (*Kiss the Boys Good-bye*, p. vii). However, her critics failed to see it that way. They viewed it as an attack on her sex and insisted that she had written a hilarious but wicked lampoon on all women.

Luce believed that women of her generation had "the most and the best." In an interview she said that "one cannot conceive of a greater time" (Interview, 1977). Her philosophy is perhaps best summarized in her comments to Marshall Berges: "My early disadvantages spurred me on to accept the challenges of life, to look for avenues of expression, to be the best I could be in whatever I tried. Coming as far as I have, I see each day's dawning as a triumph, with the curtain rising on a tremendously exciting show. I love every minute of it" (Berges, p. 12).

Clare Boothe Luce lived in Honolulu after Henry Luce died in 1967, traveling back and forth to the mainland to fulfill committee obligations and speaking engagements. She returned to Washington, D.C., in 1983 and lived at the Watergate Complex. She served for some time on President Reagan's unpaid Foreign Intelligence Advisory Board. She died on Ocober 9, 1987, at the age of eighty-four.

Information was supplied by Clare Boothe Luce in an interview at her Watergate apartment in Washington, D.C., in 1977. The biographies that give the fullest accounts of her life, she says, are full of inaccuracies which she has not bothered to correct. See Alden Hatch, *Ambassador Extraordinary—Clare Boothe Luce* (1956), and Stephen Shadegg, *Clare Boothe Luce: A Biography* (1970). Comments about her life, ideas, and career appear in her preface to *Kiss the Boys Goodbye* and in the numerous interviews she has given: Christopher P. Anderson, "Clare Luce, the Wicked Wit of Waikiki and Watergate, is Her Own Toughest Critic," *People* (July 25, 1977); Marshall Berges, "Clare Boothe Luce in Hawaii," *National Retired Teachers Association Journal* (July-August, 1979); and "What's Happening to America's Values: A Conversation with Clare Boothe Luce," *U. S. News and World Report* (June 24, 1974). Periodical and newspaper items are extensive, for example: Kris Sherman, "At 76, Clare Boothe Luce Still as Witty, Outspoken as Ever," *Cincinnati Enquirer* (November 21, 1979); and Betty Beale, "Inside Washington," *Cincinnati Enquirer* (November 26, 1978). Her ideas and opinions can be examined in her own articles, such as "Equality Begins at Home," *Saturday Evening Post* (October 1977), and "Is the New Morality Destroying America?" *Family Circle* (September 1976). Luce's obituary appeared in the *New York Times* on October 10, 1987. Luce is included in *Current Biography, 1953* (1954); *Twentieth Century Authors*, First Supplement (1955); *The Authors and Writers Who's Who* (1971); *American Authors and Books* (1972, under Boothe); *The McGraw-Hill Encyclopedia of World Drama*, Vol. I (1972, under Boothe); *Who's Who in America, 1972–1973*, Vol. I (1972); *Contemporary Authors*, Vols. 45–48 (1974); *Notable Names in the American Theatre* (1976); *American Women Writers* (1981); *The Oxford Companion to American Literature* (1983); and *The Oxford Companion to American Theatre* (1984).

Lucille M. Pederson

LYNN, Margaret E. ("Skippy") (April 28, 1924–): administrator, producer, director, actress, and originator of the worldwide Army Music and Theatre Program, was born Margaret Eleanor Linskie, one of the three children of John Joseph and Zoda (Dorsa) Linskie. Her mother, born in Palermo, Italy, migrated to Naples and then to America about 1886. John Linskie's parents were born and raised in counties Cork and Mayo in Ireland; he was born in America.

Margaret Lynn's sister, Dr. Rosella Linskie, an expert in education, served on General Douglas MacArthur's staff in Japan, performing so successfully that she was decorated by the Japanese government, and was subsequently recognized by Presidents John F. Kennedy and Lyndon B. Johnson for achievements in advancing international multicultural educational programs for the young. Margaret Lynn's brother, George Anthony Linskie, an engineer, has gained prominence throughout the Southwest for his work on many landmark buildings.

Originally intent upon a career as a concert pianist, Margaret Lynn took early training in dance and theatre as well as in music. She studied at Northwestern University in Evanston, Illinois, and Southern Methodist University in Dallas, Texas, receiving a Bachelor of Arts degree from SMU in 1942. In 1965, when SMU celebrated its fiftieth anniversary and inaugurated its "Women of Achievement" program, Margaret Lynn was selected as the woman of achievement to represent the decade of the 1940s. Following her graduation Lynn went to the Catholic University of America in Washington, D.C., studying under Walter Kerr and Alan Schneider, and earning a Master of Arts degree in speech and drama in 1943.

In the next few years, Margaret Lynn danced with the **Martha Graham** Company and appeared in seven Broadway shows, including *Oklahoma!* (1943), *Carousel* (1945), Michael Todd's *Mexican Hayride* (1944), and *Something for the Boys* (1943)—in which she performed the ingénue lead and understudied **Ethel Merman**. She was also a Rockette and dance captain at Radio City Music Hall. In 1945 she was chosen by **Peggy Wood** to be in the initial group of civilian actress technicians who went to work with army troops overseas. Under commanding officer and stage director Joshua Logan, she began creative work on the first of what would be dozens of productions for the military.

In 1947 she returned to the Department of the Army in Washington to prepare and conduct musical and theatrical workshops and programs planned to determine whether it would be appropriate and beneficial for the U.S. Army to hire civilian staff entertainment directors for bases in the United States. Her efforts led to the establishment thereafter of the worldwide Army Music and Theatre Program, which employs two-hundred full-time civilian directors and as many additional part-time directors and produces hundreds of plays and musical performances each year. Lynn herself conceived and directed productions during the Korean War, bringing entertainment, sometimes under artillery fire, to military personnel of various United Nations units involved in that conflict. Returning to the United States, she created for the Department of the Army a show called *Rolling Along*, which toured various parts of the world between 1955 and 1961. In 1962 she became director of the Army Music and Theatre Program worldwide.

In addition to the concept of "soldiers entertaining soldiers," Lynn stressed the benefits of including dependent wives and children actively in the performing arts and the desirability of involving civilians from nearby towns to counteract, where possible, the social isolation of service personnel working far from home. Under her guidance, numerous workshops, showcases, worldwide competitions, and scholarships were established to discover and encourage talented members of the military. Proscenium stages, "black box" theatre studios, and dinner theatres were established in unused army movie houses, barracks, and other surplus facilities, where colonels, corporals, and civilians created theatre together. Not content with makeshift "soldier shows," her directors produced variety bills, Broadway musicals, comedy, serious drama, and occasionally Shakespeare. The calibre and breadth of the army music and theatre activities from the 1950s into the 1980s are a tribute to Lynn and to the many professionals whom she involved, inspired, and supported at hundreds of installations at home and overseas.

In 1971 Walt Disney Productions "borrowed" Lynn from the Department of the Army to assist in arrangements for the World Symphony Orchestra, which brought together 145 musicians from 66 countries to perform concerts in New York City at Lincoln Center for the Performing Arts and the John F. Kennedy Center for the Performing Arts and to celebrate in Orlando, Florida, the opening of Walt Disney World. In 1982 she became general manager of the World Showcase Festival Program for the Disney organization. In this capacity Lynn brought more than 1,100 performing artists from 23 countries to Florida for the opening of the Walt Disney EPCOT Center (the Experimental Prototype Community of Tomorrow).

Lynn has lived and worked in more than two dozen foreign countries, has taught in more than a dozen foreign universities, has lectured widely, and has for many years given courses at the University of Virginia and Falls Church Regional Center. She is also a member of the board of directors of the National Theatre in Washington, D.C. She is founder of the Army Theatre Arts Association and has served as its president. She has been vice president for administration of the American Theatre Association (1979–1981) and executive director of that organization (1982–1986).

In the spring of 1985 Margaret Lynn was named general director of the Consortium of Nations for Cultural Exchange (CNCE). There are 126 member nations in CNCE, an organization that has grown out of the work that Lynn has done with these countries in connection with the International Seminars Program, the Walt Disney World, EPCOT Center, and the World Showcase Festival Program. CNCE sponsors activities to encourage cultural exchanges between nations.

Lynn has received numerous awards from the Department of the Army, including the Decoration for Meritorious Service from the Secretary of the Army. She has also been honored by the National Catholic Theatre Conference, the National Federation of Music Clubs, and the American Society of Composers, Authors, and Publishers, among others. She is the recipient of the Lioness Award of the Ethiopian Army, is an honorary member of both the Academy of the Olympians in Vicenza, Italy, and the International Theatre of Berlin, Germany, and is a Fellow of the American Theatre Association.

Margaret "Skippy" Lynn was the central force in developing for the United States Army what the *Washington Post* called "the largest producing organization of theatre and music in the world" (May 30, 1976)—an extensive program with hundreds of performing arts centers in far-flung parts of the world. Indeed, her efforts have provided, for many thousands of service personnel, artistic experiences far beyond those they might have known at home. Lynn's program and her encouragement aided many participants to move on to distinguished professional success in theatre and music.

An interview with Margaret Lynn and a description of the Army program that she developed are given by Richard L. Coe in "Theatre On the Front," the *Washington Post* (May 30, 1976). Extensive documentation is available in the Margaret E. Lynn Army Music and Theatre Collection at the New York Public Library Performing Arts Research Center at Lincoln Center. She is included in *Who's Who of American Women, 1968– 1969* (1967).

Donn B. Murphy

— M —

MAJOR, Clare Tree (c. 1880–October 9, 1954): outstanding entrepreneur of children's theatre, producer, director, educator, and playwright, was born in London, England, into a famous theatrical family. She trained for the theatre at the Royal Academy of Dramatic Art (RADA) and worked thereafter for a time with the company run by her relative, Sir Herbert Beerbohm-Tree. By the time she emigrated to the United States in 1914, she had been married, had borne a daughter, and had been widowed. The next year she became associated with the Washington Square Players in New York City, who in 1916 asked her to direct their newly founded school. Opening in October of 1916, the dramatic school ran in conjunction with the Players' repertory season, its pupils receiving training plus small parts with the company to enhance their theatre experience. Major's work with the dramatic school led to her interest in the need for theatrical experiences, in both performance and entertainment, for New York City's young people.

In 1921 Major formed her own company, the Threshold Players, for the express purpose of promoting quality theatre for young audiences. This company worked first in the theatre of the Heckscher Foundation on Fifth Avenue, then at the Princess Theatre, and finally in its own space on 34th Street. It was in this company that the most noteworthy accomplishments of those early years took place. Major's initial theatrical successes were adaptations of such works as *Treasure Island*, *Hansel and Gretel*, and *Pinocchio*, performed on a subscription basis for audiences who paid twenty-five cents a seat. In this way Major's early theatre for young audiences flourished. She was not the first to offer children's plays by a professional company in New York, but she certainly became one of the most successful. Significantly, she was the first to prove that theatre for children could be a profit-making venture. Her work in the 1930s stimulated others to follow her example and to aim quality professional theatre at a new, younger set of theatregoers.

In 1923 the Threshold Players became officially the Clare Tree Major Children's Theatre, and in 1928 Major added a new and amazingly successful feature. In that year she inaugurated a season of touring shows to augment the regular theatrical season in New York. In so doing she became the first entrepreneur to establish a touring theatrical company devoted to performing for young audiences. No one previously had risked such a venture, and few have done so since with such success. The general procedures employed by the Major acting company called for up to six touring shows, each sent out separately, following each other into cities at four-to five-week intervals. Eventually each city on the schedule would have the opportunity to view all of that season's offerings. Saturday was normally used for performances in large cities and weekdays for smaller towns. The four to six acting troupes toured the country from October to May with the entire operation overseen by Major. By 1938, the fifteenth year of the Clare Tree Major Children's Theatre, the company headquarters had been moved out of New York City to the more spacious environs of Chappaqua, New York; and the tours had been expanded for the first time to include performances on the West Coast, western Canada, and the Southwest. That year also witnessed Major's unique promotional tie-in with the community booksellers of each city in which the troupes were to appear. Through this ingenious advertising ploy, Clare Tree Major's name was spread across America. This self-proclaimed "World's Foremost Authority on Theatre for Children" had, because of this and other solid promotional practices, no trouble filling auditoriums with enthusiastic juveniles and their parents. In the 1930s and early 1940s, while many other financial ventures were collapsing or barely breaking even, Major expanded her successful company and its operation to far greater proportions than could have been dreamed of ten years earlier.

The prosperity achieved by Major and her disciplined, artistic repertory companies during the late 1920s and through the 1930s allowed her to expand operations once again in the 1940s. She added a National Classic Theatre wing which, as another touring arm of the Major company, performed works for students on high school and college stages. Concerned more and more with the training of future performers, she opened the National Academy of Theatre Arts in Pleasantville, New York. Reminiscent of the relationship of the old Washington Square dramatic school curricula, this new National Academy offered students a two-year course of study to prepare for professional theatre work in her company and elsewhere. A secondary summer program also offered theatrical training for educators. Meanwhile, the touring companies continued. By the late 1940s, seven companies were touring seven plays: *Alice in Wonderland*, *The Sleeping Beauty*, *Robin Hood*, *Penrod*, *Heidi*, *Hans Brinker*, and *Mrs. Wiggs of the Cabbage Patch*. From Maine to California the name of Clare Tree Major meant the best in professional theatre for children. It would remain so until her death in 1954.

Clare Tree Major was twice married. Her first husband died in England before she came to America. Her second husband, theatrical manager John Kenderdine (who was as supportive and energetic in Major's cause as she), worked with the theatre throughout its existence; her daughter, Dorothy, also worked with the theatre group. All who came within the aura of Clare Tree Major, whether they were family or employees, were indelibly marked by the woman's personality and demeanor. Some of her former actors called her "the Queen Mother," and almost all freely admitted being afraid of her. She had absolute power over her companies.

In addition to her touring activities, Clare Tree Major developed several scripts for children's theatre. In the early days of the company, Major quickly recognized the problem of the existing lack of quality children's plays and, to remedy this situation, adapted scripts to suit her production needs. The majority of her plays were adaptations of classic children's stories, wholesome fare meant both to stimulate and entertain the young people coming to view them. The *New York Times* (October 9, 1954) characterized them as "swift moving, full of action, and vivid characterization. There is utter sincerity, much humor, no terror, and few tears, except pleasant ones easily dried." Classics of the American theatre, however, they were not. They were consciously penned as intelligent drama for an intelligent, though young, group of theatre patrons.

The Clare Tree Major Theatrical Enterprises, as her company became known, closed upon her death in 1954. During its last season much of the organizational management had been transferred to her daughter, Dorothy, because of Major's failing health. When Clare Tree Major, the "Queen Mother" of professional American children's theatre, died on October 9, 1954, she had given thirty-one of her seventy-four years to the promotion and execution of quality drama for an audience all but ignored before her coming. Her uncompromising vision and tireless work brought children's theatre to a new height; she has been the model studied and imitated by others in the field of professional children's theatre.

For an introduction to the life, work, and impact of Major, see Nellie McCaslin's *Theatre for Children in the United States: A History* (1971). Two short but useful *Children's Theatre Review* articles by Michael W. Gamble are "An Analysis of the Playwriting Techniques of Clare Tree Major" (1977), and "Clare Tree Major's Popular Traveling Theatre for Children" (1978). The most complete study of Major and her theatre is Michael W. Gamble's "Clare Tree Major: Children's Theatre, 1923–1954" (Unpublished Ph.D. dissertation, New York University, 1976). Major herself published several articles including "Children's Theatre," *New York State Education* (October 1934), and three articles in the *Columbia University Institute of Arts and Sciences Magazine*: "A Children's Theatre at Columbia" (October 1929), "A Saturday Morning Children's Theatre" (May 1929), and "Playing Theatre" (February 1931). See also her "Child's Play," *Theatre Arts Monthly* (October 1952). For further insight into Major's playmaking, consult *Playing Theatre: Six Plays For Children*, edited by Clare Tree Major (1930). The Clare Tree Major Theatre Collection, containing correspondence, manuscripts, and Major's theatre memorabilia, is housed within the Theatre Collection of the New York Public Library

Performing Arts Research Center at Lincoln Center. Major is listed in *The Oxford Companion to American Theatre* (1984).

                                                                      Douglas Street

MALECZECH, Ruth (January 8, 1938–): stage and film actress, director, recording artist, founding member of the Mabou Mines Company, was born Ruth Sophia Reinprecht to Yugoslavian immigrant parents, Frank Reinprecht and Elizabeth (Maletich) Reinprecht. Maleczech was the eldest in a family of four children. When she was eight, her family moved to Phoenix, Arizona, to help her father overcome a bronchial disability contracted from working in the steel industry in Ohio. From that age also, Maleczech dates her ambition to become a performer. She is the only member of her immediate family to have entered the arts.

Graduating from Phoenix's Camelback High School in 1956, Maleczech entered the University of California at Los Angeles where she majored in theatre while working to pay for tuition, room, and board. Maleczech appeared in *The Crucible* in her second year, and in productions mounted in 3K7, a theatre in which all productions were written, directed, performed, and managed by students. Maleczech regards this early understanding that a theatre artist could control her own work as having helped shape her later career with the Mabou Mines collaborative. At the University of California at Los Angeles Maleczech met her future collaborator and husband Lee Breuer. In 1958 Maleczech (still using her maiden name Ruth Reinprecht) and Breuer moved to San Francisco where for the next six years she experimented with a wide variety of theatrical training and performance styles. She studied commedia dell'arte, French pantomime, and American comic mime with R. G. Davis of the R. G. Davis (later San Francisco) Mime Troupe, becoming a member of its second company and performing in both original and commedia dell'arte works. In this period she also worked at the San Francisco Actors' Workshop with directors Jules Irving and Herbert Blau, where she was exposed to European classical and experimental theatre, performing the Ballad Singer's Wife in Bertolt Brecht's *Galileo* (1961), Dame Pliant in Ben Jonson's *The Alchemist* (1962), and Martirio in Garcia Lorca's *The House of Bernarda Alba* (1963). At the Interplayers (another theatre group) she played Emily in *Our Town* (1960) and the Medium in *Rashomon* (1962).

Perhaps Maleczech's most fruitful San Francisco association, from the point of view of her later accomplishments as a founder of the American performance art movement, was with the San Francisco Tape Music Center, which was beginning at this time to experiment with forms of mixed media performance. She studied there with dancer Anna Halprin and made other important artistic associations. There in 1962 Maleczech performed in an improvised experimental ensemble theatre piece, *Event for Actors*, directed by Breuer. Co-performers were her future Mabou Mines collaborators **JoAnne Akalaitis** and Bill Raymond. In 1963 Maleczech performed the role of Solange in a production of Jean Genêt's

The Maids, directed by Lee Breuer, with settings by painter Judy Raphael and music composed and performed by William Spencer. This production of *The Maids* for the first time combined conceptual daring with freedom from textual linearity. These were to become characteristic of Maleczech's later undertakings. The next year she performed in an original work by Lee Breuer, *The Run*, which incorporated an animal puppet created by sculptor Bill Hamm and projections designed by Elias Romero.

In late 1964 Maleczech gave her final performance in San Francisco as the Countess Geschwitz in *Lulu*, a linking of Frank Wedekind's two Lulu plays: *Earth Spirit* and *Pandora's Box*, directed by Lee Breuer. Shortly thereafter Maleczech departed for Europe with Breuer, where she was to stay for the next five years. It was in Europe that Maleczech chose her professional name (meaning "little Czech"). After nine months in Greece, Maleczech and Breuer traveled to Paris, where Maleczech was cast in an English-language production of LeRoi Jones's *Dutchman*. As a result of this performance she was hired to do English dubbing of French films, which provided a living. JoAnne Akalaitis and the British actor David Warrilow collaborated on Samuel Beckett's work titled *Play*, at the American Centre. This collaboration, with Breuer directing and Philip Glass providing a musical score, marked the beginning of one of the most prolific and enduring partnerships in contemporary American theatre history. Out of it the Mabou Mines collaborative was founded in 1970.

Her observation of great performers has influenced Maleczech's work. At the University of California at Los Angeles she saw the Greek actress Astasia Papaphanasiou perform with the Greek National Theatre. In 1967 she and Breuer traveled to East Berlin to observe rehearsals and performances at the Berliner Ensemble, where she was deeply impressed by the acting of the premier Brecht actor, Ekkehardt Schall. They returned to Paris to mount a production of *Mother Courage and Her Children*, in which Maleczech played the mute Katrin and David Warrilow played the Chaplain. Future Mabou Mines collaborator Frederick Neumann also performed. The following year Maleczech, Neumann, Warrilow, and Breuer collaborated on a group dialectic theatre work based on Brecht's *Messingkauf Dialogues*, Antonin Artaud's *The Theatre and its Double*, and Constantin Stanislavsky's *An Actor Prepares*. This piece, called *The Messingkauf Dialogues*, was performed at the Traverse Theatre Club on the Fringe at the Edinburgh Festival in 1968.

A seminal influence on Maleczech's acting was Jerzy Grotowski, with whom she and JoAnne Akalaitis studied in Aix-en-Provence in 1969. Afterwards, Maleczech traveled with Breuer and Warrilow to see Grotowski's Laboratory Theatre in Wroclaw, Poland, where Ryszard Cieslak, the company's principal actor, made an indelible impression on her. Shortly afterwards, in September 1969, Maleczech gave birth to her and Lee Breuer's first child, a daughter when they called Clove 333 Galilee Breuer.

In December 1969, Maleczech, Breuer, and Warrilow came to New York at the invitation of JoAnne Akalaitis and Philip Glass. In 1970 Maleczech, Akalaitis, and Warrilow presented the first of the Mabou Mines animal-metaphor theatre pieces, the *Red Horse Animation*, written and directed by Lee Breuer with sound score by Glass. This work was to set the pattern for the narrative and lyric Mabou Mines works of performance poetry that were to follow for the next several years. The first version of this short piece, made from Muybridge's *Animals in Motion*, and influenced by Grotowskian ideas of physical performance, was given at the Paula Cooper Gallery in the spring of 1970. As an immediate result, the group was invited to join La Mama Experimental Theatre Club as a resident company, where it presented revised versions of the Paris production of Beckett's *Play*, *Come and Go*, and other works.

In the summer of 1970 the group went to Nova Scotia to complete the *Red Horse Animation*, formally adopting the name of the town, Mabou Mines, as their company name. As a La Mama resident company, the group performed principally in museums and galleries over the next few seasons, presenting *Red Horse Animation* and, with a larger group of performers, the *B. Beaver Animation*. In the early 1970s as well, the group participated in various performance art collaborations, such as *The Saint and the Football Players* at Pratt Institute, Brooklyn, in 1974.

In the summer of 1975 Maleczech's and Breuer's son, Lute Ramblin' Breuer, was born. Shortly afterwards, in the fall of 1975, Mabou Mines burst upon the New York Theatre scene with its program, ''Mabou Mines Performs Samuel Beckett,'' consisting of *Play*, *Come and Go*, and *The Lost Ones*, presented at the Theatre for the New City. The group won its first *Village Voice* Off-Broadway (Obie) Award for this production in 1976. Impressed by these performances, Joseph Papp, in 1976, invited Mabou Mines to take up residence at The Public Theatre, where a succession of now legendary theatre pieces followed for the next seven years. Maleczech performed in five of these: *Dressed Like an Egg*, based on the works of Colette, and the *B. Beaver Animation* in 1977; the *Shaggy Dog Animation* in 1978; *Dead End Kids* in 1980, in which Maleczech played Mme. Curie; and the performance poem *Hajj*, with Maleczech as the solo performer. Breuer wrote and directed the *Animations* and *Hajj*, and Akalaitis directed the other productions. In the 1982–1983 season, Maleczech won her first Obie award in the ''Best Performance'' category for *Hajj*, and another ''Best Performance'' in the Downtown Theatre Awards given by *The Villager*.

In 1978 Maleczech and writer-producer Lee Breuer married, celebrating their personal and professional relationship of two decades. The following year they founded the experimental theatre workshop, Re.Cher.Chez. From her work there with Beverly Brown emerged Maleczech's direction at the Theatre for the New City in January 1980 of *Vanishing Pictures*, based on an Edgar Allan Poe story, for which Maleczech shared an Obie Award in design with Julie Archer. In 1981, at the Public Theatre, Maleczech directed her first major production, *Wrong Guys*, based on the novel by Jim Strahs, a production notable for its spare but sophisticated visual scheme using screens, strings, and incandescent light bulbs. For this production Maleczech won the Best Director Award from *The Villager*.

In 1984 Maleczech directed a theatrical adaptation at the Performing Garage of Beckett's 12-minute prose piece *Imagination Dead Imagine*, which represented the first theatrical use of large-scale holography.

In recent years Maleczech has emerged increasingly as a film and stage performer in dramatic roles. In 1979 she appeared in Richard Foreman's film *Strong Medicine*, and in 1982 she played the part of Anna in Jill Godmilow's *Far From Poland*. In 1983 she appeared as Mrs. Malone in the Hollywood film *C.H.U.D.* and performed in the film version of *Dead End Kids*, written and directed by JoAnne Akalaitis. In 1984 Maleczech created the role of Annette (Martha in the German original) in Franz Xaver Kroetz's *Through the Leaves*, directed by JoAnne Akalaitis and co-produced by the Women's Interart Theatre and Mabou Mines. For this stylized, mask-like, yet naturalistic portrayal of Kroetz's female butcher Maleczech again won the Obie Award for best performance.

Maleczech launched a recording collaboration with actress-director Valeria Wasilewki in which they perform as The Android Sisters. The Android Sisters speak the text for the award-winning animated film *Boomtown*. Their first record release was made by Vanguard in 1984. Maleczech and Wasilewki are co-producing and co-directing *The Censorship Project*, a Chinese opera about censorship in America as seen through the eyes of members of the court of the Emperor Ch'in in 210 B.C. In 1986 Maleczech appeared in Franz Xaver Kroetz's *Help Wanted*, directed by JoAnne Akalaitis and presented by the Mabou Mines at Theatre for the New City.

In 1987 Maleczech appeared with David Warrilow at the Brooklyn Academy of Music's Majestic Theatre in *Zangezi*, a 1923 futurist drama by Velimir Khlebnikov. Also in 1987 Maleczech tried one of her most unusual acting roles by playing Lear in the gender-crossed adaptation of Shakespeare's great tragedy. The play, adapted by Lee Breuer and featuring members of the Mabou Mines troupe, was set in the American South in the 1950s. *Lear* premiered at the George Street Playhouse in New Brunswick, New Jersey, before moving to the Theatre Institute at Storm King.

In February 1989 Maleczech's multimedia musical, *Sueños*, opened at the Triplex Theatre in Manhattan. Using words from some of Latin America's most famous writers and images from the contemporary Mexican painter Eduardo Carillo, *Sueños* explores the effects of dictatorship and patriarchy in Latin America during the 17th and 18th centuries. The work was adapted and directed by Maleczech and was a production of the Mabou Mines troupe and INTAR Hispanic American Arts Center, in association with Boston Musica Viva.

Maleczech has taught workshops in experimental theatre techniques for actors, directors, and playwrights at colleges and theatre centers all over the country and in Europe. In addition she has toured extensively both in the United States and abroad, including the Festival d'Automne in Paris, the Nancy Festival, the Adelaide Festival, and the Toga-Mura International Theatre Festival in Japan. During the Humana Festival of New American Plays presented by the Actors

Theatre of Louisville, Ruth Maleczech was named the 1989 recipient of the Zeisler Award for distinguished achievement in the nonprofit professional theatre.

Maleczech has been in the forefront of the first generation of American experimental theatre artists to expand the art of theatre into a new art of performance incorporating many artistic disciplines, popular and traditional. Yet the work retains the psychological and humanistic coloring that sets it apart as theatre. Her work, like that of others in the movement, combines a broad range of non-American classical and avant-garde performance techniques with diverse American influences. In turn, her generation of American experimental theatre artists is the first to make a significant impact beyond American borders. Within this movement a number of creative women have shifted their emphasis almost wholly to directing, but Maleczech has retained a primary commitment to performance and has emerged in recent years as a leading actress of the American experimental theatre.

Useful for additional information about Ruth Maleczech are Kathleen Helser, "Ruth Maleczech: Pushing the Limits," *American Theatre* (September 1986); "Parallel Fantasies," an interview with Alisa Solomon, *Village Voice* (October 2, 1984); Don Shewey, "The Many Voices of Mabou Mines," *American Theatre* (June 1984); Don Shewey, "Mining New Media," *American Film* (January-February 1983); Ross Wetzsteon, "New Directors," *New York Magazine* (February 23, 1981); John Howell, "Performance in the Theatre, Performance in the Art World," *Performance Arts Magazine* (1980); and "Acting/Nonacting," an interview with John Howell, *Performance Arts Magazine* (1979). Arthur Holmberg contrasts Lee Breuer's *Lear* with Tadashi Suzuki's *The Tale of Lear* in "The Liberation of Lear" in *American Theatre* (July/August 1988).

Elinor Fuchs

MALINA, Judith (June 4, 1926–): co-founder of The Living Theatre, director, producer, and actress, was born in Kiel, Germany, the daughter of Max and Rosel (Zamora) Malina. She moved to the United States with her parents when she was three. Her father was a rabbi and her mother had been an actress. At seventeen, when she met actor and director Julian Beck, Malina already knew she wanted to be an actress. She and the former Yale University student and painter shared an intense involvement with theatre and the allied arts. In 1945 Malina enrolled in the Dramatic Workshop at the New School for Social Research, where she studied directing and acting for two years with Erwin Piscator. Malina and Beck married in 1948, one year after they had chosen to name their future collective "The Living Theatre." They had two children, Garrick and Isha Manna. Their collaboration was unbroken until Beck's death in New York City on September 14, 1985.

From the outset, Malina and Beck committed themselves to nontraditional, anti-establishment, avant-garde theatre which soon incorporated pacifist and politically revolutionary concepts. For them, theatre was life and life was theatre. After presenting a bill of one-acts in their living room, they moved their ensemble to the Cherry Lane Theatre in Greenwich Village, opening in 1951 with Gertrude Stein's *Dr. Faustus, Light the Lights*. Plays by Alfred Jarry, Bertolt Brecht,

Garcia Lorca, and others followed until the New York City Fire Department closed their building in 1952. In 1954 they opened again in a basement in Wooster Street, where they played until 1959, moving in that year to a converted second-floor loft on 14th Street, where they had their first sensational success with Jack Gelber's *The Connection*. Trouble with the city authorities and the Internal Revenue Service caused them to move to Europe in 1964. From that time forward, the Living Theatre has been itinerant, playing in many cities in Europe, in South America, and returning occasionally to New York.

The anarchist/pacifist philosophies of Malina and Beck have been a central part of their theatre from the beginning, and have involved the group in skirmishes with various authorities, including a famous imprisonment for tax evasion in 1964. Malina served thirty days in Passaic County Jail and Beck sixty days in Danbury Federal Penitentiary. Malina was involved in the earliest protests against nuclear proliferation and was often arrested for taking part in pacifist demonstrations, including those against civil defense exercises. In the late sixties, Malina and Beck began to incorporate forms of political activism into their theatre work, in order to generate militancy in their audience to direct viewers. Malina and Beck combined political commitment with a keen interest in the avant-garde, including artists like John Cage, William Carlos Williams, Jackson MacLow, and Merce Cunningham. The earliest Living Theatre productions in the Malina/Beck living room and at the Cherry Lane Theatre featured scripts with strong poetic language, experimental and/or abstract structures, and improvisatory possibilities. Malina directed most of the productions and acted in many, including Jean Racine's *Phaedra*, which she also translated. Beck designed most of the productions, and directed occasionally.

The Living Theatre's productions of *The Connection* by Jack Gelber (1959) and *The Brig* by Kenneth Brown (1963), both of which Malina directed, were two of their most controversial and characteristic works from this early period. In *The Connection* Malina began to explore actors playing themselves—the deliberate breaking down of actor/character distinctions. Because the play deals with jazz musicians (real) and drug addicts, reality and fiction are blended. Malina explains, "When a jazz musician plays his music, he enters into *personal* contact with the public; when he goes home after he has played, one who talks to him knows that there is no difference between the way he is now and the way he was on stage. . . . *The Connection* represented a very important advance for us in this respect: from then on, the actors began *to play themselves*," (*The Living Theatre*, p. 48. The emphasis is Malina's). For *The Brig*, which is about intolerable oppression inside a Marine prison, Malina developed a rehearsal discipline approximating some of the techniques of depersonalization which appear in the play. She insisted on strict attendance and punctuality. Actors could not talk to each other except about the rehearsal work, could not eat during rehearsal time, could not wear clothes of their own choice. Punishment in the form of chores was meted out for infractions. Howard Taubman called Malina's ultrarealism a "painful evening in the theatre," predicting that the audience members would have nightmares about the white lines over which the prisoners could not step without permission or punishment (*New York Times*, May 16, 1963).

After 1964, when the Living Theatre moved to Europe, Malina did not return to the United States until the 1968–1969 tour (except for a three-month prison term resulting from the 1963 trial). The repertory of the company's American tour included *Mysteries and Smaller Pieces* and *Paradise Now* (both developed by the company collectively) and *Frankenstein* and *Antigone* (reworked by the company from extant plays). The major innovation of this period was the development of their own scripts, which were frequently collages drawn from many sources. *Antigone* was the most "traditional" of the pieces, based on the *Modellbuch* for Bertolt Brecht's *Antigone*, translated by Malina and interpreted by the company. In The Living Theatre production the auditorium was always designated Argos, so that the audience became implicated in the action, treated as the Argive enemies. Of all the productions in the 1968–1969 American tour, *Paradise Now* received the most attention. Notoriety came in part from the second performance of *Paradise Now* at Yale University, where Beck, Malina, and several others were arrested on charges of indecent exposure (they were later acquitted). Partly, *Paradise Now* was also sensational because it involved the audience in direct action; in this case the company led the audience into the street for a celebration of "Paradise Now."

In 1970, after returning to Europe, the group split into four "cells" to do theatre in a variety of places and with different objectives. Specifically, The Living Theatre now found theatre buildings confining. Malina was also concerned about reaching a wider population, not just bourgeois and homogeneous theatre audiences. The need for a greater unity between their art and their politics took the company to Brazil in 1971, where they attempted to play in various small villages for the native people.

The Living Theatre returned to the United States in September 1971 and spent the next two years working on *The Destruction of the Money Tower*, part of a projected cycle of 150 plays titled *The Legacy of Cain*. These plays were intended for performance in various public environments such as parks, factories, schools, and hospitals. *Money Tower* was performed on a 20-foot by 20-foot, five-level pyramid with a green neon dollar sign on top. Different social classes inhabited the levels, beginning with the poorest and most oppressed on the bottom and ending with corporate magnates at the top. The play developed through 726 rehearsals in Vermont and Brooklyn in a semi-leaderless rehearsal process where the company participated in the development of the script (*Village Voice*, April 21, 1975). Other pieces dating from this period include *Six Public Acts* and *Seven Meditations on Political Sado-Masochism*. After a series of performances during ten months in Pittsburgh, Malina returned to Europe with her company, settled in Rome, and continued to work on pieces for public places and heterogeneous audiences.

After 1975 The Living Theatre developed two major new pieces for traditional theatre spaces: *Prometheus at the Winter Palace* and Ernst Toller's *Masse Mensch*. Malina had first read *Masse Mensch* while studying with Piscator at the New School: she had wanted to do the play since 1945. "It is a play that has always been an ideal for me because the central figure is a woman who is both anarchistic, pacifistic, and politically committed...." (Interview with Mark Amitin, *Performing Arts Journal, 14*, Vol. V, no. 2 [August 1980], p. 31).

When the Living Theatre returned to New York in 1984, they brought four pieces including *Masse Mensch*. In addition to reviving *Antigone*, they presented *The Archeology of Sleep*, which investigated the process of dreaming; and *The Yellow Methuselah*, a kind of synthesis between George Bernard Shaw and Vassily Kandinsky. While the work of the group has always been highly controversial, New York critics were almost entirely inhospitable to the new repertory, criticizing The Living Theatre for repeating themselves, often with what appeared to be a poorly trained company. The cool American response led to the company's decision to live abroad again. However, after 15 years of commuting from country to country, Judith Malina and Julian Beck themselves moved back to a West End Avenue apartment on Manhattan's upper West Side. Beck appeared in the film *The Cotton Club* (1984) shortly before his death.

Malina insists that the Living Theatre is now in New York to stay, even though they do not have a permanent home. To support herself and to subsidize new works, Malina often teaches and directs in Europe. In 1988 she directed a new opera, *Kassandra*, at the Frankfurt Opera in Germany. She also worked on a play with the students of Bologna University in Italy. In New York she directed **Karen Malpede's** *Us* at the Theatre for the New City. This was the first scripted American play that she had directed for the Living Theatre since *The Brig* in 1963. Once again, the Living Theatre stirred controversy over the play's eroticism, its showing of domestic and sexual violence, and its suggestions of the possibility of nuclear war. After the short run of *Us*, Malina and the Living Theatre began work on *Poland 1931*, a play based on the poetry of Jerome Rothenberg and adapted by Hanon Reznikov. One of Malina's most recent projects is the directing of a new play by Elsa Lasker-Schuler at LaMama ETC. *Ich und Ich (I and I)* is about the division of the self and is set in Hell. Washington, D. C.'s Living Stage Theatre Company received a small grant from the National Endowment for the Arts Theatre Program to support the production of *I and I* at their theatre during the 1988–1989 season. Malina and Hanon Reznikov are scheduled to direct.

Judith Malina has won two *Village Voice* Off-Broadway (Obie) awards, one in 1969 for best actress for her performance of the title role in Brecht's *Antigone* and one in 1975 for her lifetime achievement in the theatre. In 1985 Malina was made a Guggenheim Fellow.

Malina's working methods reveal themselves in the myriad of sketches and charts she uses to clarify various concepts for The Living Theatre productions.

Sometimes she sketches groupings of actors for particular moments or scenes; sometimes she makes a detailed chart or map for an entire production. These sketches serve to clarify both the ideas informing the productions and the visual images she will use. Her manner of working with actors has always allowed maximum freedom while still achieving precision. Beck has described her work as follows: "Judith's directing, which includes most of the plays, has exceptional precision, in my opinion. I am quite imaginative and have lots of ideas, but I do not have Judith's eye for focusing rightly on the beats of the matter" (*The Living Theatre*, p. 34). Over the years, Malina has sought to play down her role as director in keeping with her commitment to anarchism and leaderless creation. But her leadership is always evident, even in a note urging the company to be (in essence) its own director: "Listen during rehearsal for what is unfinished. FIND OUT BY YOURSELF what work is needed. WORK OUT FOR YOUR-SELF how to consolidate and organize for this work. If you do it by yourself, it will be more profound" (*Yale/Theatre*, Spring 1969, p. 131).

Judith Malina's work is most remarkable for the combination of intellectual leadership with creative talent within the context of a theatre collective—The Living Theatre. She does much of the meticulous research which goes into the company's pieces, often translating or adapting particular texts. For over thirty years she has maintained as actress, producer, and director continual aesthetic experimentation guided by a deep political commitment to nonviolent revolutionary change.

Several books are available on The Living Theatre, including Pierre Biner's *The Living Theatre* (2nd edition, 1970), which gives the history of the troupe through the 1968 American tour. See Renfreu Neff, *The Living Theatre/USA* (1970), *The Diaries of Judith Malina 1947–1957* (1984), and James Roose-Evans, *Experimental Theatre from Stanislavsky to Peter Brook* (1984). Also see *We, The Living Theatre*, by Aldo Rostagno and Gianfranco Mantegna with Julian Beck and Judith Malina (1970). *Yale/Theatre* (Spring 1969) is a special issue on The Living Theatre. Rachel Koenig's "Malina Steers New Path for the Living Theatre" in *American Theatre* (March 1988) discusses Malina's recent activities. Published scripts are available for various productions, including *The Connection*, *The Brig*, *Paradise Now*, and *Frankenstein*. Many of the recent scripts have been published in journals. *The Destruction of the Money Tower* appears in *The Drama Review* (June 1974), and *Prometheus* appears in *Performing Arts Journal, 14*, Vol. V, no. 2 (August 1980). Video tapes are also available of *The Connection*, *The Brig*, *Paradise Now*, and *Signals Through The Flames* (a documentary about the company). *Village Voice* has followed the Living Theatre over the years and provides the best source of popular critical reactions. Malina is listed in *The Biographical Encyclopaedia and Who's Who of the American Theatre* (1966), *Notable Names in the American Theatre* (1976), and *Who's Who in the Theatre* (1981). The Living Theatre (Malina and Beck) is listed in *The Oxford Companion to the Theatre* (1983) and *The Oxford Companion to American Theatre* (1984).

Janelle Reinelt

MALPEDE, Karen (June 29, 1945–): playwright and author of other works, was born in Wichita Falls, Texas, to Joseph James Malpede and Doris Jane (Liebschutz) Malpede. She has a twin brother, John David Malpede, who is a performance artist and a carpenter. When she was six months old the family moved to Illinois; she grew up in Evanston and Wilmette. Her father, who was from an Italian mining family, earned his living as an accountant. He died of cancer. Her maternal grandmother, Myrtle Liebschutz, had been an actress in Chicago. Her mother, Doris Jane Liebschutz, also an actress, had her own radio show in Chicago.

Karen Malpede obtained a Bachelor of Science degree with Honors in 1967 from the University of Wisconsin, Madison, and a Master of Fine Arts in 1971 from Columbia University's School of the Arts, Theatre Arts Division, in theatre history and criticism. She now lives with Burl Hash, producer-director and co-founder of The New Cycle Theatre in Brooklyn, for which her plays constitute the principal repertoire. Their daughter, Carrie Sophia Malpede-Hash, was born on January 20, 1980, in New York City.

Karen Malpede has written three books on theatre. Her first, *People's Theatre in Amerika*, with a preface by John Howard Lawson (1972), is a study of the radical theatre movement in America. Her second, *Three Works by the Open Theatre* (1974), edited with an introduction by Malpede and director's notes by Joseph Chaikin, provides an analysis of works by the Open Theatre; and her third, *Women in Theatre; Compassion and Hope* (1983), edited with a special introduction by Malpede, is an anthology of collected writings by Augusta Gregory, **Gertrude Stein**, Ellen Terry, Barbara Ann Teer, and **Rosamond Gilder**.

In 1981 Malpede was the recipient of a P.E.N. Writer's Grant to finish a work-in-progress, and a Creative Artists Public Service (CAPS) Award for playwriting in 1982–1983. She has taught at various colleges, but is primarily known as the co-founder and playwright for the New Cycle Theatre in Brooklyn, New York. Malpede is also a co-founder of the Woman's Salon in New York City in 1975 and member of the P.E.N. American Center. She has written the following plays: *A Lament For Three Women* (1974), *Rebeccah* (1976), *The End of War* (1977), *Making Peace: A Fantasy* (1979), *A Monster Has Stolen The Sun* (1981), and *Sappho and Aphrodite* (1983). Most of Malpede's plays are based upon historical events that have special relevance to our time. Her plays have been produced and read at the New Cycle Theatre; Cummington Community of the Arts; the Open Mind Theatre, Soho; the New Theatre Festival, Stony Brook; Prospect Park Free For All; the All-Craft-Center Theatre, Manhattan; St. Ann's Church, Brooklyn; and Richland College, Dallas.

Malpede's theatrical works are lyrical epic dramas embracing the political and ethical positions of feminism, anarchism, and pacifism. As a poetic writer she is inspired by the language of William Shakespeare, the mythic vision of William Butler Yeats, and the political ideas of Bertolt Brecht. Her first play, *A Lament for Three Women*, deals with the death of the central male in the lives of three women, and, symbolically, the death of patriarchy. It was produced at Cummington Community of the Arts and at the Open Mind Theatre in Manhattan in 1974. *Rebeccah*, set in the Depression years, portrays the new heroine who survives the death of her infant son in a pogrom in Europe and the death of her daughter in the Triangle Shirtwaist Factory Fire in America, and who rises out of this holocaust to found a shanty town. The play was produced at Playwrights Horizon in New York in the 1976–1977 season.

The End of War, which deals with the connection between rape and war, was produced at Richland College in Dallas, Texas, in 1977; at the New Cycle Theatre in Park Slope, Brooklyn, in November 1977; and at the Arts at St. Ann's in Brooklyn in 1982. Set at the time of the Russian Revolution, the play revolves around the patriarchal hero of the Anarchist movement, Nestor Makhno, who often raped women after battle. In this play two women who are in love with him slowly withdraw their allegiance from the male hero and turn to each other for support.

Making Peace: A Fantasy, set in America in the 1840s, is a visionary piece in which Mother Ann Lee, the founder of the Shakers, Charles Fourier, and Mary Wollstonecraft gather together in the heavenly precincts to watch the generations of future women invent peace and end sexism and racism by rejecting the patriarchal, political, and religious systems that oppress them. It was produced at the New Cycle Theatre and at the All-Craft-Center Theatre in Manhattan during the 1979–1980 season. For *Making Peace* Karen Malpede collaborated with Roberta Kosse, noted for her opera *The Return of The Great Mother*. This collaboration illustrates the way feminists in the arts have begun to merge their talents to enrich each other's work. Kosse's music for Malpede's play has turned important scenes into oratorio arias. The women also collaborated on *A Monster Has Stolen The Sun*, for which Kosse again composed music. It is a play set in Celtic Ireland which reveals the conflict between the ancient pagan woman-centered philosophy which revered the cycles of nature, and the Christian/patriarchal/monotheistic world-view in which the body is considered impure and generations are pitted against each other. Part I of *Monster* was performed at The New Cycle Theatre in 1981 and also at St. Ann's Church in Brooklyn. Malpede's newest play, *Sappho and Aphrodite*, is set in Sappho's School on the isle of Lesbos, where young women come to learn poetry. It is about the linking of creativity and love in a woman-centered world. Rehearsed at Smith College, Northampton, it opened in 1983 in Brooklyn and in Manhattan with music by Roberta Kosse. Malpede's *Us* was given by the Living Theatre at the Theater for the New City in New York in 1988.

In all of Karen Malpede's plays, women turn to each other for comfort and knowledge. They imagine or create a new dramatic action, one that produces joy rather than pain. Malpede defines the highest moments of human drama as compassion rather than catharsis, as caring rather than cruelty, as transformation rather than tragedy. Her plays express a new feminist-humanist vision in which the contradictions between political and poetic theatre, between social and spiritual theatre, and between verbal and visionary theatre are abolished. Her New Cycle Theatre is named for the new cycle of history which women entered in the 1970s and 1980s, as well as for the cyclical processes in which women exercise past grief and sorrow by joining forces and working towards the establishment of new values.

Karen Malpede is currently a visiting lecturer in the Theatre Department at Smith College. She has been an adjunct professor at the John Jay College of Criminal Justice and a lecturer at the Pratt Institute, Brooklyn. She has taught in the Goddard Graduate Program at Norwich University, Vermont, and assisted playwriting students at Empire State College, New York. She has given lectures, playreadings, and workshops at many universities on the East Coast. Karen Malpede is one of an active group of women whose goal is to sensitize American theatre and the American public to women's concerns and to the contributions women are making to American culture.

Malpede's major publications are *People's Theatre in Amerika* (1972), (with Joseph Chaikin) *Three Works by The Open Theatre* (1974), and *Women in Theatre: Compassion and Hope* (1983, 1985). She has also written "On Being a Verse Playwright," *Italian-American Women's Writing*, ed. Kathleen Betsko and Rachel Koenig (1986); "An Interview with Karen Malpede," *Interviews with Contemporary Women Playwrights*, ed. Kathleen Betsko and Rachel Koenig (1987); "A Talk for the Conference on Feminism and Nonviolence," *Reweaving the Web of Life*, ed. Pam McAllister (1983); and "Rebeccah Rehearsal Notes," *Women in American Theatre*, ed. Helen Krich Chinoy and Linda Walsh Jenkins (1981). Malpede's play *A Lament for Three Women* appears in *A Century of Plays by American Women*, ed. Rachel France (1979). *A Monster Has Stolen the Sun and Other Plays* (1987) includes *The End of War* and *Sappho and Aphrodite*. See "Malina Steers New Path for the Living Theatre" in *American Theatre* (March 1988) for a brief description of the Living Theatre's production of Malpede's *Us*. Her articles, essays, and reviews have appeared in the *Soho News*, *Book Forum*, *Feminist Review of Literature*, *Performance*, *Social Policy*, *Win*, *St. Louis Post-Dispatch*, *Theatrework*, and *Performing Arts Journal*. Reviews, articles, and essays about Malpede's plays and books have appeared in the *New York Times*, *Boston Globe*, *Village Voice*, *Soho News*, *Brooklyn Phoenix*, *The Villager*, *Womannews*, *New York Native*, *Prospect Press*, *Theatre Journal*, *New Directions for Women*, and *Book Forum*. She is listed as Karen Malpede Taylor in *Contemporary Authors*, Vols. 45–48 (1974).

Gloria Orenstein

MANN, Emily (April 12, 1952–): playwright and director, was born in Boston, Massachusetts, the youngest daughter of Arthur and Sylvia (Blut) Mann. Emily Mann's upbringing was Jewish and intellectual; her family was profoundly affected by Western European history in the twentieth century. Her paternal grandparents had lived in Buscovina, an area now in Russia, and her maternal grandparents came to America from Ostrolenka, Poland. Mann's maternal grandparents were already in America when the Nazis entered Ostrolenka, and, according to Mann's autobiographical play, *Annulla Allen: Autobiography of a Survivor*, her great grandfather, a much loved elder of the community, was humiliated by the Nazis before they killed him along with the entire community. At the time of Emily Mann's birth the family had one child, Carol Mann, born July 23, 1949. Arthur Mann taught in Boston at Massachusetts Institute of

Technology (MIT) until Emily was three, and then moved to Smith College in Northampton. The family went to Chicago in 1966 when Arthur Mann became a Professor of American History at the University of Chicago, where he still teaches. Sylvia Mann is currently a reading specialist in Chicago.

Emily Mann attended the University of Chicago Laboratory High School, an experimental school where, in the midst of the political crises in the late 1960s and early 1970s, an inspired and radical young teacher sparked her interest in theatre arts and literature. After graduation in 1970 Mann attended Harvard and Radcliffe, where she studied English and French literature, made Phi Beta Kappa, and received the Bachelor of Arts degree in 1974. It is material from the summer of 1974, when Mann visited London with a friend, that is documented in her first play, *Annulla Allen: Autobiography of a Survivor* (1974). In the current version of the play, revised by the author and published as *Annulla: an Auto-biography* (1986), Mann describes "knapsacking around London," and going to Hampstead Heath to visit Annulla Allen, an aunt of a friend. Of this experience the author writes, "I needed to go to someone else's relative in order to under-stand my own history because by this time my only living relative of that generation was my grandmother—my mother's mother—and she had almost no way to communicate complex ideas. She'd lost her language. . . . This is not uncommon for immigrants of her generation. So I went to Annulla, who had the language" (p. 3). In the play, Annulla tells the story of her life and relates how her husband had been imprisoned in and released from Dachau. Annulla has survived the horrors of history and now, alone, is trying to write a play. Mann, who is the "voice" of the play, finds an historical self-consciousness and community through the narrated experiences of the older woman.

Following the summer of 1974, Mann won a directing fellowship to the Guthrie Theater in Minneapolis and attended the University of Minnesota, receiving a Master of Fine Arts degree in Theatre Arts in 1976. During her five years at the Guthrie she directed the première of *Annulla* at the Guthrie Theater's Guthrie 2 in 1977. The play was selected for the Theatre Communication Group's *Plays in Process* series. The play has also been presented in Chicago, St. Louis, and Atlanta. Finally, in 1988 New Yorkers were able to see it at the New Theatre of Brooklyn with Linda Hunt playing the aging survivor of the Holocaust. Mann again directed the play.

Mann wrote her second play, *Still Life*, a three-character performance con-taining interwoven monologues. Mann based this play on her conversations with Vietnam veterans during that summer. The play premièred in 1980 at the Good-man Studio Theatre in Chicago, and then moved in February 1981 to the Amer-ican Place Theatre in New York City. The latter production, directed by Mann herself, received five *Village Voice* Off-Broadway (Obie) awards for direction, playwriting, and best production.

Mann's third play, *Execution of Justice*, commissioned by the Eureka Theatre Company, San Francisco, was a co-winner of Actors Theatre of Louisville's 1983 Great American Play Contest and was first produced there under the co-direction of Oscar Eustis, Anthony Taccone, and Mann. With the aid of a Guggenheim fellowship Mann had done exhaustive research and interviewing about Dan White's murder of San Francisco Mayor George Moscone and City Supervisor Harvey White on November 7, 1978. Trial transcripts, newspaper clippings, and material from the interviews went into the play's construction. The result Mann terms "theatre of testimony," a dramatic blending of historical facts, personal narratives, and constructed material in which, she states, "Each character struggles with his traumatic memory of events, and the play as a whole is my traumatic blending of their accounts" (Jim O'Quinn, "*Execution of Justice* Documents a City's Nightmare," *Theatre Communications*, p. 3).

Highly successful at Actors Theatre of Louisville, *Execution of Justice* was subsequently produced by other regional theatres, among them the Arena Stage in Washington, D.C., the Empty Space in Seattle, Center Stage in Baltimore, the Guthrie Theater in Minneapolis, Eureka Theatre Company in association with Berkeley Repertory Theatre, and San Jose Repertory Company. The play, under the direction of the author, had a limited Broadway run in 1986. A new play by Mann, *Nights and Days*, had a staged reading at the New Dramatists in New York during the 1984–1985 season. In 1989 Mann collaborated with playwright/poet **Ntozake Shange** and jazz trumpeter and composer Baikida Carroll in a dramatization of Shange's novel, *Betsey Brown*. The play opened the 1989 season of The American Music Theater Festival, playing at the Forum Theatre in Philadelphia.

Emily Mann ranks, furthermore, as one of the very few successful women directors in the American theatre. Having been resident director of the Guthrie Theater and associate director of the Guthrie 2, she has also directed at the Cincinnati Playhouse in the Park, Actors Theatre of Louisville, the St. Nicholas Theatre and Goodman Theatre in Chicago, the Empty Space in Seattle, Theatre in the Round in Minneapolis, the Mark Taper Forum in Los Angeles, and the American Place Theatre in New York. She spent two seasons directing *He and She* and *Oedipus the King* at the Brooklyn Academy of Music Theatre Company (BAM).

In 1982 Mann directed her first Ibsen play, *a Doll's House*, at the Oregon Contemporary Theatre in Portland. In 1986 for Connecticut's Hartford Stage Company she directed the play in a new translation by her husband, Gerry Bamman, who worked from a literal translation by Irene Berman. In 1987 Mann directed *Hedda Gabler* at La Jolla Playhouse in California, and in the spring of 1988 she directed it for the Hartford Stage Company.

Mann is a member of New Dramatists and has received a 1983 Guggenheim fellowship, a Creative Artists Public Service (CAPS) grant, a 1983 National Endowment for the Arts artists grant, and a 1985 McKnight fellowship. Mann received the **Rosamond Gilder** Award in 1983 from the New Drama Forum for "outstanding creative achievement in the theatre." Mann was one of five writers named winners of the 1986 Playwrights U.S.A. awards for outstanding work produced in a noncommercial theatre during the 1983–1984 and 1984–1985 seasons. Her award was for *Execution of Justice.*

Mann married actor and writer Gerry Bamman on August 12, 1981. Their son, Nicholas Isaac Bamman, was born in New York City on September 15, 1983. Mann currently lives with her husband and son in Rockland County, New York.

Emily Mann's plays and their blend of the personal and the political have suggested new conventions and a renewed political awareness in the American theatre, demonstrated by the rapidity with which numbers of important regional theatres have been willing to take on a play having the size and the scope of *Execution of Justice.* (It requires a minimum of 18 actors.) Mann's unusual contributions as both playwright and director are a part of the new feminist sensibility making itself felt in American theatre.

Emily Mann's published works include *Annulla: An Autobiography*, her revised first play, printed in *Plays in Process* (1985); *Still Life* (1980), published in Theatre Communication Group's *New Plays U.S.A.* (1982) and in *Coming to Terms: American Plays and the Vietnam War* (1985); and *Execution of Justice* (1983), complete text published in *American Theatre* (November 1985) and in *New Plays U.S.A. 3*, ed. James Leverett and M. Elizabeth Osborn (1986). Sources of information about Mann include her autobiographical work, *Annulla, an Autobiography* (1985); Gillian Brake, "Irrepressible Voices: Three Women Playwrights at Arena," *America's Arena* (June 17, 1985); three articles edited by Jim O'Quinn: "*Execution of Justice* Documents a City's Nightmare," *Theatre Communications* (January 1984); "Directors at Work," *American Theatre* (September 1985); and "About Emily Mann," *American Theatre* (November 1985). In "Redressing Ibsen" in *American Theatre* (November 1987), Janice Paran interviews three women directors of Ibsen's plays, including Mann. "A Survivor's Voice" by Amy Hersh in *American Theatre* (November 1988) is about the 1988 production of *Annulla*. An interview with Mann appears in *Interviews with Contemporary Women Playwrights*, ed. Kathleen Betsko and Rachel Koenig (1987). Mann is listed in *Contemporary Theatre, Film, and Television* (1984).

Ann Gavere Kilkelly

MANSFIELD, Portia (November 19, 1887–January 29, 1979): dancer, choreographer, educator, writer, and filmmaker, was born in Chicago, the daughter of Edward Ricker and Myra (Mansfield) Swett. She attended Miss Morgan's School in New York City and studied dance at the Chalif Normal School of Dancing (1911), the Cambridge Normal School of Dancing (1912), and later at La Scala, in Milan. In 1910 Mansfield received her Bachelor of Arts degree from Smith College. Her first professional engagement as a dancer was in the Pavley Oukrainsky Ballet Company (1914) in New York City. She later danced in vaudeville as a partner of Vernon Castle.

Shortly after graduation from Smith College, Mansfield and her lifelong friend, **Charlotte Perry**, began teaching dance in Omaha and Chicago. By the summer of 1913 they had saved between them $200. Wanting to establish a camp where dance could be studied in a healthful and natural environment, they found property in Eldora, Colorado, with a spectacular view and a few ramshackle buildings. For the next few years Mansfield and Perry established a pattern: during the winter they taught and saved so that each summer they could make improvements at the camp, which was somewhat primitive during these early years. Because of their tight budget Mansfield and Perry were able to hire only one handyman. The two women shared the work of the camp as well as the teaching; they hauled water, cooked, repaired old buildings, and constructed new ones. In addition, they offered classes in dance, swimming, horseback riding, and hiking. All the dance instruction was given by Mansfield; it varied from classical Greek to the popular social dances of the day, such as the One-step, Canter, and Hesitation Waltz.

Within five years, the Perry-Mansfield camp, as it was now called, boasted two separate departments operating each summer from June 28 to August 19: a professional school of dance and a recreational camp. By the 1960s the camp had moved to Steamboat Springs, Colorado, and expanded to ninety acres. The facilities included a theatre, dance studios, and dormitory space for two hundred students and fifty faculty members and counselors. The programs of study had widened to include drama, art, choreography, and music for dance. Guest teachers included some of the great names in American modern dance: Doris Humphrey, **Hanya Holm**, Charles Weidman, **Helen Tamaris**, **Agnes de Mille**, and Louis Horst. In 1961, academic credit, hitherto granted by the University of Wyoming, was taken up by Stephens College in Columbia, Missouri. Throughout the 1960s the administration of the camp was gradually transferred to Stephens until, by 1967, the camp changed its name from the Perry-Mansfield School of Theatre Arts to the Perry-Mansfield School and Camp of Stephens College.

Each summer from 1920 to 1926, following classes and rehearsals at the camp, a Perry-Mansfield group toured the Keith, Orpheum, Pantages, or Loew vaudeville circuits. Choreographed by Mansfield, the acts presented by the Perry-Mansfield dancers included *Squirrels and Girls* (1923), *Rhythm and Color* (1924), *Saturnalia* (1925), *Romantic Anglers* (1925), *Is Happiness Sin?* (1925), *Picnic Day in Holland* (1925), *From an Etruscan Screen* (1925), *Hymn of Joy* (1925), *The Sculptor's Dream* (1925), *Dutch Love* (1925), *Trepak* (1925), *Castillian Tango* (1925), *Bolero* (1926), *Komansrai* (1926), *The Fall of Babylon* (1926), *Squares and Diagonals* (1926), *Two Preludes* (1926), *Ouiji* (1926), and *Pia and Francette* (1926). The money accumulated from these engagements was invested in the camp. In 1926, after the tours ended, Mansfield returned to graduate school. In 1933 she received her Master of Arts degree from New York University and in 1953 her Doctorate of Education. She produced, in partial fulfillment of her doctorate, a film on the dances of the Conchero Indians of Mexico. At the same time she taught and directed the dance programs of a number of schools, including the Peabody Conservatory in Baltimore, Maryland.

Between 1948 and 1958 Portia Mansfield published, with composer and teacher Louis Horst, *Dance and Rhythmic Body Mechanics*, a six-volume collection of exercises. In addition to her many teaching and writing activities,

Mansfield was the producer, photographer, and editor of Perry-Mansfield Motion Picture Productions, founded in 1951. She made a series of color sound films on dance, body mechanics, and the dance training of the Perry-Mansfield Camp, as well as films on horsemanship. In 1957 Mansfield founded a school of mountain climbing for boys, which she supervised until 1971.

Portia Mansfield died in March 1979 at the age of 91. Throughout her long and varied career, she believed that dance should be studied in conjunction with other art forms, that its study involved a total commitment, and that dance training should be pursued in a natural environment. By creating the Perry-Mansfield Camp at Steamboat Springs, Colorado, Mansfield provided the ideal surroundings for generations of students and teachers of modern dance.

Although no biographical study of Portia Mansfield has been written, the Dance Collection in the New York Public Library's Performing Arts Research Center at Lincoln Center has a number of scrapbooks, clippings, and films about the Perry-Mansfield School of Theatre and Dance at Steamboat Springs, Colorado, as well as a clipping file on Mansfield. The collection also holds a number of copies of the ''Perry-Mansfield News,'' a newsletter published about the camp's activities. Mansfield's Ph.D. dissertation, ''The Conchero Dances of Mexico'' (New York University, 1953), is available from University Microfilms, University of Michigan, Ann Arbor, Michigan. Her *Dance and Rhythmic Body Mechanics*, co-authored with Louis Horst and published between 1948 and 1958, is also available, as well as journal articles. See *Dancemagazine* (May 1962) for her article on professional dance training in colleges, and ''Let Us Help Them Move Young,'' *Dancemagazine* (August 1966), for an article about exercises for women over fifty-five. See also Charlotte Perry's article on the evolution of the Perry-Mansfield School in *Dancemagazine* (April 1963). For an account of Mansfield's theories on dance training, see Theodore Orchard's article ''Portia Mansfield, Practical Theories'' in *Dancemagazine* (June 1931). Her obituary appeared in *Dancemagazine* (May 1979). Brief biographies of Mansfield appear in *Who's Who of American Women, 1964–1965* (1963); *The Biographical Encyclopaedia and Who's Who of the American Theatre* (1966); *Notable Names in the American Theatre* (1976); and *The Dance Encyclopedia* (1978).

Barbara Barker

MARBURY, Elisabeth (June 19, 1856–January 22, 1933): first dramatist's agent in the United States, producer, personal manager, and playwright, was born in Manhattan into an old New York family. Her parents, Francis Ferdinand Marbury and Elizabeth (McCoun) Marbury, had four sons before Elisabeth, their only daughter, was born. Her father, a leading admiralty lawyer and staunch supporter of the Tammany Hall Democratic organization, was descended from an English family that settled in the United States in the seventeenth century. Elizabeth Marbury's maternal grandfather, William Townsend McCoun, often told her how, as a child, he was taken to see General George Washington. Her maternal grandmother, a woman of Huguenot descent, was on the reception committee of a ball given for the Marquis de Lafayette on one of his visits to New York during the Revolutionary era.

Marbury stated in her autobiography, *My Crystal Ball* (1923), that she felt fortunate to have been taught sound bookkeeping skills by her genteel mother;

her father taught her to read Latin at the age of seven and exposed her to Greek drama, Plato, and Shakespeare. Her education also included a weekly trip to the theatre. Marbury spent winters at the family's home on Irving Place and summers at the McCoun farm in Oyster Bay, Long Island, where she was friendly with the young Theodore Roosevelt. Although brought up a Presbyterian, Marbury converted to Roman Catholicism in middle life. She never married, but lived for forty years with her friend Elsie de Wolfe, the actress turned decorator. In 1933 Marbury died of heart failure (after minor surgery on her leg) at her home, 13 Sutton Place, in New York City.

Elisabeth Marbury began her theatre career theatre by managing benefit performances for charity. In these early years she co-authored *A Wild Idea*, a one-act play produced in 1889, and adapted a French play, *Fin de Siècle*, staged in 1892 under the title *Merry Gotham*. In 1885, when one of her benefits netted $5,000, she came to the attention of producer Daniel Frohman, who advised her to make a career as a business woman in the theatre. In 1888 she became business manager for **Frances Hodgson Burnett**, who was about to dramatize her novel *Little Lord Fauntleroy*. From the beginning, Marbury attended to business matters, but also had a hand in the artistry of a production. For *Little Lord Fauntleroy* she helped with casting and rehearsed the actors for the various companies. It was in 1890, while arranging for a French production of this play, that Marbury met playwright Victorien Sardou, who engaged her as sole agent in the American and English markets for the French authors' organization, Société des Gens de Lettres. She persuaded Sardou that it would be more profitable for French playwrights to have their plays produced on a royalty basis than to sell the plays outright for a flat sum, as was then the custom. It was this association with the French playwrights that initiated Marbury's worldwide business as a literary representative.

As dramatist's agent, or "play broker," her title at the outset of her career, Marbury served as the link between playwright and manager, using her persuasive skills to bring play, actors, and manager together for a successful production. In 1897 she persuaded James M. Barrie to rewrite *The Little Minister* to satisfy the needs of Daniel Frohman's producer-brother Charles, who was looking for a play for **Maude Adams**. Barrie had written the play originally for a male lead. At a later date Marbury suggested that a French play involving a love triangle among a man and two women could be altered to meet American requirements by describing the man as a bigamist who had wickedly deceived two trusting women. Thus rewritten, the play was accepted by William Gillette under the title *All the Comforts of Home*.

As the first agent to represent playwrights in this country, Marbury's business expanded rapidly, with offices in Paris, London, Berlin, Madrid, and Moscow. Her New York office was located for several years in the Empire Theatre Building at Broadway and 40th Street, just above the offices of producer Charles Frohman, who acquired most of his plays from her. Among the French dramatists Marbury represented were Edmond Rostand, Georges Feydeau, Jean Richepin, Alexandre

Bisson, and Victorien Sardou. Clyde Fitch was probably her best known American client. She also represented James M. Barrie, Jerome K. Jerome, and W. Somerset Maugham and became George Bernard Shaw's agent early in his career, sending him generous profits for such productions as those by Richard Mansfield of *The Devil's Disciple* and *Arms and the Man*. Another client, Oscar Wilde, sent to her from prison the manuscript of *The Ballad of Reading Gaol*. New York publishers would have nothing to do with Wilde's poem; she finally sold it to *The World* for $250.

In 1914 Marbury, along with John W. Rumsey, took over the clients and purchased all the stock rights of Selwyn and Company, and formed The American Play Company, which exists today on West 44th Street in Manhattan. Always quick to anticipate a trend, Marbury capitalized on the pre-World War I dance craze by promoting the careers of Vernon and Irene Castle. With financial assistance from her New York society friends, she opened Castle House, a ballroom-dancing school patronized by the "smart set." She booked the two instructors all over the country, and through her management they became international stars.

In 1915 Marbury became a producer. With various partners and her friends Elsie de Wolfe and Anne Morgan, the daughter of the financier J. P. Morgan, she helped to create the intimate musical. These shows, which were performed at the Princess Theatre in New York and became known as the Princess Musicals, advanced the fledgling careers of Jerome Kern, Cole Porter, Guy Bolton, and P. G. Wodehouse. The Princess Musicals, by focusing on plot and character, were the first real advance in the development of the modern American musical, which up to that time had consisted largely of a series of extravagant but unrelated numbers.

Marbury was particularly interested in the function of the chorus, and these productions had ensembles instead of choruses and small-part players rather than chorus boys and girls. No two members of a Marbury ensemble were ever dressed alike; each had a unique costume, and each usually had at least one line of dialogue. Marbury produced the first of the Princess Musicals, *Nobody Home* (1915) and *Very Good Eddie* (1915), in association with F. Ray Comstock; *See America First* (1916) by herself; and *Love O'Mike* (1917) with Lee Shubert. Elsie de Wolfe worked on these productions, designing either costumes or sets. During her producing years Marbury advanced the welfare of the chorus girls in her employ, anticipating some of the later work of Actors' Equity Association.

Marbury and de Wolfe shared three successive homes in Manhattan and one in France. In the early days they lived in a small house on 17th Street said once to have been owned by Washington Irving; next they moved to a larger house on East 55th Street and finally to Sutton Place, where Marbury lived alone after de Wolfe married Sir Charles Mendl in 1924. In 1903 Marbury purchased for less than $12,000 the Villa Trianon, a mansion which had been built for the surgeon of Marie Antoinette at Versailles. Marbury and de Wolfe were joined by Anne Morgan each summer at Villa Trianon. Marbury was at the hub of an artistic circle; her Sunday salons in New York and Versailles were important gathering places for artists, and she and de Wolfe were credited with being the first hostesses to mingle actors with New York high society.

During the latter part of her career, Marbury was involved in politics. In 1918 she was asked to head the women's division of the citizens' campaign committee for the election of Alfred E. Smith as governor of New York. In 1920 she was sent as a delegate-at-large to the Democratic Convention in San Francisco, where she was elected a national committeewoman, a post she held at her death.

With her ample figure, peaches-and-cream complexion, and Pompadour hair style, Marbury was an imposing, incredibly vital woman. She slept six hours each night, smoked heavily her own special brand of cigarettes, was known for her biting wit, and demanded that her first name be spelled with an "s," not a "z." As an author's agent Marbury was responsible for introducing and protecting the work of many European and American playwrights at the beginning of the twentieth century. She is believed to have been the first agent to negotiate a percentage of box office receipts for her clients. She helped to change the course of the American musical theatre with the Princess Musicals, and she managed the careers of many successful performers.

Her obituary appeared on page one of most New York newspapers, and her funeral, held at St. Patrick's Cathedral on Fifth Avenue, was attended by scores of dignitaries from politics, show business, and society. Marbury's reputation during her lifetime is evident from the following introduction to an article in *Metropolitan Magazine* (February 1911): "The three estates of the dramatic world are playwright, actor, and manager. The fourth is Miss Elisabeth Marbury. She is an institution without precedent, without a possible successor, self-evolved, autogenerated."

The Berg Collection at the New York Public Library contains various business records and contracts of the American Play Company plus earlier contracts between (from 1897 on) playwrights and producers negotiated by Marbury, all catalogued under American Play Company. Clippings from magazines and newspapers documenting all aspects of Marbury's career are in the Billy Rose Theatre Collection at the New York Public Library Performing Arts Research Center at Lincoln Center, as are many business letters from Marbury to playwrights and producers. There are 259 business letters from the playwright Paul Kester to Marbury in the Manuscript Division of the New York Public Library. Information concerning the Princess Musicals appears in Crosby Gaige's *Footlights and Headlights* (1948), Cecil Smith's *Musical Comedy in America* (1950), and Stanley Green's *The World of Musical Comedy* (1974). Both *My Crystal Ball* (1923), Marbury's autobiography; and *After All* (1935), Elsie de Wolfe's account of her own life, provide little more than a chronology of the events of the two women's lives. Jane Smith's *Elsie de Wolfe, A Life in the High Style* (1982) provides an insightful account of the personal as well as the professional life of Elsie de Wolfe; a similar account of the personal life of Marbury has yet to be written. Marbury's obituary appeared in the *New World Telegram*, the *New York Times*, and the *New York Herald Tribune* (January 23, 1933). There are biographical accounts of Marbury in *The Oxford Companion to the Theatre* (1967);

Notable American Women, Vol. II (1971); *Notable Names in the American Theatre* (1976); and *The Oxford Companion to American Theatre* (1984).

Rebecca Strum

MARLOWE, Julia (September 23, 1866–November 12, 1950): actress who with her husband Edward Hugh Sothern toured the country with outstanding Shakespearean productions, was born Sarah Frances Frost in Upton Caldbeck, Cumberland, England, and came to the United States as a small child. Her father, John Frost, a shoemaker, believing he had accidentally blinded a man, fled England for Kansas in 1870. He changed his name to Brough. He then sent for his wife, Sarah (Hodgson) Frost, and his children, and by 1874 the Brough family had settled in Cincinnati where Sarah Brough operated a hotel. The Broughs were later divorced and Sarah Brough married a baker named Hess.

As a child, Fanny Brough (later Julia Marlowe) attended public schools and also frequented Cincinnati's National Theatre. She made her stage debut in 1880 as a member of a juvenile opera company under the management of Colonel R. E. J. Miles. The troupe toured for nine months in *H.M.S. Pinafore*, *The Chimes of Normandy*, and *The Little Duke*. Fanny Brough had small supporting roles in the productions. In 1882 she appeared as Heinrich in Robert McWade's company of *Rip Van Winkle*. She later played small roles in a Shakespearean touring company managed by Colonel Miles. Instead of continuing her career in touring companies, she left the stage in 1884 to study with Ada Dow, a well-known stock company actress. For three years Dow coached the young actress in voice, movement, and dramatic literature in order to develop her skills as a Shakespearean performer. In 1887, as Julia Marlowe, she returned to the stage in a starring role, Parthenia in *Ingomar*, debuting in New London, Connecticut, and touring briefly. She made her New York debut in the same role on October 20, 1887, at the Bijou Theatre in a special matinee.

The success of the special matinee led to a regular New York engagement at the Star Theatre in December 1887, where she appeared in *Romeo and Juliet* and *Twelfth Night*. For the next ten years Marlowe toured the country as a star in plays like *As You Like It*, *She Stoops to Conquer*, *The Hunchback*, and *The Rivals* and became one of the chief proponents of the classical repertory at a time when romantic melodrama was the mainstay of the professional theatre. In 1894 she married her leading man, Robert Taber. They were divorced in 1900.

Marlowe became a leading actress, under the management of C. B. Dillingham, with the Theatrical Syndicate in 1897, starring in a series of historical romances and enriching her fortune as well as her reputation. She appeared in such plays as *For Bonnie Prince Charles* (1897), *Colinette* (1899), and *Barbara Frietchie* (1901) and became one of the top box office attractions in the country, both for her acting and for her portrayal of virtuous characters. Her greatest popular success came in 1902 as Mary Tudor in *When Knighthood was in Flower*. She returned to the classics in 1904, under the aegis of Daniel Frehman. Her co-star, Edward Hugh Sothern, was a noted romantic actor who had also returned to classical roles. They were married that same year and became the chief exponents of Shakespearean drama in America. They toured in *Much Ado About Nothing*, *Hamlet*, *Macbeth*, and *The Merchant of Venice* and produced matinee performances for schoolchildren. In 1907 they appeared in London to great critical acclaim and on November 8, 1909, they opened the New Theatre in New York, in a production of *Antony and Cleopatra*. Though the New Theatre was started as a permanent resident company, it depended upon stars like Sothern and Marlowe for the theatre's success.

During the 1914–1915 season, Julia Marlowe was taken ill, and Sothern toured alone that season as well as the next. In 1916 they announced their retirement from the stage. During World War I, Julia Marlowe made appearances at rallies and bond drives; and both actors entertained the troops in England and Scotland. In 1921 Sothern and Marlowe returned to the stage with their Shakespearean repertory. After their retirement in 1924, Julia Marlowe and her husband traveled widely until Sothern's death in 1933. In 1921 Marlowe was presented with an honorary Doctor of Letters by George Washington University and in 1943 received an honorary doctorate from Columbia University. She died at her home in New York City on November 12, 1950.

Julia Marlowe was widely praised for her championing of Shakespeare and for her performances in classical plays. Her greatest success came with characters like Rosalind in *As You Like It* and Viola in *Twelfth Night* which showed her beauty, feminine charm, and melodious voice to best advantage. A. C. Wheeler, writing in *The Criterion* (November 18, 1899), described her Viola: "There are many women of Shakespeare's creation who demand for their incarnation more passion, more variety, more ability, perhaps than Viola; but there are none that demand more womanliness, and it is a womanliness which has to be interpreted and sustained, and when it is, it is the very quintessence of femininity in that aspect which men most admire . . . in Miss Marlowe's performance of Viola there was but one *tour de force*, and that was Viola in her completeness." John Dennis, Jr., wrote that he "had yet to hear her strike one artificial note, or one note not perfectly natural, intelligent, harmonious, and effective" (New York *World*, February 21, 1897).

Julia Marlowe was a meticulous artist who studied her roles intensely and blended movement and gesture into subtle, restrained characterization. She believed in artistic excellence and moral uplift in the theatre, a goal she pursued in both the choice and the staging of her plays. Her repertoire and her management of her career demonstrated that she felt acting was an acceptable career for a woman; she further believed that the theatre had an obligation to enlighten the public. She was also a strong advocate of a national theatre. Unlike most performers of her time she became a star through her own efforts and played in a repertory of her own choosing. In her career Julia Marlowe showed that it was possible to maintain high artistic standards and also to be a popular and successful performer.

Marlowe's career is chronicled in *Julia Marlowe's Story* by E. H. Sothern, edited by Fairfax Downey (1954). Detailed information on particular phases of her career can be found in Sallie Mitchell, "The Early Career of Julia Marlowe: The Making of a Star" (Unpublished Ph.D. dissertation, University of Illinois, 1976) and in A. Sogliuzzo, "Edward Sothern and Julia Marlowe: Shakespearean Producers" (Unpublished Ph. D. dissertation, Indiana University, 1967). Charles Edward Russell, *Julia Marlowe, Her Life and Art* (1926) is an authorized biography. John D. Barry's *Julia Marlowe* (1899) is an illustrated sketch of her early career. She is included in Lewis C. Strang, *Famous Actresses of the Day in America*, First Series (1899), and Second Series (1902); in William Winter, *The Wallet of Time*, Vol. II (1913), and *Vagrant Memories* (1916); and in John Ranken Towse, *Sixty Years of the Theatre* (1916). The Theatre Collection in the New York Public Library Performing Arts Research Center at Lincoln Center has clippings and other memorabilia about Julia Marlowe and about the Shakespearean productions of Sothern and Marlowe. Modern reference books which include Marlowe are *Notable American Women*, Vol. II (1971); William C. Young, *Famous Actors and Actresses on the American Stage*, Vol. II (1975); *Who Was Who in the Theatre*, Vol. III (1978); *The Oxford Companion to the Theatre* (1983); and *The Oxford Companion to American Theatre* (1984).

Rita M. Plotnicki

MARRANCA, Bonnie (April 28, 1947–): critic, founding editor of the *Performing Arts Journal*, and winner of the George Jean Nathan Award, was born in Elizabeth, New Jersey, to businessman Angelo Joseph Marranca and Evelyn (Mirabelli) Marranca. After she received her Bachelor of Arts degree from Montclair State College, New Jersey, in 1969, she attended the University of Copenhagen and in 1973 began graduate work at City University of New York. She received a Master of Arts degree in theatre in 1976 from Hunter College of the City University of New York and proceeded to the Ph.D. program in theatre at the Graduate School, where she has completed all requirements except the dissertation. On August 1, 1975, Marranca married critic Gautam Dasgupta.

In addition to teaching theatre in 1974 and 1976 at City University, Marranca worked a variety of theatre-related jobs. As an undergraduate in 1963 she was assistant to Max Eisen, a New York City press agent. In 1970 she served as administrative assistant for the New York City Theatre in Education Project. Her next job was with playwright-producer Irv Bauer in 1970–1971. Two years later the New York City Department of Cultural Affairs hired her as an assistant in the Street Theatre Division. From 1975 to 1977 she worked as theatre critic for *Soho Weekly News*.

In 1975 Marranca and Dasgupta founded Performing Arts Journal Publications, because they felt that there was no public forum for good, solid, analytical writings on the performing arts. Together they have co-edited since 1975 the *Performing Arts Journal*, to which Marranca has contributed numerous articles. She has also published reviews and articles in such diverse places as *Rolling Stone*, *Nation*, and *Theatre Journal*.

Marranca edited her first book in 1977, *The Theatre of Images*, which included scripts of Richard Foreman's *Pandering to the Masses: A Misrepresentation* and Robert Wilson's *A Letter for Queen Victoria*, along with drawings from Lee

Breuer's *The Red Horse Animation*. Of Marranca's introductory essays, one reviewer from *Choice* wrote, "These introductions are so clear and helpful that they extend the usefulness of the book beyond any merely esoteric level" (*Choice*, 1978, p. 694.) Those publications were followed in 1979 by her books *Theatre of the Ridiculous* and *Animations: A Trilogy for Mabou Mines*, both released by Performing Arts Journal Publications. In 1981 Marranca published *American Dreams: The Imagination of Sam Shepard*, a collection of fifteen essays, which were well received by critics: "Marranca's 'Introduction' not only whets the appetite for the works of Shepard, but provides the sauce that blends and contrasts the portions that follow" (Gerard Molyneaux, *Library Journal*, September 15, 1981, p. 1750). A *Theatre Journal* critic offers similar praise, "Marranca's introduction is more than an appetizer; she presents strong, fully developed ideas of her own" (Peter Grego, May 1982, p. 278).

Marranca collaborated with Dasgupta on another 1981 publication, *American Playwrights: A Critical Survey*, a collection of essays discussing the themes and styles of eighteen Off- and Off-off-Broadway dramatists from before 1967. Several reviewers criticized the book for being less than scholarly, but one critic called it "cogent, written with excitement and verve" (Bettina L. Knapp, *Journal of Modern Literature, 1981–1982 Annual Review*, p. 392).

In 1984 Marranca published *Theatre Writings*, for which she received the George Jean Nathan Award for 1983–1984, being only the second woman (after **Elizabeth Hardwick**) to receive this prestigious award. In the winter term of 1984 Marranca was Visiting Associate Professor at the University of California at San Diego, and in the Fall of 1985 she was awarded a Guggenheim Fellowship to support a new work which is to be titled *The Theatricalization of American Society*.

Marranca states that she believes in an American aesthetic: "Whenever I am dealing with American theatre I try to emphasize its American roots, not out of patriotic feelings, but because I feel that critics have too often overlooked our American artistic heritage in favor of praising European influences" (*Contemporary Authors, New Revision Series*, Vol. 9, p. 357). She has supported this conviction by periodically publishing short anthologies of American plays with critical introductions. To date several have been issued by Performing Arts Journal Publications and more are scheduled for publication. Through her writing and editing, Bonnie Marranca has become one of the critical champions of the new American theatrical avant-garde.

Bonnie Marranca is best known through her published works. She edited *The Theatre of Images* (1977); wrote, with Gautam Dasgupta, *American Playwrights: A Critical Survey* (1981); edited *American Dreams: The Imagination of Sam Shepard* (1981); and edited *Theatre Writings* (1984). Marranca has also written "Peter Handke's My Foot My Tutor: Aspects of Modernism," *Michigan Quarterly Review*, no. 3 (Summer 1977). Many of her articles have appeared in the *Performing Arts Journal*, including "Berlin Theatertreffen 1978," Vol. III, no. 3 (1979); (with Gautam Dasgupta and Michael Earle) "A Life in the Theatre?" Vol. IV, nos. 1 and 2 (1979); "Meredith Monk's Recent Ruins:

The Archeology of Consciousness: Essaying Images,'' Vol. IV, no. 3 (1980); ''Alphabetical Shepard: The Play of Words,'' Vol. V, no. 2 (1981); ''The Politics of Performance,'' Vol. VI, no. 1 (1982); ''Nuclear Theatre,'' Vol. VI, no. 3 (1982); ''Pirandello,'' Vol. VII, no. 2 (1983); ''The Real Life of María Irene Fornés,'' Vol. VIII, no. 1, (1984); ''Acts of Criticism,'' Vol. IX, no. 1 (1985); and ''PAJ: A Personal History,'' Vol. IX, nos. 2 and 3 (1985). Bonnie Marranca is listed in *Contemporary Authors, New Revision Series*, Vol. 9 (1983).

Dusky Loebel

MARSHALL, Armina (1900?–): actress, playwright, and producer long associated with the Theatre Guild, was born at the turn of the century in the Cherokee Strip in the Indian territory of Oklahoma to Chalmers and Elizabeth (Armina) Marshall. Her father was sheriff of Pawnee County, but after a shooting duel with a famous bandit in the town of Keystone he moved his family to Anaheim, California, where Armina Marshall finished high school and then attended the University of California at Los Angeles for two years. Displaying early her pioneering spirit, she taught for two years in a one-room schoolhouse at the edge of the desert, riding horseback eighteen miles each day for that purpose. Summer school in Berkeley and participation in its Greek Theatre productions whetted her appetite for a career in the theatre. Having saved enough money for tuition and combated the strong opposition of both parents, she traveled to New York City to enroll in the American Academy of Dramatic Arts. She then became part of the young acting group of the Theatre Guild. Her first acting assignment was the part of the Nun in *The Tidings Brought to Mary* (1922). She played the Troll King's daughter and understudied Helen Westley in *Peer Gynt* (1923). She played in *Fata Morgana* (1924), *Merchants of Glory* (1925), *Right You Are If You Think You Are* (1927), *Man's Estate* (1929), *Mr. Pim Passes By* (1929), *Those We Love* (1930), *Pillars of Society* (1931), *The Bride the Sun Shines On* (1931), *The Noble Prize* (1933), and *If This Be Treason* (1935).

In 1925 she married Lawrence Langner, co-founder with **Theresa Helburn** of the Theatre Guild, and eventually acted only intermittently, turning her attention to other theatrical pursuits. In 1933 she co-authored with Langner *Pursuit of Happiness*, which became a success both in New York and London. Other collaborations by the pair were *On to Fortune* (1935), *Susanna and the Elders* (1940), and an adaptation of Jules Romains's *Doctor Knock* (1936). Together, they founded in 1931 the Westport Country Playhouse in Connecticut, in order to establish a repertory company of their own to produce new plays by American and European playwrights. The Playhouse opened with Dion Boucicault's Victorian melodrama, *The Streets of New York*, which became a rousing success for the company both there and later in New York. Another play of their first season was *As You Like It* with Armina Marshall as Rosalind. Their son Philip, born in 1926, took over the management of the Playhouse in 1951 after a joyous celebration of its twentieth season.

Marshall produced for the Theatre Guild George Bernard Shaw's *The Millionairess* in 1938 and in 1939 served as the Guild's assistant director. During

World War II she co-directed the Stage Door Canteen in Washington, D.C. In 1945 she supervised the production of Philip Barry's *Foolish Notion* at the Martin Beck Theatre, and in 1946 Eugene O'Neill's *The Iceman Cometh* at the same theatre. After the death of the Guild's executive director Theresa Helburn in 1959, Marshall became co-director with her husband. In 1974 the Guild produced *Absurd Person Singular*, in 1975 *A Musical Jubilee*, in 1977 *Golda*, and after that an Off-Broadway play, *Mecca*.

When the Theatre Guild decided to produce a radio program, *Theatre Guild on the Air*, Marshall became associate director. She continued as such during eight years on radio (1948–1956) and eight additional years with the television program *The United States Steel Hour* (1956–1964). Armina Marshall is now co-director of the Guild with Philip and Marilyn Langner, as well as chair of the Theatre Guild-American Theatre Society. She is director and one of the founders of the American Shakespeare Theatre in Stratford, Connecticut, and also a director of the American Academy of Dramatic Arts, the American Theatre Wing, and the Actor's Fund.

Marshall is prominent among women in the American theatre for her expertise in several areas. She has done acting and management for stage, radio, and television productions. She has succeeded as writer, and as an organizer in the arts. With her husband she has worked to bring dramas of high quality to New York and regional stages, never cheapening the art by box-office demands. She and her husband pursued the original intention of the Theatre Guild, which was to produce plays of artistic merit not ordinarily produced by commercial managers. For this purpose they built a theatre in New York and set up a permanent company with a repertory of plays. Along with Helburn, Marshall knew Eugene O'Neill and George Bernard Shaw intimately and presented the plays of those two playwrights, as well as those of Shakespeare. Marshall and Langner were proud of the fact that they were producing at both the Guild and Westport Country Playhouse a larger number of Shaw's plays than any other management team. Marshall's belief in American playwrights led to her encouragement of new playwrights on the commercial stage; her energy and optimism have kept her theatre involvement continuous and vital.

The most important source on Armina Marshall's career is Lawrence Langner's *The Magic Curtain* (1951), which contains interesting and vivid details about their work with the Theatre Guild and the Westport Country Playhouse. Biographical sketches are included in *The Biographical Encyclopaedia and Who's Who of the American Theatre* (1966), *Notable Names in the American Theatre* (1976), and *Who's Who in the Theatre* (1981).

Nelda K. Balch

MARTIN, Judith (August 1918–): director, dancer, actress, playwright, and creator of the famous Paper Bag Players, was born and grew up in Newark, New Jersey. Her grandparents were working class Russian-Jewish immigrants, but her parents had achieved upper-middle class status. Judith Martin had one sister and two brothers, but she was the only one in her family to pursue a career in the arts. Her father and siblings all worked in business.

Martin remembers her lonely early childhood, from which she withdrew into a fantasy world that eventually brought her into the theatre. While attending public schools in Newark, she commuted to New York City to take dance and drama classes. After high school she studied for two years at the Neighborhood (Playhouse) School of Theatre, where she worked with the Stanislavsky method under acting-teacher Maria Ouspenskaya. During those same years, she and a friend, Diana Merliss, studied children's theatre under Lazar Galpern at the New Theatre School. Galpern had been trained in the classic Russian approach to dramatizing fairy tales with song, dance, and fantasy. Martin was taken with Galpern's romantic, creative process.

After graduation from the Neighborhood School of Theatre Martin directed the dance project of the National Youth Administration in New York. She created *America Dances* for them, a production which toured for two years throughout metropolitan New York City. When the National Youth Administration was discontinued, Martin and Diana Merliss founded the New York Theatre for Children. They obtained studio space at the Henry Street Settlement House, where they rehearsed for an entire season. Productions for the New York Theatre for Children were based on original stories created by Martin, such as *The Runaway Horse*. Though the productions were professional and charming, Martin and Merliss had difficulties obtaining bookings. The lack of bookings, plus Martin's marriage to her first husband, soon ended her first venture in children's theatre.

When Martin's husband was drafted during the Second World War, she went with him to Miami, Florida, and then to Shreveport, Louisiana. However, she soon returned to New York to pursue her career, and the marriage ended in divorce. Upon her return to New York in the early 1940s, Martin concentrated on modern dance. She achieved her early professional success in dance rather than in theatre. She studied with **Martha Graham** and was asked to join her company. Though flattered by the invitation, Martin knew that she could never completely subordinate herself and her work to the strong technique and personality of another artist. She danced with several innovative companies, including the **Anna Sokolow** Dance Company and the Merce Cunningham Company, in which she was choreographer, director, and lead dancer. In 1951 Martin won the Dance Auditions for solo dancers at the 92nd Street YM-YWHA, and it was as a solo dancer that she created a work for children titled *The Story of Dancing Feet*, her first work for a child audience since the New York Theatre for Children closed.

Concurrent with her professional dance career, Martin taught dance for a livelihood to both adults and children in recreation programs and settlement houses on the Lower East Side of New York, at the Union Settlement House in East Harlem, Adelphi College, the Turtle Bay Music School, the American Academy of Dramatic Arts, and the YMCA in Ridgeland. Martin was inspired by the discovery of what children could do from their own creative impulses, and she began to experiment with improvisation. Her teaching experiences fed her own creative work, and she steadily developed improvisation both as a way of teaching dance and as a way of creating dance and theatre material for performance.

In 1956 Martin's career paused briefly when she married Soloman Miller, an anthropologist who taught at Hofstra University and did field work in Latin America. She left New York for a year and a half to travel with her husband, first to Urbana, Illinois, and then on an expedition to Peru. In 1969 the couple adopted Daisy, their only child.

Upon returning to New York Martin's interest grew in creating a theatre form for children based on improvisation, dance, and stage movement. In 1958 she invited a variety of women artists to join her improvisation sessions: Shirley Kaplan, a talented and successful young painter; Susie Bond, an accomplished Broadway actress; and Joyce Aaron, a promising young actress. These four women formed an experimental theatre group which later evolved into the Paper Bag Players. They were joined by two men, Daniel Jahn, a musician who served as the accompanist and composer for the group, and Remy Charlip, an artist, dancer, and author-illustrator of children's books. Charlip served the group first as a consultant and later joined as a co-founder, co-director, and performer. By 1965 all these, except Martin herself, had left the group and been replaced by others. Martin continued to be the major creative force of the Paper Bag Players, directing, designing, writing, and acting in all productions. She was a pioneer in creating a new form of American children's theatre at a time when the field was dominated by the traditional fairy tale approach. In the format created by Martin and the Paper Bag Players there was no tight-plotting or character-development but rather a loose revue style which joined together a number of separate dances, songs, and sketches. The separate pieces were enacted through a combination of singing, dancing, acting, pantomime, and painting and drawing done on stage. Unity was achieved through movement and music, by a highly theatrical and comedic acting style, and by the artistic transformation of paper, cardboard, and paint into props and costumes which were visually exciting and particularly apt for the psychological truth of the presentation. This transformation of simple materials into innovative theatre has become the trademark of the Paper Bag Players.

The company is noted for other technical innovations as well. They pioneered in performing in basic "uniforms" in front of a simple, curtained background. This practice, widespread during the late 1960s and the 1970s, was almost unheard of in 1958, when the norm for children's theatre was elaborately costumed, traditional proscenium productions. The company also challenged the existing stereotype that young audiences could identify only with youthful and beautiful protagonists, played by young and attractive actors. The Paper Bag productions used individuals of all ages, sizes, and physical characteristics. Their assumption was that children can identify more readily with heroes and heroines who share the looks, fortunes, foibles, and frailties of ordinary people. Judith Martin and the Paper Bag Players were also early experimenters in the use of audience participation and in direct actor-audience relationships.

Nevertheless, the contemporary content developed by Martin was key to the Paper Bag Players' impact on child audiences and critics. What Martin discovered was a way to abstract and express in a poetic, often humorous way, the psychological truth of a situation, exploring the child's internal, perhaps even unconscious, feelings toward the subject. In the works that resulted, classic stories and fairy tales were replaced by original contemporary skits, songs, and dances based on a child's own everyday experiences, on humor, and on a world-view in which there is no overwhelming evil, a world in which individuals, even children, can influence those around them. The theatre of the Paper Bag Players uses contemporary fantasy, heightened reality, and modern-day comic allegories. For example, *Hot Feet* celebrates the problems and joys of urban living; *Dandelion* deals with evolutionary theory, explaining how we are part of the life cycle and of nature's continuing adaptive process; *I Won't Take A Bath* concerns childhood fantasies; *Grandpa* deals with the life process of growing, changing, and aging; *Everybody, Everybody* shows how to accept and live with the differences among people; and *Mama's Got A Job* explores the changing nature of the American family. The many other provocative titles *The Runaway Presents* and *The Lost and Found Christmas*.

From the outset the Paper Bag Players have been recognized as outstanding innovators in their field. An early review called them "probably the best, certainly the most original children's theatre group in this country" (*Newsweek*, December 28, 1964, p. 55). Another called the Paper Bag Players "the most successful and enduring troupe around," referring to their plays as "classics to be revisited in the company of children" (*New York Times* March 28, 1973). Critics have consistently noted their imagination and ingenuity, the appeal and insight of their contemporary content, the intelligence and respect accorded their audiences, the freshness and clarity with which they appeal equally to preschoolers and adults, and the infectious nature of their humor. Among their commendations are the following firsts for a children's theatre: the first to perform at Lincoln Center in New York; the first *Village Voice* Off-Broadway (Obie) Award; the first Jenny Heiden Award from the American Theatre Association; and the first grant from the National Endowment for the Arts to a children's theatre.

Coming from the innovative, ground-breaking world of modern dance in the 1940s and 1950s, Judith Martin brought to American children's theatre an openness to fresh, innovative ideas and an understanding of the artistic freedom found in improvisation, combined with discipline, rigorous technique, and high professionalism. In The Paper Bag Players she succeeded in creating a theatre which critics recognized not only as the most innovative and long-lasting children's repertory theatre of its time, but also as an excellent example of quality contemporary Off-Broadway theatre.

A complete bibliography of Judith Martin's work can be found in Georgia Parchem, "The Development of A Unique American Children's Theatre, The Paper Bag Players of New York: 1958–1981'' (Unpublished Ph.D. dissertation, Ohio State University, 1982). Archival resources on the Paper Bag Players and Martin are housed at the office and studio of The Paper Bag Players (50 Riverside Drive, New York City). They include correspondence; financial and business files; programs and posters; educational materials; slides, films, video and audio tapes; scripted materials; and scrapbooks containing all articles and reviews. There is an incomplete file of articles, programs, films, and video tapes at the Performing Arts Research Center of the New York Public Library at Lincoln Center. Relevant texts include Anne Hollister, "Judith Martin's Act," *People Weekly* (December 22, 1975); Marcia Marks, "The Paper Bag Players," *Dancemagazine* (June 1964); Judith Liss and Nancy Lloyd, "The Paper Bag Players," *Theatre for Young Audiences*, ed. Nellie McCaslin (1978); and Martin's own published books, plays, and records, which are available through the Paper Bag Players, Baker's Plays, and the Anchorage Press.

Georga Larsen Parchem

MARTIN, Mary (December 1, 1913–): actress and musical comedy star most famous as Peter Pan in the musical version, was born in Weatherford, Texas. Her father, Preston "Pet" Martin, was a successful attorney in Weatherford. Mary Virginia Martin inherited her considerable musical gifts from her mother, Juanita (Presley) Martin, who, from the impressively young age of seventeen, had been a violin instructor at Weatherford Seminary, later Weatherford College. Martin's older sister, Geraldine, also stimulated the younger girl's interest in dance.

Mary Martin's hometown produced an extraordinary influence on her life. Family and neighbors early encouraged her penchant for performing. She made her stage debut when five years old at a local fireman's ball. At the age of twelve she began taking voice lessons and gave a successful recital. Her voice coach then and later in New York was Helen Fouts Cahoon, whose strength lay in teaching breath control and economical use of vocal power.

In 1930 Mary Martin attended Ward Belmont Finishing School in Nashville, Tennessee, for three months. While there she married Benjamin Jackson Hagman. The couple returned to Weatherford, and on September 21, 1931, Mary Martin gave birth to a boy, Larry Martin Hagman. She subsequently graduated from the local high school, with her first stage credit: leading role in the senior play. Upon graduation she opened, at her sister's suggestion, a dancing school in a grain storage loft, but soon realized that she herself required advanced instruction. Encouraged once more by her parents, she entered the Fanchon and Marco School of the Theatre in Hollywood, California. From the one summer's experience the actress became "hooked" on the excitement of show business. The Mary Hagman School of the Dance of Weatherford, Texas, expanded to three schools.

In the summer of 1935 Martin returned to Fanchon and Marco and began her effort to enter show business. Meanwhile, in Weatherford, her father had arranged an amicable divorce between Hagman and his daughter, and Martin moved to Hollywood. She sang on national radio programs and for various clubs. She auditioned for Oscar Hammerstein II (with whom she would later make theatre history in *South Pacific*) and Jerome Kern. She also tested, unsuccessfully, for Paramount, Twentieth Century-Fox, Universal, and MGM. In the summer of 1937 she sang at the Trocadero Nightclub, and Broadway producer Lawrence Schwab offered her a contract in New York for *Ring Out the News*, but there were problems and the show never opened. Unknown in New York, Martin was compelled to audition again, winning the role of the girl who sings "My Heart Belongs to Daddy" in Cole Porter's *Leave It to Me* (1938). With coaching from Sophie Tucker and performing with Gene Kelly, Martin became identified with the song and with the show. In fact, she emerged as Broadway's sweetheart.

After *Leave It to Me* she returned to Hollywood, making her motion picture debut in *The Great Victor Herbert* (1939), starring Allan Jones. During the next three years she starred in no less than ten films, including *Rhythm on the River* (1940) with Bing Crosby; *Love Thy Neighbor* (1940) with Jack Benny and Fred Allen; *Kiss the Boys Good-Bye* (1941) with Don Ameche and Oscar Levant; *New York Town* (1941) with Fred MacMurray and Robert Preston; and *Happy Go Lucky* (1943) with Dick Powell and Rudy Vallee. In 1940 she met her second husband, Richard Halliday, an editor and executive for Paramount Pictures.

In 1943 Martin returned to Broadway in producer **Cheryl Crawford**'s *One Touch Of Venus*, requesting and receiving a large wardrobe designed by Mainbocher. After the Broadway run Martin played in the national tour of this highly successful show. She also appeared in another play, *Lute Song* (1946), which Sydney Howard and Will Irwin prepared especially for her during the war years, in adaptation of a Chinese classic, *Pi-Pa-Ki*. In 1946 she made her London debut in Noel Coward's *Pacific 1860*, another play written for her, but the show and her performance received unenthusiastic reviews. Upon her return to America Martin appeared on national tour (1947–1948) in the role that **Ethel Merman** had created on Broadway in *Annie Get Your Gun*, by Irving Berlin. She also appeared again in this musical in one of her television specials (1957).

On April 7, 1949, Mary Martin and Ezio Pinza opened at New York's Majestic Theatre in *South Pacific*. Richard Rodgers, Oscar Hammerstein II, and director Joshua Logan had created one of the best musicals in American stage history. Martin's role as Ensign Nellie Forbush, and her singing of "I'm in Love with a Wonderful Guy" and "I'm Gonna Wash that Man Right Out of My Hair" became legendary. When the show played London (1951–1953), her second appearance there—unlike that of 1946—was a triumph. She then appeared opposite Charles Boyer in the considerably less successful *Kind Sir* (1953), and opposite **Helen Hayes** and George Abbott, she recreated the role of Sabina in a revival of Thornton Wilder's *The Skin of Our Teeth* (1955). Throughout the 1950s she also took part in some lesser shows, including a television special with Ethel Merman, and discovered her own island paradise in Brazil, where she moved with her husband.

Another triumph of this decade was her appearance with Cyril Ritchard in a new musical version of *Peter Pan* in 1954. Martin considered her playing of the title role the most important thing she had ever done in the theatre. As a result of that Broadway run and the two national telecasts, millions of children grew up with Mary Martin forever etched in their minds and in their hearts as Peter Pan. Success followed success, for from 1959 to 1961, Martin played and sang the role of Maria in *The Sound of Music*, preparing for the role by becoming well acquainted with her real life counterpart, the Baroness Maria Von Trapp. In 1965–1966, as the title character in *Hello, Dolly!*, she made a tour of the Orient, giving a controversial and dangerous series of performances for troops in Vietnam. She then returned to the Broadway stage in yet another hit, *I Do, I Do* (1966), with Robert Preston. She appeared again in a Broadway comedy, *Do You Turn Somersaults?* (1978), about a middle-aged woman who has a romance with a doctor; and in 1986 teamed up with **Carol Channing** in *Legends* on national tour.

Although Mary Martin's first marriage as a child bride was dissolved in favor of her career, her second marriage grew into one of the great love stories of the twentieth century stage. Married to Richard Halliday on May 5, 1940, she was by his bedside when he died March 3, 1973. From the day they wed, Halliday had worshipped his bride. He quit his own successful career to act as his wife's manager, advisor, consultant, and agent. Their daughter, Heller, played on stage with her mother from the age of five until she was fourteen. Now married to Bromley DeMeritt, Martin's daughter lives with her four children in Houston, Texas. Martin's actor son, Larry Hagman, is famous for his character, J. R. Ewing, the greedy oil baron in the popular television series, *Dallas*. Martin now makes her home in Palm Springs. Currently she hosts a PBS talk show out of San Francisco about the elderly, titled *Over Easy*.

Famous for her performances on Broadway, in New York, and on nationwide tours, Martin's significance to the American theatre lies in the impact of her starring roles, and the manner in which she became identified with the plays in which she appeared, in particular, *One Touch of Venus*, *South Pacific*, *Peter Pan*, and *The Sound Of Music*. She advanced the significance of the performer in the American musical. In the pre-production period of *South Pacific*, Martin suggested ideas for songs which became "I'm Gonna Wash that Man Right Out'a My Hair" and "Honey-Bun." She also helped choreograph several dance numbers. Mary Martin has left a permanent imprint on our great American culture. Her portrayals of Nellie Forbush in *South Pacific*, and of Peter Pan— that child within us all—have helped to unite us.

Mary Martin's memoir, *My Heart Belongs* (1976), remains a primary source for her life and work, and serves to clarify the development of such Broadway musicals as *South Pacific* and *The Sound of Music*. In collaboration with her husband, Richard Halliday, Martin is the author of *Needlepoint* (1969), which includes some interesting personal anecdotes. Newspaper clippings, reviews, magazine articles, and interviews cover Mary Martin's career from her Broadway debut as Dolly Winslow in *Leave It to Me* on November 9, 1938, to *Legends* in 1986. Choice selections include articles in *Life* (April 14, 1947), *Theatre Arts* (January 1949), *Esquire* (April 1968), *American Home* (August 1961), *Good*

Housekeeping (January 1963), and *The Saturday Evening Post* (March 28, 1959). Summaries of her life and work can be found in *The Biographical Encyclopaedia and Who's Who of the American Theatre* (1966); *Notable Names in the American Theatre* (1976); *Who's Who in America, 1978–1979*, Vol. II (1978–1979); *Who's Who in the Theatre* (1981); *The Oxford Companion to the Theatre* (1983); and *The Oxford Companion to American Theatre* (1984).

Donald Ray Schwartz

MAY, Elaine (April 21, 1932–): actress, director, and playwright, was born Elaine Berlin in Philadelphia, Pennsylvania. She began performing on stage and radio—often with her father, Yiddish actor Jack Berlin—while she was still a child. Her family moved many times while she was growing up because of her parents' theatrical careers; after they finally settled in Los Angeles, Elaine Berlin attended school there until the age of fourteen, when she dropped out. Three years later she attended classes and various events at the University of Chicago, though she never enrolled as a student. While in Chicago she met and married Marvin May. The marriage ended in divorce. Their daughter, the actress Jeannie Berlin, has appeared most notably in *The Heartbreak Kid* (1972), a film her mother directed. Elaine May married lyricist Sheldon Harnick in 1962; they divorced a year later.

After studying acting with Maria Ouspenskaya, Elaine May became the technical director for *Bruno and Sidney* in New York (1949). Thereafter she performed with the Playwright's Theatre in Chicago, where she met Mike Nichols. Together with four other performers May and Nichols formed an improvisational theatre group that appeared at the Compass Theatre from 1954 until 1957. Nichols and May moved to New York in 1957 and performed skits as a comedy team at the Village Vanguard and the Blue Angel. Although they had several standard routines, most of their sketches were improvisational, and audiences were often called upon to suggest subjects and styles. The year they arrived in New York, they made their television debut on the *Jack Paar Show*. Nichols and May appeared on many television shows of the late 1950s and early 1960s, including those of Dinah Shore, Perry Como, and Steve Allen, *The Fabulous Fifties*, *Omnibus*, and their own specials. In 1960 they made their New York stage debut in *An Evening with Mike Nichols and Elaine May*. Among their popular comedy record albums are *Improvisations to Music* (1960), *Highlights from the Broadway Production of An Evening with Mike Nichols and Elaine May* (1964), and *The Best of Mike Nichols and Elaine May* (1965).

Though perhaps most famous for her performances with Mike Nichols, Elaine May is a successful writer, actress, and director as well. In the 1960s she wrote three plays including *A Matter of Position* (1962), *Not Enough Rope* (1962), and *Adaptation* (1969), the last of which she directed. For *Adaptation* May received a Drama Desk Award as a promising playwright and an Outer Circle Award for directing and writing. In 1971 she wrote the screenplay for *Such Good Friends* from the novel by Lois Gould, and in 1983 she wrote a play titled

Better Part of Valor. She began in film by acting in Carl Reiner's *Enter Laughing* (1967) and in Murray Schisgal's *Luv* (1967). May wrote the screenplay for *A New Leaf* (1970); she directed the production and played the principal role of Henrietta Lowell, a sweetly dimwitted and unworldly heiress opposite Walter Matthau. She directed *The Heartbreak Kid* (1972). She wrote the screenplay for *Mickey and Nicky* (1976) and directed *Heaven Can Wait* (1978), featuring Warren Beatty. In 1980 May and Mike Nichols worked together again in a production of *Who's Afraid of Virginia Woolf?* at the Long Wharf Theatre in New Haven, Connecticut. In 1982 May wrote and played a role in a one-act play, *Hot Line*, included on a triple bill at the Goodman Theatre in Chicago. In 1987 she wrote the screenplay and directed *Ishtar*, which starred Warren Beatty and Dustin Hoffman.

With Mike Nichols, May developed a witty and pointed style of improvisational humor in which comedy emerged from character and situation rather than from one-liners. An excellent mimic and actress, she has portrayed a wide variety of characters, including a social-climbing party-goer who chattily claims to know Albert Einstein, Adolf Hitler, and God; a clubwoman snootily initiating her friends into the mysteries of culture; a funeral director who offers several ice-cold, pragmatic options to her grief-stricken client; and a series of variously nasal and bureaucratic telephone company employees. Nichols and May delighted audiences with their satire; they were censored from television's 1960 Emmy Awards because the sponsor, a manufacturer of home hair permanents, was offended by their skit which mocked home "perms." Their improvisational comedy influenced generations of actors and comedians who emerged from the Second City troupe in Chicago. As a writer and director, May has shown a deep appreciation of lost, ludicrous characters, as well as situations laced with hilarity and poignance. To her multiple careers as comic, actress, writer, and director for both stage and film, May has brought a unique wit, sensitivity, and skill.

Most sources discuss Elaine May as half of the famous Nichols and May comedy team. *Joe Franklin's Encyclopedia of Comedians* (1979) describes their unique brand of improvisational humor. An early review of Nichols and May in *Time* (June 2, 1958) also explores their style and provides a brief biography of May. *Time* (September 26, 1960) and *Look* (June 21, 1960) examine the personal style and humor of Nichols and May. She is included in *Women in Comedy* by Linda Martin and Kerry Segrave (1986). *Contemporary Dramatists* (1977) lists and briefly analyzes her plays in terms of theme and content; this reference also provides a list of the plays, films, and cabarets in which she performed. *Current Biography, 1961–1962* (1961) discusses May's personal history and quotes reviews as well as interview material. She is also listed in *The Biographical Encyclopaedia and Who's Who of the American Theatre* (1966); *Notable Names in the American Theatre* (1976); *Contemporary Dramatists* (1977); *Who's Who in the Theatre* (1981); and *Who's Who in America, 1984–1985*, Vol. II (1984).

Beth Kalikoff

MAYLEAS, Ruth Rothschild (January 9, 1925–): arts executive and consultant, was born in New York City, the daughter of Anna Beatrice (Cohen) Rothschild, a native New Yorker, and Alfred Rothschild, a businessman and writer who immigrated to the United States from Germany. Her father co-edited a Bantam Shakespeare series. Ruth and her sister Joan, who is now a professor of political science, were raised in Manhattan, where their culturally minded parents early and regularly exposed them to the arts. From May 4, 1952, until they divorced in 1964, Ruth Rothschild was married to William M. Mayleas, a real estate executive. The couple had one daughter, Alexandra Rothschild Mayleas (b. 1957). After graduation from Cornell University with a Bachelor of Arts degree in English literature (1946), Mayleas broadened her education at the Alliance Française in Paris and at the **Hanya Holm** School of Dance in New York City. She also held a number of what she calls "the usual post-college jobs" (Personal interview, 1985). She worked, for example, for Time, Inc. It would be five years before she found the position which would launch her distinguished career as an arts consultant and administrator.

In 1951 Mayleas came to the American National Theatre and Academy (ANTA), which, among other things, was the only nongovernmental theatre organization founded but not financed by Congress. By 1955 Mayleas had become Director of ANTA's National Theatre Service and was also associated with the United States Center of the International Theatre Institute. She worked with these organizations until 1966. Among her advisors and mentors during this period were fellow ANTA/ITI leaders **Rosamond Gilder** and Elizabeth Burdick as well as W. McNeil Lowry, who from 1957 to 1975 directed the arts program of the Ford Foundation. At ANTA, Mayleas administered the Academy's information program, its publications division, and its advisory service to the fledgling nonprofit theatre movement.

Her next career step placed her in the position from which she has significantly affected to the development of American theatre. In 1966 she joined the newborn National Endowment for the Arts, then headed by Roger L. Stevens. Initially, she was in charge of both the Theatre and the Dance Programs. For two years she helped shape the latter program, but as the field grew more vigorous a full-time director was needed, and in 1968 that post went to June Arey. Mayleas continued to pilot the NEA's Theatre Program for thirteen crucial years, in which the number of nonprofit resident theatres grew from 30 to 200 and her budget from a few hundred thousand dollars to $7,500,000. In structuring the Theatre Program, Mayleas formulated major policy goals. Since the federal project was funded by taxpayers, it was necessary to serve the public along with the theatrical community. Mayleas strove also to support the aims and the often pressing needs of the developing regional theatres themselves. She also hoped to promote their greater stability in terms of institutional longevity and fiscal equilibrium, meanwhile stimulating growth towards artistic maturity. One key concept she originated to address some of these issues was that of peer review of grant proposals submitted to NEA. "Working with the field's outstanding professionals," she explains, "I developed consultant and panel review systems. . . . Spreading from theatre to other NEA programs, these systems eventually served as general models for the agency" (Mayleas, résumé).

The most important achievement of her tenure at the Endowment was, Mayleas believes, "building a solid program that recognized the continuing requirements of nonprofit theatre institutions, large and small, for *general* support of their ongoing work. . . . We tried to avoid gimmicky grant-making where projects needed to be invented just to get the money. Our program very deliberately avoided that. . . . What was built there was, I feel, a program that was flexible enough yet strong enough to be maintained by my successors—not totally without change, naturally, but nonetheless . . . the foundation is still there, or so it seems to me" (Personal interview).

When Mayleas and many other longtime NEA staff members were obliged to relinquish their offices at the inception of President Jimmy Carter's administration in 1978, she first became an independent arts consultant to foundations, arts service organizations, and educational institutions. Among her clients from 1978 to 1982 were the Theatre Development Fund, Cornell University, the State University of New York, and the Theatre Communications Group. However, from 1982 to the present, Mayleas has been with the Ford Foundation as director of their Education and Culture Program. In contrast to her broad, national NEA mandate with its emphasis on core support, here Mayleas has identified special areas which have been sporadically supported by other funding sources. Under her guidance the Education and Culture Program focuses on performing arts, stressing three complementary priorities: 1) the development of new work, including "cross-disciplinary collaborations" which bridge "formal barriers between art forms;" 2) encouragement of "pluralism and diversity" to enable minority artists and arts organizations to achieve artistic growth and institutional stability; and 3) archival documentation of performances and the artists who create them (Mayleas, discussion paper).

Mayleas's activities have been widespread. In 1984 she participated in the Assembly of "The Arts and Public Policy in the United States;" from 1981 until 1984 she was on the Steering Committee of the League of Professional Theatre Women; from 1980 until 1983 she was a trustee of the National Theatre Conference; and from 1980 until 1982 she was on the Board of Directors of the New Drama Forum. She was a national adjudicator for the American College Theatre Festival in 1980 and in 1979 a guest judge for the *Village Voice* Off-Broadway (Obie) awards. She has been chairperson of the Board of Visitors, School of Theatre Arts for Boston University; and Advisory Committee member for the Center for the Performing Arts at Cornell University. She has been a delegate to international congresses in Warsaw, Tel Aviv, New York, Prague, and London and a Department of State delegate to the International Conference of English Speaking Theatre. In 1979 she was a member of the Theatre Directors Delegation sent by the United States International Communications Agency to Western Europe.

She has been the recipient of the Ford Foundation Travel and Study Grant (1963); the National Theatre Conference Annual Award for distinguished contribution to the American theatre (1973); the Long Wharf Theatre Award for dedicated leadership of professional theatre (1974); the League of Resident Theatres Award for devotion to the professional theatre (1978); the Dance Theatre Workshop, New York Dance and Performance Award (Bessie), and a Special Citation to former directors of the NEA's Dance Program (1985). She has been editor, ANTA *News Bulletin*; U.S. correspondent, *World Premières Mondiales* (Paris: III); editor, regional theatre section, *Best Plays of 1964*; editor, "The Condition of Professional Training and Career-Development Opportunities in the Dance, Opera, Musical Theatre, and Theatre Fields" (Theatre Development Fund); and guest contributor to publications of the Theatre Communications Group, 1980. She has published various articles in *Yale/Theater*, *Performing Arts Journal*, and other professional periodicals. She has given seminars and lectures for the Smithsonian Institution, Yale University, the University of North Carolina, and the University of Illinois, as well as for various professional associations and in other public forums.

Mayleas is most notable in American theatre for her leadership in the not-for-profit resident theatre movement as both spokesperson and consultant. Her administration of the Theatre Program of the National Endowment for the Arts gave critical years of leadership for the American theatre.

Most of the information used in this essay has been obtained from a personal interview with Ruth Mayleas in the fall of 1985 and from her resumé. The following writings by Mayleas have also been consulted: "The Education and Culture Program's Work in the Arts," a discussion paper for the Ford Foundation (September 1985); "Resident Theatres as National Theatres," *Theater* (Summer 1979); "The Politics of Inspiration: American Theatre in Flux," a round-table discussion which included Mayleas, *Performing Arts Journal 14*, Vol. V, Number 2 (1981). Mayleas is included in *The Biographical Encyclopaedia and Who's Who of the American Theatre* (1966) and *Notable Names in the American Theatre* (1976).

C. Lee Jenner

McCANN, Elizabeth I. (March 26, 1931–): producer, was born in New York City and grew up in Manhattan's garment district. She was an only child; her whose father was a subway motorman and her mother a housewife. An Irish Catholic, she attended parochial schools and Manhattanville College in Purchase, New York. At Manhattanville she worked on school plays and developed a taste for theatre. After a trip to see Rosalind Russell in *Wonderful Town* she said that she was forever "hooked" on the theatre. She received a Master of Arts degree in English literature with a minor in Restoration drama at Columbia University. She became a production secretary at age thirty but decided to go into theatrical law. She attended Fordham Law School where she received her law degree. She worked with Maurice Evans Productions and with producers Arnold Saint-Subber and Harold Prince. In 1967 producer James Nederlander hired her as managing director for his enterprises.

In 1976 she and **Nelle Nugent**, who was assistant managing director for Nederlander, founded McCann and Nugent, a production and management firm. Each of the partners handled the work that she liked best. Nugent with a fine eye for details, worked with designers and crews and supervised technical matters, such as lighting and scenery. McCann negotiated contracts with actors, directors, and authors; supervised artistic development and advertising; and managed all merchandising/marketing aspects. Deeply analytical, McCann deals well with people.

In 1978 McCann and Nugent became consultants and then general managers of Lincoln Center's Vivian Beaumont Theatre. *Variety* referred to the two women as "the new generation" of Broadway producers, which consisted of managers who came up through the ranks acquiring indispensable experience in handling creative talent, union relationships, and promotional know-how. They also knew the business from the theatre operator's side. They saw themselves as catalysts for upgrading Broadway theatre and expanding its audience. "We must make Broadway commercially viable for serious dramatists," said McCann (*New York Times Magazine*, February 1, 1981).

By 1985 McCann and Nugent had received 58 nominations and 20 Antoinette Perry (Tony) awards. To date they have produced twenty-two Broadway productions, including *Dracula, The Elephant Man, Morning's At Seven, Home, Amadeus, Piaf, Nicholas Nickleby, The Dresser, Rose, Mass Appeal, Pilhobus Dance Theatre, Night and Day, All's Well That Ends Well, Good, Total Abandon, The Glass Menagerie, The Lady and the Clarinet, The Gin Game, Crimes of the Heart, Pacific Overtures, Painting Churches,* and *Leader of the Pack.* Critical acclaim included Tony awards for *Dracula, The Elephant Man, Morning's at Seven, Amadeus,* and *Nicholas Nickleby*; the New York Drama Critics Awards for *The Elephant Man* and *Nicholas Nickleby*; and the Drama Desk awards for *Amadeus, The Elephant Man,* and *Nicholas Nickleby*.

McCann is an active consultant to the Rockefeller Foundation and is on the executive board of the League of New York Theatres and Producers. She is also on the boards of the Joffrey Ballet and the New Dramatists. She was the 1981 recipient of the Justice Award of the Catholic Interracial Council of New York.

In May 1985 *Variety* reported that McCann and Nugent were seeking independent producing projects (May 29, 1985). Nugent has relocated in Hollywood film producing projects, and McCann has continued as a legitimate theatre producer in New York.

Articles on Elizabeth McCann and Nelle Nugent as producers are "Broadway Long Shots," *Playbill* (November 1980); "Presenting McCann and Nugent," *New York Times Magazine* (February 1, 1981); "Broadway's Golden Ladies," *Time* (March 9, 1981), which gives some biographical data; and "The Robb Report," *Eastern Airlines Magazine* (February 1985). *Variety* (May 29, 1985), as noted above, announced the current professional activities of McCann and Nugent. Some material for this essay was obtained by a telephone interview with Nelle Nugent on October 28, 1985.

Patricia Sternberg

McCASLIN, Nellie (August 20, 1914–): theatre educator, author, and specialist in children's theatre, was born in Cleveland, Ohio. Her parents, Paul Giles McCaslin and Nellie (Wagner) McCaslin, had grown up in western Pennsylvania and settled in Cleveland as young adults. Prior to his marriage, her father had been an actor touring in Shakespearean productions, but his career was short-lived due to his dissatisfaction with the ''spear-carrier'' roles in which he was cast. Upon his return from ''the road,'' his parents convinced him to become a businessman. Stories of her father's theatrical experiences were shared with Nellie McCaslin as she grew up. Her only sibling, June, was six years younger than her sister. Although June had no abiding interest in theatre, Nellie persuaded her to assist with basement puppet shows performed for neighborhood children on Saturday mornings for nearly seven years.

In 1936 Nellie McCaslin received her Bachelor of Arts degree in English from Western Reserve University in Cleveland; at that time the University did not offer an undergraduate major in theatre. She was awarded a graduate fellowship by Western Reserve and earned her Master of Arts degree in theatre in 1937. Following graduation McCaslin began her teaching career at a girls' preparatory school, the Tudor Hall School in Indianapolis. Here she had the opportunity to work with children of all ages (nursery through 12th grade) in dramatic activities. After seven years of teaching experience there, she determined that it was better not to put small children into scripted productions. The children with whom she worked began to express a desire for scripted plays only at the 7th grade level. In the mid–1940s McCaslin spent a summer in Hollywood attending a workshop taught by Maria Ouspenskaya, whose focus was solely upon improvisational work. This workshop became an important link to McCaslin's later work in creative drama.

Her next position was at the National College of Education in Evanston, Illinois, where she taught undergraduate education majors. In teaching theatre, one of her prime emphases was upon theatre for children. Noting a lack of quality theatre for children, McCaslin began to adapt children's stories for performance. She formed a children's theatre company with her students which toured northern Illinois. During her tenure at the National College of Education in Evanston, McCaslin became a good friend of **Winifred Ward**, a leading figure in the reform of children's theatre. Like McCaslin, Ward wanted to change the concept of children's theatre from the ''school assembly program'' to theatre for audiences of children.

In the early 1950s McCaslin began work on her doctorate in the Dramatic Arts program of New York University's School of Education. In 1957 she completed the Ph.D. degree at New York University under the guidance of Fred Blanchard. Her dissertation, which later evolved into a published book (1971), was written on the history of theatre for children in the United States. That same year she began teaching at Mills College of Education in New York City, where she remained for twelve years. During that time she developed a Saturday morning theatre workshop for children, which gave her students the opportunity to work within a laboratory setting for the teaching of creative drama. McCaslin's skill in teaching creative drama and conducting workshops for children led to an invitation to teach part-time at the Teacher's College of Columbia University.

After Mills College of Education closed in 1972, McCaslin was invited to teach at New York University's Program in Educational Theatre. In addition to her professorship in Educational Theatre, McCaslin became director in 1976 of New York University's "University Without Walls," a nontraditional alternative to university education. She retired in 1985 and is at present Adjunct Professor of Educational Theatre. Her career has been marked by a series of publications which have become landmarks in the literature of her chosen field, and have made her name synonymous with all that is best in American theatre for children and youth.

McCaslin has been an active member of the American Theatre Association and past president of the Children's Theatre Association of America. She also served on the advisory boards of the Anchorage Press, St. Martin's Press, Periwinkle Productions, the American Mime Theatre, and the Imagination Theatre of Chicago. She has been an invited participant in conferences all over the United States, Canada, and England. She traveled twice to Sibenik, Yugoslavia, to participate in the Festival of the Arts for Children. She has visited children's theatres in Russia, and participated there in an international children's theatre conference of the International Association of Theatre for Children and Youth (ASSITEJ).

McCaslin has received many awards. In 1976 she was given the Jennie Heiden Award for excellence in children's theatre, and in 1977 she was named to the College of Fellows of the American Theatre Association. In 1978 she was honored as advisor of the year and in 1985 was awarded a Certificate of Distinction by the New York University Gallatin Division. In 1985 she also received the Newton D. Baker Award for distinguished service from the Western Reserve University Alumni Association. In 1986 New York University conferred on her its Great Teacher Award.

McCaslin's contributions to theatre in the United States include teaching techniques of creative drama for over 30 years, writing volumes of plays for children's theatre productions, editing and contributing to anthologies about children's theatre, and writing a history of children's theatre in the United States. She remains in the top rank of those who have devoted their lives to children's theatre and creative drama.

Nellie McCaslin has published collections of stories suitable for creative dramatization by children, including *Legends in Action* (1945), *More Legends in Action* (1950), *Pioneers in Petticoats* (1961), *Tall Tales and Tall Men* (1956), *The Little Snow Girl* (1963), and *The Rabbit Who Wanted Red Wings* (1963). Her works on children's theatre and creative dramatics include *Theatre for Children in the United States: a History* (1971), *Shows on a Shoestring* (1979), *Children and Drama* (second edition, 1981), and *Creative Drama in the Classroom* (fourth edition, 1984). McCaslin has written two handbooks for teachers: *Creative Drama in the Primary Grades* (1986) and *Creative Drama in the Intermediate Grades* (1986). Her *Historical Guide to Children's Theatre in America* was published in 1988. McCaslin has also written numerous articles, book reviews, and introductions to or chapters in books on children's theatre. She is listed in *The Directory of American Scholars*, Vol. II (1982), and *Who's Who of American Women 1977–1978* (1977–1978).

Much of the information for this entry came from a personal interview with Nellie McCaslin.

Barbara Ann Simon

McCLENDON, Rose (August 27, 1884–June 12, 1936): distinguished actress, once known on Broadway as "the Negro race's first lady," was born Rosalie Virginia Scott in Greenville, South Carolina. When she was about six years old her parents, Sandy and Tena (Jenkins) Scott, moved Rosalie and her brother and sister to New York City. Her parents worked as coachman and housekeeper for a wealthy family in the city. In New York Rosalie attended Public School No. 40, Manhattan. At the age of twenty, on October 27, 1904, she married Dr. Henry Pruden McClendon. Although a licensed chiropractor, Dr. McClendon worked primarily as a Pullman porter for the Pennsylvania Railroad.

Rose McClendon became totally committed to the theatre after 1916, when she won a scholarship to the American Academy of Dramatic Art. There she studied with Frank Sargent and her first professional role soon followed. It was a small part in *Justice* by John Galsworthy, performed during the 1919–1920 season by the Bramhall Players in the Davenport Theatre in New York. Her role as Octavie in Lawrence Stallings's *Deep River*, which opened in Philadelphia in September of 1926 and moved to New York in October, brought her peer recognition and critical success. During a performance in Philadelphia, the noted director Arthur Hopkins urged **Ethel Barrymore** to stay through the performance and "watch Rose McClendon come down those stairs. She can teach some of our most hoity-toity actresses distinction." After viewing McClendon's performance, Barrymore remarked, "She can teach all of them distinction" (*Journal of Negro History*, January 1937, p. 131).

After her success with *Deep River*, McClendon was featured in Paul Green's 1926 Pulitzer-prize-winning play, *In Abraham's Bosom*. Two years later, she played Serena in Dorothy and DuBose Heyward's *Porgy*. DuBose Heyward himself believed that "Rose McClendon was perfect as the Catfish Row aristocrat Serena" (Heyward, *Porgy*, p. 13). Soon McClendon became known on Broadway as "the Negro race's first lady." Still, she remained modest and often stated that her recognition came quite undeserved (Bond, *The Negro and the Drama*, p. 84).

Her theatrical career continued to flourish in the early 1930s. In 1931 she played Big Sue in *The House of Connelly*, another play written by Paul Green. The following year she portrayed Mammy in *Never No More*, a play about lynching produced by the Group Theatre. During the 1933 season, she worked on radio in the "John Henry Sketches." All this time she remained deeply committed to promoting the needs of her fellow black actors and actresses. She fought with the actors' union for more opportunities for blacks and formed a small black theatre group. When **Hallie Flanagan** began organizing the Black Federal Theatre Project troupe in New York City in 1935, Rose McClendon played a significant part in the planning. In fact, the first meeting was held in McClendon's home.

In 1935 Rose McClendon starred as Cora in the Broadway production of Langston Hughes's *Mulatto*, the longest running play on Broadway by a black author before *A Raisin in the Sun*. In this role she received extremely favorable reviews from the New York critics. Doris Abramson believed the play's high quality of acting, particularly that of McClendon, was a major factor in its successful run. Unfortunately, during the production of *Mulatto*, McClendon became extremely ill with pleurisy and was forced to leave the cast. One year later, after a continued bout with sickness, she died of pneumonia on July 12, 1936.

Still, her spirit has managed to live on. In the year after her death, a black theatre group named the Rose McClendon Players was organized in her memory. Rose McClendon was a champion for her race and for her chosen craft, the theatre.

For reviews of Rose McClendon's performances see "In Abraham's Bosom," *Theatre Magazine* (August 1927); the *Afro-American*, New York (April 30, 1932); *National News* (March 24, 1932); *Amsterdam News* (March 25, 1931 and March 24, 1934); and *The New York Daily Mirror* (April 10, 1934). For additional information see Doris Abramson, *Negro Playwrights* (1969); Frederick Bond, *The Negro and the Drama* (1940); DuBose Hayward, *Porgy* (1929); *The Crisis* (April 1927); James Weldon Johnson, *Black Manhattan* (1930); and the *Journal of Negro History*, Vol. 22 (1937). Langston Hughes and Milton Meltzer, in *Black Magic* (1967), reprint photographs of Rose McClendon in some of her starring roles. The Rose McClendon Scrapbook and clippings about her are in the Schomburg Collection at the 135th Street branch of the New York Public Library. Obituaries of McClendon appeared in the *Journal of Negro History* (January 1937), *Opportunity* (August 1936), the *Afro-American* (April 30, 1932), the New York *Amsterdam News* (July 18, 1936), and the *New York Times* (July 14, 1936). McClendon is included in *Notable American Women*, Vol. II (1971), and *The Oxford Companion to American Theatre* (1984).

Harry Elam

McCULLERS, Carson (February 19, 1917–September 29, 1967): playwright and novelist, was born Lula Carson Smith, the daughter of Marguerite (Waters) Smith and Lamar Smith, a craftsman and jeweler. As the Smiths' firstborn, she was named after her maternal grandmother, Lula Caroline Waters, with whom they were living at the time of her birth in Columbus, Georgia.

Marguerite Waters and Lamar Smith had married in Jacksonville, Georgia, on February 14, 1910. They had three children—Lula Carson, Lamar (b. May 13, 1919), and Margarita Gachet (b. August 2, 1922). Their mother, who was studious and a music enthusiast, believed her firstborn to be a very special child who was destined to become an outstanding musician. To this end she stimulated the child's imaginative and creative disposition with fanciful stories and enrolled her in kindergarten at age four and a half, encouraging her to be "different." The child also had an enthusiasm for books even before she was enrolled in school, and her mother promoted her intellectual growth by giving her books, reading aloud to her, and offering clothing from the mother's own wardrobe for creative games. This encouragement stimulated Lula to exercise her imagination by developing plots, skits, and pantomimes for her playmates. In spite of such encouragement, Lula Carson was an unhappy child. Throughout her life she was pensive and chose solitude more often than companionship. Lamar Smith died of an acute coronary attack on August 1, 1944, and Marguerite Waters Smith died unexpectedly on June 10, 1950.

As a teen-ager Lula Carson was determined to become a concert pianist, and her mother provided weekly piano lessons with Mrs. Kendrick Kierce, a leading piano teacher in Columbus, Georgia, with whom she studied for approximately four years. She continued lessons with Mary Tucker until 1934. After she had spent the summer of 1930 in Cincinnati with her mother's relatives, Lula Carson Smith renounced her first name and implored others, including those responsible for her school records in Georgia, to address her as Carson Smith. From then until her death she was known as Carson, the name of her maternal great-grandmother. In the winter of 1932, Carson was confined to bed with rheumatic fever (misdiagnosed at the time as pneumonia) and was placed in a sanitarium to rest. During her convalescence she disclosed to her close friend, Helen Jackson, her new obsession: her determination to become a writer.

Carson was unpopular at Columbus High School, disliked by teachers who believed she had no interest in academics and by peers who ridiculed her peculiar attire and eccentric behavior. Carson's mother and piano teacher had already assumed that she would attend Juilliard to study music upon graduating from high school. She graduated in June 1933 during the depression, which made such an undertaking financially impossible without a scholarship, for which she declined to compete. She decided instead to continue study with Mrs. Tucker. In addition to studying piano, she read Greek philosophy and drama, French and German literature in translation, the works of the nineteenth-century Russian realists, and most British and American novels. Carson's mother and father were always supportive of her artistic endeavors, so when Carson told them she wanted to go to New York to study music at Juilliard and writing at Columbia University they sold two family heirlooms to finance her trip.

Carson Smith arrived in New York by steamship in September 1934, staying with her pen pal, Claire Sasser (also from Columbus), who had agreed with Carson's parents to look after her in New York. After having paid most of her tuition to study creative writing at Columbia, Carson and her new roommate lost on the subway all the money they possessed. Sasser, feeling responsible for the loss, wired her father for money for both of them, but Carson preferred to take various jobs to support herself while she attended evening writing classes. These she began in February 1935 with Dorothy Scarborough and Helen Rose Hull at Columbia. Carson returned home to Columbus during the summer.

It was during this visit that Carson's only male friend, Edwin Peacock, introduced her to his friend James Reeves McCullers, a colonel in the United

States Army. Peacock had written Carson about Reeves during their frequent correspondence, and he talked even more frequently to Reeves about Carson. The three became inseparable friends, sharing similar interests in music and literature. Reeves McCullers and Carson Smith were married September 20, 1937, at the Smith residence in Columbus. In spite of their love for each other, their common interests, and kindred spirits, their marriage was mercurial. Carson McCullers, a disciplined writer, however, continued to write daily despite marital distractions. By 1940 she had published *The Heart is a Lonely Hunter*, and was considered by critics to be one of the important new American writers. From 1940, and every year of her life thereafter, she was invited to a writers' colony where throughout the years she made friends with writers of note. Carson and Reeves McCullers were estranged by 1941, remarried in 1945, divorced in 1950, and reunited in 1951. Carson's final separation from her husband occurred during the summer of 1953 after many separations and reconciliations. Reeves McCullers committed suicide in Paris on November 19, 1953. They had no children.

Although Carson McCullers suffered from physical disabilities throughout her life, she continued to be a prolific writer best known for her novels. After studying creative writing at New York University with Sylvia Chatfield Bates in 1935 and at Columbia with Whit Burnett in 1936, McCullers became ill and was confined to bed during the winter of 1936. In December of the same year her short story, "Wunderkind," was published in *Story Magazine*. She had begun her first novel, *The Heart is a Lonely Hunter*, on her honeymoon in Charlotte, North Carolina, in 1937 during the happiest period of her marriage. In 1938 she submitted six chapters and an outline of a second novel to Houghton Mifflin, for which she received a contract and the promise of a five-hundred-dollar advance. Houghton Mifflin published three of McCullers's novels: *The Heart is a Lonely Hunter* (1940); *Reflections in a Golden Eye* (1941); and *The Member of the Wedding* (1946).

Three of McCullers's works were dramatized. Upon the suggestion of Tennessee Williams, she wrote the dramatization of her novel *The Member of the Wedding*. It opened on Broadway January 5, 1950, and ran 501 performances. It won the New York Drama Critics Circle Award and the Donaldson Award, and McCullers was given a Gold Medal by the Theatre Club, Inc., as the best playwright of the year. Both the Broadway play and the 1953 film featured **Ethel Waters** as the cook and **Julie Harris** as the twelve-year-old motherless child, Frankie Addams. McCullers' second play, titled *The Square Root of Wonderful*, opened on Broadway in October 30, 1957, but closed after 45 performances. According to Sara Nalley, the play had undergone numerous revisions, several of them guided by McCullers's close friend, producer Arnold Saint-Subber. "By the time it opened on Broadway it had been subjected to a series of directors and many rewrites.... Advance ticket sales kept it running for forty-five performances" (*Twentieth Century American Dramatists* Vol. II, p. 73). After this failure McCullers never wrote another play except her adaptation, in collaboration with Mary Rodgers, of a musical version of *The Member of the Wedding*, which was completed by Theodore Mann and produced Off-Broadway as *F. Jasmine Addams* for twenty performances in May 1971. The Glasgow Theatre, Scotland, presented *The Square Root of Wonderful* at the Palace of Art in 1963, where it was well received by critics. Edward Albee dramatized her novella *The Ballad of the Sad Café* in 1963, an adaptation which McCullers encouraged, but found disappointing. It opened on Broadway October 30, 1963, and closed after 123 performances. *Reflections in a Golden Eye* was produced as a film, but not released until October 11, 1967. *The Heart is a Lonely Hunter* went into film production one day before McCullers was buried. The film featured **Cicely Tyson**, Alan Arkin, and Stacey Keach. Carson McCullers suffered a cerebral hemorrhage and died on September 29, in the Nyack Hospital, New York; she was buried on October 3, 1967, in Oak Hill Cemetery on the bank of the Hudson River in Nyack.

Throughout her prolific writing career McCullers suffered three paralyzing strokes, respiratory diseases, a mastectomy, a heart attack, and acute depression. Indeed, by the age of 28 she had already suffered two strokes which paralyzed the left side of her body. She did not allow these serious illnesses to affect her writing. While writing novels, she also wrote short stories and nonfiction prose pieces which were published in various magazines, including *The New Yorker*, *Harper's Bazaar*, *Vogue*, *Theatre Arts*, *Mademoiselle*, *Esquire*, and *Redbook*.

People have described Carson McCullers in various ways: withdrawn, shy, eccentric, sensitive, and loyal. Tennessee Williams, her long-time friend, described her best in the preface to *The Lonely Hunter: A Biography of Carson McCullers*; he wrote, "She owned the heart and the deep understanding of it, but in addition she had that 'tongue of angels' that gave her power to sing of it, to make of it an anthem." And finally, "Carson's heart was often lonely and it was a tireless hunter for those to whom she could offer it, but it was a heart that was graced with light that eclipsed its shadows" (pp. XVIII and XIX).

McCullers was awarded two Guggenheim Fellowships, an Arts and Letters Grant from the American Academy of Arts and Letters, and membership in the National Institute of Arts and Letters, along with her theatre awards for best play and best playwright. She was inducted *in absentia* into the National Institute of Arts and Letters in 1952 and awarded the Prize of the Younger Generation by *Die Welt*, a newspaper in Hamburg, Germany. In 1966 she was the winner of the Henry Bellamann Award, a $1000 grant in recognition of her "outstanding contribution to literature." Although not primarily a playwright, McCullers contributed several memorable characters to American theatre in dramatizations which have become legendary.

Carson McCullers' work is represented by *The Heart is a Lonely Hunter* (1940, film version, 1967); *Reflections in a Golden Eye* (1941, film version, 1967); *The Member of the Wedding* (1946, dramatization by McCullers, 1951, and film version, 1952); *The Ballad of the Sad Café and Other Works* (1951, dramatization by Edward Albee, 1963); *The Ballad of the Sad Café and Collected Short Stories* (1952, 1955); *The Square Root of Wonderful* (1958); *Clock Without Hands* (1961); *Sweet As a Pickle and Clean As a*

Pig: Poems (1964); and *The Mortgaged Heart*, ed. Margarita G. Smith (1971). *Carson McCullers: A Descriptive Listing and Annotated Bibliography of Criticism* by Adrian M. Shapiro, Jackson R. Bryer, and Kathleen Field, includes comprehensive listings on and by Carson McCullers. The definitive biography of McCullers is *The Lonely Hunter: A Biography of Carson McCullers* by Virginia Spencer Carr (1975, 1985). Oliver Evans's *The Ballad of Carson McCullers* is a sympathetic biography which presents evaluations of her works. McCullers' obituary appeared in the *New York Times* (September 30, 1967). Biographical information about McCullers appears in *Current Biography, 1940* (1940, renewed 1968, reissued 1971); *Contemporary American Novelists* (1964); *The Biographical Encyclopaedia and Who's Who of the American Theatre* (1966); *Contemporary Authors*, Vols. 5–6 (1963) and Vols. 25–28 (1971); *American Writers*, ed. L. Unger (1972); *Dictionary of Literary Biography*, Vol. II, *American Novelists Since World War II* (1978); *Southern Writers: A Biographical Dictionary* (1979); *American Women Writers*, Vol. III (1981); and *Twentieth Century American Dramatists*, Vol. II (1981).

Elizabeth Hadley Freydberg

McILRATH, Patricia Anne (January 25, 1917–): educator, director, and founding artistic director of the Missouri Repertory Theatre, was born in Kansas City, the third of five children of George David and Ethel (Howard) McIlrath. Her father, of Protestant Northern Irish descent, was studying law at the University of Chicago when he met her mother, a contralto preparing for grand opera, whose Catholic family had come from Limerick and Tipperary. They settled in Kansas City, where her father practiced law for the rest of his life. In 1921 the family moved into the house on East 72nd Street where Patricia McIlrath still lives. The close-knit family enjoyed many athletic and artistic activities together, as her father had excelled in five sports and her mother was accomplished in drawing and writing as well as music.

Patricia McIlrath graduated from Paseo High School in 1933, studied for two years at Kansas City Junior College, and, at eighteen, transferred to Grinnell College, in Iowa, where she earned her Bachelor of Arts degree in history in 1937, with a certificate in education and minors in philosophy and English. Her first teaching job was at Englewood Elementary School in North Kansas City, where she organized choral speaking activities for first through fourth grades; later she taught English and directed dramatic arts programs at high schools in Webster Groves and Houston, Missouri, and in Batavia, Illinois. While completing a Master's degree in Speech and Theatre at Northwestern University in Evanston in 1946, she directed Thorne Hall Theatre on the university's downtown campus. From 1946 to 1954 she was a member of the Speech and Theatre faculty at the University of Illinois in Urbana, becoming an assistant professor and member of the Graduate College in 1952. On leave from that position in 1948–1949, she was a lecturer in speech at Stanford University in California, where she earned her doctorate in 1951.

Before McIlrath's father died of cancer in June 1954, he asked her to try to do something for Kansas City. He felt that the city had been good to him and that he had not done enough in return. She then inquired about possible openings at the University of Kansas City and was offered a position as director of the University Playhouse and chair of a theatre department newly separated from radio, television, and speech. Although her mentors could not understand such a move, she never regretted her decision to settle in Kansas City. The private University of Kansas City, which in 1963 became the University of Missouri-Kansas City, had a well-established tradition of involving professional and community theatre people in the academic production program; and this particularly appealed to McIlrath at a time when many universities regarded with disfavor any interaction with professional theatre.

A turning point in her life came in February 1959, when she directed a professional production of Sophocles' *Electra* at the Rita Allen Theatre in New York City. Judith Evelyn had performed the title role in an earlier production at the University Playhouse and had urged the Off-Broadway undertaking. But McIlrath's academic training had not prepared her for the professional bickering that she encountered. "All I could think was, if that's the purgatory we're sending our kids into, somehow we've got to get people in the academic theatre aware of it. . . . I knew something better could evolve if the academic and professional would talk and work with each other" (Interview with James Kindall, Kansas City *Star*, February 17, 1985). She became obsessed with the idea that the educational theatre must have professional theatre training programs.

McIlrath realized her abiding passion that academic theatre be placed within the totality of theatre when she founded, in 1964, a professional summer repertory theatre offering two productions at the University Playhouse. In its second season, Missouri Repertory Theatre produced four plays in rotating repertory, and in 1966 it became an Equity company. In 1968 an Equity touring wing, Missouri Vanguard Theatre, began taking two productions each year to various towns in Missouri, and eventually, in cooperation with the Mid-America Arts Alliance, to Kansas, Oklahoma, and Nebraska as well. By 1977 Missouri Repertory Theatre had expanded to an eight-play season. In 1979, culminating McIlrath's first fifteen years of leadership, the company moved into the new 733-seat Helen F. Spencer Theatre in UMKC's Center for the Performing Arts. That same year, Missouri Repertory Theatre became a nonprofit corporation related to but incorporated separately from the University of Missouri-Kansas City. Continuing her visionary role as artistic director of MRT, Patricia McIlrath saw that the new corporate structure came as close to a union of academic and professional theatre as any university and community had yet achieved.

Missouri Repertory Theatre is one of only a few professional theatres in the nation that still offer performances in rotating repertory, a system which McIlrath believes stretches both actors' and technicians' abilities. Working with two different directors, she believes, requires adaptability and gives actors diversified insights into both plays. The format has attracted internationally renowned directors such as Michael Langham, Erik Vos, Cedric Messina, John Reich, John Houseman, Alan Schneider, Albert Marre, Ellis Rabb, Cyril Ritchard, Alexis

Minotis, Vincent Dowling, Gerald Gutierrez, Adrian Hall, and Bramwell Fletcher.

In addition to her work as producing director, McIlrath has herself directed sixteen MRT productions as well as over fifty major productions in the academic theatre program. The artistry of her productions of *Look Homeward, Angel* in 1980, *Picnic* in 1981, and *Nicholas Nickleby* in 1984 exemplify her directorial skill in achieving a seamless blend of atmospheric lyricism and earthy realism. Her directorial strengths have been described as a combination of perceptive intelligence about the text and a great humanity in dealing with actors.

Despite her success with MRT, educational theatre remains vitally important to McIlrath. In 1980 she achieved another of her long-standing goals with the institution of Master of Fine Arts degrees in acting and directing and in design and technology, for which students proceed on a three-year program through professional theatre apprenticeships, internships, and residencies with MRT. Her strong commitment to education is also evident in her organizational memberships: American Theatre Association, National Theatre Conference, American Association of University Professors, Speech Communication Association of America, Speech Association of Missouri, American Association of University Women, and Central States Speech Association. Her uninterrupted twenty-eight-year tenure as director of University Theatres and as chair of the UMKC Department of Theatre attests to the lasting esteem of her staff, which now includes fifteen full-time faculty members. Among her many awards and honors are the Avila Medal for outstanding contribution in the theatre arts; the Matrix Award of Theta Sigma Phi; American College Theatre Festival Medal of Excellence; Pro Meritus Award of Rockhurst College; Germaine Monteil Beautiful Activist Award; Fellow of the American Theatre Association; charter member of the Missouri State Council on the Arts; Board of Directors, University Resident Theatre Association, 1970–1973; advisory consultant, Kansas City Arts Council; Theatre Panel member, National Endowment for the Arts, since 1979. She has received honorary Doctor of Humane Letters degrees from three institutions: Grinnell College in 1978, Park College in 1980, and William Jewell College in 1981. McIlrath retired as chair of the University of Missouri-Kansas City Theatre Department at the end of the 1983–1984 academic year. She stayed on one more year as artistic director of the Missouri Repertory Theatre, retiring from that position in June of 1985. Among other honors bestowed upon Patricia McIlrath at that time was the university's prestigious Thomas Jefferson Award.

Ron Schaeffer, production manager for Missouri Repertory Theatre, said of McIlrath, "This is her life. This is a total dedication." James Assad, a director and actor who has worked with McIlrath since he took a theatre course from her in 1964, has said, "If you can call someone Miss Theater or Mr. Theater, it certainly has to be Patricia McIlrath. There aren't even any other pretenders to the throne" (quoted by James C. Fitzpatrick in the *Kansas City Times*, February 11, 1984).

Further information about Patricia McIlrath may be found in *Players* (October-November 1968), which gives an early account of the founding of the Missouri Repertory

Theatre. The best personal profile articles are those of Jean Haley in *The Kansas City Star* (June 16, 1977), Rob Eisele in *City Magazine* (August 1977), James C. Fitzpatrick in the *Kansas City Times* (February 11, 1984), and James Kindall in *Star, The Weekly Magazine* (February 17, 1985). *Notable Names in the American Theatre* (1976) provides a list of major dates and accomplishments.

Felicia Hardison Londré

McINTYRE, Barbara M. (May 30, 1916–): specialist in theatre and drama for young people, was born in Moosejaw, Saskatchewan, Canada. She was the second of six children, and the oldest girl. Her father traveled a great deal in his work for an oil and gas company. Occasionally he took the children on his long drives; storytelling brought the tedious hours to life. Family dramas at holidays were part of Barbara McIntyre's growing up. Her brothers and sisters have since achieved prominence in their own right—two as doctors and one as a Canadian Supreme Court Justice. Upon graduation from Normal School, McIntyre began work as an elementary school teacher. Even without formal training in drama, she recognized its potential as she employed dramatic techniques in her classroom. A summer course in theatre from a visiting lecturer piqued her interest. Accompanied by her best friend, she crossed United States the border in 1945 and headed for Minneapolis. Staying in the YWCA when funds were short, she enrolled in the University of Minnesota and received her Bachelor of Arts degree in theatre in 1947. She earned her master's degree in children's theatre in 1950; her doctoral work was done at the University of Pittsburgh, where she earned her Ph.D. degree in Speech and Hearing in 1957.

McIntyre's professional experience reveals a lifetime of dedication to theatre and drama for young people. After completing her master's degree, she worked with **Winifred Ward** as a teacher of creative dramatics in the Evanston Public Schools. She spent her summers from 1948 to 1954 with **Dina Rees Evans** as a director of the innovative and successful Cain Park Creative Playshop in Cleveland Heights, Ohio. After teaching drama to high school students at the Mary Institute in St. Louis for two years, she took the first steps which would lead to her long career as a university professor. She began teaching at the University of Pittsburgh as an instructor while working on her doctorate. She joined the faculty as an assistant professor of speech and theatre arts in 1955, was promoted to associate professor in 1960, and remained with that university until 1966. She then joined the faculty of Northwestern University as an associate professor of speech in 1966 where she taught until 1971. She was appointed to the rank of Professor at the University of Victoria in 1971, and was chair of the Department of Theatre from 1972 until her retirement in 1981. She was asked to assume the responsibilities of department chair again in 1983–1984 and remains active as a Professor Emeritus. A recently contructed theatre bearing her name pays tribute to the excellence of her teaching at the University of Victoria.

McIntyre was an early and articulate advocate of empirical research to document statistically the influence of drama activities on children. While many lauded the potential of drama with and for children, few had made any attempt to support their claims scientifically. McIntyre's study, demonstrating that the articulation errors of a group of elementary children were significantly reduced as a result of drama and creative activities, represents a pioneer effort in the application of scientific principles to the field of child drama. At the 1958 convention of the Children's Theatre Conference she reported the results of her study. McIntyre chaired of the Children's Theatre Conference Research Committee from 1962 to 1964; she is credited with laying the groundwork for much of the important research done in the following decades. McIntyre was national chair of the Children's Theatre Conference (now the Children's Theatre Association of America) from 1967 to 1969. She was actively involved in the creation of ASSITEJ (the International Association of Theatre for Children and Youth), and was one of those responsible for its first organizational meeting in 1964. She has continued to promote its ideals throughout her career.

She played an active role in bringing the teachings of Brian Way and Dorothy Heathcote to this country from England. She traveled to England to observe firsthand Way's innovative methods of sociodrama and participation theatre. Having learned of Heathcote's unique and powerful style of teaching creative drama (a style very different from that practiced in the United States), McIntyre invited her to teach for a summer at Northwestern University in 1972. This marked the beginning of Heathcote's very influential work in the United States.

A longstanding advocate of the incorporation of drama into the language arts curriculum for all children, McIntyre is also acknowledged as one of the first to recognize and articulate the value of drama for exceptional children. In addition, her text *Informal Dramatics: A Language Arts Activity for the Special Pupil* (1963) appears to be the first book-length work on creative drama intended specifically for slow learners.

Because she has taught at the graduate level for more than two decades, McIntyre's legacy may best be seen in the leaders she has trained. By precept and by example, she has done much to further the theory and performance of child drama.

Barbara McIntyre's books include *Creative Drama in the Elementary School* (1974), *Count Down for Listening*, a phonodisc with 24 recorded lessons in speech improvement for the intermediate grades (1969), and *Informal Dramatics: A Language Arts Activity for the Special Pupil* (1963). She has also written "Creative Dramatics for Exceptional Children" in *Effective Language Arts Practices in Elementary School*, edited by Harold Newman (1972); "The Link Between Children's Theatre and Creative Dramatics," *Speech and Drama* (Autumn 1965); "Creative Dramatics in Programs for Exceptional Children," *Children's Theatre and Creative Dramatics* (1961); and "The Effect of Creative Activities on the Articulation Skills of Children," *Speech Monographs* (1958).

                                                                                    Rives B. Collins

MEADOW, Lynne (November 12, 1946–): producer and artistic director of the Manhattan Theatre Club in New York City, was born Carolyn Meadow in New Haven, Connecticut, the younger of two daughters of Franklin and Virginia

(Ribakoff) Meadow. Her parents fostered in her an affinity with things theatrical. Franklin Meadow was employed by United Artists in film distribution, while Virginia Meadow was writing plays and musicals for the family's Jewish temple in New Haven and acting in productions staged at nearby Yale University. In one of these productions, *Grand Tour*, by Richard Maltby, Jr., and David Shire, Virginia Meadow's twelve-year-old daughter, Lynne, appeared in a chorus of school children. Later, as artistic director of New York's Manhattan Theatre Club, that former twelve-year-old was to reunite Maltby and Shire for a series of successful ventures. Although her first experience with theatre was in acting, Meadow's interest has always been in directing and producing. Even as a child, she relates, "I was the kind of kid who liked to tell everybody else what to do . . . captain of the volleyball team and all that . . . ." (Personal interview, June 1980). The take-charge-and-do-it attitude has enabled her to build the Manhattan Theatre Club into a viable and generative force in American theatre today.

Her childhood love for theatre led Meadow to Bryn Mawr College where she majored in theatre, graduating *cum laude* in 1968 with a Bachelor of Arts degree. Following graduation Meadow applied to the Yale School of Drama, but she was not accepted into the directing program. Desperately wanting to attend Yale, she wrote an impassioned letter asserting her desire and her feeling that she was being discriminated against because she was a woman, not because she did not meet their qualifications. She was ultimately accepted and attended as a Herbert Brodkin Fellow until 1970. Meadow's accrued knowledge and personal alliances from Yale continue to serve her well. During her first year at Yale, Meadow met director Nikos Psacharopoulos, artistic director of the Williamstown Theatre Festival in Massachusetts, who assessed her abilities and advised her to go out and direct plays. He encouraged her not merely to work but to establish through effort and experience her own personal criteria of quality.

In 1970 Meadow went to live and study for a year in France. There met the influential Henry Pillsbury, director of the American Center in Paris, advised her to focus her energies and abilities. Upon her return to New York, Meadow began her career in earnest. Psacharopoulos appointed her as director of the Apprentice School at his Williamstown Theatre Festival. Teaching, Meadow found, was one way to nurture her theatrical aspirations. Since that time she has also taught at the State University of New York at Stony Brook, at the Circle in the Square Theatre School, and at Yale University. But chiefly, Meadow pursued her directing career in New York City. One avenue of investigation led to Marshall W. Mason, artistic director of New York's Circle Repertory Theatre, who offered her a position as stage manager. Recalling the advice of Psacharopoulos and Pillsbury, Meadow declined the offer. Her first opportunity to direct came in the 1971–1972 season with the production of Alfred Jarry's *Ubu Roi* at St. Clement's Church in New York starring a fellow Yale student, Henry Winkler. The show had only minor success. Afterwards Meadow met with a series of rejections. Little money, coupled with no directing work, forced her to take a job as an editorial assistant for Harper and Row. She continued looking for directing opportunities and found one, by taking a play that a friend had written, *All Through the House*, to a theatre that some businessmen had tried to establish in 1970 as an alternative to commercial theatre. Impressed with Meadow's talent and youthful energy, Gerald Freund, one of the founders of the theatre and then dean of Arts and Humanities at Hunter College, proposed her name to the board of directors of the new theatre for the position of artistic director. Meadow laughingly relates that the board was looking for the most naive person they could find in New York, "And they found me!" (Personal interview).

But the situation at the theatre she agreed to head was no laughing matter. In 1972, faced with creditors and a $75,000 deficit, Lynne Meadow, at the age of twenty-five, assumed the reins as artistic director. Initially naming the theatre the New York Theatre Strategy, the ambitious young director and the company produced a season of sixty-five plays. Their philosophy was based on a decision to do new plays by some of New York's most controversial playwrights: Sam Shepard, Terence McNally, Ed Bullins, **Maria Irene Fornés**, and Lanford Wilson. In one six-week period called the "New York Theatre Strategy Festival," twenty-three plays were produced, giving the young producer-director and her company the heady sense that they could do anything they set their minds to do. In the ensuing years they changed the theatre's name and created the Manhattan Theatre Club.

Since 1972, under Meadow's leadership, the MTC has premièred both American and foreign plays which have found a receptive testing-ground in the New York theatre world. MTC has become the chief local outlet for such European writers as Istvan Orkeny, Brian Friel, Peter Nichols, and Pam Gems. Producing twenty-five to thirty plays per year on MTC's three stages, Meadow provides playwrights with what they most need: a chance to test their work through a quality production with good actors, good directors, and good designers. Whether it is premièring Austin Pendleton's direction of Milton Stitt's *The Runner Stumbles* or Brian Murray's acting in *Artichoke* by Joanna M. Glass, or a cabaret series by Maltby and Shire, Meadow's decisive, quality-conscious choices have given the American theatre some of its most vital work in the last decade.

Her contributions both as producer and director are many. Nurtured by Meadow, the MTC has sent *Ain't MisBehavin'*, *Ashes*, *Mass Appeal*, and *Crimes of the Heart* on to successful Broadway runs. Under Meadow's guidance MTC has become "one of the principal discoverers of new plays, playwrights, actors, directors, and designers, and Meadow has become a figure of consequence in the American theatre" (Mel Gussow, *New York Times*, June 18, 1978). Her philosophy of theatre as stated in the *MTC Handbook* reveals the reason for this success, indicating her "strong commitment to producing new works for the theatre . . . . We look first for an urgent voice rather than a flawless form, . . . quality and integrity rather than commercial appeal." Nonetheless, many MTC productions have achieved critical acclaim and commercial success.

In 1980 a *Village Voice* Off-Broadway (Obie) was awarded to MTC as a special citation for excellence in theatre. *Crimes of the Heart* by **Beth Henley**, staged in the 1980–1981 season at MTC, won the coveted Pulitzer Prize for drama. *Ain't MisBehavin'* by Richard Maltby, Jr., won three Antoinette Perry (Tony) awards, an Obie, two Drama Desk awards, and both the Drama Critics Circle Award and the Outer Critics Circle Award for best musical of the 1977–1978 season. In the 1976–1977 season *Ashes*, by David Rudkin (directed by Meadow), had won an Obie for best play, best playwright, and best actor and actress (Brian Murray and Roberta Maxwell). That same year *Children*, by A. R. Gurney, Jr., had earned an Obie for its director, Melvin Bernhardt. Almost yearly an MTC production is named in *Time*'s Ten Best Plays of the Season list. Clearly the MTC has a producer for all seasons in Lynne Meadow. That "most naive person in New York" at twenty-five has grown into a managerial decision-maker upon whom the doyens of the New York theatre world look with respect, depending upon Meadow for the testing of possible products for their commercial Broadway theatres.

Indisputably, Meadow has used her creative energies as a producer to influence the course of American theatre. Nevertheless, she considers herself to be, first and foremost, a director. Her style of management is reflected in her style of directing. Meadow refers to her own work as "seamless" (Personal interview). She reflects proudly that her work does not contain the overbearing presence of a director's hand. Meadow directs one or two productions each season for MTC. In 1989 she directed *Eleemosynary* by Lee Blessing at MTC's Stage II at City Center. Additionally, she has been a guest director at the Eugene O'Neill Playwrights Conference, the Promenade Theatre, the Phoenix Repertory Company, and the New York Shakespeare Festival.

Besides producing, directing, and teaching, Lynne Meadow has served on many panels and committees which service the American theatre. From 1976 until 1979 she served on the Theatre Advisory Panel for the National Endowment for the Arts, co-chairing the panel in 1979. Also in 1979, Meadow served on the National Endowment for the Arts' Opera/Musical Theatre Advisory Panel. In 1977 the Ford Foundation sponsored an advisory panel for its support of new plays, and Meadow served on it. She has also been on the board of directors of the Theatre Communications Group.

For her work she has received a number of accolades: an Outer Circle Critics Award for perceptive and supportive contribution to American theatre; a Citation of Merit from the National Council of Women; a Drama Desk Award jointly shared with managing director Barry Grove; and, most of all, the respect and admiration of the powerful New York theatre community. Through her guidance the theatre itself, and its directors, designers, and actors have won dozens of prestigious theatre awards. But for Meadow it is not the awards that are important, but getting people to be and to do their best.

With the economic uncertainty which perpetually plagues the Broadway theatre, with the risking of hundreds of thousands of dollars on a single production, producers are going to continue to monitor the choices of Meadow and her Manhattan Theatre Club. She provides in New York the testing ground for new American and European playwrights, allowing them that freedom from commercial pressures which is necessary for creativity to flourish.

Yolanda Fleischer has written on Lynne Meadow in "An Assessment and Analysis of the Development of Selected Contemporary Women Directors in Professional Theatre" (Unpublished Ph.D. dissertation, Wayne State University, Detroit, 1983). See also Jeremy Gerard, "How a 'Chamber Theater' Grew to Fill the Orchestra," the *New York Times* (November 9, 1986). Other biographical information can be found in New York newspaper articles, including the *New York Times* (June 24, 1979, June 18, 1978, and April 24, 1977); *New York East Side Express* (October 6, 1977 and July 15, 1976); *Manhattan Daily News* (May 8, 1981); *New York Tribune* (March 27, 1978); and *New York Daily News* (September 27, 1977). There is a clipping file on Meadow in the Performing Arts Research Center of the New York Public Library at Lincoln Center. Information was also obtained from Meadow's personal resume and biographical data supplied by the Manhattan Theatre Club, New York. She is listed in *Notable Names in the American Theatre* (1976) and *Who's Who in the Theatre* (1981).

Yolanda Fleischer

MEDINA, Louisa Honor de (1813?–November 12, 1838): house playwright for New York's Bowery Theatre, was by her own account born in Europe, the daughter of a Spanish businessman who went bankrupt. Nevertheless, his daughter had either enough relatives or money to obtain an education, including the study of classical languages, logic, and algebra. She claimed a successful contribution to a London literary annual at the age of twelve, and reported spending her years from fourteen to seventeen traveling and studying in Ireland and Spain.

In 1831 or 1833 Medina came to America, worked in New York as a teacher of French and Spanish, and began to contribute poems and stories to journals and to write plays for the theatre. She is credited with the authorship of 34 plays between 1833 and 1838, of which eleven have so far been established with certainty as her work. These eleven plays and their production première dates are: *Wacousta; or, the Curse* (December 30, 1833); *Kairrissah; or, the Warrior of Wanachtiki* (September 11, 1834); *The Last Days of Pompeii* (February 9, 1835); *O'Neill the Rebel* (May 11, 1835); *Norman Leslie* (January 11, 1836); *Rienzi* (May 23, 1836); *Lafitte, Pirate of the Gulf* (September 19, 1836); *Nick of the Woods* (February 5, 1838 and May 6, 1839); *Ernest Maltravers* (March 28, 1838); *The Statue Fiend; or, the Curse of the Avenger* (May 18, 1840); and *The Collegians* (December 26, 1842, and July 3, 1843). In addition to these eleven plays, sources credit Medina with adaptations not appearing under her name, such as a reworking of Eugene Scribe's *The Jewess* (March 7, 1836) and Shakespeare's *Pericles*, and with adaptations of the novels *Giafar al Barmeki* and *Il Maledetto*.

Louisa Medina was house playwright for the Bowery Theatre, where but one of all her documented plays premiered. The Bowery was leased, managed, and/ or owned by Thomas S. Hamblin from 1830 to his death in 1853, and specialized in spectacular melodramas adapted from popular novels. Medina excelled at adaptation and was frequently adjudged to have strengthened a novel's original plot in the course of dramatizing it. Her knowledge of the theatre was extensive. Actor-manager Lester Wallack considered her "one of the most brilliant women I ever met. She was very plain, but a wonderfully bright woman, charming in every way" (*Memories of Fifty Years*, p. 119).

Medina's association with Hamblin was personal as well as professional. It is likely that they were married in 1837; from the end of that year until Medina's death she is referred to in court records and in the press as Hamblin's wife, though she continued to write as Louisa H. Medina. The legality of their marriage is questioned because Hamblin's divorce from his first wife forbade him to marry again so long as she lived (she died in 1849). The acrimony surrounding the divorce, Hamblin's association after it with Naomi Vincent, the hysteria early in his marriage to Medina concerning their protégée Louisa Missouri Miller, and Hamblin's personality colored Medina's life and career no less than Hamblin's, with scandal. She inherited many of Hamblin's enemies, which led to the disparagement of her character and work in the popular press of the 1830s and in some stage histories (notably Joseph Ireland's and George C. D. Odell's).

The quality of Medina's work may be ascertained by comparing her three extant plays—*The Last Days of Pompeii, Nick of the Woods*, and *Ernest Maltravers*—to their sources in fiction and to other plays of the period. That most of Medina's plays were popular is substantiated by theatrical records. In a theatrical period during which a play that ran three times in a week was considered successful, *The Collegians*, produced well after Medina's death, is the only one of her plays that failed to hit that mark. *Wacousta* and *Kairrissah* enjoyed a week's uninterrupted run, as did *Ernest Maltravers, Nick of the Woods*, and *The Statue Fiend*. Following the initial run, *Maltravers* and *Nick* continued to run intermittently through the month and remained in the Bowery repertory for years; indeed *Nick* was still played regularly up to 1882.

Of particular interest are the 29 consecutive performances of *The Last Days of Pompeii*, the longest run in New York theatrical history to that date (the play was still in the Bowery repertory in 1868), the 25 consecutive performances of *Norma Leslie*, and the 25 consecutive performances of *Rienzi*. *Lafitte* would surely have enjoyed a similar success had the Bowery Theatre not burned on September 21, 1836. It did not reopen under Hamblin's management until May 1839. The achievement of a month's uninterrupted run in 1835 and 1836 indicated an awesome success. Indeed, the $40,000 Hamblin cleared from the 1835–1836 season enabled him to become part owner of the Bowery Theatre building and to overcome the previous years of struggle and accumulated losses.

If Hamblin owed his financial success in the late 1830s in large part to Medina's plays, a condition he tried repeatedly and unsuccessfully to duplicate after her death by employing other house playwrights, Louisa Medina owed much of her success to Hamblin's careful and costly production of her plays. He had learned press agentry from his Bowery predecessor, Charles Gilfert, and spared no expense or verbiage to launch a promising work. Once it opened, Hamblin kept a popular work running, for as Odell points out (*Records of the New York Stage*, Vol.III, p. 515), "The Bowery, before any other theatre in New York, started the custom of continuous runs for successful plays." This policy—a beautifully mounted play kept before the public until well established, then regularly revived—insured Medina's place in theatrical history in two respects: she became one of the more popular playwrights of her day, and her success suggests the long run can be dated with accuracy to the 1830s rather than to the more commonly cited 1840s.

Louisa Medina was a rarity in her day—a woman living by her pen and succeeding as a playwright without also being an actress or manager. She was among the most prolific professionally produced American female playwright of the nineteenth century.

Louisa Medina's three surviving plays may be located as follows: *The Last Days of Pompeii* is #146 of *French Standard Drama* (New York, 1856); *Nick of the Woods* is #62 of *Spencer's Boston Theatre* (Boston, 1850s); and *Ernest Maltravers* is #379 of *Dick's Standard Plays* (London, 1880s). Among the most useful newspaper sources dealing with her life or works are *The Spirit of the Times* (September 10, 1836, and October 1, 1836), *The New York Mirror* (January 23, 1836, February 20, 1836, August 20, 1836, and April 28, 1838), *The Ladies Companion and Literary Expositor* (April, May, and June 1837). She is mentioned in Joseph Ireland, *Records of the New York Stage from 1750 to 1860* (1866, reprinted 1966); T. A. Brown, *A History of the New York Stage, 1727–1901* (1903); George C. D. Odell, *Annals of the New York Stage* (1927–1949); and Lester Wallack, *Memories of Fifty Years* (1889, reprinted 1969). An abusive account of the life of Thomas Hamblin is "A Concise History of the Life and Amours of Thomas S. Hamblin, Late Manager of the Bowery Theatre, as Communicated by His Legal Wife, Mrs. Elizabeth Hamblin, to Mr. M. Clarke" (n.d., but probably 1837), to be found in the Boston Public Library. See Rosemarie K. Bank, "Theatre and Narrative Fiction in the Work of the Nineteenth-Century American Playwright Louisa Medina," *Theatre History Studies* (1983). Medina is listed in James Rees, *The Dramatic Authors of America* (1845), Robert L. Sherman, *Actors and Authors with Composers Who Helped Make Them Famous* (1951), and *The Oxford Companion to American Theatre* (1984).

Rosemarie K. Bank

MENKEN, Adah Isaacs (June 15, 1835?–August 10, 1868): actress, who was most famous for her role as Mazeppa, in which she appeared in flesh-colored tights in an age unaccustomed to seeing the female form revealed, was probably born near New Orleans, Louisiana. Although various stories concerning her background list her real name as Delores Adios Fuertes and her father's occupation as a Presbyterian minister, she was, in fact, born Adah Bertha Theodore and was raised in the Jewish faith. Her father died when she was two years old, and her mother married a man named Josephs shortly thereafter. Josephs died in 1853, the same year that Adah and her sister Josephine made their stage debut as dancers at the French Opera House in New Orleans. The two sisters were great favorites and toured Cuba, Texas, and Mexico. Following the tour, Adah

Theodore retired from the stage to study the classics. She learned to speak fluent French, Hebrew, German, and Spanish, later taught Latin and French in a private girls' school, and in 1856 published (according to her) the first collection of her poems titled *Memories*.

In Galveston, Texas, on April 3, 1856 (or 1858), she married Alexander Isaacs Menken, a musician and the son of a Cincinnati dry-goods merchant. They lived together for a few months, and then were divorced. Adah Isaacs Menken returned to the stage, making her debut at the New Orleans Varieties as Bianca in H. H. Milman's *Fazio*, supported by Edwin Booth, James E. Murdoch, and James H. Hackett. She played Bianca and other roles, such as Pauline in *The Lady of Lyons* on tour in Shreveport, Cincinnati, and Louisville. Following this tour she again retired from the theatre and moved to Columbus, Ohio, to study sculpture.

On March 1, 1859, still retaining her married name of Adah Isaacs Menken, she returned to the stage as Widow Cheerly in *The Soldier's Daughter*, making her New York debut at Purdy's National Theatre. In September 1859, thinking that Alexander Menken had divorced her, she secretly married the boxer John Carmel Heenan. A scandal followed when it was discovered that there was no divorce. The Heenans settled in New York City. There Menken frequented Pfaff's, a "Bohemian Rendezvous," where she met Walt Whitman, Ada Clare, and other notable American writers. Following the death of their infant son in 1860, the Heenans separated. A few months later, Menken's mother died in New Orleans. The Heenans' divorce was finalized in 1862.

The following year Menken made her first appearance as Mazeppa at the Green Street Theatre in Albany, New York, to a packed house. *Mazeppa; or, The Wild Horse of Tartary* was a spectacular melodrama based on a popular poem by Lord Byron. Just before the end of the first act, the villain cries, "Bring forth the untamed steed," and to ominous music a horse is brought on stage, "restrained with difficulty," according to the stage directions. Mazeppa, the Tartar youth, is bound to the horse's back. In Act Two the horse, with Mazeppa on its back, gallops up a zigzag ramp to a place high above the stage. For years the play had been presented with a dummy strapped to the horse's back for the dangerous ride which was accompanied by lightning and thunder effects. On the night of June 7, 1861, Adah Isaacs Menken, dressed in flesh colored tights and a loincloth, made the ride on the horse's back. She also made stage history. For that audience and for the many thereafter who saw her ride the "fiery steed" she appeared to be naked. From then on she was called "the naked lady," and for the rest of her life she capitalized on the play, *Mazeppa*, or similar plays that allowed her to expose her body in flesh colored tights. Evidently, hers was a beautiful body that threw audiences, unaccustomed to the public display of the unclad female figure, into pandemonium.

In 1863 Menken married Robert Henry Newell, a journalist and humorist of the day. They sailed for San Francisco in July of 1863, and Menken appeared at Maguire's Opera House that August, again captivating audiences. In San Francisco she met Bret Harte and Joaquin Miller, both of whom were fascinated by the flamboyant actress. In Virginia City her Mazeppa was seen by Mark Twain. In 1864 the Newells sailed for England. Robert Newell returned shortly, but Menken remained and opened in London on October 3, creating a sensation as Mazeppa. At the Westminster Palace Hotel she met Charles Dickens, Dante Gabriel Rossetti, and Algernon Swinburne, the latter claiming Menken as his mistress. After her divorce from Newell in 1865, she returned to New York for a short engagement at Wood's Broadway Theatre, again playing to packed houses. She toured the West for a while; and, upon returning to New York in August 1866, married for the fourth time, to James Paul Barclay (or Barkley). A few days later she sailed for Europe alone; and in November in Paris, she gave birth to a son named Louis Dudevant Victor Emanuel Barclay, in honor of his godmother, Georges Sand (Aurore Dudevant). A month later Menken made her Paris debut at the Théatre de la Gaietaa, in *Les Pirates de la Savane*, one of the greatest successes ever achieved by an American actress in nineteenth century Paris. This melodrama also included a daring horseback ride on the stage.

At her apartment at the Hôtel de Suez, Menken met with Théophile Gautier, Georges Sand, and Alexandre Dumas, *père*, who later became her lover. She toured to Vienna and, after a brief return to Paris, went to London. On May 30, 1868, at Sadler's Wells, Adah Isaacs Menken gave the last performance of her career. Less than two months later, while rehearsing for a revival of *Les Pirates* in Paris, on July 9, 1868, she collapsed, and was sent home to rest. When, after some days, she failed to report to rehearsal, the producers filed suit in court for her return. On August 10, 1868, when the court officials went to serve her papers, they found her in her apartment, dead at the age of thirty-three. She was buried in the Jewish section of Père Lachaise Cemetery in Paris, and on April 21, 1869, Edwin James had her body removed and re-interred at Montparnasse Cemetery. Baron Lionel de Rothschild erected a marble monument in her honor, bearing the inscription ''Thou Knowest,'' from a poem by Swinburne. A collection of her poetry titled *Infelicia* (edited by John Thomson, Swinburne's secretary, and dedicated to Charles Dickens) was published posthumously in London on August 18, 1868.

Adah Isaacs Menken was not a great dramatic star, but her flamboyant style and extraordinary beauty were responsible for her extreme popularity. Her greatest success was *Mazeppa*, for she was the first actress to play the role in flesh-colored tights, strapped to a horse in a ''state of virtual nudity.'' Although she performed many other roles during her career, the name of Adah Isaacs Menken will always be synonymous with that of Mazeppa.

Menken was vague about her family life, but she was quite proud of her Jewish heritage. She was sometimes militant in her statements and in 1857 protested against the exclusion of Jews from the British House of Commons. It was said that she never performed on the Day of Atonement and that she slept with a Hebrew Bible under her pillow.

Adah Isaacs Menken's two books of poems are *Memories* (1856) and *Infelicia* (1868). She has been a favorite subject for biographers. The earliest biographies are G. Lippard

Barclay, ed., *The Life and Remarkable Career of Adah Isaacs Menken* (1868), and Edwin James, *The Biography of Adah Isaacs Menken* (1881). More recent accounts of her life are Richard Northcott, *Adah Isaacs Menken* (1921); Bernard Falk, *The Naked Lady* (1934, revised in 1952); Nathaniel S. Fleischer, *Reckless Lady* (1941); Allen Lesser, *Enchanting Rebel* (1947); and Paul Lewis, *Queen of the Plaza* (1964). Menken's unreliable "Notes of My Life," which appeared in the *New York Times* (September 6, 1868), is reprinted in the appendix of the Allen Lesser biography. Richard Moody includes some details of Menken's career, especially the *Mazeppa* episodes, in *America Takes the Stage* (1955). See also T. Allston Brown, *History of the American Stage* (1870); George C. D. Odell, *Annals of the New York Stage*, Vols. VI and VII (1931); Constance Rourke, *Troupers of the Gold Coast* (1928); and Helen Beal Woodward, *The Bold Women* (1953, reprinted 1971). Menken's obituary appeared in the *New York Times* and the *New York Tribune* (August 12, 1868). William C. Young in *Famous Actors and Actresses on the American Stage*, Vol. II (1975), quotes Mark Twain's description of a performance of *Mazeppa*. Brief biographies of Menken appear in *The Dictionary of American Biography*, Vol. VI (1933); Robert L. Sherman, *Actors and Authors with Composers Who Helped Make Them Famous* (1951); *Who Was Who in America, Historical Volume 1607–1896* (1963); *Notable American Women*, Vol. II (1971); *Victorian Actors and Actresses in Review*, ed. Donald Mullin (1983); *The Oxford Companion to American Literature* (1983); *The Oxford Companion to the Theatre* (1983); and *The Oxford Companion to American Theatre* (1984).

Penny M. Landau

MERMAN, Ethel (January 16, 1909–February 15, 1984): leading musical comedy star, was born Ethel Agnes Zimmermann in Astoria, Long Island, New York, to accountant Edward Zimmermann and his wife Agnes (Gardner) Zimmermann. She was educated at Public School No. 4 and graduated from the William Cullen Bryant High School, where she studied stenography and typing. While working as a stenographer, Merman appeared in cabaret (1928), after which she sang at Les Ambassadeurs, the New York night club, and at the Palace Theatre. She made her Broadway debut as a singing actress in *Girl Crazy* in 1930, and over the next forty years she appeared in fourteen musicals, establishing herself along the way as the quintessential musical comedy star. During her long and illustrious career she married four times: William R. Smith (1940–1941); Robert D. Levitt (1941–1952), the father of Ethel Merman Levitt (who died 1967) and Robert D. Levitt, Jr.; Robert F. Six (1953–1960); and Ernest Borgnine (1964–1965).

Merman's stage credits include Kate Fothergill in *Girl Crazy* (1930), *George White's Scandals of 1931* (1931), Wanda Brill in *Take a Chance* (1932), Reno Sweeney in *Anything Goes* (1934), Nails O'Reilly Duquesne in *Red, Hot, and Blue!* (1936), Jeanette Adair in *Stars in Your Eyes* (1939), May Daly and Du Barry in *Du Barry Was a Lady* (1939), Hattie Maloney in *Panama Hattie* (1940), Blossom Hart in *Something for the Boys* (1943), Annie Oakley in *Annie Get Your Gun* (1946), Sally Adams in *Call Me Madam* (1950), Liz Livingston in *Happy Hunting* (1956), Mama Rose in *Gypsy* (1959), and Dolly Levi Gallagher in *Hello, Dolly!* (1970).

Principally a stage performer, Merman also appeared in films and television, though not always to her greatest advantage. Her film credits include *Follow the Leader* (1930), *We're not Dressing* (1934), *Kid Millions* (1934), *Strike Me Pink* (1936), *Anything Goes* (1936), *Happy Landing* (1938), *Stage Door Canteen* (1943), *Call Me Madam* (1953), *There's No Business Like Show Business* (1954), *It's a Mad, Mad, Mad, Mad World* (1963), and *The Art of Love* (1965). Television proved to be a happier medium for Merman than motion pictures. She and **Mary Martin** provided a lengthy medley of their hit songs on the *Ford Fiftieth Anniversary Show* (1953), and in the same year Merman appeared in a tabloid version of *Anything Goes* on the *Colgate Comedy Hour*. In 1956 she played dramatic roles in *Reflected Glory* and *Honest in the Rain*, which were followed in 1960 by *Ethel Merman on Broadway*. Merman again donned buckskins for a reprise of *Annie Get Your Gun* in 1967 following the successful Broadway revival of that show. She performed in segments of *That Girl*, *Batman*, and *Tarzan* as well as with Judy Garland, Red Skelton, Lucille Ball, and Ed Sullivan. In addition to appearances on numerous talk and game shows, Merman sang "There's No Business Like Show Business" for the *Night of 100 Stars* (1982).

Merman's career went from some earlier loosely-structured musical comedy productions into more tightly-knit musical dramas. In her earlier roles she was praised largely for her exuberant singing, magnetic stage presence, and comic timing, but as her talent matured, her acting ability received critical commendation, especially in *Gypsy*.

As a young performer Merman introduced songs by the best American composers and lyricists: George and Ira Gershwin (*Girl Crazy*), Cole Porter (*Anything Goes*; *Red, Hot, and Blue!*; *Du Barry Was a Lady*; *Panama Hattie*, and *Something for the Boys*), and Irving Berlin (*Annie Get Your Gun* and *Call Me Madam*). Jule Styne and Stephen Sondheim provided her numbers in *Gypsy*. Once Merman sang a popular song, it became wholly identified with her, as has been the case with "I Got Rhythm," "I Get a Kick Out of You," "Anything Goes," "Blow, Gabriel, Blow," "Doin' What Comes Natur'lly," "You're Just in Love," and "Everything's Coming up Roses," to name but a few. These are all "Merman songs," including the unofficial anthem of her profession, "There's No Business Like Show Business." Perhaps her most memorable moment on the stage was her rendition of *Gypsy*'s "Rose's Turn," called by Martin Gottfried "the single most effective number ever done in a musical" (*Broadway Musicals*, p. 105).

For over fifty years critics have tried to analyze Merman's style of singing. Her response to such academic discussions was that she was not concerned with style; she merely tried to keep her singing honest and insure that audiences heard the lyrics. She was blessed with a powerful voice, natural breath control, and mastery of articulation; Merman's listeners heard every syllable of her lyrics.

Commentators have exhausted the thesaurus in their attempts to describe the Merman voice, basically a rich contralto of unique timbre and focus. Her clarion sound was often likened to a trumpet, but Arturo Toscanini, an auditor of undeniable credentials, concluded that her voice was like "another instrument in the band" (*Merman*, p. 9). Merman's tonal quality and vocal power were indispensable in the cavernous Broadway theatres in the days before amplification was widespread, but the very magnitude of her vocal renditions was sometimes poorly adapted to the amplification used in today's Broadway theatres. The same observation may be made of her larger-than-life stage characterizations, which frequently overwhelmed movie and television screens. Merman's true milieu was the stage; her artistry required the vastness of the theatre and the immediacy of an audience to achieve its full effect. Known and sometimes criticized as a "belter" of songs, Merman's delivery of such lyrical ballads as "How Deep Is the Ocean?," "Down in the Depths of the 90th Floor," "Let's Be Buddies," "Do I Love You?," and "Small World" revealed great tenderness and poignant sentiment.

Most of Merman's roles were tailored to her typical stage *persona*, so she did not exhibit in her career a wide range of character types. She portrayed a gambler's wife (*Girl Crazy*), two nightclub singers (*Anything Goes, Du Barry Was A Lady*), two "soiled doves" (*Take a Chance, Panama Hattie*), a rancher suspected of being a "soiled dove" (*Something for the Boys*), two political hostesses (*Red, Hot, and Blue!, Call Me Madam*), a movie siren (*Stars in Your Eyes*), a sharpshooter (*Annie Get Your Gun*), a matchmaker (*Hello, Dolly!*), and the stereotypic stage mother (*Gypsy*). In each of these roles, Merman played a brassy woman, ever ready with a wisecrack, ever vulnerable to heartbreak. Despite the inanity of some of the early musical comedy plots, Merman's character elicited sympathy because she was instantly recognizable for her earthy humanity. *Gypsy* was her first "book-show," and though her special requirements were considered in its creation, the character of "Mama Rose" remained faithful to the stage mother of Gypsy Rose Lee's memoirs. In this role Merman alternated between victimizing everyone with whom she came in contact and tugging at the audience's heartstrings as she exhibited her own frustration and vulnerability, culminating in her electrifying performance of "Rose's Turn."

When in 1930 Merman first met George Gershwin, who came to hear her in *Girl Crazy*, the composer gallantly offered to alter the songs to suit her style. She did not request any alterations, but she would not be so easily satisfied in the future. Soon Merman was challenging composers and lyricists to rise to the potential of her vocal talents. As her stature as a musical comedy star grew, producers and directors saw the wisdom of providing the dramatic material and technical support to enhance her vocal characterizations. Merman the actress emerged, and the quality of her vehicles improved. *Annie Get Your Gun, Call Me Madam, Hello, Dolly!* (which was written for her but first performed by Carol Channing), and *Gypsy* are structurally sophisticated and representative of the mature American musical.

When Merman entered the profession in 1928, the musical stage was dominated by men—Al Jolson, Eddie Cantor, George M. Cohan. As a consummate professional she helped to put women into important roles on the musical stage. Merman's professional seriousness was also reflected in her allegiance to the directors with whom she worked: Howard Lindsay, Joshua Logan, Edgar MacGregor, George Abbott, Abe Burrows, and Jerome Robbins, among others. Once her performance had been approved by her director, Merman did not vary it. This characteristic was particularly noteworthy in view of Merman's long-running plays.

Ethel Merman received two American Theatre Wing Antoinette Perry (Tony) awards: for *Call Me Madam* in 1951 and for career achievement in 1972. She was cited by the *Variety* New York Drama Critics Poll for *Something for the Boys* (1943), *Annie Get Your Gun* (1946–1947), and *Gypsy* (1959). She received the Donaldson Award for *Annie Get Your Gun* (1946–47), the Barter Theatre of Virginia Award for *Happy Hunting* (1957), and the Drama Desk Award for *Hello, Dolly!* (1969–1970). After a concert at Carnegie Hall on May 10, 1982, Merman was surprised by the appearance of Hal David, Frank Sinatra, and Barbra Streisand on stage to confer the American Society of Composers, Authors and Publishers' (ASCAP) Pied Piper Award for her contributions to American music; Sinatra and Streisand had been previous recipients.

In April of 1983 Ethel Merman underwent surgery to remove a brain tumor. On February 15, 1984, she was found dead of natural causes in her Manhattan apartment. Her body was cremated. She is survived by her son, Robert Levitt.

Martin Gottfried has correctly assessed Merman's theatrical importance. "What is it about Ethel Merman?" he asked. "It, of course, is the most indefinable, intangible, and important quality a stage performer can have: dynamism. . . . There is no performer who has so inspired our stage composers because there is none who so magnificently exemplified exactly what the Broadway musical is all about. . . . The musical theatre is the Ethel Merman [who was] so innocently obsessed with gripping the audience that she felt no embarrassment as she strode downstage, planted both feet squarely beneath her, reared back, and blasted the back wall of the balcony" (*Broadway Musicals*, pp. 277, 343). As generations of theatregoers might ask, "Who could ask for anything more?"

Ethel Merman's first autobiography, *Who Could Ask for Anything More?* (1955), written in collaboration with Pete Martin, though highly romanticized, is anecdotal and informative. Her second autobiography, aided by George Eells, *Merman: An Autobiography* (1978), is more candid. A recent biography of Merman is Bob Thomas, *I Got Rhythm! The Ethel Merman Story* (1985). Merman's career is an indispensable ingredient of all histories of the American musical, including Martin Gottfried's *Broadway Musicals* (1979) and Maurice Zolotow, *No People Like Show People* (1951). Merman's obituary appeared in the *New York Times* (February 16, 1984). She is listed in *Who's Who in America, 1954–1955* (1954), *Current Biography, 1955* (1955–1956); *The Biographical Encyclopaedia and Who's Who of the American Theatre* (1966); *Notable Names in the American Theatre* (1976); *Who's Who in the Theatre* (1981); *The Oxford Companion to the Theatre* (1983); *The Oxford Companion to American Theatre* (1984); and *Contemporary Theatre, Film, and Television*, Vol. I (1984).

George B. Bryan

MERRY, Anne Brunton (May 30, 1769–June 28, 1808). actress and manager, was born in Drury Lane, Westminster, England. Her father, John Brunton, was an actor and the manager of the Theatre Royal in Norwich, England. Her mother's maiden name was Friend. John Brunton had come to London originally to serve an apprenticeship term, but remained to appear in a benefit performance at Covent Garden. Thus, Anne Brunton was born in London. She first appeared on stage at the Theatre Royal at Bath on February 17, 1785, playing opposite her father. She had received her formal education from her mother, but her father encouraged her to memorize Shakespeare, even though it seems that he did not intend her to be an actress. Her debut piece was the sentimental drama, *The Grecian Daughter*, a favorite of Sarah Siddons, then one of London's leading actors. The part was ideal for a young female performer, enabling her to emote, rebel, kill a despot, and hold her dying father in her arms. Anne Brunton evidently met the challenge of the role, winning much acclaim for her performance.

After learning her craft by performing in provincial theatres, Brunton was invited to London, making her debut there as Horatia in William Whitehead's *The Roman Father*. She then spent seven years at the Covent Garden Theatre, training during the summer months in the provinces. Summer touring seemed to strengthen her style; she became more adventuresome and broadened her selection of roles. At first, she had performed only ingénues and tragic characters, but later she tried her hand at comic roles and again met with great success.

On August 27, 1791, Anne Brunton married Robert Merry. It is believed that the couple had been introduced when she appeared in a pantomime which he had written. Robert Merry who belonged to an aristocratic English family, was liberally educated and admired for his poetry. His friends and acquaintances found him charming and witty; he was welcome in good society. His liberal views, however, made him unpopular politically, and their marriage affected Anne Brunton Merry's career; she was not rehired at Covent Garden. About this time, Thomas Wignell, who was in London recruiting performers for the American stage, offered her a contract to perform at the Chestnut Street Theatre in Philadelphia. She quickly accepted.

Anne Merry first appeared on the American stage in 1796 as Juliet, and was immediately acclaimed a success. Her reputation had preceded her, and American audiences were not disappointed. When the Chestnut Street Theatre closed during the summer for fear of yellow fever, she toured New York, Baltimore, and Annapolis.

In December of 1798 Robert Merry died of an apparent stroke at the age of forty-three. At the time, Anne Merry was twenty-nine years of age and a well-established American star. She first considered returning to England, but, after her years in America, that seemed inadvisable, particularly since she was invited by William Dunlap to join the prestigious American Company in New York. She declined, however, and after a suitable period of mourning returned to Thomas Wignell's company at the Chestnut Street Theatre in Philadelphia. She soon became an outstanding interpreter of roles in the plays of August von Kotzebue and in the more mature roles of Shakespeare. She also took some time to visit New York and to appear at William Dunlap's Park Theatre. On January 1, 1803, Merry married Thomas Wignell. They had already long enjoyed a close relationship, but their marriage lasted only seven weeks; Wignell died on February 2, 1803. Anne Merry thereupon became manager of the company, and continued as its leading performer. In the fall she also gave birth to a daughter, Elizabeth, but quickly rejoined the company, enforcing the discipline that she personally practiced. She demanded precise and accurate rehearsals and proper behavior in the greenroom.

On August 28, 1806, Anne Merry married another long-time friend and confidant, William Warren, an actor famous for such roles as Sir Toby Belch in *Twelfth Night* and Sir Peter Teazle in *The School for Scandal*. Together, Merry and Warren managed the Chestnut Street Theatre while Merry continued to act. As usual she immersed herself in a hectic schedule, including appearances in New York. Her roles now included Belvidera in *Venice Preserved*, Rosamund in *Abaelino*, Julia in *The Rivals*, Beatrice in *Much Ado About Nothing*, Calista in *The Fair Penitent*, Lady Teazle in *The School for Scandal*, Lady Macbeth, and the more mature characters of Kotzebue. Anne Brunton Merry died on June 28, 1808, at the age of thirty-nine, in Alexandria, Virginia, after a dangerous and difficult pregnancy and delivery.

From all accounts the rapidly developing American stage had lost a great contributor. All her reviewers praised her work. She acted everything from tragic Juliet to sophisticated Lady Teazle. All her reviewers were amazed at her precision and truthful portrayal of subtle sentiments. Every reviewer and many theatregoers commented on her elegance and presence and, most especially, her melodic and correct voice. William Dunlap—dramatist, diarist, critic, and theatre historian—commented on her New York debut in August 1797 "The performance was highly approved, and I believe Mrs. Merry has made a lasting impression" (*Diary*, letter to John Hodgkinson, p. 138). He further mentioned that in September he saw her Juliet "with much more delight." The next evening he thought her playing of Desdemona was "enchanting" (*Diary*, pp. 144, 150). Dunlap felt that audiences coming to see a girl whom they considered a novice, saw, instead, a graceful and accomplished actress. He further observed that the year 1808 was noteworthy in theatrical history, being the year of Anne Merry's death. Dunlap believed that at thirty-nine Merry was still in full possession of those eminent qualifications which made her second only to Sarah Siddons. He argued that Siddons worked a lifetime to achieve those qualities that Merry realized at the outset of her career.

Anne Brunton Merry's influence as actress and manager was great in the American theatre. She was one of those transitional actresses who brought the classical traditions of the London theatre to the American stage. Through extraordinary application and discipline, she added excellence and professionalism to the burgeoning American theatre.

The Career of Mrs. Anne Brunton Merry in the American Theatre (1971) by Gresdna Ann Doty is the definitive work on Merry. William Dunlap's *Diary* (1930) is a gossipy account of the New York, Boston, and Philadelphia theatres. He was enamored of Mrs. Merry and her work as an actress. *History of the American Theatre* (1832), also by William Dunlap, has many admiring references to Merry. Arthur Hornblow, *A History of the Theatre in America* (1919) also refers to her in complimentary terms. See also William B. Wood, *Personal Recollections of the Stage* (1855); Joseph N. Ireland, *Records of the New York Stage*, Vol. I (1866); John Bernard, *Retrospections of America, 1797–1811* (1877); George C. D. Odell, *Annals of the New York Stage*, Vols. I and II (1927); and Thomas Clark Pollock, *The Philadelphia Theatre in the Eighteenth Century* (1833). Merry's Covent Garden career is recorded in John Genest, *Some Account of the English Stage*, Vols. VI and VII (1832). William C. Young, *Famous Actors and Actresses of the American Stage*, Vol. II (1975), contains her picture and reprints some reviews of her work. Garff B. Wilson comments on Mrs. Merry in *Three Hundred Years of American Drama and Theatre* (1973). Biographical accounts of Anne Brunton Merry are included in *Dictionary of American Biography*, Vol. VI (1933, renewed 1961); *Who Was Who in America, Historical Volume, 1607–1896* (1963); *Notable American Women*, Vol. II (1971); *The Oxford Companion to the Theatre* (1983); and *The Oxford Companion to American Theatre* (1984).

Catherine B. McGovern

MILES, Julia (1930?–): director and producer, was the second child born to John Cornelius Hinson (a farmer) and Saro (Jones) Hinson. She spent her childhood in Pelham, Georgia, where she attended Brenau Academy. She graduated in 1951 from Northwestern University in Evanston, Illinois, with a Bachelor of Science degree in theatre. After graduation she immediately moved to New York with hopes of becoming an actress. Once there, she met and married writer and actor William Miles, with whom she had two children, Stacey Priscilla (b. 1952) and Lisa Pratt (b. 1956). Her marriage to William Miles ended in 1958. In 1962 she married Samuel C. Cohn, a casting agent with International Creative Management. They have a daughter, Marya Ruth (b. 1964), and from Cohn's previous marriage, a son, Peter (b. 1955).

In the early years of her career, Miles acted and produced. The process of seeking work, caring for her first baby, and acting, led her to start a theatre where she and her collaborators could spend most of their time working rather than seeking work. In 1961 at St. Ann's Church in Brooklyn Heights, Miles acted in and produced Arnold Weinstein's *The Red Eye of Love*. With the success of that production, Miles, John Wulp, and Sam Cohn gathered money and took a long-time lease on the Maidman Theatre on 42nd Street and produced three plays in the 1961–1962 season: Kenneth Koch's *George Washington Crossing the Delaware*, Elaine May's *Not Enough Rope*, and a revival of Weinstein's *The Red Eye of Love*. For the next few years Miles was involved with Happenings (improvisational performance pieces) until her concern for working with the written and spoken word drew her to other projects.

Gradually, Miles began to perform less and to produce more frequently. She acted for a time in several of her own productions, and appeared on *Love of Life*, *Dupont Show of the Month*, *The Defenders*, and other television shows. Miles said, however, about her final withdrawal from acting, "I found that for the time and concentration it takes, it wasn't giving me back enough. It was like a disease that I got over and I don't miss at all. Acting is really about selling, and I'm not good at that'' (Personal interview).

In 1964 Miles volunteered to work with a new theatre group at St. Clement's Church headed by Wynn Handman. This group nurtured new American playwrights and plays and soon became the American Place Theatre. Within a year Miles was named its associate director, a post she still holds. In this administrative and producing position she reads scripts, discusses and advises on play choices, negotiates contracts, and plans fund raisers. Both she and director Wynn Handman have been responsible for showcasing works of Sam Shepard, Ronald Ribman, Robert Lowell, Ed Bullins, Jules Feiffer, and Steve Tesich—now well-known writers who may never have graced a stage without the support of the American Place Theatre.

A turning point in Miles's work took place in 1978. As she recalls, she couldn't figure out what the clamor in the women's movement was all about; she had never personally experienced prejudice in her work, and she had successfully combined motherhood, marriage, and a career. "What's such a big deal?" she thought. However, looking over the number of plays submitted by women to American Place Theatre, she discovered that they were far fewer than those written by men. In an effort to revise this trend Miles, with a grant from the Ford Foundation, founded and became director of the Women's Theatre Project at the American Place Theatre. The Project was designed to identify and nurture the work of women playwrights and directors. As it blossomed into its eighth season, the Project had developed plays from rehearsed readings to studio productions, and, in a few cases, to main-stage productions for the American Place Theatre.

The Project has been supported by performers such as **Colleen Dewhurst**, Tammy Grimes, Linda Hunt, and Carrie Nye and by the leadership of its board of directors, which includes Dewhurst, Sam Cohn, and Steve Tesich, among others. In eight seasons, the Project had presented 150 scripts as rehearsed readings, produced 35 plays, and published two anthologies of plays written by Project members. Kathleen Collins, **Emily Mann**, Lavonne Mueller, and Nadja Tesich are key writers who have already emerged through the Project.

Miles's commitment to finding women directors for the Project has been fraught with difficulty. Directors, she feels, need to be visually oriented, highly knowledgeable about various intellectual issues, and capable of functioning as psychiatrists. The Women's Project exists to bring women directors together with a playwright, a stage, and some actors. Miles's efforts to identify directors has paid off. Joan Macklin-Silver, Ellie Renfield, Amy Saltz, Joan Vail Thorne, Claudia Weill, and Bryna Wortman are just a few of the directors who have developed through the Project and are taking on significant work in both commercial and regional theatre and in film.

Even stronger than her desire for the development of women directors is Miles's concern for the plight of women playwrights. In addition to providing a way for playwrights to see their work realized on stage, she initiated the Play Bank. Funded by the Ford Foundation and supported by the Women's Program of the American Theatre Association, the Play Bank contains scripts by women playwrights distributed upon request to professional and university theatres. Women playwrights whose plays have been published or produced by a professional or university theatre may submit plays for inclusion in the Bank.

In addition to these responsibilities, Miles has begun to produce commercial films under her logo, Four Women Productions. Miles believes that playwrights need to be writing for film for two reasons: to attain financial solvency and to reach a mass audience. She does not limit the productions to women's themes. She encouraged Steve Tesich, for instance, to write the script for *Four Friends*, a film which explored the working class point of view in the 1960s, Miles is admittedly drawn, however, to scripts exploring relationships between mothers and daughters, to those depicting women in a new light, and to those exploring women in connection with social issues.

Miles's concern for the artist and for social issues has extended her influence to various professional associations. Her service to the arts encompasses memberships in the National Theatre Conference, Theatre Communications Group, and the New York State Council on the Arts Theatre Panel, which she has chaired. Her concern for women artists drove her to become a founding member of the American Theatre Association's Women's Program and a founder of the networking organization, Women in Theatre/New York. Miles also serves as a board member for The Bridge (a musical theatre in France) and for Performing Artists for Nuclear Disarmament.

Although, like many theatre people, Miles believes that luck and timing often determine people's careers, in her own case these elements were superseded by her deep concern for the quality of artistic life. This concern has spurred her to nurture the creative process for playwrights, actors, directors, and especially for women in those professions. Her former co-administrator Amy Ober has written, "I see Julia Miles helping to rear a new generation of professional women equipped with the healthy assumption that the theatre has a place for us. The fact is, Julia Miles picks up where our mothers left off, giving women the kind of support that leads not to dependency, but to professional growth" ("The Women's Project Journal," 1980, no pagination). Since she is now in mid-career Miles's nurturing of young talent for the American theatre can only continue. Appropriately, the Drama Guild Committee of Women in June 1985 presented Julia Miles with an award for Outstanding Contribution to Women in Theatre.

Julia Miles's work includes editing *The Women's Project 1* (1980) and *The Women's Project 2* (1984), published by the *Performing Arts Journal* and the American Place Theatre. Material for this essay was drawn principally from "The Women's Project Journal" (one-time newsletter, 1980), the vertical files in the Theatre Collection Performing Arts Research Center at the New York Public Library at Lincoln Center, and telephone interviews with Julia Miles on August 31, 1982, and December 22, 1985.

Miles is listed in *Notable Names in the American Theatre* (1976) and *Contemporary Theatre, Film, and Television* (1984).

Kathleen Conlin

MILLAY, Edna St. Vincent (February 22, 1892–October 19, 1950): poet, playwright, actress, and director with the Provincetown Players, was born in Rockland, Maine, the eldest of three daughters of Cora Lounella (Buzzell) Millay and Henry Tolman Millay a charming, but undependable insurance agent, later a school teacher and superintendent. Called "Vincent" by her family, Millay always spoke of her childhood as "extraordinarily happy," even though her parents divorced in 1900 after her poker-playing father had brought the family to near bankruptcy. Millay's mother, of old New England stock, moved her daughters in 1904 to Camden, Maine, where she worked as a practical nurse. Mrs. Millay, herself a musician and writer of verse, encouraged the girls' artistic inclinations, providing them with books, musical instruments, lessons, and art supplies even when money for necessities was in short supply.

Edna St. Vincent Millay's youthful talents were devoted in equal measure to music, drama, and writing. For a time she trained as a concert pianist, but relinquished this goal when it was determined that her hands were too small. During high school she was recognized for her acting abilities in school plays and other amateur theatricals and was at times hired to fill in for stock companies traveling through Camden. Though music and drama were important to her throughout her career Millay was to become known primarily as a poet. She was taught verse at the age of four by her mother; and her first poem was published in 1906 in the *St. Nicholas Magazine*, which continued to publish her poetry until 1910, when she became too old to hold membership in the St. Nicholas League. During her high school years in Camden (1905–1909), she wrote for her school magazine, *The Megunticook*, and became its editor-in-chief.

After graduation from high school in 1909, Millay, unable to afford college, remained at home and wrote poetry. At eighteen she wrote "Renascence," the poem which was to launch her literary career. In 1911, at the prompting of her mother, she entered "Renascence" in a competition sponsored by *The Lyric Year*, a projected anthology of contemporary poetry. After reading the poem, Ferdinand Earle, the editor, all but promised her the first prize of $500. The other judges did not agree, however, and Millay was awarded a fourth prize but no money. When "Renascence" appeared in *The Lyric Year* in November 1912, it attracted national attention. Earlier in the summer of 1912 Millay had played the piano and read her poems, including "Renascence," in an evening program at the Whitehall Inn in Camden where her sister was working as a waitress. Present in the audience was Caroline B. Dow, executive secretary of the New York Y.W.C.A.'s National Training School, who encouraged Millay to apply for a scholarship to Smith or Vassar College, promising her that money for other expenses would be provided. To prepare for her entrance into Vassar in the fall of 1913, Millay moved to New York City in February and enrolled in Barnard

College, where she read literature for one semester and was introduced to the cultural life of the city.

During the Vassar years (1913–1917), Millay not only continued to write and publish romantic lyrics, which were soon to make her famous, but established herself as an actress and playwright. Each year she played increasingly important roles in Vassar productions. She also enrolled in a playwriting course, where she wrote three of her six plays: *The Princess Marries the Page* (produced at Vassar in 1917 with Millay in the leading role), *The Wall of Dominoes* (her only play in prose, published in the *Vassar Miscellany*, May 1917), and *Two Slatterns and a King*. Her achievements as an actress at Vassar led her to seek a career on the stage when she had completed her studies. Immediately following graduation in 1917, Millay applied, unsuccessfully, for a number of acting jobs before accepting $50 from the Bennett School for coaching productions of her own *Two Slatterns and a King* and *The Princess Marries a Page*. During this time also, Millay began to give public performances of her poetry. In December 1917, Millay read for the ingénue role in Floyd Dell's *The Angel Intrudes* and got the part but at no salary. The play opened on December 28, 1917, at the Playwright's Theatre (home of the Provincetown Players) on Macdougal Street in Greenwich Village. Pleased with Millay's performance in *The Angel Intrudes*, Dell offered her a part in his next play, *Sweet and Twenty*, and Millay became known as "the beautiful young actress at the Provincetown."

Millay then moved to Greenwich Village, where her mother and sisters soon joined her. There she became associated with an avant-garde circle of feminists, freethinkers, political radicals, and artistic bohemians, including many whose names would become famous in later years. With the publication in 1917 of her *Renascence and Other Poems* and because of her association with the Provincetown Players, Millay was soon one of the most visible members of the "Village" set during its heyday. In its 1918–1919 season the Provincetown Players opened with three one-act plays, including Millay's *The Princess Marries the Page*, in which she once again took an acting part and directed. She also played in the George Cram Cook-**Susan Glaspell** satire, *Tickless Time*, and had a Japanese role in *The String of the Samisen* in January 1919. In December 1919 Millay directed the first performance of her own *Aria da Capo*, judged to be the most distinguished presentation of the Provincetown's 1919–1920 season. This play, along with its expressionistic staging and its lyrical satirization of the folly and greed of humankind, was performed widely in little theatres across the country and was published in *Reedy's Mirror*.

In spite of her theatrical triumphs during this time, the theatre was not supplying Millay with a livelihood. The income she derived from her "Nancy Boyd" stories published in *Ainslee's Magazine* allowed her to continue writing poetry and acting, but by April 1920 she was exhausted and in poor health. That year marks the end of her acting career, and in the fall of 1920 she accepted an offer from Frank Crowninshield to go to Europe on salary as a foreign correspondent for *Vanity Fair*. Before sailing for France in January 1921, she saw published her second collection of poems, *A Few Figs From Thistles*. Millay remained in Europe for two years, traveling in France, Italy, Albania, Austria, and England and writing magazine pieces, but little poetry. She brought out her third volume of poems, *Second April*, in 1921 and completed in Paris her longest, most ambitious play, *The Lamp and the Bell*, commissioned by the Vassar College Alumnae Association for its fiftieth anniversary celebration on June 18, 1921. In February 1923, she returned to America. Later in the same year she received the Pulitzer Prize for Poetry for her *Ballad of the Harpweaver*.

In the spring of 1923 Millay met Eugen Jan Boissevain, twelve years her senior and a widower, and married him on July 18. On the afternoon of the wedding Millay checked into a New York hospital for an operation which left her convalescing through the summer. During her recovery, she made an adaptation, under the title of *Launzi*, of Ferenc Molnar's play, *Heavenly and Earthly Love*, and readied *The Harp-Weaver and Other Poems* for publication. Millay's marriage was a happy one; convinced of the significance of her literary work, Boissevain relieved her of all mundane tasks so that she might devote herself completely to writing. In early 1924 Millay did a series of highly successful reading tours of the Midwest, after which she and her husband toured the Orient. The following year she was awarded an honorary degree by Tufts University, the first of many such honors. In 1925 she and Boissevain purchased Steepletop, a seven-hundred-acre farm in Austerlitz, New York, in the southern Berkshires. There she and Boissevain spent the remainder of their lives, alternating periods of complete isolation with periods of entertaining friends. One of these friends was Deems Taylor, the composer with whom she collaborated on *The King's Henchmen*, commissioned by New York City's Metropolitan Opera Company. The opera premiered at the Met on February 17, 1927, with Lawrence Tibbett in the leading role, and was very successful. It subsequently toured for several months and was played at the Met fourteen times during three seasons. By November 1927 the libretto was in its eighteenth printing.

During the 1920s Millay was at the height of her popularity and critical acclaim. She continued to publish volumes of poetry in relatively quick succession throughout the next decade: *The Buck in the Snow* (1928); *Fatal Interview*, a sonnet sequence dedicated to Elinor Wylie (1931); *Wine From These Grapes* (1934); *Huntsman, What Quarry?* (1939). Though these volumes were not greeted with the universal applause which her earlier work prompted, Millay could still count on the approval of the general public. On December 25, 1932, she began a series of eight very successful readings of her poetry on national radio. She also garnered honorary degrees from the University of Wisconsin in 1933 and New York University and Colby College in 1937. In the summer of 1935 she collaborated with George Dillon on a translation of Baudelaire's *Flowers of Evil*, published in 1936. In May 1936, the only copy of the manuscript of *Conversation at Midnight*, on which she had been working for two years, was destroyed in a hotel fire at Sanibel Island, Florida. Millay reconstructed the work, partly from memory, and published it in 1937. It is a verse debate or symposium among seven men of diverse social, political, and religious backgrounds. Though not originally meant to be played, it was presented on stage for the first time in Los Angeles in November 1961 and ran for sixteen weeks before its New York engagement.

A changing poetic climate in the late 1930s, stimulated in part by the appearance of T. S. Eliot's *The Waste Land*, began a trend toward a lower critical estimate of Millay's work as romantic and facile. The war years accelerated the decline in her reputation, largely because she cooperated with the Writer's War Board in the production of propaganda verse subsequently published as *Make Bright the Arrows* (1940). In 1941 she recorded poems for RCA Victor and in 1942 she published *The Murder of Lidice*, a long dramatic narrative in verse commemorating the Czechoslovakian village exterminated by the Nazis. The poem was broadcast over NBC in October 1942, read by Alexander Woollcott, Paul Muni, and Clifton Fadiman. Millay referred to her propaganda verse as the "acres of bad poetry" she had written during the war; her only defense was that it contributed to the perpetuation of a world in which poetry could remain viable. For five years she had produced little else.

In the late 1940s she was at work on her new collection of poems—her last, as it turned out. In 1949 her husband died in Boston of a stroke following an operation for lung cancer. Millay returned to Steepletop alone, where she apparently drank excessively, ignored her health, and worked too hard. On October 19, 1950, she was found dead of a heart attack on the stairs of her home. After a small private service, she was buried at Steepletop. *Mine the Harvest* was published posthumously in 1954 and her *Collected Poems* in 1956.

The current critical neglect of Millay's poetry and drama does not obscure her contributions to the American theatre. As actress, playwright, and occasional director, Millay contributed significantly to the success of the Provincetown Players, a company credited by many with providing a regenerating force in American theatre. In its eight seasons (1915–1922), the Provincetown produced ninety-seven plays by forty-seven American authors. Millay was acclaimed as an actress in a number of these plays, had three of her own plays produced (including the avant-garde *Aria da Capo*, one of the Provincetown's greatest successes), and served for several seasons on the company's executive committee. At the Provincetown Players, only seven other playwrights, including Eugene O'Neill, had more plays produced than Millay. Through her close involvement with the Provincetown Players, then, Millay attended at the birth of a serious American drama and helped to create an atmosphere in which it could flourish.

General accounts of Millay's life and works include Elizabeth Atkins, *Edna St. Vincent Millay and Her Times* (1936), Vincent Sheean, *The Indigo Bunting* (1951), Toby Shafter, *Edna St. Vincent Millay: America's Best Loved Poet* (1957), Miriam Gurko, *Restless Spirit* (1962), and Jean Gould, *The Poet and Her Book* (1969). Norman A. Brittin, *Edna St. Vincent Millay* (1967) offers biographical information as well as perceptive critical discussions of her poetry and plays. Robert Sarlos, *Jig Cook and the Provincetown Players*

(1982), and Anne Cheney, *Millay in Greenwich Village* (1975), provide information about Millay's involvement with the Provincetown Players. John Joseph Patton, "Edna St. Vincent Millay as a Verse Dramatist" (Unpublished Ph.D. dissertation, University of Colorado, 1962) provides an analysis and evaluation of Millay's verse drama. Millay's letters, edited by Allan Ross Macdougall, were published in 1952, and Karl Yost's bibliography of her works appeared in 1937. Judith Nierman, *Edna St. Vincent Millay: A Reference Guide* (1977) is an annotated bibliography of the writings on Millay. The largest collections of Millay's papers are at the Library of Congress, in the Berg Collection of the New York Public Library, and at the Beinecke Library of Yale University. Her obituary appeared in the *New York Times* (October 20, 1950). Biographical information on Millay may be found in Siegfried Melchinger, *The Concise Encyclopedia of Modern Drama* (1964); *Notable American Women*, Vol. II (1971); Myron Matlaw, *Modern World Drama: An Encyclopedia* (1972); *American Writers*, Vol. III (1974); *American Women Writers*, Vol. III (1981); *The McGraw-Hill Encyclopedia of World Drama*, Vol. III (1984); and *Dictionary of Literary Biography*, Vol. 45, *American Poets, 1880–1945*, First Series (1986).

Lucien L. Agosta

MILLER, Ann (April 12, 1923–): dancer and star in the old Hollywood tradition, began her career by lying about her age, and the resulting confusion about her birthdate persisted in many press releases and biographies until her own autobiography, *Miller's High Life*, set the record straight in 1972. She was born Johnnie Lucille Collier in Houston, Texas, the daughter of Clara and John Alfred Collier, a criminal lawyer. When her parents' marriage broke up in 1934, Johnnie Lucille Collier had to use her only salable skill—tap dancing—to support herself and her mother. The pair moved to Hollywood, where Collier already had performed as a movie extra. As Anne (the final "e" was later dropped) Miller, she eventually landed an engagement at the Bal Tabarin Club in San Francisco, where an RKO talent scout spotted her in 1936. To sign with RKO, however, Ann had to be of age. Her father accordingly sent her a false birth certificate, which stated that Lucy Ann Collier had been born in Chireno, Texas, on April 12, 1919. It was, Miller remembers, "the only kind thing my father ever did for me" (*Miller's High Life*, p. 58).

When she danced in the RKO film, *The Life of the Party*, *Variety* praised her by comparing her to Eleanor Powell, the tap dance star of MGM. In her next films Miller worked with many movie greats, including **Katharine Hepburn** and Ginger Rogers in *Stage Door* (1937), with Frank Capra in *You Can't Take It With You* (1938), and with Lucille Ball and the Marx Brothers in *Room Service* (1938). However, these movies did not showcase Miller's dancing talents, and her agents suggested that she travel to New York for a featured role in *George White's Scandals of 1939*. In true Hollywood movie fashion she stopped the show with her "Mexiconga," and film studios immediately began bidding for her services. Ann Miller accordingly returned to the West Coast in 1940 and worked for RKO, Republic, and Columbia studios. She remained with Columbia until 1948, making a total of ten pictures. Most of these were short black-and-white musicals with wartime settings and titles like *Reveille with Beverly* (1943) and *True to the Army* (1942), in which she allegedly danced 840 taps to the minute.

On February 16, 1946, Miller married steel heir Reese Llewellan Milner, and agreed to give up her career once she completed her Columbia contract. Milner, however, was alcoholic and abusive. Miller fell or was knocked down a staircase when nine months pregnant, lost the baby, and injured her spine. Rehabilitating herself with enormous will power, she returned to pictures to dance with Fred Astaire in MGM's *Easter Parade* (1948). In this film Miller briefly gave up her ''machine-gun taps'' for Astaire's more fluid style in their duet, ''It Only Happens When I Dance With You.'' She remained with MGM until 1958, making thirteen pictures, including *On the Town* (1949) with Gene Kelly and Frank Sinatra, and *Kiss Me, Kate* (1953) with Katharine Grayson and Howard Keel. During this decade she replaced the retired Eleanor Powell as MGM's star tap dance artist. But MGM could not make Ann Miller into the same caliber of star that Eleanor Powell had been. Television was undermining the big studios, and lavish musicals were now too expensive to produce. Worse, early television producers found taps too difficult to record, so the art could not yet reach the new mass audience. Finally, tap dancing gradually slid out of fashion during the 1950s, replaced on Broadway by modern and jazz styles.

Meanwhile, Miller undertook two more marriages: the first, in 1958, to Texas oilman William Moss; the second, in 1961, to another oil millionaire, Arthur Cameron. The latter marriage was annulled in 1962 after a spectacular lawsuit which developed when Cameron claimed there had been no legal marriage ceremony. Thus, Miller had to make yet another comeback to show business. Television had now learned to record tap dancing, and in 1964 she began a series of appearances on variety programs like the *Hollywood Palace* and the *Ed Sullivan Show*, specials like *The Bell Telephone Hour*, and numerous game and talk shows. She also appeared in various stock productions, including the title role of *Mame* in Florida. As a result of these appearances, Miller replaced **Angela Lansbury** in the Broadway production of *Mame*, performing from May 1969 to January 1970. In this role Clive Barnes discovered in Miller ''a vivacity . . . that made her stand out from the somewhat languid stars of the late Forties and early Fifties'' (*New York Post*, October 9, 1979).

Ann Miller had succeeded in keeping herself in the public eye during the decline of the Hollywood musical and the brief eclipse of tap dancing. Now she rode the wave of returning interest in, and nostalgia for, those two arts. In 1971 she danced in a Heinz Soup commercial which was a one-minute musical extravaganza done in the old Hollywood musical tradition. Later that year, she appeared in a television production of *Dames at Sea*, a musical spoof of that same tradition. In 1974 and again in 1976 United Artists put together *That's Entertainment, I* and *II*, showcasing, among others, the dancing stars of the forties. Finally, in 1979 Ann Miller joined Mickey Rooney on Broadway in *Sugar Babies*. Critics disagreed about the overall value of this affectionate reproduction of burlesque, but were delighted to see Miller "in stunning shape at whatever age she must be" (*New York Times*, October 9, 1979). The show closed in August 1982, and in October Miller and Rooney undertook a two-year national tour of *Sugar Babies*.

In 1972 Ann Miller had referred to herself as the "near-click" of show business, never quite the big star she could have been (Shipman p. 146). But her relative youth—she is ten years younger than tap greats Ginger Rogers and Eleanor Powell—along with her start at twelve years old, has helped her to stay in the public eye longer than other female dance stars. She continues to project, and believe in, her old-style "star" image, always appearing with perfectly groomed hair and a sunny smile. Predictably, some modern critics object to this packaging. *The Village Voice*, for example, noted wearily during an interview that she wore "enough makeup on her face to cover the White House," and "hair that's been sculpted by the savage messiah." Furthermore, the *Voice* discovered Miller was no intellect: her autobiography was, in its breathless style, "hilarious." But in the end, the worldly journalist succumbed to her charm, concluding that "she was dipsy and funny and glamorous and sweet and very Ann Miller" (December 21, 1972). This style, combined with her spectacular dancing, creates her nostalgic appeal to today's audiences. It was best summed up by Charles Goodman, who wrote that even as Ann Miller talks with you, you see that "somewhere she is still in technicolor—tap dancing to Cole Porter's tunes in *Kiss Me, Kate*" (*Applause*, October 6, 1971).

For biographical information on Ann Miller, see her autobiography, *Miller's High Life* (1972), written in collaboration with Norma Lee Browning; and a biography by Jim Connor, *Ann Miller: Tops in Taps* (1981). See also Jerry Ames and Jim Siegleman, *The Book of Tap* (1977); David Shipman, *The Great Movie Stars: The International Years* (1972); and Gerald Bordman, *American Musical Revue: from The Passing Show To Sugar Babies* (1985). Newspaper articles and reviews of interest include Clive Barnes, "Rooney's the Icing on *Sugar Babies*," *New York Post* (October 9, 1979); Charles Goodman, "Ann Miller: Technicolor, Cinemascope, and Stereophonic Sound," *Applause* (October 6, 1971); Walter Kerr, "Sugar Babies, Burlesque is Back," *New York Times* (October 9, 1979); and *The Village Voice* (December 21, 1972). There is a clipping file on Ann Miller in the Billy Rose Theatre Collection in the New York Public Library Performing Arts Research Center at Lincoln Center. She is listed in *Who's Who in the Theatre* (1981) and *International Motion Picture Almanac*, ed. Richard Gertner (1986).

Judith Pratt

MILLER, Marilyn (September 1, 1898–April 7, 1936): musical comedy star, dancer, and actress, was born Mary Ellen Reynolds in Evansville, Indiana, the third and youngest daughter of Edwin D. Reynolds, an electrician, and Ada (Thompson) Reynolds. Her mother divorced Reynolds and married Oscar Miller, an actor. By the time of her first Broadway success at the age of twenty-two, Mary Ellen Reynolds had changed her name in three ways. She took the last name of her stepfather, Oscar Miller, substituted Lynn for her middle name, and on the advice of Florenz Ziegfeld, dropped the second "n" in Lynn and added the second name to her first, making Marilyn Miller her stage name.

Miller's parents and two older sisters, Ruth and Claire, were known in the vaudeville circuit of the Midwest as "The Four Columbians." The four became five in 1904, when the six-year-old Marilyn joined the act. She was billed as "Mlle. Sugarplum," a dancing "infant prodigy" who also played the drums in the family musical act. This popular family toured during the early 1900s throughout the United States, Canada, the West Indies, and England. Although Miller's life from early on was constantly "on the road" in the entertaining profession, her upbringing was strict; she attributed to her early training the hard work and self-discipline visible in every aspect of her later career. She was "discovered" at the age of fifteen by Lee Shubert, who saw her performing at the Embassy Club in London as a solo act doing impressions of **Elsie Janis**, Bessie McCoy, Stella Mayhew, Fritzi Scheff, and Bert Williams. Shubert was so taken with the young talented beauty that he offered her an engagement at New York's Winter Garden Theatre in his *Passing Show of 1914*. Miller agreed, and made her first New York appearance as Miss Jerry in the Winter Garden's annual revue. She was a hit and stayed with the Shuberts for the next three years, starring as First Love in the *Passing Show of 1915*, as the leading dancer of the "Burmese Ballet" in *The Show of Wonders* (1916), and in several roles in the *Passing Show of 1917*.

Although the Shuberts could take credit for discovering Miller, it was Florenz Ziegfeld who made her a "star." She became one of his *Follies* girls in 1918 and starred as a dancer in "Syncopated Time," "A Yankee Doodle Dance," "Mine was a Marriage of Convenience," "Poor Little Me," and "A Dream Dance." In the last piece, she danced with Frank Carter, a young actor-dancer whose career was developing under Ziegfeld's management. Marilyn Miller and Frank Carter were married in May 1919, but their happiness was cut short by his death in a car accident barely a year later. In 1922 Miller married Jack Pickford, brother of Mary Pickford. An often rocky marital road finished in divorce in 1927.

Ziegfeld had decided that Miller should be more than a chorus girl and occasional featured dancer, and he provided her with singing and acting lessons. Her success in the 1918 *Follies* brought hopeful predictions from the critics: "Freshness, youthfulness, and a pretty blonde comeliness are hers, and also enough proudness in the technique of her work to carry her well outside the vaudevillian stratum" (*Boston Evening Transcript*, September 17, 1918). Miller had brought with her to Broadway a thorough training in classical dance, which she incorporated into the contemporary numbers. Her dancing dazzled the audiences from the beginning; and, with Ziegfeld's patronage, her acting and singing eventually gained critical praise as well.

Praised for her bright presence and talented toes in *Fancy Free* (1918) and the 1919 *Follies*, Miller "bloomed from a vaudeville bud into one of musical comedy's fairest blossoms" when she starred in *Sally* (according to Percy Stone of the *New York Herald Tribune*, November 10, 1924). This Ziegfeld production at the New Amsterdam Theatre was the story of a girl who goes from dishwasher to dancer—a Cinderella fable of a foundling who becomes a Follies girl. The Guy Bolton and Jerome Kern story, with production design by Joseph Urban, and co-starring Leon Errol, premièred on December 21, 1920, commanding the top ticket price of the day: $3.50. *Sally* became the most popular show of the decade, with a Broadway box-office record of over 570 performances in its two-year run, followed by a tour to Boston and Chicago. Miller stopped the show every night when she sang "Look for the Silver Lining." Although *Sally* enhanced Miller's status as a star, she was surprised at, but quite unchanged by, her success. In an interview near the end of the show's run, she maintained, "I cannot but think of the other hundreds of worthy girls who are struggling as I have struggled to win the place I have won" (Unidentified clipping, New York, 1922).

After *Sally*, Miller broke with Ziegfeld over monetary and contractual matters, and his rival, Charles Dillingham, quickly engaged Broadway's hottest new star. Dillingham offered her the role of Peter Pan, and her assumption of the part was personally approved by James M. Barrie. The play opened on November 6, 1924, at the Knickerbocker Theatre, and included Leslie Banks as Captain Hook. Inevitably, Miller's performance was compared to that of the incomparable Maude Adams, who had originated the role. Since Miller did not have Adams's ethereal charm, pathos, and wistfulness, she received her first negative criticism, even though her grace and effort were acknowledged. She was accused of being mechanical and uncertain, and having an "unlovely" speaking voice. The "spirituality," said the critics, that Adams had brought to the part was replaced by Miller's "gaiety of the musical comedienne" (*Boston Herald*, February 22, 1925). The Peter Pan role, lasting into 1925, was Miller's only diversion from the musical comedy stage.

In September of 1925, Dillingham found another song and dance vehicle for Miller. *Sunny*, by Otto Harbach, Oscar Hammerstein, and Jerome Kern, co-starred Jack Donahue and played for fifteen months in New York, Boston, and Philadelphia. Miller played an English circus performer who made her first appearance in the show on a horse. Her popular songs from the show, "Who?" and "Do You Love Me?", were published as best-selling sheet music. The production, called a "hippodramatic vaudeville" by Gilbert Gabriel of the *New York Sun* (September 23, 1925), was full of Miller's "infectious" zest. The *Boston Transcript* critic praised her dancing as an "instinct with a graphic sense of proportion and a rhythmic accuracy truly remarkable" (December 1, 1927). With this show, Miller became the highest paid musical comedy star up to that time at $3,000 a week.

In 1927 Miller reconciled her differences with Ziegfeld and returned to his organization. He produced George Gershwin and Sigmund Romberg's *Rosalie* in January of 1928 at the New Amsterdam Theatre. It was "part operetta, part musical comedy, and part strutting-star vehicle" for the Marilyn Miller and Jack

Donahue team (Mordden, *Better Foot Forward*. p. 80). This story of a princess who disguises herself as a cadet in order to see the West Pointer she loves, ran for over ten months in New York, then toured. With *Rosalie*, Miller came into her own again as the most magnetic, most accomplished, and most popular of musical stars. Her magic was in her magnificent dancing and her ability to give her audiences "happiness and the joy of life expressed in love and laughter and songs and dances as light and sweet as apple blossoms fluttering" (Walter Kingsley, unidentified clipping).

Her charm first appeared on film in 1929, when she starred in the movie version of her first hit, *Sally*. The following year she was back on Broadway in *Smiles*, produced by Ziegfeld, and also starring the dancers Fred and Adele Astaire. It was the story of a French orphan who comes to New York and joins the Salvation Army. In 1930 she returned to Hollywood to make two more films, *Sunny* and *Her Majesty, Love*, which starred W. C. Fields. Miller's last Broadway show was *As Thousands Cheer* (Music Box Theatre, September 30, 1933), a satirical review of contemporary politics by Moss Hart and Irving Berlin, which also starred Clifton Webb and **Ethel Waters**. Miller's most popular numbers were those in which she impersonated Joan Crawford and **Lynn Fontanne**. In 1934 she married Chester O'Brien, a young actor in the show. A contractual dispute caused both to quit the show before the end of its 400-performance run. She officially announced her retirement, and after that her husband, content to live on her wealth, made only occasional efforts to secure work as an actor or dancer. In the spring of 1936, one of Miller's frequent sinus infections was severe enough to put her in the hospital. A toxic condition developed from the infection, and she died on April 7, at the age of thirty-seven.

Although she died relatively young, Marilyn Miller had left her mark on the American theatre. She once said, "I am more interested in dancing than anything else in the world" (*New York Herald Tribune*, March 23, 1930). One of the classiest stars of the 1920s and 1930s, Miller was a dancer first, and her contribution to the American musical stage lies in her gift of ballet to Broadway. Her legacy was a new appreciation of dance as part of musical theatre. She brought a range of styles to her performances—from classical to clog to contemporary. It was her dancing, far more than her other talents, that made her a great box-office attraction and the "Pavlova of the tired business man, the Taglioni of the world of musical comedy and of jazz, the Fanny Elssler of a whole generation of college boys in search of diversion" (*Boston Transcript*, April 11, 1936). She was later recognized as a "pioneer ballet exponent on the legitimate stage" (*Christian Science Monitor*, July 19, 1972). Had she lived, she might have contributed more to Broadway's dance through teaching or choreography.

The primary sources on Marilyn Miller's career are the news clippings, articles, programs, photographs, and sheet music in the Harvard Theatre Collection, Harvard University, and the Theatre Collection of the New York Public Library Performing Arts Research Center at Lincoln Center. Her biography is *The Other Marilyn* by Warren G.

Harris (1985). Jeanne Perkins, "Mary Martin," *Life* (December 27, 1943) includes pictures of Marilyn Miller in some of her famous roles. See also *Cosmopolitan* (November 1914), *American Magazine* (May 1921), and *Motion Picture Magazine* (October 1923, October 1929, and September 1931). Miller's obituary appeared in the *New York Times* (April 8, 1936). She is mentioned in Marjorie Farnsworth, *The Ziegfeld Follies* (1956); Ethan Mordden, *Better Foot Forward: The History of American Musical Theatre* (1976); Gerald Bordman, *American Musical Theatre* (1978); Cecil Smith, *Musical Comedy in America* (1980); and Gerald Bordman, *American Musical Revue: From the Passing Show to Sugar Babies* (1985). Miller is included in *Who's Who in the Theatre* (1936); Robert L. Sherman, *Actors and Authors With Composers Who Helped Make Them Famous* (1951); *Notable American Women*, Vol. II (1971); *Who Was Who in the Theatre*, Vol. III (1978); and *The Oxford Companion to American Theatre* (1984).

Noreen Barnes

MILLS, Florence (January 25, 1895–November 1, 1927): stage performer, singing comedienne, and dancer, was born in Washington, D.C., the youngest of the three daughters of John and Nellie (Simon) Winfrey. She performed in the homes of Washington diplomats as "Baby Florence" at an early age. She made her first stage appearance at the age of five in Bert Williams and George Walker's *Sons of Ham* (1900), a performance about which the *Washington Star* noted, "Baby Florence made a big hit and was *encored* for dancing" (quoted in *Black Manhattan*, p. 198).

Mills continued to perform after her family moved to Harlem in 1903. In 1910 she joined with her two sisters, Olivia and Maude, in a musical group called the Mills Sisters, which toured the country in various vaudeville troupes. In 1923 she married a dancer named Ulysses S. ("Slow Kid") Thompson and then left her sisters to perform as a singer and dancer with her husband. Mills's breakthrough as an adult artist occurred when Noble Sissle and Eubie Blake's *Shuffle Along* lost its leading lady, Gertrude Saunders, in 1921 and Florence Mills delighted audiences in her place, especially with the song "I'm Crazy for that Kind of Love." *Shuffle Along* was presented at the Sixty-Third Street Theatre, since no Broadway theatre was available. The show was so popular that there were traffic jams on Sixty-Third Street every night. Mills became known as "Little Twinks," for she was a small, delicate woman, described as "pixie-ish," "birdlike and beautiful." Poet and critic James Weldon Johnson said of her, "She could be whimsical, she could be almost grotesque; but she had the good taste that never allowed her to be coarse. She could be *risqué*, she could be seductive; but it was impossible for her to be vulgar, for she possessed a naiveté that was alchemic" (*Black Manhattan*, p. 199). Her gifts included pantomime in addition to song, dance, and comedy. When on July 17, 1922, after a long and successful engagement at the Plantation Club nightclub *The Plantation Revue* opened on Broadway, Mills's talents became known to the theatrical world at large; and she was in demand internationally almost at once.

Mills performed in Paris and London in 1923 and 1924 in a show called *From Dover to Dixie*, and Sir John Irvine wrote of her, "She is by far the most artistic person London has had the good fortune to see" (*Black Manhattan*, p. 198). Later in 1924 she returned to the United States, and on October 29 opened on Broadway as the star of the show now titled *From Dixie to Broadway*, in which she shattered the tradition that black musicals should have as central characters two male comedians. Fresh from this triumph, she took the leading role in Lew Leslie's *Blackbirds* (1926), which was written especially for her, and which contained the song that became her trademark, "I'm Just a Blackbird Looking for a Bluebird." After a triumphant six-week engagement at the Alhambra Theatre in Harlem, Mills went with *Blackbirds* back to Paris and London. Her name and photograph were famous over Europe, and the Prince of Wales was said to have seen her performance sixteen times and to have pronounced her "ripping."

When she returned to Harlem in 1927, Mills checked into a hospital for an appendectomy that she had previously postponed; she died several days later. Her sudden death stunned theatregoers who had looked forward to seeing her *Blackbirds* performance. Her funeral inspired one of the largest crowds and outpourings of grief in the history of Harlem. Five thousand people were packed in Mother Zion Church, while 150,000 waited outside for the funeral procession. "She was more their idol," said James Weldon Johnson, "than any other artist of the race" (*Black Manhattan*, p. 200).

A testimony to the stature of Florence Mills can be found in Ethel Waters' autobiography, *His Eye Is On the Sparrow* (1951). Waters made no effort to conceal the high opinion she had of her own artistic gifts; however, after substituting for Mills in *Shuffle Along*, at that time the premiere showcase of black musical talent, Waters did not even think about the possibility of outshining Mills and perhaps stealing her role, because "Broadway and all downtown belonged to Florence Mills" (p. 225).

Since there are no vocal recordings nor many artists who point to Florence Mills as their teacher (she died at the age of 32), and since she excelled in a theatrical form not usually associated with lasting significance, it is difficult to measure her contribution. Writers speak of an indefinable quality in Florence Mills, one for which the most carefully chosen words are unsuitable. What cannot fail to strike wonder is the sheer magnitude of the respect and love that she seemed to call forth from her audiences, both American and European.

The most comprehensive background on Florence Mills is in James Weldon Johnson's *Black Manhattan* (1968). Donald Bogle gives an overview of her life and lists her theatre credits in "Florence Mills: Make way for Little Twinks" in *Brown Sugar: Eighty Years of America's Black Female Superstars* (1980). See also Langston Hughes and Milton Meltzer, *Black Magic: A Pictorial History of Black Entertainers in America* (1967); Loften Mitchell, *Black Drama: The Story of the American Negro in the Theatre* (1967); and Lindsay Patterson, *International Library of Negro Life and History: Anthology of the American Negro in the Theatre* (1968). See also Charles B. Cochran's memoirs, *The Secrets of a Showman* (1926). Mills's obituary and other appreciative articles after her death appeared in the *New York Times* (November 2, 4, and 7, 1927). There are clippings about Mills in the Harvard Theatre Collection and in the Theatre Collection of the New York Public Library Performing Arts Research Center at Lincoln Center. There are biographical accounts of Florence Mills in *Who's Who in the Theatre* (1925); *Notable American Women*, Vol. II (1971); *Who Was Who in the Theatre*, Vol. III (1978); and *The Oxford Companion to American Theatre* (1984).

Elizabeth Hadley Freydberg

MITCHELL, Maggie (June 14, 1832–March 22, 1918): actress renowned in the role of Fanchon, was born Margaret Julia Mitchell in New York City, the daughter of Charles S. and Anna Dodson Mitchell. Both parents encouraged Maggie and her sisters Mary and Emma to pursue careers in the theatre. In 1851, when she was nineteen, Mitchell had the opportunity to fill a vacancy in the cast of *The Soldier's Daughter* at Burton's Theatre in New York. She was carefully coached in the part and performed with marked success. By the next season she was hired at the Bowery Theatre at a salary of four dollars a week, playing mostly boys' roles, including the Prince of Wales in Shakespeare's *Richard III* and Oliver Twist, an audience favorite. Following a disagreement with the management, Mitchell left the Bowery and went to perform in Baltimore, Boston, Cleveland, Philadelphia, and other cities in a wide repertoire of male and female roles. These included Claude Melnotte in *The Lady of Lyons*, Richard III, Young Norval in *Douglas*, Margery in *A Rough Diamond*, Gertrude in *The Loan of a Lover*, Paul in *The Pet of the Petticoats*, Harry Halcyon in *A Middy Ashore*, the Countess in *The Wild Irish Girl*, and Dot in *The Cricket on the Hearth*. A starring tour followed. One of her new plays written especially for her, was *Our Maggie*.

In 1860 Mitchell came across *Fanchon, the Cricket*, a dramatization by August Waldauer from a German version of George Sand's story, *La Petite Fadette*. The play was first produced January 19, 1861, at the St. Charles Theatre in New Orleans. *The Picayune's* reviewer noted that "the applause . . . which was constant throughout the performance, was at once a tribute to the merits of the piece and the manner in which it was acted" (quoted by Kendall, *The Golden Age of New Orleans Theatre*, p. 319). Until *Fanchon* Mitchell had been just one of many clever comediennes, but after *Fanchon* she was considered a truly notable American actress, according to John Kendall (*The Golden Age of New Orleans Theatre*, p. 318).

From New Orleans, Mitchell embarked on a Southern tour with *Fanchon*, but this was cut short by the outbreak of the Civil War. Mitchell took the play to the Boston Museum Theatre, where it opened June 3, 1861. In New York *Fanchon* was performed for the first time on June 9, 1862, at the New Olympic Theatre, where it ran for six weeks. Then Mitchell continued to enlarge her repertory with *Little Barefoot*, *The Pearl of Savoy*, *Lorle*, *Mignon*, *Jane Eyre*, and *Ray*. However, audiences in New York and Boston looked forward to *Fanchon* each season. The popularity of *Fanchon* over the other plays in Mitchell's repertoire is reflected by a return visit she paid to New Orleans in 1870.

She performed for two weeks again at the St. Charles Theatre, which was filled for performances of *Fanchon* but was nearly empty for *Jane Eyre* and *Lorle*.

The public never seemed to grow tired of *Fanchon*, and so eminent a person as Ralph Waldo Emerson wrote some verses praising Mitchell's performance as the piquant country girl. Mitchell returned annually to perform *Fanchon* at the Boston Theatre. Here she was seen by German tragedian Bogumil-Dawison, who was unfamiliar with English but knew the story. He was so delighted with Mitchell that he offered to take the actress and the company to Germany for a protracted engagement, but Mitchell declined the offer. Henry Wadsworth Longfellow, who admired her *Jane Eyre*, urged her to take that play to England. The popular actress, **Charlotte Cushman**, also urged Mitchell to play *Fanchon* abroad. It is a tribute to Mitchell's performance that the rash of imitations and reproductions from a stolen prompt book of *Fanchon* never diminished the luster and popularity of the original as presented by Maggie Mitchell.

Like many of her contemporaries, Mitchell achieved success in a single role, which she returned to again and again for twenty-five years. Luther Holden described her success with this role: "If we examine Miss Mitchell's stage art to discover the secret of her really wonderful success, we readily find that naturalness and a seeming absence of art are its essential qualities. . . . Her portrayals were unique, and yet nothing more than the holding of the mirror before nature's self. She had the rare faculty of painting the picture of maidenly purity and nobility of soul most deftly; and her audience laughed when she laughed, and wept when she wept" (*Famous American Actors of Today*, p. 319). According to Holden, Mitchell was a small and "elfish creature with a wealth of sunny, golden hair, whose nervous energy and sprightliness, no less than an exquisite form and face, gave picturesque presence to the line of child heroines she made peculiarly her own" (*Famous American Actors*, p. 115).

Mitchell's performance of the youthful Fanchon appears to have endured despite the actress's own advancing age. When Mitchell was forty-five years old *The Spirit of the Times* reviewed a performance of *Fanchon* on March 30, 1878: "She is not alone a hoyden, moved by shallow impulses; she conveys the impression of having caught something of the mysterious influences of the night that she invokes. . . . Her pleading, coaxing tone is inimitable; it belongs very clearly to Maggie Mitchell's self. . . . " Mitchell continued to play Fanchon until her last appearance at the age of fifty-eight in 1892.

Mitchell was married three times. The first marriage was a youthful romantic interlude which led to a swift divorce. She married Henry T. Paddock in 1868 and was divorced 20 years later. In 1889 she married Charles Abbott (Charles Mace), the leading man in her company during her last years on the stage. Unlike some other actors, she managed her money well and retired from the stage with a small fortune. She died of a stroke in 1918 and was buried as Margaret Julia Mace in Greenwood Cemetery, Brooklyn.

The major biographical information about Maggie Mitchell is found in *Players of the Present*, Part II, by John B. Clapp and Edwin Francis Edgett (1900). Commentary on her acting is found in Luther Holden's chapter on Mitchell in *Famous American Actors of Today*, edited by Frederic Scott McKay and Charles E. L. Wingate (1896). A description of the New Orleans premiere of *Fanchon* appears in John S. Kendall's *The Golden Age of New Orleans Theater* (1952). Other contemporary accounts of Mitchell are included in T. Allston Brown, *History of the American Stage* (1870) and H. P. Phelps, *Players of a Century* (1880). See also J. N. Ireland, *Records of the New York Stage from 1750 to 1860* (1867) and George C. D. Odell, *Annals of the New York Stage*, Vols. VI-XV (1931 - 1949). There are clippings about Maggie Mitchell in the Harvard Theatre Collection. Her obituary appeared in the *New York Times* (March 23 and 25, 1918) and the *New York Tribune* (March 23, 1918). She is included in Dixie Hines and Harry Prescott Hanaford, eds., *Who's Who in Music and Drama* (1914); *Dictionary of American Biography*, Vol. VII, Part 1 (1934); Robert L. Sherman, *Actors and Authors With Composers Who Helped Make Them Famous* (1951); *Who Was Who in America: Vol. I: 1897–1942* (1966); *Notable American Women*, Vol. II (1971); and *The Oxford Companion to American Theatre* (1984).

Susan S. Cole

MODJESKA, Helena (October 12, 1840–April 8, 1909): actress, was born in Krakow, Poland. In childhood she was known as Helena Opid. Her mother, Jozefa (Misel) Benda, had been a widow for ten years at the time of Helena's birth. Michael Opid, a music teacher, resided in the Benda household, but it is uncertain whether or not he was Helena's father or not. The vivacious, intelligent, and willful girl was taught, along with her brothers and sisters, by Gustave Sinmayer, a German, who became resident tutor in the household after Opid's death. Sinmayer, who was avidly interested in the theatre, saw Helena Opid's potential as an actress and tutored her in dramatic literature and the German language to prepare her for a stage career. She made her stage debut in the provincial Polish theatre in 1861, the same year she gave birth to Rudolf, her son by Sinmayer. When she went on the stage she adopted the name Modrezejewska (later Americanized as Modjeska), the name Sinmayer used in theatrical circles. A daughter, Maria, was born in 1862 and died three years later. When Helena Modjeska moved to America her son Rudolf came with her as Ralph Modjeska. He later became a successful civil engineer.

By 1868 Modjeska had become one of the stars of the Krakow stage, after refining her acting in the provincial theatres. In Krakow she met Karol Chlapowski, eight years her senior, brought up in a wealthy and aristocratic family. They were married on September 12, 1868, in spite of his family's objections.

From Krakow, Modjeska moved to Warsaw, the largest city in Poland, where she became one of the most popular stars of the Imperial Theatre, renowned for her performances in Shakespeare and classics of the Polish stage. Having reached the height of her profession in Poland, she began to consider expanding her career to another country. Maurice Neville, an American with whom she played in *Hamlet* in 1874, urged her to try the New York stage. The Chlapowskis left Poland in 1875 with a small group of their friends, including the noted author Henryk Sienkiewicz, all of whom were frustrated by the political conditions in

Poland; they settled on a farm in Anaheim, California. In America, Chlapowski was often called "Count Bozenta," though the title belonged to another branch of the family. Modjeska was often given the title of Countess. Chlapowski toured with his wife, helped manage her career, and took care of their ranch in California. Modjeska helped with the farm for a time and then began an intensive study of English to prepare for her new career. Though she became fluent in the language, she never lost her accent. For her American debut she chose one of the staples of her Polish repertory, *Adrienne Lecouvreur*, and made her first American appearance in San Francisco on August 20, 1877. She was an instant success and, after a tour of California, she made her New York debut in the same play on December 22, 1877, at the Fifth Avenue Theatre.

For the next thirty years Modjeska toured America playing in a repertory that included *Macbeth*, *Henry VIII*, *Mary Stuart*, *As You Like It*, *Camille*, and *Odette*. During that time she remained one of the top stars in the country, In her excellent companies were future stars like Maurice Barrymore and Otis Skinner. In Louisville on December 7, 1883, she presented *Thora*, a version of Henrik Ibsen's *A Doll's House*, but the experiment was poorly received and the play was dropped from the repertory. During the season of 1889–1890 she toured with Edwin Booth, who, at the end of his career, was making his last extended tour of the country.

Modjeska frequently returned to Poland to visit and to play occasional engagements in her native country. She also appeared successfully on the London stage. Though she wanted to become director of a resident company in either Europe or America, she never was offered a suitable troupe. As a result, she continued the touring, though she disliked it. Modjeska retired from the stage at the end of the 1906–1907 season, though she later gave occasional readings for the numerous charities she supported. She devoted herself to her many friends and relatives until her death on April 8, 1909, of Bright's disease, at her home in Bay Island, California. Her husband, son, and three grandchildren survived her. She was buried in her native city of Krakow.

Though she learned her craft in Europe, Modjeska spent most of her career in America, where she enriched the stage with her interpretations of the classics at a time when great classical performers were scarce. Her repertory included both tragic and comic heroines from Shakespeare. To parts like Rosalind (her most famous role) in *As You Like It*, Viola in *Twelfth Night*, and Juliet in *Romeo and Juliet*, she brought lyricism and poetry through her beauty, grace, and refinement. Critics praised the way she used her voice to give emphasis and clarity to her characters. William Winter remembered " . . . her presence of tender, poetic beauty, winning refinement, and perfect grace" (*The Wallet of Time*, Vol. I, p. 360).

Modjeska's eminent theatrical success in Poland spurred her to risk beginning anew in another country with a different language, but with hard work she prospered again in her adopted country. Remembering her own struggle, she gave freely of her time and talent to help other Polish people settle in America. Modjeska was a great international actress of her time.

Before her death Modjeska completed her autobiography, *Memories and Impressions of Helena Modjeska* (1910). Her American career is chronicled in Marion Moore Coleman, *Fair Rosalind: The American Career of Helena Modjeska* (1969). Though somewhat sensational, Antoni Gronowicz's *Modjeska, Her Life and Loves* (1956) contains some material not available elsewhere, including extracts from her journal while she was touring with Edwin Booth. Her niece supplied information for Arthur P. Coleman and Marion M. Coleman, *Wanderers Twain: Modjeska and Sienkiewicz: A View From California* (1964). Contemporary views of Modjeska may be found in Lewis Strang, *Famous Actresses of the Day in America*, Vol. I (1899); John B. Clapp and Edwin Frances Edgett, *Players of the Present*, Part 2 (1900); *The Green Room Book or Who's Who on the Stage, 1909* (1909); and William Winter, *The Wallet of Time*, two volumes (1913). Stephen M. Archer, *American Actors and Actresses* (1983), lists books and magazine articles about Modjeska. Of special interest are Jameson Torr Altemus, *Helena Modjeska* (1883), a biographical sketch and reprints of published criticism and of her article, "Success on the Stage," reprinted from the *North American Review* (December 1882); J. Rankin Towse, "Madame Modjeska," *Century* (November 1883); Edward A. Dithmar, "Helena Modjeska," *Harper's Bazaar* (January 11, 1890); and Marion Moore Coleman, *American Debut: Source Materials on the First Appearance of the Polish Actress Helena Modjeska on the American Stage* (1965). Upon Modjeska's death, *Theatre* (May 1909) carried an article of appreciation, "A Brilliant Career Closes for Helena Modjeska." Clippings and other memorabilia are in the Theatre Collection of the New York Public Library Performing Arts Research Center at Lincoln Center. Some of her papers are at the Charles W. Bowers Museum in Santa Ana, California. Helena Modjeska is included in the *Dictionary of American Biography*, Vol. VII (1934, renewed 1962); Robert L. Sherman, *Actors and Authors With Composers Who Helped Make Them Famous* (1951); *Who Was Who in America, Historical Volume: 1607–1896* (1963); *The Oxford Companion to American Literature* (1965); *Who Was Who: Vol. I: 1897–1915* (1967); *Notable American Women*, Vol. II (1971); William C. Young, *Famous Actors and Actresses on the American Stage* (1975); Donald Mullin, *Victorian Actors and Actresses in Review* (1983); *The Oxford Companion to the Theatre* (1983); and *The Oxford Companion to American Theatre* (1984.

Rita M. Plotnicki

MOISEIWITSCH, Tanya (December 3, 1914–): designer, was born in London, England, the first of two daughters of Benno and Daisy (Kennedy) Moiseiwitsch. Her mother, born in Australia, was a violinist, while her father, born in Odessa, Russia, was a pianist world-famous for his interpretations of the Romantic musical literature. Tanya studied the Irish harp and the piano only to decide, in her late teens, that she was not intended for the concert stage. Her parents divorced by the time she was fifteen, and her mother married the famous poet and playwright, John Drinkwater. His greatest success, *Abraham Lincoln*, had premièred in 1919. With her stepfather and her mother, Tanya went to the theatre often in her adolescent years.

After realizing that she had no special musical gifts, Tanya Moiseiwitsch studied art at the Central School of Arts and Crafts, London. Before a year had passed, she began her training for the theatre with scene painters at the Old Vic. She then became assistant to Ruth Keating, designer at the Westminister Theatre, London, where Moiseiwitsch designed her first set in 1934 for a production of *The Faithful*. The next year she began an affiliation with the Abbey Theatre, Dublin, that lasted three years, during which time she designed more than fifty productions. Her first West End assignment was *The Golden Cuckoo* (1940) at the Duchess Theatre, London. While working at the Oxford Playhouse during World War II, she met and married Felix Krish, then on leave from the Royal Air Force. Within months of their marriage he was killed in a crash (1942). She has not remarried.

Moiseiwitsch began in 1945 an association with the Old Vic that placed her among the top theatrical designers in Britain. Her reputation soon became international. Today she is known primarily as a costume designer, but has earned distinction for her scenic design as well. Her credits, which number well into the hundreds, constitute a nearly complete list of the classic dramatic literature performed by such important institutional companies as the Edinburgh Festival (Scotland); the Old Vic, the National Theatre, the Stratford Memorial Theatre (all in England); the Habimah Theatre (Tel Aviv, Israel); the Piccolo Theatre (Milan, Italy), the Stratford Shakespeare Festival (Canada); and the Tyrone Guthrie Theatre (Minneapolis). She has seldom undertaken the design of contemporary plays for commercial managements, instead devoting her career to productions of Greek tragedy, Restoration and eighteenth-century comedies, Molière, Chekhov, Marlowe, Ibsen, Shaw, and most of the Shakespearean canon. She has returned to some plays repeatedly: *Volpone*, *The Miser*, *Cyrano de Bergerac*, *The Cherry Orchard*, *Twelfth Night*, *Measure for Measure*, and Shakespeare's histories. For the world's opera stages she has rendered sets and/ or costumes for *The Marriage of Figaro*, *The Beggar's Opera*, *Don Giovanni*, and *Peter Grimes*.

Tanya Moiseiwitsch's most significant work has been in collaboration with director Tyrone Guthrie, whom she now considers to be the greatest influence on her career. Until Guthrie's death in 1971, they worked together on nearly thirty projects, including the design of two thrust stages, one in Canada and the other in Minneapolis. Both Guthrie and Moiseiwitsch had been fascinated by the prospect of an ''open'' or thrust stage. Guthrie had experimented with this unique actor-audience relationship in the Presbyterian Assembly Hall at the Edinburgh Festival in 1949. Moiseiwitsch in 1951 devised for the Shakespeare Memorial Theatre in Stratford, England, one setting to serve *Richard II*, both parts of *Henry IV*, and *Henry V*. It included stairways, platforms, and galleries constructed in timber. This permanent set, suggestive of an Elizabethan theatre, pushed the action out in front of the proscenium arch onto an apron jutting into the audience. In designing Shakespearean productions, Moiseiwitsch came to see the need to break through the proscenium.

It was at Stratford, Canada, that the move away from the proscenium arch was completed. A Shakespeare festival was organized there in 1953 with Tyrone

Guthrie as director and Tanya Moiseiwitsch as designer. Together, they designed a thrust stage in which the audience, arranged on steeply tiered seats, surrounded the acting area on three sides; no vestige of the proscenium arch remained. Their now famous stage is wedge-shaped with a two-level permanent architectural façade at the rear. No audience member is farther than seventy feet from the stage, though the theatre seats about 2,200. Costumes, properties, and lighting essentially replace traditional scenery, allowing multiscened plays, like those of Shakespeare, to be staged fluidly. Critic Brooks Atkinson of the *New York Times* called the Stratford, Canada, stage "the most vital instrument in the production of Shakespeare most of us have ever seen" (quoted in *Current Biography, 1955*, p. 425). This stage was initially covered by a tent. Moiseiwitsch collaborated in 1957 on the permanent theatre building which replaced the temporary tent and in 1961 on the adjustments that were made to the permanent stage structure.

American critics were quick to lionize the Canadian festival and Moiseiwitsch's costumes for such plays as *Richard III*, *The Taming of the Shrew*, *Measure for Measure*, *Julius Caesar*, and *The Merchant of Venice* in the early seasons. Brooks Atkinson used the adjectives "bold and beautiful" and "stunning" to describe her costumes. Walter Kerr of the *New York Herald Tribune* called them "breathtaking," saying they "achieve a near-sculptured effect" (quoted in *Current Biography, 1955*, p. 423). In the first four years of the festival, Moiseiwitsch designed the costumes and properties for all nine productions. The dimensional effect Kerr admired was, in part, a solution to a technical problem at Stratford. In their rolling repertory production schedule, there was not sufficient time to change the colored filters on the lights from show to show. herefore, white light was used. To compensate, Moiseiwitsch painted colored shading into the folds of the costumes to achieve the noted sculptural richness.

The design hallmark that Moiseiwitsch began to develop in England became clear in Canada. This imprint, called "poetic realism" by some observers, is especially evident in her costumes for Shakespeare's male characters. While the selection of silhouette and line is based on thorough research and is thus realistic, the manipulation of proportion and the control of decorative motif is imaginative. Larger than life characters, for example, are given a monumental appearance by the use of an exaggerated, sculptured shoulder treatment. Decorative detail on the chest and shoulders focuses attention upward to the actor's face. The tapered line of the lower body is controlled so that the legs do not seem spindly. Frequently fabric is painted to create an appropriate sense of realistic wear or to enhance the draping. The total effect is subtle, graceful, and organic.

Though Moiseiwitsch has designed over thirty productions for the Canadian festival, she is best known for the Tyrone Guthrie production of *Oedipus Rex* in 1954. Moiseiwitsch elaborated upon the scant clues found in ancient Greek sources to create an imaginative, mythic stage picture. The actors were dressed in masks, platform shoes, and massive robes. The masks, larger than the actor's head, were tapered to meet the lips, but the chin and mouth were uncovered so that clarity of speech was not sacrificed. The effect, awesome in its grandeur, literally made the characters of Sophocles larger than life. It was a controversial production; some critics thought the masks and robes unnecessarily inhibited the actors while others found it the most exciting production of the play ever seen. Despite the controversy, pictures from this production are frequently reproduced, and it has come to be synonymous in the popular imagination with Greek tragedy in production.

In 1963 Tyrone Guthrie was invited to establish a theatre in Minneapolis, Minnesota, which now bears his name. Moiseiwitsch collaborated with Guthrie and the architect on the design of the thrust stage for the building, and then remained in Minneapolis to become the company's principal designer in its early years. The Minnesota Theatre Company performed a broader selection of plays than the festival in Canada, so while Moiseiwitsch designed *Hamlet* and *As You Like It*, she also designed *Saint Joan*, *The Way of the World*, *The Three Sisters*, and *The Skin of Our Teeth*. Her most memorable production there, however, was again a Greek tragedy directed by Tyrone Guthrie. Guthrie staged in 1967 *The House of Atreus*, an adaptation by John Lewin of *The Oresteia* by Aeschylus. With one notable exception, the production concept was much like the one devised more than a decade earlier for *Oedipus Rex* at Stratford. While the Canadian production used female actors, all of the principal roles in *The House of Atreus* were played by men. A grand mask obscured all but the actor's mouth and chin, the upper torso was broadened by padding, and platform shoes increased the actor's stature. In addition, Moiseiwitsch devised a hugh puppet-like apparatus for the goddess Athena that was much admired.

The House of Atreus was moved to Broadway in 1968 where it played a limited run at the Billy Rose Theatre. Although the script and Tyrone Guthrie's direction received a mixed critical reception, Tanya Moiseiwitsch's set and costumes were lavishly praised. Clive Barnes wrote that Moiseiwitsch ''has produced a beautiful and apt permanent setting for the blood-stained 'Oresteia' and richly fanciful costumes. . . . She has also designed some striking masks and her structure for the appearance of the goddess Athena was a superb piece of stagecraft'' (*New York Times*, December 18, 1968). John Chapman thought the production was designed on a ''grand scale. . . . The platform set is spare enough but the costumes one sees upon it from the shroud-like garb of the many Athenians to the golden radiance of Apollo and the massive majesty of Athena are part of a majestic whole'' (*Daily News*, December 18, 1968). Moiseiwitsch won the Drama Desk Award for her designs.

Prior to *The House of Atreus* little of Moiseiwitsch's work had been seen in New York. Thornton Wilder's *The Matchmaker*, originally produced at the Edinburgh Festival under Guthrie's direction, was moved to the Royale Theatre (New York) in 1955. The play and its star **Ruth Gordon**, together with Moiseiwitsch's sets and costumes, were greatly praised. Two Stratford (Canada) productions in the fifties were moved to Broadway: *Tamburlaine* (1956) and *Twelfth Night* (1957). Her production of *The Misanthrope* for the National Theatre of Britain was moved to the St. James Theatre (New York) in 1975. For the Metropolitan Opera she designed *Peter Grimes* (1967) and *Rigoletto* (1977). Her other work in the United States included a stint as guest designer at the Mark Taper Forum (Los Angeles) from 1967 until 1969. She designed the sets for the American Shakespeare Festival's *Antony and Cleopatra* (Stratford, Connecticut) in 1967.

Though Tanya Moiseiwitsch is now over seventy, she still finds work to claim her enthusiasm, including the film of *King Lear* (1984) starring Laurence Olivier. She continues to design for the Stratford Shakespeare Festival (Canada) and elsewhere. Her numerous honors include Commander of the British Empire, 1976; *Diplôme D'Honneur*, Canadian Conference of the Arts; Honorary Doctor of Literature, Birmingham University (England), 1964; and Honorary Fellow, Ontario (Canada) College of Art, 1979. In April 1987 she received the United States Institute for Theatre Technology distinguished service award at the organization's conference in Minneapolis. She was honored for her fifty years of contributions to theatre.

Representative photographs of Moiseiwitsch's sets and costumes can be found in *Stratford Memorial Theatre*, a series of yearbooks published in 1951, 1953, 1956, and 1959 that document over a decade of English Shakespearean production. Examples of her costume designs are reproduced in full color in *Thrice the Brindled Cat Hath Mew'd* (1955), a collection of essays by Robertson Davies, Tyrone Guthrie, Boyd Neel, and Tanya Moiseiwitsch that discuss the 1955 season of the Canadian Shakespeare Festival; two books by Tyrone Guthrie, *A Life in the Theatre* (1960) and *A New Theatre* (1964), include material on their collaborations. For further biographical information and lists of Tanya Moiseiwitsch's design credits, see *Current Biography, 1955* (1955–1956); *The Biographical Encyclopaedia and Who's Who of the American Theatre* (1966); John Russell Taylor, *The Penguin Dictionary of the Theatre* (1970); *Notable Names in the American Theatre* (1976); *Who's Who in the Theatre* (1981); and *The Oxford Companion to the Theatre* (1983).

James A. Patterson

MONK, Meredith (November 10, 1943–): experimental performer, director, choreographer, filmmaker, and innovator in performance art, was born to Audrey (Zellman) Monk (whose stage name was Audrey Marsh) and Theodore Glenn Monk in Peru, where her mother was touring as a popular singer. One grandmother was a concert pianist; one grandfather was a Jewish cantor, a singer and violinist for Russia's last Czar, and founder of the Harlem School of Music. Monk often comments that she sang before she talked and read music before she read words. At the age of three, she began dance training with Lola Rohn, a teacher of Emile Jacques Dalcroze's eurythmics. No other event could have forecast so well the direction of Monk's future creativity; her interest in an interdisciplinary approach to performance extended Dalcroze's holistic technique of teaching music through rhythmic movement.

Monk's training in dance, musical performance, and theory continued. She began composing at sixteen, and choreographed a musical for her high school in Bucks County, Pennsylvania. In 1964 she was graduated from Sarah Lawrence College in Bronxville, New York, with an emphasis on dance, feeling indebted to Bessie Schoenberg (Monk calls her a "genius teacher"), and to a program that allowed interdisciplinary work in dance, music, and theatre. She had studied classical ballet, Humphrey/Weidman modern dance, and had worked briefly with Alwin Nikolais and Merce Cunningham.

In 1964 Monk arrived in New York City, just as the Judson dance group was moving from an initial sense of revolt to a quieter consolidation. Although she became a part of the Judson scene for a time, she developed a different aesthetic. By 1969 she could say, "I don't really call myself a dancer anymore," preferring instead the terms "performer," or "nonverbal actress" (*New York Times*, November 7, 1969). Participation in Happenings, in Off-Broadway shows, and early collaboration with Kenneth King strengthened her interest in the theatrical. She has called King a "seminal thinker," saying of him, "He taught me a great deal about theatre, and I taught him a great deal about dance" (*The Drama Review*, September 1976, p. 53). Monk also composed both vocal and instrumental music for her performances. In 1968 she organized the group, Meredith Monk/The House, with which she created composites of dance, music, theatre, and film, naming each result according to the particular combination of disciplines. "Nonverbal opera," "theatre cantata," "live movie," dance theatre," "mosaic theatre," and "psychic tapestry," are all names she and others have applied to her work.

Monk has defined her aesthetic purpose as "a spiritual thing of trying to get back to a whole," of trying to capture "simultaneous realities" (*New York Times*, March 28, 1976, and *The Drama Review*, March 1972, p. 96). Every aspect of a Monk performance, beginning with its interdisciplinary approach, reflects her holistic concern. She emphasizes the mythical and archetypal and creates a series of elusive, fragmented images, but balances the abstract with some character specificity and referential movement. Characters with a mythological aura about them often appear—kings, witches, hermaphrodites, an ancestress, Death and her companion—as well as other emblematic but less specifically defined personas based on a particular actor's experiences. When Monk moves close to specific character portrayal, she tries to preserve the archetypal dimension by developing a "*persona*," as opposed to a psychologically motivated "character," universalizing by blending several characters into one and by approaching character through "gesture and movement" instead of "psychology or situation" (*The Drama Review*, September 1976, pp. 54–56). She uses a variety of movement styles, from everyday gestures to pure dance. Often the referential and the abstract combine in "non-specific mime," gestures that look "like familiar activities" such as "sewing, or hammering, or kneading and molding," yet are "never totally identifiable" (*Dancemagazine*, July 1972). She also combines a variety of rhythmic qualities, performing one action or scene in a "timeless" slow motion, so that the gesture becomes momentous, but following with another action or scene of intense energy. Sometimes she further combines "simultaneous realities" by using a mundane action, such as drinking water from a glass, as the basis for the slow motion.

Monk's work presents a totality of disciplines and a balance of opposites in an effort to capture wholeness. Her disciplinary crossings and her creation of performances without pre-existing texts ally her with artists such as Robert Wilson, Richard Foreman, Joseph Chaikin; and, like them, she creates imagistic rather than narrative theatre, dedicated to suggestive fragments evoking moods, memories, sensations, and thoughts. Yet Monk defines an important distinction in her style: her background in dance gives her work a rhythmic, kinetic focus distinct from the works of the others whose primary training is in the visual arts or in theatre (*The Drama Review*, September 1976, p. 53).

Since beginning her professional career, Monk has created and performed in more than fifty original works from individual disciplines or combinations of disciplines. Early performances were often solos or duets, such as *Break* (1964), which Monk performed to her own nonverbal sounds, to short phrases such as "watch out," and to a tape of automobiles being wrecked. *16 mm Earrings* (1966), a personal favorite of Monk's, was a mixed-media solo about attempts to harmonize body and mind—film projections onto Monk's face and body combining the "projected" or pretended with the "real."

Blueprint (1) and *Overload/Blueprint (2)* (1967) began Monk's extended-time works, presenting two sections played one month apart and in different locations. She also began to exploit sound more fully, singing, vocalizing nonverbally, playing the organ, recording and replaying her voice. In 1969 her casts sometimes expanded to as many as one hundred performers, and she began a series of "specific site" works adapted to an existing environment such as the Smithsonian Museum of Natural History, Chicago's Museum of Modern Art, and various college campuses. *Juice* (1969) combined the extended-time and specific-site approaches by playing on three separate days at three separate locations, and *Vessel* (1971) transported the audience to different areas on the same evening.

In 1976 Monk's *Village Voice* Off-Broadway (Obie) Award-winning *Quarry* established her reputation with a wider audience. More than any previous piece, it depended on a loosely narrative framework involving a fragilely ill young girl's reaction to World War II, which incomprehensibly intruded into her life through radio broadcasts. The images of the girl's mind, which were performed by the company, became increasingly confused and exaggerated, until finally she began a fearful journey into that outside world.

Specimen Days (1981) extended Monk's fame. Borrowing a title from Walt Whitman, Monk organized the piece around the American Civil War. A pianist and a photographer (based on Louis Gottschalk who toured in concert during the time and on Matthew Brady whose photographs documented the struggle) wandered in and out of the action. The central action focused on a Northern and Southern family presented simultaneously on separate sides of the stage. As in many Monk performances, scenes from the present intersected those from the past, recognizable dramatic situations and images combined with pure dance, and film loops interrupted the live action.

In 1984 Monk's collaboration with Ping Chong, titled *The Games*, opened the Brooklyn Academy of Music's New Wave Festival; it was a revision of an earlier première in West Berlin. In 1985 the Whitney Museum of American Art in New York City screened a film/video retrospective in celebration of twenty years of creative work, and La Mama Experimental Theatre Club revived *Quarry*. In 1986 *Quarry* was given at the Kennedy Center for the Performing Arts in Washington, D.C.

From the early days of Monk's performing career, most critics have recognized her importance. In 1979 John Rockwell attested to her growing influence by writing that "anyone interested in the future of theatre, dance or music" should not miss her work (*New York Times*, November 18, 1979). In addition to her theatrical works, she has presented concerts and made recordings of her highly original music; in 1978 she organized Meredith Monk and Vocal Ensemble to perform her compositions. She has created an award-winning film and collaborated in video productions. She is now an internationally renowned artist, winning awards and prizes both in the United States and abroad, including Guggenheim Fellowships, a Brandeis Creative Arts Award, two *Village Voice* Off-Broadway (Obie) awards, and Villager and ASCAP awards for her music.

A film of Monk's *Quarry* is in the Theatre Collection of the New York Public Library Performing Arts Research Center at Lincoln Center. The collection also provides limited access to films of other Monk works. Monk comments on her early performances in *Dancemagazine* (June 1968). Interviews appear in *The Drama Review* by C. Koenig (September 1976), and by Brooks McNamara (March 1972). Excellent summaries of Monk's work are Robb Baker, "Landscapes and Telescopes: A Personal Response to the Choreography of Meredith Monk," *Dancemagazine* (April 1976); Deborah Jowitt, "Meredith Monk's Gift of Vision," the *Village Voice* (October 9, 1984); and Sally Banes, "The Art of Meredith Monk," *Performing Arts Journal* (Spring/Summer 1978). Reviews of specific works appear in *Dancemagazine*, *The New York Times*, and the *Village Voice*. Outstanding analyses of *Recent Ruins* are in *Theater* (Spring 1980) and *Performing Arts Journal* (Winter 1980). Meredith Monk is included in Don McDonagh, *The Complete Guide to Modern Dance* (1976); Mary Clarke and David Vaughan, eds., *The Encyclopedia of Dance and Ballet* (1977); *The Biographical Dictionary of Dance* (1982); and *The Concise Oxford Dictionary of Ballet* (1982).

Erlene Hendrix

MOOREHEAD, Agnes (December 6, 1900–April 30, 1974): actress of stage, screen, radio, and television, famous as one of the First Drama Quartette, was born in Clinton, Massachusetts, the daughter of Reverend John Henderson Moorehead and Marie (McCauley) Moorehead. John Moorehead was a Presbyterian minister and Marie Moorehead was a singer. Agnes was the first of two daughters, and during her childhood years the family resided in Reedsburg, Wisconsin; Hamilton, Ohio; and St. Louis, Missouri. Her grandparents from Scotland, London, Wales, and Ireland had settled in Pennsylvania and Ohio, where the Moorehead family owned a 320-acre farm. Agnes Moorehead's education included a Bachelor of Arts degree from Muskingum College in Ohio (1928); a Master of Arts degree from the University of Wisconsin in English and public speaking; and actor-training at the American Academy of Dramatic Arts, Columbia University, and the University of Wisconsin. She also studied pantomime with Marcel Marceau in Paris. Much later she was to receive an honorary Doctor of Drama degree from Muskingum College and an honorary Doctor of Literature degree from Monmouth College. On June 6, 1930, Agnes Moorehead married actor John Griffith Lee. They had an adopted son, Sean, born in 1949. In June 1952 they were divorced. She then married actor Robert Gist in 1953; they were divorced in 1958. Moorehead died in 1974 of cancer in Rochester, Minnesota, and was buried in Ohio. Her professional contributions to American theatre were primarily as an actress though she was also active in teaching drama. She is remembered for her ability to develop characters of various types and ages, and she is respected for her range of accomplishment in comedy and tragedy on stage, screen, and radio.

As a child, Moorehead performed in church plays; she first appeared professionally at the age of ten in St. Louis as a singer and dancer with the municipal opera. There in subsequent years, she performed in approximately forty other productions. She acted for the Dramatic Club of Muskingum College; and while studying at the Academy of Dramatic Arts in New York (1927–1929), she had roles in Broadway plays, including the Theatre Guild productions of *Marco Millions*, *Scarlet Pages*, *All the King's Horses*, *Soldiers and Women*, and *Candelight*.

Her most noted performance on the live stage was in the role of Doña Ana in *Don Juan in Hell* with Charles Laughton, Charles Boyer, and Cedric Hardwicke. These four premièred as the First Drama Quartette in 1951 in California (Claremont College), played at Carnegie Hall in New York, and toured the United States from coast to coast with appearances at high schools, community halls, and churches. Critics gave Moorehead favorable notices for this role and cited the *Don Juan in Hell* production as a distinguished contribution to theatre in the 1951–1952 season. An often quoted critical comment is that of William Hawkins, "The actress has the crisp, clean elegance of a lily. She falls into exquisite poses and moves like a self-appointed queen, to give the play its chief visual distraction. It is a lovely performance" (*New York World Telegram*, October 23, 1951). Walter Kerr described her as "striking to watch" (*Herald Tribune*, October 23, 1951) and *Life* magazine referred to the production as "sensationally popular in a long tour around the U.S." (November 5, 1951). The significance of the success of these four performers is enhanced by their demonstration that the staged reading format was a valid theatrical approach, one to which audiences and critics reacted favorably. Textbooks in readers' theatre include this production as an historic landmark in the development of oral performance.

Some of Moorehead's other roles included the Shade of Eleanor West in *The Pink Jungle* (1959) in San Francisco; Claire Flemming in *Prescription: Murder* (1962), also in San Francisco; and Miss Swanson in *Lord Pengo* (1962), in New York and on tour. Moorehead performed a one-woman show, *The Redhead*, a script formed from a variety of pieces. She toured this show for ten years and also performed it in Cairo, Egypt, in 1960 and at the Israeli Festival in 1963.

In 1973 *Don Juan in Hell* was revived with Moorehead and co-stars Paul Henreid, Ricardo Montalban, and Edward Mulhare. It opened at the Palace Theatre on Broadway on January 15 and closed February 4 after 24 performances. The *Daily News* reviewer wrote, "It is good to find that mettlesome actress Agnes Moorehead back as Doña Ana" (January 16, 1973), and T. E. Kalem described her Doña Ana as "all that could be asked" (*Time*, January 29, 1973). Her final stage appearance was in the revival of *Gigi*, which opened at the Uris Theatre in New York on November 13, 1973. Her role was Aunt Alicia, noted by reviewer Richard Watts as a "delightful portrayal" (*New York Post*, November 14, 1973). However, ill health prevented her completing the run of 103 performances.

In addition to her stage work Moorehead achieved national recognition for acting on radio, television, and film. Some of her most significant performances were in radio plays, including *Sorry, Wrong Number* (1943), and numerous roles in series, such as *The Shadow*, *The March of Time*, and *Cavalcade of America*. Moorehead received television's Emmy Award for best actress in a single performance for her role in an episode of *Wild, Wild West* (December 13, 1967). Evidence of her success in television was her role as Endora in *Bewitched*, which earned five nominations for Emmy awards. She was also seen in episodes from a variety of serials, such as *The Twilight Zone*, *Gunsmoke*, *Wagon Train*, and *Night Gallery*. Memorable roles in films indicate the range of characters Moorehead was capable of playing in all theatrical media: Kane's mother in *Citizen Kane* (1941), spinster Aunt Fanny in *The Magnificent Ambersons* (1942), a Chinese peasant in *Dragon Seed* (1944), a woman over one-hundred years old in *The Lost Moment* (1947), and Mrs. Snow in *Pollyanna* (1960). She received four nominations for the Academy (Oscar) Award as best supporting actress in *The Magnificent Ambersons* (1942), *Mrs. Parkington* (1944), *Johnny Belinda* (1946), and *Hush, Hush Sweet Charlotte* (1964).

Although her achievements as an actress were her major contribution, Moorehead also served American theatre as an educator. Her career began as a high school coach in Soldiers Grove, Wisconsin. In the fifties she held private acting classes at her home in Beverly Hills, California. At the conclusion of her career she toured colleges with acting lectures and taught in her own acting school. For acting preparation, she stressed the significance of a soundly based program in voice, speech, ballet, interpretive reading, pantomime, and scene work (Mike Steen, *Hollywood Speaks*, p. 108). Impressive in appearance, thoroughly in command of acting technique, Agnes Moorehead, over the course of her career, contributed many memorable characterizations to the portrait gallery of American theatre.

A biographical work has been written on Agnes Moorehead by Warren Sherk, titled *Agnes Moorehead, A Very Private Person* (1976). A chapter on Moorehead is included in *Scream Queens* by Calvin Thomas Beck (1978). An interview with her is in *Hollywood Speaks* by Mike Steen (1974). Reference to the original *Don Juan in Hell* is included in *The Readers Theatre Handbook* (1973) by Leslie Irene Coger and Melvin White. *Theatre World*, Volumes 29 and 30, contains program information on the 1973 revival of *Don Juan in Hell* and *Gigi* (1973). Moorehead's obituary appeared in the *New York Times* (May 1, 1974). Agnes Moorehead is included in *Who's Who in America, 1952–1953* (1952); *Current Biography, 1952* (1953); *The Biographical Encyclopaedia and Who's Who of the American Theatre* (1966); Eric Johns, ed., *British Theatre Review, 1974* (1975); and *Who's Who in the Theatre* (1977). An annotated bibliography appears in Marsha McCreadie's entry on Moorehead in *Notable American Women*, Vol. IV: *The Modern Period* (1980). There are discrepancies in the reported year of Moorehead's birth. It is often reported as 1906; however, McCreadie indicates verification of the 1900 date by birth certificate (see *Notable American Women*).

Phyllis Scott Carlin

MORGAN, Agnes (October 31, 1879–May 25, 1976): director, playwright, actress, and producer, was born in Le Roy, New York, to Frank H. Morgan, an editor, and Sarah L. (Cutler) Morgan, a teacher. Morgan studied at Radcliffe College, receiving her Bachelor of Arts degree in 1901 and her Master of Arts degree in 1903. She attended George Pierce Baker's 47 Workshop at Harvard in 1904.

After leaving Harvard University, Morgan worked on the publicity staff of the Shubert theatrical producing organization. Her first play, *When Two Write History*, was produced in Chicago in 1910 and received favorable reviews. Two years later, she began her association with the Neighborhood Players, a theatre company established by **Alice** and **Irene Lewisohn** as an adjunct to the Grand Street Settlement House on the Lower East Side of New York City. Morgan directed the Players' first dramatic production, *The Shepherd*, in collaboration with the actress Sarah Cowell LeMoyne. When the Lewisohn sisters opened the Neighborhood Playhouse in 1915, Agnes Morgan joined the staff as a full-time director and playwright. She also acted in a few productions. Over the twelve years of the Playhouse's existence she directed or co-directed thirty-five productions including plays by George Bernard Shaw, John Galsworthy, James Joyce, **Susan Glaspell**, and Percy MacKaye. She also wrote or adapted the scripts for several productions, including five editions of *The Grand Street Follies*, the satirical review offered by the Playhouse at the end of each season.

In 1922 Morgan, in collaboration with Alice Lewisohn, directed Parts I and II of Shaw's *Back to Methuselah* for the Theatre Guild. The New York critics were generally unimpressed with the five-part, three-night presentation of Shaw's play, but reserved their most enthusiastic comments for the directors, Morgan and Lewisohn. After the Neighborhood Playhouse closed in 1927, Morgan formed a producing organization called Actors-Managers, Inc. During the 1930s she directed plays on Broadway, in the Newport (Rhode Island) Casino Theatre, and for the Federal Theatre Project. The Federal Theatre Project production of *American Holiday* in 1936 benefited in the critics' estimation from Morgan's ability to handle large groups of actors with varied backgrounds and levels of expertise. In 1940 she joined Frank Carrington in the management of the Paper Mill Playhouse in Millburn, New Jersey, a position she held until her retirement in 1968. She also directed many of the Playhouse's productions. She died of heart disease in California in 1976, and her remains were cremated.

Agnes Morgan was one of the few women able to sustain a long career as a director in the New York professional theatre. Unfortunately, since New York drama critics almost never included an assessment of the director's work in their reviews during the first three decades of this century, it is difficult to learn anything specific about Morgan's directorial style and techniques. However, her versatility as a director is indicated by the range of productions she staged, from the stark realism of John Galsworthy's *The Mob*, to the brittle satire of Richard Brinsley Sheridan's *The Critic*, to the bright nonsense of *The Grand Street Follies*. Perhaps her most imaginative production was a 1924 revival of *The Little Clay Cart*, a 1500-year-old Hindu drama that Morgan adapted and staged with a swirl of color and movement. As a playwright Morgan contributed little of lasting value, but her satirical sketches for *The Grand Street Follies* were considered by most critics to be the most sophisticated and venomous parodies of their time.

Primary materials are available in the Agnes Morgan Collection at the Theatre Collection of the New York Public Library Performing Arts Research Center at Lincoln Center. Morgan's work at the Neighborhood Playhouse is documented in Alice Lewisohn Crowley, *The Neighborhood Playhouse: Leaves from a Theatre Scrapbook* (1959). Her contributions to *The Grand Street Follies* are discussed in Margaret Knapp, "Theatrical Parody in the Twentieth-Century American Theatre: *The Grand Street Follies*," *Educational Theatre Journal* (October 1975). Several of the sketches written by Morgan for *The Grand Street Follies* are in the Library of Congress. Agnes Morgan is included in *The Biographical Encyclopaedia and Who's Who of the American Theatre* (1966) and *Notable Names in the American Theatre* (1976).

Margaret M. Knapp

MORGENTHAU, Rita Wallach (March 4, 1880–April 8, 1964): theatre educator, director, and administrator, was born in New York City, the only daughter of Leopold and Teresa Wallach. Her father, an attorney, was from a financially successful family with an ethic of public service. Rita Wallach went to the Saxon School for Girls and taught in the New York public school system before her marriage to Maximilian Morgenthau. The Morgenthaus had one daughter, now deceased. Maximilian Morgenthau was a cousin of Henry Morgenthau, United States Treasurer. It was through Henry Morgenthau's wife, Elinor, that Rita Morgenthau met Lillian Wald, director of the Henry Street Settlement and became a volunteer there. When Lillian Wald asked her to become director of club work with girls, she answered that she did not feel qualified. She went to Teachers College at Columbia University and studied with John Dewey; then she took over as director of the children's club and class work at Henry Street. She is described by **Alice Lewisohn** (Crowley) as "an aspiring friend of every child." She found no child ugly or dull, and yet "there was no suggestion of false sentimentality in her relations with them. She could discipline without disciplining, for whatever she administered in the way of punishment had also the grace of humor" (*The Neighborhood Playhouse*, pp. 12–13). This quality of stern caring was to be Morgenthau's trademark as an educator throughout her career at the Henry Street Settlement and as director of The Neighborhood Playhouse School of the Theatre in New York City beginning in 1928, the year she and Maximilian Morgenthau were divorced.

The association that would lead to the founding of this two-year intensive theatre school, which numbers among its graduates theatre and movie personalities such as Tony Randall, Joanne Woodward, Tammy Grimes, Gregory Peck, and many others, began when two sisters whose interests were equally divided between a passion for acting and a social conscience, **Irene** and **Alice Lewisohn**, became leaders of the Dramatic Club at Henry Street, working under Rita Morgenthau's supervision. In 1913 the three produced an event that Morgenthau always heralded as the beginning of the style that would be unique to the famed Neighborhood Playhouse at 466 Grand Street. The 1913 street fair encompassed a history of the area in a highly stylized, colorful pageant planned for a cast of five hundred—an event attended by ten-thousand people from the Henry Street neighborhood. In a report on "The Henry Street Settlement, 1893 to 1913," edited and largely written by Morgenthau, she advocated a fellowship with boys, girls, men, and women in neighborhoods to increase concern for the dignity of human beings. The street pageant led the way for the celebration of that ethic and to the characteristic difference in style between the Neighborhood Playhouse (founded in 1915 under the direction of Alice and Irene Lewisohn) and the two other contemporary theatres that pioneered an American renaissance in theatre in the early part of the century—the Provincetown Players and The Washington Square Players. The Neighborhood Playhouse was less interested in drama as literature than in what the theatre and theatrical presentation could accomplish as an independent art. Also, the Neighborhood Playhouse utilized song, dance, and ritual to express the beauty and joy of life. Among the best public productions at the Playhouse performed between 1915 and 1928 were *The Little Clay Cart* and *The Dybbuk*.

During the years of the Neighborhood Playhouse (1914–1928), Morgenthau served on the board of advisors and administered many of the classes that were used as training for the productions. When the Neighborhood Playhouse closed its doors in 1928, Irene Lewisohn and Rita Morgenthau founded the Neighborhood Playhouse School of the Theatre, as "an attempt to form an organic language out of a collection of different techniques; acting, movement, mime, speech" (*The Neighborhood Playhouse*, p. 247). While at Henry Street, Morgenthau had formed a close association with Martha Graham and Louis Horst and helped in the founding of Graham's own company. Graham and Horst taught at the Neighborhood Playhouse School from its inception, as did Laura Elliot, whose experimental work in choral speech had been a feature of Playhouse productions. In 1935 Sanford Meisner became head of the acting department and brought with him from the Group Theatre the American approach to the teachings of Constantin Stanislavsky.

Every student at the Neighborhood Playhouse School of the Theatre was conscious of the small lady with the brown face and shrewd eyes who would take in every detail of each visitor as he or she walked toward her desk. From 1928 until her retirement in 1963, each student had annual interviews with Morgenthau. The students knew that from her office on the top of the building she was aware of them as individuals and as members of the collective entity that made up the intensely disciplined school. Interest in a broad base of education continued for Rita Morgenthau during her long tenure as administrator of the Neighborhood Playhouse School of the Theatre. She was the first vocational counselor for the Vocational Advisory Service in New York City and subsequently its vice president. She edited "Skylines for Youth" and "Vocational Services for Juniors" through the advisory service.

Rita Morgenthau, who died of cancer in 1964, was an educator who brought her own version of the firm yet liberal educational principles of John Dewey to the administration of a professional theatre school. Her unique contribution to the theatre student was intense discipline coupled with a clear-eyed approach to vocational guidance. The necessity of education not just as an actor but as a total theatre person was instilled in the faculty and became the hallmark of a graduate of the Neighborhood Playhouse School of the Theatre, which today remains one of the eminent professional schools for theatre education.

The major source of information for this article was a personal interview with Alice Owens, librarian for the Neighborhood Playhouse School of the Theatre. The author also interviewed Anna Sokolow, and Harold Baldridge. Baldridge was a student during Rita Morgenthau's association with the playhouse and is now director of the school. Other factual material about Morgenthau may be found in *The Neighborhood Playhouse* by Alice Lewisohn Crowley (1959) and *Report on Henry Street Settlement, 1893–1913* by Mrs. Max Morgenthau, Jr. Morgenthau's obituary appeared in the *New York Times* (April 9, 1964). She is listed in *The Biographical Encyclopaedia and Who's Who of the American Theatre* (1966).

Judith Edwards

MORRIS, Clara (March 17, 1847?–November 20, 1925): popular star in nineteenth century melodrama, was born in Toronto, Canada, though she frequently claimed Cleveland, Ohio, as her birthplace in order to be considered an American actress. Morris was apparently the eldest of three children born to the bigamous union of Sarah Jane Proctor, an American servant of Scottish and English descent, and Charles La Montagne, a French-Canadian taxi driver. On learning of her husband's other marriage, Sarah Proctor gave her two younger children up for adoption and took her mother's maiden name of Morrison before journeying with the three-year-old Clara to serve as farm hand, domestic, and practical nurse in various parts of Ohio and Illinois, settling at last in Cleveland after La Montagne's death. During her impoverished and insecure childhood, Clara Morrison attended school only intermittently, but read widely on her own.

When her mother accepted a housekeeping job in a Cleveland boarding house frequented by actors, thirteen-year-old Clara Morrison was encouraged to apply for the *corps de ballet* at John Ellsler's Cleveland Academy of Music. Under the name of Clara Morris, she served a long apprenticeship in ballet followed by years of playing small parts and serving as understudy, all at the wages of a ballet girl. In Cleveland and Columbus she appeared on stage with some of the greatest actors of her day, including Charles W. Couldock, Joseph Jefferson, E. L. Davenport, Lawrence Barrett, James E. Murdoch, and Edwin and John Wilkes Booth.

There was little chance of advancement in Ellsler's company, so in 1869 Clara Morris moved to Wood's Theatre in Cincinnati where she remained for one season as leading lady. After a summer engagement in Halifax, Nova Scotia, she accepted Augustin Daly's offer to come to his Fifth Avenue Theatre in New York, even though an offer from San Francisco would have paid more. Daly pronounced her a comic actress, but when Agnes Ethel refused the leading role of Anne Sylvester in Wilkie Collins' *Man and Wife*, the opening play of the season, Daly asked Morris to act the part. On September 14, 1870, Clara Morris scored the first of many opening night triumphs with New York audiences. During her three seasons at Daly's Fifth Avenue Theatre, Morris was praised for her emotional roles in contemporary French domestic melodrama. Her success in *Man and Wife* was repeated in 1871 when she played Madame D'Artigues in *Jezebel*. She was acclaimed one of the greatest emotional actresses of her day after her April 1872 opening as Cora, a disfigured and betrayed octoroon who goes mad in the sensational French play, *L'Article 47*. In preparation for this role, she made a study of insanity both in asylums and in medical books. According to Joseph Daly (*The Life of Augustin Daly*, p. 110), Morris reached "the height of her achievement" in this play's mad scene; her passage "through the stages of fear, cunning, and loss of control to raving madness was electrifying; and when the curtain fell she was the mistress of the American stage." Her Cora was the sensation of the day, though some critics decried the "adulterous drama from the French" on moral grounds. Morris continued her realistic portrayals of unhappy women in *Alixe* (1873) and in *Madeleine Morel* (1873). In the latter she played a jilted and betrayed nun who dies trampling her crucifix and calling down curses on the head of her seducer. Though critics praised her acting abilities and her magnetic power to move her audience to tears, they criticized these plays as morbid, unwholesome, and morally repulsive.

Following a contract dispute, Morris left Daly's Fifth Avenue Theatre for a successful starring tour before returning to New York and signing with A. M. Palmer, manager of the Union Square Theatre, known as "The Home of Refined

Melodrama.'' There, in 1874, she triumphed in *Camille*. The critics considered her the equal of Sarah Bernhardt and of **Helena Modjeska** in realistic pathos, but not in art. Her performance in the death scene is reported to have caused Bernhardt to exclaim that she was not acting but suffering. This reaction was precisely the impression Morris wished from her audiences. She fortified the impression of her stage suffering by having a physician in attendance backstage. Audiences believed that she had to be medicated during excessively prolonged intermissions. Consequently, when she played a suffering heroine, the audience assumed that Morris was enduring her own suffering for the sake of her performance.

On November 30, 1874, Clara Morris married Frederick C. Harriott, the young scion of two wealthy and politically powerful New York families—the Havemeyers and the Harriotts. He was to remain her agent and constant companion until his death in May 1914. Although she was acclaimed a ''histrionic genius'' by many critics, she was nevertheless denied the title of ''great actress'' by some because she had not yet acted the great roles. Accordingly, in 1875 she opened at Booth's Theatre as a tragic actress, playing in *Evadne, Jane Shore*, and *Macbeth*. In none of these roles was she a critical success, though her Lady Macbeth occasioned wide critical comment for its originality. Departing from the monumental and declamatory high-tragedy style of Sarah Siddons and **Charlotte Cushman**, Morris played Lady Macbeth as a seductive and guileful siren, tender and fair, though mastered by ambition. The critics pronounced her interpretation intelligent but on the whole unsound and, finally, a failure because of its lack of tragic elevation.

In 1876 Morris returned to domestic drama and scored one of the greatest successes of her career in the Union Square Theatre production of *Miss Multon*, a French version of Mrs. Henry Wood's *East Lynne*, a sensational novel about a faithless wife who returns as governess to her own children. Morris's acting in this play is described by critic William Winter: ''Contortions of the body, convulsions of the face, disproportionate attitudes, extravagant gestures, spasmodic starts and changes, and indescribable wild moans and cries were commingled in that singular embodiment with moments of sweet dignity, lovely tenderness, and exalted fortitude. Over the whole effort there was the lawlessness of a genius that is a law to itself; and the effect of the effort was that of deep pathos'' (*The Wallet of Time*, Vol. I, p. 572).

During the late 1870s and through the 1880s Morris toured with her own company and continued to act in New York in the roles which had made her famous, adding to her repertoire the leading female parts in such plays as *Jane Eyre* (1878), *Conscience* (1881), *The New Magdalen* (1882), *La Morte Civile* (1883), and *Denise* (1885). With the rise of realism in the American theatre, audiences turned away from the exaggerated emotional school of French domestic melodrama with which Morris was identified, and her popularity waned. During the 1890s she gave up regular performance, though she did occasional public lectures, acted in vaudeville, and made returns to the stage for various revivals and benefits. Toward the end of her acting career, her always precarious health began to fail severely. She made her last stage appearance in the 1904 revival of *The Two Orphans* at the New Amsterdam Theatre in New York. In retirement she wrote often unreliable articles on the theatre for various magazines and newspapers in addition to producing six volumes of fiction and three volumes of personal memoirs. Her writing career seems to have been prompted by financial difficulties. These difficulties were compounded by five years of temporary blindness, though her eyesight was partially restored about 1915. Known popularly as "the woman of sorrows," Morris was the recipient of at least one benefit, well attended by audiences made aware of the real-life sufferings of an actress who had so often suffered in her stage roles. Her last years were spent alone following the deaths of her husband in 1914 and her mother, who had always lived with her, in 1917. She had no children.

Clara Morris died of chronic endocarditis on November 20, 1925, at New Canaan, Connecticut. She was buried in Kensico Cemetery, Valhalla, New York, after services in New York City's Episcopal Church of the Transfiguration (the "Little Church Around the Corner"), then frequented by theatre people.

Critics essentially agree that Morris triumphed as an actress in spite of numerous flaws. She was not a remarkable beauty. She had a peculiar nasal intonation and what critics called barbarous pronunciations. Worse, she was seen as crude in her mannerisms and postures, and her gestures were frequently condemned as stereotypical and tiresome. However, though her acting was uneven and full of eccentricities, her magnetic, almost hypnotic power over audiences was universally acknowledged. Adept at stormy scenes of passion and at convincing portrayals of suffering, she was credited with rendering emotional crises so realistically as to seem at one with the characters she portrayed. She always claimed that she was able to move her audiences only if she "felt" her parts intensely. Consequently, in spite of her forethought for costume and for line delivery, Morris was judged a "natural" or "born" actress blessed with the "sacred fire," who achieved her effects through spontaneous inspiration, as opposed to more studied and self-conscious artistry. Her instinctive, undisciplined acting methods probably contributed as much to her eclipse as did the turning of audiences away from melodrama to the new plays of Henrik Ibsen, Anton Chekhov, and their contemporaries. During her reign on the American stage, however, Clara Morris was acclaimed as America's greatest emotional actress.

Clara Morris's published memoirs, *Life on the Stage* (1901), *Stage Confidences* (1902), *The Life of a Star* (1906), are anecdotal and engaging but unreliable. Her manuscript diaries are in the Schlesinger Library, Radcliffe College, and other memorabilia are in the Robinson Locke Collection of Dramatic Scrapbooks, New York Public Library Performing Arts Research Center at Lincoln Center. Contemporary accounts of her performances are included in Frederick E. McKay and Charles E. L. Wingate, eds., *Famous American Actors of Today* (1896); William Winter, *The Wallet of Time*, Vol. I (1913); John Ranken Towse, *Sixty Years of the Theatre* (1916); and Joseph F. Daly, *The Life of*

Augustin Daly (1917). See also George C. D. Odell, *Annals of the New York Stage*, Vols. VIII-XV (1937–1949). Mildred Langford Howard, "The Acting of Clara Morris" (Unpublished Ph.D. dissertation, University of Illinois at Urbana-Champaign, 1956) offers a sound assessment of her acting. Also see Garff B. Wilson, "Queen of Spasms: The Acting of Clara Morris," *Speech Monographs* (November 1955). The sources conflict concerning her early family history. Clara Morris's date of birth is variously reported as 1846, 1848, or 1849, though her death record has it as March 17, 1847. Morris is included in *Notable American Women*, Vol. II (1971); William C. Young, *Famous Actors and Actresses of the American Stage*, Vol. I (1975); *The Oxford Companion to the Theatre* (1983); and *The Oxford Companion to American Theatre* (1984).

Lucien L. Agosta

MORRIS, Mary (June 24, 1895–January 16, 1970): actress and educator, attained the rare distinction of achieving success in both professional and educational theatre. In 1924 she made American theatre history by originating the role of Abbie Putnam in Eugene O'Neill's *Desire Under the Elms*. In 1939, at the age of 44, she began her career in educational theatre, serving twenty years as a drama professor at the famous drama school of the Carnegie Institute of Technology (now Carnegie-Mellon University) in Pittsburgh.

Born in the resort town of Swampscott, Massachusetts, she was the daughter of George Perry Morris, an editor, and Martha Sophia (Turner) Morris. She had one brother, Ellison (b. 1897). She was encouraged in her acting aspirations by her mother who took her to a dinner of the Millenium Society at which she met the guests of honor, Minnie Maddern Fiske and George Arliss. (In later years she was to appear with Arliss in *Alexander Hamilton*.) Mary Morris attended high school in Brookline, Massachusetts, and enrolled at Radcliffe College as a special or non-degree student in 1912. While a student at Radcliffe, she studied Shakespeare with George Kittredge and participated in George Pierce Baker's 47 Workshop. She later recalled the workshop as one of the most important parts of her life.

She left Radcliffe in 1915 and went to New York, where, with support from her parents, she made the rounds of theatrical agencies. A letter of introduction from Baker won her a place with the Washington Square Players, where she served as "understudy, prop girl, and general factotum" (*The Record Radcliffe*, 1941, p. 58). She made her New York debut with this group in 1916, playing the farm wife (Mary Trask) in Lewis Beach's *The Clod* and winning recognition from the critics. Following Baker's advice, she then spent two years in stock companies, including one season in Northampton, Massachusetts, with Jessie Bonstelle's municipally supported theatre. In 1918 she went on tour with George Arliss in *Alexander Hamilton*. "I played a small part, and understudied two leads," she remembered. "Mr. Arliss sometimes conducted understudy rehearsals, which was of great benefit to us younger players" (*The Record Radcliffe*, 1941, p. 58).

During World War I she acted in a series of one-act plays in the military camps around New York. She spent from 1920 to 1923 in California playing one year of stock with the San Francisco Stage Guild (where she played leading roles in the plays of George Bernard Shaw, James M. Barrie, and Henrik Ibsen), and two years in the Greek Theatre productions at the University of California, Berkeley, under Sam Hume. In 1924 she joined the Provincetown Theatre (then under the direction of Robert Edmond Jones, Eugene O'Neill, and Kenneth Macgowan), where she played the Dark Lady in August Strindberg's *The Ghost Sonata* and Gertrude in **Anna Cora Mowatt**'s *Fashion*. During this same year she was cast to play Abbie Putnam opposite Walter Huston in *Desire Under the Elms*. In later years she wrote, "I never worked so hard as at rehearsals of *Desire Under the Elms*. It was eight hours a day going into the psychology of the characters and no play has ever seemed difficult to me since then" (Ormsbee, *New York Herald Tribune*, February 2, 1941). O'Neill cast her for the role of Abbie Putnam without having her read for the part. In a letter to Kenneth Macgowan he wrote, "The important thing is her whole attitude and conception and there she's O.K." (O'Neill in Bryer, p. 60). She continued to play Abbie through 1925 and 1926. In 1927 she played Ellen Faring in *Hidden*, directed by David Belasco. Other noteworthy roles were Dorimene in **Eva Le Gallienne**'s Civic Repertory production of *Le Bourgeois Gentilhomme* (1928), Barbara in *The Cross Roads*, directed by Guthrie McClintic (1929), and Irina in Michael Afanasyev Bulgakov's production of *The Sea Gull* (1930). In 1931 under the direction of Lee Strasberg and **Cheryl Crawford**, she played Mrs. Connelly in the Group Theatre's production of Paul Green's *House of Connelly*. Under the direction of Robert Edmond Jones in 1932, she played with **Lillian Gish** in a Central City, Colorado, revival of *Camille*. One of her most famous roles was the sinister Victoria Van Brett in the 1933 production of Elizabeth McFadden's *Double Door*. She recreated this role in the 1934 film version of that play. In the 1935–1936 season she played The Old Woman in Sean O'Casey's *Within the Gates*, directed by Melvin Douglas, and Mrs. Clemm in **Sophie Treadwell**'s *Plumes in the Dust*, directed by Arthur Hopkins. In 1936–1937 she played the leading role of Mrs. Smith in *Suspect* at the St. Martin Theatre, London, and in 1938 she appeared as Empress Elizabeth in *Empress of Destiny* at the St. James Theatre, New York.

In 1939 Morris was appointed assistant professor of drama at the Carnegie Institute's School of Fine Arts, but she continued to perform by giving readings and appearing in summer theatres throughout the country. She was also granted leave from teaching to appear on Broadway in 1941 as Mrs. Sawters in Lynn Riggs's *The Cream in the Well* and again in 1949 as The Nurse in August Strindberg's *The Father* with Raymond Massey. She was also granted leave in 1951 to play the Nurse in **Judith Anderson**'s *Medea* at the International Theatre Festival in Berlin and in 1956 to play Anna in Ivan Turgenev's *A Month in the Country* with **Uta Hagen**. In 1941 she had written, "It is fine to be in a place so liberal that they will let me get away to act once in a while" (*The Record Radcliffe*, 1941, p. 58).

As a teacher and director of young actors, Mary Morris relied on her years of training in professional theatre while gaining experience in her new role of drama professor. In a 1941 interview she said, "Teaching is new to me and I am unacademic, but I know the greatest joy a teacher can have is to find ability in a student. . . . As for criticizing the work of the students, I have found that they will take any amount of adverse comment if you first let them understand that you believe in them and want to help them" (Ormsbee, *New York Herald Tribune*, February 2, 1941). Always stressing the importance of solid training and experience, she felt the demise of stock companies provided a hardship for young actors and advised her students not to head for New York but to work in any group that is putting on plays. "I am a believer in little theatres, experimental theatres, and experimental acting groups as substitutes for the stock company. . . . There ought to be experimental groups all over the country" (Ormsbee, *New York Herald Tribune*, February 2, 1941). She supported efforts to bring live theatre into neighborhoods, towns, and cities throughout the country, and she appeared with the Artillery Lane Players of St. Augustine, Florida, in their 1948 production of *Hedda Gabler*, and at the Cincinnati Summer Playhouse as the Dowager Empress in a 1956 production of *Anastasia*.

While at Carnegie, Mary Morris directed more than thirty plays. She also helped to develop and direct the National Theatre Conference's Tryout Studio. Originally conducted in 1947 at the Hunter College Playhouse, the studio gave outstanding young actors just graduating from schools and colleges the opportunity to be seen by those who could best help them find employment. Joining her in developing this student showcase were George Freedley, curator of the New York Public Library's Theatre Collection, and **Rosamond Gilder**, editor of *Theatre Arts*.

Morris was made a full professor at Carnegie in 1949 and became Professor Emeritus upon her retirement in 1960. Throughout her career she also represented her peers by serving on the council of Actors' Equity Association (1932–1937), the executive board of the National Theatre Conference (1940–1950), and the American National Theatre and Academy (ANTA) board of directors. Morris was married to Reginald Richard in 1918; they were divorced in 1922. In 1924 she married James Meighan, Jr., in Provincetown, but that marriage ended in divorce in 1925. Her one son Richard was killed in an accident on June 4, 1943, at age twelve, while he was riding his bicycle to school.

It is interesting to note that in September 1959, one year before her retirement, she played the role of Grand Duchess Anastasia in a production of *The Student Prince* at Musicarnival in Warrensville Heights, Ohio. During 1961–1962, the year after her retirement from Carnegie, she joined the faculty of the American Shakespeare Festival Theatre in Stratford, Connecticut. In 1964 she entered the convalescent wing of the Percy Williams Home, Islip, Long Island, as a guest of the Actor's Fund. She continued to live there until her death at the age of 74 on January 16, 1970, at Roosevelt Hospital in New York. There were no immediate survivors; no funeral services were held; and her body was willed to Columbia University's Medical School for scientific study.

Mary Morris devoted her entire life to the theatre. In both professional and educational settings, she sought to understand and practice the powers of that art. In the midst of World War II she wrote, "Now, if ever, is the time for the theatre, along with all the other great arts which serve life, to make itself of worth and significance in the world. Theatre can speak to mankind as no other art can speak, most directly, most movingly. People are hungry for the word that illumines, the idea that inspires, the emotion that warms and strengthens. Now is the time for all to go forward who believe in the theatre as a place of revelation and communication" (*Theatre Arts*, July 1941, p. 486). The life of Mary Morris provided a model for both the practicing artist and the teacher. Her career demonstrated a full integration of the professional and the educational.

The Clipping File in the Theatre Collection, New York Public Library Performing Arts Research Center at Lincoln Center contains programs, reviews, interviews, and articles covering Mary Morris's entire career as well as obituaries from *The New York Times*, *Variety*, and *The New York Daily News*. This collection also contains Mary Morris, "A Letter from Mr. Baker," in *Radcliffe Quarterly* (February 1961) and Mary Morris, *The Record Radcliffe—1916* (1941), a reunion report written by Mary Morris in 1941 which reviews her career. See also: Mary Morris, "This Ancient and Magical Art," *Theatre Arts* (July 1941), which discusses her career and her philosophy of theatre; Bess Kimberly, "Carnegie-Mellon University, College of Fine Arts, Department of Drama, Seventy Years of Performance," which lists all Drama Department Alumni from 1917 to 1984 and all plays produced by the department through 1984; "Star Among Stars," *The Pittsburgh Press*, Roto Magazine section (January 1, 1956); Helen Ormsbee, "Arliss, Belasco, Jessie Bonstelle Taught an Actress How to Teach," *New York Herald Tribune* (February 2, 1941), which best demonstrates her integration of professional and educational theatre. William Hawkins, "Mary Morris Gives Young Actors a Chance" in the *New York World Telegram* (September 2, 1947) discusses the National Theatre Conference's Tryout Studio. The most recent publication containing references to her is Jackson R. Bryer, ed., *The Theatre We Worked For: The Letters of Eugene O'Neill to Kenneth Macgowan* (1982). Morris is listed in *Who's Who in the Theatre* (1939), *The Biographical Encyclopaedia and Who's Who of the American Theatre* (1966), and *Who Was Who in the Theatre*, Vol. III (1978).

Judith L. Stephens

MORTON, Martha (October 10, 1865?–February 18, 1925): playwright and founder of the Society of Dramatic Authors, was born in New York City into a family whose English ancestry included playwrights John Maddison Morton and Alfred Sutro, and novelist-critic Edward Arthur Morton. Her brother, Michael Morton, was an actor and a playwright. Martha Morton's mother had memorized most of Shakespeare's plays and encouraged her children's interest in dramatic literature. Well-read in French and German literature, Martha Morton first published imitative stories in magazines, but Edward Arthur Morton told her to write about the life that she knew. She never forgot that advice; as a playwright she often spoke of her dedication to the ideal of the thoughtful yet entertaining realistic play that would reflect contemporary American life, including the role of women in that life.

Educated in New York City public schools and the Normal (now Hunter) College, Martha Morton was prevented by ill health from completing her studies at the latter institution. Her first attempt at playwriting was a parody of David Belasco's 1884 play, *May Blossom*, which her parents had taken her to see. A friend who heard her read the play called it to the attention of Daniel Frohman, who arranged a performance of the little spoof for a charity benefit at the Academy of Music. Its success prompted Morton's decision to become a playwright and persuaded her parents to give her a tour abroad to study European culture.

On her return to America, Martha Morton attempted to find a manager who would produce her play *Helene*. Unsuccessful in the search (possibly because she was a woman), she mounted the play at her own expense for one performance only, on April 30, 1888, at the Fifth Avenue Theatre. The happy result was that actress **Clara Morris** bought it as a vehicle for herself for the following season. Again unable to find a producer for her next play, a Wall Street drama titled *The Merchant*, Morton submitted it under a male pseudonym to the *New York World*'s playwriting competition. It won first prize and was produced, starring **Rose Coghlan**, at the Madison Square Theatre in 1891. Morton supervised rehearsals of all her plays but was never credited with the title "director." Nearly twenty years later, she recalled the prejudice she faced while rehearsing *The Merchant*: "The men shook their heads. They said drama was going to the dogs. Then they crept in through the stage door and watched that 'green girl' direct the rehearsal and one of them came up to me and said, 'Are you going to make a business out of this?'... I looked him straight in the eye and answered fervently, 'God help me, I must!' Then he put out a friendly hand, crushed my fingers into splinters and gave me the comforting assurance that a woman would have to do twice the work of a man to get one-half the credit" (*Green Book Album*, September 1910, p. 633).

She found a considerate and discerning producer, Augustus Pitou, for her subsequent play, *Geoffrey Middleton, Gentleman*, which was a popular success at the Union Square Theatre in 1892. Then she wrote a series of plays for comedian William H. Crane: *Brother John* (1893), *His Wife's Father* (1895), *A Fool of Fortune* (1896, revived in 1899 and 1912), and *The Senator Keeps House* (1911). In 1896 she wrote *A Bachelor's Romance* for comedian Sol Smith Russell, who considered it one of his greatest hits. Another comedy, *The Triumph of Love*, won *The Theatre Magazine*'s playwriting competition in 1904. With fourteen plays professionally produced in New York between 1888 and 1911, Martha Morton truly deserves to be called "America's pioneer woman playwright," and "the dean of women playwrights."

In private life Martha Morton was the wife of Hermann Conheim (1858–1927), a leader in the American Zionist movement and a wealthy importer of bristles. Their home on West 90th Street near Riverside Drive featured a three-thousand-volume library with custom-made furniture of the same black wood and red velvet as the woodwork and wall coverings. She became known not only for her philanthropic work, but also for her professional generosity in helping younger women playwrights to avoid the difficulties she herself had encountered. Because women were not admitted to the American Dramatists Club when she began her career, Morton organized the Society of Dramatic Authors in 1907 with a charter membership of thirty women. Soon the older group became eager for consolidation, and Morton became vice-president of the resulting Society of American Dramatists and Composers. Reviews of her plays were often harsh, even vicious in tone, but her persistence—buoyed by box-office success—blazed the way for the many women playwrights who emerged from 1910 until 1930.

The Martha Morton file in the Theatre Collection at the New York Public Library Performing Arts Research Center at Lincoln Center includes some material on her early career, such as the interview in *New York Dramatic Mirror* (November 7, 1891). Articles that appeared after she was an established playwright include those by Virginia Frame in *Theatre Magazine* (October 1906); Lucy France Pierce in *World To-Day* (July 1908); Ada Patterson in *The Theatre* (1909); Shirley Burns in *Green Book Album* (September 1910); Lucy France Pierce in *Green Book Album* (May 1912); Alan Dale in *The Delineator* (February 1917). Other contemporary accounts of Morton are given in Dixie Hines and Harry Prescott Hansford, eds., *The Green Room Book or Who's Who on the Stage* (1909), *Who's Who in Music and Drama* (1914); and *Who's Who in the Theatre* (1925). Morton's obituary appeared in the *New York Times* (February 20, 1925). Rosemary Gipson has written "Martha Morton: America's First Professional Woman Playwright," *Theatre Survey* (November 1982). Gipson gives Morton's birth date as 1870. A complete list of Morton's plays is included with Felicia Hardison Londré's entry in *American Women Writers*, Vol. 3 (1981). Morton is included in *The Oxford Companion to American Theatre* (1984).

Felicia Hardison Londré

MOWATT, Anna Cora Ogden (March 5, 1819–July 21, 1870): actress, playwright, novelist, often called the first successful woman playwright in America, was born in Bordeaux, France, where her father, Samuel Gouverneur Ogden, was residing with his family while on business related to his import-export company. Samuel Ogden was the son of the Reverend Doctor Uzal Ogden, a distinguished cleric. Anna Cora Ogden's mother was Eliza Lewis, the granddaughter of Francis Lewis, one of the signers of the Declaration of Independence. Anna Cora Ogden (called Lily by her family) was seven when the Ogdens returned to New York City in 1826. She was educated primarily at home. An avid reader, she had read Shakespeare's plays many times over by the time she was ten years old. The large family was devoted to amateur theatricals, and Anna Cora Ogden became the adapter, producer, and leading actress in their private productions. When she was thirteen she met James Mowatt, a wealthy New York attorney, thirteen years her senior. Before she was fifteen, James Mowatt proposed marriage. Six months later she married him secretly because her father had insisted that she wait until she was seventeen to marry. James Mowatt bought Melrose, an estate in Flatbush, Long Island, and there Anna

Cora Mowatt continued her studies under the supervision of her husband. Inspired by her reading of poetry and of history, she wrote a long, romantic epic poem set in Spain, titled *Pelayo; or, the Cavern Cavadonga*, which was published by her husband in 1836. In 1837 Mowatt, whose health had always been delicate, was diagnosed as a consumptive; a sea voyage was recommended. Accompanied by her aunt she sailed for Europe. In London she saw the actress Madame Lucia Vestris at the Olympic Theatre, and in Paris she frequently saw the famous actress Rachel at the Théâtre Français. Before leaving Paris, she composed a poetic play in six acts titled *Gulzara; or, the Persian Slave* for an Ogden family performance. In August of 1840, Mowatt and her husband, who had joined her in Europe, sailed for New York. At a grand ball given to celebrate their return, Mowatt and her sisters presented *Gulzara*, and in 1841 it was published in *The New World*.

About this time James Mowatt began to lose his eyesight and was soon unable to practice law. Then in the fall of 1841 he lost his entire fortune through speculation. Anna Cora Mowatt, resolving that she would have to support her husband and herself, surveyed her talents and decided that she could give public readings of poetry. Encouraged by her friend, Epes Sargent, she initiated her new career with three evenings of readings at the Masonic Temple in Boston. The program began with Walter Scott's *The Lay of the Last Minstrel* and continued with other popular poems of the time. Fashionable Boston audiences were delighted. She then performed in Providence and in New York intermittently throughout the winter of 1841–1842. The schedule was, however, a strain on her delicate health, and she could not continue. In any event, she had become America's first female elocutionist, and she was followed by a number of imitators.

Seeking a cure for her illness, she consulted William Francis Channing, a mesmeric healer, whose treatments seemed to help her, and she began to regain her strength. She also began to write for popular women's magazines. Before the winter was over she had become a regular contributor to *Godey's*, *The Democratic Review*, *The Ladies Companion*, *Graham's*, *The Columbian*, and other periodicals. Her articles included sketches of celebrities she had met, essays contrasting the manners of Europeans and Americans, and even articles on housekeeping, etiquette, and needlework, most of these published under the pseudonym of Helen Berkley. With *The Fortune Hunter* she also won a contest for the best original novel in one volume. Most lucrative were articles on housekeeping which she ghostwrote for a "Mrs. Ellis." James Mowatt, thinking that he might be able to make a bigger profit from his wife's writings, decided to publish them himself. The firm of Mowatt and Company published a *Life of Goethe* and *Memoirs of Madame D'Arblay*, both by Anna Cora Mowatt. These were not successful, and she had to return to the writing of manuals of useful information. Mowatt also wrote a two-volume novel, *Evelyn* (1845), but before it was published she had already made her entrance into the theatre as a playwright.

In 1845 Mowatt's friend Epes Sargent, who had been highly entertained by Mowatt's description and imitation of the *nouveaux riches* in New York society, suggested that she write a play on the subject. Within a few weeks she had written *Fashion*, a lively social comedy satirizing those who would put fashion and the imitation of foreign ways above native American virtues. The play opened at the Park Theatre on March 24, 1845. Because of Mowatt's social standing the opening night audience was made up of the best of New York society, and the play was a brilliant success, running for three weeks. Edgar Allan Poe wrote two reviews of *Fashion*. His review in the *Broadway Journal* for March 29, 1845, first states that the play has the "usual routine of stage characters and stage maneuvers—but there is not one particle of any nature beyond green-room nature, about it." However, he continues: "It must be understood that we are not condemning Mrs. Mowatt's comedy in particular, but the modern drama in general. Comparatively, there is much merit in 'Fashion,' and in many respects (and those of a *telling* character) it is superior to any American play. It has, in especial, the very high merit of simplicity in plot. . . . The colloquy in Mrs. Mowatt's comedy is spirited, generally terse, and well seasoned at points with sarcasm of much power."

While still playing in New York, *Fashion* was also produced at the Walnut Street Theatre in Philadelphia. However, all the profits from the play had to be used to pay off the debts that had accumulated from the failure of James Mowatt's publishing business. So Anna Cora Mowatt decided to go on the stage herself. On June 13, 1845, she made her debut as Pauline in Edward George Bulwer-Lytton's *The Lady of Lyons*. The audience and the critics were ecstatic about the new star. Nearly everyone commented upon Mowatt's naturalness. "Pauline has not been played till now," wrote the critic of *The Sunday Mercury* (quoted by Barnes, *The Lady of Fashion*, p. 171). Thus, with no formal training, but with much experience in amateur theatricals and much acquaintance with drama, Mowatt began her professional career as a star. On a tour of the United States during her first year as a professional actress, she mastered twenty roles and played two hundred nights. Edgar Allan Poe gives us a delightful picture of Mowatt as an actress. Writing about the "Literati of New York City" in *Godey's Lady's Book* (June 1846), he describes Mowatt: "Indeed, the great charm of her manner is its naturalness. She looks, speaks and moves with a well-controlled impulsiveness, as different as can be conceived from the customary rant and cant, the hack conventionality of the stage. Her voice is rich and voluminous. . . . Her utterance is singularly distinct. . . . Her reading could scarcely be improved. Her action is distinguished by an ease and self-possession which would do credit to a veteran. Her step is the perfection of grace."

For her second season Mowatt chose E. L. Davenport as her leading man. During the summer after her second year as an actress, Mowatt wrote *Armand, the Child of the People*, a romantic play in blank verse set in eighteenth century France, with the roles of the heroic Armand and the beautiful Blanche tailored to suit the talents of E. L. Davenport and herself. *Armand* opened at the Park

Theatre on September 27, 1847, "with marked favor." In November 1847, Anna Cora, James Mowatt, and E. L. Davenport sailed for England, planning to play briefly in the provinces prior to a London appearance. Although British audiences and critics did not usually look favorably on American actors at this period, by the end of the Manchester engagement the two American actors had pleased both audiences and critics. The *Manchester Guardian* wrote of Mowatt that she had "an ensemble of personal requisites not excelled by anyone on the stage," and "she is the most refined American actor whom we have yet seen" (quoted by Barnes, p. 247). The provincial success led to an engagement at the Princess's Theatre in London, and a starring contract for the entire next season at the Marylebone Theatre, where Walter Watts, the manager, spared no expense to present plays with historical accuracy. Mowatt's *Armand* was given a grand staging with the sub-title changed from "the Child of the People" to "the Peer and the Peasant," in order to satisfy the Royal Licenser. At the final curtain Mowatt received her first great London ovation, and the play ran to full houses for twenty-one nights. Mowatt was the talk of London, and that season the Marylebone became the most popular theatre in the city.

Optimistically, the Mowatts invested money in Walter Watts's attempt to take over the Olympic Theatre for the next season. Then James Mowatt was sent by his doctors to the West Indies for his health, his wife remaining in London to perform. Disaster struck on March 2, when Walter Watts was arrested for fraud and misappropriation of funds. Anna Cora Mowatt collapsed; the next four months were a blank for her. It was found that Watts had stolen from the insurance company where he had been a clerk. He had used the stolen money to present the plays at the Marylebone Theatre the previous season and to lease the Olympic Theatre. Watts was tried and sentenced to transportation for ten years; the night after his sentencing, he hanged himself. James Mowatt returned to England, but once again the Mowatts faced financial difficulties. Their investment in the Olympic Theatre had been lost with Watts's ruin. Needing desperately to earn some money, Anna Cora Mowatt embarked on a tour to Dublin and then Newcastle, where she received word of her husband's death. She returned to London, saw her husband buried, and on July 9, 1851, sailed for New York.

In August Mowatt played at Niblo's Garden Theatre, and from there she went on tour. In Boston she was welcomed as a national heroine whose triumphs in England had raised the prestige of America. In January she appeared in Richmond, and there she met the editor of *The Richmond Enquirer*, William Foushee Ritchie. Ritchie was ceaseless in his attentions to Mowatt, following her by letter, by telegram, or in person wherever she went on tour.

Mowatt's next season's tour ended abruptly in Memphis when she became very ill and returned to her father's home to recuperate. As soon as she was able she began to write *The Autobiography of an Actress*, published in 1854 in Boston. This book provides an invaluable picture of the theatre in the 1840s and 1850s. Late in 1853 Mowatt began her farewell tour. Night after night in city after city the theatres were thronged with people who had come to see this remarkable woman. On June 2, 1854, she made her last appearance in Boston, where she had first stepped on a stage to give her poetry readings. The next day at Niblo's Garden Theatre in New York she made her final stage appearance. Three days later she married William Foushee Ritchie and moved with him to Richmond.

In Richmond Mowatt continued writing and in 1856 published *Mimic Life*, a collection of three fictionalized stories based on her own experiences in the theatre. The next year she published a novel, *Twin Roses*. She was also active in the movement led by Ann Pamela Cunningham to acquire Mount Vernon for a national shrine; and when the Mount Vernon Ladies' Association was granted a charter, she became its vice regent for Virginia.

This second marriage proved an unhappy one, and at the outbreak of the Civil War Mowatt left her husband to live with her family in the North. In 1861 she went to live in Europe, first in Florence and then in England. Always plagued by financial difficulties, Mowatt continued to write even though she was seriously ill. She sent articles home to American newspapers and published two novels, *Fairy Fingers* and *The Mute Singer*. In 1868 she gathered together some of her essays that had been written earlier and published them under the title, *The Clergyman's Wife and Other Sketches*. On July 29, 1870, at Twickenham, England, Anna Cora Mowatt Ritchie died of tuberculosis. She was buried in Kensal Green Cemetery, London, beside her first husband, James Mowatt.

Contemporary descriptions of Anna Cora Mowatt mention her slight and delicate figure and her graceful bearing, which reflected her refinement and breeding. She had an exquisite complexion, blue eyes, and masses of soft curls. She had a gentle voice of "silvery sweetness," that was capable of great variety. She had a fine feeling for poetry. Mowatt was at her best in the comedies of Shakespeare; Rosalind, Viola, and Beatrice were among her favorites. She also played Juliet, Desdemona, Lady Teazle in *The School for Scandal*, Mrs. Haller in *The Stranger*, and many of the heroines of the romantic plays of the day. In England she played some of the roles made famous by the French actress Rachel. One of Mowatt's favorite roles and one that she sometimes chose for her benefits was Parthenia in Mrs. Lovell's translation of *Ingomar*, a play that she called almost a woman's rights drama. As an actress Mowatt impressed the English as had no other American before her.

Mowatt's play, *Fashion*, was not America's first social comedy, but its quality and its success make it the first significant one. However, Mowatt's influence upon the theatre was greater than upon the drama. She proved to an America still under Puritan influences that a woman of breeding and social standing could succeed on the stage and yet remain "untainted" by the evils that so many people associated with the theatre.

Eric W. Barnes, *The Lady of Fashion* (1954), gives full details of Anna Cora Mowatt's life and work and includes an extensive bibliography. Principal sources are Mowatt's *Autobiography of an Actress* (1854) and her other writings. There is a small collection of her letters in the Schlesinger Library, Radcliffe College. Other sources are memoirs of her by Mary Howitt in *Howitt's Journal* (March 4, 11, and 18, 1918), and by Bayle Bernard in *Tallis's Drawing Room Table Book* (1851). Marion Harland wrote "Personal Recollections of a Christian Actress," published in *Our Continent* (March 15, 1882), and *Marian Harland's Autobiography* (1910) contains a chapter on Mowatt. Poe's review of *Fashion* has been reprinted in *The Complete Works of Edgar Allan Poe*, Vol. XII, *Literary Criticism*, edited by James A. Harrison (1965); and his description of Mowatt as an actress has been reprinted in *Edgar Allan Poe, Essays and Reviews* (1984). Two unpublished sources are Marius Blesi's "The Life and Letters of Anna Cora Mowatt" (Unpublished Ph.D. dissertation, University of Virginia, 1938) and Imogene McCarthy's "Anna Cora Mowatt and Her American Audience" (Unpublished M. A. thesis, University of Maryland, 1952). The following memoirs and histories of the theatre contain information: Arthur Hobson Quinn, *A History of the American Drama From the Beginning to the Civil War* (1923); George C. D. Odell, *Annals of the New York Stage*, Vols. IV and V (1928–1931); Brander Matthews and Laurence Hutton, eds., *Actors and Actresses of Great Britain and the United States* (1886); Laurence Hutton, *Curiosities of the American Stage* (1891); and William W. Clapp, *A Record of the Boston Stage* (1853). Anna Cora Mowatt is included in *Dictionary of American Biography*, Vol. VII (1934, renewed 1962); eds. Stanley J. Kunitz and Howard Haycraft *American Authors 1600–1900* (1938, reprinted 1964); *Who Was Who in America, Historical Volume, 1607–1896* (1963); Robert J. Sherman, *Actors and Authors with Composers Who Helped Make Them Famous* (1951); *Notable American Women*, Vol. II (1971); *Famous Actors and Actresses on the American Stage*, Vol. II (1975); ed. Donald Mullin, *Victorian Actors and Actresses in Review*, (1983); *The Oxford Companion to the Theatre* (1983); *The Oxford Companion to American Literature* (1983); *The McGraw-Hill Encyclopedia of World Drama*, Vol. III (1984); and *The Oxford Companion to American Theatre* (1984).

Alice McDonnell Robinson

MUSSER, Tharon Myrene (January 8, 1925–): lighting designer and theatre consultant, was born to George C. and Hazel (Riddle) Musser in Roanoke, Virginia, where her father was a clergyman. She graduated from Berea College in Kentucky in 1946 with a Bachelor of Arts degree. As an undergraduate she designed the college's production of Henrik Ibsen's *Ghosts*. She earned the Master of Fine Arts degree from the Yale University School of Drama in 1950, working both at Wellesley College and for the Provincetown Playhouse in New York City before graduation.

From 1950 to 1951, Musser worked as the stage manager-lighting designer at the YMHA, New York City, where much of her time was devoted to dance lighting. This experience led to a job as stage manager-lighting designer for José Limon in the 1953–1954 season. Musser's first Broadway lighting assignment was for a revival of Eugene O'Neill's *Long Day's Journey into Night* in 1956, starring Jason Robards, Jr. Her international career began the following year when she designed the lights for the show's Paris production. She then went to Israel in 1958 to light *The First Born*.

Musser has had an outstanding lighting career in musicals. Her first was *Shinbone Alley* in 1957. Some of the more prominent shows since then include *Once Upon a Mattress* (1959), *Golden Boy* (1964), *Applause* (1970), *Follies*

(1971), *The Boy Friend* (1970), *A Little Night Music* (1973), *Mack and Mabel* (1974), *Candide* (1974), *The Wiz* (1975), *A Chorus Line* (1975), *Pacific Overtures* (1976), *Ballroom* (1978), *42nd Street* (1980), *Dream Girls* (1981), and *Merlin*, which opened in February 1983 with what Brendan Gill in *The New Yorker* called a "fierce bedazzlement of lighting." In 1986 Musser designed the lighting for Neil Simon's *Broadway Bound* (Broadhurst Theatre). Musser has received any number of Antoinette Perry (Tony) Award nominations for musicals, and she was a winner with *Follies*, *A Chorus Line*, and *Dream Girls*. The Los Angeles Drama Critics Circle Award went to her for *Follies*, *Pacific Overtures*, and *A Chorus Line*.

Musser lights all other forms of theatre, too. She began lighting for the American Shakespeare Festival Theatre in Stratford, Connecticut, with *Much Ado About Nothing* in 1957, followed by many plays there through the mid–1960s. In 1969 she became staff designer for the Dallas Civic Opera and in 1970 for the Los Angeles Center Theatre Group at the Mark Taper Forum, where she designed *Dream on Monkey Mountain*, which won the Los Angeles Drama Critics Circle Award.

During 1975, a typical Musser year, she designed lights for *A Chorus Line* on Broadway and productions of *A Little Night Music* in London, Vienna, and Johannesburg. She also did *Once in a Lifetime* at the Mark Taper Forum in Los Angeles, *Tales of Hoffman* at the Dallas Civic Opera, and *The Flying Dutchman* for the Miami Opera Guild. The same year she designed the Broadway productions of *The Wiz*, *Same Time, Next Year*, *A Chorus Line* and *Me and Bessie*.

Although there would seem to be time for little else than designing shows, Musser is a frequent lighting consultant to architects. She helped in the restoration of Ford's Theatre in Washington, D.C., and then lighted the related production celebrating the event. She worked on renovations for Radcliffe College, The American Academy of Dramatic Arts, the Chicago Auditorium, and the Shubert Theatre in Los Angeles. She was the consultant on the Berea College Dramatic Arts Center, for which her alma mater gave her an honorary doctorate. Emerson College in Boston also awarded her an honorary degree in 1980.

Musser has lectured for the New York Teachers' Association, 1957–1958; the American National Theatre and Academy National Convention, 1958; Vassar College, 1961; Yale University School of Drama, 1962 and 1969; the Polakov Studio of Design, 1962–1964; Bridgeport (Connecticut) University Student Center, 1967; the State University of New York at Purchase, 1969; Bucknell University, 1973; Rhode Island College, 1974; Carnegie-Mellon University, 1980; and Rutgers University, 1982. She was also on the Visiting Committee at Harvard University's Loeb Drama Center, 1974–1976.

The United States Institute for Theatre Technology gave Tharon Musser a special award for Art and Technology in Theatre Lighting in 1976. This award from her peers in technical theatre illustrates her eminent position in the profession. With *A Chorus Line* Musser brought computerized lighting control to Broadway for the first time. Resistance dimmers were still being used in 1975.

Also, with *A Chorus Line* she became part of a production team unique in the commercial theatre. The collaborators were Michael Bennett (director, choreographer), Robin Wagner (set designer), **Theoni Aldredge** (costume designer), and Tharon Musser (lighting designer). They have collaborated on *A Chorus Line*, *Ballroom*, and *Dream Girls*. Musser continues to be one of the busiest designers in the lighting world.

Tharon Musser has written "Cutting Lighting Without Losing Concept," *Theatre Crafts* (November/December 1969.). Articles about Musser and her lighting designs include Patricia MacKay, "Mack and Mabel—Silent Era Sound Stage Recreated," *Theatre Crafts* (November/December 1974); Patricia MacKay, "A Chorus Line—Computerized Lighting Comes to Broadway," *Theatre Crafts* (November/December 1975); *Pacific Overtures*: Veteran designer Boris Aronson creates a vision of 19th Century Japan," *Theatre Crafts* (January/February 1976), and Patricia MacKay, "Ballroom—Tharon Musser Lights the Ballroom Floor," *Theatre Crafts* (March/April 1979). "The Dream Team on Collaboration; or, Five Designers in Search of an Author," *Theatre Crafts* (August/September 1982) discusses the collaboration of Michael Bennett, Robin Wagner, Tharon Musser, Theoni Aldredge, and Bob Avian on *A Chorus Line*, *Ballroom*, and *Dream Girls*. Musser is listed in *The Biographical Encyclopaedia and Who's Who of the American Theatre* (1966); *Who's Who of American Women, 1966–1967* (1967); *Notable Names in the American Theatre* (1976); *Who's Who in Opera* (1976); *Who's Who in the Theatre* (1977); and *Who's Who in America, 1982–1983*, Vol. II (1983).

Richard K. Knaub

N

NAZIMOVA, Alla (June 4, 1878–July 13, 1945): actress famous for her interpretations of Henrik Ibsen's heroines, was born in Yalta, Russia, the daughter of pharmacist Jacob Leventon and Sophia (Hervit) Leventon. Nazimova was educated in Switzerland, returning to Russia at the age of twelve, when she studied violin in Odessa. She entered the dramatic school of the Philharmonic Society of Moscow at the age of seventeen, studying under Vladimir Nemirovich-Danchenko, and joining the Moscow Art Theatre's school Constantin Stanislavsky and Nemirovich-Danchenko opened it in 1898. After several years in stock companies in Kislovodski, Kostroma, and Vilna, Nazimova played the leading lady in Ibsen's *Ghosts* in St. Petersburg (1903–1904) with actor-manager Paul Orleneff. She then took the lead role in his production of Evgeni Chirikov's *The Chosen People* on tour in Berlin and London. Nazimova made her American debut at New York's Herald Square Theatre (March 23, 1905), performing *The Chosen People* in Russian for a series of matinees.

Although critically hailed, Orleneff's company was a commercial failure and soon returned to Russia. Nazimova remained in the United States; her acting had been praised for its realistic intensity, which, combined with her striking appearance, attracted the attention of commercial managements. After she learned English in approximately six months, the Shuberts sponsored her in *Hedda Gabler* (under Henry Miller's management) for a series of matinees beginning November 13, 1906. Her performance in *A Doll's House* (January 1907) was a critical and commercial success, launching the Russian actress on a starring career; *Hedda Gabler* was revived in March 1907, and she was also hailed as Hilda Wangel in *The Master Builder* the same year.

The Shuberts built the Nazimova Theatre (later the 39th Street Theatre) for her in New York, which she opened with *Little Eyolf* in 1910. However, in addition to the Ibsen roles that gained her critical fame, the Shuberts placed her in melodramatic vehicles like *Comtesse Coquette* and *The Comet* (both 1907) that stressed her exotic good looks and ability to portray passionate emotion. Nazimova signed with Charles Frohman in 1912, only to play another exotic heroine in *Bella Donna* (1912). She then toured in a pacifist play, *War Brides* (1915). Rewritten as an anti-German propaganda piece, the play served as her film debut in 1916. For the next several years, Nazimova was a major screen star; her roles—ironically in the same vein as the popular plays that had led her to break with the Shuberts—made her for a while a leading portrayer of the "vamp" image. She returned to the legitimate theatre briefly in 1918 to play in Ibsen's *The Wild Duck*.

Nazimova's film career, which at its height paid her $13,000 weekly and gave her artistic control of her movies, faltered in the 1920s, especially after it was revealed that her 1913 marriage to actor-manager Charles Bryant had been invalid. Nazimova maintained that an early marriage in Russia—either to Sergei Golovin (a fellow student at the Moscow Art Theatre Academy) in 1898 or to Paul Orleneff shortly before the tour that brought her to New York—had never been dissolved for lack of a divorce law in Russia.

Nazimova returned to Broadway in *Dagmar* (1923), which was excoriated by critics as a cheap melodrama. She then played in vaudeville for several years, creating a stir when her sketch *The Unknown* was banned from the Keith-Orpheum circuit in the autumn of 1923 because of its criticism of the New York divorce law. The actress then joined **Eva Le Gallienne**'s Civic Repertory Theatre (in 1928) and began a second, and final, period as a major stage figure. With Le Gallienne's troupe, Nazimova appeared in a series of starring roles as a mature performer, most notably in a major revival of Anton Chekhov's *The Cherry Orchard* (1928) and in Leonid Andreyev's *Katerina* (1929). She also appeared briefly in Chekhov's one-act play *On the High Road* (1929).

In 1930 Nazimova joined the Theatre Guild, for which she acted Natalya Petrovna in Ivan Turgenev's *A Month in the Country*. She won the role of Christine Mannon in the guild's production of Eugene O'Neill's *Mourning Becomes Electra* in 1931, then one of the most sought-after roles for mature performers. This part secured her reputation as one of the most brilliant of realistic actresses in her era. For the Theatre Guild, Nazimova also acted in *The Good Earth* (1932) and in the American première of George Bernard Shaw's *The Simpleton of the Unexpected Isles* (1935). Her last major starring role, also for the Theatre Guild, was the 1935 production of *Ghosts*; again, as the Ibsen heroine Mrs. Alving, Nazimova scored a brilliant success. She revived *Hedda Gabler* in 1936; her final stage appearance was in Karl Capek's *The Mother* (April 25, 1939), which played only four performances.

In the late 1930s, Nazimova returned to Hollywood, playing character roles in a series of films, including *Escape* (1940), *Blood and Sand* (1944), *The Bridge of San Luis Rey* (1944), and *Since You Went Away* (1944). She died of a heart attack in 1945 at the Good Samaritan Hospital in Hollywood; her ashes were interred at Forest Lawn Memorial Park, Glendale, California.

Nazimova was widely regarded from the early years of her stage career as the first notable practitioner of the Stanislavskian approach to acting. The convincing style with which she portrayed passion on the stage, coupled with her exotic attractiveness, helped to make her a major figure in the interpretation of both Ibsen and Chekhov. The Shuberts and Frohman tended to present her in exotic vehicles of far lesser quality, helping to create the femme fatale image that she successfully played for a time on screen. She combined great technical skill with spontaneity. She approached each character she played by analyzing the person's inner psychology, maintaining that "once you know what she *is*, what she *does* becomes easy to interpret" (Eustis, *Players at Work*, p. 53). The power and clarity of her characterizations, controlled by masterly technique, made her one of the more influential performers in the first part of the twentieth century; her scenes were often watched from the wings by other members of her companies. Her early work helped to confirm Ibsen's status as a major modern writer for American audiences, while her later starring career did the same for Chekhov and helped make *Mourning Becomes Electra* one of the most highly respected of O'Neill's mature plays. She was one of the few star actresses of the period able to make the transition to mature roles and to retain a starring status during three decades on the stage.

Alla Nazimova's own account of her childhood is "My Yesterdays," *Bohemian* (June 1907). This can be found in the clipping file in the Theatre Collection of the New York Public Library Performing Arts Research Center at Lincoln Center. Other collections of material about Nazimova are in the Harvard Theatre Collection, the library of the Academy of Motion Picture Arts and Sciences in Los Angeles, and the Samuel Stark Collection at Stanford University. There are references to her in Frank P. Morse, *Backstage with Henry Miller* (1938); Emma Goldman, *Living My Life* (1931); Eva Le Gallienne, *With a Quiet Heart* (1935); and William A. Brady, *Showman* (1937). Her obituary appeared in the *New York Times* (July 14, 1945). The major scholarly work devoted to Nazimova is Clifford Ashby's "Alla Nazimova and the Advent of the New Acting in America," *Quarterly Journal of Speech* (April 1959), while a full account of her life is in Alexander Kirkland's "The Woman from Yalta," *Theatre Arts* (December 1949). Her ideas on acting are collected in Morton Eustis, *Players at Work* (1937, reprinted 1969). A complete bibliography of popular periodical literature is in Stephen Archer, *American Actors and Actresses* (1983). Nazimova is included in *The National Encyclopedia of American Biography*, Vol XXXVI (1950, reprinted 1967); *Who Was Who in America: Vol II, 1943–1950* (1966); *Notable American Women*, Vol. II (1971), William C. Young, *Famous Actors and Actresses on the American Stage*, Vol. II (1975); *Who Was Who in the Theatre*. Vol. III (1978); *The Oxford Companion to the Theatre* (1983); and *The Oxford Companion to American Theatre* (1984).

Alan Woods

NICHOLS, Anne (November 26, 1891?–September 15, 1966): playwright, director, producer, actress, most remembered for writing *Abie's Irish Rose*, was born in Dales Mill, Georgia, to George Nichols, a lawyer, and Julia (Bates)

Nichols. Her parents were strict Baptists, but as an adult she converted to Roman Catholicism. Reared in Philadelphia, she attended Central High School for two years and Strayer's Business College for six months. In January 1914, she married Henry Duffy, an actor and theatrical producer. They had one child, Henry D. Nichols, before the marriage was dissolved in 1924. Anne Nichols died of a heart attack at the Cliff House Nursing Home in Englewood Cliffs, New Jersey, and was buried in Valhalla, New York.

Despite a rigid religious upbringing, Nichols's childhood ambition was to become an actress, and at sixteen she ran away from home with thirty-six dollars in her purse in order to pursue a career in the theatre. With five dollars left of her original funds, she landed a job in a touring Biblical extravaganza called *The Shepherd King*. Then came several years of stock and vaudeville engagements and marriage to Henry Duffy in 1914. She decided to try writing when she realized that she and Duffy had no money to buy vaudeville sketches in which to perform. Her first effort, a melodramatic tear-jerker, inadvertently turned out to be funny, and audiences laughed hysterically. The delighted theatre manager offered Nichols her first important contract, launching her career as a professional playwright.

She wrote her first full-length play, *Heart's Desire*, in 1916, in collaboration with Adelaide Matthews. For various touring companies she wrote *The Man From Wicklow* (1917), *The Happy Cavalier* (1918), *A Little Bit Old-Fashioned* (1918), and *Springtime in Mayo* (1919). She also wrote the books for several musicals in 1919, among them *Linger Longer Letty*, which was constantly revived throughout the twenties and thirties. For Fiske O'Hara, with whose company she had toured as far back as 1915, she wrote *Down Limerick Way* (1920) and *Marry in Haste* (1921). She again collaborated with Adelaide Matthews to write *Just Married*, which opened in New York on April 26, 1921, and broke all extant stock company records there as well as in Chicago and London. It was apparently made into a movie three times. However, it was *Abie's Irish Rose*, an amusing but unpretentious comedy about religious tolerance, that was to overshadow all her other work and gradually dominate her life. The play opened on Broadway on May 23, 1922, after considerable difficulties. It had been rejected by every producer from New York to Hollywood, even after having a successful run on the West Coast. In order to give *Abie* a chance in New York, Nichols mortgaged her home and produced the play herself at the Fulton Theatre. The reviews were mixed—some favorable, some downright hostile—and box-office receipts suffered. However, Nichols put every cent she had into the production, the actors took a salary cut, ticket prices were reduced, and *Abie* managed to survive for two shaky months until it suddenly "caught on" with theatre audiences. *Abie's Irish Rose* set a record for consecutive performances (2,327) and held that record for fourteen years. It is estimated that Anne Nichols, as sole owner of the play, earned from this single work a million dollars in royalties as author and millions more as producer. The movie rights alone brought in two million. "There were weeks when I made $180,000 net profit," she once told a reporter. "I bought stocks and bonds and most of Flushing" (*New York Times*, May 21, 1962). In addition to the Broadway production there were performances of *Abie* all over the United States and Canada, in London, and in Sydney, Australia. The play was performed in Europe in French, German, Swedish, Portuguese, Spanish, and Russian. It played eight months to packed houses in Berlin. It was even produced in China with an all-Chinese cast. There were two New York revivals (1937 and 1954), two film versions (1928 and 1946), and a weekly radio show in the early 1940s.

The tremendous success of the play proved a mixed blessing for the author, who eventually came to feel "haunted" by her creation. She went on with her career as an active producing manager and later wrote, directed, and produced about half a dozen other plays, such as *Pre-Honeymoon* in 1936. However, she gradually found herself forced to devote more and more time to the play that critic George Jean Nathan called "the fourth biggest industry in the United States" (*Materia Critica*, p. 229). Her motives, however, were not entirely financial. She genuinely loved and believed in her play and felt compelled to keep a managerial eye on it. "No matter what else I was trying to work on, I had a compulsion to check up on the various companies," she said. "And invariably I'd find that the minute my back was turned, the actors would start distorting the play by ad-libbing lines for laughs. I had to travel back and forth across the country constantly to keep them in check. I hardly found time to write any more" (*New York Times*, May 21, 1962).

Numerous legal battles also consumed her time and energy, starting with Oliver Morosco's attempt to get an injunction to stop the play's opening in New York. He failed, but there was trouble with contracts, booking agents, and dishonest managers. In 1929 she sued Universal Pictures Corporation, charging that they had used her play as the basis for their film *The Cohens and the Kellys*. She lost the case when George Jean Nathan testified that the theme of young lovers thwarted by their parents could be found as early as Shakespeare's *Romeo and Juliet*. The court then ruled that Nichols's idea was in the public domain. Eventually, Anne Nichols attempted to write her autobiography, but peace and quiet continually eluded her. Still pursued by would-be interviewers, she attempted to work in seclusion in Harwich, Massachusetts, in the 1960s. She had lost a substantial part of her fortune in the Great Depression, and medical bills reduced what was left. In 1966, fighting poor health, she entered the Actors' Fund Home in Englewood, and later a nursing home. She died with her autobiography, tentatively titled *Such is Fame*, still unfinished.

Anne Nichols's significance lies not only in the fact that she is the author of a play that proved to be one of the greatest commercial success stories in the history of the American theatre, but also in the fact that her theatrical career was a particularly active and creative one. In addition to *Abie*, she wrote over twenty other plays, plus numerous vaudeville sketches, film scenarios, and a radio serial (*Dear John*, NBC, 1938–1942). She proved that a woman could operate successfully as a director and theatrical producer in New York City; she disproved George Jean Nathan's contention that women playwrights were somehow "inferior to their boy-friends" (*The Entertainment of a Nation*, p. 34). She withstood the hostility of critics and conclusively demonstrated that a well-constructed play could survive without their approval. (Some critics relentlessly hounded *Abie* for the entire five years of the play's New York run.) Though her greatest success was to distort her life and reputation, she nevertheless continued to love and support the play for which she once mortgaged her home and of which she said it "has never stopped playing somewhere."

Major sources on Anne Nichols's life and career are Doris Abramson and Laurilyn Harris, "Anne Nichols: Million Dollar Playwright," *Players* (April/May, 1976); "Anne Nichols Is Dead at 75: Author of *Abie's Irish Rose*," *New York Times* (September 16, 1966); Mary Braggiotti, "Abie's Rose Grows an Olive Leaf," *New York Post* (June 26, 1943); Arthur Gelb, "Author of *Abie's Irish Rose* Reviews 40 Years," *New York Times* (May 21, 1962); Jean Meegan, "Old Man Abie, He Just Goes Rolling," *Milwaukee Journal* (October 3, 1943); and "Anne Nichols, The Million Dollar Hit," *Theatre Arts Magazine* (July 1924). George Jean Nathan mentioned the great popularity of *Abie's Irish Rose* in *Materia Critica* (1924) and *The Entertainment of a Nation* (1942). There is disagreement about Nichols's date of birth. The *New York Times* obituary (September 16, 1966) lists her age as seventy-five, which would make her birth date 1891. Other sources state that she was born on November 26, 1896. Anne Nichols is included in *Who's Who in the Theatre* (1952); *The Reader's Encyclopedia of American Literature* (1962); *Everyman's Dictionary of Literary Biography, English and American* (1962); *The Biographical Encyclopaedia and Who's Who of the American Theatre* (1966); *Who Was Who in America, Vol. IV 1961–1968* (1968); Myron Matlaw, *Modern World Drama: An Encyclopedia* (1972); *American Women Writers*, Vol. III (1981); *The Oxford Companion to American Theatre* (1984); and *The McGraw-Hill Encyclopedia of World Drama*, Vol. III (1984).

Laurilyn J. Harris

NORMAN, Marsha (September 21, 1947–): Pulitzer Prize-winning playwright, is in the forefront of the contemporary surge of American women successfully writing for the stage. The oldest of four children born to Billie and Bertha Williams, she grew up in Louisville, Kentucky, where her father sold insurance. She recalls a lonely childhood in a fundamentalist household. A scholarship took her to Agnes Scott College in Decatur, Georgia, between 1965 and 1968, where she earned a Bachelor of Arts degree in philosophy. Three years later she received her master's degree in education from the University of Louisville. Her marriage to Michael Norman, an educator whom she knew from her native city, lasted from 1968 to 1973. She wed for a second time in 1978. Her husband, Dann Byck, Jr., was a founder of the Actors Theatre of Louisville. Formerly involved in his family-owned business, a Louisville women's specialty store chain, he became a theatrical producer. However, this marriage also ended in divorce.

Before embarking on her playwriting career, Marsha Norman held several positions involving children. These include two years as a volunteer in the pediatric burn unit at Grady Memorial Hospital in Atlanta. After completing her bachelor's degree she taught severely disturbed children at Kentucky Central State Hospital. From 1970 to 1972 she worked with gifted students in the Jefferson County (Kentucky) school system. This last experience, she says helped her to understand the isolation she had felt as a gifted child in the Kentucky schools. From 1972 to 1974 Norman conducted film classes for the Kentucky Arts Commission. This position allowed her to study in New York during two summers at the Center for Understanding Media. Immersed there in film and video work, she found the center's environment extremely stimulating. Subsequently, an appointment to the position of arts administrator enabled her to develop a special arts project for the Kentucky Arts Commission. Marsha Norman's early professional writing background included free-lancing as a book reviewer and editing the *Louisville Times*'s Saturday children's section, the *Jellybean Journal*. During this period—from 1974 to 1978—she also contributed to Kentucky Educational Television's workbook for a remedial reading series.

The Actors Theatre of Louisville, where she became writer-in-residence for the 1978–1979 season, figured importantly in Norman's full-time commitment to playwriting. Artistic director Jon Jory encouraged her to write her first drama, which she did. *Getting Out* opened in Louisville in November 1977. The play concerns a woman newly released from prison who must dispel the destructive elements of her personality and come to some hard decisions about her life. An unusual feature is the simultaneous depiction of the present-day heroine, Arlene, and her former teenage self, Arlie. *Getting Out* was voted the best new regional play by the American Theatre Critics Association. After a second production at the Mark Taper Forum in Los Angeles in February 1978, the play opened in New York's Phoenix Theatre on October 19, 1978, for a limited run of twenty-two performances. It reopened as an independent Off-Broadway production at the Theatre De Lys on May 15, 1979, for an additional 237 performances. The play earned Norman several awards. The Rockefeller Foundation included Marsha Norman among eight recipients of the Playwrights-in-Residence Awards for 1979–1980, and the Outer Critics Circle gave her the John Gassner New Playwrights Medallion Award. She received the first George Oppenheimer-Newsday Playwriting Award for a new American playwright whose work was produced in New York or on Long Island. Critical reaction was enthusiastic. John Simon, writing in the *Hudson Review* (Spring 1979), called the simultaneous presentation of Arlie and Arlene "a brilliant dramatic stratagem" (p. 82). T. E. Kalem declared that *Getting Out* promised to be "one of the prides of Off-Broadway" (*Time*, May 28, 1979, p. 28), and Jack Kroll labeled it a "superb first play" (*Newsweek*, May 28, 1979, p. 103).

Third and Oak, a bill of two related one-act plays set respectively in a laundromat and a pool hall, opened to good reviews in March 1978 at the Actors Theatre of Louisville. It was later taped for National Public Radio's "Earplay" series. The first of the one-acts, *The Laundromat*, has been produced around the country, for instance, at New York's Ensemble Studio Theatre, where it was part of a program titled *The Invitational*, from November 14 to December 30, 1979. Less well received was *Circus Valentine*, the story of a failing family circus. The play opened in February 1979 at the Actors Theatre of Louisville and ran for eleven performances. Despite the lack of enthusiasm generated by the production, Norman has been told that monologues from *Circus Valentine* are frequently used as audition pieces. Written during Norman's Rockefeller grant and later revised several times, *The Holdup* was performed in workshop at the Actors Theatre of Louisville during the summer of 1980. It was subsequently presented by the Circle Repertory Company in New York. A more recent production of *The Holdup*, at the American Conservatory Theatre in San Francisco, opened in April 1983.

Norman's most successful play to date, the Pulitzer Prize-winning *'night, Mother*, displays the crisis moment when a woman informs her mother of her determination to commit suicide. In an interview in *USA Today*, the playwright said, "Jessie thinks she cannot have any of the other things she wants from her life, so what she will have is control, and she will have the courage to take that control. Mama, a woman completely unprepared for this moment, is ready to fight with everything she has to keep her alive" (May 5, 1983, p. 5D). This two-character study of the mother-daughter relationship, constructed, according to Norman, in classic sonata form, received a staged reading at the Circle Repertory in November 1981. Following a full production at the American Repertory Theatre in Cambridge, Massachusetts, it moved to Broadway's John Golden Theatre, opening on March 31, 1983.

A devastating ninety minutes without intermission, *'night, Mother*, by its uniqueness, sharply contrasted with most other Broadway offerings, and the initial ticket sales were not brisk. After being awarded the Pulitzer Prize on April 18, 1983, however, the play tripled its box-office receipts. In addition to the Pulitzer for *'night, Mother*, Norman received the fifth annual Susan Smith Blackburn Prize. Critics viewed *'night, Mother* as a fulfillment of the promise apparent in *Getting Out*. Mel Gussow called it "one of the season's major dramatic events" (*New York Times Magazine*, May 1, 1983, p. 22). Jack Kroll wrote, "If there is such a thing as a benign explosion, this is it: it detonates with startling quietness, showering us with truth, compassion and uncompromising honesty" (*Newsweek*, January 3, 1983, p. 41). John Simon summarized the play as "honest, uncompromising, lucid, penetrating, well-written, dramatic, and as unmanipulatively moving as we expected from the author of the remarkable *Getting Out*" (*New York Magazine*, April 11, 1983, p. 56).

Norman's next play centered around a life crisis experienced by a brilliant cancer researcher who, despite his unusual gifts, cannot save someone close to him. *Traveler in the Dark*, starring Sam Waterston as the doctor and Hume Cronyn as his father, a rural revivalist preacher, opened in February 1984 at Cambridge's American Repertory Theatre, where *'night, Mother* had first been performed. The play received mixed reviews. *Newsweek*'s Kroll stated: "In *'night, Mother*, the play's shattering resonance developed inexorably from the piling on of one piercingly observed detail after another. In *Traveler in the Dark*, the action seems whipped up under the lash of Norman's urgent need to dramatize a crisis of faith'' (*Newsweek*, February 27, 1984, p. 76). Although the work is "far too clever," writes *Time*'s critic, "still, *Traveler in the Dark* has emotional power, an insight into men that matches Norman's previously demonstrated understanding of women, and a hearteningly grand ambition" (*Time*, February 27, 1984, p. 101).

One of Norman's more recent theatrical undertakings is a musical about a Kentucky Shaker community in 1857. *Winter Shakers* features music by Norman L. Berman with book and lyrics by Norman. The Actors Theatre of Louisville commissioned a new play from Norman for their 1988 Humana Festival of New Plays. The play, *Sarah and Abraham*, takes place in a regional theatre where the characters' situation begins to mirror that of the Biblical characters. *Sarah and Abraham* was given a lively workshop production. Also in 1988 Norman was one of six playwrights awarded commissions by the American Playwright Project. Norman has not restricted herself to drama, and in 1987 her novel, *The Fortune Teller*, was published.

Because she has achieved so much success in a field long dominated by men, Norman has often been asked to comment on women playwrights. The following quotation from a *New York Times Magazine* article is a representative statement, "Plays require active central characters. Until women could see themselves as active, they could not really write for the theatre. We are the central characters in our lives. That awareness had to come to a whole group before women could write about it" (May 1, 1983, p. 26).

In addition to her theatrical works, Norman has written the video script, *It's a Willingness*, a depression era story set in the Kentucky hills. It appeared in 1979 on National Educational Television's *Visions* series. She also contributed *In Trouble at Fifteen* to the NBC series *Skag*. Norman's foray into film has not yet proved as successful as her other projects. Her 1979 screenplay for Columbia, *The Children with Emerald Eyes*, about a woman who works with disturbed youngsters, has not been produced. Similarly, scripts based on the building of the Verrazano Narrows Bridge (requested by Joseph E. Levine Presents) and on Gay Talese's best seller *Thy Neighbor's Wife* (for United Artists) remain unfilmed. Norman wrote the screenplay for the televised version of *'night, Mother* (1986), starring Cissy Spacek and **Anne Bancroft**.

Norman has recently written articles about other playwrights. "Sam Shepard, the Inaccessible Man," appeared in the February 1984 *Vogue*, and her interview with **Lillian Hellman** was featured in the May 1984 issue of *American Theatre*.

Marsha Norman is a member of the Dramatists Guild and has served for three years on the council for that organization. She is also a member of the Writers Guild of America. In 1986 Norman was inducted into the American Academy and Institute of Arts and Letters in recognition of her achievements as an award-winning writer in America's commercial and nonprofit theatre.

Marsha Norman's *Four Plays* (1988) contains *Getting Out*, *Third and Oak*, *The Holdup*, and *Traveler in the Dark*. Some of the information in this entry was obtained through telephone interviews with Marsha Norman on November 15, 1981, and January 12, 1982. For reviews of *Getting Out*, see Walter Kerr, "A Pinch of Variety Never Hurts," *New York Times* (June 3, 1979); Stanley Kauffmann, "All New, All American," *New Republic* (July 7 and 14, 1979); and Richard Elder, "Stage: 'Getting Out' by Marsha Norman," *New York Times* (May 16, 1979). See also Judy Klemesrud's portrait of Norman, "She Had Her Own 'Getting Out' to Do," *New York Times* (May 27, 1979). For *'night, Mother*, see Frank Rich, "Theater: Suicide Talk in *'night, Mother*," *New York Times* (April 1, 1983). Articles appearing after the Pulitzer Prize announcement include Mel Gussow, "Women Playwrights: New Voices in the Theater," *New York Times Magazine* (May 1, 1983); Nancy Malitz, "Marsha Norman Plays It Her Way," *USA Today* (May 5, 1983); Allan Wallach, "Marsha Norman: A Model Modern Playwright," *Newsday* (May 8, 1983); Amy Gross, "Marsha Norman: Pulitzer Prize-Winner," *Vogue* (July 1983); Elizabeth Stone, "Playwright Marsha Norman: An Optimist Writes about Suicide, Confinement and Despair," *Ms.* (July, 1983); and Kate Stout, "Marsha Norman: Writing for the 'Least of Our Brethren,' " *Saturday Review* (September-October 1983). An interview with Norman is included in *Interviews with Contemporary Women Playwrights*, eds. Kathleen Betsko and Rachel Koenig (1987) and also in *In Their Own Words: Contemporary American Playwrights*, ed. David Savran (1988). Norman is included in *Contemporary Authors*, Vol. 105 (1982); *Current Biography, 1984* (1984–1985); and *The Oxford Companion to American Theatre* (1984).

Susan M. Steadman

NUGENT, Nelle (May 24, 1939–): producer and manager, was born in Jersey City, New Jersey, the daughter of John Patrick Nugent and Evelyn Adelaide (Stern) Nugent. Her father is an attorney and her one brother is a salesman. Married twice before, she is currently married since April 7, 1982, to Jolyon Fox Stern. Nugent's interest in theatre developed in high school and college. As a drama major at Skidmore College in Saratoga Springs, New York, she studied dramatic literature, theatre production, and the history of theatre, as well as English and art history. She attributes her present understanding of scene analysis and structure to her English courses. "Structure is what playwriting is about," she emphasizes (Interview, October 28, 1985). Her art history studies gave her a visual appreciation of composition, content, and color. Her college career, culminating in a bachelor's degree in 1960, included college productions that incorporated professional actors and theatre workers along with students. After graduation she was an Off-Broadway stage manager from 1960 to 1963. From 1964 to 1969 she was a stage manager on Broadway, and from 1968 to 1970 she served as vice president for Theatre NOW, Inc., an Off-Broadway producing organization. In 1971 she became the associate managing director of the Nederlander organization, a major producer of Broadway shows.

In 1976 Nugent and **Elizabeth I. McCann** formed McCann and Nugent Productions, a production and management firm. By 1982 their various shows had received fifty-eight nominations and twenty **Antoinette Perry** (Tony) awards. To date they have produced twenty-two shows, including *Dracula, The Elephant Man, Morning's At Seven, Home, Amadeus, Piaf, Rose, Nicholas*

Nickleby, *The Dresser*, *Mass Appeal*, *Pilobolus Dance Theatre*, *Night and Day*, *All's Well That Ends Well*, *Good*, *Total Abandon*, *The Glass Menagerie*, *The Lady and the Clarinet*, *The Gin Game*, *Crimes of the Heart*, *Pacific Overtures* (revival), *Painting Churches*, and *Leader of the Pack*.

Critical acclaim for Nugent includes the Antoinette Perry (Tony) Award for *Dracula*, *The Elephant Man*, *Morning's at Seven*, *Amadeus*, and *Nicholas Nickleby*; the New York Drama Critics Award for *The Elephant Man* and *Nicholas Nickleby*; and the Drama Desk Award for *Amadeus*, *The Elephant Man* and *Nicholas Nickleby*. Nugent was also named the Entrepreneurial Woman of the Year in 1981 and received the Los Angeles Critics Award.

Nelle Nugent and Elizabeth McCann have been leading members of a new generation of Broadway producers who came up through the ranks. Their professional know-how, such as their ability to handle creative talent and union relationships, has developed through experience. "I was a top Off-Broadway production stage manager but couldn't get a job on Broadway. There was a lot of prejudice against women, so I went backwards to go forwards," says Nelle Nugent. "I learned shorthand and became a production assistant. And my persistence paid off. I was hired as a stage manager" (Interview).

She credits many important professional associations and acquaintances with helping her on the way to success. Among them is Rowena Stevens of the Pocono Playhouse. Nugent says, "She helped me believe I could do it. She took me under her wing. She was a very smart lady, a pioneer in summer stock. She had a style and trained herself rigorously." Another woman who helped Nelle Nugent was Lucia Victor. Nugent describes her this way, "A brilliant stage manager who taught me you don't have to keep your nose to the grindstone all the time. Sometimes it's better to take a walk around the block to relieve the pressure." Charles Blackwell also helped. These friends recommended her for jobs. Nugent goes on to say, "**Cheryl Crawford**, the greatest of the greats, who . . . showed me that theatre could be passionate and still be commercial." Next came "Jimmy Nederlander, who taught me what it was like on the other side—the theatre owner's side—a whole different world" (Interview).

"And, of course, my beloved Liz McCann, who taught me that two heads are better than one. What we did to make it was to give the play every chance. We never compromised on the look. We made sure the production values were top drawer. We offered a creative atmosphere where creative people can do their best work, and we felt very strongly about the business end of theatre. As Henry Irving said, 'If it doesn't succeed as a business, it won't succeed as art' " (Interview).

Nelle Nugent and her former partner Elizabeth McCann became successful producers in a largely male world. They came up through the ranks unlike most of their male counterparts. They took chances on producing shows that other producers said could not be done. It is said that they produce the impossible. "We produce plays because we love them," Nugent says. "I think we have made it possible for some good plays to be seen that might not otherwise have been produced'' (Interview).

Currently Nelle Nugent is in California, where she is producing films for Walt Disney Productions. Her former partner, Elizabeth McCann, has remained in New York.

An article on Nelle Nugent and Elizabeth McCann titled "Broadway Long Shots" appeared in *Playbill* (November 1980, p. 94). A feature article in the *New York Times Magazine* (February 1, 1981) titled "Presenting McCann and Nugent" deals with their incredible rise to success as producers. There is a piece in *Time* (March 9, 1981) titled "Broadway's Golden Ladies," which gives some biographical data. Another article, taken from "The Robb Report" and reprinted in *Eastern Airlines Magazine* (February 1985), points out their business acumen. An article in *Variety* (May 29, 1985) announces that Nugent will become involved with film projects in Hollywood while McCann will continue as a producer in New York. Additional material for this article was obtained during a telephone interview with Nelle Nugent on October 28, 1985. Nugent is listed in *Contemporary Theatre, Film, and Television*, Vol. I (1984).

Patricia Sternberg

O'CONNOR, Sara Andrews (April 5, 1932–): managing director of the Milwaukee Repertory Theatre, was born in Syracuse, New York, and grew up in Canastota, New York, where her father, Harlan F. Andrews, was a stockbroker and her mother, Ethel (Hoyt) Andrews, was a contralto with the local opera company and active in girl scouting. She attended Swarthmore College in Pennsylvania, graduating in 1954 with a Bachelor of Arts degree (with high honors) in art history. She then studied at Tufts University in Massachusetts, where she was granted a master's degree in drama in 1955. She married Boardman O'Connor, a designer, in 1955. The marriage lasted until 1968. She has two sons: Ian (b. December 1, 1956), who constructs properties for the Hartford Stage Company, Connecticut, and Douglas (b. October 23, 1958), who is in the Navy medical corps.

Sara O'Connor is one of the most influential arts managers in the United States, providing leadership and vision coming from her work at the Milwaukee Repertory Theatre since 1974, and from her experience in other management and directorial capacities before that. At the Milwaukee Repertory Theatre she has worked with artistic director John Dillon to build an interracial resident company and to develop touring exchanges with Japanese theatres. She has managed the planning and financing of a facility at a cost of more than twelve million dollars. It contains a 720-seat theatre; a 200-seat theatre; a 100-seat cabaret space; 2 rehearsal halls; a studio for laboratory work; scene, paint, property, and costume shops; offices; and other support space. The project has catalyzed a one-hundred-million-dollar downtown development in Milwaukee, involving a hotel, restaurants, an office tower, cinemas, and other businesses. In addition to her management endeavors, she has begun translating plays from French for production at the Milwaukee Repertory Theatre and elsewhere.

From her position in Milwaukee, O'Connor has provided major leadership for the field of nonprofit theatre in the United States. For the League of Resident Theatres (LORT), she has served as president (1984–1987), vice president (1971–1978), chair of the Minority Hiring Committee, and member of the Actors' Equity Negotiating Committee. For the Theatre Communications Group (TCG), she has served as president (1980–1982), member of the board of directors, and member of the Japan Touring Committee. For the National Endowment for the Arts, she has served on the Large Theatres Grants Panel, the Theatre Policy Panel, the architecture program (Cultural Facilities Grants Panel), the international program (Japan Fellowship Panel), the Symposium on Touring, and the Discussion Group/Ongoing Ensembles. She has worked with the International Theatre Institute/United States as a member of its board of directors and as delegate to its World Congress, Madrid, 1981. She has also served on the Ohio Arts Council and the Wisconsin Arts Board. She has held management consultancies for the New American Theatre, the North Carolina Readers' Theatre, the Actors Theatre of St. Paul, and the Arkansas Repertory Theatre. In addition, she has belonged to the American Theatre Association's Theatre Development Commission, the Japan Society Performing Arts Advisory Committee, the Bank of Delaware Commonwealth Awards Committee, the American Arts Alliance board of directors, and many other boards and committees.

O'Connor began her theatre career as an actress at Swarthmore College. She performed in student productions, in a summer non-Equity company in Rome, New York (where she also was a stage manager), and in the summer Tufts Arena Theatre. Her career goal was clearly fixed on theatre at this point, and it became focused on directing when she directed a student musical in her junior year. She went to Tufts University for a master's degree, concentrating on directing. Her thesis on repertory companies in the United States prior to 1955 fixed her sights on becoming an artistic director and founding a repertory company outside New York, preferably one with rotating repertory on the European model. (She has since learned that that model does not necessarily transplant well to this country.) In her thesis research she had a "lifechanging" interview with **Eva Le Gallienne** that showed her "what the power of belief can be" (Personal interview).

O'Connor's subsequent shift from directing to management occurred as she observed the need for management, began doing management work herself, and realized she was both very good at it and very excited by its challenges. But the transition from director to managing director took nearly twenty years. After her marrying Boardman O'Connor in 1955 she went with him to the Old Globe in San Diego, where he had been hired as a designer. She assisted in its production shops and also directed community theatre.

In 1957 the family moved to Chicago, where her husband was first a lighting designer, then an operations manager, for television's Channel 11. There she and her husband, along with two friends, formed the Company of the Four, which was headquartered initially at the First Unitarian Church in Hyde Park, but also performed at the Studebaker Theatre and the University of Chicago. In the first years of its existence it presented twenty productions, of which O'Connor directed eight. The Company of the Four contributed significantly to her career development: she successfully negotiated a part-time contract with Actors' Equity Association (possibly the forerunner of the Chicago Off-Loop Theatre contract, 1972–1983). The company casts parts interracially, and she managed the group because she was the only one at home during the day. She discovered that she loved management, which for her is "making the impossible happen" (Interview).

Although she continued to see herself as a director, she became increasingly involved in management. This transition period from director to manager lasted until 1971. She was stage manager for the Harper Theatre (Chicago) in 1964, after first having been hired as wardrobe mistress. Then she had an Equity stage management assignment in Chicago. In 1965, after massive layoffs at Channel 11, the family moved to Boston, where O'Connor began a significant involvement with the Theatre Company of Boston (David Wheeler, artistic director). She was first a stage manager, then general manager, then associate producer (until 1968), although she continued to direct. In 1968 the family moved to New Orleans, where she worked briefly in audience development and public relations for the Repertory Theatre of New Orleans. When the O'Connors divorced, she went north with the children to work for a company in Rhode Island; the company dissolved before she got there. As a result, she took a management job at the Cherry County Playhouse, and returned in 1969 to Boston as producer for the Theatre Company.

In 1971 she accepted a management challenge from the Cincinnati Playhouse—to eradicate a six-hundred-thousand-dollar debt. She met the challenge and stopped thinking of directing as a career; she was now clearly a manager. In 1974 she joined the Milwaukee Repertory Theatre, a company that "is not far from what I always wanted" (Interview).

O'Connor feels that she is now doing exactly what she wants to do: meeting the challenges of winning board and audience support for a theatre's vision and having a real effect on the artistic future of a significant theatre. The Milwaukee Repertory Theatre has become a pacesetter for other American resident companies in its commitment to new play development in a laboratory theatre, its maintenance of a resident company, its close interactions with the business community, its introduction of Japanese and European writers and theatres, its diverse and challenging seasons, and its commitment to interracial casting. Her own long devotion to interracial casting has helped educate Milwaukee audiences and is providing a vision for other theatres. She argues that "theatres are denying themselves great talent . . . if they ignore minority talent" (Interview). Sara O'Connor has been a driving force behind the building of the Milwaukee Repertory's new theatre complex which opened for the 1988 season.

In recent years, O'Connor has tried her hand at translating plays from the French. With Daniel A. Stein, she translated *The Workroom* by Jean-Claude Grumberg, published in 1984 by Samuel French. The play has been produced in Baltimore, Seattle, Los Angeles, New York, Little Rock, Philadelphia, and Evanston. Her translation of *At Fifty, She Discovered the Sea* by Denise Chalem was produced Off-off-Broadway. *Numbered Crosses* by Georges Duhamel was adapted by John Leicht for the Lab Theatre at the Milwaukee Repertory (1985–1986). *Them* (*On Vacation* and *The Brawl*) by Gremberg was produced by the Court Street Theatre at the Milwaukee Repertory Theatre in 1985. *A Flea in Her Ear* by Georges Feydeau was produced during the 1986–1987 Milwaukee Repertory Theatre season and at StageWest, Springfield, Massachusetts.

Sara O'Connor's expertise in theatre management is often sought, and she has spoken at many conferences and symposia both in the United States and abroad. In June 1988 her contributions to the theatre were recognized at the Theatre Communications Group's National Conference when she was named the 1988 recipient of the Zeisler Award for distinguished service in administration to the nonprofit professional theatre. The Theatre Communication Group's director Peter Zeisler noted that "O'Connor has made a career practicing the fine art of theatre management and, in the process, has inspired generations of younger arts managers."

Sara O'Connor has written an article on American theatre in a Japanese publication (unavailable in this country). Her article on fiscal management was published by *Theatre Crafts* (February 1981). An account of her receiving the Zeisler Award appears in *American Theatre* (September 1988). Most of the information about O'Connor used in this essay was secured by a personal interview with her by the author.

Linda Walsh Jenkins

OLIVER, Edith (August 11, 1913–): drama critic, was born in New York City, the daughter of Samuel and Maude (Biow) Goldsmith. She attended Horace Mann High School, graduated in 1931, and then attended Smith College, Northampton, Massachusetts, from 1931 until 1933. She later studied acting privately with Mrs. Patrick Campbell, Laura Elliott, and Frances Robinson Duff. She started her acting career at the Berkshire Playhouse in Stockbridge, Massachusetts, and became assistant to the director (1932–1933). She acted on radio programs like *Gangbusters, True Detective, Crime Doctor,* and *Philip Morris Playhouse* from 1937 until 1941 (frequently using her low-pitched voice to portray gun molls) and later branched out into casting for the Biow Advertising Agency (1944–1946) and writing and producing radio quiz shows (*Take It or Leave It, The 64 Dollar Question,* 1940–1952).

She began her career in journalism in 1948 when she joined the editorial staff of *The New Yorker.* During a staff shakeup in 1961 she became that magazine's Off-Broadway critic, a position she still holds. She is one of a relatively small number of women critics for New York publications and is unique in the length of her tenure. She is a member of the New York Drama Critics Circle and New Drama Forum, as well as the National Arts Club, the Cosmopolitan Club, and the Coffee House. She has periodically served on the juries for the Pulitzer Prize and the *Village Voice* Off-Broadway (Obie) awards and since 1972 has been a dramaturg each summer at the National Playwrights Conference at the Eugene O'Neill Theatre Center in Waterford, Connecticut.

Edith Oliver's reviews are invariably succinct, perceptive, and appreciative of new talent. Through them she has become an influential figure in the avant-garde American theatre. She has brought to the attention of nationwide cosmopolitan readers the Off-Broadway works of emerging American playwrights, among them Sam Shepard, **Marsha Norman**, and **Wendy Wasserstein**, and she has done this consistently for over two decades.

Edith Oliver's criticisms have not been collected, and it is necessary to refer to many issues of *The New Yorker* for a complete view of her work. Biographical information is available in M. E. Comtois, *Contemporary American Theatre Critics* (1977); *Who's Who in the Theatre* (1981); and *Who's Who in America, 1984–1985*, Vol. II (1984).

Gayle Austin

ORDWAY, Sally (January 5, 1939–): playwright, was born in Lafayette, Alabama. The daughter of Charles B. Ordway, a chemist, and Mary (Tucker) Ordway, a teacher, Sally Ordway attended Hollins College, where she received her Bachelor of Arts degree in 1959. She was awarded an American Broadcasting Corporation Fellowship in writing for the camera at the Yale Drama School, 1967–1968. During this time she completed a short documentary film, *Street Corner*, about the corner of Eighth Street and Sixth Avenue in New York City. After attending Hunter College of the City University of New York, Ordway received her Master of Arts degree in theatre in 1970. Ordway has held numerous jobs in theatrical production. Although she taught English at Mitchell Junior College, New Haven, Connecticut, from 1967 to 1975, her main work has been as a playwright.

Ordway is a member of the Dramatists Guild and the Authors League of America. Her membership in the New York Redstockings, a radical feminist association, influenced her philosophy and her writings. One of the original members of the Westbeth Playwrights' Feminist Collective, formed initially in 1970 as a tenants' collective at the Westbeth Artists' Residence in New York City, Ordway contributed frequently to this group's readings. Actor-tenants read plays written by playwright-residents to help the playwrights better understand and develop their plays. Gradually the consciousness-raising of the group led to the writing and production of plays about women. The first play actually produced by the Westbeth Playwrights' Feminist Collective (consisting of Sally Ordway, **Susan Yankowitz**, Dolores Walker, Gwendolyn Gunn, Patricia Horan, and Chryse Maile) was *Rape-In* at the Assembly Theatre in May of 1971. Another major production of Westbeth, *Up! An Uppity Review* (March 1972), dealt with the problems created by the roles women are forced to play. As a part of this cabaret production Ordway contributed *Family, Family*, a short piece that follows the growth of Margaret, the daughter of a nuclear family, from childhood to womanhood. Innovatively, male performers played the parts of Margaret and the Mother, and female performers played the roles of Father and Son in order to strengthen the gender differences. As an active member of Westbeth until 1974, Ordway wrote sections of *We Can Feed Everybody Here*, *Sex Warfare*, and *All Them Women* (January 1974). The latter included work by **Megan Terry** in addition to the members of Westbeth. After 1974 Ordway moved away from cabaret theatre, the type of writing produced by the Westbeth group, and began work on her long play, *S.W.A.K.*

Ordway joined with Susan Yankowitz, Helen Duberstein, Richard Foreman, Mario Fratti, Arthur Sainer, Robert Patrick, and others to form the Playwrights' Cooperative in 1972. This group organized as a united front to help produce works by group members. However, Stanley Nelson in *The Scene/2* (December 18, 1974) points out that the cooperative was formed to compete with the New York Theatre Strategy. In an interview, Ordway confirmed Nelson's contention. She also noted that for Off-off-Broadway, "knowing someone" helped a playwright get produced (Personal interview, 1976).

Ordway's plays have been produced quite extensively. *Free! Free! Free!*, produced in the spring of 1965 at Theatre Genesis in New York, was later produced in a full-length version at Hunter College of the City University of New York in the spring of 1969 as part of their Playwrights' Project. In September 1966, Theatre Genesis produced *There's a Wall Between Us, Darling*. This short play, representative of Ordway's themes, presents a wife, Celia, during the final stages of walling up her husband, Sam, into a section of their cellar, having decided to wipe the slate clean and begin anew. Other plays by Ordway present similar themes, such as the friction between the sexes and the problem of roles established for women by society, especially by men. Her plays concern the maturing of the individual and the adaptations people make when faced with problems. Set in a Barbie Doll boudoir, *Playthings*, presented at the Theatre for the New City, attacks the Barbie Doll that teaches girls to be consumers and sex objects. *Sex Warfare*, produced by Westbeth (1974), presents a twenty-minute history of women that documents the historical change from matriarchy to patriarchy.

In November of 1971 the New York Theatre Ensemble presented *The Lay of the Land*, which included four short plays by Ordway: *We Agree*, *Australia Play*, *Movie, Movie on the Wall*, and *San Fernando Valley*. The last two plays form the East and West Coast sections of the play published as *Cross Country* in *Scripts 2* (December 1971). Selected as a member of the O'Neill Theater Center's National Playwrights Conference in Waterford, Connecticut, Ordway presented *A Passage through Bohemia* (Summer 1966) and *Movie, Movie on the Wall* (Summer 1968). The latter play was also produced at the Mark Taper Forum in Los Angeles (Fall 1968). The recipient of fellowships at Yaddo, MacDowell Colony, and the Edward Albee Foundation, Sally Ordway also received a National Endowment for the Arts grant and a New York Arts Council Grant in 1978.

Two other notable short plays by Sally Ordway are *Crabs* (produced at the Company Theatre of Los Angeles in May 1972, and at the Almost Free Theatre in London in 1973) and *The Hostess* (produced in April 1975, by the Westbeth Playwrights' Feminist Collective and later by the Royal Court Theatre, London). In the full-length play *S.W.A.K.*, cinematically structured and presented at the Phoenix Theatre (1978) and Playwrights Horizons, New York City, Ordway moved wholly away from the cabaret style of writing. In *S.W.A.K.* ("sealed with a kiss"), Ordway began to explore her southern roots. The play concerns three single New York women who struggle to cope with unloving lovers, intense therapy, mother-daughter relationships, and the discovery of their new strengths. It uses facts, "herstory," and myths to inform and enlighten the audience with a new perspective on women. Other plays by Ordway include *A Desolate Place Near a Deep Hole*, produced at Café Cino in August 1965, and *Allison*, which formed part of the Peace Festival at Westbeth and at the Music Barn Theatre (1970). *The Chinese Caper* was performed at the Theatre for the New City (1973), while *War Party* and *Memorial Day* were produced at St. Clement's Theatre in 1974. In 1979 a staged reading of *Film Festival* was presented by Playwrights Horizon. In 1980 *Promise Her Anything* was presented by the Columbia University Theatre in New York, and in 1981 *No More Chattanooga Choo Choo* was given by the Women's Project at the American Place Theatre. In 1982 *A Pretty Passion* was presented by Women's Interart and *Binoculars* by the Amateur Comedy Club, both in New York City. In 1984 and 1985 Ordway wrote *Translators* and *Ike and Mamie, A Nuclear Romance*, respectively.

Ordway has received favorable reviews for her plays. Michael Feingold of the *Village Voice* (June 21, 1973) liked her futuristic twist to the old revue-sketch situation of husband and wife bickering in *San Fernando Valley*. He commented appreciatively about the "warmth hidden under the acerbic jabs at people." Howard Thompson of the *New York Times* (May 26, 1973) found *Family, Family* the "freshest, funniest, and best sketch" of the short plays presented by the Joseph Jefferson Theater Company in May 1973. Marilyn Stasio of *Cue* (June 12, 1971) described Ordway's work as possessing "wry, insightful humor" and as being "really sophisticated in its grasp of dramatic character." To her, *Crabs* was a "howlingly funny look at emancipated woman" and *There's A Wall Between Us, Darling* was "a delightfully bitchy view of marriage." The two plays, Stasio summarized, "mark Ordway as a playwright with a genuine, even remarkable talent."

Most of Sally Ordway's plays have not been published. The exceptions are *There's a Wall Between Us, Darling*, which appeared in *Yale/Theatre* (Summer 1968); *Crabs* and *Cross Country* in *Scripts/2* (December 1971); and *Family, Family* in *The Scene/2* (1974). Some of the plays are available from the Joe Cino Memorial Collection at the New York Public Library Performing Arts Research Center at Lincoln Center. Ordway also wrote a screenplay from a novel, *Wait 'til the Sun Shines, Nellie*, for Rastar Productions (Columbia Pictures) in 1969. For additional information about Ordway, see Helen Krich Chinoy and Linda Walsh Jenkins, eds., *Women in American Theatre* (1981, 1987); and Albert Poland and Bruce Mailman, eds., *The Off-Off Broadway Book* (1972). See also "Westbeth Playwrights' Feminist Collective" in *Women's Movement Media: A Source*

Guide by Cynthia Ellen Harrison (1975) and "Westbeth Playwrights' Feminist Collective" in *The New Woman's Survival Catalog*, Kirsten Grimstad and Susan Rennie, eds. (1973). Reviews include Michael Feingold, "Doris Day Among the Buffoons," *Village Voice* (June 21, 1973); Howard Thompson, "Theater: An Original?," *New York Times*, (May 26, 1973); Marilyn Stasio, "Rape-In: An Evening of Feminist Theater," *Cue* (June 12, 1971); Toni Blevins, "Town Hall Evening of Feminist Theater," *Soho: The Weekly News* (December 20, 1973). Additional material for this entry was obtained in an interview with Sally Ordway at the Westbeth Residence, November 22, 1976. Sally Ordway is included in *Contemporary Authors*, Vols. 57–60 (1976); *National Playwrights Directory* (1981); *Who's Who in the Theatre* (1981); and *Contemporary Theatre, Film, and Television*, Vol. I (1984).

Carolyn Karis

OWENS, Rochelle (April 2, 1936–): poet, playwright, translator, critic, and writer of short fiction, was born Rochelle Bass in Brooklyn, New York, the daughter of Maxwell Bass, a postal clerk, and Molly (Adler) Bass. She attended public schools in New York City and later took courses at the Herbert Berghof Studio and the New School for Social Research. In 1956 she married David Owens; they were divorced in 1960. In 1962 she married George Economou, a poet and university professor. Before gaining success as a poet and playwright, Owens worked as a saleswoman for Park-Bernet Galleries, as a store detective, and as a perfume tester for a whaling company.

Owens has achieved success both as a playwright and as a poet. Her poetry, originally published in magazines and journals, has been collected into several published volumes: *I Am the Babe of Joseph Stalin's Daughter: Poems, 1961–1971* (1972), *Poems from Joe's Garage* (1973), *The Joe Eighty-Two Creation Poems* (1974), *Joe Chronicles—Part 2* (1979), and *Salt and Core* (1982). For playwriting she received a Rockefeller Foundation grant in 1965. In 1967 she received the *Village Voice* Off-Broadway (Obie) Award for Distinguished Playwriting for *Futz!* She was awarded an American Broadcasting Corporation Fellowship in film writing at the Yale School of Drama in 1968 and a Guggenheim Fellowship in 1971. Owens's *The Karl Marx Play* was nominated for an Obie Award for best play in 1973.

Owens has been called one of the most inventive of the new playwrights. Clive Barnes termed her a "Baroque artist" whose plays shock "to further a moral cause" (*New York Times*, June 14, 1968). However, Ross Wetzsteon in the *Village Voice* (December 19, 1968) said that she was the "anthropologist of the impulses," a poet-playwright in a Brechtian style and with the quality of Jean Genêt. Most critics have seen her work as being closely aligned with Antonin Artaud's theatre of cruelty: some have called her a female Marquis de Sade. Henry Hewes in his critique of *Beclch*, produced at Theatre of the Living Arts, Philadelphia, January 1967, noted that the play contained "much ruthless and horrifying detail," but the "events emerge with a sense of the poetic" (*Saturday Review*, January 7, 1967). Rochelle Owens stated her philosophy of playwriting and theatre in her introduction to *Spontaneous Combustion* (1972): "We won't be decorative playwrights, laying on falseness over the false emotional structure of false people: authentic theatre oscillates between joyousness and fiendishness. . . . We want to ease the human soul's tension. We write for the sake of your spirit. . . . We are mystics; we are contrary people.''

Owens's plays break usual stereotypes. They are about the total human experience, not about sexism or any other ''ism.'' Her wild imagination and fantasy are displayed in the contents of the plays that are sometimes very ugly and horrifying. She explores the subjects of bestiality, of the phony bloodlessness of civilization, of obsession and fetishism, of power and domination (the need to rule and to be ruled, treated in sexual, racial, religious, and political terms), of murder, of sex, and of love. In *Futz!* (first produced in Minneapolis at the Tyrone Guthrie Theatre Workshop in 1965, later performed at the La Mama Experimental Theatre Club in New York in 1967, and made into a controversial film in 1969), the sexually repressed inhabitants of a rural community destroy Cyrus Futz when they discover his physical passion for his pig, Amanda. In *Beclch* (first produced in 1967, at the Philadelphia Theatre of the Living Arts and televised later), the title character Beclch (pronounced ''beklek'' and meaning ''roots'') convinces her husband Yago to contract elephantiasis so that he may become king of the African natives. In *Kontraption* (1970) Abdal and Hortten murder Strauss, the German laundry man, and calmly roll a cigarette. The Chemist, the powerful changer, transforms Abdal and Hortten into ''contraptions.'' *Istanboul*, three-time Obie winner (first produced at Judson Poets' Theater in New York in September 1965), presents a Crusader named Godfrigh who buys a shrine on the road to Jerusalem and installs a resident holy person whom he calls St. Mary of Egypt. She is a particularly hairy woman who fulfills both his commercial needs and his own personal lust.

Owens's plays draw upon primitive myths and on Biblical and mythological impulses: *Beclch* evokes an African white mother goddess with overtones of Greek mythology; *Istanboul* mixes Saracen and Christian images. Thus they appeal to the psychic and mythic soul of audiences. Although they have many diverse scenes and exotic locales, the narrative structure is straightforward and actually rather conventional. It is the settings, the situations, the characters' actions and motivations, the images and symbols that are surreal. Some of her works, such as the plays in her second anthology, *The Karl Marx Play and Others* (1974), and the play *Emma Instigated Me* (1976), seem at first to be more historical and less surreal, but their themes and concepts still show Owens's unusual mind and creative powers. In *The Karl Marx Play* (first presented at the American Place Theatre in 1973), Owens presents Marx as a Jewish black with a Chinese collaborator, Frederick Engels. *Emma Instigated Me* presents the historical Emma Goldman, the nineteenth-century revolutionary and anarchist, in confrontation with the author who has been researching the character of Emma for thirty-eight years. The play was produced at the American Place Theatre in 1976. It uses recorded voices, a play within a play within a play, and the distortion of history to present truth.

There have been productions of Owens's plays throughout the world. The chief early producers of her plays were the Judson Poets' Theatre (*String Game*, 1965), the Tyrone Guthrie Theatre in Minneapolis (*Futz!*, 1965), the La Mama Experimental Theatre Club in New York (*The Queen of Greece* and *Homo*, 1969), and the American Place Theatre (*The Karl Marx Play*, 1973, and *Emma Instigated Me*, 1976). Her plays have been seen in Stockholm, at the Edinburgh Festival, and at the Ambience Lunch-Hour Theatre Club in London. In 1981 the Theatre for the New City presented her one-character play, *Chucky's Hunch*, about a broken 1950s artist writing recriminating letters to his third ex-wife.

Owens was one of the founding members of *Scripts/Performance*, two magazines of the theatre arts, first appearing in 1971, but no longer published. She was on the Advisory Board for the *Performing Arts Journal*, which started publication in the Spring of 1976, and which published the script of *Emma Instigated Me*. She was also a founding member of the Women's Theatre Council (1972), an organization formed so that women playwrights might have a greater chance of being produced. The WTC also included **Julie Bovasso**, **Megan Terry**, **Maria Irene Fornés**, **Rosalyn Drexler**, and **Adrienne Kennedy**. Owens was also a founding member of the New York Theatre Strategy (1972).

Rochelle Owens has earned the respect of many critics. Some have been disappointed with productions of her works, but this disappointment seems to arise more from the production than from the writing. William Packard writes, "Surely Rochelle Owens is doing something unique in the American theatre, writing plays that take place in the never-never-land of unconscious allegory. She is exploring the archetypes of all our fantasies and projections, and in doing so she achieves extraordinary insights into how women see men. This is very difficult to portray effectively on stage. And now that I think back on the three plays by Rochelle Owens that I have seen produced, I have a disquieting sense that her work has not yet been fully explored in stage terms" (*Contemporary Authors*, First Revision, 1976).

Owens's plays can be found in several publications: *Futz! and What Came After*, with Introduction by Jerome Rothenberg (1968), contains *Futz!*, *The String Game*, *Beclch*, *Istanboul*, and *Homo*. *Spontaneous Combustion: Eight New American Plays*, edited by Owens (1972), contains an introduction by Owens and *He Wants Shih!* *The Karl Marx Play and Others* (1974) contains an introduction titled "Mustard Gas: Interaction," *The Karl Marx Play*, *Kontraption*, *He Wants Shih!*, *Farmer's Almanac*, *Coconut Folk-Singer*, and *O.K. Certaldo*. *Emma Instigated Me* is published in *Performing Arts Journal* (Spring 1976); *The Queen of Greece* in *Yale/Theatre* (Summer 1964); *The Widow and the Colonel* in *The Best Short plays 1977* (1977); *Mountain Rites* in *The Best Short Plays 1978* (1978); and *Chucky's Hunch* in *Wordplays 2* (1983). *A Game of Billiards* and *Who Do You Want, Peire Vidal?* are available in manuscript. Reviews of *Futz!* by Douglas Watt, Richard Watts, Jack Kroll, and Martin Gottfried appear in *New York Theater Critics Reviews* (1968). Other reviews of plays include Henry Hewes, "Futz!", *Saturday Review* (June 22, 1968); Ross Wetzsteon, "*Beclch*," *Village Voice* (December 19, 1968); Henry Hewes, "*Beclch*," *Saturday Review* (January 7, 1967); Richard L. Fisher, "*Beclch*," the *Montgomery Post*, Norristown, Pennsylvania, (December 25, 1966); Julius Novick, "Theatre

Afield, Cruelty in Philadelphia (*Beclch*)," *Village Voice* (January 5, 1967); Elenore Lester, "Only Rochelle Escaped to Tell Us," *New York Times* (July 21, 1968); Irving Wardle, "The Plays of Rochelle Owens," *Times Saturday Review* (London) (December 7, 1968); Joan Goulianos, "Getting rid of thou shalt not," *Village Voice* (February 4, 1971); Michael Feingold, "Commedia, Clutching, Futz! and Fun," *Yale/Theatre* (Winter, 1968); and "People: the Play's Her Thing," *Viva* (December, 1976). *The Off-Off-Broadway Book: The Plays, People, Theatre* (1972), ed. Albert Poland and Bruce Mailman, contains *Futz!* and biographical information. See also Julius Novick, *Beyond Broadway* (1968); Robert Brustein, *The Third Theatre* (1969); and Walter Kerr, *God on the Gymnasium Floor* (1969). An interview with Owens is included in *Interviews with Contemporary Women Playwrights*, ed. Kathleen Betsko and Rachel Koenig (1978). The Boston University Mugar Library and the library of the University of California at Davis contain collections of Rochelle Owens's manuscripts and correspondence. Owens is listed in *Contemporary Authors*, Vols. 17–20 (1976); *Notable Names in the American Theatre* (1976); *Contemporary Literary Criticism*, Vol. 8 (1978); *American Women Writers*, Vol. III (1981); *Who's Who in the Theatre* (1981); and *Contemporary Dramatists* (1982).

Carolyn Karis

—— P ——

PAGE, Geraldine (October 22, 1924–June 13th, 1987): actress and famous member of the Actors Studio, was born in Kirksville, Missouri, to Pearl (Maize) Page and Leon Page, a doctor. After graduating from the Englewood High School in Chicago, she attended the Goodman Theatre Dramatic School (1942–1945), thus permanently shifting from her teen-age devotion to music and the piano to a career in acting for theatre, film, and television. Her first public appearance on stage had been in 1940, in a performance of *Excuse My Dust* at the Englewood Methodist Church in Chicago—an experience that convinced her that acting was more rewarding than playing the piano and required less work. Upon finishing at the Goodman School she went to New York City, making her first stage appearance there on October 25, 1945, at the Blackfriars Guild in their production of *Seven Mirrors*. She also undertook further study with **Uta Hagen** at the Berghof Studios and at the Theatre Wing School, and she studied voice with Alice Hermes. She returned to Illinois for summer stock seasons at Lake Zurich and at Marengo, where Vincent Canby remembers seeing her for the first time in *Rain* (*New York Times*, April 6, 1946). She spent two seasons at the Woodstock (Illinois) Winter Playhouse (1947–1949).

Page was married twice: first to Alexander Schneider, and then for the last twenty-five years to Rip (Elmore) Torn. They had three children, now grown: their daughter Angelica and twin sons Anthony and Jonathan.

It was her performance as Alma in Tennessee Williams' *Summer and Smoke* that catapulted Page into public prominence. In her first appearance with the new Circle in the Square company in New York, in the fall of 1951, she played the Pagan Crone in Garcia Lorca's *Yerma* to no critical notice whatsoever. But in April 1952, Brooks Atkinson of the *New York Times* journeyed down to Sheridan Square in Greenwich Village and was struck by her performance in

Summer and Smoke. Thus was Geraldine Page "discovered," and the next year her name was in lights on Broadway. She played Lily Barton in Vina Delmar's *Midsummer*, opening at the Vanderbilt Theatre on January 21, 1953, winning for her the Theatre World Award, the Donaldson Award, and the New York Drama Critics Award for that season. From that date she was seldom out of public view. She created a memorable series of characterizations on the stage, acted in a long list of films, and appeared on television. She had a long and illustrious career.

On the strength of her discovery and her personal triumph in *Midsummer*, she did a series of "Best Plays" on radio in 1953—*Summer and Smoke*, *Ethan Frome*, and *The Glass Menagerie*—and was invited by Hollywood to play opposite John Wayne in *Hondo*, a Warner Brothers 3-D epic that earned her an Academy of Motion Picture Arts (Oscar) nomination as best supporting actress for 1954. She would not appear again in Hollywood for seven years. She returned to Broadway to open in *The Immoralist* on February 8, 1954, at the Royale Theatre; then played Lizzie Curry in *The Rainmaker*, opening at the Cort Theatre on October 28, 1954, with a performance described as "fresher than the play and equally funny" (*New York Times*, October 29, 1954). At the close of the Broadway run, the show toured through the spring of 1955 and played in London in May 1956, after Page's short run in *The Innkeepers* at the John Golden Theatre in New York in February 1956. The last three months of 1956 she spent at the Studebaker Theatre in Chicago, playing in repertory in *Desire Under the Elms*, *A Month in the Country*, and *The Immoralist*. In July of 1958 Page replaced Margaret Leighton in *Separate Tables*, which was playing at the Music Box Theatre in New York, and she went on tour with the show.

Then came another triumph with a cluster of awards. The play was Tennessee Williams's *Sweet Bird of Youth* (Martin Beck Theatre, March 10, 1959), for which she won both the Donaldson and the New York Drama Critics awards and a nomination for the Antoinette Perry (Tony) Award, as well as Chicago's Sarah Siddons Award. Playing the flamboyant Alexandra del Lago opposite Paul Newman, she was called "fabulous" by Brooks Atkinson (*New York Times*, March 10, 1959). The show ran for 375 performances; then Page and Newman went to Hollywood for the MGM film version, which was released in 1962, and for which Page won her third Oscar nomination. (Her second was for Alma in *Summer and Smoke*, with Laurence Harvey, released by Paramount in 1961.)

During her long career, Page appeared in dozens of stage plays and a long list of films, rather consistently alternating work in the theatre and in Hollywood. She was nominated for the Oscar seven times, finally winning the best actress award in 1985 for her sensitive performance in *The Trip to Bountiful*. It was in 1982 that she won the Tony for her performance in *Agnes of God* on Broadway. She had earlier twice won television's Emmy Award for her performance in ABC's *A Christmas Memory* (1966–1967) and *The Thanksgiving Visitor* (1968–1969). But awards are a mere by-product to this actress. She said: "I would like to live to be about 132 and to work all the time. . . . My total ambition is to follow one project with another project and another project—an endless succession in which I can use different facets of the human state and communicate it and learn as I'm going" (Amitin interview, February 28, 1983). From her earliest triumphs to her latest she succeeded in an amazing variety of roles, bringing to each an unusual intensity and commitment. One of her most interesting projects was her involvement with the Actors Studio in the 1960s, when its director, Lee Strasberg, mounted Studio productions on Broadway. Page played Nina Leeds in Eugene O'Neill's *Strange Interlude* under the direction of José Quintero (Hudson Theatre, March 11, 1963) for 94 performances; and Olga, then Masha, in Anton Chekhov's *The Three Sisters*, directed by Strasberg himself (Morosco Theatre, June 22, 1964) for 119 performances. She particularly enjoyed the latter because, as she said some years later, "People like Chekhov and Shakespeare are really expressing more densely and more complicatedly, getting more information across per second on stage than most about humanness: who we are and what we do" (Amitin interview, February 28, 1983).

Additional leading roles on Broadway were in *P. S. I Love You* (1964), *The Great Indoors* (1966), *Black Comedy* (1967), *Angela* (1969), *Absurd Person Singular* (1974), *Clothes for a Summer Hotel* (1980), *Mixed Couples* (1981), and *Blithe Spirit* (1987). She also performed in other venues. She appeared at the Locust Theatre in Philadelphia in *The Umbrella* (1962); at Philadelphia's Playhouse in the Park in Chekhov's *The Marriage Proposal* and *The Boor* (1971); at the Academy Festival in Lake Forest, Illinois, as Regina Giddens in **Lillian Hellman**'s *The Little Foxes* (1974) and Blanche DuBois in Williams's *A Streetcar Named Desire* (1976); at the Hudson Guild Theatre in New York as Tekla in August Strindberg's *Creditors* (1977); and at the Promenade Theatre in New York as Lorraine in Sam Shepard's *A Lie of the Mind* (1985). She was a member of The Mirror Repertory Company, an acclaimed Off-Broadway group, and the Sanctuary Theatre, an acting ensemble founded by Page and her husband Rip Torn. Page based her acceptance of film roles on whether or not the character she was being invited to play was an interesting one that she would enjoy doing. She expressed her attitude toward film acting while working on Woody Allen's *Interiors* (United Artists, 1978), for which she won an Oscar nomination as best actress. She says, "As I explained to Mary Beth Hurt, in film you have no responsibility. Say to yourself all day, 'it's not my fault.' You must constantly remind yourself, 'I had nothing to do with this, and its up to them to paste it together in a way that makes sense.' Just go ahead and enjoy whatever task he [Woody Allen] sets up. Let *him* figure it out" (Amitin interview, February 28, 1983). In such a fashion she obviously enjoyed her small role in *Pete 'n Tillie* (Universal, 1972), for which she was again nominated for a best supporting actress Award, as she had been for the role of the mother in Frank Coppola's *You're a Big Boy Now* (Warner, 1967). At last, in 1985, Geraldine Page was awarded an Oscar for her role as Carrie Watts in the film *The Trip to Bountiful*.

Geraldine Page died of a heart attack on June 13, 1987. She was appearing on Broadway as Madame Arcate in *Blithe Spirit* at the time of her death.

Page's long and active career was marked by her constant curiosity about human characteristics as embodied in a variety of roles. A devoted student of Stanislavsky and "The Method" as practiced at the Actors Studio, she once said, "Stan the Man. I'm so fond of him. He wrote all the stuff down . . . so you can keep working at it. After I graduated from Goodman I assumed . . . that I knew all about it. And then to find out that if I studied for the next ninety years I'd just be scratching the surface was divine. It's like suddenly being handed a bottomless cup" (*Tulane Drama Review*, Winter 1964, p. 130). This attitude, which Page maintained throughout her career, gave zest to her performances. Perhaps the final word on Page belongs to Tennessee Williams, in whose plays she performed so brilliantly: "She is the most disciplined and dedicated of actresses, possibly the one that fate will select as the American Duse" (*Where I Live*, 1978, p. 129).

A long interview with Page, "The Bottomless Cup" by Richard Schechner, in the *Tulane Drama Review* for Winter 1964, is very revealing of Page's methods of work. It is reprinted in Helen Krich Chinoy's *Actors on Acting* (1970). The unpublished interview (February 28, 1983) with Mark Hall Amitin shows that Page's work methods and points of view remained fairly constant throughout her career. Vincent Canby's feature article "Out of Marengo, Illinois, and Bound for Glory" (*New York Times*, April 6, 1986) is an interesting assessment of her career. Reviews of her numerous stage appearances can be found in the various chronological volumes of the *New York Times Theatre Reviews* and of the *New York Drama Critics Reviews*. An announcement of Page's death appeared on the first page of the *New York Times* on June 14, 1987. The next day the *New York Times* published her obituary and an appreciation of Page written by the drama critic Mel Gussow. Geraldine Page is included in *Current Biography, 1953* (1954); *The Biographical Encyclopaedia and Who's Who of the American Theatre* (1966); William C. Young, *Famous Actors and Actresses on the American Stage*, Vol. II (1975); *Notable Names in the American Theatre* (1976); *Who's Who in the Theatre* (1981); *Who's Who in America, 1984–1985*, Vol. II (1984); *The Oxford Companion to American Theatre* (1984); and *Contemporary Theatre, Film, and Television*, Vol. I (1984).

Vera Mowry Roberts and
Mark Hall Amitin

PARKER, Dorothy Rothschild (August 22, 1893–June 7, 1967): poet, short-story writer, critic, and playwright, was born to parents who lived in New York City but were vacationing at the time of her birth in West End, New Jersey. Her father, Henry Rothschild, who was in the garment industry, was Jewish, and her mother, Eliza A. (Marston) Rothschild, was of Scottish descent. Parker was the youngest of three children by several years and was never close to her older sister and brother. Her mother died when Parker was still a young child, and Rothschild remarried, this time to a woman who was Roman Catholic. In later years the author recalled her urban childhood as unpleasant and stifling and her father and stepmother as oppressive. She began her education, probably through the influence of her stepmother, at the Blessed Sacrament Convent in

New York and subsequently attended and graduated in 1911 from Miss Dana's School in Morristown, New Jersey.

Soon after her father's death in 1912, Parker entered the world of the New York working girl about which she was later to write often in poems and stories. In 1916 she went to work for *Vogue*, writing advertising copy, and the following year joined the staff of *Vanity Fair*. In 1919 she was promoted to drama critic but was dismissed the following year for writing damning reviews that angered the theatrical interests whose advertisements helped to support the magazine. However, she had a sound critical judgment, capable of distinguishing the good work and the fine performance from the mediocre or the bad, a virtue that was in no way diminished by her derisive wit. Certainly she might stoop to wise-cracking, but wit was her forte, and she always wanted to be considered a satirist rather than a mere humorist.

For a few years after her dismissal from *Vanity Fair*, Parker contributed poems, stories, sketches, and reviews to several magazines, including the *Saturday Evening Post*. In 1925, when Harold Ross founded *The New Yorker*, Parker became a member of its staff, writing a variety of things, including drama reviews when regular critic Robert Benchley was on vacation. Although she did not remain a member of the staff after 1926, she was to be associated with *The New Yorker* in one way or another for the rest of her life. For several years she contributed a book review column under the title "Constant Reader" in addition to theatre reviews and short stories, all marked by her keen eye and ear, her clever and satirical touch, and her concise style.

It was during the 1920s that Parker became associated with a number of writers and other intellectuals, including Ross, Benchley, Robert Sherwood, James Thurber, Franklin P. Adams, George S. Kaufman, and **Edna Ferber**. With these friends and others she founded the famous Round Table at the Algonquin Hotel. They met over lunch at a table reserved for them to exchange critical views and humorous anecdotes and other items of wit. Although the number of original members and their identities are disputed, Parker was a prime mover in the organization of the Round Table and is generally recognized as having been their leader until she left the circle in 1930. It is not an exaggeration to say that no greater collection of wits was ever gathered together anywhere in the United States, and the anecdotes that have emanated from their meetings are the stuff of legend.

This period was a time of great friendships and exciting career moves for Dorothy Parker: in 1926 she published her first collection of verse, *Enough Rope*, which became a best seller, and by then she had already had a play produced on Broadway. However, it was also a troubled period in her personal life. In 1917 she had married Edward Pond Parker II. His background and Wall Street job were at odds with her career and her liberal politics, and their troubled union ended in divorce in 1928. During the latter half of the marriage, the author had engaged in several affairs, usually with handsome younger men who, in the view of her friends, often seemed to her friends to be using her. She had undergone an abortion and twice attempted suicide; and as her friend **Lillian Hellman** pointed out, she felt herself to be unworthy, inadequate, a failure. Another major source of bitterness in her life at this point was the execution of Sacco and Vanzetti in 1927. Like other writers—**Edna St. Vincent Millay**, Katherine Anne Porter, and John Dos Passos among them—she had actively campaigned for their lives to be spared and was arrested for her participation in a protest march. At some point she began to drink heavily, a practice that continued until the end of her life and, indeed, probably contributed to her death.

The decade of the 1930s saw Parker involved with Hollywood, writing screenplays, a task that she found not to her liking, but lucrative. There in 1933 she met and married her second husband, Alan Campbell, a screen actor with whom she collaborated on scripts. Their best known efforts for the movies included *Big Broadcast of 1936* (1935), the first *A Star is Born* (1937), *Sweethearts* (1938), and *Mr. Skeffington* (1944). Their best work, perhaps, was the writing of some dialogue and scenes for Lillian Hellman's screenplay of her drama *The Little Foxes* (1941). Despite the work they produced, however, this marriage was surely as turbulent as the first one. They divorced in 1947, then remarried in 1950 and remained together until Campbell's death, apparently by suicide, in 1963. In their early years together, she had become pregnant, but the couple's joy at the prospect of a child ended when she suffered a miscarriage.

Ironically, given the fact of her continued association with the cafe society of New York, Parker continued to be involved in leftist politics, even to the point of openly acknowledging that she was a Communist. During the Hollywood years, she was an active worker with the Screen Actors' Guild's attempt to unionize the film industry. In the late 1930s she went to Spain to work for the Loyalist cause during the Civil War and there demonstrated her abilities as a serious journalist. For these and other political activities, she, like other illustrious writers of the time, was blacklisted in Hollywood in the 1950s and was called to testify before the House Un-American Activities Committee, which cited her for contempt.

Despite personal sorrows and disappointments, however, Parker had a productive career. Between 1926 and 1939, she had published four books of poetry and three collections of short stories in addition to countless reviews of plays and books, humorous sketches, and other short works. Most of her best prose and poetry, of course, is distinguished by her sophisticated, caustic, tough though elegant approach. Her style, sometimes compared favorably to Hemingway's, was always sparse and lean and simple, saying what she had to say in the fewest (but choicest) possible words. Her settings were realistic, her eye for sharp detail made stories such as "Big Blonde" memorable, and her dialogue, among the best by American writers of her time, was credible and convincing. Her themes involved the position of women in a society she often viewed as phony and shallow, the alienation of human beings in the modern world, and the sorrow of love gone wrong. Her satirical analyses of high society people and practices are among the most perceptive of any writer in this country.

The same virtues and strengths are to be found in her association with the theatre. In addition to writing drama reviews for *Vanity Fair* and *The New Yorker* and producing more than twenty screenplays, Parker had a career as a playwright stretching from 1924 to 1956. Her first play, a collaboration with Elmer Rice, was a satirical examination of life in the suburbs titled *Close Harmony*, which opened at the Gaiety Theatre in New York, December 1, 1924, for a brief run. The same year, she produced lyrics for a revue titled *Round the Town*, as she did for another revue, *Shoot the Works*, in 1931. She also wrote a one-act play, *Here We Are*, in 1931. A 1934 revue, *After Such Pleasures*, was adapted by Parker from her own stories. Following the Hollywood period, she wrote a play based on the life of Charles Lamb, *The Coast of Illyria*, which was produced in Dallas, Texas, in 1949. *Ladies of the Corridor*, a collaboration with Arnaud d'Usseau, was her last full-length play. It received a New York production in 1953 but was unsuccessful. In recent years it has been adapted for television in a version that shows the dramatic force the play possesses. Bringing to bear upon her subject matter—the interrelationships of a group of women living in a residence hotel—her feelings and empathy for the problems of some women in the urban environment, their loneliness, their sense of isolation, aimlessness, and often despair, Parker produced a moving dramatic vehicle. The characterization is strong, the dialogue authentic and revealing. *Ladies of the Corridor* in its thematic content seems a fitting final play for her to have created. Her last contribution to American drama, however, occurred in 1956 when, along with John La Touche and Richard Wilbur, she contributed lyrics for the momentous musical *Candide*, with book by Lillian Hellman and with score by Leonard Bernstein.

For the last decade of her life, she produced almost no literature. Her final years were lonely and unhappy. Although she taught English briefly at Los Angeles State University in the early 1960s, she remained for the most part out of the public eye. When she died in 1967, she made one last strong political statement with her will: her entire estate was left to Dr. Martin Luther King, Jr., a man she had never met but whose cause she espoused.

Parker belongs to that group of writers—including figures as diverse as Samuel Johnson and Oscar Wilde—who are remembered more for what they said than for any piece of literature they ever produced. There are, of course, many readers who remember well specific works of Parker's—her short story "Big Blonde," which won the O. Henry Prize, or *Ladies of the Corridor*, perhaps her most successful play—but many more will recall isolated verses ("Men seldom make passes/ At girls who wear glasses") or the conversational one-liners attributed to her. Her sharp tongue and painfully accurate wit, which could pin an unsuspecting victim to the wall in an instant, made her a celebrity and a public figure in the 1930s, and for the last half-century, quoting her puns, epigrams, and putdowns has been a favorite cocktail party pastime among intellectuals. Lillian Hellman devotes one chapter of her autobiographical *An Unfinished Woman* to Parker, her long-time friend and collaborator. Along with delightful anecdotes and quotations, it contains a tribute that reveals much about the woman who hid behind the mask of barbed comments: Dorothy Parker's "view of people was original and sharp, her elaborate over-delicate manners made her a pleasure to live with, she liked books and was generous about writers, and the wit, of course, was so wonderful that neither age not illness ever dried up the spring from which it came fresh each day" (p. 187).

Books by Dorothy Parker include *Enough Rope* (1926), *Sunset Gun* (1928), *Laments for the Living* (1930), *Death and Taxes* (1931), *After Such Pleasures* (1933), *Not So Deep as a Well* (1936), *Here Lies* (1939), *The Portable Dorothy Parker* (1944), and *The Collected Dorothy Parker* (1973). John Keats has written a biography of Parker, *You Might as Well Live: The Life and Times of Dorothy Parker* (1972), and Arthur F. Kinney has written *Dorothy Parker* (1978). See also Lillian Hellman's *An Unfinished Woman: A Memoir* (1969); James R. Gaines, *Wits End: Days and Nights of the Algonquin Round Table* (1977); and Brenda Gill, *Here at The New Yorker* (1975). Alexander Woollcott has a chapter, "Our Mrs. Parker," in *While Rome Burns* (1934). Dorothy Parker's obituary appeared in the *New York Times* (June 8, 1967). Her papers are the property of the National Association for the Advancement of Colored People. Letters and memorabilia are owned by several American university libraries. Most are at the Houghton Library at Harvard University. Parker is listed in *Who Was Who: Vol. VI: 1961–1970* (1972); *Contemporary Authors*, Vols. 93–96 (1980); *American Women Writers*, Vol. III (1981); *Dictionary of Literary Biography, Vol. 11: American Humorists, 1800–1950*, Part 2 (1982); *The Oxford Companion to American Literature* (1983); *The Oxford Companion to American Theatre* (1984); and *Dictionary of Literary Biography, Vol. 45: American Poets, 1880–1945*, First Series (1986).

W. Kenneth Holditch

PARKS, Hildy (March 12, 1926–): actress, writer, producer in partnership with Alexander H. Cohen, was born in Washington, D.C. Named Hilda de Forrest Parks, she was the daughter of Steve McNeill Parks, a high school principal, and Cleo (Scanland) Parks, a concert singer. Hildy, as she was called, was raised in Virginia, graduating from Thomas Jefferson High School in Richmond in 1942 and in 1945 from Mary Washington College of the University of Virginia, completing the degree in three years. Parks would later be honored by Mary Washington College when it gave her its Distinguished Alumnus Award in 1978 and when it elected her to membership in Phi Beta Kappa (1981). Her education continued, even in the midst of a busy theatrical career. From 1963 to 1964 she attended Danbury State Teachers' College in Connecticut, receiving a teaching certificate that she has never used.

Immediately after graduation from Mary Washington College, Hildy Parks went to New York and immersed herself in theatre with a group at the New School for Social Research that was under the supervision of Erwin Piscator. This group, led by Peter Frye, included such young actors as Martin Balsam and Nehemiah Persoff. Parks made her stage debut with this group in John Steinbeck's *Of Mice and Men* (1945). In 1946 she married Sidney Morse, a talent representative. Her Broadway debut was made as Shari in *Bathsheba* (1947) opposite James Mason. Other early Broadway appearances were in Tennessee Williams' *Summer and Smoke* (1948) and *Magnolia Alley* (1949). In 1950 she went to London to appear in *Mister Roberts* with Tyrone Power and Jackie Cooper. Now divorced from her first husband, she married Jackie Cooper, but this marriage also was short-lived. In New York again, Hildy Parks appeared on Broadway in *To Dorothy, a Son* (1951), *Be Your Age* (1953), and *The Tunnel of Love* (1957). She also appeared in William Saroyan's *The Time of Your Life* at the Brussels World's Fair in 1958. At the same time she was performing in such films as *The Night Holds Terror* (Columbia 1955), *Seven Days in May* and *Fail Safe* (Columbia 1964), and *The Group* (United Artists 1966). Television, in the fabled "Golden Age" provided her with frequent appearances on programs such as *Studio One*, *Philco Playhouse*, *Playhouse 90*, *Danger*, *You Were There*, *Omnibus*, and *General Electric Theatre*; and for five years she played a continuing role in the daytime soap opera *Love of Life*.

On February 24, 1956, Parks married her third husband, Alexander H. Cohen, producer, and her life and career began to change direction. Two sons, Gerry and Christopher, and a home in the country outside New York, plus two active theatre careers, necessitated some juggling, some compromise. Cohen suggested that Parks also become his partner in production, and this partnership proved to be successful. For some ten years the family spent half the year in London and half in New York, with Parks working primarily on casting and with writers. In 1967 Cohen decided to produce the annual **Antoinette Perry** (Tony) awards on television from New York and asked his wife to write the show, which she has done annually since then, being credited since 1977 as "Producer/Writer." The Broadway shows that she has co-produced with Cohen include *I Remember Mama* (1980) with Liv Ullmann, *A Day in Hollywood/A Night in the Ukraine* (1981), and the Peter Brook version of *Carmen* (1984). She worked as associate producer on *Baker Street* (1965), *Ivanov* (1966) with John Gielgud and Vivien Leigh, *A Time for Singing* (1966), *Little Murders* (1967), *The Unknown Soldier and His Wife* (1967), *Dear World* (1969) with **Angela Lansbury**, *Home* (1970) with John Gielgud and Ralph Richardson, *Ulysses in Nighttown* (1974) with Zero Mostel, and *Anna Christie* (1977) with Liv Ullmann.

As a television writer in the 1970s, Parks wrote *William* (1973), an introduction to Shakespeare for children, starring John Gielgud, Ralph Richardson, Lynn Redgrave, and Paul Jones, which was shown on television both in England and in the United States. She wrote *A World of Love*, a children's party in the General Assembly of the United Nations, starring Shirley MacLaine, Julie Andrews, Audrey Hepburn, Harry Belafonte, Bill Cosby, and others. She wrote the thirtieth anniversary Emmy Awards show and the week-long celebration, *CBS: On the Air, a Celebration of 50 Years*. A major project in February 1982 was *The Night of 100 Stars*, a three-hour live celebration from the stage of Radio City Music Hall in New York, commemorating the 100th anniversary of the Actors' Fund of America. The show was televised by ABC and was legendary as a feat of endurance for all concerned, including the audience. In 1984 *The Night of 100*

Stars—II was produced, again in Radio City Music Hall. In addition to co-producing, she has also written the Emmy Awards shows of 1984 and 1985.

Any assessment of Hildy Parks's career would have to take into account breadth—theatre, television, and film—and its diversity—acting, writing, and producing. Another the ease with which Parks works with great numbers of highly individualistic, creative persons to produce successful shows. Her own lively intelligence and flexibility, plus her thorough knowledge of theatre's many aspects, have been her greatest strengths. It is no small measure of credit to her that the Tony Awards shows and other specials have received praise from critics and audiences alike for being literate, entertaining, and honest.

For additional information on Hildy Parks, see Daniel Blum, *Theatre World*, Vols. 8 and 9 (1952, 1953); *The Biographical Encyclopaedia and Who's Who of the American Theatre* (1966); *Notable Names in the American Theatre* (1976); and *Contemporary Theatre, Film, and Television*, Vol. I (1984).

Roger Kenvin

PATON, Angela (January 11, 1930–): actress, director, founder and artistic director of the Berkeley Stage Company, was born in Brooklyn, New York, the only child of William Paton and Winnifred (Giles) Paton. Her mother worked as a registered British nurse, and her father was a merchant marine captain in the British navy. Paton graduated from Public School 85 in Brooklyn and the Philadelphia School for Girls, where her stage experience began. Her first acting roles were in the all-girl high school where she played the men's roles "because I was such a strong actress" (Personal interview). Paton continued her acting at the School of the Arts at the Carnegie Institute of Technology (now Carnegie-Mellon University), where she received her Bachelor of Fine Arts degree in 1951. Upon graduation, she was the first actress hired for the new repertory company at Washington's Arena Stage. She worked there until 1952, when she married Robert Goldsby, a young director from the Yale School of Drama. Goldsby accepted a position at Columbia University, and Paton accompanied him to New York, leaving occasionally between 1953 and 1957 to play in professional stock companies in Chicago and along the East Coast.

In 1957 Goldsby became a professor of drama at the University of California at Berkeley. Paton moved with him to the San Francisco Bay Area, where they continue to reside today. From 1957 to 1964, Paton left the theatre world to have three children and to work as a full-time mother. Though Paton and Goldsby spend most of their time in the world of theatre, only their son Matthew has pursued a career on the stage, and he has been cast in a major motion picture. Their oldest child, Wendy, is completing a doctoral degree in chemistry at the University of California, San Diego; and their youngest child, Robert, is in a college chemistry program.

In 1964 Paton returned to the stage to act for **Margaret Webster** one of the leading woman directors of the time. Paton starred in *Antony and Cleopatra* in the Berkeley Greek Theatre to capacity audiences and good reviews. Once back on the stage, Paton accepted the position as a leading actress at San Francisco's American Conservatory Theatre in 1966. She worked there until 1970, playing twelve leading roles in four years, including Mary Tyrone in *Long Day's Journey Into Night*, Olga in *The Three Sisters*, and Gertrude in *Hamlet*. Aside from her performances as Cleopatra, Paton has generally been cast as a of mother, an independent single woman, or in character parts.

A strong actor, both on the stage and off, she decided that she "had a talent for solving dramatic problems" herself and that she could be "helpful to other actors in finding solutions" (Personal interview). So from 1970 to 1974, Paton began directing in Bay Area theatres, primarily at the Berkeley Repertory Company. She directed plays by William Shakespeare, George Bernard Shaw, and Noel Coward. In fact, most of her work in theatre until 1974 was either in the classics or in standard repertory fare. In 1974, being eager to promote new plays and playwrights and tired of "doing what I was told and not doing what I really felt" (Interview), Paton joined her husband in founding the Berkeley Stage Company. This company was dedicated to presenting new plays, using a production style that is an alternative to that of large, commercial Equity theatres. Berkeley Stage Company (BSC) was a ninety-nine-seat Equity waiver house located in a converted garage in the heart of the Berkeley ghetto. In spite of its crude construction and dangerous location, it was one of the most successful small theatres in the Bay Area. In 1975, when BSC was only one year old, it was endowed by a continuing National Endowment for the Arts grant and invited to take its production of David Rabe's *Sticks and Bones* to the Venice Biennial. The theatre began by hiring a staff with government-funded Comprehensive Employment and Training Act (CETA) salaries, but in 1979 it was healthy enough to absorb into its own budget the salaries of its entire full-time staff. In 1976 it began its first season of six productions a year. The 1981–1982 season was an exception and included eleven productions. The theatre was awarded eight Bay Area Theatre Critics Circle Awards and received critical acclaim for many productions in local newspapers as well as in such international journals as the Yale *Theater* magazine and the Berlin *Theater Heute*.

The play selection, determined primarily by Paton and Goldsby, included such European playwrights as Samuel Beckett, Bertolt Brecht, Peter Handke, and Heiner Müller, such American playwrights as David Rabe and Albert Innaurato, and such local playwrights as Michael McClure and Sam Shepard. The plays ranged from realism to modernism and from political drama to light comedy. The criteria for selection included no preference either in political perspective or form of production. The only requirement was that the plays be theatrical and honest. However, like all small theatres that produce new plays, BSC had its share of dissatisfied critics and audiences. In addition, since the theatre company was not an ensemble, it depended on a group of transient directors, actors, and designers, whose sometimes slight loyalty to the company often caused a change in production personnel mid-rehearsal, or even mid-run. It was Paton who then searched for replacements, cajoled them into staying, or did the work herself.

When asked how she was able to keep the theatre together against these odds, she replied that her experience as a mother taught her how to "seem to make concessions without actually making any" (Interview).

Paton also created a unique composition in the staff of her theatre. It was composed equally of men and women; more interestingly, women were placed in positions typically held by men. The production manager was always a woman, and many of the stage managers and designers were women. Many women in the Bay Area wanted to work at BSC because of its demonstrated respect for women.

Paton's acting provided the backbone of support for the theatre. She helped to draw audiences with her performances and brought distinction to the theatre with awards and good reviews, as when she won the Bay Area Critics' outstanding actress award for her role in *Earthworms* by Albert Innaurato. When that production closed, Innaurato took Paton to New York to star in his new Off-Broadway production of *Passione*. The play was so successful that Paton played in it on Broadway at the Morosco Theatre in 1980. Paton's directing was also important to the BSC; her success with McClure's *Minnie the Mouse Singer* led her to direct it Off-off-Broadway.

In addition to providing a full-time professional theatre for adults, Paton created theatre outreach programs in the schools. In 1976 she founded the Poetry Playhouse, which annually produced ten dramatizations of poetry in the Berkeley Public Schools. The program was awarded a National Endowment for the Arts grant as well as three Golden Eagle Awards, given by the Council on International Nontheatrical Events. One of the programs, *Catch A Falling Star*, was bought for National Educational Television. In the 1981–1982 season of productions, Paton starred in two plays and directed one. In spite of all this activity and acclaim, the Berkeley Stage Company began to suffer financial difficulties, and in February 1985 the company closed its doors for lack of funds.

After the Berkeley Stage Company closed, Angela Paton resumed her career as an actress in Los Angeles. She appeared in the opening production of *The Three Sisters* at the Los Angeles Theatre Center and starred in the one-woman show *Elizabeth Dead* by George W. S. Trow at the Stages Theatre. She has also begun working in television in addition to appearing on stage with various West Coast companies. She played Essie Miller in *Ah, Wilderness!* and Mary Tyrone in *Long Day's Journey Into Night* (1988) in Berkeley Theatre productions. She also appeared in *The Sea Gull* at Los Angeles Theatre Center and in Tom Strelich's *Dog Logic* at the South Coast Repertory in Costa Mesa. Hers has been, and continues to be, an active and productive career in the American regional theatre. She is distinguished as an actress as well as a founding artistic director of a significant regional theatre.

Most of the material on Angela Paton and the Berkeley Stage Company was obtained directly from Paton and the theatre's records. Articles and reviews mentioned include "San Francisco und zurück" in *Theater Heute* (October 1980), "Theater in Berkeley" in *Theater* (Fall/Winter 1979), and "*Cement* in Berkeley" in *Brecht-Jahrbuch 1980*.

Reviews of the Berkeley Stage Company productions may be found in the San Francisco *Chronicle* and the *Examiner*, *The Berkeley Barb*, *Express*, and *Gazette* from 1974 to 1985. See also Paton, Angela. "Long Day's Journal: An Actress Chronicles Her Intimate Encounter with O'Neill's Mary Tyrone." *American Theatre* (December 1988).

Sue Ellen Case

PEABODY, Josephine Preston (May 30, 1874–December 4, 1922): playwright and poet most famous for her poetic drama, *The Piper*, was born in Brooklyn, New York, the second of three daughters of Charles Kilham Peabody and Susan Josephine (Morrill) Peabody. Through her paternal grandparents, Francis and Hannah Kilham (Preston) Peabody, she was descended from Francis Peabody, who had come to America in 1635 from St. Albans, England, and settled in Topsfield, Massachusetts. Her first eight years were happy ones, as her parents devoted themselves entirely to developing the artistic sensibilities of their daughters. Mrs. Peabody coached the children in painting and kept them supplied with books by the best authors. The Peabodys, who lived in Brooklyn, were avid New York theatregoers, and the children loved to hear their parents' detailed discussions of the productions they saw. Their father, a merchant who had memorized much of Shakespeare, led the family's favorite before-bedtime activity: acting out scenes from great plays.

The joy went out of Josephine Peabody's childhood after the deaths of her younger sister, Florence, in 1882 and of her father in 1884. Financial hardship forced their mother to take Josephine and her older sister, Marion, to live with their maternal grandmother in Dorchester, Massachusetts. Josephine detested the public school in the suburbs of Boston. Her loneliness at school and her mother's lingering grief over her husband's death left the child to her own resources. She soon turned to writing poetry and, at fourteen, had published seven poems in magazines like *The Woman's Journal*. From 1889 to 1892 she attended Girls' Latin School in Boston, but ill health prevented her graduation. The diary she kept from early childhood until her death reveals a continual longing for books and symphony tickets during those years of poverty.

Her charming request for constructive criticism in 1893 initiated a long correspondence with Horace Scudder, editor of the *Atlantic Monthly*, who first published one of her poems in 1894 and who was instrumental in getting a local philanthropist to support her as a special student at Radcliffe College from 1894 to 1896. Her verse soon appeared in the most important periodicals of the day. Her first book, *Old Greek Folk Stories* (1897), was followed by *The Wayfarers* (1898), the first of her five volumes of poetry; poems also fill out a volume containing her one-act play *Fortune and Men's Eyes* (1900). Her major literary inspiration was the English Renaissance, which she used as the background of her first full-length play, *Marlowe*, published in 1901. It was produced at Radcliffe College in 1905 with George Pierce Baker in the title role. Her choric idyll, *Pan*, was set to music by C. A. E. Harriss and performed at a State Concert in Ottawa in 1904. From 1901 to 1903 she held a lectureship in poetry and literature at Wellesley College, Massachusetts.

On June 21, 1906, Josephine Preston Peabody married Lionel S. Marks, an English-born professor of mechanical engineering at Harvard University. After a trip to England and the Low Countries, they settled in Cambridge, Massachusetts. They had two children, Alison Peabody, born July 30, 1908, and Lionel Peabody, born February 10, 1910. The sixteen years following Josephine Peabody's marriage were the happiest and most productive of her life. Soft-spoken and graceful of manner, she always looked younger than her years; she was often likened to a Dresden china figurine because of her pale complexion and dainty appearance. Long periods of illness in the last years of her life did not deter her from taking part in liberal reform movements; she was an advocate of women's suffrage and of pacifism. In January 1922 she fell into a coma caused by hardening of the arteries leading to the brain. She was able to take up her creative work again that summer but died in December at forty-eight years of age.

Josephine Preston Peabody's most memorable achievement was winning the $1,500 Stratford-on-Avon Shakespeare Memorial Prize in 1910 for her poetic drama *The Piper*. Actor Otis Skinner had suggested that she dramatize for him Robert Browning's poem about the Pied Piper of Hamelin, but Skinner was bound by other commitments when she had completed her play. After fruitless attempts to find an American producer, she heard about a competition for plays in English, prose or poetry, set in any period before 1800. She submitted *The Piper* and eventually received a cable informing her that the play was one of two finalists selected from 315 submissions; the final decision was to be made by the Duke of Argyll. On a whim, she asked Shakespeare what would happen: she opened her bedside volume and pointed to a verse at random. It was from *A Midsummer Night's Dream*: "Not a word of me. All that I will tell you is that the Duke hath din'd. Get your apparel together, good strings to your beards, new ribands to your pumps; meet presently at the palace." This reference to a Duke augured well and seemed even more pointed when her husband came and turned the page to complete the speech: "Every man look o'er his part; for the short and the long is, our play is preferred." She learned of her triumph on March 10, her son's one-month birthday. Her subsequent diary entries were: "March 11, 1910. Cables, telegrams, motors, callers, letters, flowers, all day long. 'Tis much like waking up to find one's self famous. A dizzying dream. Benign and patriotic cab-driver calls after Lionel in the street, 'Professor Marks, your wife's ALL RIGHT.' March 15. And still it keeps on—this delicious unhoped-for thing that people (and papers) take it as an honor for the country, and a Banner for the cause of womankind. Oh—oh—and I wanted to be something or other for these in some manner, some day!" (*Diary*, p. 227).

One condition of the award was that the winner attend the première performance of the play following the annual end-of-April Shakespeare festival. Josephine Peabody traveled to England with Alison, two-month-old Lionel, and a nurse, while her husband finished his academic term. Using her "necromantic method," she called on Shakespeare to see if her play would be a success, but the random selection, from *Richard III*, seemed inappropriate: "Edward, my lord, thy son, our king, is dead!" She wrote to her husband that Shakespeare was not a dependable prophet after all. Then came the news of King Edward VII's death and the production was postponed until summer. Marks joined his wife and they traveled in Switzerland, leaving the children with his parents in Birmingham. In August, as a special privilege, the infant Lionel was christened in the Stratford Church "in the *old* font, where Shakespeare himself and his own children were christened, and which only *one* other baby had been permitted to use for 150 years!" (*Diary*, p. 234).

The Piper opened in the Stratford Memorial Theatre on July 26, 1910, produced by Frank Benson, who played the title role. Seated in a box to one side of the stage, the author saw "straight through the wall of that theatre, with my inner eye" the panorama of "the Avon River and the church where you are forbidden to dig certain dust. When the play had begun and I knew that it held the thought and the heart of the audience, that they had forgotten me, I sat all by myself, as it were, looking up the quiet river to his church (*Diary*, p. 234). At the end of the performance she was showered with bouquets and presented with her prize money in the form of a check inside "a solid silver casket with four tiny legs, the whole richly chased and monogrammed." In her gracious acceptance speech, she told a charmed audience that she did not think of herself as a foreigner, since England's Shakespeare is *our* Shakespeare, and Americans take as much pride as their British kin in the development of a common literature.

The New York première of *The Piper*, on January 30, 1911, at the New Theatre, was produced by Winthrop Ames, who had previously been unwilling to take a chance on poetic drama. The playwright was unhappy with the casting of actress Edith Wynne Mattheson in the male role of the Piper, but the play was a critical and popular success. It was revived in March 1920 in New York with English actor A. E. Anson as the Piper. Although stringent child labor laws prevented widespread American production of the play (with its five speaking roles for children and numerous extra children required), *The Piper* remained in print for many years, going into its twenty-first edition in 1920. Published in French, Danish, German, Swedish, and Russian, it was favorably compared with Maurice Maeterlinck's *The Bluebird*.

Josephine Preston Peabody's other published plays are: *The Wings* (1907), a one-act play set in Northumbria in A.D. 700; *The Wolf of Gubbio* (1913), a full-length play about St. Francis of Assisi; *The Chameleon* (1917), a prose comedy; and *Portrait of Mrs. W.* (1922), about Mary Wollstonecraft's marriage to William Godwin. In 1914 Josephine Preston Peabody was elected an honorary member of Phi Beta Kappa at Tufts College in Medford, Massachusetts. For a decade following her death she was remembered as one of America's finest poets.

The Diary and Letters of Josephine Preston Peabody, edited by Christina Hopkinson Baker (1925), is the best source of information, but other good profiles are the Foreword by George Pierce Baker to *The Collected Plays of Josephine Preston Peabody* (1927); the Foreword by Katherine Lee Bates to *The Collected Poems of Josephine Preston Peabody* (1927); and the chapter on Peabody in Jessie B. Rittenhouse, *The Younger American Poets* (1904). Useful articles are Mary Stoyell Stimpson, *New England Magazine* (May 1910); J. S. Harbour, *Theatre* (August 1910); *Hampton Magazine* (October 1910); Walter Prichard Eaton, *The Metropolitan Magazine* (May 1911); Abbie Farwell Brown, *Bookman* (May 1923); and *Atlantic Monthly* (December 1927). Specific biographical data and lists of her works appear in *The National Cyclopaedia of American Biography*, Vol. 19 (1926); *Notable American Women*, Vol. III (1971); *American Women Writers*, Vol. III (1981); and *The Oxford Companion to American Theatre* (1984).

                                                                                    Felicia Hardison Londré

PERRY, Antoinette (June 27, 1888–June 28, 1946): actress, director, and producer, in whose honor the annual Tony awards are named, was born in Denver, Colorado. Her father was William Russell Perry, a lawyer, and her mother was Minnie Betsy (Hall) Perry, whose father Charles L. Hall went west from Iowa to Colorado in an 1859 wagon train and made a fortune in mining. Mary Antoinette Perry received her education at Miss Wolcott's School in Denver and was a Christian Scientist throughout her life; her mother and maternal grandmother are said to have taken this religion with them to Colorado in 1886. Perry married Frank Wheatcroft Frueauff on November 30, 1909. Three daughters were born to them: Margaret Hall (1913); Virginia Day (1917), who died in infancy; and Elaine Storrs (1921). Margaret and Elaine Perry followed their mother's lead and had active theatrical careers as performers and directors. Perry died in her Park Avenue home in New York in 1946 of heart failure and overwork, at age fifty-eight, and was buried beside her husband in Woodlawn Cemetery.

Antoinette Perry had many talents. Though trained as a singer, she began her career in acting in 1905 in *Mrs. Temple's Telegram* at the Powers' Theatre in Chicago; she was just turning seventeen. Her New York debut followed later that year with her performance as Mrs. Frank Fuller in the same play at the Madison Square Theatre. The following season she appeared in *Lady Jim*, *The Music Master* (with David Warfield), and in late 1907 as Hallie in *A Grand Army Man* (again with David Warfield). During the 1906–1907 and 1908–1909 seasons she toured in *The Music Master*. She left the stage in 1909, following her marriage to Frank Frueauff. The Frueauffs were prominent socially, and as a socialite Perry was involved in the Liberty Bond drives for World War I.

Two years after the death of her husband in 1922, Antoinette Perry returned to the stage as Rachel Arrowsmith in *Mr. Pitt* (with Walter Huston) and went on to play Lil Corey in *Minick* (1924), Ma Huckle in *The Dunce Boy* (1925), Belinda Treherne in *Engaged* (1925), Judy Rose in *Caught* (1925), Sophia Weir in *The Masque of Venice* (1926), Margaret in *The Ladder* (1926), and Clytemnestra in *Electra* (with **Margaret Anglin**, 1927).

In 1928 she shifted her career focus and began directing and producing, primarily in association with Brock Pemberton. The Pemberton-Perry production team was to last many years; during this period she directed *Goin' Home* (1928);

Strictly Dishonorable (1929), her first notable success; *Personal Appearance* (1934); *Ceiling Zero* (1935); *Red Harvest* (1937); *Kiss the Boys Goodbye* (1938); *Lady in Waiting* (1940); *Janie* (1942); and *Harvey* (1944), which won the Pulitzer Prize for playwright **Mary Chase**, among many other awards. As a director, Antoinette Perry was known for her attention to detail, her skill in analyzing scripts, and her great respect for actors.

Though clearly Antoinette Perry was a talented actress and a skillful director, she was perhaps best known and has made her greatest contribution to the American theatre in areas other than these. It has been suggested that she spent two-thirds of her professional life in the service of others. During the years preceding World War II and during the war years themselves, her participation in numerous professional theatrical organizations affected the lives of untold numbers of Americans, both in and out of the theatre. From 1937 to 1939 as chair of the committee on the Apprentice Theatre, under the auspices of the American Theatre Council, she organized and conducted auditions for 5,000 aspiring actors in an effort to bring new talent into the American theatre. These efforts were recognized at a testimonial dinner in 1938, at which time she received a Gold Cross "for distinguished service in the theatre." In 1941 she served as president of the Experimental Theatre, sponsored by Actors' Equity Association, an early opportunity for younger members of the acting profession to display their talent.

From 1940 to 1944 Perry aided in the development of the American Theatre Wing and served first as its secretary and later as chair of the board of directors. Her work with the American Theatre Wing resulted in the creation of Stage Door Canteens, which provided entertainment and hospitality for servicemen on leave in cities across the country. Wing activities also included hospital entertainment for the wounded, touring productions overseas, and a Speakers' Bureau. At the peak of World War II there were fifty-four separate American Theatre Wing projects. Most famous of her wartime productions was *The Barretts of Wimpole Street*, with **Katharine Cornell** and Brian Aherne, which played to Allied troops in Europe in 1944–1945. At the time of her death Perry was busy organizing a drama school for returning war veterans. She was a trustee of the Actors' Fund of America and also supported the Stage Relief Fund and the Actors' Thrift Shop.

After her death in 1946, the American Theatre Wing instituted the Antoinette Perry Awards in memory of her tremendous service to the American theatre and her devotion to young artists and to artistic excellence. The awards, referred to as Tonys after her nickname, are presented annually to theatre artists who have made noteworthy contributions during the preceding season.

The Antoinette Perry Clipping File in the Theatre Collection, New York Public Library Performing Arts Research Center at Lincoln Center consists of newspaper clippings, reviews, and articles from the 1930s to her death in 1946. Collections of photographs are included in the American Theatre Wing Scrapbook and the Vincent Sardi Collection, both in the Lincoln Center Library. Perry's obituary appeared in the *New York Times*

(June 29, 1946). Lists of theatre credits are contained in *National Cyclopaedia of American Biography*, Vol. 37 (1967); *Notable American Women*, Vol. III (1971); *Who Was Who in the Theatre* (1978); and *The Oxford Companion to American Theatre* (1984).

Suzanne Trauth

PERRY, Charlotte (December 21, 1890–October 28, 1983): educator, designer, and director, was born in Denver, Colorado, to Samuel M. and Lottie (Matson) Perry. Her father, a surveyor, was instrumental in building the railroad that opened up Northern Colorado, where she was raised. After graduation from Kent High School in Denver in 1907, she went east to Smith College in Northampton, Massachusetts, where she received a Bachelor of Arts degree in English literature and botany in 1911. At Smith, she worked in the college theatre, designing student plays and dance performances, many choreographed by her lifelong friend and companion **Portia Mansfield**. Perry took Mansfield with her to Colorado where, in 1913, they founded a summer camp/student theatre. They shared responsibility for building the camp facilities (including the proscenium theatre that is still in use) and raising funds for development through teaching in the winter months. Mansfield led the dance training program, which employed such modern dance pioneers as Doris Humphrey and **Helen Tamiris**. Perry directed, designed, and supervised productions. She promoted shared responsibilities among all campers so that actors and directors worked on production crews and student designers participated in scene study classes and rehearsals. Perry also designed sets and costumes for tours by the Perry-Mansfield Dancers from 1920 to 1926. Perry and Mansfield maintained the independence of the camp and theatre program until 1967, when Stephens College in Columbia, Missouri, assumed its administration. The Perry-Mansfield Camp had been granted academic credit since 1946 in cooperation with the University of Wyoming.

Perry taught in the Northeast each winter from 1913 to 1955. She directed drama programs at public and independent secondary schools in New York and Connecticut until 1946. That year, she joined the faculty of Hunter College (now a unit of the City University of New York) where she taught and directed the adult theatre workshop. Part of her work at that college was the supervision of drama teacher training in the Hunter Campus Schools—a program that prepared students for the entire New York City public school system. Perry continued her own training while teaching. She studied at the New School for Social Research and the Bank Street Cooperative Bureau of Education (now Bank Street College) and received a master's degree from New York University. She also continued her professional training in acting classes with Maria Ouspenskaya (1943–1944) and directing workshops with Erwin Piscator (1947) and Lee Strasberg (1947–1948). In 1955 Perry moved west to become the director of drama at the Santa Catalina School in Monterey, California, and head of children's theatre activity for the Cherry Foundation in nearby Carmel. She retired in 1982.

Her final project was the conversion of a train depot into a community arts center in Steamboat Springs, Colorado.

The Perry-Mansfield Camp fostered young talent in acting, playwriting, design, and dance through a system involving cooperation and shared responsibilities in theatre production. Over a long lifetime, Charlotte Perry brought her talent, energy, and creativity to both nonprofit and educational theatre, with an influence that spread to both coasts. Through her own work, and her innovations in teaching drama pedagogy, she had a wide and lasting influence.

The history of the Perry-Mansfield Camp is well documented in the scrapbooks and holdings of the Dance Collection of the New York Public Library Performing Arts Research Center at Lincoln Center. Clipping files on Perry herself are housed in the Billy Rose Theatre Collection at the same institution. Many articles on the camp have appeared in dance magazines since the 1930s, among them Perry's own ''Reminiscences and Plans'' in the April 1963 *Dancemagazine*. See also *Dancemagazine* (April 1954 and June 1931) and *Dance Observer* (February 1961, October 1952, May 1942, and May 1940). A brief biographical entry on Charlotte Perry appears in *The Biographical Encyclopaedia and Who's Who of the American Theatre* (1966).

Barbara Cohen-Stratyner

PICON, Molly (February 28, 1898–): actress and author, was born Margaret Pyckoon in New York City. Her family were Russian and Polish Jewish immigrants. Her mother, Clara (Ostrow) Pyckoon, was a dressmaker and wardrobe mistress, first at Philadelphia's Columbia Theatre, later at the Arch Street Theatre. Her father, Louis Pyckoon, was a ne'er-do-well scholar, dreamer, and eccentric. When Molly was born, he stopped speaking to his wife for a year because she had failed to produce a son. Three years later Mrs. Pyckoon compounded the insubordination with the birth of Helen, the Pyckoon's second and last child. Outraged, her husband moved to a separate residence.

Molly Picon's theatrical career began in 1903 on a Philadelphia trolley where she sang to passengers ''I'm Afraid to Go Home in the Dark,'' the number for which she would win a five-dollar gold piece in an amateur contest at the Bijou Theatre. She made her professional debut in the summer of 1904 as Baby Margaret in a vaudeville act playing nickelodeon theatres in the Philadelphia area. Subsequently, she and her sister became child performers in Yiddish repertory. The sisters attended the Northern Liberties School, then William Penn High School, which Molly Picon left after her sophomore year to play the role of Winter in a touring vaudeville troupe called the Four Seasons.

When the Four Seasons folded in Boston early in 1919, Jacob (Yonkel) Kalich, manager of the Yiddish company that played Boston's Grand Opera House on Saturday nights, gave her a job. Among her fellow actors were Menashe Skulnik, playing bits and filling in as prompter, and a young character actor, Muni Weisenfreund, later known as Paul Muni. Before long Kalich proposed to his new soubrette and they were married in Philadelphia on June 29, 1919. The bride wore a wedding dress made by her mother from a discarded Arch Street Theatre curtain and the groom a cutaway that he had once used on the London stage. The marriage, a professional as well as a domestic partnership, lasted fifty-six years until Kalich's death in 1975. The couple's only issue was a stillborn daughter (1920), but they eventually adopted four foster children.

Kalich, born in Poland, was an established actor and director of Yiddish theatres in eastern Europe and in England before he emigrated to the United States in 1914. After their marriage he merged his career with his wife's, serving as her producer, director, manager, fellow performer, coach, and lyricist. He also wrote or adapted scores of star vehicles for her—comedies, dramas, operettas, and revues with titles like *Tzipke*, *Mamele*, and *Oy Is Dus a Leben*. One of his best-loved plays was *Yonkele*, in which Molly Picon launched her New York career at the Second Avenue Theatre on December 24, 1923. The title role, a Jewish Peter Pan, became the cornerstone of her Yiddish Theatre reputation both in America and abroad, a reputation that would earn her the affectionate title "Sweetheart of Second Avenue." So popular was she in the part that she performed it some three thousand times across four continents. Excerpts from *Yonkele* were still included in the concerts, one woman shows, and autobiographical revues that she toured successfully into the 1980s.

Molly Picon made her English language debut not in legitimate theatre but in vaudeville, playing New York's famous Palace Theatre in 1929 on the same bill with Sophie Tucker. Her first Broadway role was in *Morning Star* (Longacre Theatre, 1940), which folded after a brief run. She would be in her sixties before she achieved Broadway success in *Milk and Honey* (Martin Beck Theatre, 1961). This musical opened during the same season in which Molly Picon published her first book, a memoir titled *So Laugh a Little* (1962), and made her first Hollywood film, *Come Blow Your Horn*, starring Frank Sinatra. Picon appeared in comedies and musicals such as *A Majority of One*, *Dear Me, the Sky is Falling*, *The Rubaiyat of Sophie Klein*, *How to Be a Jewish Mother*, *Paris is Out*, and *Hello, Dolly!* She is also remembered for the radio show, *Mr. and Mrs.*, that she and her husband broadcast for over twenty years, as well as for her numerous television appearances.

The diminutive, four-foot, eleven-inch actress, described as "adorably impish" and "an irresistible scamp and waif," is one of the many Second Avenue favorites who entered mainstream American theatre. She brought with her the flavor of Yiddish operetta and the versatility its fans demanded. She could act, sing, dance, compose music, write lyrics, play several musical instruments, and perform acrobatic stunts.

Adept linguistically, she acted in Yiddish, English, German, Spanish, Rumanian, Polish, and, once, in Zulu. She toured from the Arctic Circle to Argentina, from "the grain elevator circuit" of the Middle West to the court of Queen Marie of Rumania. She estimated that she performed in every venue, except burlesque and the circus. She and her husband were the first American actors to bring entertainment to the Jewish refugees in Europe following World War II, traveling on a flatbed truck to the displaced persons camps in Poland during the summer of 1946. Now near the close of a legendary life, Molly Picon lives with her sister in New York City.

Molly Picon wrote two autobiographical books: *So Laugh a Little* (1962) and *Molly* (1980). Louis Nizer's memoir, *Between You and Me* (1978), contains useful anecdotes. For reviews and articles about Picon see *Cue* (April 20, 1940), the *New York Herald Tribune* (April 7, 1940, October 11, 1942, and November 14, 1948), and the *New York Times* (October 2, 1946, and November 13, 1949). Picon donated memorabilia to the American Jewish Historical Society at Brandeis University and the Theatre Collection, Museum of the City of New York. She is listed in *Universal Jewish Encyclopedia* (1948); *Current Biography, 1951* (1952); *The Biographical Encyclopaedia and Who's Who of the American Theatre* (1966); *Notable Names in the American Theatre* (1976); *Who's Who in the Theatre* (1981); and *The Oxford Companion to American Theatre* (1984).

C. Lee Jenner

PONS, Helene Weinncheff (1898–): costume designer and technician, the first to view costume design as painting and sculpture, was born in Tiflis in the south of Russia in the Caucasus near Iran, between the Black and Caspian Seas. Her mother was a pianist and her father a self-made man of business who became Russia's minister of food. She was one of six children, three boys and three girls. Helene Weinncheff's early life kept her moving between Russia and Switzerland. In 1905, at the age of seven, she began to study art. She returned to Russia after the 1905 Revolution, but was forced to leave again to fight tuberculosis. She returned to Russia again, but in 1919 was forced to flee with her family during the turmoil following the Russian Revolution. When she was twenty-one years old, Helene Weinncheff met her future husband, George Pons, in Paris, where he was a technician on tour with the Moscow Art Theatre. He had been a pupil of Constantin Stanislavsky and had worked with the Moscow Art Theatre since the age of fifteen. George Pons was a highly skilled and imaginative technician as well as an intellectual whose other interests included, composing a dictionary of language sources. After their marriage George Pons trained his wife in theatrical design. She learned easily, already having a substantial background in painting and sculpture as well as a natural eye for the character and fall of fabric. In 1922 the impresario Michael Guest brought Nikita Balieff's *Chauve Souris* to New York. George Pons was the technical director, and Helene Pons had created the dolls used in a window display for the play. The Ponses stayed in the United States and soon opened the Pons Studio for costume construction. In what amounts to on-the-job training, Helene Pons developed a philosophy about costume design that revolutionized the approach to costume construction in the American theatre. The marriage produced one daughter, and almost forty years of theatrical collaboration.

Pons's belief that costumes should be impressionistic rather than realistic, and that their major function was to make the characters believable, led to her process of painting, aging, and dyeing as a means of achieving this end. She was influenced by the practices of Henry Dreyfuss, who at the age of eighteen had become a pupil of designer Norman Bel Geddes. Henry Dreyfuss believed that details were not important, but that color and line were the most significant elements in costume design. When the Pons Studio was contracted to build costumes for *Kiss Me, Kate* (1948), the hallmarks of the Pons Studio—namely, imagination and economy—made it possible to build beautiful, stylish, and appropriate costumes on a minimal budget. Helene Pons believed that if the play was designed and built to look like a painting rather than a realistic event, the resulting emphasis on color, shape, and line would succeed where traditional dressmaking would not in making the design appropriate and affordable. Of these costumes, Robert Coleman said that they "are happily complimentary to the players, and at least two of Kate's flamboyant gowns drew gasps from the première audience" (*Daily Mirror*, December 31, 1948).

Helene and George Pons did the painting and dyeing for the Pons Studio, which executed the designs of other artists as well as their own. When they were contracted to build a thousand costumes for *Damascus Road*, they were forced to hire seventy-five new people and rent another floor of the building that housed the Pons Studio in order to carry out the dyeing in wash tubs. The Pons Studio's reputation for imagination and economy was put to a severe test in this production, for which the one thousand costumes were budgeted at twenty-six dollars each.

"Great designers were my friends," Helene Pons says (Personal interview). She was also the friend of designers because of her commitment to the execution of their visions. The great designers went to the Pons Studio assured that in Helene Pons they would find a true collaborator because she refused to do anything that she did not believe in. They found that at the Pons Studio they did not have to supervise the work closely because they could rely on Helene Pons's grasp of design and her imaginative interpretation. The Pons Studio also became a training ground for future costume designers and technicians. Pons asserted that practical, on-the-job training for designers and technicians was the most valuable. She accepted numerous graduates from the Yale School of Drama's design program to apprentice under her critical eye.

As a designer in her own right, Pons created costumes for approximately eighty productions. The studio executed those as well as about one hundred and fifty other theatre, opera, dance, and film productions over a period of forty years. Pons particularly enjoyed designing for such operas as *Don Carlos*, *La Bohème*, and *Faust* for the Metropolitan Opera because she loved singers. She appreciated their discipline and believed they were happier than other artists because they had music in their lives. Over the course of her career Pons worked for nearly every notable producer and director as well as most of the prominent designers in New York.

Pons attributes her success and the success of the Pons Studio to George Pons, to hard work, and to luck. She believed that she could never have achieved what she did without the early training she received from her husband and his support, skill, and collaboration in later years. His death in 1959 resulted in the loss not only of her husband but of her business partner and mentor. After the death of

George Pons, Helene Pons closed the studio and moved to Rome to be near her only daughter, her four grandchildren, and her great grandchildren. She resumed her painting and exhibited in various galleries in Europe and New York. After losing her apartment in Rome, Pons joined her sister for a time in Santa Fe, New Mexico. When she required cataract surgery she went to Sacramento, California, for the surgery and decided to remain near her doctors. In Sacramento, Pons continued to paint and to write her autobiography. She has frequently visited her family in Rome, where she plans to return to live some day.

Helene Pons, as president of the Pons Studio, was the first costumer truly to collaborate with the designer in the interpretation of design drawings. Her background as a painter, rather than as a seamstress or dressmaker, brought a new viewpoint to the execution of costume designs. Costumes built by the Pons Studio emphasized costumes as part of a painting or a sculpture that conveyed an idea about the character rather than stressing historical detail.

Most of the information in this essay is from personal interviews with Helene Pons and Ben Edwards. There is little printed material about Pons except for short biographical sketches in *The Biographical Encyclopaedia and Who's Who of the American Theatre* (1966); *Notable Names in the American Theatre* (1976); and the *Enciclopedia dello spettacolo*, Vol. VIII (1961). Reviews of the plays that Pons designed provide few details about her work.

Marianne Custer

PREER, Evelyn (1896–November 18, 1932): stage and film actress, was born in Vicksburg, Mississippi, the daughter of Frank and Blanche (Jarvis) Preer. Following the death of her father, when Preer was about two years old, she moved with her mother and an older sister and younger brother to Chicago because her mother felt that the city would be more congenial for them. In Chicago Evelyn Preer attended public grammar and high schools. In high school she took part in an organization named "The Lady Amateur Minstrels," which gave her an interest in theatre. After graduating from high school, she made a tour with the Orpheum circuit to the Pacific Coast starring as a prima donna with Charley Johnson's vaudeville company.

Upon her return to Chicago she cheerfully joined her mother, who was a devout member of the Black Apostolic Church, in trying to raise the necessary capital to start a branch of that church in Chicago. Mrs. Preer, who had become an effective lay preacher, took her daughter to street corners of Chicago's South Side, where their ardent and dramatic pleading with "sinners" won them an audience of willing converts. Evelyn Preer won the attention of show business people as well, and soon she was receiving offers to work on the stage. One offer she accepted was a contract with the black movie producer Oscar Micheaux, who between 1918 and 1941 produced over thirty black films that were distributed nationally and internationally. In 1918 Preer appeared in Micheaux's first black silent film, *The Homesteader*, based on a story by Micheaux. Subsequently, Preer was to star in most of Micheaux's productions, notably in *The Brute*,

Within Our Gates (1920), *Deceit, The Gunsaulus Mystery* (1921), *Birthright* (1924), *The Conjure Woman, The Spider's Web*, and *The Devil's Disciple* (1925). Preer considered *The Devil's Disciple* her best work in film. Of this performance, a reviewer for *The New York Age* said, ''Very often do our people reach the heights of musical comedy stardom, but seldom do they reach the enviable position that Evelyn Preer holds in the history of dramatic art. An actress of rare ability and intelligence'' (October 24, 1925).

Preer was later to appear in several films for Paramount Studios and in 1931 worked under the director Cecil B. De Mille, who lauded her acting and her singing ability. She worked for the Christie Studios in Hollywood and starred in at least three productions for them: *The Melancholy Dame, The Framing of the Shrew, Oft in the Silly Night*, all written by Octavius R. Cohen, a writer for the *Saturday Evening Post*. From time to time she also did small roles in pictures made by Paramount, Fox, Metro-Goldwyn-Mayer, Columbia, and Warner Brothers Studios.

It was as leading lady for the famous Lafayette Players, however, that Evelyn Preer was to leave her lasting mark. When Anita Bush, dancer and singer with the renowned company of Bert Williams and Andrew Walker, stopped dancing after a back injury, she decided to open a black stock company to present legitimate drama to black audiences. The aim was to demonstrate that black actors could perform as competently in straight dramas as white actors could. She formed a group with five performers, including Evelyn Preer, and called them the Anita Bush Players. After a successful opening at the Lincoln Theatre in Harlem on West 105th Street in November 1915 and well-received subsequent performances, Bush moved her company to the rival black theatre, the Lafayette, on 132nd Street at Seventh Avenue, where the co-manager, Lester Walton, was black. On December 27, 1915, the Harlem newspaper headlined that the Lafayette Players were opening at the Lafayette in a new drama. Thereafter, despite various changes of management, the company was known as the Lafayette Players. Apart from the short-lived African Grove Theatre in the early 1800s and the Pekin Theatre of Chicago (founded in 1904), the Lafayette Players were the first professional black dramatic stock company in this country. They were to perform for seventeen years, playing not only at the Lafayette Theatre in New York but on tour around the country, at one time having four troupes on tour. They presented serious, legitimate drama during a period when blacks on the American stage appeared exclusively in musicals, vaudeville routines, and minstrel shows. The Lafayette Players set a new pattern for black performers and introduced legitimate drama to black audiences in more than twenty-five cities of the United States. The only major company of its kind, they produced dramas that attracted white audiences as well. Their repertoire of some two hundred and fifty plays included melodramas, comedies, farces, and tragedies written by the outstanding playwrights of their day. Occasionally, the company presented popular Broadway musicals, though this was not their usual fare.

The Lafayette Players were successful in attracting the serious consideration of white audiences and critics, who prior to this time had accorded the black entertainer little, if any, appreciative attention. The players, working against tremendous social and economic odds, won a place of distinction among performers of their era. They undertook the work of identifying and promoting black dramatic stars. One of the most outstanding of these was Evelyn Preer.

From time to time, Preer left the Lafayette Players to perform elsewhere. One such venture took place in 1923, when she performed the title role in Oscar Wilde's *Salome* at the Frazee Theatre on Broadway (May 7, 1923). This production was staged by Raymond O'Neil, the white director of the all-black Ethiopian Art Theatre, founded in Chicago the previous February. It had played in Chicago and Washington, D.C., before going to Broadway. This company also presented Shakespeare's *Comedy of Errors* and Willis Richardson's *The Chip-Woman's Fortune*, which was hailed as an effective folk play and the first play by a black playwright produced appear on Broadway. Preer played in all three productions, but won particular praise for *Salome* (see the *New York Times*, May 8, 1923).

Preer again ventured away briefly from the Lafayette Players in 1925, when impresario David Belasco cast her in *Lulu Belle*, along with her husband, Edward Thompson (son of composer deKoven Thompson), whom she had married in 1924. Belasco's experience with these talented black players led him to write a feature article for *Liberty Magazine* (August 7, 1926) titled "Tomorrow's Stage and the Negro," in which he stated that the black performers with whom he had worked showed "an instinctive dramatic talent that surpasses that of most trained and experienced white actors and actresses." Thus Evelyn Preer was clearly earning the "sweet kiss" of white recognition and praise. An article in the September 11, 1926, *Pittsburgh Courier* declared, "David Belasco Speaks Highly of Evelyn Preer's Talent." From this time until her death, Preer was to be identified as "a Belasco star."

Besides these performances, Preer appeared in many other dramas in which she gave memorable performances and in which she won critical acclaim from both white and black critics. Some of these were *Over the Hill to the Poorhouse* (1922), *The Taming of the Shrew* (1923), *Bought and Paid For* (1923), *Follies of Scapin* (1923), *Branded* (1924 and 1929), *Paid in Full* (1924), *The Hunchback of Notre Dame* (1926), *Rang Tang* (1927), *Rain* (1928), *Anna Christie* (1928), *On Trial* (1928), *The Cat and the Canary* (1929), *The Yellow Ticket* (1930), *Irene* (1930), *Porgy* (1931), and *Desire Under the Elms* (1932).

In June 1927 *The Pittsburgh Courier* carried a series of articles by Evelyn Preer under the title "My Thrills in the Movies." In the articles she chronicled exciting incidents during the filming of such movies as *Birthright*, *The Brute*, *Deceit*, and *Within Our Gates*. Written very simply but honestly, the articles are very entertaining and show a sense of humor on the part of the young star (June 11 through June 25, 1927).

Ina Duncan, the dancer who rose to fame in *Hot Chocolates*, wrote of Evelyn Preer in *The Pittsburgh Courier* for August 12, 1930, "Prior to the appearance of the Lafayette Players in Hollywood, race actors were refused serious parts in the movies. When the Lafayette first came to the Pacific Coast they produced the drama *Rain* (1928). At that time Gloria Swanson had just finished the drama for screen use. One night . . . about 200 white stars of Hollywood came to the Lincoln, presumably with the idea of being amusingly entertained. If they came to laugh, they remained to cheer. Following the performance they went backstage to compliment Miss Preer, her husband, Eddie Thompson, and other members of the cast. This was the dawn of a new day for the Negro in Hollywood."

Besides her theatrical and film achievements, Evelyn Preer was noted for her vocal ability and made popular jazz recordings for Victor Records, Imperial, and other well- known recording companies. Some of her most popular recorded hits were "When the Red, Red Robin Comes Bob-Bob-Bobbin' Along," "Breezing Along with the Breeze," "Bye-Bye Blackbird," "Do-do-do," "One Sweet Letter From You," "Someday, Sweetheart," and "After You've Gone." For several months during 1930 and 1931, she performed with other prominent vocal entertainers; for example, Lottie Gee and Ethel Waters, at the famous Sebastian's Cotton Club in Los Angeles, California.

In December 1931, Evelyn Preer and her husband announced that she would be starring in a real-life role of mother. It was the fulfillment of a cherished dream for the actress who had been told by numerous doctors that she could not bear a child. In April 1932, she gave birth to a daughter, whom she and her husband (combining their own names) called "Edeve." Only seven months later, on November 18, 1932, Evelyn Preer died of double pneumonia. She was ill for only four days. Her death was a great shock to members of her race, her loyal fans, and to her theatrical "family."

Oscar Micheaux, who gave Preer leading roles at the beginning of her meteoric career, said upon hearing of her death: "She was beautiful and intelligent and became immediately popular with audiences everywhere, those who saw and appreciated her work. . . . Miss Preer was a born artist and her early passing will leave her missed greatly by the profession. . . . More versatile than any actress I have ever known, Miss Preer could play any role assigned her and always did so cheerfully and without argument" (*The California Eagle*, November 26, 1932). At her funeral, one of the most impressive ever witnessed even by Hollywood standards, thousands passed Evelyn Preer's bier to pay respects. Clarence Muse, in his eulogy at Preer's funeral, concluded by saying, "Preer, go on! The Lafayette Players have profited by your visit here. The world has been uplifted" (*Pittsburgh Courier*, December 10, 1932). It was a fitting final tribute to a multitalented, dedicated artist who had made her final exit.

Much of the information contained in this entry is from the recollections of Evelyn Preer's daughter, Sister Francesca Thompson, from conversations with Preer's husband, Edward Thompson, and from an interview with Anita Bush in December 1969. Henry T. Sampson mentions Preer in *Blacks in Black and White* (1977). Newspaper articles about Evelyn Preer and her career include *New York Amsterdam News* (December 24, 1915), *Pittsburgh Courier* (September 11, 1926, April 16, 1927, June 11 through June 25, 1927, August 12, 1930, and December 10, 1932), *The New York Age* (October 17, 1925, August 14, 1926, and August 28, 1926), *The California Eagle* (November 25, 1932), and unidentified newspaper articles in Evelyn Preer's scrapbook, now in the possession of Sister Francesca Thompson.

Sister Francesca Thompson

— R —

RAWLS, Eugenia (September 11, 1916–): actress, monodramatist, and author, was born in Macon, Georgia, a year after the elopement of her parents, Louise (Roberts) and Hubert Fields Rawls. Her father, who eventually practiced law, was a student at the time, and her paternal grandmother, Mary Eugenia Cumming, took over the care of her grandchild. Two maiden aunts, Gussie Belle Rawls, a graduate of the American Academy of Dramatic Arts, and Maggie May Rawls, a graduate of the Emerson School of Oratory, gave elocution lessons in Macon, and the young Eugenia used to sit and watch and listen. This practice led to her stage debut, at which as a five-year-old she performed recitation pieces at the Grand Opera House in Macon.

Eugenia Rawls attended high school in Dublin, Georgia, and then went to Wesleyan Conservatory, where in 1932 she was named most promising student and was elected president of the Dramatic Art Club. She applied to the University of North Carolina at Chapel Hill but informed Frederick H. Koch, mentor of such writers as Maxwell Anderson, Paul Green, and Thomas Wolfe, and director of the Carolina Playmakers, that she had no math and no money. A scholarship was secured, and Rawl's dramatic training continued. It was at the University of North Carolina that she met her future husband, Donald R. Seawell, who would later become a later to be a distinguished attorney, theatre producer, chairman of the *Denver Post*, and board chairman of the Denver Center for the Performing Arts and the Denver Center Theatre Company. He is also chairman of the American National Theatre and Academy and on the board of directors of the Royal Shakespeare Company in England.

After a year in North Carolina, Rawls moved to New York and began her professional career with **Clare Tree Major**'s Children's Theatre during the 1933–1934 season. In November 1934 she made her Broadway debut as Peggy in

Lillian Hellman's *The Children's Hour*. Subsequently she played Jane Bennett in the tour of *Pride and Prejudice* and appeared in *To Quito and Back* (October 1937) and *Journeyman* (January 1938). In the summer of 1938 she performed at the Westport Country Playhouse in *Susanna and the Elders* and *The Inner Light*. In 1939 she joined **Margaret Webster**'s Shakespeare Company, playing leading roles in *As You Like It*, *A Midsummer Night's Dream*, *The Taming of the Shrew*, and *The Comedy of Errors* at the New York World's Fair. In October 1939 Rawls took over the role of Alexandra in the Broadway production of *The Little Foxes* starring **Tallulah Bankhead**. Bankhead became her lifelong friend and a godmother to her two children. They had first met when Rawls came to the theatre as the new understudy and, after scrutiny, was told by Bankhead that she looked enough like her to be her own child. After the Broadway run, the company took *The Little Foxes* on tour from February 1940 to April 1941, covering twenty-five thousand miles, and offering eighty-seven one-night stands. The last performance was in Philadelphia on April 5, 1941. Before the matinee Eugenia Rawls and Donald Seawell were married at the Holy Trinity Chapel with Bankhead as matron of honor and provider of asparagus and champagne.

Eugenia Rawls's stage career continued with Arthur Wing Pinero's *The Second Mrs. Tanqueray* and Ivor Novello's *Curtain Going Up, Harriet*, and in the spring of 1942, she returned to Broadway to take over the role of Evelyn Heath in *A Guest in the House*. At the same time she was performing in two daytime radio dramas and volunteering her time at the Stage Door Canteen. Also in 1942 Rawls and Seawell inherited a farm on the Maryland shore from Aunt Maggie May, who, in her forties, had married a Captain Hurley and moved away from Georgia. The farm is now Rawls's prime source of relaxation and the family meeting place.

In February 1943 Rawls went to Chicago for *Cry Havoc*. That summer Donald Seawell traveled to Europe as a private in the United States Army. Rawls then played Mrs. DeWinter in the 1944–1945 tour of *Rebecca* before returning to Broadway for Lillian Smith's *Strange Fruit* in 1945. Lillian Smith's work appealed to Rawls's southern sensibilities, and she was to create her fourth one-woman show from Smith's book *Memory of a Large Christmas* (1962).

Meanwhile, Donald Seawell returned from Europe, and Rawls gave birth to their first child, Eugenia Ashley Brook, on March 31, 1947. The Seawells' second child, Donald Brockman, was born on January 27, 1952.

Soon after Brockman's birth, Rawls returned to the theatre, taking over the role of Evelyn in *The Shrike*, starring José Ferrer. In 1956 she was in the Alfred Lunt-**Lynn Fontanne** production of *The Great Sebastians*, and in 1961 she played in *All The Way Home* at Philadelphia's Playhouse in the Park, with her son Brockman. In 1965 she played the role of Amanda Wingfield in *The Glass Menagerie* at Cincinnati's Playhouse-in-the-Park, the first of six productions in which she has played that role. Rawls then joined Stuart Vaughan's company at the Repertory Theatre of New Orleans for the 1966–1967 season. She returned to New York to appear in *The Poker Session* at the Martinique and then went on tour with Sean O'Casey's *Pictures in the Hallway*. She was Artist-in-Residence at the University of Denver, Colorado, during the 1967–1968 season.

In 1975–1976 Rawls appeared in the New York production of *Sweet Bird of Youth* with **Irene Worth** and Christopher Walken. In 1977 she was suddenly called upon to learn to shimmy, shake, and stand on her head in order to stand by for **Mary Martin** in *Do You Turn Somersaults?* The next year she played in *Daughter of the Regiment* with Opera New England and *Just the Immediate Family* at the Hudson Guild Theatre in New York.

Eugenia Rawls is also no stranger to television audiences. In 1954 she played Mrs. Elvsted to Tallulah Bankhead's *Hedda Gabler*. She was in *Magnificent Yankee* with the Lunts and appeared in productions for *Armstrong Circle Theatre*, the *DuPont Show of the Month*, the *U.S. Steel Hour*, and others, and has had roles on *The Doctors*, *The Nurses*, *Love of Life*, and *Guiding Light*. She also worked on radio with Voice of America and has recorded approximately two hundred and fifty Talking Books for the American Foundation for the Blind, including all the works of Eudora Welty.

In 1961 the Museum of the City of New York commissioned Rawls to create a one-woman show. After six years of research and writing, she produced *Affectionately Yours, Fanny Kemble*, which has now played all over the United States and the United Kingdom. A second one-woman show, *Tallulah, A Memory*, was soon added to her repertory. When she was pregnant with Brockman, Rawls had written *The Story of a Friendship*, and on Bankhead's death had written "Another Tallulah" for *Equity Magazine*. These writings became the basis for her one-woman show. She has become a storyteller par excellence, performing her one-woman shows in major theatres, including Britain's National Theatre and America's John F. Kennedy Center for the Performing Arts, Folger Theatre, National Portrait Gallery in Washington, D.C., in small theatres, libraries, museums, embassies, stately homes, clubs, town halls, universities, schools, army bases, and in the middle of the Atlantic Ocean, aboard the *Queen Elizabeth II*. In 1969 the British Arts Council presented Rawls in her Fanny Kemble show in London. She alternated performances with Dame Sybil Thorndike's one-woman show on Ellen Terry. In 1972 Rawls became the first American to perform at Dublin's Abbey Theatre, where she gave her Fanny Kemble portrait. The extensive research that Rawls undertook to prepare *Affectionately Yours, Fanny Kemble* has made her a leading expert on the actress and the Kemble family. In 1977 her research led her to Fanny Kemble Wister, Kemble's great-granddaughter, who resides near Philadelphia. Rawls received her blessing and help.

Now in her sixth decade as a professional actress, Eugenia Rawls is a constant traveler on two continents, fulfilling bookings, primarily for her Fanny Kemble and Tallulah Bankhead portraits. She has also added a third one-woman show, *Women of the West*, described as a female *Profiles in Courage*. The fourth show, based on Lillian Smith's *Memory of a Large Christmas*, receives seasonal bookings.

Eugenia Rawls has received wide acknowledgement, most particularly for her one-woman shows, in which she perpetuates the art of dramatic storytelling and through which she reaches a wide audience of all backgrounds and ages. In 1973 she received the Gold Chair Award of the Central City Opera Association. In 1979 she received an honorary doctorate from the University of Northern Colorado, and in 1982 an honorary Doctor of Fine Arts from Wesleyan College, Georgia, her alma mater. The citation stated, "You have succeeded in elevating storytelling to an esteemed art form. We applaud you for your devotion to authenticity, dedication to the theatre, and total commitment to the arts."

Material on Eugenia Rawls may be found in the New York Public Library Performing Arts Research Center at Lincoln Center. Her book *Tallulah, A Memory* was published in 1979 by the University of Alabama Press, and in 1984 the Denver Center published a book of her poetry, *A Moment Ago*. Rawls is listed in *Notable Names in the American Theatre* (1977) and *Who's Who in the Theatre* (1981).

Elizabeth Swain

REHAN, Ada Delia (April 22, 1857–January 8, 1916): leading actress with Augustin Daly's company, was born in Limerick, Ireland, the daughter of Thomas and Harriett (Ryan) Crehan. She spent most of her childhood in Brooklyn where her family settled when she was five. Crehan was her family name, but through an error on a playbill she became known as Ada C. Rehan. The Crehan family had no prior connection with the theatre until Kate, the eldest daughter, married Oliver Doud Byron, an actor-manager and playwright, and joined his company. Harriet, the middle daughter, later joined the troupe, and Arthur, one of three sons, also became an actor.

Ada Rehan, the youngest daughter, after some haphazard schooling, joined her sisters on tour in 1873, but not as a performer. When an actress became ill in Newark, New Jersey, the young girl went on as Clara in *Across the Continent*. That evening her family held a conference and decided that she should also become an actress. She toured in *Across the Continent* for the remainder of the season and made her New York debut in *Thoroughbred* in the spring of 1873 at Wood's Museum. For the next two seasons she was a member of **Louisa Lane Drew**'s stock company at the Arch Street Theatre in Philadelphia, where she appeared with stars like Edwin Booth and John McCullough. She also spent a season in Louisville, Kentucky, and two in Albany, New York, with other stock companies. In 1879, while she was appearing in New York with **Fanny Davenport**'s company in *Pique*, she attracted the attention of Augustin Daly, the noted producer, who signed her for his company. She made her debut with Daly's company in May of 1879 as Big Clemence in *L'Assommoir*.

Rehan remained with Daly's company for the next twenty years. She soon became one of the leading actors of the troupe, and one of Daly's "Big Four," along with John Drew, **Anne Hartley Gilbert**, and James Lewis. Ada Rehan played the vivacious young American girl in a string of comedies including *Divorce*, *Cinderella*, *The Royal Youth*, *Odette*, *The Squire*, and *The Country*

Girl. When Daly's theatrical activities extended to London in June 1884 Rehan made her London debut. For the remainder of her work with Daly, she was to appear in both New York and London.

To showcase his leading comedienne, Daly began a series of revivals of classic comedies in 1886 with *The Merry Wives of Windsor*, in which Rehan appeared as Mistress Ford. The following year she appeared as Katherine in *The Taming of the Shrew*, one of her most famous roles. Of her Katherine portrayal, the author of Rehan's obituary in the *New York Times* (January 9, 1916) wrote, "She raised the character of Shakespeare's Shrew from the level of turbulent farce, and made it a credible, consistent, continuously interesting and ultimately sympathetic image of human nature." She also won renown in *A Midsummer Night's Dream*, *As You Like It*, *Twelfth Night*, *The School for Scandal*, and *The Hunchback*. The same article states further, "She was the best Rosalind ever seen in our time, . . . and I confidently believe that within her special field—of archness, raillery, sentiment, coquetry, and noble, woman-like feelings—she has seldom been equaled and never excelled." Daly's revivals of these plays focused on Ada Rehan and made her the leading member of his company. Daly's death, on June 7, 1899, was a shock to Rehan, and she did not act for over a year.

She returned to the theatre on November 28, 1900, in *Sweet Nell of Old Drury* and played in the piece for the season. Her mother died in 1901, and again she retired from the stage for a year. When she returned in 1903 she toured the country with Otis Skinner for a season in a repertory of classic comedies. The following season she toured by herself, but illness forced her to quit the stage in May 1905. During the last ten years of her life she lived in New York and, though still in poor health, took yearly trips to Europe. Ada Rehan never married. When she died in New York on January 8, 1916, of arterial disease, she was survived by two sisters and a nephew.

As an actress, Ada Rehan was known for her energy, high spirits, and full, clear voice. Tall and graceful, with reddish hair, she projected her personality into her roles and played them with zest. Like all Daly's stars, she appeared natural and spontaneous in roles that were light and artificial. Without Daly's guidance her style seemed exaggerated, and she was less successful after his death. Though not considered a great Shakespearean actress, Ada Rehan brought energy and sincerity to Katherine and Rosalind and made them two highly successful roles. For twenty years she was one of the most popular comediennes on the American stage, and Daly launched his series of Shakespearean revivals explicitly to display her spirited, larger-than-life acting.

William Winter's *Ada Rehan* (1891, revised 1898) was commissioned by Daly and glorifies the actress. Winter also includes Rehan in *The Wallet of Time*, Vol. II (1913). Lewis C. Strang, *Famous Actresses of the Day in America* (1899) also praises Rehan. She is included in John B. Clapp and Edwin F. Edgett, *Players of the Present*, Part III (1901). See also Fola LaFollette, "Ada Rehan: Some Personal Recollections," *Bookman* (July 1916). Rehan is discussed in Marvin Feldheim, *The Theater of Augustin Daly* (1958) and in Richard Harlan Andrew, "Augustin Daly's Big Four: John Drew, Ada Rehan, John Lewis, and Mrs. G. H. Gilbert" (Unpublished Ph.D. dissertation, University of Illinois, Urbana, 1971). Material can also be found in Otis Skinner, *Footlights and Spotlights* (1924); Cornelia Otis Skinner, *Family Circle* (1948); W. Graham Robertson, *Life Was Worth Living* (1931); and John Drew, *My Years on Stage* (1922). Also of interest is Sylvia Golden, "The Romance of Ada Rehan," *Theatre* (January 1931). Clippings, programs, and other memorabilia are held in the Theatre Collection of the New York Public Library Performing Arts Research Center at Lincoln Center. Rehan's obituary appeared in the *New York Times* (January 9, 1916). Rehan is listed in Walter Browne and E. de Roy Koch, *Who's Who on the Stage, 1908* (1908); Dixie Hines and Harry Prescott Hanaford, eds., *Who's Who in Music and Drama* (1914); *Who's Who in the Theatre* (1916); *Who Was Who in America*, Vol. I: 1887–1942 (1966); *Notable American Women*, Vol. III (1971); William C. Young, *Famous Actors and Actresses on the American Stage*, Vol. II (1975); *Who Was Who in the Theatre*, Vol. IV (1978); Donald Mullin, ed., *Victorian Actors and Actresses in Review* (1983); *The Oxford Companion to the Theatre* (1983); and *The Oxford Companion to American Theatre* (1984).

Rita M. Plotnicki

REIGNOLDS, Kate (May 16, 1836–July 11, 1911): star performer and author, was born near London. She was christened Catherine Mary Reignolds and was the granddaughter of an English soldier who had been among the first killed at the Battle of Waterloo. Her father, Robert Gregory Taylor Reignolds, died young, leaving his widow, Emma (Absolon) Reignolds, to rear three daughters, of whom Catherine Mary was the eldest. In 1850 Emma Reignolds and her daughters left England for the United States, where they settled in Chicago. They were employed by theatre manager John B. Rice. For four years the Reignolds family attempted to earn a living on the Chicago stage. Kate Reignolds's memoirs recall these difficult years and suggest that, as an adolescent, she carried most of the burden of support for the family. By 1855 Catherine Mary, now known as Kate Reignolds, moved to New York, where she arranged to meet Edwin Forrest, the famous actor. Forrest gave her an audition and hired her to play the ingénue Virginia to his title role in Sheridan Knowles's *Virginius*, one of his most celebrated roles. On April 7, 1855, Kate Reignolds made her New York debut with Forrest at the Broadway Theatre; there followed almost fifteen years of uninterrupted employment in the theatre.

In the fall and early winter of 1855, Reignolds appeared at Burton's theatre in New York; she then joined **Laura Keene**'s company and appeared in sixteen productions there between late December and June 1856. Next Reignolds moved to the Bowery Theatre under the management of John Brougham, and between June and December of 1856 she appeared in twenty-six productions. In March 1857 Reignolds returned to Laura Keene's company, where she remained until autumn, at which time she joined Ben De Bar's company at the St. Louis Opera House. During the winter months De Bar's organization regularly moved to the St. Charles Theatre in New Orleans, and Reignolds performed in the stock company that provided support to visiting stars. In December 1857 she married

Henry Farran, another member of the company. In February 1858, at the St. Charles Theatre, Reignolds performed Juliet to the Romeo of **Charlotte Cushman**. In her memoirs, Reignolds praises the great Cushman's patience and willingness to coach others in their roles. Other stars with whom Reignolds appeared at this time were **Matilda Heron**, **Matilda Vining Wood**, James E. Murdoch, and James Hackett, all of whom, along with Ben De Bar, are described in Reignolds's memoirs.

On January 8, 1860, Henry Farran died, leaving Reignolds a widow at the age of twenty-four. Reignolds returned to New York, where she appeared at the Winter Garden Theatre in July in the role of Anna Chute in Dion Boucicault's *The Colleen Bawn*, the farewell production for star **Agnes Robertson**. Subsequently, Reignolds refused an offer to join Irish star Barry Sullivan as leading lady in an international tour, and instead joined the Boston Museum stock company for five years, playing many leading roles such as Desdemona, Juliet, Lydia Languish, Laetitia Hardy, Lady Gay Spanker, and Peg Woffington. While performing at the Boston Museum, Reignolds appeared opposite visiting actor John Wilkes Booth, whom she described in her memoirs as violent and uncontrolled, an actor who left her frightened on Desdemona's deathbed and bedraggled in Juliet's torn costume. While in Boston Reignolds married Erving Winslow, a Boston businessman from an old New England family.

In January 1865, Kate Reignolds gave her last performance as a member of the Boston Museum company. During the late 1860s she toured the United States in a repertoire that included plays by Shakespeare, classic English comedies, and popular contemporary plays. From time to time she appeared in New York and Boston, where she was now considered a visiting star. With her reputation established in this country, Reignolds traveled to England in 1868. She appeared at the Princess's Theatre in London and then toured in Manchester, Liverpool, Glasgow, Weymouth, and Exeter. While appearing in *Nobody's Daughter* in Exeter, Reignolds injured her back in a fall on stage. The remainder of her tour was canceled, and she returned to the United States. From this point on, her appearances and tours gradually diminished. In 1877 her son, Charles Edward Amory Winslow, was born. He later became a professor of Public Health at Yale University and a translator of European plays.

In 1886, then known as Mrs. Reignolds-Winslow, she began to present dramatic readings for Boston charities. In 1889 she appeared in matinees at Boston's Columbia Theatre in staged readings of Henrik Ibsen's plays, and during the same year she presented dramatic readings at the Berkeley Lyceum in New York. In 1890 she performed her program of readings at New York's Hotel Brunswick, and on April 1, 1890, she appeared at Madison Square Garden. She also returned to London at this time to present a reading of Ibsen's *An Enemy of the People* at the Haymarket Theatre.

After retiring from her active stage career, Reignolds taught elocution to young women interested in acting. In addition she enjoyed various successes in publishing. Her memoirs, *Yesterdays with Actors*, is based on a series of articles originally published in the *Boston Herald* and released in book form in 1887. Chapters are devoted to many of the famous persons who helped her in her career: Charlotte Cushman, Edwin Forrest, John Brougham, and Laura Keene, among others. She also edited a two-volume work titled *Readings from Old English Dramatists* (1895), which combines interpretive essays by Reignolds with illustrative examples from representative plays ranging from medieval miracle plays to eighteenth century dramas. Reignolds's writings also appeared in Boston newspapers, an example of which is a lengthy tribute to Edwin Forrest published in the *Boston Evening Transcript* on March 19, 1907, the centennial anniversary of Forrest's birth.

During a severe New England heat wave on July 11, 1911, Catherine Mary Reignolds-Winslow died of heat prostration at her summer home in Concord, Massachusetts. She was buried in the Springfield Cemetery.

Kate Reignolds achieved stardom as an actress during the 1860s. With intelligence and versatility, she later made notable contributions to Boston's cultural life as a teacher and author.

Kate Reignolds's autobiography, *Yesterdays with Actors* (1887), provides the best source of information about her life as well as giving information about many of the people associated with her stage career. Her essays in *Readings from Old English Dramatists* (1895) are interesting in giving her interpretations of the material. John B. Clapp and Edwin F. Edgett, *Players of the Present*, Part III (1901), shows how Reignolds was regarded in her era. See also T. Allston Brown, *History of the American Stage* (1870), and George C. D. Odell, *Annals of the New York Stage*, Vols. VI-VIII (1931–1936). Obituary notices appeared in the *Boston Evening Transcript* (July 12, 1911), the *Boston Herald* (July 12, 1911), and the *New York Dramatic Mirror* (July 19, 1911). There is a collection of clippings about Kate Reignolds in the Harvard University Theatre Collection. A biographical account of her life is given in *Notable American Women*, Vol. III (1971).

Edna J. Clark

ROBBINS, Carrie (February 7, 1943–): award-winning costume designer, was born in Baltimore, Maryland, the daughter of Sidney W. Fishbein, a high school history teacher, and Bettye A. (Berman) Fishbein. From the time she could hold a crayon Carrie Fishbein drew on her bedroom walls. Dismayed, her parents enlisted professional help. The doctor encouraged her parents to guide their child's behavior along positive channels, so in 1946, at the age of three, Carrie was enrolled in her first art class. For the next fifteen years she attended various art schools in the Baltimore area, most notably the Maryland Institute of Art. During these years her interest in theatre developed through involvement in school and summer camp theatrical productions.

As a 1960 graduate of Baltimore's Forest Park High School, Carrie Fishbein wanted to pursue degrees in both art and theatre. Pennsylvania State University agreed to accept her in both programs. While at Penn State she designed scenery and played leading roles in *The Bells Are Ringing* and *Bye Bye Birdie*; in her senior year she was resident scenic designer at the Playhouse and Pavilion Theatre there. She graduated (Phi Beta Kappa) in 1964 with a Bachelor of Science degree in applied arts and a Bachelor of Arts degree in theatre arts.

Carrie Fishbein next enrolled in the Master of Fine Arts design program at the Yale University School of Drama. There she shifted her focus from scenic to costume design. She assisted Michael Annals on costumes for *Prometheus Bound* (1965) and designed costumes for *Tartuffe* (1966) and *Pantagleize* (1967). While at Yale she drafted for the George Izenour theatre lab and designed costumes for three productions at the Studio Arena in Buffalo, New York. In 1967 she received her graduate degree from Yale and was accepted into the United Scenic Artists union, Local 829.

Directly after graduation she secured the position of resident costume designer for the Inner City Cultural Center in Los Angeles, California. André Gregory, then artistic director at Inner City, was impressed with her work and recommended her as costume designer for his forthcoming Broadway production of *Leda Had a Little Swan* (1968). With portfolio in hand, Carrie Fishbein traveled back across the country to interview with renowned scenic designer Oliver Smith. She was hired, but *Leda Had a Little Swan* never opened. The next nine months proved professionally discouraging and financially difficult. In order to pay the bills, she resorted to illustrating dental equipment, a job that she found both frustrating and demoralizing. A well-meaning friend resolved to improve her life by finding her a husband. Reluctantly, Carrie agreed to meet physician Richard D. Robbins. To their mutual surprise they enjoyed each other's company and continued to see one another. Before agreeing to marry him, she insisted that Robbins witness firsthand the demands her work would force upon their relationship. When she signed a contract with the Studio Arena Theatre in Buffalo to design costumes for *The Lion in Winter* (October 1968), Robbins accompanied her and saw the hectic schedule involved in theatre production. Nevertheless, they were married on February 15, 1969, only two months before Carrie's next show, *Trainer, Dean, Liepolt, and Company*, opened Off-Broadway.

In March 1969, *Inner Journey* opened at New York's Lincoln Center. Carrie F. Robbins (as she named herself professionally) designed the costumes and worked for the first time with artistic director Jules Irving. Their mutual respect accelerated Robbins's career over the next few years as they collaborated on *The Year Boston Won the Pennant* (1969), *The Time of Your Life* (1969), *The Good Person of Setzuan* (1970), *An Enemy of the People* (1971), *Narrow Road to the Deep North* (1972), *The Crucible* (1972), and *The Plough and the Stars* (1973). During these four years Robbins also designed Broadway's *Look to the Lilies*, Bell Telephone's film *Flight of Fantasy*, and the Minneapolis Guthrie Theatre's Aztec version of *Julius Caesar*. Most significantly, she designed costumes for the Broadway musical *Grease*, for which she won both the 1971–1972 Antoinette Perry (Tony) Award for best costumes and the Drama Desk Award. One month after *Grease*, *The Beggar's Opera* opened (1972) under artistic director Robert Kalfin at the Brooklyn Academy of Music, and Robbins's costumes won another Drama Desk Award.

As with Jules Irving at Lincoln Center's Vivian Beaumont Theatre, Carrie Robbins established a working relationship with Robert Kalfin at the Brooklyn Academy of Music (Chelsea Theatre Center). They worked together on numerous successful productions, including *Sunset* (1972), *Yentl, The Yeshiva Boy* (1974), which moved to Broadway in 1975 as *Yentl*, and *Polly* for which she won the 1975 Maharam Award for Design. In 1974 she won the Drama Desk Award for a revival of *The Iceman Cometh* and for *Over Here*; the latter also earned her a second Tony Award.

Both her Tony Award-winning designs (*Grease* and *Over Here*) were for productions directed by Tom Moore, a fellow Yale School of Drama graduate. She continued her director-designer relationship with Tom Moore on Broadway in *Frankenstein* (1981) and *The Octette Bridge Club* (1985), for which she was nominated for a Drama Desk Award. They also collaborated at the American Conservatory Theatre in San Francisco and at the Mark Taper Forum in Los Angeles. *A Flea In Her Ear* (1982) won the Los Angeles Dramalogue Critics Award for costume design.

With inexhaustible enthusiasm Carrie Robbins has designed costumes for over nineteen Broadway and five Off-Broadway productions; four shows for the New York Shakespeare Festival; ten for Lincoln Center; seven for the Chelsea Theatre Center; three for the Acting Company at the Juilliard School of Drama; five for WNET and cable television; and fifteen shows for regional theatres, including the Guthrie Theatre, the Mark Taper Forum, Center Stage, Studio Arena, Seattle Repertory, and the American Conservatory Theatre. Moreover, her work in opera encompasses such productions as San Francisco Opera's *Samson et Dalila*, starring Placido Domingo, and the United States première of *Russlann and Ludmilla* for Sarah Caldwell's Opera Company in Boston. International credits include the Hamburg (West Germany) State Opera Company's production of *West Side Story* in 1979 and Canada's Shaw Festival production of *Sisters of Mercy* in 1973. She was awarded the Silver Medal for design by the sixth Triennial of Theatre Design in Novisad, Yugoslavia, in 1981. She was one of three designers responsible for creating the United States exhibit at the 31-nation Prague Quadrennial Scenic and Costume Design exhibition in 1987. Along with scenic designers Douglas Schimdt and John Lee Beatty, she helped to create four environmental work spaces which attempted to present design as a process, not an end in itself. The design won the Quadrennial's top honors for the best national exhibition. Robbins' drawings have been featured in numerous galleries, including the Cooper Hewitt Museum, the Wright-Hepburn Gallery, Center Falls Gallery, and the Scottsdale Arts Center (Arizona).

In addition to establishing a career in costume design, Robbins has maintained an active career in interior design. Her early interest in scenic design and spatial relationships, along with her art background, led to free-lance employment in interior design. She is a member of the American Society of Interior Design and also belongs to the Society of Scribes and the Graphic Artists' Guild. In order to coordinate her free-lance jobs in interior design, graphic art, and costume design, in 1982 she established her own business, Carrie Robbins Designage, Inc.

Currently a master teacher of costume design at New York University's Tisch School of the Arts, where she joined the faculty in 1971, Robbins has also lectured at various universities including Oberlin College, the University of California at Los Angeles, and the University of Illinois. Since 1977, she has served as a member of the steering committee for the League of Professional Theatre Training Programs. Her commitment to education is evident not only in her teaching but in her articles in *Theatre Crafts* on designer training. Recently, Robbins has ventured into the designing of uniforms for elegant restaurants like the Rainbow Room in New York City and Caesar's Palace in Los Vegas. For the uniforms that she has designed she is able to use custom work and detail that would not be seen in a theatre.

Robbins's designs are characterized by her devotion to detail, her strong sense of period, and her concern for and attention to the director's and the actor's visual understanding of a play. According to Robbins, "Everything in the visual world is relevant to our work as designers for the stage. And consequently, we have to look at and take in everything" ("Training," *Theatre Crafts*, November/December 1977, p. 71). Along with their visual skills, she emphasizes that designers should develop verbal skills. Robbins herself continues to learn by attending lectures and taking classes between jobs. "The more knowledge we can bring to the decisions we make, the more credible our field becomes, the more worthy our contribution, and the more that the people we work with see why they pay us for what we do," she writes (*Theatre Crafts*, April 1981, p. 72).

Carrie F. Robbins's philosophy of costume design can be found in her articles for *Theatre Crafts*, "Training the Costume Designer: A Curriculum Proposal" (April 1981), and "Portfolio Review for Costume Designers" (November/December 1977). Her work can be seen in two *Theatre Crafts* articles: "Re-creating the Deep South on Costumes for 'Rebel Women,' " by Carrie Robbins (September 1976), "The Audience Should Not Leave Whistling the Costumes," by Patricia J. MacKaye (January/February 1974), and "Carrie Robbins, Dressing Up a Rainbow and a Palace" by Michael Sommers (November 1988). See also Deborah Dryden, *Fabric Painting and Dyeing for the Theatre* (1981) and Barbara and Cletus Anderson, *Costume Design* (1984). The Time-Life Series, *The Encyclopedia of Collectibles*, Vol. 15, reprints one of her designs. Personal information was supplied by Carrie F. Robbins in an interview in March 1985. Robbins is included in *Notable Names in the American Theatre* (1976); *Who's Who in the Theatre* (1981); *Who's Who of American Women, 1985–1986* (1984); and *Who's Who in America, 1984–1985*, Vol. II (1984).

Diane R. Berg

ROBERTS, Vera Mowry (October 21, 1918–): theatre educator, administrator, and director, was born in Pittsburgh, Pennsylvania, to interior decorator Joseph E. and Emma C. (Steinmann) Mowry. She was the middle of three daughters. Her family went to the theatre frequently and formed an acting troupe putting on productions for their friends. Educated in her native Pittsburgh, Vera Mowry received a Bachelor of Science degree in 1938, a Master of Arts degree in 1945, and a Ph.D. degree in 1951 from the University of Pittsburgh. She also studied at Pennsylvania College for Women (now Chatham College) and the School of Fine Arts, Carnegie Institute of Technology (now Carnegie-Mellon University).

Vera Mowry juggled studies and war service between 1943 and 1946, while earning the rank of lieutenant senior grade in the United States Naval Reserves and serving as a production officer on the rocket development program in the Bureau of Ordnance in Washington, D.C. She began her teaching career in Washington, D.C., as an assistant professor from 1946 to 1954 in the English Department at George Washington University.

Active in educational, community, and professional theatre, Vera Mowry directed plays for George Washington University, the Children's Theatre, and the Mount Vernon Players in Washington; for the Little Theatre of Alexandria and the Cross-Roads Theatre, both in Virginia; and for the Port Players in Wisconsin. Her doctoral dissertation had been on ''Satire in American Drama,'' and being fond of American theatre history, she gave stage life to it in productions like *A Texas Steer*, Charles Hale Hoyt's popular vaudeville comedy of the late nineteenth century. Her taste for revivals was catholic, however, as shown in her resurrection of George Coleman's *The Jealous Wife*, a 1761 British Restoration-style comedy for the Little Theatre of Alexandria, and a season at the Mount Vernon Players of world classics, beginning with *The Brothers Menaechmus*. She comments, ''I specialized in reviving plays that had suffered neglect but were very playable'' (Personal interview).

While exploring Western theatre's riches from the past, Vera Mowry also helped establish a treasure for its future. In 1950 she was one of six founders of Washington's Arena Stage. She directed, designed sets and costumes, and acted in Arena Stage productions until 1955, when she moved to New York City.

In January 1951 she married actor Pernell E. Roberts. Their son, J. Christopher, was born in October 1951. The couple divorced in 1960.

Joining the Department of Speech and Dramatic Arts at Hunter College of the City University of New York in 1955, Vera Mowry Roberts attained the rank of full professor in 1969 and became chair of the new Department of Theatre and Film in 1970, serving for ten years in that capacity. She drew up the plan for the department's master's degree program in 1962, was one of three developers of the City University of New York Graduate School's Ph.D. program in theatre (serving one term in the 1980s as its executive officer), and was instrumental in securing a one-million-dollar National Endowment for the Humanities grant for Hunter College's Division of Humanities and Arts for 1978–1982. During her tenure at Hunter, Roberts also wrote two textbooks—*On Stage, A History of the Theatre* (1962) and *The Nature of Theatre* (1972)—and brought the number of plays she had directed to over one hundred. She recalls, ''Three of the best productions I ever directed were at Hunter—*Othello*, *The Skin of Our Teeth*, and *Tiger at the Gates*'' (Interview).

A member of the American Theatre Association since the mid-fifties, Roberts served the organization in numerous capacities. She started an association project to bring prominent theatre professionals from Europe to lecture in America and chaired a restructuring committee to broaden the association's base and to encourage more grassroots participation—resulting in the organization's 1970 change of name from the American Educational Theatre Association to the American Theatre Association.

Roberts spent her sabbatical leave in 1973 as president of ATA, traveling some eighty-five thousand miles around America to attend conferences, give speeches, and work toward unity among the various academic, community, armed services, children's, and professional theatre elements of the organization. She appointed a task force, which became the ATA Women's Project, and another group to work with theatre by, for, and with the aging—which became the Senior Adult Theatre Project. Roberts also served as chair of ATA's Committee on Awards and Honors and its Commission on Standards and Accreditation. The latter, which Roberts led from 1976 until 1980, issued in 1978—for the first time in ATA history—a paper on standards for degree programs in theatre. In 1969 Roberts was elected an ATA Fellow. This honorary distinction was awarded for her conspicuous contributions to the association and to the theatre world in general. She is also active in the American Society for Theatre Research and the National Theatre Conference and was for six years (1977–1983) on the National Joint Commission on Theatre and Dance Accreditation.

Roberts's variety of interests is exemplified in her membership on the boards of several New York theatres: Nuestro Teatro, a bilingual company; Playwrights Horizons, a forum for new plays; Periwinkle Productions, a children's theatre; and Direct Theatre, a forum for experimental work. She also helped to found the American College Theatre Festival, an annual event held in Washington, D.C., to showcase the range and quality of college theatre productions, and served on its central committee for four years.

Roberts is the recipient of the Phi Delta Gamma National Achievement Award and the American College Theatre Festival's Gold and Silver Medallions as well as the Award of Excellence from the president of Hunter College. Long active in the Presbyterian Church, she became a Presbyterian Elder in 1960 and in 1975 was the first woman to be elected Moderator of the New York City Presbytery in its 200-year history.

Frequently a consultant and evaluator or speaker at nationwide panels, councils, and conferences, Roberts observes, ''One of my convictions—and I've acted on this all my life—is that one must be an artist as well as a teacher, and one must continuously practice one's art in order to teach it. I think I have been instrumental over the years in erasing the false distinction between what is called the real world of the theatre and academic theatre. One of my satisfactions over time has been to see that dichotomy diminish'' (Interview).

Vera Mowry Roberts's books are *On Stage, A History of Theatre* (1962, 1974) and *The Nature of Theatre* (1972). Both are standard college texts. In addition, Roberts has written a monograph entitled *One Third of a Nation* and has contributed articles to the McGraw-Hill *Encyclopedia of World Drama, Collier's Encyclopedia*, the *Dictionary of Literary Biography, Educational Theatre Journal, Quarterly Journal of Speech, Clearing House, Marquee, Speech Monographs*, the *Washington Post*, the *Phi Delta Gamma Journal*, and the *ACA Bulletin*. Roberts is listed in *The Biographical Encyclopaedia and Who's Who of the American Theatre* (1966); *Who's Who in American Education* (1968); *Directory of American Scholars*, Vol. II (1982); and the *International Who's Who* (1982). Additional information and quotations are from an interview with Roberts in New York City on March 4, 1982.

Holly Hill

ROBERTSON, Agnes Kelly (December 25, 1833–November 6, 1916): actress, was born in Edinburgh, Scotland. Her father was Thomas Robertson, an art publisher. Agnes began her stage career at the age of ten as a singer at the Theatre Royal, Aberdeen, and also acted in the play *The Spoiled Child*. Not long after her first appearance on the stage, the Robertson family moved to Dublin, and Robertson later wrote that she considered herself more Irish than Scottish. She appeared in provincial companies in Manchester, Hull, Liverpool, and Glasgow, playing with Fanny Kemble, William Macready, and the Terry family. While in Liverpool she acted with Mr. and Mrs. Charles Kean, and when Kean took over the Princess's Theatre in London, he invited her to join the company. Since she was only seventeen, she lived with the Keans and became their temporary ward. She made her first appearance in London on October 16, 1850, playing a page in *A Wife's Secret*. Although she usually played light comedy parts, she also appeared as Nerissa, Hero, and Ophelia in Kean's Shakespearean revivals.

While at the Princess's Theatre, Robertson met house dramatist Dion Boucicault, already a successful writer in London. For the Keans' benefit in 1852 Boucicault wrote an afterpiece called *The Vampire*. Robertson appeared in this play, and Boucicault himself played the Phantom. Her beauty and charm attracted Boucicault, and he wrote for her a two-act sentimental play, *The Prima Donna*. An argument between Kean and Boucicault resulted in Boucicault's resignation; in addition, Robertson movied out of the Keans' home and withdrew from the company. She joined Madame Lucia Elizabeth Vestris at the Lyceum Theatre, but the season at the Lyceum was a failure, and Robertson found herself out of work. Boucicault arranged for Robertson to play a season at Burton's Theatre in New York, where his plays had been very popular. On August 17, 1853, she sailed for New York, and three weeks later Boucicault also left for America.

Before her New York engagement, Robertson played at the Theatre Royal in Montreal, opening on September 19, 1853, in *The Young Actress*, Boucicault's adaptation of Edward Lancaster's play *The Manager's Daughter*. Essaying five roles in this production, Robertson performed as singer, dancer, and actress, playing to packed houses. News of her success brought offers from every major city in the United States. She went to New York, opening at Burton's Theatre on October 22, 1853, in *The Young Actress*. A week later she appeared as Master Bob Nettles in *To Parents and Guardians* and then in a new play, *The Fox Hunt*, by Boucicault, now her husband and manager.

After three very successful months in New York, Robertson accepted a two-week engagement at the Boston Museum, which was such a success that it was extended to nine weeks. While in Boston, Boucicault wrote another young boy role for her, this time an Irish lad called Andy Blake, in a play by that name. From Boston, Robertson and Boucicault traveled to Washington, Philadelphia, Baltimore, Chicago, Rochester, and Buffalo. Robertson played to full houses everywhere. Returning with her to Boston, Boucicault made his American acting debut on September 22, 1854, in *The Irish Artist*. Their next engagement was in New York at the Broadway Theatre, where Robertson, in a comic sketch written by Boucicault, sang, danced, and interpreted five characters. The audiences once again were delighted with the dainty Agnes Robertson and gave her the nickname, "The Fairy Star," from the title of this piece. During this engagement Boucicault made his first New York appearance, along with his wife, in the play *Used Up*. Thereafter, the Boucicaults were to appear frequently together.

During 1855 the Boucicaults traveled to Mobile and New Orleans, where Robertson appeared in a play designed to make the most of her popularity, *Agnes Robertson at Home*. In New Orleans their first child, Dion William, was born. Within a month after the baby's birth Robertson was playing in Philadelphia. Shortly thereafter, they presented Boucicault's new play, *Grimaldi; or, Scenes in the Life of an Actress*, in Cincinnati. After an unsuccessful attempt to manage a theatre in New Orleans, the family returned to New York, where Robertson and Boucicault were signed up for a summer season at Wallack's Theatre. This summer season, made up almost exclusively of Boucicault's plays, was so successful that they were retained for the autumn season (1857) and Boucicault was hired as the general manager. During this season they added *Old Heads and Young Hearts* and *London Assurance* to their repertoire. *London Assurance* had been Boucicault's first successful play at the Princess's Theatre in London, but he had never played in it. In this production, Boucicault played Dazzle and Robertson played Grace.

Robertson's next great success was as Jessie Brown in her husband's play *Jessie Brown; or, The Relief of Lucknow*, which opened at Wallack's Theatre on February 22, 1858, and became the hit of the season. Boucicault played the villainous Sepoy Nana Sahib, and Robertson gave one of her long-remembered performances as the courageous young Scottish girl who kept up the spirits of the besieged Europeans by claiming she could hear the pipes of a Scottish regiment coming to rescue them. Another Boucicault play, *Pauvrette*, with the author and Robertson in the leading roles, also proved successful that season.

In September 1859 Robertson played the title role in *Dot*, Boucicault's dramatization of Charles Dickens' novel, *The Cricket on the Hearth*, with Joseph

Jefferson as Caleb Plummer. This play opened the season at the remodeled Union Square Theatre, now called the Winter Garden. That same season Robertson played the pitiful, abused Smike in her husband's adaptation of Dickens's *Nicholas Nickleby*. One of the sensations of this season was the play *The Octoroon*, in which Robertson played Zoe, the girl with one-eighth Negro blood who is put up for auction as a slave. This play by Boucicault dealt with the current attitudes of both Northerners and Southerners toward slavery. The play opened on December 6, four days after John Brown had been hanged.

In 1860 Robertson and Boucicault joined **Laura Keene**'s theatre, where they played in *Jeanie Deans*, Boucicault's adaptation of Sir Walter Scott's novel *The Heart of Midlothian*. The role of Jeanie Deans was another triumph for Robertson. Only a few weeks later Robertson made a great success of *The Colleen Bawn*, a play by Boucicault based on a true incident that had recently taken place in Ireland. Robertson played Eily O'Connor, the Colleen Bawn (which means the fair-haired girl), a simple girl married to a wealthy husband who tries to have her murdered. Boucicault played the comic Irish hero, Myles-na-Coppaleen.

Having received many offers from London theatre managers, the Boucicaults decided that it was time to make a triumphant return to London. They opened in *The Colleen Bawn* at the Adelphi Theatre on September 10, 1860. This play was the biggest success seen in London for decades. It was presented every night for ten months, with only a short break in April, the longest run to that time in the history of the English stage. Boucicault sent out touring companies of the play, and in April he and Robertson appeared in it at the Theatre Royal, Dublin, where they were lionized by audiences. On November 18, 1860, the Boucicaults presented *The Octoroon* in London, with Robertson repeating her role as Zoe. English audiences would not accept Zoe's death at the the end of the play, and Boucicault wrote a new last act that allowed Zoe to live. The Boucicaults once again presented *The Colleen Bawn*, this time at Drury Lane, where night after night the theatre was packed.

On November 7, 1864, Robertson opened in Dublin in another Irish play, *Arrah-na-Pogue*. This play by Boucicault played to wild enthusiasm in Dublin and then moved to London, where it was the hit of the season, running for 164 nights. Robertson played Arrah-na-Pogue, or Arrah of the Kiss, and Boucicault was Shaun the Post. In 1866 Robertson played Jane Learoyd in her husband's *The Long Strike*, one of the earliest examples of a play based on a labor dispute. *The Long Strike* had a successful run at the Lyceum Theatre in London. Robertson and Boucicault continued to act in Boucicault's plays both in England and Ireland until 1868, when they announced their retirement from the stage. For two years they remained in retirement. Robertson was busy rearing their five children. In 1869 Abrey, their sixth and last child, was born. Boucicault's new plays were not successful, and in 1871 Robertson and Boucicault acted again in *The Colleen Bawn* in Manchester. Then they agreed to play a season of Boucicault's Irish plays at the Gaiety Theatre in London. This engagement was extended for a second season.

In 1872 the Boucicaults, leaving their children in school in London, sailed for the United States. On September 23 they began an engagement at Booth's Theatre with *Arrah-na-Pogue*. It was twelve years since they had left the United States, but New York turned out to welcome them back. They added *Jessie Brown* and *Night and Morning* (renamed *Kerry*) to the bills and had a very successful eight-week run before beginning a short tour to Boston and other cities. Their enthusiastic reception convinced them to stay in the United States, and early in 1873 they applied for and received American citizenship. However, their marriage was breaking up. Boucicault had had a number of mistresses, and one of them, Katharine Rogers, had followed them to the United States. In March 1873, Robertson sailed alone for England.

In August 1875, Boucicault brought his successful new Irish play, *The Shaughraun*, to London. The play had been much acclaimed in the United States, where Boucicault won high praise for his role as the Shaughraun, or vagabond. In London, he persuaded Robertson to play Moya in the play, and once again the partnership of Robertson and Boucicault worked its magic on the stage. On the final evening of the production, the Boucicaults' oldest child, Willie, now a young man of twenty, was killed in a train accident. The grief of the parents brought them together for a short time, but in July 1876 Boucicault sailed alone for America. Over the next few years, Robertson made three trips to America to try to effect a reconciliation with Boucicault, but in 1885 he went with a company to Australia. While there he married a young actress in the company, Louise Thorndyke. When news of the marriage reached Robertson in London, she declared that she was still married to Boucicault. He contended that they had never been married. In June 1888, the court ruled that Boucicault and Robertson had been married in New York in 1853 and that his marriage to Louise Thorndyke was bigamous. Robertson received the final decree for her divorce in 1889. Boucicault died on September 18, 1890.

Two months after Boucicault's death, Robertson was once again in the United States, and a benefit was arranged for her at the Fifth Avenue Theatre in New York. E. H. Sothern, Maurice Barrymore, **Lillian Russell**, and Nina Boucicault, their daughter, appeared; Robertson herself acted with J. H. Stoddart in a scene from *The Long Strike*. She returned to England, where she continued to act occasionally, making her last appearance in London in 1896 in the role of Mrs. Cregan in a revival of *The Colleen Bawn*. She died in London on November 6, 1916, and was buried at Brompton Cemetery.

Agnes Robertson was described as small and delicate. Early pictures of her and descriptions by friends attest to her striking beauty. Her voice was described as sweet, and a critic for the *New York Times* wrote that "she had the prettiest of ballad voices" and "was always unaffected in the use of it" (July 4, 1875). In the juvenile comedy of her early career and in the breeches' parts she was bright and bewitching, but it was in serious and sad roles that she won the hearts of her audience. "Her sweetness, her susceptibility, her submission under suffering, her uncomplaining courage and repining resignation beneath undeserved persecution'' made her ideal for such roles as Dot, Eily O'Connor, Jeanie Deans, and the wretched, beaten Smike (*Actors and Actresses*, Vol. VI, pp. 83–86). In the representation of simple Scottish and Irish peasant girls, Agnes Robertson has probably never been surpassed. To the popular melodramas of the day she brought charm, naturalness, and simplicity.

Agnes Robertson has written about her early life in "In the Days of My Youth" in *M.A.P. (Mainly About People*, July 1, 1899). Contemporary views of the Boucicaults may be found in J. B. Matthews and Laurence Hutton, *The Life and Art of Edwin Booth and His Contemporaries* (1886); J. B. Matthews and Laurence Hutton, *Actors and Actresses of Great Britain and the United States*, Vol. VI (1886); John B. Clapp and Edwin Francis Edgett, *Players of the Present*, Part 3 (1901); and Montrose J. Moses, *Famous Actor-Families in America* (1906, reprinted 1968). See also Jane Ellen Frith Panton, *Leaves from a Life* (1908); George C. D. Odell, *Annals of the New York Stage*, Vols, VI, VII (1931), Vol. IX (1937), Vol. XIV (1945); and Arthur Hobson Quinn, *A History of the American Drama From the Beginning to the Civil War* (1943). Such biographies as Richard Fawkes's *Dion Boucicault* (1979); Robert Hogan's, *Dion Boucicault* (1969); and Townsend Walsh's, *The Career of Dion Boucicault* (1915, reprinted 1967); contain information on Robertson's life and career. Robertson's obituary appeared in the *New York Times* (November 7, 1916) and in the London *Times* (November 7, 1916). An article about Robertson also appeared in the *New York Times* on November 26, 1916. The Robinson Locke Collection of Dramatic Scrapbooks in the New York Public Library Performing Arts Research Center at Lincoln Center contains clippings about the Boucicaults, as does the Harvard Theatre Collection. Robertson is included in *Who's Who in the Theatre* (1916); William C. Young, *Famous Actors and Actresses on the American Stage*, Vol. II (1975); *Who Was Who in the Theatre*, Vol. I (1978, under Boucicault); *Victorian Actors and Actresses in Review*, ed. Donald Mullin (1983); *The Oxford Companion to the Theatre* (1983, under Boucicault); *The Oxford Companion to American Theatre* (1984).

Alice McDonnell Robinson

ROSENTHAL, Jean (March 16, 1912–May 1, 1969): preeminent lighting designer, also scene designer, consultant, and producer, was born Eugenie Rosenthal in New York City, to Dr. Morris Rosenthal and Dr. Pauline (Scharfman) Rosenthal. Both parents had emigrated from Rumania in the 1880s. Eugenie was the middle child; her brothers were Ivan and Leon Rosenthal. Her mother, a psychiatrist, was a progressive-minded parent who enrolled her three children in William Fincke's Manumit School in Pawling, New York, where Jeannie, as she was called, took readily to the vast numbers of independent projects available to students. She long remembered that an important lesson she learned there was how to walk into a chicken house without disturbing the chickens. People who worked with her later came to know how emblematic this story was of Rosenthal's quiet but precise way of working in the theatre.

At Manumit, one of Rosenthal's class projects was George Bernard Shaw's play *Arms and the Man*. She was both director and stage manager, and she cast her brother Ivan in the lead. She discovered then that she loved working with lights, properties, and scenery; and she could easily relate these theatrical elements to the world in which she lived, for Jean Rosenthal's world in the 1920s was a vibrant, stimulating New Yorker's world. Her parents saw to it that her days were full of plays, operas, symphonies, and museums. At the Museum of Modern Art she was introduced to the shimmering world of the French Impressionists and their obsession with light.

After William Fincke died, the Manumit School was closed, and the Rosenthal children were enrolled at Friends' Seminary, just around the corner from their brownstone on East 15th Street in Manhattan. Upon graduation Jean Rosenthal attended the Neighborhood Playhouse School of the Theatre "to enlarge her horizons" (*Magic of Light*, p. 13), because, as her parents put it, she as yet had no firm idea of what she really wanted to do with her life. At the Neighborhood Playhouse, founded in the 1920s by **Irene** and **Alice Lewisohn**, and still in its formative years, Rosenthal came into contact with a young dance teacher who was to have the strongest influence on her life and way of thinking about art— **Martha Graham**. Rosenthal said of her, "She was a woman of imagination, of total purpose toward what she wished to achieve, and she was busy creating a new language in the dance. I was fortunate enough to grow up with her as it developed. My association with her was really the first I had in terms of lighting design, and it still continues" (*Magic of Light*, p. 13). Martha Graham, in turn, described Rosenthal in this way: "When she came to me at the Neighborhood Playhouse, Jean was a little, pop-eyed girl, enamoured of the theatre, and she did not know what she wanted to do. Or maybe she did. She wanted to 'make theatre' " (*Magic of Light*, p. 13). At the Neighborhood Playhouse, Louis Horst taught styles of dance; Laura Elliott, voice production and speech; Irene Lewisohn, lyric theatre production; Martha Graham, modern dance; and **Aline Bernstein**, design. Rosenthal showed no talent as a performer or dancer, so she became technical assistant to Martha Graham, an association that was to become a lifelong one.

Rosenthal was never quite sure how the next move in her life developed. After a year and a half at the Neighborhood Playhouse, she was interviewed by George Pierce Baker and enrolled in the Yale University School of Drama. She spent the next three years at Yale, where she studied theatre history with George Pierce Baker, scene design with Donald Oenslager, and costume design with Frank Bevin. Her most important teacher at Yale, however, was Stanley McCandless, whom she was pleased to call "the granddaddy of us all" (*Magic of Light*, p. 16). McCandless taught lighting and was the author of *A Method for Lighting the Stage* (1932), a seminal handbook on lighting. Rosenthal felt that McCandless's teaching supplemented her instinctive knowledge. She especially admired his theory that there had to be a technique and a method for organizing ideas on lighting. Later, she would feel that her ability to organize and to find a method would be her strongest gift.

At Yale Rosenthal was learning theories and techniques from teachers who also were active in the professional theatre. She felt that those years (1930 to 1933) represented a transition from the older theatre of Arthur Wing Pinero and

Clyde Fitch to the theatre of Philip Barry and Eugene O'Neill. To have gone through so many contrasting styles in such a short space of time delighted Rosenthal. "I really could not have been better placed in history. I waltzed through an entire span of dramatic changes in a period of about three years" (*Magic of Light*, p. 16).

After Yale, Rosenthal went to New York, where she met director-actor-producer John Houseman. Through him she joined the Federal Theatre Project. Now twenty-one years old, Rosenthal worked in the One-Act Project as a technician in charge of setting up and moving theatre productions from one city park to another. She learned to work under pressure and claims that she learned technical theatre well because "there was no time to be artistic about art" (*Magic of Light*, p. 17). Houseman was soon made producer for one of the projects in the Federal Theatre, and he asked for Rosenthal as a technical assistant. Now began an extraordinary period in her life where she worked with Orson Welles as director and with such actors as Joseph Cotton, Arlene Francis, Bil Baird, and Hiram Sherman, all just beginning their careers. She also had the opportunity to work with Houseman on Leslie Howard's production of *Hamlet* (1936) on Broadway and then to tour with this show across the United States.

While she was with the Federal Theatre Project, Rosenthal experienced the joy of instant success with the project's high-style farce *Horse Eats Hat* (1936), and she was at the very center of the storm over Marc Blitzstein's *The Cradle Will Rock* (1937) when, in the face of government opposition to that play's opening in New York, Orson Welles, along with Blitzstein, Rosenthal, cast members, *and* audience, all marched up Broadway and Seventh Avenue to 58th Street, where they put on a hastily improvised performance at the Venice Theatre. This revolt of actors against the United States government became a theatrical legend. Because of this illicit performance, both Welles and Houseman were fired from the Federal Theatre—as was Rosenthal—but Welles and Houseman soon recovered and retaliated by founding the Mercury Theatre, hiring Jean Rosenthal as their technical director.

Rosenthal's experience with the Mercury Theatre, a repertory company, was an important one for her. Recognizing the genius of Orson Welles, she wrote, "For all of us, working under the dominant direction of Orson Welles was clear-cut, stimulating, and rewarding" (*Magic of Light*, p. 22). The Mercury Theatre productions were all fascinating adventures. There was for instance, Shakespeare's *Julius Caesar* (1937), done in a contemporary Nazi style. Then by contrast, came Thomas Dekker's *Shoemaker's Holiday* (1938), a warm, genial comedy, followed by George Bernard Shaw's *Heartbreak House* (1938) with Welles himself playing Captain Shotover. Next came *Five Kings* (1938–1939), a hugely ambitious show concocted from Shakespeare's histories, which was toured outside New York. Finally, *Too Much Johnson* (1938), a bizarre production that baffled its audiences, was given in Connecticut during the summer but never taken to New York. Rosenthal provided more than the lighting and technical expertise for these productions. John Houseman said of her, "She was not only very good at lighting and an extremely able technical expert, but she kept up the morale when too much was being asked of human beings, particularly of the electricians. Jean kept up their spirits, kept the whole thing going. We could not have survived at the Mercury without the particular combination of talents she brought to us'' (*Magic of Light*, p. 23). Houseman and Welles were unfortunately lured soon afterwards to Hollywood, and the Mercury Theatre dissolved.

In the late 1930s modern dance was gaining momentum in New York. Rosenthal was still working for Martha Graham, but she now began with Lincoln Kirstein and his Ballet Society an association that was to last eighteen years. In 1940 she also opened a firm called Theatre Production Service, offering complete design services for shows and theatres. Her partners in this venture were two Yale Drama School friends, Helen March and Eleanor Wise.

Rosenthal now began to understand that her special kind of theatre was one in which she could paint with light even as choreographers provided patterns of movement and musicians patterns of sound. Kirstein's Ballet Society blossomed and became the New York City Ballet at City Center. Rosenthal designed the lighting for Gian-Carlo Menotti's operas *The Medium* (1947), *The Telephone* (1947), *The Saint of Bleecker Street* (1954), and for musicals like *Show Boat* (1954), *Die Fledermaus* (1954), *House of Flowers* (1954), *The King and I* (1956), and *Kiss Me, Kate* (1956). For five years, between 1953 and 1958, she again worked with her old friend John Houseman at the American Shakespeare Festival in Stratford, Connecticut, where she was technical director. Among the shows she designed lighting for in this period were *Much Ado About Nothing* (1957) and *The Merchant of Venice* (1957), both starring **Katharine Hepburn**.

Other Broadway shows that featured "lighting by Jean Rosenthal" were *West Side Story* (1957), *Jamaica* (1957), *The Dark at the Top of the Stairs* (1957), *The Disenchanted* (1958), *Redhead* (1958), *Destry Rides Again* (1959), *The Sound of Music* (1959), *A Taste of Honey* (1960), *Night of the Iguana* (1961), *A Funny Thing Happened on the Way to the Forum* (1962), *Hello, Dolly!* (1964), *Fiddler on the Roof* (1964)—the list is a veritable compendium of the best on Broadway. Jean Rosenthal also found herself in demand as a consultant on lighting systems—not all of them connected with theatres. She worked on the Los Angeles Music Center, Canada's national theatres, the Pan American building at John F. Kennedy International Airport, the Juilliard School of Music and Drama at Lincoln Center, the Guthrie Theatre in Minneapolis, the Boscobel Restoration in Garrison, New York, and many others.

Rosenthal had received the Henrietta Lord Memorial Award from the Yale School of Drama in 1932. In 1968–1969 she received the Outer Critics Circle Award for her contributions to stage design. Unfortunately, her career and life were drawing to an early close; by 1968 she had cancer and, after a major operation, never recovered her health. Her ending was what the theatre had come to expect of Jean Rosenthal. On April 20, 1969, Martha Graham's *Archaic Hours* opened at the New York City Center. The program proudly announced

"Production and lighting by Jean Rosenthal." In the audience that night, against the wishes of her doctors and friends, was Jean Rosenthal, who had come to see that all went well, that all lighting cues were executed properly.

On May 1, 1969, Jean Rosenthal died in a New York hospital, and in 1972 Lael Wertenbaker published the book on which she had been collaborating with Rosenthal titled *The Magic of Light*, in which the designer wrote, "For the first time, on the [Martha's] Vineyard, I have had the time—for time seems to stretch itself as I do, within its cradle of seas—to consider and sum up my lifetime in light" (*Magic of Light*, p. 26).

The best source of information about Jean Rosenthal is *The Magic of Light* (1972) by Jean Rosenthal and Lael Wertenbaker. Reviews of her work can be found in the *New York Times Directory of the Theatre* (1973). Winthrop Sargeant wrote a biographical account of Rosenthal in "Please, Darling, Bring Three to Seven," *The New Yorker* (February 4, 1956). See also "Personality of the Month: Jean Rosenthal," *Dancemagazine* (October 1959), and John Houseman, *Entertainers and the Entertained* (1986). Rosenthal's obituary appeared in the *New York Times* (May 2, 1969). The Jean Rosenthal Papers are at the Wisconsin Center for Theatre Research in Madison. There are some lighting plots and other papers in the Billy Rose Theatre Collection in the New York Public Library Performing Arts Research Center at Lincoln Center. Rosenthal is listed in *The Biographical Encyclopaedia and Who's Who of the Theatre* (1966) and *Notable American Women*, Vol IV: *The Modern Period* (1980).

Roger Kenvin

ROWSON, Susanna Haswell (1762–November 2, 1824): playwright, actress, novelist, and educator, was born in Portsmouth, England. Her mother, Susanna (Musgrave) Haswell, died in giving birth to the child. Her father, William Haswell, was a lieutenant and later a captain in the Royal Navy. His ancestors had been workers in the shipyards at Portsmouth. Shortly after the birth of his child and the death of his wife, Lt. Haswell, leaving his baby with relatives in England, came to America as a collector of royal customs. He settled in Nantasket, Massachusetts, and some time later married Rachel Woodward of Boston. By his second wife he had three sons, all of whom went to sea. In 1767 Lt. Haswell went to England to bring Susanna and her nurse to America, narrowly escaping shipwreck in Boston Harbor. In Nantasket the Haswell family was acquainted with James Otis, who took an interest in Susanna and called her "my little scholar" because of her interest in books. As tensions rose between the Tories and the Patriots, Susanna's father, as an officer of the Crown, was looked upon with suspicion by his neighbors. In 1775 his property was confiscated, and he and his family were interned. In 1778 Haswell and his impoverished family were returned to England.

Susanna Haswell was soon hired as a governess by the Duchess of Devonshire and was thus able to tour Europe and become acquainted with the private lives of the aristocracy. During this time she also began to write and publish stories and poems. In 1786 she dedicated her first novel, *Victoria*, to her patroness. In 1787 she met and married William Rowson, a handsome London hardware merchant and a trumpeter in the Royal Horse Guards. In 1791 Susanna Rowson published her major novel, *Charlotte Temple*, which was wildly popular in both England and America. When her husband's business failed the next year, Susanna and William Rowson and William's sister, Charlotte, determined to earn money by going on the stage. During the 1792–1793 season, they toured England and Scotland. In Edinburgh they were seen by Thomas Wignell, who had come to Britain to recruit actors for his New Theatre on Chestnut Street in Philadelphia. The Rowsons joined Thomas Wignell's company and sailed for America. When they arrived in December 1793, yellow fever was raging in Philadelphia; so the acting company opened in Annapolis and then played Baltimore. The Philadelphia opening was delayed until February 1794. Susanna and William Rowson remained with the Chestnut Street Theatre company until 1796, when they joined the Federal Street Theatre in Boston. On May 1, 1797, at the age of thirty-five, Susanna Rowson made her farewell appearance on stage.

In her few years in the theatre Susanna Rowson played 129 roles in 126 different productions. R. W. G. Vail in his *Bibliographic Study* of Susanna Rowson has listed her roles. She usually played secondary or character parts. Occasionally she played serious roles like Lady Capulet in *Romeo and Juliet* and the Duchess of York in *Richard III*, but her specialty was comedy. She played Audrey in *As You Like It*, Mrs. Quickly in *The Merry Wives of Windsor*, Lucy in *The Rivals*, and Lady Sneerwell in *The School for Scandal*. Her first biographer, Elias Nason, who knew her personally, wrote that she had clear enunciation and a "good reading" of her lines. He also described her as having "a face beaming with expression, an easy and polite manner, and retentive memory" (Nason, p. 73). Rowson was also a dancer and is said to have been the first female Harlequin in America. She and her husband also appeared with Ricketts' circus, for which she danced the hornpipe in the role of a sailor.

In addition, Rowson could sing and play the harpsichord and the guitar, and Nason wrote that she could improvise "a song or speech with equal skill and beauty" (Nason, p. 73). This musical ability made her a valuable member of the company, and she also became popular as a writer of song lyrics. Her songs were set to music by Alexander Reinagle, one of the managers of the company at the Chestnut Street Theatre; by James Hewitt of the John Street Theatre, New York; by Peter Albrecht Van Hagen, Jr., conductor of the orchestra at the Haymarket Theatre in Boston; by Benjamin Carr, conductor, performer, teacher, and publisher; and by other popular musicians of the time. The American Antiquarian Society has a collection of sixteen of Rowson's songs. Some of her lyrics later appeared in her book, *Miscellaneous Poems* (1804). Most of her songs are patriotic, but she also wrote love songs like "Will You Rise, My Love?"

Rowson was not content to write only isolated lyrics; in March 1794, she and Alexander Reinagle and William Francis, a dancer, produced a "pantomimical dance" called *The Sailor's Landlady*. This piece proved very popular and contained Rowson's most famous song, "America, Commerce and Freedom," which remained a popular drinking song for twenty-five years, although it was originally intended to promote a belief in American maritime power.

On June 30, 1794, Susanna Rowson's first musical play, *Slaves in Algiers*, was presented in Philadelphia, and during the next few years in Baltimore, New York, Boston, Hartford, and Charleston. It was printed in Philadelphia in 1794 and in Boston in 1796. The play was so outspoken on liberty and human rights and on America's great destiny that it was bitterly criticised in *A Kick for a Bite* by the spokesman for the Federalists, William Cobbett, writing under the name of Peter Porcupine. An anonymous writer defended the play in *A Rub from Snub* and called Rowson "a bright ornament to female science" (*A Rub from Snub*, 1795). The major characters are women. *Slaves in Algiers* is a romantic three-act play interspersed with songs about Americans held captive by the Barbary pirates. The music was composed by Alexander Reinagle, and when the play was first produced, Susanna Rowson played the major role of Olivia.

In January 1795, Rowson's second play, *The Volunteers*, inspired by the 1794 Whiskey Insurrection in Western Pennsylvania, was produced in Philadelphia. The play with music was evidently published, but only the songs and Reinagle's vocal score are extant. In 1795 Susanna Rowson also wrote an address in poetic form called "The Standard of Liberty," which was frequently spoken from the stage. In the same year, 1795, Rowson made an adaptation of Philip Massinger's *Bondman*, which was produced as *The Female Patriot; or, Nature's Rights*. It was never printed. For her last appearance on the stage in 1797, Rowson wrote a comedy, *Americans in England*, printed in 1796 and revived in 1800 by John Hodgkinson at the Park Theatre in New York under the title *The Columbian Daughter; or, Americans in England*. Although the script has not survived, the cast list infers that the Americans, Mr. and Mrs. Freedom, are contrasted with such British ladies as Mrs. Manners and Mrs. Prattle.

When Rowson retired from the stage in 1797 she established a school for young ladies on Federal Street in Boston. By 1800 the Ladies' Academy had outgrown its building, and Rowson moved it to Medford, then in 1803 to Newton, Massachusetts. In 1807 she moved back to Boston, and there the school remained. Rowson retired in 1822, leaving the school in charge of her niece, Susan Johnston, and her adopted daughter, Fanny Mills. She had also reared William B. Rowson, the illegitimate son of her husband who had become a customs clerk after 1797.

Rowson was one of the first educators in Boston to own a piano, and she hired excellent music teachers like Peter Von Hagen and Gotlieb Graupner to teach this new instrument to her young ladies. She was also one of the first teachers of young women to include instruction in public speaking, declamation, and dramatics. In 1811 she published *A Present for Young Ladies*, a book that contained addresses, poems, and dialogues that had been used in the teaching of her pupils. During her years as a school mistress, she published textbooks on geography, history, and spelling; she edited a magazine, *The Boston Weekly*;

and she contributed to magazines like the *Monthly Anthology* and the *New England Galaxy*. She also continued to write poetry, songs, and novels.

Rowson is remembered today especially for her novel *Charlotte, a Tale of Truth*, later called *Charlotte Temple*. There have been over two hundred editions of this novel; it was America's first best seller. Another novel that proved popular was *Rebecca, or the Fille de Chambre*. She also published a novel in four volumes, *Trials of the Human Heart* (1795), and the historical novel *Reuben and Rachel* (1798). In 1804 Rowson's *Miscellaneous Poems* was published, and in 1813 *Sarah, the Exemplary Wife*, a series of fictionalized moral tracts. At the time of her death in Boston, Rowson had completed *Charlotte's Daughter; or, the Three Orphans*, which was published in 1828 and included a memoir about Mrs. Rowson by her friend Samuel L. Knapp. This book, later published as *Lucy Temple*, had at least thirty-one editions. Rowson was buried in the family vault of her friend Gotlieb Graupner, in St. Matthew's Church, South Boston. When St. Matthew's Church was demolished in 1866, Rowson's remains were transferred to Mount Hope Cemetery in Dorchester.

Susanna Rowson was born in England and reared in a Loyalist family, yet became an early spokesperson for American ideals. She helped to promote the arts, especially music and theatre, and she was a progressive educator. She was one of the first American writers to express openly through her novels and her plays a protest against the subordinate status of women.

The earliest account dealing with Susanna Rowson's life is Samuel L. Knapp's "Memoir" in the preface to *Charlotte's Daughter* (1828). One of the early biographies is Elias Nason's *A Memoir of Mrs. Susanna Rowson* (1870). R. W. G. Vail lists the roles played by Rowson, many of the songs written by her, and most of the editions of her books in his *Susanna Haswell Rowson, the Author of Charlotte Temple: A Bibliographical Study* (1933), published in the *Proceedings of the American Antiquarian Society* (Vol. 42, April 1932, pp. 47–160). Francis W. Halsey's introduction to the 1905 edition of *Charlotte Temple* contains a biography of Rowson, as does also the more recent edition for the modern reader by Clara M. and Rudolf Kirk (1964). Dorothy Weil's *In Defense of Women: Susanna Rowson (1762–1824)* (1976) discusses Rowson's aims and attitudes as reflected in her writings. The book also contains a listing of Rowson's works. See also Joseph T. Buckingham, *Personal Memoirs and Recollections of Editorial Life*, Vol. I (1852), and *Anthony Haswell, Printer-Patriot-Ballader* (1925), which contains an account of the Haswell family. For Rowson's theatrical career, see Arthur Hobson Quinn's *A History of the American Drama from the Beginning to the Civil War* (1923, 1943); Charles Durang, "The Philadelphia Stage from the Year 1749 to the Year 1855," *Philadelphia Sunday Dispatch* (May 7, 1854, June 29, 1856, and July 8, 1860); William Clapp, Jr., *A Record of the Boston Stage* (1853); George O. Seilhamer, *The History of the American Theatre*, Vol. III (1891); Julian Mates, *The American Musical Stage Before 1800* (1962); and Constance Rourke, *The Roots of American Culture and Other Essays* (1942). Rowson's papers may be found at the American Antiquarian Society, the New York Public Library, the Harvard College Library, the Library of Congress, the University of Chicago Library, the Boston Public Library, the New York Historical Society, the British Museum Library, the Yale University Library, Brown University Library, the Watkinson Library at Trinity College, Hartford, Connecticut, and the New York State Library, Albany.

Susanna Haswell Rowson is included in James Rees, *The Dramatic Authors of America* (1845); T. Allston Brown, *History of the American Stage* (1870); *Dictionary of American Biography*, Vol. VIII (1935, renewed 1963); *Notable American Women*, Vol. III (1971); James Vinson, ed., *American Literature to 1900* (1980); *American Women Writers*, Vol. IV (1982); *The Oxford Companion to American Literature* (1983); and *Dictionary of Literary Biography*, Vol. 37, *American Writers of the Early Republic* (1985).

Alice McDonnell Robinson

RUSSELL, Lillian (December 4, 1861–June 6, 1922): preeminent musical comedy star, was born Helen Louise Leonard in Clinton, Iowa. Her father was Charles E. Leonard, a moderately successful publisher of the weekly *Clinton Herald*. Helen Louise was the youngest of five daughters. For reasons unknown, Leonard nicknamed his baby daughter "Nellie." Her mother, Cynthia Howland (Van Name) Leonard, was an ardent feminist. Clinton, Iowa, proved too provincial for her influence to be felt in the suffrage and equal rights movement. Sometime between 1863 and 1865, probably at the insistence of Cynthia Leonard, the family relocated in Chicago, where her influence could be properly exercised. She proceeded to organize the women of the city, and soon her various feminist societies became a thorn in the sides of the city fathers.

Cynthia Leonard's strong belief that a person's sex should not determine her place in society extended to the home front. "Nellie," already an extraordinarily beautiful child, received a private education at the Sacred Heart School, and later at the Park Institute, a fashionable finishing school. The nuns and teachers at these schools encouraged the girl's singing ability. In addition she studied voice with a Professor Gill in Chickering Hall. By the time Nellie Leonard reached the age of fourteen, it was clear to her mother that the girl had grown into an exceptionally beautiful young woman, who was independent, charming, and the possessor of a crystalline, lilting soprano voice. Over the next few years, Cynthia Leonard became convinced that her daughter could be an opera star. In 1878 she took Helen Louise to New York and sought the best vocal teacher available for her daughter, while at the same time pursuing her own feminist interests. She selected Leopold Damrosch, a noted Brooklyn voice coach, who heard the seventeen-year-old girl sing and accepted her at once as his pupil. Her voice was a clear, true soprano effortlessly capable of attaining high "C." Mother and teacher began to prepare the girl for a career in grand opera, but Helen Leonard had learned independence from her mother. At eighteen, she began to demonstrate that independence along with a certain degree of resistance to the years of arduous voice study ahead of her. Surreptitiously, she auditioned for and received a chorus part in Edward E. Rice's American production of *H. M. S. Pinafore* (1879). Soon she was fighting off stage-door Johnnies, as well as the dismay of her mother and Damrosch over her less refined professional debut. Nevertheless, she proved a willing captive of orchestra conductor Harry Braham, whom she married in 1880. The match was short-lived. In 1883 following the tragic loss of their infant son, each blaming the other for the tragedy, the couple divorced.

During the 1880s, Tony Pastor, one of the major impresarios of his day, presided over the Casino Theatre. As retold by the actress herself, the story goes that Pastor heard her sing at the home of a friend and hired her on the spot. She knew that her mother disapproved of her singing at music halls, but Pastor told her not to worry; he would give her a stage name and bill her as being from overseas. Thus, on November 22, 1880, the producer introduced "Miss Lillian Russell, the English ballad singer, a vision of loveliness and a voice of gold." With her perfect complexion, her perfect hourglass figure, and her perfect soprano voice, she was on her way to becoming the greatest comic opera star of her time.

During the 1880s on both coasts and on both sides of the Atlantic, triumph followed triumph. Men across the country fell in love with her, sight seen or sight unseen. She played in Edwin Andrau's *The Great Mogul* (1881) and in Gilbert and Sullivan operettas. Unfortunately, she also established a temperamental reputation with theatre managers. In 1883 Russell eloped to England with her second husband, Edward Solomon, another pit musician and would-be composer of comic opera. This marriage produced a daughter, Dorothy, who became a writer.

Russell made her London debut in 1883 in her husband's *Virginia and Paul*, which was greeted with praise for Russell, in spite of a second-rate script. In 1885 Russell returned to America in triumph, only to learn shortly thereafter that Solomon had been sued by an Englishwoman for bigamy, and Russell had her second marriage annulled.

She was married for a third time in January 1894 to John Haley Augustin Chatterton, a foppish narcissist. He used Russell and their marriage to forward his own musical career, pompously entitling himself "Signor Perugini." Unwilling, or unable, to consummate the marriage, Signor Perugini denounced Russell publicly for stealing his street makeup to enhance her own complexion. Five months following the ceremony, Russell walked out. About this time, she made the acquaintance of Diamond Jim Brady. By all accounts, Brady's congeniality matched his gargantuan appetites, and he never let his wealth get in the way of his friendships. By all evidence never lovers, Brady and Russell became lifelong companions and enduring friends.

For the six seasons prior to 1904, Russell was the happy star of vaudeville/burlesques at Weber and Fields' Music Hall, appearing in such revues as *Fiddle-dee-dee* and *Whoop-dee-doo*. Weber and Fields disbanded their company in 1904. Russell achieved some success in the title role of *Lady Teazle* in a musical version of *The School for Scandal* in 1904. She toured with F. F. Proctor's vaudeville company in 1905 and 1906. However, minor surgery on her throat had caused some deterioration of her voice, and under contract to Joseph Grooks she undertook some straight comedy roles. In 1907 she appeared in *Butterfly* and in 1908 in *Wildfire*. Her straight acting roles were not very successful, and she soon returned to vaudeville. In 1912 she experienced the first and most successful of several comebacks. Weber and Fields reconciled their differences and took Russell on their triumphal national tour of *Hokey-Pokey*, her last performance in a musical. Later the same year, she was married for the fourth, time, successfully at last, to Alexander Pollock Moore, publisher of the *Pittsburgh Leader* and, after her death, United States ambassador to Spain.

During the last ten years of her life, she lived out her parents' interests. Like her father she became a newspaper columnist; like her mother she became a political activist. She wrote beauty and feminine advice columns for the women's sections of the *Chicago Herald* and the *Chicago Daily Tribune*; she stumped the country for Liberty Loans and the American Red Cross; she campaigned vigorously for Warren G. Harding. During the course of a brief political appointment from Harding, she fell while aboard a transatlantic ship. Sometime later, due to complications from the fall, Lillian Russell died at her home in Pittsburgh.

Lillian Russell was a phenomenon: her profile appeared on those ubiquitous masculine properties, the cigar band and the matchbox cover; she was known popularly as "The American Beauty," adored by men and women alike; in fact, she was without question the most celebrated of what later became known as a pinup girl, a love goddess. Even today the name Lillian Russell conjures up the image of a woman of magical feminine charms. More significantly, Russell was instrumental in establishing the dignity and the art of the American musical theatre. Effortlessly attaining eight high "C's" an evening, an accomplishment of which any opera prima donna might be proud, Russell brought to the music hall, the operetta, and Weber and Fields' burlesques the concept that refined talent, exquisite beauty, and singular charm were not exclusive to the opera house. Russell was an original, and she helped to pave the way for the development of the American musical as a uniquely American phenomenon.

Surprisingly little coherent biographical material about Russell exists, largely due, no doubt, to her untimely death while she was writing her memoirs. Still, autobiographical material can be gleaned from her "reminiscences," which appeared in various issues of *Cosmopolitan* magazine from February through September of 1922. Other source information must be drawn from various periodical and newspaper clippings, especially the *New York Tribune* (June 8, 1883; April 2, 1886; September 24, 1886; October 1, 1886; February 10, 1891; August 30, 1893; November 15, 1893; November 17, 1893; January 20, 1894; January 22, 1894; May 21, 1897; June 24, 1898; July 1, 1898; October 23, 1898; and October 9, 1906), *Green Book Album* (February 1909), the *New York Herald* (June 6, 1922), the *New York Times* (June 6, 1922), and the *New York World* (June 7, 1922), *The National Magazine* (July 1922), *Literary Digest* (April 22, 1922, and June 24, 1922). There are scrapbooks in the Robinson Locke Dramatic Collection in the New York Public Library Performing Arts Research Center at Lincoln Center, and there are also clippings in the Harvard Theatre Collection. Other contemporary accounts concerning Russell can be found in works by one of her more loyal producers, Rudolph Aronson, in his *Theatrical and Musical Memoirs* (1913); by her colleague and good friend, Marie Dressler, in her autobiography, *My Own Story* (1934); and by her self-proclaimed fan Lewis C. Strang, in his *Famous Prima Donnas* (1900). Parker Morrell wrote a biography, *Lillian Russell* (1940). Philip C. Lewis's *Trouping: How the Show Came to Town* (1973) provides some colorful glimpses of the Russell legend, including one of the best portrait photographs of her in any source. See also Martin Gottfried, *In Person: The Great Entertainers* (1985). The best and most accurate secondary source remains John Burke, *Duet in Diamonds: The Flamboyant Saga of Lillian Russell and Diamond Jim Brady in America's Gilded Age* (1972). Lillian Russell is listed in Walter Browne and E. de Roy Koch, *Who's Who on the Stage, 1908* (1908); Dixie Hines and Harry Prescott Hanaford, eds., *Who's Who in Music and Drama* (1914); *Who's Who in the Theatre* (1922); *Notable American Women*, Vol. III (1971); William C. Young, *Famous Actors and Actresses on the American Stage*, Vol. II (1975); *Who Was Who in the Theatre*, Vol. IV (1978); and *The Oxford Companion to American Theatre* (1984).

Donald Ray Schwartz

S

SCHAFFNER, Caroline Hannah (June 24, 1901–): actress, entertainer, playwright, businesswoman, and museum curator, was born in Orange, Texas, the daughter of Helen Ridgway (Jones) Hannah and Charles Lee Hannah. She grew up in DeRidder, Louisiana, and attended Louisiana State University, Baton Rouge. She then became the first graduate of the School of Expression of the Horner Institute of Fine Arts in Kansas City, Missouri. In 1924, while appearing at the Lyric Theatre in Fort Dodge, Iowa, with ''Al Russell and His Sizzling Cuties,'' Caroline Hannah met Neil E. Schaffner, manager of the J. S. Angell's Comedians. On April 26, 1925, she joined that tent repertory company in Murray, Iowa, and three months later married Neil Schaffner in Sioux City, Iowa. After the summer season of 1925 they formed the Neil and Caroline Schaffner Players and opened at the Strand Theatre in Fort Dodge, Iowa, on October 10, 1925. For ten years the Schaffner players trouped through Iowa, playing theatres and opera houses, except for sixteen weeks each summer when they performed in a tent. During the summer of 1926, a son, Rome Lee, was born.

In 1926 the Schaffner Players was one of 400 repertory companies playing in theatres and under canvas tents, employing about 6,400 persons and playing to a total audience of over 18,000,000. By 1935 the depression had taken its toll on traveling repertory theatres. The Schaffner Players managed to survive with quality entertainment and wise business practices. For example, in the fall of 1935 Neil and Caroline Schaffner appeared on WCAZ radio in Carthage, Illinois, as Toby and Susie, a freckle-faced yokel and his girlfriend. They presented a daily fifteen-minute comedy show concerning the comings and goings in the office of *The Bugtussle News*. These shows were presented free to WCAZ in exchange for advertising the appearances of the Schaffner Players. During the winter season of 1936 ''Toby and Susie'' took their *Bugtussle News* to the *National Barn Dance* on NBC Radio in Chicago. For eight years, beginning in

1938 under the sponsorship of the Peterson Baking Company of Omaha, Nebraska, "Toby and Susie" appeared on a Midwest network of radio stations out of Cedar Rapids, Iowa. The program was renamed *The Corntussle News* with Toby Toliver, editor, and Susie B. Sharp, assistant. Thus, the Schaffner Players survived the depression, and "Toby and Susie" gained nationwide popularity on radio. Schaffner and her husband continued their summer tent theatre appearances throughout Iowa, Illinois, and Missouri, and during the 1950s, they appeared on television. First came the *Omnibus* showing of *Toby in the Tall Corn*, which won the Edinburgh Film Festival Award as best television documentary of 1954, and later came *Wide Wide World* with *Sounds of Laughter* in 1958. Also in 1958 the Schaffners were the subjects of Ralph Edward's *Neil Schaffner, This Is Your Life*. In 1961 they appeared on the *DuPont Show of the Week* in *Laughter, U.S.A.*

Between 1926 and their farewell tour in 1962, Caroline and Neil Schaffner appeared together in some three hundred plays for over five thousand performances and played to a minimum of one hundred thousand paid admissions per summer season. The Schaffners wrote forty plays and adapted over one hundred others. They wrote dramas, mysteries, comedies, farces, and musical reviews. Although Neil Schaffner wrote the final draft of the scripts, the plays were thoroughly "talked" through by both. As each play went into production Caroline Schaffner gave her approval or disapproval. Her husband stated, "She is an expert 'No' woman. When she gives her approval, it means the audience is going to like it" (Morris, p. 61). Schaffner plays were also popular with other theatre companies. In 1969 Dale Kittle provided a list of 173 companies that leased and featured these plays. The most popular Schaffner play in 1929 was *The Vulture*, which in that year was staged by more schools and colleges than any other play except George M. Cohan's *Seven Keys to Baldpate*. Many Schaffner plays continue to be leased through Caroline Schaffner or from Samuel French, Publisher. The most popular Schaffner play in 1981 was *Natalie Needs A Nightie*, which is widely used by community theatre groups and professional theatre companies.

Through the years Caroline and Neil Schaffner dreamed of a museum devoted to their kinds of theatre: opera house, tent, touring stock, and Chautauqua. The dream became a reality in 1973 when the Museum of Repertoire Americana opened in Mount Pleasant, Iowa, with Caroline Schaffner as curator. This unique museum houses memorabilia from the golden age of the Schaffners' type of theatre: scripts, backdrops, costumes, heralds, properties, and so forth. Caroline Schaffner has guided the collecting, cataloguing, and displaying of thousands of items from dozens of private collections of theatre professionals and fans. The museum displays are popular attractions for anyone interested in theatre. In addition, the museum is a treasury for scholars of popular entertainment. The museum also includes a theatre where appropriate plays and programs are presented throughout the year. The annual meeting there of the National Society for the Preservation of Tent, Folk, and Repertoire Theatre provides professionals, fans, and scholars an opportunity to share this theatre legend. Although Caroline Schaffner's influence was widespread as a performer and playwright, her long-range legacy will be the museum and its unique collection. Caroline Schaffner also shares her knowledge by publishing and by presenting papers to a variety of groups across the nation. Her many papers and presentations include programs for conferences at Lincoln Center, C. B. Post Center on Long Island, and the International Platform Association. In addition she has published a number of articles in *Variety*. In this way Schaffner continues her commitment as a professional in repertory theatre.

Caroline Schaffner's honors are many. The walls of her office are decorated with plaques, awards, and keys to cities presented during the 1962 farewell tour of the Schaffner Players. In 1979 she was guest lecturer and special guest at the University of Texas, Austin, for the première performance of a Toby play for children. That same year she gave the commencement address at Iowa Wesleyan College, Mount Pleasant, and her lifelong contributions to her profession were recognized with an honorary degree, Doctor of Humane Letters.

Caroline Schaffner is an eminent theatrical phenomenon and a very special person: performer, playwright, businesswoman, wife, mother, teacher, and scholar. Through all the struggles and successes, she has remained dignified and professional. Her high moral and ethical standards have upheld the theme of the Schaffner plays: good does triumph over evil.

Caroline Schaffner's collected press clippings, photographs, letters, scrapbook items, and play scripts are housed in her office and in the Museum of Repertoire Americana in Mount Pleasant, Iowa. Dolores Dorn-Heft, "Toby: The Twilight of a Tradition," *Theatre Arts* (August 1985), and Joe Alex Morris, "Corniest Show on the Road," *Saturday Evening Post* (September 17, 1955) include brief, informal accounts of the Schaffner Players. Two scholarly dissertations, Russell Dale Kittle, "Toby and Susie: The Show-Business Success of Neil and Caroline Schaffner, 1925–1962" (Unpublished Ph.D. dissertation, Ohio State University, 1969) and Martha Frances Stover Langford, "The Tent Repertoire Theatre of Neil and Caroline Schaffner: A Case Study in Tent Repertoire Theatre as Communication" (Unpublished Ph.D. dissertation, University of Colorado, Boulder, 1978), provide more definitive accounts of the Schaffners. Although *The Fabulous Toby and Me* (1968), Neil Schaffner's autobiography, it includes information about Caroline Schaffner and her career in show business. In addition, Caroline Schaffner reports her experiences in "Hicksville Opera House, A Recall of Repertoire," *Variety* (January 14, 1981), and "Trouping With The Schaffners," *American Popular Entertainment*, ed. Myron Matlaw (1977).

                                                          Frances Langford Johnson

SEGAL, Vivienne (April 19, 1897–): actress in musical comedy, light opera, and vaudeville, most notable for her role in *Pal Joey*, was born in Philadelphia to a socially prominent Philadelphia family. Her father, Bernard Segal, was a physician. Her mother, Paula (Hahn) Segal, saw in her daughter Vivienne the chance to fulfill her own lost dreams of an acting career and became the typical stage mother. Segal studied voice in Philadelphia with Mrs. Phillip Jenkins and went to school at the Sisters of Mercy Academy, where she studied music and drama. She sang in several amateur productions of the Philadelphia Operatic Society. Her most notable performance in the society's productions was the lead in *Carmen* at the age of eighteen. In 1915 she appeared on Broadway at the Casino Theatre in the Shubert production of *The Blue Paradise*, which established her in New York; it was rumored that her well-to-do father underwrote the cost of the production. Her sister Louise followed her to New York and also appeared in several productions. Vivienne Segal was known as "the little girl with the big voice," and in 1923 she teamed up with lyricist Harry Carroll to tour the B. F. Keith vaudeville circuit.

Early in Segal's career **Ethel Barrymore** came backstage after her performance in an ill-suited tragic role in *The Wise Child* and remarked, "My child, you're going to be a comedienne someday" (*New York Times*, November 23, 1952). Also in her early career she became known for the following productions: *Tangerine* (1921), *The Yankee Princess* (1922), *Adrienne* (1923), *The Desert Song* (1926), and *The Three Musketeers* (1928). In the thirties and forties she played her most notable roles as Nanette in *No, No, Nanette* (1938), Vera Simpson in *Pal Joey* (1940 and again in 1952), and Queen Morgan Le Fay in *A Connecticut Yankee* (1943). In 1952 she won the Donaldson Award and the New York Drama Critics Award for best actress in the revival of *Pal Joey*. In a 1952 *New York Times* interview, Segal commented that playing Vera Simpson had saved her from being typecast as the perpetual ingénue. Of *Pal Joey* the *New York Times* critic observed, "Again Miss Segal presides over the sordid affairs of an astringent tale with humor, reserve and charm" (January 4, 1953). Meeting the peculiar requirements of each of the media, she performed in films from 1929 to 1934, on the radio in the 1930s, and on television in the 1950s. Her last public performance was in *Alfred Hitchcock Presents* in 1961.

Segal married twice. In 1923 while appearing in *Adrienne*, she eloped with a twice-divorced actor, Robert Downing Ames. They were divorced in 1926. In 1950 she married Hubbell Robinson, Jr., a television executive. In an interview with the *San Francisco Chronicle* in 1923, she had answered the question, "What type of man makes the best husband?" with, "I'd rather have a perfect lover for a year than a bore for a lifetime." She was popular with the public as a fashion trendsetter and was an effective sponsor of a variety of products ranging from an outfit she wore in *Adrienne* to lemon face cream. She believed in physical fitness and reportedly carried a trunk full of athletic equipment around with her. She was referred to in one newspaper review as "115 pounds of solid muscle." She was superstitious about the color blue, thinking it lucky, and introduced the song "Bluebird." Her long career demonstrates her staying power in show business and her ability to adapt to changing media and public tastes.

The Robinson Locke scrapbook collection in the New York Public Library Performing Arts Research Center at Lincoln Center contains many clippings concerning Vivienne Segal's early stage career and background. See also the *New York Times* discussions of *Pal Joey* (November 23, 1952, January 4, 1952, February 17, 1952, and June 17, 1952). Segal is listed in *Who's Who in the Theatre* (1961); *The Biographical Encyclopaedia and Who's Who of the American Theatre* (1966); *Notable Names in the American Theatre*

(1976); *Who Was Who in the Theatre*, Vol. IV (1978); and *The Oxford Companion to American Theatre* (1984).

Pamela Hewitt

SELDES, Marian (August 23, 1928–): actress, director, teacher, and writer, was born in New York City, one of the two children of Gilbert and Alice (Hall) Seldes. She grew up in a house on Henderson Place among a family known for its literary and philosophical accomplishments. Her grandfather had created a utopian community in Alliance, New Jersey; her uncle George Seldes was a noted journalist; and her father was one of the earliest and most influential writers on the popular arts. Her brother Timothy became a literary agent. The household was often full of visiting writers and artists, and when the young Marian Seldes expressed a desire to be an actress her father simply arranged for her to meet with his friend and neighbor, scenic designer Robert Edmond Jones. Seldes attended the School of American Ballet and the Dalton School, a private academy from which she graduated in 1945. Another family friend, director-producer Guthrie McClintic, advised her to attend the Neighborhood Playhouse School of the Theatre, and she finished at that institution in 1947. McClintic and his wife, **Katharine Cornell**, remained mentors to young Seldes, and in 1949 she played Cornell's daughter in *That Lady*.

Although some directors saw her height of five feet, eight inches as a handicap in casting, Marian Seldes made her professional debut in October 1947 as an attendant in John Gielgud's production of *Medea* with **Judith Anderson** in the title role. This auspicious beginning was followed by roles such as Douania in *Crime and Punishment* with Gielgud (1949), Electra in *The Tower Beyond Tragedy* opposite Anderson's Clytemnestra (1950), Bertha in Alfred Lunt's *Ondine* with Audrey Hepburn (1954), and Olivia in *The Chalk Garden* with Siobhan McKenna and Fritz Weaver (1955).

In November of 1953, Seldes married Julian Arnold Claman (1918–1969), then vice president of Talent Associates. Claman was producer of a number of television shows, including *Playhouse 90*, and *Have Gun Will Travel*; his one play, *A Quiet Place*, closed out of town in 1955. A daughter, named for Katharine Cornell, was born in April 1956. The couple divorced in August of 1961.

During the 1950s Seldes appeared in a number of plays in Los Angeles, and in 1955 worked as artist-in-residence at Stanford University. She also entered upon a brief film career, taking the lead role in *The Lonely Night* (1951), a documentary drama on mental illness produced by the Mental Health Film Board. Other films include *Mr. Lincoln* (1952), *Crime and Punishment USA* (1959), *The Big Fisherman* (1959), and *The Greatest Story Ever Told* (1964). Seldes made her television debut in September of 1950 as the Gentlewoman in *Macbeth* and appeared on programs such as *Omnibus*, *Playhouse 90*, and *The Defenders*. Although she received generally positive reviews for her work in the media, Seldes has always preferred live theatre and still refuses to make television commercials. In her autobiography, *The Bright Lights* (1978), she affirms her devotion to the theatre. Though she is a consummate professional, who in five years never missed one of the 1,809 performances of *Deathtrap*, Seldes still retains her childhood awe for the stage.

Seldes's youthful promise as an actress began to be realized during the decade of the 1960s. In 1964 she won a *Village Voice* Off-Broadway (Obie) Award for her portrayal of Miss Frost in *The Ginger Man*. She received a 1967 Antoinette Perry (Tony) Award for Julia in *A Delicate Balance*, in spite of the formidable competition of Estelle Parsons, Diana Rigg, and **Maureen Stapleton**. Her other awards include a Tony nomination and the Drama Desk Award for *Father's Day* (1971), an Obie for *Isadora Duncan Sleeps with the Russian Navy* (1976), a Tony nomination for *Deathtrap* (1978), and the Outer Critics Circle Award for *Painting Churches* (1984).

Despite such acclaim Seldes has remained a supporting player and a character actress. Although her classic features and graceful figure give her a leading lady's presence, the intensity of her style seems better suited to character roles. Critics are not lukewarm about Seldes: her intense work creates vigorous responses. Clive Barnes has praised her acting as "nervily brilliant" (*New York Post*, February 27, 1978), but Stanley Kauffmann has objected to what he calls "ethereal attitudinizing" (*New Republic*, November 22, 1969). Her strong character choices and passionate style led to uniform praise of her two scenes as Queen Margaret in *Richard III* (Delacorte Theatre, 1983) but garnered her mixed reviews in the longer role of Fanny in *Painting Churches* (1983–1984). Of the latter production, Frank Rich complained in the *New York Times* that "Miss Seldes has gone off the deep end" with an "arsenal of stylized arm gestures and vocal flourishes" (November 23, 1983). A clipping from the *Long Island Press* of March 17, 1971, sums up her work in simple terms: "She overdoes it now and then, but somehow you forgive her and kind of love her." Seldes's performance in the 1987 revival of Tennessee Williams's *The Milk Train Doesn't Stop Here Anymore* (WPA Theatre, New York) also received mixed reviews.

Marian Seldes is often called "an actor's actor," always a working professional but never a star. For example, after thirty years of constant work in the theatre, Seldes wrote in her autobiography, "I had never been asked my opinion by an interviewer; . . . I hadn't had my caricature drawn for Sardi's" (*The Bright Lights*, p. 118). Not until her appearance in *Equus*—first as Hester Salomon (1974–1976), then as Dora Strang (1976–1977)—did she acquire those accoutrements of fame. She followed these roles by playing the wife in *Deathtrap* for five years, at which point she discovered to her surprise that she possessed, "for the first time, more money than I needed to live on," and traveled to Europe on her earnings (*New York Times*, May 8, 1983). *Deathtrap* also gave her the confidence to write her autobiography, *The Bright Lights*, which was published in 1978. *The New Yorker* praised it as "not the usual theatrical biography," but a "perspicacious" study of "the chemistry of acting and of the stage" (January 29, 1979, p. 25).

Seldes's interest in writing predates *The Bright Lights* and probably harkens back to her childhood days surrounded by her father's literary circle. She began doing poetry readings on the *Today* show and now does them for many groups.

In 1968, for example, she read Nelly Sachs's *O the Chimneys* for the Jewish Theological Seminary; in 1976 at the Inner Circle she read Yiddish poems in memory of writers murdered by Stalin. She has produced various albums for Folkways records, including a reading of Racine's *Phèdre*. Her book reviews often appear in the *New York Times*, and in 1981 she published a novel, *A Time Together*.

When John Houseman asked Seldes to join the drama faculty of New York's Juilliard School in 1969, she feared the invitation meant Houseman considered her acting days to be over. Nevertheless, she committed herself to teaching with the same intensity she brought to acting and by 1980 told John Corry, "I love teaching. . . . There are only a few things I'm sure of in my life: that I can write, that I can teach, and that I belong in the theatre" (*New York Times*, June 25, 1976). Houseman's original Acting Company was made up of students from her first class. Later, she directed Patti LuPone, star of the musical *Evita*, in a Juilliard production of *Next Time I'll Sing To You* that traveled to Broadway in 1974. Seldes joined the Juilliard dance faculty in 1972 and continues to teach in the theatre program. She also continues to act. In 1987 she appeared in a revival of Tennessee Williams' *The Milk Train Doesn't Stop Here Anymore* at the WPA Theatre in New York.

Her teaching and performing bridge two generations of actors. Early in her career she performed with famous mentors such as Katharine Cornell, Judith Anderson, and John Gielgud. Now she performs with her often famous students: with Steve Basset in *Deathtrap*, with Kevin Kline in *Richard III*, and with Elizabeth McGovern in *Painting Churches*. Seldes once said that she teaches no special method of acting, except for a belief that there is no acting problem that cannot be solved. As artist and as teacher of the art, Marian Seldes not only has contributed a gallery of memorable stage portraits to American theatre but has shared her enthusiasm and experience with a rising generation of theatre artists.

The Billy Rose Theatre Collection at the New York Public Library Performing Arts Research Center at Lincoln Center has clipping and photo files on Marian Seldes, Gilbert Seldes, the Juilliard School, and Julian Claman, the latter including various scrapbooks on *A Quiet Place*. Particularly useful in this material were two interviews with Seldes by John Corry, *New York Times* (June 25, 1976, and June 20, 1980); an interview with Carol Lawson, *New York Times* (July 29, 1983); and the *New York Times* obituary of Gilbert Seldes (September 30, 1970). Extensive reviews of Seldes's work are available in *The New York Times Theater Reviews* (1971) and *New York Times Film Reviews* (1970). Seldes' autobiography, *The Bright Lights: A Theatre Life*, was published in 1978. Also useful is John Houseman's *Final Dress* (1983). See also "The Talk of the Town" in *The New Yorker* (January 29, 1979). Marian Seldes is listed in *The Biographical Encyclopaedia and Who's Who of the American Theatre* (1966); *Notable Names in the American Theatre* (1976); *Who's Who in the Theatre* (1981); and *Contemporary Theatre, Film, and Television*, Vol. II (1986).

Judith Pratt

SELZNICK, Irene Mayer (April 2, 1907–): theatrical producer, was the younger of two daughters born to Louis B. and Margaret (Shenberg) Mayer. She was born in Massachusetts and spent some of her early years in Haverhill, where her father managed a theatre, which he called the Orpheum. The family moved to Brookline just outside of Boston, where Irene attended the public schools. In 1918 the family moved to Hollywood, California, where Irene and her sister attended the private Hollywood School for Girls. She married film producer David O. Selznick on April 29, 1930. The marriage was dissolved in 1948, the decree becoming final in January 1949. She has two sons: Lewis Jeffrey Selznick (b. 1932), now a film producer in Europe, and Daniel Mayer Selznick (b. 1936). She is the author of an autobiography, *A Private View* (1983), and currently resides in New York City. In her autobiography Selznick states that "I've had three lives—one as the daughter of my father, another as the wife of my husband. The theatre furnished me with a third act" (*A Private View*, p. 384). The "third act," which established her as a dedicated, meticulous producer of landmark dramas such as *A Streetcar Named Desire* and *The Chalk Garden*, appears to have crept up on her unexpectedly; despite her extensive background in the film community and her numerous friends in the worlds of both cinema and theatre, any career in show business initially seemed unlikely for the strictly-brought-up daughter of conservative, traditionalist movie executive Louis B. Mayer. That she eventually became a noted "produttrice teatrale di vari spettacoli" (*Enciclopedia dello spettacolo*, s.v. "Selznick," Vol. 8, p. 1822) is a tribute to her courage, talent, and innate independence.

As a child she was taught the values of economy, discipline, and organization by her autocratic father, who ruled both his family and Metro-Goldwyn-Mayer with the same loving ruthlessness. Careers and professions were not considered suitable for the Mayer daughters, and "college went by default" (*A Private View*, p. 52). Her sole childhood ambition was to marry and have two sons; this she attained by marrying cinema entrepreneur David O. Selznick and producing the requisite offspring. Her role was to give her husband support and encouragement, especially during the turbulent years in which he was producing *Gone With the Wind* (1936–1939). He evidently valued her advice and constantly solicited her opinions about his work. Though she was listed as an "executive" with Selznick International Pictures (*The Biographical Encyclopaedia and Who's Who of the American Theatre*, p. 816), she "never mixed into the business," preferring by her own admission "reflected glory" rather than active participation (*A Private View*, pp. 260, 159). Other than the movie business, the couple had little in common; and by 1945, when the pressure caused by David Selznick's recklessness, extravagance, and compulsive gambling ruptured the marriage, the couple had already separated. "For the very first time," she says, "I took my life into my own hands" (*A Private View*, p. 269). Uncertain about her future and thinking only that she would inevitably remarry, she went in September 1945 to New York, a city she had always found stimulating. The visit was extended indefinitely as she obeyed an irresistible underlying urge to "do something in the theatre" (*A Private View*, p. 279).

Irene Selznick had been interested in live theatre ever since a childhood trip to the Hippodrome in New York. She had always enjoyed the company of playwrights like S. N. Behrman and Clifford Odets, and was friendly with actors and actresses like Spencer Tracy and **Katharine Hepburn**. Encouraged by Hepburn and playwright Moss Hart, she rented an office in the Henry Miller Theatre in New York in 1946, hired the experienced Irving Schneider as general manager, and embarked on a career as a producer. Her aim was modest: simply to help "neglected playwrights or, better still, fledglings" (A Private View, p. 286). However, her own talents and the realities of Broadway soon brought into being the Irene M. Selznick Company, a production enterprise with a formidable reputation for excellence, while observers pointed to Selznick herself as "a dame to watch" (Max Siegel, as quoted in A Private View, p. 294).

Inundated with manuscripts, she chose Heartsong, a new play by the relatively unknown Arthur Laurents. She used her own money to back the play, helped the playwright with rewrites, and secured the talented **Shirley Booth** for a leading character role. The play opened in New Haven on February 27, 1947, but insurmountable problems forced an out-of-town closing in Philadelphia on March 29. After this unpromising beginning, Selznick was surprised when literary agent **Audrey Wood** offered her Tennessee Williams's newest play, A Streetcar Named Desire, in 1947. Wood had been impressed by Selznick's energy, diligence, and protective attitude toward playwrights and her wise though painful decision not to bring a flawed production into New York. Though the play was "bigger than I wanted, earlier than I wanted" (A Private View, p. 296), Selznick signed the contracts and thus joined the ranks of major Broadway producers. She gave all her attention to the play—bolstering actors, supporting the playwright, tirelessly raising money, and quelling backstage insurrections led by director Elia Kazan. The production weathered lukewarm notices in New Haven and finally opened in New York on December 3, 1947, to a standing ovation and rave reviews. Selznick was elected to the board of governors of the League of New York Theatres, and Williams won the Pulitzer Prize. She then co-produced the play in London (with H. M. Tennent, Ltd.) and organized and monitored the United States road company to visit Chicago, Madison, Indianapolis, and Kansas City.

For the 1950–1951 fall season she chose John van Druten's Bell, Book and Candle. Lilli Palmer agreed to play the female lead, but twenty-two actors turned down the leading male role. With Selznick's encouragement and advice, van Druten rewrote the play so effectively that Rex Harrison, Palmer's husband, agreed to star. The production was another major success for the Irene M. Selznick Company, opening in New York City on November 14, 1950, and in London on October 5, 1954. Selznick now had a waiting list of investors, and in 1951 she decided to produce George Tabori's Flight into Egypt. Elia Kazan again agreed to direct, and another hit appeared to be in the offing. But Kazan, unnerved by the investigations of the House Committee on Un-American Activities, constantly changed the script to remove all lines that might conceivably be viewed with suspicion by the committee. Selznick viewed the script alterations with alarm and postponed the opening at her own expense in order to give Kazan the chance to restore the original script. Kazan failed to do so, and after he named names to the House Committee, Selznick comforted the stricken cast and quietly closed the show after a brief run in the spring of 1952.

Enid Bagnold's *The Chalk Garden* presented a whole new set of problems. Initially Selznick turned down the play. Selznick began a correspondence with the author, a noted novelist, suggesting, criticizing, and analyzing. Much correspondence and numerous trips to England followed, a structured script emerged, and Selznick found herself committed to produce the result of their joint efforts. Despite a difficult cast and a change of directors, the show opened in New York on October 26, 1955, and in London on April 12, 1956. While a qualified success in New York (it ran for five months with good notices), the play packed the Haymarket Theatre in London for twenty-three months and was greeted with dazzling reviews by the English critics.

The final production of the Irene M. Selznick Company was Graham Greene's *The Complaisant Lover*, to which Tennent Ltd. had offered her the New York production rights. Because of various casting problems, the show took two years to produce and, though a smash hit in London, ran only three months in New York in 1961. At this point, Selznick, who had been totally immersed in her work, decided to reconsider her commitment. She came to the conclusion that her career had gone far beyond "helping out a few struggling playwrights" and that she "resented being a prisoner of my office and [feeling] guilty if I wasn't there" (*A Private View*, p. 356). She decided therefore to stop producing plays, closed her office, and retired as a producer in the mid-sixties, donating her collection of theatrical papers to the Boston University Library. She continued to live in New York, traveled extensively, and enjoyed a broad network of friends both in and out of the theatre.

Irene Selznick's importance as a producer lies not only in the stature of the plays she produced but in the stature she herself achieved in a difficult, male-dominated profession. As a professional theatrical producer she balanced sharp curiosity with sound judgment. Her critical abilities, honed by years of assessing film scripts for her father and her husband, made her a shrewd judge of dramatic material, able to evaluate the weaknesses and strengths of a script and to suggest directions for improvement. Yet she imposed nothing; she restricted herself to encouraging and suggesting without limiting the artistic freedom of the writer. The same policy held true for the directors, actors, and designers involved in her productions. Conscientious and dedicated, she attended every rehearsal possible but did not take unwarranted advantage of her position to force interpretations on cast and crew. She placed a high value on the playwrights' participation and never froze them out of rehearsals. She was also concerned about her investors, and tried to stop the unions from featherbedding successful productions. Her greatest success was with the American Federation of Musicians, who accepted her proposal to establish a formula by which producers could determine musical costs in advance instead of suffering arbitrary and expensive decisions after their productions opened.

Perhaps her most significant accomplishment as a producer was to insist always on the priority of the show. To ensure the success of her productions, she was willing to endure the difficult temperaments of performers such as the unpredictable, moody Marlon Brando in *A Streetcar Named Desire* and the icy, imperious Gladys Cooper in *The Chalk Garden*. When noted Irish star Siobhan McKenna accepted a major role in *The Chalk Garden* and then vanished to a remote island off the Irish coast, Selznick sent a man in a rowboat to contact her instead of firing her. Because Kazan's talents as a director suited *Streetcar*, she acceded to his outrageous demands for money (part of which came out of her share as producer). She even hired Cecil Beaton to design *The Chalk Garden*, despite the fact that he was responsible for an anti-Semitic *Vogue* illustration in which her name was prominently featured. Likewise, she did not hesitate to fire her old friend George Cukor when his directing talents proved incompatible with Bagnold's comedy. Her system of priorities, in which her own ego was constantly subordinated to the needs of the play, ensured the best possible intermixture of theatrical talent, and her high standards of production set an outstanding example for those who followed her.

The most valuable source for information about Irene Mayer Selznick is her autobiography, *A Private View* (1983), which corrects a number of misconceptions and errors about her and her family and provides fascinating insights into the theatrical period 1946–1961. More general sources such as *The Biographical Encyclopaedia and Who's Who of the American Theatre* (1966) and *Who's Who of American Women, 1972–1973* (1971) are helpful in establishing the order and dates of the plays she produced but perpetuate several errors, the most common being the place and date of her birth, which are often given as New York City, 1910. Other useful sources include *Celebrity Register*, U.S. edition (1959); *Celebrity Register* (1963); and *Variety International Showbusiness Reference* (1981).

Laurilyn J. Harris

SHANGE, Ntozake (October 18, 1948–): playwright, poet, actress, and important contributor to the development of black feminist drama, is the daughter of Paul T. and Eloise Williams. She was born in Trenton, New Jersey, and was named Paulette, "after [her] father because he wanted a boy" (*Time*, July 19, 1976, p. 44). She moved with her family five times before she was thirteen: from Trenton to upstate New York, to Alabama, back to Trenton, then to St. Louis, and back again to Trenton. Despite her family's comparative affluence— her father was a surgeon, her mother a psychiatric social worker—Shange did not escape the cruelties of American racism. Living in St. Louis when she was eight years old, she was taken by bus to a previously all-white school, where she was subjected to racial harassment by some of the white children. Nevertheless, her family's comparative wealth provided Shange with advantages few other black children enjoyed. From an early age she studied the violin, and her family—Shange has two sisters and one brother—had regular poetry readings and variety shows on Sunday afternoons. Her parents traveled widely outside the United States, and Shange was accustomed to having her parents' friends from many foreign countries visit in her home. She reports growing up with the sounds of "many languages, [and] many different kinds of music" around her (*Ms.*, December 1977, p. 70).

In 1970 Shange graduated cum laude with a Bachelor of Arts degree in American Studies from Barnard College in New York. That same year she moved to California, where in 1971 she took the name "Ntozake Shange." The two African words mean "She comes with her own thing" and "She who walks like a lion" (*Ebony*, August 1977, p. 136). In 1973 she received her master's degree in American Studies from the University of Southern California. Shange then continued her studies at Sonoma State College in the Women's Studies Program. Her experiences and friendships there greatly influenced the development of her poetry and drama.

Shange has been a member of the faculty of Sonoma State College (1973–1975), Mills College (1975), City College of the City University of New York (1975), Douglass College of Rutgers University (1978), and Rice University (1983). From 1984 to 1986 she was an associate professor and head of the drama department's playwriting program at the University of Houston, University Park. She has lectured widely at institutions such as Brown University, the University of Connecticut, Howard University, New York University, and Yale University. In addition to her work in the theatre, she has published poems, essays, and short stories in numerous magazines and anthologies, including *APR*, *Black Maria*, *Black Scholar*, *Broadway Boogie*, *The Chicago Review*, *Chrysalis*, *Essence*, *Invisible City*, *Margins*, *Ms.*, *Shocks*, *Third World Women*, *Time to Greez*, *West End Magazine*, and *Yardbird Reader*.

Shange is best known for the innovative dramas that she calls "choreopoems." Her most important and successful work has been *for colored girls who have considered suicide/when the rainbow is enuf: a choreopoem*, begun in the summer of 1974 as a series of seven poems first performed at the Bacchanal, a women's bar outside Berkeley, California. The performances continued, with the addition of music and dance, and moved through several bars, cafés, and poetry centers. From San Francisco, Shange took "the show" to the Studio Rivbea in New York City. After playing in a series of cafés, the show—under Oz Scott's direction—was produced Off-off-Broadway by Woodie King, Jr., as an Actors' Equity Showcase, at the Henry Street Settlement's New Federal Theatre. Joseph Papp then produced it at the New York Shakespeare Festival's Public Theatre in June of 1976. Three months later the show opened on Broadway (September 15, 1976) at the Booth Theatre, with set designed by Ming Cho Lee. *For colored girls . . .* was a huge success, winning an Antoinette Perry (Tony) Award nomination for best play. Trazana Beverley won a Tony Award for best featured actress for her role as the Lady in Red. The play ran for two years on Broadway, then toured the United States, Canada, and the Caribbean. In 1979 it opened in London at the Royalty Theatre, and a production for public television was videotaped on location in and around Miami.

In its final form, *for colored girls* . . . comprises twenty poems that are recited, sung, and danced by seven black actresses, identified only by the colors in which they are dressed—brown, yellow, red, green, purple, blue, orange—the colors of the rainbow, plus brown. The women's anonymity makes their experiences seem less those of seven individual women and more the collective experience of Every(black)woman. Shange's term "choreopoem" refers to the play's form—the loosely connected poems or vignettes acted to music and dance. The choreopoem is her answer to what she sees as the artificial aesthetics of the perfect play, a form Shange considers "a truly European framework for European psychology [that] cannot function efficiently for those of us from this hemisphere" (*Black Scholar*, July-August 1979, p. 7). Controversial for its form, *for colored girls* . . . was accused of using Amos 'n' Andy stereotypes in its verbal depictions of black men. Shange replied that she intended to portray the realities of (black) women's lives, regardless of the effect that portrayal had on men, black or white.

For colored girls . . . is among the important and successful feminist plays with a positive—even joyous—ending. In the final poem of the play, the seven Ladies of Color discover and affirm their self-worth as they repeat to themselves and then sing together: "i found god in myself/ & i loved her/ i loved her fiercely." That strong affirmation of women's experience places Shange in the forefront of the women's movement.

In addition to *for colored girls* . . . , Shange has written six other plays that have been produced. Three have been published: *negress* (1977); *where the mississippi meets the amazon* (1977); and *from okra to greens: a different love story* (1978). The remaining three, collected in Shange's anthology *three pieces*, have had varying degrees of commercial success. *A photograph* was first produced by Joseph Papp in a workshop production for the New York Shakespeare Festival in 1977. Directed by Oz Scott, that production of the play was known as *a photograph: a still life with shadows/a photograph: a study in cruelty*. In 1979 the play was presented in revised form as *a photograph: lovers in motion* at the Equinox Theatre, Houston, under the direction of Shange. Like her best-known work, this play includes poetry, music, and dance, but the cast has five characters, two men and three women. *Boogie woogie landscapes* was first presented as a one-woman piece on December 18, 1978, as part of the New York Shakespeare Festival's *Poetry at the Public* series. On June 26, 1979, it was produced in play form, directed by Avery Brooks, at the Symphony Space Theatre, as a fund raiser for the Frank Silvera Writers' Workshop. On June 17, 1980, the play opened at the John F. Kennedy Center for the Performing Arts Terrace Theatre in Washington, D.C., and then toured Philadelphia, Chicago, and Detroit. It has a cast of seven, four women and three men. The central character, Layla, is in her bedroom sleeping; the other six characters move into and out of her bedroom, bringing with them scenes and thoughts from her earlier life. First presented as a workshop production in May 1979, the sixth play, *magic spell #7* was later revised and produced as *spell #7* by Joseph Papp's New

York Shakespeare Festival's Public Theatre/Other Stage in the summer of 1979. Once again Oz Scott directed. In its published form in *three pieces*, *spell #7* is given the subtitle *geechee jibara quik magic trance manual for technologically stressed third world people* and is identified as "a theatre piece." Nine characters—four men and five women—act out poems or vignettes from their lives. A huge blackface minstrel's mask hangs over the stage, and the framing device is a minstrel magician.

Shange's newest play, *Betsey Brown*, is a collaboration with playwright **Emily Mann** and jazz trumpeter and composer Baikida Carroll. The play is based on Shange's novel about a teenage girl coming of age in a middle-class black family in the 1950s. *Betsey Brown* opened the 1989 season of The American Music Theater Festival, playing at the Forum Theatre in Philadelphia in April of 1989.

Shange has also received critical attention for her directing and adaptations. Her directing debut was of her own adaptation of Richard Wesley's *The Mighty Gents*, on August 17, 1979, at Joseph Papp's New York Shakespeare Festival's Mobile Theatre. In the summer of 1980 she adapted Bertolt Brecht's *Mother Courage and Her Children*. In addition to her work in the theatre, Shange has published *Sassafrass* (1976), a novella; two collections of poetry, *Happy Edges* (1978) and *A Daughter's Geography* (1983); two novels, *Sassafrass, Cypress & Indigo* (1982) and *Betsey Brown* (1985); and *See No Evil: Prefaces, Essays & Accounts, 1976–1983* (1984), which includes the reprinted prefaces to *for colored girls*... and *three pieces*, as well as an essay on her adaptation of Brecht's *Mother Courage* called "How I Moved Anna Fierling to the Southwest Territories or My Personal Victory Over the Armies of Western Civilization."

Shange has received several awards, including the Outer Critics Circle Award (1977), the *Village Voice* Off-Broadway (Obie) Award (1977), the Audelco Award (1977), and the Frank S. Silvera Writers' Workshop Award (1978). More recently, in 1981, she won the poetry category in the Los Angeles *Times* Book Prizes competition for *three pieces*, and she was awarded both a Guggenheim Fellowship and Columbia University Medal of Excellence. Shange's greatest contribution to American theatre is the beautiful and terrifying expression she has given to black women's pain, rage, and joy.

Shange's *for colored girls*... has been included in *Plays from the New York Shakespeare Festival*, with an introduction by Joseph Papp (1987). Additional biographical details about Ntozake Shange are available in magazine articles about her, such as "Success Requires Talent and Drive—Ntozake Shange: Playwright," *Ebony* (August 1977); "Trying to Be Nice," *Time* (July 19, 1976); and "Ntozake Shange Interviews Herself," *Ms.* (December 1977). Henry Blackwell's "An Interview with Ntozake Shange," in *Black American Literature Forum* (Winter 1979), provides important information about Shange's development as a writer and her intentions in *for colored girls*... Shange talks about herself in "Unrecovered Losses/Black Theatre Traditions," *The Black Scholar* (July-August 1979), which has been reprinted as the Foreword to *three pieces*. Jeffrey Elliot details the genesis and development of *for colored girls*... in "Ntozake Shange: Genesis of a Choreopoem," *Negro History Bulletin* (January-February 1978). Two important and opposing critiques of *for colored girls*... are Erskine Peters's "Some Tragic

Propensities of Ourselves: The Occasion of Ntozake Shange's 'for colored girls who have considered suicide/when the rainbow is enuf,' " in *The Journal of Ethnic Studies* (1978), and Carol P. Christ's "'i found god in myself . . . & I loved her fiercely': Ntozake Shange," in *Diving Deep and Surfacing: Women Writers on Spiritual Quest* (1980). Sandra L. Richards's essay "Conflicting Impulses in the Plays of Ntozake Shange," in *Black American Literature Forum* (Summer 1983), discusses the influence of Frantz Fanon, Bertolt Brecht, Antonin Artaud, Amiri Baraka, and the African world view on Shange's plays. An interview with Ntozake Shange is included in *Interviews with Contemporary Women Playwrights*, edited by Kathleen Betsko and Rachel Koenig (1987). She is included in *9 Plays by Black Women*, edited by Margaret B. Wilkerson (1986), and in *Women in American Theater* edited by Helen Krich Chinoy and Linda Walsh Jenkins (1981, 1987). Shange is listed in *Who's Who Among Black Americans, 1980–1981* (1981); *Who's Who in America, 1982–1983* (1982); and *Who's Who of American Women, 1983–1984* (1983).

Anne Hudson Jones

SHANK, Adele Edling (April 9, 1940–): playwright, was born in Litchfield, Minnesota, the oldest child of Elwood R. Edling and Gladys Miriam (Parsons) Edling, both the children of Swedish emigrants who arrived in Minnesota during the last quarter of the nineteenth century. Shank's father holds a bachelor's degree from the University of Minnesota in agriculture, a line of work to which he devoted himself in both public and private agencies and as a working farmer. Her mother studied nursing for two years before abandoning her training to care for her family, which by 1942 included a second daughter, Susan Katherine, who today is an attorney practicing in Sacramento, California. Shank was raised on a farm near Dassel, Minnesota, and attended the local country school. It was a true one-room schoolhouse: some thirty pupils ranging from first through twelfth grades were taught simultaneously by one teacher, Mrs. Helen Johnson. "I particularly remember her," says Shank, "because I still could not read when we moved to Dassel and I was in the third grade. I thought there was something wrong with me, that I was stupid. Everybody else could read and write. Mrs. Johnson rapidly taught me to do both. I think one reason I continue to read and write avidly is that it meant so much to me when I learned" (Interview).

The Edlings moved to Pasadena, California, when Adele was in the eighth grade; they relocated in Sacramento a few months later. Shank graduated from Norte Del Rio High School; then she entered the University of California, Davis. She began as a biology major specializing in endocrinology but graduated with a Bachelor of Arts degree in dramatic art and speech (1963), which she followed with a master's degree in playwriting (1966). After a year of teaching junior high school, Adele Edling married Theodore Shank on Christmas Day, 1967. While the couple has no issue, her husband has two children from a previous marriage: Theodore Stanley, a photographer, and Kendra Ann, a musician.

A director, playwright, critic, and dramaturg, Theodore Shank had been Adele Edling's first playwriting professor at the University of California, Davis, and, consequently, exercised an early influence on her writing, one which would gather strength after their marriage. Adele Shank feels that his influence and their travels together to see experimental theatre both in the United States and abroad significantly shaped her future work as a dramatist. Starting in 1980, another important factor was her continuing artistic affiliation with the Magic Theatre in San Francisco.

Although she was committed to becoming a playwright, a decade passed between Shank's marriage and the outset of her professional career. "I spent a lot of time thinking about and seeing theatre," she explains, "but I stopped writing plays partly because I no longer knew what I wanted to write about or how" (Interview). Adele Shank resumed playwriting in an effort to help her husband update the text of Ben Jonson's *Volpone*, which he had agreed to direct. The result was *Fox & Co.* (University of California, Davis, 1978), a contemporary adaptation of Ben Jonson's classic, heavily indebted to director Richard Foreman's work. "Some of the avant-garde plays I had seen," Shank explains, "had taught me a fresh way of addressing my writing. People like Foreman and Robert Wilson were creating a non-linear, less empathic theatre in which the visual component was not just scenery but a vital aspect that actually carried meaning" (Interview).

Since *Fox & Co.*, Shank has written a new play every year, most of them incorporating her own variation on the visual arts perspective she absorbed from experimentalists of the 1960s and 1970s. Her next play, *Sunset/Sunrise* (University of California, Davis, 1979; Actors Theatre of Louisville, 1980), began as another contemporary comedy, set in a back yard around a swimming pool. In search of a style for her idea, Shank was helped by her husband's suggestion that she look to super real paintings. She went on to transpose the super real aesthetic into stage terms and called her new approach "theatrical hyperrealism." To date she has produced an interlocking six-play cycle in this style, called "the California Series." Together these plays explore the gap between the material satisfaction promised by the American dream and the amorphous dissatisfaction of characters who have achieved it. In addition to *Sunset/Sunrise*, the cycle includes *Winterplay* (American Place Theatre, New York, staged reading, Spring 1980, and Magic Theatre, San Francisco, September 1980); *Stuck: A Freeway Comedy* (Magic Theatre, October 1981); *Sand Castles* (Magic Theatre, October 1982); *The Grass House* (Magic Theatre, October 1983); and *Tumbleweed* (Los Angeles Theatre Center, 1985).

Like super real paintings, theatrical hyperrealism is part of the post-modern resurgence of realistic and naturalistic impulses in all of the arts. Although the term "hyperreal" has been applied to the plays of other neonaturalistic dramatists, notably Franz Xaver Kroetz, Shank is the only such American playwright to have consciously developed a coherent hyperreal dramaturgy. In common with pictorial art forms, Shank's California plays are characterized by a photographically detailed examination of the surface qualities of commonplace objects and scenes, conducted from an emotionally detached perspective, and designed to focus attention on elements of life so familiar that they ordinarily pass unnoticed. Both paintings and plays avoid narrative tendencies; instead each records visual or behavioral data in order to present a portrait of the human condition. To capture the perspective of super real paintings, Shank uses a complex of distancing devices intended to undercut empathy. Most important among these is her promotion of realistic detail of stage behavior and setting from background to foreground. This is an unusual use of realistic illusion, which traditionally fosters subjective involvement instead of holding it at bay.

From 1981 through the winter quarter of 1984, Adele Shank was a visiting lecturer at both the San Diego and Davis branches of the University of California. In the spring of 1984 she was appointed associate professor in charge of the Playwriting Program for the Department of Drama at University of California— San Diego, La Jolla.

In 1980 *Sunset/Sunrise* was co-winner of the Great American Play Contest sponsored by the Actors Theatre of Louisville. Shank received a Rockefeller Foundation Playwrights-in-Residence grant and a National Endowment for the Arts Playwriting Fellowship for 1981–1982. In 1985 she received one of five first place awards from the Foundation for the Dramatists Guild/Columbia Broadcasting System New Plays Program. In the same year the publication called *Hollywood Drama-Logue* gave her its Critics Award for outstanding achievement in theatre for the play *War Horses*, produced at San Francisco's Magic Theatre. Shank is on the board of directors of the SOON 3 Theatre in San Francisco, the San Francisco International Theatre Festival, and the Welfare State Theatre in England. She is also on the advisory board of the Bay Area Playwrights Festival (Marin County, California) and on the 1986–1987 Theatre Advisory Panel of the National Endowment for the Arts. Several of her plays have been translated into Polish, Serbo-Croatian, Dutch, and French. Her work has introduced a new style—hyperrealism—to the modern American theatre.

Shank's plays include *The Mayor of Normington* (1960); *To Those Who Don't Survive* (1962); *The Games* (1963); untitled manuscript (1966); Fernando Arrabal's *The Architect and the Emperor of Assyria*, translated with Everard d'Harnoncourt (1969); *Fox & Co.* (1977); *Sunset/Sunrise* in *West Coast Plays 4* (1979); *Dry Smoke* (1981); *Winterplay* in *Plays in Process* (1981) and *New Plays USA* (1982); *Stuck: A Freeway Comedy* in *Plays in Process* (1982) and Polish translation by Margaret Semil; *Dialog* (1983); *Innocence Abroad* (1983); *Sand Castles* in *West Coast Plays 15/16* (1983); *The Grass House* in *Plays in Process* (1983); *War Horses* (1984); and *Tumbleweed* (1984). Some articles about Adele Shank and hyperrealism include Michael Carrier, "Talking Shop II: Beyond the Conventional," *The Birdcage Review* 247 (October 1985); Adele Edling Shank, program notes for productions of her California Series Plays in the Magic Theatre's *Newsletter* (San Francisco), Vols. 1–4 (1980–1983); Adele Edling Shank, "Theatrical Hyperrealism," *Call Board* (San Francisco, 1980); Theodore Shank, "Hyperrealism in the Theatre: Shank Interviews Shank," *West Coast Plays* (1979); Theodore Shank, "*Stuck* on a California Freeway," *Theatre Design and Technology* (Summer 1982); Bernard Weiner, "The Success of a 'Sunrise,' " *San Francisco Chronicle* (December 15, 1979); and Stephen Winn, "A Radical Turn Into Suburbia," *San Francisco Chronicle* (October

1980). Quotations from Adele Shank are from personal interviews. Adele Edling Shank is listed in *The National Playwrights Directory* (1981).

C. Lee Jenner

SHARAFF, Irene (1910?–): costume designer, was born in Boston, Massachusetts, and studied art at the New York School of Fine and Applied Arts, the New York Art Students' League and La Grande Chaumière in Paris. During a career spanning fifty years, she created the costume designs for more than twenty ballets, thirty movies, and sixty productions on Broadway. Throughout her career Irene Sharaff's name has been synonymous with excellence in design and has carried with it an aura of elegance. For her efforts she has been rewarded with a Donaldson Award for *The King and I*, an **Antoinette Perry** (Tony) Award for *The King and I*, and five Academy Awards for *An American in Paris*, *The King and I*, *West Side Story*, *Cleopatra*, and *Who's Afraid of Virginia Woolf?* She has had fourteen Oscar nominations.

While still a student she was introduced to **Aline Bernstein**, at that time art director of **Eva Le Gallienne**'s Civic Repertory Theatre, and became her assistant for costumes, scenery, and properties. In 1928 she assisted Bernstein there on sets and costumes for *L'Invitation au Voyage* and *The Cherry Orchard*. In 1929 she assisted on the productions of *The Lady From Alfaqueque*, *On the High Road*, *A Sunny Morning*, and *Mademoiselle Bourrat*. The following year she again assisted Bernstein with *The Open Door*, *The Women Have Their Way*, *Romeo and Juliet*, *The Green Cockatoo*, and co-designed both *Siegfried* and *Alison's House*. Her own talents, combined with an intense three-year internship Bernstein, were excellent preparation for a creative and successful career designing costumes.

With the temporary closing of the Civic Repertory Theatre due to economic conditions in 1931, Sharaff traveled to Paris with the intention of spending a year abroad. While there she was exposed to the best of European design and to *haute couture*. This influenced her rapidly developing style by adding an undeniable richness and exotic flavor to her designs. Eva Le Gallienne visited her in Paris and asked her to design *Alice in Wonderland* for the re-opening of the Civic Repertory Theatre. Sharaff made her designs after careful study of the story and of the illustrations by Tenniel that were to be adapted for the stage. The costumes were very successful and were acclaimed by public and critics alike. In his review of the opening, Brooks Atkinson stated, "In designing the costumes Miss Sharaff has reverenced the illustrations, adding to them colors that give the production a disarmingly lovely appearance" (*New York Times*, December 12, 1932). Writing in *Theatre Arts Monthly* (February 1933), Morton Eustis complimented Sharaff on both her ingenuity and her perfection of design.

Such accolades from respected theatre critics were only the first Sharaff would receive during her career. In the following year, after the permanent closing of the Civic Repertory Theatre, she made her Broadway debut with the opening of *As Thousands Cheer* (1933), directed by Hassard Short.

In the years that followed, the success of many productions was due in part to Sharaff's creations. Writing in the *New York Times* after the opening of *Count Me In* (1942), Brooks Atkinson began his review with the following words: "If *Count Me In* looks like a show it is not difficult to tell the reason why. Irene Sharaff has designed the costumes. For several years she has been imparting gaiety and electricity to musical shows by the use of design and color. But what she has done for the musical comedy that arrived at the Ethel Barrymore last evening deserves a prize. It is wonderfully imaginative; it is brilliant and stunning. Miss Sharaff has even discovered how to make Uncle Sam's unobtrusive and eminently practical Army uniform blend into the fantasy of a musical show" (October 9, 1942).

When Sharaff began her career, costumes were usually part of the responsibility of the scenic designer, and in her early years she designed both sets and costumes for productions. As specialization in theatre increased, she turned her attention entirely to costumes and was one of those talented people who contributed to the emergence of costume design as an art in its own right. Her credits through the years are varied. In 1933, in addition to *As Thousands Cheer* she designed *Union Pacific*. In 1934, her designs included *Life Begins at 8:40* and *The Great Waltz*. Subsequent costume creations include *Crime and Punishment* (also scenery), *Parade* (with Constance Ripley, Billy Livingston, and Lee Simonson), *Jubilee*, and *Rosmersholm* (costumes and scenery) in 1935. In 1936 she created costumes for *Idiot's Delight*, *On Your Toes*, and *White Horse Inn*; and in 1937, *Virginia* (with John Hambleton) and *I'd Rather Be Right*. In 1938 she designed *The Boys from Syracuse*; in 1939, *The American Way*, *Streets of Paris*, *Gay New Orleans*, and *From Vienna*. In 1940 she designed costumes for *Boys and Girls Together* and *All In Fun* (with Hattie Carnegie); in 1941 her designs included both sets and costumes for *Lady in the Dark*, as well as costumes for *The Land is Bright*, *Sunny River*, *Mr. Bib*, and *Banjo Eyes*. In 1942 she designed *By Jupiter*, *Star and Garter*, and *Count Me In*.

Following this last production, Sharaff took a hiatus from theatre design to work in Hollywood, beginning her film career with *Girl Crazy* in 1943. After several movies she returned to New York in 1945 to design *Billion Dollar Baby* and *Hamlet*. In 1946 she did the costumes for both *The Would-Be Gentleman* and *G.I. Hamlet*. While commuting to the West Coast for films in 1948, she also designed the New York productions for the pre-Broadway tryout of *Bonanza Bound*, and *Magdalena*. In subsequent years she designed the following: 1949, *Montserrat*; 1950, *Dance Me a Song* and *Mike Todd's Peepshow*; 1951, *The King and I* (Donaldson Award, Antoinette Perry Award) and *A Tree Grows in Brooklyn*. Her successful theatre work made her the obvious choice for the film versions of both as well. In 1952 she designed the revival of *Of Thee I Sing*. In 1953 Sharaff designed *Me and Juliet* and the London production of *The King and I*. Following years saw her design for *By The Beautiful Sea*, the revival of *On Your Toes* (1954), *Shangri-la*, *Candide*, *Happy Hunting* (1956), *Small War on Murray Hill* and the noteworthy *West Side Story* (1957). Thereafter, she was less active but did create costumes for many outstanding productions, such as *Flower Drum Song* (1958), *Juno* (1959), *Do Re Mi* (1960), *Jenny* (1963), *The Girl Who Came To Supper* (1963), *The Boys From Syracuse* (London Production, 1963), *Funny Girl* (1964), with Barbra Streisand, the revival of *The King and I* (1964), *Sweet Charity* (1965), *Hallelujah, Baby* (1967), and *Irene* (1972). In 1976 Sharaff wrote a book about her lifework titled *Broadway and Hollywood: Costumes Designed by Irene Sharaff*. The book is illustrated with photographs and renderings and is filled with lively commentary. In 1980 the revival of *West Side Story* was the culmination of her career in the theatre, though she has designed occasionally since. In March 1985, the United States Institute of Theatre Technology honored Sharaff for her distinguished career.

The best source of information on Irene Sharaff is her own book, *Broadway and Hollywood: Costumes Designed by Irene Sharaff* (1976). Articles in *Theatre Arts Monthly* (February 1933) and the *New York Times* (December 12, 1932) are helpful for her early career. See also B. O'Connell, "Irene Sharaff Recreates Joan Crawford," *Theatre Crafts* (January 1982); "Venezuelan Venture: Costuming of Montserrat," *Theatre Arts* (November 1949); and "Color is an Invitation to be Inventive," *House and Garden* (September 1952). She is mentioned in *Aline* (a biography of Aline Bernstein) by Carole Klein (1979). Additional information is available in *The Biographical Encyclopedia and Who's Who of the Theatre* (1966); *Who's Who in the Theatre* (1971–1977); *Notable Names in the American Theatre* (1976); *Who's Who in America, 1982–1983*, Vol. II (1982); *Costume Design in the Movies* (1977); *Who's Who of American Women, 1974–1975* (1973); and *The Oxford Companion to American Theatre* (1984).

Bobbi Owen

SHAW, Mary G. (January 25, 1854–May 18, 1929): actress famous for her performances in plays by Henrik Ibsen and George Bernard Shaw, and dedicated feminist, grew up in Boston, the daughter of Levi W. Shaw and Margaret (Keating) Shaw. Her father had come from Wolfboro, New Hampshire, to Boston, where he was for many years the assistant inspector of buildings. Mary Shaw grew up in Boston's South End, graduating from Girls' Highland Normal School in 1871. Louis Strang, in his biographical sketch of Shaw, explains that her initial interest in theatre resulted from losing her voice while teaching in Boston, so that she was led to study elocution (*Famous Actresses of the Day*, pp. 210–211). She performed with various amateur groups in Boston until, in 1879, she joined the Boston Museum stock company. Years later she confided to the *Dramatic Mirror* that her father's influence had been the critical factor in gaining her an introduction to Mr. Field, the Boston Museum company manager, who apparently hoped that friends of the Shaws would become regular patrons (June 26, 1897). While at the Boston Museum, Shaw supported **Fanny Davenport**, who was a visiting star in *Pique*. Davenport was so impressed with Shaw that she subsequently arranged for her to join Augustin Daly's company in New York for the 1882–1883 season.

Mary Shaw's career on the stage was to bridge two important eras in the development of American acting. Her early work exposed her to many of the great names of the nineteenth-century American stage. During the years up to the turn of the century she supported such famous actresses and actors as **Helena Modjeska**, **Fanny Janauschek**, Joseph Jefferson, **Julia Marlowe**, E. H. Sothern, and **Minnie Maddern Fiske**. During the latter part of her career she worked with **Helen Hayes** and **Eva Le Gallienne**, collaborated with George Bernard Shaw, and performed Ibsen.

Her earliest appearance in New York was in December of 1881, when she supported Fanny Davenport in a repertory including *As You Like It* (as Audrey) and *Camille*. In 1882 she participated in *The School for Scandal* (as Mrs. Sneerwell). In 1883 she performed in a short-lived run of *Sergaa Panine* with Augustin Daly's troupe. Strang records that after her season with Davenport, Shaw performed in *The Young Mrs. Winthrop*, by Bronson Howard, under the management of Daniel Frohman. In February 1884 Shaw joined Modjeska's production of *Twelfth Night* (as Maria); her other shows with Modjeska included *Camille*, *Much Ado About Nothing*, *Odette*, *Measure for Measure*, and *Cymbeline*. A more important role was that of Elizabeth opposite Modjeska's Mary Queen of Scots in Frederick Schiller's *Mary Stuart*, which opened January 5, 1886. She continued to play with Modjeska until 1888, when she joined Julia Marlowe in repertory for one season, playing Celia in *As You Like It*, Cynisca in *Pygmalion and Galatea*, and Helen in *The Hunchback*. In 1890 Shaw took the title role in what was probably the first in her long sequence of feminist plays, namely *Mary Lincoln, M.D.* by Charles Barnard. She had by this time left Modjeska's company and was acting in independent productions.

In December of 1892 she enrolled as a charter member of the Professional Women's League, which had been founded with the idea of having established actresses offer help to beginning actresses "in the spirit of the elder and helpful sister" (*The Theatre*, Vol. 2, August 1902, p. 21). Eventually the club was to include women engaged in literary and musical careers as well. Shaw's next recorded production was a benefit for the League; she played Rosalind in an all-woman cast of *As You Like It* (with Janauschek as Jacques) in November of 1893, and again in the spring of 1894. In 1895 she originated the part of Roxy in the adaptation of Mark Twain's *Pudd'nhead Wilson*. In 1896 she toured with Joseph Jefferson, playing Gretchen in *Rip Van Winkle*. In the fall of 1897 she played Marian in Minnie Maddern Fiske's touring production of *Tess of the D'Urbervilles*. In December of 1899 Shaw gained considerable critical recognition for her work as Amrah, the slave, in *Ben Hur*; but the landmark production of that year was her performance as Mrs. Alving in Ibsen's *Ghosts* on May 29, 1899, at the Carnegie Lyceum. She became associated with this part in many revivals (the first in 1902, a thirty-seven-week tour in 1903–1904, a revival in 1917, and one in 1922).

The year 1899 was an important year for Mary Shaw for another reason: she was delegate to the International Women's Congress in London, representing women of the American stage. Shaw wrote later that she had been under considerable pressure not to mix politics with art: a "widely influential manager" warned her that "an actress must be an actress and nothing else, to the public. The moment she appeared before them as a lecturer, she forfeited that exclusiveness, that fascination of mystery, which is the most potent instrumentality of her art" (*The Theatre*, August 1902, p. 21). This imposed separation between art and life constituted a direct challenge to Mary Shaw's philosophy of theatre. Theatre, she believed, was a powerful educational tool for religious and political issues as well as feminist ones. She once said that the drama is "an engrossing form of instruction in the vital truths of life" (*New York Tribune*, January 27, 1903). At any rate, she ignored the influential manager's advice, attended the Congress, and on June 30, 1899, in London, in the company of such notables as Susan B. Anthony, she delivered a paper on "Drama as a Field for Women," in which she declared: "There is an axiom in my profession that the most successful plays and players are the ones that please women. . . . It is truth pregnant with meaning for women [which] will rouse, perhaps, some new and strange convictions as to women's influence and responsibility toward the drama (*Dramatic Mirror*, July 15, 1899).

In the years that followed, Shaw's name became increasingly associated with feminist causes and with plays that confronted the truths of women's condition in the world and the need for reform. In an interview in the *New York Times* in 1903, Shaw explained her reasons for performing Ibsen: "Say what you will of Ibsen; he stands for a reform of our social system. What more powerful argument in favor of divorce . . . could be devised than *Ghosts*?" William Winter, among others, belittled her seriousness and referred to her work in *Ghosts* scathingly as a "reformatory crusade" (*Tribune*, January 27, 1903). Her work in *Hedda Gabler* in 1904 and her well-publicized feminist explanation for Hedda's behavior were greeted coldly by the critics. But her growing reputation as a feminist had attracted one very powerful ally, George Bernard Shaw, whose collaboration was to culminate in the most controversial production of her career.

In an interview in 1914, Mary G. Shaw described her work with George Bernard Shaw as dating from an early interest on her part in performing *Candida*, which had resulted in a flurry of letters from him. Shaw did not play Candida, but on October 30, 1905, she appeared in the American première of *Mrs. Warren's Profession* at the Garrick Theatre in New York. The play was closed by the police as "revolting, indecent, and nauseating." Following a favorable decision by the State Supreme Court, the play was announced for another production in 1907, starring **Rose Coghlan**. George Bernard Shaw, however, would not release the rights to the production unless Mary Shaw played Mrs. Warren; therefore she performed the role for the second time in 1907. This role and that of Mrs. Alving in Ibsen's *Ghosts* are probably her most outstanding characterizations.

Another important area of Shaw's concern first voiced publicly at the 1899 Women's Congress in London was her repeated claim that "the woman's point of view" was usually not respected by either manager, producer, or actor. This failing on the part of directors resulted in the appearance on stage of heroines who "talk and act not as real women would, but as men think that women ought to talk and act" (*Harper's Weekly*, May 8, 1915). Moreover, since all published criticism was written by men who at no point consulted the women constituting four/fifths of most audiences about what *they* felt was good drama, the "feminine sensibility" was completely disregarded.

In the years following *Mrs. Warren's Profession*, Shaw's political and reform activities increased as her popularity and influence as an actress gradually decreased and her acting met with respectful but lukewarm reviews. She appeared in *The Silent System* (1907), Elizabeth Robins's *Votes for Women* (1909), Paul Bourget's *Divorce* (1909), and *New York* (1910). None of these productions was a critical success, though the opening night of *Votes for Women* apparently created tremendous excitement because of the play's topicality. Much of her work in the years that followed was either in touring companies or in revivals. Very few of the plays have endured. After a brief stint in vaudeville in 1907 and 1908, she played in *Mother* (1911), *The Seventh Chord* (1914), *The Dicky Bird* (1915), *The Melody of Youth* and *The Travelling Man* (1916), revivals of *Ghosts* (1917) and *Mrs. Warren's Profession* (1920), *Back Pay* and *Idle Run* (1921), another revival of *Mrs. Warren's Profession* and *Ghosts* (1922, this time with her own son Arthur Shaw playing Jacob Engstrand), *The Rivals* (1923, in which Shaw achieved modest critical success as Mrs. Malaprop), *We Moderns* (1924, with Helen Hayes), and finally *Cradle Song* (1927–1928, a tour with Eva Le Gallienne's Civic Repertory Company). The only play that Shaw is known to have directed was August Strindberg's *Countess Julia* (*Miss Julie*) that opened April 28, 1913, at the 48th Street Theatre.

Some modern critics suggest that Shaw's politics marred her career and that her insistence on producing feminist dramas resulted in critical failures which injured her popularity and ended her star billing. But it is probably more true that tastes in acting style had changed over her lifetime, and that her work, largely based on her classical training in Shakespeare under Modjeska, was characterized by a broader style of performance than the highly detailed, understated work of performers like Mrs. Fiske, for example, whose work was finding a wider audience. Shaw's warmest reviews, especially after the turn of the century, tended to be for her work in comedy, particularly in *The Rivals*, about which John Corbin wrote: "The Mrs. Malaprop of Mary Shaw finely eschewed artificiality and had, indeed, moments of electric inspiration" (*New York Times*, June 6, 1922). In 1924 Corbin compared her comic delivery and timing in *We Moderns* to that of Helen Hayes (March 12, 1924). The impression given by her many reviews is that her style of acting, which was well suited to romantic and classical works, was not as effective in the "new realism."

Shaw's activities outside the theatre during the last two decades of her life deserve special mention. On July 13, 1913, she founded the Gamut Club, whose early members included **Lillian Russell** and Billie Burke. The club was to provide a meeting place for busy professional women, and its goal was to represent in its membership the full gamut of arts and professions (*The Theater*, October

1914, p. 187). A year after its founding, on August 29, 1914, the Gamut Club led a protest march of over fifteen thousand women opposed to what they saw as "the slaughter" of World War I. In December 1914, Shaw was featured in a week's program of addresses sponsored by the Women's Political Union in support of women's suffrage. Other speakers included such notables as Dorothea Dix and Walter Lippman, then of the *New Republic*. She also functioned as a fund raiser for the cause. With Jessie Bonstelle, actress and director-manager of stock companies, Shaw also worked to raise funds for a Women's National Theatre, which was intended to produce plays with a "feminist sensibility" independent of the predominantly male commercial establishment. This project finally floundered for lack of sufficient funding, but until the end of her life, Shaw was an outspoken supporter of the need for women's influence in the theatre, so that it might better meet women's needs and represent the real conditions of women's lives. Her conviction was that a vital relationship existed between the theatre and the possibility for feminist reform; it is for this conviction that she has won her place in American theatre history.

Shaw was married twice: the first marriage, to Henry G. Leach, ended in divorce in 1883; the second, in 1885 to the Duc de Brissac, an actor-director and a member of Modjeska's company, also ended in divorce. Her only child, the actor Arthur Shaw, was born of her first marriage.

Shaw died of heart disease at age seventy-five at her residence in the Wellington Hotel in New York. Her funeral on May 21, 1929, was attended by many theatrical notables and representatives of Actors' Equity, The Actors' Fund, the Lamb's Club, and the Gamut Club. On April 27, 1930, members of the Gamut Club unveiled a window in memory of Mary Shaw at the Little Church Around the Corner in New York. A spokesperson at the unveiling said, "The dominant interest of Mary Shaw's life ... was her love for her fellow woman. Women ever had in her a fighting champion" (*Equity Magazine*, May 1930).

Robert Schanke writes a particularly informative and interesting article on Mary Shaw called "Mary Shaw: A Fighting Champion" in *Women in American Theatre* (1981, 1987), edited by Helen Krich Chinoy and Linda Walsh Jenkins. Contemporary periodical articles about Shaw are included in the *New York Dramatic Mirror* (June 26, 1897), *The Theatre* (August, 1902), *McClure's Magazine* (April 1912), *Harper's Weekly* (May 8, 1915), and *Equity Magazine* (May, 1930). Shaw is also mentioned in "Actresses' Clubs in America," *The Theatre* (October 1914). Her speech to the International Women's Congress is summarized in the *London Times* (July 1, 1899) and quoted in full by the *New York Dramatic Mirror* (July 15, 1899). Her performances are widely reviewed, notably in the *New York Tribune* (January 27, 1903) and the *New York Times* (October 31, 1905, February 27, 1907, November 30, 1909, March 24, 1914, June 6, 1922, and March 12, 1924). Other volumes that are useful but occasionally inaccurate in details are T. Allston Brown, *A History of the New York Stage* (1903); John B. Clapp and Edwin F. Edgett, *Players of the Present* (1901); Helena Modjeska, *Memories and Impressions* (1910); and Eugene Tompkins and Quincy Kilby, *The History of the Boston Theatre, 1854–1901* (1908). More reliable are Lewis Strang's *Famous Actresses of The Day in America* (1900) and George C. D. Odell's *Annals of the New York Stage*, Vols. 11–15

(1927–1949). There is a clipping file on Mary Shaw in the Harvard Theatre Collection. There are entries on Shaw in Walter Browne and E. de Roy Koch, *Who's Who on the Stage, 1908* (1908); *The Green Room Book or Who's Who on the Stage* (1909); *The Dramatic List: Who's Who in the Theatre* (1925); *The Dictionary of American Biography*, Vol. IX (1935–1936); *Who Was Who in America*, Vol. I, 1897–1942 (1966), *Notable American Women*, Vol. III (1971); *Who Was Who in the Theatre*, Vol. IV (1978); and *The Oxford Companion to American Theatre* (1984).

Ellen Donkin

SIKS, Geraldine Brain (February 11, 1912–): theatre educator, author, playwright, and pioneer in the field of child drama, was born in Thorp, Washington, to George Brain and Alice Pearl (Ellison) Brain. Her father, of Irish and English descent, was a farmer who struggled through the depression years to provide for his family and educate the children. Her mother, of Swedish, Scottish, and Pennsylvania Dutch ancestry, won the 1966 Mother of the Year Award of the state of Washington for her life of service and influence on the education of her children. Geraldine Brain was the second of five children. In early childhood she and her two sisters, Hazel and Phyllis, and two brothers, George and Warren Eugene, were encouraged by their mother to act out plays improvisationally. They dramatized folk tales, myths, stories from history, and stories of their own creation. Later, while attending the Thorp schools, the Brain children participated in plays, in forensic contests, in county drama festivals, and in Chautauqua children's programs.

After graduating from Thorp High School in 1929, Geraldine Brain attended Washington State Normal School in Ellensburg, receiving her teaching certificate in 1931. For the next five years she taught in public schools in Kittitas and Toppenish, Washington, while taking classes at Central Washington University, from which she received her Bachelor of Arts degree in 1936. She and her older sister, Hazel, then went to Northwestern University in Evanston, Illinois, to study creative dramatics and children's theatre with Winifred Ward, the leading authority in the field at that time. During her years at Evanston (1936–1945), Geraldine Brain was a drama specialist with the Evanston Public Schools and associate director of the Children's Theatre of Evanston. She also wrote her first play, *Marco Polo*, under the guidance of **Charlotte Chorpenning** at the Goodman School of Theatre in Chicago's Art Institute. She designed, directed, and produced *Marco Polo* for the fifteenth anniversary of the Children's Theatre of Evanston, a production done in partial fulfillment of her master's degree in theatre and speech, which she received in 1940 from Northwestern University. During her years in Evanston, she met and married Charles J. (Karlis Janis) Siks, the Latvian vice consul in Chicago. When the Russians annexed Latvia in 1941, the consulate was closed; in 1945 Siks and her husband moved to Seattle, where he worked in the export-import trade. They had two children: Jan Karlis Siks (b. 1942,) who is a practicing veterinarian; and Mark Dean Siks (b. 1946), a dentist.

After moving to Seattle, Geraldine Siks became, in 1948, an instructor at the University of Washington School of Drama. She remained there until her retirement in 1977. On the occasion of her retirement, Siks and her long-time colleague at the University of Washington, **Agnes Haaga**, were honored by the university, their colleagues, and their friends from all over the world for their services to the development of child drama. At that time, the Seattle Junior Theatre, Inc. established the Agnes Haaga/Geraldine Siks Scholarship Fund in recognition of the efforts and achievements of both women.

Siks has published six books in the field of educational drama. Her first text, in collaboration with Ruth G. Lease, *Creative Dramatics in Home, School, and Community* (1952), provided a practical guide for parents, teachers, and community leaders. Widely used, the book was selected by the United States Information Services of UNESCO as one of five books to be distributed in 1952 to United States libraries in foreign countries. Her second text, *Creative Dramatics: An Art for Children* (1958), published after ten years of teaching experience at the university, extended and clarified practices based on Winifred Ward's philosophy. It, too, became a standard text in the field, and in 1975 was translated into Japanese for use in the educational system of Japan.

Siks's next book was written under the auspices of the American Educational Theatre Association with the cooperation of its Children's Theatre Conference (later the American Theatre Association and Children's Theatre Association of America). A collection of twenty-five essays by leaders in the field, it is titled *Children's Theatre and Creative Dramatics* (1961), edited in collaboration with Siks's sister, Hazel Brain Dunnington. Siks's fourth text, *Children's Literature for Dramatization: An Anthology* (1964), provided fifty stories and eighty poems strong in dramatic action for use in creative drama programs.

It was ten years before her next book was published. For Siks, that decade was one of exploration and discovery concerning the relationship of dramatic process to the principles of child development. In 1965 Siks received a contract with the United States Office of Education to study educational drama in seventeen European countries. For a year she observed and conferred with creative drama practitioners in Europe. In May 1966 that study tour culminated with the First International Assembly of the Association of Theatre for Children and Young People (ASSITEJ) in Prague, Czechoslovakia. Siks returned from Europe by way of the Orient, eventually teaching graduate courses in creative drama theory and practice at the University of Hawaii in Honolulu during the summer of 1966. During this year of study, Siks became convinced that traditional creative drama practices, emphasizing creative self-expression, placed little emphasis on the need for children to acquire the conscious skills and concepts necessary to participate in dramatic forms. In the summer of 1967 she was invited to attend a six-week seminar at the Central Atlantic Regional Educational Laboratory, which had been charged with the task of writing ''Behavioral Objectives in the Arts for Early Childhood Education.'' With some of her graduate students at the University of Washington, Siks began the task of identifying the most fundamental elements and concepts of drama that could be understood and enjoyed by children. A five-year test program of the new concepts resulted in two books: *Spotlight on Drama, K–6* (1975), edited and partly written by Siks, and *Drama with Children* (1977, translated into Japanese in 1978 and revised in 1983). This was the first text in the field to present a conceptual approach for teaching the art of drama to children.

An active member of the American Theatre Association, Siks was chairperson of the Children's Theatre and Creative Dramatics Presidential Monograph Committee, 1957–1960; served on the board of directors and executive committee, 1961–1963; and was a member of the Commission on Theatre Education, 1980–1982. In 1976 Siks was elected to the association's College of Fellows. In addition she served on various committees of the Children's Theatre Association of America. She was Children's Theatre Editor of the *Educational Theatre Journal* (1955–1957) and was associate editor for the *Children's Theatre Review* (1979–1981). During her professional career Siks has conducted more than five hundred creative drama workshops and lecture demonstrations throughout the state of Washington, the nation, and in foreign countries. In addition, she has conducted over seven hundred creative drama demonstrations with children. Siks received the Children's Theatre Association Creative Dramatics for Human Awareness Award in 1977; and in 1985, in recognition of her eminent, ongoing contributions, the American Theatre Association presented her with its highest honor—the Award of Merit for Distinguished Service to Educational Theatre. In addition, Siks has received honorary membership in the Delta Kappa Gamma Society (1956), the Distinguished Service Award of Zeta Phi Eta (the National Professional Speech Arts Fraternity for Women) (1967), and the Theta Alpha Phi Medallion of Honor (1979); she was selected by the Central Washington University Alumni Association as the Distinguished Alumnus of 1982.

Siks's contributions as a playwright include nine plays for audiences of children and youth. Four of these, produced by the Children's Theatre of Evanston and published by the Anchorage Press, are *Marco Polo* (1941), *Prince Fairyfoot* (1947), *The Sandalwood Box* (1954, translated into Arabic, 1960), and *The Nuremberg Stove* (1956). During her forty years working in child drama, Siks has been an effective advocate for including dramatic arts in the education of children and youth. In higher education, Siks has been a leader in curriculum change and the development of educational drama. She has advocated the need to train teachers and leaders so they are qualified to teach drama as an art in education and to use it as a methodology to educate children. Through her teaching, research, publications, and public service, Siks has influenced the evolution of drama education at elementary and higher education levels both nationally and internationally.

Geraldine Brain Siks has written or edited six major books on creative dramatics and theatre for children. They are *Creative Dramatics in Home, School, and Community* (1952) with Ruth G. Lease; *Creative Dramatics: An Art for Children* (1958); *Children's Theatre and Creative Dramatics* (1961) with Hazel Brain Dunnington; *Children's Lit-*

erature for Dramatization: An Anthology (1964); *Spotlight on Drama, K–6* (1975); and *Drama With Children* (1977, second edition, 1983). Much of the material included in this article is based on the personal collection of Geraldine Brain Siks and files at the University of Washington, Seattle. Siks has now donated her personal accumulation of material to the Child Drama Special Collection at Arizona State University, Tempe. Siks is listed in *The Biographical Encyclopaedia and Who's Who of American Theatre* (1966); *Who's Who of American Women, 1966–1967* (1965); *The World Who's Who of Women: Dictionary of International Biography* (1973); *Notable Names in the American Theatre* (1976); *Contemporary Authors*, Vol. 25 (1977); and *Dictionary of American Scholars* (1978).

Lou Furman

SINCLAIR, Catherine Norton (February 20, 1817–June 9, 1891): actress and theatre manager, was born in London, the eldest of four children of John and Catherine (Norton) Sinclair. Her parents were natives of Edinburgh, Scotland. When they were married in 1816, they went to the Continent, where John Sinclair studied music before settling in London. He was an accomplished, though second-rate, vocalist, and his wife was an actress of small consequence. He had managed to acquire some prominence in opera, however, by the time the pair toured America from 1831 to 1833. At home in London Catherine, their eldest daughter, had grown into a great beauty with natural charm and vivacity. She had apparently inherited her father's musical taste and was fluent in French; the resulting social poise was irresistible to the great American actor, Edwin Forrest, when he met her during his starring engagement in London in 1836. Though Forrest bridled at the impertinence of her father's inquiry into the actor's intentions regarding Catherine and what settlement he would make on her, Forrest was sufficiently undeterred to make her his bride at St. Paul's, Covent Garden, on June 23, 1837. They honeymooned on the Continent.

As Mrs. Edwin Forrest, Catherine Sinclair's next ten years were spent in seeming domestic bliss, as consort to America's greatest theatrical star and contender for the title of "foremost English-speaking actor of the age." His rivalry with William Charles Macready for that honor culminated in the famous Astor Place Riot in 1849, ironically only a few weeks after the Forrests' marriage had disintegrated. Throughout the 1840s Catherine Forrest either traveled with her husband on the circuits, mending his costumes and attending to his every need, or remained in New York City to manage their fashionable, well-staffed townhouse on West 22nd Street. This idyll was shattered by the deaths of all four of their children at birth, and thereafter they both continually sought affection outside of the home: he with his "amazon" leading lady, **Josephine Clifton**, and she with George Jamieson, a handsome actor who had supported Forrest on occasion. Finally, in the spring of 1849 Forrest charged his wife with infidelity and withdrew to Fonthill, a massive stone castle he was building on the Hudson River. She left the New York townhouse during the week of the Astor Place Riot and moved in with her friends, the Parke-Goodwins. Their friends' many attempts to reconcile them were futile.

The divorce trial—running from December 1851 to January 1852—was marked by mutual charges of flagrant infidelity and her lurid testimony. The newspapers took up the story and gave it sensational coverage and the dimensions of a national scandal without precedent. Catherine Forrest's name became a household word in its own right, just as Edwin Forrest's had been for nearly two decades. Though she won the case and was awarded alimony of $3000 a year, Forrest withheld payment and kept the case in appeal for sixteen years until he was forced to settle for $68,000 in arrears and $4,000 a year thereafter. She netted a scant $15,000 from the settlement, having consumed the rest in legal fees. At his death in 1872 she received a final $100,000 from his estate.

Using her maiden name, Catherine Sinclair, she began her theatrical career predicated on this newly won notoriety. In the last few weeks of the trial in 1852, she enlisted the services of actor George Vandenhoff to coach her for her acting debut. She apparently had no previous experience as an actress, and Vandenhoff was frankly dubious of her chances (and also complained of being "severely out of pocket" for his pains). Billed as "Mrs. C. N. Sinclair, the late Mrs. Forrest," she made her debut at Brougham's Lyceum in New York on February 2, 1852, as Lady Teazle in *The School for Scandal*. Her beauty, charm, and vivacity were noted by the critics, but so were her weak voice and lack of any genuine ability. Subsequent performances of Pauline in *The Lady of Lyons* and Beatrice in *Much Ado About Nothing* failed to impress the judicious but drew excellent business anyway. Later in the season she made an unusual appearance playing in French in *Elle Est Folle*. The next season she toured intermittently over the eastern seaboard and as far south as New Orleans, then turned to California in the summer of 1853. Her own management of a stock company at the Metropolitan Theatre in San Francisco, opening on December 24 of that year, is a feminist landmark in the American theatre; **Laura Keene**, an English actress newly arrived in America, began her own management of the Charles Street Theatre in Baltimore on the same night. Jointly, therefore, they both appeared to be the first actress-managers of consequence in America. Catherine Sinclair's management in San Francisco ran until June 1855 and is said to have earned her over $250,000. She continued management at the Sacramento and Forrest Theatres in Sacramento throughout the winter season of 1855–1856; a member of her company was the young, and as yet unknown, Edwin Booth. After a season in Australia, Catherine Sinclair made her London debut in September 1857 at the Haymarket Theatre and then made a tour of the English provinces. She retired from the stage on December 18, 1859, at New York's Academy of Music, her fame and notoriety apparently spent.

The last thirty years of her life were exceedingly private. She lived on Staten Island with her sister, Virginia Sedley, and her sister's husband Henry—an actor and critic. After her sister's death in 1869, Sinclair moved in with the Sedleys' son in New York City, where she remained until her death on June 9, 1891, at the age of seventy-four. The cause of death was given as a cerebral embolism, and she was buried in Staten Island's Silver Mount Cemetery.

Catherine Norton Sinclair was probably the first woman to move from the divorce court to the dramatic stage. **Mrs. Leslie Carter** would do the same—and with somewhat more artistic success—thirty-eight years later. Sinclair's marketability as an actress undoubtedly rested on the fame and notoriety of her divorce from the famous Forrest rather than on any genuine abilities, but her management of the theatres in California left a distinct landmark in the gradual development of the American actress-manager tradition.

Biographical material is scant. Of the five Forrest biographies—James Rees, *Life of Edwin Forrest* (1874); William R. Alger, *Life of Edwin Forrest* (1877); Laurence Barrett, *Edwin Forrest* (1881); Montrose Moses, *The Fabulous Forrest* (1929); and Richard Moody, *Edwin Forrest: First Star of the American Theatre* (1960)—only Moody gives a fair and unprejudiced account of Sinclair. George Vandenhoff's *Leaves of An Actor's Notebook* (1860) is a primary but hostile account of her training and debut as an actress. The *San Francisco Theatre Research—W.P.A. Project*, Vol. 11 (March, 1940), edited by Lawrence Estavan, features monographs on Forrest and Sinclair and is an exhaustive source regarding the divorce trial and her California management. Helpful news clippings include those in *Gleason's Pictorial* (Boston, April 24, 1852) as well as George Morton's "Memoirs of Mrs. Catherine Norton Sinclair," *New York Clipper* (February 18, 1911). She is listed in *The Era Almanack and Annual, 92* (1892) and under the name of Forrest in *Notable American Women*, Vol. I (1971).

James C. Burge

SKINNER, Cornelia Otis (March 30, 1901–July 9, 1979): actress, monologuist, author, and playwright, was born in Chicago, Illinois, the daughter of Otis Skinner and Maud (Durbin) Skinner. Both parents had acted on the stage before her birth; her father continued in that career and was acclaimed as one of the outstanding actors of the twentieth century. Although he left his family in Bryn Mawr, Pennsylvania, while he traveled with his company around the United States, his many letters to them, detailing his experiences as a touring actor, and his frequent and warm visits gave his daughter Cornelia a close acquaintance with the stage and influenced her in the choice of a career. Her mother devoted her life to making a home for the family and a place for them in society. Cornelia went to Baldwin School in Bryn Mawr for her preparatory education, was a student for a time, class of 1922, at Bryn Mawr College, and then went to France to study at the Comédie Française, under Emile Dehelly, and at the Jacques Copeau School. She married Alden Sanford Blodget on October 2, 1928, and had one son, Otis Skinner Blodget, now of London, and two stepchildren, Alden S. Blodget, Jr., and Mrs. Peter Whitman.

Cornelia Otis Skinner made her first professional appearance in 1921 with her father's company in Buffalo, New York, in a small role in *Blood and Sand* and her first appearance in New York at the Empire Theatre on September 20, 1921, in the same part. In 1923 she played the Maid of Honor in *Will Shakespeare*. Over the next several years she appeared in four more or less forgettable plays, gaining experience but little acclaim as an actress until 1935, when she played the title role in George Bernard Shaw's *Candida*.

Meanwhile, she found a métier in the writing and performing of character sketches in which she played all the roles, an art she perfected after studying **Ruth Draper** as a model. She presented these solo performances all over the United States and in London, appearing in the latter city for the first time in June 1929. In 1931 she presented *The Wives of Henry VIII* in London and in 1932 *The Empress Eugénie*. In New York in 1933 she added *The Loves of Charles II* to her repertoire, and in 1937, *Edna, His Wife*, a series of monologues based on Margaret Ayer Barnes's novel; she toured with it in 1938. In 1952 she opened a revue in New York, titled *Paris 90*, playing all fourteen characters; she took the production to London two years later. In all of these productions she succeeded in deftly transforming herself, with often only a simple property or one piece of costume, into a series of different people.

In addition to her solo performances, she continued to appear in stage productions in New York, in summer theatre, and on tour across the country. In the 1940s and 1950s she found roles in a number of noteworthy plays that revealed her talent: *Theatre* (1941), *The Searching Wind* (1944), *Lady Windermere's Fan* (1946), *Major Barbara* (1956), and *The Pleasure of His Company* (1958). In the last-named play, her performance as Jessica's mother pleased Brooks Atkinson, who wrote, "She plays it with taste and distinction and also with wit—wit not only in the edging of phrases but also in posture, movement and in the silent language of her eyes. In all respects this is her finest performance" (*New York Times*, October 23, 1958). The play ran for more than a year in New York and then went on tour.

Skinner's first attempt at writing a play was *Captain Fury* in 1925. This was followed by many lighthearted, witty books that were based on personal experiences: vignettes on traveling, backstage comportment, domestic problems, and social situations. Among them are *Tiny Garments* (1932), *Excuse It, Please* (1936), *Dithers and Jitters* (1938), *Soap Behind the Ears* (1941), *Nuts in May* (1950), and *The Ape in Me* (1959). *Our Hearts Were Young and Gay*, which she co-authored with Emily Kimbrough in 1942, related a youthful trip abroad and sold a million copies, with a motion picture version appearing in 1944. In 1948 **Jean Kerr** adapted it into a popular play. Reviews spoke of it as "joyous from beginning to end." In 1959 she and S. A. Taylor wrote the highly successful play *The Pleasure of His Company*, and in 1966 she published *Madame Sarah*, a vivid and affectionate biography of Sarah Bernhardt, the French actress. In *Harper's Magazine* Clive Barnes commented, "Miss Skinner is an authority on this period of French theatre, and in addition to the story of Madame Bernhardt, the book also contains lots of information about the stage of the period." Her last book, *The Life of Lindsay and Crouse*, was published in 1976. Throughout her life Skinner wrote sundry articles, sketches, and verse for various magazines such as *Vogue*, *The New Yorker*, *Scribner's*, and *Theatre Arts*. She wrote scripts for the radio and appeared on radio and television and in films. During World War II she presented her monologues for servicemen under the auspices of the American Theatre Wing.

Despite her heavy performance schedule, she found time to serve on many committees and was given special awards for her contributions to American culture. She received the Barter Theatre Award in 1952 and in 1954 was invested as an Officer de Académie in Paris. She also received honorary degrees from the University of Pennsylvania, New York University, Tufts University, Emerson College, Bryn Mawr College, Mills College, and several others.

Cornelia Otis Skinner died July 9, 1979, in New York City, from a cerebral hemorrhage. The *New York Times* (July 10, 1979) carried a long and glowing account of her accomplishments, indicating that she was "one of the favorite stage personalities of devoted audiences for more than thirty-five years because of her ability to provoke laughter that was balm for her barbs." Skinner was certainly an accomplished actress and one recognized not only throughout this country but abroad as well. She made a significant contribution to the theatre through the productions of her monologues. These entertainments she presented on tours ranging across the country, often exciting the imagination of audiences in rural communities who had seen few stage plays. Always willing to meet with admiring school girls after a performance or to chat with the townspeople brought into the host's home, she inspired many to explore a career in the theatre. In her essays and vignettes she entertained many readers as a sophisticated commentator of the day. Critics recognized her as a serious writer in her later works. Her book *Elegant Wits and Grand Horizontals* (1962); describing life in Paris at the turn of the century, was praised by Rose MacMurray in the *Washington Post* (October 21, 1962): "As we read Mrs. Skinner's lively prose, we are compelled by her headlong narrative, beguiled by her humor, and likely to forget that we are in the presence of genuine scholarship." André Maurois, a serious biographer, praised *Madame Sarah*, and theatre historians treasure her autobiographical books for the personal record of the life and acting style of her father, Otis Skinner. She brought grace, wit, and charm to the American stage, for which she was a dedicated and meticulous worker. The seeming effortlessness of her writing and her acting characterizes the art of which she was mistress.

Cornelia Otis Skinner has written several autobiographical books and articles. "Father" in *Harper's Bazaar* (August 1941) describes her childhood. *Family Circle* (1984) tells of her life up until the time of her New York debut. *Our Hearts Were Young and Gay* (1942), written with Emily Kimbrough, recounts in a humorous way her experiences on her first trip to Europe. "I Saw Your Father in Kismet," *Theatre Arts* (October 1941), tells how her father's fame as an actor. Skinner has also published *One-Woman Show: Monologues as Originally Written and Performed by Cornelia Otis Skinner* (1974). She has written three biographies; *Madam Sarah* (1967), a biography of Sarah Bernhardt; *Maud Durbin Skinner* (1939), a biography of Skinner's mother; and *The Life of Lindsay and Crouse* (1976). Allen H. Smith has written "Cornelia Otis Skinner," *Cosmopolitan* (April 1942). Skinner's obituary appeared in the *New York Times* (July 10, 1979). Skinner is listed in Stanley J. Kunitz, ed., *Twentieth Century Authors*, First Supplement (1955); *Current Biography, 1964* (1964–1965); *Who's Who in America, 1964–1965* (1964); *Who's Who of American Women, 1954–1965* (1963); *The Biographical Encyclopaedia and Who's*

Who of the American Theatre (1966); Robin May, *A Companion to the Theatre: The Anglo-American Stage from 1920* (1973); *Notable Names in the American Theatre* (1976); *Who's Who in the Theatre* (1977); *Contemporary Authors*, Vols. 89–92 (1980); *American Women Writers*, Vol. IV (1982); *The Oxford Companion to American Literature* (1983); and *The Oxford Companion to American Theatre* (1984).

Nelda K. Balch

SKINNER, Edith Warman (September 22, 1902–July 25, 1981): speech teacher and coach, was born in Moncton, New Brunswick, Canada, the third of four daughters of Herbert Havelock Warman and Agnes Lynn (Orr) Warman. Her father worked with a furniture company and later an insurance firm, and her mother was a public school teacher; but theatre seems to have been a strong family interest, with two of the daughters subsequently pursuing professional careers—Edith as a renowned teacher and her older sister Margaret Hewes as a successful Broadway and regional producer in the 1920s and early 1930s. After graduating from the Edith Cavell High School in 1920, Edith Warman moved to the United States and began working as head of the drama program at the Beechwood School for Girls in Jenkintown, Pennsylvania. She was also enrolled at the Leland Powers School of the Spoken Word in Boston, from which she received a diploma in 1923.

It was at the Leland Powers School that Edith Warman met her first mentor, Margaret Prendergast McLean, at that time a leading American speech teacher and subsequently author of two respected texts, *Good American Speech* and *Oral Interpretation of Forms of Literature*. McLean was a disciple of phonetician William Tilly, then teaching at Columbia University and himself a student of Henry Sweet, the British dialectician said to have been George Bernard Shaw's model for Henry Higgins in *Pygmalion*. With McLean's encouragement Edith Warman began to spend summers studying with Tilly in New York, becoming his personal assistant for his extension division classes in 1926. For the next two years she divided her time between New York and Boston, assisting McLean at the Leland Powers School and continuing her work with Tilly. In 1928 she enrolled full-time at Teachers' College, Columbia University, completing her bachelor's degree by 1930 and her master's degree the following year. For the next four years she continued to work closely with Tilly and McLean, as both teaching assistant and student. Various New York teaching jobs and assistantships provided income and experience during this period, including assignments at Packer Collegiate Institute, Hunter College, and the Bonstelle School of Drama. McLean also brought her into contact with the work of Richard Boleslavsky's Laboratory Theatre.

Beginning in 1928, Margaret Hewes produced professional summer seasons at the Wharf Theatre in Provincetown, Massachusetts, and Edith Warman spent her summers coaching the company. After 1930 she also instructed apprentices in a full-scale training program—one of the first models for actor-training efforts within a professional company in the United States. It was at Provincetown that she met actor Neil Skinner, the company's resident juvenile. They were married in 1932. He worked with some success as a stock and touring actor, and she continued to teach, study, and assist Tilly and McLean. In 1935 Hewes, following her second marriage, turned the Wharf Theatre over to her sister and brother-in-law, Edith and Neil Skinner, who produced summer seasons for the next few years. As personal difficulties developed between them, leading to a 1939 divorce, Edith Skinner began to run the theatre herself as managing director, while simultaneously directing a constantly expanding training program. Among her productions in this period was an acclaimed revival of Eugene O'Neill's *Ah, Wilderness!*, starring writer Sinclair Lewis, whose plays she also produced.

During the winter she continued to teach, assisting McLean in a comparative phonetics course for the New York City Board of Education in early 1935 and spending the 1935–1936 season at the Cornish School in Seattle. In 1937, after enthusiastic recommendations from Tilly and McLean, she was invited to join the faculty of the Department of Drama at the Carnegie Institute of Technology (now Carnegie-Mellon University) in Pittsburgh. She did not intend to stay beyond that first year; she did not leave until 1974. It was here that she found her niche, beginning a life's work that would have a profound effect on American theatre, theatre training, and generations of American actors. In the words of American Conservatory Theatre's general director William Ball, "Edith Skinner alone did more than any single person in modern history to change the course of American theatre by elevating the standard of speech for American actors" ("Dedication" to *Newsletter 80/81*, Department of Drama, Carnegie-Mellon University, 1981). She began as an instructor and progressed over the next thirty-seven years to full professor, continuing to work beyond the retirement age as Andrew Mellon lecturer and visiting Andrew Mellon professor. Writing of Skinner, Drama Department head Earle R. Gister called her "this country's leading teacher of speech" (*Alumni Magazine*, Carnegie-Mellon University, 1981, p. 23).

Skinner did not teach trainers; she taught actors how to work on their own speech problems but not necessarily how to convey Skinner's concepts and methodology to others. In the last years of her career she was deeply concerned about the survival of her work and concentrated on the training of several young instructors in the teaching of her methods. Most of these have gone on to successful teaching careers. She also prepared two book-and-cassette publications, *Good Speech for the American Actor* and, in the last year of her life, *The Seven Points for Good Speech in Classic Plays*. The latter is also available on videotape that gives the viewer at least some impression of Skinner's personality and authority. Her work was based on the International Phonetic Alphabet, using a meticulous "narrow transcription" that enabled the student to identify minute variation in spoken sound. Through this system she trained her students in a standard form of American English. Her "standard" was not British, nor did she agree with the notion of "mid-Atlantic" speech. The speech she taught was American, but it was an American speech free of regionalism—the "pure" set of sounds used to form words in the spoken language. Dialects were taught, with the aid of phonetics, by making specific adjustments in sounds within the "standard" system. She taught sounds to her students not merely through mimicry but through specific analysis of lip, tongue, teeth, throat, and roof-of-mouth positions, the absence of vocal tension, and efficient use of the articulation and respiratory system. She was also acclaimed as a text coach, particularly in Shakespeare, where her work was based on relative sound lengths, strong and weak word forms, rhythmic thought groupings, and the mechanisms of scansion.

Skinner was a popular and ultimately revered teacher, and like many outstanding teachers, she was as much cherished for her personal eccentricities as she was respected for her knowledge and skill. Throughout the years at Carnegie she also continued her professional coaching work, first with the Pittsburgh Playhouse and later, as former student actors and directors required her skills, in New York, California, and throughout the country. During World War II she taught summer sessions for the School of Education at New York University, and such guest engagements at other colleges and drama schools continued throughout her career. With McLean she did extensive work on a pronouncing dictionary of American English, which remained unpublished. She did, however, publish two standard texts, *Dialects for the Theatre* (1963) and *Speak with Distinction* (1942).

By the mid–1950s some of her students had moved into positions of importance in the theatre, and in 1957 she coached the Siobhan McKenna *Hamlet* produced for the American National Theatre and Academy (ANTA) Matinee Series at New York's Theatre de Lys. In the spring of 1964 Tyrone Guthrie summoned her to Minneapolis for intensive work with his new repertory company; then she spent that summer coaching former student Ellis Rabb's Association of Producing Artists (APA Repertory Company) in New York. In the fall and winter she began working with William Ball (also a former student) at his newly formed American Conservatory Theatre, then in residence at the Pittsburgh Playhouse. In 1966 she rejoined Rabb's company in New York and Los Angeles, taking her only leave of absence in her thirty-seven years of teaching at Carnegie Mellon to remain with the company throughout the 1966–1967 season on a Rockefeller Foundation grant as voice and speech coach. In 1967 the *Pittsburgh Post-Gazette* named her one of the year's "Outstanding Pittsburgh Women."

By this time, Skinner had reached the normal academic retirement age; she nevertheless kept working. At this point John Houseman invited her to join the faculty of the soon-to-be-established Juilliard School of Drama in New York. Skinner, whom Houseman later described in the third volume of his autobiography as "the most esteemed speech teacher in America," was one of his very first faculty appointments. "Her reputation," he noted, "was enormous and her presence on our faculty brought us instant prestige" (John Houseman, *Final Dress*, p. 345). Skinner's speech class subsequently opened the first day of the new school. She taught at Juilliard on Mondays and Tuesdays and returned to Pittsburgh and Carnegie Mellon on Tuesday evening for three days of teaching and the weekend at her home. During these years she also worked periodically in St. Louis, at Webster College and the then affiliated Loretto-Hilton Repertory Company, and with the McCarter Theatre at Princeton. Other assignments included that of dialect coach for Ellis Rabb's Lincoln Center production of *A Streetcar Named Desire*.

In 1974 when a change in departmental administration ended her relationship with Carnegie she moved to New York, where her modest Juilliard salary and small pension from Carnegie-Mellon provided an income that she attempted to augment with private teaching and professional coaching, notably with the Theatre Company at the Brooklyn Academy of Music. In 1977 and 1978 William Ball invited her to teach at the Summer Training Congress of his American Conservatory Theatre, now firmly established in San Francisco. Her success was such that Ball urged her to begin a permanent relationship with the A.C.T. professional company. At age seventy-five she thus began a bi-coastal career, dividing her time between Juilliard in New York and A.C.T. in California. In this period she also coached the dialects for Laurence Olivier's Broadway production of *Filumena*, taught at the Banff Theatre Center in Canada, and published the first of her two cassette books.

At A.C.T. in 1980 that she organized her first workshop for the training of teachers, a project prompted by her growing concern for the survival of her work. That summer she also spoke with great success at the convention of the American Theatre Association in San Diego. It was to be a valedictory.

In 1981 she coached her last Broadway production, the Elizabeth Taylor revival of **Lillian Hellman**'s *The Little Foxes*. She continued to work at Juilliard and A.C.T. and in June went to Milwaukee to conduct a second teacher-training workshop organized through the University of Wisconsin. It was here she died of a stroke on the evening of July 25, 1981. She was sitting in bed at the time, correcting the phonetic dictation of her current students, as had been her nightly custom for decades.

Edith Warman Skinner was the author of four works: *Speak with Distinction* (1942, fifth edition, 1965), *Dialects for the Theatre* (1963), *Good Speech for the American Actor* (with cassette) (1980), and *The Seven Points for Good Speech in Classic Plays* (with cassette and videotape; posthumous release, California, 1983). Skinner's birthdate is sometimes given as 1904, but official papers at the Department of Drama, Carnegie-Mellon University, give it as 1902. The best source of information on Skinner's career is in the files of this department. Additional details were secured by interviews with her nephew Henry Hewes, who is a noted critic, Bes Kimberly of Carnegie-Mellon University, and three Skinner-trained teachers—Deborah Hecht of New York University, Chapel Hill, Timothy Monich of the Juilliard School, and Deborah Sussel of the American Conservatory Theatre. Skinner is mentioned frequently in John Houseman, *Final Dress* (1983). Obituaries or tributes appear in the *New York Times* (July 28, 1981); *Los Angeles Times* (August 2, 1981), *Newsletter 80/81*, Department of Drama, Carnegie-Mellon University (1981); and *Alumni Magazine*, Carnegie-Mellon University (1981). Skinner is listed in

Who's Who of American Women, 1964–1965 (1963); *The Biographical Encyclopaedia and Who's Who of the American Theatre* (1966); and *Notable Names in the American Theatre* (1976).

David Hammond

SKLAR, Roberta (November 24, 1940–): director and playwright, was born in Brooklyn, New York, the fourth child and fourth daughter of five children born to a first generation American working class couple, whose parents were from eastern Russia near Odessa. Graduation from Erasmus Hall High School in Brooklyn, Roberta Sklar studied at Hunter College, from which she received her bachelor's degree in literature in 1962. She subsequently completed the Master of Arts degree at the City University of New York (1972), as well as additional graduate study at Columbia University. Over the ensuing years she also engaged in extensive study and dialogue with **Uta Hagen**, **Kristin Linklater**, **JoAnne Akalaitis**, Peter Brook, Julian Beck, and Jerzy Grotowski. A native New Yorker, she has lived there all her life, residing now on New York's Upper West Side with her child, Jesse.

A founding member of the Off-off-Broadway movement, Sklar has worked primarily in experimental theatre; since 1972 she has emphasized in her work thematic material in which women are central to dramatic content. She has been prominent in bringing the concerns of women and the lives of women—as seen by women themselves—into the theatre and establishing that perspective as a part of theatre. Her approach in experimental theatre can be seen as the search for a theatrical form to express the experience of women.

Sklar began directing plays while an undergraduate student at Hunter and was the first woman there to be awarded the University Fellowship in theatre (1963–1966). During this time she was also active in the nascent Off-off-Broadway movement, directing some twenty original scripts at the Café Cino and the La Mama Experimental Theatre Club by such American playwrights as Lanford Wilson, Robert Patrick, and Harry Katoukas, as well as the plays of Bertolt Brecht, Jean Genêt, and Eugene Ionesco.

Sklar was introduced to Joseph Chaikin of the Open Theatre by *Village Voice* critic Michael Smith, and in 1968 she joined the Open Theatre as co-director with Chaikin. In this role, she worked with the actors, developed improvisatory material, and was central to the creation of the dramatic structure of the collaborative works. She was responsible for the training of the acting company in Saturday workshops, which she and Chaikin conducted on alternate weekends for two years. She developed with Chaikin the patterns for the daily improvisational sessions; and she chose what was to be used from the materials brought in by actors and writers. She likens their collaboration to a relay situation: one carrying the ball, then handing it off to the other to run with it. Because of Chaikin's five years' prior experience with the company, his role was stronger in relating directly to the actors. Sklar's work included collaboration with writers

Megan Terry, Jean-Claude van Itallie, Sam Shepard, and **Susan Yankowitz** (essentially in the role of dramaturg) as well as directing and actor training.

Sklar's credits as co-director from 1968 to 1974 include, from the Open Theatre's major collaborative works: *The Serpent*, *Terminal*, *The Mutation Show*, and *America Hurrah/Interview*, which played not only in the Public Theatre and the St. Clements Theatre in New York, but toured nationally and internationally. For the company, she also directed Samuel Beckett's *Endgame*, with Chaikin playing Hamm (1969), and the world premiére of Luciano Berio's *Opera*, for which she took ten Open Theatre actors to Santa Fé (1970), where the work was first presented.

In an interview with Cornelia Brunner, Sklar observed: "The struggle to articulate a sense of self becomes evident to me when I look back to the creation of the last directorial work I did at the Open Theatre, *The Mutation Show*. For me, it was really the beginning of my feminist expression, and it was the piece about which there was the greatest struggle between Chaikin and me. During the earlier pieces, I worked much the way women did in the peace movement and in the student movement: we did a lot of the work, got little of the credit, and didn't realize yet that there was a major section missing in the political analysis—the section that was about us" (*The Drama Review*, June 1980).

Sklar and the Open Theatre were co-recipients of numerous awards, including *Village Voice* Off-Broadway (Obie) Awards for outstanding contribution to experimentation in theatre for *The Serpent* (1968) and *The Mutation Show* (1971); the Vernon Rice Drama Desk Award for *The Serpent* (1968); the Brandeis Citation in Theatre Arts (1970); the Bitif, Yugoslavia Festival Award (1971); and the New England Theatre Conference Award (1972). She also individually received a New York Drama Desk Award for direction in 1972 for *The Mutation Show*; and when she accepted it, she pointed out to the assembled press that she had been consistently referred to as "Robert" Sklar and had come to receive the reward in person "to let you know I am Roberta."

In 1971 Sklar began to teach an all-women's course at Bard College, which evolved into a group called the Women's Unit. With that group she developed the play *Obscenities and Other Questions*. By 1974 she was ready to leave the Open Theatre. To Brunner, she acknowledged, "It was hard to leave the Open Theatre, but I had to find a new way of working. Another part of my life took over: the advancement of a deep connection with women" (*The Drama Review*, June 1980). Now she would go outside theatre to bring back to the theatre the experience of women, by gathering oral histories of groups of women and integrating them into dramatic work.

In 1974 Sklar joined the Womanrite Theatre Ensemble, whose members, she told Brunner, "were 'just women' rather than actors. I had come to suspect, given the experience at Bard, that my previous ideas about who belongs on stage and who belongs in the audience were not necessarily correct. I knew that it requires skill to theatrically analyze human behavior and to project your analysis, but more than anything else it requires interest'' (*The Drama Review*, June 1980). She worked with this group for three years as teacher and as director.

In 1976 she founded with Clare Coss, poet, playwright, and psychotherapist, and Sondra Segal, actress and writer, the Women's Experimental Theatre. Between that year and 1985, Sklar directed and co-authored *The Daughters Cycle Trilogy: Daughters, Sister/Sister*, and *Electra Speaks*; and three works on food: *Food, Foodtalk*, and *Feast or Famine*, all produced at the Interart Theatre in New York and subsequently toured to other cities and to universities. In 1986 Sklar became assistant to the commissioner for cultural affairs in New York City.

Sklar's work with the Women's Experimental Theatre has earned the group grants from the National Endowment for the Arts, the New York State Council of the Arts, and the Women's Fund. She has collaborated with various video artists in bringing her work to the media. At the Open Theatre, she helped adapt for television *The Serpent, Terminal*, and *The Mutation Show*. Parts of the later *Electra* and of *Feast or Famine* have also been produced for television. Sklar is a busy guest lecturer, panelist, and workshop leader in addition to her continuing work as a theatre practitioner. "We seek a theatre that has been revolutionized by feminism and women's vision, . . . not only feminist theatres . . . but the theatre as an institution. The impact of the full inclusion of women would change the face of theatre as we know it. There is no way for any of us to understand what that could mean,'' says Sklar (*The Drama Review*, Winter 1983). Sklar is unquestionably one of the most important modern theatre professionals who are working with experimental forms and feminist materials.

Materials concerning Roberta Sklar's work are to be found in Cornelia Brunner, "Roberta Sklar: Towards a Women's Theatre," *The Drama Review* (June 1980); Clare Coss, Sondra Segal, Roberta Sklar, "Separation and Survival: Mothers, Daughters, Sisters," *The Scholar and the Feminist*, Vol. I: *The Future of Difference*, ed. by H. Eisenstein and A. Jardine (1980); "Notes on the Women's Experimental Theatre," *Women in Theatre: Compassion and Hope*, ed. by Karen Malpede (1983); Debra Gorlin, "Dramatic Transformations: The Work of Roberta Sklar, Playwright, Director," *Valley Advocate* (December 2, 1981); Sondra Segal and Roberta Sklar, "Without the Participation of Women There is No Revolution," *Womanews* (March 1984); and "The Women's Experimental Theatre," *The Drama Review* (Winter 1983); and "Reflections" by Roberta Sklar in *Women in American Theatre*, ed. by Helen Krich Chinoy and Linda Walsh Jenkins (1981, 1987).

Saraleigh Carney

SMITH, Betty (December 15, 1904–January 18, 1972): playwright and novelist, was born Elizabeth Wehner in Brooklyn, New York. She was the daughter of two first generation Americans, John and Catherine (Hummel) Wehner. Smith's father died when she was eleven, and her mother later married Michael Keogh. After completing the eighth grade at P.S. 23 in Greenpoint, New York, Smith left school and worked for a time in factory, retail, and clerical jobs in New York City. Her first contact with the theatre came through community activities with the local Williamsburg Y.M.C.A., where she acted in several amateur plays. At the age of twenty she married George H. E. Smith, a law student at the University of Michigan, Ann Arbor. They had two daughters, Mary and Nancy Smith. Her interest in the theatre was stimulated in the early years of this marriage, when she was admitted as a special student at the University of Michigan where she audited several English courses. In 1930, while a student at the University of Michigan, Smith wrote her first full-length play. Written in the social-conscious style of the 1930s, it was called *Francie Nolan* and won the first prize of one thousand dollars from the Avery Hopwood competition drama.

From 1927 to 1930 Smith wrote and published one-act plays, worked as a feature writer for the newspaper syndicate NEA, and wrote columns for the *Detroit Free Press*. From 1931 to 1934 she attended the Yale Drama School, where she studied under George Pierce Baker and Walter Pritchard Eaton. After leaving Yale, Smith became an actress and playwright in association with the Federal Theatre Project and also worked as a radio actress. As a member of the Federal Theatre she met playwright Paul Green, who persuaded her to move to Chapel Hill, North Carolina, to write.

In the mid–1930s, she became a visiting lecturer in the Department of English at the University of North Carolina—Chapel Hill as well as a special lecturer in drama in the Department of Dramatic Art. In the summers she made guest appearances in Green's outdoor drama, *The Lost Colony*, and worked in various stock companies. While at Yale, she had been awarded the Rockefeller Dramatists Guild Playwriting Fellowship, and at North Carolina she received a second Rockefeller grant.

In 1938 Betty Smith divorced her first husband and five years later married Joseph Piper Jones, a private in the army who later became an assistant editor of the *Chapel Hill Weekly*. They were divorced in 1951, and six years later she married Robert Finch with whom she collaborated on many of her plays. Finch died just a year and a half after their marriage.

By 1940 Smith had published seventy-five one-act plays and two full-length plays in collaboration with Finch. Following this prolific dramatic outpouring, Smith decided to write a novel. The original draft of her ''novel'' was 800 pages of dialogue and stage directions divided into scenes and acts, amounting to nearly eight full-length plays. For two years she worked on converting this playscript into her novel *A Tree Grows in Brooklyn* (1943). In 1945 her novel was made into a movie, but Smith declined to work on the screenplay adaptation. In 1949 George Abbott and Robert Fryer acquired the movie and planned to make a musical from it; despite her initial reluctance, Smith began working with Abbott on the adaptation. Arthur Schwartz and Dorothy Fields were engaged to do the music and lyrics, Jo Mielziner the set, and **Irene Sharaff** the costumes.

On April 19, 1951, *A Tree Grows in Brooklyn* opened on Broadway at the Alvin Theatre. Smith's novel about the suffering of a poor family in Brooklyn was drastically revised for the Broadway show. Francie Nolan, the bright and ambitious heroine of the novel, is overshadowed in the musical by **Shirley**

Booth's starring role as Aunt Cissy, who by simulating birth and passing the infant off as her boyfriend's, tricks the boyfriend into agreeing to adopt it. Nothing in Smith's novel, a rather somber look at the rasping poverty of a tenement family, suggests such broad comedy; Smith evidently had to forego her more serious purpose for the exigencies of the new genre. The musical was a great success; Brooks Atkinson called it "one of those happy inspirations that the theatre dotes on" (*New York Times*, April 20, 1951).

Most of Betty Smith's nonmusical plays reflect a strong Christian didacticism. Many of the one-acts, such as *Room for a King* (a Christmas play) and *The Silvered Rope*, are modernized versions of medieval miracle plays. They adhere strictly to a parable form and usually employ one allegorical figure in the person of a wayfaring stranger who forces a moral recognition. In *The Far-Distant Shore*, Smith uses the same form to present a more topical message. Written at a time when there was a strong feeling of apathy in America about fighting what seemed an inevitable wave of racial discrimination, this play is an allegory in which a disheartened Jew finds renewed spirit through the visitation of a stranger who reminds him of the hope promised in God's choice of a Hebrew for his son. *Western Night*, which won the silver cup offered by the Theatre Guild for the best one-act play of 1938, is also an allegory, in which death comes to claim the life of an injured cowboy and opens up the promise of heaven to his surviving friends. In *Freedom's Bird* (1945), Smith uses the Harrison/Tyler campaign of 1840 as a setting to expose the corrupt political practices of American politicians and to criticize the American public, who are only interested in a "good show." *Gander Sauce* (1942) is a clever comedy based on a series of complex recognition scenes involving one man and his many mistresses. Here Smith uses the medium to express a need for women to band together to deter of one man's manipulative devices. On November 12, 1947, Smith's play *The First in Heart* premièred at the Yale School of Drama. Suggested by the novel *And Never Yield* by Elinor Pryor, this play is concerned with Mormonism during the years 1840–1841 and powerfully exposes the problems of multiple marriage. *Heroes Just Happen* is typical of Smith's moralistic pieces for high school students. The majority of her plays follow this didactic pattern, which she employs to comment upon a wide range of topics from politics to personal relationships. Their common concern is always to strip away false appearances and to uncover dangers. Her contributions to the American theatre give voice to a strong social consciousness and a sustained effort to reach a widely varied audience.

Betty Smith was named "Woman of the Year" in 1943. She also received a certificate of merit from the New York Museum of Science and Industry for Outstanding Achievement in the Arts, and the Carolina Playmakers Alumni Award (1964). She died in a New York City convalescent home on January 18, 1972, survived by her two daughters and six grandchildren.

There exists very little commentary on Betty Smith's career as a dramatist. See *Contemporary Authors*, Vol. 5–6 (1969) for a detailed list of her plays. For a listing of single editions and plays in collections, see *An Index to One-Act Plays*, second supplement, 1932–1940, by Hannah Logasa and Winifred Ver Nooy (1941). A number of Smith's collaborations with Robert Finch can be found in his *Plays of the American West* (1947). See also *Twenty-Five Non-Royalty One-Act Plays for All-Girl Casts* (1942), Betty Smith, editor and contributor. Smith compiled and contributed to *Twenty Prize-Winning Non-Royalty One-Act Plays*. See also *The New Yorker*, 19: 16–17 (October 9, 1943), and *Newsweek* (February 24, 1958) for professional profiles and biographical detail. For an interview with Betty Smith, see Robert Van Gelder, "Betty Smith on Fame and Money: an Interview with the Author of *A Tree Grows in Brooklyn* and *Tomorrow Will Be Better*," *Vogue* (April 1949). Also see Walter Spearman, *The Carolina Playmakers: The First Fifty Years* (1970). Betty Smith's collected letters, typescripts, articles, short stories, novels, clippings, scrapbooks, photographs, posters, short writings, and an unfinished autobiography are held in Wilson Library at the University of North Carolina—Chapel Hill. Smith's obituary appeared in the *New York Times* (January 18, 1972). Harry Redcay Warfel, *American Novelists of Today* (1951) contains a biographical sketch of Smith. She is also included in *Current Biography, 1943* (1944); *Twentieth Century Authors, First Supplement* (1955); *The Biographical Encyclopaedia and Who's Who of the American Theatre* (1966); *Contemporary Authors*, Vols. 5–8 (1963, 1969); *Who Was Who in America with World Notables, Vol. V, 1969–1973* (1973); *Contemporary Literary Criticism*, Vol. 19 (1981); *American Women Writers*, Vol. IV (1982); *Dictionary of Literary Biography Yearbook: 1982* (1983); and *The Oxford Companion to American Literature* (1983).

Lynda Hart

SOKOLOW, Anna (February 20, 1913, or February 9, 1915–): dancer and choreographer, was born in Hartford, Connecticut. Her parents, recent emigrants from eastern Europe, were the subjects of many of her important works, but Sokolow will not give biographical data on them or verify her own exact birth date. She moved to New York City as a child with her mother, an organizing member of the International Ladies' Garment Workers' Union. Living on the Lower East Side, Anna discovered dance and theatre through classes and projects sponsored by local settlement houses. Sokolow began her dance training with Bird Larson and took classes in dance composition with **Martha Graham**, Blanche Talmud, and Louis Horst, assisting Horst in his Pre-Classic Dance Forms classes to pay for the instruction she received. She made her professional debut as a dancer in a Neighborhood Playhouse project in 1927 and joined the Martha Graham company in 1930. In nine years Sokolow appeared in many of the most influential works in Graham's repertory; among them, *Primitive Mysteries*, *Tragic Patterns*, *American Provincials*, and *American Lyric*. She began creating dances while in the company and received the first Bennington College Fellowship in Choreography. Sokolow shared recitals with the New Dance League (later called the New Dance Group). Although she composed primarily in solo forms, some of her pieces like *We Remember* (1935), were created collectively, and others were co-choreographed with other dancers, among them *Challenge*, with Sophie Maslow and Jane Dudley. Her pieces invariably communicated her political views on bigotry, poverty, and industrialization as they have affected domestic life and on the destruction of Europe in the Nazi era. In 1939 Sokolow was invited by the Mexican Ministry of Fine Arts to choreograph, perform, and teach in Mexico. She remained there until 1943 and, for decades after, scheduled annual tours and seasons there. She used Mexican folk forms in many works, most notably *Retablo* (1949).

Sokolow has worked with her own American companies, notably the Dance Unit in the 1930s and 1950s, but more often she choreographs for professional and student groups in Mexico, Israel, Europe, and the United States. Many of her works relate to specific historical events—from the Dance League recital solos on the Spanish Civil War and the fascist governments of Italy to the more abstracted concentration camp nightmare called *Dreams* (1961), the monumental *Tribute to Martin Luther King* (1968), and *Ellis Island* (1976), her bicentennial tribute to her parents and their fellow immigrants. Some pieces are pure abstractions set to 1950s jazz scores (the *Session* and *Opus* series). She has also used the music of Aleksandr Scriabin (*Ballade*, 1965 and *Homage*, 1979) and George Gershwin (*Four Pieces*, 1984). Her best-known works deal with alienation in contemporary life. Those depicting anxiety and fear in the 1950s, such as *Rooms* (1955), are as current and arresting as the more recent *Come, Come Travel with Dreams* (1974), created for her students at the Juilliard School. Examples of all Sokolow's styles survive in the active repertoires of ballet and modern dance companies on four continents.

Sokolow has also had a successful career as a choreographer and director in the dramatic and lyric theatre. She has worked with equal success on plays such as the original production of *Camino Real* (1953) and rock musicals such as the original production of *Hair* (1968). Her movement patterns for *The Dybbuk* (1951) and *The Brig* (1971) have been especially admired. She has also choreographed dance numbers and movement for actors for many American operas, including *Street Scene* (1947) and *Regina* (1949), and served as choreographer-in-residence for the original Lincoln Center Repertory Theatre in 1963.

Sokolow's influence on dancers of the last four decades is inestimable. She has taught widely in Europe, Israel, and the United States, with commitments to create new works annually for student companies. She has also sponsored dancers for study when they could not receive sufficient training or artistic freedom in their homelands. For example, choreographer Ze'eva Cohen and Kei Takei each came to New York under Sokolow's aegis. She has also been tireless in supporting the established companies and has shared the recitals of dancers and former students, many of whom now direct or serve as choreographers-in-residence for their own groups. Her impact on dance itself has been extraordinary. She has helped to keep the fervor of political and social ethics alive in American dance. Even those critics, dancers, and audience members who do not wish to see realities of their lives exposed on stage honor her total commitment to her vision. While maintaining that vitality associated with the birth of American modern dance, she has reached every generation of new performers and creators and affected their dance experience.

Chapters on Anna Sokolow's works can be found in Margaret Lloyd's *The Borzoi Book of Modern Dance* (1949) and Selma Jeanne Cohen's *The Modern Dance: Seven Statements of Belief* (1966). Reviews and feature articles concerning Sokolow's choreography and teaching appear in *Dancemagazine* (February 1970, March 1947, April 1956, June 1956, January 1961, March 1962, February 1963, May 1963). Interviews appear in *Impulse* (1958), *Dance and Dancers* (1967), and *American Dancer* (February 1938 and April 1938). The Dance Collection of the New York Public Library Performing Arts Research Center at Lincoln Center has clippings, programs, photographs, and films of her work. Entries on Sokolow appear in *The Biographical Encyclopaedia and Who's Who of the American Theatre* (1966) and *Notable Names in the American Theatre* (1976), as well as the 1949 and 1967 editions of the *Dance Encyclopedia*. A long entry with a full chronology of dance and theatre works appears in the *Biographical Dictionary of Dance* (1983).

Barbara Cohen-Stratyner

SONTAG, Susan (January 16, 1933–): critic, novelist, screenwriter, film and stage director, was born in New York City to middle-class Jewish parents (a traveling salesman and a teacher); she is the older of two daughters. She grew up in Tucson, Arizona, and the Los Angeles suburb of Canoga Park in California. In an interview with Nora Ephron of the New York *Post* (September 23, 1967), she said that she had "no complaints" about the way her parents reared her: "They treated me as if my life was my own affair."

She was a prodigy and, at fifteen (1948), entered the University of California at Berkeley but transferred to the University of Chicago a year later. She graduated with a Bachelor of Arts degree in philosophy in 1951. While studying at the University of Chicago, she married social psychologist Philip Rieff in 1950. They collaborated on the book *Freud: The Mind of the Moralist*; by mutual agreement only Rieff's name appeared on the title page when it was published in 1959. The couple had one son, David, born in 1952. They separated in 1957 and were divorced in 1959. Sontag did graduate study in English and philosophy at Harvard University. She received the Master of Arts degree in English in 1954, and the Master of Arts degree in philosophy in 1955 from Harvard; she was a Ph.D. candidate there from 1955–1957, completing all requirements except the dissertation.

In the late 1950s, Sontag seemed to be headed for a career in academe. In 1957 she attended St. Anne's College at Oxford in England. Then from 1957 until 1959, she studied at the University of Paris on a grant from the American Association of University Women. After a brief stint as editor of *Commentary* in 1959, she taught philosophy at City College of the City University of New York for one year, at Sarah Lawrence College for another, and became an instructor of religion for four years (1960–1964) at Columbia University. She was also a writer-in-residence for one year at Rutgers University (1964–1965).

Sontag had been writing essays, poems, and plays since she was eight years old; at twenty-eight she sat down to write her first novel, *The Benefactor*. She also began publishing criticism in literary journals and little magazines, including *Partisan Review*, *Harper's Bazaar*, *Commentary*, *New York Review of Books*, *Book Week*, *Esquire*, *Vogue*, *The New Yorker*, *The Tulane Drama Review*,

Evergreen Review, *Saturday Review*, *Ramparts Magazine*, *Moviegoer*, *Nation*, *Film Quarterly*, and *Vanity Fair*.

Out of relative obscurity she burst onto the arts scene with "Notes on Camp," published in *Partisan Review* in 1964, and became a celebrity of pop culture almost overnight. In that essay, she attempted the first public description of a sensibility, or taste, that had long been the private code among small, effete urban cliques. She defined the essence of "Camp" as the love of the unnatural, of artifice, and of exaggeration. "The hallmark of Camp," she wrote, "is the spirit of extravagance. Camp is a woman walking around in a dress made of three million feathers" (*Against Interpretation*, p. 283).

The essay on camp, along with twenty-six other essays published between 1962 and 1965, were collected in her book *Against Interpretation*, nominated for the National Book Award. This collection contains her writings on French novels and films and the avant-garde theatre. In the title essay, she strikes a blow at the assumptions of modern literary and theatrical criticism, calling for an end to the kind of literary and artistic criticism that concentrates on content and looks to meaning. This essay, titled "Against Interpretation," has become a seminal piece of modern criticism. She argues against the tendency of some critics to reduce works of art to their contents or messages. "The function of criticism," she wrote, "should be to show *how it is what it is*, and even *that it is what it is*, rather than to show *what it means*" (p. 14).

Her criticism, like her politics, is liberal and left-wing. Since adolescence Sontag has been a liberal of the political left, expressing, for example, a passionate opposition to the Vietnam War. She visited North Vietnam for two weeks in 1968; the journal of her experiences and observations there became the basis for "Trip to Hanoi," first published in *Esquire Magazine* (December 1968). It was included along with seven other essays in *Styles of Radical Will* (1969), a collection of essays that traces the shift in Sontag's interest away from literature to film.

Sontag's theatre criticism has centered on the avant-garde, including playwrights Antonin Artaud and Bertolt Brecht and director Peter Brook. In the essay "Marat/Sade/Artaud" (1965), published in *Against Interpretation*, she scrutinized the genius of Peter Brook's interpretation of the play *Marat/Sade* by German playwright Peter Weiss. She has also edited and written the introduction for *Antonin Artaud: Selected Writings* (1976), calling Artaud modern literature's most didactic and uncompromising hero of self-exacerbation.

Today, Sontag lives half the year in New York and the other half in Paris. She travels widely (to China, India, and Israel), and is the recipient of many awards. She has been a Rockefeller Foundation Fellow (1965, 1974), a Guggenheim Fellow (1966, 1975), a recipient in 1966 of the George Polk Memorial Award "for contribution toward better appreciation of theatre, motion pictures, and literature," and a recipient of the Ingram Merrill Foundation Award in Literature in the field of American letters (1976). In 1976 she received the Creative Arts Award from Brandeis University and in 1976 the Arts and Letters

Award of the American Academy of Arts and Letters. *On Photography* received the National Book Critic's Circle Award for the best work of criticism in 1977. Moreover, she is a member of the American Institute of Arts and Letters.

Since the early sixties, Susan Sontag has been central to new forms in literature, culture, art, film, and theatre. Through her essays on camp, "happenings," "style," avant-garde theatre, French movies, post-abstract painting, and pornography, she has identified a new aesthetic in which style and pleasure are established as values in their own right, apart from the norms of morality and academic exegesis. She has called her essays "case studies" for a theory of her own sensibility. Those case studies have been collected in *Against Interpretation and Other Essays* (1966), *Trip to Hanoi* (1969), *Styles of Radical Will* (1969), *On Photography* (1977), and *Under the Sign of Saturn* (1980). In addition, she has written short stories, two novels, and three screenplays and directed two full-length films and a documentary on Israel.

In *On Photography*, published in 1977, she demonstrated her interest in the camera as an art form. A collection of six previously published essays on individual photographers such as Diane Arbus and Richard Avedon, it concentrates on "the art of photography" as a means of access to contemporary ways of feeling and thinking. In 1978 she turned her critical sensibility toward her own struggle with cancer and wrote a remarkable essay called *Illness as Metaphor*. In short, Susan Sontag in her mid-forties achieved status as a culture figure. Critic **Elizabeth Hardwick** has called Sontag the "most interesting American woman of her generation" (*Vogue*, June 1978, p. 184).

In the 1980s Sontag has shifted from writing theatre criticism and screenplays to directing films, thus turning her artistic sensibilities largely to photography, film making, and directing for the stage. In 1980 in Italy she directed her first play, Luigi Pirandello's *As You Desire Me*. For the American Repertory Theatre in Boston, she translated and made her American directing debut in 1984 with Czech novelist Milan Kundera's play *Jacques and His Master* (adapted from the novel by Denis Diderot). Of her immediate experience of the theatre as a director she has said, "What I cherish in the theatre are those dazzling visual images the stage can generate that rattle inside your head for ever. . . . The theatre liberates. It frees our deepest feelings" (*Performing Arts Journal*, 25, Vol. 9, November 1985, p. 30).

Sontag's body of work encompasses the arts of literature, criticism, filmmaking, photography, and theatre. In whatever medium, she raises important and exciting questions with passion, clarity, skepticism, and a rare intelligence.

Susan Sontag's works include novels: *The Benefactor* (1963), *Death Kit* (1967); short stories: *I, Etcetera* (1978); essays: *Against Interpretation* (1966), *Trip to Hanoi* (1969), *Styles of Radical Will* (1969), *On Photography* (1977), *Illness as Metaphor* (1978), *Under the Sign of Saturn* (1980), *A Susan Sontag Reader* (1981); edited works: *Selected Writings of Artaud* (1976), *A Barthes Reader* (1981); preface: *Maria Irene Fornés: Plays* (1986); screenplays *Duet for Cannibals* (1969), *Brother Carl* (1971), *The Spiral* (1979); directed films: *Duet for Cannibals* (1969), *Brother Carl* (1971), *Promised Lands* (documentary)

(1974); and directed plays: *As You Desire Me* (1980), *Jacques and His Master* (1984). Recent work includes a short story, "The Way We Live Now," published in *The Best American Short Stories, 1987* (1988) and *AIDS and Its Metaphor* (1989). Sontag is listed in *Modern American Literature*, Vol. 3 (1969); *The Penguin Companion to American Literature* (1971); *Celebrity Register* (1973); *The Reader's Adviser: A Layman's Guide to Literature* (1974); *Women Who Make Movies* (1975); *World Authors* (1975); *A Dictionary of American Fiction Writers* (1976); *International Authors and Writers Who's Who* (1976); *The Oxford Companion to Film* (1976); *Political Profiles: The Johnson Years* (1976); *Who's Who in Twentieth Century Literature* (1976); *Contemporary Authors*, Vols. 17–20 (1976); *The Blue Book: Leaders of the English Speaking World* (1976); *The Lincoln Library of Language Arts* (1978); *Dictionary of Literature in the English Language* (1978); *Liberty's Women* (1980); *Novels and Novelists: A Guide to the World of Fiction* (1980); *Contemporary Novelists* (1982); *The International Dictionary of Women's Biography* (1982); *Dictionary of Literary Biography: American Novelists Since World War Two*, Vol. 2 (1978–1984); and *The Writers Directory* (1984–1986).

Milly S. Barranger

SPENCER, Sara (February 18, 1908–February 9, 1977): founding publisher and editor of Anchorage Press, was born in Louisville, Kentucky. Her father, Phelps Spencer, was a merchant in both Jefferson and Fayette Counties, Kentucky. Her mother, Mary Julia (Vaughan) Spencer, was a teacher. Spencer was descended on her father's side from the Spencer and Phelps families of England; her mother's family was of the Fields and Vaughans of England and France. On both sides were numerous American patriots. As an infant, Sara Spencer was stricken with polio but steadfastly maintained an active life, wearing steel braces on both legs, admitting no weakness, acknowledging no impediment. She attended elementary schools in Louisville and secondary schools in Charleston, West Virginia. She entered Vassar College, studying literature and drama under distinguished professor **Hallie Flanagan**, receiving the Bachelor of Arts degree in 1930. She entered the professional theatre and, despite her severe physical handicap, earned performing opportunities in New York City and the Northeast. Her rich voice was her chief dramatic asset. Throughout her life she recorded for the blind. When not performing, she served as stage manager or property mistress for several summer stock companies in New England.

In the early 1930s, at the depth of the Great Depression, she became aware, as she once described it, "of world crisis, the international monetary conference in London, the rise of Fascism in Italy and Germany, stark need in America," and concluded, "I must do something more important with my life than the humoring of my personal ambition" (Arizona State University Archives). Completing her obligations to the theatre company with which she was working at the time on Cape Cod, she resolved to return to Charleston. En route she paused in New York to visit the national offices of the Junior Leagues of America. She sought advice as to what she could do with her training and interest in theatre and was advised to create a theatre for children in Charleston. She subsequently founded the Charleston Children's Theatre, which in 1982 celebrated its fiftieth anniversary. She quickly discovered a dearth of good plays for children and created for the stage several adaptations of beloved books. She began corresponding with other children's theatres affiliated with the Junior League, seeking the exchange of play scripts. Her brothers, Vaughan and Phelps, were publishers in Charleston, and Sara Spencer determined to establish a publishing house to serve the specialized area of children's theatre.

In 1935 she founded the Children's Theatre Press (the name was changed to Anchorage Press, Inc. in 1962) to broaden options of publications for the theatre and immediately published ten plays for children. Three of these titles were her own adaptations of *Mary Poppins*, *The Adventures of Tom Sawyer*, and *Little Women*. The latter two remain staples of American children's theatre after nearly half a century.

Thereafter, endowing the little press with her idealism and spirit (and her means, for she did not pay herself a salary as editor for the first thirty-three years, and then only modestly), she set about the task of enriching children's writing theatre by promoting skillful playwriting and stage production. She sought out people concerned with dramatics for children, whether, like **Winifred Ward** of Northwestern University, they hoped the power of drama would lead young viewers to use their own creative potential or, like **Charlotte Chorpenning** of the Goodman Theatre in Chicago, these specialists wanted children to enjoy the excitement of learning as they watched plays of literary value performed by professionals. Spencer worked closely with Hallie Flanagan, who at that time, as director of the Federal Theatre Project, was encouraging plays for children and searching for authors. She worked to foster literate stage plays and encouraged their production in places as disparate as the new Palo Alto Children's Theatre (the first theatre constructed in the country solely for that purpose), community theatres, university and college theatres, recreational centers, and professional theatres in New York City. The Children's Theatre Press became the catalyst for the influence of scholars upon generations of students and also upon those producing plays, whether from an educational, a recreational, or a professional theatre viewpoint.

Sara Spencer was one of a few pioneers—also including Winifred Ward, Charlotte Chorpenning, **Dina Rees Evans** of Cleveland Heights, Hazel Glaister Robertson of Palo Alto, **Isabel Burger** of Baltimore—who in 1944 formed the Children's Theatre Committee (later the Children's Theatre Conference) within the American Educational Theatre Association (later the American Theatre Association). As the first corresponding secretary of the new organization, Sara Spencer originated its newsletter, thus binding together the small group of teachers, scholars, producers, and playwrights with information and ideas. As one of the early presidents of the new conference, she worked to obtain its parity with other segments of the large association, gaining independent organizational status for children's theatre in 1952. With keen foresight and convincing observations, she quietly encouraged college and university professors to produce plays for children and to train directors to understand artistic productions for this most vital of audiences. Her persuasive powers were augmented with warm Kentucky hospitality and an open bar at her suite at national conferences for more than a generation. Slowly the number of courses including drama and productions for young audiences increased.

Spencer's heart, nevertheless, remained with professionals. In the post-World War II era she was a strong supporter of the Children's World Theatre, a New York-based professional touring company founded by Monte Meacham. She maintained cordial relationships with the professional theatre throughout the country. From 1958 to 1965 she was a member of the executive board of the American National Theatre and Academy. She was a staunch patron of Actors Theatre of Louisville from its founding and a friend of artistic director Jon Jory. She was patron and advisor to the Kentucky-based Everyman Players, a classical repertory company that toured the world with *Job*, *The Tempest*, *The Pilgrim's Progress*, and works for children.

In 1958 Spencer co-founded with Campton Bell of Denver the Children's Theatre Foundation, to advance the professional status of children's theatre and creative drama in the United States. She chaired the foundation until her death and made it the chief beneficiary of her estate, bestowing the proceeds of the sale of the Anchorage Press for the advancement of its aims. She was the initiator of American involvement in the founding and organization of the International Association of Theatre for Children and Youth (ASSITEJ) based in Paris. She led the exploratory conference in London in 1964 and the writing of the ASSITEJ constitution in Paris in 1965. She chaired the United States Center for ASSITEJ initially and headed the committee that hosted the Third International ASSITEJ Congress and Festival at Montreal and Albany in June of 1972. Most people agree that the bial of ASSITEJ was highly important for children's theatre in the United States and a worthy sequel to the 1944 formation of the Children's Theatre Conference.

Spencer's chief commitment, however, was to the creation of a world repertoire for children and young people. For the forty-two years she headed Anchorage Press, she tirelessly traveled the United States, Britain, and Europe (Russia included), seeking the best work available. In Charlotte Chorpenning, a successful Broadway playwright who had learned her craft in the famed 47 Workshop of George Pierce Baker at Harvard University, she found the major talent of the quarter-century from 1930 to 1955. She encouraged students of Chorpenning, including James Norris and Madge Miller, by publishing their works. However, Aurand Harris of New York and Hollywood was her greatest discovery. Harris, the dean of American playwrights for young people, has published nearly forty plays with a half-dozen dramatic publishers, and Anchorage Press has published more than half of his output. Spencer brought into English the works of Belgium's Arthur Fauquez, Holland's Eric Vos, and Iran's Bijan Mofid. England's Alan Cullen and Alan Broadhurst have also become favorite writers of American children. Not least, Anchorage Press moved from the realm of private philanthropy (beneath a mask of business) into the reality of a soundly based specialty publishing firm. Spencer sold it on February 1, 1977, to Orlin Corey, a theatrical producer-author, who had long advised the press about new plays and playwrights. Nine days later she died of arterial thrombosis at her home, "Cloverlot," in Anchorage, Kentucky.

Sara Spencer's true legacy is the laughter, tears, and applause of tens of thousands of young people assembled in thousands of audiences around the world who cherish such works as Harris's *Punch and Judy* and *Steal Away*, Miller's *The Land of the Dragon*, Chorpenning's *The Elves and the Shoemaker*, Fauquez's *Reynard the Fox* and *Don Quixote*, Cullen's *Trudi and the Minstrel* or *The Beeple*, Broadhurst's *The Great Cross-Country Race*. Characteristically, she never directly articulated her implicit interest in the children themselves. Once, when questioned, she said, "My commitment is to the professional producer of theatre—to see that he has the finest play that may be found" (Arizona State University Archives).

Spencer was a lifelong sustaining member of the Junior League, a member of Mayflower Descendants and the Daughters of the American Revolution, and a founding board member of the Louisville Children's Theatre and the Children's Theatre of Anchorage, Kentucky. She was prominent in the formation of the Southeastern Theatre Conference and the Kentucky Theatre Association. She was honored as a Distinguished Alumna of Vassar College and was made a Fellow of the American Theatre Association. She was the first recipient of the Susan B. Davis Award of the Southeastern Theatre Conference and in 1976 received the Jennie Heiden Award for encouraging professional excellence in theatre for children from the Children's Theatre Association of America.

In the spring of 1943, Sara Spencer married Clarence Arthur Campbell of Grosse Point, Michigan. She was widowed by his death in December 1943. There were no children. Sara Spencer is buried in the historic Lexington Cemetery at Lexington, Kentucky.

The best source of information on Sara Spencer is the collection of her papers at the National Children's Theatre Archives at Arizona State University in Tempe, Arizona, from which material for this essay has been drawn.

Orlin Corey and
Margaret Patterson

SPEWACK, Bella (March 25, 1899–): playwright, press agent, television and screenwriter, was born Bella Cohen, the daughter of Adolph Cohen and Fanny (Lang) Cohen, who emigrated to the United States from Rumania shortly after their daughter's birth. She was educated in New York City public schools and graduated from Washington Irving High School in 1917. Her career began in journalism as a reporter for the *Bronx Home News* and the *Yorkville Home News*, and for several years she was a reporter for New York's *Call*, a socialist daily, then literary editor of New York's *Evening Mail*.

On March 25, 1922, Bella Cohen married Samuel Spewack, a first generation American of Russian emigrant parentage. In the first four years of her marriage, she worked as a correspondent in Berlin for the *New York Evening World* (1922–1926). Her career in the theatre began when Morris Gest engaged her as a theatrical press agent in New York. In collaboration with her husband she began writing for the theatre in 1926 with *The Solitaire Man*, followed by *Poppa* (1928), *The War Song* (1928), *Clear All Wires* (1932), *Spring Song* (1934), *Boy Meets Girl* (1935), *Leave It To Me!* (1938), *Miss Swan Expects* (1939), *Woman Bites Dog* (1946), *Kiss Me, Kate* (1948), *My Three Angels* (1953), and *Festival* (1955). Later, she co-authored the television adaptations of *Kiss Me, Kate* (NBC, 1959) and *My Three Angels* (NBC, 1960) and the original teleplay *Enchanted Nutcracker* (ABC, 1963). The Spewacks also wrote twenty screenplays, including *Clear All Wires* (MGM, 1933), *Should Ladies Behave?* (MGM, 1933), *The Nuisance* (MGM, 1933), *The Cat and the Fiddle* (MGM, 1933), *Rendezvous* (MGM, 1935), *Vogues of 1938* (United Artists, 1937), *Boy Meets Girl* (Warner Brothers, 1938), *Three Loves Has Nancy* (MGM, 1938), *My Favorite Wife* (RKO, 1940), and *Weekend at the Waldorf* (MGM, 1945).

Bella Spewack's career in the theatre actively spanned three decades. One of her earliest plays was *Spring Song*, first produced by Max Gordon in 1934 at the Morosco Theatre in New York. This simple but skillfully written melodrama reflected the concern of the American theatre of the 1930s with the difficult social adjustments of immigrant families. *Spring Song*, a domestic tragedy, concerned the fate of Florrie Solomon who loves a braggart traveling salesman but is pregnant with her sister's fiancé's child. Mrs. Solomon takes the advice of her rabbi and forces Florrie to marry the father, a decision that brings predictable tragedy for the entire family. Brooks Atkinson's evaluation of the play as "pedestrian" reflected the general commercial failure of the piece. The Spewacks turned to comedy as the genre best suited for their social satire with the highly successful *Boy Meets Girl*, produced in 1935 by George Abbott at the Cort Theatre in New York. This lively satire on the Hollywood movie industry ran for 660 performances and won the Roi Cooper Megrue Prize (1936). In 1953 their adaptation of Albert Husson's *La Cuisine des Anges* opened at the Morosco Theatre in New York as *My Three Angels*. Revolving around the actions of three convicts who try the truth of the maxim "virtue is its own reward," the comedy ran for 344 performances. Their most successful collaboration was *Kiss Me, Kate*, an adaptation of *The Taming of the Shrew* and a memorable contribution to the American musical genre. With the sparkling addition of Cole Porter's music, *Kiss Me, Kate*—directed by Samuel Spewack—enjoyed a long Broadway run in 1948 and won the Antoinette Perry (Tony) Award. In 1970 *Kiss Me, Kate* became the first Broadway musical to be performed at the Sadler's Wells Opera in London.

Samuel Spewack died in New York in 1971. The couple had no children, and there are no close relatives surviving.

Bella Spewack's best plays indicate a skillful handling of a wide range of comedy from farce to light satire and inject a freshness and vitality into the popular entertainment arena of the American theatre. Spewack's background in journalism, television, film, and theatre combine to make her a skillful artist of the American theatre and a sympathetic critic of American institutions.

Many of the plays of Bella and Samuel Spewack have been included in anthologies. *Boy Meets Girl* is in *Twenty Best Plays of the Modern Theatre 1930–1939* (1939), ed. John Gassner. *My Three Angels* appears in *Twenty Best European Plays on the American Stage* (1957), ed. John Gassner. *Kiss Me, Kate* is in *Ten Great Musicals of the American Theatre*, ed. Stanley Richards (1973). *Theatre Arts* (December 1949) contains the text of *Two Blind Mice* and a biographical introduction. See also Samuel Spewack, "Four Years in Europe Made Me an American," *Saturday Evening Post* (May 29, 1926). *Notable Names in the American Theatre* (1976) contains a partial listing of Spewack's work in theatre, film, and television; and *Who Was Who in the Theatre*, Vol. IV (1978), offers additional biography. The best reference for commentary on Spewack's drama is in *American Women Writers*, Vol. IV (1980). For further reference, see *Women Who Make Movies* (1975), *Encyclopedia of Musical Theatre* (1976), and *The Oxford Companion to American Theatre* (1984).

Lynda Hart

SPOLIN, Viola Mills (November 7, 1906–): theatre educator, director, and actress recognized internationally for her "Theatre Games" system of actor training, was raised in a tradition of family theatre amusements, operas, and charades. Viola Spolin trained initially (1924–1926) to be a settlement worker, studying at Neva Boyd's Group Work School in Chicago. Boyd's innovative teaching in the areas of group leadership, recreation, and social group work strongly influenced Spolin, as did the use of traditional game structures to affect social behavior in inner-city and immigrant children.

While serving as drama supervisor for the Chicago branch of the Works Progress Administration's Recreational Project (1939–1941), Spolin perceived a need for an easily grasped system of theatre training that could cross the cultural and ethical barriers within the WPA project. Building upon the experience of Boyd's work, she responded by developing new games that focused upon individual creativity, adapting and focusing the concept of play to unlock the individual's capacity for creative self-expression. These techniques were later to be formalized under the rubric "Theatre Games." "The games emerged out of necessity," she has said. "I didn't sit at home and dream them up. When I had a problem [directing], I made up a game. When another problem came up, I just made up a new game" (Interview, *Los Angeles Times*, May 26, 1974).

In 1946 Spolin founded the Young Actors Company in Hollywood. Children six years of age and older were trained, through the medium of the still-developing Theatre Games system, to perform in productions. This company continued until 1955, when Spolin returned to Chicago to direct for the Playwright's Theatre Club and subsequently to conduct games workshops with the Compass, the country's first professional, improvisational acting company. From 1960 to 1965, still in Chicago, she worked with Paul Sills (her son) as workshop director for his Second City Company and continued to teach and develop Theatre Games theory. As an outgrowth of this work, she published *Improvisation for the Theatre*

(1963), consisting of approximately two hundred and twenty games/exercises. It has become a classic reference text for teachers of acting, as well as for educators in other fields. In 1965 she co-founded the Game Theatre in Chicago, again working with Sills. Open only one evening a week, the theatre sought to have its audiences participate directly in Theatre Games, thus effectively eliminating the conventional separation between improvisational actors and audiences who watched them. The experiment achieved limited success, and the theatre closed after only a few months.

In 1970–1971 Spolin served as special consultant for productions of Sills's *Story Theatre* in Los Angeles, New York, and on television. On the West Coast, she conducted workshops for the companies of the *Rhoda* and *Friends and Lovers* television series and appeared as an actress in the Paul Mazursky film *Alex in Wonderland* (MGM, 1970).

In November 1975 the publication of the *Theatre Game File* made her unique approaches to teaching and learning more readily available to classroom teachers; in 1976 she established the Spolin Theatre Game Center in Hollywood, serving as its artistic director. In 1979 she was awarded an honorary doctorate by Eastern Michigan University, and until recently she has continued to teach at the Theatre Game Center. In 1985 her new book, *Theater Games for Rehearsal: A Director's Handbook*, was published.

Spolin's Theatre Games are simple, operational structures that transform complicated theatre conventions and techniques into game forms. Each game is built upon a specific focus or technical problem and is an exercise that militates against the artifice of self-conscious acting. The playing (acting) emerges naturally and spontaneously; age, background, and content are irrelevant. The exercises are, as one critic has written, "structures designed to almost fool spontaneity into being" (Review, *Film Quarterly*, Fall/Winter 1963). By themselves, the games have a liberating effect (accounting for their wide application in self-actualization contexts); within the theatre context, each clearly fosters a facet of performance technique. There are games to free the actor's tension, games to "cleanse" the actor of subjective preconceptions of the meanings of words, games of relationship and character, games of concentration—in short, games for each of the areas with which the growing actor is concerned. Key to the rubric of Spolin games are the terms *physicalization* ("showing and not telling"), *spontaneity* ("a moment of explosion"), *intuition* ("unhampered knowledge beyond the sensory equipment—physical and mental"), *audience* ("part of the game, not the lonely looker-onners"), and *transformation* ("actors and audience alike receive. . .the appearance of a new reality"). To achieve their purpose, Theatre Games need only the rules of the game, the players (both actors and audience are considered to be players), and a space in which to play. Beyond the very tangible pleasures of "playing" which the games encompass, they also heighten sensitivity, increase self-awareness, and effect group and interpersonal communication. As a result, Spolin's games have developed currency beyond actor training, that is, in encounter techniques, self-awareness programs, and nonverbal communication studies. Viola Spolin's systems are in use throughout the country not only in university, community, and professional theatre training programs, but also in countless curricula concerned with educational interests not related specifically to theatre.

The list of Spolin's guest lectures, demonstrations, and workshops is extensive. She has introduced her work to students and professionals in theatre, elementary and secondary education, schools for gifted and talented programs, curriculum studies in English, religion, mental health, psychology, and in centers for the rehabilitation of delinquent children. She notes that "Theatre Games are a process applicable to any field, discipline, or subject matter which creates a place where full participation, communication, transformation can take place" (*Los Angeles Times*, May 26, 1984). Exemplary of the broad recognition her work has received are a 1966 New England Theatre Conference Award citing "contributions to theatre, education, mental health, speech therapy, and religion," and the 1976 award by the Secondary School Theatre Association of the American Theatre Association of its highest honor: the Founders Award. In her devotion to the development and application of Theatre Games, Spolin has made a unique contribution to American theatre.

Viola Spolin's publications are *Improvisation for the Theatre* (1963); *Theatre Game File* (1975); and *Theater Games for Rehearsal* (1985); *Theatre Games for the Classroom, Grades 1–3* (1986); and *Theatre Games for the Classroom, Grades 4–6* (1986). Selected sources of comment about Spolin's work are Hans G. Furth, *Piaget for Teachers* (1970); Jeffrey Sweet, *Something Wonderful Right Away* (1978); and *Yale Theater* (Spring 1974). See also the interview by Barry Hyams in the *Los Angeles Times* (May 26, 1984) and the review of *Theatre Games for Rehearsal*, "Playing Viola," by Joan D. Lynch in *American Theatre* (December 1985).

D. E. Moffitt

The SPOONERS. Mary Gibbs Spooner (1853?–April 12, 1940), Edna May Spooner (1875?–July 14, 1953), and Cecil Spooner (1888?–May 1953): a mother and two daughters who shared a lifetime of acting in and managing stock companies, were active in the eastern United States, chiefly in Brooklyn and Manhattan.

At one time distinguished as the only female member of the New York Theatrical Managers' Association, Mary Gibbs Spooner became highly respected in New York area theatrical circles after she cured the long-standing financial troubles of Brooklyn's Park Theatre and elevated both of her actress-daughters, Edna May and Cecil, to national prominence. Raised in the small town of Centerville, Iowa, Mary Spooner grew up community-minded and with good business sense, having absorbed during her childhood some of the work ethic, staunch Methodist faith, and small-town politics to which she was exposed. After spending several years assisting her grandfather, the town's postmaster, she observed, "The politics of the whole town went on in the post office, and I always had a finger in things" (Ormsbee article, no pagination).

A half sister of matinee idol Corse Payton, Mary Gibbs went on the stage after she married actor Sprague Spooner in the early 1870s. She became a member of Spooner's traveling company, which constantly toured the midwestern and eastern circuits. There Spooner's folksy Yankee and frontier characters were especially popular. Edna May was the Spooners' first child, born in Centerville, Iowa, in 1875. Their son Robert born soon thereafter, and a second was daughter, Cecil, arrived over a decade later, in 1888, while the Spooner Company was touring New York State. Each child was made part of the company as soon as possible.

The family was still touring together in upstate New York when Sprague Spooner died in 1900, and Mary Spooner decided to curtail the company's travels. She chose to create her own resident stock company at a time when resident stock was resurgent, especially on the East Coast and in expanding urban residential neighborhoods. Corse Payton at that time operated a prosperous troupe at Brooklyn's Lee Avenue Theatre. Upon learning of the availability of the Park Theatre (383 Fulton Street), Mary Spooner set out to duplicate her half brother's success. She persuaded the theatre's owners, the powerful Hyde and Behman organization, to rent the building to a woman—something which they had vowed not to do—because she produced ready cash and rejected all credit terms.

From the start of her management career, Mary Spooner relinquished acting to concentrate on the theatre's administration. The Spooner Stock Company was designed to feature her two daughters, Edna May as leading lady and the younger, teen-age Cecil, as soubrette. Within a week of taking possession of the Park Theatre's lease, the new company opened on February 23, 1901, with a production of *The Soldier of the Empire*. Mary Spooner followed most of the standard operational modes already established by stock companies: a weekly change of bill, low admission prices of ten to fifty cents, substantial scheduling of matinee performances, and dedication to strong community interaction. Mary Spooner, especially aware of the latter, became quite active in the Stella Chapter of the Brooklyn Order of the Eastern Star and further enhanced her position in the community by offering weekly on-stage audience receptions and by performing charitable functions for local churches, synagogues, and community organizations.

The Spooner Stock Company played season after season at the Park and became a veritable Brooklyn institution, known especially for its exceedingly moral and respectable dramas. The company focused on the needs and desires of its primarily middle-class and female audience. Edna May and Cecil Spooner became local stars of the first magnitude. The public responded to Edna May's performance in emotional roles, such as Camille, Magda, and Leah the Forsaken, and applauded the sprightly, innocent Cecil for her comedic skills and specialty song and dance routines. That Cecil Spooner also gained abilities in serious drama was attested to by playwright-critic Channing Pollock, who observed the special appeal she held for local audiences. He wrote, ''In Brooklyn it used to be a common thing to hear that Cecil Spooner was much better than **Mrs. Leslie Carter** as Zaza'' (*The Footlights Fore and Aft*, 1911, p. 366).

Cecil Spooner's popularity resulted in an invitation in 1903 to leave the Spooner Stock Company and make her Manhattan debut at Augustin Daly's Theatre in *My Lady Peggy Goes to Town*. Meanwhile, the Spooner Stock Company continued to generate such enthusiastic audience support that they secured a larger Brooklyn theatre, the Bijou, located at Smith and Livingston Streets. In 1907 Mary Spooner decided to risk transferring her company permanently to Manhattan, which had few stock companies. The motivation for the move was her desire to give her actress daughters a more prestigious Broadway status. The Spooner Stock Company opened at the Fifth Avenue Theatre in April 1907, replacing the short-lived Keith and Proctor Stock Company. That she was granted a lease to this theatre was a supreme compliment, as New York theatre owners were notoriously "cliquish" in their dealings and skeptical of resident theatrical groups. From this point on the Spooner family constantly expanded and diversified their dramatic enterprises. Cecil Spooner, who had hitherto played featured roles to her sister's leads, rose to the status of both manager and leading lady with her own company. The Cecil Spooner Stock Company became the toast of the Bronx, playing first at the Metropolis Theatre, located at Third Avenue and 142nd Street, and then at her own Cecil Spooner Theatre at 163rd Street and Southern Avenue. At approximately the same time, she married producer, playwright, and actor Charles E. Blaney, who was known for his touring melodrama and resident stock company ventures, with which his brother, Harry Clay Blaney assisted. The three formed the Blaney-Spooner Amusement Company, which acquired theatre leases and created resident stock organizations. Although Cecil preferred to concentrate her energies on the New York assets, Mary and Edna May Spooner participated in the regional activities of the new company, including management of resident troupes and theatre buildings in Baltimore, Newark, Brooklyn, Pittsburgh, and Philadelphia. Edna May managed and was the leading performer in her own Edna May Spooner Stock Company in New Orleans during 1909–1910 and at Jersey City's Orpheum Theatre for the 1910–1911 season. In 1911 and 1912 the Blaney-Spooner Stock Company at Philadelphia's American Theatre headlined Edna May Spooner as leading lady and her husband, Arthur Behrens (Whaley), as leading man.

Although Edna May and Mary Spooner confined their activities to the stock realm, Cecil often left her Bronx resident company to tour greater New York and eastern seaboard theatres. She originated the title roles in several of her husband's plays, including *The Dancer and the King*, *That Girl Raffles*, and *The Girl and the Detective*. She also toured in *The Fortunes of Betty*, *One Day*, *A Girl in Pawn*, *For Her Soul and Body*, and *The Brat*. She collaborated with Blaney on several successful comedy-dramas, in which she subsequently starred, notably *My Irish Cinderella*, *A Friendly Divorce*, and *My Wife's Gone to the Country*. Several silent film versions of her stage vehicles, such as *The Dancer and the King* and *The Prince and the Pauper*, also were added to her credit in the second decade of this century. One event of that decade brought Cecil Spooner's name to nationwide attention in December 1913, when she was arrested for producing and starring in *The House of Bondage* at her Bronx theatre. The play, on the topic of white slavery, was deemed improper by the New York City Police Department; misdemeanor charges were leveled at Cecil and the theatre's manager. The press scandalized the event, noting always the irony inherent in the Spooner family's high moral image and this unsavory development.

Mary Gibbs Spooner retired to New Canaan, Connecticut, in the 1920s, living there with the now unattached Edna May. Reversing the pattern of previous years, Edna May often appeared in secondary roles in her sister's touring vehicles. She also performed character roles in many silent films, most notably in the 1923 *Man and Wife*. By the 1930s she resided almost exclusively in Connecticut, where she participated in local amateur and church theatricals and wrote several plays marketed for amateur groups, such as *1776* and *Love is Born of a Glance*.

Although Cecil Spooner's career waned with the decline of the stock company institution, she continued to tour out of New York in comedy-dramas, such as Bernard J. McOwens's *Paid Companion* and George Spaulding's *Love on Approval*. She retired to Connecticut with her mother and sister in the late 1930s and joined them in real estate investment and development. After their mother's death in 1940, Edna May and Cecil moved to California. Both died in Sherman Oaks in 1953, Cecil's death preceding her sister's by two months.

Mary Gibbs Spooner and her daughters exemplified the importance female managers and actress-managers held in financing and producing regionally based resident theatre during the first three decades of the twentieth century. Their careers as three of the country's most famous stock company personalities were marked by a keen sensitivity to their middle-class, community-based audiences' needs, especially those of the urban homemaker. Their willingness to integrate these needs into their companies helped mold the stock institution and helped facilitate the existence of an early twentieth-century regional stage.

Sketches of Cecil Spooner appear in *The New York Dramatic Mirror*, 1900–1920 (Volume 69, April 2, 1913, and Volume 70, November 26, 1913). See also the *New York Times* (December 10, 1913). There is an unidentified, undated article by Helen Ormsbee titled "Remember Mrs. Spooner?" in the personality files of the Philadelphia Theatre Collection, The Free Library of Philadelphia at Logan Square. Other sources giving information about the Spooners include David Ragan, *Who's Who in Hollywood*, 1900–1976 (1976); John Stewart, *Filmarama*, Vol. 1 (1975); and *Theatre* (Volume 7, August 1907). Mari Kathleen Fielder has written "The Blaney-Spooner Stock Company, Philadelphia," which appears in *American Theatre Companies*, Vol. 2, edited by Weldon B. Durham (1987).

Mari Kathleen Fielder

STANISTREET, Grace M. (September 6, 1902–July 21, 1984): educator, author, and innovator in arts education for children, was born in the Kensington section of Philadelphia. In an article by Dorothy R. Disher, Stanistreet is quoted as saying about her parents, "My father was a weaver by day, a weaver of songs by night—he was an entertainer—he published—he was an inventor. My mother had tuberculosis and was expected to die. But she didn't die. She set herself to helping people—she discovered she had a gift for helping" (*The Adelphi Quarterly*, Winter 1966).

Stanistreet attended the Shoemaker School of Speech and Drama in Philadelphia and at sixteen began to explore the essentials of her lifelong work: the relationship of the dramatic process to the learning process. Her love and respect for children and her talent for teaching emerged in her church Sunday school classes. She collaborated on the development of a play designed to teach children about good health and sponsored by the National Tuberculosis Association. The play toured urban and rural Pennsylvania, and Stanistreet acted in it. At first she began teaching drama to children privately. As her classes grew she was asked to join the staff of the Shoemaker School and to develop a children's unit. From the beginning, a creative approach to teaching and performing were at the heart of her work. She was interested in drama for expression rather than for exhibition.

In 1931 she went to New York, but finding no full-time teaching opportunities, she worked in the hotel supply industry, using the love for color and fabric she had learned from her father, as well as her talents as an actress, in her selling. During the summers she worked with children at the Marble Collegiate Church Camp. Resolved to devote her full energies to teaching, she returned to Philadelphia in 1937. She was invited to a farewell party for Paul Dawson Eddy, who had seen her work with children at the Shoemaker School and at the Marble Collegiate Church. He was leaving Philadelphia to become president of Adelphi College in Garden City, New York, and talked with Stanistreet about the possibility of a children's art workshop at Adelphi. Consequently, the Adelphi Children's Theatre was born in 1937. The Saturday morning program began with forty children and a staff of two, which included Stanistreet as director and teacher. A student volunteer from the college played the piano, and another student whose specialty was folk dancing joined the staff in the spring. Grace Stanistreet believed that children should be offered variety; if acting alone did not reach a child, then other art forms might. As the numbers of children grew, so did the faculty of skilled artist-teachers. College students, parents, and others interested in her innovative work volunteered to become the leadership staff.

By the 1950s the Adelphi Children's Theatre had become an internationally known demonstration center where educators, university students, community leaders, and artists could observe and participate in the arts as education. Henry Cowell and Ruth St. Denis, who were on the faculty in the early years, often returned as guest artists. In 1953 the Children's Theatre was host to the National Children's Theatre Conference of the American Theatre Association. The Children's Theatre was renamed the Children's Centre for Creative Arts in 1961.

In addition to her teaching and administrative duties, Grace Stanistreet contributed her talent and energy to many off-campus activities. In 1962 she directed a pilot project at the Lincoln Square Neighborhood Housing Center designed to provide evidence of the value of the creative arts experience in social and educational rehabilitation programs. She was continually teaching in-service courses for teachers and giving workshops and demonstrations for schools and community organizations. At Adelphi's Suffolk campus she established the Creative Arts In Action Summer Institute in drama, music, and dance, where the concept of children and adults learning together attracted educators from all over the world.

In 1965 Paul D. Eddy, still president of Adelphi University, conferred upon Stanistreet the title of honorary professor of creative arts for children. In 1970 she retired as director of the Children's Centre but continued to teach undergraduate classes at Adelphi and to serve as a consultant to the centre. In 1972 the university honored her with the Doctor of Fine Arts degree, and in 1977 the Children's Theatre Association of America awarded her a Special Recognition Citation for achievement in the field of drama for children. After her retirement from Adelphi in 1977, Grace Stanistreet remained active in the development of innovative projects. She taught in Adelphi's Urban Education program in Manhattan and conducted creative drama classes at a senior citizen center in Roslyn, New York, which integrated the elderly with very young children.

Stanistreet was a pioneer in creative arts education in the United States. In the 1930s, at a time when most children experienced art as elocution, piano, and dancing lessons, and as unimaginative classroom music and art courses, Stanistreet was exploring the potential of drama as a resource for human development. She was concerned with the interaction of all art forms, incorporating them into her own teaching and into the experience of the children at the Centre for Creative Arts. She advocated the arts *as* education as well as *in* education and believed that the artistic experience should be an integral part of every child's learning experience. At the Adelphi Children's Centre, she focused on the development of the children and of the artists who taught them. Her recognition of the value of adults and children learning together was reflected in her work at the Children's Centre, in the Creative Arts In Action Summer Institute, and in her classes for senior citizens and children. Finally, her work with classroom teachers demonstrated her belief in their potential to use the artistic process in their approach to learning. She taught them to understand this process and to find their own ways to creative teaching.

Grace Stanistreet wrote numerous articles for professional and artistic journals, many of which are incorporated into her three books, *Teaching Is A Dialogue* (1969, 1974), *Learning Is A Happening* (1974), and *Creative Assignments* (1975), distributed by New Plays for Children, Rowayton, Connecticut. Gloria Siegel Moss's, "The Centre for Creative Arts: A Model for Arts Education" (Unpublished Ph.D. dissertation, New York University, 1980) is the best source on Stanistreet's career and philosophy of arts education.

Margaret Linney

STANLEY, Kim (February 12, 1925–): critically acclaimed actress, was born Patricia Kimberly Reid in Tularosa, New Mexico. She spent her early childhood in New Mexico where her father was a professor of philosophy at the University of New Mexico, Albuquerque. Upon her parents' divorce when Stanley was three years old, she moved to Texas with her three older brothers and her mother Ann (Miller) Reid, an interior decorator. Her parents, whom she calls "hard shell Baptists," did not encourage her interest in the theatre.

Stanley attended the University of New Mexico for two years and then transferred to the University of Texas at Austin from which she graduated in 1945 as a premed student with a major in psychology. When she was confronted with her first cadaver she made a rapid retreat from a career in medicine. Following the advice of a director from the Pasadena Playhouse who had seen her act in a college production and recognized her talent, she moved to California where she studied acting at the Pasadena Playhouse from 1945 to 1946.

After a brief stint with a Louisville stock company, Stanley arrived in New York in 1947, with twenty-one dollars in her pocket and the determination of youth. She quickly landed an acting job with a New Jersey stock company, only to find that almost two years would go by without further employment in her chosen profession. At her lowest point, waiting tables and working as a garment center model, Stanley saw **Laurette Taylor** in Tennessee Williams' *The Glass Menagerie* and was inspired to battle the odds. Her fortunes changed abruptly when she was discovered by producer Kermit Bloomgarten and television talent scouts while playing the title role in the 1949 Equity Library Theatre production of *Saint Joan*. Bloomgarten hired her to replace **Julie Harris** as Felisa in *Montserrat*, and in 1949 her Broadway career was launched. She continued her training at the Actors Studio in New York City over many years under the tutelage of such theatre luminaries as Elia Kazan and Lee Strasberg.

When Horton Foote saw Stanley play Adela in the 1951 American National Theatre and Academy (ANTA) production of Garcia Lorca's *The House of Bernarda Alba*, he requested that she read for his play *The Chase*, in which she played the lead in 1952. Following her celebrated performance in William Inge's *Picnic*, for which she won the 1953 New York Drama Critics Award, she again collaborated with Foote in *The Traveling Lady*. Her performance was so noteworthy that, in response to the critical acclaim, her name was elevated to star billing after the play opened.

Numerous Broadway successes followed, but Stanley is perhaps best remembered for her performance as Chérie in Inge's *Bus Stop*, which earned her the Donaldson and New York Drama Critics Awards in 1955. Stanley made her first appearance on the London stage as Maggie in Tennessee Williams's *Cat on a Hot Tin Roof* in 1958. Elizabeth Taylor attended this production to take notes for the film role of Maggie that she was to play. Later that year, Stanley was back on Broadway as Sara Melody in Eugene O'Neill's *A Touch of the Poet*. She played Elizabeth von Ritter, Sigmund Freud's first important patient, in *A Far Country* (1961) and Masha in the famed Actors Studio theatre production of Anton Chekhov's *The Three Sisters*, which was also performed in London's World Theatre Season.

During a period of intense professional activity, Stanley also performed the roles of wife and mother. In fact, she played the part of fifteen-year-old Millie Owen in the Broadway production of *Picnic* while pregnant with her son Jamison. Stanley's 1948 marriage to actor Bruce Franklin Hall ended in divorce, and she later married actor-director Curt Conway. The couple had one daughter and one son before their marriage was dissolved in 1956. In 1958 she wed actor Alfred Ryder, with whom she had one daughter. None of her children has pursued a career in the theatre.

Stanley's active stage career ended as abruptly as it had begun. When performing in *The Three Sisters*, she suffered an emotional breakdown and was forced to retire for a time from the demands of her professional life. She returned to New Mexico, where she taught acting and worked with young actors for many years. Of this turn in her life she says, "God had his hand on my shoulder in some way—that I'm extraordinarily good at teaching. The human exchange is fantastic—much more interesting than acting. Much!" (*New York Times*, September 20, 1979).

Amazing as is her record of performance in live theatre, Stanley concurrently performed in some fourscore television roles, winning an Emmy in 1963 for her role in *A Cardinal Act of Mercy*. Most recently she appeared as Big Mama in a television production of *Cat on a Hot Tin Roof*.

Stanley resisted film acting for many years, convinced that she did not have a "Hollywood face." In fact, many of the roles she originated in the theatre were recreated on film by movie stars such as Marilyn Monroe and Elizabeth Taylor. Stanley expresses concern for the lack of sequential rehearsal time allotted in film work, as well as the relinquishing of control to directors and editors. Nonetheless, her first film appearance in *The Goddess* in 1958 earned her an Academy Award (Oscar) nomination, and her next film, *Séance on a Wet Afternoon* (1964), won much critical praise. If movies failed to interest her in her youth, they offered her the possibility of a comeback. In 1982 she appeared as the domineering mother in *Frances*, with Jessica Lange, and in 1983 she played Pancho Barnes in *The Right Stuff*, with Sam Shepard. Recently, she has attempted to form a theatre company and return to her roots on the live stage.

Critics have rhapsodized about Stanley's work, often singling her out for praise in doomed productions. Deeply influenced by the Actors Studio approach to method acting, she thoroughly researches her roles and attempts to penetrate psychoanalytically the core of her character's motivations. Her versatility and range of characterization are remarkable. The strongest influences on her remain Lee Strasberg, whom she credits with opening up the whole world to her, and Harold Clurman, whom she saw as her "mentor." To many, Kim Stanley remains the quintessential actress of the 1950s.

Some reviews of Kim Stanley's work appeared in the *New York World Telegram* (October 23, 1954), the *New York Post Magazine* (March 13, 1955), and the *New York Times* (April 3, 1955). Interviews with Stanley are Gilbert Milstein, "Kim Stanley," *Theatre Arts* (November 1959), and John Corry, "Kim Stanley Returns, Directing Ensemble Troupe,'' *New York Times* (September 20, 1979). See also Jon Kobal, ''Dialogue on Film—Kim Stanley,'' *American Film* (June 1983). Kim Stanley is included in *Current Biography, 1955* (1955–1956), *The Biographical Encyclopaedia and Who's Who of the American Theatre* (1966), *Notable Names in the American Theatre* (1976), *Who's Who in the Theatre* (1981), and *The Oxford Companion to American Theatre* (1984).

Mira Felner

STAPLETON, Maureen (June 21, 1925–): outstanding actress on stage, screen, and television, was born in Troy, New York. Her parents, John P. Stapleton and Irene (Walsh) Stapleton, were staunch Irish Catholics, who separated when she was five years old. Maureen Stapleton and her younger brother, Jack, went to live with her mother, her maternal grandmother, three aunts, and two uncles in Troy. Her mother worked as a clerk for the New York State Department of Unemployment in Albany. Maureen Stapleton graduated from Catholic Central High School in Troy in 1942. Her first marriage was in July 1949 to Max Allentuck, general manager for producer Kermit Bloomgarden. She had two children, Daniel Vincent (b. 1950), now a filmmaker, and Catherine, (b. 1954), now working in theatre. In February 1959 Stapleton divorced Allentuck. She was married again in July 1963 to playwright David Rayfiel; that brief marriage ended in divorce as well.

Stapleton came to New York in September 1943 to fulfill her childhood aspiration to become an actress. She had been inspired by the movies of Jean Harlow and was encouraged by her uncle, Vincent Walsh, to pursue her career. To support herself and her studies, she modeled for artists Raphael Soyer and Reginald Marsh and worked the night shift as a billing machine operator at the Hotel New Yorker. She initially studied Delsarte acting technique with Frances Robinson-Duff but after a few months began taking classes with Herbert Berghof. In the summer of 1945 she worked in Berghof's summer stock company at the Greenbush Summer Theatre in Blauvelt, New York, and the following summer she performed in stock at Mount Kisco, also in New York State.

The actress's first Broadway experience was in October 1946. She convinced producer-director Guthrie McClintic to give her an audition for *The Playboy of the Western World* and was cast in the small role of Sara Tansey. At the same time she understudied the leading role of Pegeen and was given the opportunity to perform during the last week of the run. It was the beginning of an important apprenticeship with the McClintic-**Katharine Cornell** company. During 1947– 1948 she performed small roles in that company's Broadway and touring productions as Iras in *Antony and Cleopatra* and Wilson in *The Barretts of Wimpole Street*.

In October 1947 Stapleton became a charter member of the Actors Studio, where she studied with Robert Lewis and Lee Strasberg. She appeared in workshop productions and in the Studio's 1948–1949 live performances on ABC-TV. While studying at the Studio, she continued her work on the commercial stage. On March 23, 1949, she played Miss Hatch in Sydney Kingsley's *Detective*

Story at the Hudson Theatre and Emilie in Arthur Laurents's *The Bird Cage* on February 22, 1950, at the Coronet Theatre. Summing up Stapleton's abilities, Robert Lewis called her an actress who operates on an instinctive level. "Maureen Stapleton . . . is a kind of 'true believer.' She just believes in everything. It's part of her nature. It's the way she is, and that is her particular talent" (*American Theatre*, April 1986, p. 16).

Stapleton's first major success was her portrayal of the earthy Italian widow, Serafina della Rosa, in Tennessee Williams' *The Rose Tattoo*, which was produced by **Cheryl Crawford** and co-starred Eli Wallach as Alvaro. It opened February 3, 1951, at the Martin Beck Theatre on Broadway. In addition to winning the Antoinette Perry (Tony) Award for best actress, Stapleton was hailed as the "American Anna Magnani" (Magnani was the Italian actress who would make the film version of the play). The review in the New York *Morning Telegraph* (February 6, 1951), typical of the high critical acclaim Stapleton often received, described her Serafina as "lusty, brawling, brooding, hysterical, and encompassing, a performance of stunning and tremendous size. She is mistress of the role in every nuance of it and it is a joy to watch her acting."

Established at age twenty-five as a character actress of great emotional power, Stapleton has continued to display an extraordinary range, especially finding success with the intense heroines of Tennessee Williams. After her unforgettable Serafina (which she played again in the October 22, 1966, revival at the New York City Center), Stapleton created Flora Meighan in *27 Wagons Full of Cotton* (April 19, 1955, at the Playhouse) and Lady Torrance in *Orpheus Descending* (March 21, 1957, at the Martin Beck Theatre). She played Amanda Wingfield in Tennessee Williams's *The Glass Menagerie* in the May 4, 1965, revival at the Brooks Atkinson Theatre and again in the 1975 revival on December 18 at the Circle in the Square.

Since the 1950s Stapleton's stage career has encompassed a broad spectrum of classic and contemporary drama. December 9, 1953, she played Anne in *Richard III* with José Ferrer at the New York City Center. She premièred May 1, 1954, as Masha in the Phoenix Theatre's production of Anton Chekhov's *The Sea Gull*. In Lillian Hellman's *Toys in the Attic*, she created the role of Carrie Berniers at the Hudson Theatre (February 25, 1960). She played Georgie Elgin in *The Country Girl* by Clifford Odets, in the November 16, 1971, revival with Jason Robards, Jr., at the John F. Kennedy Center (which moved to the Billy Rose Theatre in New York, March 1972). That same year she played the title role in *The Secret Affairs of Mildred Wild* at the Ambassador Theatre (November 14, 1971). For the Mark Taper Forum in Los Angeles, she played Juno in *Juno and the Paycock* (November 7, 1974).

Stapleton began to play more comedy as she appeared as the amateur matchmaker, Aunt Ida, in S. N. Behrman's *The Cold Wind and the Warm* at the Morosco Theatre on December 8, 1958. In this production she again co-starred with Eli Wallach under the direction of Harold Clurman and was praised for her versatility. But it was in two plays by Neil Simon that Stapleton was able to display her full comedic talents. Under the direction of Mike Nichols she played three different roles in Simon's *Plaza Suite*: Karen Nash, Muriel Tate, and Norma Hubley. Richard Watts, Jr., acknowledged that Stapleton "has been widely recognized as one of America's finest actresses, and she is at the peak of her talent as a dowdy wife, a not-too-guileless young woman from New Jersey, and a distraught mother" in the *New York Post* (February 15, 1968). Martin Gottfried claimed that Stapleton proved "for the first time to me that an Actors Studio-trained actor can play comedy" (*Women's Wear Daily*, February 15, 1968). For her next Simon role, that of Evy Meara in *The Gingerbread Lady*, Stapleton was awarded the Antoinette Perry (Tony) Award and the Drama Desk Award and was a winner in *Variety*'s New York Drama Critics Poll. The comedy premièred at the Plymouth Theatre on December 13, 1970, and Clive Barnes said, "Maureen Stapleton, as the battered, baffled lush thrush has probably the part of her career, and she is quite wonderful" (*New York Times*, December 14, 1970).

Stapleton replaced **Jessica Tandy** in *The Gin Game* (1978) and went on to portray Birdie Hubbard in the 1981 New York revival of Lillian Hellman's *The Little Foxes*, starring Elizabeth Taylor. Director Austin Pendleton remarked that the secret to her acting lies in her amazing ability to concentrate, that "she has that gift, that gift of just being there. . . . She has a capacity to make the audience believe everything she says" (*New York Times*, June 21, 1981). Liz Smith wrote in the *New York Daily News* (May 11, 1981) that "a special word must be said for Maureen Stapleton who is one of the finest actresses in the entire world. She does her usual practically perfect job as the faded Southern belle who would like just one more day of complete happiness in her life and has no expectation of getting it. Maureen is a true national treasure, one of those unique performers who make the theatre so special" (*New York Daily News*, May 11, 1981).

Stapleton's tremendous range and versatility have carried over to her numerous film and television roles. The actress performed in NBC's *Goodyear Playhouse*, *Philco Playhouse*, and *Armstrong Circle Theatre* (1953–1956). She won Emmy awards in 1967 and 1968 for *Save Me a Place at Forest Lawn* and *Among the Paths to Eden*. Among her numerous specials are the 1959 *For Whom the Bell Tolls*, in which she played the gypsy Pilar for *Playhouse 90*, and *Cat On A Hot Tin Roof*, in which she played Big Mama opposite Laurence Olivier (1976). Stapleton received Emmy nominations for her roles in *The Queen of the Stardust Ballroom* (1975) and *The Gathering* (1977). In 1983 she played the White Queen in the public television special *Alice in Wonderland*. Stapleton's experience in film began in 1958 with *Lonelyhearts* and has included the film version of *Orpheus Descending*, titled *The Fugitive Kind* (1960); *A View from the Bridge* and *Bye Bye Birdie* (1962); *Trilogy* (1969); *Airport* (1970); *Plaza Suite* (1971); *Interiors* (1978); *The Runner Stumbles* (1979); and *The Fan* and *On the Right Track* (1981). She received the Golden Globe Award for *Airport* in 1971, and in 1981 she received the National Society of Film Critics Award as well as the Academy (Oscar) Award for best supporting actress for her portrayal of Emma

Goldman in *Reds*. Stapleton's recent film roles include *Johnny Dangerously* (1984), *Cocoon* (1985), *Lost and Found* (1985), *The Money Pit* (1986), and *Heartburn* (1986).

Throughout her career, Stapleton has retained a down-to-earth attitude toward the theatre and the media. In the *New York Journal American* (February 16, 1959) she was quoted as saying, "Acting's a trade, an illogical trade, and you have to have a completely illogical need to follow it." And follow it she has—because of her celebrated fear of flying, she has made up to ten transcontinental trips a year in trains and buses and even taken freighters across the Atlantic to reach filming locations. Her first love is still the stage, and she would like the financial security to stay in her New York home and not have to travel again. In an interview in *The New Yorker* she expressed her belief that the "aspiration to act is so great, so deep, so complete, that you give yourself not ten years, not twenty, but your whole lifetime to realize it" (October 28, 1961, p. 132).

On April 5, 1981, Stapleton was inducted into the Theatre Hall of Fame—a fitting tribute to a versatile actress who has created so many vivid, diverse images of Italian, Jewish, Irish, and southern women on the American stage and screen. Melody Kimmel, in an interview in *Films in Review*, summed up the extraordinary contribution of Maureen Stapleton by saying that as "an actress of great versatility, Miss Stapleton plays comedy with terrific timing and energy while remaining a notable dramatic performer. She is able to summon up grief, pathos, sweetness—all with a depth of feeling that has made her one of the preeminent actresses of our time" (February 1982, p. 71).

Information about Stapleton's life and career is to be found in Suzanne Edelson, "Interview with Maureen Stapleton," *People Weekly* (May 3, 1982); Melody Kimmel, "Interview with Maureen Stapleton," *Films in Review* (February 1982); Robert Lewis, "Discovering 'The Life of Our Times,' " *American Theatre* (April 1986); "New Star," *The New Yorker* (February 24, 1951); and Lillian Ross, "Profiles," *The New Yorker* (October 28, 1961). She is also discussed in *The Kindness of Strangers: The Life of Tennessee Williams* (1985) by Donald Spoto. Significant reviews of her work are those in the *New York Daily News* (May 11, 1981), the *New York Journal-American* (February 16, 1959), the *New York Times* (December 14, 1970, and June 21, 1981), the (New York) *Morning Telegraph* (February 6, 1951), the *New York Post* (February 15, 1968), and *Women's Wear Daily* (February 15, 1968). Entries on Stapleton are included in *Current Biography, 1959* (1959–1960); *Notable Names in the American Theatre* (1976); *Who's Who in the Theatre* (1981); *The Oxford Companion to American Theatre* (1984); and *Who's Who of American Women, 1985–1986* (1986).

Jeannie M. Woods

STASIO, Marilyn (1939?–): critic, was born in Revere, Massachusetts, near Boston, into a family of which some members were involved in the newspaper business. She holds a Bachelor of Arts degree from Regis College and a Master of Arts degree from Columbia University in comparative literature (1962). She married Richard J. Hummler in 1971 and has no children. Her first job in New York was as editor of the weekly *Brooklyn Graphic*, and in 1965 she became feature editor at *Cue* magazine, replacing Emory Lewis in 1968 as first-string reviewer for *Cue*, a position she held until 1978. She wrote weekly reviews as well as monthly "think pieces" on the theatre, which were notable for their well-stated insights. During this period she also served as contributing editor for *Ingénue*, *Penthouse*, *Politicks*, and *I-AM* (Italian-American) magazines. In March 1978 she left *Cue* to become first-string theatre critic for the newly formed *The (New York) Tribune*, but the paper folded before printing any of her reviews. If it had materialized, the position would have been the first time in several decades that a woman was a first-string critic on a New York daily. That fall she became second-string critic for the New York *Post*.

Stasio has contributed articles to the *Los Angeles Times*, *Harper's*, *New York Magazine*, *Village Voice*, *Soho Weekly News*, *Christopher Street*, and other publications. She has also published a book of criticism, *Broadway's Beautiful Losers* (1972), a novel (1974), and recently a monthly syndicated book review column. She was a regular on the arts segment of PBS *Special Edition* with Marilyn Berger in the 1979–1980 season.

In 1974 Stasio became a co-founder of the New Drama Forum, an alternative organization to the Drama Desk, to which she had belonged from 1968 to 1974. She has also been a member of the New York Drama Critics Circle, the League of Professional Theatre Women/New York, the nominating committees for the Antoinette Perry (Tony) awards (five times since 1970) and for the *Village Voice* Off-Broadway (Obie) awards (three times since 1970), as well as the advisory board of the Theatre Collection of the New York Public Library Performing Arts Research Center at Lincoln Center.

Stasio has also been a dramaturg at the Eugene O'Neill Theatre Center's National Playwrights Conference (1976–1980) and at Shenandoah Valley Playwrights Retreat, where she set up a dramaturgy program in 1982. She has been a lecturer at the National Critics Institute at the O'Neill Center (1970–1984), a lecturer and dramaturg at Virginia Polytechnic Institute and State University (1980–1984), and a consultant to the Empire State Institute for the Performing Arts (1983–1985). She has been a national adjudicator for the American College Theatre Festival of the American Theatre Association from 1978 to 1985.

At mid-point now in her active career, Stasio is one of the few women who have become important theatre critics.

Besides Stasio's own *Broadway's Beautiful Losers* (1972), the best sources for her work are the various pieces in the magazines mentioned above. She is included in M. E. Comtois, *Contemporary American Theatre Critics* (1977). She is reticent about the details of her birth and childhood.

Gayle Austin

STEIN, Gertrude (February 3, 1874–June 27, 1946): playwright and poet, was born to Daniel and Amelia (Keyser) Stein, both of German-Jewish descent, in Allegheny (now a part of Pittsburgh), Pennsylvania, the last of seven children. Her father was an emigrant from Weigergruben, Germany, settling with his family in Baltimore in 1841. A few years later, he and his brother Solomon moved to Allegheny to set up a clothing business. His first-born child was a son, Michael; then came two children who died in infancy, then Simon, Bertha, Leo, and Gertrude Stein, the latter two making up the complement of five that Daniel Stein had determined to have. As soon as the infant Gertrude could travel, her father moved the family to Europe. They spent the next five years in Gemunden, Vienna, Paris, and briefly in London. They returned to Baltimore in 1879, then moved in 1880 to East Oakland, California, into a large house on ten acres of land. Stein's recollections of her childhood centered on this place, and here she and Leo formed the close companionship that would last through their college days and their early years in Paris. They had a mutual interest in books, in talking and arguing, and in theatre. At the local theatre Gertrude and Leo Stein saw touring companies present George L. Aiken's *Uncle Tom's Cabin* and William Gillette's *Secret Service*. They saw Edwin Booth and Sarah Bernhardt. At the San Francisco opera they saw *Faust* and *Lohengrin*. The Stein children attended public schools but also had at home a governess and occasional tutors.

In 1888 Stein's mother died, and when her father died in 1891 her oldest brother Michael became head of the family. He successfully disposed of his father's business interests and arranged for each of the siblings to have an independent income for life. In 1892 Bertha, Gertrude, and Leo were sent to Baltimore to live with their mother's sister, Fanny Bachrach, Leo transferring from the University of California to Harvard. In 1893 Gertrude, never having completed high school, applied as a special student to the Harvard Annex (now Radcliffe College). She took a broad range of subjects and in 1898 received her Bachelor of Arts degree, magna cum laude. Stein then entered the Johns Hopkins University Medical School, having been recommended by her Harvard psychology professor, William James. However, she progressively lost interest in medical subjects, and in the spring of 1902 she joined her brother Leo in Italy where he had gone in 1900 to pursue a career in aesthetics. That summer they took rooms in London at 20 Bloomsbury Square, spending much of their time at the British Museum. In late summer Stein had a series of lively conversations at Friday's Hill, Bernard Berenson's country house, with her host Berenson and Bertrand Russell. These discussions started her thinking about the nature of America and how she valued it, a subject that would occupy the expatriate writer for the rest of her life. She eventually came to be certain that to see her homeland truly, she could not live there. Nevertheless, in 1902, in the face of a dreary London winter, she sailed to New York, settled in with Mabel Weeks, Harriet Clark, and Estelle Rumbold at 100th Street and Riverside Drive, and began to write.

In October 1903 she rejoined Leo, who was now living at 27 Rue de Fleurus in Paris and pursuing a career in painting. Soon after Gertrude Stein's arrival, the two began exploring art galleries with plans to collect some Cézanne paintings. In a short time they had bought not only several Cézannes but paintings by Matisse, Renoir, Manet, Gauguin, Rousseau, Braque, Picasso, and others. Within a few years the eccentric American couple had put together an astounding collection and had made the acquaintance of a vast society of artists, critics, and writers. To accommodate the volume of visitors to their collection, the Steins instituted the Saturday evening salon, greatly accelerating the rise to fame of the painters they promoted, while their own notoriety grew likewise.

Meanwhile, Gertrude Stein had been quietly pursuing her own career as a writer. Her first book *Q. E. D.*, published posthumously in 1950 as *Things As They Are*, was completed within a month of her arrival in Paris; it described a lesbian relationship much like one in which she had been recently involved. *Three Lives* (published in 1909 to critical acclaim) was written in 1905–1906. Leo Stein, silent on the subject of his sister's writing, eventually disapproved, and it was Alice B. Toklas, lately arrived from San Francisco and destined to be Stein's lifelong companion and lover, who would provide the support system for Stein's full pursuit of writing. By 1909 Toklas had joined the household and was typing the mammoth manuscript of *The Making of Americans*, Stein's attempt to write a psychological history of "everyone who can or is or was or shall be living." She also experimented with a form in which she tried to capture the essential quality of the person at whom she looked. The portrait form first accomplished in "Ada," wherein Toklas was the subject, eventually led to Stein's efforts at playwriting. *The Making of Americans* was completed in 1911 but not published until 1925. Together with her portraits, in particular a collection titled *Tender Buttons* (1914), *Three Lives* (1909) signaled a new style in Stein's writing, which brought her a reputation as a difficult and eccentric writer for the remainder of her career. In August 1912 her portraits of Matisse and Picasso appeared in *Camera Work*, confirming her association with the artists of the notorious Armory Show in New York and garnering her considerable fame. The next year Leo and Gertrude finally separated, dividing up their paintings, and in that year also Stein's first of seventy-seven plays, *What Happened: A Play*, was written. It renders the images, rhythms, and qualities of an evening dinner party without suggesting a story line. Typical of her first period of playwriting, it is an attempt to capture the essence of relationships and subtle movements between things without telling what happened, but rather to make a play the essence of what happened. Stein distinguished her plays from her portraits by their ability to present relationships instead of single people or things and by her implicit assumption that they would be performed. Stein wrote thirty plays over the next nine years, all of them sharing the general characteristics of *What Happened: A Play*, capturing in essence moments in Stein's own life (though her presence as a character is never explicitly stated) and providing an admirable record of her life and times.

Stein and Toklas spent much of World War I in Spain, and upon their return to France in 1917, drove a supply truck for the American Fund for French Wounded. By 1922 Stein was being sought out by other budding writers, including Sherwood Anderson and Ernest Hemingway. That same year she published her first collection of plays, *Geography and Plays*, and began her second playwriting period, which lasted until 1931. Her "landscape plays" are spatially arranged, not vertically progressive. They depend upon relationships and are expressed in the overtly spatial terms of a physical landscape.

In May of 1926 Stein delivered the lecture "Composition As Explanation" at Cambridge and Oxford universities. Perhaps the most complete explication she ever made of her writing, it was very well received, winning for her new understanding and acceptance. Soon after, Stein and Toklas visited Belley in the French countryside, which they enjoyed so much that they leased a house nearby at Bilignin, where they were to spend every summer and fall from 1929 on.

The year 1932 marked the beginning of Stein's third and last period of playwriting, her narrative period, within which she depended for the first time upon some sort of story. Nevertheless, these plays depend less on causal connections between story elements than on sustained views of each element, subverting overt movement to the quality of the scene at hand. Not surprisingly, these plays—*The Mother of Us All* (1945–1946) and *Yes Is For a Very Young Man* (1944–1946)—are the most frequently produced because they allow more concessions to traditional playwriting. The year 1932 also marked Toklas and Stein's publication of *Operas and Plays*, which contained Stein's landscape plays. That same year her best seller, *The Autobiography of Alice B. Toklas*, was published. This was Stein's version, through the eyes of Toklas, of their lives together. In 1933 Virgil Thompson found backers for his and Stein's long-planned opera, *Four Saints in Three Acts*, for which Thomson wrote the score. The successful Broadway production of the opera in early 1934 and Stein's overwhelming popular success with the *Autobiography* prompted her to make a triumphal tour of America in October of 1934. She delivered a series of lectures that dispelled any notion that she was a crank or an impostor. She returned to France a celebrity.

In 1937 Lord Gerald Berners produced a ballet, *A Wedding Bouquet*, based on one of her landscape plays. After seeing the ballet and traveling through Provence, Stein settled at her Bilignin home to live out World War II. She and Toklas returned to Paris in 1944, moving into a new home on the Rue Christine. There they held court to hundreds of American servicemen who wanted to meet the controversial and influential heroine she had become. In 1946, en route to the country with Toklas, she became ill. On July 19 she was admitted to the American Hospital at Neuilly-sur-Seine, where she died of cancer on July 27. She is buried at Père Lachaise Cemetery in Paris, where her gravestone informs visitors that she was born in "Allegheny" and died on July 29.

If Gertrude Stein remains the least read giant of modern literature, she is surely the least acclaimed major playwright of all time. Having no more respect for traditional theatre than she had for traditional literature, she bowed to few dramaturgical conventions. It is no surprise that her plays and their productions, when they occur, appeal to a select audience. The theatre that Stein enjoyed and respected was concrete, dynamic, and absolutely present, capturing in essence what traditional theatre was content to describe linearly. Her youthful experiences at the theatre in San Francisco and in later life, and her own experiments in writing, had taught her to distrust climactic, linear structure. Stein entered playwriting as a *naïf* and considered it, as she did literature, a wholly solitary pastime. Part of no playwright's club, she nevertheless knew theatrical figures such as Jean Cocteau, Roger Vitrac, Avery Hopwood, and Virgil Thomson and had a tremendous influence upon another contemporary, Thornton Wilder, who felt sure Stein would take the theatre in new directions. Her influence has grown over the years rather than diminished. Her groundbreaking experiments in nonreferentiality and nonlinearity in literature and theatre are directly evident in work by theatre artists like Richard Foreman and Robert Wilson, and in poets like Dick Higgins and Jackson MacLow, all of whom acknowledge her influence.

Whether the movement in recent theatre toward immediacy and physicality and away from traditional referential language can be attributed solely to Gertrude Stein's work is another question. She was, after all, responding in her work to a disconnection in the world also obvious to her contemporaries—the symbolists, surrealists, dadaists, and futurists—all of whom rejected traditional linear form for different reasons and in different ways. Stein's work, while forming an important segment of modernism, is not synonymous with it; but the innovators of recent American theatre, with their stress on physicality, immediacy, multi-dimensionality, and political and social message, owe a debt to the heritage of modernism to which Gertrude Stein contributed.

The American Literature Collection of Yale University is the chief repository for manuscripts, typescripts, letters, diaries, notebooks, and memorabilia pertaining to Gertrude Stein. There is a new edition of Stein's *Operas and Plays* (1987). The majority of her plays are published in three volumes: *Geography and Plays* (1922), *Operas and Plays* (1932), and *Last Operas and Plays* (1949). Her most important theoretical writings are *Lectures in America* (1935), *How To Write* (1931), *Narration* (1935), *The Geographical History of America, or the Relation of Human Nature to the Human Mind* (1936), and "Composition As Explanation," published in *Selected Writings of Gertrude Stein* (1945). There is as yet no full-length published work on Stein's plays or theatre, though two dissertations—Wilford Leach's "Gertrude Stein and the Modern Theatre" (1956) and Betsy Ryan's "Gertrude Stein's Theatre of the Absolute" (1980) (Unpublished Ph.D. dissertations, University of Illinois, Champaign—Urbana) fill that gap. The most valuable critical studies to address her writings are Richard Bridgman, *Gertrude Stein in Pieces* (1970); Michael Hoffman, *Gertrude Stein* (1976); Donald Sutherland, *Gertrude Stein: A Biography of Her Work* (1951); and Norman Weinstein, *Gertrude Stein and the Literature of Modern Consciousness* (1970). Biographical material includes Stein's *Autobiography of Alice B. Toklas* (1933) and *Everybody's Autobiography* (1937), in addition to James Mellow, *Charmed Circle* (1974), and John Malcolm Brinnin, *The Third Rose; Gertrude Stein and Her World* (1959). A short biography of Stein appears in *Notable American Women*, Vol. III (1971), and in *The Oxford Companion to American Theatre* (1984). She was also the subject of a one-woman show titled *Gertrude Stein, Gertrude Stein, Gertrude Stein* (New York, 1979). The principal bibliographic studies are Robert B. Haas and Donald C. Gallup, *A Catalog of the Published and Unpublished Writings of Gertrude Stein* (1941); Julian Sawyer, *Gertrude Stein: A Bibliography* (1940); and Robert Wilson, *Gertrude Stein: A Bibliography* (1974).

Betsy Ryan

STERNBERG, Patricia Ann Sikes (July 16, 1930–): playwright, director, actress, and specialist in child drama, was born in Detroit, Michigan. She was an only child and when her father died in 1941, she and her mother moved to Springfield, Ohio, to live with her grandmother. At the age of twelve, she joined the Springfield Junior Civic Theatre, where she acted in plays.

Her mother married Raymond Harris in 1946, and Patricia Sikes had a dream come true because her stepfather had three children from a previous marriage and Patricia was an only child no longer. She continued acting in high school and was also involved in debate contests. When she chose to continue her theatre training at Bowling Green State University in Ohio, she was a national oratory winner and appeared in *The Little Foxes*, *Three Men on a Horse*, and *The Skin of Our Teeth*. In 1952 with a Bachelor of Arts degree in speech and drama, Patricia Sikes decided to pursue an acting career in New York, where she studied with Lee Strasberg and Wynn Handmann. She was able to support herself making television commercials for such products as Johnson's Wax and Oxydol, as well as acting Off-Broadway with Martin Landau in *Laura* and with Lauritz Melchior in *Arabian Nights*.

In 1956 Patricia Sikes married Richard Sternberg, a New Yorker in the garment business. She told Gloria Kremer of the *Jewish Exponent* that after four years of struggling to support herself with acting and commercials, "I thought I would be satisfied with the life of a housewife and mother" (January 27, 1978). However, in 1957, six months after her son David was born, she decided to return to the theatre. Patricia Sternberg founded the Riverdale Children's Theatre at this time and began a career in children's theatre that has established her as a significant figure in the field. Dissatisfied with the material available for children, she also began to write plays. Before establishing the Riverdale Community Theatre, she wrote and produced more than a dozen children's plays, including *The Curious Adventure* (1963) and *The Witch in the Moon* (1962).

While at the Riverdale Community Theatre, Sternberg realized that she enjoyed directing as well as writing and acting. By then she was a mother of three, having given birth to two daughters, Ruth in 1959, and Anne in 1966. In 1968, under a grant from the New York Council on the Arts, she directed a number of Magic Wand productions that toured Bronx ghetto areas. Surprised by the response of these underprivileged children, she said that "once they allowed themselves to get into it, they wanted to be a part of it" (Interview).

When it was necessary for Sternberg to move to Philadelphia because of her husband's work, she wrote to Pennsylvania State University, where a program in recreation and parks had been developed. She was asked to prepare a course in creative dramatics for recreation leaders. She found she loved teaching but soon discovered that she would need a master's degree to continue teaching at the university level. Thus, she enrolled at Villanova University in Pennsylvania, where she studied playwriting and cinematography with David Rabe. In 1974, twenty years after receiving her bachelor's degree, Sternberg earned her master's degree in theatre.

As a university teacher she continued to write plays for both children and adults and in 1976 became associated with the Germantown Theatre Guild. She and her partner, Dolly Beechman, wrote the children's plays *Circle of Freedom*, *The Treaty Never Broken*, and *Sojourner*, which had a national tour in 1978 for the Germantown Theatre Guild. At this time she also wrote a series of four plays called *History Through the Theatre*, a project funded by the Pennsylvania Council on the Arts. During this period Sternberg also began work as a drama therapist at Eugenia Hospital, a private psychiatric hospital in Lafayette Hill, Pennsylvania. Her experiences there prompted her to write a book on friendship, *Be My Friend—The Art of Good Relationships*, in 1983.

During Sternberg's life, at one time or another, she has earned a living in practically all areas of the theatre. Her children's play, *The Treasure Makers*, was presented at the 1982 American Theatre Association convention and was subsequently published by Samuel French. In addition to writing plays, teaching creative dramatics, and directing, she has appeared in feature films and on television on the *Milton Berle Show* and the *Jackie Gleason Show*; she has also published books and scholarly articles on creative drama and arts for the handicapped. She is currently the head of developmental drama at Hunter College of the City University of New York, where she teaches children's theatre and creative dramatics. She is also director of the Mad Hatter's Children's Theatre Company, and for this company she wrote *The Princess and the Pauper*, which toured the New York elementary schools in the fall of 1983.

Patricia Sternberg, who calls children's theatre her first love, is and has been a motive force in the development of creative dramatics in the United States.

Books by Patricia S. Sternberg include *Theatre Accessibility for the Disabled Playgoer* (1980), *Creative Dramatics Handbook* (1981), *Arts for the Handicapped* (1981), *On Stage (How to Put on a Play)* (1982), and *Speak Up! A Guide to Public Speaking* (1984). Information on Sternberg was obtained through an interview by the author of this essay. Sternberg is listed in *Contemporary Authors* (1985).

                                                                                                        Juli Thompson

STEWART, Ellen (1920?–): theatrical producer and founder of Café La Mama (now La Mama Experimental Theatre Club) in New York City. When asked about her life before she started her theatre in 1961, Café La Mama, Ellen Stewart gave few details and said that she prefers to be identified by her work in the theatre. She may have been born in New Orleans or Chicago, since she has relatives in Louisiana and in Illinois. She has one son and is a grandparent. In interviews, Stewart does, however, tell anecdotes about her arrival in New

York from Chicago and of her eventual founding of her Off-off-Broadway theatre.

Stewart arrived in New York in the early 1950s to learn fashion design. Earlier, she had studied at the University of Arkansas. She told interviewer Patricia Bosworth for the *New York Times* (March 30, 1969) that "a Negro can't study design in Louisiana; that's impossible. My first job in New York was snipping threads off brassieres at Saks Fifth Avenue. I didn't know anybody and I couldn't get into art school because I was black. I used to travel the subways on Sunday. What else is there to do when you're lonely?" One Sunday she found herself down on Orchard Street, where there were carts full of rolls of material. Abraham Diamond, an elderly merchant, befriended her. He had a fabric store, and he kept encouraging her to design. They had a regular ritual. Each Sunday he would give her a package of cloth, and she would go back to her room where she had a sewing machine, and make a new outfit. When she came to see Diamond and his family the following Sunday, she would be wearing the new outfit. He would then take her around to his friends on Orchard Street and introduce her as "my daughter, the artist." This story about the Orchard Street merchant is Stewart's prelude to how she became a designer of sportswear at Saks Fifth Avenue. Customers started asking her where she got the clothes she wore to work there, and she was eventually discovered as a designer. She worked in the design department at Saks until she became ill and had to quit the job.

Some years later, at a low emotional ebb, Stewart went to Tangiers with a friend; while there, she decided to give a new direction to her life. She would earn her living as a free-lance fashion designer, but she would also start a theatre. Back in New York, Stewart teamed up with struggling playwright Paul Foster, rented a basement in 1961 at 321 East Ninth Street, and opened a boutique *cum* theatre in which her dress designs were on display during the day, and a twenty-five-seat theatre operated in the evenings. Two or three new plays were presented each week, written by Foster, Bruce Kessler, Don Julian, and others. The idea was unique, for the Café Cino (founded by Joe Cino in December 1958) had not yet concentrated exclusively on producing new plays and would not do so until August 1963. Stewart's friends called her "La Mama." Thus her theatre was known as Café La Mama. Precarious finances, city fire marshals, and housing authorities precipitated hasty moves. After a year in the basement on 9th Street, Café La Mama moved to 82 Second Street, and then in 1964 to a space one flight up from a dry cleaner's at 122 Second Avenue and Eighth Street, where its capacity expanded to seventy-four seats.

La Mama (as the theatre is known today) began as a coffee house, a private club whose members paid dues of one dollar each week. Although coffee and pastries have not been served at the theatre in years, technically La Mama is a private club. In 1966 Stewart made the *New York Times* in a dispute with Actors' Equity Association over salaries. She announced in the *Times* that she was closing her theatre because Equity had forbidden its members to perform at La Mama unless they were paid. After hearing Stewart plead the theatre's case, Equity rescinded its earlier decision. The union, according to the *Times*, recognized the importance of experimental theatre in general. As long as La Mama remained technically a private club, Equity members would be allowed to perform there without salary under the union's "showcase and workshop production" contract.

By 1968 Stewart's energy and personal magnetism had found La Mama its fourth (and permanent) location in a former meat packing plant at 74A East Fourth Street. This move was made possible by a grant from the Ford Foundation (under W. McNeil Lowry's stewardship) for purchase of the building and renovation. A Rockefeller Foundation grant subsidized salaries and production expenses. Of this move into permanent quarters Stewart said, "We hope to make it possible for playwrights, actors, and directors and all those interested in any aspect of the theatre to enjoy and make a creative contribution to the arts" (*New York Times*, July 24, 1968). Renovation proceeded on the four-story building, but before the renovation could be completed, Stewart became seriously ill and was hospitalized. When she was discharged from the hospital she found that the renovation had fallen behind schedule and that the theatre was, as yet, unfit to open. The La Mama company performed that season at 9 St. Marks Place. The building and the new theatres were finally opened on April 3 and 4, 1969, as a testament to Stewart's vision, determination, and stamina.

The first-floor theatre of the La Mama Experimental Theatre Club opened on April 3, 1969, with Tom Eyen's *Caution: A Love Story*; the third-floor theatre opened with the La Mama Company's performance of **Julie Bovasso**'s *Gloria and Esperanza*. Against all odds, Stewart was now in command of a permanent home with a group of new playwrights, actors, and directors committed to her vision of alternative theatre. By this time Stewart had become what one critic called the "doyenne of Off-off-Broadway." Moreover, a "La Mama tradition" was now recognized; that is, there was never enough money at La Mama for salaries, equipment, and productions; everyone worked for nothing. Above all else, La Mama was a playwrights' theatre. The list of new American playwrights associated with La Mama is impressive: Tom Eyen, Paul Foster, **Rochelle Owens**, Lanford Wilson, Julie Bovasso, Sam Shepard, Leonard Melfi, Jean-Claude van Itallie, Robert Patrick, **Megan Terry**, Elizabeth Swados, and many more. Of this aspect of producing Stewart said in an interview with the *New York Times*: "People sometimes wonder at my choice of plays. I've been criticized for choosing amateurish writing. . . . I happen to think I am right. If a script 'beeps' to me, I do it. Audiences may hate these plays but I believe in them. The only way I can explain my 'beeps' is that I'm no intellectual but my instincts tell me automatically when a playwright has something. Some of the plays we do have been called crashing bores. But with them the playwright learns. He learns that he can fail and his soul won't be crushed for it. In our culture playwrights can be eaten alive by the success-failure syndrome. I've never believed in long runs for that reason. Long runs tend to corrupt and to get the writer caught up in that success-failure hang-up which has nothing to do with his development as a writer. Before you fail, you try—and after you fail you must be encouraged to try again until something beautiful comes out. The ability to create is a dangerous and wonderful thing'' (March 30, 1969).

In the 1970s Stewart's work took on a greater international flavor. Since 1965 the La Mama Company has toured Europe and Scandinavia. The tours began, in part, as a means of attracting the attention of New York critics and publishers; but the company also succeeded in exerting influence abroad with the New York alternative theatre movement. Taking part at various times in the touring companies were professionals like Tom O'Horgan, Robert Wilson, and Joseph Chaikin. In West Berlin in 1967, for instance, the La Mama group performed Rochelle Owens's *Futz*, Paul Foster's *Tom Paine*, and Sam Shepard's *Melodrama Play*. In effect, Ellen Stewart has been responsible for taking to European audiences some of the best artists and plays from the American avant-garde of the 1960s. Also, she has brought European companies to New York. Throughout the 1970s, both American and foreign theatre artists came to La Mama to observe the inner workings of the theatre and its many components. Stewart was now producing an average of five new plays a month. In the La Mama Plexus workshop, actors were developing physical strength and flexibility plus what Stewart has called "that umbilical, emotional thing with the group" (*New York Times*, April 5, 1970). Under her auspices Rumanian director Andrei Serban came to the United States, as well as Yugoslavia's leading playwright, Aleksandar Popovic.

The extension of La Mama into an annex two doors away, at 66–68 East Fourth Street, in 1974 was a sign of the theatre's expanding activities. Always in need of more rehearsal and performance space, Stewart had become interested in the building when it was taken over by the city for urban development. That year, the city gave her a dollar-a-month renewable lease. The La Mama Annex opened in October 1974 with a trilogy of Greek plays directed to critical acclaim by Andrei Serban. Again, a grant from the Ford Foundation had made the renovation possible. In the decade of the 1970s, Stewart focused on developing ensemble companies, some of them ethnic (Black, Puerto Rican, and Native American). In 1972 she instituted a series of repertory seasons to nurture and showcase ensemble companies. Tom O'Horgan and Andrei Serban are perhaps the best-known directors to have emerged from La Mama's repertory seasons.

"Internationalism," the fostering of a cross pollination of theatrical ideas between cultures, remains one of Stewart's most passionately held credos. Since 1965 she has toured the company to more than twenty countries, nurturing La Mama-affiliated groups in some eight cities from Tokyo to Paris to Bogota. She has brought foreign artists to the United States and invited Polish, Portuguese, Japanese, Dutch, Italian, and Yugoslavian companies to perform in their native languages on La Mama's stages. Peter Brook's company—called the International Centre for Theatre Research—from Paris performed to critical acclaim at La Mama in 1980. Of these activities Stewart has said, "Certainly America has a lot to give, but it also has a lot to learn. . . . But I believe in what I'm doing. I believe that theatre can go beyond language, that there is a special energy when there are many different nationalities on stage at once. I won't change" (*New York Times*, April 5, 1980).

To the hundreds of actors, directors, and playwrights who have gotten their start at La Mama, Ellen Stewart *is* La Mama. Her inborn creativity and courageous spirit have nourished their work. When asked about the homage that these artists pay to her, she explains, "I'm just an instrument through which La Mama functions. I never dictate. . . . Maybe it's fatalistic, but I know La Mama has its own spirit and if that spirit wishes to keep going, it will. All I can do is be a part of it" (*New York Times*, April 5, 1980). Among Ellen Stewart's numerous awards and citations are the American Theatre Association/International Theatre Institute Award, 1975; the **Margo Jones** Award for the encouragement of new playwrights, 1979; a Village Voice Off Broadway (Obie) Award and Special Citation for her career work, 1980; the Edwin Booth Award for contributions to New York theatre from the Graduate School of the City University of New York, 1984; and for Ellen Stewart and La Mama a special citation from Dance Theatre Workshop, 1987.

Since 1961 and its beginnings, Café La Mama, with Ellen Stewart as producer, has been a nucleus for new playwrights, directors, actors, and companies. She is the energetic driving force that has secured a performance space and atmosphere where theatre artists could develop their talents apart from the commercial environment of Broadway. As a producer, Ellen Stewart believes in the playwright's inspiration and the dramatic text as a starting point. She has said that the written text must be used to inspire movement, dance, and music in performance. Her legacy to the American theatre is still being developed and evaluated. The 1986–1987 season at La Mama marks the twenty-fifth anniversary of this seminal Off-off-Broadway theatre. The Silver Season reprises *Carmilla* by Wilford Leach; *The Architect and the Emperor of Assyria* directed by Tom O'Horgan; and the Andrei Serban/Elizabeth Swados trilogy—Euripides' *Medea*, *Electra*, and *The Trojan Women*.

Ellen Stewart has perhaps best summed up her contributions to the American theatre as her ability to choose new plays and the people to work with those plays. Over the years, no matter how precariously, she has also provided a physical space to do plays and an environment free of commercial pressures.

The most interesting articles to be found in the *New York Times* about Ellen Stewart and her La Mama Experimental Theatre Club are those in the issues for July 24, 1968, March 30, 1969, April 5, 1970, and April 5, 1980. See also "La Mama Celebrates 20 Years," *Performing Arts Journal 17* (1982), and Elizabeth Swados, "Sketching Boundaries: the Merlin of La Mama," *New York Times* (October 6, 1986). Ellen Stewart is listed in *Current Biography, 1973* (1973–1974); *Biography News* (1974); *Notable Names in the American Theatre* (1976); *Directory of Blacks in the Performing Arts* (1978); *Who's Who in America, 1978*, Vol. II (1976–1978), *Who's Who in America, 1978–1979*; Vol. II (1978–1979), *The Black and White* (1980), and *Who's Who in the Theatre* (1981).

                                                                                      Milly S. Barranger

SULLAVAN, Margaret Brooke (April 16, 1911–January 1, 1960): actress of stage and screen, was born in Norfolk, Virginia, to Cornelius Hancock and Garland (Council) Sullavan. Her early life was spent in a gracious Tidewater environment; it included education at private schools, dancing classes, summer camps, hunting expeditions with her father, parties, debuts, and always lots of beaux for the vivacious, talented "Peggy," as she was always called. She had a brother, Cornelius, Jr., and an older stepsister, Lewise.

The charismatic Peggy Sullavan began her dramatic career by providing recitations in the family parlor at the age of six. Photographs show her at later ages, now imitating Isadora Duncan in striking dance poses, now hanging fetchingly from a tree as Peter Pan. In these years she was proudest of four accomplishments: winning the "best all-round athlete" award at Camp Aloha one summer, being chosen salutatorian of her class at Chatham Episcopal Institute (now Chatham Hall), being elected president of the student council, and being voted "most talented" in her class. Following these triumphs, Peggy Sullavan spent a year at Sullins College in Bristol, Virginia, where she was voted "most popular" in her class.

Anxious to launch a dancing career, Sullavan went to Boston, Massachusetts, where she stayed with her stepsister Lewise. She spent three weeks at the Denishawn School of Dance, which convinced her that dancing was not really her forte. She then enrolled in the E. E. Clive Dramatic School and earned her way by selling books at the Harvard Cooperative Society. In May 1929 she landed a role in the Harvard Dramatic Society's show, *Close Up*, where she met two who were to play significant roles in her life, Joshua Logan and Henry Fonda. These two men were members of the University Players Guild, a group of college students mostly from Princeton, Harvard, and Smith, who produced plays at Falmouth on Cape Cod. Sullavan was invited to join them, and she spent several seasons with them at their theatre at Old Silver Beach. Joshua Logan recalled, "Peggy became, within an instant, an accomplished actress. She went through thirty, forty, fifty shows with us over the years, playing every kind of part, every age, mostly leading ladies or ingénues, but the extraordinary thing was she'd never really had a great deal of training. If there was ever a natural, she was it. She had, from the beginning, that magic, that indescribable, quality that is just extremely rare and immediately makes a star of a person. She was a true star. . . . The audiences in Falmouth fell madly in love with her" (*Haywire*, pp. 187– 188). Henry Fonda added, "And very early it became obvious she was a brilliant actress. I don't know what kind of experience she'd had: I don't think any. She had presence, which is something you're born with, you don't acquire. You don't learn it. . . . Soon it was clear she was the talent; she played all the good parts" (*Haywire*, p. 188).

In 1930 Margaret Sullavan's professional career began in earnest when she was offered the role of the understudy in Preston Sturges's successful play *Strictly Dishonorable*. She toured the South with this play and then rejoined the University Players. Her interview with Lee Shubert at this time is theatrical legend. Suffering from a heavy cold and plagued with laryngitis, she was astonished when the great man hired her on the spot. He was enamored of her husky, attractive voice and told her that she sounded like Helen Morgan and **Ethel Barrymore**. Her daughter, Brooke Hayward, reported that her mother joked that "after that interview with Mr. Shubert, she coddled her laryngitis into permanent hoarseness by standing in every available draft" (*Haywire*, p. 189). Nevertheless, Margaret Sullavan's voice became a finely tuned instrument, like a viola or cello, which she used to advantage in her later roles.

May 1931 marked Margaret Sullavan's Broadway debut in *A Modern Virgin*, produced by Lee Shubert, who had put her under contract. Critic John Mason Brown prophesied a happy future for her in his review in the New York *Post*: "Miss Sullavan is in reality what the old phrase calls a 'find.' She has youth, beauty, charm, vivacity and intelligence. She has a bubbling sense of comedy and acts with a veteran's poise. . . . Last night the evening was hers, as many other evenings should be in the future" (New York *Post*, May 21, 1931). Typically, she rejoined her friends in the University Players after the show closed, working with them in Baltimore, where they had moved, and on December 25, 1931, she and Henry Fonda were married at the Kernan Hotel in Baltimore.

Other plays in which she appeared on Broadway in the early 1930s included *Chrysalis* (1932), opposite Humphrey Bogart; *Dinner at Eight* (1932); and *Bad Manners* (1933). She also acquired an agent in 1931, Leland Hayward, who would later become her third husband and the father of her three children. During the run of *Dinner at Eight*, Universal Pictures signed her to a film contract for three years for two films a year with summers free for theatre work. Her motion picture debut in *Only Yesterday* (1933) with John Boles and Billie Burke was a repeat of her personal success on the stage; the film, directed by John Stahl, opened at Radio City Music Hall in New York.

After her second film, *Little Man, What Now?* (1934, Frank Borzage, director), she again returned to the stage for the summer, playing Norma Besant in *Coquette* at Mount Kisco, New York. Her marriage to Henry Fonda had by this time foundered. Her third film was a version of Ferenc Molnar's play *The Good Fairy* (1935, William Wyler, director). During the making of this film she married Wyler in Yuma, Arizona, but this marriage also was short-lived. *Next Time We Love* (1936, Edward H. Griffith, director) was a significant film for an old friend from her University Players' days. She persuaded the casting director to test a gangly youth trying to make it as an actor, and he won the prized role opposite Sullavan. His name was Jimmy Stewart, and this film was the first of four that he made with Sullavan, for the two had become an irresistible combination on the screen. Other films from this period included *So Red the Rose* (1935, King Vidor, director), a film that prefigured *Gone with the Wind* and featured Sullavan as a flirtatious southern belle; and *The Moon's Our Home* (1936, William A. Seiter, director), notable because **Dorothy Parker** and Alan Campbell wrote additional dialogue for it and Sullavan starred in it with her ex-husband, Henry Fonda.

When the Universal contract expired, Margaret Sullavan returned to the stage to create the role of Terry Randall in *Stage Door* (1936). This play established her as one of the most compelling actresses on the American stage that season. Her intelligence, originality, and naturalness as an actress galvanized Broadway audiences. It should also be noted that Sullavan was one of only a handful of stars—along with Fredric March, Katharine Hepburn, and Paul Muni—who in this period could command the highest critical and popular respect in both theatre and film. Margaret Sullavan married her agent, Leland Hayward, in Newport, Rhode Island, during the run of this play. Their children were Brooke (1937), Bridget (1939–1960), and William Leland Hayward (1941).

After her third marriage, Sullavan, now called "Maggie," made a series of films, including *Three Comrades* (1938, Frank Borzage, director, F. Scott Fitzgerald, screenplay), for which she received the New York Film Critics Award for "best actress" plus an Academy Award (Oscar) nomination; *The Shopworn Angel* (1938, H. C. Potter, director), with Jimmy Stewart; *The Shining Hour* (1938, Frank Borzage, director); *The Shop Around the Corner* (1940, Ernst Lubitsch, director), again with Jimmy Stewart; *So Ends Our Night* (1941, John Cromwell, director), with Fredric March; *Back Street* (1941, Robert Stevenson, director), with Charles Boyer; *Appointment for Love* (1941, William A. Seiter, director), with Charles Boyer; and *Cry Havoc* (1943, Richard Thorpe, director). Of these, *The Shop Around the Corner* has become a classic Lubitsch film—a Broadway musical, *She Loves Me*, was based on it—and *Three Comrades*, *The Mortal Storm*, and *Cry Havoc* are all regarded as films from the World War II period that had lasting worth.

In December 1943, following her usual pattern, Sullavan returned to Broadway to star in John Van Druten's three-character play *The Voice of the Turtle*, which became one of Broadway's longest-running comedies. True to form, Sullavan's work elicited the highest praise. Howard Barnes, critic for the New York *Herald Tribune*, described her as "impeccably right . . . little short of magnificent." He continued, "She reads her lines and plays her business so aptly that there is no questioning the fact that one is witnessing the finest actress of our day in the theatre" (*New York Herald Tribune*, December 9, 1943). Sullavan was awarded the *Variety* Drama Award in 1944 as best actress for her role as Sally Middleton. The producer, Alfred de Liagre, hoped to duplicate the New York success of *The Voice of the Turtle* in London, and so in 1947 Margaret Sullavan opened in Manchester and played a run in London, leaving her family behind for six months. The separation was a critical one, and upon her return, she separated from and then divorced Leland Hayward.

For a brief period, personal problems seemed overwhelming. She was troubled about her own ambivalence: she wanted to be both a wife/mother and a leading actress; she began to be troubled by deafness and eventually had a delicate but successful operation. Then in 1950, with the full approval of her children, she married her fourth husband, Kenneth Wagg, an English executive in the Horlick's Malted Milk Company. He was a widower with four sons, and he was completely devoted to Margaret Sullavan. In 1950, Sullavan also made her last film, *No Sad Songs for Me* (Rudolph Mate, director), which was regarded as a "brave" film about a woman dying from cancer.

Sullavan had transplanted her family to Connecticut in 1945 to escape what she felt were insidious Hollywood influences, and in 1952 she decided to return to the stage in Terence Rattigan's play *The Deep Blue Sea*. The next year, 1953, she dazzled Broadway audiences (although she was now forty-four) by playing once again the archetypal Sullavan ingénue in the comedy *Sabrina Fair*, with Joseph Cotton, Scott McKay, and Catherine Nesbitt. Again, the old Sullavan magic worked. But in 1955, two of her children, now teen-agers, chose to live with their father, Leland Heyward; only Brooke remained with her mother. Sullavan was devastated. Although she had signed to appear in Carolyn Green's play *Janus* on Broadway with Robert Preston and Claude Dauphin, she left the show and was replaced by Claudette Colbert. In September of that year she undertook a live television show for CBS, *The Pilot*, but the dress rehearsal was a shambles, and Sullavan mysteriously disappeared; the show was canceled. Because of depression, she spent two and a half months at the Austen Riggs Foundation in Stockbridge, Massachusetts, trying to regain her health, which she did sufficiently to revive *Sabrina Fair* with Joseph Cotton under the auspices of Harold Kennedy at the Grist Mill Theatre, Andover, New Jersey, in the summer of 1958. In 1959 she called the *New York Times* to tell the drama editor of a wonderful new play she had found called *Sweet Love Remembered* by Ruth Goetz, which she felt would mark her return to the Broadway theatre. In December 1959 *Sweet Love Remembered* opened its tryout at the Shubert Theatre in New Haven, Connecticut; the reviews called Sullavan eloquent but had reservations about the play itself. There were rumors that Kenneth Wagg was trying to buy her out of the play. On New Year's Day 1960, Sullavan was found dying in her room at the Hotel Taft, apparently from an overdose of sleeping pills. A memorial service was held for her later in Greenwich, Connecticut; her body was cremated, and her ashes were interred near her parents at St. Mary's White Chapel, in Lively, Lancaster County, Virginia. Ten months later her daughter, Bridget, took her own life.

Margaret Sullavan's acting was intuitively right in every role she played. She invariably appeared to be carefully listening to or observing the people with whom she appeared, and much of her acting consisted of her reactions to what was being said or done. Her films stand up remarkably well even today because everything she said or did as an actress seemed right and natural. Along with Bette Davis and Olivia de Havilland, Sullavan insisted that women in films should be presented as intelligent individuals, not as cowering simpletons or as sex objects. One could wish that Sullavan had played some of the great roles, but she herself often proclaimed that she was really no pillar of the theatre. She read twice for the role of Blanche DuBois in Tennessee Williams's *A Streetcar Named Desire*, but twice Williams turned her down. Yet every film or play she was in owed much of its success to her acting; her fierce, proud intelligence and good humor informed every role she played, and she continues to hold a leading place in United States film and stage history.

The best source of information about Margaret Sullavan is *Haywire* by Brooke Hayward (1977). Reviews of her plays may be found in *The New York Times Directory of the*

Theater (1973). Reviews of special interest are found in the *New York Post* (May 21, 1931) and the *Herald Tribune* (December 9, 1943). Sullavan's obituary appeared in the *New York Times* (January 2, 1960). Margaret Sullavan is listed in *Current Biography, 1944* (1945); *Who's Who in the Theatre* (1957); *Who Was Who in America*, Vol. III, 1951–1960 (1966); *Who Was Who in the Theatre*, Vol. IV (1978); *The Oxford Companion to the Theatre* (1983); and *The Oxford Companion to American Theatre* (1984).

Roger Kenvin

——— T ———

TAMIRIS, Helen (April 24, 1902?–August 4, 1966): dancer and choreographer, was born Helen Becker in New York City. She was the only daughter and the youngest of five children of Isor and Rose (Simoneff or Simonov) Becker, who were Russian Jewish emigrants. Her father worked as a tailor. Early in her dance career, she adopted her stage name from a poem about an ancient Persian queen: ''Thou are Tamiris, the ruthless queen who banishes all obstacles.''

A vital force in the development of modern dance in America, Tamiris was one of the few major dancer-choreographers of her time who did not receive her initial training at the Denishawn School. She began her dance training with Irene Lewisohn at the Henry Street Settlement in New York City, where she studied creative dance. She later studied modern dance with followers of Isadora Duncan and ballet with Michel Fokine and Rosina Gill of the Metropolitan Opera Ballet School.

During the summer of 1923, Tamiris toured South America. Returning to the United States she began appearing in nightclubs and revues. In 1924 she appeared in the *Music Box Revue of 1924* in New York with Fanny Brice and Bobby Clark. However, in 1927 she decided to leave her career in musical revues for the concert stage, and she produced her first solo program on October 9, 1927, at the Little Theatre in New York. In her second solo concert on January 29, 1928, she danced to two Negro spirituals. Later her dances for spirituals became her most famous works.

In 1928 Tamiris traveled to Europe, dancing in Paris, at the Salzburg Festival in Austria, and finally in Berlin in 1929. Later that same year, Tamiris founded her own school in New York. As the director of the School of the American Dance, she was able to use its facilities to explore and develop her own unique movement vocabulary.

From 1930 until 1939 Tamiris was active in the development of the new art form called modern dance. With **Martha Graham**, Doris Humphrey, and Charles Weidman she formed the Dance Repertory Theatre. The organization lasted two seasons (1930 and 1931). When the Federal Theatre Project was founded in 1935, Tamiris organized the Dance Association and convinced **Hallie Flanagan**, the project's director, that dancers should be recognized as a separate group. Through the Dance Project, Tamiris brought modern dance with social themes to a wide audience. Among her dances were *How Long, Brethren?* (1937), based on seven Negro songs of protest, and *Adelante* (1939) whose theme is the Spanish civil war.

In 1937 Tamiris's Dance Association merged with two other dance groups to form the American Dance Association (ADA), with Tamiris becoming its first president. In that same year, she received the first *Dancemagazine* award for her group choreography *How Long, Brethren?''*

During the Second World War, Tamiris choreographed dances dealing with wartime problems, such as black marketeering. A strong Franklin Delano Roosevelt supporter, Tamiris choreographed a pro-Roosevelt revue for his 1944 presidential campaign. After the war Tamiris expanded her involvement in the theatre and became a motivating force for change in musical comedy, as did other ballet and modern choreographers such as **Agnes de Mille**, **Hanya Holm**, Jerome Robbins, and Michael Kidd. She felt that it was the responsibility of a choreographer to enhance and further the story line of a musical production and to make dance an integral part of the show.

Helen Tamiris first achieved recognition and success on Broadway in 1945 with her choreography for *Up in Central Park*. Especially commended was the effect of a Currier and Ives print that she achieved in the ice-skating sequence. *Up in Central Park* ran for over five hundred performances in New York, was made into a film in 1945, and then toured nationally during 1946 and 1947. In 1946 Tamiris choreographed two successful Broadway musicals—a revival of *Showboat* and *Annie Get Your Gun* the latter starring **Ethel Merman**. In 1949 she won the **Antoinette Perry** (Tony) Award for the best choreography of the season for *Touch and Go*. In 1954 she choreographed *Fanny* and in 1955 *Plain and Fancy*.

In 1960 Helen Tamiris and her husband, Daniel Nagrin, also a dancer, founded the Tamiris-Nagrin Dance Company. Tamiris was the primary choreographer, and Nagrin was a leading dancer of the company. The company disbanded when Tamiris and Nagrin separated.

Tamiris's last work as a choreographer was *The Lady from Colorado*, presented in 1964 by the Central City (Colorado) Opera Association. In 1963 Tamiris was artist-in-residence at Indiana University, Bloomington. Later that same year she entered the Jewish Memorial Hospital in New York City, suffering from cancer. She died there in August of 1966. In her will she left one-third of her estate for the advancement of American modern dance, and the Tamiris Foundation was established to continue her contributions to dance in America.

As a choreographer Tamiris felt that dance should deal with contemporary concerns. Some of her pieces exemplifying this philosophy include *Women's Song*, concerning the emotions of womanhood, *How Long, Brethren?* dealing with equal rights, and *Memoirs*, contrasting tempestuous slum life with a serene Jewish family Sabbath. Some of her other pieces are *The Individual and the Mass*, *Negro Spirituals*, *Dance of War*, *Walt Whitman Suite*, and *Liberty Song*. These pieces were direct statements of her radical beliefs in social reform. Her advocacy of such social improvements through novel dance forms added much to the American theatre.

Biographical information on Helen Tamiris can be found in *Dancemagazine* (May 1961). An overview of her career is briefly covered in *Dancemagazine* (May 1965). Information concerning her repertoire of pieces may be found in *Dancemagazine* (January 1961, January 1962, and June 1967). Her contributions to musical comedy dance forms is discussed in *Theatre Arts* (November 1960). *Dancemagazine* (May 1965) gives details concerning her views on theatre dance. A review of the film *Negro Spirituals* appears in *Dancemagazine* (April 1959). The most complete study of Tamiris is Christena L. Schlundt, *Tamiris, A Chronicle of Her Dance Career, 1927–1955* (1972). Tamiris is discussed in John Martin, *America Dancing* (1968); Joseph Mazo, *Prime Movers: The Makers of Modern Dance in America* (1977); Don McDonagh, *The Complete Guide to Modern Dance* (1976); and Walter Terry, *The Dance in America* (1971). See also John Martin, "The Dance: Tamiris," the *New York Times* (December 1, 1946). The Tamiris scrapbooks and all of her papers are in the Dance Collection in the New York Public Library Performing Arts Research Center at Lincoln Center. Some printed sources give 1905 as her birthdate; however, Daniel Nagrin says that she was born in 1902. Tamiris is listed in *The Biographical Encyclopaedia and Who's Who of the American Theatre* (1966); *Who Was Who in the Theatre*, Vol. IV (1978); *Notable American Women*, Vol. IV: *The Modern Period* (1980); and *Biographical Dictionary of Dance* (1982).

Deborah Nadell

TANDY, Jessica (June 7, 1909–): actress, was born Jessie Alice Tandy in Upper Clapton, London, the youngest of three children of Harry Tandy, a commercial traveler for a rope-manufacturing firm, and Jessie Helen (Horspool) Tandy, headmistress of a school for retarded children. Her father died when she was twelve, and her mother subsequently took additional employment doing clerical work and teaching evening classes for adults. The family lived in a six-room house in the shabby northeast London district of Hackney, while Mrs. Tandy struggled to provide for the education of her children, instilling in all of them an interest in literature, art, and the theatre. Home theatricals and trips to museums were popular family pastimes, and money was carefully saved for visits to plays and pantomimes.

The two Tandy boys, Arthur Harry ("Michael") and Edward James ("Tully"), were both to win scholarships to Oxford, but childhood bouts with tuberculosis forced their sister to miss school frequently, making higher education and a teaching career seem unrealistic goals for her. Fortunately, she had an alternative. At the age of thirteen she had begun to accompany her mother to night school, enrolling in adult courses in Shakespeare, poetry, dancing, and calisthenics to avoid being left alone at home while Mrs. Tandy taught. She continued the Shakespeare classes for two years, and with her mother's encouragement, she began working on Saturdays with a private drama coach. At age fifteen she enrolled full-time at London's Ben Greet Academy of Acting, where instructor Lillian E. Simpson was to be a powerful influence in guiding Tandy's emerging talent.

Upon completing her studies three years later, Tandy began professional work immediately, making her debut at age eighteen on November 22, 1927, in *The Manderson Girls* at Playroom Six in Soho. The next season she joined the Birmingham Repertory Company, appearing in *Alice Sit-by-the-Fire* and *The Comedy of Good and Evil*. These were followed by a tour in *Yellow Sands* and, at the Court Theatre on February 21, 1929, a West End debut as Lena Jackson in *The Rumour*.

She now worked steadily, playing a wide variety of roles. Within the next year she had been seen as The Typist in *The Theatre of Life*, Maggie in *Water*, and Aude in *The Unknown Warrior*. She first appeared in New York at the Longacre Theatre, on March 18, 1930, as Toni Rakonitz in *The Matriarch*. The following summer she played her first Shakespearean role, appearing with the Oxford University Dramatic Society as Olivia in *Twelfth Night*. She then returned briefly to Broadway, as Cynthia Perry in *The Last Enemy*. In the next two years she appeared in six London productions, notable among them being *Autumn Crocus*, in which she enjoyed her first extended West End run. In 1931 she played her first film role in the British production of *The Indiscretions of Eve* (released the next year). In the spring of 1932 she joined the Cambridge Festival Theatre for a repertory season of classic and contemporary plays. She appeared in *Troilus and Cressida*, *See Naples and Die*, *The Witch*, *Rose Without a Thorn*, *The Inspector General*, and *The Servant of Two Masters* before returning to the West End as Carlotta in *Mutual Benefit*. On October 7, 1932, she appeared at the Duchess Theatre as Manuela in *Children in Uniform*; it was this performance that firmly established her reputation as a distinguished young actress. In that same year she was married to the actor Jack Hawkins. Their daughter Susan was born in 1934.

Now began a period of distinguished work on the British stage, with Tandy balancing performances in over a dozen popular West End plays with an increasing number of appearances in classical roles. In 1933 she followed her appearances in *Lady Audley's Secret* and *Midsummer Fires* with a performance as Titania in *A Midsummer Night's Dream* at the Open Air Theatre in Regents Park, London. Subsequent Shakespearean roles included Viola in *Twelfth Night* and Anne Page in *The Merry Wives of Windsor* in 1934 at the Hippodrome in Manchester, England. In November of that year she was an acclaimed Ophelia to John Gielgud's Hamlet at the New Theatre in the West End, London. Other West End performances followed; then in 1937 she joined the Old Vic company in London, playing both Viola and Sebastian in *Twelfth Night* and a memorable

Katharine to Laurence Olivier's Henry V, both productions staged by Tyrone Guthrie. The following year she made her American film debut in *Murder in the Family*.

Tandy appeared again on Broadway in 1938 as Kay in J.B. Priestley's *Time and the Conways*, following this with the West End production of *Glorious Morning*. In 1939 she enjoyed a modest success as Nora in *The White Steed*. She then returned to the Regents Park Open Air Theatre for another Viola, after which she joined a repertory company tour of Canada. She played again in New York in January of 1940 in the short-lived *Geneva* and then returned in the spring to the Old Vic, appearing as Cordelia to Gielgud's Lear under the direction of Harley Granville-Barker and as Miranda in *The Tempest*.

In September of 1940 Tandy again traveled to New York, accompanied by her six-year-old daughter, to appear in A. J. Cronin's *Jupiter Laughs*. With her now estranged husband serving in the wartime British army, she decided to stay in the United States and attempt to establish a full-time career in New York and Hollywood. She would become a naturalized American citizen in 1954. It was in the early 1940s that she met Canadian-born actor Hume Cronyn, who became her second husband after both had settled in Hollywood in 1942.

In several years on the West Coast, Cronyn worked with some frequency as a character actor and occasional screenwriter, while Tandy, under contract with Twentieth Century-Fox, found few opportunities. "On loan" to MGM, she appeared with her husband and Spencer Tracy in *The Seventh Cross* and played supporting roles in *The Valley of Decision* and *The Green Years*. Under her Twentieth Century-Fox contract she played in *Dragonwyck* and *Forever Amber* and, a few years later, in *The Desert Fox*. A leading role finally came with *A Woman's Vengeance*, released by Universal-International in 1947.

After five years of relative inactivity in minor film roles, Tandy was hungry for work. In the summer of 1946 Cronyn, who held under option several early works by Tennessee Williams, directed his wife in a Los Angeles Actor's Laboratory Theatre production of the playwright's one-act play *Portrait of a Madonna*. Tandy's performance received widespread acclaim and standing ovations from Hollywood audiences. This success did not change her status in the cinema, but it led directly to her being cast as Blanche DuBois in the 1947 Broadway production of Williams's *A Streetcar Named Desire*, a performance that resurrected her career and established her as a preeminent actress of the American stage. Brooks Atkinson, writing in the *New York Times*, described her work as "one of the most perfect marriages of acting and playwriting" (*New York Times*, December 4, 1947). The play was awarded the Pulitzer Prize and the New York Drama Critics Circle award, and Tandy received her first **Antoinette Perry** (Tony) Award and the Twelfth Night Club Award. Ironically, despite a performance unanimously acknowledged by critics as the vital component of the play's success, she was not asked to repeat her role in the subsequent *Streetcar* film, in which her Broadway colleagues Marlon Brando, **Kim Hunter**, and Karl Malden performed under the play's original director, Elia Kazan.

She concentrated now on the theatre, working frequently with her husband. Their joint appearance in Jan de Hartog's two-character play *The Fourposter* in 1951 established them firmly in the public mind as a performing duo. Their subtle teamwork and beautifully complementary styles in this series of vignettes recounting thirty-five years of a marriage earned high praise, with Tandy and Cronyn sharing a Commoedia Matinee Club Bronze Medallion for their performances. Following the New York run at the Ethel Barrymore Theatre, the Cronyns toured the play extensively.

Despite their subsequent popularity as a theatrical team, however, Tandy and Cronyn continued to appear separately. They have also contributed, throughout their individual and joint careers, to the early stages of several major theatrical movements. The developing Off-Broadway theatre, for example, gained immeasurable stature when Tandy and Cronyn joined the new Phoenix Theatre in 1953 for its opening production of Sidney Howard's *Madam, Will You Walk*. In a similar spirit, they repeated their performances in *The Fourposter* at reduced salaries for the New York City Center's popularly priced revival series in 1955. In 1961 Tandy joined the American Shakespeare Festival to play Lady Macbeth in repertory with Cassandra in *Troilus and Cressida*. The couple's most significant and far-reaching contribution may well have been their decision in 1963 to join Tyrone Guthrie's Minnesota Theatre Company in Minneapolis for its initial season, in which Tandy appeared as Gertrude in *Hamlet*, Olga in *The Three Sisters*, and Linda in *Death of a Salesman*. They were the first major American stars to join a regional theatre on a full-time basis, and Guthrie's pioneering effort to establish an American regional theatre gained impetus and legitimacy through their presence. They returned to the Guthrie Theatre in 1965, when Tandy appeared as Ranyevskaya in *The Cherry Orchard*, Lady Wishfort in *The Way of the World*, and the Mother-in-Law in *The Caucasian Chalk Circle*. During the summer of 1982 she played there in a pre-Broadway trial of *Foxfire*.

In other regional theatre work the couple joined the Center Theatre Group at the Mark Taper Forum in Los Angeles for a 1968 version of Molière's *The Miser*, based on a production in which Cronyn had first appeared in Minneapolis. The following summer Tandy joined the Shaw Festival at Niagara-on-the-Lake in Canada, playing Hesione Hushabye in *Heartbreak House*. Tandy also joined New York's struggling Repertory Theatre of Lincoln Center in 1970 to play Marguerite Gautier in Tennessee Williams's *Camino Real* and returned to Lincoln Center with her husband for a Samuel Beckett Festival directed by Alan Schneider in 1972, appearing in *Happy Days* and in *Not I*. She received the Drama Desk Award for both plays and a *Village Voice* Off-Broadway (Obie) Award for *Not I*, with which she subsequently toured. For Ontario's Stratford Shakespeare Festival, under the direction of Robin Phillips, Tandy appeared as Titania to Cronyn's Bottom in *A Midsummer Night's Dream*, as Lady Wishfort in *The Way of the World*, and in the première of *Eve*. She attracted major critical attention to Phillips's subsequent repertory attempt at the Theatre London in Ontario, where she gave a shattering performance as Mary Tyrone in Eugene O'Neill's *Long Day's Journey into Night*, a role she later repeated at Stratford.

On the Broadway stage the Cronyns followed *The Fourposter* with several joint efforts, including *The Honeys* and *A Day by the Sea* in 1955, *The Man in the Dog Suit* in 1958, and the 1959 *Triple Play* (a bill of one-acts, in which Tandy repeated her *Portrait of a Madonna* performance together with roles in two short plays by Sean O'Casey). In December of 1959 Tandy appeared at the Music Box Theatre under John Gielgud's direction in Peter Shaffer's *Five Finger Exercise*, winning critical praise and the Delia Austrian Medal of the New York Drama League for her performance as Louise Harrington, a role in which she subsequently toured. This was followed by two productions with Cronyn, including *Big Fish, Little Fish*, in which she joined him in a supporting role when the 1962 New York production moved to the Duke of York's Theatre in London, and Friedrich Durrenmatt's critically esteemed but unsuccessful *The Physicists* at New York's Martin Beck Theatre in 1964. On September 12, 1966, the couple returned to the Martin Beck as Agnes and Tobias in Edward Albee's *A Delicate Balance*. The much-praised production, directed by Alan Schneider, won a Pulitzer Prize for its author and a Leland Powers Honor Award for Tandy. Both Cronyn and Tandy stayed with the play for its tour.

In January 1971 Tandy joined the Broadway cast of David Storey's *Home*, a production imported from London's Royal Court Theatre, and in it she was reunited with old friends John Gielgud and Ralph Richardson. Later that same season she and Cronyn appeared under Gielgud's direction in another Albee play, *All Over*, which closed after forty-two performances at the Morosco Theatre despite excellent reviews for its cast. The couple next played together in *Promenade All*, on tour and in New York, then opened at New York's Ethel Barrymore Theatre in a popular production of *Noel Coward in Two Keys*, two Coward one-acts in which both played pairs of beautifully contrasted roles as different occupants of the same hotel suite. The Broadway performances were followed once more by a successful tour.

In 1977 Cronyn was shown a script of D. L. Coburn's *The Gin Game*, originally produced by the Actors Theatre of Louisville in Kentucky. The two-character play was its author's first produced work, but Cronyn did not hesitate to option the script. With Mike Nichols directing, *The Gin Game* opened at the John Golden Theatre on October 6, 1977, with only Tandy and Cronyn on stage as two lonely inmates of a nursing home. The production was to be one of the high points of both their careers; their performance was described by Jack Kroll of *Newsweek* (October 17, 1977) as "professionalism raised to the level of incandescence." For her work in *The Gin Game* Tandy received her second Tony Award, another Drama Desk Award, and on the subsequent tour, the Los Angeles Drama Critics Circle Award and the Chicago Sarah Siddons Award. Playwright Coburn was awarded the 1978 Pulitzer Prize. The Cronyns also toured with the play to Moscow, Leningrad, and London. A videotape of the play, recorded during actual performances in London, was later broadcast on American public television to widespread acclaim.

In 1981 Tandy accepted a supporting role in Andrew Davies' play *Rose*, which had been brought to New York from London as a starring vehicle for Glenda Jackson. The play was not a success, but Tandy's performance, limited to two scenes in the production, received enthusiastic critical attention and brought her a Tony nomination as best actress in a supporting role. In 1982 the Cronyns appeared together again, in the gentle and spirit-affirming *Foxfire*, written by Susan Cooper and Hume Cronyn and inspired by the *Foxfire Books* series, anthologies of anecdotes and interviews collected by high school teacher Elliot Wigginton and his students in southern Appalachia. The play had received trial productions at the Stratford Festival in Ontario and the Guthrie Theatre in Minneapolis before opening at the Ethel Barrymore Theatre on November 11, 1982. Critical response to the play was mostly favorable, if not unanimously enthusiastic, but Tandy's performance as elderly mountain woman Annie Nations, confronting a changing world while simultaneously reassessing her own past, was hailed as a consummate achievement. "Everything this actress does is so pure and right that only poets, not theatre critics, should be allowed to write about her," stated Frank Rich in the *New York Times* (November 12, 1982). The performance earned Tandy another Drama Desk Award and another Outer Circle Critics Award. In addition, she received her third Tony Award at a nationally broadcast ceremony, which included a memorable standing ovation from her colleagues.

That same season brought the death of Tennessee Williams. At the playwright's memorial service in New York the most moving moment for many in the audience was Tandy's stepping to the front of the stage, pushing aside the waiting microphone, and transforming herself again into Blanche DuBois to perform a monologue from *A Streetcar Named Desire*, thirty-four years after her initial appearance in the play. The next year she played Amanda Wingfield in a Broadway revival of Williams's *The Glass Menagerie*. The production was generally greeted as a flawed effort, but her performance was critically esteemed.

Tandy's recent appearances have included performances in Louise Page's *Salonika* at New York's Public Theatre, and in a 1985 revival of *Foxfire*, again opposite Cronyn, at the Ahmanson Theatre in Los Angeles and in a televised version in 1987. Tandy and Cronyn have also toured widely in concert readings, notably in *Face to Face* in 1954 and *The Many Faces of Love* twenty years later. In 1965 they were invited by President and Mrs. Lyndon B. Johnson to perform at the White House in their program *Hear America Speaking*, later returning to appear in recital before President and Mrs. Gerald Ford. In 1986 Tandy and Cronyn again appeared together in a two-person play, *The Petition*, by Brian Clark, at the Golden Theatre for which Tandy received a Tony award nomination for best actress of the season.

Tandy has continued to work in films, appearing, in addition to those already mentioned, in *September Affair* (1950), *The Light in the Forest* (1958), *Adven-*

tures of a Young Man (1962), *The Birds* (1963), and the acclaimed *Butley* (1972). In recent years she has begun to appear on the screen with greater frequency. After 1981's *Honky Tonk Freeway*, David Denby wrote "Jessica Tandy, eyes glittering with the love of performing after more than 50 years in show business, steals the movie in a small role as an alcoholic lady driving to a retirement home with her husband (Hume Cronyn, of course)" (*New York*, September 7, 1981). Other recent films include the three 1982 releases *Still of the Night*, *Best Friends*, and *The World According to Garp* (in which she again appears with Cronyn). She was highly praised for her work in *The Bostonians* (1984), and she and Cronyn enjoyed critical and popular success in *Cocoon* (1985) and in *Batteries Not Included* (1987).

Tandy first appeared on television in England in 1939. She performed with Cronyn on NBC radio and television in their series *The Marriage* for two years, beginning in 1953, and has continued to appear occasionally. She has done recorded versions of her stage performances in *The Cherry Orchard* and *Heartbreak House* and has participated in studio productions of *The Glass Menagerie*, *Coriolanus*, and, with Cronyn, *The Wind in the Willows*.

The Cronyns have a son, Christopher, and a daughter, Tandy, who have forged their own careers as a film production manager and an actress, respectively. The couple has had several homes. Most recently, after a period of residence at New York's Wyndham Hotel, they moved to a house in Connecticut.

Tandy and Cronyn were both inducted into the Theatre Hall of Fame in 1979. Other honors have included a Brandeis University Creative Arts Award, an Honorary L.L.D. from the University of Western Ontario, and an Honorary L.H.D. from Fordham University. Tandy was named a recipient of the 1986 annual award by the John F. Kennedy Center for the Performing Arts for "artistic achievement as a performer."

Reviews of Jessica Tandy's performances are too numerous to list. Those quoted are identified in the text. The following articles are also of particular interest: Dan Sullivan, "The Actors's Art: Jessica Tandy," *Los Angeles Times "Calendar"* (March 25, 1984); John Simon and Rhoda Koenig, "Theatre: Jessica Tandy," *New York* (September 19, 1983); Chris Chase, "Tandy and Cronyn are Wed to the Theatre, Too," *New York Times* (March 24, 1974); Chris Chase, "Jessica Tandy Shuttles from Stage to Screen," *New York Times* (April 10, 1981); Timothy White, "Theatre's First Couple," *New York Times Magazine* (December 26, 1982); Leota Diesel, "Round-the-Clock with the Cronyns," *Theatre Arts* (February 1952); and Michael Kernan, "Jessica Tandy, Between the Lines," the *Washington Post* (December 23, 1982). An interview with Tandy and Cronyn is included in Alfred Rossi's book on Tyrone Guthrie, *Astonish Us in the Morning* (London, 1977). Jessica Tandy is listed in *The Biographical Encyclopaedia and Who's Who of the American Theatre* (1966); Normal Olin Ireland, *Index of Women of the World from Ancient to Modern Times: Biographies and Portraits* (1970); *Celebrity Register* (1973); *A Concise Encyclopedia of the Theatre* (1974); Leslie Halliwell, *The Filmgoer's Companion* (1974); *Notable Names in the American Theatre* (1976); *International Motion Picture Almanac* (1977); *Who's Who in the Theatre* (1981); *Current Biography, 1984* (1984, 1985); *The*

Oxford Companion to American Theatre (1984); and *Contemporary Theatre, Film, and Television*, Vol. I (1984).

David Hammond

TANGUAY, Eva (August 1, 1878–January 11, 1947): the "I Don't Care" girl, vaudeville and musical comedy entertainer, was born in Marbleton, Quebec, the daughter of Octave and Adele (Pajean) Tanguay. Before she was six, the family moved to Holyoke, Massachusetts, where her father died shortly thereafter. The early career of this popular performer is not well documented. Tanguay was a child actress, dancer, and singer who made her professional debut at about the age of eight in the role of Cedric Errol in *Little Lord Fauntleroy*, which toured for five years. She first attracted the attention of the New York public in 1898 with her appearance in *In Gotham*, a burlesque of *Rip Van Winkle*. For the next three decades, Eva Tanguay would be a familiar presence on the musical-comedy stage and a reigning favorite of the vaudeville circuit. She sang some show-stopping numbers on Broadway, and many of her songs from there went with her on her record-breaking vaudeville tours.

In 1901 she made a brief appearance in *My Lady*, a burlesque of *The Three Musketeers*. In 1902 she received favorable mention for her role as Claire de Lune in *The Office Boy*, which starred Frank Daniels. It was Tanguay's third major production, *The Chaperons* by Witmark, and the show's hit song, "My Sambo," that made her a star. Reviews of her early performances in these roles referred to Tanguay as "an eccentric but lively actress" (*Buffalo Evening News*, September 15, 1903), whose dancing, "while it does not at any time suggest the poetry of motion, has a quality of abandon that many people like just as much" (*New York Times*, March 11, 1903).

In 1904 Tanguay scored another hit as Carlotta Dashington, an American singer in Paris, in *The Sambo Girl*. One of its songs, "I Don't Care," became a best-selling "single" of 1905 and subsequently Tanguay's trademark. Other favorites from the show, such as "The Banjo Serenade," and "The Love Song," were sold as sheet music with Tanguay's picture and endorsement. One of the show's most memorable moments came during a drinking song in which Tanguay "soaked her hair with champagne and probably ruined her dress" (*Boston Transcript*, September 5, 1905). She was encored for every song and cited by the critics as a "vivacious soubrette" of "irresistible mirth" (*Boston Transcript*, September 5, 1905), who "sparkled and danced and made a noise like singing" (*New York Times*, October 16, 1905).

Tanguay continued for the next decade to alternate her appearances in musical-comedy productions with vaudeville performances, on tour and in New York. She toured in *A Good Fellow* (1906), *The Sun-Dodgers* (1912), and *Miss Tabasco* (1914). She also starred in the *Follies of 1909* and was distinguished by being the only performer ever to have her name advertised in letters as large as those of the show's title. Another Broadway success for Tanguay came in 1916 with *The Girl Who Smiles*. She played Phonette Duttier, a cook who joins a group of Bohemians. Tanguay's lavish and daring costumes brought gasps and applause from the audience, and her songs "T-A-N-G-U-A-Y" and "I'm Here to Stay" called forth numerous encores.

As a vaudeville headliner, Tanguay was noted for her contribution to the 1908 craze of the Salomé dance, as she "really busted things wide open for Salomé dancers when she discarded all seven veils" (Laurie, p. 41). Of all the single-woman acts of vaudeville, none involved greater costume expenditure, nor did any exceed Tanguay's act in popularity and controversy. She was well known for her publicity stunts, which included selling newspapers on street corners with a trained elephant, and, when Lincoln pennies were new, wearing a mail suit of them in her act, and throwing twelve hundred a day to her audiences. A temperamental star, she elicited both shock and affection from audiences. She was "good newspaper copy, always doing something to pump blood into the box office" (Laurie, p. 58). Acknowledged as being full of the "true spirit of vaudeville," Tanguay had, like most of her contemporaries, risen to the top through persistence, personality, and performances that depended less on her actual talent than on her forceful and winning presence. Her various vaudeville billings illustrate this emphasis on her personality: "The Girl Who Made Vaudeville Famous," "Cyclonic Eva Tanguay," "Mother Eve's Merriest Daughter," "The Genius of Mirth and Song," "America's Champion Comedienne," "Our Own Eva," "America's Idol," "The Girl the Whole World Loves," "Vaudeville's Greatest Drawing Card," and "The One Best Bet." At the height of her career in 1910 Tanguay was the highest paid star of the day. She made as much as $3,500 a week, said to be a sum more than even President William Howard Taft was paid.

Tanguay's vaudeville and musical-comedy performances included a variety of musical styles, and the songs written for her reflect both novelty and sentiment as the two most popular modes. The best sellers included "Eva Tanguay's Love Song," from Sambo Girl, noted for its eight encores nightly (1904); the ten-verse hit "I Don't Care" (1905); "I Can't Help It If I'm Fidgety" (1908); "Nothing Bothers Me" (1908); "The Tanguay Rag" (1910); "I'd Like to Be an Animal in the Zoo" (1910); "M-O-T-H-E-R" (1915); "If You Had All the World and Its Gold" (1916); and "Give an Imitation of Me" (1910).

With Mae West, herself a great admirer of Tanguay, the "I Don't Care" girl was indeed the most imitated star of the day. Her frizzy hair, energetic movements, piercing voice, and form-fitting outfits of spangles, lace, and feathers were favorite objects of parody by other vaudeville acts. But no one could imitate her boundless energy. A pedometer once showed that she had covered over three miles in the course of her act.

Well known as a tough, assured, carefree, and egotistical lady, Tanguay delighted her consistently packed houses. Her shouting, shrieking, and strutting were popular, though neither polished nor graceful. However, she was the favorite of Variety and the occasional darling of the Dramatic Mirror. The fact that Tanguay was an unexceptional performer with immense popularity puzzled her critics. Outraged by her tasteless singing and miming of the "Marseillaise" in 1918, the *Tribune* named her the "parsnip of performers." Despite "no voice, no artistry, no deftness," critics did acknowledge that her one talent was the greatest of all—that "from the moment she bounced upon the stage, the audience was hers" (*New York Herald-Tribune*, January 12, 1947).

Though a vital presence on the stage, Tanguay's off-stage life was plagued by marital instability as well as monetary and health problems. In 1913 she married John Ford but divorced the future film director three years later. She married her pianist Alexander Booke (or Allan Parado) in 1927 but quickly divorced him a few months later when she was disappointed to learn that his real name was Chandos Ksiazkewacz. In the financial crash of 1929 Tanguay lost over two million dollars in real estate and stock. Tanguay's health also was on an irreversible decline, beginning in 1908 with a nervous breakdown and illness. In 1925, after over twenty-five years as a headlining performer, she developed cataracts, and, unknown to her audiences, she had to be led by hand from her dressing room to the stage wings before her entrances. Later, her physical difficulties were compounded by heart problems, Bright's disease, and arthritis. Tanguay spent the last years of her life in near seclusion in Hollywood, supported by the charity of old vaudevillians and an occasional benefit performance. She died at the age of sixty-eight, nearly blind, and confined to her bed. She was buried at the Hollywood Mausoleum.

As the "I Don't Care" star Eva Tanguay had brought a new spirit to the early twentieth-century American theatre—a refreshing, aggressive one that captured the hearts of audiences and exemplified the newly found independence of the woman of the age.

The primary sources on Eva Tanguay are the news clippings, articles, photographs, and sheet music in the Theatre Collection of the New York Public Library Performing Arts Research Center at Lincoln Center, the Harvard University Theatre Collection, and the private Frank Lenthall Collection. Of special interest are the reviews in the *New York Dramatic Mirror* (January 27, 1915) and the *Boston Herald* (September 25, 1932). Tanguay is mentioned in Caroline Caffin, *Vaudeville* (1914); Albert F. McLean, Jr., *American Vaudeville as Ritual* (1965); John E. Dimeglio, *Vaudeville U.S.A.* (1973); Gerald Bordman, *American Musical Theatre* (1978); Martin Gottfried, *In Person: The Great Entertainers* (1985); and Linda Martin and Kerry Segrave, *Women in Comedy* (1986). Tanguay's obituary appeared in the *New York Times* (January 12, 1947). Eva Tanguay is listed in *Who's Who in the Theatre* (1922); *Notable American Women*, Vol. III (1971); *Who Was Who in the Theatre*, Vol. IV (1978); and *The Oxford Companion to American Theatre* (1984).

Noreen Barnes

TAYLOR, Laurette Cooney (April 1, 1884–December 7, 1946): actress, was born Loretta Cooney, the daughter of James and Elizabeth (Dorsey) Cooney in Harlem, New York City, when her mother was only sixteen. She was the oldest of three children and the only member of her family to display a talent for acting. The success of her mother's dressmaking business supplemented her father's harness-making endeavors. Loretta Cooney's first public appearances involved declamations of such soul-stirring poetic masterpieces as "The Wreck of the Hesperus," "The Charge of the Light Brigade," and "Curfew Shall Not Ring To-Night." As Roman Catholics for many generations, the members of her family expressed some of the commonly held prejudices against the stage: for her father, the stage was a dreadful thing worthy of eternal damnation; for her grandmother, the stage did not exist. Her mother, however, approved of a theatrical career and encouraged her daughter to participate in the performing arts program at Public School No. 68 in Harlem. There Loretta Cooney did play the piano, sing, dance, and perform impersonations in both black and white face. Many of her teachers also lent support, predicting a platform career for their talented pupil.

From piece-speaking at school and church, she moved on to vaudeville, where she gave imitations of such personalities as Eddie Foy and **Anna Held**. Her initial vaudeville performances in 1896 as "La Belle Laurette" in Lynn and Gloucester, Massachusetts, were not a success. Three years later she joined the vaudeville section of the Boston Athenaeum.

She was still in her teens when on May 1, 1901, she married Charles Alonzo Taylor, who was twenty years her senior and one of the most successful writers and producers of melodrama. During the next six years Laurette Taylor learned every aspect of the stage, from making costumes to managing the box office. The couple had two children, Dwight and Marguerite. In 1901 Taylor acted the soubrette roles in the road company productions of her husband's melodramas *The King of the Opium Ring* and *Child Wife*. She embarked on a long tour from city to city with little time for rest. The couple finally settled in the Pacific Northwest, where Taylor played additional soubrette parts for a melodrama stock company that excelled in such popular plays as *The Queen of the White Slaves* and *Scotty, the King of the Desert Mines*. Eventually she joined the acting troupe at the Seattle Theatre and made her first appearance in "a long dress part" as Marguerite in *Faust*. Over the next two years she performed in almost fifty plays and musical comedies, including *East Lynne*, *Camille*, *Carmen*, *Our Boys*, *Romeo and Juliet*, *Uncle Tom's Cabin*, *Michael Strogoff*, and *She*.

Working nightly performances plus four weekly matinees finally took its toll on Taylor, and she collapsed from overwork and anxiety. She later declared, "The good Lord sent me nervous prostration after two years of it, which compelled a bed for months, and quiet, quiet, and still more quiet" (*The American Magazine*, October 1913, p. 51). When she was well again, she went back to the same company but had difficulty learning lines, so she returned to New York and her family. Further personal and financial problems caused Taylor to separate from her husband in 1907; they were divorced in 1911.

Taylor's first appearance on the New York stage was in *From Rags to Riches* (1903), a popular melodrama that enabled her to tour the cheaper circuits. Alexander Woollcott related that she became the girl "engaged to be rescued nightly from predicaments fraught with peril, and to utter such sentiments as 'Rags are royal raiment when worn for virtue's sake' '' (*Everybody's Magazine*, May 1920, pp. 78–79). This inauspicious beginning in New York was followed by a long list of successes between 1903 and 1910: *The Great John Ganton*, *Alias Jimmy Valentine*, *The Girl in Waiting*, *The Seven Sisters*, and *The Bird of Paradise*. The part of Rose Lane in *Alias Jimmy Valentine* (1910) gave her instant success; the role of the Hawaiian princess Luana in *The Bird of Paradise* (1912) crowned her with fame. It was her next play, however, that was to win the unqualified admiration of Sarah Bernhardt and make Taylor a star in New York and London. On December 21, 1912, John Cort opened his new Broadway theatre with J. Hartley Manners's *Peg o' My Heart*, a play written especially for Laurette Taylor. The little Irish-American waif, Peg, and her scraggly Irish terrier, Michael, immediately won the hearts of their audiences. Of her performance, Walter Prichard Eaton reported that her madcap Peg "is so human, underneath the gay spirits so lonely and homesick; because the laugh is never far from a tear" (*American Magazine*, October 1913, p. 51). The play and the player were applauded for their skillful handling of young love amidst social claptrap. Alexander Woollcott celebrated Laurette Taylor as a first-rate actress, asserting that "any role she plays, . . . at once becomes so colored by her qualities as a person, so defined by her method, and so complicated both by her distinct limitations and her all-conquering charm, that it seems like an invention of her own and begets the ever-recurrent legend that she really does much of the writing herself" (*Everybody's Magazine*, May 1920, p. 79).

Peg o' My Heart ran in New York for over six hundred performances and then traveled to London, where it ran for another five hundred. During the New York run, Taylor and Author J. Hartley Manners had a highly publicized controversy with Oliver Morosco, the producer of *Peg o' My Heart*, because the leading ladies of the road companies playing *Peg o' My Heart* were receiving rave reviews and excellent publicity. Taylor and Manners wanted Morosco not to feature these actresses in any way. In May of 1913 Taylor gave a special 11:00 A.M. performance of *Peg* for Sarah Bernhardt, who formed an audience of one. Bernhardt predicted, "Within five years Laurette Taylor will be the greatest actress on the American stage" (*New York Dramatic Mirror*, December 16, 1916, p. 5).

Before *Peg* had opened on Broadway in 1912, Taylor and J. Hartley Manners were married, thereby officially sealing a partnership that was to last for seventeen years. In his affectionate dedication of *Peg*, he states that he is offering this play to her as a wedding present. *Peg* had established Taylor as a great actress and J. Hartley Manners as one of the most prosperous playwrights of his time. Throughout their marriage he continued to write and produce successful plays in which she starred. From 1916 to 1928, she appeared primarily in his plays. One notable exception was a series of special matinees devoted to scenes from Shakespeare in which she played Juliet, Katharina, and Portia. During this twelve-year period, her many popular roles included Sylvia in *The Harp of Life* (1916), Aunt Annie in *Out There* (1917), Madame L'Enigme in *One Night in*

Rome (1919), Marian Hale in *The National Anthem* (1921), Sarah Kantor in *Humoresque* (1923), Nell Gwynne in *Sweet Nell of Old Drury* (1923), and Rose Trelawney in *Trelawney of the "Wells"* (1925). In praising her husband for teaching her much about acting, she said that he gave her "a sense of the fitness of things, a sense of proportion" (*Everybody's Magazine*, May 1920, p. 79). With townhouses in New York and London and another home in southern France, Taylor and her husband entertained lavishly and made their homes centers for literary and theatrical life. Their good friend Noel Coward was so charmed by their lifestyle that he wrote *Hay Fever* (1925), a play based on the delightful idiosyncrasies of this amusing family.

When in 1927 Hartley Manners became seriously ill and died the following year, the tragedy proved too much for his wife. Taylor sold their house on Riverside Drive as well as their estate in East Hampton, Long Island. She withdrew from the theatre; she avoided friends; she wandered aimlessly; she became an alcoholic. Some five years later, her desire to write finally pulled her out of her depression. Two of her plays were produced (one in Florida, the other in Maine), and her short stories and personal sketches appeared in *Vogue* and *Town and Country*. In 1938, ten years after Hartley Manners' death she once again found a role that challenged her imagination—Mrs. Midget in Sutton Vane's *Outward Bound*. Her sensitive portrayal of the charwoman-mother of a wayward son revealed to a new generation of theatregoers the magical powers of this great actress. Of her performance, Brooks Atkinson wrote that she gave "a glow and a heartbeat to the old charwoman's humility," thus convincing the audience that "God is in His heaven and all's right with the celestial beyond" (*New York Times*, December 23, 1938). This highly praised characterization won her the Barter Award in 1939.

When she premièred as Amanda Wingfield in Tennessee Williams' *The Glass Menagerie* on March 31, 1945, her triumph was complete. As the faded, vain, pathetic Amanda Wingfield, she achieved her greatest acting triumph. That she had come to terms with herself as well as her character may be seen in an interview she gave to Thyra Samter Winslow: "You see, the woman I play is really two parts," explained Taylor. "First she is a shrew. Then she remembers— and you see her as she remembers herself—as a young girl." When asked why she gave Amanda Wingfield bangs, she replied, "Because, alas, I have too good a brow for a brainless woman—and the woman in the play has no brains" (*Stage Pictorial*, Autumn 1945, pp. 48 and 21). In his review of *The Glass Menagerie* for the *New Republic*, Stark Young attempted to define the acting style that contributed to this tour de force performance, "Hers is naturalistic acting of the most profound, spontaneous, unbroken continuity and moving life. There is an inexplicable rightness, moment by moment, phrase by phrase, endlessly varied in the transitions. Technique, which is always composed of skill and instinct working together, is in this case so overlaid with warmth, tenderness, and wit that any analysis is completely baffled" (April 16, 1945). Lewis Nicholas, theatre critic for the *New York Times*, observed, "She plays softly and part of the time seems to be mumbling—a mumble that can be heard at the top of the gallery. Her accents, like the author's phrases, are unexpected; her gestures are vague and fluttery. There is no doubt she was a southern belle; there is no doubt she is a great actress'' (April 2, 1945).

Early in her career Taylor wrote an article for the *Green Book* titled ''The Quality You Need Most,'' which stated her credo for successful acting, ''It isn't beauty or personality or magnetism that make a really great actress. It is imagination'' (April 1914). Thirty-one years later, she showed that her imagination could still enable her to create the role of Amanda Wingfield. With this artistic creation she gave the theatre world one of its greatest performances.

Laurette Taylor died of a coronary thrombosis shortly after leaving the highly successful Broadway run of *The Glass Menagerie*. She had been weakened by a throat ailment that grew gradually worse. She died on December 7, 1946, and was buried in Woodlawn Cemetery, New York City, beside J. Hartley Manners.

The Hoblitzelle Theatre Arts Library at the University of Texas in Austin has an excellent holograph file for Laurette Taylor. Margaret Courtney's *Laurette* (1955) and John Mason Brown's ''The Woman Who Came Back'' in his *Seeing Things* (1946) provide useful biographical information. Laurette Taylor's ''*The Greatest of These* ——'' (1918), ''From Seattle to Broadway: My Experiences in Finding a Good Place on the Stage'' in *The American Stage* (Autumn 1945), and ''The Quality You Need Most'' in *Green Book* (April 1914) give important information about her acting style, stage relationships, and personal life. Her son Dwight Taylor's *Blood-and-Thunder* (1962) discusses the turn-of-the-century melodramas of her first husband, Charles Alonzo Taylor, melodramas in which Laurette Taylor often played the starring role. Notable among the hundreds of articles about Laurette Taylor are Carol Bird, ''A Dressing Room Chat with 'Peg,' '' *Theatre Magazine* (May 1921); Walter Prichard Eaton, ''The Theatre: Carrying on the Torch,'' *The American Magazine* (October 1913); Oliver Morosco, ''Artistic Temperament: Some of Its Manifestations and Some of Its Results,'' *Green Book* (September 1914); Ada Patterson, ''Playing Under Fire,'' *Theatre* (March 1916); and Alexander Woollcott, ''A Partnership of the Theatre,'' *Everybody's Magazine* (May 1920). See also Norris Houghton, ''Laurette Taylor,'' *Theatre Arts* (December 1945). Laurette Taylor's obituary appeared in the *New York Times* (December 8, 1946). Taylor is included in *Current Biography, 1945* (1946); *Who's Who in the Theatre* (1947); *Who Was Who in America*, Vol. II, 1943–1950 (1966); *The Oxford Companion to the Theatre* (1967); *Notable American Women*, Vol. III (1971); *Dictionary of American Biography*, Supplement Four, 1946–1950 (1974); William C. Young, *Famous Actors and Actresses of the American Stage*, Vol. II (1975); *Who Was Who in the Theatre*, Vol. IV (1978); and *The Oxford Companion to American Theatre* (1984).

Colby H. Kullman

TAYMOR, Julie (December 15, 1952–): designer, director, puppeteer, was born in Boston, Massachusetts, the youngest of the three children of gynecologist Melvin Lester Taymor and his wife Elizabeth (Bernstein) Taymor. By the time she graduated from Newton High School in 1970 at the age of sixteen, Julie Taymor had already been involved in theatre for half of her life, and her interest in Eastern culture, which would influence her career, had been formed. She began acting with the Boston Children's Theatre when she was eight, eventually moving on to the young people's division of Julie Portman's Theatre Workshop in Boston, headed by Portman's partner, Barbara Linden. Through the Experiment for International Living program, Taymor traveled at the age of fifteen to India and Sri Lanka, an area of the world to which she would return to study and work.

Sensing a need to discipline her imagination, she enrolled at Jacques Le Coq's École du Mime in Paris. There she trained in movement, masks, and puppetry for a year before entering Oberlin College in Ohio in the fall of 1971. Taymor spent her sophomore year engaging in independent studies in New York City. She took acting classes at the Herbert Berghof Studio and apprenticed with the Chelsea Theatre at the Brooklyn Academy of Music, the Open Theatre, and— with most direct effects on her career—Peter Schumann's Bread and Puppet Theatre. With Schumann she expanded ideas she was forming about the uses of puppets and masks and learned about methods and materials for constructing both.

At Oberlin College, Taymor worked with Kraken, Herbert Blau's professional theatre company. Kraken, also known as the Oberlin Group, experimented with ensemble-created, environmental approaches that Taymor still uses in her work. At this time she was also exposed to Chinese shadow puppetry; and in the summer of 1973 she studied Japanese and Javanese puppetry, dance, and wood carving at the American Society for Eastern Arts in Seattle. The skills and aesthetic principles she absorbed there influenced her first design assignments: puppets and costumes for campus productions. Taymor graduated from Oberlin in 1974 with a major in folklore and mythology.

On a Watson Traveling Fellowship following graduation, Taymor was so taken with Indonesian theatre forms that her visit to the islands turned into a four-year residency, sponsored by the Ford Foundation and the United States Department of State, which appointed her a cultural consultant on Indonesian art. On Bali she organized a multinational theatre company, Teatr Loh, which experimented with eclectic training and performance techniques ranging from Western approaches such as Constantin Stanislavsky's Method, or Jerzy Growtowski's plastiques, improvisation, and mime, to Indonesian dances, masks, and storytelling traditions.

Despite bureaucratic difficulties, language and cultural barriers, malaria, and earthquakes, Taymor and her troupe built two complex imagistic works for masked actors and puppets: *Way of Snow* (1976) and *Tirai* (1978). Both were subsequently produced in New York during the 1980–1981 season, the former at the Ark Theatre, the latter at La Mama Experimental Theatre Club. *Way of Snow*, which was also presented at the World Puppet Festival in Washington, D.C., that same season, brought Taymor particularly excellent personal notices that stressed her visual gifts.

Among Taymor's other stage credits are an adaptation of Homer's *The Odyssey*, Center Stage, Baltimore, 1979 (sets, costumes, masks); Elizabeth Swados's *The Haggadah*; Joseph Papp's New York Shakespeare Festival, 1980, along with revivals in 1981 and 1982 (sets, puppets, masks, and puppet/mask choreography); *Black Elk Lives*, an adaptation of the book, *Black Elk Speaks*, Entermedia, 1981 (sets, masks, puppets); *La Gioconda and Si-u*, the Talking Band, 1981–1982 (sets and puppets); Christopher Hampton's *Savages*, Center Stage, Baltimore, 1982 (puppets). She was resident designer for the 1982–1983 season at the American Place Theatre. In 1984 she created the visual concepts as well as puppet and mask choreography for *The King Stag* at the Sundance Institute. She worked with Theatre for a New Audience (New York) on two projects in 1984, as well as designing scenery for the American Place Theatre's production of *Do Lord Remember Me*. In 1985 she co-authored, directed, and designed *Liberty's Token*. In 1986 she directed *The Tempest* for Theatre for a New Audience using a Bunraku puppet for Ariel. Her 90 minute adaptation of the play was presented at New York's CSC Repertory, the American Shakespeare Festival in Stratford, Connecticut, and in high schools. Also in 1986 Taymor adapted Thomas Mann's *The Transposed Heads*, which played at Lincoln Center Theatre during October and November. In 1988 Taymor designed puppetry and masks for *Juan Darien*, a play inspired by Horacio Quiroga's short story and co-authored by Taymor and Elliot Goldenthal. The play was produced at St. Clement's Church, New York City. At the 1987–1988 Obie Awards ceremony Taymor and Goldenthal were presented special citations for *Juan Darien*.

Julie Taymor has received the Villager Theatre Award, 1979–1980, for distinguished prop/set designs and puppets for *The Haggadah*; the Maharam Theatre Design Award, 1979–1980, for *The Haggadah*; the Villager Theatre Award, 1980–1981, "For the art of play direction for *Way of Snow*;" and the Creative Artists Public Service Award (CAPS), 1982. In 1985 she was awarded a *Village Voice* Off-Broadway (Obie) Award for *Visual Magic*. In 1988 an exhibition of Taymor's sculpted figures, Bunraku, rod and leather puppets, masks, costumes, renderings, and photographs was held at the New York Public Library and Museum of the Performing Arts at Lincoln Center.

Julie Taymor is one of a growing school of young American artists who are comfortable wearing a number of theatrical hats: conceiving, designing, directing, or performing with equal facility and sometimes assuming a number of these roles within a single production. Like her contemporaries and occasional collaborators, actor/clown Bill Irwin and puppeteer Bruce Schwartz, she uses time-honored theatrical traditions to make innovative but still widely accessible theatre, which tends to favor visual imagery over language and to couple humor with complex themes.

The most comprehensive articles on Taymor's work to date are C. Lee Jenner, "Puppet Love," *Other Stages* (March 26 and April 8, 1981); Gerri Kobren, "Puppet Odyssey: Myth in Masks," *Baltimore Sun* (September 30, 1979); Don Shewey, "Bali Highs and

Soho Lows,'' *Soho Weekly News* (June 11, 1980); and Taymor's own report, ''Teatr Loh, Indonesia, 1977–1978,'' *The Drama Review* (June 1979). Julie Taymor is included in *Contemporary Theatre, Film, and Television*, Vol. I (1984).

C. Lee Jenner

TERRY, Megan (July 22, 1932–): playwright, was born in Seattle, Washington, the daughter of Joseph Duffy, Jr., and Marguerite Cecelia (Henry) Duffy. Though christened Josephine by her parents, she later changed her name to Megan Terry to emphasize her Welsh heritage. Terry was educated in theatre design at the Banff School of Fine Arts, the University of Alberta, Edmonton, and the University of Seattle, Washington, where she studied drama and received a bachelor's degree in 1956. She trained in all aspects of theatre at the Seattle Repertory Playhouse, where, at the age of fourteen, she ''hung around and begged to clean up and to sort nuts and bolts'' (*The Drama Review*, December, 1977, p. 60). Later she taught drama at the Cornish School of Allied Arts (1954–1956) and reorganized the Cornish Players, touring the Northwest for two years.

In 1956 Terry moved from the Northwest to New York City, an event that marked the beginning of the first half of her playwriting career. She was awarded a writer-in-residence fellowship at the School of Drama at Yale University in 1966. Terry was a founding member of the New York Open Theatre, where she was a playwright-in-residence (1963–1968), working with Joseph Chaikin, Jean-Claude van Itallie, **Roberta Sklar**, and others. The most important of her eight works there was *Viet Rock: A Folk War Movie* (1966), one of the first rock musicals, which she also directed. The play was produced at various locations in Manhattan, at Yale, and later, around the country. The montage-like structure of *Viet Rock* grew out of her previous experiments in playwriting, particularly *Comings and Goings* (1966), a nonlinear sequence of two-character ''open'' scenes. Twenty years later *Comings and Goings* is still frequently produced around the world and, according to Terry, earns the most royalties of all her plays. Her awards while in New York include a Stanley Drama Award (1965), two grants from the Office of Advanced Drama Research at the University of Minnesota (1965), two Rockefeller grants (1968), a New York Arts Council Fellowship, and a Literature Fellowship from the National Endowment for the Arts. Her most favorably reviewed play while in New York City was *Approaching Simone*, which presented Terry's first feminist ''role model'' heroine, Simone Weil, the French religious philosopher who perished of a hunger strike in protest of the Nazi occupation of her country. The play was awarded a *Village Voice* Off-Broadway (Obie) Award in 1970 after only five performances. Terry is also a founding member of the New York Theatre Strategy (1971) and the Women's Theatre Council, New York (1971).

Terry left New York in 1974 and has since made her permanent home in Omaha, Nebraska, as the playwright-in-residence of the Magic Theatre, a small storefront portion of a building converted into an environmental theatre space. Terry moved from New York to work with the Magic Theatre's artistic director, former Open Theatre actress Jo Ann Schmidman. Also impelling her move were difficulties with Actors' Equity in New York over her last-minute withdrawal of *Hothouse* prior to an Equity showcase production in 1974. Though the Magic Theatre has had difficulty securing consistent support from the Nebraska Arts Council, Terry has been extremely productive in her new environment. She explains, "I get so much work done in Omaha. Understand that the noise in New York comes right through the walls. And in New York it's not just noise. The very vibrations in the air have a way of assaulting you" (Personal interview).

Terry's most popular Omaha play is *Babes in the Bighouse* (1974), an exhaustively researched documentary musical fantasy about life inside a women's prison. Similar in nonlinear form to *Viet Rock*, *Babes in the Bighouse* deals with the women inmates and their male guards. In 1982 Terry wrote *Kegger*, a play about teen-agers and alcohol abuse, which has subsequently toured the Midwest and reached a much larger audience than her Omaha theatre facility can serve. In Omaha, Terry was adjunct professor of theatre at the University of Nebraska, Omaha, until 1978; she has given numerous playwriting seminars throughout the United States. She has served on the faculty of the Squaw Valley Community of Writers (1976 and 1977), as a member of the Theatre Policy Panel of the National Endowment for the Arts, as adjudicator for the American College Theatre Festival New Play Contest (1977), and as co-chair for the Playwrights' Project Committee for the American Theatre Association's 1977 convention. She has also recently received another Advanced Drama Research grant and a Guggenheim Fellowship. More than twenty of her fifty-three plays have been translated, and many have enjoyed major productions outside the United States.

Terry's dramas fall into four categories. Her early realism consists of plays such as *Hothouse* (1955), *Attempted Rescue on Avenue B* (1958), and *Ex-Miss Copper Queen on a Set of Pills* (1959). These plays demonstrate Terry's fundamental mastery of realism. More importantly, they reveal her embryonic awareness of transformational characterization. They also express her predilection for a fragmentary, montage-like structure and the political possibilities of satire.

Terry's role model and family dramas are best represented by *Approaching Simone* (1970) and *Mollie Bailey's Traveling Family Circus: Featuring Scenes from the Life of Mother Jones* (1981). Terry has often expressed concern over the need for female role models like Simone Weil and union activist Mother Jones. "Women haven't had the time or the opportunity" says Terry, "or just haven't taken the power into their own hands to create a model outside of themselves of what's in here, of what they really know. They've imitated masculine models" (Interview with Phyllis Jane Wagner, *Approaching Simone*, 1973).

Terry's political and public service dramas began with *Viet Rock* in 1966. After *Babes in the Bighouse* (1974), Terry shifted her political satire to polemics about community problems. She illustrates family and domestic violence in *Goona Goona* (1979) and teen-age alcohol abuse in *Kegger* (1982). These musical dramas feature broad satire, grotesque characters, and an episodic plot that parodies the well-made play. Terry's play *Sleazing Toward Athens*, about the materialism she sees reshaping young people's values, was produced at the Omaha Magic Theatre in 1986.

Critics most often cite Terry as the chief pioneer in developing transformational drama, in which the established realities or given circumstances of the scene change several times during the course of the action. Her transformational dramas began with *Calm Down Mother* (1965) and *Keep Tightly Closed in a Cool Dry Place* (1965). With *Massachusetts Trust* (1968), a play about Robert Kennedy's assassination, and *The Tommy Allen Show* (1970), in which a talk-show host is represented by four characters simultaneously, Terry begins to merge the relativistic, subconscious qualities of pure transformation with political issues, forming a drama of "public dreams." This style is best represented by *Brazil Fado* (1977), which employs transformational techniques to investigate the 1970s human rights violations in Brazil, juxtaposing violent images of right-wing oppression with a long monologue spoken by a "post-modern" American woman who practices sadomasochism with her husband in her ranch-style home.

Even though audiences in Omaha are small, and the Magic Theatre company suffers from meager local recognition, Terry continues to write plays, asserting that she is a participant in the decentralization of American theatre away from New York City. The stridency of her early feminist years has mellowed into a humanistic concern for local community problems. Meanwhile, she still displays innovativeness in her structural experimentation and her avant-garde explorations of language and theatrical image-making, especially in those dramas that merge transformational techniques with political issues. She is certainly one of the most interesting and prolific of America's "new" playwrights.

Megan Terry's published plays include *Ex-Miss Copper Queen on a Set of Pills* (1966), *Keep Tightly Closed in a Cool Dry Place* (1966), *The Gloaming, Oh My Darling* (1967), *Comings and Goings* (1967), *Viet Rock* (1967), *The Magic Realists* (1969), *The People vs. the Ranchman* (1970), *Calm Down Mother* (1970), *One More Little Drinkie* (1971), *Tommy Allen Talk Show* (1971), *Maps: India Collage* (1972), *Megan Terry's Home, or Future Soap* (1972), *Sanibel and Captiva* (1972), *American Wedding Ritual* (1973), *Approaching Simone* (1973), *Hothouse* (1975), *Nightwalk*, (written with Sam Shepard and Jean-Claude van Itallie) (1975), *The Pioneer* (1975), *Pro Game* (1975), *Women and the Law* (1976), *Willa-Willie-Bill's Dope Garden* (1977), *American King's English for Queens* (1978), *Babes in the Bighouse* (1978), *100,001 Horror Stories of the Plains*, (written with James Larson and Judith Katz) (1978), *Attempted Rescue on Avenue B* (1979), *Brazil Fado* (1979), *Fireworks* (1980), *Goona Goona* (1980), *Mollie Bailey's Traveling Family Circus: Featuring Scenes from the Life of Mother Jones* (1983), *Fifteen Million Fifteen-Year-Olds* (1984), and *Disko Ranch* (1986). Other writings by Megan Terry include "Two Pages a Day," *The Drama Review* (December 1977); "An Interview with Megan Terry," *The Performing Arts Journal* (Fall 1977); "Cool Is Out! Up-Tight Is Out!," *New York Times* (January 14, 1968); "Who Says Only Words Make Great Drama?," *New York Times* (November 10, 1968). For information about the playwright and her plays, see Robert Asahina, "The Basic Training of American Playwrights: Theatre and the Vietnam War," *Theater*, 9, ii (Spring 1978); Ruby Cohn, "Camp, Cruelty, Colloquialism," *Comic Relief: Humor in Contemporary American Literature* (1977); Helene Keyssar, *Feminist Theatre* (1984); James Larson, "Megan Terry: Artsperson," *Spectacle* (November 1976); James Larson, "Public Dreams: A Critical Investigation of the Plays of Megan Terry, 1955–1986" (Unpublished Ph.D. dissertation, University of Kansas, 1986); Bonnie Marranca, *American Playwrights: A Critical Survey* (1981); Richard Schechner, "Megan Terry: The Playwright as Wrighter," *Public Domain* (1969). A recent interview with Terry is included in Kathleen Betsko and Rachel Koenig, eds., *Interviews With Contemporary Women Playwrights* (1987) and in David Savran, ed., *In Their Own Words: Contemporary American Playwrights (1988). Megan Terry is included in Crowell's Handbook of Contemporary Drama* (1971); *Prize Winning Drama: A Bibliographic and Descriptive Guide* (1973); *Notable Names in the American Theatre* (1976); *Contemporary Dramatists* (1977); *Contemporary Authors*, Vols. 77–80 (1979); *Contemporary Literary Criticism*, Vol. 19 (1981); *Dictionary of Literary Biography*, Vol. 7; *Twentieth-Century American Dramatists*, Part 2 (1981); *Who's Who in the Theatre* (1981); and *American Women Writers*, Vol. 4 (1982).

James Larson

THARP, Twyla (July 1, 1941–): one of the most innovative choreographers in contemporary dance, was born in Portland, Indiana, and named Twyla because her mother thought Twyla would look good on a theatre marquee. Her mother, a professional musician, started her daughter on piano lessons at the age of two. By the age of four, Tharp was taking dance lessons. Starting with tap, she later took lessons in ballet, acrobatics, baton, and musical instruments, including the violin and viola. Tharp attended Barnard College (1960–1964) in New York City, where she majored in art history. While in college, she studied modern dance at both the **Martha Graham** and Merce Cunningham studios, classical ballet at American Ballet Theatre, and jazz with Luigi. She studied extensively with Merce Cunningham, whom she considered to be her master teacher. Just before graduating from college she joined the Paul Taylor Dance Company but left after only one year to form her own company in 1965.

Tank Dive, one of her first pieces, was performed at Hunter College of the City University of New York shortly after her company was formed. A short piece for one dancer and four nondancers, *Tank Dive* lasted only four minutes. Two months later, the state of Alaska commissioned a work, *Stage Show*, for its New York World's Fair Pavilion. By the fall of 1965 she had choreographed *Stride*, a quartet in five sections designed for film. In the winter of that same year, she returned to Hunter College, where she presented *Cede Blue Lake* and *Unprocessed*, both pieces for three dancers. Some observers noted an affinity to painting in these presentations and saw a kind of "coolness" in the performance. Tharp then became interested in manipulations of time, space, repetition, variation, and structure. *Disperse* was an example of her manipulations of space. Another piece, *Dancing in the Streets of Paris and London, Continued in Stockholm and Sometimes Madrid*, consisted of dances occurring simultaneously in separate rooms visually connected through closed circuit television. Tharp tended to break away from the traditional proscenium stage typically used for dance and to work in nontheatrical spaces. By 1967 her company had performed in a wide variety of places—from the Judson Memorial Church in Greenwich Village to the Kunstverein Museum in Stuttgart, Germany.

In dealing with music, Tharp either ignored it altogether, or chose unusual modes of accompaniment, such as the metronome or clicking heels on a "miked" stage or popular music. She used no scenery at first, and later added a minimal amount. In addition to the concise, crisp cleanliness of her 1960s pieces, she used a unisex approach to choreography. There was basically no division in the types of steps executed by men and women, nor was there physical contact among dancers during her earlier choreography. To Tharp, this represented a kind of democracy—all parties equal. Her work gradually changed as she "came to be more interested in how objects could support one another and in the physical problems of balance and tension. Beyond that she apprehended an emotional problem—when one person is supporting another, what does that convey to an audience?" (*Dancemagazine*, March 1980). In an interview with Alan M. Kriegsman of the *Washington Post* she said, "I wanted to find out what dance, as sheer movement, could accomplish on its own" (July 28, 1973).

During the late 1960s, Twyla Tharp's company accepted several brief teaching residencies at various colleges and universities in the United States. These residencies, sponsored by state and national arts councils, resulted in several pieces geared towards the university environment. While at the University of Massachusetts, Amherst, for example, she created *Rose's Cross-Country*, a dance intended to be performed while crossing campus, and *The Fugue*, a series of variations on a twenty-count phrase. As a part of the National Educational Television Coordinated Touring Company residency, she choreographed an *Hour's Work for Children*, consisting of a series of dance games designed to bring together children of diverse social, economic, and racial backgrounds.

In January 1971 Tharp premièred *Eight Jelly Rolls* at Oberlin College and, by October of that same year, presented a revised version at the Delacorte Theatre in Central Park, New York City. Set to the jazz music of Jelly Roll Morton, the dance was declared to be an astounding masterpiece. Using popular dance forms in her nonchalant, loose-jointed, throwaway style, Tharp created a piece appealing to dance and nondance audiences alike.

Another of Tharp's jazz or "pop" ballets was *The Bix Pieces*. First presented in November of 1971 for the Ninth International Festival of Dance in Paris, it was a suite of five dances to the music of Bix Biederbecke, played by Paul Whiteman's Orchestra. More than a dance about America's jazz age, it was designed to be followed by a lecture-demonstration explaining how the dance was composed. The finale of *The Bix Pieces* was performed to Thelonius Monk's "Abide With Me." The entire work was televised on CBS-TV's *Camera Three* on October 7, 1973.

The Raggedy Dances, yet another of her jazz ballets, was presented in October 1972 at the City Center American Dance Marathon at the American National Theatre and Academy Theatre in New York City. Tharp used a combination of Scott Joplin rags and Wolfgang Amadeus Mozart variations for this dance, and it was extremely successful and popular. Clive Barnes felt that the piece was "quintessentially American in its laconic ease and deliberately underplayed bravado" (*New York Times*, November 5, 1972).

After Tharp's enormous success with *The Bix Pieces* and *The Raggedy Dances*, Robert Joffrey asked her to choreograph a dance for the Joffrey Ballet. Using music recorded by the Beach Boys over the last ten years, she created *Deuce Coupe*, which combines the formality of ballet and a stylized version of the social dances of the 1960s. First premièred on February 8, 1973, at the Auditorium Theatre in Chicago, Illinois, it was an instant success and was later revised to be danced by the Joffrey Ballet without Tharp and her company. One critic, Peter Rosenwalk, said of Tharp's new form of dance theatre, "'Deuce Coupe' says more about the integration of classic and modern dance movement, dance theatre, [and] free group expression through movement than the collected works of a half dozen critics" (*Guardian*, January 12, 1974). The following fall, the Joffrey Ballet commissioned another work. This time, Tharp choreographed *As Time Goes By* to the classical music of Franz Joseph Haydn's "Symphony No. 45" (the last two movements). These two major works, plus her many other innovative creations, brought Tharp international acclaim.

In the summer of 1975, Tharp choreographed *Ocean's Motion*, set to the rock music of Chuck Berry; the production premièred at the Festival of Two Worlds in Spoleto, Italy. *Sue's Leg*, set to tunes played by Fats Waller, was presented as a major work on the PBS *Great Performances* series in 1976. Her next major work, *Push Comes to Shove* (January 1976), was choreographed for the American Ballet Theatre. It is a parody of ballet in general and of George Balanchine in particular, choreographed to Franz Joseph Haydn's "82nd Symphony," and its première performance featured American Ballet Theatre dancers Mikhail Baryshnikov, Mariane van Hamel, and Marianna Tcherkassky. The next piece in what has been referred to as Tharp's "uniquely American dance" was *Give and Take* (March 1976), regarded by critics as one of her more sedate pieces, neither so brash as *Deuce Coupe* nor as brilliant as *Push Comes to Shove*. Tharp also choreographed the film version of the rock musical *Hair*, which premièred in March 1979. By this time Tharp's company had become one of the most popular dance groups in the country.

With a reputation as one of the most versatile and innovative of choreographers, Tharp headed for Broadway. There, she adapted verses by A. A. Milne and choreographed a work combining all the theatrical elements—music, dialogue, and dance. An original score was composed by Paul Simon, and narration and dialogue were written by playwright Thomas Babe. Tharp felt that adding dialogue to dance was a perfectly natural progression. She said, "We started out just with movement, then we put in some music, then some costumes, then scenery, and now we're adding words. How will the words color the audience's perception? It's always the question of perception that interests me—that's why I almost became a psychiatrist'' (*Dancemagazine*, March 1980). This adaptation of Milne's verse resulted in a play titled *When We Were Very Young*. The dialogue was delivered by Babe and a nine-year-old child from a platform above the stage. As they reminisced, Tharp and her company danced the story. Critics greeted this performance with mixed reactions, feeling that the three artists did not always complement one another in their dancing.

A recent piece choreographed by Tharp is *The Catherine Wheel*. In mime and dance, Tharp tells the sordid, soap opera-like story of an American family. The piece tends more towards theatre than dance, using a quasi-Greek chorus of masked dancers to react seriously to events, contrasted with the grotesque family caricatures portrayed. This eighty-minute work is set to a rock score written by David Byrne of the Talking Heads. The sets, by Santo Loquasto, consist of rooms and various trappings that are lowered to divide the action. In 1987 Tharp introduced new works at the Brooklyn Academy of Music including *Ballare* and *In the Upper Room*, with score by Philip Glass and lighting by **Jennifer Tipton**.

In addition to the 1976 performance of *Sue's Leg* on television, Tharp did a special for WNET-TV, New York, in 1977, titled *Making Television Dance*. In 1981 cable television broadcast three of her works in a show called *Confessions of a Corner Maker*; they were *Bach Duet* and *Baker's Dozen*, especially adapted for the medium, and *Short Stories*, especially choreographed for television. Perhaps the most unusual of her contributions to television was the showing on NBC-TV's *Today* show (December 1970) of part of *The Willie Smith Series*, a videotape record of Tharp's pregnancy as it affected her dance movement. In the late 1960s Tharp had married Robert Huot, an artist who had designed costumes for her company during the earlier years; they were divorced sometime after the birth of their son. In 1985 Tharp made her Broadway directing debut with a stage version of *Singing in the Rain*.

Tharp has been called the Busby Berkeley of the 1970s, a modern Nijinsky, a female Balanchine, a Bette Midler of dance. She tends to be eclectic, using a combination of dance forms. An extremely prolific choreographer, she has created well over fifty works. A number of these, such as *Eight Jelly Rolls*, *Sue's Leg*, *Baker's Dozen*, and *Deuce Coupe*, are considered major works of art by many critics. For her excellence in the field of dance, Twyla Tharp was awarded the Brandeis University Creative Arts Award in 1972, and in 1978 the California Institute of the Arts presented her with an honorary doctorate in performing arts. In 1981 she received the *Dancemagazine* Award—''because as an American choreographer she has captured the essence of our time and place in an original symbiosis of movement and music.''

A biographical overview of Twyla Tharp can be found in *Time* (January 19, 1976) and *Dancemagazine* (April 1973 and March 1980). Descriptions of her movement style are covered in *Vogue* (June 1975 and March 1976), *Commonwealth* (April 27, 1979), *Nation* (March 26, 1973, and March 15, 1975), *Dancemagazine* (April 1973, December 1973,

June 1976, March 1980, and April 1981). See also discussions of her use of costume and music in *Dancemagazine* (April 1969, April 1973, December 1973, June 1976, and March 1980). Tharp's pieces are discussed at great length in *Dancemagazine* (April 1973, March 1980, and April 1981). Several of Tharp's pieces taped for television are briefly covered in *Dancemagazine* (September 1977 and October 1981). Her expansion into theatre is detailed in *Newsweek* (October 19, 1981), *Dancemagazine* (December 1973 and March 1980), *New Republic* (February 12, 1977), and *Newsweek* (April 7, 1980). Many critics have reviewed Tharp's works and excerpts of these can be found in *Newsweek* (April 7, 1980), *Time* (January 19, 1976), and *Dancemagazine* (March 1980). Her many awards and grants are listed in *Dancemagazine* (April 1981, April 1973, and April 1974), *Time* (January 19, 1976), and the *New York Times* (June 9, 1985). Twyla Tharp is included in *Current Biography, 1975* (1975–1976); *Bibliographic Guide to Dance, 1975*, Vol. 2 (1976); Don McDonogh, *The Complete Guide to Modern Dance* (1976); Mary Clarke and David Vaughan, eds., *The Encyclopedia of Dance and Ballet* (1977); and *The Concise Oxford Dictionary of Ballet* (1982).

Deborah Nadell

THOMPSON, Sada (September 27, 1929–): actress, was born in Des Moines, Iowa, to Hugh Woodruff Thompson and Corlyss Elizabeth (Gibson) Thompson. When Sada was five years old, her father, a magazine editor, moved the family to Fanwood, New Jersey. Thompson was educated at Scotch Plains High School in New Jersey, then attended the drama school of the Carnegie Institute of Technology (now Carnegie-Mellon University) in Pittsburgh, graduating with a Bachelor of Fine Arts degree. While at Carnegie she met her future husband, Donald E. Stewart, who was also a student actor. They married on December 18, 1948, and Stewart subsequently became a businessman. The couple had one daughter, Liza, in 1951.

Sada Thompson made her stage debut in 1945 in a college production of William Saroyan's *The Time of Your Life* as Nick's Ma. She began her professional career on June 30, 1947, in another Saroyan play, *The Beautiful People*, as Harmony Blueblossom at the University Playhouse in Mashapee, Massachusetts. She remained with the company for the next two years, playing a wide range of roles, including Lady Bracknell in Oscar Wilde's *The Importance of Being Earnest* (1947), Eileen in *Where Stars Walk* by Michael MacLiammoir (1948), Leda in Jean Giraudoux's *Amphitryon 38* (1948), Nina in Anton Chekhov's *The Sea Gull* (1948), and Ruth in *Thunder on the Left* by Richard Pryce (1948).

In the fall of 1948, Thompson returned to Pittsburgh, appearing in the title role of Maxwell Anderson's *Joan of Lorraine* at the Pittsburgh Playhouse (October 7, 1948) and as Mrs. Phelps in a production of Sidney Howard's *The Silver Cord* at the Morris Kaufmann Memorial Theatre (March 29, 1948). In the summer of 1949 she joined the stock company at the Henrietta Hayloft Theatre in Rochester, New York, returning the following year. She appeared there in such roles as Mrs. Higgins in George Bernard Shaw's *Pygmalion*, Emily Webb in Thornton Wilder's *Our Town*, Madame Arcati in Noel Coward's *Blithe Spirit*, Billy Dawn in Garson Kanin's *Born Yesterday*, and Birdie Hubbard in **Lillian Hellman**'s *The Little Foxes*. Perhaps Thompson's most popular role during her early career was Peg in J. Hartley Manners's *Peg o' My Heart*, an American comedy classic. Thompson acted the role four times, first at the University Playhouse (July 14, 1947), next in summer stock at the Henrietta Hayloft Theatre in Rochester, New York (July 13, 1948), again at the Pittsburgh Playhouse (February 23, 1952), and finally at the Totem Pole Playhouse in Fayetteville, Pennsylvania (July 5, 1954).

Having proven herself a versatile actress, Sada Thompson made her New York stage debut in 1953, when she was called upon to take several parts in a staged reading of Dylan Thomas's *Under Milk Wood* at the Kaufmann Auditorium (May 14, 1953). She appeared in several New York productions thereafter, including Mrs. Heidelberg in David Garrick's *The Clandestine Marriage* at the Province-town Playhouse (October 2, 1954), then Cornelia in John Webster's *The White Devil* (March 14, 1955), and Feng Nan in *The Carefree Tree* by Aldyth Morris (October 11, 1955), both at the Phoenix theatre. Recognition finally came in 1956 when the actress won the Drama Desk's Vernon Rice Award for her performance as Eliante in Molière's *The Misanthrope* at Theatre East (November 12, 1956). She won the same award the following year for her role as Valerie Barton in Charles Morgan's *The River Line* at the Carnegie Hall Playhouse (January 2, 1957). Thompson also appeared regularly at the American Shake-speare Festival in Stratford, Connecticut, playing the majority of Shakespeare's secondary female roles. She acted in the company in the summers of 1957, 1959, 1960, and 1962, returning in 1971 as Christine Mannon in Eugene O'Neill's *Mourning Becomes Electra*.

During the 1960s Thompson continued to expand her repertoire, appearing in many productions in New York and on tour. In 1965, she received *The Village Voice* Off-Broadway (Obie) Award for her rendition of Dorine in Molière's *Tartuffe* at the Washington Square Theatre (January 14, 1965). The next year she repeated the role at the American Conservatory Theatre in San Francisco, where she also appeared in a production of *Dear Liar*. In 1970 Sada Thompson achieved great success with her role as Beatrice, the mother in Paul Zindel's *The Effects of Gamma Rays on Man-in-the-Moon Marigolds*, at the Mercer-O'Casey Theatre, an Off-Broadway house. Clive Barnes proclaimed, "Sada Thompson's Beatrice, embittered, beleaguered, cynical and yet, despite herself, supremely pitiable, is among the best things in the current New York theatre" (*New York Times*, April 8, 1970). The actress was awarded the Drama Desk Award, an Obie, *Variety*'s Poll of Off-Broadway Critics Award, and the *Best Plays* citation as best actress for the 1969–1970 season. The following year she topped this achievement with her appearance in George Furth's *Twigs*. The play was structured as four linked sketches, each with a strong female character played by Thompson. Walter Kerr declared, "Sada Thompson does not simply give a stunning performance. She gives four of them" (*New York Times*, November 21, 1971). Her separate roles of Emily, Celia, Dorothy, and Ma won her the prestigious Sarah Siddons Award, another Drama Desk Award, *Variety*'s Poll of New York Critics Award, another *Best Plays* citation, and her first Antoinette Perry (Tony) Award for best actress of the 1971–1972 season. One of Thompson's most recent stage appearances has been as Miss Daisy in the Chicago production of Alfred Uhry's 1987 Pulitzer Prize winning *Driving Miss Daisy*.

In addition to her numerous stage performances, Thompson has also acted in films and television. Her film credits include *You Are Not Alone* (1961), *The Pursuit of Happiness* (1971), and *Desperate Characters* (1971). On television, she has performed in such series as *The Kraft Theatre*, *Camera Three*, *Big Story*, *Lamp Unto My Feet*, and in special presentations of Carl Sandburg's *Lincoln* and Thornton Wilder's *Our Town*. From 1976 to 1979 she was a regular on the dramatic series *Family*.

During her extensive career, Sada Thompson has appeared in over ninety productions on stage, film, and television. She has proved her acting abilities in young and old roles, in both comedy and tragedy, and in a wide variety of leading and character parts. She has performed in classic plays and not so classic plays, yet has managed always to bring characters to life in a unique way. Sada Thompson has "that special sympathy for life, that expansiveness, that not only makes stars but also makes audience idols" (Clive Barnes, *New York Times*, November 15, 1971). There is no doubt that her talent as an actress has secured her a significant place in the history of the American theatre.

Critical reviews of Sada Thompson's work include Clive Barnes, "Paul Zindel Melodrama at Mercer-O'Casey," *New York Times* (April 8, 1970); Walter Kerr, "Kerr on Sada Thompson in 'Twigs': Couldn't Take My Eyes Off Her," *New York Times* (November 21, 1971); Jack Kroll, "Four Faces of Sada," *Newsweek* (November 29, 1971); and Gerald Weales, "Fall Prospect," *Commonweal* (October 9, 1970). For additional information on Thompson's stage career, consult *The New York Times Directory of the Theatre* (1973) using the Personal Name Index, which includes a complete list of her acting credits, as well as a comprehensive list of her *New York Times* reviews. Sada Thompson is included in *The Biographical Encyclopaedia and Who's Who of the American Theatre* (1966); *Current Biography, 1973* (1973–1974); *Notable Names in the American Theatre* (1976); Leslie Halliwell, *Halliwell's Filmgoer's Companion* (1980); *Who's Who in the Theatre* (1981); and *The International Motion Picture Almanac* (1985).

Roberta L. Lasky

TIPTON, Jennifer (September 11, 1937–): lighting designer, was born in Columbus, Ohio, to Samuel Ridley Tipton and Isabel (Hansen) Tipton. Her father was a professor of zoology and her mother a professor of physics. Both parents taught at the University of Tennessee, Knoxville, before their retirement. Jennifer Tipton wanted to be a dancer, and at the age of fifteen she began attending the Connecticut College School of Dance during the summers. She attended Cornell University, graduating in 1958 with a Bachelor of Arts degree in English. She studied at the **Martha Graham** school and danced with a group called the Merry-Go-Rounders, which performed mainly for children. She studied lighting design with Thomas Skelton at Connecticut College and later served as his assistant. She traveled with the Paul Taylor Dance Company, rooming with dancer **Twyla Tharp** as she began her career as a lighting designer in 1965. She continues today to light works of both the Taylor and the Tharp companies.

Tipton did the lighting of her first Shakespeare production, *Macbeth*, for the American Shakespeare Festival, Stratford, Connecticut, in 1967. Her work was highly praised, and she proceeded to design the lights for *Richard II* and *Love's Labour's Lost* the next year. She also lighted modern dance performances for her friend Dan Wagoner and the Dan Wagoner Dancers, and less modern presentations at both the Pennsylvania Ballet Company and the Harkness Ballet Company. During the late sixties Tipton lighted such stage plays as *Horseman, Pass By* and *Our Town* in New York while lighting for the dance companies Les Grands Ballets Canadiens, Yvonne Rainer, and the Robert Joffrey Ballet.

During the 1970s Tipton continued to light for leading dance companies. One of the high points was *Celebration: The Art of the Pas De Deux* by Jerome Robbins, performed at the Festival of Two Worlds, Spoleto, Italy. Tipton also lighted works for the American Ballet Theatre, the San Francisco Ballet, and for José Limón. In addition she has designed for Frederick Ashton, Mikhail Baryshnikov, John Cranko, David Gordon, and Anthony Tudor. She won the Drama Desk Award in 1976 for her lighting of Ntozake Shange's *for colored girls who have considered suicide/when the rainbow is enuf*. She began working with Joseph Papp and the New York Shakespeare Festival in 1974, lighting *The Tempest*, *Macbeth*, and *A Midsummer Night's Dream*. This association has continued and over the years Tipton has lighted such plays as *The Cherry Orchard*, *Agamemnon*, and *The Pirates of Penzance*. The production of *Landscape of the Body*, first done in Illinois and brought to New York under the auspices of the New York Shakespeare Festival, won Tipton the Joseph Jefferson Award in Chicago in 1977. Her colleagues honored her with the Antoinette Perry (Tony) Award for *The Cherry Orchard* the same year. She has worked with such provocative directors as Liviu Ciulei, Andrei Serban, Jonathan Miller, Robert Wilson, and **JoAnne Akalaitis**.

Jennifer Tipton's more recent lighting designs include *Leonce and Lena (and Lenz)*. JoAnne Akalaitis' merging of Georg Buchner's prose work *Lenz* with his comedy *Leonce and Lena*, presented at the Guthrie Theater in Minneapolis in 1987, and Eugene O'Neill's *Long Day's Journey Into Night* and *Ah, Wilderness!*, produced for the O'Neill centennial first at the Yale Repertory Theatre and then at the Neil Simon Theatre in New York in 1988.

Tipton's lighting assignments have taken her around the United States and most of Europe. She has provided lighting for *The Goodbye People* at the Westport Playhouse, Connecticut; Baryshnikov's *Don Quixote* for the American Ballet Theatre; *The Pirates of Penzance* in London's West End, and *Falstaff* at Covent Garden—such productions suggest the diverse requirements she faces. She has lighted *Svadebka* and *Songs of a Wayfarer* for Jiri Kylian at the Nederlands Dans Theatre, The Hague. She lighted *An Evening of Dance* for Jerome Robbins at the Spoleto Festival, Italy, and did a workshop in dance lighting in

Rennes, France. In 1979 Tipton went to Chicago to light *Two Part Inventions* and *Bosoms and Neglect* for the Goodman Theatre, beginning an association with that theatre that continues to this day. She is now an associate director at the Goodman Theatre. She has been an associate professor at the Yale School of Drama. She has lighted productions for the Yale Repertory Theatre and the American Repertory Theatre, Cambridge. Recently she has expanded her activities to include theatre consulting, as the consultant for Cornell University's new Performing Arts Center. In 1988 she became a contributing editor for *American Theatre* magazine

The high quality of Tipton's work for the New York Shakespeare Festival organization was recognized with a *Village Voice* Off-Broadway (Obie) Award in recognition of her sustained excellence in lighting at the Public Theatre in 1979. Brandeis University gave her the Creative Arts Award Medal in Dance in 1982. In 1985 she was awarded a grant from the National Endowment for the Arts as an artistic associate with the Mabou Mines of New York, and in 1986 she was given a Guggenheim Fellowship to write a book on theatrical lighting design. In 1987 Tipton received a New York Dance and Performance Award from Dance Theatre Workshop for her lighting design for *Circumstantial Evidence*. In 1989 she received the Common Wealth Award of Distinguished Service in Dramatic Arts for her "excellence of achievement and high potential for future contributions." Also in 1989 she received the Drama Desk award for lighting for *Jerome Robbins' Broadway, Long Day's Journey Into Night*, and *Waiting for Godot*.

Tipton began her career primarily as a lighting artist for dance, although she quickly expanded to theatre. Arnold Aronson has suggested that if there is a Tipton style it is characterized by "textured and sculptured space" (*American Theatre*, January 1986, p. 16). In dance lighting she feels that she is continuing the tradition of Jean Rosenthal but has made innovations in the use of a palette based on white. Jennifer Tipton's talents are such that she is one of the most sought-after lighting artists in the world today, and her career continues to flourish.

Jennifer Tipton wrote "Lighting for the Dance," *Theatre Crafts* (September 1973). For further information on Tipton, see "Illuminating Lady," *Ballet News* (July 1982); Patricia MacKay, "Jennifer Tipton, Lighting Designer," *Theatre Crafts* (April 1983); Jane Ann Crum, "Three Generations of Lighting Designers: An Interview with Peggy Clark Kelley, Jennifer Tipton and Danianne Mizzy," *Theatre* (Winter 1985); and Arnold Aronson, "The Facts of Light," *American Theatre* (January 1986). Tipton's professional résumé was consulted in compiling this biography. Jennifer Tipton is listed in *Who's Who in America, 1984–1985*, Vol. 2 (1984).

Richard K. Knaub

TREADWELL, Sophie (October 3, 1885?–February 20, 1970): playwright, most noted as the author of *Machinal*, was born Sophie Anita Treadwell in Stockton, California, to Alfred Benjamin Treadwell, an attorney, and Nettie

(Fairchild) Treadwell. Her mother's lineage was Scottish, her father's Spanish and English. Treadwell attended a number of public and private schools, finally graduating from Girls' High School in San Francisco in 1902. She attended the University of California from 1902 until 1906 in a liberal arts curriculum, earning good grades, while at the same time working at various money-making jobs to help pay her expenses. By her senior year the strain of steady work and intensive participation in campus theatrical activities almost caused a physical breakdown. Her earliest plays were written for campus production: an untitled one-act and *A Man's Own*, a one-act stressing equality for women. She also wrote some comic sketches and songs during her college years. She graduated in the spring of the great earthquake (1906) with a Bachelor of Letters degree. Treadwell had hoped for a stage career, but with the necessity of earning her own living, she had trained herself in journalism. The first year after graduation Treadwell taught in a one-room school at Yankee Jim's in Placer County, using the long winter nights to write her first full-length play, *Le Grand Prix*, along with feature articles for the *San Francisco Sunday Chronicle*.

In the fall of 1907 Treadwell and her mother went to Los Angeles, where she began her stage career as an extra, then as a vaudeville performer, meanwhile making friends with newspaper folk. In the spring of 1908 she took over from Constance Skinner the compilation of **Helena Modjeska**'s memoirs, moving for four months to the Modjeska ranch. During this sojourn Treadwell wrote her second full-length play, *The Right Man*, and began her third play, *Constance Darrow*. Curiously enough, Modjeska's *Memoirs* make no mention of Treadwell, nor do the two biographies of Modjeska.

Treadwell returned to San Francisco in the fall of 1908 as a full-time staff member on the *San Francisco Bulletin*, covering police beats, sports, and theatre. At the *Bulletin* she met reporter William O'Connell McGeehan, whom she married on January 27, 1910, although she retained her maiden name throughout her life. After her marriage, Treadwell continued writing plays as well as newspaper articles and book reviews. More importantly, she regularly reported events of the Mexican Revolution (1910–1920) for American newspapers. As the first American woman war correspondent, she reported the rule, overthrow, flight, and murder of Carranza. She interviewed General Obregon, who assumed power from Carranza, and she covered the murder of Felipe Carillo in the Yucatán. Treadwell was the only reporter to get an interview with Pancho Villa in Mexico—an international scoop. Meanwhile, on January 31, 1915, *Sympathy*, the first of Treadwell's plays to be produced, opened at the Pantages Theatre in San Francisco.

In 1916 Treadwell sailed for France as a war correspondent covering World War I battles. When she returned home in 1918, she and her husband settled in New York City, where she wrote *Madame Bluff* from her war experiences. She also took a job with the *New York American* but continued to write plays. She was to complete seven one-acts and two more full-length plays in the next few years. On December 22, 1922, Treadwell's play *Gringo*, based on her experiences in Mexico, opened at the Comedy Theatre in New York. Directed by Guthrie McClintic, this melodrama received mixed notices and had a short run. Her next produced play, *Loney Lue*, opened on November 5, 1923, under the auspices of George C. Tyler, with **Helen Hayes** playing the leading role. After its Atlantic City première, Tyler did not take the show to New York. In 1925 Treadwell produced the play herself in New York, as *Oh Nightingale*. It is Treadwell's funniest play, a comedy in which Cinderella comes to New York from the Midwest to act Juliet but finds Prince Charming instead.

Treadwell's enduring enchantment with Edgar Allan Poe was expressed in a biographical play, *Plumes in the Dust*, which she began writing in 1922. Unfortunately, the play brought litigation and anguish. Treadwell approached John Barrymore to play the role of Poe. Barrymore read the play and liked it. Michael Strange, Barrymore's wife, then wrote a play about Poe, titled *Dark Crown*, as a vehicle for her husband. Treadwell sued; Barrymore and Strange counter-sued. The decision was in Treadwell's favor, but the years of publicity before the decision in 1924 prevented the production of both plays, while probably stigmatizing Treadwell as intransigent and difficult. *Plumes in the Dust* was ultimately produced in 1936 with Henry Hull in the lead.

Treadwell's twin careers peaked in her play *Machinal* (1928), an expressionist tragedy in nine episodes. In John Gassner's words, it was "one of the most unusual plays of the twenties" (*Twenty-Five Best Plays of the Modern American Theatre*, p. 494). Treadwell had reported Ruth Snyder and Judd Gray's sensational trial for the murder of Snyder's husband, both defendants finally receiving the death penalty. Treadwell, in describing the dramatic goals of *Machinal*, said, "It is all in the title-Machine-al—machine-like. A young woman—ready—eager—for life—for love . . . but deadened—squeezed—crushed by the machine-like quality of the life surrounding. She is a woman who must love and be loved. And she goes through life trying to satisfy this. She reaches out to her mother—to a man to marry—to having a child—a lover—searching for that living 'somebody.' She cannot reach to God, and she dies with this call—'somebody.' She finds her answer once—in the lover. And in this scene comes her blossoming—she is complete—like a flower" (Letter dated March 14, 1955, in the Treadwell Papers). Produced September 7, 1928, directed by Arthur Hopkins with Robert Edmond Jones as scene designer, *Machinal* was a critical and commercial success. Zita Johann starred as the Young Woman, George Still as the Husband, and the role of the lover was performed so well by Clark Gable that it brought him to the attention of Hollywood producers. In 1931 foreign productions of *Machinal* took Treadwell to London, Paris, and Moscow. After a successful run in the Kamerny Theatre in Moscow, the play toured the provinces. Treadwell was the first United States playwright known to have earned royalties in rubles that she was obliged to spend in the U.S.S.R. *Machinal* was revived in 1960 in New York at the Gate Theatre.

On October 1, 1929, Treadwell's *Ladies Leave* premièred. In it, Zizi Powers takes a lover, confesses her error to her indulgent husband, who forgives her as she departs alone on a trip to Vienna. Exploring the subject of adultery in a seriocomic, psychoanalytical manner, *Ladies Leave* is Treadwell's least successful play, running only fifteen performances. On March 3, 1933, Treadwell herself produced *Lone Valley*, a play about a prostitute who seeks a new life and fails to find it. The play failed. This disappointment and the death of her husband on November 29, 1933, along with Treadwell's inability to interest producers in her plays, cast her into a profound depression.

Treadwell's travels in Russia had inspired *Promised Land* (1933), a slice-of-life drama depicting post-Revolutionary lives, including that of a Communist party official. With her husband's assistance, she had written *Million-Dollar Gate* (1930) about corruption in boxing. *For Saxophone* (1934) was an innovative script with music and dance, which Robert Edmond Jones highly praised. But these plays were never published or produced. In 1936 Arthur Hopkins produced Treadwell's play about Edgar Allan Poe, *Plumes in the Dust*, with Henry Hull in the leading role. The play was well received by audiences, but critics found the dialogue artificial. It closed after eleven performances.

In 1937 Treadwell took a steamer trip around the world, coming home with a completed novel, titled *Hope for a Harvest* (1938). By 1940 she had revised the novel and rewritten it as a play. Lawrence Langner and **Theresa Helburn** of the Theatre Guild became interested in the play as a vehicle for Frederic March and his wife, **Florence Eldridge**. Rehearsals began in January 1941. The tryout was in New Haven, Connecticut. After its success there, the Marches toured with *Harvest* to Boston, Pittsburgh, Baltimore, and Washington, D.C., earning plaudits all the way. It opened in New York on November 26, 1941, but the reviews were lukewarm, and the play ran for only thirty-eight performances. Ten years later, the play was televised on the United States Steel Hour.

Highway, a comedy about a young woman who tends a chili-stand on a Texas highway, found its way to production on television on February 16, 1954, after Treadwell had tried for years to sell it to play producers in the United States and abroad. It was the next-to-last of her plays to be produced, though she continued to write. *The Last Border*, a drama set in the Spanish Civil War; *A String of Pearls*, a mystery; and *Andrew Wells' Lady* (later titled *Judgment in the Morning*), depicting the moral anguish of an attorney during a trial, were competently written plays that never saw production. In 1953 she copyrighted *Siren*, an anti-Russian play about a male spy in American disguise. It was never produced or published. Yet another unproduced work, *Loving Lost*, about a male ex-convict, was written in television format. Her one successful venture in these years was a novel, *One Fierce Hour and Sweet*, published in 1959. After her retirement to Tucson, Arizona, her play *Now He Doesn't Want to Play*, a comedy placed in a Mexican boarding house, was performed July 26–29, 1967, at the University of Arizona Theatre. Sadly, the play was not the success Treadwell hoped for. She died of cerebrovascular failure on February 20, 1970, in Tucson.

Amazingly little is documented about Treadwell's personality, friends, and family ties. Apparently her volatile temperament, her frankness, and assertiveness did little to foster her career as a playwright. Her lack of shining success as a dramatist had many possible causes: she wrote plays whose subject matter was truly new and untried; her styles were often innovative and not geared to pleasing audiences; her dramaturgy often included film between the acts or music and dance within the act; her major characters were often foreign-born. These innovations frequently puzzled audiences. Treadwell never won a Pulitzer Prize for drama, as did her peers **Zona Gale**, **Susan Glaspell**, and **Zoë Akins**. However, she was the first American woman playwright to write the international political play, the experimental (surrealistic) play, the play with a sexually liberated woman, and, most importantly, the play with a nonheroic male protagonist. She was unquestionably an agent for change in the content and the structure of American drama in the first half of the twentieth century.

The Sophie Treadwell Papers at the University of Arizona Library hold all her plays, letters, and clippings. The Theatre Collection in the New York Public Library Performing Arts Research Center at Lincoln Center includes programs and a few scripts. *Machinal* may be read in *Twenty-Five Best Plays of the Modern American Theatre: Early Series*, ed. John Gassner (1949), and in *Plays By American Women: 1900–1930*, ed. Judith E. Barbour (1986). *Hope for a Harvest* is Treadwell's only play published in book form (1942). For a photograph of Treadwell, see Dan Pavillard's "A New Treadwell" in the *Tucson Daily Citizen* (June 24, 1967). The best source of information about Sophie Treadwell is "Sophie Treadwell, The Career of a Twentieth-Century American Feminist Playwright" by Nancy Wynne (Unpublished Ph.D. dissertation, City University of New York, 1982). As a journalist, Treadwell is mentioned by Isabel Ross in *Ladies of the Press* (1936). Treadwell's obituary appeared in the *New York Times* (February 24, 1970). Short biographies of Sophie Treadwell appear in *The Concise Encyclopedia of Modern Drama* (1964); *McGraw Hill Encyclopedia of World Drama*, Vol. 4 (1972); *Modern World Drama: an Encyclopedia* (1972); and *American Women Writers*, Vol. IV (1982). *Machinal* is listed in *The Oxford Companion to American Theatre* (1984). Treadwell's birth date is debatable. Her own handwritten application to the University of California cites October 3, 1885. However, 1890 is cited in all documentary sources.

Louise Heck-Rabi

TRIPLETT, Jane Dinsmoor (August 5, 1918–): children's theatre director and playwright, was born in St. Mary's, West Virginia, to James Denton Dinsmoor, an oil man, and Nelle (Gallaher) Dinsmoor, a nursery woman and clothes designer. Her parents were both musical and encouraged each of their five children to play and sing. They frequently had family sing-alongs with her mother playing the piano, her father playing the piano or violin, and each of the children playing or singing. Poetry recitals were also a family tradition. Jane Dinsmoor was an excellent student and was advanced two grades. She attended Thomas Jefferson High School in San Antonio, Texas, and graduated in 1935. After graduating from high school, she attended Gulf Park Junior College in Gulfport, Mississippi, receiving her associate degree in 1937 with a major in speech and dance. She and several of her classmates followed one of their professors, Nadine Shepherdson, to Northwestern University in Evanston, Illinois. In 1939 Dinsmoor received her Bachelor of Science degree, and in 1940 she received her Master of Arts degree with a major in theatre and a minor in interpretation. While at Northwestern she studied acting with **Alvina Krause**, lighting with Theodore Fuchs, and radio with Albert Crews.

In 1940 Jane Dinsmoor married Dr. William Carryl Triplett, an old friend from St. Mary's, who was then beginning his internship in Wheeling, West Virginia. While in Wheeling, Jane Triplett taught stage movement at a drama school, directed, acted, presented dramatic monologues, and did some acting on radio. In 1941 the Tripletts moved to Corpus Christi, Texas, where their son, William Carryl, II (now a lawyer in Washington, D.C.), was born in 1942. During the Second World War Triplett continued her work in radio, giving her dramatic monologues, and writing weekly half-hour broadcasts for the American Red Cross. Her daughter, Jan Frances (now a media director-consultant), was born in 1950. In 1955, Triplett became an active member of the Corpus Christi Little Theatre and the Parish Players Guild of the Good Shepherd Episcopal Church. She acted in productions for the Little Theatre and was production designer for the Parish Players.

After a divorce in 1961, Jane Triplett and the children moved to Evanston, Illinois, where she began work on a doctoral degree in theatre at Northwestern University and was director of "The Lyrics," a singing group. With her former teacher, Alvina Krause, she also worked, alternatively, as stage manager, costumer, choreographer, or assistant director at the Harper Theatre in Chicago during the winters and at Eagles Mere Playhouse in Eagles Mere, Pennsylvania, during the summers. To support her family and to put her son through college, she earned a teaching and supervisory certificate from the state of Illinois and began teaching creative dramatics to elementary school students. She later taught in junior high schools and in college. She also began directing plays for the Children's Theatre of Evanston, which had been founded by **Winifred Ward** in 1925. Early in 1967, **Rita Criste**, then director of the theatre, asked Triplett to become her assistant. At that time, the theatre was performing two series of children's plays (three plays per series) for children from kindergarten through third grade and for fourth grade through eighth. These plays, mostly fairy tales, were performed by child actors, a departure from most children's theatres, which usually used adult actors.

When Criste retired in 1967, Triplett became executive director of the theatre, which had been renamed Theatre 65 for the school district that supported it financially. Under her direction and with the aid of a highly trained professional staff, including artistic director Edgar P. Van De Vort, Theatre 65 endeavored to find a broader base of support while maintaining its high caliber of production. Triplett instituted a program of audience research and analysis, one device being "Theatre Day." This was a touring exhibit that visited all the schools in the district. Eleven thousand students saw the exhibit, which was designed for students with little or no background or experience in theatre. Each student individually saw, touched, and worked with properties, lighting, costumes, and scenery. Another method was an alteration in the presentation and the content of the plays, from an emphasis on verbal qualities to an emphasis on visual presentation. The content of the plays was changed from a moralistic emphasis to fantasy or day-to-day situations. Curriculum guides were developed for each play, which were sent to teachers responsible for the children for whom the play was intended. The guides included activities and ideas relating the play to school subjects, such as math, science, and language arts. In addition, a "family night" was instituted on Friday evenings to encourage families to come to the theatre together. The changes proved very successful, and plays were performed for about sixty thousand spectators per year in Evanston alone.

To maintain the theatre's momentum, Triplett and her staff offered a summer workshop in theatre beginning in 1968. The children, who were selected by audition, were given training in writing, acting, movement, voice, costume, and set design and construction. They developed an original production, which they then performed free of charge in the Evanston parks. The group was known as "Plays on Wheels." A few years later a high school and college group, known as "Shakespeare in Your Park," was formed to present free performances of Shakespeare's plays. By 1971 Theatre 65 was touring on a regional basis from Wisconsin to Ohio.

In 1970 Triplett established the first theatre school for the gifted. Thirty talented eighth-graders, who were selected through auditions and interviews with each of the staff members, were transferred to Chute Junior High School. There they took core courses in the morning and then walked to Theatre 65, which was nearby. At the theatre they studied theatre history, acting, movement, historical styles, voice, directing, oral interpretation, writing, radio, television, costume, and set design and construction. As part of the curriculum they performed plays that were toured to area schools.

Theatre 65 had always had college students as interns in costume, set design and construction, lighting, and as actors to play the older roles in the series of plays for older children. In 1971, however, Triplett broadened this program by establishing a touring repertory company made up of Northwestern University students. Three to four plays were maintained in the repertory, and the company toured from Wisconsin to Ohio. Participants received college credit and a stipend for their work. Several of the plays they performed were televised either locally or nationally, including two original musicals, *Please Don't Call the 'El' the Subway*, a history of Chicago, and *Yankee Doodle was a Travellin' Man*, with book by Triplett and Van De Vort and lyrics by Ken Hosie. *Yankee* was televised and appeared on ABC's *Make a Wish* program in 1972.

When Theatre 65 lost partial funding in 1971 because a bond issue failed, Triplett was able to keep the theatre going and growing through funding from various private foundations, as well as the National Endowment for the Arts. For one of the National Endowment projects, Triplett wrote and field-tested scripts (based on her background in radio) which could be performed by physically handicapped children in hospitals. In 1975 Triplett established the Communication Arts Center at Kendall College in Evanston, Illinois. It combined the theatre school and repertory company, as well as a high school repertory company, and added a new area—communications skills for disadvantaged adults. In 1976 Triplett moved to Austin, Texas, where, under her maiden name, Jane Porter Dinsmoor, she and Van De Vort began "Designs for Living," a firm that helps young people develop poise and social skills and also advises clients on the use of living space and work space.

Through Jane Triplett's efforts, Theatre 65 was recognized both nationally and internationally. The International Association of Theatres for Children and Youth (ASSITEJ) invited Triplett and her staff to participate as delegates in the 1972 International Convention held in Albany, New York. In addition, the theatre was one of the semi-finalists chosen nationwide to perform at that convention. Through her teaching, consulting, and appearances at numerous conventions, Jane Triplett has helped to disseminate innovative ideas about what children's theatre and creative dramatics can and should be.

Triplett is the author or co-author of fifteen plays and musicals for children, all of which have been performed successfully by Theatre 65 and elsewhere. She has published poetry in national and regional poetry magazines. She also wrote the preface to *Six New Plays for Children* by Christian Moe and Darwin Reid Payne (1969). She is working on a volume of six plays for children, which expounds her philosophy of play selection, acting, and directing for children.

Jan Frances Triplett

TYSON, Cicely (December 19, 1933–): stage, screen, and television actress, was born in East Harlem to Theodosia Tyson, a domestic worker, and William Tyson, carpenter, house painter, and pushcart peddler. Her parents emigrated separately from the West Indies, met in New York City, and married. They had three children—Cicely, Emily, and a son known as Tyson. Making a living in Harlem was a difficult task for the Tyson family. While the mother was working as a domestic and the father at various jobs, Cicely at age nine sold shopping bags on street corners to assist the family financially. During her spare time she would ride the bus beyond Harlem to see what the rest of the world had to offer. Cicely was a frail, sickly child, and her father's favorite. He spoiled her, concocted nutritious remedies to help her gain weight, and took her for long, early-morning walks. The Tysons divorced when Cicely was eleven years old; William Tyson died in 1962.

After the divorce Theodosia Tyson raised the three children alone. She was a God-fearing woman who rarely permitted her children to play with other children in the neighborhood, forbade them to attend movies, and sent them to church (Episcopal and Baptist) to keep them out of trouble. The only films the children saw were religious films presented in the church. Cicely Tyson taught Sunday school, played the church piano and organ, and sang in the choir. After finishing elementary school at P.S. 121, she attended Margaret Knox Junior High School and Charles Evans Hughes High School, from which she graduated.

She then found a job as a secretary and attended classes at New York University. When Walter Johnson, her hairdresser, asked her to model some wigs in a show for him, she decided to pursue modeling. She enrolled in the Barbara Watson Modeling School and began a successful modeling career, appearing in such respected magazines as *Vogue* and *Harper's Bazaar*. Between modeling engagements Tyson earned additional income as a typist. Her mother did not mind her modeling career because she associated it with having a well-groomed, socially accepted daughter. Theodosia Tyson died in 1974. Tyson's first marriage at age eighteen ended with the death of her husband, and it was not until 1981 that she married a long-time friend, jazz trumpeter Miles Davis. She has no children.

Tyson's career as an actress began when, at a modeling interview, an actress arrived in the same office. The actress remarked that Tyson "looked perfect for" a certain movie role and ought to audition for it. After much encouragement from her agent, she auditioned, made an impression, but the film was never completed because of financial problems. Tyson did, however, become interested in acting. She began to study acting with Lloyd Richards, director of the famous 1959 Broadway production of **Lorraine Hansberry**'s *A Raisin in the Sun*. She also studied with Paul Mann, and at the Actors Studio. Her decision to become an actress caused a break in her close relationship with her mother. The conflict lasted for two years, and Tyson moved permanently out of her mother's house. In 1958 Tyson played the role of Barbara Allen in **Vinette Carroll**'s production of *The Dark of the Moon* as her stage debut. Her first television production came shortly thereafter when she appeared in Paule Marshall's *Brown Girl, Brown Stones*, which led to appearances in Sunday morning dramas and a Camera Three production titled *Between Yesterday and Today*. Tyson then played the role of Virtue in Jean Genêt's *The Blacks* (1961), whose cast included **Maya Angelou**, Billy Dee Williams, James Earl Jones, Esther Rolle, Louis Gossett, Jr., and others; she won the Vernon Rice Award and the Drama Desk Award as outstanding Off-Broadway performer of the year. The following year she won the Vernon Rice Award for her performance as Mavis in *Moon on a Rainbow Shawl* (1962). George C. Scott saw Tyson in *The Blacks* and recruited her as his co-star in the television series *East Side, West Side* (1963), the first black woman to have a continuing major role in a television series.

The 1950s and 1960s were busy years for Tyson, during which she was performing almost constantly on stage, on television, and in films. Most notable of her stage performances were Celeste in *Tiger, Tiger, Burning Bright* (1962); Rev. Marion in *Trumpets of the Lord* (1963, 1969), with the American Conservatory Theatre; *In White America, Tartuffe*; *A Servant of Two Masters*; *The Apollo of Bellac* (1966); *To Be Young, Gifted and Black* (1969); and *Desire Under the Elms* (1974). Her television credits included appearances in *Slattery's People*, *I Spy*, *The Guiding Light*, *Cowboys in Africa*, and *The FBI*. Her film credits included *Twelve Angry Men* (1957), *The Last Angry Man* (1959), *Odds Against Tomorrow* (1959), *A Matter of Conviction* and *Who Was That Lady?*

(1960), *A Man Called Adam* (1966), *The Heart is a Lonely Hunter* (1968). From 1968 to 1972 Tyson did no films although she continued to appear on television. She spent much of that time with Miles Davis, but after Davis left America for a European tour, Tyson made a triumphant return to the film screen as the strong, persevering black woman Rebecca Morgan, in *Sounder* (1972), for which she won an Academy (Oscar) Award nomination. This film was followed by a made-for-television movie, *The Autobiography of Miss Jane Pittman* (1974), for which she won two Emmys. Returning to the film world, in which black women were consistently employed as prostitutes, concubines, drug addicts, machine-gun- and knife-wielding "vindictive Mamas," Tyson refused to play such stereotypes and chose only roles that depicted the nobility, strength, and endurance of specific renowned black women. She portrayed Harriet Tubman in *A Woman Called Moses* (1978), for which she was also the executive producer; Coretta Scott King, in *King* (1978); and Chicago educator Marva Collins, in *The Marva Collins Story* (1981). Tyson also co-starred with Richard Pryor in the feature film *Bustin' Loose* (1981), co-produced by Pryor and Michael S. Glick.

In a 1979 *Redbook* interview with Joel Dreyfuss, Tyson stated, "One of the things that I think important is to get to a point where I am considered for a part simply because I am a good actress rather than because I am a black actress" (October, 1979). This determination caused a ten-year absence from the stage, to which she returned in the leading role of Miss Moffat in *The Corn is Green*, which opened at the Lunt-Fontanne Theatre on August 22, 1983. This short-lived production, produced by the Elizabeth Theatre Group (Zev Bufman and Elizabeth Taylor, producers), received lukewarm reviews from critics. Maintaining that Tyson's color was not an issue, they nonetheless mentioned color in every review. The play closed September 18, 1983. It concluded in a lawsuit filed by Cicely Tyson against Elizabeth Taylor for breach of contract. Tyson had missed a performance because of a delayed airline flight and had been dismissed from the show. In 1985, Actors' Equity Association and the League of New York Theatres and Producers ruled in Tyson's favor.

Many distinguished awards have been bestowed on Cicely Tyson: the Vernon Rice Award (1961 and 1962), the Best Actress Awards of the Atlanta Film Festival (1972), Screen World's Most Promising Personality Award (1972) for *Sounder*, and two National Academy of Television Arts and Sciences (Emmy) Awards (1974) for *The Autobiography of Miss Jane Pittman*. She has received awards from the National Association for the Advancement of Colored People (NAACP) and the National Council of Negro Women. Tyson has also been accorded honorary doctorates from Atlanta, Loyola, and Lincoln Universities; and Harvard University honored her with "Cicely Tyson Day" (April 18, 1974). Marymount College presented her with an honorary degree in Fine Arts (1979). Cicely Tyson, from her first appearance on stage, has consistently done work of the highest caliber. She has refused to accede to black stereotypes and has done much to elevate the position of black actresses in the American theatre.

A good source for Cicely Tyson's childhood, her career, her objectives, and her aspirations for the future is "Cicely Tyson: Reflections on a Lone Black Rose," *Ladies*

Home Journal (February 1977). Additional personal and career information is in "Cicely Tyson, a Very Unlikely Movie Star," an interview with Louis Robinson, *Ebony* (May 1974), and "Cicely Tyson: She Can Smile Again After a Three-Year Ordeal," an interview with Charles S. Saunders, *Ebony* (January 1979). See also Donald Bogle's article, "Cicely Tyson: The Incorruptible Black Artist," in *Brown Sugar: Eighty Years of America's Black Female Superstars* (1980). "Cicely Tyson, a Communicator of Pride," in *Black Collegian* (November/December 1978), is a comprehensive interview by Kalamu ya Salaam. "A Woman Called Cicely," *Redbook* (October 1979), is an interview with Joel Dreyfuss. See also "Cicely Tyson: Hollywood's advocate of positive Black images talks about the 'Bo Derek' look rip-off, her new movie, being typecast as an actress and her love for Miles Davis," an interview with Lynn Norment, *Ebony* (February 1981). In "The Importance of Cicely Tyson," *Ms.* (August 1974), the author Yvonne describes several ways in which Cicely Tyson has influenced young black women. "Miles Davis' Miraculous Recovery From Stroke," *Ebony* (December 1982), by Leonard Feather, mentions his marriage to Cicely Tyson. Edward Rothstein's article "625,000 Sought by Cicely Tyson," *New York Times* (November 22, 1983), is a discussion of Tyson's suit against Elizabeth Taylor. "Cicely Tyson Awarded $607,000 in Theatre Suit," *Jet* (April 29, 1985), is an announcement of the settlement of Tyson's lawsuit against Taylor. Cicely Tyson is listed in *The Biographical Encyclopaedia and Who's Who of the American Theatre* (1966); *Actor's Television Credits, 1950–1972* (1973), Supplement I (1978); *Ebony Success Library*, Vols. I and II (1973); *Who's Who in America, 1974–1975*, Vol. II (1974); *Current Biography, 1975* (1975–1976); *Notable Names in the American Theatre* (1976); *Who's Who in the Theatre* (1981); and *Contemporary Theatre, Film, and Television* (1984).

Elizabeth Hadley Freydberg

— V —

VANCE, Nina (October 22, 1914–February 18, 1980): founder and artistic director of Houston's Alley Theatre, was born Nina Eloise Whittington to Calvin Perry and Minerva (Dewitt) Whittington in Yoakum, Dewitt County, Texas. Her father was a cotton broker; her mother was a direct descendant of Green Dewitt, the pioneer who settled the county that bears his name. By the time Nina Whittington had graduated with a Bachelor of Arts degree from the University of Texas in 1935, she had decided that she wanted to be a director. She then attended the University of Southern California (1936), Columbia University (1937), and the American Academy of Dramatic Art in New York. Nina Whittington discovered that New York, unfortunately, was not at all interested in her as a director. Her reaction to this indifference she described to an interviewer from *Time* (February 14, 1964): "You know the story about how if you're in college and can't get into a sorority, you can always start your own. That's what I did."

Nina Whittington returned to Houston, married Milton Vance, a Houston attorney, and became assistant to **Margo Jones** at the Houston Community Players. In 1944 Nina Vance was asked by Vivien Altfeld, a dance instructor, to teach some adult acting classes at the Jewish Center in Houston. Three years later Vivien Altfeld and her husband Bob discussed at length with Vance and her husband the feasibility of producing plays themselves. Vivien Altfeld volunteered her dance studio for a public meeting and Nina Vance bought and sent 214 penny postcards representing the amount of change in her pocketbook when this decision was made). The postcard read, "It's a beginning. Do you want a new theatre for Houston? Meeting 3617 Main Street. Bring a friend. Tuesday, October 7, 8:00 p.m. Nina Vance." More than a hundred people attended that meeting and the Alley Theatre was born. Thirty-seven people gave twenty dollars each to begin a season of plays. On November 18, 1947, Harry Browne's *A*

Sound of Hunting opened and ran for ten nights. The Alley's first home was condemned in 1949, and they moved to an abandoned fan factory that Bob Altfeld had found. February 8, 1949, saw the first production in the fan factory. In the early 1950s, a controversy arose in the group over the continued use of amateur performers. By arguing the impossibility of getting volunteers to work full-time, Vance was able to persuade the Alley's board of directors to permit the payment of semi-professional actors.

On August 23, 1952, the Alley changed its amateur status to semiprofessional, much to the distress of many community persons who had worked for five years to make the Alley a success. From that moment, Bob Altfeld, the president of the group that had given birth to the Alley, a man who himself had worked in the theatre from its early years, disappeared from the Alley's recorded history; it became Nina Vance's theatre.

The overriding consideration for Vance was her determination to create a resident theatre in Houston that would equal, indeed surpass, any other regional theatre. On February 23, 1954, the Alley Theatre became a fully professional association through Actors' Equity. Vance judged correctly that visibility beyond the boundaries of Houston and association with professional groups such as Actors' Equity and the American National Theatre and Academy were essential to achieving her goal. In May 1958 the Alley Theatre was selected by the national television show *Wide, Wide World* to represent regional theatre at a professional level; the show brought national recognition to the Alley. Also in 1958, an invitation from the Department of State to participate in the Brussels World's Fair moved Vance another step toward her goal. In that same year Vance received a grant from the English Speaking Union to observe and report on theatre conditions in England; this event drew still wider attention to the Alley Theatre and its director.

In 1959 Vance received a Ford Foundation grant of $10,000 enabling her to travel and study on theatre on a wide scale. In December 1959 the Alley Theatre was selected for participation in the Ford Foundation Program for Actors. A grant of $156,000 for the three-year program was set up to determine if *top* professional actors would leave the commercial centers of New York and the West Coast to perform in the regional theatre. The grant was matched by Houstonians, and the result was a fine resident company at the beginning of the 1960–1961 season.

In May 1962 Houston Endowment, Inc., the philanthropic foundation established by the late Mr. and Mrs. Jesse H. Jones, made a gift to the Alley Theatre of a half-block of land in downtown Houston to house the Alley's new theatre and academy. Close upon the heels of this gift, the Ford Foundation in October 1962 announced a major step to strengthen repertory in the United States with grants totaling $6.1 million to nine theatre companies across the nation. The Alley Theatre received $2.1 million, the largest grant ever made to a theatre, for construction and development assistance over a ten-year period. The *Houston Post* and the *Houston Chronicle* gave generous coverage to the Ford proposal and enthusiastically urged the public to respond. By August 1963 over $900,000 had been contributed for the new theatre building. In May 1964 another 21,000 square feet of land was purchased, making available approximately five-sixths of a downtown block. As the Alley's prime motivator, Vance found these expressions of public interest and financial support greatly encouraging. In order to construct a new building she canceled the 1965–1966 season. This strategy was partly motivated by the fact that the actors' salaries grant was no longer available and the Ford Foundation funds could be used for operations only in the new building.

In July 1964, Ulrich Franzen, one of the leading modern architects in the nation, was contracted as architect for the new Alley Theatre. In reality the new building was to house two theatres. The Arena in the new Alley Theatre was to be a rectangle bordered on four sides by an audience of 300. The larger fan-shaped theatre was to seat 800. The completed structure was lavishly praised as an important theatrical statement. The architect's rendering of the interior and exterior of the new Alley is strikingly innovative and somehow appropriate for the young director who turned rejection by New York into the creation of her own theatre. The theatre that opened in 1968 cost far more than its original estimate. The Ford Foundation gave the Alley an additional $1.4 million to complete the construction of the building. By 1973 the Alley's budget had tripled, but this giant increase was offset by a rise in the regular subscription audience to more than 20,000 Houstonians—a figure far in excess of Vance's expressed goal of 12,000 subscribers for the new theatre.

Vance is credited with the direction of 125 of the 277 shows produced at the Alley Theatre during her tenure. Moreover, she was a shrewd businesswoman and, as J. W. Ziegler puts it, "a brilliant master of institutional propulsion." Her practice of producing, as she explained it, "Broadway flops—that is, plays that were critically successful in New York but not commercially so," found an appreciative audience in Houston (*Regional Theatre*, p. 31).

Eventually, Vance moved from producing revivals to including new plays in the repertoire. The most notable of these was Paul Zindel's *The Effect of Gamma Rays on Man-in-the-Moon Marigolds*, which went on to Broadway and won a Pulitzer Prize in 1971. In 1978 Vance offered as a step in cultural détente a Russian play, *Echelon*, directed by a Russian and using American actors. Vance occasionally guest-directed at other theatres, like the Playhouse in the Park in Philadelphia and Arena Stage in Washington, D.C.

In 1960 Nina Vance was given the Matrix Award from Theta Sigma Phi in recognition of her outstanding contribution to the field of fine arts. In May 1969 she was given an honorary Doctor of Literature degree from the University of St. Thomas, Houston.

Nina Eloise Whittington Vance died of cancer in Houston, Texas, on February 18, 1980. A memorial service was held on February 19, 1980, at the First Presbyterian Church in Houston. Her marriage to Milton Vance had ended in 1960. They had no children.

Nina Vance achieved her personal goal as artistic director of a major regional theatre. The fact that she operated at a time, in a place, and in a climate favorable to the establishment of theatre was, for her, most auspicious. Her work made a significant contribution to decentralizing of professional theatre in America and to the regional theatre movement.

For further information on Nina Vance and the Alley Theatre, see *The Alley Theatre: Four Decades in Three Acts* (1987) by Ann Hitchcock Holmes. See also the chapter "Resident Theatres" in *Theatre in America: Impact of Economic Factors, 1870–1967* by Jack Poggi (1968), and "Equity Revising Theatre Canons" by Cecil Smith, which appeared in the *Los Angeles Times* (December 30, 1965). An Alley Theatre monograph titled "Alley Theatre: History and General Information" (1965) is a rich source of information as is Alley's file of favorable press comments. Although the comments made in *Regional Theatre: The Revolutionary Stage* by J. W. Ziegler (1973) derive largely from *Thresholds: The Story of Nina Vance's Alley Theatre* by William Beeson (1968), they should not be overlooked. See also *Best Plays of 1964–1965*, which contains the essay "Season at the Alley: A Two Part Drama," contributed by Nina Vance. See also Vance's obituaries in the *New York Times*, the *Houston Chronicle*, and the *Houston Post* (February 19, 1980). Nina Vance is included in *The Biographical Encyclopaedia and Who's Who of the American Theatre* (1966) and *Notable Names in the American Theatre* (1976).

Florence M. Lea

VERDON, Gwen (January 13, 1926–): stage and film actress and dancer, was born in Culver City, California, to Joseph W. Verdon, an MGM studio electrician, and Gertrude Verdon, a dancer. Verdon's mother taught her ballet and acrobatics as rehabilitation therapy for childhood rickets, and she soon found work as a "baby" dancer and tumbler. She was married in adolescence to Hollywood columnist and film critic Jim Heneghan; they had a son, James, now an actor-producer. Verdon studied ballet with Los Angeles-based Ernest Belcher and with Carmelita Maracchi. Studies with dancer-choreographer Jack Cole after the breakup of her marriage led to participation in his Columbia Studio workshops and employment as his assistant and demonstrator. She partnered him in *Bonanza Bound* (1948, closed out of town in Philadelphia) and *Alive and Kicking* (1950), and assisted him in choreographing and dance-coaching many Columbia and Twentieth Century-Fox films, among them *On the Riviera* (1951) and his greatest hit, *Gentlemen Prefer Blondes* (1953).

Verdon left Jack Cole in 1953 to dance for Michael Kidd as Claudine, the Apache soloist in *Can-Can*. Though she had few lines and appeared only in a short dance number, she stopped the show. Claudine was her only supporting role—her five other Broadway shows have all featured her as a star. As Lola in *Damn Yankees* (1955), Anna Christie in *New Girl in Town* (1957), Essie in *Redhead* (1959), Charity Valentine in *Sweet Charity* (1966), and Roxy Hart in *Chicago* (1975), Verdon demonstrated her ability to woo an audience while performing the intricate rhythms and fluid movements of choreographer Bob Fosse. She was given Antoinette Perry (Tony) Awards for her roles in *Damn*

Yankees, *New Girl in Town*, and *Redhead*, and received the Film Daily Award for her performance as Lola in the 1958 Warner Brothers movie version of *Damn Yankees*. She received the *Dancemagazine* Award in 1962.

Since retiring from Broadway, Verdon has appeared infrequently on stage—mostly at benefits, though she continues to appear as a popular guest artist at the Tony Awards presentations. She has coached the Fosse and Cole styles as dance captain for *Dancin'* (1979–1980), and has been guest teacher for the American Dance Machine. Her teaching schedule has taken her to China (with the Houston Ballet staff) and many times around the country. Verdon has also acted in dramatic roles on television, most notably as the choreographer in *Legs*, a 1983 movie about Radio City Music Hall. Gwen Verdon married Bob Fosse in 1960. Their daughter, Nicole, has appeared on Broadway with the Cleveland Ballet and in the film version of *A Chorus Line* (1983).

One of the most popular performers in the American musical theatre, Gwen Verdon has combined charm and sexuality with an absolute precision of technique, placement, and movement that choreographers and audiences adore. Her impact on musical comedy dance has gone beyond her immediate theatre audiences through her film appearances, her participation in retrospectives on Broadway's best, and her extensive coaching and teaching.

Since 1955 Gwen Verdon has been profiled in almost every general-interest, film, dance, and theatre magazine. Biographical entries on Verdon appear in *The Biographical Encyclopaedia and Who's Who of the American Theatre* (1966), *Motion Picture Performers* (1971), *Who's Who in Hollywood* (1976), *Encyclopedia of the Musical Theatre* (1976), *Notable Names in the American Theatre* (1976), and *Who's Who in the Theatre* (1981).

Barbara Cohen-Stratyner

VOLLMER, Lulu (1898?–May 2, 1955): playwright who used folk themes and characters, most notably in *Sun-Up*, was born in Keyser, North Carolina, to William Sherman Vollmer and Virginia (Smith) Vollmer. William Vollmer, a lumberman, traveled through the South, taking his wife and three girls with him. The summer vacations spent among the mountaineers of North Carolina were the seminal influence on the young writer. Raised as an Episcopalian, Vollmer was educated at the Normal and Collegiate Institute (later Asheville College) in Asheville, North Carolina. Though the school did not consider theatre part of a proper education, Vollmer, inspired by classroom recitations of Shakespeare, began to write one-act plays for her classmates. Her sketches were produced clandestinely in the gymnasium while the teachers were at dinner. When she was eighteen, Vollmer saw her first professional play, a melodrama, *The Curse of Drink*, while on Christmas holiday in New Orleans, Louisiana. She decided to spend the rest of her life writing plays.

Vollmer worked as a newspaper reporter in Atlanta, Georgia, before moving to New York, where she was employed in the box office of the Theatre Guild at the Garrick Theatre when her first, best, and most successful play, *Sun-Up*, was produced. Apart from a brief, unhappy stint in Hollywood as a scriptwriter, Vollmer, who never married, spent most of her adult life in Greenwich Village, where she died at her home at 1 MacDougal Alley at the age of fifty-seven. She was buried in Attalla, Alabama.

Vollmer's major contribution to American theatre was a series of regional folk dramas set in the North Carolina mountains. The plays focused on inarticulate, uneducated protagonists caught up in events they understand, much less control. At their best, Vollmer's plays demonstrated a new sympathy toward a segment of American society cut off from world affairs and suggested the common denominators of basic human feelings which link all people. At their worst, her plays were melodramatic, clumsy, and flat.

Sun-Up, which Vollmer wrote in 1918, was not produced until May 1923, when Alice Krauser bought it for the Provincetown Playhouse. Starring Lucille LaVerne, *Sun-Up* was an immediate success and thrust Vollmer into a temporary prominence. Suggested by a story Vollmer had heard of a southern boy who, upon arriving in an army camp, had exclaimed, "Air this hyar France?," *Sun-Up* dramatizes provincialism at its most innocent and sentimental within the larger context of a nation at war. The central character, the mother, Widow Cagle, tries to resist abstract forces she cannot comprehend: a law that killed her moonshiner husband and a war that threatens to kill her son. Though now considered crude and flawed by excessive local color, *Sun-Up* had the advantage of novelty when it appeared, and critics were receptive to the subject matter and the fine acting. After running for two years in New York and eight months in London, *Sun-Up* went to Paris, Amsterdam, and Budapest. Vollmer consigned her royalties of over forty thousand dollars from these productions for educational work among the mountaineers, thereby returning the rewards to the people who inspired the play.

Though Vollmer never again enjoyed the success she had with *Sun-Up*, her next two works, *The Shame Woman* (1923) and *The Dunce Boy* (1925), had reasonable receptions. The critics, however, were beginning to attack Vollmer's improbably melodramatic plots and detailed realism while still praising her lofty intentions and compelling themes. In *The Shame Woman*, Vollmer's most decidedly feminist play, an older woman kills the man who had seduced her and then, twenty years later, seduced her adopted daughter. The mother chooses to die in the electric chair rather than let her daughter, though dead, suffer the ignominy of being a "shame woman." *The Dunce Boy* deals with sexual impulses in the mentally retarded and a mother's desperate need to protect her son as well as the woman he desires.

Vollmer's later plays could not match her earlier efforts either in subject or style. *Trigger* (1927), a confused and sentimental play set in rural North Carolina, later was adapted as a film, *Spitfire*, in 1934. Lulu Vollmer and Jane Murfin wrote this adapation as a vehicle for **Katharine Hepburn** (her fifth movie). Hepburn's performance as the hoydenish girl given to alternate fits of physical violence and fanatical praying received as much adverse criticism as the script, which was dismissed as nonsensical and oversimplified. Vollmer's only other collaborative effort was *Green Stones* (1927) with G. G. Dawson-Scott.

Troyka (1930) signaled a departure from Vollmer's usual mode. Adapted from the Hungarian play by Imre Fazekas, *Troyka* starred Zita Johann, who had become famous in **Sophie Treadwell**'s *Machinal*. Set against the background of a prison camp on the eve of the Russian Revolution, the play focused on the love triangle of one woman and two men. While acknowledging that the ideas about love in a political context were important and genuine, critics found the writing hackneyed and cliché-ridden.

Vollmer fared no better with her last plays, *Sentinels* (1931), *Shining Blackness* (1932), *In a Nutshell* (1937), and *The Hill Between* (1938), all of which were written in her by now predictable folk idiom. *Sentinels*, a study in loyalty of an old Negress to the family to which she belonged, suffered from tedious and elaborate exposition and was panned by Brooks Atkinson, the *New York Times* reviewer. By 1938 mountain people were no longer fresh material; *The Hill Between*, about a wholesome mountain boy who is destroyed when he goes to the evil city, received little notice.

Vollmer turned from stage plays to radio serials and short stories as her popularity in the theatre waned. Her subjects were the Carolina mountain people. The short stories "The Road that Led Afar," "She Put Out to Go," "According to the Prophet," "Ghost Shoes," and "Things Hoped For" appeared in the *Saturday Evening Post* between 1939 and 1942. The radio show, *Moonshine and Honeysuckle*, a series of sketches focusing on a rural Romeo and Juliet, ran from 1930 to 1933; *Grits and Gravy* during 1934; *The Widow's Son* from 1935 to 1937. Her last work, *The American Story* (1949), was a radio series written for the National Association of Manufacturers.

Vollmer's most ardent supporter, theatre historian Arthur Hobson Quinn, extolled her early plays for characters worthy of the Russian stage and found in her regional portraits a potential gold mine for a national art. Vollmer's plays were part of a brief, uncoordinated national interest in regional folk drama that climaxed in the mid-twenties and got lost in the more interesting wave of theatrical experimentation influenced by European movements. At first heralded as a serious contender for Eugene O'Neill's title as a leading American dramatist, Vollmer quickly fell from prominence. She should be remembered for her two important contributions to regional folk theatre: first, she took a sympathetic view of simple people, always refusing to use them as comic subjects and insisting that her sophisticated, cosmopolitan audiences accord them the dignity and attention they deserved; second, she dealt with difficult social topics such as sexuality in women and the handicapped, topics not often confronted directly in the drama of the twenties.

Sun-Up has been widely reprinted. See Samuel Marion Tucker, ed., *Modern American and British Plays* (1931); Burns Mantle, ed., *The Best Plays of 1923/24 and the Yearbook of the Drama in America*; and Arthur Hobson Quinn, ed., *Representative American Plays*, revised edition (1938). For discussions of Vollmer's early work, see A. H. Quinn, *A*

History of the American Drama from the Civil War to the Present, revised edition (1980); Helen Krich Chinoy and Linda Walsh Jenkins, eds., *Women in American Theatre* (1981); and Burns Mantle, *American Playwrights of Today* (1929), and *Contemporary American Playwrights* (1938). Vollmer's obituary appeared in the *New York Times* (May 3, 1955). This was followed by a tribute to her in the *New York Times* on May 15, 1955. Lulu Vollmer is included in Siegfried Melchinger, *The Concise Encyclopedia of Modern Drama* (1964); *Who Was Who in America, Vol. 3: 1951–1960* (1966); *Who's Who in the Theatre* (1967); Myron Matlaw, *Modern World Drama: An Encyclopedia* (1972); and *The Oxford Companion to American Literature* (1983).

Susan Harris Smith

WARD, Winifred (October 29, 1884–August 16, 1975): producer, educator, and writer in children's theatre and creative drama, was born in Eldora, Iowa. Her father, George William Ward, was an established lawyer, and her mother, Frances Allena (Dimmick) Ward, was deeply involved in civic affairs. The Ward children were given a strict yet multifaceted education that included theatre and the arts. These early experiences, coupled with a memorable visit to her grand-parents' home in Washington, D.C., at which time she witnessed her first professional theatrical performance in a major commercial theatre, led Winifred Ward to recognize the value of a theatrical education for the young. After high school graduation in 1902, she enrolled in the Cumnock School of Oratory in Evanston, Illinois, later to be incorporated into the Northwestern University School of Speech. Her oratory instructors, particularly Robert Cumnock and Agnes Law, had a profound influence upon the young woman from Iowa. She received her degree from the Cumnock School in 1905 and returned home to Eldora, where she began her teaching career as instructor of oratory and theatre. In 1907 she returned to the Cumnock School for postgraduate work, and in 1908 she accepted a position in Adrian, Michigan.

Ward spent eight fruitful years working in the Adrian public schools, coaching everything from public speaking to calisthenics, before setting out to further her college education at the University of Chicago. A bachelor's degree in English, a master's degree with honors, and an invitation to join the Cumnock School faculty prepared the way for an illustrious teaching career spanning thirty-two years at Cumnock before and after it became part of Northwestern University. She was noted at Northwestern for her exhilarating classes, enriched with frequent appearances by noteworthy writers, artists, and performers like poet Carl Sand-burg and the ventriloquist team of Edgar Bergen and Charlie McCarthy.

By the year 1924 Ward, remembering the value of theatrical activity in her own development, succeeded in implementing a creative dramatics curriculum for the elementary schools of Evanston. So committed was she to both the concept and its continued development in Evanston that for the next twenty-five years she conscientiously served as supervisor of that program along with her regular university duties. Her experiences in the creative drama activities of the Evanston schools significantly influenced the direction of creative drama theory and research in this country. Her work with schoolchildren was chronicled in her book *Playmaking With Children* (1947).

In 1925, the year after her entrance into the public schools, Ward founded, along with associates Ralph Dennis and Alexander Dean, the Children's Theatre of Evanston. *Snow White and the Seven Dwarfs*, directed and produced by Ward, inaugurated this institution, which was to become a paradigm of the American children's theatre movement. While the Children's Theatre provided children of North Chicago with dramatic entertainment, it also broke with tradition by allowing and encouraging many of its juvenile patrons to assume roles in its productions, thus adding to the experience of theatregoers that of theatre performers. The Children's Theatre was revolutionary for its time in yet another fashion. Primarily because of Ward's several affiliations, it was one of the first examples of such a working relationship between Northwestern University and the Evanston Public Schools. The joint sponsorship was formalized in 1927 and lasted until Ward's retirement in 1950. This relationship is still held to be a model of university, public school, and community cooperation in the fostering and administering of a community arts program for children.

In all aspects of production and administration, Ward was a tireless worker. Over the decades of four-play annual seasons and two-a-day performances, Ward distinguished herself as a director, designer, writer, and teacher whose energies seemed boundless and whose adherence to quality in all areas of production was unswerving. As her devotion to the theatre and creative drama for the young blossomed in her university classrooms, in her continued supervision of the public school programs, and in her Children's Theatre work, her name became synonymous with the children's drama movement in America through the thirties and early forties. When the developing American Educational Theatre Association (later the American Theatre Association) recognized a need for exploring its children's theatre branches, it was Ward who rallied her comrades in 1944 into what became the Children's Theatre Conference (now Children's Theatre Association of America). For the first time in the United States practitioners of children's drama nationwide, in the classrooms and on the stages, had an organization wherein they could exchange information and ideas, keep abreast of the theatre scene throughout the continent, and link themselves to the body of academic and commercial theatre professionals. Ward assembled her colleagues on the Northwestern campus during the summer of 1944 under the original title, the Children's Theatre Committee of the American Educational Theatre Association. From the initial eighty-three individuals attending that first CTC meeting, the organization's membership grew to nearly two thousand in less than fifteen years. Ward's involvement had provided the needed impetus for affiliation by many new members.

In 1950 Ward retired from academic life at Northwestern and from her myriad professional activities in Evanston. It was noted that she had given twenty-three years of service and supervision to the Evanston Public Schools, twenty-five years to the directorship of the Children's Theatre of Evanston, and thirty-two years to the faculty of speech and drama at Northwestern University. Ostensibly retired, Ward proceeded to do more writing and to carry out a full schedule of lectures and workshops around the nation. She had published her first major work, *Creative Dramatics*, in 1930. This initial publication defined the approach for subsequent practitioners and theorists in child drama. Her second volume, *Playmaking with Children* (1947), also became a standard text by which others in the field have since been measured. Her publications appearing after her retirement were equally important and influential. Her second edition of *Playmaking with Children*, in which she reexamined ideas in the first printing and developed them further or updated them, appeared in 1957. A year later Ward incorporated her earlier writings into the still timely book *Theatre for Children*. Ward's particular contribution was to set down in print for the first time the art and science of children's theatre. Mainly because of her insights and elaborations, many formal academic theatre programs that had long excluded children's theatre as a "legitimate" branch began to reassess in the late 1950s the true worth and artistry of the area and welcome it into academic programs. In 1960 Ward published her UNESCO monograph on *Drama With and For Children*, which details both creative dramatics and children's theatrical activities. This was followed by several critical reassessments and studies of the current status of the field in the sixties. Other books and articles of varying import punctuated the prolific publication career of Winifred Ward. As calculated by chronicler Jan Guffin (Unpublished Ph.D. dissertation, 1975), Ward contributed more articles about children's drama than any other single writer to the entire spectrum of periodical literature published during the first seventy years of the twentieth century—no small accomplishment for one woman simultaneously tied to several major careers in theatre and education. In addition to her prolific writing, speaking, and workshop activities, Winifred Ward took upon herself during these post-retirement years the duties of resource specialist with UNESCO, board member with the American National Theatre and Academy, and chairperson of the Religious Drama Committee of the American Educational Theatre Association.

Winifred Ward died in Evanston on August 16, 1975. She was ninety years old, and until a few months before her death was still active in the pursuits that had consumed her interests since she left her home in Iowa for the Cumnock School on the northside of Chicago. Along the way she had done more to influence the development of drama in education than anyone before her. The impact of Winifred Ward on American educational theatre is summed up in a *Children's Theatre Review* recollection by Nellie McCaslin, herself a major figure in educational drama: "Though times have changed and children's theatre and creative dramatics today are not what they were even a decade ago, there is no doubt that Winifred Ward changed the course of drama in education for children in our country, and as a consequence, for the adults working with them."

See Winifred Ward's four major works for critical insight into the woman and her theories: *Creative Dramatics in the Upper Grades and Junior High School* (1930); *Playmaking With Children*, second Edition (1957); *Stories to Dramatize* (1952); and *Theatre for Children*, third Revised Edition (1958). The only substantial biography available is Jan A. Guffin's unpublished Ph.D. dissertation, "Winifred Ward: A Critical Biography" (Duke University, 1975). Information can also be gleaned from Ruth Beall Heinig's edited collection of articles, *Go Adventuring! A Celebration of Winifred Ward: America's First Lady of Drama for Children* (1977), and the "Winifred Ward Memorial Issue" of the *Children's Theatre Review*, 25, no. 2 (1976). Ward's place in the history of children's theatre may be seen in Geraldine Brain Siks and Hazel Brain Dunnington, eds., *Children's Theatre and Creative Dramatics* (1961), and in Nellie McCaslin, *Theatre for Children in the United States: A History* (1971). Further resources for the investigation of Ward's writing and practice in theatre may be had by consulting the *Children's Theatre Review Index* for 1951 to 1975, under Ward, published in *CTR* 30(1980), pp. 51 and 54; a full listing of her numerous articles for that publication is given. Ward's manuscripts, correspondence, and memorabilia are housed in the Winifred Ward Archives in the library at Northwestern University in Evanston, Illinois. Her obituary appeared in the *Chicago Tribune* (August 20, 1975). Winifred Ward is included in *Notable American Women*, Vol. IV: *The Modern Period* (1980).

Douglas Street

WARREN, Mercy Otis (September 25, 1728–October 19, 1814): playwright, poet, patriot, and historian, was born in Barnstable, Massachusetts, the third child and first daughter of James and Mary (Allyne) Otis. James Otis was the fourth generation of Otises in New England. He was a farmer, merchant, and lawyer, who served as judge of the County Court of Common Pleas and as colonel of the militia. Mary Allyne Otis was a great-granddaughter of Edward Dotey, who came to America as a servant on the *Mayflower*. James Otis met and married Mary Allyne in Wethersfield, Connecticut. Portraits of both James and Mary Allyne Otis survive, painted by John Singleton Copley. Mercy Otis was three years younger than her brother, the patriot James Otis. She was allowed to study under her uncle, the Reverend Jonathan Russell, when he prepared her brothers for college. In her uncle's library she became familiar with Cicero, Shakespeare, Milton, Dryden, Pope, and with Sir Walter Raleigh's *History of the World*. When James Otis went to Harvard University, he seems to have shared much of his learning and many of his ideas with his sister.

When Mercy Otis was sixteen, she attended her brother's graduation, and she may have met his friend James Warren at that time. James Otis spent much of the next two years at home studying for his master's degree, and he seems to have guided his sister's studies, for Mercy was by now a confirmed scholar. On November 14, 1754, James Warren and Mercy Otis were married. James Warren was the fifth generation Warren to live in Plymouth. The first Richard Warren had come to America on the *Mayflower*. Mercy Otis was twenty-six when she settled with her husband into the Warren family home on the Eel River near Plymouth.

James and Mercy Warren had five sons: James (b. 1757), Winslow (b. 1759), Charles (b. 1762), Henry (b. 1764), and George (b. 1766). Three of the sons died before their parents. James Warren greatly admired his wife's intellectual bent and encouraged her in her studies and in her writing. After her marriage she continued to study and to write poems on nature, friendship, philosophy, and religion. She was also actively involved in lively political discussions, many of which took place in her home. James Otis, Samuel Adams, and John Adams were frequent visitors. James Otis, excitable and occasionally irrational, was one of the most outspoken of the early patriots. In 1769 he published his opinion of certain customs officials who had printed scurrilities against him. The next evening he was attacked with canes and swords by his enemies. Some speculate that this attack helped precipitate his mental breakdown in December of 1771; for Mercy Warren, her beloved brother was the first martyr to American freedom.

In 1772 Warren began her series of polemical writings. On March 26 and April 23, 1772, excerpts from her first propaganda play, *The Adulateur*, appeared anonymously in the radical newspaper, the *Massachusetts Spy*. A revised five-act version of the play was published in pamphlet form in 1773. Her purpose, as she later wrote, was to "strip the Vizard from the Crafty" (These words appear in the papers of Mercy Warren preserved by the Massachusetts Historical Society. They are also quoted by Alice Brown in her biography, *Mercy Warren*, pp. 177–178). The politicians against whom she directed her satirical pen were the wealthy Tory oligarchs who represented the British king and opposed the elected assembly. Chief of these was Thomas Hutchinson, called Rapatio in the play. Opposed to the Tories were the Patriots, led by James Otis, called Brutus. The real names of the characters were not printed but were easily identified by readers. The characters were drawn in strong contrast—the villainous Tories and the heroic Patriots. Mercy Warren's primary purpose in writing the play was to arouse the Patriots and unite them once again as they had been two years before at the time of the Boston Massacre.

In 1773 Warren published in the *Boston Gazette* some excerpts from her second propaganda play, *The Defeat*. This play was evidently never published in pamphlet form. Once again Rapatio appears in the play, and he and his cohorts are opposed by members of the Massachusetts Assembly. In *The Defeat* Mrs. Warren optimistically prophesied victory for the Patriots. In December 1773, the Boston Tea Party took place, prompting Warren, urged on by John Adams, to write a poem, "The Squabble of the Sea Nymphs," which appeared on the front page of the *Boston Gazette* for March 21, 1774. In June 1774, another poem by Warren appeared in the *Royal American Magazine*, satirizing women who refused to give up their imported luxuries.

Early in 1775, Warren wrote her most popular propaganda play, *The Group*, attacking the sixteen councilors who had been appointed by the king and who had refused to resign their commissions despite threats from the mobs. The first two scenes of this play were printed in the *Boston Gazette* on January 23, 1775, and reprinted three days later in the *Massachusetts Spy*. The play, with four scenes and an epilogue, came out in pamphlet form in April. A short time later pamphlet editions were published in New York and Philadelphia, but these editions included only the two scenes that had appeared in the newspapers and may have been pirated.

The Group seems to be the last of Warren's satires in dramatic form, written for publication, not for production. Some scholars have credited her with two more propaganda plays, but there is no proof that she wrote either of them. Their style is very different from *The Adulateur* and *The Group*. The first of these plays is *The Blockheads; or, the Affrighted Officers*, written about the retreat by sea of the British soldiers and Tories from Boston in March of 1776. The second is called *The Motley Assembly*, published anonymously in 1779. It satirizes the *nouveaux riches* who in the latter years of the war began to imitate the social customs of the British and Tories. Warren did write a poem on this theme called ''O Tempora! O Mores!'' It appeared on the front page of the *Boston Gazette* on October 5, 1778.

In 1790 Mercy Warren published her first signed work, *Poems, Dramatic and Miscellaneous*, printed in Boston and dedicated to George Washington. The book contained some of her earlier poems and two long plays that she had just completed. The two plays were written in blank verse and followed rules of the neoclassic drama. *The Ladies of Castile* is based on Spanish history and tells the story of a people's uprising against tyranny. For the first time Warren used female characters, and her heroine is the wife of one patriot and the sister of another. *The Sack of Rome* takes up one of Warren's favorite themes, the danger of luxury and pride. Here the leading woman character is a mixture of heroine and villain. Warren sent this play to her old friend John Adams, who was the American ambassador in London, to see if he could find a producer. Adams did try, but he tactfully wrote Warren that ''nothing American sells here.'' The plays make dull reading today; however, they do show great progress in form and style over her early propaganda plays.

In the 1770s Warren had begun her major literary work, a history of the American Revolution, finally published in three volumes in 1805–1806: *History of the Rise, Progress and Termination of the American Revolution, Interspersed with Biographical, Political, and Moral Observations*. Of most interest to present-day readers are her descriptions of the leaders of the time, because she was writing from personal knowledge of many of them.

On November 27, 1808, Warren's husband, James Warren, died. In 1814 her last and youngest brother died. Three of her five sons had also died. At last, on October 19, 1814, the frail, white-haired, eighty-six-year-old Puritan lady with the fighting republican spirit died at her home in Plymouth. She was buried beside her husband in the old Pilgrim cemetery, Burial Hill, in Plymouth.

Through her propaganda plays and poems, Mercy Otis Warren helped to discredit the Tories and unify the Patriots. She was one of the most democratic of the Revolutionary leaders, and her plays stress the dignity of the common man. She was one of the first writers to use the word "independence" and one of the first to write of a united nation that would some day achieve great things. Warren attempted for the first time in American drama to define "true" Americans as they differed from Englishmen. Royall Tyler was to create a very similar "true" American in his professionally produced American play *The Contrast* (1786). The writers of the propaganda plays, of whom Mercy Warren was the first, started the American drama on the course it was to follow for many years. It was to continue to be journalistic in subject matter, to be a medium for the discussion of current issues, and a means of propagating ideas and urging action. The drama and the theatre were to be a strong force for unifying the people of the new country.

Mercy Warren thought that women were fully capable of participating in many activities that were in her time restricted to men, and in her own life she proved this. Her long history of the Revolution was a most unusual accomplishment for a woman of the eighteenth century. Mercy Otis Warren was greatly respected and admired by her contemporaries for her intelligence and her literary skills.

The Massachusetts Historical Society in Boston has the Mercy Otis Warren Papers and the Mercy Otis Warren Letter-Book. The Massachusetts Historical Society has published the *Warren-Adams Letters* (*Collections*, fifth series, Vols. LXXII and LXXIII, 1917–1925) and "Correspondence between John Adams and Mercy Warren Relating to her *History of the American Revolution*" (*Collections*, Vol. IV, 1878, pp. 315–511). The Library of Congress has copies of the pamphlet editions of *The Adulateur* and *The Group*. *The Adulateur* was reprinted in *The Magazine of History* (Vol. XVI, extra number 63, 1918, pp. 255–259), and the first two scenes of *The Group* were reprinted by Montrose J. Moses in *Representative Plays by American Dramatists, from 1765 to the Present Day* (Vol. I, 1925–26). Norman Philbrick believes it probable that Mercy Warren wrote *The Blockheads* and *The Motley Assembly*; he has reprinted them in *Trumpets Sounding, Propaganda Plays of the American Revolution* (1972). A portrait of Mercy Otis Warren by John Singleton Copley is in the Museum of Fine Arts in Boston. There are two full-length biographies: *Mercy Warren* by Alice Brown (1896) in the *Women of Colonial and Revolutionary Times* series and *First Lady of the Revolution: The Life of Mercy Otis Warren* by Katharine Anthony (1958). *Cast for a Revolution* (1972) by Jean Pritz is a composite biography of James Otis, Mercy and James Warren, and John and Abigail Adams. Maud M. Hutcheson gives a short account of Warren's life in *William and Mary Quarterly* (July 1953). See also "Mrs. Warren's 'The Group,' " by Worthington C. Ford, *Massachusetts Historical Society Proceedings*, Vol. LXII (1930), and Charles Warren's "Elbridge Gerry, James Warren, Mercy Warren and the Ratification of the Federal Constitution in Massachusetts" (*Massachusetts Historical Society Proceedings*, Vol. LXIV (1932). William R. Smith analyzes Warren's *History* in *History as Argument: Three Patriot Historians of the American Revolution* (1966). Arthur Hobson Quinn discusses Warren's propaganda plays in Chapter II of his *A History of the American Drama from the Beginning to the Civil War* (1923 and 1943). Alice McDonnell Robinson has written of the propaganda plays in "Mercy Warren: Satirist of the Revolution" in *Women in American Theatre* (1981), edited by Helen Krich Chinoy and Linda Walsh Jenkins. Alice McDonnell Robinson, "The Developing Ideas of Individual Freedom and National Unity as Reflected in American Plays and the Theatre, 1772–1819" (Unpublished Ph.D. dissertation, Stanford University, 1965) discusses all the propaganda plays written during the Revolution. See also Gerald Weales, "The Quality of Mercy, or Mrs. Warren's Profession," *Georgia Review* (Winter 1979), and Walter J. Meserve, *An Emerging Entertainment: The Drama of the American People to 1828* (1977). Mercy Otis Warren is included in Stephen Jones, *Biographica Dramatica; or, A Companion to the Playhouse*, Vol. III (1912); S. Austin Allibone, *A Critical Dictionary of English Literature and British and American Authors Living and Deceased from the Earliest Accounts to the Latter Half of the Nineteenth Century* (1858–1871, reprint 1965); *Cyclopaedia of American Literature*, Vol. I (1875, reprint 1965); *A Dictionary of American Authors* (1904, reprint 1969), *Dictionary of American Biography*, Vol. X (1936); Stanley J. Kunitz and Howard Haycroft, eds., *American Authors, 1600–1900* (1938); *A Dictionary of North American Authors Deceased Before 1950* (1951, reprint 1968); William Rose Benet, *The Reader's Encyclopedia* (1965); John Gassner and Edward Quinn, eds., *The Reader's Encyclopedia of World Drama* (1969); *Notable American Women*, Vol. III (1971); *Great Writers of the English Language—Dramatists* (1979); *American Women Writers*, Vol. IV (1982); *The Oxford Companion to American Literature* (1983); and *Dictionary of Literary Biography*, Vol. 31, *American Colonial Writers, 1735–1781* (1984).

                                                          Alice McDonnell Robinson

WASSERSTEIN, Wendy (October 18, 1950–): playwright, is the youngest of five children of Morris W. Wasserstein, a textile manufacturer, and Lola (Schleifer) Wasserstein, a dancer. Born in Brooklyn and named after the heroine in James M. Barrie's *Peter Pan*, Wendy Wasserstein and her family moved to Manhattan when she was thirteen; she attended the Calhoun School and studied with the June Taylor School of Dance. Later she attended Mount Holyoke College in South Hadley, Massachusetts, where she majored in history, earning a Bachelor of Arts degree in 1971. Although her parents encouraged her to become a lawyer, she chose to enter the master's degree program in creative writing at City College of the City University of New York. Her first produced play, *Any Woman Can't* (written in 1971), belongs to this period. The play deals with a woman who retreated from career and personal conflicts into marriage. In 1973 Playwrights Horizons, one of New York's Off-Broadway theatres, produced *Any Woman Can't* as well as Wasserstein's musical, *Montpelier Pa-Zazz*. These productions at Playwrights Horizons marked the beginning of a long and continuing affiliation. Wasserstein feels that her association with Playwrights brought inspiration and vitality to her craft. Since then Wasserstein has become a member of the theatre's artistic board of directors.

     After earning her master's degree in 1973, Wasserstein entered the Master of Fine Arts degree program in playwriting at the Yale University School of Drama, graduating in 1976. At Yale, she worked with playwright Christopher Durang on *When Dinah Shore Ruled the Earth*, which was produced in the Yale Cabaret.

For her master's thesis she wrote *Uncommon Women and Others*, which was produced in 1977 at the Eugene O'Neill National Playwrights Conference in Waterford, Connecticut. The play was given a reading at Playwrights Horizons and produced at the Phoenix Theatre, New York, opening on November 21, 1977. The play is a study of well-educated women charged with the responsibility of becoming uncommon contributors to the world without compromising traditions of gentility and refinement. Six years after their graduation from Mount Holyoke, the five heroines gather to discuss in witty dialogue their respective careers in law, insurance, writing, and school, along with their live-in arrangements, their problems of solitude, and their marriages. Wasserstein received a *Village Voice* Off-Broadway (Obie) Award and also the Joseph Jefferson, Dramalogue, and Inner Boston Critics awards for the various productions of *Uncommon Women and Others* from New York to Boston to San Francisco. In 1978 Wasserstein adapted the play for the PBS *Theatre in America* series; the television production featured Meryl Streep and Swoozie Kurtz.

Renewing her association with PBS in 1980, Wasserstein adapted John Cheever's short story "The Sorrows of Gin" for the *Great Performances* series. In 1981 Wasserstein and Christopher Durang again collaborated on an unfilmed screenplay titled *The House of Husbands*. That same year she and Durang, along with other actors, writers, cartoonists, artists, and salespeople, acted in Wallace Shawn's caustic farce *The Hotel Play* at **Ellen Stewart**'s La Mama Experimental Theatre Club, Off-off-Broadway.

In 1980 Wasserstein began writing her second major work, *Isn't It Romantic*. The play elaborates the dilemmas confronting modern women that Wasserstein treated earlier in *Uncommon Women and Others*. *Isn't It Romantic* examines the bonds between two women, their parents, and the men in their lives, and battles with the question how women can attain uncompromising independence and fulfillment without sacrificing romance. The play was produced by the Phoenix Theatre in 1981 but received mixed reviews; many considered the plot too episodic and the characters underdeveloped. A revised version opened in 1983 at Playwrights Horizons for a run just short of two years.

The year 1983 was typically productive for Wasserstein. Her one-act play *Tender Offer* was presented at New York's Ensemble Studio Theatre. The play is about a father who misses his daughter's dance recital, realizes that he has committed a serious offense, and commences the sensitive work of building up a reconciliation with her. Also in 1983 Wasserstein received a Guggenheim Foundation Fellowship. Since that time she, along with six other playwrights including **Maria Irene Fornés**, contributed to *Orchards: Seven American Playwrights Present Stories by Chekhov*—Wasserstein adapted "The Man in a Case"—produced by the Acting Company at the Krannert Center for the Performing Arts (Champaign-Urbana, Illinois) on September 19, 1985, and on tour. She collaborated with Jack Feldman and Bruce Sussman on *Miami*, a musical produced by Playwrights Horizons (1986), and she wrote *Maggie/Magalita*, produced by the Lamb's Theatre Company, New York City (1986). In December

1987 Wasserstein's play, *The Heidi Chronicles*, opened to rave reviews at the tiny Off-Broadway Playwrights Horizon theatre. After a sold-out three month run the play was moved to Broadway. *Time* magazine critic Walter Shapiro wrote that in this play Wasserstein "has written a memorable elegy for her own lost generation" (March 27, 1989). The play won the 1989 Pulitzer Prize for Drama and the Drama Desk and **Antoinette Perry** (Tony) awards for best new play.

In the 1980s, Wendy Wasserstein, who like many of her heroines has so far chosen a career over marriage, is regarded as one of the brightest playwriting talents at work in the United States. Central to her plays are contemporary women's hopes, dilemmas, and ambitions expressed with tender comic warmth by characters who are at once vulnerable and courageous. Wasserstein's plays demonstrate that it is possible to laugh and be compassionate, to explore unknown territory and remain good-natured, to describe hard emotional truths and retain an unabashed sense of romance.

Articles on Wendy Wasserstein include reviews of *Uncommon Women and Others*, such as Harold Clurman, *The Nation* (December 17, 1977); Richard Eder, "Dramatic Wit and Wisdom Unite in 'Uncommon Women and Others,' " the *New York Times* (November 22, 1977); and T. E. Kalem, "Stereotopical," *Time* (December 5, 1977). See also *New York Theatre Critics' Reviews, 1977: Off-Broadway Supplement*, Vol. IV (1977). For *Isn't It Romantic*, see *Vogue* (March 1984), *Time* (December 26, 1983), the *New York Times* (June 15, 1981), *Variety* (June 17, 1981), the *New York Times* (June 28, 1981), *The New Yorker* (June 22, 1981 and December 26, 1983), and *New York Magazine* (June 29, 1981). For *Tender Offer*, see *The New Yorker* (June 13, 1983). Other articles on Wasserstein include Leslie Bennett, "An Uncommon Dramatist Prepares Her New York," the *New York Times* (May 24, 1981), and Benedict Nightingale, "There Really Is a World Beyond 'Diaper Drama,' " the *New York Times* (January 1, 1984). Benedict Nightingale discusses Wasserstein in *Fifth Row Center: A Critic's Year On and Off Broadway* (1986). See also Mervyn Rothstein, "After the Revolution, What?" the *New York Times* (December 11, 1988) and Walter Shapiro, "Chronicler of Frayed Feminism," *Time* (March 27, 1989). Wasserstein's article, "New York Theatre: Isn't It Romantic?" appeared in the *New York Times* (January 11, 1987); with Terence McNally she wrote " 'The Girl From Fargo': A Play," the *New York Times* (March 8, 1987); and her adaptation of "The Man in a Case" is published in *Orchards: Seven American Playwrights Present Stories by Chekhov* (1986). Wasserstein is included in *Interviews with Contemporary Women Playwrights*, ed. Kathleen Betsko and Rachel Koenig (1987). She is listed in *Contemporary Theatre, Film, and Television*, Vol. I (1984); *Contemporary Literary Criticism*, Vol. 32 (1985); and *Who's Who of American Women 1985–1986* (1986).

Nancy Backes

WATERS, Ethel (October 31, 1900?–September 1, 1976): actress and singer, was born in Chester, Pennsylvania. Her mother, Louise Anderson, gave birth at age thirteen to Ethel Waters after a sexual assault by John Waters. Louise Anderson was scarred for life by the experience. Ethel Waters was raised by her grandmother, Sally Anderson, a housemaid, along with her grandmother's children Viola, Edith, and Charlie. As a child, Waters worked at various jobs, including chores at local brothels, cleaning hotel rooms, and washing dishes. Even after her professional career had begun, she made certain that these jobs would be kept for her in the intervals between professional engagements. Her dream, even after much early success, was to become a lady's maid and companion to some wealthy woman who would take her on travels around the world.

Waters's religious affiliation was Roman Catholic. Her allegiance to that church had been cemented by the humane treatment received at a Catholic school in Philadelphia, and she contributed to Catholic charities throughout her career. Her deeply religious nature sustained her through both triumphs and setbacks. In 1957, during a low point in her professional and personal fortunes, she joined the Billy Graham Crusade, with which she remained associated for the rest of her life. Ethel Waters was married twice: first to Buddy Purnsley when she was thirteen years old (whom she left after less than one year), and while in the prime of her career to Eddie Matthews (a marriage that was also short lived). She left no children of her own, though she did provide financial support for approximately twenty needy young girls.

Waters began her show business career as a singer billed as "Sweet Mama Stringbean," in a Philadelphia nightclub in 1911. She then toured as the third member of the Hill Sisters and became the first woman to sing the W. C. Handy classic "St. Louis Blues." Her initial performance of this song at the Lincoln Theatre in Baltimore, Maryland, in 1913 brought a shower of money to the stage along with the enthusiastic applause. After many years of performing as a singer (during which time she became well known for "shimmying" as well as for her vocal abilities), she appeared on Broadway in *Dancer* and Hayward's all-black revue, *Africana* (1927), for which she received an excellent notice in *Variety*. Waters went on to perform in her first film, *On With the Show* (1929), in which she sang "Am I Blue?" As a result of her performance in *Africana*, she appeared in Lew Leslie's *Blackbirds of 1930* (1930) and *Rhapsody in Black* (1931), two other all-black revues.

Upon hearing her sing "Stormy Weather" at Harlem's Cotton Club, Irving Berlin invited Waters to play in his Broadway show *As Thousands Cheer* (1933), with Clifton Webb, **Marilyn Miller**, and Helen Broderick, making her the first black performer in an otherwise all-white cast to appear on Broadway. The show featured Waters singing "Suppertime," the dirge of a black woman who is preparing dinner for her family on the day that her husband has been lynched, the first such song to reach a wide audience. She remained in the hit show for two years (1933–1935). *As Thousands Cheer* was the vehicle that carried Ethel Waters to stardom on Broadway, where she was to become a highly paid performer. When the show went to the South, she became the first black to co-star with whites on the southern stage. During the success of this show, she was hired by the Amoco Gas Company to be the vocalist for the Sunday night radio broadcast of Jack Denny's orchestra, thus becoming the first black to star on a commercial coast-to-coast radio program. She continued to enjoy success as a singer and recording artist after leaving the show.

In 1935–1936, she co-starred with Beatrice Lillie in *At Home Abroad* (which was Vincent Minnelli's first directing job) and received glowing notices from Brooks Atkinson of the *New York Times*. In spite of her success she received no further offers to perform as an actress. She then joined trumpeter Eddie Malloy's band as a vocalist for two years while waiting for her theatrical fortunes to rise again. In 1939, long frustrated with the failure of her theatrical career to develop and confronted by people who regarded her as exclusively a musical performer, she created the dramatic role of Hagar in Dorothy and DuBose Heyward's *Mamba's Daughters*, which opened on January 3, 1939. This role made her the first black actress to star on Broadway in a dramatic play. The character, which bore striking similarities to Waters's mother, enabled Waters to explore and express emotional depths that had been long suppressed. Her performance brought nearly universal rave reviews. The one discordant critic, the same Brooks Atkinson who had praised her four years earlier, was moved to recant his criticism after a notice was taken out in the *New York Times* by theatre notables such as **Tallulah Bankhead**, **Dorothy Gish**, and Burgess Meredith urging him to take a second look at the performance. One day during the run of *Mamba's Daughters*, Ethel Waters learned that her mother, who needed medical attention but was legally sane, was to be confined to a mental institution because no facility in Pennsylvania that could provide appropriate care would accept black patients. After providing home care for her mother, Waters noted the cruel irony: she was being hailed by thousands of sympathetic spectators for her vivid portrayal of an oppressed black character, which she patterned after her mother, while her mother, a real human being, was being callously refused medical care less than one hundred miles away.

After starring in the musical stage production of *Cabin in the Sky* (1940) and a variety revue titled *Laugh Time*, her theatre career languished for nearly a decade. So also did her career in motion pictures after she had appeared in *Cairo* (1942), *Tales of Manhattan* (1942) with Paul Robeson, and *Stage Door Canteen* (1943). Though still in demand as a singer, she received little attention as an actress.

However, in 1949 her career took another favorable turn when she played the role of the grandmother in the film *Pinky*, for which she received an Academy Award (Oscar) nomination. She then gave a memorable performance as Berenice Sadie Brown, the compassionate servant and surrogate mother to **Julie Harris**'s portrayal of tomboy Frankie Addams, in **Carson McCullers**'s *The Member of the Wedding* in 1950, for which she received the New York Drama Critics Circle Award. She was nominated for an Oscar for the same role in the 1955 film version. During preproduction consultations Waters had insisted as a condition for accepting the role that McCullers alter the character of the maid. Carson McCullers agreed that Waters could bring ''God'' and ''hopefulness'' to the character, qualities that were missing from both the novel and the play. Langston Hughes said of her performance: ''She gave an additional human dimension to the conventional 'Mammy' of old—one of both dignity and gentleness—that endeared her to theatregoers without the use on stage of the handkerchief-head dialect and broad humor of former days. In her portrayals of illiterate Negro mothers of the South, Ethel Waters was a mistress of the 'laughter through tears' technique which she brought to perfection in her highly hailed performance of Berenice in Carson McCullers' *The Member of the Wedding*" (*Black Magic*, p. 198). In the twilight of her career Waters played a few guest spots on television shows and was the star of the first "Beulah" series; however, most of her time was dedicated to the Billy Graham Crusade.

Ethel Waters was in no sense a political radical or an agitator for racial equality in the theatrical profession, though in her personal dealings she was a tough negotiator and one who would brook no assaults on her dignity. She was even critical of black political groups who would question the accuracy of the way blacks were portrayed on the American stage and screen. She maintained that there were thieves and murderers and wife-beaters among her people as well as geniuses and saints and that it was therefore misguided to protest the depiction of the former. If the theatrical roles she created reflected the stereotyped perceptions more than the complex realities of American life for blacks, she nevertheless brought an unquestioned sincerity and talent to her work.

Ethel Waters, *His Eye Is on the Sparrow* (1951), is a poignant autobiography. Waters's later autobiography, *To Me It's Wonderful* (1972), discusses primarily her life as a Billy Graham Crusader. Twila Knaack, *Ethel Waters/I Touched a Sparrow* (1978), also covers Waters's career with Billy Graham. See also Donald Bogle, "Ethel Waters: Sweet Mama Goes Legit" in *Brown Sugar: Eighty Years of America's Black Female Superstars* (1980), and Donald Bogle, "Ethel Waters: Earth Mother for an Alienated Age," in *Toms, Coons, Mulattoes, Mammies, and Bucks: An Interpretive History of Blacks in American Films* (1974). Waters is included in Langston Hughes and Milton Meltzer, *Black Magic: A Pictorial History of Black Entertainers in America* (1967); James Weldon Johnson, *Black Manhattan* (1968); Phyllis Rauch Klotman, *Frame by Frame: A Black Filmography* (1979); Loften Mitchell, *Black Drama: The Story of the American Negro in the Theatre* (1967); and Gerald Bordman, *American Musical Revue: From The Passing Show To Sugar Babies* (1985). She is listed in *Notable Names in the American Theatre* (1976), *Who's Who in the Theatre* (1977), and *The Oxford Companion to American Theatre* (1984). Ethel Waters's birth date is often given as 1896, but her autobiography gives 1900.

Elizabeth Hadley Freydberg

WATSON, Lucile (May 27, 1879–June 24, 1962): stage and screen actress, was born in Quebec, Canada, the daughter of Charles Thomas Watson, a major in the Royal Sherwood Foresters, and his wife Leila (Morlet) Watson. Though her early education was with private tutors, she later attended the Ursuline Academy (Quebec) before entering New York's American Academy of Dramatic Arts in 1900. Her first professional stage appearance was in *The Wisdom of the Wise* (1902). Early in her career she had the good fortune of catching the eye of the great producer-manager Charles Frohman. Under his patronage she was ensured a steady career in productions of high quality. Several of the plays were written by the renowned dramatist Clyde Fitch, whose play *The City* gave Watson a two-year run (1909–1911), astonishing at that time.

An early supporter of the Theatre Guild, Watson first appeared under its auspices as Lady Utterwood in George Bernard Shaw's *Heartbreak House* (1920). During the 1920s, Lucile Watson starred in many important New York productions, including Henrik Ibsen's *Ghosts* and Oscar Wilde's *The Importance of Being Earnest*. In 1925 she added a London season to her growing list of credentials, starring in *Dancing Mothers*. In 1934 she made her film debut in James M. Barrie's *What Every Woman Knows*. For the next seven years she alternated between stage and screen. In this first phase of her film career, she had featured roles in such pictures as *A Woman Rebels* (1936), starring **Katharine Hepburn**; *The Garden of Allah* (1936), with Charles Boyer and Marlene Dietrich; and the classic "four-handkerchief weeper" *Waterloo Bridge* (1940), starring Vivien Leigh and Robert Taylor. One of her best and most typical roles was in *The Women* (1939), an adaptation of Clare Boothe Luce's stage hit. As Norma Shearer's mother, Watson was in her element delineating a character that was warm, wise, and sympathetic, yet capable of making piquant observations on the true character of Shearer's friends.

With the outbreak of World War II in Europe (1939), Lucile Watson, along with such notables as Josephine Hull, **Rachel Crothers**, Gertrude Lawrence, and **Antoinette Perry**, became a board member of the American Theatre Wing War Service, at that time a branch of the British War Relief Society. Following the bombing of Pearl Harbor, the service became an independent organization. Watson was chairwoman of the workroom committee, thus in no small way assisting the service to achieve its aim of helping to sell war bonds, entertaining members of the armed forces both in this country and abroad, and collecting food and clothing for the war effort.

In the spring of 1941, Lucile Watson opened on Broadway in what was to be her best-known and most acclaimed role: Mrs. Fanny Farrelly in **Lillian Hellman**'s timely exposé of creeping fascism, *Watch on the Rhine*, directed by Herman Shumlin and with costumes by **Helene Pons**. As the indomitable matriarch of a family that comes to realize, in joltingly personal terms, both the evils of fascism and the valiant efforts of those fighting for democracy, Watson delivered the play's most pungent line: "Well, we've finally been shaken out of the magnolias!" Lucile Watson returned to Hollywood to re-create her role in the film version of *Watch on the Rhine* (1943), for which she received an Academy (Oscar) Award nomination for best supporting actress. The next seven years (1943–1950) were spent working in films. Once again, she had featured roles in many distinguished films, including *Song of the South* (1946), *The Razor's Edge* (1946), and *Little Women* (1949). Her last picture was *My Forbidden Past* (1951).

Returning to the stage in 1950, Watson was featured in Christopher Fry's adaptation of Jean Anouilh's *Ring Around the Moon*. Three years later, after a run in the comedy *Late Love*, she announced her retirement. Brooks Atkinson of the *New York Times* commented, "There are countless theatregoers who have not had enough of her crackling mind, her peppery speech, her fluffy hair, her grand manners" (October 14, 1953).

Lucile Watson had married playwright Louis E. Shipman in 1928. He died five years later. Upon her retirement, Watson led a quiet life in her New York brownstone. Looking back on her career, she reflected that the "Lucile Watson parts" were "high comedy, with feeling, with pathos, funny, gay, kind, tart, and naughty" (quoted in *Current Biography, 1953*, p. 647). When asked about the chances of resuming her career, Watson answered that that would be ungracious. She died on June 25, 1962. In 1950 *The New Yorker* critic Wolcott Gibbs had summed up Lucile Watson's great ability as a comedy actress, "She is one of the most extraordinary comediennes in the theatre, impeccable in timing and delivery, getting her effects with a wonderful economy of gesture and admirable vocal restraint" (December 2, 1950).

Lucile Watson's character roles have received many complimentary comments by the critics. Among the most interesting are those in the *New York Times* for *Pride and Prejudice* (November 3, 6, 17, 1935), for *Yes, My Darling Daughter* (February 10, 1937), for *Watch on the Rhine* (April 2 and 13, 1941), for *Ring Around the Moon* (November 24, 1950), and for *Late Love* (October 14, 1953). See also *The New Yorker* (December 2, 1950). Watson's obituary appeared in the *New York Times* (June 25, 1962). Biographical information on Lucile Watson may be found in *Current Biography, 1953* (1954), *Who's Who in the Theatre* (1961), and *Who Was Who in the Theatre*, Vol. IV (1978). See also *The American Movies Reference Book: The Sound Era* (1969) and Isabelle Stevenson, *The Tony Award* (1975).

William Lindesmith

WEBSTER, Margaret (March 15, 1905–November 13, 1972): director, actress, writer, and co-founder of the American Repertory Theatre, was the final member of four generations active in British and American theatre. Her great-grandfather, B. N. Webster, was an actor and theatre manager of London's Haymarket Theatre in the early nineteenth century. Her father, Benjamin Webster, though admitted to the bar, became an actor in theatre and silent film. His marriage to actress Mary Louisa (Dame May Whitty) Webster in 1892 continued the family's devotion to both the artistic and organizational aspects of the theatre. Peggy Webster, christened Margaret, was born in New York City while her parents were on tour from London. She thus held and maintained dual citizenship, which, during the 1950s McCarthy era, was to her distinct advantage. During her first three years Margaret Webster frequently was left in the care of family friends and her aunt Gretchen while her parents appeared on Broadway and on tour, often in different cities. In 1908 the family returned to London, where she was educated in private schools and graduated from Queen Anne's School, Caversham, in 1923. While her parents did not insist on theatre as a career, they certainly encouraged it by offering their daughter three months in Paris when she was considering attending Oxford University on a scholarship to study the classics. Upon her return from Paris she enrolled in the Etlinger Dramatic School, managed by her mother, whose energy for committees, causes, and the theatre seemed without limits. Weight problems of late adolescence and eye glasses prevented Margaret Webster from playing ingénue parts; she became the aunt or mother-in-law of the young characters. Eye surgery finally corrected her sight, and maturity and diet her weight problems.

Webster's professional theatre debut was as a member of the chorus in Euripides' *The Trojan Women* in October 1924. Shortly thereafter she was the leader of the chorus in *Hippolytus* and played several small parts in John Barrymore's *Hamlet* (1925). Prior to her professional engagements she had made many amateur appearances, one of them as Puck on a program honoring Shakespeare's birthday with the great actress Ellen Terry portraying Portia.

The ten years from 1925 to 1935 were years that Margaret Webster spent working and learning to be an actress. London's West End theatres offered a place to test one's abilities, albeit for little or no money. She understudied Sybil Thorndike in *St. Joan* in 1925, and she and Laurence Olivier were both understudies in a production of *Henry VIII*. After her twenty-first birthday she joined the Macadona Players, first with minor roles, then major ones, in their George Bernard Shaw repertory. After touring England for a year, she joined the Oxford Players, directed by J. B. Fagan, and played in Anton Chekhov's *Uncle Vanya*. In 1928 she joined the Ben Greet Shakespeare Company for a "pastoral tour." The plays were staged out-of-doors, often without rehearsal, and they varied in quality. This experience gave Webster a foundation from which she established in the 1950s her own touring Shakespearean company. In 1929 she was invited to join the prestigious company at the Old Vic under the direction of Harcourt Williams. She played a variety of roles and finally in the 1932–1933 season played Lady Macbeth. Margaret Webster was active in the 1930s in British Actors' Equity Association. For three years she chaired the editorial board that produced British Equity's first magazine. In the United States she served on the board of Actors' Equity for ten years (1941–1951).

In 1934 Webster agreed, as her first major directing task to manage some eight hundred performers in an outdoor production of *Henry VIII*. Her career now took a significant turn towards directing rather than acting. During 1935 and 1936 she directed nine plays, all new (with the exception of a revival of Henrik Ibsen's *Lady from the Sea*), for tryout theatres and Sunday societies. As she achieved notice as a director, she became linked with Shakespeare; consequently, when a former colleague, British actor Maurice Evans, decided to play *Richard II* in New York in 1937, he asked Webster to direct the production. With some trepidation she accepted, arriving in New York with five weeks to cast and mount the Shakespeare play. Webster was praised by the critics for her brilliant, versatile, and powerful production. This success established Webster's career in America as a director, particularly of Shakespeare. During this same year, 1937, Webster's mother, Dame May Whitty, came to Hollywood and at the age of seventy-one embarked upon a career in film. Her best known film is Alfred Hitchcock's *The Lady Vanishes*, made in 1938.

A brief sojourn in London to do *Old Music* at the St. James Theatre (1937) ended for eighteen years Margaret Webster's work in England. She returned to New York to direct Maurice Evans in *Hamlet* (1938). After months of study and textual analysis, she set aside the academic minutiae and "applied an actor's ear and knowledge of stage practices to the arguable points . . . and tried to make myself a channel of communication through which something greater than I might speak" (*Don't Put Your Daughter on the Stage*, p. 26). Webster directed a *Hamlet* that audiences could understand and enjoy. Although some critics complained that she stressed the theatrical values of Shakespeare to the detriment of the intellectual content, Brooks Atkinson wrote, "Miss Webster is all for putting the master out of schoolrooms and museums and setting him on the stage for modern enjoyment" (*New York Times*, November 20, 1940). The response to *Hamlet* was overwhelming; cheers from audiences and accolades from critics caused the play to run for ninety-six performances and to go on two national tours. The Evans-Webster team went on to do *Henry IV, Part I* (1939), *Twelfth Night* (1940) with **Helen Hayes** as Viola, *Macbeth* (1941) with Evans as Macbeth and **Judith Anderson** as Lady Macbeth, and *The Taming of the Shrew* (1951).

In 1939 Webster directed condensed versions of four Shakespeare comedies in a replica of the "Globe Theatre in the Merrie England concession of the New York World's Fair. In the same year she directed her father, who played the elder Disraeli in an unsuccessful production of *Young Mr. Disraeli*. She also directed *Family Portrait* with Judith Anderson in 1938 and Sidney Howard's last play, *Madam, Will You Walk* (1939).

Like many Broadway actors and directors, Webster responded to the siren call of Hollywood. After having convinced her parents to return from prewar England to Hollywood, Margaret Webster accepted a contract with Paramount Pictures. During the first six months she was without a specific assignment but was expected to learn the craft of motion pictures. Her career in film never developed, and after five months she returned to Broadway to produce two plays for the Theatre Guild: Shakespeare's *Twelfth Night* (1940) and *Battle of Angels* (1941), by emerging playwright Tennessee Williams. She then directed *The Tempest* and *The Cherry Orchard* with **Eva Le Gallienne** and two war plays in 1942, *Flare Path* and *Counterattack*. Also during this time she had the opportunity to direct her mother in *Therese* (1945) and in *The Trojan Women* (1941). Her father died in 1947 and her mother in 1948.

Webster, an active proponent of civil rights, raised considerable hostility and predictions of doom by casting a black actor, Paul Robeson, as Othello in 1942. As it turned out, the play made social and theatrical history. Robeson was the first black Othello in the United States, and his performance broke box office records (295 performances). Webster herself played Emilia, José Ferrer Iago, and **Uta Hagen** Desdemona; Webster garnered much praise for her casting and directing. In 1945 Webster joined Eva Le Gallienne to do *The Tempest* at the Alvin Theatre. The next year Webster, Le Gallienne, and producer **Cheryl Crawford**, with great optimism, founded the American Repertory Theatre. They produced a largely classic repertory including *Henry VIII* and *Androcles and the Lion*. The American Repertory Theatre gave opportunities to new performers, like Anne Jackson, Eli Wallach, and **Julie Harris**, the last of these playing the White Rabbit to Webster's the Cheshire Cat and the Red Queen in Lewis Carroll's *Alice in Wonderland* (1947). Webster not only contributed her efforts in fund raising and management but acted, directed, and invested her own money in the project. However, the theatre was able to sustain itself only until May 1948.

Webster then convinced the impresario Sol Hurak to assist her in organizing a truck and bus caravan to be known as the Margaret Webster Shakespeare Company, consisting of twenty-one actors and eight staff members who took Shakespeare across America on the "gymnasium circuit" for two years. Convinced by a previous lecture tour (1942) that good theatre must travel across America, Webster braved high school audiences who munched popcorn and candy, endured transportation breakdowns, played on stages of all sizes and conditions, was subject to union-nonunion crew squabbles, and coped with arrivals only a few hours before curtain time. The troupe presented *Hamlet, Macbeth, Julius Caesar*, and *The Taming of the Shrew* in thirty-six states and four Canadian provinces to audiences who had little or no previous exposure to professional theatre, or to Shakespeare. Despite its popular success the company, wracked by financial troubles, disbanded in 1950. Webster wrote, "The commercial success was nil; the other rewards were enormous. I have not the slightest doubt that it was the most valuable contribution I ever made to theatre in America" (*Don't Put Your Daughter on the Stage*, p. 173).

In 1950 Webster's career made another shift when she accepted an invitation by Rudolf Bing, the new manager of the Metropolitan Opera, to stage *Don Carlos*, the first opera of his opening season. Aware that she would be the first woman to direct at the Met, she began with some trepidation the task of directing performers who saw themselves as vocal soloists. She also had to plan stage action for a ninety-five-member chorus. Using boxes of toy soldiers sent by friends, she planned stage movement on ground plans of the sets. Since full rehearsals had not been a regular practice at the Met, her methods of directing surprised both cast members and chorus; extras and chorus members were particularly grateful for her attention to details of staging. *Don Carlos* was a complete success. She went on to direct *Aida* (1951) and *Simon Boccanegra* (1960) at the Met and *Troilus and Cressida* (1951), *Macbeth* (1957), *The Taming of the Shrew* and *The Silent Woman* (both 1958) at the New York City Opera.

Acting, however, was Webster's first love, and although she continued to act over the years, critics were less likely to praise her acting than to commend her directing skills. Critics were favorable to her characterization of Masha in an Alfred Lunt-**Lynn Fontanne** production of Anton Chekhov's *The Sea Gull* (1938), to her portrayal of Mrs. Borkman in Henrik Ibsen's *John Gabriel Borkman* (1946), and for her portrayal of a nun-detective in *The High Ground* (1951). Webster did not adhere to a particular theory of acting, having learned her craft from observation and understudy of the great actors and actresses of British theatre.

In 1950 Margaret Webster saw her name, along with those of other theatre professionals, published in *Red Channels*, and her battle with McCarthy's House Committee on Un-American Activities began. When the Department of State was hesitant to issue her a passport to attend a UNESCO conference in Paris, she made the trip on her British passport, having maintained her dual citizenship. She was called before the House Committee on Un-American Activities in May of 1953. Despite her clearance on all charges, fears of new accusations or even imprisonment plagued her. Like many, including Lillian Hellman, her career suffered. She lost assignments on radio and in film, and no offers of work in the theatre were forthcoming. Webster went to France, wrote some articles, and worked on a script of *The Strong are Lonely* (1953), which she directed in England and later in New York. In England she directed *The Merchant of Venice* (1956) for the Shakespeare Festival Theatre at Stratford-on-Avon, *Measure for Measure* (1957) for the Old Vic, and Noel Coward's *Waiting in the Wings* (1960) in the West End. In 1964 she gave a solo performance based on the life and works of the Brontës.

By the 1960s the stigma from the House Committee on Un-American Activities had lessened, and Webster was sent to South Africa for three months by the United States Department of State under the American Specialists Program. She lectured, gave recitals and interviews, and directed a production of Eugene O'Neill's *A Touch of the Poet*, which played across the country for both black and white audiences. She returned a year later to do *A Man for All Seasons* in New York. She also toured Australia in 1968 for the Department of State. In 1963 with Maurice Evans, she directed *The Aspern Papers*, which closed after ninety-three performances. Her final Broadway production was Graham Greene's *Carving A Statue* (1968), which closed after twelve performances.

Also during the 1960s Webster was a visiting professor at the University of California at Berkeley, Boston University, and the University of Wisconsin. She found academic theatre uncertain, whether its mission was to train actors or to bring theatre to the community. Webster was amazed to find herself the subject of three doctoral dissertations and was probably just as surprised when, over the years, five colleges and universities bestowed upon her honorary degrees. Webster wrote some forty-five articles and three books: *The Same Only Different* (1969), about her family's history; *Don't Put Your Daughter on the Stage* (1972), an autobiography; and *Shakespeare Without Tears* (1942), which was revised in 1957 and also published in Great Britain under the title *Shakespeare Today* (1957).

Webster's approach to Shakespeare was not scholarly; she grew up with a living poet who was performed in the theatre on a regular basis. At her mother's knee she learned to love the beauty and power of the language and sought to convey this in production. Like Granville-Barker, she saw the classics as theatre, not as literature. Emphasis was placed upon a clean text and a good story, an uncluttered stage, speed and fluency of language, and strong, credible characters. Such practices sometimes led Margaret Webster to ignore the psychological aspects of contemporary works that she directed; nonetheless, she unquestionably created a new interest in classical drama and revitalized Shakespeare on the American stage.

Margaret Webster's papers are in the Margaret Webster Theatre Collection in the Library of Congress. Additional materials are in the British Museum Library, the Harvard Theatre Collection, and the Theatre Collection of the New York Public Library Performing Arts Research Center at Lincoln Center. The Beinecke Library at Yale University has materials on Webster's Theatre Guild association. Studies of Webster include Ely Silverman, "Margaret Webster's Theory and Practice of Shakespearean Production in the United States, 1937–1953" (Unpublished Ph.D. dissertation, New York University, 1969); Janet Carroll, "A Promptbook Study of Margaret Webster's Production of *Othello*" (Unpublished Ph.D. dissertation, Louisiana State University, Baton Rouge, 1977); Robert Worsley, "Margaret Webster: A Study of Her Contributions to American Theatre" (Unpublished Ph.D. dissertation, Wayne State University, Detroit, 1973); and Amanda Sue Rudisill, "The Contributions of Eva Le Gallienne, Margaret Webster, Margo Jones and Joan Littlewood to the Establishment of Repertory Theatre in the United States and Great Britain" (Unpublished Ph.D. dissertation, Northwestern University, Evanston, Illinois, 1972). In addition, there is David Fenema's "The Problem of the Touring Company, Margaret Webster's Touring Company, 1948–1950" (Unpublished master's thesis, University of Wisconsin, 1968). A bibliography on Webster appears in *Cumulated Dramatic Index 1909–1949*. The books written by Webster are cited in the text. She also adapted a play from the German, *Royal Highness* (1949), and wrote *Shakespeare and the Modern Theatre*, fifth Lecture on the Helen Kenyon lectureship at Vassar College (1944). Obituaries appeared in the *New York Times* (November 14, 1972) and *The Times* (November 14, 1972). Eva Le Gallienne wrote a tribute to Margaret Webster in the *New York Times* (November 26, 1972), and Laurence Olivier wrote one for *The Times* (November 16, 1972). A biographical essay about Webster appeared in *The New Yorker* (May 20, 1944). Margaret Webster is included in *Who's Who in the Theatre* (1947); *Who's Who in America, 1950–1951* (1950); *Who's Who, 1950* (1950); *Current Biography, 1950* (1951); *The Biographical Encyclopaedia and Who's Who of the American Theatre* (1966); *American Women 1939–1940* (1974); *Notable American Women*, Vol. IV: *The Modern Period* (1980); *The Oxford Companion to the Theatre* (1983); and *The Oxford Companion to American Theatre* (1984).

Fran Hassencahl

WEST, Mae (August 17, 1892?–November 22, 1980): actress, playwright, screenwriter, novelist, and famous "Sex Goddess," was born Mary Jane West in Brooklyn, New York. Her father, John West, of English and Irish ancestry, was known as "Battling Jack," an ex-prizefighter who ran a livery stable business. Her mother, Matilda Delker (Dolger) West, had been born in Bavaria, Germany, and came to the United States as a young girl. Before her marriage she had been a corset and fashion model. Little Mae was the first child; five years after her a sister, Beverly, was born and a year later a brother, John Edwin. Mae West was privately tutored and briefly attended two public schools, but her formal education ceased when she was thirteen. She began dance lessons at the age of seven and made a successful debut as "Baby Mae" in a song and dance act in an amateur night at the Royal Theatre, Brooklyn. A determined and independent child, she demanded and got her own spotlight at the Royal Theatre. Later she would insist on rewriting scripts, changing scenes and costumes, and adding her own personal touches to plays and films. Eventually she wrote and produced her own material.

At age eight, after successfully making the rounds of amateur nights in local theatres, she joined a theatre stock company to play child parts. This apprenticeship lasted until, at the age of eleven, she began to outgrow child parts. She continued to perform in vaudeville and at age seventeen met and teamed up with Frank Wallace. They put together a song and dance act and began a road tour. In Milwaukee on April 11, 1911, they were secretly married. Upon returning to New York, West dissolved the act and then the marriage by getting Wallace a forty-week job with a touring company. In 1942 they were divorced; she never married again.

After performing at the Columbia Theatre on Broadway in 1911, West received job offers from Florenz Ziegfeld and from Ned Wayburn. She based her choice on the size of the theatre. She found that she was most successful in a smaller theatre where she could work more closely with audiences. "The entire effect of my personality depends on audiences being able to see my facial expressions, gestures, slow, lazy comic mannerisms, to hear me properly" (*Goodness Had Nothing to Do With It*, p. 31). West was seeking stardom and being one of Ziegfeld's Follies girls would not bring her individual attention. She went with Wayburn, and *A la Broadway and Hello Paris* opened on September 22, 1911. West was unknown, but she, as she often would do in the future, she rewrote her part of an Irish maid and added songs; in effect she stole the scenes and received great applause from audiences and compliments from reviewers. The surprised and pleased author was William Le Baron, who later produced some of her films.

In November 1911, West appeared in a Shubert show, *Vera Violetta*, at the Winter Garden Theatre. When it closed after 152 performances, West teamed up with two male dancers to be billed as "Mae West and the Gerard Brothers" and returned to the vaudeville circuit with star billing and a top agent, Frank Bohn, from the United Booking Office. Her salary rose from $350 to $750 a week. Although nudity was never part of her act, she was developing a sexually seductive wiggle in her routine, and she adorned herself with elaborate satin and velvet gowns, rhinestones, furs, and feathers. West was also developing a lusty style that both parodied and glorified conventional sexuality. She became adept in the use of double-entendre. She wrote, "It wasn't what I did, but how I did it. It wasn't what I said, but how I said it and how I looked when I did it and said it. I had evolved into a symbol and didn't even know it" (*Goodness*, p. 43). She did little to discourage the media from giving her the title, "America's Sex Goddess." In fact, she encouraged it by the content and style of her performances. West was a comedienne who poked fun at conventional morality and had great fun doing it. Such behavior inevitably brought her into conflict with the censors.

During her years on the road with vaudeville acts (1912–1916) West became interested in jazz and visited black cafés in Chicago, where she observed blacks dancing the Shimmy. When she returned to New York on October 4, 1918, to play the lead, Mamie Dyne, opposite Ed Wynn, in Arthur Hammerstein and Rudolph Friml's *Sometime*, she introduced her version of the shimmy dance. After 283 performances, she returned to vaudeville in *Demi-Tasse* (1919) and the *Mimic World* (1921). Her shimmy dance amused and titillated audiences and critics, but she soon ran afoul of the Society for the Suppression of Vice in New York City.

West had long taken liberties with lines and lyrics in her performances. When she was unable to find a role she liked, she wrote her own. Undaunted by J. J. Shubert's rejection of her first play (*Sex*), she teamed up with her mother, her mother's attorney, James Timony, and veteran producer C. W. Morganstern to produce it herself. Her business relationship with Timony lasted until his death in 1954. *Sex* opened at Daly's Theatre in New York on April 26, 1926. Because of the title, newspapers refused to carry ads, but a poster campaign and word of mouth made the show a success. West played the lead, Margie LaMont, a waterfront prostitute. In its forty-first week the play was closed by the Society for the Suppression of Vice. Mayor James (Jimmie) Walker was on vacation and his vice mayor, Joseph V. "Holy Joe" McKee, decided to crack down on pornography. In court, unable to establish that the text was obscene, the prosecutor secured a conviction on the basis that West, fully clothed in a tight metallic evening gown, moved her navel in an obscene way when she danced. She was sentenced to serve eight days in prison at Welfare Island for "corrupting the morals of youth." Her protests at the coarse texture of the prison-issued underwear were duly reported in the *New York Times*. While in prison she wrote an article for *Liberty Magazine* and made a donation of $1,000 to the prison library.

West's second play, *The Drag* (1926), produced in Patterson, New Jersey, condemned current views of homosexuality and asked for tolerance and understanding. Advised because of censorship problems not to bring the play to Broadway, West wrote another play, *The Wicked Age* (1927), which was an exposé of bathing beauty contests with their crooked operations and fixed winners. West's greatest success was *Diamond Lil* (1928), a comic melodrama with a gay nineties theme set in New York's Bowery. West, as was her custom, wrote the leading role for herself. Diamond Lil became the personification of Mae West as she was and wished to be and solidified the type of role she would play when she moved to Hollywood. West realized that Diamond Lil, descending the stairs of a western dance hall, clad in extravagant turn-of-the-century costumes, lying in a golden bed reading the *Police Gazette*, spoofing the Salvation Army, love, and marriage, and belting out the popular ballad, "Frankie and Johnny," was her other self and wrote in her autobiography that "Lil in her various incarnations—play, novel, motion picture—and I have been one" (*Goodness*, p. 115).

Diamond Lil opened in Brooklyn at the Shubert Theatre in 1928, moved to Broadway a week later on April 9, and continued there until January 1929, when it went on tour to Chicago and other major cities. Meanwhile, West's *Pleasure Man* (1928) opened at the Biltmore but was closed by the police. West went to court and won, but she did not reopen the show. On the road she also revived *Sex* and wrote *Babe Gordon* (1930), a novel about "an amoral lady of pleasure," whose career takes her from the dives of Harlem to the smart circles of New York and Paris. The book became a play, *The Constant Sinner*, which opened on Broadway in 1931 and ran into the summer of 1932.

A reviewer for the *New York Times* had found *Sex* "feeble and disjointed," ineptly written, and cheaply produced by a cast of unknowns (*New York Times*, April 27, 1926). Later critics found *Diamond Lil* to be more professionally staged, the writing improved, and the play no thinner in plot line than many others. "It uses every tried and trusted trick, hokum, motive, and stage expectation, but always shrewdly" (*New Republic*, June 27, 1928). *The Constant Sinner* was also seen as melodramatic and dull and the main character, Babe Gordon, the scarlet woman, with "her exploitation of blonde buxomness—all these grow pretty tiresome through repetition" (*New York Times*, September 15, 1931). West's plays, never "classics" of the theatre, have nevertheless aged well. When West revived *Diamond Lil* twenty-one years later, critics saw the play as a part of American folklore like the minstrel show and burlesque, compared it to the dime novel, and praised it as "a triumph of nostalgic vulgarity" (*New York Times*, February 7, 1949, and November 30, 1948). Thus, in more ways than one, West had wiggled into popular culture.

West's performance carried her shows. She wrote them as vehicles for herself; thus, the roles emphasized her strengths as an actress. Critics in the 1920s and 1930s, unimpressed by her scripts, were entertained by her performances, her timing, her voice, and her ability to captivate and hold an audience. Even in film, West played as though the audience were just beyond the footlights. She dazzled them with her costumes and her slow, sensual movements, and she shocked audiences with her insolence. Her ability to give a quick one-line response, often laden with sexual overtones, was reminiscent of her vaudeville days. Reviewers puzzled over whether to take her seriously and whether or not she took herself seriously. They decided that it really didn't matter because she should be seen as comparable to and bringing back all of the glamour of **Lillian Russell**. What shocked censors of the 1920s was no longer shocking to later critics. The sex was suggestive. Love scenes were burlesqued and ended with a wisecrack or a clever line before they were even begun. Viewers were left to project their own wishes and sexual feelings upon West who remained the earthy but remote sex object. In 1948 Brooks Atkinson, reviewer for the *New York Times*, asked what all the patrol wagon ruckus was about twenty years earlier because Mae's burlesque of sex (*Diamond Lil*) was "about as wicked as a sophomore beer night and smoker" (*New York Times*, November 30, 1948).

Ever aware of changing tastes and fortunes in the entertainment business, West had decided to accept a $5,000 a-week contract from Paramount Pictures in 1932. She starred in twelve pictures. Nine were screenplays that she had written. It was in her first picture, *Night After Night*, that she ad-libbed an answer to the admiring remark, "Goodness, what beautiful diamonds," saying "Goodness has nothing to do with it, dearies" (*Films of Mae West*, p. 65, and *Goodness*, pp. 156–157). This line became the title of her autobiography, written in 1959 and revised in 1970. West went on to make seven pictures for Paramount: *She Done Him Wrong* (1933), *I'm No Angel* (1933), *Belle of the Nineties* (1934), *Goin' to Town* (1935), *Go West Young Man* (1936), *Klondike Ann* (1936), and *Every Day's A Holiday* (1937). Her pictures rescued Paramount from financial malaise, made a star of the unknown Cary Grant, and made West the highest-paid star in Hollywood. In 1938 West teamed up with comedian W. C. Fields to make a mock western, *My Little Chickadee* (1940). West wrote the script, leaving room for Fields's improvisations. The film has become a classic.

West returned to Broadway with a new play, *Catherine Was Great* (1944), and revivals of *Diamond Lil* in New York (1949 and 1951) and in London (1948). West, in her sixties, surrounded by young muscle-men, many of whom fought for her affections both off and on stage, made a nightclub tour from 1954 until 1956. She also produced three records: *The Fabulous Mae West* (Decca, 1955), *Way Out West*, and *Wild Christmas* (Tower, 1966).

At the age of seventy-seven, West returned to Hollywood to make the film *Myra Breckinridge* (1970). Reviewer Vincent Canby said, "Mae got short shrift in a junk picture" (*New York Times*, June 25, 1970), and wondered if this was really West or just a caricature of her. As she aged, she found the prospect that she was no longer young difficult to accept. Her last film, *Sexette*, made when she was eighty-seven years old, was a disaster. Makeup and costumes could not hide her age. Her voice cracked, she walked with difficulty, and one eye, weakened from a stroke, sagged. Reviewers were irritated at her presumption, and Canby suggested that she was a tragic reminder "of how a disembodied ego can survive total physical decay and loss of common sense" (*New York Times*, June 8, 1979).

Audience response to Mae West was always strong. During World War II, pilots of the British Royal Air Force put Mae West in the dictionary by naming an inflatable life jacket after her. United States Army soldiers referred to twin-turreted combat tanks as "Mae Wests." Audiences today know West primarily through her films. Revivals of her films from the 1960s on college campuses made her part of the "camp" culture and established her place in film history as a comedienne in the company of the Marx Brothers, W. C. Fields, Abbott and Costello, Red Skelton, Bob Hope, and Martin and Lewis. Like Fields and the Marx Brothers, West was in the iconoclastic tradition of Mack Sennet, Charlie Chaplin, and Buster Keaton, who ridiculed the sweet, the nice, the polite, and the accepted social customs. A supreme egoist, West cut a wide swath through early twentieth-century American theatre and became something of a legend.

Mae West's career can be followed through her reviews, popular magazine articles about her, and interviews, most particularly in *Esquire* (July 1967), *Saturday Evening Post* (November 14, 1964), *TV Guide* (February 27, 1965), and the *New York Times Magazine* (November 2, 1969), as well as her autobiography, *Goodness Had Nothing To Do With It* (1959, revised in 1970). A popular book, *The Wit and Wisdom of Mae West* (1967) by Joseph Weintraub is an illustrated collection of her many witticisms. *Mae West* by George Eells and Stanley Musgrove (1982) and *The Films of Mae West* by Jon Juska (1973) also chronicle her Broadway and Hollywood career. Obituaries appeared in the *New York Times* (November 23, 1980) and *Time Magazine* (December 1, 1980). West's birth date appears in some biographies as 1893. Mae West is included in Robert L. Sherman, *Actors and Authors with Composers Who Helped Make Them Famous* (1951); *The Biographical Encyclopaedia and Who's Who of the American Theatre* (1966); *Current Biography, 1967* (1967–1968); Myron Matlaw, *Modern World Drama: An Encyclopedia* (1972); William C. Young, *Famous Actors and Actresses on the American Stage*, Vol. II (1975); *Notable Names in the American Theatre* (1976); *Who's Who in the Theatre* (1981); and *The Oxford Companion to American Theatre* (1984).

Fran Hassencahl

WESTLEY, Helen (March 28, 1875–December 12, 1942): stage and film actress, long associated with the Theatre Guild, was born Henrietta Remsen Meserole Manney in Brooklyn, New York. She was the younger of two children and the only daughter of Charles Palmer and Henrietta (Meserole) Manney. At an early age, she decided on an acting career. With a dedication of purpose that was to become a lifelong characteristic, she pursued her higher education, studying at the Brooklyn School of Oratory, Boston's Emerson College of Oratory, and finally at the American Academy of Dramatic Arts in New York.

Billing herself as Helen Ransom, she joined the touring stock company of Rose Stahl, making her New York debut in *The Captain of the Nonsuch* (1897). This early training in stock companies, where an actress would have to undertake a wide variety of roles in the period of a few weeks, coupled with her formal training, helped turn her into a highly skilled actress in a relatively short time. On October 31, 1900, she married the actor Jack Westley (John Wesley Wilson Conroy), and their marriage produced one child, Ethel. During her twelve years of marriage Helen Westley subordinated her career to the demands of domesticity. After separating from her husband in 1912, she became a member of Greenwich Village's Liberal Club, which counted Sinclair Lewis, Theodore Dreiser, **Susan Glaspell**, and Lawrence Langner among its members. In 1915 Westley, Langner, and others founded the Washington Square Players, a troupe that did not hesitate to satirize contemporary issues or figures. An early target was one of the then current darlings of the intelligentsia, Belgian dramatist Maurice Maeterlinck. That first season, Westley appeared as the Oyster in a one-act play titled *Another*

Interior, a takeoff on Maeterlinck's *Interior*. More seriously, in 1916 she appeared in the Washington Square Players' production of *The Sea Gull*.

In 1918, after various New York engagements, Helen Westley helped found the Theatre Guild, an organization she served until a year before her death. A direct, honest, and often outspoken woman, she was unswerving in her quest for perfection. Neither the size nor showiness of a role was important to her; whether or not it was good theatre was her main concern. In her years with the Guild, she took mainly supporting parts, such as Mrs. Zero in Elmer Rice's *The Adding Machine* (1923), Ftatateeta in George Bernard Shaw's *Caesar and Cleopatra* (1925), Mrs. Higgins in *Pygmalion* (1926), Lady Britomart in *Major Barbara* (1928), and Mrs. Evans in Eugene O'Neill's *Strange Interlude* (1931).

In 1934 Helen Westley started an eight-year screen career that encompassed nearly thirty films. No longer young and never a conventional beauty, she was nevertheless in great demand as a character actress. Of medium height, Westley could appear as either fat and slatternly or large and imposing. Like her build, her screen personality ran between tart but warm-hearted on one end of the spectrum to downright shrewish on the other. Among her better-known films are *The House of Rothschild* (1934); two Irene Dunne classics, *Roberta* (1935) and *Showboat* (1936); *Heidi* (1937), in which Westley may have had her best screen role, as the asp-tongued but loving Parthy Hawks; and *Alexander's Ragtime Band* (1938). Her last film, *My Favorite Spy*, was completed less than a year before her death.

Having made a final stage appearance in *The Primrose Path* (1939), heart disease forced Westley to curtail her activities. She resigned from the board of the Theatre Guild in 1942, its twenty-fourth year, and retired to New Jersey. While there she suffered a heart attack and died on December 12, 1942.

Lawrence Langner remembered Helen Westley as "one of the most refreshing personalities in the theatre, as well as one of its most talented character actresses. But what made Helen Westley invaluable to the Washington Square Players and later to the Theatre Guild, was her simple, direct enthusiasm for the greatest plays, her incisive mind which cut through any meretricious work like a surgeon's scalpel, her disregard for appearances, her dislike of mediocrity, and her unwillingness to sacrifice art for money . . . '' (*The Magic Curtain*, p. 93).

There is a clipping file on Helen Westley in the Harvard University Theatre Collection. Some newspaper and magazine articles of interest are *Theatre Magazine* (August 1922), *The New Yorker* (March 27, 1926), the *New York World-Telegram* (March 24, 1930, and August 18, 1931), and the *New York Times* (December 12 and 13, 1937). See also Walter Prichard Eaton, *The Theatre Guild: The First Ten Years* (1929); Lawrence Langner, *The Magic Curtain* (1951); and Theresa Helburn, *A Wayward Quest* (1960). Westley's obituary appeared in the *New York Times* (December 13, 1942). Biographical accounts of Helen Westley appear in *Who's Who in the Theatre* (1939); *Notable American Women*, Vol. III (1971); *Dictionary of American Biography, Supplement Three, 1941–1945* (1973); *Who Was Who in the Theatre*, Vol. IV (1978); and *The Oxford Companion to American*

Theatre (1984). Her birth date is sometimes given as 1879, but her death certificate (under the name of Henrietta Manney Conroy) verifies the year of birth as 1875.

William Lindesmith

WHITE, Ruth (April 24, 1914–December 3, 1969): actress, was born in Perth Amboy, New Jersey, the daughter of Charles V. and Jane A. (Gibbons) White. Her father was an industrial designer and her mother an amateur actress. She had two brothers and two sisters. Both her sisters and one of her brothers sang, but not professionally. Her younger brother, Charles, became a professional actor. The Whites were frequent theatregoers, and fireside storytelling, recitations, and musicales were part of their family life. Ruth White, a Roman Catholic, attended St. Mary's High School in Perth Amboy. She received a Bachelor of Arts degree from Douglass College, majoring in speech and dramatics. In 1962 Douglass awarded her an honorary Master of Arts degree. In New York she studied acting with Maria Ouspenskaya from 1938 to 1940.

White began her theatrical activities early in life. At the age of seventeen she toured New England in a mystery play titled *The Trial of the Century*. She also performed her own original material in one-woman shows at clubs, community centers, and churches. Even long after she was well established, she continued directing amateur theatricals. She explained that since acting was such self-centered work, she was grateful for the chance to give of herself a little in the area that she knew so well. She also taught at Perth Amboy High School and Seton Hall University.

From 1940 on, White became active in professional theatre. Her first Broadway-bound venture was as Mary Todd Lincoln in *Stove-Pipe Hat*, which closed in its Boston tryout in 1944. White was subsequently cast in two other productions, which failed to open on Broadway: *Mardi Gras* in 1947 and *Catstick* in 1956. In 1945 she toured Alaska and the Aleutian Islands for the USO as Miss Eggleston in *What A Life*. It was at this time that she formed an association with the Bucks County Playhouse as resident actress. This association lasted until 1956. Among her most noted roles were Amanda Wingfield in *The Glass Menagerie* and Birdie Hubbard in *The Little Foxes*.

White made her Broadway debut in 1947 in *The Ivy Green*, but it wasn't until 1956 that she was seen there again as Teacake Magee in *The Ponder Heart*. She was also featured that year as Mrs. Duke in *The Happiest Millionaire*. Subsequent productions in which she took part, both on Broadway and Off-Broadway, were *Rashomon*, where she appeared as the Mother (1959); *The Warm Peninsula*, as Iris Floria (1959); *Whisper To Me*, as Lucille Mary Purdy (1960); *Big Fish, Little Fish*, as Edith Maitland (1961), for which she had won the Philadelphia Drama Critics Award the previous season; *Happy Days*, as Winnie, for which she won a *Village Voice* Off-Broadway (Obie) Award in 1962; *Lord Pengo*, as Mrs. Drury (1962); *Absence of a Cello*, as Celia Pilgrim (1964); and *The Birthday Party*, as Meg (1967). For the last play, she was nominated for the Antoinette

Perry (Tony) Award in 1968. She did the voice-over narrations for *Motel* in 1966 and *Box Mao Box* in 1968.

Against the advice of her peers, her agent, and even Actors' Equity, Ruth White was one of the first Broadway-calibre actresses to perform in experimental plays for what is now known as Off-off-Broadway. The gesture earned her the title "Queen of the Avant-Garde." In this capacity she appeared in plays by Samuel Beckett, Harold Pinter, Jean-Claude Van Itallie, and Edward Albee.

White also established a career on television and in films. As early as 1950 she appeared on television in *Suspense* and *Rocky King*. Other shows included *Ben Casey*, *Dr. Kildare*, *You Are There*, *The Alcoa Hour*, *U.S. Steel Hour*, *Philco Playhouse*, and *Hallmark Hall of Fame*. She received an Emmy Award from the National Academy of Television Arts and Sciences for her portrayal of Mrs. Mangan in the *Hallmark Hall of Fame* production of *Little Moon of Alban* in 1964. She also appeared in such films as *Edge of the City* (MGM, 1957), *The Nun's Story* (Warner, 1959), *To Kill a Mockingbird* (Universal International, 1962), *Up the Down Staircase* (Warner, 1967), *Hang 'em High!* (United Artists, 1969), and *The Pursuit of Happiness* (Columbia, 1970). She died of cancer during the filming of *The Reivers* and was buried in Perth Amboy.

Ruth White was known as an actor's actor; she had a visible following among her peers. At a memorial given for her at the Circle In The Square Theatre shortly after her death, literally hundreds of actors and directors turned out to reminisce. Among the speakers was Harold Clurman, who in 1965 had directed her as Mary Tyrone in a Japanese-sponsored production of *Long Day's Journey Into Night* in 1965. He began by exclaiming, "To praise Ruth White is like praising the Atlantic Ocean—she was a force of nature!" Alan Schneider, who had directed Ruth White a half-dozen times, wrote in the obituary in the *New York Times* (December 14, 1969), "In any other theatrical civilization, Ruth White would not have been dismissed as a 'character actress,' whatever that means, nor as a 'star.' . . . She would have been appreciated long ago as an actress of the first rank."

There is a clippings file on Ruth White in the Billy Rose Collection at the New York Public Library Performing Arts Research Center at Lincoln Center. Among the many clippings are her obituaries from *Variety* (December 10, 1969), the *New York Post* (December 4, 1969), the *Newark Evening News* (December 4, 1969), a notice in the *New York Times* (December 18, 1969, announcing her memorial service), and an article by Alan Schneider, which appeared in the *New York Times* (December 14, 1969). Additional information was supplied by Ruth White's surviving brother, actor Charles White. Basic information about Ruth White's life is contained in *The Biographical Encyclopaedia and Who's Who of the American Theatre* (1966).

                                                                    Constance Clark

WOOD, Audrey (February 28, 1905–December 27, 1985): literary representative and agent, was born in New York City, the only child of William H. and Ida (Gaubatz) Wood. The Woods had come to New York from Milwaukee in order to further William Wood's career as a theatrical producer and manager.

He managed the Broadway Theatre at Fortieth and Broadway from the turn of the century until 1912. In 1912, when the Broadway was converted to a silent movie house, he became the manager of the Palace, a theatre designed especially for vaudeville stars. Sarah Bernhardt, **Ethel Barrymore**, W. C. Fields, Douglas Fairbanks, Sophie Tucker, and Bert Williams all headlined at the Palace, and as the manager's daughter, Audrey Wood saw all of them. She and her mother also frequented other Broadway theatres, where, out of professional courtesy, they had free passes.

In 1916 William Wood became the manager of a stock company housed in the Hudson Theatre in Union Hill, New Jersey. The bill changed frequently, and as a result, Audrey Wood saw an even greater variety of plays. She also often read the unproduced manuscripts sent to her father. Besides going to the theatre, Wood attended grammar school on Fiftieth Street (in what was even then known as ''Hell's Kitchen'') and went on to Washington Irving High School. There she became editor of the school magazine, *The Sketch Book*, and its first theatre critic. She graduated in 1925 and enrolled at Hunter College (now a unit of the City University of New York). She withdrew after three months, however. College did not suit her, and her father had had a stroke. Until his death, Wood worked as a secretary. She then attempted to support the family by becoming an actress, as her father had always hoped she would do.

Although she had grown up around the theatre, she had very little professional experience. When she was sixteen, her father had cast her in a small role at the Hudson Theatre, which was followed by some bit parts at the Brooklyn Stock Company. What she lacked in credentials, however, she possessed in self-confidence and influence. Working through her father's friends, she got an offer to act in a company in Chicago. She turned down the job, however, when she realized that she would never be able to support the family on an actor's small salary. In 1927 Wood began working for the Century Play Company, a highly successful agency that acted on behalf of playwrights. She began as what we would now call a free-lance reader, writing reports (for three dollars each) on the commercial potential of unsolicited manuscripts. She later convinced Gus Diehl, a friend of the family who handled much of the paperwork for Century, to hire her as his assistant, and from there she moved into the new plays department.

As a play agent Wood had a chance to strike out in new directions. Rather than wait for new plays to arrive on her desk, she went out looking for them. Unintimidated by her own lack of experience or reputation, she contacted George Pierce Baker, the dean of the Yale Drama School. Wood met with Baker (who had recently moved his ''47 Workshop,'' in which he taught playwriting, from Harvard to Yale) and convinced him to refer promising graduates to her agency. This led to her representation of playwrights such as Joseph Kesselring (*Arsenic and Old Lace*), Harry Segall (*Heaven Can Wait*), and Arnold Sundgaard (*Everywhere I Roam*).

Wood stayed with Century Plays for seven years. When the agency folded in the early thirties, she was offered a job with Leland Hayward's agency, a prestigious firm that represented such talents as **Katharine Hepburn** and Fred Astaire. She turned down the offer, however, when Hayward informed her that he would have the last word on all scripts. Nothing came of her interviews with other agencies, so when Doris Frankel (a friend and a client) offered Wood free office space in return for a partnership in her own agency, Wood accepted. The Audrey Wood Agency opened with a small list of clients and so little income that the young agent was forced to go to her mother for bus fare.

Wood was struggling to keep the agency alive when she was contacted by William Liebling, a noted Broadway casting agent, who was interested in opening a new play department and wanted to hire Wood as its director. Despite her financial problems, she put Liebling on hold, not wanting to give up her business or disappoint her partner. Not long after, Doris Frankel pulled out of the partnership, leaving Wood free to join forces with Liebling. The two chose April 23 (Shakespeare's probable birthday) to open the Liebling-Wood Agency at 30 Rockefeller Plaza. Only two months later, in June 1937, they had their first big hit (*Room Service*, a comedy by John Murray and Allen Boretz), and the problem of finding clients was solved.

The business merger was only the beginning of their partnership. Less than one year after the agency opened, they decided to marry. They knew that their mothers would be troubled by the interfaith marriage (Liebling was Jewish while Wood was Lutheran), so they decided to marry first and face the consequences later. They married secretly on February 28, 1938, and continued to live apart until March 24, when Audrey Wood decided that the only way to make things right would be to marry again in the presence of her mother. Ida Wood attended the second ceremony, which was held in the parsonage of the Little Church Around the Corner. Liebling's mother died without ever knowing that her son had married.

Liebling and Wood were a formidable team. Together they attended countless plays and readings, always actively seeking out new talent. Each was equally intent on a career, and they lived in the Royalton Hotel at West 44th Street in order to accommodate their busy lifestyle. Audrey Wood's clients included Dubose and Dorothy Heyward, Tennessee Williams, Robert Anderson, William Inge, Truman Capote, Arthur Kopit, **Carson McCullers**, Preston Jones, Brian Friel, and many others. Her most publicized and turbulent professional relationship was with Tennessee Williams, whom she discovered through a play contest held by the Group Theatre. Wood immediately recognized Williams' talent, and she helped him find grants and jobs so that he could keep on writing. Even after his first play failed in Boston, Wood supported him and, convinced of the merits of *The Glass Menagerie*, promoted the script for six years until it finally opened on Broadway. She continued to be his agent until the early 1970s, when Williams turned against Wood, blaming her for the failure of his 1960s plays. The experience was painful for Wood, who felt that she had always been loyal to Williams. She severed their professional and personal relationship, breaking the silence only in 1980, when the playwright's mother died.

Liebling-Wood became so successful that in 1954 the couple decided to sell the agency to the Music Corporation of America (MCA), thereby allowing Liebling to pursue producing while Wood remained an associate at MCA. In 1962 MCA developed legal problems, and Wood moved to Ashley-Steiner, which was to become a part of International Creative Management (ICM). In 1965 Wood became an advisor to the Eugene O'Neill Memorial Theatre Foundation, and in 1967 she taught a playwriting course at Wesleyan University in conjunction with the foundation. In 1970 she was honored by the New Dramatists Committee, a new playwrights organization that she ardently supported, and by Florida State University in Tallahassee, which awarded her an honorary Doctor of Humane Letters degree.

Wood and her husband had been living in Florida during the 1960s because Liebling's health was failing. The couple had taken a house in Sarasota, from which Audrey Wood would commute in order to continue to represent her clients. On December 29, 1969, William Liebling died after a long illness, and Wood moved back to the Royalton Hotel in New York, which she had always considered her home. She continued to work at ICM and also began taping her memoirs. She filled twenty cassettes with reminiscences that became the basis for her autobiography, *Represented by Audrey Wood*. On April 28, 1981, Audrey Wood went over the final manuscript with Max Wilks, her collaborator. She never saw the published book, however. On April 30 she stepped out of a cab at the Royalton Hotel and collapsed. She was taken to Mount Sinai Hospital, where it was discovered she had suffered a cerebral hemorrhage and had lapsed into an irreversible coma.

When Wood was eventually moved from Mount Sinai Hospital to a nursing home in Connecticut, it became more difficult to visit her. Nevertheless, she was not forgotten. In October 1981, although she was unable to be present, she received the Richard L. Coe Award at the John F. Kennedy Center for the Performing Arts in Washington, D.C., for her contributions to the theatre. In 1982 a scholarship fund for aspiring dramatists was established in her name at the Yale School of Drama and Repertory Theatre. On October 22, 1984, the Audrey Wood Theatre was dedicated at 359 West 48th Street. In 1984 Arthur Kopit also paid a personal tribute to Wood, writing her in as a character in his play *End of the World*. Wood died in the nursing home in Fairfield, Connecticut, on December 27, 1985.

Audrey Wood was a tiny woman, under five feet tall, who managed to command attention and respect both in artistic and business circles. She was able to bring outstanding American playwrights to the stage because she could recognize and deal with genius. As Tennessee Williams wrote in 1981: "Theatrical people are often impossible people. No one understood them better than Audrey or knew so well that understanding was so essential to their existence" *(Represented by Audrey Wood*, p. 325).

The best source of information on Audrey Wood's life and career is her autobiography, *Represented by Audrey Wood* (1981). Clippings, programs, and photographs are available at the New York Public Library Performing Arts Research Center at Lincoln Center. Wood's collection of books and scripts is in the Wood-Leibling Library at the O'Neill Theater Center in Waterford, Connecticut. There are also a number of excellent articles on Audrey Wood, including "The Agent as Catalyst" by Tennessee Williams and David Newman in *Esquire* (December 1963), and "Devotion to the Stage Was Her Hallmark" by Samuel G. Freedman in the *New York Times* (August 1, 1984). Her relationship with Tennessee Williams is described at length in *Tennessee Williams: An Intimate Biography* (1983) by Dakin Williams and Shepherd Mead and in *The Kindness of Strangers: The Life of Tennessee Williams* (1985) by Donald Spoto. Wood's obituary appeared in the *New York Times* on December 28, 1985. A short biography of Audrey Wood is included in *The Biographical Encyclopaedia and Who's Who of the American Theatre* (1966) and in *Notable Names in the American Theatre* (1976).

Brenda Gross

WOOD, Mrs. John (November 6, 1831–January 10,1915): outstanding actress and theatre manager during the mid-nineteenth century, was born Matilda Charlotte Vining in Liverpool, England. Her parents, Mr. and Mrs. Henry Vining, were both actors in the English provinces. Henry Vining, son of silversmith Charles Vining, was one of eight children all of whom pursued theatrical careers. Matilda Vining was the second of his two daughters, both of whom joined the Vining theatrical tradition. A cousin, Fanny Elizabeth Vining, married the American actor E. L. Davenport.

In 1841 at age nine, Matilda Vining made her stage debut in Brighton. For the next thirteen years she acted in English provincial theatres, principally Manchester, where for several years she was engaged to play leading comic roles at the Theatre Royal. In May 1854, after marrying actor John Wood, the young Matilda Vining Wood, together with her new husband, contracted for the first season of the Boston Theatre, Massachusetts. Thomas Barry, recruiting for the new theatre, hired John Wood for the first low comedy line and Matilda Vining Wood for the chambermaids. He claimed that they were great favorites and were generally considered equal to any artists on the English stage. The Woods sailed for Boston in August, and, on September 11, 1854, they made their American debut. John Wood played Bob Acres in *The Rivals* and Matilda Wood appeared as Gertrude in J. R. Planchaa's *The Loan of a Lover*.

Mr. and Mrs. Wood remained with the Boston Theatre company for three seasons. Mrs. Wood's repertoire was extensive and varied. She had played such roles as Ariel in *The Tempest* and Puck in *A Midsummer Night's Dream*, but she also excelled in burlesque and farce.

The couple made their first New York appearance on September 4, 1856, in Planché's *The Invisible Prince* at the Academy of Music, in a benefit for W. M. Fleming. On December 25, 1856, the Woods also began a for a three-week engagement at Wallack's Theatre in New York. George C. D. Odell states that Christmas night "brought to New York the gift of the joyous Mrs. John Wood"

(Vol. VI, p. 533). Mrs. Wood appeared in the Charles Melton Walcot burlesque *Hiawatha, or Ardent Spirits and Laughing Waters*, a vehicle in which she was to succeed for many years. *Hiawatha* ran without interruption until January 13, 1857. The Woods' stay at Wallack's concluded on January 21, and they returned to the Boston Theatre until the end of May.

By July 1857 the Woods were once again at Wallack's Theatre in New York. Mrs. Wood recaptured the critics' hearts in Francis Talfourd's burlesque *Shylock, or The Merchant of Venice Preserved*. By the end of their engagement in August, it was apparent that Matilda Wood surpassed John Wood in critical acclaim. He was still regarded as a competent comic actor, but Mrs. Wood was being heralded as the queen of comedy.

In September 1857 the Woods set out for San Francisco, playing theatres in St. Louis and New Orleans en route to the West Coast. Their San Francisco première took place on January 18, 1858, at Maguire's Opera House in the musical comedy *Josephine; or, The Fortune of War*. Long-time San Francisco actor Walter Leman claimed of Matilda Wood that "no more popular actress ever visited the Pacific Coast; her first engagements at the Opera House were a series of triumphs" (*Leman*, pp. 283–284). Mrs. Wood left San Francisco in March to tour various theatres on the California circuit, including Sacramento, where she briefly managed the Forrest Theatre. By August 1858 she had returned to San Francisco, and the controversial *Love's Disguises* at Maguire's provided Mrs. Wood with one of the many male (breeches) roles for which she became famous. In March 1859 the American Theatre was newly renovated, and Mrs. Wood enjoyed another foray into theatrical management. It was during the California tour that she became estranged from her husband. When she left San Francisco for New York in the summer of 1859, she left her husband, their daughter Florence, and her mother in California. John Wood died in Victoria, British Columbia, on May 28, 1863. Daughter Florence later married dramatist Ralph Lumley.

In September 1859 Mrs. Wood joined Dion Boucicault at the Winter Garden Theatre in New York. In addition to Boucicault, the company included Joseph Jefferson III and Boucicault's wife **Agnes Robertson**. In *Dot*, Boucicault's version of *The Cricket on the Hearth*, Mrs. Wood had the role of Tilly Slowboy. George C. D. Odell claimed that Mrs. Wood "kept the audience in a continuous roar. Her performance and Jefferson's were more especially Dickensy then any of the others" (*Odell*, Vol. VII, p. 211). The association was not entirely harmonious, however. James H. Stoddart reports that Mrs. Wood had a misunderstanding and withdrew from the company. For the next three years she toured leading theatrical centers, including Philadelphia, Boston, New Orleans, and New York.

On October 8, 1863, Mrs. John Wood began a three-year reign as actress-manager of the Olympic Theatre in New York. The theatre, leased by John Duff, Augustin Daly's father-in-law, had formerly been **Laura Keene**'s Theatre. Mrs. Wood headed a company including E. L. Davenport, **Mrs. G. H. Gilbert**,

William Davidge, and James H. Stoddart. The last of these characterized her tenure at the Olympic as "brilliant." Her American managerial career concluded on June 30, 1866, after which she sailed for England and a London première.

Mrs. John Wood's first appearance upon the London stage took place at the Princess's Theatre on November 12, 1866. Her reception as Miss Miggs in *Barnaby Rudge* on that date was less than enthusiastic. She had to face the existing English prejudice against American artists, since the audience had the mistaken impression that Mrs. Wood was an American-born actress. In October 1869 she undertook the management of London's St. James's Theatre, which *The Times* of London described as being, at the time, "a despised and unlucky house." Under Mrs. John Wood it "quickly rose into favour. She made it comfortable and attractive, and drew around her a fine company" (January 15, 1915). She continued to perform there at St. James's until her return tour to the United States in 1872–1873. On March 4, 1872, Wood appeared on the New York stage in a production of *La Belle Sauvage* at Niblo's Garden Theatre. Her engagement at Niblo's Garden ended April 20, 1872, but she joined the company of Daly's Grand Opera House on August 26, 1872, with the political burlesque *King Carrot*. She remained with the Daly company until April 26, 1873, when she played Peachblossom in Daly's own *Under the Gaslight* for her final New York performance.

Mrs. Wood returned to London in 1873 and resumed both acting and managing responsibilities. She was seen in productions at the Criterion, the Gaiety, the Haymarket, and St. James's theatres. In 1883 she began a connection, first as actress and later as manager, with the Court Theatre, where she played several of her most memorable performances in Arthur Wing Pinero's farces and in dramas by her son-in-law, Ralph Lumley. Except for occasional productions, Mrs. Wood left the theatre after retiring from management in 1893. Her next stage role thereafter was in the 1905 production of *The Prodigal Son*. On January 10, 1915, she died at age eighty-three at her Birchington home after being in poor health for five years.

Mrs. John Wood's reputation as a comic actress of rare merit, excelling in burlesque and farce, is well documented by her theatrical colleagues on both sides of the Atlantic. Singing and dancing complemented her comedic skill. Ann Hartley Gilbert, who acted with Mrs. Wood in New York and London, declared, "She is the most absolutely funny woman I have ever seen, both on and off stage. The fun simply bubbled up in her. Then she could sing and dance a bit, and in the burlesques and farces she did . . . she was inimitable" *Stage Reminiscences of Mrs. Gilbert*, pp. 78–79). Her competence and fairness as a manager were also noted by those who worked with her. As both actress and manager, Mrs. John Wood helped sustain the comic and farcical traditions of the English-speaking stage for over half a century.

Specific facts and information about Matilda Vining Wood must be gathered from theatre histories and personal reminiscences. Eugene Tompkins, *The History of the Boston Theatre 1854–1901* (1908), suggests the circumstances of the American debut of John and Matilda Wood. The New York career of the actress-manager can be followed through George C. D. Odell, *Annals of the New York Stage*, Vols. VI-IX (1931–1937), and T. Allston Brown, *A History of the New York Stage* (1903). The best personal account of Mrs. Wood's reign at the Olympic Theatre is provided by James H. Stoddart, *Recollections of a Player* (1902). Edmond Gagey's *The San Francisco Stage* (1950) and George R. MacMinn's *The Theatre of the Golden Era in California* (1941) mention Wood's appearance on the West Coast, while Walter M. Leman, *Memories of an Old Actor* (1886), provides a glowing account of her success in San Francisco. Insight into her comedic skill can be gleaned from Catherine Mary Reignolds-Winslow, *Yesterdays with Actors* (1887); Charlotte M. Martin, *The Stage Reminiscences of Mrs. Gilbert* (1901); John H. Barnes, *Forty Years on the Stage* (1914); and Clement Scott, *The Drama of Yesterday and Today* (1899). See also T. Allston Brown, *History of the American Stage* (1870); Charles Eyre Pascoe, ed., *Our Actors and Actresses: The Dramatic List* (1880); Erskine Reid and Herbert Compton, *The Dramatic Peerage, 1891* (1891); *The Green Room Book or Who's Who on the Stage, 1909* (1909); and *The New Dramatic List: Who's Who in the Theatre* (1914). Matilda Vining Wood is included in *Notable American Women*, Vol. III (1971); *Who Was Who in the Theatre*, Vol. IV (1978); *The Oxford Companion to the Theatre* (1983); and *The Oxford Companion to American Theatre* (1984). *Who Was Who in the Theatre* gives Wood's birth date as 1833.

Jane T. Peterson

WOOD, Peggy (February 9, 1892–March 18, 1978): actress and author, was born Margaret Wood in Brooklyn, New York, the only child of Eugene and Mary (Gardner) Wood. Eugene Wood, a newspaperman, believed that if a parent could not give his offspring a large inheritance, the least he could do was see that his child possessed a skill whereby she could earn a living. With this concern in mind Eugene Wood began training his daughter for a singing career. Margaret Wood studied voice with Arthur Van der Linde, Eleanor McLellan, and the renowned opera star Madame Emma Calvé. Her performing career began in 1910, the year following her graduation from Manual Training High School in Brooklyn, New York.

Margaret Wood was married twice; first to the novelist, poet, and playwright John Van Alstyn Weaver, on February 14, 1924. In September 1927, their son David Weaver was born. John Weaver died on June 18, 1938. Wood then married printing executive William A. Walling on October 1, 1946, remaining with Walling until his death in 1973. In her final years Wood resided at a retirement home in Stamford, Connecticut, where she died at the age of eighty-six of a cerebral hemorrhage.

Wood entered theatrical life in 1910 as a chorus member in Victor Herbert's operetta *Naughty Marietta*. During this production she changed her name from Margaret to Peggy, since there were eight other Margarets in the chorus. Wood continued as a singer, chorus member, and understudy through 1914, when she was cast in the leading role in a touring production of the musical *Adela*. That year she also performed in George M. Cohan's revue *Hello Broadway*, which set the style for the modern American musical revue by dispensing with all pretense of a plot. In 1915 Wood had a leading role in a nonmusical, the George M. Cohan production of *Young America*, and in 1917 she opened in the Shubert production of Sigmund Romberg's *Maytime*. This appearance established her as a musical-comedy star. The musical's immense popularity made it unique in theatrical history: within a year after its August 1917 première at the Shubert Theatre, a second company opened with the same production at the 44th Street Theatre, almost directly across the street. It, too, played to sold-out houses.

In 1919 Wood went to Hollywood to co-star with Will Rogers in the silent film *Almost A Husband*. When she was offered another starring role in the Shubert Broadway musical *Buddies*, she left Hollywood with little hesitation, even though her film had been favorably received. During the summer of 1921 Wood starred in a play that she co-authored with Sam Merwin, *Artist's Life*, about the life of Johann Strauss, performed at the Shubert-Murat Theatre in Indianapolis, Indiana. She returned to Broadway in 1922, starring in the popular musicals *Marjolaine* and *The Clinging Vine*. During the run of *The Clinging Vine* she developed an illness termed "hysterical aphonia," or loss of voice for no physical reason. Her dream of becoming an opera star was subsequently destroyed. One doctor suggested that Wood's inability to sing during performances or under pressure might be a result of a subconscious reaction to the paternalism of the show's producer. Wood's father once tried to force her as a child to sing in front of company—a traumatic experience from which she never fully recovered. No longer confident of her ability to achieve excellent vocal production, Wood tried a new path. In 1924 she created her first straight comedy role on Broadway in *The Bride*. Indeed, the 1920s marked many firsts for Peggy Wood. In 1925 she starred in her first dramatic role, Candida in George Bernard Shaw's play. The following year she successfully attempted her first Shakespearean role, Lady Percy in *Henry IV, Part I*. She toured with John Drew's company in Arthur Wing Pinero's *Trelawney of the "Wells"* in 1927. Inspired by her contact with Drew, she wrote her first book, *A Splendid Gypsy*, which chronicled episodes from Drew's career. In 1928 she played Portia in the critically acclaimed George Arliss production of *The Merchant of Venice*.

In 1929 Wood starred in the successful London production of Noel Coward's *Bitter Sweet* and reappeared on the London stage in 1932 in the Jerome Kern and Otto Harback operetta *The Cat and the Fiddle*. Wood returned to Hollywood in 1934, where she once again co-starred with Will Rogers, this time in a "talkie," *Handy Andy*. In 1937 she appeared in David O. Selznick's film *A Star is Born*.

In 1938 Wood returned to the London stage where she starred in Coward's *Operette*, which opened to mixed reviews for Coward and rave reviews for Wood. While in London she appeared on television, performing in variety shows and plays. Following *Operette*, Wood appeared in the **Edna Ferber**-George S. Kaufman comedy *Theatre Royal*, more commonly known in the United States as *The Royal Family*. Returning to the United States, she co-starred with **Jane**

Cowl in John Van Druten's Broadway comedy *Old Acquaintance* (1940). The following year Wood and Coward proved again to be a winning combination, taking New York by storm with the opening of Coward's *Blithe Spirit* (1941) at the Morosco Theatre, where the play ran for 650 performances. The cast then went on a national tour for almost a year, followed by a World War II European USO tour from October 1944 to June 1945. In all, Wood performed in this production for almost four years.

In 1949 Peggy Wood began a television series that introduced her to thousands of households across the nation. *Mama* was based on the John Van Druten play, *I Remember Mama*, and the Kathryn Forbes diary by the same name. Wood played the title role of a warm and witty Norwegian immigrant, living with her family in San Francisco at the beginning of the century. The major contribution of the series to television history was that it set the pattern for many of the family situation comedies that followed. *Mama* occupied most of Wood's professional life between 1949 and 1957. During the late 1950s and 1960s she performed in regional theatre productions, in Broadway and Off-Broadway plays, in film, and on television. None of these productions reached the critical acclaim of her 1941 hit, *Blithe Spirit*, or her successful television series, *Mama*.

Wood's involvement with theatrical organizations dominated the latter part of her career. In 1959 Peggy Wood became the president of the American National Theatre and Academy (ANTA). She served as president through 1965. During her presidency Wood was instrumental in the founding of the American College Theatre Festival (ACTF), which still takes place each spring at the John F. Kennedy Center for the Performing Arts in Washington, D.C. Another project that Wood nurtured during her presidency of ANTA was the subsidizing of Broadway theatre tickets for New York City school children. Wood stated that the future of our theatre depended upon the youth of our nation.

In 1963 Wood testified at an inquiry conducted by New York State's attorney general Louis Lefkowitz, investigating the financing and ticket distribution practices of the New York legitimate theatre. Her testimony, along with that of songwriter Richard Rodgers, helped to create the Theatrical Syndication Financing Act. This law states that all producers of Broadway and Off-Broadway shows must file a prospectus with the attorney general's office for each theatrical production. The licensing of box-office personnel also came about through this inquiry. The Theatrical Syndication Financing Act is significant because it protects a show's investors, creators, and artistic staff, whose financial returns are based upon a percentage of the box-office receipts.

In 1959 Wood spearheaded the drive to restore the Goodspeed Opera House, a playhouse in East Haddam, Connecticut. This revitalized regional theatre has provided Broadway with several major musicals, including *Man of La Mancha*, *Very Good Eddie*, *Shenandoah*, and *Annie*.

Wood's lifelong theatrical activities promoted positive international understanding. As early as 1929, when she performed in Noel Coward's *Bitter Sweet*, a leading London critic wrote that one could seldom hear English so well spoken.

Wood's portrayal of Mama (on the CBS television series) was so loved by Norwegian immigrants that in 1951 the Norwegian ambassador to the United States presented Wood with the medal of the Order of Saint Olaf, Norway's patron saint. Norway's King Haakon selected Wood because he felt that her portrayal of "Mama" contributed to the betterment of international understanding. Wood also served on the permanent advisory drama panel of the United States State Department's Cultural Presentation Program. As part of this program she undertook several lecture tours, during which she described the acting profession in the United States and promoted cultural exchange. In addition to the Royal Order of St. Olaf medal (1951), Wood received the Kelcey Allen Award in 1964 for her unselfish contributions to the American theatre. (Kelcey Allen was a highly respected drama critic with *Women's Wear Daily*). In 1965 Wood was nominated for an Academy (Oscar) Award for her portrayal of the Mother Abbess in the film musical *The Sound of Music*. In May of 1966 she received an award from the National Council on the Arts and Government for her championing of government aid to the arts. She was selected to become the first recipient of the Agnes J. Futterer Lecture Chair at the State University of New York (SUNY) at Albany in September 1966. In September of 1970 Wood was presented with the Theatre La Salle Award in honor of her distinguished service to the American theatre outside New York. In 1974 she was honored with the American Theatre Association's Distinguished Service to the American Theatre Award for a lifetime of dedication and commitment to the betterment of American theatre. She received honorary degrees from Lake Erie College (1950), Hobart College (1959), Hamilton College (1964), and Mount Holyoke College (1967). She was named Fellow of Timothy Dwight College, Yale University (1967), and Westminster Choir College (1969).

An actress of considerable fame during her performing career, Wood was also a committed theatre activist, participating in and leading causes and projects that added to the effectiveness of American theatre in ways that endured beyond her lifetime.

Peggy Wood's published works include *The Flying Prince* (1927), a play written in collaboration with Eugene Wood; *The Splendid Gypsy* (1928), theatrical reminiscences of John Drew's life; *Actors and People* (1930), Wood's conversations with George Bernard Shaw and Emma Calvé during her 1922 visit to France and Italy; *The Star Wagon* (1936), a novel; *How Young You Look* (1941), the first segment of Wood's autobiography; and *Arts and Flowers* (1963), the second segment of Wood's autobiography, which describes her life between 1941 and 1963. Articles about Wood include Maude S. Cheatham, "Peggy Wood on Her Way to Popularity," *Motion Picture Classic* (October 1919); Harold B. Clemko, "The Armchair Spectator Meets Peggy Wood," *TV Guide* (May 9, 1952); George Freedley, "Peggy Wood," *Chapter One* (Fall 1960); "Why Miss Wood Walked Out," *New York Times* (December 22, 1964); and Eugene Wood, "The Childhood of a Star," *Pictorial Review* (June 1964). Peggy Wood's obituary appeared in the *New York Times* (March 19, 1978). She is listed in *Current Biography, 1953* (1954); *The Biographical Encyclopaedia and Who's Who of the American Theatre* (1966); William C. Young, *Famous Actors and Actresses of the American Stage* (1975); *Notable Names in the American Theatre* (1976); *Who's Who in the Theatre* (1977); and *The Oxford Companion to American Theatre* (1984).

Barbara Ann Simon

WORTH, Irene (June 23, 1916–): actress, was born in Omaha, Nebraska, but moved to California at the age of one when her father, a superintendent of schools, secured a new position there. At twenty-one she graduated with a Bachelor of Education degree from the University of California at Los Angeles and taught kindergarten for two years. Despite her opera singing and her lack of dramatic training, Irene Worth set out on a theatre career in 1942 with the road company of *Escape Me Never*, directed by the Russian director, Theodore Komisarjevsky. The following year she made her Broadway debut in *The Two Mrs. Carrolls*, with Elizabeth Bergner. Most young actresses would have been delighted with their good fortune and remained in New York to capitalize on their success, but not Irene Worth. In 1944 she responded to advice from Elizabeth Bergner and left New York for England to broaden her experience of English classical theatre and to study with the voice teacher Elsie Fogerty in London. As she told Robert Wahls in an interview for the *New York Sunday News* (March 13, 1960), "In those days we had no Off-Broadway, no Phoenix Theatre, no stock companies, not even a Stratford Connecticut Shakespeare Festival. Nothing but Broadway." It was a fortuitous move. She very quickly found employment in the English theatre, and for the next thirty years Irene Worth made her home in London playing a diverse range of roles on stage, radio, television, and film, with actors and actresses of the stature of Laurence Olivier, John Gielgud, Sybil Thorndike, Ralph Richardson, Alec Guinness, and Peggy Ashcroft, and earning a reputation as one of the great actresses of her generation.

In 1975 Worth returned to New York and decided to make her home once more in the United States. The occasion was her appearance in Tennessee Williams's *Sweet Bird of Youth*, for which she won her second **Antoinette Perry** (Tony) Award. As she said to Eileen Blumenthal of the *Village Voice* (August 27, 1979), "It went so well that I couldn't leave. I got all these offers and so many things happened. Then I found out the theatre here was frightfully stimulating." Perhaps, too, she decided it was time for another change. Since then she has resided in a modest apartment in mid-Manhattan, devoted to her work, and spending her leisure time listening to music, collecting and refinishing antiques, making pottery, or dining quietly with friends. She is reluctant to talk about her personal life, remarking to Mark Ginsburg, "I have no way of telling you where I come from. I have no curiosity about it either. I'm interested in the future. I'm not a great one for looking back" (*Interview*, October 1977).

If Worth does look back, she must contemplate a rich professional life spanning the past forty years. Worth's first London appearance was at the Lyric Theatre, Hammersmith, London, as Elsie in *The Time of Your Life* (1946), followed by a substantial number of roles, including Donna Pascuala in *Drake's Drum* (1947),

Olivia Brown in *Love in Idleness* (1948), and Eileen Perry in *Edward, My Son* (1948). She subsequently toured as Lady Fortrose in *Home is Tomorrow* (1948) and as Olivia Raines in *Champagne for Delilah* (Edinburgh Festival, 1948), but it was the critical acclaim she received for her portrayal of Celia Copplestone in *The Cocktail Party* at the Edinburgh Festival in 1949 that confirmed her position as one of the most sensitive, intelligent, and dynamic actresses on the English stage. She repeated the role in New York and London (1950), drawing the approval of Brooks Atkinson, who wrote, "Irene Worth finds the lonely depths in the character of the other woman in a remarkably skillful, passionate and perceptive performance" (*New York Times*, January 23, 1950). She then joined the prestigious Old Vic Company and, during her first season (1951–1952), appeared as Desdemona in *Othello*, Helena in *A Midsummer Night's Dream*, and Catherine Vausselles in *The Other Heart*. She toured South Africa with the Old Vic Company in 1952 in the same parts, with the addition of Lady Macbeth. On her return to London in 1953 she appeared with the same company as Portia in *The Merchant of Venice*. Then she joined Tyrone Guthrie at the creation of the Shakespeare Festival Theatre in Stratford, Ontario, Canada (1953), appearing in the opening season as Queen Margaret in *Richard III* and as Helena in *All's Well That Ends Well*. Recalling that opening season Worth said, "When we arrived in 1953 the theatre was just a hole in the ground. We played under a tent. The theatre started with so many odds against it, so many financial crises; even the acoustics were absolutely terrible. All the cement flooring had to be covered with coconut matting. And then it rained and the tent leaked. But you see, it survived" (*Christian Science Monitor*, July 3, 1959).

Returning to London she played Francis Farrar in *A Day By the Sea* (1953) and created the roles of Argia in *The Queen and the Rebels* (Coventry and London, 1955), Alcestis in Thornton Wilder's *A Life in the Sun* (Edinburgh Festival, 1955), and Marcelle in *Hotel Paradiso* (1956). In 1957 she made a triumphant appearance in the United States as the heroine *Mary Stuart*, adapted by Jean Stock Goldstone and John Reich. Critics were unanimous in their praise for her performance. Richard Watts claimed in the *New York Post* (October 20, 1957), "Irene Worth is an ideal Mary, beautiful, proud, fiery, and immensely touching in her doomed courage, . . . and henceforth I'll always see Mary as Irene Worth." After performing the role of Sara Callifer in *The Potting Shed* (London, 1958), she repeated her New York triumph in *Mary Stuart* at the Edinburgh Festival and at the Old Vic Theatre (1958) in a new adaptation by Stephen Spender. She appeared again at the Stratford Shakespeare Festival, Ontario, in 1959, playing Rosalind in *As You Like It*, followed by a return visit to New York as Albertine Prine in Lillian Hellman's *Toys in the Attic* (1960), for which she won the New York Page One Award. Nevertheless, her loyalty to the British classical theatre remained, and she joined the Royal Shakespeare Company in 1962 to play Goneril in Peter Brook's critically acclaimed *King Lear*, with Paul Scofield. In 1964 this production embarked on a world tour. It went first to Northern and Eastern Europe and next to the United States, where, with *Much Ado About Nothing*, it opened the New York State Theatre in April 1964. Irene Worth remained in New York to display her extraordinary emotional range in Edward Albee's *Tiny Alice* (1964), a performance for which she was awarded her first Antoinette Perry (Tony) Award (1965). Returning to London she received the Evening Standard Award for the Noel Coward trilogy, *A Suite in Three Keys* (1966), in which she co-starred with Lilli Palmer and the author, but as Gerard Fay noted, "Irene Worth . . . act[s] everybody off the stage in the first twenty minutes" (*Gaurdian*, April 15, 1966). After gaining a further award from the Variety Club of Great Britain for Hesione Hushabye in *Heartbreak House* (Chichester and London, 1967), she played Jocasta in the controversial Old Vic production of Seneca's *Oedipus* (1968), directed by Peter Brook. Of this production she said to Mark Ginsburg, "If a work of art doesn't have danger in it, it's not worth looking at. Everything has to change" (*Interview*, October 1977). That her experience with Brook was an enriching one was confirmed by Martin Esslin, who wrote, "Irene Worth displays a strength which seems new even in this powerful actress" (*New York Times*, March 31, 1968); while of her next performance as Hedda Gabler at Stratford, Ontario, in 1970, Walter Kerr claimed, "She is quite possibly the best actress in the world" (quoted by Kevin Kelly, *Boston Sunday Globe*, July 23, 1978). In 1971 she again joined Peter Brook in his experimental *Orghast in Persepolis*, commissioned for the Arts Festival in Iran. On her return to London she was involved in a further experiment at the Greenwich Theatre, playing the three matriarchs in *Hamlet*, *Ghosts*, and *The Sea Gull* (1974). This mammoth undertaking, however, marked the ended her long stay in her adopted homeland. She returned to the United States in 1975 to play the Tony Award-winning role of Alexandra Del Lago in *Sweet Bird of Youth* and has remained ever since.

Her two major roles after her return were Madame Ranevskaya in *The Cherry Orchard* (for which she won the Drama Desk Award, 1977) and Winnie in *Happy Days* (1979), both directed by the Rumanian, Andrei Serban. She had first met Serban in Iran, and, as she told Eileen Blumenthal (*Village Voice*, August 27, 1979), she was convinced he had "a very powerful imagination and a brilliant, brilliant mind." His reputation for re-interpreting the classics, his boldness and inventiveness, were the attraction. "It renews energy, and it renews youth, as it renews one's joy in living. And, if I may say it, the joy of acting" (*Village Voice*, August 27, 1979). Characteristically, at the same time as her New York successes, she took part in three productions at the Lake Forest Festival, Illinois: *Misalliance* (1976), *Old Times* (1977), and *After the Season* (1978). Her next Broadway appearances were in *The Lady from Dubuque* and *The Physicists*, both in 1980, the year she was invited to become a member of Broadway's Hall of Fame. In 1982 she played with Constance Cummings in *The Chalk Garden* at the Roundabout Theatre, New York; in 1984 she appeared in New York in *The Golden Age*; and in 1986 in London she appeared in *The Bay at Nice* at the National Theatre. During the 1988–1989 season she appeared in *Coriolanus*, presented by the New York Shakespeare Festival Public Theatre and directed by Steven Berkoff.

Irene Worth's appearances, however, have not been limited to the stage. She is also an experienced performer on radio, television, and film. Many of her media roles have been repeats of outstanding stage performances. Notable BBC radio portrayals include Cleopatra in *Goddess and God* (1953), Anna Petrovna in *Ivanov* (1954), Lady Godiva in *Scandal at Coventry* (1964), and Lucille in *Duel of Angels* (1964). In a 1984 BBC television series shown in the United States, she has appeared in the title roles of *Antigone* (1949), *Candida* (1955), and *The Duchess of Malfi* (1949 and 1955), and as Volumnia in *Coriolanus* (1983). On American television she has played Elizabeth Cady Stanton, an early feminist, in *Under the Sky* (1979), and in 1988 she appeared in a PBS production of Clifford Odets' *The Big Knife*. Her film work is less extensive, though she won the British Film Academy Award (the British Oscar) for her role in *Order to Kill* (1958). Other film credits include *The Scapegoat* (1959), *King of the Seven Seas* (1961), *Deathtrap* (1981), and *Room With a View* (1986).

She has also given a series of solo and dramatic readings, including *Excerpts from Samuel Beckett* (Harvard, 1977); *Letters of Love and Affection* (Stratford, Ontario, 1979, and New York, 1982), a personal selection of letters from the Pierpoint Morgan Library; *Irene Worth in Chelsea* (1984), which included readings from the diaries of Virginia Woolf and Molly Bloom's soliloquy from *Ulysses*; and *Shakespeare Sonnets*, with an extract from *Venus and Adonis* (1984). With John Gielgud she has performed a tribute to T. S. Eliot and Edith Sitwell (1965) and *Men and Women of Shakespeare* (Washington and New York, 1967).

Irene Worth has received many honors, but especially notable is the honorary award of Commander of the British Empire, presented by Queen Elizabeth in 1975 for her distinguished contribution to dramatic art. She received an honorary Doctor of Fine Arts degree in 1986 from Queens College, New York. As a performer she has been an inspiration not only to fellow actors and actresses but to the many directors who have benefited from her dedication and commitment. She is devoted to her art and acknowledges that she has at times sacrificed financial stability, fame, and a secure family life for the theatre. She is passionately interested in the craft of acting, and in her interviews she gives selflessly of her knowledge and experience for the benefit of young performers. She deprecates the assumption that actors cannot (and should not) read, write, or think too much. "They should study painting and sculpture and music. They should know what Titian was doing; what a Bellini sky is like; they should know the cast of a Giotto figure. They should know history. . . . They should know what is going on in terms of human values and human experience" (*Village Voice*, August 27, 1979). Above all, Irene Worth is a fine human being, whose talents have touched whole generations of dedicated playgoers. Of her chosen profession she has said, "Everything I have done has always been a choice, and I don't regret what I've chosen. I'm very rich inwardly, I've had such a fulfilled career, even if I were to never act again" (*Women's Wear Daily*, March 7, 1984).

Significant articles on Irene Worth's career are "Worth: Actress Not for Sale," *Cue* (January 17, 1976); "Irene Worth Talks About Art, Energy—Even Acting," *New York Times* (February 5, 1976); "A Chat with the World's Greatest Actress," *Boston Sunday Globe* (July 23, 1978); "Irene Worth, the stage's leading lady talks, to Mark Ginsburg," *Interview* (October 1977); "Irene Worth Finds Beckett Uplifting," *New York Times* (June 1, 1979); "Irene Worth Has Time on Her Side," *Village Voice* (August 27, 1979); "Irene Worth: Where Theatre Is You'll Find Her," *Christian Science Monitor* (November 5, 1979); "America's Gift to the Classical Theatre," *The Westsider* (November 22, 1980); and "Acting for All She's Worth," *Women's Wear Daily* (March 7, 1984). Irene Worth is included in *The Biographical Encyclopaedia and Who's Who of the American Theatre* (1966); *Current Biography, 1968* (1968–1969); *Notable Names in the American Theatre* (1976); *Who's Who in the Theatre* (1981); *Who's Who of American Women, 1983–1984* (1983); *The Oxford Companion to the Theatre* (1983); *The Oxford Companion to American Theatre* (1984); and *Who's Who, 1984–1985* (1984).

Sam McCready

WYCHERLY, Margaret (October 26, 1884–June 6, 1956): actress, producer, and director, was born in London, England, the daughter of Dr. and Mrs. J. L. DeWolfe. When the family came to the United States is not known, but Wycherly was educated at the Boston Latin School and went on to study at the American Academy of Dramatic Art in New York City. She married Bayard Veiller in 1901 and had one son, Anthony Veiller. They were divorced in 1922.

Margaret Wycherly made her acting debut in New York in 1898 with **Fanny Janauschek** in *What Dreams May Come*; then she appeared as Juanita in *The Dawn of Freedom* and spent three months with the **Jessie Bonstelle** Stock Company in Rochester, New York. Wycherly toured extensively throughout her career and played in stock at the Alcazar Theatre in San Francisco. She also appeared as Olivia in *Twelfth Night* under the management of Ben Greet. Subsequently, she moved to Boston, where in 1905 she produced a series of new plays by William Butler Yeats, including *The Land of Heart's Desire*, *The Hour Glass*, *Kathleen-Ni-Houlihan*, and *The Countess Cathleen*. Wycherly was in fact instrumental in introducing Yeats as a playwright to America and in 1907–1908 helped to revive his plays in New York. She also played many leading roles in George Bernard Shaw's plays with Arnold Daly's company, including the title role in *Candida* and Raina in *Arms and the Man*. She also created the role of Lydia in Shaw's *Cashel Byron's Profession* in 1906, about which the *New York Times* reported, "Miss Wycherly is charmingly girlish, and there is a good deal of attractive sweetness about her method" (January 9, 1906). At Winthrop Ames's New Theatre in New York, she played Light in Maurice Maeterlinck's *The Blue Bird* in 1910. The *New York Times* again singled her out for praise. Between the years 1912 and 1917 she acted in numerous productions in New York and Boston.

In 1917 she became active in the newly established Provincetown Players and directed Pendleton King's very successful *Cocaine* at the Playwright's Theatre. In 1921 she also appeared there as Claire, the lead in Susan Glaspell's extraordinary play, *The Verge*, about a nonconforming woman. Wycherly continued to expand the scope of her roles, playing the Mother in Luigi Pirandello's *Six Characters in Search of an Author* at the Princess Theatre in New York in 1922, Daisy Devore in Elmer Rice's *The Adding Machine* in 1923, Rebecca West in Henrik Ibsen's *Rosmersholm* at the 52nd Street Theatre in 1925 (Stark Young said, in the *New York Times*, May 6, 1975, "Her depth as an actress showed itself"), Mrs. Amos Evans in Eugene O'Neill's *Strange Interlude* in 1929, and Ada Lester in Jack Kirkland's *Tobacco Road*, which ran for 3,182 performances between 1933 and 1935. Later in her career she replaced **Laurette Taylor** as Amanda Wingfield in Tennessee Williams's *The Glass Menagerie* (1946), and shortly before her death she played the Dowager Duchess of York in Shakespeare's *Richard III* at the City Center in New York (1953). From 1941 to 1946 Wycherly appeared in films in Hollywood, among them *Sergeant York* (1941).

Margaret Wycherly's acting career was extensive. Making her debut at the age of fourteen, she appeared on stage and in films for over fifty years and acted in significant classical and modern plays, introducing the plays of Henrik Ibsen, William Butler Yeats, and Luigi Pirandello to American audiences and originating roles in plays by Elmer Rice and Eugene O'Neill.

For further information on Margaret Wycherly, see Burns Mantle, *The Best Plays, 1899–1956* (1957), the *New York Times* (January 9, 1906, October 2, 1910, and May 6, 1925), and Robert K. Sarlos, *Jig Cook and the Provincetown Players: Theatre in Ferment* (1982). Wycherly's obituary appeared in the *New York Times* (June 7, 1956). She is listed in *The Green Room Book; or, Who's Who on the Stage* (1909); *Who's Who in the Theatre* (1956); *Who Was Who in the Theatre*, Vol. IV (1978); and *The Oxford Companion to American Theatre* (1984).

Robert K. Sarlós and
Roberta L. Lasky

——— Y ———

YANKOWITZ, Susan (February 20, 1941–): playwright and novelist, was born in Newark, New Jersey. The daughter of Irving N. Yankowitz and Ruth (Katz) Yankowitz, she received her Bachelor of Arts degree from Sarah Lawrence College, Bronxville, New York, in 1963 and her Master of Fine Arts degree from the Yale School of Drama in 1968. In 1978 she married Herbert Leibowitz; they have one son, Gabriel.

Susan Yankowitz has received many awards for her writing of plays (for stage, television, and radio), a film scenario (*The Land of Milk and Funny or Portrait of a Scientist as a Dumb Broad*, 1968), and a novel, *Silent Witness* (1976). Her awards include the Joseph E. Levine Fellowship in screenwriting, 1968–1969; the Vernon Rice Drama Desk Award for most promising playwright, 1969; the MacDowell Colony Fellowship, 1971 and 1973; a National Endowment for the Arts Creative Writing Fellowship, 1972; a Rockefeller Foundation grant in 1973 for writing a play for the Long Wharf Theatre in New Haven; and a Guggenheim Fellowship in playwriting, 1975.

Susan Yankowitz has been associated with the Open Theatre, which included other emerging women dramatists of her generation such as **Megan Terry**, **Roberta Sklar**, and **Karen Malpede**. Several of Yankowitz's plays, such as *Transplant* (1971), have been presented at the Magic Theatre in Omaha, Nebraska, founded by Megan Terry and Jo Ann Schmidman, also a former member of the Open Theatre. As a member of the Playwrights' Cooperative, formed in 1972, Yankowitz associated with Nancy Fales, Sally Ordway, Sharon Thei, Nancy Walter, and others. As a reader for *Scripts*, a valuable but short-lived magazine that published new plays in the 1970s, Yankowitz worked with **Julie Bovasso**, **Rosalyn Drexler**, **Maria Irene Fornés**, **Myrna Lamb**, **Rochelle Owens**, Sonia Sanchez, Megan Terry, and Nancy Walter.

Yankowitz was also an active member of New York's Westbeth Playwrights Feminist Collective, a group started in 1970 as a tenants' bargaining alliance, which became instrumental in encouraging women playwrights and in assisting production of plays by women. Yankowitz wrote a series of monologues for the Westbeth production *The Wicked Women Revue* (1973). For the 1972 production *Up!* she wrote the one-act play *Positions*.

Plays by Yankowitz have been produced in New York, London, Paris, Algeria, Israel, and Iran. Her teleplay *Prison Game* appeared as part of the *Visions* series on KCET-TV in 1976. This was followed in 1977 by the production of her musical teleplay *The Land of Milk and Funny* as part of the *Visions* series. *Slaughterhouse Play*, a major work by Yankowitz, was produced by Joseph Papp at the New York Shakespeare Festival Public Theatre in 1971; it shows American society as a greedy, bloodthirsty culture that vicitimizes minorities.

Yankowitz's subjects include death, racism, sexism, injustice and brutality in the prison system, the lack of concern about individual rights, the restrictions of gender roles, and the violence of society. She has said that her work is "generally informed by the social and political realities which impinge on all our lives" (*Contemporary Dramatists*, 1977, p. 886). Her concern about politics and the moral life of people may have been developed through her early work with the Open Theatre. *Terminal* evolved from that group's concern about death and their meditations on death, and from the actors' responses to their own mortality. Although playwrights were always present during the collaborative creation of the Open Theatre pieces, scant attention was paid to them by the media, which generally focused on director Joseph Chaikin. After the Open Theatre's production of *The Mutation Show*, many of the women left the group.

The Ha-Ha Play, a children's play by Yankowitz, was first produced at the Cubiculo Theatre, New York, in November 1970. *Boxes*, a play produced at the Magic Theatre in Berkeley, California, in 1972, comments on the roles people play, on the lack of individuality, and on the inhumanity of a largely urban society. The "boxes" are literal boxes on stage as well as apartment dwellings; they symbolize the lives and personalities that people adopt or that society forces them to accept. *A Knife in the Heart*, presented at the Eugene O'Neill Theatre Center in Waterford, Connecticut, in August 1982, and at the Williamstown Theatre Festival (Massachusetts) in August 1983, is a play about a mass murderer and the effect of his actions on his family. The play develops in a series of vignettes with twenty-four characters, many of whom "unleash subconscious terror" (Frank Rich, *New York Times*, August 1, 1982). Yankowitz's film scenario, *The Land of Milk and Funny or Portrait of a Scientist as a Dumb Broad*, presents the exploits of Velma Vavoom, a closet (literally) scientist who has discovered a formula to transform nuclear energy into milk.

Works by Yankowitz, including her novel *Silent Witness*, reveal a concern for problems of injustice and inequality. These themes are evident in all her plays: *The Cage*, a one-act, first produced in 1965 in New York at the Omar Khayyam Café; *Nightmare*, a one-act produced at Yale University in 1967; *That*

Old Rock-A-Bye, a one-act produced at Cooper Square Arts Theatre in 1968; *The Lamb*, a one-act produced at the Academy Theatre in Atlanta, Georgia, in 1973; *Wooden Nickels*, produced in New York in 1973; *American Piece*, written with the Provisional Theatre and produced in Los Angeles in 1974; *Still Life*, a full-length play produced at the Interart Theatre (a mainly feminist theatre in New York) in 1976; *True Romances*, a full-length play produced at the Mark Taper Lab in Los Angeles in 1978; *Qui est Anna Marks?*, a full-length play, produced in Paris, France, in 1979; *A Knife in the Heart*, first produced at the O'Neill Theatre Conference, 1982; and *Baby*, produced on Broadway, 1984. Although Yankowitz turned away from playwriting for a time to write fiction, a medium in which only language is necessary, the main focus of her writing has been plays for the stage, where collaboration is essential. Her early work on *Terminal* with the Open Theatre taught her much about collaboration. Yankowitz's concerns are political, and all are established on a moral foundation. Arthur Sainer notes that her writings all display an "impulse toward ritual, toward rhetorical and choral language, toward allegory, toward fluid action dictated by the unconscious" (*Contemporary Dramatists*, 1973, p. 842). Yankowitz is a significant member of the theatrical avant-garde.

Susan Yankowitz's *Terminal* has been printed in *Scripts 1*, New York Shakespeare Festival Public Theatre (November 1971), in Karen Malpede's *Three Works by the Open Theatre* (1974), and in Arthur Sainer's *The Radical Theater Notebook* (1975). *The Ha-Ha Play* is in *Scripts 10* (October 1972); *Slaughterhouse Play* is in *Yale/Theatre* (1974); and *Boxes* is in *Playwrights for Tomorrow*, edited by Arthur Ballet (1973). The following plays are in manuscripts: *A Knife in the Heart* (1982), *Qui est Anna Marks?* (1979), *True Romances* (1978), *Still Life* (1976), *The American Piece* (1974), *Wooden Nickels* (1973), *Acts of Love* and *Positions* (1972), *Sideshow*, *Transplant*, *The Lamb* and *The Old Rock-A-Bye* (1968), *Basics* and *Nightmare* (1976), and *The Cage* (1965). Knopf published the novel *Silent Witness* in 1976. Also of interest is an interview with Yankowitz by Arthur Sainer in *The Radical Theatre Notebook* (1975). A more recent interview with Yankowitz is included in Kathleen Belsko and Rachel Koenig, *Interviews with Contemporary Women Playwrights* (1987). See also "Westbeth Playwrights' Collective" in *Women's Movement Media: A Source Guide* by Cynthia Ellen (1975). Katha Pollitt reviewed *Silent Witness* in the *New York Times* (June 27, 1976). Susan Yankowitz is included in *Contemporary Authors*, Vols. 45–48 (1974); *Notable Names in the American Theatre* (1976); *National Playwrights Directory* (1981); *Contemporary Dramatists* (1977 and 1982); and *Contemporary Authors: New Revised Series*, Vol. 1 (1981) and Vol. 17, 1986).

Carolyn Karis

YOUNG, Margaret Mary (April 24, 1909–): distinguished community theatre designer and producer, was born in Viola, Iowa, to Samuel Andrew and Mary (Lacy) Anderson. She attended Mount Mercy Academy in Cedar Rapids, where her interest in theatre was nurtured. From Mount Mercy Academy, Margaret Mary Anderson studied at the University of Iowa in one of the country's most exciting drama departments, directed by E. C. Mabie. There she met John Wray Young, and on October 5, 1929, they were married. After John Young's graduation in 1929, Mabie helped the two get positions at the Sioux City Little Theatre, where Margaret Mary Young designed the productions and also worked in children's theatre. In 1931 Mabie invited the Youngs to join the University of Iowa theatre faculty and asked Margaret Mary Young to found and direct the Iowa Children's Theatre.

The next year Gilmor Brown invited the Youngs to the Pasadena Playhouse, where John Young directed and Margaret Mary Young was a guest instructor. In the fall of 1933 they went to the Duluth Playhouse, where Young not only designed all productions but alternated with her husband as director during the summer seasons. In the summer of 1936 they founded the Duluth Summer School of Theatre. Their school received wide praise, and subsequently they were invited by the Shreveport Little Theatre in Louisiana to design and direct there.

In October 1936 the Youngs opened the first of their thirty-seven seasons in Shreveport. Working together as a designer-director team, Margaret Mary Young and John Young presented some 320 productions. Since their plays averaged at least two sets per production, Margaret Mary Young estimates that she must have designed nearly seven hundred settings. She worked closely with her husband, the director, to achieve a complete harmony between the concept of the play and the set. Margaret Mary Young will not admit to any favorite type of play to design, believing that a broad interest and knowledge is essential for the scene designer. Along with her design career she found time for two children, John Wray Young, III, and Margaret Mary Young, Jr.

In the summer of 1959 the Youngs began *LAGNIAPPE*, the distinguished Second Series of the Shreveport Little Theatre. This summer program was an inspiration of Margaret Mary Young, who had decided that it was time someone changed the traditional, inept matter of community theatres' "Second Programs," which are called workshops or given other apologetic names. She wanted a series having as much rehearsal as the Membership Series and therefore being worth the full admission charge.

LAGNIAPPE opened in 1959 with a production of Samuel Beckett's *Waiting for Godot* and continued until 1969, having produced thirty-one plays. It concluded with the production of one of twelve original plays produced during its operation. *LAGNIAPPE* did the best of the avant-garde plays and occasional classics, in addition to premières of new plays. The program served as a model for many community theatres across the country and helped to improve the caliber of productions given in Second Series summer programs.

As an actress in Shreveport, Margaret Mary Young starred in *Angel Street*, *Mr. and Mrs. North*, *Pygmalion*, *State of the Union*, *Candida*, *Still Life*, *The Great Sebastians*, *The Village Wooing*, and *Dear Liar*. A member of the American National Theatre and Academy, she did important work in the founding of the Southwest Theatre Conference and served on the board of the American Theatre Association from 1957 until 1959. She was a board member for the American Community Theatre Association from 1962 until 1964. In addition to her other publications, she and her husband wrote *How to Produce the Play* (thirteenth printing, 1981).

The Youngs have received twenty-six regional and national awards. Of these, twelve were for Margaret Mary Young's distinguished work in community theatre. In partnership with her husband, she has produced, designed, or directed 320 major plays over the last 50 years. Margaret Mary Young has become a legend in American community theatres everywhere.

Scores of photographs of Margaret Mary Young's settings, more than 300 playbills, and 108 published articles co-authored by the Youngs are in the Norton Museum and the Archives of Louisiana State University in Shreveport. Margaret Mary Young is listed in *The Biographical Encyclopaedia and Who's Who of the American Theatre* (1966); *Who's Who of American Women, 1970–1971* (1969); and *Notable Names in the American Theatre* (1976).

John Wray Young

YOUNG, Rida Johnson (February 28, 1875?–May 8, 1926): playwright and lyricist, was born in Baltimore, Maryland, the daughter of William A. and Emma (Stuart) Johnson. Her father was a prominent resident of Baltimore, and her mother was the granddaughter of a Hungarian nobleman named Mayer, who had married a Rothschild. Rida Johnson was educated at Wilson College in Chambersburg, Pennsylvania.

After publishing a number of poems and stories in local newspapers, she wrote a play and decided to take it in person to New York. Her parents reluctantly gave her the money for the short visit, but she immediately began to support herself there with a four-dollar-a-week job selling furniture polish. She offered her lengthy, hundred-character play about Omar Khayyam to all the leading actors of the day; one of them, E. H. Sothern, took an interest in her and got her an interview with producer Daniel Frohman, who in turn gave her a walk-on role in *The Three Musketeers*. She was by her own admission a poor actress, but she continued acting for four years, including a season with E. H. Sothern. In 1898 she toured the South with a youthful company whose handsome leading man, James Young, Jr., was the son of the senator from Maryland. She married the actor in 1904, but they were eventually divorced. *Lord Byron*, a play she wrote for Young, was added to the touring company's repertoire, and this renewed her interest in writing. Young subsequently left the stage and went to work for Whitmark Music Publishing Company, where for two years she did publicity work and wrote song lyrics. "We worked as a factory works," she recalled, "turning out songs at a rate that was bewildering. When someone singing in vaudeville made a hit, and an order came in for an encore verse, or two or three, or half a dozen, I sat down and wrote them. When a song was needed to fit a particular play or concert or actor, someone wrote the music and I fitted the words to it; or I wrote the words and someone fitted the music" (*The American Magazine*, December 1920, p. 185). Including her dozen musical comedies with about twenty songs each, she estimated in 1920 that she had written five hundred songs. Her most successful were "Mother Machree" from *Barry of Ballymore* (1911), "When Love Is Young in Springtime" from *Brown of Harvard* (1906), "I'm Falling in Love with Someone" from *Naughty Marietta* (1910), and "Sweethearts" from *Maytime* (1917).

Her first successful play, *Brown of Harvard* (1906), was written for her actor-husband, but the director insisted upon casting in his place a better-known actor, Harry Woodruff, who made a hit of the comedy. In 1908 she condensed the play into a farcical sketch, which her husband performed in vaudeville. That same year Daniel Frohman sent her on her first trip abroad to study the British academic life at Oxford University as the basis for another "college play," a genre for which she had started a vogue.

In eighteen years Rida Johnson Young had twenty-six plays and musical comedies produced in New York. Among the composers with whom she collaborated were Victor Herbert (*Naughty Marietta*, 1910, and *The Dream Girl*, 1924), Jerome Kern (*The Red Petticoat*, 1912), Sigmund Romberg (*Maytime*, 1917), and Rudolf Friml (*Sometime*, 1918). With her royalties she bought a summer home at Bellhaven, New York, and an estate at Stamford, Connecticut. She had a weakness for automobiles and jewels, but her greatest interest was gardening, a subject that crops up in most interview articles about her. She was consistently modest about her work, saying, "I have never undertaken anything really big; I have contented myself with writing plays that are popular and within my ability" (*The American Magazine*, December 1920, p. 187).

Rida Johnson Young died in 1926 in her home at Southfield Point, near Stamford, Connecticut.

Plays by Rida Johnson Young include *Brown of Harvard* (1906); *The Boys of Company B* and *The Lancers* (1907); *Glorious Betsy* (1908); *Naughty Marietta* (1910); *Barry of Ballymore* and *Next* (1911); *The Red Petticoat* (1912); *The Isle o' Dreams* and *The Girl and the Pennant* (1913); *Shameen Dhu* and *Lady Luxury* (1914); *Captain Kidd, Jr.* and *Her Soldier Boy* (1916); *His Little Widows* and *Maytime* (1917); *Sometime* and *Little Simplicity* (1918); *Little Old New York* and *Macushla* (1920); *The Front Seat* (1921); *The Rabbit's Foot*, *The Dream Girl*, and *Cock o' the Roost* (1924). Young's novels are *Brown of Harvard* (1907), *Out of the Night* (1925), and *Red Owl* (1927). Clippings in the Theatre Collection of the New York Public Library Performing Arts Research Center at Lincoln Center are the major source of information about Young. She is the subject of a few major articles including those of Shirley Burns in *Green Book Album* (September 1910), Helen Ten Boeck in *The Theatre* (April 1917), and Helen Christine Bennett in *The American Magazine* (December 1920). Felicia Hardison Londré's entry in *American Women Writers*, Vol. 4 (1982), includes a complete list of her plays. Rida Johnson Young is included in Dixie Hines and Harry Prescott Hanaford, eds., *Who's Who in Music and Drama* (1914); *Who's Who in the Theatre* (1925); Robert L. Sherman, *Actors and Authors With Composers Who Helped Make Them Famous* (1951); *Who Was Who in America, Vol. I: 1897–1942* (1966); *The ASCAP Biographical Dictionary of Composers, Authors and Publishers* (1966 and 1980); and *The Oxford Companion to American Theatre* (1984).

The ASCAP Biographical Dictionary of Composers, Authors and Publishers gives Young's birth date as February 28, 1869.

                                                    Felicia Hardison Londré

YURKA, Blanche (June 19, 1887?–June 6, 1974): actress, was born in St. Paul, Minnesota, to Anton and Karolina (Novak) Jurka. Her parents, part of a wave of immigrants from Czechoslovakia, had settled in Chicago, where there was a large Czech colony. Her father, trained as a surveyor in Czechoslovakia, worked on a Czech newspaper in Chicago and later taught Czech children in an elementary school in St. Paul. By a previous marriage, Karolina Jurka had one daughter, Mila, who lived with a grandmother in Chicago. Mila was later united with the family in New York City and became a close confidante to Blanche Yurka and supporter of her career. Blanche was the third child; and she, her older sister Rosa, and her two brothers, Charles and Tony, were a close-knit family. Yurka's father was supportive of his daughter's career, because as a young man in Bohemia he had been discouraged from being an actor, and he later had found an outlet as an amateur in Chicago's Czech theatre.

Blanche Yurka had just completed grade school in St. Paul when her father lost his teaching job. In a move that delighted her, but displeased her mother, the family moved in 1900 to New York City, where her father accepted a position as executive secretary for the Czech Benevolent Society. Shortly after arriving in New York, Yurka began singing lessons with the Czech Sokol singing society. A major role in the society's production of Balfe's *The Bohemian Girl* encouraged her interest in performance and supplied a title for her autobiography (1970). In 1901 she entered Wadleigh High School, but aside from classes in English and French, the studies failed to capture her attention. In 1903 she was given the Heinrich Conried scholarship and enrolled in the Metropolitan Opera School. She made her debut as the Grail Bearer in a 1903 Metropolitan production of *Parsifal*. In her enthusiasm she failed to take care of her developing voice and injured it singing the role of Leonora in an amateur production of *Il Trovatore*. Her scholarship was discontinued. A second chance to salvage her voice and continue her musical career was offered in 1905 at the Institute of Musical Art. During this period she supported herself by singing in a choir directed by Leopold Stokowski at St. Bartholomew's Church. While she made considerable progress, she felt it was not enough to justify continued study, and she left the institute in 1907.

Broadway seemed a closed world to her. She lacked training and experience, but she knocked on doors until one was opened for her by David Belasco in 1906. Her lessons in music, French, and German had produced a strong clear voice with good enunciation and timbre that impressed Belasco, who decided to take a chance on her potential to develop as an actress. Yurka wrote, "What I eventually learned about acting was acquired through watching the work of players whose performances I admired. And eventually I came to learn from those most exacting teachers: paying audiences" (*Bohemian Girl*, p. 35). Her first roles in 1906 were bit parts in *Grand Army Man* and *The Rose of the Rancho*; she received a contract as a general understudy for the 1907 season at $25.00 a week. It was apparently at this time that she changed the spelling of her last name. After a summer trip to Europe she alternated between a stock company and touring productions. Yurka found her first road tour with *The Warrens of Virginia* (1907) to be a great adventure, and instructive as well, because one of the actresses in Belasco's touring production was sixteen-year-old Mary Pickford, who "took charge of my backstage ignorance" (*Bohemian Girl*, p. 50).

Ten years later, still waiting for the play that would bring her critical notice, Blanche met her second mentor, **Jane Cowl**, who offered her the lead in *Daybreak* (1917). It ran twelve weeks and then went on tour. The two women became close friends, and Yurka commented that this "refutes the notion that generosity and goodwill cannot exist among women of the theatre" (*Bohemian Girl*, p. 70). In 1918 she returned to New York to act in a war play, *Allegiance*, which closed after forty-four performances. During the 1972 run of a society melodrama, *The Law Breaker*, she met Ian Keith Ross, who used Ian Keith as his stage name. After their marriage in Chicago in September 1922, they had great visions of acting together. This dream was quickly marred by a mother-in-law who opposed the marriage, and by Ross's jealousy of his wife's career, which was in a more advanced stage than his. The newly-weds also quarreled over her professional use of her maiden name. After an effort to repair the marriage and a joint appearance in a summer stock company's production of Maurice Maeterlinck's *Monna Vanna* and Oscar Wilde's *An Ideal Husband*, they separated in the fall of 1925 and divorced in 1928.

In 1922 Yurka played a youthful Gertrude to John Barrymore's Hamlet for 125 performances and earned notice from reviewers in a play dominated by its leading man. Yurka sometimes took roles that she was not particularly fond of to tide her through financially until a better role became available. Such was the case when she began what she thought would be a two-week run of a melodrama, *The Squall* (1926). Surprisingly, it became a commercial success and ran for a year on Broadway and for another year on the road.

It was in classical theatre, particularly those productions staged by the Actors' Theatre, that Yurka made her major contributions as both performer and director during the 1920s and 1930s. Jane Cowl appointed Yurka to the board of the Actors' Theatre. Her role as Gina in Henrik Ibsen's *The Wild Duck* (1925) established her as an able performer, and Stark Young in the *New York Times* praised her performance and interpretation of the play. In the fall of 1928, after she had completed an Ibsen season in Minneapolis, Lee Shubert asked her to direct and star in three Ibsen plays in New York. She again played Gina in *The Wild Duck* (1928), followed by *Hedda Gabler* (1929) and *The Lady From the Sea* (1929). Her efforts served to popularize Ibsen and to create an identity for her as an actress. Brooks Atkinson, reviewing *Hedda Gabler* in the *New York Times*, praised Yurka as an "actress of great depth of emotion, blessed with a voice of almost eerie timbre. . . . Although the design of her acting may not seem bold enough to sustain the part, you quickly perceive that she has not flung it impulsively upon the stage, but has planned it intelligently with a view to the frightened climaxes of the third and fourth acts'' (February 4, 1929).

Yurka, having had experience of theatre outside New York, went to Ann Arbor, Michigan, in 1931 and to Boston, then back to New York, to play Sophocles' *Electra*. Early in 1932 she took over the title role in Aristophanes' *Lysistrata*, which Norman Bel Geddes had opened two years earlier in New York. She played the role for five months. During the 1932–1933 season she played Portia in *The Merchant of Venice*, staged in Detroit. In December 1932 she was praised for her role in **Katharine Cornell**'s production of André Obey's play *Lucrèce*, first in Cleveland, then in New York City. After *Lucrèce* closed, Yurka played one of her favorite roles, Eleanor, in Susan Glaspell's *Comic Artist* (1933). In 1935 she took over from Edith Evans the role of the nurse in *Romeo and Juliet*, with Katharine Cornell as Juliet. In 1936, troubled by a lack of good roles, she assembled a one-woman show, ''The Arc of the Theatre,'' and gave readings from classic plays on college campuses and in civic centers and auditoriums across the United States. Not only was she well received, but she found a new strength in the solo performance that ''kept my acting muscles exercised, my contact with audiences very much alive'' (*Bohemian Girl*, p. 260).

Hollywood beckoned. Her successful first role as Madame De Farge in Metro-Goldwyn-Mayer's production of *A Tale of Two Cities* (1935) was never equaled in the small parts she played in twenty-one subsequent films. Yurka was now forty-eight years old; few parts other than character roles existed in film for older women. After playing in 1939 a mother of mobsters in *Queen of the Mob* (Paramount, 1940) and a Nazi concentration camp nurse in *Escape* (MGM, 1940), she decided, against the advice of her agent, to return to New York to perform in two war plays, *The Wind is Ninety* (1945) and *Temper the Wind* (1946). Her final film was *Thunder in the Sun* (Paramount, 1959), a ''mediocre little film,'' according to the reviewer, who nonetheless praised Yurka for her characterization of a French Basque woman (*New York Times*, April 9, 1959).

Yurka also found a paucity of good plays on Broadway in the 1950s, so in 1954 she went to Greece under the auspices of the United States International Exchange of Artists to appear in the Greek Drama Festival and gave a reader's theatre performance of Edith Hamilton's translation of Aeschylus's *Prometheus Bound*. In 1958 she returned to Broadway in a dramatization of Charlotte Brontë's *Jane Eyre*, titled *The Master of Thornfield*. In 1960 Yurka received a citation from the Washington Theatre Club for high achievement in the theatre, and in 1961 she was given an honorary membership in Equity Library Theatre for her performance as Miss Moffat in a revival of Emlyn Williams's *The Corn is Green*. Few good roles came her way in her later years. Her part in George S. Kaufman and Edna Ferber's *Dinner at Eight* (1966) was a tiny one. Her final appearance in a production of Jean Giraudoux's *The Madwoman of Chaillot* (1970) earned her praise from Clive Barnes for her past work in American theatre (*New York Times*, March 23, 1970). Although Yurka was not a political activist, she supported the actors' strike of 1919, the Federal Theatre Project, and the American National Theatre and Academy (ANTA), and defended American actors against the frequent disparaging remarks based on comparison with the ability and training of British actors. Ever mindful of her heritage, she expressed great concern over Hitler's invasion of Czechoslovakia and tried to raise interest in the plight of her parents' native country by trying to get together a season of plays by the Czechoslovakian playwright, Karel Capek. During the war she participated in a recording of **Edna St. Vincent Millay**'s long poem "The Murder of Lidice."

Yurka's book *Dear Audience* (1959) presented a series of personal and historical anecdotes to illustrate the basic principles of theatre. She edited *Three Scandinavian Plays* in 1962 and *Three Classic Greek Plays* in 1964. Her autobiography, *Bohemian Girl: Blanche Yurka's Theatrical Life*, appeared in 1970.

Blanche Yurka's theatre was not limited by centuries, by Broadway, by genre, or by media. She was at home playing on Broadway or in Saginaw, Michigan, and she could play comedy or tragedy. The tall blonde who learned by doing will be best remembered for her portrayal of Henrik Ibsen's strong-willed women. Yurka died on June 6, 1974, in New York City.

Information about Yurka's life and career is in the Blanche Yurka Collection in the Billy Rose Theatre Collection and the Robinson Locke Scrapbooks in the New York Public Library Performing Arts Research Center at Lincoln Center. There is also a file on Yurka in the Harvard University Theatre Collection. Her autobiography, *Bohemian Girl: Blanche Yurka's Theatrical Life* (1970), has some errors in dates and sequences of events, but it is the most complete book on her life. *Dear Audience*, written by Yurka in 1959, gives information about her acting style and her approach to developing a character. See also Louis Sheaffer's interview in the *New York Times* (November 6, 1955), the review in *Opera News* (April 3, 1971), and Arthur William Row's "A Star Who is a Luminary" in *Poet Lore* (Spring 1928). John Mason Brown mentions Yurka in *Two on the Aisle* (1938). The *New York Times* contains reviews of her major films and plays. Yurka's obituary appeared in the *New York Times* (June 7, 1974). Blanche Yurka is included in *The Biographical Encyclopaedia and Who's Who of the American Theatre* (1966); *Who's Who in the Theatre* (1967); William C. Young, *Famous Actors and Actresses of the American Stage*, Vol. II (1975); *Notable American Women*, Vol. IV: *The Modern Period* (1981); and *The Oxford Companion to the Theatre* (1983). Both *Who's Who in the Theatre* and Young's *Famous Actors and Actresses of the American Stage* give Yurka's birth date as 1893.

Fran Hassencahl

—Z—

ZIPPRODT, Patricia (February 25, 1925–): costume designer, was born in Evanston, Illinois, and grew up in Kenilworth, Illinois, where her parents moved soon after her birth. Herbert Edward Zipprodt, her father, was a businessman who owned an advertising agency in Chicago. Her mother, Irene (Turpin) Zipprodt, had served as a yeoman in the medical corps during World War I. Patricia was the first born of three daughters. One sister, Barbara, is now deceased. The third sister, Constance Zipprodt Yonka, is the owner of a public relations firm in Chicago. The Zipprodt family is of German-Swiss descent and emigrated from the Weimar-Neuchâtel area of Switzerland during the 1820s.

Patricia Zipprodt attended art school from the age of ten. Though she always thought she would be a painter, she submitted to parental pressure and attended Bradford Junior College. She intended to return after two years to her art studies at the Chicago Art Institute. She remained at Bradford only one year and then transferred to Wellesley College in Massachusetts, where she earned a Bachelor of Arts degree in sociology. After graduation Zipprodt, much to the dismay of her family, became a puppeteer for a dental hygiene program in Pennsylvania. After a year she moved to New York, where she continued to study painting while holding a series of part-time jobs. She did some free-lance writing, waited on tables at Schraffts, and ushered at Carnegie Hall and City Center, where she became fascinated by dance; she contemplated making a living by painting dance scenes with color and form. She fell in love with the New York City Ballet and the wonderful netting creations of Barbara Karinska, the costume designer George Balanchine had brought with him from Russia. It was Karinska's netting, colors, and painting that lured Patricia Zipprodt into the theatre.

Determined to learn the craft of costume design, Zipprodt applied to the Fashion Institute of Technology in New York, where she received a scholarship. She studied there for a year and a half, learning to cut, sew, and drape. Upon the completion of her studies she spent a period of apprenticeship to couturier Charles James and began to sew for Off-off-Broadway shows. Zipprodt believes that the best way to learn the art and craft of costume design is to work for the designer whose work one most admires. She obtained her United Scenic Artists card and began to look for jobs assisting designers like Barbara Karinska, **Irene Sharaff**, and Rouben Ter-Arutunian, whom she admired for their strong, clear, conceptual designs and sense of color.

Zipprodt eventually was chosen to design her own shows—first at Circle in the Square with director José Quintero. Here she brought sewing machines into the theatre, hired people to cut and sew, and created her own costume shop. She subsequently became the resident designer at the Phoenix Theatre in the 1960s. It was here that she met two young directors, Jerome Robbins and Harold Prince, who would play an important part in her career. Because they had worked earlier with Zipprodt as a costume designer, Robbins and Prince sought her out as a designer to create the costumes for *Cabaret* and *Fiddler on the Roof* in the 1960s. Scene designers Jo Mielziner and Boris Aronson also had a significant influence on Zipprodt's career. As they watched her develop as a designer, they would frequently suggest Zipprodt to producers of plays for which they were employed as scenic designers.

Zipprodt's designs are fresh, inventive, and audacious. She takes costume designs beyond the realm of real clothes to what her fellow artists consider art. Her fresh use of old fabrics, unique materials, and inventive designs are only part of what has made Patricia Zipprodt one of the most interesting and challenging designers in the United States. She also has the ability to stimulate a director with not only the strength of her intellect and artistry but the electricity of her personality. She creates in odd fits and starts with an innocent, open enthusiasm that is fun and kinetic for the director. Her personality and her energy are combined in whatever she designs. She is a thinking designer, who does not rubber stamp the director's ideas. Instead she surprises directors with solutions to their ideas about costumes for a production. She designs with enthusiasm and commitment that never wane, whether she is working on Broadway or in regional theatre.

Zipprodt's designs may be characterized as having a bite and an undertone. She has designed for many of the more socially conscious productions of the third quarter of the twentieth century and has used costume design as an element to underscore the various levels of meaning in those productions. Costumes for *The Balcony* (1960), *The Blacks* (1961), *Fiddler on the Roof* (1964), *Cabaret* (1966), *Chicago* (1975), and *Pippin* (1972) particularly illuminate the dramatic action, not merely the objective facts of time, place, and characterization.

Recent designs by Zipprodt include the costumes for *Into the Woods*, designed in collaboration with Ann Hould-Ward. The Stephen Sondheim/James Lapine musical about various fairytale characters was first staged at the Old Globe in San Diego and then moved to the Martin Beck Theatre on Broadway in September 1987. Also in 1987 Zipprodt designed the costumes for Euripides' *The Bacchae* at the Guthrie Theatre in Minneapolis. The play was directed by Liviu Ciulei. In 1988 Zipprodt designed the costumes for the production of *Macbeth*, starring Christopher Plummer and Glenda Jackson.

Zipprodt's ability to articulate her art and her processes of creation have made her a leading figure in the profession of costume design in the United States. She was chosen, for instance, to present the costume point of view for the 1979 Antoinette Perry (Tony) Awards presentation, and was elected to the scenography commission of the International Organization of Scenographers and Theatre Technicians in 1976. She is a desired speaker at diverse conferences, including those of the United States Institute for Theatre Technology.

Zipprodt's designs have won a long list of awards. These include Tony awards for best costumes, *Fiddler on the Roof*, 1965, and *Cabaret*, 1967; Tony nominations for best costumes, *Mack and Mabel*, 1974, and *Chicago*, 1975; the Joseph Maharam Foundation Award for best costumes, *1776*, 1969; the nomination for best costumes, *Fools*, 1981; the Outer Critics Circle Award for best costumes, *1776*, 1969, and *Zorba*, 1969; the *Variety* Critics Award for best costumes, *Cabaret*, 1967; the Drama Desk Award for best costumes, *King of Hearts*, 1978; the Tony Award for best costumes, *Sweet Charity*, 1986; and a nomination by the Joseph Maharam Foundation Award for her designs, *Big Deal*, 1986.

Patricia Zipprodt as a costume designer broke the tradition of costume as "clothes." She took the art and craft of costume design beyond dressmaking and into a world of exciting color palettes, layers of textures, and unexpected fabrics. She developed through costume design a visual language for the second half of the twentieth century.

Most of the information on Patricia Zipprodt in this essay is from personal interviews with Zipprodt and Hal Prince. Zipprodt has written "Designing Costumes for Broadway and Hollywood," *Theatre Crafts* (January/February 1973), and "Designing Costumes," *Contemporary Stage Design, U.S.A.* (1974). Patricia Zipprodt is included in *Notable Names in the American Theatre* (1976), *Who's Who in the Theatre* (1981), and *Contemporary Theatre, Film, and Television*, Vol. 2 (1984).

Marianne Custer

APPENDIX 1
Listing by Place of Birth

THE UNITED STATES

Alabama

Viola Allen
Tallulah Bankhead
Milly S. Barranger
Sally Ordway

Arkansas

Esther Jackson
Fay Templeton

California

Eve Adamson
Mary Anderson
Laura Hope Crews
Joan Holden
Willa Kim
Anita Loos
Pauline Lord
Sophie Treadwell
Gwen Verdon

Colorado

Helen Bonfils
Mary Chase
Antoinette Perry
Charlotte Perry

Connecticut

Harriet French Ford
Katharine Hepburn
Lynne Meadow
Anna Sokolow

District of Columbia

Ina Claire
Helen Hayes
Florence Mills
Hildy Parks

Florida

Nancy Hanks

Georgia

Georgia Douglas Johnson
Carson McCullers
Julia Miles
Anne Nichols
Eugenia Rawls

Illinois

JoAnne Akalaitis
Nora Bayes?
Claudia Cassidy
Rachel Crothers

Katherine Dunham
Dina Rees Evans
Loie Fuller
Alice Gerstenberg
Lorraine Hansberry
Julie Haydon
Rowena Jelliffe
Portia Mansfield
Cornelia Otis Skinner
Patricia Zipprodt

Indiana

Marilyn Miller
Twyla Tharp

Iowa

Irene Corey
Susan Glaspell
Amy Leslie
Lillian Russell
Sada Thompson
Winifred Ward
Margaret Mary Young

Kentucky

Mrs. Leslie Carter
Anne Crawford Flexner
Elizabeth Hardwick
Marsha Norman
Sara Spencer

Louisiana

Lucinda Ballard
Minnie Maddern Fiske
Lillian Hellman
Adah Isaacs Menken?

Maine

Maxine Elliott
Edna St. Vincent Millay

Maryland

Kate Bateman
Hazel Bryant
Isabel Burger
Peggy Clark
Mildred Dunnock
Carrie Robbins
Rida Johnson Young

Massachusetts

Jane Alexander
Dorothy Coit
Jane Cowl
Charlotte Cushman
Millia Davenport
Zelda Fichandler
Rosamond Gilder
Ruth Gordon
Chrystal Herne
Marjorie Bradley Kellogg
Edith Lawrence King
Dania Krupska
Emily Mann
Agnes Moorhead
Mary Morris
Irene Selznick
Irene Sharaff
Mary G. Shaw
Marilyn Stasio
Julie Taymor
Mercy Otis Warren

Michigan

Ellen Burstyn
Edna Ferber
Julie Harris
Kim Hunter
Doris Keane
Patricia Sternberg

Minnesota

Adele Shank
Blanche Yurka

Mississippi

Ruth Ford
Mary Beth Henley
Patricia Anne McIlrath
Evelyn Preer

Missouri

Zoë Akins
Maya Angelou
Jeanne Eagels
Geraldine Page

Nebraska

Irene Worth

New Jersey

Sidney Frances Bateman?
Helen Krich Chinoy
Toby Cole
Jean Dalrymple
Julia Dean
Dorothy Fields
Myrna Lamb
Elizabeth LeCompte
Bonnie Marranca
Judith Martin
Nelle Nugent
Dorothy Parker
Ntozake Shange
Ruth White
Susan Yankowitz

New Mexico

Kim Stanley

New York

Stella Adler
Anne Bancroft
Djuna Barnes
Sidney Frances Bateman?
Barbara Bel Geddes
Gertrude Berg
Aline Bernstein
Jessie Bonstelle
Shirley Booth
Julie Bovasso
Alice Brady
Fanny Brice
Vinnette Carroll
Josephine Clifton?
Martha Coigney
Betty Comden
Charlotte Barnes Conner
Lotta Crabtree
Agnes de Mille
Helen Gahagan Douglas
Ruth Draper
Rosalyn Drexler
Florence Eldridge
Malvina Theresa Florence

Theresa Helburn
Alice Minnie Herts Heniger
Judy Holliday
Celeste Holm
Tina Howe
Fay Kanin
Wendy Kesselman
Clare Kummer
Franne Lee
Rosetta LeNoire
Alice Lewisohn
Irene Lewisohn
Olive Logan
Lucille Lortel
Clare Boothe Luce
Elisabeth Marbury
Ruth Mayleas
Elizabeth McCann
Ethel Merman
Maggie Mitchell
Agnes Morgan
Rita Morgenthau
Martha Morton
Sara O'Connor
Edith Oliver
Rochelle Owens
Angela Paton
Josephine Preston Peabody
Molly Picon
Jean Rosenthal
Marian Seldes
Roberta Sklar
Betty Smith
Susan Sontag
Mary Gibbs Spooner
Cecil Spooner
Maureen Stapleton
Helen Tamiris
Laurette Taylor
Cicely Tyson
Wendy Wasserstein
Margaret Webster
Mae West
Helen Westley
Audrey Wood
Peggy Wood

North Carolina

Winona Fletcher
Lulu Vollmer

Ohio

Ruby Cohn
Cheryl Crawford
Ruby Dee
Ketti Frings
Dorothy Gish
Lillian Gish
Elsie Janis
Nellie McCaslin
Jennifer Tipton

Oklahoma

Armina Marshall

Oregon

Blanche Bates

Pennsylvania

Ethel Barrymore
Mary Boland
Fanny Bradshaw
Josephine Clifton?
Rita Criste
Mae Desmond
Marie Doro
Rose Eytinge
Martha Graham
Adrienne Kennedy
Jean Kerr
Elaine May
Very Mowry Roberts
Vivienne Segal
Grace Stanistreet
Gertrude Stein
Ethel Waters

Rhode Island

Martha Boesing
Cordelia Howard

South Carolina

Jane Chambers
Alice Childress
Rose McClendon

South Dakota

Hallie Flanagan

Tennessee

Agnes Marie Haaga
Ann Hill

Texas

Rose Franken
Margo Jones
Margaret "Skippy" Lynn
Karen Malpede
Mary Martin
Ann Miller
Caroline Schaffner
Nina Vance

Utah

Maude Adams
Lucy Barton

Virginia

Tharon Musser
Margaret Sullavan

Washington

Carol Channing
Kate Drain Lawson
Geraldine Brain Siks
Megan Terry

West Virginia

Jane Dinsmoor Triplett

Wisconsin

Angna Enters
Mary Jane Evans
Zona Gale
Edith Isaacs
Alvina Krause

State Unknown

Charlotte Chorpenning
Beverly Emmons
Eliza Tukes Hallam?
Gypsy Rose Lee
Ruth Maleczech?
Louisa Medina?
Viola Spolin
Ellen Stewart

AUSTRALIA

Judith Anderson
Agnes Booth
Zoe Caldwell

CANADA

Margaret Anglin
Colleen Dewhurst
Marie Dressler
June Havoc
May Irwin
Barbara McIntyre
Clara Morris
Edith Skinner
Eva Tanguay
Lucile Watson

CHINA

Tisa Chang

CUBA

Maria Irene Fornés

CZECHOSLOVAKIA

Fanny Janauschek

EGYPT

Sylvie Drake

ENGLAND

Frances Hodgson Burnett
Rose Coghlin
Fanny Davenport
Louisa Lane Drew
Mary Ann Duff
Clara Fisher
Lynne Fontanne
Anne Jane Hartley Gilbert
Jane Greenwood
Mrs. Lewis Hallam, Sr.?
Rosemary Harris
Laura Keene
Angela Lansbury
Eva Le Gallienne
Clare Tree Major
Julia Marlowe
Ann Brunton Merry

Tanya Moiseiwitsch
Kate Reignolds
Susanna Haswell Rowson
Catherine Sinclair
Jessica Tandy
Mrs. John Wood
Margaret Wycherly

FRANCE

Anna Held?
Anna Cora Mowatt

GERMANY

Katharine Cornell
Uta Hagen
Hanya Holm
Judith Malina

GREECE

Theoni Aldredge

IRELAND

Geraldine Fitzgerald
Katharine Corcoran Herne
Matilda Heron
Ada Rehan

PERU

Meredith Monk

POLAND

Anna Held?
Helena Modjeska

PUERTO RICO

Miriam Colón

ROMANIA

Bella Spewack

RUSSIA

Alla Nazimova
Helene Pons

SCOTLAND

Kristin Linklater
Agnes Robertson

APPENDIX 2
Listing by Profession

ACTRESSES

Adams, Maude
Adamson, Eve
Adler, Stella
Akalaitis, JoAnne
Alexander, Jane
Allen, Viola
Anderson, Judith
Anderson, Mary
Anglin, Margaret
Bancroft, Anne
Bankhead, Tallulah
Barrymore, Ethel
The Batemans
Bates, Blanche
Bel Geddes, Barbara
Berg, Gertrude
Boland, Mary
Booth, Agnes
Booth, Shirley
Brady, Alice
Burstyn, Ellen
Caldwell, Zoe
Carter, Mrs. Leslie
Chang, Tisa
Channing, Carol
Claire, Ina
Clifton, Josephine

Coghlan, Rose
Colón, Miriam
Cornell, Katharine
Cowl, Jane
Crabtree, Lotta
Crews, Laura Hope
Cushman, Charlotte
Davenport, Fanny
Dean, Julia
Dee, Ruby
Desmond, Mae
Dewhurst, Colleen
Doro, Marie
Douglas, Helen Gahagan
Draper, Ruth
Dressler, Marie
Drew, Louisa Lane
Duff, Mary Ann
Dunnock, Mildred
Eagels, Jeanne
Eldridge, Florence
Elliott, Maxine
Eytinge, Rose
Fisher, Clara
Fiske, Minnie Maddern
Fitzgerald, Geraldine
Florence, Malvina Theresa
Fontanne, Lynn

Ford, Ruth
Gilbert, Anne Jane Hartley
Gish, Dorothy
Gish, Lillian
Gordon, Ruth
Hagen, Uta
Hallam, Mrs. Lewis, Sr.
Hallam, Eliza Tukes
Harris, Julie
Harris, Rosemary
Havoc, June
Haydon, Julie
Hayes, Helen
Hepburn, Katharine
Herne, Chrystal
Herne, Katharine Corcoran
Heron, Matilda
Holliday, Judy
Holm, Celeste
Howard, Cordelia
Hunter, Kim
Janauschek, Fanny
Keane, Doris
Keene, Laura
Lansbury, Angela
Le Gallienne, Eva
LeNoire, Rosetta
Linklater, Kristin
Logan, Olive
Lord, Pauline
Maleczech, Ruth
Malina, Judith
Marlowe, Julia
Marshall, Armina
Martin, Judith
Martin, Mary
May, Elaine
McClendon, Rose
Menken, Adah Isaaks
Merman, Ethel
Merry, Ann Brunton
Miller, Ann
Miller, Marilyn
Mitchell, Maggie
Modjeska, Helena
Monk, Meredith
Moorhead, Agnes

Morris, Clara
Morris, Mary
Mowatt, Anna Cora
Nazimova, Alla
Page, Geraldine
Paton, Angela
Perry, Antoinette
Picon, Molly
Preer, Evelyn
Rawls, Eugenia
Rehan, Ada
Reignolds, Kate
Robertson, Agnes
Rowson, Susanna Haswell
Schaffner, Caroline
Segal, Vivienne
Seldes, Marian
Shaw, Mary G.
Sinclair, Catherine
Skinner, Cornelia Otis
Spooner, Mary Gibbs, Edna May, and Cecil
Stanley, Kim
Stapleton, Maureen
Sullavan, Margaret
Tandy, Jessica
Taylor, Laurette
Thompson, Sada
Tyson, Cicely
Verdon, Gwen
Waters, Ethel
Watson, Lucile
Webster, Margaret
West, Mae
Westley, Helen
White, Ruth
Wood, Mrs. John
Wood, Peggy
Worth, Irene
Wycherly, Margaret
Yurka, Blanche

AGENTS

Cole, Toby
Marbury, Elisabeth
Wood, Audrey

CHILDREN'S THEATRE SPECIALISTS

Burger, Isabel
Chorpenning, Charlotte
Coit, Dorothy
Criste, Rita
Evans, Dina Rees
Evans, Mary Jane
Haaga, Agnes
Heniger, Alice Minnie Herts
Hill, Ann
King, Edith Lawrence
Major, Clare Tree
Martin, Judith
McCaslin, Nellie
McIntyre, Barbara
Siks, Geraldine Brain
Spencer, Sara
Stanistreet, Grace
Sternberg, Patricia
Triplett, Jane Dinsmore
Ward, Winifred

CRITICS

Cassidy, Claudia
Drake, Sylvie
Gilder, Rosamond
Hardwick, Elizabeth
Isaacs, Edith
Leslie, Amy
Logan, Olive
Malpede, Karen
Marranca, Bonnie
Oliver, Edith
Parker, Dorothy
Sontag, Susan
Stasio, Marilyn

DANCERS/CHOREOGRAPHERS

De Mille, Agnes
Dunham, Katherine
Enters, Angna
Fuller, Loie
Graham, Martha
Holm, Hanya
Krupska, Dania

Monk, Meredith
Sokolow, Anna
Tamiris, Helen
Tharp, Twyla
Verdon, Gwen

DESIGNERS

Aldredge, Theoni
Ballard, Lucinda
Barton, Lucy
Bernstein, Aline
Clark, Peggy
Corey, Irene
Davenport, Millia
Emmons, Beverley
Fuller, Loie
Greenwood, Jane
Kellogg, Marjorie Bradley
Kim, Willa
Lawson, Kate Drain
Lee, Franne
Moiseiwitsch, Tanya
Musser, Tharon
Pons, Helene
Robbins, Carrie
Rosenthal, Jean
Sharaff, Irene
Taymor, Julie
Tipton, Jennifer
Young, Margaret Mary
Zipprodt, Patricia

DIRECTORS

Adamson, Eve
Adler, Stella
Akalaitis, JoAnne
Anglin, Margaret
Boesing, Martha
Bonstelle, Jessie
Bovasso, Julie
Caldwell, Zoe
Carroll, Vinnette
Chang, Tisa
Coit, Dorothy
Colón, Miriam
Crawford, Cheryl
Crews, Laura Hope

Crothers, Rachel
Dewhurst, Coleen
Fichandler, Zelda
Fiske, Minnie Maddern
Fitzgerald, Geraldine
Flanagan, Hallie
Fornes, Maria Irene
Franken, Rose
Havoc, June
Hellman, Lillian
Jones, Margo
Keane, Laura
Le Gallienne, Eva
LeNoire, Rosetta
Lewisohn, Alice and Irene
Linklater, Kristin
Maleczech, Ruth
Malina, Judith
Mann, Emily
Martin, Judith
May, Elaine
McIlrath, Patricia
Meadow, Lynne
Miles, Julia
Monk, Meredith
Morgan, Agnes
O'Connor, Sara
Paton, Angela
Perry, Antoinette
Sklar, Roberta
Sontag, Susan
Spolin, Viola
Vance, Nina
Webster, Margaret

EDUCATORS/SCHOLARS

Adams, Maude
Adler, Stella
Barranger, Milly S.
Barton, Lucy
Bradshaw, Fanny
Chinoy, Helen Krich
Cohn, Ruby
Coit, Dorothy
Cole, Toby
Corey, Irene
Criste, Rita
Davenport, Millia

Evans, Dina Rees
Evans, Mary Jane
Fichandler, Zelda
Flanagan, Hallie
Fletcher, Winona
Haaga, Agnes
Hagen, Uta
Jackson, Esther
King, Edith Lawrence
Krause, Alvina
Linklater, Kristin
Mansfield, Portia
McCaslin, Nellie
McIlrath, Patricia
McIntyre, Barbara
Morgenthau, Rita
Morris, Mary
Perry, Charlotte
Roberts, Vera Mowry
Seldes, Marian
Siks, Geraldine Brain
Skinner, Edith
Spolin, Viola
Stanistreet, Grace
Sternberg, Patricia
Ward, Winifred

PATRONS

Hanks, Nancy
Hill, Ann
Lewisohn, Alice and Irene
Lortel, Lucille
Perry, Antoinette
Spencer, Sara
Stewart, Ellen

PLAYWRIGHTS/LYRICISTS/ LIBRETTISTS

Akins, Zoë
Angelou, Maya
Barnes, Charlotte (also listed under Conner)
Barnes, Djuna
Berg, Gertrude
Boesing, Martha
Bovasso, Julie
Burnett, Frances Hodgson
Carroll, Vinette

Chambers, Jane
Chase, Mary
Childress, Alice
Chorpenning, Charlotte
Comden, Betty
Conner, Charlotte Barnes
Cowl, Jane
Crothers, Rachel
Drexler, Rosalyn
Ferber, Edna
Fields, Dorothy
Fiske, Minnie Maddern
Flanagan, Hallie
Flexner, Anne Crawford
Ford, Harriet French
Ford, Ruth
Fornés, Maria Irene
Franken, Rose
Frings, Ketti
Gale, Zona
Gerstenberg, Alice
Glaspell, Susan
Gordon, Ruth
Hansberry, Lorraine
Havoc, June
Hellman, Lillian
Henley, Mary Beth
Holden, Joan
Howe, Tina
Johnson, Georgia Douglas
Kanin, Fay
Kennedy, Adrienne
Kerr, Jean
Kesselman, Wendy
Kummer, Clare
Lamb, Myrna
LeCompte, Elizabeth
LeNoire, Rosetta
Logan, Olive
Loos, Anita
Luce, Clare Boothe
Malpede, Karen
Mann, Emily
Marshall, Armina
Martin, Judith
May, Elaine
McCullers, Carson
Medina, Louisa

Millay, Edna St. Vincent
Morton, Martha
Mowatt, Anna Cora
Nichols, Anne
Norman, Marsha
Ordway, Sally
Owen, Rochelle
Parker, Dorothy
Peabody, Josephine Preston
Picon, Molly
Rowson, Susanna Haswell
Schaffner, Caroline
Shange, Ntozake
Shank, Adele
Skinner, Cornelia Otis
Smith, Betty
Spewack, Bella
Stein, Gertrude
Sternberg, Patricia
Terry, Megan
Treadwell, Sophie
Vollmer, Lulu
Warren, Mercy Otis
Wasserstein, Wendy
West, Mae
Yankowitz, Susan
Young, Rida Johnson

PRODUCERS/MANAGERS/ADMINISTRATORS

Adamson, Eve
Akalaitis, JoAnne
Anglin, Margaret
Barranger, Milly S.
Bateman, Sidney Frances Cowell
Boesing, Martha
Bonfils, Helen
Bonstelle, Jessie
Bryant, Hazel
Carroll, Vinette
Chang, Tisa
Coigney, Martha
Colón, Miriam
Cornell, Katharine
Crawford, Cheryl
Crothers, Rachel
Cushman, Charlotte
Dalrymple, Jean

Davenport, Fanny
Desmond, Mae
Draper, Ruth
Drew, Louisa Lane
Elliott, Maxine
Fichandler, Zelda
Fiske, Minnie Maddern
Flanagan, Hallie
Gilder, Rosamond
Glaspell, Susan
Hanks, Nancy
Havoc, June
Helburn, Theresa
Heniger, Alice Minnie Herts
Hill, Ann
Jelliffe, Rowena
Jones, Margo
Keane, Laura
Le Gallienne, Eva
LeNoire, Rosetta
Lewisohn, Alice and Irene
Linklater, Kristin
Lortel, Lucille
Lynn, Margaret "Skippy"
Major, Clare Tree
Malina, Judith
Mansfield, Portia
Marbury, Elisabeth
Marshall, Armina
Mayleas, Ruth
McCann, Elizabeth
McIlrath, Patricia
Meadow, Lynne
Merry, Ann Brunton
Miles, Julia

Monk, Meredith
Morgan, Agnes
Morgenthau, Rita
Nichols, Anne
Nugent, Nelle
O'Connor, Sara
Parks, Hildy
Paton, Angela
Perry, Antoinette
Perry, Charlotte
Schaffner, Caroline
Selznick, Irene
Sinclair, Catherine
Sklar, Roberta
Spooner, Mary Gibbs, Edna May, and Cecil
Stewart, Ellen
Vance, Nina
Ward, Winifred
Webster, Margaret
Wood, Mrs. John
Young, Margaret Mary

SINGERS/VARIETY PERFORMERS

Bayes, Nora
Brice, Fanny
Held, Anna
Irwin, May
Janis, Elsie
Lee, Gypsy Rose
Miller, Ann
Mills, Florence
Russell, Lillian
Tanguay, Eva
Templeton, Fay

Index

Page numbers of actual entries appear in **bold face** type.